NCE D.H.LAWRENCE D.H.LAWRENCE D.H.LAWREN
RENCE D.H.LAWRENCE D.H. H.LAWI
NCE D.H.LAWRENCE D.H. LAWREN
RENCE D.H.LAWRENCE D.H.LAWRENCE D.H.LAWI
NCE D.H.LAWRENCE D.H.LAWRENCE D.H.LAWREN
RENCE D.H.LAWRENCE D.H.LAWRENCE D.H.LAWI
NCE D.H.LAWRENCE D.H.LAWRENCE D.H.LAWREN
RENCE D.H.LAWRENCE D.H.LAWRENCE D.H.LAWI
NCE D.H.LAWRENCE D.H.LAWRENCE D.H.LAWREN
RENCE D.H.LAWRENCE D.H.LAWRENCE D.H.LAWI
NCE D.H.LAWRENCE D.H.LAWRENCE D.H.LAWREN
RENCE D.H.LAWRENCE D.H.LAWRENCE D.H.LAWI
NCE D.H.LAWRENCE D.H.LAWRENCE D.H.LAWREN
RENCE D.H.LAWRENCE D.H.LAWRENCE D.H.LAWI
NCE D.H.LAWRENCE D.H.LAWRENCE D.H.LAWREN
RENCE D.H.LAWRENCE D.H.LAWRENCE D.H.LAWI
NCE D.H.LAWRENCE D.H.LAWRENCE D.H.LAWREN
RENCE D.H.LAWRENCE D.H.LAWRENCE D.H.LAWI
NCE D.H.LAWRENCE D.H.LAWRENCE D.H.LAWREN
RENCE D.H.LAWRENCE D.H.LAWRENCE D.H.LAWI
NCE D.H.LAWRENCE D.H.LAWRENCE D.H.LAWREN
RENCE D.H.LAWRENCE D.H.LAWRENCE D.H.LAWI
NCE D.H.LAWRENCE D.H.LAWRENCE D.H.LAWREN
RENCE D.H.LAWRENCE D.H.LAWRENCE D.H.LAWI
NCE D.H.LAWRENCE D.H.LAWRENCE D.H.LAWREN
RENCE D.H.LAWRENCE D.H.LAWRENCE D.H.LAWI
NCE D.H.LAWRENCE D.H.LAWRENCE D.H.LAWREN
RENCE D.H.LAWRENCE D.H.LAWRENCE D.H.LAWI
NCE D.H.LAWRENCE D.H.LAWRENCE D.H.LAWREN
RENCE D.H.LAWRENCE D.H.LAWRENCE D.H.LAWI
NCE D.H.LAWRENCE D.H.LAWRENCE D.H.LAWREN
RENCE D.H.LAWRENCE D.H.LAWRENCE D.H.LAWI
NCE D.H.LAWRENCE D.H.LAWRENCE D.H.LAWREN
RENCE D.H.LAWRENCE D.H.LAWRENCE D.H.LAWI

D.H. Lawrence

Women in Love

The Ladybird

The Man Who Died

The Captain's Doll

The Rainbow

D.H. Lawrence

Heinemann / Octopus

Women in Love first published in Great Britain in 1921
by Martin Secker Limited
The Ladybird first published in Great Britain in 1923
by Martin Secker Limited
The Man Who Died first published in Great Britain in 1931
by Martin Secker Limited
The Captain's Doll first published in Great Britain in 1923
by Martin Secker Limited
The Rainbow first published in Great Britain in 1915
by Methuen & Co. Limited

This edition first published in Great Britain
in 1980 jointly by

William Heinemann Limited
10 Upper Grosvenor Street
London W1

Martin Secker & Warburg Limited
54 Poland Street
London W1

and

Octopus Books Limited
59 Grosvenor Street
London W1

ISBN 0 905712 52 8

Printed in the United States of America

Contents

Women in Love

Chapter One

Sisters

Ursula and Gudrun Brangwen sat one morning in the window-bay of their father's house in Beldover, working and talking. Ursula was stitching a piece of brightly-coloured embroidery, and Gudrun was drawing upon a board which she held on her knee. They were mostly silent, talking as their thoughts strayed through their minds.

'Ursula,' said Gudrun, 'don't you *really want* to get married?' Ursula laid her embroidery in her lap and looked up. Her face was calm and considerate.

'I don't know,' she replied. 'It depends how you mean.'

Gudrun was slightly taken aback. She watched her sister for some moments.

'Well,' she said, ironically, 'it usually means one thing! But don't you think, anyhow, you'd be—' she darkened slightly – 'in a better position than you are in now.'

A shadow came over Ursula's face.

'I might,' she said. 'But I'm not sure.'

Again Gudrun paused, slightly irritated. She wanted to be quite definite.

'You don't think one needs the *experience* of having been married?' she asked.

'Do you think it need *be* an experience?' replied Ursula.

'Bound to be, in some way or other,' said Gudrun, coolly. 'Possibly undesirable, but bound to be an experience of some sort.'

'Not really,' said Ursula. 'More likely to be the end of experience.'

Gudrun sat very still, to attend to this.

'Of course,' she said, 'there's *that* to consider.' This brought the conversation to a close. Gudrun, almost angrily, took up her rubber and began to rub out part of her drawing. Ursula stitched absorbedly.

'You wouldn't consider a good offer?' asked Gudrun.

'I think I've rejected several,' said Ursula.

'*Really!*' Gudrun flushed dark – 'But anything really worth while? Have you *really?*'

'A thousand a year, and an awfully nice man. I liked him awfully,' said Ursula.

'Really! But weren't you fearfully tempted?'

'In the abstract but not in the concrete,' said Ursula. 'When it comes to the point, one isn't even tempted – oh, if I were tempted, I'd marry like a shot. I'm only tempted *not* to.' The faces of both sisters suddenly lit up with amusement.

'Isn't it an amazing thing,' cried Gudrun, 'how strong the temptation is, not to!' They both laughed, looking at each other. In their hearts they were frightened.

There was a long pause, whilst Ursula stitched and Gudrun went on with her sketch. The sisters were women, Ursula twenty-six, and Gudrun twenty-five. But both had the remote, virgin look of modern girls, sisters of Artemis rather than of Hebe. Gudrun was very beautiful, passive, soft-skinned, soft-limbed. She wore a dress of dark-blue silky stuff, with ruches of blue and green linen lace in the neck and sleeves; and she had emerald-green stockings. Her look of confidence and diffidence contrasted with Ursula's sensitive expectancy. The provincial people, intimidated by Gudrun's perfect sang-froid and exclusive bareness of manner, said of her: 'She is a smart woman.' She had just come back from London, where she had spent several years, working at an art-school, as a student, and living a studio life.

'I was hoping now for a man to come along,' Gudrun said, suddenly catching her underlip between her teeth, and making a strange grimace, half sly smiling, half anguish. Ursula was afraid.

'So you have come home, expecting him here?' she laughed.

'Oh my dear,' cried Gudrun, strident, 'I wouldn't go out of my way to look for him. But if there did happen to come along a highly attractive individual of sufficient means – well—' she tailed off ironically. Then she looked searchingly at Ursula, as if to probe her. 'Don't you find yourself getting bored?' she asked of her sister. 'Don't you find, that things fail to materialise? *Nothing materalises!* Everything withers in the bud.'

'What withers in the bud?' asked Ursula.

'Oh, everything – oneself – things in general.' There was a pause, whilst each sister vaguely considered her fate.

'It does frighten one,' said Ursula, and again there was a pause. 'But do you hope to get anywhere by just marrying?'

'It seems to be the inevitable next step,' said Gudrun. Ursula pondered this, with a little bitterness. She was a class mistress herself, in Willey Green Grammar School, as she had been for some years.

'I know,' she said, 'it seems like that when one thinks in the abstract. But really imagine it: imagine any man one knows, imagine him coming home to one every evening, and saying "Hello", and giving one a kiss—'

There was a blank pause.

'Yes,' said Gudrun, in a narrowed voice. 'It's just impossible. The man makes it impossible.'

'Of course there's children— ' said Ursula doubtfully.

Gudrun's face hardened.

'Do you *really* want children, Ursula?' she asked coldly. A dazzled, baffled look came on Ursula's face.

'One feels it is still beyond one,' she said.

'*Do* you feel like that?' asked Gudrun. 'I get no feeling whatever from the thought of bearing children.'

Gudrun looked at Ursula with a mask-like, expressionless face. Ursula knitted her brows.

'Perhaps it isn't genuine,' she faltered. 'Perhaps one doesn't really want them, in one's soul – only superficially.' A hardness came over Gudrun's face. She did not want to be too definite.

'When one thinks of other people's children— ' said Ursula.

Again Gudrun looked at her sister, almost hostile.

'Exactly,' she said, to close the conversation.

The two sisters worked on in silence. Ursula having always that strange brightness of an essential flame that is caught, meshed, contravened. She lived a good deal by herself, to herself, working, passing on from day to day, and always thinking, trying to lay hold on life, to grasp it in her own understanding. Her active living was suspended, but underneath, in the darkness, something was coming to pass. If only she could break through the last integuments! She seemed to try and put her hands out, like an infant in the womb, and she could not, not yet. Still she had a strange prescience, an intimation of something yet to come.

She laid down her work and looked at her sister. She thought Gudrun so *charming*, so infinitely charming, in her softness and her fine, exquisite richness of texture and delicacy of line. There was a certain playfulness about her too, such a piquancy or ironic suggestion, such an untouched reserve. Ursula admired her with all her soul.

'Why did you come home, Prune?' she asked.

Gudrun knew she was being admired. She sat back from her drawing and looked at Ursula, from under her finely-curved lashes.

'Why did I come back, Ursula?' she repeated. 'I have asked myself a thousand times.'

'And don't you know?'

'Yes, I think I do. I think my coming back home was just *reculer pour mieux sauter.*'

And she looked with a long, slow look of knowledge at Ursula.

'I know!' cried Ursula, looking slightly dazzled and falsified, and as if she did *not* know. 'But where can one jump to?'

'Oh, it doesn't matter,' said Gudrun, somewhat superbly. 'If one jumps over the edge, one is bound to land somewhere.'

'But isn't it very risky?' asked Ursula.

A slow mocking smile dawned on Gudrun's face.

'Ah!' she said, laughing. 'What is it all but words!' And so again she closed the conversation. But Ursula was still brooding.

'And how do you find home, now you have come back to it?' she asked.

Gudrun paused for some moments, coldly, before answering. Then, in a cold truthful voice, she said:

'I find myself completely out of it.'

'And father?'

Gudrun looked at Ursula, almost with resentment, as if brought to bay.

'I haven't thought about him: I've refrained,' she said coldly.

'Yes,' wavered Ursula; and the conversation was really at an end. The sisters found themselves confronted by a void, a terrifying chasm, as if they had looked over the edge.

They worked on in silence for some time, Gudrun's cheek was flushed with repressed emotion. She resented its having been called into being.

'Shall we go out and look at that wedding?' she asked at length, in a voice that was too casual.

'Yes!' cried Ursula, too eagerly, throwing aside her sewing and leaping up, as if to escape something, thus betraying the tension of the situation and causing a friction of dislike to go over Gudrun's nerves.

As she went upstairs, Ursula was aware of the house, of her home round about her. And she loathed it, the sordid, too-familiar place! She was afraid at the depth of her feeling against the home, the milieu, the whole atmosphere and condition of this obsolete life. Her feeling frightened her.

The two girls were soon walking swiftly down the main road of Beldover, a wide street, part shops, part dwelling-houses, utterly formless and sordid, without poverty. Gudrun, new from her life in Chelsea and Sussex, shrank cruelly from this amorphous ugliness of a small colliery town in the Midlands. Yet forward she went, through the whole sordid gamut of pettiness, the long amorphous, gritty street. She was exposed to every stare, she passed on through a stretch of torment. It was strange that she should have chosen to come back and test the full effect of this shapeless, barren ugliness upon herself. Why had she wanted to submit herself to it, did she still want to submit herself to it, the insufferable torture of these ugly, meaningless people, this defaced countryside? She felt like a beetle toiling in the dust. She was filled with repulsion.

They turned off the main road, past a black patch of common-garden, where sooty cabbage stumps stood shameless. No one thought to be ashamed. No one was ashamed of it all.

'It is like a country in an underworld,' said Gudrun. 'The colliers bring it above-ground with them, shovel it up. Ursula, it's marvellous, it's really marvellous – it's really wonderful, another world. The people are all ghouls, and everything is ghostly. Everything is a ghoulish replica of the real world, a replica, a ghoul, all soiled, everything sordid. It's like being mad, Ursula.'

The sisters were crossing a black path through a dark, soiled field. On the left was a large landscape, a valley with collieries, and opposite hills with cornfields and woods, all blackened with distance, as if seen through a veil of crape. White and black smoke rose up in steady columns, magic within the dark air. Near at hand came the long rows of dwellings, approaching curved up the hill-slope, in straight lines along the brow of the hill. They were of darkened red brick, brittle, with dark slate roofs. The path on which the sisters walked was black, trodden-in by the feet of the recurrent colliers, and bounded from the field by iron fences; the stile that led again into the road was rubbed shiny by the moleskins of the passing miners. Now the two girls were going between some rows of dwellings, of the poorer sort. Women, their arms folded over their coarse aprons, standing gossiping at the end of their block, stared after the Brangwen sisters with that long, unwearying stare of aborigines; children called out names.

Gudrun went on her way half dazed. If this were human life, if these were human beings, living in a complete world, then what was her own world, outside? She was aware of her grass-green stockings, her large grass-green velour hat, her full soft coat, of a strong blue colour. And she felt as if she were treading in the air, quite unstable, her heart was contracted, as if at any minute she might be precipitated to the ground. She was afraid.

She clung to Ursula, who, through long usage, was inured to this violation of a dark, uncreated, hostile world. But all the time her heart was crying, as if in the midst of some ordeal: 'I want to go back. I want to go away, I want not to know it, not to know that this exists.' Yet she must go forward.

Ursula could feel her suffering.

'You hate this, don't you?' she asked.

'It bewilders me,' stammered Gudrun.

'You won't stay long,' replied Ursula.

And Gudrun went along, grasping at release.

They drew away from the colliery region, over the curve of the hill, into the purer country of the other side, towards Willey Green. Still the faint glamour of blackness persisted over the fields and the wooded hills, and seemed darkly to gleam in the air. It was a spring day, chill, with snatches of sunshine. Yellow celandines showed out from the hedge-bottoms, and in the cottage gardens of Willey Green, currant-bushes were breaking into leaf, and little flowers were coming white on the grey alyssum that hung over the stone walls.

Turning, they passed down the high-road, that went between high banks towards the church. There, in the lowest bend of the road, low under the trees, stood a little group of expectant people, waiting to see the wedding. The daughter of the chief mine-owner of the district, Thomas Crich, was getting married to a naval officer.

'Let us go back,' said Gudrun, swerving away. 'There are all those people.'

And she hung wavering in the road.

'Never mind them,' said Ursula, 'they're all right. They all know me, they don't matter.'

'But must we go through them?' asked Gudrun.

'They're quite all right, really,' said Ursula, going forward. And together the two sisters approached the group of uneasy, watchful common people. They were chiefly women, colliers' wives of the more shiftless sort. They had watchful, underworld faces.

The two sisters held themselves tense, and went straight towards the gate. The women made way for them, but barely sufficient, as if grudging to yield ground. The sisters passed in silence through the stone gateway and up the steps, on the red carpet, a policeman estimating their progress.

'What price the stockings!' said a voice at the back of Gudrun. A sudden fierce anger swept over the girl, violent and murderous. She would have liked them all annihilated, cleared away, so that the world was left clear for her. How she hated walking up the churchyard path, along the red carpet, continuing in motion, in their sight.

'I won't go into the church,' she said suddenly, with such final decision that Ursula immediately halted, turned round, and branched off up a small side path which led to the little private gate of the Grammar School, whose grounds adjoined those of the church.

Just inside the gate of the school shrubbery, outside the churchyard, Ursula sat down for a moment on the low stone wall under the laurel bushes, to rest. Behind her, the large red building of the school rose up peacefully, the windows all open for the holiday. Over the shrubs, before her, were the pale roofs and tower of the old church. The sisters were hidden by the foliage.

Gudrun sat down in silence. Her mouth was shut close, her face averted. She was regretting bitterly that she had ever come back. Ursula looked at her, and thought how amazingly beautiful she was, flushed with discomfiture. But she caused a constraint over Ursula's nature, a certain weariness. Ursula wished to be alone, freed from the tightness, the enclosure of Gudrun's presence.

'Are we going to stay here?' asked Gudrun.

'I was only resting a minute,' said Ursula, getting up as if rebuked. 'We will stand in the corner by the fives-court, we shall see everything from there.'

For the moment, the sunshine fell brightly into the churchyard, there was a vague scent of sap and of spring, perhaps of violets from off the graves. Some white daisies were out, bright as angels. In the air, the unfolding leaves of a copper-beech were blood-red.

Punctually at eleven o'clock, the carriages began to arrive. There was a stir in the crowd at the gate, a concentration as a carriage drove up, wedding guests were mounting up the steps and passing along the red carpet to the church. They were all gay and excited because the sun was shining.

Gudrun watched them closely, with objective curiosity. She saw each one as a complete figure, like a character in a book, or a subject in a picture, or a marionette in a theatre, a finished creation. She loved to recognise their various characteristics, to place them in their true light, give them their own surroundings, settle them for ever as they passed before her along the path to the church. She knew them, they were finished, sealed and stamped and finished with, for her. There was none that had anything unknown, unre-solved, until the Criches themselves began to appear. Then her interest was piqued. Here was something not quite so preconcluded.

There came the mother, Mrs. Crich, with her eldest son Gerald. She was a queer unkempt figure, in spite of the attempts that had obviously been made to bring her into line for the day. Her face was pale, yellowish, with a clear, transparent skin, she leaned forward rather, her features were strongly marked, handsome, with a tense, unseeing, predative look. Her colourless hair was untidy, wisps floating down on to her sac coat of dark blue silk, from under her blue silk hat. She looked like a woman with a monomania, furtive almost, but heavily proud.

Her son was of a fair, sun-tanned type, rather above middle height, well-made, and almost exaggeratedly well-dressed. But about him also was the strange, guarded look, the unconscious glisten, as if he did not belong to the same creation as the people about him. Gudrun lighted on him at once. There was something northern about him that magnetised her. In his clear northern flesh and his fair hair was a glisten like sunshine refracted through crystals of ice. And he looked so new, unbroached, pure as an arctic thing. Perhaps he was thirty years old, perhaps more. His gleaming beauty, maleness, like a young, good-humoured, smiling wolf, did not blind her to the significant, sinister stillness in his bearing, the lurking danger of his unsubdued temper. 'His totem is the wolf,' she repeated to herself. 'His mother is an old, unbroken wolf.' And then she experienced a keen paroxysm, a transport, as if she had made some incredible discovery, known to nobody else on earth. A strange transport took possession of her, all her veins were in a paroxysm of violent sensation. 'Good God!' she exclaimed to herself, 'what is this?' And then, a moment after, she was saying assuredly, 'I shall know more of that man.' She was tortured with desire to see him again, a nostalgia, a necessity to see him again, to make sure it was not all a mistake, that she was not deluding herself, that she really felt this strange and overwhelming sensation on his account, this knowledge of him in her essence, this powerful apprehension of him. 'Am I *really* singled out for him in some way, is there really some pale gold, arctic light that enveloped only us two?' she asked herself. And she could not believe it, she remained in a muse, scarcely conscious of what was going on around.

The bridesmaids were here, and yet the bridegroom had not come. Ursula wondered if something was amiss, and if the wedding would yet all go wrong. She felt troubled, as if it rested upon her. The chief bridesmaids had arrived. Ursula watched them come up the steps. One of them she knew, a tall, slow, reluctant woman with a weight of fair hair and a pale, long face. This was Hermione Roddice, a friend of the Criches. Now she came along, with her head held up, balancing an enormous flat hat of pale yellow velvet, on which were streaks of ostrich feathers, natural and grey. She drifted forward as if scarcely conscious, her long blanched face lifted up, not to see the world. She was rich. She wore a dress of silky, frail velvet, of pale yellow colour, and she carried a lot of small rose-coloured cyclamens. Her shoes and stockings were of brownish grey, like the feathers on her hat, her hair was heavy, she drifted along with a peculiar fixity of the hips, a strange unwilling motion. She was impressive, in her lovely pale-yellow and brown-ish-rose, yet macabre, something repulsive. People were silent when she passed, impressed, roused, wanting to jeer, yet for some reason silenced. Her long, pale face, that she carried lifted up, somewhat in the Rossetti fashion, seemed almost drugged, as if a strange mass of thoughts coiled in the darkness within her, and she was never allowed to escape.

Ursula watched her with fascination. She knew her a little. She was the most remarkable woman in the Midlands. Her father was a Derbyshire Baronet of the old school, she was a woman of the new school, full of intellectuality, and heavy, nerve-worn with consciousness. She was passion-ately interested in reform, her soul was given up to the public cause. But she was a man's woman, it was the manly world that held her.

She had various intimacies of mind and soul with various men of capacity. Ursula knew, among these men, only Rupert Birkin, who was one of the school-inspectors of the county. But Gudrun had met others, in London. Moving with her artist friends in different kinds of society, Gudrun had already come to know a good many people of repute and standing. She had met Hermione twice, but they did not take to each other. It would be queer to meet again down here in the Midlands, where their social standing was so diverse, after they had known each other on terms of equality in the houses of sundry acquaintances in town. For Gudrun had been a social success, and had her friends among the slack aristocracy that keeps touch with the arts.

Hermione knew herself to be well-dressed; she knew herself to be the social equal, if not far the superior, of anyone she was likely to meet in Willey Green. She knew she was accepted in the world of culture and of intellect. She was a *Kulturträger*, a medium for the culture of ideas. With all that was highest, whether in society or in thought or in public action, or even in art, she was at one, she moved among the foremost, at home with them. No one could put her down, no one could make mock of her, because she stood among the first, and those that were against her were below her, either in rank, or in wealth, or in high association of thought and progress and understanding. So, she was invulnerable. All her life, she had sought to make herself invulnerable, unassailable, beyond reach of the world's judgment.

And yet her soul was tortured, exposed. Even walking up the path to the church, confident as she was that in every respect she stood beyond all vulgar judgment, knowing perfectly that her appearance was complete and perfect, according to the first standards, yet she suffered a torture, under her confidence and her pride, feeling herself exposed to wounds and to mockery and to despite. She always felt vulnerable, vulnerable, there was always a secret chink in her armour. She did not know herself what it was. It was a lack of robust self, she had no natural sufficiency, there was a terrible void, a lack, a deficiency of being within her.

And she wanted someone to close up this deficiency, to close it up for ever. She craved for Rupert Birkin. When he was there, she felt complete, she was sufficient, whole. For the rest of time she was established on the sand, built over a chasm, and, in spite of all her vanity and securities, any common maid-servant of positive, robust temper could fling her down this bottomless pit of insufficiency, by the slightest movement of jeering or contempt. And all the while the pensive, tortured woman piled up her own defences of aesthetic knowledge, and culture, and world-visions, and disinterestedness. Yet she could never stop up the terrible gap of insufficiency.

If only Birkin would form a close and abiding connection with her, she would be safe during this fretful voyage of life. He could make her sound and triumphant, triumphant over the very angels of heaven. If only he would do it! But she was tortured with fear, with misgiving. She made herself beautiful, she strove so hard to come to that degree of beauty and advantage, when he should be convinced. But always there was a deficiency.

He was perverse too. He fought her off, he always fought her off. The more she strove to bring him to her, the more he battled her back. And they had been lovers now, for years. Oh, it was so wearying, so aching; she was so tired. But still she believed in herself. She knew he was trying to leave her. She knew he was trying to break away from her finally, to be free. But still she believed in her strength to keep him, she believed in her own higher knowledge. His own knowledge was high, she was the central touchstone of truth. She only needed his conjunction with her.

And this, this conjunction with her, which was his highest fulfilment also, with the perverseness of a wilful child he wanted to deny. With the wilfulness of an obstinate child, he wanted to break the holy connection that was between them.

He would be at this wedding; he was to be groom's man. He would be in the church, waiting. He would know when she came. She shuddered with nervous apprehension and desire as she went through the church-door. He would be there, surely he would see how beautiful her dress was, surely he would see how she had made herself beautiful for him. He would understand, he would be able to see how she was made for him, the first, how she was, for him, the highest. Surely at last he would be able to accept his highest fate, he would not deny her.

In a little convulsion of too-tired yearning, she entered the church and looked slowly along her cheeks for him, her slender body convulsed with agitation. As best man, he would be standing beside the altar. She looked slowly, deferring in her certainty.

And then, he was not there. A terrible storm came over her, as if she were drowning. She was possessed by a devastating hopelessness. And she approached mechanically to the altar. Never had she known such a pang of utter and final hopelessness. It was beyond death, so utterly null, desert.

The bridegroom and the groom's man had not yet come. There was a growing consternation outside. Ursula felt almost responsible. She could not bear it that the bride should arrive and no groom. The wedding must not be a fiasco, it must not.

But here was the bride's carriage, adorned with ribbons and cockades. Gaily the grey horses curvetted to their destination at the church-gate, a laughter in the whole movement. Here was the quick of all laughter and pleasure. The door of the carriage was thrown open, to let out the very blossom of the day. The people on the roadway murmured faintly with the discontented murmuring of a crowd.

The father stepped out first into the air of the morning, like a shadow. He was a tall, thin, careworn man, with a thin black beard that was touched with grey. He waited at the door of the carriage patiently, self-obliterated.

In the opening of the doorway was a shower of fine foliage and flowers, a whiteness of satin and lace, and a sound of a gay voice saying:

'How do I get out?'

A ripple of satisfaction ran through the expectant people. They pressed near to receive her, looking with zest at the stooping blonde head with its flower buds, and at the delicate, white, tentative foot that was reaching down to the step of the carriage. There was a sudden foaming rush, and the bride like a sudden surf-rush, floating all white beside her father in the morning shadow of trees, her veil flowing with laughter.

'That's done it!' she said.

She put her hand on the arm of her careworn, sallow father, and frothing her light draperies, proceeded over the eternal red carpet. Her father, mute and yellowish, his black beard making him look more careworn, mounted the steps stiffly, as if his spirit were absent; but the laughing mist of the bride went along with him undiminished.

And no bridegroom had arrived! It was intolerable for her. Ursula, her heart strained with anxiety, was watching the hill beyond; the white, descending road, that should give sight of him. There was a carriage. It was running. It had just come into sight. Yes, it was he. Ursula turned towards the bride and the people, and, from her place of vantage, gave an inarticulate cry. She wanted to warn them that he was coming. But her cry was inarticulate and inaudible, and she flushed deeply, between her desire and her wincing confusion.

The carriage rattled down the hill, and drew near. There was a shout from the people. The bride, who had just reached the top of the steps, turned round gaily to see what was the commotion. She saw a confusion among the people, a cab pulling up, and her lover dropping out of the carriage, and dodging among the horses and into the crowd.

'Tibs! Tibs!' she cried in her sudden, mocking excitement, standing high on the path in the sunlight and waving her bouquet. He, dodging with his hat in his hand, had not heard.

'Tibs!' she cried again, looking down to him.

He glanced up, unaware, and saw the bride and her father standing on the path above him. A queer, startled look went over his face. He hesitated for a moment. Then he gathered himself together for a leap, to overtake her.

'Ah-h-h!' came her strange, intaken cry, as, on the reflex, she started, turned and fled, scudding with an unthinkable swift beating of her white feet and fraying of her white garments, towards the church. Like a hound the young man was after her, leaping the steps and swinging past her father, his supple haunches working like those of a hound that bears down on the quarry.

'Ay, after her!' cried the vulgar women below, carried suddenly into the sport.

She, her flowers shaken from her like froth, was steadying herself to turn the angle of the church. She glanced behind, and with a wild cry of laughter and challenge, veered, poised, and was gone beyond the grey stone buttress. In another instant the bridegroom, bent forward as he ran, had caught the angle of the silent stone with his hand, and had swung himself out of sight, his supple, strong loins vanishing in pursuit.

Instantly cries and exclamations of excitement burst from the crowd at the gate. And then Ursula noticed again the dark, rather stooping figure of Mr. Crich, waiting suspended on the path, watching with expressionless face the flight to the church. It was over, and he turned round to look behind him, at the figure of Rupert Birkin, who at once came forward and joined him.

'We'll bring up the rear,' said Birkin, a faint smile on his face.

'Ay!' replied the father laconically. And the two men turned together up the path.

Birkin was as thin as Mr. Crich, pale and ill-looking. His figure was narrow but nicely made. He went with a slight trail of one foot, which came only from self-consciousness. Although he was dressed correctly for his part, yet there was an innate incongruity which caused a slight ridiculousness in his appearance. His nature was clever and separate, he did not fit at all in the conventional occasion. Yet he subordinated himself to the common idea, travestied himself.

He affected to be quite ordinary, perfectly and marvellously commonplace. And he did it so well, taking the tone of his surroundings, adjusting himself quickly to his interlocutor and his circumstance, that he achieved a verisimilitude of ordinary commonplaceness that usually propitiated his onlookers for the moment, disarmed them from attacking his singleness.

Now he spoke quite easily and pleasantly to Mr. Crich, as they walked along the path; he played with situations like a man on a tight-rope: but always on a tight-rope, pretending nothing but ease.

'I'm sorry we are so late,' he was saying. 'We couldn't find a button-hook, so it took us a long time to button our boots. But you were to the moment.'

'We are usually to time,' said Mr. Crich.

'And I'm always late,' said Birkin. 'But to-day I was *really* punctual, only accidentally not so. I'm sorry.'

The two men were gone, there was nothing more to see, for the time. Ursula was left thinking about Birkin. He piqued her, attracted her, and annoyed her.

She wanted to know him more. She had spoken with him once or twice, but only in his official capacity as inspector. She thought he seemed to acknowledge some kinship between her and him, a natural, tacit understanding, a using of the same language. But there had been no time for the understanding to develop. And something kept her from him, as well as attracted her to him. There was a certain hostility, a hidden ultimate reserve in him, cold and inaccessible.

Yet she wanted to know him.

'What do you think of Rupert Birkin?' she asked, a little reluctantly, of Gudrun. She did not want to discuss him.

'What do I think of Rupert Birkin?' repeated Gudrun. 'I think he's attractive – decidedly attractive. What I can't stand about him is his way with other people – his way of treating any little fool as if she were his greatest consideration. One feels so awfully sold, oneself.'

'Why does he do it?' said Ursula.

'Because he has no real critical faculty – of people, at all events,' said Gudrun. 'I tell you, he treats any little fool as he treats me or you – and it's such an insult.'

'Oh, it is,' said Ursula. 'One must discriminate.'

'One *must* discriminate,' repeated Gudrun. 'But he's a wonderful chap, in other respects – a marvellous personality. But you can't trust him.'

'Yes,' said Ursula vaguely. She was always forced to assent to Gudrun's pronouncements, even when she was not in accord altogether.

The sisters sat silent, waiting for the wedding party to come out. Gudrun was impatient of talk. She wanted to think about Gerald Crich. She wanted to see if the strong feeling she had got from him was real. She wanted to have herself ready.

Inside the church, the wedding was going on. Hermione Roddice was thinking only of Birkin. He stood near her. She seemed to gravitate physically towards him. She wanted to stand touching him. She could hardly be sure he was near her, if she did not touch him. Yet she stood subjected through the wedding service.

She had suffered so bitterly when he did not come, that still she was dazed. Still she was gnawed as by a neuralgia, tormented by his potential absence from her. She had awaited him in a faint delirium of nervous torture. As she stood bearing herself pensively, the rapt look on her face, that seemed spiritual, like the angels, but which came from torture, gave her a certain poignancy that tore his heart with pity. He saw her bowed head, her rapt face, the face of an almost demoniacal ecstatic. Feeling him looking, she lifted her face and sought his eyes, her own beautiful grey eyes flaring him a great signal. But he avoided her look, she sank her head in torment and shame, the gnawing at her heart going on. And he too was tortured with shame, and ultimate dislike, and with acute pity for her, because he did not want to meet her eyes, he did not want to receive her flare of recognition.

The bride and bridegroom were married, the party went into the vestry. Hermione crowded involuntarily up against Birkin, to touch him. And he endured it.

Outside, Gudrun and Ursula listened for their father's playing on the organ. He would enjoy playing a wedding march. Now the married pair were coming! The bells were ringing, making the air shake. Ursula wondered if the trees and the flowers could feel the vibration, and what they thought of it, this strange motion in the air. The bride was quite demure on the arm of the bridegroom, who stared up into the sky before him, shutting and opening his eyes unconsciously, as if he were neither here nor there. He looked rather comical, blinking and trying to be in the scene, when emotionally he was violated by his exposure to a crowd. He looked a typical naval officer, manly, and up to his duty.

Birkin came with Hermione. She had a rapt, triumphant look, like the fallen angels restored, yet still subtly demoniacal, now she held Birkin by the arm. And he was expressionless, neutralised, possessed by her as if it were his fate, without question.

Gerald Crich came, fair, good-looking, healthy, with a great reserve of energy. He was erect and complete, there was a strange stealth glistening through his amiable, almost happy appearance. Gudrun rose sharply and went away. She could not bear it. She wanted to be alone, to know this strange, sharp inoculation that had changed the whole temper of her blood.

Chapter Two

Shortlands

The Brangwens went home to Beldover, the wedding party gathered at Shortlands, the Criches' home. It was a long, low old house, a sort of manor farm, that spread along the top of a slope just beyond the narrow little lake of Willey Water. Shortlands looked across a sloping meadow that might be a park, because of the large, solitary trees that stood here and there, across the water of the narrow lake, at the wooded hill that successfully hid the colliery valley beyond, but did not quite hide the rising smoke. Nevertheless, the scene was rural and picturesque, very peaceful, and the house had a charm of its own.

It was crowded now with the family and the wedding guests. The father, who was not well, withdrew to rest. Gerald was host. He stood in the homely entrance hall, friendly and easy, attending to the men. He seemed to take pleasure in his social functions, he smiled, and was abundant in hospitality.

The women wandered about in a little confusion, chased hither and thither by the three married daughters of the house. All the while there could be heard the characteristic, imperious voice of one Crich woman or another calling 'Helen, come here a minute,' 'Marjory, I want you – here.' 'Oh, I say, Mrs. Witham—' There was a great rustling of skirts, swift glimpses of smartly-dressed women, a child danced through the hall and back again, a maidservant came and went hurriedly.

Meanwhile the men stood in calm little groups, chatting, smoking, pretending to pay no heed to the rustling animation of the women's world. But they could not really talk, because of the glassy ravel of women's excited, cold laughter and running voices. They waited, uneasy, suspended, rather bored. But Gerald remained as if genial and happy, unaware that he was waiting or unoccupied, knowing himself the very pivot of the occasion.

Suddenly Mrs. Crich came noiselessly into the room, peering about with her strong, clear face. She was still wearing her hat, and her sac coat of blue silk.

'What is it, mother?' said Gerald.

'Nothing, nothing!' she answered vaguely. And she went straight towards Birkin, who was talking to a Crich brother-in-law.

'How do you do, Mr. Birkin,' she said, in her low voice, that seemed to take no count of her guests. She held out her hand to him.

'Oh Mrs. Crich,' replied Birkin, in his readily-changing voice, 'I couldn't come to you before.'

'I don't know half the people here,' she said, in her low voice. Her son-in-law moved uneasily away.

'And you don't like strangers?' laughed Birkin. 'I myself can never see why one should take account of people, just because they happen to be in the room with one: why *should* I know they are there?'

'Why indeed, why indeed!' said Mrs. Crich, in her low, tense voice. 'Except that they *are* there. *I* don't know people whom I find in the house. The children introduce them to me – "Mother, this is Mr. So-and-so." I am no further. What has Mr. So-and-so to do with his own name? – and what have I to do with either him or his name?'

She looked up at Birkin. She startled him. He was flattered too that she came to talk to him, for she took hardly any notice of anybody. He looked down at her tense clear face, with its heavy features, but he was afraid to look into her heavy-seeing blue eyes. He noticed instead how her hair looped in slack, slovenly strands over her rather beautiful ears, which were not quite clean. Neither was her neck perfectly clean. Even in that he seemed to belong to her, rather than to the rest of the company; though, he thought to himself, he was always well washed, at any rate at the neck and ears.

He smiled faintly, thinking these things. Yet he was tense, feeling that he and the elderly, estranged woman were conferring together like traitors, like enemies within the camp of the other people. He resembled a deer, that throws one ear back upon the trail behind, and one ear forward, to know what is ahead.

'People don't really matter,' he said, rather unwilling to continue.

The mother looked up at him with sudden, dark interrogation, as if doubting his sincerity.

'How do you mean, *matter?* ' she asked sharply.

'Not many people are anything at all,' he answered, forced to go deeper than he wanted to. 'They jingle and giggle. It would be much better if they were just wiped out. Essentially, they don't exist, they aren't there.'

She watched him steadily while he spoke.

'But we don't imagine them,' she said sharply.

'There's nothing to imagine, that's why they don't exist.'

'Well,' she said, 'I would hardly go as far as that. There they are, whether they exist or no. It doesn't rest with me to decide on their existence. I only know that I can't be expected to take count of them all. You can't expect me to know them, just because they happen to be there. As far as *I* go they might as well not be there.'

'Exactly,' he replied.

'Mightn't they?' she asked again.

'Just as well,' he repeated. And there was a little pause.

'Except that they *are* there, and that's a nuisance,' she said. 'There are my sons-in-law,' she went on, in a sort of monologue. 'Now Laura's got married, there's another. And I really don't know John from James yet. They come up to me and call me mother. I know what they will say – "How are you, mother?" I ought to say, "I am not your mother, in any sense." But what is the use? There they are. I have had children of my own. I suppose I know them from another woman's children.'

'One would suppose so,' he said.

She looked at him, somewhat surprised, forgetting perhaps that she was talking to him. And she lost her thread.

She looked round the room, vaguely. Birkin could not guess what she was looking for, nor what she was thinking. Evidently she noticed her sons.

'Are my children all there?' she asked him abruptly.

He laughed, startled, afraid perhaps.

'I scarcely know them, except Gerald,' he replied.

'Gerald!' she exclaimed. 'He's the most wanting of them all. You'd never think it, to look at him now, would you?'

'No,' said Birkin.

The mother looked across at her eldest son, stared at him heavily for some time.

'Ay,' she said, in an incomprehensible monosyllable, that sounded profoundly cynical. Birkin felt afraid, as if he dared not realise. And Mrs. Crich moved away, forgetting him. But she returned on her traces.

'I should like him to have a friend,' she said. 'He has never had a friend.'

Birkin looked down into her eyes, which were blue, and watching heavily. He could not understand them. 'Am I my brother's keeper?' he said to himself, almost flippantly.

Then he remembered, with a slight shock, that that was Cain's cry. And Gerald was Cain, if anybody. Not that he was Cain, either, although he had slain his brother. There was such a thing as pure accident, and the consequences did not attach to one, even though one had killed one's brother in such wise. Gerald as a boy had accidentally killed his brother. What then? Why seek to draw a brand and a curse across the life that had caused the accident? A man can live by accident, and die by accident. Or can he not? Is every man's life subject to pure accident, is it only the race, the genus, the species, that has a universal reference? Or is this not true, is there no such thing as pure accident? Has *everything* that happens a universal significance? Has it? Birkin, pondering as he stood there, had forgotten Mrs. Crich, as she had forgotten him.

He did not believe that there was any such thing as accident. It all hung together, in the deepest sense.

Just as he had decided this, one of the Crich daughters came up, saying: 'Won't you come and take your hat off, mother dear? We shall be sitting down to eat in a minute, and it's a formal occasion, darling, isn't it?' She drew her arm through her mother's, and they went away. Birkin immediately went to talk to the nearest man.

The gong sounded for the luncheon. The men looked up, but no move was made to the dining-room. The women of the house seemed not to feel that the sound had meaning for them. Five minutes passed by. The elderly manservant, Crowther, appeared in the doorway exasperatedly. He looked with appeal at Gerald. The latter took up a large, curved conch shell, that lay on a shelf, and without reference to anybody, blew a shattering blast. It was a strange rousing noise, that made the heart beat. The summons was almost magical. Everybody came running, as if at a signal. And then the crowd in one impulse moved to the dining-room.

Gerald waited a moment, for his sister to play hostess. He knew his mother would pay no attention to her duties. But his sister merely crowded to her seat. Therefore the young man, slightly too dictatorial, directed the guests to their places.

There was a moment's lull, as everybody looked at the *hors d'oeuvres* that were being handed round. And out of this lull, a girl of thirteen or fourteen, with her long hair down her back, said in a calm, self-possessed voice:

'Gerald, you forget father, when you make that unearthly noise.'

'Do I?' he answered. And then, to the company, 'Father is lying down, he is not quite well.'

'How is he, really?' called one of the married daughters, peeping round the immense wedding cake that towered up in the middle of the table shedding its artificial flowers.

'He has no pain, but he feels tired,' replied Winifred, the girl with the hair down her back.

The wine was filled, and everybody was talking boisterously. At the far end of the table sat the mother, with her loosely-looped hair. She had Birkin for a neighbour. Sometimes she glanced fiercely down the rows of faces, bending forwards and staring unceremoniously. And she would say in a low voice to Birkin:

'Who is that young man?'

'I don't know,' Birkin answered discreetly.

'Have I seen him before?' she asked.

'I don't think so. *I* haven't,' he replied. And she was satisfied. Her eyes closed wearily, a peace came over her face, she looked like a queen in repose. Then she started, a little social smile came on her face, for a moment she looked the pleasant hostess. For a moment she bent graciously, as if everyone were welcome and delightful. And then immediately the shadow came back, a sullen, eagle look was on her face, she glanced from under her brows like a sinister creature at bay, hating them all.

'Mother,' called Diana, a handsome girl a little older than Winifred, 'I may have wine, mayn't I?'

'Yes, you may have wine,' replied the mother automatically, for she was perfectly indifferent to the question.

And Diana beckoned to the footman to fill her glass.

'Gerald shouldn't forbid me,' she said calmly, to the company at large.

'All right, Di,' said her brother amiably. And she glanced challenge at him as she drank from her glass.

There was a strange freedom, that almost amounted to anarchy, in the house. It was rather a resistance to authority, than liberty. Gerald had some command, by mere force of personality, not because of any granted position. There was a quality in his voice, amiable but dominant, that cowed the others, who were all younger than he.

Hermione was having a discussion with the bridegroom about nationality.

'No,' she said, 'I think that the appeal to patriotism is a mistake. It is like one house of business rivalling another house of business.'

'Well, you can hardly say that, can you?' exclaimed Gerald, who had a real *passion* for discussion. 'You couldn't call a race a business concern, could you? – and nationality roughly corresponds to race, I think. I think it is *meant* to.'

There was a moment's pause. Gerald and Hermione were always strangely but politely and evenly inimical.

'*Do* you think race corresponds with nationality?' she asked musingly, with expressionless indecision.

Birkin knew she was waiting for him to participate. And dutifully he spoke up.

'I think Gerald is right – race is the essential element in nationality, in Europe at least,' he said.

Again Hermione paused, as if to allow this statement to cool. Then she said with strange assumption of authority:

'Yes, but even so, is the patriotic appeal an appeal to the racial instinct? Is it not rather an appeal to the proprietary instinct, the *commercial* instinct? And isn't this what we mean by nationality?'

'Probably,' said Birkin, who felt that such a discussion was out of place and out of time.

But Gerald was now on the scent of argument.

'A race may have its commercial aspect,' he said. 'In fact it must. It is like a family. You *must* make provision. And to make provision you have got to strive against other families, other nations. I don't see why you shouldn't.'

Again Hermione made a pause, domineering and cold, before she replied: 'Yes, I think it is always wrong to provoke a spirit of rivalry. It makes bad blood. And bad blood accumulates.'

'But you can't do away with the spirit of emulation altogether?' said Gerald. 'It is one of the necessary incentives to production and improvement.'

'Yes,' came Hermione's sauntering response. 'I think you can do away with it.'

'I must say,' said Birkin, 'I detest the spirit of emulation.' Hermione was biting a piece of bread, pulling it from between her teeth with her fingers, in a slow, slightly derisive movement. She turned to Birkin.

'You do hate it, yes,' she said, intimate and gratified.

'Detest it,' he repeated.

'Yes,' she murmured, assured and satisfied.

'But,' Gerald insisted, 'you don't allow one man to take away his neighbour's living, so why should you allow one nation to take away the living from another nation?'

There was a long slow murmur from Hermione before she broke into speech, saying with a laconic indifference:

'It is not always a question of possessions, is it? It is not all a question of goods?'

Gerald was nettled by this implication of vulgar materialism.

'Yes, more or less,' he retorted. 'If I go and take a man's hat from off his head, that hat becomes a symbol of that man's liberty. When he fights me for his hat, he is fighting me for his liberty.'

Hermione was nonplussed.

'Yes,' she said, irritated. 'But that way of arguing by imaginary instances is not supposed to be genuine, is it? A man does *not* come and take my hat from off my head, does he?'

'Only because the law prevents him,' said Gerald.

'Not only,' said Birkin. 'Ninety-nine men out of a hundred don't want my hat.'

'That's a matter of opinion,' said Gerald.

'Or the hat,' laughed the bridegroom.

'And if he does want my hat, such as it is,' said Birkin, 'why, surely it is open to me to decide, which is a greater loss to me, my hat, or my liberty as a free and indifferent man. If I am compelled to offer fight, I lose the latter. It is a question which is worth more to me, my pleasant liberty of conduct, or my hat.'

'Yes,' said Hermione, watching Birkin strangely. 'Yes.'

'But would you let somebody come and snatch your hat off your head?' the bride asked of Hermione.

The face of the tall straight woman turned slowly and as if drugged to this new speaker.

'No,' she replied, in a low inhuman tone, that seemed to contain a chuckle. 'No, I shouldn't let anybody take my hat off my head.'

'How would you prevent it?' asked Gerald.

'I don't know,' replied Hermione slowly. 'Probably I should kill him.'

There was a strange chuckle in her tone, a dangerous and convincing humour in her bearing.

'Of course,' said Gerald, 'I can see Rupert's point. It is a question to him whether his hat or his peace of mind is more important.'

'Peace of body,' said Birkin.

'Well, as you like there,' replied Gerald. 'But how are you going to decide this for a nation?'

'Heaven preserve me,' laughed Birkin.

'Yes, but suppose you have to?' Gerald persisted.

'Then it is the same. If the national crown-piece is an old hat, then the thieving gent may have it.'

'But *can* the national or racial hat be an old hat?' insisted Gerald.

'Pretty well bound to be, I believe,' said Birkin.

'I'm not so sure,' said Gerald.

'I don't agree, Rupert,' said Hermione.

'All right,' said Birkin.

'I'm all for the old national hat,' laughed Gerald.

'And a fool you look in it,' cried Diana, his pert sister who was just in her teens.

'Oh, we're quite out of our depths with these old hats,' cried Laura Crich. 'Dry up now, Gerald. We're going to drink toasts. Let us drink toasts. Toasts – glasses, glasses – now then, toasts! Speech! Speech!'

Birkin, thinking about race or national death, watched his glass being filled with champagne. The bubbles broke at the rim, the man withdrew, and feeling a sudden thirst at the sight of the fresh wine, Birkin drank up his glass. A queer little tension in the room roused him. He felt a sharp constraint.

'Did I do it by accident, or on purpose?' he asked himself. And he decided that, according to the vulgar phrase, he had done it 'accidentally on purpose'. He looked round at the hired footman. And the hired footman came, with a silent step of cold servant-like disapprobation. Birkin decided that he detested toasts, and footmen, and assemblies, and mankind altogether, in most of its aspects. Then he rose to make a speech. But he was somehow disgusted.

At length it was over, the meal. Several men strolled out into the garden. There was a lawn, and flower-beds, and at the boundary an iron fence shutting off the little field or park. The view was pleasant; a highroad curving round the edge of a low lake, under the trees. In the spring air, the water gleamed and the opposite woods were purplish with new life. Charming Jersey cattle came to the fence, breathing hoarsely from their velvet muzzles at the human beings, expecting perhaps a crust.

Birkin leaned on the fence. A cow was breathing wet hotness on his hand.

'Pretty cattle, very pretty,' said Marshall, one of the brothers-in-law. 'They give the best milk you can have.'

'Yes,' said Birkin.

'Eh, my little beauty, eh, my beauty!' said Marshall, in a queer high falsetto voice, that caused the other man to have convulsions of laughter in his stomach.

'Who won the race, Lupton?' he called to the bridegroom, to hide the fact that he was laughing.

The bridegroom took his cigar from his mouth.

'The race?' he exclaimed. Then a rather thin smile came over his face. He did not want to say anything about the flight to the church door. 'We got there together. At least she touched first, but I had my hand on her shoulder.'

'What's this?' asked Gerald.

Birkin told him about the race of the bride and the bridegroom.

'H'm!' said Gerald, in disapproval. 'What made you late then?'

'Lupton would talk about the immortality of the soul,' said Birkin, 'and then he hadn't got a button-hook.'

'Oh, God!' cried Marshall. 'The immortality of the soul on your wedding day! Hadn't you got anything better to occupy your mind?'

'What's wrong with it?' asked the bridegroom, a clean-shaven naval man, flushing sensitively.

'Sounds as if you were going to be executed instead of married. *The immortality of the soul!*' repeated the brother-in-law, with most killing emphasis.

But he fell quite flat.

'And what did you decide?' asked Gerald, at once pricking up his ears at the thought of a metaphysical discussion.

'You don't want a soul to-day, my boy,' said Marshall. 'It'd be in your road.'

'Christ! Marshall, go and talk to somebody else,' cried Gerald, with sudden impatience.

'By God, I'm willing,' said Marshall, in a temper. 'Too much bloody soul and talk altogether—'

He withdrew in a dudgeon, Gerald staring after him with angry eyes, that grew gradually calm and amiable as the stoutly-built form of the other man passed into the distance.

'There's one thing, Lupton,' said Gerald, turning suddenly to the bridegroom. 'Laura won't have brought such a fool into the family as Lottie did.'

'Comfort yourself with that,' laughed Birkin.

'I take no notice of them,' laughed the bridegroom.

'What about this race then – who began it?' Gerald asked.

'We were late. Laura was at the top of the churchyard steps when our cab came up. She saw Lupton bolting towards her. And she fled. But why do you look so cross? Does it hurt your sense of the family dignity?'

'It does, rather,' said Gerald. 'If you're doing a thing, do it properly, and if you're not going to do it properly, leave it alone.'

'Very nice aphorism,' said Birkin.

'Don't you agree?' asked Gerald.

'Quite,' said Birkin. 'Only it bores me rather, when you become aphoristic.'

'Damn you, Rupert, you want all the aphorisms your own way,' said Gerald.

'No. I want them out of the way, and you're always shoving them in it.'

Gerald smiled grimly at this humorism. Then he made a little gesture of dismissal with his eyebrows.

'You don't believe in having any standard of behaviour at all, do you?' he challenged Birkin, censoriously.

'Standard – no. I hate standards. But they're necessary for the common ruck. Anybody who is anything can just be himself and do as he likes.'

'But what do you mean by being himself?' said Gerald. 'Is that an aphorism or a cliché?'

'I mean just doing what you want to do. I think it was perfect good form in Laura to bolt from Lupton to the church door. It was almost a masterpiece in good form. It's the hardest thing in the world to act spontaneously on one's impulses – and it's the only really gentlemanly thing to do – provided you're fit to do it.'

'You don't expect me to take you seriously, do you?' asked Gerald.

'Yes, Gerald, you're one of the very few people I do expect that of.'

'Then I'm afraid I can't come up to your expectations here, at any rate. You think people should just do as they like.'

'I think they always do. But I should like them to like the purely individual thing in themselves, which makes them act in singleness. And they only like to do the collective thing.'

'And I,' said Gerald grimly, 'shouldn't like to be in a world of people who acted individually and spontaneously, as you call it. We should have everybody cutting everybody else's throat in five minutes.'

'That means *you* would like to be cutting everybody's throat,' said Birkin.

'How does that follow?' asked Gerald crossly.

'No man,' said Birkin, 'cuts another man's throat unless he wants to cut it, and unless the other man wants it cutting. This is a complete truth. It takes two people to make a murder: a murderer and a murderee. And a murderee is a man who is murderable. And a man who is murderable is a man who in a profound if hidden lust desires to be murdered.'

'Sometimes you talk pure nonsense,' said Gerald to Birkin. 'As a matter of fact, none of us wants our throat cut, and most other people would like to cut it for us – some time or other—'

'It's a nasty view of things, Gerald,' said Birkin, 'and no wonder you are afraid of yourself and your own unhappiness.'

'How am I afraid of myself?' said Gerald; 'and I don't think I am unhappy.'

'You seem to have a lurking desire to have your gizzard slit, and imagine every man has his knife up his sleeve for you,' Birkin said.

'How do you make that out?' said Gerald.

'From you,' said Birkin.

There was a pause of strange enmity between the two men, that was very near to love. It was always the same between them; always their talk brought them into a deadly nearness of contact, a strange, perilous intimacy which was either hate or love, or both. They parted with apparent unconcern, as if their going apart were a trivial occurrence. And they really kept it to the level of trivial occurrence. Yet the heart of each burned from the other. They burned with each other, inwardly. This they would never admit. They intended to keep their relationship a casual free-and-easy friendship, they were not going to be so unmanly and unnatural as to allow any heart-burning between them. They had not the faintest belief in deep relationship between men and men, and their disbelief prevented any development of their powerful but suppressed friendliness.

Chapter Three

Class-room

A school-day was drawing to a close. In the class-room the last lesson was in progress, peaceful and still. It was elementary botany. The desks were littered with catkins, hazel and willow, which the children had been sketch-ing. But the sky had come over dark, as the end of the afternoon approached: there was scarcely light to draw any more. Ursula stood in front of the class, leading the children by questions to understand the structure and the meaning of the catkins.

A heavy, copper-coloured beam of light came in at the west window, gilding the outlines of the children's heads with red gold, and falling on the wall opposite in a rich, ruddy illumination. Ursula, however, was scarcely conscious of it. She was busy, the end of the day was here, the work went on as a peaceful tide that is at flood, hushed to retire.

This day had gone by like so many more, in an activity that was like a trance. At the end there was a little haste, to finish what was in hand. She was pressing the children with questions, so that they should know all they were to know, by the time the gong went. She stood in shadow in front of the class, with catkins in her hand, and she leaned towards the children, absorbed in the passion of instruction.

She heard, but did not notice the click of the door. Suddenly she started. She saw, in the shaft of ruddy, copper-coloured light near her, the face of a man. It was gleaming like fire, watching her, waiting for her to be aware. It startled her terribly. She thought she was going to faint. All her suppressed, subconscious fear sprang into being, with anguish.

'Did I startle you?' said Birkin, shaking hands with her. 'I thought you had heard me come in.'

'No,' she faltered, scarcely able to speak. He laughed, saying he was sorry. She wondered why it amused him.

'It is so dark,' he said. 'Shall we have the light.'

And moving aside, he switched on the strong electric lights. The class-room was distinct and hard, a strange place after the soft dim magic that filled it before he came. Birkin turned curiously to look at Ursula. Her eyes were round and wondering, bewildered, her mouth quivered slightly. She looked like one who is suddenly wakened. There was a living, tender beauty, like a tender light of dawn shining from her face. He looked at her with a new pleasure, feeling gay in his heart, irresponsible.

'You are doing catkins?' he asked, picking up a piece of hazel from a scholar's desk in front of him. 'Are they as far out as this? I hadn't noticed them this year.'

He looked absorbedly at the tassel of hazel in his hand.

'The red ones too!' he said, looking at the flickers of crimson that came from the female bud.

Then he went in among the desks, to see the scholars' books. Ursula watched his intent progress. There was a stillness in his motion that hushed the activities of her heart. She seemed to be standing aside in arrested silence, watching him move in another concentrated world. His presence was so quiet, almost like a vacancy in the corporate air.

Suddenly he lifted his face to her, and her heart quickened at the flicker of his voice.

'Give them some crayons, won't you?' he said, 'so that they can make the gynaecious flowers red, and the androgynous yellow. I'd chalk them in plain, chalk in nothing else, merely the red and the yellow. Outline scarcely matters in this case. There is just the one fact to emphasise.'

'I haven't any crayons,' said Ursula.

'There will be some somewhere – red and yellow, that's all you want.'

Ursula sent out a boy on a quest.

'It will make the books untidy,' she said to Birkin, flushing deeply.

'Not very,' he said. 'You must mark in these things obviously. It's the fact you want to emphasise, not the subjective impression to record. What's the fact? – red little spiky stigmas of the female flower, dangling yellow male catkin, yellow pollen flying from one to the other. Make a pictorial record of the fact, as a child does when drawing a face – two eyes, one nose, mouth with teeth – so—' And he drew a figure on the blackboard.

At that moment another vision was seen through the glass panels of the door. It was Hermione Roddice. Birkin went and opened to her.

'I saw your car,' she said to him. 'Do you mind my coming to find you? I wanted to see you when you were on duty.'

She looked at him for a long time, intimate and playful, then she gave a short little laugh. And then only she turned to Ursula, who, with all the class, had been watching the little scene between the lovers.

'How do you do, Miss Brangwen,' sang Hermione, in her low, odd, singing fashion, that sounded almost as if she were poking fun. 'Do you mind my coming in?'

Her grey, almost sardonic eyes rested all the while on Ursula, as if summing her up.

'Oh no,' said Ursula.

'Are you *sure?*' repeated Hermione, with complete sang froid, and an odd, half-bullying effrontery.

'Oh no, I like it awfully,' laughed Ursula, a little bit excited and bewildered, because Hermione seemed to be compelling her, coming very close to her, as if intimate with her; and yet, how could she be intimate?'

This was the answer Hermione wanted. She turned satisfied to Birkin.

'What are you doing?' she sang, in her casual, inquisitive fashion.

'Catkins,' he replied.

'Really!' she said. 'And what do you learn about them?' She spoke all the while in a mocking, half teasing fashion, as if making game of the whole business. She picked up a twig of the catkin, piqued by Birkin's attention to it.

She was a strange figure in the class-room, wearing a large, old cloak of greenish cloth, on which was a raised pattern of dull gold. The high collar, and the inside of the cloak, was lined with dark fur. Beneath she had a dress of fine lavender-coloured cloth, trimmed with fur, and her hat was close-fitting, made of fur and of the dull, green-and-gold figured stuff. She was tall and strange, she looked as if she had come out of some new, bizarre picture.

'Do you know the little red ovary flowers, that produce the nuts? Have you ever noticed them?' he asked her. And he came close and pointed them out to her, on the sprig she held.

'No,' she replied. 'What are they?'

'Those are the little seed-producing flowers, and the long catkins, they only produce pollen, to fertilise them.'

'Do they, do they!' repeated Hermione, looking closely.

'From those little red bits, the nuts come; if they receive pollen from the long danglers.'

'Little red flames, little red flames,' murmured Hermione to herself. And she remained for some moments looking only at the small buds out of which the red flickers of the stigma issued.

'Aren't they beautiful? I think they're so beautiful,' she said, moving close to Birkin, and pointing to the red filaments with her long, white finger.

'Had you never noticed them before?' he asked.

'No, never before,' she replied.

'And now you will always see them,' he said.

'Now I shall always see them,' she repeated. 'Thank you so much for showing me. I think they're so beautiful – little red flames—'

Her absorption was strange, almost rhapsodic. Both Birkin and Ursula were suspended. The little red pistillate flowers had some strange, almost mystic-passionate attraction for her.

The lesson was finished, the books were put away, at last the class was dismissed. And still Hermione sat at the table, with her chin in her hand, her elbow on the table, her long white face pushed up, not attending to anything. Birkin had gone to the window, and was looking from the brilliantly-lighted room on to the grey, colourless outside, where rain was noiselessly falling. Ursula put away her things in the cupboard.

At length Hermione rose and came near to her.

'Your sister has come home?' she said.

'Yes,' said Ursula.

'And does she like being back in Beldover?'

'No,' said Ursula.

'No, I wonder she can bear it. It takes all my strength, to bear the ugliness of this district, when I stay here. Won't you come and see me? Won't you come with your sister to stay at Breadalby for a few days? – do—'

'Thank you very much,' said Ursula.

'Then I will write to you,' said Hermione. 'You think your sister will come? I should be so glad. I think she is wonderful. I think some of her work is really wonderful. I have two water-wagtails, carved in wood, and painted – perhaps you have seen it?'

'No,' said Ursula.

'I think it is perfectly wonderful – like a flash of instinct—'

'Her little carvings *are* strange,' said Ursula.

'Perfectly beautiful – full of primitive passion—'

'Isn't it queer that she always likes little things? – she must always work small things, that one can put between one's hands, birds and tiny animals. She likes to look through the wrong end of the opera-glasses, and see the world that way – why is it, do you think?'

Hermione looked down at Ursula with that long, detached scrutinising gaze that excited the younger woman.

'Yes,' said Hermione at length. 'It is curious. The little things seem to be more subtle to her—'

'But they aren't, are they? A mouse isn't any more subtle than a lion, is it?'

Again Hermione looked down at Ursula with that long scrutiny, as if she were following some train of thought of her own, and barely attending to the other's speech.

'I don't know,' she replied.

'Rupert, Rupert,' she sang mildly, calling him to her. He approached in silence.

'Are little things more subtle than big things?' she asked, with the odd grunt of laughter in her voice, as if she were making game of him in the question.

'Dunno,' he said.

'I hate subtleties,' said Ursula.

Hermione looked at her slowly.

'Do you?' she said.

'I always think they are a sign of weakness,' said Ursula, up in arms, as if her prestige were threatened.

Hermione took no notice. Suddenly her face puckered, her brow was knit with thought, she seemed twisted in troublesome effort for utterance.

'Do you really think, Rupert,' she asked, as if Ursula were not present, 'do you really think it is worth while? Do you really think the children are better for being roused to consciousness?'

A dark flash went over his face, a silent fury. He was hollow-cheeked and pale, almost unearthly. And the woman, with her serious, conscience-harrowing question tortured him on the quick.

'They are not roused to consciousness,' he said. 'Consciousness comes to them, willy-nilly.'

'But do you think they are better for having it quickened, stimulated? Isn't it better that they should remain unconscious of the hazel, isn't it better that they should see as a whole, without all this pulling to pieces, all this knowledge?'

'Would you rather, for yourself, know or not know, that the little red flowers are there, putting out for the pollen?' he asked harshly. His voice was brutal, scornful, cruel.

Hermione remained with her face lifted up, abstracted. He hung silent in irritation.

'I don't know,' she replied, balancing mildly. 'I don't know.'

'But knowing is everything to you, it is all your life,' he broke out. She slowly looked at him.

'Is it?' she said.

'To know, that is your all, that is your life – you have only this, this knowledge,' he cried. 'There is only one tree, there is only one fruit, in your mouth.'

Again she was some time silent.

'Is there?' she said at last, with the same untouched calm. And then in a tone of whimsical inquisitiveness: 'What fruit, Rupert?'

'The eternal apple,' he replied in exasperation, hating his own metaphors.

'Yes,' she said. There was a look of exhaustion about her. For some moments there was silence. Then, pulling herself together with a convulsed movement, Hermione resumed, in a sing-song, casual voice.

'But leaving me apart, Rupert; do you think the children are better, richer, happier, for all this knowledge; do you really think they are? Or is it better to leave them untouched, spontaneous. Hadn't they better be animals, simple animals, crude, violent, *anything*, rather than this self-consciousness, this incapacity to be spontaneous.'

They thought she had finished. But with a queer rumbling in her throat she resumed, 'Hadn't they better be anything than grow up crippled, crippled in their souls, crippled in their feelings – so thrown back – so turned back on themselves – incapable—' Hermione clenched her fist like one in a trance – 'of any spontaneous action, always deliberate, always burdened with choice, never carried away.'

Again they thought she had finished. But just as he was going to reply, she resumed her queer rhapsody – 'never carried away, out of themselves, always conscious, always self-conscious, always aware of themselves. Isn't *anything* better than this? Better be animals, mere animals with no mind at all, than this, this *nothingness*—'

'But do you think it is knowledge that makes us unliving and self-conscious?' he asked irritably.

She opened her eyes and looked at him slowly.

'Yes,' she said. She paused, watching him all the while, her eyes vague. Then she wiped her fingers across her brow, with a vague weariness. It irritated him bitterly. 'It is the mind,' she said, 'and that is death.' She raised her eyes slowly to him: 'Isn't the mind—' she said, with the convulsed movement of her body, 'isn't it our death? Doesn't it destroy all our spontaneity, all our instincts? Are not the young people growing up to-day, really dead before they have a chance to live?'

'Not because they have too much mind, but too little,' he said brutally.

'Are you *sure?*' she cried. 'It seems to me the reverse. They are over-conscious, burdened to death with consciousness.'

'Imprisoned within a limited, false set of concepts,' he cried.

But she took no notice of this, only went on with her own rhapsodic interrogation.

'When we have knowledge, don't we lose everything but knowledge?' she asked pathetically. 'If I know about the flower, don't I lose the flower and have only the knowledge? Aren't we exchanging the substance for the shadow, aren't we forfeiting life for this dead quality of knowledge? And what does it mean to me after all? What does all this knowing mean to me? It means nothing.'

'You are merely making words,' he said; 'knowledge means everything to you. Even your animalism, you want it in your head. You don't want to *be* an animal, you want to observe your own animal functions, to get a mental thrill out of them. It is all purely secondary – and more decadent than the most hide-bound intellectualism. What is it but the worst and last form of intellectualism, this love of yours for passion and the animal instincts? Passion and the instincts – you want them hard enough, but through your head, in your consciousness. It all takes place in your head, under that skull of yours. Only you won't be conscious of what *actually* is: you want the lie that will match the rest of your furniture.'

Hermione set hard and poisonous against this attack. Ursula stood covered with wonder and shame. It frightened her, to see how they hated each other.

'It's all that Lady of Shalott business,' he said, in his strong abstract voice.

He seemed to be charging her before the unseeing air. 'You've got that mirror, your own fixed will, your immortal understanding, your own tight conscious world, and there is nothing beyond it. There, in the mirror, you must have everything. But now you have come to all your conclusions, you want to go back and be like a savage, without knowledge. You want a life of pure sensation and "passion".'

He quoted the last word satirically against her. She sat convulsed with fury and violation, speechless, like a stricken pythoness of the Greek oracle.

'But your passion is a lie,' he went on violently. 'It isn't passion at all, it is your *will*. It's your bullying will. You want to clutch things and have them in your power. You want to have things in your power. And why? Because you haven't got any real body, any dark sensual body of life. You have no sensuality. You have only your will and your conceit of consciousness, and your lust for power, to *know*.'

He looked at her in mingled hate and contempt, also in pain because she suffered, and in shame because he knew he tortured her. He had an impulse to kneel and plead for forgiveness. But a bitterer red anger burned up to fury in him. He became unconscious of her, he was only a passionate voice speaking.

'Spontaneous!' he cried. 'You and spontaneity! You, the most deliberate thing that ever walked or crawled! You'd be verily deliberately spontaneous – that's you. Because you want to have everything in your own volition, your deliberate voluntary consciousness. You want it all in that loathsome little skull of yours, that ought to be cracked like a nut. For you'll be the same till it *is* cracked, like an insect in its skin. If one cracked your skull perhaps one might get a spontaneous, passionate woman out of you, with real sensuality. As it is, what you want is pornography – looking at yourself in mirrors, watching your naked animal actions in mirrors, so that you can have it all in your consciousness, make it all mental.'

There was a sense of violation in the air, as if too much was said, the unforgivable. Yet Ursula was concerned now only with solving her own problems, in the light of his words. She was pale and abstracted.

'But do you really *want* sensuality?' she asked puzzled.

Birkin looked at her, and became intent in his explanation.

'Yes,' he said, 'that and nothing else, at this point. It is a fulfilment – the great dark knowledge you can't have in your head – the dark involuntary being. It is death to one's self – but it is the coming into being of another.'

'But how? How can you have knowledge not in your head?' she asked, quite unable to interpret his phrases.

'In the blood,' he answered; 'when the mind and the known world is drowned in darkness – everything must go – there must be the deluge. Then you find yourself in a palpable body of darkness, a demon—'

'But why should I be a demon—?' she asked.

' "*Woman wailing for her demon lover*"—' he quoted – 'why, I don't know.'

Hermione roused herself as from a death – annihilation.

'He is such a *dreadful* satanist, isn't he?' she drawled to Ursula, in a queer resonant voice, that ended in a shrill little laugh of pure ridicule. The two women were jeering at him, jeering him into nothingness. The laugh of the shrill, triumphant female sounded from Hermione, jeering him as if he were a neuter.

'No,' he said. 'You are the real devil who won't let life exist.'

She looked at him with a long, slow look, malevolent, supercilious.

'You know all about it, don't you?' she said, with slow, cold, cunning mockery.

'Enough,' he replied, his face fixing fine and clear like steel. A horrible despair, and at the same time a sense of release, liberation, came over Hermione. She turned with a pleasant intimacy to Ursula.

'You are sure you will come to Breadalby?' she said, urging.

'Yes, I should like to very much,' replied Ursula.

Hermione looked down at her, gratified, reflecting, and strangely absent, as if possessed, as if not quite there.

'I'm so glad,' she said, pulling herself together. 'Some time in about a fortnight. Yes? I will write to you here, at the school, shall I? Yes. And you'll be sure to come? Yes. I shall be so glad. Good-bye! Good-bye!'

Hermione held out her hand and looked into the eyes of the other woman. She knew Ursula as an immediate rival, and the knowledge strangely exhilarated her. Also she was taking leave. It always gave her a sense of strength, advantage, to be departing and leaving the other behind. Moreover she was taking the man with her, if only in hate.

Birkin stood aside, fixed and unreal. But now, when it was his turn to bid good-bye, he began to speak again.

'There's the whole difference in the world,' he said, 'between the actual sensual being and the vicious mental-deliberate profligacy our lot goes in for. In our night-time, there's always the electricity switched on, we watch ourselves, we get it all in the head, really. You've got to lapse out before you can know what sensual reality is, lapse into unknowingness, and give up your volition. You've got to do it. You've got to learn not-to-be, before you can come into being.

'But we have got such a conceit of ourselves – that's where it is. We are so conceited, and so unproud. We've got no pride, we're all conceit, so conceited in our own papier-mâché realised selves. We'd rather die than give up our little self-righteous self-opinionated self-will.'

There was silence in the room. Both women were hostile and resentful. He sounded as if he were addressing a meeting. Hermione merely paid no attention, stood with her shoulders tight in a shrug of dislike.

Ursula was watching him as if furtively, not really aware of what she was seeing. There was a great physical attractiveness in him – a curious hidden richness, that came through his thinness and his pallor like another voice, conveying another knowledge of him. It was in the curves of his brows and his chin, rich, fine, exquisite curves, the powerful beauty of life itself. She could not say what it was. But there was a sense of richness and of liberty.

'But we are sensual enough, without making ourselves so, aren't we?' she asked, turning to him with a certain golden laughter flickering under her greenish eyes, like a challenge. And immediately the queer, careless, terribly attractive smile came over his eyes and brows, though his mouth did not relax.

'No,' he said, 'we aren't. We're too full of ourselves.'

'Surely it isn't a matter of conceit,' she cried.

'That and nothing else.'

She was frankly puzzled.

'Don't you think that people are most conceited of all about their sensual powers?' she asked.

'That's why they aren't sensual – only sensuous – which is another matter. They're *always* aware of themselves – and they're so conceited, that rather than release themselves, and live in another world, from another centre, they'd—'

'You want your tea, don't you,' said Hermione, turning to Ursula with a gracious kindliness. 'You've worked all day—'

Birkin stopped short. A spasm of anger and chagrin went over Ursula. His face set. And he bade good-bye, as if he had ceased to notice her.

They were gone. Ursula stood looking at the door for some moments. Then she put out the lights. And having done so, she sat down again in her chair, absorbed and lost. And then she began to cry, bitterly, bitterly weeping: but whether for misery or joy, she never knew.

Chapter Four

Diver

The week passed away. On the Saturday it rained, a soft drizzling rain that held off at times. In one of the intervals Gudrun and Ursula set out for a walk, going towards Willey Water. The atmosphere was grey and translucent, the birds sang sharply on the young twigs, the earth would be quickening and hastening in growth. The two girls walked swiftly, gladly, because of the soft, subtle rush of morning that filled the wet haze. By the road the blackthorn was in blossom, white and wet, its tiny amber grains burning faintly in the white smoke of blossom. Purple twigs were darkly luminous in the grey air, high hedges glowed like living shadows, hovering nearer, coming into creation. The morning was full of a new creation.

When the sisters came to Willey Water, the lake lay all grey and visionary, stretching into the moist, translucent vista of trees and meadow. Fine electric activity in sound came from the dumbles below the road, the birds piping one against the other, and water mysteriously plashing, issuing from the lake.

The two girls drifted swiftly along. In front of them, at the corner of the lake, near the road, was a mossy boat-house under a walnut tree, and a little landing-stage where a boat was moored, wavering like a shadow on the still grey water, below the green, decayed poles. All was shadowy with coming summer.

Suddenly, from the boat-house, a white figure ran out, frightening in its swift sharp transit, across the old landing-stage. It launched in a white arc through the air, there was a bursting of the water, and among the smooth ripples a swimmer was making out to space, in a centre of faintly heaving motion. The whole otherworld, wet and remote, he had to himself. He could move into the pure translucency of the grey, uncreated water.

Gudrun stood by the stone wall, watching.

'How I envy him,' she said, in low, desirous tones.

'Ugh!' shivered Ursula. 'So cold!'

'Yes, but how good, how really fine, to swim out there!' The sisters stood watching the swimmer move farther into the grey, moist, full space of the water, pulsing with his own small, invading motion, and arched over with mist and dim woods.

'Don't you wish it were you?' asked Gudrun, looking at Ursula.

'I do,' said Ursula. 'But I'm not sure – it's so wet.'

'No,' said Gudrun, reluctantly. She stood watching the motion on the bosom of the water, as if fascinated. He, having swum a certain distance, turned round and was swimming on his back, looking along the water at the two girls by the wall. In the faint wash of motion, they could see his ruddy face, and could feel him watching them.

'It is Gerald Crich,' said Ursula.

'I know,' replied Gudrun.

And she stood motionless gazing over the water at the face which washed up and down on the flood, as he swam steadily. From his separate element he saw them and he exulted to himself because of his own advantage, his possession of a world to himself. He was immune and perfect. He loved his own vigorous, thrusting motion, and the violent impulse of the very cold water against his limbs, buoying him up. He could see the girls watching him a way off, outside, and that pleased him. He lifted his arm from the water, in a sign to them.

'He is waving,' said Ursula.

'Yes,' replied Gudrun. They watched him. He waved again, with a strange movement of recognition across the difference.

'Like a Nibelung,' laughed Ursula. Gudrun said nothing, only stood still looking over the water.

Gerald suddenly turned, and was swimming away swiftly, with a side stroke. He was alone now, alone and immune in the middle of the waters, which he had all to himself. He exulted in his isolation in the new element, unquestioned and unconditioned. He was happy, thrusting with his legs and all his body, without bond or connection anywhere, just himself in the watery world.

Gudrun envied him almost painfully. Even this momentary possession of pure isolation and fluidity seemed to her so terribly desirable that she felt herself as if damned, out there on the high-road.

'God, what it is to be a man!' she cried.

'What?' exclaimed Ursula in surprise.

'The freedom, the liberty, the mobility!' cried Gudrun, strangely flushed and brilliant. 'You're a man, you want to do a thing, you do it. You haven't the *thousand* obstacles a woman has in front of her.'

Ursula wondered what was in Gudrun's mind, to occasion this outburst. She could not understand.

'What do you want to do?' she asked.

'Nothing,' cried Gudrun, in swift refutation. 'But supposing I did. Supposing I want to swim up that water. It is impossible, it is one of the impossibilities of life, for me to take my clothes off now and jump in. But isn't it *ridiculous*, doesn't it simply prevent our living!'

She was so hot, so flushed, so furious, that Ursula was puzzled.

The two sisters went on, up the road. They were passing between the trees just below Shortlands. They looked up at the long, low house, dim and glamorous in the wet morning, its cedar trees slanting before the windows. Gudrun seemed to be studying it closely.

'Don't you think it's attractive, Ursula?' asked Gudrun.

'Very,' said Ursula. 'Very peaceful and charming.'

'It has form, too – it has a period.'

'What period?'

'Oh, eighteenth century, for certain; Dorothy Wordsworth and Jane Austen, don't you think?'

Ursula laughed.

'Don't you think so?' repeated Gudrun.

'Perhaps. But I don't think the Criches fit the period. I know Gerald is putting in a private electric plant, for lighting the house, and is making all kinds of latest improvements.'

Gudrun shrugged her shoulders swiftly.

'Of course,' she said, 'that's quite inevitable.'

'Quite,' laughed Ursula. 'He is several generations of youngness at one go. They hate him for it. He takes them all by the scruff of the neck, and fairly flings them along. He'll have to die soon, when he's made every possible improvement, and there will be nothing more to improve. He's got *go*, anyhow.'

'Certainly, he's got go,' said Gudrun. 'In fact I've never seen a man that showed signs of so much. The unfortunate thing is, where does his *go* go to, what becomes of it?'

'Oh I know,' said Ursula. 'It goes in applying the latest appliances!'

'Exactly,' said Gudrun.

'You know he shot his brother?' said Ursula.

'Shot his brother?' cried Gudrun, frowning as if in disapprobation.

'Didn't you know? Oh yes! – I thought you knew. He and his brother were playing together with a gun. He told his brother to look down the gun, and it was loaded, and blew the top of his head off. Isn't it a horrible story?'

'How fearful!' cried Gudrun. 'But it is long ago?'

'Oh yes, they were quite boys,' said Ursula. 'I think it is one of the most horrible stories I know.'

'And he of course did not know that the gun was loaded?'

'Yes. You see it was an old thing that had been lying in the stable for years. Nobody dreamed it would ever go off, and of course, no one imagined it was loaded. But isn't it dreadful, that it should happen?'

'Frightful!' cried Gudrun. 'And isn't it horrible too to think of such a thing happening to one when one was a child, and having to carry the responsibility of it all through one's life. Imagine it, two boys playing together – then this comes upon them, for no reason whatever – out of the air. Ursula, it's very frightening! Oh, it's one. of the things I can't bear. Murder, that is thinkable, because there's a will behind it. But a thing like that to *happen* to one—'

'Perhaps there *was* an unconscious will behind it,' said Ursula. 'This playing at killing has some primitive *desire* for killing in it, don't you think?'

'Desire!' said Gudrun, coldly, stiffening a little. 'I can't see that they were even playing at killing. I suppose one boy said to the other, 'You look down the barrel while I pull the trigger, and see what happens.' It seems to me the purest form of accident.'

'No,' said Ursula. 'I couldn't pull the trigger of the emptiest gun in the world, not if someone were looking down the barrel. One instinctively doesn't do it – one can't.'

Gudrun was silent for some moments, in sharp disagreement.

'Of course,' she said coldly. 'If one is a woman, and grown up, one's instinct prevents one. But I cannot see how that applies to a couple of boys playing together.'

Her voice was cold and angry.

'Yes,' persisted Ursula. At that moment they heard a woman's voice a few yards off say loudly:

'Oh damn the thing!' They went forward and saw Laura Crich and Hermione Roddice in the field on the other side of the hedge, and Laura Crich struggling with the gate, to get out. Ursula at once hurried up and helped to lift the gate.

'Thanks so much,' said Laura, looking up flushed and amazon-like, yet rather confused. 'It isn't right on the hinges.'

'No,' said Ursula. 'And they're so heavy.'

'Surprising!' cried Laura.

'How do you do,' sang Hermione, from out of the field, the moment she could make her voice heard. 'It's nice now. Are you going for a walk? Yes. Isn't the young green beautiful? So beautiful – quite burning. Good morning – good morning – you'll come and see me? thank you so much – next week – yes – good-bye, g-o-o-d-b-y-e.'

Gudrun and Ursula stood and watched her slowly waving her head up and down, and waving her hand slowly in dismissal, smiling a strange affected smile, making a tall queer, frightening figure, with her heavy fair hair slipping to her eyes. Then they moved off, as if they had been dismissed like inferiors. The four women parted.

As soon as they had gone far enough, Ursula said, her cheeks burning:

'I do think she's impudent.'

'Who, Hermione Roddice?' asked Gudrun. 'Why?'

'The way she treats one – impudence!'

'Why, Ursula, what did you notice that was so impudent?' asked Gudrun rather coldly.

'Her whole manner. Oh, it's impossible, the way she tries to bully one. Pure bullying. She's an impudent woman. "You'll come and see me," as if we should be falling over ourselves for the privilege.'

'I can't understand, Ursula, what you are so much put out about,' said Gudrun, in some exasperation. 'One knows those women are impudent – these free woman who have emancipated themselves from the aristocracy.'

'But it is so *unnecessary* – so vulgar,' cried Ursula.

'No, I don't see it. And if I did – *pour moi elle n'existe pas*. I don't grant her the power to be impudent to me.'

'Do you think she likes you?' asked Ursula.

'Well, no, I shouldn't think she did.'

'Then why does she ask you to go to Breadalby and stay with her?'

Gudrun lifted her shoulders in a low shrug.

'After all, she's got the sense to know we're not just the ordinary run,' said Gudrun. 'Whatever she is, she's not a fool. And I'd rather have somebody I detested than the ordinary woman who keeps to her own set. Hermione Roddice does risk herself in some respects.'

Ursula pondered this for a time.

'I doubt it,' she replied. 'Really she risks nothing. I suppose we ought to admire her for knowing she *can* invite us – school teachers – and risk nothing.'

'Precisely!' said Gudrun. 'Think of the myriads of women that daren't do it. She makes the most of her privileges – that's something. I suppose, really, we should do the same, in her place.'

'No,' said Ursula. 'No. It would bore me. I couldn't spend my time playing her games. It's infra dig.'

The two sisters were like a pair of scissors, snipping off everything that came athwart them; or like a knife and a whetstone, the one sharpened against the other.

'Of course,' cried Ursula suddenly, 'she ought to thank her stars if we will go and see her. You are perfectly beautiful, a thousand times more beautiful than ever she is or was, and to my thinking, a thousand times more beautifully dressed, for she never looks fresh and natural, like a flower, always old, thought-out; and we are more intelligent than most people.'

'Undoubtedly!' said Gudrun.

'And it ought to be admitted, simply,' said Ursula.

'Certainly it ought,' said Gudrun. 'But you'll find that the really chic thing is to be so absolutely ordinary, so perfectly commonplace and like the person in the street, that you really are a masterpiece of humanity, not the person in the street actually, but the artistic creation of her—'

'How awful!' cried Ursula.

'Yes, Ursula, it *is* awful, in most respects. You daren't be anything that isn't amazingly *à terre*, so much *à terre* that it is the artistic creation of ordinariness.'

'It's very dull to create oneself into nothing better,' laughed Ursula.

'Very dull!' retorted Gudrun. 'Really, Ursula, it *is* dull, that's just the word. One longs to be high-flown, and make speeches like Corneille, after it.'

Gudrun was becoming flushed and excited over her own cleverness.

'Strut,' said Ursula. 'One wants to strut, to be a swan among geese.'

'Exactly,' cried Gudrun, 'a swan among geese.'

'They are all so busy playing the ugly duckling,' cried Ursula, with mocking laughter. 'And I don't feel a bit like a humble and pathetic ugly duckling. I do feel like a swan among geese – I can't help it. They make one feel so. And I don't care what *they* think of me. *Je m'en fiche.*'

Gudrun looked up at Ursula with a queer, uncertain envy and dislike.

'Of course, the only thing to do is to despise them all – just all,' she said.

The sisters went home again, to read and talk and work, and wait for Monday, for school. Ursula often wondered what else she waited for, besides the beginning and end of the school week, and the beginning and end of the holidays. This was a whole life! Sometimes she had periods of tight horror, when it seemed to her that her life would pass away and be gone, without having been more than this. But she never really accepted it. Her spirit was active, her life like a shoot that is growing steadily, but which has not yet come above ground.

Chapter Five

In the Train

One day at this time Birkin was called to London. He was not very fixed in his abode. He had rooms in Nottingham, because his work lay chiefly in that town. But often he was in London, or in Oxford. He moved about a great deal, his life seemed uncertain, without any definite rhythm, any organic meaning.

On the platform of the railway station he saw Gerald Crich, reading a newspaper, and evidently waiting for the train. Birkin stood some distance off, among the people. It was against his instinct to approach anybody.

From time to time, in a manner characteristic of him, Gerald lifted his head and looked round. Even though he was reading the newspaper closely, he must keep a watchful eye on his external surroundings. There seemed to be a dual consciousness running in him. He was thinking vigorously of something he read in the newspaper, and at the same time his eye ran over the surfaces of the life round him, and he missed nothing. Birkin, who was watching him, was irritated by his duality. He noticed too, that Gerald seemed always to be at bay against everybody, in spite of his queer, genial, social manner when roused.

Now Birkin started violently at seeing this genial look flash on to Gerald's face, at seeing Gerald approaching with hand outstretched.

'Hallo, Rupert, where are you going?'

'London. So are you, I suppose.'

'Yes—'

Gerald's eyes went over Birkin's face in curiosity.

'We'll travel together if you like,' he said.

'Don't you usually go first?' asked Birkin.

'I can't stand the crowd,' replied Gerald. 'But third'll be all right. There's a restaurant car, we can have some tea.'

The two men looked at the station clock, having nothing further to say.

'What were you reading in the paper?' Birkin asked.

Gerald looked at him quickly.

'Isn't it funny, what they *do* put in the newspapers,' he said. 'Here are two leaders—' he held out his *Daily Telegraph*, 'full of the ordinary newspaper cant—' he scanned the columns down – 'and then there's this little – I dunno what you'd call it, essay, almost – appearing with the leaders, and saying there must arise a man who will give new values to things, give us new truths, a new attitude to life, or else we shall be a crumbling nothingness in a few years, a country in ruin—'

'I suppose that's a bit of newspaper cant, as well,' said Birkin.

'It sounds as if the man meant it, and quite genuinely,' said Gerald.

'Give it to me,' said Birkin, holding out his hand for the paper.

The train came, and they went on board, sitting on either side of a little table, by the window, in the restaurant car. Birkin glanced over his paper, then looked up at Gerald, who was waiting for him.

'I believe the man means it,' he said, 'as far as he means anything.'

'And do you think it's true? Do you think we really want a new gospel?' asked Gerald.

Birkin shrugged his shoulders.

'I think the people who say they want a new religion are the last to accept anything new. They want novelty right enough. But to stare straight at this life that we've brought upon ourselves and rejected, absolutely smash up the old idols of ourselves, that we sh'll never do. You've got very badly to want to get rid of the old before anything new will appear – even in the self.'

Gerald watched him closely.

'You think we ought to break up this life, just start and let fly?' he asked.

'This life. Yes I do. We've got to bust it completely, or shrivel inside it, as in a tight skin. For it won't expand any more.'

There was a queer little smile in Gerald's eyes, a look of amusement, calm and curious.

'And how do you propose to begin? I suppose you mean, reform the whole order of society?' he asked.

Birkin had a slight, tense frown between the brows. He too was impatient of the conversation.

'I don't propose at all,' he replied. 'When we really want to go for something better, we shall smash up the old. Until then, any sort of proposal, or making proposals, is no more than a tiresome game for self-important people.'

The little smile began to die out of Gerald's eyes, and he said, looking with a cool stare at Birkin:

'So you really think things are very bad?'

'Completely bad.'

The smile appeared again.

'In what way?'

'Every way,' said Birkin. 'We are such dreary liars. Our one idea is to lie to ourselves. We have an ideal of a perfect world, clean and straight and sufficient. So we cover the earth with foulness; life is a blotch of labour, like insects scurrying in filth, so that your collier can have a pianoforte in his parlour, and you can have a butler and a motor-car in your up-to-date house, and as a nation we can sport the Ritz, or the Empire, Gaby Deslys and the Sunday newspapers. It is very dreary.'

Gerald took a little time to re-adjust himself after this tirade.

'Would you have us live without houses – return to nature?' he asked.

'I would have nothing at all. People only do what they want to do – and what they are capable of doing. If they were capable of anything else, there would be something else.'

Again Gerald pondered. He was not going to take offence at Birkin.

'Don't you think the collier's *pianoforte*, as you call it, is a symbol for something very real, a real desire for something higher, in the collier's life?'

'Higher!' cried Birkin. 'Yes. Amazing heights of upright grandeur. It makes him so much higher in his neighbouring collier's eyes. He sees himself reflected in the neighbouring opinion, like in a Brocken mist, several feet taller on the strength of the pianoforte, and he is satisfied. He lives for the sake of that Brocken spectre, the reflection of himself in the human opinion. You do the same. If you are of high importance to humanity you are of high importance to yourself. That is why you work so hard at the mines. If you can produce coal to cook five thousand dinners a day, you are five thousand times more important than if you cooked only your own dinner.'

'I suppose I am,' laughed Gerald.

'Can't you see,' said Birkin, 'That to help my neighbour to eat is no more than eating myself. "I eat, thou eatest, he eats, we eat, you eat, they eat" – and what then? Why should every man decline the whole verb. First person singular is enough for me.'

'You've got to start with material things,' said Gerald. Which statement Birkin ignored.

'And we've got to live for *something*, we're not just cattle that can graze and have done with it,' said Gerald.

'Tell me,' said Birkin. 'What do you live for?'

Gerald's face went baffled.

'What do I live for?' he repeated. 'I suppose I live to work, to produce something, in so far as I am a purposive being. Apart from that, I live because I am living.'

'And what's your work? Getting so many more thousands of tons of coal out of the earth every day. And when we've got all the coal we want, and all the plush furniture, and pianofortes, and the rabbits are all stewed and eaten, and we're all warm and our bellies are filled and we're listening to the young lady performing on the pianoforte – what then? What then, when you've made a real fair start with your material things?'

Gerald sat laughing at the words and the mocking humour of the other man. But he was cogitating too.

'We haven't got there yet,' he replied. 'A good many people are still waiting for the rabbit and the fire to cook it.'

'So while you get the coal I must chase the rabbit?' said Birkin, mocking at Gerald.

'Something like that,' said Gerald.

Birkin watched him narrowly. He saw the perfect good-humoured callousness, even strange, glistening malice, in Gerald, glistening through the plausible ethics of productivity.

'Gerald,' he said, 'I rather hate you.'

'I know you do,' said Gerald. 'Why do you?'

Birkin mused inscrutably for some minutes.

'I should like to know if you are conscious of hating me,' he said at last. 'Do you ever consciously detest me – hate me with mystic hate? There are odd moments when I hate you starrily.'

Gerald was rather taken aback, even a little disconcerted. He did not quite know v. hat to say.

'I may, of course, hate you sometimes,' he said. 'But I'm not aware of it – never acutely aware of it, that is.'

'So much the worse,' said Birkin.

Gerald watched him with curious eyes. He could not quite make him out.

'So much the worse, is it?' he repeated.

There was a silence between the two men for some time, as the train ran on. In Birkin's face was a little irritable tension, a sharp knitting of the brows, keen and difficult. Gerald watched him warily, carefully, rather calculatingly, for he could not decide what he was after.

Suddenly Birkin's eyes looked straight and overpowering into those of the other man.

'What do you think is the aim and object of your life, Gerald?' he asked.

Again Gerald was taken aback. He could not think what his friend was getting at. Was he poking fun, or not?

'At this moment, I couldn't say off-hand,' he replied, with faintly ironic humour.

'Do you think to live is the be-all and the end-all of life?' Birkin asked, with direct, attentive seriousness.

'Of my own life?' said Gerald.

'Yes.'

There was a really puzzled pause.

'I can't say,' said Gerald. 'It hasn't been, so far.'

'What has your life been, so far?'

'Oh – finding out things for myself – and getting experiences – and making things *go*.'

Birkin knitted his brows like sharply moulded steel.

'I find,' he said, 'that one needs some one *really* pure single activity – I should call love a single pure activity. But I *don't* really love anybody – not now.'

'Have you ever really loved anybody?' asked Gerald.

'Yes and no,' replied Birkin.

'Not finally?' said Gerald.

'Finally – finally – no,' said Birkin.

'Nor I,' said Gerald.

'And do you want to?' said Birkin.

Gerald looked with a long, twinkling, almost sardonic look into the eyes of the other man.

'I don't know,' he said.

'I do – I want to love,' said Birkin.

'You do?'

'Yes. I want the finality of love.'

'The finality of love,' repeated Gerald. And he waited for a moment.

'Just one woman?' he added. The evening light, flooding yellow along the fields, lit up Birkin's face with a tense, abstract steadfastness. Gerald still could not make it out.

'Yes, one woman,' said Birkin.

But to Gerald it sounded as if he were insistent rather than confident.

'I don't believe a woman, and nothing but a woman, will ever make my life,' said Gerald.

'Not the centre and core of it – the love between you and a woman?' asked Birkin.

Gerald's eyes narrowed with a queer dangerous smile as he watched the other man.

'I never quite feel it that way,' he said.

'You don't? Then wherein does life centre, for you?'

'I don't know – that's what I want somebody to tell me. As far as I can make out, it doesn't centre at all. It is artificially held *together* by the social mechanism.'

Birkin pondered as if he would crack something.

'I know,' he said, 'it just doesn't centre. The old ideals are dead as nails – nothing there. It seems to me there remains only this perfect union with a woman – sort of ultimate marriage – and there isn't anything else.'

'And you mean if there isn't the woman, there's nothing?' said Gerald.

'Pretty well that – seeing there's no God.'

'Then we're hard put to it,' said Gerald. And he turned to look out of the window at the flying, golden landscape.

Birkin could not help seeing how beautiful and soldierly his face was, with a certain courage to be indifferent.

'You think it's heavy odds against us?' said Birkin.

'If we've got to make our life up out of a woman, one woman, woman only, yes, I do,' said Gerald. 'I don't believe I shall ever make up *my* life, at that rate.'

Birkin watched him almost angrily.

'You are a born unbeliever,' he said.

'I only feel what I feel,' said Gerald. And he looked again at Birkin almost sardonically, with his blue, manly, sharp-lighted eyes. Birkin's eyes were at the moment full of anger. But swiftly they became troubled, doubtful, then full of a warm, rich affectionateness and laughter.

'It troubles me very much, Gerald,' he said, wrinkling his brows.

'I can see it does,' said Gerald, uncovering his mouth in a manly, quick, soldierly laugh.

Gerald was held unconsciously by the other man. He wanted to be near him, he wanted to be within his sphere of influence. There was something very congenial to him in Birkin. But yet, beyond this, he did not take much notice. He felt that he, himself, Gerald, had harder and more durable truths than any the other man knew. He felt himself older, more knowing. It was the quick-changing warmth and vitality and brilliant warm utterance he loved in his friend. It was the rich play of words and quick interchange of feelings he enjoyed. The real content of the words he never really considered: he himself knew better.

Birkin knew this. He knew that Gerald wanted to be *fond* of him without taking him seriously. And this made him go hard and cold. As the train ran on, he sat looking at the land, and Gerald fell away, became as nothing to him.

Birkin looked at the land, at the evening, and was thinking: 'Well, if mankind is destroyed, if our race is destroyed like Sodom, and there is this beautiful evening with the luminous land and trees, I am satisfied. That which informs it all is there, and can never be lost. After all, what is mankind but just one expression of the incomprehensible? And if mankind passes away, it will only mean that this particular expression is completed and done. That which is expressed, and that which is to be expressed, cannot be diminished. There it is, in the shining evening. Let mankind pass away – time it did. The creative utterances will not cease, they will only be there. Humanity doesn't embody the utterance of the incomprehensible any more. Humanity is a dead letter. There will be a new embodiment, in a new way. Let humanity disappear as quick as possible.'

Gerald interrupted him by asking:

'Where are you staying in London?'

Birkin looked up.

'With a man in Soho. I pay part of the rent of a house, and stop there when I like.'

'Good idea – have a place more or less your own,' said Gerald.

'Yes. But I don't care for it much. I'm tired of the people I am bound to find there.'

'What kind of people?'

'Art – music – London Bohemia – the most pettifogging calculating Bohemia that ever reckoned its pennies. But there are a few decent people, decent in some respects. They are really very thorough rejecters of the world – perhaps they live only in the gesture of rejection and negation – but negatively something, at any rate.'

'What are they? – painters, musicians?'

'Painters, musicians, writers – hangers-on, models, advanced young people, anybody who is openly at outs with the conventions, and belongs to nowhere particularly. They are often young fellows down from the University, and girls who are living their own lives, as they say.'

'All loose?' said Gerald.

Birken could see his curiosity roused.

'In one way. Most bound, in another. For all their shockingness, all on one note.'

He looked at Gerald, and saw how his blue eyes were lit up with a little flame of curious desire. He saw too how good-looking he was. Gerald was attractive, his blood seemed fluid and electric. His blue eyes burned with a keen, yet cold light, there was a certain beauty, a beautiful passivity in all his body, his moulding.

'We might see something of each other – I am in London for two or three days,' said Gerald.

'Yes,' said Birkin, 'I don't want to go to the theatre, or the music-hall – you'd better come round and see what you can make of Halliday and his crowd.'

'Thanks – I should like to,' laughed Gerald. 'What are you doing to-night.'

'I promised to meet Halliday at the Pompadour. It's a bad place, but there is nowhere else.'

'Where is it?' asked Gerald.

'Piccadilly Circus.'

'Oh yes – well, shall I come round there?'

'By all means, it might amuse you.'

The evening was falling. They had passed Bedford. Birkin watched the country, and was filled with a sort of hopelessness. He always felt this, on approaching London. His dislike of mankind, of the mass of mankind, amounted almost to an illness.

'"Where the quiet coloured end of evening smiles
    Miles and miles—"'

he was murmuring to himself, like a man condemned to death. Gerald, who was very subtly alert, wary in all his senses, leaned forward and asked smilingly:

'What were you saying?' Birkin glanced at him, laughed, and repeated:

'"Where the quiet coloured end of evening smiles,
    Miles and miles,
Over pastures where the something something sheep
    Half asleep—"'

Gerald also looked now at the country. And Birkin, who, for some reason was now tired and dispirited, said to him:

'I always feel doomed when the train is running into London. I feel such a despair, so hopeless, as if it were the end of the world.'

'Really!' said Gerald. 'And does the end of the world frighten you?'

Birkin lifted his shoulders in a slow shrug.

'I don't know,' he said. 'It does while it hangs imminent and doesn't fall. But people give me a bad feeling – very bad.'

There was a roused glad smile in Gerald's eyes.

'Do they?' he said. And he watched the other man critically.

In a few minutes the train was running through the disgrace of outspread London. Everybody in the carriage was on the alert, waiting to escape. At last they were under the huge arch of the station, in the tremendous shadow of the town. Birkin shut himself together – he was in now.

The two men went together in a taxi-cab.

'Don't you feel like one of the damned?' asked Birkin, as they sat in a little, swiftly-running enclosure, and watched the hideous great street.

'No,' laughed Gerald.

'It is real death,' said Birkin.

Chapter Six

Creme de Menthe

They met again in the café several hours later. Gerald went through the push doors into the large, lofty room where the faces and heads of the drinkers showed dimly through the haze of smoke, reflected more dimly, and repeated ad infinitum in the great mirrors on the walls, so that one seemed to enter a vague, dim world of shadowy drinkers humming within an atmosphere of blue tobacco smoke. There was, however, the red plush of the seats to give substance within the bubble of pleasure.

Gerald moved in his slow, observant, glistening-attentive motion down between the tables and the people whose shadowy faces looked up as he passed. He seemed to be entering in some strange element, passing into an illuminated new region, among a host of licentious souls. He was pleased, and entertained. He looked over all the dim, evanescent, strangely illuminated faces that bent across the tables. Then he saw Birkin rise and signal to him.

At Birkin's table was a girl with bobbed, blonde hair cut short in the artist fashion, hanging straight and curving slightly inwards to her ears. She was small and delicately made, with fair colouring and large, innocent, blue eyes. There was a delicacy, almost a floweriness in all her form, and at the same time a certain attractive grossness of spirit, that made a little spark leap instantly alight in Gerald's eyes.

Birkin, who looked muted, unreal, his presence left out, introduced her as Miss Darrington. She gave her hand with a sudden, unwilling movement, looking all the while at Gerald with a dark, exposed stare. A glow came over him as he sat down.

The waiter appeared. Gerald glanced at the glasses of the other two. Birkin was drinking something green, Miss Darrington had a small liqueur glass that was empty save for a tiny drop.

'Won't you have some more—?'

'Brandy,' she said, sipping her last drop and putting down the glass. The waiter disappeared.

'No,' she said to Birkin. 'He doesn't know I'm back. He'll be terwified when he sees me here.'

She spoke her r's like w's, lisping with a slightly babyish pronunciation which was at once affected and true to her character. Her voice was dull and toneless.

'Where is he then?' asked Birkin.

'He's doing a private show at Lady Snellgrove's,' said the girl. 'Warens is there too.'

There was a pause.

'Well, then,' said Birkin, in a dispassionate protective manner, 'what do you intend to do?'

The girl paused sullenly. She hated the question.

'I don't intend to do anything,' she replied. 'I shall look for some sittings to-morrow.'

'Who shall you go to?' asked Birkin.

'I shall go to Bentley's first. But I believe he's angwy with me for running away.'

'That is from the Madonna?'

'Yes. And then if he doesn't want me, I know I can get work with Carmarthen.'

'Carmarthen?'

'Frederick Carmarthen – he does photographs.'

'Chiffon and shoulders—'

'Yes. But he's awfully decent.' There was a pause.

'And what are you going to do about Julius?' he asked.

'Nothing,' she said. 'I shall just ignore him.'

'You've done with him altogether?' But she turned aside her face sullenly, and did not answer the question.

Another young man came hurrying up to the table.

'Hallo, Birkin! Hallo, Minette, when did you come back?' he said eagerly.

'To-day.'

'Does Halliday know?'

'I don't know. I don't care either.'

'Ha-ha! The wind still sits in that quarter, does it? Do you mind if I come over to this table?'

'I'm talking to Wupert, do you mind?' she replied, coolly and yet appealingly, like a child.

'Open confession – good for the soul, eh?' said the young man. 'Well, so long.'

And giving a sharp look at Birkin and at Gerald, the young man moved off, with a swing of his coat skirts.

All this time Gerald had been completely ignored. And yet he felt that the girl was physically aware of his proximity. He waited, listened, and tried to piece together the conversation.

'Are you staying at the house?' the girl asked, of Birkin.

'For three days,' replied Birkin. 'And you?'

'I don't know yet. I can always go to Bertha's.' There was a silence.

Suddenly the girl turned to Gerald, and said, in a rather formal, polite voice, with the distant manner of a woman who accepts her position as a social inferior, yet assumes intimate *camaraderie* with the male she addresses:

'Do you know London well?'

'I can hardly say,' he laughed. 'I've been up a good many times, but I was never in this place before.'

'You're not an artist, then?' she said, in a tone that placed him an outsider.

'No,' he replied.

'He's a soldier, and an explorer, and a Napoleon of industry,' said Birkin, giving Gerald his credentials for Bohemia.

'Are you a soldier?' asked the girl, with a cold yet lively curiosity.

'No, I resigned my commission,' said Gerald, 'some years ago.'

'He was in the last war,' said Birkin.

'Were you really?' said the girl.

'And then he explored the Amazon,' said Birkin, 'and now he is ruling over coal-mines.'

The girl looked at Gerald with steady, calm curiosity. He laughed, hearing himself described. He felt proud too, full of male strength. His blue, keen eyes were lit up with laughter, his ruddy face, with its sharp fair hair, was full of satisfaction, and glowing with life. He piqued her.

'How long are you staying?' she asked him.

'A day or two,' he replied. 'But there is no particular hurry.'

Still she stared into his face with that slow, full gaze which was so curious and so exciting to him. He was acutely and delightfully conscious of himself, of his own attractiveness. He felt full of strength, able to give off a sort of electric power. And he was aware of her blue, exposed-looking eyes upon him. She had beautiful eyes, flower-like, fully opened, naked in their looking at him. And on them there seemed to float a curious iridescence, a sort of film of disintegration, and sullenness, like oil on water. She wore no hat in the heated café, her loose, simple jumper was strung on a string round her neck. But it was made of rich yellow crêpe-de-chine, that hung heavily and softly from her young throat and her slender wrists. Her appearance was simple and complete, really beautiful, because of her regularity and form, her shiny yellow hair falling curved and level on either side of her head, her straight, small, softened features, provoking in the slight fullness of their curves, her slender neck and the simple, rich-coloured smock hanging on her slender shoulders. She was very still, almost null, in her manner, apart and watchful.

She appealed to Gerald strongly. He felt an awful, enjoyable power over her, an instinctive cherishing very near to cruelty. For she was a victim. He felt that she was in his power, and he was generous. The electricity was turgid and voluptuously rich, in his limbs. He would be able to destroy her utterly in the strength of his discharge. But she was waiting in her separation, given.

They talked banalities for some time. Suddenly Birkin said:

'There's Julius!' and he half rose to his feet, motioning to the newcomer. The girl, with a curious, almost evil motion, looked round over her shoulder without moving her body. Gerald watched her fair, close hair swing over her ears. He felt her watching intensely the man who was approaching, so he looked too. He saw a swarthy, slender young man with rather long, solid black hair hanging from under his black hat, moving cumbrously down the room, his face lit up with a smile at once naïve and warm, and vapid. He approached towards Birkin with a haste of welcome.

It was not till he was quite close that he perceived the girl. He recoiled, went green, and said, in a high squealing voice:

'Minette, what are *you* doing here?'

The café looked up like animals when they hear a cry. Halliday hung motionless, an almost imbecile smile flickering palely on his face. The girl only stared at him with an ice-cold look in which flared an unfathomable hell of knowledge, and a certain impotence. She was limited by him.

'Why have you come back?' repeated Halliday, in the same high, hysterical voice. 'I told you not to come back.'

The girl did not answer, only stared in the same ice-blank, heavy fashion, straight at him, as he stood recoiled, as if for safety, against the next table.

'You know you wanted her to come back – come and sit down,' said Birkin to him.

'No, I didn't want her to come back, and I told her not to come back. What have you come for, Minette?'

'For nothing from *you*,' she said in a heavy voice of resentment.

'Then why have you come back at *all*?' cried Halliday, his voice rising to a kind of squeal.

'She comes as she likes,' said Birkin. 'Are you going to sit down, or are you not?'

'No, I won't sit down with Minette,' cried Halliday.

'I won't hurt you, you needn't be afraid,' she said to him, very curtly, and yet with a sort of protectiveness towards him, in her voice.

Halliday came and sat at the table, putting his hand on his heart, and crying:

'Oh, it's given me such a turn! Minette, I wish you wouldn't do these things. Why did you come back?'

'Not for anything from you,' she repeated.

'You've said that before,' he cried in a high voice.

She turned completely away from him, to Gerald Crich, whose eyes were shining with a subtle amusement.

'Were you ever vewy much afwaid of the savages?' she asked in her calm, dull, childish voice.

'No – never very much afraid. On the whole they're harmless – they're not born yet, you can't feel really afraid of them. You know you can manage them.'

'Do you weally? Aren't they very fierce?'

'Not very. There aren't many fierce things, as a matter of fact. There aren't many things, neither people nor animals, that have it in them to be really dangerous.'

'Except in herds,' interrupted Birkin.

'Aren't there really?' she said 'Oh, I thought savages were all so dangerous, they'd have your life before you could look round.'

'Did you?' he laughed. 'They are over-rated, savages. They're too much like other people, not exciting, after the first acquaintance.'

'Oh, it's not so very wonderfully brave then, to be an explorer?'

'No. It's more a question of hardships than of terrors.'

'Oh! And weren't you ever afraid?'

'In my life? I don't know. Yes, I'm afraid of some things – of being shut up, locked up anywhere – or being fastened. I'm afraid of being bound hand and foot.'

She looked at him steadily with her naïve eyes, that rested on him and roused him so deeply, that it left his upper self quite calm. It was rather delicious, to feel her drawing his self-revelations from him, as from the very innermost dark marrow of his body. She wanted to know. And her eyes seemed to be looking through into his naked organism. He felt, she was compelled to him, she was fated to come into contact with him, must have the seeing him and knowing him. And this roused a curious exultance. Also he felt, she must relinquish herself into his hands, and be subject to him. She was so profane, slave-like, watching him, absorbed by him. It was not that she was interested in what he said; she was absorbed by his self-revelation, by *him*, she wanted the secret of him, the experience of his male being.

Gerald's face was lit up with an uncanny smile, full of light and rousedness, yet unconscious. He sat with his arms on the table, his sun-browned, rather sinister hands, that were animal and yet very shapely and attractive, pushed forward towards her. And they fascinated her. And she knew, she watched her own fascination.

Other men had come to the table, to talk with Birkin and Halliday. Gerald said in a low voice, apart, to Minette:

'Where have you come back from?'

'From the country,' replied Minette, in a very low, yet fully resonant voice. Her face closed hard. Continually she glanced at Halliday, and then a flare came over her eyes. The heavy, fair young man ignored her completely; he was really afraid of her. For some moments she would be unaware of Gerald. He had not conquered her yet.

'And what has Halliday to do with it?' he asked, his voice still muted.

She would not answer for some seconds. Then she said, unwillingly:

'He made me go and live with him, and now he wants to throw me over. And yet he won't let me go to anybody else. He wants me to live hidden in the country. And then he says I persecute him, that he can't get rid of me.'

'Doesn't know his own mind,' said Gerald.

'He hasn't any mind, so he can't know it,' she said. 'He waits for what somebody tells him to do. He never does anything he wants to do himself – because he doesn't know what he wants. He's a perfect baby.'

Gerald looked at Halliday for some moments, watching the soft, rather degenerate face of the young man. Its very softness was an attraction; it was a soft, warm nature, into which one might plunge with gratification.

'But he has no hold over you, has he?' Gerald asked.

'You see he *made* me go and live with him, when I didn't want to,' she replied. 'He came and cried to me, tears, you never saw so many, saying *he couldn't* bear it unless I went back to him. And he wouldn't go away, he would have stayed for ever. He made me go back. Then every time he behaves in this fashion. And now I'm going to have a baby, he wants to give me a hundred pounds and send me into the country, so that he would never see me nor hear of me again. But I'm not going to do it, after—'

A queer look came over Gerald's face.

'Are you going to have a child?' he asked incredulous. It seemed, to look at her, impossible, she was so young and so far in spirit from any childbearing.

She looked full into his face, and her blue, inchoate eyes had now a furtive look, and a look of a knowledge of evil, dark and indomitable. A flame ran secretly to his heart.

'Yes,' she said. 'Isn't it beastly?'

'Don't you want it?' he asked.

'I don't,' she replied emphatically.

'But—' he said, 'how long have you known?'

'Ten weeks,' she said.

All the time she kep her eyes full upon him. He remained silent, thinking. Then, switching off and becoming cold, he asked, in a voice full of considerate kindness:

'Is there anything we can eat here? Is there anything you would like?'

'Yes,' she said, 'I should adore some oysters.'

'All right,' he said. 'We'll have oysters.' And he beckoned to the waiter.

Halliday took no notice, until the little plate was set before her. Then suddenly he cried:

'Minette, you can't eat oysters when you're drinking brandy.'

'What has it got to do with you?' she asked.

'Nothing, nothing,' he cried. 'But you can't eat oysters when you're drinking brandy.'

'I'm not drinking brandy,' she replied, and she sprinkled the last drops of her liqueur over his face. He gave an odd squeal. She sat looking at him, as if indifferent.

'Minette, why do you do that?' he cried in panic. He gave Gerald the impression that he was terrified of her, and that he loved his terror. He seemed to relish his own horror and hatred of her, turn it over and extract every flavour from it, in real panic. Gerald thought him a strange fool, and yet piquant.

'But Minette,' said another man, in a very small, quick Eton voice, 'you promised not to hurt him.'

'I haven't hurt him,' she answered.

'What will you drink?' the young man asked. He was dark, and smooth-skinned, and full of a stealthy vigour.

'I don't like porter, Maxim,' she replied.

'You must ask for champagne,' came the whispering gentlemanly voice of the other.

Gerald suddenly realised that this was a hint to him.

'Shall we have champagne?' he asked, laughing.

'Yes, please, dwy,' she lisped childishly.

Gerald watched her eating the oysters. She was delicate and finicking in her eating, her fingers were fine and seemed very sensitive in the tips, so she put her food apart with fine, small motions, she ate carefully, delicately. It pleased him very much to see her, and it irritated Birkin. They were all drinking champagne. Maxim, the prim young Russian with the smooth, warm-coloured face and black, oiled hair was the only one who seemed to be perfectly calm and sober. Birkin was white and abstract, unnatural, Gerald was smiling with a constant bright, amused, cold light in his eyes, leaning a little protectively towards Minette, who was very handsome, and soft, unfolded like some fair ice-flower in dreadful flowering nakedness, vainglorious now, flushed with wine and with the excitement of men. Halliday looked foolish. One glass of wine was enough to make him drunk and giggling. Yet there was always a pleasant, warm naïveté about him, that made him attractive.

'I'm not afwaid of anything except black-beetles,' said Minette, looking up suddenly and staring with her round eyes, on which there seemed an unseeing film of flame, fully upon Gerald. He laughed dangerously, from the blood. Her childish speech caressed his nerves, and her burning, filmed eyes, turned now full upon him, oblivious of all her antecedents, gave him a sort of licence.

'I'm not,' she protested. 'I'm not afraid of other things. But black-beetles – ugh!' she shuddered convulsively, as if the very thought were too much to bear.

'Do you mean,' said Gerald, with the punctiliousness of a man who has been drinking, 'that you are afraid of the sight of a black-beetle, or you are afraid of a black-beetle biting you, or doing you some harm?'

'Do they bite?' cried the girl.

'How perfectly loathsome!' exclaimed Halliday.

'I don't know,' replied Gerald, looking round the table. 'Do black-beetles bite? But that isn't the point. Are you afraid of their biting, or is it a metaphysical antipathy?'

The girl was looking full upon him all the time with inchoate eyes.

'Oh, I think they're beastly, they're horrid,' she cried. 'If I see one, it gives me the creeps all over. If one were to crawl on me, I'm *sure* I should die – I'm sure I should.'

'I hope not,' whispered the young Russian.

'I'm sure I should, Maxim,' she asseverated.

'Then one won't crawl on you,' said Gerald, smiling and knowing. In some strange way he understood her.

'It's metaphysical, as Gerald says,' Birkin stated.

There was a little pause of uneasiness.

'And are you afraid of nothing else, Minette?' asked the young Russian, in his quick, hushed, elegant manner.

'Not weally,' she said. 'I am afwaid of some things, but not weally the same. I'm not afwaid of *blood.*'

'Not afwaid of blood!' exclaimed a young man with a thick, pale, jeering face, who had just come to the table and was drinking whisky.

Minette turned on him a sulky look of dislike, low and ugly.

'Aren't you really afraid of blood?' the other persisted, a sneer all over his face.

'No, I'm not,' she retorted.

'Why, have you ever seen blood, except in a dentist's spittoon?' jeered the young man.

'I wasn't speaking to you,' she replied rather superbly.

'You can answer me, can't you?' he said.

For reply, she suddenly jabbed a knife across his thick, pale hand. He started up with a vulgar curse.

'Show's what you are,' said Minette in contempt.

'Curse you,' said the young man, standing by the table and looking down at her with acrid malevolence.

'Stop that,' said Gerald, in quick, instinctive command.

The young man stood looking down at her with sardonic contempt, a cowed, self-conscious look on his thick, pale face. The blood began to flow from his hand.

'Oh, how horrible, take it away!' squealed Halliday, turning green and averting his face.

'D'you feel ill?' asked the sardonic young man, in some concern. 'Do you feel ill, Julius? Garn, its nothing, man, don't give her the pleasure of letting her think she's performed a feat – don't give her the satisfaction, man – it's just what she wants.'

'Oh!' squealed Halliday.

'He's going to cat, Maxim,' said Minette warningly. The suave young Russian rose and took Halliday by the arm, leading him away. Birkin, white and diminished, looked on as if he were displeased. The wounded, sardonic young man moved away, ignoring his bleeding hand in the most conspicuous fashion.

'He's an awful coward, really,' said Minette to Gerald. 'He's got such an influence over Julius.'

'Who is he?' asked Gerald.

'He's a Jew, really. I can't bear him.'

'Well, he's quite unimportant. But what's wrong with Halliday?'

'Julius's the most awful coward you've ever seen,' she cried. 'He always faints if I lift a knife – he's tewwified of me.'

'H'm!' said Gerald.

'They're all afwaid of me,' she said. 'Only the Jew thinks he's going to show his courage. But he's the biggest coward of them all, really, because he's afwaid what people will think about him – and Julius doesn't care about that.'

'They've a lot of valour between them,' said Gerald good-humouredly.

Minette looked at him with a slow, slow smile. She was very handsome, flushed, and confident in dreadful knowledge. Two little points of light glinted on Gerald's eyes.

'Why do they call you Minette? Because you're like a cat?' he asked her.

'I expect so,' she said.

The smile grew more intense on his face.

'You are, rather; – or a young, female panther.'

'Oh God, Gerald!' said Birkin, in some disgust.

They both looked uneasily at Birkin.

'You're silent to-night, Wupert,' she said to him, with a slight insolence, being safe with the other man.

Halliday was coming back, looking forlorn and sick.

'Minette,' he said, 'I wish you wouldn't do these things—Oh!' He sank in his chair with a groan.

'You'd better go home,' she said to him.

'I *will* go home,' he said. 'But won't you all come along. Won't you come round to the flat?' he said to Gerald. 'I should be so glad if you would. Do – that'll be splendid. I say?' He looked round for a waiter. 'Get me a taxi.' Then he groaned again. 'Oh, I do feel – perfectly ghastly! Minette, you see what you do to me.'

'Then why are you such an idiot?' she said with sullen calm.

'But I'm not an idiot! Oh, how awful! Do come, everybody, it will be *so* splendid. Minette, you are coming. What? Oh, but you *must* come, yes, you must. What? Oh, my dear girl, don't make a fuss now, I feel perfectly – Oh, it's so ghastly—Ho! – er! Oh!'

'You know you can't drink,' she said to him, coldly.

'I tell you it isn't drink – it's your disgusting behaviour, Minette, it's nothing else. Oh, how awful! Libidnikov, do let us go.'

'He's only drunk one glass – only one glass,' came the rapid, hushed voice of the young Russian.

They all moved off to the door. The girl kept near to Gerald, and seemed to be at one in her motion with him. He was aware of this, and filled with demon-satisfaction that his motion held good for two. He held her in the hollow of his will, and she was soft, secret, invisible in her stirring there.

They crowded five of them into the taxi-cab. Halliday lurched in first, and dropped into his seat against the other window. Then Minette took her place, and Gerald sat next to her. They heard the young Russian giving orders to the driver, then they were all seated in the dark, crowded close together, Halliday groaning and leaning out of the window. They felt the swift, muffled motion of the car.

Minette sat near to Gerald, and she seemed to become soft, subtly to infuse herself into his bones, as if she were passing into him in a black, electric flow. Her being suffused into his veins like a magnetic darkness, and concentrated at the base of his spine like a fearful source of power. Meanwhile her voice sounded out reedy and nonchalant, as she talked indifferently with Birkin and with Maxim. Between her and Gerald was this silence and this black, electric comprehension in the darkness. Then she found his hand, and grasped it in her own firm, small clasp. It was so utterly dark, and yet such a naked statement, that rapid vibrations ran through his blood and over his brain, he was no longer responsible. Still her voice rang on like a bell, tinged with a tone of mockery. And as she swung her head, her fine mane of hair just swept his face, and all his nerves were on fire, as with a subtle friction of electricity. But the great centre of his force held steady, a magnificent pride to him, at the base of his spine.

They arrived at a street of quiet houses, went up a garden path, and presently a door was being opened for them by a dark-skinned servant. Gerald looked in surprise, wondering if he were a gentleman, one of the Orientals down from Oxford, perhaps. But no, he was the man-servant.

'Make tea, Hasan,' said Halliday.

'There is a room for me?' said Birkin.

To both of which questions the man grinned, and murmured.

He made Gerald uncertain, because, being tall and slender and reticent, he looked like a gentleman.

'Who is your servant?' he asked of Halliday. 'He looks a swell.'

'Oh yes – that's because he's dressed in another man's clothes. He's anything but a swell really. We found him in the road, starving. So I took him here, and another man gave him clothes. He's anything but what he seems to be – his only advantage is that he can't speak English and can't understand it, so he's perfectly safe.'

'He's very dirty,' said the young Russian swiftly and silently.

Directly, the man appeared in the doorway.

'What is it?' said Halliday.

The man grinned and murmured shyly:

'Want to speak to master.'

Gerald watched curiously. The fellow in the doorway was good-looking and clean-limbed, his bearing was calm, he looked elegant, aristocratic. Yet he was half a savage, grinning foolishly. Halliday went out into the corridor to speak with him.

'What?' they heard his voice. 'What? What do you say? Tell me again. What? Want money? Want *more* money? But what do you want money for?' There was the confused sound of the Arab's talking, then Halliday appeared in the room, smiling also foolishly, and saying:

'He says he wants money to buy underclothing. Can anybody lend me a shilling? Oh thanks, a shilling will do to buy all the underclothes he wants.' He took the money from Gerald and went out into the passage again, where they heard him saying, 'You can't want more money, you had three and six yesterday. You mustn't ask for any more. Bring the tea in quickly.'

Gerald looked round the room. It was an ordinary London sitting-room in a house evidently taken furnished, rather haphazard but pleasant. But there were several statues, wood-carvings from the West Pacific, strange and disturbing, the carved natives looked almost like the foetus of a human being. One was a woman sitting naked in a strange posture, and looking tortured, her abdomen stuck out. The young Russian explained that she was sitting in child-birth, clutching the ends of the band that hung from her neck, one in each hand, so that she could bear down, and help labour. The strange, transfixed, rudimentary face of the woman again reminded Gerald of a foetus, it was also rather wonderful, conveying the suggestion of the extreme of physical sensation, beyond the limits of mental consciousness.

'Aren't they rather obscene?' he asked, disapproving.

'I don't know,' murmured the other rapidly. 'I have never defined the obscene. I think they are very good.'

Gerald turned away. There were one or two new pictures in the room, in the Futurist manner; there was a large piano. And these, with some ordinary London lodging-house furniture of the better sort, completed the whole.

Minette had taken off her hat and coat, and was seated on the sofa. She was evidently quite at home in the house, but uncertain, suspended. She did not quite know her position. Her alliance for the time being was with Gerald, and she did not know how far this was admitted by any of the men. She was considering how she should carry off the situation. She was determined to have her experience. Now, at this eleventh hour, she was not to be baulked. Her face was flushed as with battle, her eye was brooding but inevitable.

The man came in with tea and a bottle of Kümmel. He set the tray on a little table before the couch.

'Minette,' said Halliday, 'pour out the tea.'

She did not move.

'Won't you do it?' Halliday repeated, in a state of nervous apprehension.

'I've not come back here as it was before,' she said. 'I only came because the others wanted me to, not for your sake.

'My dear Minette, you know you are your own mistress. I don't want you to do anything but use the flat for your own convenience – you know it, I've told you so many times.'

She did not reply, but silently, reservedly reached for the tea-pot. They all sat round and drank tea. Gerald could feel the electric connection between him and her so strongly, as she sat there quiet and withheld, that another set of conditions altogether had come to pass. Her silence and her immutability perplexed him. *How* was he going to come to her? And yet he felt it quite inevitable. He trusted completely to the current that held them. His perplexity was only superficial, new conditions reigned, the old were surpassed; here one did as one was possessed to do, no matter what it was.

Birkin rose. It was nearly one o'clock.

'I'm going to bed,' he said. 'Gerald I'll ring you up in the morning at your place – or you ring me up here.'

'Right,' said Gerald, and Birkin went out.

When he was well gone, Halliday said in a stimulated voice, to Gerald: 'I say, won't you stay here – oh do!'

'You can't put everybody up,' said Gerald.

'Oh but I can, perfectly – there are three more beds besides mine – do stay, won't you. Everything is quite ready – there is always somebody here – I always put people up – I love having the house crowded.'

'But there are only two rooms,' said Minette, in a cold, hostile voice, 'now Rupert's here.'

'I know there are only two rooms,' said Halliday, in his odd, high way of speaking. 'But what does that matter? There is the studio—'

He was smiling rather foolishly, and he spoke eagerly, with an insinuating determination.

'Julius and I will share one room,' said the Russian in his discreet, precise voice. Halliday and he were friends since Eton.

'It's very simple,' said Gerald, rising and pressing back his arms, stretching himself. Then he went again to look at one of the pictures. Every one of his limbs was turgid with electric force, and his back was tense like a tiger's with slumbering fire. He was very proud.

Minette rose. She gave a black look at Halliday, fierce and deadly, which brought the rather foolish, pleased smile to that young man's face. Then she went out of the room, with a cold Good-night to them all generally.

There was a brief interval, they heard a door close, then Maxim said, in his refined voice:

'That's all right.'

He looked significantly at Gerald, and said again, with a silent nod:

'That's all right – you're all right.'

Gerald looked at the smooth, ruddy, comely face, and at the strange, significant eyes, and it seemed as if the voice of the young Russian, so small and perfect, sounded in the blood rather than in the air.

'*I'm* all right then,' said Gerald.

'Yes! Yes! You're all right,' said the Russian.

Halliday continued to smile, and to say nothing.

Suddenly Minette appeared again in the door, her small, childish face looking sullen and vindictive.

'I know you want to catch me out,' came her cold, rather resonant voice. 'But I don't care, I don't care how much you catch me out.'

She turned and was gone again. She had been wearing a loose dressing-gown of purple silk, tied round her waist. She looked so small and childish and vulnerable, almost pitiful. And yet the looks of her eyes made Gerald feel drowned in some potent darkness that almost frightened him.

The men lit another cigarette and talked casually.

Chapter Seven

Totem

In the morning Gerald, woke late. He had slept heavily. Minette was still asleep, sleeping childishly and pathetically. There was something small and curled up and defenceless about her, that roused an unsatisfied flame of passion in the young man's blood, a devouring avid pity. He looked at her again. But it would be too cruel to wake her. He subdued himself, and went away.

Hearing voices coming from the sitting-room, Halliday talking to Libidnikov, he went to the door and glanced in. He had on a silk wrap of a beautiful bluish colour, with an amethyst hem.

To his surprise he saw the two young men by the fire, stark naked. Halliday looked up, rather pleased.

'Good-morning,' he said. 'Oh – did you want towels?' And stark naked he went out into the hall, striding a strange, white figure between the unliving furniture. He came back with the towels, and took his former position, crouching seated before the fire on the fender.

'Don't you love to feel the fire on your skin?' he said.

'It *is* rather pleasant,' said Gerald.

'How perfectly splendid it must be to be in a climate where one could do without clothing altogether,' said Halliday.

'Yes,' said Gerald, 'if there weren't so many things that sting and bite.'

'That's a disadvantage,' murmured Maxim.

Gerald looked at him, and with a slight revulsion saw the human animal, golden skinned and bare, somehow humiliating. Halliday was different. He had a rather heavy, slack, broken beauty, dark and firm. He was like a Christ in a Pietà. The animal was not there at all, only the heavy, broken beauty. And Gerald realised how Halliday's eyes were beautiful too, so hazel-yellow and warm and confused, broken also in their expression. The fireglow fell on his heavy, rather bowed shoulders, he sat slackly crouched on the fender, his face was uplifted, weak, perhaps slightly disintegrate, and yet with a moving beauty of its own.

'Of course,' said Maxim, 'you've been in hot countries where the people go about naked.'

'Oh really!' exclaimed Halliday. 'Where?'

'South America – Amazon,' said Gerald.

'Oh but how perfectly splendid! It's one of the things I want most to do – to live from day to day without *ever* putting on any sort of clothing whatever. If I could do that, I should feel I had lived.'

'But why?' said Gerald. 'I can't see that it makes so much difference.'

'Oh, I think it would be perfectly splendid. I'm sure life would be entirely another thing – entirely different, and perfectly wonderful.'

'But why?' asked Gerald. 'Why should it?'

'Oh – one would *feel* things instead of merely looking at them. I should feel the air move against me, and feel the things I touched, instead of having only to look at them. I'm sure life is all wrong because it has become much too visual – we can neither hear nor feel nor understand, we can only see. I'm sure that is entirely wrong.'

'Yes, that is true, that is true,' said the Russian.

Gerald glanced at him, and saw him, his suave, golden coloured body with the black hair growing fine and freely, like tendrils, and his limbs like smooth plant-stems. He was so healthy and well-made, why did he make one ashamed, why did one feel repelled? Why should Gerald even dislike it, why did it seem to him to detract from his own dignity. Was that all a human being amounted to? So uninspired! thought Gerald.

Birkin suddenly appeared in the doorway, in white pyjamas and wet hair, and a towel over his arm. He was aloof and white, and somehow evanescent.

'There's the bath-room now, if you want it,' he said generally, and was going away again, when Gerald called:

'I say, Rupert!'

'What?' The single white figure appeared again, a presence in the room.

'What do you think of that figure there? I want to know,' Gerald asked.

Birkin, white and strangely ghostly, went over to the carved figure of the savage woman in labour. Her nude, protuberant body crouched in a strange, clutching posture, her hands gripping the ends of the band, above her breast.

'It is art,' said Birkin.

'Very beautiful, it's very beautiful,' said the Russian.

They all drew near to look. Gerald looked at the group of men, the Russian golden and like a water-plant, Halliday tall and heavily, brokenly beautiful, Birkin very white and indefinite, not to be assigned, as he looked closely at the carven woman. Strangely elated, Gerald also lifted his eyes to the face of the wooden figure. And his heart contracted.

He saw vividly with his spirit the grey, forward-stretching face of the savage woman, dark and tense, abstracted in utter physical stress. It was a terrible face, void, peaked, abstracted almost into meaninglessness by the weight of sensation beneath. He saw Minette in it. As in a dream, he knew her.

'Why is it art?' Gerald asked, shocked, resentful.

'It conveys a complete truth,' said Birkin. 'It contains the whole truth of that state, whatever you feel about it.'

'But you can't call it *high* art,' said Gerald.

'High! There are centuries and hundreds of centuries of development in a straight line, behind that carving; it is an awful pitch of culture, of a definite sort.'

'What culture?' Gerald asked, in opposition. He hated the sheer barbaric thing.

'Pure culture in sensation, culture in the physical consciousness, really ultimate *physical* consciousness, mindless, utterly sensual. It is so sensual as to be final, supreme.'

But Gerald resented it. He wanted to keep certain illusions, certain ideas like clothing.

'You like the wrong things, Rupert,' he said, 'things against yourself.'

'Oh, I know, this isn't everything,' Birkin replied, moving away.

When Gerald went back to his room from the bath, he also carried his clothes. He was so conventional at home, that when he was really away, and on the loose, as now, he enjoyed nothing so much as full outrageousness. So he strode with his blue silk wrap over his arm and felt defiant.

Minette lay in her bed, motionless, her round, blue eyes like stagnant, unhappy pools. He could only see the dead, bottomless pools of her eyes. Perhaps she suffered. The sensation of her inchoate suffering roused the old sharp flame in him, a mordant pity, a passion almost of cruelty.

'You are awake now,' he said to her.

'What time is it?' came her muted voice.

She seemed to flow back, almost like liquid, from his approach, to sink helplessly away from him. Her inchoate look of a violated slave, whose fulfilment lies in her further and further violation, made his nerves quiver with acutely desirable sensation. After all, his was the only will, she was the passive substance of his will. He tingled with the subtle, biting sensation. And then he knew, he must go away from her, there must be pure separation between them.

It was a quiet and ordinary breakfast, the four men all looking very clean and bathed. Gerald and the Russian were both correct and *comme il faut* in appearance and manner, Birkin was gaunt and sick, and looked a failure in his attempt to be a properly dressed man, like Gerald and Maxim. Halliday wore tweeds and a green flannel shirt, and a rag of a tie, which was just right for him. The Arab brought in a great deal of soft toast, and looked exactly the same as he had looked the night before, statically the same.

At the end of the breakfast Minette appeared, in a purple silk wrap with a shimmering sash. She had recovered herself somewhat, but was mute and lifeless still. It was a torment to her when anybody spoke to her. Her face was like a small, fine mask, sinister too, masked with unwilling suffering. It was almost midday. Gerald rose and went away to his business, glad to get out. But he had not finished. He was coming back again at evening, they were all dining together, and he had booked seats for the party, excepting Birkin, at a music-hall.

At night they came back to the house very late again, again flushed with drink. Again the Arab – who invariably disappeared between the hours of ten and twelve at night – came in silently and inscrutably with tea, bending in a slow, strange, leopard-like fashion to put the tray softly on the table. His face was immutable, aristocratic-looking, tinged slightly with grey under the skin; he was young and good-looking. But Birkin felt a slight sickness, looking at him, and feeling the slight greyness as an ash or a corruption, in the aristocratic inscrutability of expression a nauseating, bestial stupidity.

Again they talked cordially and rousedly together. But already a certain friability was coming over the party, Birkin was mad with irritation, Halliday was turning in an insane hatred against Gerald, Minette was becoming hard and cold, like a flint knife, and Halliday was laying himself out to her. And her intention, ultimately, was to capture Halliday, to have complete power over him.

In the morning they all stalked and lounged about again. But Gerald could feel a strange hostility to himself in the air. It roused his obstinacy, and he stood up against it. He hung on for two more days. The result was a nasty and insane scene with Halliday on the fourth evening. Halliday turned with absurd animosity upon Gerald, in the café. There was a row. Gerald was on the point of knocking-in Halliday's face; when he was filled with sudden disgust and indifference, and he went away, leaving Halliday in a foolish state of gloating triumph, Minette hard and established, and Maxim standing clear. Birkin was absent, he had gone out of town again.

Gerald was piqued because he had left without giving Minette money. It was true, he did not know whether she wanted money or not. But she might have been glad of ten pounds, and he would have been *very* glad to give them to her. Now he felt in a false position. He went away chewing his lips to get at the ends of his short clipped moustache. He knew Minette was merely glad to be rid of him. She had got her Halliday whom she wanted. She wanted him completely in her power. Then she would marry him. She wanted to marry him. She had set her will on marrying Halliday. She never wanted to hear of Gerald again; unless, perhaps, she were in difficulty; because after all, Gerald was what she called a man, and these others, Halliday, Libidnikov, Birkin, the whole Bohemian set, they were only half men. But it was half men she could deal with. She felt sure of herself with them. The real men, like Gerald, put her in her place too much.

Still, she respected Gerald, she really respected him. She had managed to get his address, so that she could appeal to him in time of distress. She knew he wanted to give her money. She would perhaps write to him on that inevitable rainy day.

Chapter Eight

Breadalby

Breadalby was a Georgian house with Corinthian pillars, standing among the softer, greener hills of Derbyshire, not far from Cromford. In front, it looked over a lawn, over a few trees, down to a string of fish-ponds in the hollow of the silent park. At the back were trees, among which were to be found the stables, and the big kitchen garden, behind which was a wood.

It was a very quiet place, some miles from the high-road, back from the Derwent Valley, outside the show scenery. Silent and forsaken, the golden stucco showed between the trees, the house-front looked down the park, unchanged and unchanging.

Of late, however, Hermione had lived a good deal at the house. She had turned away from London, away from Oxford, towards the silence of the country. Her father was mostly absent, abroad, she was either alone in the house, with her visitors, of whom there were always several, or she had with her her brother, a bachelor, and a Liberal member of Parliament. He always came down when the House was not sitting, seemed always to be present in Breadalby, although he was most conscientious in his attendance to duty.

The summer was just coming in when Ursula and Gudrun went to stay the second time with Hermione. Coming along in the car, after they had entered the park, they looked across the dip, where the fish-ponds lay in silence, at the pillared front of the house, sunny and small like an English drawing of the old school, on the brow of the green hill, against the trees.

There were small figures on the green lawn, women in lavender and yellow moving to the shade of the enormous, beautifully balanced cedar tree.

'Isn't it complete!' said Gudrun. 'It is as final as an old aquatint.' She spoke with some resentment in her voice, as if she were captivated unwillingly, as if she must admire against her will.

'Do you love it?' asked Ursula.

'I don't *love* it, but in its way, I think it is quite complete.'

The motor-car ran down the hill and up again in one breath, and they were curving to the side door. A parlour-maid appeared, and then Hermione, coming forward with her pale face lifted, and her hands outstretched, advancing straight to the new-comers, her voice singing:

'Here you are – I'm so glad to see you—' she kissed Gudrun – 'so glad to see you—' she kissed Ursula and remained with her arm round her. 'Are you very tired?'

'Not at all tired,' said Ursula.

'Are you tired, Gudrun?'

'Not at all, thanks,' said Gudrun.

'No—' drawled Hermione. And she stood and looked at them. The two girls were embarrassed because she would not move into the house, but must have her little scene of welcome there on the path. The servants waited.

'Come in,' said Hermione at last, having fully taken in the pair of them. Gudrun was the more beautiful and attractive, she had decided again, Ursula was more physical, more womanly. She admired Gudrun's dress more. It was of green poplin, with a loose coat above it, of broad, dark-green and dark-brown stripes. The hat was of a pale, greenish straw, the colour of new hay, and it had a plaited ribbon of black and orange, the stockings were dark green, the shoes black. It was a good get-up, at once fashionable and individual. Ursula, in dark blue, was more ordinary, though she also looked well.

Hermione herself wore a dress of prune-coloured silk, with coral beads and coral-coloured stockings. But her dress was both shabby and soiled, even rather dirty.

'You would like to see your rooms now, wouldn't you! Yes. We will go up now, shall we?'

Ursula was glad when she could be left alone in her room. Hermione lingered so long, made such a stress on one. She stood so near to one, pressing herself near upon one, in a way that was most embarrassing and oppressive. She seemed to hinder one's workings.

Lunch was served on the lawn, under the great tree, whose thick, blackish boughs came down close to the grass. There were present a young Italian woman, slight and fashionable, a young, athletic-looking Miss Bradley, a learned, dry Baronet of fifty, who was always making witticisms and laughing at them heartily in a harsh, horse-laugh, there was Rupert Birkin, and then a woman secretary, a Fräulein März, young and slim and pretty.

The food was very good, that was one thing. Gudrun, critical of everything, gave it her full approval. Ursula loved the situation, the white table by the cedar tree, the scent of new sunshine, the little vision of the leafy park, with far-off deer feeding peacefully. There seemed a magic circle drawn about the place, shutting out the present, enclosing the delightful, precious past, trees and deer and silence, like a dream.

But in spirit she was unhappy. The talk went on like a rattle of small artillery, always slightly sententious, with a sententiousness that was only emphasised by the continual crackling of a witticism, the continual spatter of verbal jest, designed to give a tone of flippancy to a stream of conversation that was all critical and general, a canal of conversation rather than a stream.

The attitude was mental and very wearying. Only the elderly sociologist, whose mental fibre was so tough as to be insentient, seemed to be thoroughly happy. Birkin was down in the mouth. Hermione appeared, with amazing persistence, to wish to ridicule him and make him look ignominious in the eyes of everybody. And it was surprising how she seemed to succeed, how helpless he seemed against her. He looked completely insignificant. Ursula and Gudrun, both very unused, were mostly silent, listening to the slow, rhapsodic sing-song of Hermione, or the verbal sallies of Sir Joshua, or the prattle of Fräulein, or the responses of the other two women.

Luncheon was over, coffee was brought out on the grass, the party left the table and sat about in lounge chairs, in the shade or in the sunshine as they wished. Fräulein departed into the house, Hermione took up her embroidery, the little Contessa took a book, Miss Bradley was weaving a basket out of fine grass, and there they all were on the lawn in the early summer afternoon, working leisurely and spattering with half-intellectual, deliberate talk.

Suddenly there was the sound of the brakes and the shutting off of a motor-car.

'There's Salsie!' sang Hermione, in her slow, amusing sing-song. And laying down her work, she rose slowly, and slowly passed over the lawn, round the bushes, out of sight.

'Who is it?' asked Gudrun.

'Mr. Roddice – Miss Roddice's brother – at least, I suppose it's he,' said Sir Joshua.

'Salsie, yes, it is her brother,' said the little Contessa, lifting her head for a moment from her book, and speaking as if to give information, in her slightly deepened, guttural English.

They all waited. And then round the bushes came the tall form of Alexander Roddice, striding romantically like a Meredith hero who remembers Disraeli. He was cordial with everybody, he was at once a host, with an easy, off-hand hospitality that he had learned for Hermione's friends. He had just come down from London, from the House. At once the atmosphere of the House of Commons made itself felt over the lawn: the Home Secretary had said such and such a thing, and he, Roddice, on the other hand, thought such and such a thing, and had said so-and-so to the P.M.

Now Hermione came round the bushes with Gerald Crich. He had come along with Alexander. Gerald was presented to everybody, was kept by Hermione for a few moments in full view, then he was led away, still by Hermione. He was evidently her guest of the moment.

There had been a split in the Cabinet; the Minister for Education had resigned owing to adverse criticism. This started a conversation on education.

'Of course,' said Hermione, lifting her face like a rhapsodist, 'there *can* be no reason, no *excuse* for education, except the joy and beauty of knowledge in itself.' She seemed to rumble and ruminate with subterranean thoughts for a minute, then she proceeded: 'Vocational education *isn't* education, it is the close of education.'

Gerald, on the brink of discussion, sniffed the air with delight and prepared for action.

'Not necessarily,' he said. 'But isn't education really like gymnastics, isn't the end of education the production of a well-trained, vigorous, energetic mind?'

'Just as athletics produce a healthy body, ready for anything,' cried Miss Bradley, in hearty accord.

Gudrun looked at her in silent loathing.

'Well—' rumbled Hermione, 'I don't know. To me the pleasure of knowing is *so* great, so *wonderful* – nothing has meant so much to me in all life, as certain knowledge – no, I am sure – nothing.'

'What knowledge, for example, Hermione?' asked Alexander.

Hermione lifted her face and rumbled –

'M – m – m – I don't know. . . . But one thing was the stars, when I really understood something about the stars. One feels so *uplifted*, so *unbounded.* . . .'

Birkin looked at her in a white fury.

'What do you want to feel unbounded for?' he said sarcastically. 'You don't want to *be* unbounded.'

Hermione recoiled in offence.

'Yes, but one does have that limitless feeling,' said Gerald. 'It's like getting on top of the mountain and seeing the Pacific.'

'Silent upon a peak in Dariayn,' murmured the Italian, lifting her face for a moment from her book.

'Not necessarily in Darien,' said Gerald, while Ursula began to laugh.

Hermione waited for the dust to settle, and then she said, untouched:

'Yes, it is the greatest thing in life – *to know*. It is really to be happy, to be *free.*'

'Knowledge is, of course, liberty,' said Mattheson.

'In compressed tabloids,' said Birkin, looking at the dry, stiff little body of the Baronet. Immediately Gudrun saw the famous sociologist as a flat bottle, containing tabloids of compressed liberty. That pleased her. Sir Joshua was labelled and placed for ever in her mind.

'What does that mean, Rupert?' sang Hermione, in a calm snub.

'You can only have knowledge, strictly,' he replied, 'of things concluded, in the past. It's like bottling the liberty of last summer in the bottled gooseberries.'

'*Can* one have knowledge only of the past?' asked the Baronet, pointedly. 'Could we call our knowledge of the laws of gravitation for instance, knowledge of the past?'

'Yes,' said Birkin.

'There is a most beautiful thing in my book,' suddenly piped the little Italian woman. 'It says the man came to the door and threw his eyes down the street.'

There was a general laugh in the company. Miss Bradley went and looked over the shoulder of the Contessa.

'See!' said the Contessa.

'Bazarov came to the door and threw his eyes hurriedly down the street,' she read.

Again there was a loud laugh, the most startling of which was the Baronet's, which rattled out like a clatter of falling stones.

'What is the book?' asked Alexander, promptly.

'Fathers and Sons, by Turgenev,' said the little foreigner, pronouncing every syllable distinctly. She looked at the cover, to verify herself.

'An old American edition,' said Birkin.

'Ha! – of course – translated from the French,' said Alexander, with a fine declamatory voice. *'Bazarov ouvra la porte et jeta les yeux dans la rue.'*

He looked brightly round the company.

'I wonder what the "hurriedly" was,' said Ursula.

They all began to guess.

And then, to the amazement of everybody, the maid came hurrying with a large tea-tray. The afternoon had passed so swiftly.

After tea, they were all gathered for a walk.

'Would you like to come for a walk?' said Hermione to each of them, one by one. And they all said yes, feeling somehow like prisoners marshalled for exercise. Birkin only refused.

'Will you come for a walk, Rupert?'

'No, Hermione.'

'But are you *sure?*'

'Quite sure.' There was a second's hesitation.

'And why not?' sang Hermione's question. It made her blood run sharp, to be thwarted in even so trifling a matter. She intended them all to walk with her in the park.

'Because I don't like trooping off in a gang,' he said.

Her voice rumbled in her throat for a moment. Then she said, with a curious stray calm:

'Then we'll leave a little boy behind, if he's sulky.'

And she looked really gay, while she insulted him. But it merely made him stiff.

She trailed off to the rest of the company, only turning to wave her handkerchief to him, and to chuckle with laughter, singing out:

'Good-bye, good-bye, little boy.'

'Good-bye, impudent hag,' he said to himself.

They all went through the park. Hermione wanted to show them the wild daffodils on a little slope. 'This way, this way,' sang her leisurely voice at intervals. And they had all to come this way. The daffodils were pretty, but who could see them? Ursula was stiff all over with resentment by this time, resentment of the whole atmosphere. Gudrun, mocking and objective, watched and registered everything.

They looked at the shy deer, and Hermione talked to the stag, as if he too were a boy she wanted to wheedle and fondle. He was male, so she must exert some kind of power over him. They trailed home by the fish-ponds, and Hermione told them about the quarrel of two male swans, who had striven for the love of the one lady. She chuckled and laughed as she told how the ousted lover had sat with his head buried under his wing, on the gravel.

When they arrived back at the house, Hermione stood on the lawn and sang out, in a strange, small, high voice that carried very far:

'Rupert! Rupert!' The first syllable was high and slow, the second dropped down. 'Roo-o-opert.'

But there was no answer. A maid appeared.

'Where is Mr. Birkin, Alice?' asked the mild straying voice of Hermione. But under the straying voice, what a persistent, almost insane *will!*

'I think he's in his room, madame.'

'Is he?'

Hermione went slowly up the stairs, along the corridor, singing out in her high, small call:

'Ru-oo-pert! Ru-oo-pert!'

She came to his door, and tapped, still crying: 'Roo-pert.'

'Yes,' sounded his voice at last.

'What are you doing?'

The question was mild and curious.

There was no answer. Then he opened the door.

'We've come back,' said Hermione. 'The daffodils are *so* beautiful.'

'Yes,' he said, 'I've seen them.'

She looked at him with her long, slow, impassive look, along her cheeks.

'Have you?' she echoed. And she remained looking at him. She was stimulated above all things by this conflict with him, when he was like a sulky boy, helpless, and she had him safe at Breadalby. But underneath she knew the split was coming, and her hatred of him was subconscious and intense.

'What were you doing?' she reiterated, in her mild, indifferent tone. He did not answer, and she made her way, almost unconsciously into his room. He had taken a Chinese drawing of geese from the boudoir, and was copying it, with much skill and vividness.

'You are copying the drawing,' she said, standing near the table, and looking down at his work. 'Yes. How beautifully you do it! You like it very much, don't you?'

'It's a marvellous drawing,' he said.

'Is it? I'm so glad you like it, because I've always been fond of it. The Chinese Ambassador gave it me.'

'I know,' he said.

'But why do you copy it?' she asked, casual and sing-song. 'Why not do something original?'

'I want to know it,' he replied. 'One gets more of China, copying this picture, than reading all the books.'

'And what do you get?'

She was at once roused, she laid as it were violent hands on him, to extract his secrets from him. She *must* know. It was a dreadful tyranny, an obsession in her, to know all he knew. For some time he was silent, hating to answer her. Then, compelled, he began:

'I know what centres they live from – what they perceive and feel – the hot, stinging centrality of a goose in the flux of cold water and mud – the curious bitter stinging heat of a goose's blood, entering their own blood like an inoculation of corruptive fire – fire of the cold-burning mud – the lotus mystery.'

Hermione looked at him along her narrow, pallid cheeks. Her eyes were strange and drugged, heavy under their heavy, drooping lids. Her thin bosom shrugged convulsively. He stared back at her, devilish and unchanging. With another strange, sick convulsion, she turned away, as if she were sick, could feel dissolution setting-in in her body. For with her mind she was unable to attend to his words; he caught her, as it were, beneath all her defences, and destroyed her with some insidious occult potency.

'Yes,' she said, as if she did not know what she were saying. 'Yes,' and she swallowed, and tried to regain her mind. But she could not, she was witless, decentralised. Use all her will as she might, she could not recover. She suffered the ghastliness of dissolution, broken and gone in a horrible corruption. And he stood and looked at her unmoved. She strayed out, pallid and preyed-upon like a ghost, like one attacked by the tomb-influences which dog us. And she was gone like a corpse, that has no presence, no connection. He remained hard and vindictive.

Hermione came down to dinner strange and sepulchral, her eyes heavy and full of sepulchral darkness, strength. She had put on a dress of stiff old greenish brocade, that fitted tight and made her look tall and rather terrible, ghastly. In the gay light of the drawing-room she was uncanny and oppressive. But seated in the half-light of the dining-room, sitting stiffly before the shaded candles on the table, she seemed a power, a presence. She listened and attended with a drugged attention.

The party was gay and extravagant in appearance, everybody had put on evening dress except Birkin and Joshua Mattheson. The little Italian Contessa wore a dress of tissue, of orange and gold and black velvet in soft wide stripes, Gudrun was emerald green with strange net-work, Ursula was in yellow with dull silver veiling, Miss Bradley was of grey, crimson and jet, Fräulein März wore pale blue. It gave Hermione a sudden convulsive sensation of pleasure, to see these rich colours under the candle-light. She was aware of the talk going on, ceaselessly, Joshua's voice dominating; of the ceaseless pitter-patter of women's light laughter and responses; of the brilliant colours and the white table and the shadow above and below; and she seemed in a swoon of gratification, convulsed with pleasure, and yet sick, like a *revenant*. She took very little part in the conversation, yet she heard it all, it was all hers.

They all went together into the drawing-room, as if they were one family, easily, without any attention to ceremony. Fräulein handed the coffee, everybody smoked cigarettes, or else long warden pipes of white clay, of which a sheaf was provided.

'Will you smoke? – cigarettes or pipe?' asked Fräulein prettily. There was a circle of people, Sir Joshua with his eighteenth-century appearance,

Gerald the amused, handsome young Englishman, Alexander tall and the handsome politician, democratic and lucid, Hermione strange like a long Cassandra, and the women lurid with colour, all dutifully smoking their long white pipes, and sitting in a half-moon in the comfortable, soft-lighted drawing-room, round the logs that flickered on the marble hearth.

The talk was very often political or sociological, and interesting, curiously anarchistic. There was an accumulation of powerful force in the room, powerful and destructive. Everything seemed to be thrown into the melting-pot, and it seemed to Ursula they were all witches, helping the pot to bubble. There was an elation and a satisfaction in it all, but it was cruelly exhausting for the new-comers, this ruthless mental pressure, this powerful, consuming, destructive mentality that emanated from Joshua and Hermione and Birkin and dominated the rest.

But a sickness, a fearful nausea gathered possession of Hermione. There was a lull in the talk, as it was arrested by her unconscious but all-powerful will.

'Salsie, won't you play something?' said Hermione, breaking off completely. 'Won't somebody dance? Gudrun, you will dance, won't you? I wish you would. *Anche tu, Palestra, ballerai?* – *si, per piacere.* You too, Ursula.'

Hermione rose and slowly pulled the gold-embroidered band that hung by the mantel, clinging to it for a moment, then releasing it suddenly. Like a priestess she looked, unconscious, sunk in a heavy half-trance.

A servant came, and soon reappeared with armfuls of silk robes and shawls and scarves, mostly Oriental, things that Hermione, with her love for beautiful extravagant dress, had collected gradually.

'The three women will dance together,' she said.

'What shall it be?' asked Alexander, rising briskly.

'Vergini Delle Rocchette,' said the Contessa at once.

'They are so languid,' said Ursula.

'The three witches from Macbeth,' suggested Fräulein usefully. It was finally decided to do Naomi and Ruth and Orpah. Ursula was Naomi, Gudrun was Ruth, the Contessa was Orpah. The idea was to make a little ballet, in the style of the Russian Ballet of Pavlova and Nijinsky.

The Contessa was ready first, Alexander went to the piano, a space was cleared. Orpah, in beautiful Oriental clothes, began slowly to dance the death of her husband. Then Ruth came, and they wept together, and lamented, then Naomi came to comfort them. It was all done in dumb show, the women danced their emotion in gesture and motion. The little drama went on for a quarter of an hour.

Ursula was beautiful as Naomi. All her men were dead, it remained to her only to stand alone in indomitable assertion, demanding nothing. Ruth, woman-loving, loved her. Orpah, a vivid, sensational, subtle widow, would go back to the former life, a repetition. The inter-play between the women was real and rather frightening. It was strange to see how Gudrun clung with heavy, desperate passion to Ursula, yet smiled with subtle malevolence against her, how Ursula accepted silently, unable to provide any more either for herself or for the other, but dangerous and indomitable, refuting her grief.

Hermione loved to watch. She could see the Contessa's rapid, stoat-like sensationalism, Gudrun's ultimate but treacherous cleaving to the woman in her sister, Ursula's dangerous helplessness, as if she were helplessly weighted, and unreleased.

'That was very beautiful,' everybody cried with one accord. But Hermione writhed in her soul, knowing what she could not know. She cried out for more dancing, and it was her will that set the Contessa and Birkin moving mockingly in Malbrouk.

Gerald was excited by the desperate cleaving of Gudrun to Naomi. The essence of that female, subterranean recklessness and mockery penetrated his blood. He could not forget Gudrun's lifted, offered, cleaving, reckless, yet withal mocking weight. And Birkin, watching like a hermit crab from its hole, had seen the brilliant frustration and helplessness of Ursula. She was rich, full of dangerous power. She was like a strange unconscious bud of powerful womanhood. He was unconsciously drawn to her. She was his future.

Alexander played some Hungarian music, and they all danced, seized by the spirit. Gerald was marvellously exhilarated at finding himself in motion, moving towards Gudrun, dancing with feet that could not yet escape from the waltz and the two-step, but feeling his force stir along his limbs and his body, out of captivity. He did not know yet how to dance their convulsive, rag-time sort of dancing, but he knew how to begin. Birkin, when he could get free from the weight of the people present, whom he disliked, danced rapidly and with a real gaiety. And how Hermione hated him for this irresponsible gaiety.

'Now I see,' cried the Contessa excitedly, watching his purely gay motion, which he had all to himself. 'Mr. Birkin, he is a changer.'

Hermione looked at her slowly, and shuddered, knowing that only a foreigner could have seen and have said this.

'*Cosa vuol'dire*, Palestra?' she asked, sing-song.

'Look,' said the Contessa, in Italian. 'He is not a man, he is a chameleon, a creature of change.'

'He is not a man, he is treacherous, not one of us,' said itself over in Hermione's consciousness. And her soul writhed in the black subjugation to him, because of his power to escape, to exist, other than she did, because he was not consistent, not a man, less than a man. She hated him in a despair that shattered her and broke her down, so that she suffered sheer dissolution like a corpse, and was unconscious of everything save the horrible sickness of dissolution that was taking place within her, body and soul.

The house being full, Gerald was given the smaller room, really the dressing-room, communicating with Birkin's bedroom. When they all took their candles and mounted the stairs, where the lamps were burning sub-duedly, Hermione captured Ursula and brought her into her own bedroom, to talk to her. A sort of constraint came over Ursula in the big, strange bedroom. Hermione seemed to be bearing down on her, awful and inchoate, making some appeal. They were looking at some Indian silk shirts, gorgeous and sensual in themselves, their shape, their almost corrupt gorgeousness. And Hermione came near, and her bosom writhed, and Ursula was for a moment blank with panic. And for a moment Hermione's haggard eyes saw the fear on the face of the other, there was again a sort of crash, a crashing down. And Ursula picked up a shirt of rich red and blue silk, made for a young princess of fourteen, and was crying mechanically:

'Isn't it wonderful – who would dare to put those two strong colours together—'

Then Hermione's maid entered silently and Ursula, overcome with dread, escaped, carried away by powerful impulse.

Birkin went straight to bed. He was feeling happy, and sleepy. Since he had danced he was happy. But Gerald would talk to him. Gerald, in evening dress, sat on Birkin's bed when the other lay down, and must talk.

'Who are those two Brangwens?' Gerald asked.

'They live in Beldover.'

'In Beldover! Who are they then?'

'Teachers in the Grammar School.'

There was a pause.

'They are!' exclaimed Gerald at length. 'I thought I had seen them before.'

'It disappoints you?' said Birkin.

'Disappoints me! No – but how is it Hermione has them here?'

'She knew Gudrun in London – that's the younger one, the one with the darker hair – she's an artist – does sculpture and modelling.'

'She's not a teacher in the Grammar School, then – only the other?'

'Both – Gudrun art mistress, Ursula a class mistress.'

'And what's the father?'

'Handicraft instructor in the schools.'

'Really!'

'Class-barriers are breaking down!'

Gerald was always uneasy under the slightly jeering tone of the other.

'That their father is handicraft instructor in a school! What does it matter to me?'

Birkin laughed. Gerald looked at his face, as it lay there laughing and bitter and indifferent on the pillow, and he could not go away.

'I don't suppose you will see very much more of Gudrun at least. She is a restless bird, she'll be gone in a week or two,' said Birkin.

'Where will she go?'

'London, Paris, Rome – heaven knows. I always expect her to sheer off to Damascus or San Francisco; she's a bird of paradise. God knows what she's got to do with Beldover. It goes by contraries, like dreams.'

Gerald pondered for a few moments.

'How do you know her so well?' he asked.

'I knew her in London,' he replied, 'in the Algernon Strange set. She'll know about Minette and Libidnikov and the rest – even if she doesn't know them personally. She was never quite that set – more conventional, in a way. I've known her for two years, I suppose.'

'And she makes money, apart from her teaching?' asked Gerald.

'Some – irregularly. She can sell her models. She has a certain réclame.'

'How much for?'

'A guinea, ten guineas.'

'And are they good? What are they?'

'I think sometimes they are marvellously good. That is hers, those two wagtails in Hermione's boudoir – you've seen them – they are carved in wood and painted.'

'I thought it was savage carving again.'

'No, hers. That's what they are – animals and birds, sometimes odd small people in everyday dress, really rather wonderful when they come off. They have a sort of funniness that is quite unconscious and subtle.'

'She might be a well-known artist one day?' mused Gerald.

'She might. But I think she won't. She drops her art if anything else catches her. Her contrariness prevents her taking it seriously – she must never be too serious, she feels she might give herself away. And she won't give herself away – she's always on the defensive. That's what I can't stand about her type. By the way, how did things go off with Minette after I left you? I haven't heard anything.'

'Oh, rather disgusting, Halliday turned objectionable, and I only just saved myself from jumping in his stomach, in a real old-fashioned row.'

Birkin was silent.

'Of course,' he said, 'Julius is somewhat insane. On the one hand he's had religious mania, and on the other, he is fascinated by obscenity. Either he is a pure servant, washing the feet of Christ, or else he is making obscene drawings of Jesus – action and reaction – and between the two, nothing. He is really insane. He wants a pure lily, another girl, with a Botticelli face, on the one hand, and on the other, he *must* have Minette, just to defile himself with her.'

'That's what I can't make out,' said Gerald. 'Does he love her, Minette, or doesn't he?'

'He neither does nor doesn't. She is the harlot, the actual harlot of adultery to him. And he's got a craving to throw himself into the filth of her. Then he gets up and calls on the name of the lily of purity, the baby-faced girl, and so enjoys himself all round. It's the old story – action and reaction, and nothing between.'

'I don't know,' said Gerald, after a pause, 'that he does insult Minette so very much. She strikes me as being rather foul.'

'But I thought you liked her,' exclaimed Birkin. 'I always felt fond of her. I never had anything to do with her, personally, that's true.'

'I liked her all right, for a couple of days,' said Gerald. 'But a week of her would have turned me over. There's a certain smell about the skin of those women, that in the end is sickening beyond words – even if you like it at first.'

'I know,' said Birkin. Then he added, rather fretfully, 'But go to bed, Gerald. God knows what time it is.'

Gerald looked at his watch, and at length rose off the bed, and went to his room. But he returned in a few minutes, in his shirt.

'One thing,' he said, seating himself on the bed again. 'We finished up rather stormily, and I never had time to give her anything.'

'Money?' said Birkin. 'She'll get what she wants from Halliday or from one of her acquaintances.'

'But then,' said Gerald, 'I'd rather give her her dues and settle the account.'

'She doesn't care.'

'No, perhaps not. But one feels the account is left open, and one would rather it were closed.'

'Would you?' said Birkin. He was looking at the white legs of Gerald, as the latter sat on the side of the bed in his shirt. They were white-skinned, full, muscular legs, handsome and decided. Yet they moved Birkin with a sort of pathos, tenderness, as if they were childish.

'I think I'd rather close the account,' said Gerald, repeating himself vaguely.

'It doesn't matter one way or another,' said Birkin.

'You always say it doesn't matter,' said Gerald, a little puzzled, looking down at the face of the other man affectionately.

'Neither does it,' said Birkin.

'But she was a decent sort, really—'

'Render unto Caesarina the things that are Caesarina's,' said Birkin, turning aside. It seemed to him Gerald was talking for the sake of talking. 'Go away, it wearies me – it's too late at night,' he said.

'I wish you'd tell me something that *did* matter,' said Gerald, looking down all the time at the face of the other man, waiting for something. But Birkin turned his face aside.

'All right then, go to sleep,' said Gerald, and he laid his hand affectionately on the other man's shoulder, and went away.

In the morning when Gerald awoke and heard Birkin move, he called out: 'I still think I ought to give Minette some money.'

'Oh, God!' said Birkin, 'don't be so matter-of-fact. Close the account in your own soul, if you like. It is there you can't close it.'

'How do you know I can't?'

'Knowing you.'

Gerald meditated for some moments.

'It seems to me the right thing to do, you know, with the Minettes, is to pay them.'

'And the right thing for mistresses: keep them. And the right thing for wives: live under the same roof with them. *Integer vitae scelerisque purus—*' said Birkin.

'There's no need to be nasty about it,' said Gerald.

'It bores me. I'm not interested in your peccadilloes.'

'And I don't care whether you are or not – I am.'

The morning was again sunny. The maid had been in and brought the water, and had drawn the curtains. Birkin, sitting up in bed, looked lazily and pleasantly out on the park, that was so green and deserted, romantic, belonging to the past. He was thinking how lovely, how sure, how formed, how final all the things of the past were – the lovely accomplished past – this house, so still and golden, the park slumbering its centuries of peace. And then, what a snare and a delusion, this beauty of static things – what a horrible, dead prison Breadalby really was, what an intolerable confinement, the peace! Yet it was better than the sordid scrambling conflict of the present. If only one might create the future after one's own heart – for a little pure truth, a little unflinching application of simple truth to life, the heart cried out ceaselessly.

'I can't see what you will leave me at all, to be interested in,' came Gerald's voice from the lower room. 'Neither the Minettes, nor the mines, nor anything else.'

'You be interested in what you can, Gerald. Only I'm not interested myself,' said Birkin.

'What am I to do at all, then?' came Gerald's voice.

'What you like. What am I to do myself?'

In the silence Birkin could feel Gerald musing this fact.

'I'm blest if I know,' came the good-humoured answer.

'You see,' said Birkin, 'part of you wants Minette, and nothing but Minette, part of you wants the mines, the business, and nothing but the business – and there you are – all in bits—'

'And part of me wants something else,' said Gerald, in a queer, quiet, real voice.

'What?' said Birkin, rather surprised.

'That's what I hoped you could tell me,' said Gerald.

There was a silence for some time.

'I can't tell you – I can't find my own way, let alone yours. You might marry,' Birkin replied.

'Who – Minette?' asked Gerald.

'Perhaps,' said Birkin. And he rose and went to the window.

'That is your panacea,' said Gerald. 'But you haven't even tried it on yourself yet, and you are sick enough.'

'I am,' said Birkin. 'Still, I shall come right.'

'Through marriage?'

'Yes,' Birkin answered obstinately.

'And no,' added Gerald. 'No, no, no, my boy.'

There was a silence between them, and a strange tension of hostility. They always kept a gap, a distance between them, they wanted always to be free each of the other. Yet there was a curious heart-straining towards each other.

'*Salvator femininus,*' said Gerald, satirically.

'Why not?' said Birkin.

'No reason at all,' said Gerald, 'if it really works. But whom will you marry?'

'A woman,' said Birkin.

'Good,' said Gerald.

Birkin and Gerald were the last to come down to breakfast. Hermione liked everybody to be early. She suffered when she felt her day was diminished, she felt she had missed her life. She seemed to grip the hours by the throat, to force her life from them. She was rather pale and ghastly, as if left behind, in the morning. Yet she had her power, her will was strangely pervasive. With the entrance of the two young men a sudden tension was felt.

She lifted her face, and said, in her amused sing-song:

'Good morning! Did you sleep well? I'm so glad.'

And she turned away, ignoring them. Birkin, who knew her well, saw that she intended to discount his existence.

'Will you take what you want from the sideboard?' said Alexander, in a voice slightly suggesting disapprobation. 'I hope the things aren't cold. Oh no! Do you mind putting out the flame under the chafing-dish, Rupert? Thank you.'

Even Alexander was rather authoritative where Hermione was cool. He took his tone from her, inevitably. Birkin sat down and looked at the table. He was so used to this house, to this room, to this atmosphere, through years of intimacy, and now he felt in complete opposition to it all, it had nothing to do with him. How well he knew Hermione, as she sat there, erect and silent and somewhat bemused, and yet so potent, so powerful! He knew her statically, so finally, that it was almost like a madness. It was difficult to believe one was not mad, that one was not a figure in the hall of kings in some Egyptian tomb, where the dead all sat immemorial and tremendous. How utterly he knew Joshua Matheson, who was talking in his harsh, yet rather mincing voice, endlessly, endlessly, always with a strong mentality working, always interesting, and yet always known, everything he said known beforehand, however novel it was, and clever. Alexander the up-to-date host, so bloodlessly free-and-easy, Fräulein so prettily chiming in just as she should, the little Italian Countess taking notice of everybody, only playing her little game, objective and cold, like a weasel watching everything, and extracting her own amusement, never giving herself in the slightest; then Miss Bradley, heavy and rather subservient, treated with cool, almost amused contempt by Hermione, and therefore slighted by everybody – how known it all was, like a game with the figures set out, the same figures, the Queen of chess, the knights, the pawns, the same now as they were hundreds of years ago, the same figures moving round in one of the innumerable permutations that make up the game. But the game is known, its going on is like a madness, it is so exhausted.

There was Gerald, an amused look on his face; the game pleased him. There was Gudrun, watching with steady, large, hostile eyes; the game fascinated her, and she loathed it. There was Ursula, with a slightly startled look on her face, as if she were hurt, and the pain were just outside her consciousness.

Suddenly Birkin got up and went out.

'That's enough,' he said to himself involuntarily.

Hermione knew his motion, though not in her consciousness. She lifted her heavy eyes and saw him lapse suddenly away, on a sudden, unknown tide, and the waves broke over her. Only her indomitable will remained static and mechanical, she sat at the table making her musing, stray remarks. But the darkness had covered her, she was like a ship that has gone down. It was finished for her too, she was wrecked in the darkness. Yet the unfailing mechanism of her will worked on, she had that activity.

'Shall we bathe this morning?' she said, suddenly looking at them all.

'Splendid,' said Joshua. 'It is a perfect morning.'

'Oh, it is beautiful,' said Fräulein.

'Yes, let us bathe,' said the Italian woman.

'We have no bathing-suits,' said Gerald.

'Have mine,' said Alexander. 'I must go to church and read the lessons. They expect me.'

'Are you a Christian?' asked the Italian Countess, with sudden interest.

'No,' said Alexander, 'I'm not. But I believe in keeping up the old institutions.'

'They are so beautiful,' said Fräulein daintily.

'Oh, they are,' cried Miss Bradley.

They all trailed out on to the lawn. It was a sunny, soft morning in early summer, when life ran in the world subtly, like a reminiscence. The church bells were ringing a little way off, not a cloud was in the sky, the swans were like lilies on the water below, the peacocks walked with long, prancing steps across the shadow and into the sunshine of the grass. One wanted to swoon into the by-gone perfection of it all.

'Good-bye,' called Alexander, waving his gloves cheerily, and he disappeared behind the bushes, on his way to church.

'Now,' said Hermione, 'shall we all bathe?'

'I won't,' said Ursula.

'You don't want to?' said Hermione, looking at her slowly.

'No. I don't want to,' said Ursula.

'Nor I,' said Gudrun.

'What about my suit?' asked Gerald.

'I don't know,' laughed Hermione, with an odd, amused intonation. 'Will a handkerchief do – a large handkerchief?'

'That will do,' said Gerald.

'Come along then,' sang Hermione.

The first to run across the lawn was the little Italian, small and like a cat, her white legs twinkling as she went, ducking slightly her head, that was tied in a gold silk kerchief. She tripped through the gate and down the grass, and stood, like a tiny figure of ivory and bronze, at the water's edge, having dropped off her towelling, watching the swans, which came up in surprise. Then out ran Miss Bradley, like a large, soft plum in her dark-blue suit. Then Gerald came, a scarlet silk kerchief round his loins, his towels over his arms. He seemed to flaunt himself a little in the sun, lingering and laughing, strolling easily, looking white but natural in his nakedness. Then came Sir Joshua, in an overcoat, and lastly Hermione, striding with stiff grace from out of a great mantle of purple silk, her head tied up in purple and gold. Handsome was her stiff, long body, her straight-stepping white legs, there was a static magnificence about her as she let the cloak float loosely away from her striding. She crossed the lawn like some strange memory, and passed slowly and statelily towards the water.

There were three ponds, in terraces descending the valley, large and smooth and beautiful, lying in the sun. The water ran over a little stone wall, over small rocks, splashing down from one pond to the level below. The swans had gone out on to the opposite bank, the reeds smelled sweet, a faint breeze touched the skin.

Gerald had dived in, after Sir Joshua, and had swum to the end of the pond. There he climbed out and sat on the wall. There was a dive, and the little Countess was swimming like a rat, to join him. They both sat in the sun, laughing and crossing their arms on their breasts. Sir Joshua swam up to them, and stood near them, up to his arm-pits in the water. Then Hermione and Miss Bradley swam over, and they sat in a row on the embankment.

'Aren't they terrifying? Aren't they really terrifying?' said Gudrun. 'Don't they look saurian? They are just like great lizards. Did you ever see anything like Sir Joshua? But really, Ursula, he belongs to the primeval world, when great lizards crawled about.'

Gudrun looked in dismay on Sir Joshua, who stood up to the breast in the water, his long, greyish hair washed down into his eyes, his neck set into thick, crude shoulders. He was talking to Miss Bradley, who, seated on the bank above, plump and big and wet, looked as if she might roll and slither in the water almost like one of the slithering sea-lions in the Zoo.

Ursula watched in silence. Gerald was laughing happily, between Hermione and the Italian. He reminded her of Dionysus, because his hair was really yellow, his figure so full and laughing. Hermione, in her large, stiff, sinister grace, leaned near him, frightening, as if she were not responsible for what she might do. He knew a certain danger in her, a convulsive madness. But he only laughed the more, turning often to the little Countess, who was flashing up her face at him.

They all dropped into the water, and were swimming together like a shoal of seals. Hermione was powerful and unconscious in the water, large and slow and powerful, Palestra was quick and silent as a water-rat, Gerald wavered and flickered, a white natural shadow. Then, one after the other, they waded out, and went up to the house.

But Gerald lingered a moment to speak to Gudrun.

'You don't like the water?' he said.

She looked at him with a long, slow inscrutable look, as he stood before her negligently, the water standing in beads all over his skin.

'I like it very much,' she replied.

He paused, expecting some sort of explanation.

'And you swim?'

'Yes, I swim.'

Still he would not ask her why she would not go in then. He could feel something ironic in her. He walked away, piqued for the first time.

'Why wouldn't you bathe?' he asked her again, later, when he was once more the properly-dressed young Englishman.

She hesitated a moment before answering, opposing his persistence.

'Because I didn't like the crowd,' she replied.

He laughed, her phrase seemed to re-echo in his consciousness. The flavour of her slang was piquant to him. Whether he would or not, she signified the real world to him. He wanted to come up to her standards, fulfil her expectations. He knew that her criterion was the only one that mattered. The others were all outsiders, instinctively, whatever they might be socially. And Gerald could not help it, he was bound to strive to come up to her criterion, fulfil her idea of a man and a human being.

After lunch, when all the others had withdrawn, Hermione and Gerald and Birkin lingered, finishing their talk. There had been some discussion, on the whole quite intellectual and artificial, about a new state, a new world of man. Supposing this old social state *were* broken and destroyed, then, out of the chaos, what then?

The great social idea, said Sir Joshua, was the *social* equality of man. No, said Gerald, the idea was, that every man was fit for his own little bit of a task – let him do that, and then please himself. The unifying principle was the work in hand. Only work, the business of production, held men together. It was mechanical, but then society *was* a mechanism. Apart from work they were isolated, free to do as they liked.

'Oh!' cried Gudrun. 'Then we shan't have names any more – we shall be like the Germans, nothing but Herr Obermeister and Herr Untermeister. I can imagine it – "I am Mrs. Colliery-Manager Crich – I am Mrs. Member-of-Parliament Roddice. I am Miss Art-Teacher Brangwen." Very pretty that.'

'Things would work very much better, Miss Art-Teacher Brangwen,' said Gerald.

'What things, Mr. Colliery-Manager Crich? The relation between you and me, *par exemple?*'

'Yes, for example,' cried the Italian. 'That which is between men and women—!'

'That is non-social,' said Birkin, sarcastically.

'Exactly,' said Gerald. 'Between me and a woman, the social question does not enter. It is my own affair.'

'A ten-pound note on it,' said Birkin.

'You don't admit that a woman is a social being?' asked Ursula of Gerald.

'She is both,' said Gerald. 'She is a social being, as far as society is concerned. But for her own private self, she is a free agent, it is her own affair, what she does.'

'But won't it be rather difficult to arrange the two halves?' asked Ursula.

'Oh no,' replied Gerald. 'They arrange themselves naturally – we see it now, everywhere.'

'Don't you laugh so pleasantly till you're out of the wood,' said Birkin.

Gerald knitted his brows in momentary irritation.

'Was I laughing?' he said.

'*If*,' said Hermione at last, 'we could only realise that in the *spirit* we are all one, all equal in the spirit, all brothers there – the rest wouldn't matter, there would be no more of this carping and envy and this struggle for power, which destroys, only destroys.'

This speech was received in silence, and almost immediately the party rose from the table. But when the others had gone, Birkin turned round in bitter declamation, saying:

'It is just the opposite, just the contrary, Hermione. We are all different and unequal in spirit – it is only the *social* differences that are based on accidental material conditions. We are all abstractly or mathematically equal, if you like. Every man has hunger and thirst, two eyes, one nose and two legs. We're all the same in point of number. But spiritually there is pure difference and neither equality nor inequality counts. It is upon these two bits of knowledge that you must found a state. Your democracy is an absolute lie – your brotherhood of man is a pure falsity, if you apply it further than the mathematical abstraction. We all drank milk first, we all eat bread and meat, we all want to ride in motor-cars – therein lies the beginning and the end of the brotherhood of man. But no equality.

'But I, myself, who am myself, what have I to do with equality with any other man or woman? In the spirit, I am as separate as one star is from another, as different in quality and quantity. Establish a state on *that*. One man isn't any better than another, not because they are equal, but because they are intrinsically *other*, that there is no term of comparison. The minute you begin to compare, one man is seen to be far better than another, all the inequality you can imagine is there by nature. I want every man to have his share in the world's goods, so that I am rid of his importunity, so that I can tell him: "Now you've got what you want – you've got your fair share of the world's gear. Now, you one-mouthed fool, mind yourself and don't obstruct me." '

Hermione was looking at him with leering eyes, along her cheeks. He could feel violent waves of hatred and loathing of all he said, coming out of her. It was dynamic hatred and loathing, coming strong and black out of the unconsciousness. She heard his words in her unconscious self, *consciously* she was as if deafened, she paid no heed to them.

'It *sounds* like megalomania, Rupert,' said Gerald, genially.

Hermione gave a queer, grunting sound. Birkin stood back.

'Yes, let it,' he said suddenly, the whole tone gone out of his voice, that had been so insistent, bearing everybody down. And he went away.

But he felt, later, a little compunction. He had been violent, cruel with poor Hermione. He wanted to recompense her, to make it up. He had hurt her, he had been vindictive. He wanted to be on good terms with her again.

He went into her boudoir, a remote and very cushiony place. She was sitting at her table writing letters. She lifted her face abstractedly when he entered, watched him go to the sofa, and sit down. Then she looked down at her paper again.

He took up a large volume which he had been reading before, and became minutely attentive to his author. His back was towards Hermione. She could not go on with her writing. Her whole mind was a chaos, darkness breaking in upon it, and herself struggling to gain control with her will, as a swimmer struggles with the swirling water. But in spite of her efforts she was borne down, darkness seemed to break over her, she felt as if her heart was bursting. The terrible tension grew stronger and stronger, it was most fearful agony, like being walled up.

And then she realised that his presence was the wall, his presence was destroying her. Unless she could break out, she must die most fearfully, walled up in horror. And he was the wall. She must break down the wall – she must break him down before her, the awful obstruction of him who obstructed her life to the last. It must be done, or she must perish most horribly.

Terrible shocks ran over her body, like shocks of electricity, as if many volts of electricity suddenly struck her down. She was aware of him sitting silently there, an unthinkable evil obstruction. Only this blotted out her mind, pressed out her very breathing, his silent, stooping back, the back of his head.

A terrible voluptuous thrill ran down her arms – she was going to know her voluptuous consummation. Her arms quivered and were strong, immeasurably and irresistibly strong. What delight, what delight in strength, what delirium of pleasure! She was going to have her consummation of voluptuous ecstasy at last. It was coming! In utmost terror and agony, she knew it was upon her now, in extremity of bliss. Her hand closed on a blue, beautiful ball of lapis lazuli that stood on her desk for a paper-weight. She rolled it round in her hand as she rose silently. Her heart was a pure flame in her breast, she was purely unconscious in ecstasy. She moved towards him and stood behind him for a moment in ecstasy. He, closed within the spell, remained motionless and unconscious.

Then swiftly, in a flame that drenched down her body like fluid lightning and gave her a perfect, unutterable consummation, unutterable satisfaction, she brought down the ball of jewel stone with all her force, crash on his head. But her fingers were in the way and deadened the blow. Nevertheless, down went his head on the table on which his book lay, the stone slid aside and over his ear, it was one convulsion of pure bliss for her, lit up by the crushed pain of her fingers. But it was not somehow complete. She lifted her arm high to aim once more, straight down on the head that lay dazed on the table. She must smash it, it must be smashed before her ecstasy was consummated, fulfilled for ever. A thousand lives, a thousand deaths mattered nothing now, only the fulfilment of this perfect ecstasy.

She was not swift, she could only move slowly. A strong spirit in him woke him and made him lift his face and twist to look at her. Her arm was raised, the hand clasping the ball of lapis lazuli. It was her left hand, he realised again with horror that she was left-handed. Hurriedly, with burrowing motion, he covered his head under the thick volume of Thucydides, and the blow came down, almost breaking his neck, and shattering his heart.

He was shattered, but he was not afraid. Twisting round to face her he pushed the table over and got away from her. He was like a flask that is smashed to atoms, he seemed to himself that he was all fragments, smashed to bits. Yet his movements were perfectly coherent and clear, his soul was entire and surprised.

'No you don't, Hermione,' he said in a low voice. 'I don't let you.'

He saw her standing tall and livid and attentive, the stone clenched tense in her hand.

'Stand away and let me go,' he said, drawing near to her.

As if pressed back by some hand, she stood away, watching him all the time without changing, like a neutralised angel confronting him.

'It is no good,' he said, when he had gone past her. 'It isn't I who will die. You hear?'

He kept his face to her as he went out, lest she should strike again. While he was on his guard, she dared not move. And he was on his guard, she was powerless. So he had gone, and left her standing.

She remained perfectly rigid, standing as she was for a long time. Then she staggered to the couch and lay down, and went heavily to sleep. When she awoke, she remembered what she had done, but it seemed to her, she had only hit him, as any woman might do, because he tortured her. She was perfectly right. She knew that, spiritually, she was right. In her own infallible purity, she had done what must be done. She was right, she was pure. A drugged, almost sinister religious expression became permanent on her face.

Birkin, barely conscious, and yet perfectly direct in his motion, went out of the house and straight across the park, to the open country, to the hills. The brilliant day had become overcast, spots of rain were falling. He wandered on to a wild valley-side, where were thickets of hazel, many flowers, tufts of heather, and little clumps of young fir-trees, budding with soft paws. It was rather wet everywhere, there was a stream running down at the bottom of the valley, which was gloomy, or seemed gloomy. He was aware that he could not regain his consciousness, that he was moving in a sort of darkness.

Yet he wanted something. He was happy in the wet hill-side, that was overgrown and obscure with bushes and flowers. He wanted to touch them all, to saturate himself with the touch of them all. He took off his clothes, and sat down naked among the primroses, moving his feet softly among the primroses, his legs, his knees, his arms right up to the arm-pits, lying down and letting them touch his belly, his breasts. It was such a fine, cool, subtle touch all over him, he seemed to saturate himself with their contact.

But they were too soft. He went through the long grass to a clump of young fir-trees, that were no higher than a man. The soft sharp boughs beat upon him, as he moved in keen pangs against them, threw little cold showers of drops on his belly, and beat his loins with their clusters of soft-sharp needles. There was a thistle which pricked him vividly, but not too much, because all his movements were too discriminate and soft. To lie down and roll in the sticky, cool young hyacinths, to lie on one's belly and cover one's back with handfuls of fine wet grass, soft as a breath, soft and more delicate and more beautiful than the touch of any woman; and then to sting one's thigh against the living dark bristles of the fir-boughs; and then to feel the light whip of the hazel on one's shoulders, stinging, and then to clasp the silvery birch-trunk against one's breast, its smoothness, its hardness, its vital knots and ridges – this was good, this was all very good, very satisfying. Nothing else would do, nothing else would satisfy, except this coolness and subtlety of vegetation travelling into one's blood. How fortunate he was, that there was this lovely, subtle, responsive vegetation, waiting for him, as he waited for it; how fulfilled he was, how happy!

As he dried himself a little with his handkerchief, he thought about Hermione and the blow. He could feel a pain on the side of his head. But after all, what did it matter? What did Hermione matter, what did people matter altogether? There was this perfect cool loneliness, so lovely and fresh and unexplored. Really, what a mistake he had made, thinking he wanted people, thinking he wanted a woman. He did not want a woman – not in the least. The leaves and the primroses and the trees, they were really lovely and cool and desirable, they really came into the blood and were added on to him. He was enrichened now immeasurably, and so glad.

It was quite right of Hermione to want to kill him. What had he to do with her? Why should he pretend to have anything to do with human beings at all? Here was his world, he wanted nobody and nothing but the lovely, subtle, responsive vegetation, and himself, his own living self.

It was necessary to go back into the world. That was true. But that did not matter, so one knew where one belonged. He knew now where he belonged. This was his place, his marriage place. The world was extraneous.

He climbed out of the valley, wondering if he were mad. But if so, he preferred his own madness, to the regular sanity. He rejoiced in his own madness, he was free. He did not want that old sanity of the world, which was become so repulsive. He rejoiced in the new-found world of his madness. It was so fresh and delicate and so satisfying.

As for the certain grief he felt at the same time, in his soul, that was only the remains of an old ethic, that bade a human being adhere to humanity. But he was weary of the old ethic, of the human being, and of humanity. He loved now the soft, delicate vegetation, that was so cool and perfect. He would overlook the old grief, he would put away the old ethic, he would be free in his new state.

He was aware of the pain in his head becoming more and more difficult every minute. He was walking now along the road to the nearest station. It was raining and he had no hat. But then plenty of cranks went out nowadays without hats, in the rain.

He wondered again how much of his heaviness of heart, a certain depression, was due to fear, fear lest anybody should have seen him naked lying against the vegetation. What a dread he had of mankind, of other people! It amounted almost to horror, to a sort of dream terror – his horror of being observed by some other people. If he were on an island, like Alexander Selkirk, with only the creatures and the trees, he would be free and glad, there would be none of this heaviness, this misgiving. He could love the vegetation and be quite happy and unquestioned, by himself.

He had better send a note to Hermione: she might trouble about him, and he did not want the onus of this. So at the station, he wrote saying:

'I will go on to town – I don't want to come back to Breadalby for the present. But it is quite all right – I don't want you to mind having biffed me, in the least. Tell the others it is just one of my moods. You were quite right, to biff me – because I know you wanted to. So there's the end of it.'

In the train, however, he felt ill. Every motion was insufferable pain, and he was sick. He dragged himself from the station into a cab, feeling his way step by step, like a blind man, and held up only by a dim will.

For a week or two he was ill, but he did not let Hermione know, and she thought he was sulking; there was a complete estrangement between them. She became rapt, abstracted in her conviction of exclusive righteousness. She lived in and by her own self-esteem, conviction of her own rightness of spirit.

Chapter Nine

Coal-dust

Going home from school in the afternoon, the Brangwen girls descended the hill between the picturesque cottages of Willey Green till they came to the railway crossing. There they found the gate shut, because the colliery train was rumbling nearer. They could hear the small locomotive panting hoarsely as it advanced with caution between the embankments. The one-legged man in the little signal-hut by the road stared out from his security, like a crab from a snail-shell.

Whilst the two girls waited, Gerald Crich trotted up on a red Arab mare. He rode well and softly, pleased with the delicate quivering of the creature between his knees. And he was very picturesque, at least in Gudrun's eyes, sitting soft and close on the slender red mare, whose long tail flowed on the air. He saluted the two girls, and drew up at the crossing to wait for the gate, looking down the railway for the approaching train. In spite of her ironic smile at his picturesqueness, Gudrun liked to look at him. He was well set and easy, his face with its warm tan showed up his whitish, coarse moustache, and his blue eyes were full of sharp light as he watched the distance.

The locomotive chuffed slowly between the banks, hidden. The mare did not like it. She began to wince away, as if hurt by the unknown noise. But Gerald pulled her back and held her head to the gate. The sharp blasts of the chuffing engine broke with more and more force on her. The repeated sharp blows of unknown, terrifying noise struck through her till she was rocking with terror. She recoiled like a spring let go. But a glistening, half-smiling look came into Gerald's face. He brought her back again, inevitably.

The noise was released, the little locomotive with her clanking steel connecting-rod emerged on the highroad, clanking sharply. The mare rebounded like a drop of water from hot iron. Ursula and Gudrun pressed back into the hedge, in fear. But Gerald was heavy on the mare, and forced her back. It seemed as if he sank into her magnetically, and could thrust her back against herself.

'The fool!' cried Ursula loudly. 'Why doesn't he ride away till it's gone by?'

Gudrun was looking at him with black-dilated, spellbound eyes. But he sat glistening and obstinate, forcing the wheeling mare, which spun and swerved like a wind, and yet could not get out of the grasp of his will, nor escape from the mad clamour of terror that resounded through her, as the trucks thumped slowly, heavily, horrifying, one after the other, one pursuing the other, over the rails of the crossing.

The locomotive, as if wanting to see what could be done, put on the brakes, and back came the trucks rebounding on the iron buffers, striking like horrible cymbals, clashing nearer and nearer in frightful strident concussions. The mare opened her mouth and rose slowly, as if lifted up on a wind of terror. Then suddenly her fore-feet struck out, as she convulsed herself utterly away from the horror. Back she went, and the two girls clung to each other, feeling she must fall backwards on top of him. But he leaned forward, his face shining with fixed amusement, and at last he brought her down, sank her down, and was bearing her back to the mark. But as strong as the pressure of his compulsion was the repulsion of her utter terror, throwing her back away from the railway, so that she spun round and round on two legs, as if she were in the centre of some whirlwind. It made Gudrun faint with poignant dizziness, which seemed to penetrate to her heart.

'No—! No—! Let her go! Let her go, you fool, you *fool*—!' cried Ursula at the top of her voice, completely outside herself. And Gudrun hated her bitterly for being outside herself. It was unendurable that Ursula's voice was so powerful and naked.

A sharpened look came on Gerald's face. He bit himself down on the mare like a keen edge biting home, and *forced* her round. She roared as she breathed, her nostrils were two wide, hot holes, her mouth was apart, her eyes frenzied. It was a repulsive sight. But he held on her unrelaxed, with an almost mechanical relentlessness, keen as a sword pressing into her. Both man and horse were sweating with violence. Yet he seemed calm as a ray of cold sunshine.

Meanwhile the eternal trucks were rumbling on, very slowly, treading one after the other, one after the other, like a disgusting dream that has no end. The connecting chains were grinding and squeaking as the tension varied, the mare pawed and struck away mechanically now, her terror fulfilled in her, for now the man encompassed her; her paws were blind and pathetic as she beat the air, the man closed round her, and brought her down, almost as if she were part of his own physique.

'And she's bleeding! She's bleeding!' cried Ursula, frantic with opposition and hatred of Gerald. She alone understood him perfectly, in pure opposition.

Gudrun looked and saw the trickles of blood on the sides of the mare, and she turned white. And then on the very wound the bright spurs came down, pressing relentlessly. The world reeled and passed into nothingness for Gudrun, she could not know any more.

When she recovered, her soul was calm and cold, without feeling. The trucks were still rumbling by, and the man and the mare were still fighting. But she herself was cold and separate, she had no more feeling for them. She was quite hard and cold and indifferent.

They could see the top of the hooded guard's-van approaching, the sound of the trucks was diminishing, there was hope of relief from the intolerable noise. The heavy panting of the half-stunned mare sounded automatically, the man seemed to be relaxing confidently, his will bright and unstained. The guard's-van came up, and passed slowly, the guard staring out in his transition on the spectacle in the road. And through the man in the closed wagon Gudrun could see the whole scene spectacularly, isolated and momentary, like a vision isolated in eternity.

Lovely, grateful silence seemed to trail behind the receding train. How sweet the silence is! Ursula looked with hatred on the buffers of the diminishing wagon. The gate-keeper stood ready at the door of his hut, to proceed to open the gate. But Gudrun sprang suddenly forward, in front of the struggling horse, threw off the latch and flung the gates asunder, throwing one-half to the keeper, and running with the other half forwards. Gerald suddenly let go the horse and leaped forwards, almost on to Gudrun. She was not afraid. As he jerked aside the mare's head, Gudrun cried, in a strange, high voice, like a gull, or like a witch screaming out from the side of the road:

'I should think you're proud.'

The words were distinct and formed. The man, twisting aside on his dancing horse, looked at her in some surprise, some wondering interest. Then the mare's hoofs had danced three times on the drum-like sleepers of the crossing, and man and horse were bounding springily, unequally up the road.

The two girls watched them go. The gate-keeper hobbled thudding over the logs of the crossing, with his wooden leg. He had fastened the gate. Then he also turned, and called to the girls:

'A masterful young jockey, that'll have his own road, if ever anybody would.'

'Yes,' cried Ursula, in her hot, overbearing voice. 'Why couldn't he take the horse away, till the trucks had gone by? He's a fool, and a bully. Does he think it's manly, to torture a horse? It's a living thing, why should he bully it and torture it?'

There was a pause, then the gate-keeper shook his head, and replied:

'Yes, it's as nice a little mare as you could set eyes on – beautiful little thing, beautiful. Now you couldn't see his father treat any animal like that – not you. They're as different as they welly can be, Gerald Crich and his father – two different men, different made.'

Then there was a pause.

'But why does he do it?' cried Ursula, 'why does he? Does he think he's grand, when he's bullied a sensitive creature, ten times as sensitive as himself?'

Again there was a cautious pause. Then again the man shook his head, as if he would say nothing, but would think the more.

'I expect he's got to train the mare to stand to anything,' he replied. 'A pure-bred Harab – not the sort of breed as is used to round here – different sort from our sort altogether. They say as he got her from Constantinople.'

'He would!' said Ursula. 'He'd better have left her to the Turks, I'm sure they would have had more decency towards her.'

The man went in to drink his can of tea, the girls went on down the lane, that was deep in soft black dust. Gudrun was as if numbed in her mind by the sense of indomitable soft weight of the man, bearing down into the living body of the horse: the strong, indomitable thighs of the blond man clenching the palpitating body of the mare into pure control; a sort of soft white magnetic domination from the loins and thighs and calves, enclosing and encompassing the mare heavily into unutterable subordination, soft-blood-subordination, terrible.

On the left, as the girls walked silently, the coal-mine lifted its great mounds and its patterned head-stocks, the black railway with the trucks at rest looked like a harbour just below, a large bay of railroad with anchored wagons.

Near the second level-crossing, that went over many bright rails, was a farm belonging to the collieries, and a great round globe of iron, a disused boiler, huge and rusty and perfectly round, stood silently in a paddock by the road. The hens were pecking round it, some chickens were balanced on the drinking trough, wagtails flew away in among trucks, from the water.

On the other side of the wide crossing, by the road-side, was a heap of pale-grey stones for mending the roads, and a cart standing, and a middle-aged man with whiskers round his face was leaning on his shovel, talking to a young man in gaiters, who stood by the horse's head. Both men were facing the crossing.

They saw the two girls appear, small, brilliant figures in the near distance, in the strong light of the late afternoon. Both wore light, gay summer dresses. Ursula had an orange-coloured knitted coat, Gudrun a pale yellow. Ursula wore canary yellow stockings, Gundrun bright rose. The figures of the two women seemed to glitter in progress over the wide bay of the railway crossing, white and orange and yellow and rose glittering in motion across a hot world silted with coal-dust.

The two men stood quite still in the heat, watching. The elder was a short, hard-faced energetic man of middle age, the younger a labourer of twenty-three or so. They stood in silence watching the advance of the sisters. They watched whilst the girls drew near, and whilst they passed, and whilst they receded down the dusty road, that had dwellings on one side, and dusty young corn on the other.

Then the elder man, with the whiskers round his face, said in a prurient manner to the young man:

'What price that, eh? She'll do, won't she?'

'Which?' asked the young man, eagerly, with a laugh.

'Her with the red stockings. What d' you say? I'd give my week's wages for five minutes; what! – just for five minutes.'

Again the young man laughed.

'Your missis 'ud have summat to say to you,' he replied.

Gudrun had turned round and looked at the two men. They were to her sinister creatures, standing watching after her, by the heap of pale grey slag. She loathed the man with whiskers round his face.

'You're first class, you are,' the man said to her, and to the distance.

'Do you think it would be worth a week's wages?' said the younger man, musing.

'Do I? I'd put 'em bloody-well down this second—'

The younger man looked after Gudrun and Ursula objectively, as if he wished to calculate what there might be, that was worth his week's wages. He shook his head with fatal misgiving.

'No,' he said. 'It's not worth that to me.'

'Isn't?' said the old man. 'By God, if it isn't to me!'

And he went on shovelling his stones.

The girls descended between the houses with slate roofs and blackish brick walls. The heavy gold glamour of approaching sunset lay over all the colliery district, and the ugliness overlaid with beauty was like a narcotic to the senses. On the roads silted with black dust, the rich light fell more warmly, more heavily, over all the amorphous squalor a kind of magic was cast, from the glowing close of day.

'It has a foul kind of beauty, this place,' said Gudrun, evidently suffering from fascination. 'Can't you feel in some way, a thick, hot attraction in it? I can. And it quite stupefies me.'

They were passing between blocks of miners' dwellings. In the back yards of several dwellings a miner could be seen washing himself in the open on this hot evening, naked down to the loins, his great trousers of moleskin slipping almost away. Miners already cleaned were sitting on their heels, with their backs near the walls, talking and silent in pure physical well-being, tired, and taking physical rest. Their voices sounded out with strong intonation, and the broad dialect was curiously caressing to the blood. It seemed to envelope Gudrun in a labourer's caress, there was in the whole atmosphere, a resonance of physical men, a glamorous thickness of labour and maleness, surcharged in the air. But it was universal in the district, and therefore unnoticed by the inhabitants.

To Gudrun, however, it was potent and half-repulsive. She could never tell why Beldover was so utterly different from London and the south, why one's whole feelings were different, why one seemed to live in another sphere. Now she realised that this was the world of powerful, underworld men who spent most of their time in the darkness. In their voices she could hear the voluptuous resonance of darkness, the strong, dangerous underworld, mindless, inhuman. They sounded also like strange machines, heavy, oiled. The voluptuousness was like that of machinery, cold and iron.

It was the same every evening when she came home, she seemed to move through a wave of disruptive force, that was given off from the presence of thousands of vigorous, underworld, half-automatised colliers, and which went to the brain and the heart, awaking a fatal desire, and a fatal callousness.

There came over her a nostalgia for the place. She hated it, she knew how utterly cut off it was, how hideous and how sickeningly mindless. Sometimes she beat her wings like a new Daphne, turning not into a tree but a machine. And yet she was overcome by the nostalgia. She struggled to get more and more into accord with the atmosphere of the place, she craved to get her satisfaction of it.

She felt herself drawn out at evening into the main street of the town, that was uncreated and ugly, and yet surcharged with this same potent atmosphere of intense, dark callousness. There were always miners about. They moved with their strange, distorted dignity, a certain beauty, and unnatural stillness in their bearing, a look of abstraction and half resignation in their pale, often gaunt faces. They belonged to another world, they had a strange glamour, their voices were full of an intolerable deep resonance, like a machine's burring, a music more maddening than the sirens' long ago.

She found herself, with the rest of the common women, drawn out on Friday evenings to the little market. Friday was pay-day for the colliers, and Friday night was market night. Every woman was abroad, every man was out, shopping with his wife, or gathering with his pals. The pavements were dark for miles around with people coming in; the little market-place on the crown of the hill, and the main street of Beldover were black with thickly-crowded men and women.

It was dark, the market-place was hot with kerosene flares, which threw a ruddy light on the grave faces of the purchasing wives, and on the pale abstract faces of the men. The air was full of the sound of criers and of people talking, thick streams of people moved on the pavements towards the solid crowd of the market. The shops were blazing and packed with women, in the streets were men, mostly men, miners of all ages. Money was spent with almost lavish freedom.

The carts that came could not pass through. They had to wait, the driver calling and shouting, till the dense crowd would make way. Everywhere, young fellows from the outlying districts were making conversation with the girls, standing in the road and at the corners. The doors of the public-houses were open and full of light, men passed in and out in a continual stream, everywhere men were calling out to one another, or crossing to meet one another, or standing in little gangs and circles, discussing, endlessly discussing. The sense of talk, buzzing, jarring, half-secret, the endless mining, and political wrangling, vibrated in the air like discordant machinery. And it was their voices which affected Gudrun almost to swooning. They aroused a strange, nostalgic ache of desire, something almost demoniacal, never to be fulfilled.

Like any other common girl of the district, Gudrun strolled up and down, up and down the length of the brilliant two-hundred paces of the pavement nearest the market-place. She knew it was a vulgar thing to do; her father and mother could not bear it; but the nostalgia came over her, she must be among the people. Sometimes she sat among the louts in the cinema: rakish-looking, unattractive louts they were. Yet she must be among them.

And, like any other common lass, she found her 'boy'. It was an electrician, one of the electricians introduced according to Gerald's new scheme. He was an earnest, clever man, a scientist with a passion for sociology. He lived alone in a cottage, in lodgings, in Willey Green. He was a gentleman, and sufficiently well-to-do. His landlady spread the reports about him; he *would* have a large wooden tub in his bedroom, and every time he came in from work, he *would* have pails and pails of water brought up, to bathe in, then he put on clean shirt and under-clothing *every* day, and clean silk socks; fastidious and exacting he was in these respects, but in every other way, most ordinary and unassuming.

Gudrun knew all these things. The Brangwen's house was one to which the gossip came naturally and inevitably. Palmer was in the first place a friend of Ursula's. But in his pale, elegant, serious face there showed the same nostalgia that Gudrun felt. He too must walk up and down the street on Friday evening. So he walked with Gudrun, and a friendship was struck up between them. But he was not in love with Gudrun; he *really* wanted Ursula, but for some strange reason, nothing could happen between her and him. He liked to have Gudrun about, as a fellow-mind – but that was all. And she had no real feeling for him. He was a scientist, he had to have a woman to back him. But he was really impersonal, he had the fineness of an elegant piece of machinery. He was too cold, too destructive to care really for women, too great an egoist. He was polarised by the men. Individually he detested and despised them. In the mass they fascinated him, as machinery fascinated him. They were a new sort of machinery to him – but incalculable, incalculable.

So Gudrun strolled the streets with Palmer, or went to the cinema with him. And his long, pale, rather elegant face flickered as he made his sarcastic remarks. There they were, the two of them: two elegants in one sense: in the other sense, two units, absolutely adhering to the people, teeming with the distorted colliers. The same secret seemed to be working in the souls of all alike, Gudrun, Palmer, the rakish young bloods, the gaunt, middle-aged men. All had a secret sense of power, and of inexpressible destructiveness, and of fatal half-heartedness, a sort of rottenness in the will.

Sometimes Gudrun would start aside, see it all, see how she was sinking in. And then she was filled with a fury of contempt and anger. She felt she was sinking into one mass with the rest – all so close and intermingled and breathless. It was horrible. She stifled. She prepared for flight, feverishly she flew to her work. But soon she let go. She started off into the country – the darkish, glamorous country. The spell was beginning to work again.

Chapter Ten

Sketch-book

One morning the sisters were sketching by the side of Willey Water, at the remote end of the lake. Gudrun had waded out to a gravelly shoal, and was seated like a Buddhist, staring fixedly at the water-plants that rose succulent from the mud of the low shores. What she could see was mud, soft, oozy, watery mud, and from its festering chill, water-plants rose up, thick and cool and fleshy, very straight and turgid, thrusting out their leaves at right angles, and having dark lurid colours, dark green and blotches of black-purple and bronze. But she could feel their turgid fleshy structure as in a sensuous vision, she *knew* how they rose out of the mud, she *knew* how they thrust out from themselves, how they stood stiff and succulent against the air.

Ursula was watching the butterflies, of which there were dozens near the

water, little blue ones suddenly snapping out of nothingness into a jewel-
life, a large black-and-red one standing upon a flower and breathing with
his soft wings, intoxicatingly, breathing pure, ethereal sunshine; two white
ones wrestling in the low air; there was a halo round them; ah, when they
came tumbling nearer they were orange-tips, and it was the orange that had
made the halo. Ursula rose and drifted away, unconscious like the butterflies.

Gudrun, absorbed in a stupor of apprehension of surging water-plants,
sat crouched on the shoal, drawing, not looking up for a long time, and then
staring unconsciously, absorbedly at the rigid, naked, succulent stems. Her
feet were bare, her hat lay on the bank opposite.

She started out of her trance, hearing the knocking of oars. She looked
round. There was a boat with a gaudy Japanese parasol, and a man in
white, rowing. The woman was Hermione, and the man was Gerald. She
knew it instantly. And instantly she perished in the keen *frisson* of anticipation, an electric vibration in her veins, intense, much more intense than
that which was always humming low in the atmosphere of Beldover.

Gerald was her escape from the heavy slough of the pale, underworld,
automatic colliers. He started out of the mud. He was master. She saw his
back, the movement of his white loins. But not that – it was the whiteness
he seemed to enclose as he bent forwards, rowing. He seemed to stoop to
something. His glistening, whitish hair seemed like the electricity of the sky.

'There's Gudrun,' came Hermione's voice floating distinct over the water.
'We will go and speak to her. Do you mind?'

Gerald looked round and saw the girl standing by the water's edge, looking
at him. He pulled the boat towards her, magnetically, without thinking of
her. In his world, his conscious world, she was still nobody. He knew that
Hermione had a curious pleasure in treading down all the social differences,
at least apparently, and he left it to her.

'How do you do, Gudrun?' sang Hermione, using the Christian name in
the fashionable manner. 'What are you doing?'

'How do you do, Hermione? I *was* sketching.'

'Were you?' The boat drifted nearer, till the keel ground on the bank.
'May we see? I should like to *so* much.'

It was no use resisting Hermione's deliberate intention.

'Well—' said Gudrun reluctantly, for she always hated to have her
unfinished work exposed – 'there's nothing in the least interesting.'

'Isn't there? But let me see, will you?'

Gudrun reached out the sketch-book, Gerald stretched from the boat to
take it. And as he did so, he remembered Gudrun's last words to him, and
her face lifted up to him as he sat on the swerving horse. An intensification
of pride went over his nerves, because he felt, in some way she was compelled
by him. The exchange of feeling between them was strong and apart from
their consciousness.

And as if in a spell, Gudrun was aware of his body, stretching and surging
like the marsh-fire, stretching towards her, his hand coming straight forward
like a stem. Her voluptuous, acute apprehension of him made the blood faint
in her veins, her mind went dim and unconscious. And he rocked on the
water perfectly, like the rocking of phosphorescence. He looked round at the

boat. It was drifting off a little. He lifted the oar to bring it back. And the exquisite pleasure of slowly arresting the boat, in the heavy-soft water, was complete as a swoon.

'*That's* what you have done,' said Hermione, looking searchingly at the plants on the shore, and comparing with Gudrun's drawing. Gudrun looked round in the direction of Hermione's long, pointing finger. 'That is it, isn't it?' repeated Hermione needing confirmation.

'Yes,' said Gudrun automatically, taking no real heed.

'Let me look,' said Gerald, reaching forward for the book. But Hermione ignored him, he must not presume, before she had finished. But he, his will as unthwarted and as unflinching as hers, stretched forward till he touched the book. A little shock, a storm of revulsion against him, shook Hermione unconsciously. She released the book when he had not properly got it, and it tumbled against the side of the boat and bounced into the water.

'There!' sang Hermione, with a strange ring of malevolent victory. 'I'm so sorry, so awfully sorry. Can't you get it, Gerald?'

This last was said in a note of anxious sneering that made Gerald's veins tingle with fine hate for her. He leaned far out of the boat, reaching down into the water. He could feel his position was ridiculous, his loins exposed behind him.

'It is of no importance,' came the strong, clanging voice of Gudrun. She seemed to touch him. But he reached further, the boat swayed violently. Hermione, however, remained unperturbed. He grasped the book, under the water, and brought it up, dripping.

'I'm so dreadfully sorry – dreadfully sorry,' repeated Hermione. 'I'm afraid it was all my fault.'

'It's of no importance – really, I assure you – it doesn't matter in the least,' said Gudrun loudly, with emphasis, her face flushed scarlet. And she held out her hand impatiently for the wet book, to have done with the scene. Gerald gave it to her. He was not quite himself.

'I'm so dreadfully sorry,' repeated Hermione, till both Gerald and Gudrun were exasperated. 'Is there nothing that can be done?'

'In what way?' asked Gudrun, with cool irony.

'Can't we save the drawings?'

There was a moment's pause, wherein Gudrun made evident all her refutation of Hermione's persistence.

'I assure you,' said Gudrun, with cutting distinctness, 'the drawings are quite as good as ever they were, for my purpose. I want them only for reference.'

'But can't I give you a new book? I wish you'd let me do that. I feel so truly sorry. I feel it was all my fault.'

'As far as I saw,' said Gudrun, 'it wasn't your fault at all. If there was any *fault*, it was Mr. Crich's. But the whole thing is *entirely* trivial, and it really is ridiculous to take any notice of it.'

Gerald watched Gudrun closely, whilst she repulsed Hermione. There was a body of cold power in her. He watched her with an insight that amounted to clairvoyance. He saw her a dangerous, hostile spirit, that could stand undiminished and unabated. It was so finished, and of such perfect gesture, moreover.

'I'm awfully glad if it doesn't matter,' he said; 'if there's no real harm done.'

She looked back at him, with her fine blue eyes, and signalled full into his spirit, as she said, her voice ringing with intimacy almost caressive now it was addressed to him:

'Of course, it doesn't matter in the *least*.'

The bond was established between them, in that look, in her tone. In her tone, she made the understanding clear – they were of the same kind, he and she, a sort of diabolic freemasonry subsisted between them. Henceforward, she knew, she had her power over him. Wherever they met, they would be secretly associated. And he would be helpless in the association with her. Her soul exulted.

'Good-bye! I'm so glad you forgive me. Gooood-bye!'

Hermione sang her farewell, and waved her hand. Gerald automatically took the oar and pushed off. But he was looking all the time, with a glimmering, subtly-smiling admiration in his eyes, at Gudrun, who stood on the shoal shaking the wet book in her hand. She turned away and ignored the receding boat. But Gerald looked back as he rowed, beholding her, forgetting what he was doing.

'Aren't we going too much to the left?' sang Hermione, as she sat ignored under her coloured parasol.

Gerald looked round without replying, the oars balanced and glancing in the sun.

'I think it's all right,' he said good-humouredly, beginning to row again without thinking of what he was doing. And Hermione disliked him extremely for his good-humoured obliviousness, she was nullified, she could not regain ascendancy.

Chapter Eleven

An Island

Meanwhile Ursula had wandered on from Willey Water along the course of the bright little stream. The afternoon was full of larks' singing. On the bright hill-sides was a subdued smoulder of gorse. A few forget-me-nots flowered by the water. There was a rousedness and a glancing everywhere.

She strayed absorbedly on, over the brooks. She wanted to go to the mill-pond above. The big mill-house was deserted, save for a labourer and his wife who lived in the kitchen. So she passed through the empty farm-yard and through the wilderness of a garden, and mounted the bank by the sluice.

When she got to the top, to see the old, velvety surface of the pond before her, she noticed a man on the bank, tinkering with a punt. It was Birkin sawing and hammering away.

She stood at the head of the sluice, looking at him. He was unaware of anybody's presence. He looked very busy, like a wild animal, active and intent. She felt she ought to go away, he would not want her. He seemed to be so much occupied. But she did not want to go away. Therefore she moved along the bank till he would look up.

Which he soon did. The moment he saw her, he dropped his tools and came forward, saying:

'How do you do? I'm making the punt water-tight. Tell me if you think it is right.'

She went along with him.

'You are your father's daughter, so you can tell me if it will do,' he said.

She bent to look at the patched punt.

'I am sure I am my father's daughter,' she said, fearful of having to judge. 'But I don't know anything about carpentry. It *looks* right, don't you think?'

'Yes, I think. I hope it won't let me to the bottom, that's all. Though even so, it isn't a great matter, I should come up again. Help me to get it into the water, will you?'

With combined efforts they turned over the heavy punt and set it afloat.

'Now,' he said, 'I'll try it and you can watch what happens. Then if it carries, I'll take you over to the island.'

'Do,' she cried, watching anxiously.

The pond was large, and had that perfect stillness and the dark lustre of very deep water. There were two small islands overgrown with bushes and a few trees, towards the middle. Birkin pushed himself off, and veered clumsily in the pond. Luckily the punt drifted so that he could catch hold of a willow bough, and pull it to the island.

'Rather overgrown,' he said, looking into the interior, 'but very nice. I'll come and fetch you. The boat leaks a little.'

In a moment he was with her again, and she stepped into the wet punt.

'It'll float us all right,' he said, and manoeuvred again to the island.

They landed under a willow tree. She shrank from the little jungle of rank plants before her, evil-smelling figwort and hemlock. But he explored into it.

'I shall mow this down,' he said, 'and then it will be romantic – like Paul et Virginie.'

'Yes, one could have lovely Watteau picnics here,' cried Ursula with enthusiasm.

His face darkened.

'I don't want Watteau picnics here,' he said.

'Only your Virginie,' she laughed.

'Virginie enough,' he smiled wryly. 'No, I don't want her either.'

Ursula looked at him closely. She had not seen him since Breadalby. He was very thin and hollow, with a ghastly look in his face.

'You have been ill, haven't you?' she asked, rather repulsed.

'Yes,' he replied coldly.

They had sat down under the willow tree, and were looking at the pond, from their retreat on the island.

'Has it made you frightened?' she asked.

'What of?' he asked, turning his eyes to look at her. Something in him, inhuman and unmitigated, disturbed her, and shook her out of her ordinary self.

'It *is* frightening to be very ill, isn't it?' she said.

'It isn't pleasant,' he said. 'Whether one is really afraid of death or not, I have never decided. In one mood, not a bit, in another, very much.'

'But doesn't it make you feel ashamed? I think it makes one so ashamed, to be ill – illness is so terribly humiliating, don't you think?'

He considered for some minutes.

'May-be,' he said. 'Though one knows all the time one's life isn't really right, at the source. That's the humiliation. I don't see that the illness counts so much, after that. One is ill because one doesn't live properly – can't. It's the failure to live that makes one ill, and humiliates one.'

'But do you fail to live?' she asked, almost jeering.

'Why, yes – I don't make much of a success of my days. One seems always to be bumping one's nose against the blank wall ahead.'

Ursula laughed. She was frightened, and when she was frightened she always laughed and pretended to be jaunty.

'Your poor nose!' she said, looking at that feature of his face.

'No wonder it's ugly,' he replied.

She was silent for some minutes, struggling with her own self-deception. It was an instinct in her, to deceive herself.

'But *I'm* happy – I think life is *awfully* jolly,' she said.

'Good,' he answered, with a certain cold indifference.

She reached for a bit of paper which had wrapped a small piece of chocolate she had found in her pocket, and began making a boat. He watched her without heeding her. There was something strangely pathetic and tender in her moving, unconscious finger-tips, that were agitated and hurt, really.

'I *do* enjoy things – don't you?' she asked.

'Oh yes! But it infuriates me that I can't get right, at the really growing part of me. I feel all tangled and messed up, and I *can't* get straight anyhow. I don't know what really to *do*. One must do something somewhere.'

'Why should you always be *doing*?' she retorted. 'It is so plebeian. I think it is much better to be really patrician, and to do nothing but just be oneself, like a walking flower.'

'I quite agree,' he said, 'if one has burst into blossom. But I can't get my flower to blossom anyhow. Either it is blighted in the bud, or has got the smother-fly, or it isn't nourished. Curse it, it isn't even a bud. It is a contravened knot.'

Again she laughed. He was so very fretful and exasperated. But she was anxious and puzzled. How was one to get out, anyhow. There must be a way out somewhere.

There was a silence, wherein she wanted to cry. She reached for another bit of chocolate paper, and began to fold another boat.

'And why is it,' she asked at length, 'that there is no flowering, no dignity of human life now?'

'The whole idea is dead. Humanity itself is dry-rotten, really. There are myriads of human beings hanging on the bush – and they look very nice and rosy, your healthy young men and women. But they are apples of Sodom, as a matter of fact, Dead Sea Fruit, gall-apples. It isn't true that they have any significance – their insides are full of bitter, corrupt ash.'

'But there *are* good people,' protested Ursula.

'Good enough for the life of to-day. But mankind is a dead tree, covered with fine brilliant galls of people.'

Ursula could not help stiffening herself against this, it was too picturesque and final. But neither could she help making him go on.

'And if it is so, *why* is it?' she asked, hostile. They were rousing each other to a fine passion of opposition.

'Why, why are people all balls of bitter dust? Because they won't fall off the tree when they're ripe. They hang on to their old positions when the position is overpast, till they become infested with little worms and dry-rot.'

There was a long pause. His voice had become hot and very sarcastic. Ursula was troubled and bewildered, they were both oblivious of everything but their own immersion.

'But even if everybody is wrong – where are *you* right?' she cried, 'where are you any better?'

'I? – I'm not right,' he cried back. 'At least my only rightness lies in the fact that I know it. I detest what I am, outwardly. I loathe myself as a human being. Humanity is a huge aggregate lie, and a huge lie is less than a small truth. Humanity is less, far less than the individual, because the individual may sometimes be capable of truth, and humanity is a tree of lies. And they say that love is the greatest thing; they persist in *saying* this, the foul liars, and just look at what they do! Look at all the millions of people who repeat every minute that love is the greatest, and charity is the greatest – and see what they are doing all the time. By their works ye shall know them, for dirty liars and cowards, who daren't stand by their own actions, much less by their own words.'

'But,' said Ursula sadly, 'that doesn't alter the fact that love is the greatest, does it? What they *do* doesn't alter the truth of what they say, does it?'

'Completely, because if what they say *were* true, then they couldn't help fulfilling it. But they maintain a lie, and so they run amok at last. It's a lie to say that love is the greatest. You might as well say that hate is the greatest, since the opposite of everything balances. What people want is hate – hate and nothing but hate. And in the name of righteousness and love, they get it. They distil themselves with nitro-glycerine, all the lot of them, out of very love. It's the lie that kills. If we want hate, let us have it – death, murder, torture, violent destruction – let us have it; but not in the name of love. But I abhor humanity, I wish it was swept away. It could go, and there would be no *absolute* loss, if every human being perished to-morrow. The reality would be untouched. Nay, it would be better. The real tree of life would then be rid of the most ghastly, heavy crop of Dead Sea Fruit, the intolerable burden of myriad simulacra of people, an infinite weight of mortal lies.'

'So you'd like everybody in the world destroyed?' said Ursula.

'I should indeed.'

'And the world empty of people?'

'Yes truly. You yourself, don't you find it a beautiful clean thought, a world empty of people, just uninterrupted grass, and a hare sitting up?'

The pleasant sincerity of his voice made Ursula pause to consider her own proposition. And really it *was* attractive: a clean, lovely, humanless world. It was the *really* desirable. Her heart hesitated, and exulted. But still, she was dissatisfied with *him*.

'But,' she objected, 'you'd be dead yourself, so what good would it do you?'

'I would die like a shot, to know that the earth would really be cleaned of all the people. It is the most beautiful and freeing thought. Then there would *never* be another foul humanity created, for a universal defilement.'

'No,' said Ursula, 'there would be nothing.'

'What! Nothing? Just because humanity was wiped out? You flatter yourself. There'd be everything.'

'But how, if there were no people?'

'Do you think that creation depends on *man!* It merely doesn't. There are the trees and the grass and birds. I much prefer to think of the lark rising up in the morning upon a humanless world. Man is a mistake, he must go. There is the grass, and hares and adders, and the unseen hosts, actual angels that go about freely when a dirty humanity doesn't interrupt them – and good pure-tissued demons: very nice.'

It pleased Ursula, what he said, pleased her very much, as a phantasy. Of course it was only a pleasant fancy. She herself knew too well the actuality of humanity, its hideous actuality. She knew it could not disappear so cleanly and conveniently. It had a long way to go yet, a long and hideous way. Her subtle, feminine, demoniacal soul knew it well.

'If only man was swept off the face of the earth, creation would go on so marvellously, with a new start, non-human. Man is one of the mistakes of creation – like the ichthyosauri. If only he were gone again, think what lovely things would come out of the liberated days; – things straight out of the fire.'

'But man will never be gone,' she said, with insidious, diabolical knowledge of the horrors of persistence. 'The world will go with him.'

'Ah no,' he answered, 'not so. I believe in the proud angels and the demons that are our fore-runners. They will destroy us, because we are not proud enough. The ichthyosauri were not proud: they crawled and floundered as we do. And besides, look at elder-flowers and bluebells – they are a sign that pure creation takes place – even the butterfly. But humanity never gets beyond the caterpillar stage – it rots in the chrysalis, it never will have wings. It is anti-creation, like monkeys and baboons.'

Ursula watched him as he talked. There seemed a certain impatient fury in him, all the while, and at the same time a great amusement in everything, and a final tolerance. And it was this tolerance she mistrusted, not the fury. She saw that, all the while, in spite of himself, he would have to be trying to save the world. And this knowledge, whilst it comforted her heart somewhere with a little self-satisfaction, stability, yet filled her with a certain sharp contempt and hate of him. She wanted him to herself, she hated the Salvator Mundi touch. It was something diffuse and generalised about him, which she could not stand. He would behave in the same way, say the same things, give himself as completely to anybody who came along, anybody and everybody who liked to appeal to him. It was despicable, a very insidious form of prostitution.

'But,' she said, 'you believe in individual love, even if you don't believe in loving humanity —?'

'I don't believe in love at all – that is, any more than I believe in hate, or in grief. Love is one of the emotions like all the others – and so it is all right whilst you feel it. But I can't see how it becomes an absolute. It is just part of human relationships, no more. And it is only part of *any* human relationship. And why one should be required *always* to feel it, any more than one always feels sorrow or distant joy, I cannot conceive. Love isn't a desideratum – it is an emotion you feel or you don't feel, according to circumstance.'

'Then why do you care about people at all,' she asked, 'if you don't believe in love? Why do you bother about humanity?'

'Why do I? Because I can't get away from it.'

'Because you love it,' she persisted.

It irritated him.

'If I do love it,' he said, 'it is my disease.'

'But it is a disease you don't want to be cured of,' she said, with some cold sneering.

He was silent now, feeling she wanted to insult him.

'And if you don't believe in love, what *do* you believe in?' she asked, mocking. 'Simply in the end of the world, and grass?'

He was beginning to feel a fool.

'I believe in the unseen hosts,' he said.

'And nothing else? You believe in nothing visible, except grass and birds? Your world is a poor show.'

'Perhaps it is,' he said, cool and superior now he was offended, assuming a certain insufferable aloof superiority, and withdrawing into his distance.

Ursula disliked him. But also she felt she had lost something. She looked at him as he sat crouched on the bank. There was a certain priggish Sunday-school stiffness over him, priggish and detestable. And yet, at the same time, the moulding of him was so quick and attractive, it gave such a great sense of freedom: the moulding of his brows, his chin, his whole physique, something so alive, somewhere, in spite of the look of sickness.

And it was this duality in feeling which he created in her, that made a fine hate of him quicken in her bowels. There was his wonderful, desirable life-rapidity, the rare quality of an utterly desirable man: and there was at the same time this ridiculous, mean effacement into a Salvator Mundi and a Sunday-school teacher, a prig of the stiffest type.

He looked up at her. He saw her face strangely enkindled, as if suffused from within by a powerful sweet fire. His soul was arrested in wonder. She was enkindled in her own living fire. Arrested in wonder and in pure, perfect attraction, he moved towards her. She sat like a strange queen, almost supernatural in her glowing smiling richness.

'The point about love,' he said, his consciousness quickly adjusting itself, 'is that we hate the word because we have vulgarised it. It ought to be prescribed, tabooed from utterance, for many years, till we get a new, better idea.'

There was a beam of understanding between them.

'But it always means the same thing,' she said.

'Ah, God, no, let it not mean that any more,' he cried. 'Let the old meanings go.'

'But still it is love,' she persisted. A strange, wicked yellow light shone at him in her eyes.

He hesitated, baffled, withdrawing.

'No,' he said, 'it isn't. Spoken like that, never in the world. You've no business to utter the word.'

'I must leave it to you, to take it out of the Ark of the Covenant at the right moment,' she mocked.

Again they looked at each other. She suddenly sprang up, turned her back to him, and walked away. He too rose slowly and went to the water's edge, where, crouching, he began to amuse himself unconsciously. Picking a daisy he dropped it on the pond, so that the stem was a keel, the flower floated like a little water-lily, staring with its open face up to the sky. It turned slowly round, in a slow, slow Dervish dance, as it veered away.

He watched it, then dropped another daisy into the water, and after that another, and sat watching them with bright, absolved eyes, crouching near on the bank. Ursula turned to look. A strange feeling possessed her, as if something were taking place. But it was all intangible. And some sort of control was being put on her. She could not know. She could only watch the brilliant little discs of the daisies veering slowly in travel on the dark, lustrous water. The little flotilla was drifting into the light, a company of white specks in the distance.

'Do let us go to the shore, to follow them,' she said, afraid of being any longer imprisoned on the island. And they pushed off in the punt.

She was glad to be on the free land again. She went along the bank towards the sluice. The daisies were scattered broadcast on the pond, tiny radiant things, like an exaltation, points of exaltation here and there. Why did they move her so strongly and mystically?

'Look,' he said, 'your boat of purple paper is escorting them, and they are a convoy of rafts.'

Some of the daisies came slowly towards her, hesitating, making a shy bright little cotillon on the dark clear water. Their gay bright candour moved her so much as they came near, that she was almost in tears.

'Why are they so lovely,' she cried. 'Why do I think them so lovely?'

'They are nice flowers,' he said, her emotional tones putting a constraint on him.

'You know that a daisy is a company of florets, a concourse, become individual. Don't the botanists put it highest in the line of development? I believe they do.'

'The compositae, yes, I think so,' said Ursula, who was never very sure of anything. Things she knew perfectly well, at one moment, seemed to become doubtful the next.

'Explain it so, then,' he said. 'The daisy is a perfect little democracy, so it's the highest of flowers, hence its charm.'

'No,' she cried, 'no – never. It isn't democratic.'

'No,' he admitted. 'It's the golden mob of the proletariat, surrounded by a showy white fence of the idle rich.'

'How hateful – your hateful social orders!' she cried.

'Quite! it's a daisy – we'll leave it alone.'

'Do. Let it be a dark horse for once,' she said: 'if anything can be a dark horse to you,' she added satirically.

They stood aside, forgetful. As if a little stunned, they both were motionless, barely conscious. The little conflict into which they had fallen had torn their consciousness and left them like two impersonal forces, there in contact.

He became aware of the lapse. He wanted to say something, to get on to a new more ordinary footing.

'You know,' he said, 'that I am having rooms here at the mill? Don't you think we can have some good times?'

'Oh, are you?' she said, ignoring all his implication of admitted intimacy.

He adjusted himself at once, became normally distant.

'If I find I can live sufficiently by myself,' he continued. 'I shall give up my work altogether. It has become dead to me. I don't believe in the humanity I pretend to be part of, I don't care a straw for the social ideals I live by, I hate the dying organic form of social mankind – so it can't be anything but trumpery, to work at education. I shall drop it as soon as I am clear enough – to-morrow perhaps – and be by myself.'

'Have you enough to live on?' asked Ursula.

'Yes – I've about four hundred a year. That makes it easy for me.'

There was a pause.

'And what about Hermione?' asked Ursula.

'That's over, finally – a pure failure, and never could have been anything else.'

'But you still know each other?'

'We could hardly pretend to be strangers, could we?'

There was a stubborn pause.

'But isn't that a half-measure?' asked Ursula at length.

'I don't think so,' he said. 'You'll be able to tell me if it is.'

Again there was a pause of some minutes' duration. He was thinking.

'One must throw everything away, everything – let everything go, to get the one last thing one wants,' he said.

'What thing?' she asked in challenge.

'I don't know – freedom together,' he said.

She had wanted him to say 'love'.

There was heard a loud barking of the dogs below. He seemed disturbed by it. She did not notice. Only she thought he seemed uneasy.

'As a matter of fact,' he said, in rather a small voice, 'I believe that is

Hermione come now, with Gerald Crich. She wanted to see the rooms before they are furnished.'

'I know,' said Ursula. 'She will superintend the furnishing for you.'

'Probably. Does it matter?'

'Oh no, I should think not,' said Ursula. 'Though personally, I can't bear her. I think she is a lie, if you like, you who are always talking about lies.' Then she ruminated for a moment, when she broke out: 'Yes, and I do mind if she furnishes your rooms – I do mind. I mind that you keep her hanging on at all.'

He was silent now, frowning.

'Perhaps,' he said. 'I don't *want* her to furnish the rooms here – and I don't keep her hanging on. Only, I needn't be churlish to her, need I? At any rate, I shall have to go down and see them now. You'll come, won't you?'

'I don't think so,' she said coldly and irresolutely.

'Won't you? Yes, do. Come and see the rooms as well. Do come.'

Chapter Twelve

Carpeting

He set off down the bank, and she went unwillingly with him. Yet she would not have stayed away, either.

'We know each other well, you and I, already,' he said. She did not answer.

In the large darkish kitchen of the mill, the labourer's wife was talking shrilly to Hermione and Gerald, who stood, he in white and she in a glistening bluish foulard, strangely luminous in the dusk of the room; whilst from the cages on the walls, a dozen or more canaries sang at the top of their voices. The cages were all placed round a small square window at the back, where the sunshine came in, a beautiful beam, filtering through green leaves of a tree. The voice of Mrs. Salmon shrilled against the noise of the birds, which rose ever more wild and triumphant, and the woman's voice went up and up against them, and the birds replied with wild animation.

'Here's Rupert!' shouted Gerald in the midst of the din. He was suffering badly, being very sensitive in the ear.

'O-o-h them birds, they won't let you speak—!' shrilled the labourer's wife in disgust. 'I'll cover them up.'

And she darted here and there, throwing a duster, an apron, a towel, a table-cloth over the cages of the birds.

'Now will you stop it, and let a body speak for your row,' she said, still in a voice that was too high.

The party watched her. Soon the cages were covered, they had a strange funereal look. But from under the towels odd defiant trills and bubblings still shook out.

'Oh, they won't go on,' said Mrs. Salmon reassuringly. 'They'll go to sleep now.'

'Really,' said Hermione politely.

'They will,' said Gerald. 'They will go to sleep automatically, now the impression of evening is produced.'

'Are they so easily deceived?' cried Ursula.

'Oh yes,' replied Gerald. 'Don't you know the story of Fabre, who, when he was a boy, put a hen's head under her wing, and she straight away went to sleep? It's quite true.'

'And did that make him a naturalist?' asked Birkin.

'Probably,' said Gerald.

Meanwhile Ursula was peeping under one of the cloths. There sat the canary in a corner, bunched and fluffed up for sleep.

'How ridiculous!' she cried. 'It really thinks the night has come! How absurd! Really, how can one have any respect for a creature that is so easily taken in!'

'Yes,' sang Hermione, coming also to look. She put her hand on Ursula's arm and chuckled a low laugh. 'Yes, doesn't he look comical?' she chuckled. 'Like a stupid husband.'

Then, with her hand still on Ursula's arm, she drew her away, saying, in her mild sing-song:

'How did you come here? We saw Gudrun too.'

'I came to look at the pond,' said Ursula, 'and I found Mr. Birkin there.'

'Did you? This is quite a Brangwen land, isn't it?'

'I'm afraid I hoped so,' said Ursula. 'I ran here for refuge, when I saw you down the lake, just putting off.'

'Did you! And now we've run you to earth.'

Hermione's eyelids lifted with an uncanny movement, amused but over-wrought. She had always her strange, rapt look, unnatural and irresponsible.

'I was going on,' said Ursula. 'Mr. Birkin wanted me to see the rooms. Isn't it delightful to live here? It is perfect.'

'Yes,' said Hermione, abstractedly. Then she turned right away from Ursula, ceased to know her existence.

'How do you feel, Rupert?' she sang in a new, affectionate tone to Birkin.

'Very well,' he replied.

'Were you quite comfortable?' The curious, sinister, rapt look was on Hermione's face, she shrugged her bosom in a convulsed movement, and seemed like one half in a trance.

'Quite comfortable,' he replied.

There was a long pause, whilst Hermione looked at him for a long time, from under her heavy, drugged eyelids.

'And you think you'll be happy here?' she said at last.

'I'm sure I shall.'

'I'm sure I shall do anything for him as I can,' said the labourer's wife. 'And I'm sure our mester will; so I *hope* as he'll find himself comfortable.'

Hermione turned and looked at her slowly.

'Thank you so much,' she said, and then she turned completely away again. She recovered her position, and lifting her face towards him, and addressing him exclusively, she said:

'Have you measured the rooms?'

'No,' he said, 'I've been mending the punt.'

'Shall we do it now?' she said slowly, balanced and dispassionate.

'Have you got a tape measure, Mrs. Salmon?' he said, turning to the woman.

'Yes, sir, I think I can find one,' replied the woman, bustling immediately to a basket. 'This is the only one I've got, if it will do.'

Hermione took it, though it was offered to him.

'Thank you so much,' she said. 'It will do very nicely. Thank you so much.' Then she turned to Birkin, saying with a little gay movement: 'Shall we do it now, Rupert?'

'What about the others, they'll be bored,' he said reluctantly.

'Do you mind?' said Hermione, turning to Ursula and Gerald vaguely.

'Not in the least,' they replied.

'Which room shall we do first?' she said, turning again to Birkin, with the same gaiety, now she was going to *do* something with him.

'We'll take them as they come,' he said.

'Should I be getting your teas ready, while you do that?' said the labourer's wife, also gay because *she* had something to do.

'Would you?' said Hermione, turning to her with the curious motion of intimacy that seemed to envelop the woman, draw her almost to Hermione's breast, and which left the others standing apart. 'I should be so glad. Where shall we have it?'

'Where would you like it? Shall it be in here, or out on the grass?'

'Where shall we have tea?' sang Hermione to the company at large.

'On the bank by the pond. And *we'll* carry the things up, if you'll just get them ready, Mrs. Salmon,' said Birkin.

'All right,' said the pleased woman.

The party moved down the passage into the front room. It was empty, but clean and sunny. There was a window looking on to the tangled front garden.

'This is the dining-room,' said Hermione. 'We'll measure it this way, Rupert – you go down there—'

'Can't I do it for you,' said Gerald, coming to take the end of the tape.

'No, thank you,' cried Hermione, stooping to the ground in her bluish, brilliant foulard. It was a great joy to her to *do* things, and to have the ordering of the job, with Birkin. He obeyed her subduedly. Ursula and Gerald looked on. It was a peculiarity of Hermione's, that at every moment, she had one intimate, and turned all the rest of those present into onlookers. This raised her into a state of triumph.

They measured and discussed in the dining-room, and Hermione decided what the floor coverings must be. It sent her into a strange, convulsed anger, to be thwarted. Birkin always let her have her way, for the moment.

Then they moved across, through the hall, to the other front room, that was a little smaller than the first.

'This is the study,' said Hermione. 'Rupert, I have a rug that I want you to have for here. Will you let me give it to you? Do – I want to give it you.'

'What is it like?' he asked ungraciously.

'You haven't seen it. It is chiefly rose red, then blue, a metallic, mid-blue, and a very soft dark blue. I think you would like it. Do you think you would?'

'It sounds very nice,' he replied. 'What is it? Oriental? With a pile?'

'Yes. Persian! It is made of camel's hair, silky. I think it is called Bergamos – twelve feet by seven – Do you think it will do?'

'It would *do*,' he said. 'But why should you give me an expensive rug? I can manage perfectly well with my old Oxford Turkish.'

'But may I give it to you? Do let me.'

'How much did it cost?'

She looked at him, and said:

'I don't remember. It was quite cheap.'

He looked at her, his face set.

'I don't want to take it, Hermione,' he said.

'Do let me give it to the rooms,' she said, going up to him and putting her hand on his arm lightly, pleadingly. 'I shall be so disappointed.'

'You know I don't want you to give me things,' he repeated helplessly.

'I don't want to give you *things*,' she said teasingly. 'But will you have this?'

'All right,' he said, defeated, and she triumphed.

They went upstairs. There were two bedrooms to correspond with the rooms downstairs. One of them was half furnished, and Birkin had evidently slept there. Hermione went round the room carefully, taking in every detail, as if absorbing the evidence of his presence, in all the inanimate things. She felt the bed and examined the coverings.

'Are you *sure* you were quite comfortable?' she said, pressing the pillow.

'Perfectly,' he replied coldly.

'And were you warm? There is no down quilt. I am sure you need one. You mustn't have a great pressure of clothes.'

'I've got one,' he said. 'It is coming down.'

They measured the rooms, and lingered over every consideration. Ursula stood at the window and watched the woman carrying the tea up the bank to the pond. She hated the palaver Hermione made, she wanted to drink tea, she wanted anything but this fuss and business.

At last they all mounted the grassy bank, to the picnic. Hermione poured out tea. She ignored now Ursula's presence. And Ursula, recovering from her ill-humour, turned to Gerald saying:

'Oh, I hated you so much the other day, Mr. Crich.'

'What for?' said Gerald, wincing slightly away.

'For treating your horse so badly. Oh, I hated you so much!'

'What did he do?' sang Hermione.

'He made his lovely sensitive Arab horse stand with him at the railway-crossing whilst a horrible lot of trucks went by; and the poor thing, she was in a perfect frenzy, a perfect agony. It was the most horrible sight you can imagine.'

'Why did you do it, Gerald?' asked Hermione, calm and interrogative.

'She must learn to stand – what use is she to me in this country if she shies and goes off every time an engine whistles.'

'But why inflict unnecessary torture?' said Ursula. 'Why make her stand all that time at the crossing? You might just as well have ridden back up the road, and saved all that horror. Her sides were bleeding where you had spurred her. It was too horrible—!'

Gerald stiffened.

'I have to use her,' he replied. 'And if I'm going to be sure of her at *all*, she'll have to learn to stand noises.'

'Why should she?' cried Ursula in a passion. 'She is a living creature, why should she stand anything, just because you choose to make her? She has as much right to her own being, as you have to yours.'

'There I disagree,' said Gerald. 'I consider that mare is there for my use. Not because I bought her, but because that is the natural order. It is more natural for a man to take a horse and use it as he likes, than for him to go down on his knees to it, begging it to do as it wishes, and to fulfil its own marvellous nature.'

Ursula was just breaking out, when Hermione lifted her face and began, in her musing sing-song:

'I do think – I do really think we must have the *courage* to use the lower animal life for our needs. I do think there is something wrong, when we look on every living creature as if it were ourselves. I do feel, that it is false to project our own feelings on every animate creature. It is a lack of discrimination, a lack of criticism.'

'Quite,' said Birkin sharply. 'Nothing is so detestable as the maudlin attributing of human feelings and consciousness to animals.'

'Yes,' said Hermione wearily, 'we must really take a position. Either we are going to use the animals, or they will use us.'

'That's a fact,' said Gerald. 'A horse has got a will like a man, though it has no *mind*, strictly. And if your will isn't master, then the horse is master of you. And this is a thing I can't help. I can't help being master of the horse.'

'If only we could learn how to use our will,' said Hermione, 'we could do anything. The will can cure anything, and put anything right. That I am convinced of – if only we use the will properly, intelligibly.'

'What do you mean by using the will properly?' said Birkin.

'A very great doctor taught me,' she said, addressing Ursula and Gerald vaguely. 'He told me, for instance, that to cure oneself of a bad habit, one should *force* oneself to do it, when one would not do it; – make oneself do it – and then the habit would disappear.'

'How do you mean?' said Gerald.

'If you bite your nails, for example. Then, when you don't want to bite your nails, bite them, make yourself bite them. And you would find the habit was broken.'

'Is that so?' said Gerald.

'Yes. And in so many things, I have *made* myself well. I was a very queer and nervous girl. And by learning to use my will, simply by using my will, I *made* myself right.'

Ursula looked all the while at Hermione, as she spoke in her slow, dispassionate, and yet strangely tense voice. A curious thrill went over the younger woman. Some strange, dark, convulsive power was in Hermione, fascinating and repelling.

'It is fatal to use the will like that,' cried Birkin harshly, 'disgusting. Such a will is an obscenity.'

Hermione looked at him for a long time, with her shadowed, heavy eyes. Her face was soft and pale and thin, almost phosphorescent, her jaw was lean.

'I'm sure it isn't,' she said at length. There always seemed an interval, a strange split between what she seemed to feel and experience, and what she actually said and thought. She seemed to catch her thoughts at length from off the surface of a maelstrom of chaotic black emotions and reactions, and Birkin was always filled with repulsion, she caught so infallibly, her will never failed her. Her voice was always dispassionate and tense, and perfectly confident. Yet she shuddered with a sense of nausea, a sort of sea-sickness that always threatened to overwhelm her mind. But her mind remained unbroken, her will was still perfect. It almost sent Birkin mad. But he would never, never dare to break her will, and let loose the maelstrom of her subconsciousness, and see her in her ultimate madness. Yet he was always striking at her.

'And of course,' he said to Gerald, 'horses *haven't* got a complete will, like human beings. A horse has no *one* will. Every horse, strictly, has two wills. With one will, it wants to put itself in the human power completely – and with the other, it wants to be free, wild. The two wills sometimes lock – you know that, if ever you've felt a horse bolt, while you've been driving it.'

'I have felt a horse bolt while I was driving it,' said Gerald, 'but it didn't make me know it had two wills. I only knew it was frightened.'

Hermione had ceased to listen. She simply became oblivious when these subjects were started.

'Why should a horse want to put itself in the human power?' asked Ursula. 'That is quite incomprehensible to me. I don't believe it ever wanted it.'

'Yes it did. It's the last, perhaps highest, love-impulse: resign your will to the higher being,' said Birkin.

'What curious notions you have of love,' jeered Ursula.

'And woman is the same as horses: two wills act in opposition inside her. With one will, she wants to subject herself utterly. With the other she wants to bolt, and pitch her rider to perdition.'

'Then I'm a bolter,' said Ursula, with a burst of laughter.

'It's a dangerous thing to domesticate even horses, let alone women,' said Birkin. 'The dominant principle has some rare antagonists.'

'Good thing too,' said Ursula.

'Quite,' said Gerald, with a faint smile. 'There's more fun.'

Hermione could bear no more. She rose, saying in her easy sing-song:

'Isn't the evening beautiful! I get filled sometimes with such a great sense of beauty, that I feel I can hardly bear it.'

Ursula, to whom she had appealed, rose with her, moved to the last impersonal depths. And Birkin seemed to her almost a monster of hateful arrogance. She went with Hermione along the bank of the pond, talking of beautiful, soothing things, picking the gentle cowslips.

'Wouldn't you like a dress,' said Ursula to Hermione, 'of this yellow spotted with orange – a cotton dress?'

'Yes,' said Hermione, stopping and looking at the flower, letting the thought come home to her and soothe her. 'Wouldn't it be pretty? I should *love* it.'

And she turned smiling to Ursula, in a feeling of real affection.

But Gerald remained with Birkin, wanting to prove him to the bottom, to know what he meant by the dual will in horses. A flicker of excitement danced on Gerald's face.

Hermione and Ursula strayed on together, united in a sudden bond of deep affection and closeness.

'I really do not want to be forced into all this criticism and analysis of life. I really *do* want to see things in their entirety, with their beauty left to them, and their wholeness, their natural holiness. Don't you feel it, don't you feel you *can't* be tortured into any more knowledge?' said Hermione, stopping in front of Ursula, and turning to her with clenched fists thrust downwards.

'Yes,' said Ursula. 'I do. I am sick of this poking and prying.'

'I'm so glad you are. Sometimes,' said Hermione, again stopping arrested in her progress and turning to Ursula, 'sometimes I wonder if I *ought* to submit to all this realisation, if I am not being weak in rejecting it. But I feel I *can't* – I *can't*. It seems to destroy *everything*. All the beauty and the – and the true holiness is destroyed – and I feel I can't live without them.'

'And it would be simply wrong to live without them,' cried Ursula. 'No, it is so *irreverent* to think that everything must be realised in the head. Really, something must be left to the Lord, there always is and always will be.'

'Yes,' said Hermione, reassured like a child, 'it should, shouldn't it? And Rupert –' she lifted her face to the sky, in a muse – 'he *can* only tear things to pieces. He really *is* like a boy who must pull everything to pieces to see how it is made. And I can't think it is right – it does seem so irreverent, as you say.'

'Like tearing open a bud to see what the flower will be like,' said Ursula.

'Yes. And that kills everything, doesn't it? It doesn't allow any possibility of flowering.'

'Of course not,' said Ursula. 'It is purely destructive.'

'It is, isn't it!'

Hermione looked long and slow at Ursula, seeming to accept confirmation from her. Then the two women were silent. As soon as they were in accord, they began mutually to mistrust each other. In spite of herself, Ursula felt herself recoiling from Hermione. It was all she could do to restrain her revulsion.

They returned to the men, like two conspirators who have withdrawn to come to an agreement. Birkin looked up at them. Ursula hated him for his cold watchfulness. But he said nothing.

'Shall we be going?' said Hermione. 'Rupert, you are coming to Shortlands to dinner? Will you come at once, will you come now, with us?'

'I'm not dressed,' replied Birkin. 'And you know Gerald stickles for convention.'

'I don't stickle for it,' said Gerald. 'But if you'd got as sick as I have of rowdy go-as-you-please in the house, you'd prefer it if people were peaceful and conventional, at least at meals.'

'All right,' said Birkin.

'But can't we wait for you while you dress?' persisted Hermione.

'If you like.'

He rose to go indoors. Ursula said she would take her leave.

'Only,' she said, turning to Gerald, 'I must say that, however man is lord of the beast and the fowl, I still don't think he has any right to violate the feelings of the inferior creation. I still think it would have been much more sensible and nice of you if you'd trotted back up the road while the train went by, and been considerate.'

'I see,' said Gerald, smiling, but somewhat annoyed. 'I must remember another time.'

'They all think I'm an interfering female,' thought Ursula to herself, as she went away. But she was in arms against them.

She ran home plunged in thought. She had been very much moved by Hermione, she had really come into contact with her, so that there was a sort of league between the two women. And yet she could not bear her. But she put the thought away. 'She's really good,' she said to herself. 'She really wants what is right.' And she tried to feel at one with Hermione, and to shut off from Birkin. She was strictly hostile to him. But she was held to him by some bond, some deep principle. This at once irritated her and saved her.

Only now and again, violent little shudders would come over her, out of her subconsciousness, and she knew it was the fact that she had stated her challenge to Birkin, and he had, consciously or unconsciously, accepted. It was a fight to the death between them – or to new life: though in what the conflict lay, no one could say.

Chapter Thirteen

Mino

The days went by, and she received no sign. Was he going to ignore her, was he going to take no further notice of her secret? A dreary weight of anxiety and acrid bitterness settled on her. And yet Ursula knew she was only deceiving herself, and that he *would* proceed. She said no word to anybody.

Then, sure enough, there came a note from him, asking if she would come to tea, with Gudrun, to his rooms in town.

'Why does he ask Gudrun as well?' she asked herself at once. 'Does he want to protect himself, or does he think I would not go alone?'

She was tormented by the thought that he wanted to protect himself. But at the end of all, she only said to herself:

'I don't want Gudrun to be there, because I want him to say something more to me. So I shan't tell Gudrun anything about it, and I shall go alone. Then I shall know.'

She found herself sitting on the tram-car, mounting up the hill going out of the town, to the place where he had his lodging. She seemed to have passed into a kind of dream world, absolved from the conditions of actuality. She watched the sordid streets of the town go by beneath her, as if she were a spirit disconnected from the material universe. What had it all to do with her? She was palpitating and formless within the flux of the ghost life. She could not consider any more, what anybody would say of her or think about her. People had passed out of her range, she was absolved. She had fallen strange and dim, out of the sheath of the material life, as a berry falls from the only world it has ever known, down out of the sheath on to the real unknown.

Birkin was standing in the middle of the room, when she was shown in by the landlady. He too was moved outside himself. She saw him agitated and shaken, a frail, unsubstantial body silent like the node of some violent force, that came out from him and shook her almost into a swoon.

'You are alone?' he said.

'Yes – Gudrun could not come.'

He instantly guessed why.

And they were both seated in silence, in the terrible tension of the room. She was aware that it was a pleasant room, full of light and very restful in its form – aware also of a fuchsia tree, with dangling scarlet and purple flowers.

'How nice the fuchsias are!' she said, to break the silence.

'Aren't they! Did you think I had forgotten what I said?'

A swoon went over Ursula's mind.

'I don't want you to remember it – if you don't want to,' she struggled to say, through the dark mist that covered her.

There was silence for some moments.

'No,' he said. 'It isn't that. Only – if we are going to know each other, we must pledge ourselves for ever. If we are going to make a relationship, even of friendship, there must be something final and irrevocable about it.'

There was a clang of mistrust and almost anger in his voice. She did not answer. Her heart was too much contracted. She could not have spoken.

Seeing she was not going to reply, he continued, almost bitterly, giving himself away:

'I can't say it is love I have to offer – and it isn't love I want. It is something much more impersonal and harder – and rarer.'

There was a silence, out of which she said:

'You mean you don't love me?'

She suffered furiously, saying that.

'Yes, if you like to put it like that. Though perhaps that isn't true. I don't know. At any rate, I don't feel the emotion of love for you – no, and I don't want to. Because it gives out in the last issues.'

'Love gives out in the last issues?' she asked, feeling numb to the lips.

'Yes, it does. At the very last, one is alone, beyond the influence of love. There is a real impersonal me, that is beyond love, beyond any emotional relationship. So it is with you. But we want to delude ourselves that love is the root. It isn't. It is only the branches. The root is beyond love, a naked kind of isolation, an isolated me, that does *not* meet and mingle, and never can.'

She watched him with wide, troubled eyes. His face was incandescent in its abstract earnestness.

'And you mean you can't love?' she asked, in trepidation.

'Yes, if you like. I have loved. But there is a beyond, where there is not love.'

She could not submit to this. She felt it swooning over her. But she could not submit.

'But how do you know – if you have never *really* loved?' she asked.

'It is true what I say; there is a beyond, in you,·in me, which is further than love, beyond the scope, as stars are beyond the scope of vision, some of them.'

'Then there is no love,' cried Ursula.

'Ultimately, no, there is something else. But, ultimately, there *is* no love.'

Ursula was given over to this statement for some moments. Then she half rose from her chair, saying, in a final, repellent voice:

'Then let me go home – what am I doing here?'

'There is the door,' he said. 'You are a free agent.'

He was suspended finely and perfectly in this extremity. She hung motionless for some seconds, then she sat down again.

'If there is no love, what is there?' she cried, almost jeering.

'Something,' he said, looking at her, battling with his soul, with all his might.

'What?'

He was silent for a long time, unable to be in communication with her while she was in this state of opposition.

'There is,' he said, in a voice of pure abstraction, 'a final me which is stark and impersonal and beyond responsibility. So there is a final you. And it is there I would want to meet you – not in the emotional, loving plane – but there beyond, where there is no speech and no terms of agreement. There we are two stark, unknown beings, two utterly strange creatures, I would want to approach you, and you me. And there could be no obligation, because there is no standard for action there, because no understanding has been reaped from that plane. It is quite inhuman – so there can be no calling to book, in any form whatsoever – because one is outside the pale of all that is accepted, and nothing known applies. One can only follow the impulse, taking that which lies in front, and responsible for nothing, asked for nothing, giving nothing, only each taking according to the primal desire.'

Ursula listened to this speech, her mind dumb and almost senseless, what he said was so unexpected and so untoward.

'It is just purely selfish,' she said.

'If it is pure, yes. But it isn't selfish at all. Because I don't *know* what I want of you. I deliver *myself* over to the unknown, in coming to you, I am without reserves or defences, stripped entirely, into the unknown. Only there needs the pledge between us, that we will both cast off everything, cast off ourselves even, and cease to be, so that that which is perfectly ourselves can take place in us.'

She pondered along her own line of thought.

'But it is because you love me, that you want me?' she persisted.

'No it isn't. It is because I believe in you – if I *do* believe in you.'

'Aren't you sure?' she laughed, suddenly hurt.

He was looking at her steadfastly, scarcely heeding what she said.

'Yes, I must believe in you, or else I shouldn't be here saying this,' he replied. 'But that is all the proof I have. I don't feel any very strong belief at this particular moment.'

She disliked him for this sudden relapse into weariness and faithlessness.

'But don't you think me good-looking?' she persisted in a mocking voice.

He looked at her, to see if he felt that she was good-looking.

'I don't *feel* that you're good-looking,' he said.

'Not even attractive?' she mocked, bitingly.

He knitted his brows in sudden exasperation.

'Don't you see that it's not a question of visual appreciation in the least,' he cried. 'I don't *want* to see you. I've seen plenty of women, I'm sick and weary of seeing them. I want a woman I don't see.'

'I'm sorry I can't oblige you by being invisible,' she laughed.

'Yes,' he said, 'you are invisible to me, if you don't force me to be visually aware of you. But I don't want to see you or hear you.'

'What did you ask me to tea for, then?' she mocked.

But he would take no notice of her. He was talking to himself.

'I want to find you, where you don't know your own existence, the you that your common self denies utterly. But I don't want your good looks, and I don't want your womanly feelings, and I don't want your thoughts nor opinions nor your ideas – they are all bagatelles to me.'

'You are very conceited, Monsieur,' she mocked. 'How do you know what my womanly feelings are, or my thoughts or my ideas? You don't even know what I think of you now.'

'Nor do I care in the slightest.'

'I think you are very silly. I think you want to tell me you love me and you go all this way round to do it.'

'All right,' he said, looking up with sudden exasperation. 'Now go away then, and leave me alone. I don't want any more of your meretricious persiflage.'

'Is it really persiflage?' she mocked, her face really relaxing into laughter.

She interpreted it, that he had made a deep confession of love to her. But he was so absurd in his words, also.

They were silent for many minutes, she was pleased and elated like a child. His concentration broke, he began to look at her simply and naturally.

'What I want is a strange conjunction with you—' he said quietly: '– not meeting and mingling; – you are quite right: – but an equilibrium, a pure balance of two single beings: – as the stars balance each other.'

She looked at him. He was very earnest, and earnestness was always rather ridiculous, commonplace, to her. It made her feel unfree and uncomfortable. Yet she liked him so much. But why drag in the stars.

'Isn't this rather sudden?' she mocked.

He began to laugh.

'Best to read the terms of the contract, before we sign,' he said.

A young grey cat that had been sleeping on the sofa jumped down and stretched, rising on its long legs, and arching its slim back. Then it sat considering for a moment, erect and kingly. And then, like a dart, it had shot out of the room, through the open window-doors, and into the garden.

'What's he after?' said Birkin, rising.

The young cat trotted lordly down the path, waving his tail. He was an ordinary tabby with white paws, a slender young gentleman. A crouching, fluffy, brownish-grey cat was stealing up the side of the fence. The Mino walked statelily up to her, with manly nonchalance. She crouched before him and pressed herself on the ground in humility, a fluffy soft outcast, looking up at him with wild eyes that were green and lovely as great jewels. He looked casually down on her. So she crept a few inches further, proceeding on her way to the back door, crouching in a wonderful, soft, self-obliterating manner, and moving like a shadow.

He, going statelily on his slim legs, walked after her, then suddenly, for pure excess, he gave her a light cuff with his paw on the side of her face. She ran off a few steps, like a blown leaf along the ground, then crouched unobtrusively, in submissive, wild patience. The Mino pretended to take no notice of her. He blinked his eyes superbly at the landscape. In a minute she drew herself together and moved softly, a fleecy brown-grey shadow, a few paces forward. She began to quicken her pace, in a moment she would be gone like a dream, when the young grey lord sprang before her, and gave her a light handsome cuff. She subsided at once, submissively.

'She is a wild cat,' said Birkin. 'She has come in from the woods.'

The eyes of the stray cat flared round for a moment, like great green fires staring at Birkin. Then she had rushed in a soft swift rush, half-way down the garden. There she paused to look round. The Mino turned his face in pure superiority to his master, and slowly closed his eyes, standing in statuesque young perfection. The wild cat's round, green, wondering eyes were staring all the while like uncanny fires. Then again, like a shadow, she slid towards the kitchen.

In a lovely springing leap, like a wind, the Mino was upon her, and had boxed her twice, very definitely, with a white, delicate fist. She sank and slid back, unquestioning. He walked after her, and cuffed her once or twice, leisurely, with sudden little blows of his magic white paws.

'Now why does he do that?' cried Ursula in indignation.

'They are on intimate terms,' said Birkin.

'And is that why he hits her?'

'Yes,' laughed Birkin, 'I think he wants to make it quite obvious to her.'

'Isn't it horrid of him!' she cried; and going out into the garden she called to the Mino:

'Stop it, don't bully. Stop hitting her.'

The stray cat vanished like a swift, invisible shadow. The Mino glanced at Ursula, then looked from her disdainfully to his master.

'Are you a bully, Mino?' Birkin asked.

The young slim cat looked at him, and slowly narrowed its eyes. Then it glanced away at the landscape, looking into the distance as if completely oblivious of the two human beings.

'Mino,' said Ursula, 'I don't like you. You are a bully like all males.'

'No,' said Birkin, 'he is justified. He is not a bully. He is only insisting to the poor stray that she shall acknowledge him as a sort of fate, her own fate: because you can see she is fluffy and promiscuous as the wind. I am with him entirely. He wants superfine stability.'

'Yes, I know!' cried Ursula. 'He wants his own way – I know what your fine words work down to – bossiness, I call it, bossiness.'

The young cat again glanced at Birkin in disdain of the noisy woman.

'I quite agree with you, Miciotto,' said Birkin to the cat. 'Keep your male dignity, and your higher understanding.'

Again the Mino narrowed his eyes as if he were looking at the sun. Then, suddenly affecting to have no connection at all with the two people, he went trotting off, with assumed spontaneity and gaiety, his tail erect, his white feet blithe.

'Now he will find the belle sauvage once more, and entertain her with his superior wisdom,' laughed Birkin.

Ursula looked at the man who stood in the garden with his hair blowing and his eyes smiling ironically, and she cried:

'Oh, it makes me so cross, the assumption of male superiority! And it is such a lie! One wouldn't mind if there were any justification for it.'

'The wild cat,' said Birkin, 'doesn't mind. She perceives that it is justified.'

'Does she!' cried Ursula. 'And tell it to the Horse Marines.'

'To them also.'

'It is just like Gerald Crich with his horse – a lust for bullying – a real *Wille zur Macht* – so base, so petty.'

'I agree that the *Wille zur Macht* is a base and petty thing. But with the Mino, it is the desire to bring this female cat into a pure stable equilibrium, a transcendent and abiding *rapport* with the single male. Whereas without him, as you see, she is a mere stray, a fluffy sporadic bit of chaos. It is a *volonté de pouvoir*, if you like, a win to ability, taking *pouvoir* as a verb.'

'Ah—! Sophistries! It's the old Adam.'

'Oh yes. Adam kept Eve in the indestructible paradise, when he kept her single with himself, like a star in its orbit.'

'Yes – yes—' cried Ursula, pointing her finger at him. 'There you are – a star in its orbit! A satellite – a satellite of Mars – that's what she is to be!

There – there – you've given yourself away! You want a statellite, Mars and his satellite! You've said it – you've said it – you've dished yourself!'

He stood smiling in frustration and amusement and irritation and admiration and love. She was so quick, and so lambent, like discernible fire, and so vindictive, and so rich in her dangerous flamy sensitiveness.

'I've not said it at all,' he replied, 'if you will give me a chance to speak.'

'No, no!' she cried. 'I won't let you speak. You've said it, a satellite, you're not going to wriggle out of it. You've said it.'

'You'll never believe now that I *haven't* said it,' he answered. 'I neither implied nor indicated nor mentioned a satellite, nor intended a satellite, never.'

'*You prevaricator!*' she cried, in real indignation.

'Tea is ready, sir,' said the landlady from the doorway.

They both looked at her, very much as the cats had looked at them, a little while before.

'Thank you, Mrs. Daykin.'

An interrupted silence fell over the two of them, a moment of breach.

'Come and have tea,' he said.

'Yes, I should love it,' she replied, gathering herself together.

They sat facing each other across the tea table.

'I did not say, nor imply, a satellite. I meant two single equal stars balanced in conjunction—'

'You gave yourself away, you gave away your little game completely,' she cried, beginning at once to eat. He saw that she would take no further heed of his expostulation, so he began to pour the tea.

'What *good* things to eat!' she cried.

'Take your own sugar,' he said.

He handed her her cup. He had everything so nice, such pretty cups and plates, painted with mauve-lustre and green, also shapely bowls and glass plates, and old spoons, on a woven cloth of pale grey and black and purple. It was very rich and fine. But Ursula could see Hermione's influence.

'Your things are so lovely!' she said, almost angrily.

'*I* like them. It gives me real pleasure to use things that are attractive in themselves – pleasant things. And Mrs. Daykin is good. She thinks everything is wonderful, for my sake.'

'Really,' said Ursula, 'landladies are better than wives, nowadays. They certainly *care* a great deal more. It is much more beautiful and complete here now, than if you were married.'

'But think of the emptiness within,' he laughed.

'No,' she said, 'I am jealous that men have such perfect landladies and such beautiful lodgings. There is nothing left them to desire.'

'In the house-keeping way, we'll hope not. It is disgusting, people marrying for a home.'

'Still,' said Ursula, 'a man has very little need for a woman now, has he?'

'In outer things, maybe – except to share his bed and bear his children. But essentially, there is just the same need as there ever was. Only nobody takes the trouble to be essential.'

'How essential?' she said.

'I do think,' he said, 'that the world is only held together by the mystic conjunction, the ultimate unison between people – a bond. And the immediate bond is between man and woman.'

'But it's such old hat,' said Ursula. 'Why should love be a bond? No, I'm not having any.'

'If you are walking westward,' he said, 'you forfeit the northern and eastward and southern direction. If you admit a unison, you forfeit all the possibilities of chaos.'

'But love is freedom,' she declared.

'Don't cant to me,' he replied. 'Love is a direction which excludes all other directions. It's a freedom *together*, if you like.'

'No,' she said, 'love includes everything.'

'Sentimental cant,' he replied. 'You want the state of chaos, that's all. It is ultimate nihilism, this freedom-in-love business, this freedom which is love and love which is freedom. As a matter of fact, if you enter into a pure unison, it is irrevocable, and it is never pure till it is irrevocable. And when it is irrevocable, it is one way, like the path of a star.'

'Ha!' she cried bitterly. 'It is the old dead morality.'

'No,' he said, 'it is the law of creation. One is committed. One must commit oneself to a conjunction with the other – for ever. But it is not selfless – it is a maintaining of the self in mystic balance and integrity – like a star balanced with another star.'

'I don't trust you when you drag in the stars,' she said. 'If you were quite true, it wouldn't be necessary to be so far-fetched.'

'Don't trust me then,' he said, angry. 'It is enough that I trust myself.'

'And that is where you make another mistake,' she replied. 'You *don't* trust yourself. You don't fully believe yourself what you are saying. You don't really want this conjunction, otherwise you wouldn't talk so much about it, you'd get it.'

He was suspended for a moment, arrested.

'How?' he said.

'By just loving,' she retorted in defiance.

He was still a moment, in anger. Then he said:

'I tell you, I don't believe in love like that. I tell you, you want love to administer to your egoism, to subserve you. Love is a process of subservience with you – and with everybody. I hate it.'

'No,' she cried, pressing back her head like a cobra, her eyes flashing. 'It is a process of pride – I want to be proud—'

'Proud and subservient, proud and subservient, I know you,' he retorted dryly. 'Proud and subservient, then subservient to the proud – I know you and your love. It is a tick-tack, tick-tack, a dance of opposites.'

'Are you sure?' she mocked wickedly, 'what my love is?'

'Yes, I am,' he retorted.

'So cocksure!' she said. 'How can anybody ever be right, who is so cocksure? It shows you are wrong.'

He was silent in chagrin.

They had talked and struggled till they were both wearied out.

'Tell me about yourself and your people,' he said.

And she told him about the Brangwens, and about her mother, and about Skrebensky, her first love, and about her later experiences. He sat very still, watching her as she talked. And he seemed to listen with reverence. Her face was beautiful and full of baffled light as she told him all the things that had hurt her or perplexed her so deeply. He seemed to warm and comfort his soul at the beautiful light of her nature.

'If she *really* could pledge herself,' he thought to himself, with passionate insistence but hardly any hope. Yet a curious little irresponsible laughter appeared in his heart.

'We have all suffered so much,' he mocked, ironically.

She looked up at him, and a flash of wild gaiety went over her face, a strange flash of yellow light coming from her eyes.

'Haven't we!' she cried, in a high, reckless cry. 'It is almost absurd, isn't it?'

'Quite absurd,' he said. 'Suffering bores me, any more.'

'So it does me.'

He was almost afraid of the mocking recklessness of her splendid face. Here was one who would go to the whole lengths of heaven or hell, whichever she had to go. And he mistrusted her, he was afraid of a woman capable of such abandon, such dangerous thoroughness of destructivity. Yet he chuckled within himself also.

She came over to him and put her hand on his shoulder, looking down at him with strange golden-lighted eyes, very tender, but with a curious devilish look lurking underneath.

'Say you love me, say "my love" to me,' she pleaded.

He looked back into her eyes, and saw. His face flickered with sardonic comprehension.

'I love you right enough,' he said grimly. 'But I want it to be something else.'

'But why? But why?' she insisted, bending her wonderful luminous face to him. 'Why isn't it enough?'

'Because we can go one better,' he said, putting his arms round her.

'No, we can't,' she said, in a strong, voluptuous voice of yielding. 'We can only love each other. Say "my love" to me, say it, say it.'

She put her arms round his neck. He enfolded her, and kissed her subtly, murmuring in a subtle voice of love, and irony, and submission:

'Yes – my love, yes – my love. Let love be enough then. I love you then – I love you. I'm bored by the rest.'

'Yes,' she murmured, nestling very sweet and close to him.

Chapter Fourteen

Water-party

Every year Mr. Crich gave a more or less public water-party on the lake. There was a little pleasure-launch on Willey Water and several rowing-boats, and guests could take tea either in the marquee that was set up in the grounds of the house, or they could picnic in the shade of the great walnut tree at the boat-house by the lake. This year the staff of the Grammar School was invited, along with the chief officials of the firm. Gerald and the younger Criches did not care for this party, but it had become customary now, and it pleased the father, as being the only occasion when he could gather some people of the district together in festivity with him. For he loved to give pleasures to his dependants and to those poorer than himself. But his children preferred the company of their equals in wealth. They hated their inferiors' humility or gratitude or awkwardness.

Nevertheless they were willing to attend at this festival, as they had done almost since they were children, the more so, as they all felt a little guilty now, and unwilling to thwart their father any more, since he was so ill in health. Therefore, quite cheerfully Laura prepared to take her mother's place as hostess, and Gerald assumed responsibility for the amusements on the water.

Birkin had written to Ursula saying he expected to see her at the party, and Gudrun, although she scorned the patronage of the Criches, would nevertheless accompany her mother and father if the weather were fine.

The day came blue and full of sunshine, with little wafts of wind. The sisters both wore dresses of white crêpe, and hats of soft grass. But Gudrun had a sash of brilliant black and pink and yellow colour wound broadly round her waist, and she had pink silk stockings, and black and pink and yellow decoration on the brim of her hat, weighing it down a little. She carried also a yellow silk coat over her arm, so that she looked remarkable, like a painting from the Salon. Her appearance was a sore trial to her father, who said angrily:

'Don't you think you might as well get yourself up for a Christmas cracker, an' ha' done with it?'

But Gudrun looked handsome and brilliant, and she wore her clothes in pure defiance. When people stared at her, and giggled after her, she made a point of saying loudly, to Ursula:

'*Regarde, regarde ces gens-là! Ne sont-ils pas des hiboux incroyables?*' And with the words of French in her mouth, she would look over her shoulder at the giggling party.

'No, really, it's impossible!' Ursula would reply distinctly. And so the two girls took it out of their universal enemy. But their father became more and more enraged.

Ursula was all snowy white, save that her hat was pink, and entirely without trimming, and her shoes were dark red, and she carried an orange-coloured coat. And in this guise they were walking all the way to Shortlands, their father and mother going in front.

They were laughing at their mother, who, dressed in a summer material of black and purple stripes, and wearing a hat of purple straw, was setting forth with much more of the shyness and trepidation of a young girl than her daughters ever felt, walking demurely beside her husband, who, as usual, looked rather crumpled in his best suit, as if he were the father of a young family and had been holding the baby whilst his wife got dressed.

'Look at the young couple in front,' said Gudrun calmly. Ursula looked at her mother and father, and was suddenly seized with uncontrollable laughter. The two girls stood in the road and laughed till the tears ran down their faces, as they caught sight again of the shy, unworldly couple of their parents going on ahead.

'We are roaring at you, mother,' called Ursula, helplessly following after her parents.

Mrs. Brangwen turned round with a slightly puzzled exasperated look. 'Oh indeed!' she said. 'What is there so very funny about *me*, I should like to know?'

She could not understand that there could be anything amiss with her appearance. She had a perfect calm sufficiency, an easy indifference to any criticism whatsoever, as if she were beyond it. Her clothes were always rather odd, and as a rule slip-shod, yet she wore them with a perfect ease and satisfaction. Whatever she had on, so long as she was barely tidy, she was right, beyond remark; such an aristocrat she was by instinct.

'You look so stately, like a country Baroness,' said Ursula, laughing with a little tenderness at her mother's naïve puzzled air.

'*Just* like a country Baroness!' chimed in Gudrun. Now the mother's natural hauteur became self-conscious, and the girls shrieked again.

'Go home, you pair of idiots, great giggling idiots!' cried the father inflamed with irritation.

'Mm-m-er!' booed Ursula, pulling a face at his crossness.

The yellow lights danced in his eyes, he leaned forward in real rage.

'Don't be so silly as to take any notice of the great babies,' said Mrs. Brangwen, turning on her way.

'I'll see if I'm going to be followed by a pair of giggling, yelling jackan-apes—' he cried vengefully.

The girls stood still, laughing helplessly at his fury, upon the path beside the hedge.

'Why you're as silly as they are, to take any notice,' said Mrs. Brangwen also becoming angry now he was really enraged.

'There are some people coming, father,' cried Ursula, with mocking warning. He glanced round quickly, and went on to join his wife, walking stiff with rage. And the girls followed, weak with laughter.

When the people had passed by, Brangwen cried in a loud, stupid voice:

'I'm going back home if there's any more of this. I'm damned if I'm going to be made a fool of in this fashion, in the public road.'

He was really out of temper. At the sound of his blind, vindictive voice, the laughter suddenly left the girls, and their hearts contracted with contempt. They hated his words 'in the public road'. What did they care for the public road? But Gudrun was conciliatory.

'But we weren't laughing to *hurt* you,' she cried, with an uncouth gentleness which made her parents uncomfortable. 'We were laughing because we're fond of you.'

'We'll walk on in front, if they are *so* touchy,' said Ursula, angry. And in this wise they arrived at Willey Water. The lake was blue and fair, the meadows sloped down in sunshine on one side, the thick dark woods dropped steeply on the other. The little pleasure-launch was fussing out from the shore, twanging its music, crowded with people, flapping its paddles. Near the boat-house was a throng of gaily-dressed persons, small in the distance. And on the high-road, some of the common people were standing along the hedge, looking at the festivity beyond, enviously, like souls not admitted to paradise.

'My eye!' said Gudrun, sotto voce, looking at the motley of guests, 'there's a pretty crowd if you like! Imagine yourself in the midst of that, my dear.'

Gudrun's apprehensive horror of people in the mass unnerved Ursula. 'It looks rather awful,' she said anxiously.

'And imagine what they'll be like – *imagine!*' said Gudrun, still in that unnerving, subdued voice. Yet she advanced determinedly.

'I suppose we can get away from them,' said Ursula anxiously.

'We're in a pretty fix if we can't,' said Gudrun. Her extreme ironic loathing and apprehension was very trying to Ursula.

'We needn't stay,' she said.

'I certainly shan't stay five minutes among that little lot,' said Gudrun. They advanced nearer, till they saw policemen at the gates.

'Policemen to keep you in, too!' said Gudrun. 'My word, this is a beautiful affair.'

'We'd better look after father and mother,' said Ursula anxiously.

'Mother's *perfectly* capable of getting through this little celebration,' said Gudrun with some contempt.

But Ursula knew that her father felt uncouth and angry and unhappy, so she was far from her ease. They waited outside the gate till their parents came up. The tall, thin man in his crumpled clothes was unnerved and irritable as a boy, finding himself on the brink of this social function. He did not feel a gentleman, he did not feel anything except pure exasperation.

Ursula took her place at his side, they gave their tickets to the policeman, and passed in on to the grass, four abreast; the tall, hot, ruddy-dark man with his narrow boyish brow drawn with irritation, the fresh-faced, easy woman, perfectly collected though her hair was slipping on one side, then Gudrun, her eyes round and dark and staring, her full soft face impassive, almost sulky, so that she seemed to be backing away in antagonism even whilst she was advancing; and then Ursula, with the odd, brilliant, dazzled look on her face, that always came when she was in some false situation.

Birkin was the good angel. He came smiling to them with his affected social grace, that somehow was never *quite* right. But he took off his hat and smiled at them with a real smile in his eyes, so that Brangwen cried out heartily in relief:

'How do you do? You're better, are you?'

'Yes, I'm better. How do you do, Mrs. Brangwen? I know Gudrun and Ursula very well.'

His eyes smiled full of natural warmth. He had a soft, flattering manner with women, particularly with women who were not young.

'Yes,' said Mrs. Brangwen, cool but yet gratified. 'I have heard them speak of you often enough.'

He laughed. Gudrun looked aside, feeling she was being belittled. People were standing about in groups, some women were sitting in the shade of the walnut tree, with cups of tea in their hands, a waiter in evening dress was hurrying round, some girls were simpering with parasols, some young men, who had just come in from rowing, were sitting cross-legged on the grass, coatless, their shirt-sleeves rolled up in manly fashion, their hands resting on their white flannel trousers, their gaudy ties floating about, as they laughed and tried to be witty with the young damsels.

'Why,' thought Gudrun churlishly, 'don't they have the manners to put their coats on, and not to assume such intimacy in their appearance.'

She abhorred the ordinary young man, with his hair plastered back, and his easy-going chumminess.

Hermione Roddice came up, in a handsome gown of white lace, trailing an enormous silk shawl blotched with great embroidered flowers, and balancing an enormous plain hat on her head. She looked striking, astonishing, almost macabre, so tall, with the fringe of her great cream-coloured vividly-blotched shawl trailing on the ground after her, her thick hair coming low over her eyes, her face strange and long and pale, and the blotches of brilliant colour drawn round her.

'Doesn't she look *weird!*' Gudrun heard some girls titter behind her. And she could have killed them.

'How do you do!' sang Hermione, coming up very kindly, and glancing slowly over Gudrun's father and mother. It was a trying moment, exasperating for Gudrun. Hermione was really so strongly entrenched in her class superiority, she could come up and know people out of simple curiosity, as if they were creatures on exhibition. Gudrun would do the same herself. But she resented being in the position when somebody might do it to her.

Hermione, very remarkable, and distinguishing the Brangwens very much, led them along to where Laura Crich stood receiving the guests.

'This is Mrs. Brangwen,' sang Hermione, and Laura, who wore a stiff embroidered linen dress, shook hands and said she was glad to see her. Then Gerald came up, dressed in white, with a black and brown blazer, and looking handsome. He too was introduced to the Brangwen parents, and immediately he spoke to Mrs. Brangwen as if she were a lady, and to Brangwen as if he were *not* a gentleman. Gerald was so obvious in his demeanour. He had to shake hands with his left hand, because he had hurt his right, and carried it, bandaged up, in the pocket of his jacket. Gudrun was *very* thankful that none of her party asked him what was the matter with the hand.

The steam launch was fussing in, all its music jingling, people calling excitedly from on board. Gerald went to see to the debarkation, Birkin was getting tea for Mrs. Brangwen, Brangwen had joined a Grammar-School group, Hermione was sitting down by their mother, the girls went to the landing-stage to watch the launch come in.

She hooted and tooted gaily, then her paddles were silent, the ropes were thrown ashore, she drifted in with a little bump. Immediately the passengers crowded excitedly to come ashore.

'Wait a minute, wait a minute,' shouted Gerald in sharp command.

They must wait till the boat was tight on the ropes, till the small gangway was put out. Then they streamed ashore, clamouring as if they had come from America.

'Oh, it's *so* nice!' the young girls were crying. 'It's quite lovely.'

The waiters from on board ran out to the boat-house with baskets, the captain lounged on the little bridge. Seeing all safe, Gerald came to Gudrun and Ursula.

'You wouldn't care to go on board for the next trip, and have tea there?' he asked.

'No, thanks,' said Gudrun coldly.

'You don't care for the water?'

'For the water? Yes, I like it very much.'

He looked at her, his eyes searching.

'You don't care for going on a launch, then?'

She was slow in answering, and then she spoke slowly.

'No, she said. 'I can't say that I do.' Her colour was high, she seemed angry about something.

'*Un peu trop de monde,*' said Ursula, explaining.

'Eh? *Trop de monde!*' He laughed shortly. 'Yes, there's a fair number of 'em.'

Gudrun turned on him brilliantly.

'Have you ever been from Westminster Bridge to Richmond on one of the Thames steamers?' she cried.

'No,' he said, 'I can't say I have.'

'Well, it's one of the most *vile* experiences I've ever had.' She spoke rapidly and excitedly, the colour high in her cheeks. 'There was absolutely nowhere to sit down, nowhere, a man just above sang "Rocked in the Cradle of the Deep" the *whole* way; he was blind and he had a small organ, one of those portable organs, and he expected money; so you can imagine what *that* was like; there came a constant smell of luncheon from below, and puffs of hot oily machinery; the journey took hours and hours and hours; and for miles, literally for miles, dreadful boys ran with us on the shore, in the *awful* Thames mud, going in *up to the waist* – they had their trousers turned back, and they went up to their hips in that indescribable Thames mud, their faces always turned to us, and screaming, exactly like carrion creatures, screaming " 'Ere y'are sir, 'ere y'are sir, 'ere y'are sir", exactly like some foul carrion objects, perfectly obscene; and paterfamilias on board, laughing when the boys went right down in that awful mud, occasionally throwing them a ha-penny. And if you'd seen the intent look on the faces of these boys, and the way they darted in the filth when a coin was flung – really, no vulture or jackal could dream of approaching them, for foulness. I *never* would go on a pleasure boat again – never.'

Gerald watched her all the time she spoke, his eyes glittering with faint rousedness. It was not so much what she said; it was she herself who roused him, roused him with a small vivid pricking.

'Of course,' he said, 'every civilised body is bound to have its vermin.'

'Why?' cried Ursula. '*I* don't have vermin.'

'And it's not that – it's the *quality* of the whole thing – paterfamilias laughing and thinking it sport, and throwing the ha'pennies, and materfamilias spreading her fat little knees and eating, continually eating—' replied Gudrun.

'Yes,' said Ursula. 'It isn't the boys so much who are vermin; it's the people themselves, the whole body politic, as you call it.'

Gerald laughed.

'Never mind,' he said. 'You shan't go on the launch.'

Gudrun flushed quickly at his rebuke.

There were a few moments of silence. Gerald, like a sentinel, was watching the people who were going on to the boat. He was very good-looking and self-contained, but his air of soldierly alertness was rather irritating.

'Will you have tea here then, or go across to the house, where there's a tent on the lawn?' he asked.

'Can't we have a rowing-boat, and get out?' asked Ursula, who was always rushing in too fast.

'To get out?' smiled Gerald.

'You see,' said Gudrun, flushing at Ursula's outspoken rudeness, 'we don't know the people, we are almost *complete* strangers here.'

'Oh, I can soon set you up with a few acquaintances,' he said easily.

Gudrun looked at him, to see if it were ill-meant. Then she smiled at him.

'Ah,' she said, 'you know what we mean. Can't we go up there, and explore that coast?' She pointed to a grove on the hillock of the meadowside, near the shore, half-way down the lake. 'That looks perfectly lovely. We might even bathe. Isn't it beautiful in this light! Really, it's like one of the reaches of the Nile – as one imagines the Nile.'

Gerald smiled at her factitious enthusiasm for the distant spot.

'You're sure it's far enough off?' he asked ironically, adding at once: 'Yes, you might go there, if we could get a boat. They seem to be all out.'

He looked round the lake and counted the rowing-boats on its surface.

'How lovely it would be!' cried Ursula wistfully.

'And don't you want tea?' he said.

'Oh, said Gudrun, 'we could just drink a cup, and be off.'

He looked from one to the other, smiling. He was somewhat offended – yet sporting.

'Can you manage a boat pretty well?' he asked.

'Yes,' replied Gudrun coldly, 'pretty well.'

'Oh yes,' cried Ursula. 'We can both of us row like water-spiders.'

'You can? There's a light little canoe of mine, that I didn't take out for fear somebody should drown themselves. Do you think you'd be safe in that?'

'Oh, perfectly,' said Gudrun.

'What an angel!' cried Ursula.

'Don't, for *my* sake, have an accident – because I'm responsible for the water.'

'Sure,' pledged Gudrun.

'Besides, we can both swim quite well,' said Ursula.

'Well – then I'll get them to put you up a tea-basket, and you can picnic all to yourselves – that's the idea, isn't it?'

'How fearfully good! How frightfully nice if you could!' cried Gudrun warmly, her colour flushing up again. It made the blood stir in his veins, the subtle way she turned to him and infused her gratitude into his body.

'Where's Birkin?' he said, his eyes twinkling. 'He might help me to get it down.'

'But what about your hand? Isn't it hurt?' asked Gudrun, rather muted, as if avoiding the intimacy. This was the first time the hurt had been mentioned. The curious way she skirted round the subject sent a new, subtle caress through his veins. He took his hand out of his pocket. It was bandaged. He looked at it, then put it in his pocket again. Gudrun quivered at the sight of the wrapped-up paw.

'Oh, I can manage with one hand. The canoe is as light as a feather,' he said. 'There's Rupert! – Rupert!'

Birkin turned from his social duties and came towards them.

'What have you done to it?' asked Ursula, who had been aching to put the question for the last half-hour.

'To my hand?' said Gerald. 'I trapped it in some machinery.'

'Ugh!' said Ursula. 'And did it hurt much?'

'Yes,' he said. 'It did at the time. It's getting better now. It crushed the fingers.'

'Oh,' cried Ursula, as if in pain, 'I hate people who hurt themselves. I can *feel* it.' And she shook her hand.

'What do you want?' said Birkin.

The two men carried down the slim brown boat, and set it on the water.

'You're quite sure you'll be safe in it?' Gerald asked.

'Quite sure,' said Gudrun. 'I wouldn't be so mean as to take it, if there was the slightest doubt. But I've had a canoe at Arundel, and I assure you I'm perfectly safe.'

So saying, having given her word like a man, she and Ursula entered the frail craft, and pushed gently off. The two men stood watching them. Gudrun was paddling. She knew the men were watching her, and it made her slow and rather clumsy. The colour flew in her face like a flag.

'Thanks awfully,' she called back to him, from the water, as the boat slid away. 'It's lovely – like sitting in a leaf.'

He laughed at the fancy. Her voice was shrill and strange, calling from the distance. He watched her as she paddled away. There was something childlike about her, trustful and deferential, like a child. He watched her all the while, as she rowed. And to Gudrun it was a real delight, in make-believe, to be the childlike, clinging woman to the man who stood there on the quay, so good-looking and efficient in his white clothes, and moreover the most important man she knew at the moment. She did not take any notice of the wavering, indistinct, lambent Birkin, who stood at his side. One figure at a time occupied the field of her attention.

The boat rustled lightly along the water. They passed the bathers whose striped tents stood between the willows of the meadow's edge, and drew along the open shore, past the meadows that sloped golden in the light of the already late afternoon. Other boats were stealing under the wooded shore opposite, they could hear people's laughter and voices. But Gudrun rowed on towards the clump of trees that balanced perfect in the distance, in the golden light.

The sisters found a little place where a tiny stream flowed into the lake, with reeds and flowery marsh of pink willow herb, and a gravelly bank to the side. Here they ran delicately ashore, with their frail boat, the two girls took off their shoes and stockings and went through the water's edge to the grass. The tiny ripples of the lake were warm and clear, they lifted their boat on to the bank, and looked round with joy. They were quite alone in a forsaken little stream-mouth, and on the knoll just behind was the clump of trees.

'We will bathe just for a moment,' said Ursula, 'and then we'll have tea.'

They looked round. Nobody could notice them, or could come up in time to see them. In less than a minute Ursula had thrown off her clothes and had slipped naked into the water, and was swimming out. Quickly, Gudrun joined her. They swam silently and blissfully for a few minutes, circling round their little stream-mouth. Then they slipped ashore and ran into the grove again, like nymphs.

'How lovely it is to be free,' said Ursula, running swiftly here and there between the tree-trunks, quite naked, her hair blowing loose. The grove was of beech-trees, big and splendid, a steel-grey scaffolding of trunks and boughs, with level sprays of strong green here and there, whilst through the northern side the distance glimmered open as through a window.

When they had run and danced themselves dry, the girls quickly dressed and sat down to the fragrant tea. They sat on the northern side of the grove, in the yellow sunshine facing the slope of the grassy hill, alone in a little wild world of their own. The tea was hot and aromatic, there were delicious little sandwiches of cucumber and of caviare, and winy cakes.

'Are you happy, Prune?' cried Ursula in delight, looking at her sister.

'Ursula, I'm perfectly happy,' replied Gudrun gravely, looking at the westering sun.

'So am I.'

When they were together, doing the things they enjoyed, the two sisters were quite complete in a perfect world of their own. And this was one of the perfect moments of freedom and delight, such as children alone know, when all seems a perfect and blissful adventure.

When they had finished tea, the two girls sat on, silent and serene. Then Ursula, who had a beautiful strong voice, began to sing to herself, softly:

'*Annchen von Tharau.*' Gudrun listened as she sat beneath the trees, and the yearning came into her heart. Ursula seemed so peaceful and sufficient unto herself, sitting there unconsciously crooning her song, strong and unquestioned at the centre of her own universe. And Gudrun felt herself outside. Always this desolating, agonised feeling, that she was outside of life, an onlooker, whilst Ursula was a partaker, caused Gudrun to suffer from a sense of her own negation, and made her, that she must always demand the other to be aware of her, to be in connection with her.

'Do you mind if I do Dalcroze to that tune, Hurtler?' she asked in a curious muted tone, scarce moving her lips.

'What did you say?' asked Ursula, looking up in peaceful surprise.

'Will you sing while I do Dalcroze?' said Gudrun, suffering at having to repeat herself.

Ursula thought for a moment, gathering her straying wits together.

'While you do—?' she asked vaguely.

'Dalcroze movements,' said Gudrun, suffering tortures of self-consciousness, even because of her sister.

'Oh, Dalcroze! I couldn't catch the name. *Do* – I should love to see you,' cried Ursula, with childish surprised brightness. 'What shall I sing?'

'Sing anything you like, and I'll take the rhythm from it.'

But Ursula could not for her life think of anything to sing. However, she suddenly began, in a laughing, teasing voice:

'My love - is a high-born lady—'

Gudrun, looking as if some invisible chain weighed on her hands and feet, began slowly to dance in the eurhythmic manner, pulsing and fluttering rhythmically with her feet making slower, regular gestures with her hands and arms, now spreading her arms wide, now raising them above her head, now flinging them softly apart, and lifting her face, her feet all the time beating and running to the measure of the song, as if it were some strange incantation, her white, rapt form drifting here and there in a strange impulsive rhapsody, seeming to be lifted on a breeze of incantation, shuddering with strange little runs. Ursula sat on the grass, her mouth open in her singing, her eyes laughing as if she thought it was a great joke, but a yellow light flashing up in them, as she caught some of the unconscious ritualistic suggestion of the complex shuddering and waving and drifting of her sister's white form, that was clutched in pure, mindless, tossing rhythm, and a will set powerful in a kind of hypnotic influence.

'My love is a high-born lady – she is-s-s – rather dark than shady—' rang out Ursula's laughing, satiric song, and quicker, fiercer went Gudrun in the dance, stamping as if she were trying to throw off some bond, flinging her hands suddenly and stamping again, then rushing with face uplifted and throat full and beautiful, and eyes half closed, sightless. The sun was low and yellow, sinking down, and in the sky floated a thin, ineffectual moon.

Ursula was quite absorbed in her song, when suddenly Gudrun stopped and said mildly, ironically:

'Ursula!'

'Yes?' said Ursula, opening her eyes out of the trance.

Gudrun was standing still and pointing, a mocking smile on her face, towards the side.

'Ugh!' cried Ursula in sudden panic, starting to her feet.

'They're quite all right,' rang out Gudrun's sardonic voice.

On the left stood a little cluster of Highland cattle, vividly coloured and fleecy in the evening light, their horns branching into the sky, pushing forward their muzzles inquisitively, to know what it was all about. Their eyes glittered through their tangle of hair, their naked nostrils were full of shadow.

'Won't they do anything?' cried Ursula in fear.

Gudrun, who was usually frightened of cattle, now shook her head in a queer, half-doubtful, half-sardonic motion, a faint smile round her mouth.

'Don't they look charming, Ursula?' cried Gudrun, in a high, strident voice, something like the scream of a seagull.

'Charming,' cried Ursula in trepidation. 'But won't they do anything to us?'

Again Gudrun looked back at her sister with an enigmatic smile, and shook her head.

'I'm sure they won't,' she said, as if she had to convince herself also, and yet, as if she were confident of some secret power in herself, and had to put it to the test. 'Sit down and sing again,' she called in her high, strident voice.

'I'm frightened,' cried Ursula, in a pathetic voice, watching the group of sturdy short cattle, that stood with their knees planted, and watched with their dark, wicked eyes, through the matted fringe of their hair. Nevertheless, she sank down again, in her former posture.

'They are quite safe,' came Gudrun's high call. 'Sing something, you've only to sing something.'

It was evident she had a strange passion to dance before the sturdy, handsome cattle.

Ursula began to sing, in a false quavering voice:

'Way down in Tennessee—'

She sounded purely anxious. Nevertheless, Gudrun, with her arms outspread and her face uplifted, went in a strange palpitating dance towards the cattle, lifting her body towards them as if in a spell, her feet pulsing as if in some little frenzy of unconscious sensation, her arms, her wrists, her hands stretching and heaving and falling and reaching and reaching and falling, her breasts lifted and shaken towards the cattle, her throat exposed as in some voluptuous ecstasy towards them, whilst she drifted imperceptibly nearer, an uncanny white figure, towards them, carried away in its own rapt trance, ebbing in strange fluctuations upon the cattle, that waited, and ducked their heads a little in sudden contraction from her, watching all the time as if hypnotised, their bare horns branching in the clear light, as the white figure of the woman ebbed upon them, in the slow, hypnotising convulsion of the dance. She could feel them just in front of her, it was as if she had the electric pulse from their breasts running into her hands. Soon she would touch them, actually touch them. A terrible shiver of fear and pleasure went through her. And all the while Ursula, spell-bound, kept up her high-pitched thin, irrelevant song, which pierced the fading evening like an incantation.

Gudrun could hear the cattle breathing heavily with helpless fear and fascination. Oh, they were brave little beasts, these wild Scotch bullocks, wild and fleecy. Suddenly one of them snorted, ducked its head, and backed.

'Hue! Hi-eee!' came a sudden loud shout from the edge of the grove. The cattle broke and fell back quite spontaneously, went running up the hill, their fleece waving like fire to their motion. Gudrun stood suspended out on the grass, Ursula rose to her feet.

It was Gerald and Birkin come to find them, and Gerald had cried out to frighten off the cattle.

'What do you think you're doing?' he now called, in a high, wondering vexed tone.

'Why have you come?' came back Gudrun's strident cry of anger.

'What do you think you were doing?' Gerald repeated, automatically.

'We were doing eurhythmics,' laughed Ursula, in a shaken voice.

Gudrun stood aloof looking at them with large dark eyes of resentment, suspended for a few moments. Then she walked away up the hill, after the cattle, which had gathered in a little spell-bound cluster higher up.

'Where are you going?' Gerald called after her. And he followed her up the hill-side. The sun had gone behind the hill, and shadows were clinging to the earth, the sky above was full of travelling light.

'A poor song for a dance,' said Birkin to Ursula, standing before her with a sardonic, flickering laugh on his face. And in another second, he was singing softly to himself, and dancing a grotesque step-dance in front of her, his limbs and body shaking loose, his face flickering palely, a constant thing, whilst his feet beat a rapid mocking tattoo, and his body seemed to hang all loose and quaking in between, like a shadow.

'I think we've all gone mad,' she said, laughing rather frightened.

'Pity we aren't madder,' he answered, as he kept up the incessant shaking dance. Then suddenly he leaned up to her and kissed her fingers lightly, putting his face to hers and looking into her eyes with a pale grin. She stepped back, affronted.

'Offended—?' he asked ironically, suddenly going quite still and reserved again. 'I thought you liked the light fantastic.'

'Not like that,' she said, confused and bewildered, almost affronted. Yet somewhere inside her she was fascinated by the sight of his loose, vibrating body, perfectly abandoned to its own dropping and swinging, and by the pallid, sardonic-smiling face above. Yet automatically she stiffened herself away, and disapproved. It seemed almost an obscenity, in a man who talked as a rule so very seriously.

'Why not like that?' he mocked. And immediately he dropped again into the incredibly rapid, slack-waggling dance, watching her malevolently. And moving in the rapid, stationary dance he came a little nearer, and reached forward with an incredibly mocking, satiric gleam on his face, and would have kissed her again, had she not started back.

'No, don't!' she cried, really afraid.

'Cordelia after all,' he said satirically. She was stung, as if this were an insult. She knew he intended it as such, and it bewildered her.

'And you,' she cried in retort, 'why do you always take your soul in your mouth, so frightfully full?'

'So that I can spit it out the more readily,' he said, pleased by his own retort.

Gerald Crich, his face narrowing to an intent gleam, followed up the hill with quick strides, straight after Gudrun. The cattle stood with their noses together on the brow of a slope, watching the scene below, the men in white hovering about the white forms of the women, watching above all Gudrun, who was advancing slowly towards them. She stood a moment, glancing back at Gerald, and then at the cattle.

Then in a sudden motion, she lifted her arms and rushed sheer upon the long-horned bullocks, in shuddering irregular runs, pausing for a second and looking at them, then lifting her hands and running forward with a flash, till they ceased pawing the ground, and gave way, snorting with terror, lifting their heads from the ground and flinging themselves away, galloping off into the evening, becoming tiny in the distance, and still not stopping.

Gudrun remained staring after them, with a mask-like defiant face.

'Why do you want to drive them mad?' asked Gerald, coming up with her.

She took no notice of him, only averted her face from him.

'It's not safe, you know,' he persisted. 'They're nasty, when they do turn.'

'Turn where? Turn away?' she mocked loudly.

'No,' he said, 'turn against you.'

'Turn against *me?*' she mocked.

He could make nothing of this.

'Anyway, they gored one of the farmer's cows to death the other day,' he said.

'What do I care?' she said.

'*I* cared though,' he replied, 'seeing that they're my cattle.'

'How are they yours! You haven't swallowed them. Give me one of them now,' she said, holding out her hand.

'You know where they are,' he said, pointing over the hill. 'You can have one if you'd like it sent to you later on.'

She looked at him inscrutably.

'You think I'm afraid of you and your cattle, don't you?' she asked.

His eyes narrowed dangerously. There was a faint domineering smile on his face.

'Why should I think that?' he said.

She was watching him all the time with her dark, dilated, inchoate eyes. She leaned forward and swung round her arm, catching him a light blow on the face with the back of her hand.

'That's why,' she said, mocking.

And she felt in her soul an unconquerable desire for deep violence against him. She shut off the fear and dismay that filled her conscious mind. She wanted to do as she did, she was not going to be afraid.

He recoiled from the slight blow on his face. He became deadly pale, and a dangerous flame darkened his eyes. For some seconds he could not speak, his lungs were so suffused with blood, his heart stretched almost to bursting with a great gush of ungovernable emotion. It was as if some reservoir of black emotion had burst within him, and swamped him.

'You have struck the first blow,' he said at last, forcing the words from his lungs, in a voice so soft and low, it sounded like a dream within her, not spoken in the outer air.

'And I shall strike the last,' she retorted involuntarily, with confident assurance. He was silent, he did not contradict her.

She stood negligently, staring away from him, into the distance. On the edge of her consciousness the question was asking itself, automatically:

'Why *are* you behaving in this *impossible* and ridiculous fashion.' But she was sullen, she half shoved the question out of herself. She could not get it clean away, so she felt self-conscious.

Gerald, very pale, was watching her closely. His eyes were lit up with intent lights, absorbed and gleaming. She turned suddenly on him.

'It's you who make me behave like this, you know,' she said, almost suggestive.

'I? How?' he said.

But she turned away, and set off towards the lake. Below, on the water, lanterns were coming alight, faint ghosts of warm flame floating in the pallor of the first twilight. The earth was spread with darkness, like lacquer, overhead was a pale sky, all primrose, and the lake was pale as milk in one part. Away at the landing-stage, tiniest points of coloured rays were stringing themselves in the dusk. The launch was being illuminated. All round, shadow was gathering from the trees.

Gerald, white like a presence in his summer clothes, was following down the open grassy slope. Gudrun waited for him to come up. Then she softly put out her hand and touched him, saying softly:

'Don't be angry with me.'

A flame flew over him, and he was unconscious. Yet he stammered:

'I'm not angry with you. I'm in love with you.'

His mind was gone, he grasped for sufficient mechanical control, to save himself. She laughed a silvery little mockery, yet intolerably caressive.

'That's one way of putting it,' she said.

The terrible swooning burden on his mind, the awful swooning, the loss of all his control, was too much for him. He grasped her arm in his one hand, as if his hand were iron.

'It's all right, then, is it?' he said, holding her arrested.

She looked at the face with the fixed eyes, set before her, and her blood ran cold.

'Yes, it's all right,' she said softly, as if drugged, her voice crooning and witch-like.

He walked on beside her, a striding, mindless body. But he recovered a little as he went. He suffered badly. He had killed his brother when a boy, and was set apart, like Cain.

They found Birkin and Ursula sitting together by the boats, talking and laughing. Birkin had been teasing Ursula.

'Do you smell this little marsh?' he said, sniffing the air. He was very sensitive to scents, and quick in understanding them.

'It's rather nice,' she said.

'No,' he replied, 'alarming.'

'Why alarming?' she laughed.

'It seethes and seethes, a river of darkness,' he said, 'putting forth lilies and snakes, and the *ignis fatuus*, and rolling all the time onward. That's what we never take into count – that it rolls onwards.

'What does?'

'The other river, the black river. We always consider the silver river of life, rolling on and quickening all the world to a brightness, on and on to heaven, flowing into a bright eternal sea, a heaven of angels thronging. But the other is our real reality—'

'But what other? I don't see any other,' said Ursula.

'It is your reality, nevertheless,' he said; 'that dark river of dissolution. You see it rolls in us just as the other rolls – the black river of corruption. And our flowers are of this – our sea-born Aphrodite, all our white phosphorescent flowers of sensuous perfection, all our reality, nowadays.'

'You mean that Aphrodite is really deathly?' asked Ursula.

'I mean she is the flowering mystery of the death-process, yes,' he replied. 'When the stream of synthetic creation lapses, we find ourselves part of the inverse process, the blood of destructive creation. Aphrodite is born in the first spasm of universal dissolution – then the snakes and swans and lotus – marsh-flowers – and Gudrun and Gerald – born in the process of destructive creation.'

'And you and me—?' she asked.

'Probably,' he replied. 'In part, certainly. Whether we are that, *in toto*, I don't yet know.'

'You mean we are flowers of dissolution – *fleurs du mal?* I don't feel as if I were,' she protested.

He was silent for a time.

'I don't feel as if we were, *altogether*,' he replied. 'Some people are pure flowers of dark corruption – lilies. But there ought to be some roses, warm and flamy. You know Herakleitos says "a dry soul is best". I know so well what that means. Do you?'

'I'm not sure,' Ursula replied. 'But what if people *are* all flowers of dissolution – when they're flowers at all – what difference does it make?'

'No difference – and all the difference. Dissolution rolls on, just as production does,' he said. 'It is a progressive process – and it ends in universal nothing – the end of the world, if you like. But why isn't the end of the world as good as the beginning?'

'I suppose it isn't,' said Ursula, rather angry.

'Oh yes, ultimately,' he said. 'It means a new cycle of creation after – but not for us. If it is the end, then we are of the end – *fleurs du mal*, if you like. If we are *fleurs du mal*, we are not roses of happiness, and there you are.'

'But I think I am,' said Ursula. 'I think I am a rose of happiness.'

'Ready-made?' he asked ironically.

'No – real,' she said, hurt.

'If we are the end, we are not the beginning,' he said.

'Yes, we are,' she said. 'The beginning comes out of the end.'

'After it, not out of it. After us, not out of us.'

'You are a devil, you know, really,' she said. 'You want to destroy our hope. You *want* us to be deathly.'

'No,' he said, 'I only want us to *know* what we are.'

'Ha!' she cried in anger. 'You only want us to know death.'

'You're quite right,' said the soft voice of Gerald, out of the dusk behind.

Birkin rose. Gerald and Gudrun came up. They all began to smoke, in the moments of silence. One after another, Birkin lighted their cigarettes. The match flickered in the twilight, and they were all smoking peacefully by the water-side. The lake was dim, the light dying from off it, in the midst of the dark land. The air all round was intangible, neither here nor there, and there was an unreal noise of banjoes, or suchlike music.

As the golden swim of light overhead died out, the moon gained brightness, and seemed to begin to smile forth her ascendancy. The dark woods on the opposite shore melted into universal shadow. And amid this universal under-shadow, there was a scattered intrusion of lights. Far down the lake were fantastic pale strings of colour, like beads of wan fire, green and red and yellow. The music came out in a little puff, as the launch, all illuminated, veered into the great shadow, stirring her outlines of half-living lights, puffing out her music in little drifts.

All were lighting up. Here and there, close against the faint water, and at the far end of the lake, where the water lay milky in the last whiteness of the sky, and there was no shadow, solitary, frail flames of lanterns floated from the unseen boats. There was a sound of oars, and a boat passed from the pallor into the darkness under the wood, where her lanterns seemed to kindle into fire, hanging in ruddy lovely globes. And again, in the lake, shadowy red gleams hovered in reflection about the boat. Everywhere were these noiseless ruddy creatures of fire drifting near the surface of the water, caught at by the rarest, scarce visible reflections.

Birkin brought the lanterns from the bigger boat, and the four shadowy white figures gathered round, to light them. Ursula held up the first, Birkin lowered the light from the rosy, glowing cup of his hands, into the depths of the lantern. It was kindled, and they all stood back to look at the great blue moon of light that hung from Ursula's hand, casting a strange gleam on her face. It flickered, and Birkin went bending over the well of light. His face shone out like an apparition, so unconscious, and again, something demoniacal. Ursula was dim and veiled, looming over him.

'That is all right,' said his voice softly.

She held up the lantern. It had a flight of storks streaming through a turquoise sky of light, over a dark earth.

'This is beautiful,' she said.

'Lovely,' echoed Gudrun, who wanted to hold one also and lift it up full of beauty.

'Light one for me,' she said. Gerald stood by her, incapacitated. Birkin lit the lantern she held up. Her heart beat with anxiety, to see how beautiful it would be. It was primrose yellow, with tall straight flowers growing darkly from their dark leaves, lifting their heads into the primrose day, while butterflies hovered about them, in the pure clear light.

Gudrun gave a little cry of excitement, as if pierced with delight.

'Isn't it beautiful, oh, isn't it beautiful!'

Her soul was really pierced with beauty, she was translated beyond herself. Gerald leaned near to her, into her zone of light, as if to see. He came close to her, and stood touching her, looking with her at the primrose-shining globe. And she turned her face to his, that was faintly bright in the light of the lantern, and they stood together in one luminous union, close together and ringed round with light, all the rest excluded.

Birkin looked away, and went to light Ursula's second lantern. It had a pale ruddy sea-bottom, with black crabs and sea-weed moving sinuously under a transparent sea, that passed into flamy ruddiness above.

'You've got the heavens above, and the waters under the earth,' said Birkin to her.

'Anything but the earth itself,' she laughed, watching his live hands that hovered to attend to the light.

'I'm dying to see what my second one is,' cried Gudrun, in a vibrating rather strident voice, that seemed to repel the others from her.

Birkin went and kindled it. It was of a lovely deep blue colour, with a red floor, and a great white cuttle-fish flowing in white soft streams all over it. The cuttle-fish had a face that stared straight from the heart of the light, very fixed and coldly intent.

'How truly terrifying!' exclaimed Gudrun, in a voice of horror. Gerald, at her side, gave a low laugh.

'But isn't it really fearful!' she cried in dismay.

Again he laughed, and said:

'Change it with Ursula, for the crabs.'

Gudrun was silent for a moment.

'Ursula,' she said, 'could you bear to have this fearful thing?'

'I think the colouring is *lovely*,' said Ursula.

'So do I,' said Gudrun. 'But could you *bear* to have it swinging to your boat? Don't you want to destroy it *at once?*'

'Oh no,' said Ursula. 'I don't want to destroy it.'

'Well, do you mind having it instead of the crabs? Are you sure you don't mind?'

Gudrun came forward to exchange lanterns.

'No,' said Ursula, yielding up the crabs and receiving the cuttle-fish.

Yet she could not help feeling rather resentful at the way in which Gudrun and Gerald should assume a right over her, a precedence.

'Come then,' said Birkin. 'I'll put them on the boats.'

He and Ursula were moving away to the big boat.

'I suppose you'll row me back, Rupert,' said Gerald, out of the pale shadow of the evening.

'Won't you go with Gudrun in the canoe?' said Birkin. 'It'll be more interesting.'

There was a moment's pause. Birkin and Ursula stood dimly, with their swinging lanterns, by the water's edge. The world was all illusive.

'Is that all right?' said Gudrun to him.

'It'll suit *me* very well,' he said. 'But what about you, and the rowing? I don't see why you should pull me.'

'Why not?' she said. 'I can pull you as well as I could pull Ursula.'

By her tone he could tell she wanted to have him in the boat to herself, and that she was subtly gratified that she should have power over them both. He gave himself, in a strange, electric submission.

She handed him the lanterns, whilst she went to fix the cane at the end of the canoe. He followed after her, and stood with the lanterns dangling against his white-flannelled thighs, emphasising the shadow around.

'Kiss me before we go,' came his voice softly from out of the shadow above.

She stopped her work in real, momentary astonishment.

'But why?' she exclaimed, in pure surprise.

'Why?' he echoed ironically.

And she looked at him fixedly for some moments. Then she leaned forward and kissed him, with a slow, luxurious kiss, lingering on the mouth. And then she took the lanterns from him, while he stood swooning with the perfect fire that burned in all his joints.

They lifted the canoe into the water, Gudrun took her place, and Gerald pushed off.

'Are you sure you don't hurt your hand, doing that?' she asked, solicitous. 'Because I could have done it *perfectly*.'

'I don't hurt myself,' he said in a low, soft voice, that caressed her with inexpressible beauty.

And she watched him as he sat near her, very near to her, in the stern of the canoe, his legs coming towards hers, his feet touching hers. And she paddled softly, lingeringly, longing for him to say something meaningful to her. But he remained silent.

'You like this, do you?' she said, in a gentle, solicitous voice.

He laughed shortly.

'There is a space between us,' he said, in the low, unconscious voice, as if something were speaking out of him. And she was as if magically aware of their being balanced in separation, in the boat. She swooned with acute comprehension and pleasure.

'But I'm very near,' she said caressively, gaily.

'Yet distant, distant,' he said.

Again she was silent with pleasure, before she answered, speaking with a reedy, thrilled voice:

'Yet we cannot very well change, whilst we are on the water.' She caressed him subtly and strangely, having him completely at her mercy.

A dozen or more boats on the lake swung their rosy and moon-like lanterns low on the water, that reflected as from a fire. In the distance, the steamer twanged and thrummed and washed with her faintly-splashing paddles, trailing her strings of coloured lights, and occasionally lighting up the whole scene luridly with an effusion of fireworks, Roman candles and sheafs of stars and other simple effects, illuminating the surface of the water, and showing the boats creeping round, low down. Then the lovely darkness fell again, the lanterns and the little threaded lights glimmered softly, there was a muffled knocking of oars and a waving of music.

Gudrun paddled almost imperceptibly. Gerald could see, not far ahead, the rich blue and the rose globes of Ursula's lanterns swaying softly cheek to cheek as Birkin rowed, and iridescent, evanescent gleams chasing in the wake. He was aware, too, of his own delicately coloured lights casting their softness behind him.

Gudrun rested her paddle and looked round. The canoe lifted with the lightest ebbing of the water. Gerald's white knees were very near to her.

'Isn't it beautiful!' she said softly, as if reverently.

She looked at him, as he leaned back against the faint crystal of the lantern-light. She could see his face, although it was a pure shadow. But it was a piece of twilight. And her breast was keen with passion for him, he was so beautiful in his male stillness and mystery. It was a certain pure effluence of maleness, like an aroma from his softly, firmly moulded contours, a certain rich perfection of his presence, that touched her with an ecstasy, a thrill of pure intoxication. She loved to look at him. For the present she did not want to touch him, to know the further, satisfying substance of his living body. He was purely intangible, yet so near. Her hands lay on the paddle like slumber, she only wanted to see him, like a crystal shadow, to feel his essential presence.

'Yes,' he said vaguely. 'It is very beautiful.'

He was listening to the faint near sounds, the dropping of water-drops from the oar-blades, the slight drumming of the lanterns behind him, as they rubbed against one another, the occasional rustling of Gudrun's full skirt, an alien land noise. His mind was almost submerged, he was almost transfused, lapsed out for the first time in his life, into the things about him. For he always kept such a keen attentiveness, concentrated and unyielding in himself. Now he had let go, imperceptibly he was melting into oneness with the whole. It was like pure, perfect sleep, his first great sleep of life. He had been so insistent, so guarded, all his life. But here was sleep, and peace, and perfect lapsing out.

'Shall I row to the landing-stage?' asked Gudrun wistfully.

'Anywhere,' he answered. 'Let it drift.'

'Tell me then, if we are running into anything,' she replied, in that very quiet, toneless voice of sheer intimacy.

'The lights will show,' he said.

So they drifted almost motionless, in silence. He wanted silence, pure and whole. But she was uneasy yet for some word, for some assurance.

'Nobody will miss you?' she asked, anxious for some communication.

'Miss me?' he echoed. 'No! Why?'

'I wondered if anybody would be looking for you.'

'Why should they look for me?' And then he remembered his manners. 'But perhaps you want to get back,' he said, in a changed voice.

'No, I don't want to get back,' she replied. 'No, I assure you.'

'You're quite sure it's all right for you?'

'Perfectly all right.'

And again they were still. The launch twanged and hooted, somebody was singing. Then as if the night smashed, suddenly there was a great shout, a confusion of shouting, warring on the water, then the horrid noise of paddles reversed and churned violently.

Gerald sat up, and Gudrun looked at him in fear.

'Somebody in the water,' he said angrily, and desperately, looking keenly across the dusk. 'Can you row up?'

'Where, to the launch?' asked Gudrun, in nervous panic.

'Yes.'

'You'll tell me if I don't steer straight,' she said, in nervous apprehension.

'You keep pretty level,' he said, and the canoe hastened forward.

The shouting and the noise continued, sounding horrid through the dusk, over the surface of the water.

'Wasn't this *bound* to happen?' said Gudrun, with heavy hateful irony. But he hardly heard, and she glanced over her shoulder to see her way. The half-dark waters were sprinkled with lovely bubbles of swaying lights, the launch did not look far off. She was rocking her lights in the early night. Gudrun rowed as hard as she could. But now that it was a serious matter, she seemed uncertain and clumsy in her stroke, it was difficult to paddle swiftly. She glanced at his face. He was looking fixedly into the darkness, very keen and alert and single in himself, instrumental. Her heart sank, she seemed to die a death. 'Of course,' she said to herself, 'nobody will be drowned. Of course they won't. It would be too extravagant and sensational.' But her heart was cold, because of his sharp impersonal face. It was as if he belonged naturally to dread and catastrophe, as if he were himself again.

Then there came a child's voice, a girl's high, piercing shriek:

'Di-Di-Di-Di-Oh Di-Oh Di-Oh Di!'

The blood ran cold in Gudrun's veins.

'It's Diana, is it,' muttered Gerald. 'The young monkey, she'd have to be up to some of her tricks.'

And he glanced again at the paddle, the boat was not going quickly enough for him. It made Gudrun almost helpless at the rowing, this nervous stress. She kept up with all her might. Still the voices were calling and answering.

'Where, where? There you are – that's it. Which? No – No-o-o. Damn it all, here, *here*—' Boats were hurrying from all directions to the scene, coloured lanterns could be seen waving close to the surface of the lake, reflections swaying after them in uneven haste. The steamer hooted again, for some unknown reason. Gudrun's boat was travelling quickly, the lanterns were swinging behind Gerald.

And then again came the child's high, screaming voice, with a note of weeping and impatience in it now:

'Di-Oh Di-Oh Di-Di—!'

It was a terrible sound, coming through the obscure air of the evening.

'You'd be better if you were in bed, Winnie,' Gerald muttered to himself.

He was stooping unlacing his shoes, pushing them off with the foot. Then he threw his soft hat into the bottom of the boat.

'You can't go into the water with your hurt hand,' said Gudrun, panting, in a low voice of horror.

'What? It won't hurt.'

He had struggled out of his jacket, and had dropped it between his feet. He sat bare-headed, all in white now. He felt the belt at his waist. They were nearing the launch, which stood still big above them, her myriad lamps making lovely darts, and sinuous running tongues of ugly red and green and yellow light on the lustrous dark water, under the shadow.

'Oh get her out! Oh Di, *darling!* Oh get her out! Oh Daddy, Oh Daddy!' moaned the child's voice, in distraction. Somebody was in the water, with a lifebelt. Two boats paddled near, their lanterns swinging ineffectually, the boats nosing round.

'Hi there – Rockley! – hi there!'

'Mr. Gerald!' came the captain's terrified voice. 'Miss Diana's in the water.'

'Anybody gone in for her?' came Gerald's sharp voice.

'Young Doctor Brindell, sir.'

'Where?'

'Can't see no signs of them, sir. Everybody's looking, but there's nothing so far.'

There was a moment's ominous pause.

'Where did she go in?'

'I think – about where that boat is,' came the uncertain answer, 'that one with red and green lights.'

'Row there,' said Gerald quietly to Gudrun.

'Get her out, Gerald, oh get her out,' the child's voice was crying anxiously. He took no heed.

'Lean back that way,' said Gerald to Gudrun, as he stood up in the frail boat. 'She won't upset.'

In another moment, he had dropped clean down, soft and plumb, into the water. Gudrun was swaying violently in her boat, the agitated water shook with transient lights, she realised that it was faintly moonlight, and that he was gone. So it was possible to be gone. A terrible sense of fatality robbed her of all feeling and thought. She knew he was gone out of her world, there was merely the same world, and absence, his absence. The night seemed large and vacuous. Lanterns swayed here and there, people were talking in an undertone on the launch and in the boats. She could hear Winifred moaning: *'Oh do find her Gerald, do find her,'* and someone trying to comfort the child. Gudrun paddled aimlessly here and there. The terrible, massive, cold, boundless surface of the water terrified her beyond words. Would he never come back? She felt she must jump into the water too, to know the horror also.

She started, hearing someone say: 'There he is.' She saw the movement of his swimming, like a water-rat. And she rowed involuntarily to him. But he was near another boat, a bigger one. Still she rowed towards him. She must be very near. She saw him – he looked like a seal. He looked like a seal as he took hold of the side of the boat. His fair hair was washed down on his round head, his face seemed to glisten suavely. She could hear him panting.

Then he clambered into the boat. Oh, and the beauty of the subjection of his loins, white and dimly luminous as he climbed over the side of the boat, made her want to die, to die. The beauty of his dim and luminous loins as he climbed into the boat, his back rounded and soft – ah, this was too much for her, too final a vision. She knew it, and it was fatal. The terrible hopelessness of fate, and of beauty, such beauty!

He was not like a man to her, he was an incarnation, a great phase of life. She saw him press the water out of his face, and look at the bandage on his hand. And she knew it was all no good, and that she would never go beyond him, he was the final approximation of life to her.

'Put the lights out, we shall see better,' came his voice, sudden and mechanical and belonging to the world of man. She could scarcely believe there was a world of man. She leaned round and blew out her lanterns. They were difficult to blow out. Everywhere the lights were gone save the coloured points on the sides of the launch. The bluey-grey, early night spread level around, the moon was overhead, there were shadows of boats here and there.

Again there was a splash, and he was gone under. Gudrun sat, sick at heart, frightened of the great, level surface of the water, so heavy and deadly. She was so alone, with the level, unliving field of the water stretching beneath her. It was not a good isolation, it was a terrible, cold separation of suspense. She was suspended upon the surface of the insidious reality until such time as she also should disappear beneath it.

Then she knew, by a stirring of voices, that he had climbed out again, into a boat. She sat wanting connection with him. Strenuously she claimed her connection with him, across the invisible space of the water. But round her heart was an isolation unbearable, through which nothing would penetrate.

'Take the launch in. It's no use keeping her there. Get lines for the dragging,' came the decisive, instrumental voice, that was full of the sound of the world.

The launch began gradually to beat the waters.

'Gerald! Gerald!' came the wild crying voice of Winifred. He did not answer. Slowly the launch drifted round in a pathetic, clumsy circle, and slunk away to the land, retreating into the dimness. The wash of her paddles grew duller. Gudrun rocked in her light boat, and dipped the paddle automatically to steady herself.

'Gudrun?' called Ursula's voice.

'Ursula!'

The boats of the two sisters pulled together.

'Where is Gerald?' said Gudrun.

'He's dived again,' said Ursula plaintively. 'And I know he ought not, with his hurt hand and everything.'

'I'll take him in home this time,' said Birkin.

The boats swayed again from the wash of steamer. Gudrun and Ursula kept a look-out for Gerald.

'There he is!' cried Ursula, who had the sharpest eyes. He had not been long under. Birkin pulled towards him, Gudrun following. He swam slowly, and caught hold of the boat with his wounded hand. It slipped, and he sank back.

'Why don't you help him?' cried Ursula sharply.

He came again, and Birkin leaned to help him into the boat. Gudrun again watched Gerald climb out of the water, but this time slowly, heavily, with the blind clambering motions of an amphibious beast, clumsy. Again the moon shone with faint luminosity on his white wet figure, on the stooping back and the rounded loins. But it looked defeated now, his body, it clambered and fell with slow clumsiness. He was breathing hoarsely too, like an animal that is suffering. He sat slack and motionless in the boat, his head blunt and blind like a seal's, his whole appearance inhuman, unknowing. Gudrun shuddered as she mechanically followed his boat. Birkin rowed without speaking to the landing-stage.

'Where are you going?' Gerald asked suddenly, as if just waking up.

'Home,' said Birkin.

'Oh no!' said Gerald imperiously. 'We can't go home while they're in the water. Turn back again, I'm going to find them.' The women were frightened, his voice was so imperative and dangerous, almost mad, not to be opposed.

'No,' said Birkin. 'You can't.' There was a strange fluid compulsion in his voice. Gerald was silent in a battle of wills. It was as if he would kill the other man. But Birkin rowed evenly and unswerving, with an inhuman inevitability.

'Why should you interfere?' said Gerald, in hate.

Birkin did not answer. He rowed towards the land. And Gerald sat mute, like a dumb beast, panting, his teeth chattering, his arms inert, his head like a seal's head.

They came to the landing-stage. Wet and naked looking, Gerald climbed up the few steps. There stood his father, in the night.

'Father!' he said.

'Yes, my boy? Go home and get those things off.'

'We shan't save them, father,' said Gerald.

'There's hope yet, my boy.'

'I'm afraid not. There's no knowing where they are. You can't find them. And there's a current, as cold as hell.'

'We'll let the water out,' said the father. 'Go home you and look to yourself. See that he's looked after, Rupert,' he added in a neutral voice.

'Well, father, I'm sorry. I'm sorry. I'm afraid it's my fault. But it can't be helped; I've done what I could for the moment. I could go on diving, of course – not much, though – and not much use—'

He moved away barefoot, on the planks of the platform. Then he trod on something sharp.

'Of course, you've got no shoes on,' said Birkin.

'His shoes are here!' cried Gudrun from below. She was making fast her boat.

Gerald waited for them to be brought to him. Gudrun came with them. He pulled them on his feet.

'If you once die,' he said, 'then when it's over, it's finished. Why come to life again? There's room under that water there for thousands.'

'Two is enough,' she said, murmuring.

He dragged on his second shoe. He was shivering violently, and his jaw shook as he spoke.

'That's true,' he said, 'maybe. But it's curious how much room there seems, a whole universe under there; and as cold as hell, you're as helpless as if your head was cut off.' He could scarcely speak, he shook so violently. 'There's one thing about our family, you know,' he continued. 'Once anything goes wrong, it can never be put right again – not with us. I've noticed it all my life – you can't put a thing right, once it has gone wrong.'

They were walking across the high-road to the house.

'And do you know, when you are down there, it is so cold, actually, and so endless, so different really from what it is on top, so endless – you wonder how it is so many are alive, why we're up here. Are you going? I shall see you again, shan't I? Good-night, and thank you. Thank you very much.'

The two girls waited a while, to see if there were any hope. The moon shone clearly overhead, with almost impertinent brightness, the small dark boats clustered on the water, there were voices and subdued shouts. But it was all to no purpose. Gudrun went home when Birkin returned.

He was commissioned to open the sluice that let out the water from the lake, which was pierced at one end, near the high-road, thus serving as a reservoir to supply with water the distant mines, in case of necessity. 'Come with me,' he said to Ursula, 'and then I will walk home with you, when I've done this.'

He called at the water-keeper's cottage and took the key of the sluice. They went through a little gate from the high-road, to the head of the water, where was a great stone basin which received the overflow, and a flight of stone steps descended into the depths of the water itself. At the head of the steps was the lock of the sluice-gate.

The night was silver-grey and perfect, save for the scattered restless sound of voices. The grey sheen of the moonlight caught the stretch of water, dark boats plashed and moved. But Ursula's mind ceased to be receptive, everything was unimportant and unreal.

Birkin fixed the iron handle of the sluice, and turned it with a wrench. The cogs began slowly to rise. He turned and turned like a slave, his white figure became distinct. Ursula looked away. She could not bear to see him winding heavily and laboriously, bending and rising mechanically like a slave, turning the handle.

Then, a real shock to her, there came a loud splashing of water from out of the dark, tree-filled hollow beyond the road, a splashing that deepened rapidly to a harsh roar, and then became a heavy, booming noise of a great body of water falling solidly all the time. It occupied the whole of the night, this great steady booming of water, everything was drowned within it, drowned and lost. Ursula seemed to have to struggle for her life. She put her hands over her ears, and looked at the high bland moon.

'Can't we go now?' she cried to Birkin, who was watching the water on the steps, to see if it would get any lower. It seemed to fascinate him. He looked at her and nodded.

The little dark boats had moved nearer, people were crowding curiously along the hedge by the high-road, to see what was to be seen. Birkin and Ursula went to the cottage with the key, then turned their backs on the lake. She was in great haste. She could not bear the terrible crushing boom of the escaping water.

'Do you think they are dead?' she cried in a high voice, to make herself heard.

'Yes,' he replied.

'Isn't it horrible!'

He paid no heed. They walked up the hill, farther and farther away from the noise.

'Do you mind very much?' she asked him.

'I don't mind about the dead,' he said, 'once they are dead. The worst of it is, they cling on to the living, and won't let go!'

She pondered for a time.

'Yes,' she said. 'The *fact* of death doesn't really seem to matter much, does it?'

'No,' he said. 'What does it matter if Diana Crich is alive or dead?'

'Doesn't it?' she said, shocked.

'No, why should it? Better she were dead – she'll be much more real. She'll be positive in death. In life she was a fretting, negated thing.'

'You are rather horrible,' murmured Ursula.

'No! I'd rather Diana Crich were dead. Her living somehow was all wrong. As for the young man, poor devil – he'll find his way out quickly instead of slowly. Death is all right – nothing better.'

'Yet you don't want to die,' she challenged him.

He was silent for a time. Then he said, in a voice that was frightening to her in its change:

'I should like to be through with it – I should like to be through with the death process.'

'And aren't you?' asked Ursula nervously.

They walked on for some way in silence, under the trees. Then he said slowly, as if afraid:

'There is life which belongs to death, and there is life which isn't death. One is tired of the life that belongs to death – our kind of life. But whether it is finished, God knows. I want love that is like sleep, like being born again, vulnerable as a baby that just comes into the world.'

Ursula listened, half attentive, half avoiding what he said. She seemed to catch the drift of his statement, and then she drew away. She wanted to hear, but she did not want to be implicated. She was reluctant to yield there, where he wanted her, to yield as it were her very identity.

'Why should love be like sleep?' she asked sadly.

'I don't know. So that it is like death – I *do* want to die from this life – and yet it is more than life itself. One is delivered over like a naked infant from the womb, all the old defences, and the old body gone, and new air around one, that has never been breathed before.'

She listened, making out what he said. She knew, as well as he knew, that words themselves do not convey meaning, that they are but a gesture we make, a dumb show like any other. And she seemed to feel his gesture through her blood, and she drew back, even though her desire sent her forward.

'But,' she said gravely, 'didn't you say you wanted something that was *not* love – something beyond love?'

He turned in confusion. There was always confusion in speech. Yet it must be spoken. Whichever way one moved, if one were to move forwards, one must break a way through. And to know, to give utterance was to break a way through the walls of the prison as the infant in labour strives through the walls of the womb. There is no new movement now, without the breaking through of the old body, deliberately, in knowledge, in the struggle to get out.

'I don't want love,' he said. 'I don't want to know you. I want to be gone out of myself, and you to be lost to yourself, so we are found different. One shouldn't talk when one is tired and wretched. One Hamletises, and it seems a lie. Only believe me when I show you a bit of healthy pride and insouciance. I hate myself serious.'

'Why shouldn't you be serious?' she said.

He thought for a minute, then he said sulkily:

'I don't know.' Then they walked on in silence, at outs. He was vague and lost.

'Isn't it strange,' she said, suddenly putting her hand on his arm, with a loving impulse, 'how we always talk like this! I suppose we do love each other, in some way.'

'Oh yes,' he said; 'too much.'

She laughed almost gaily.

'You'd have to have it your own way, wouldn't you?' she teased. 'You could never take it on trust.'

He changed, laughed softly, and turned and took her in his arms, in the middle of the road.

'Yes,' he said softly.

And he kissed her face and brow, slowly, gently, with a sort of delicate happiness which surprised her extremely, and to which she could not respond. They were soft, blind kisses, perfect in their stillness. Yet she held back from them. It was like strange moths, very soft and silent, settling on her from the darkness of her soul. She was uneasy. She drew away.

'Isn't somebody coming?' she said.

So they looked down the dark road, then set off again walking towards Beldover. Then suddenly, to show him she was no shallow prude, she stopped and held him tight, hard against her, and covered his face with hard, fierce kisses of passion. In spite of his otherness, the old blood beat up in him.

'Not this, not this,' he whimpered to himself, as the first perfect mood of softness and sleep-loveliness ebbed back away from the rushing of passion that came up to his limbs and over his face as she drew him. And soon he was a perfect hard flame of passionate desire for her. Yet in the small core of the flame was an unyielding anguish of another thing. But this also was lost; he only wanted her, with an extreme desire that seemed inevitable as death, beyond question.

Then, satisfied and shattered, fulfilled and destroyed, he went home away from her, drifting vaguely through the darkness, lapsed into the old fire of burning passion. Far away, far away, there seemed to be a small lament in the darkness. But what did it matter? What did it matter, what did anything matter save this ultimate and triumphant experience of physical passion, that had blazed up anew like a new spell of life. 'I was becoming quite dead-alive, nothing but a wordbag,' he said in triumph, scorning his other self. Yet somewhere far off and small, the other hovered.

The men were still dragging the lake when he got back. He stood on the bank and heard Gerald's voice. The water was still booming in the night, the moon was fair, the hills beyond were elusive. The lake was sinking. There came the raw smell of the banks, in the night air.

Up at Shortlands there were lights in the windows, as if nobody had gone to bed. On the landing-stage was the old doctor, the father of the young man who was lost. He stood quite silent, waiting. Birkin also stood and watched, Gerald came up in a boat.

'You still here, Rupert?' he said. 'We can't get them. The bottom slopes, you know, very steep. The water lies between two very sharp slopes, with little branch valleys, and God knows where the drift will take you. It isn't as if it was a level bottom. You never know where you are, with the dragging.'

'Is there any need for you to be working?' said Birkin. 'Wouldn't it be much better if you went to bed?'

'To bed! Good God, do you think I should sleep? We'll find 'em, before I go away from here.'

'But the men would find them just the same without you – why should you insist?'

Gerald looked up at him. Then he put his hand affectionately on Birkin's shoulder, saying:

'Don't you bother about me, Rupert. If there's anybody's health to think about, it's yours, not mine. How do you feel yourself?'

'Very well. But you, you spoil your own chance of life – you waste your best self.'

Gerald was silent for a moment. Then he said:

'Waste it? What else is there to do with it?'

'But leave this, won't you? You force yourself into horrors, and put a mill-stone of beastly memories round your neck. Come away now.'

'A mill-stone of beastly memories!' Gerald repeated. Then he put his hand again affectionately on Birkin's shoulder. 'God, you've got such a telling way of putting things, Rupert, you have.'

Birkin's heart sank. He was irritated and weary of having a telling way of putting things.

'Won't you leave it? Come over to my place' – he urged as one urges a drunken man.

'No,' said Gerald coaxingly, his arm across the other man's shoulder. 'Thanks very much, Rupert – I shall be glad to come to-morrow, if that'll do. You understand, don't you? I want to see this job through. But I'll come to-morrow, right enough. Oh, I'd rather come and have a chat with you than – than do anything else, I verily believe. Yes, I would. You mean a lot to me, Rupert, more than you know.'

'What do I mean, more than I know?' asked Birkin irritably. He was acutely aware of Gerald's hand on his shoulder. And he did not want this altercation. He wanted the other man to come out of the ugly misery.

'I'll tell you another time,' said Gerald coaxingly.

'Come along with me now – I want you to come,' said Birkin.

There was a pause, intense and real. Birkin wondered why his own heart beat so heavily. Then Gerald's fingers gripped hard and communicative into Birkin's shoulder, as he said:

'No, I'll see this job through, Rupert. Thank you – I know what you mean. We're all right, you know, you and me.'

'I may be all right, but I'm sure you're not, mucking about here,' said Birkin. And he went away.

The bodies of the dead were not recovered till towards dawn. Diana had her arms tight round the neck of the young man, choking him.

'She killed him,' said Gerald.

The moon sloped down the sky and sank at last. The lake was sunk to quarter size, it had horrible raw banks of clay, that smelled of raw rottenish water. Dawn roused faintly behind the eastern hill. The water still boomed through the sluice.

As the birds were whistling for the first morning, and the hills at the back of the desolate lake stood radiant with the new mists, there was a straggling procession up to Shortlands, men bearing the bodies on a stretcher, Gerald going beside them, the two grey-bearded fathers following in silence. Indoors the family was all sitting up, waiting. Somebody must go to tell the mother, in her room. The doctor in secret struggled to bring back his son, till he himself was exhausted.

Over all the outlying district was a hush of dreadful excitement on that Sunday morning. The colliery people felt as if this catastrophe had happened directly to themselves, indeed they were more shocked and frightened than if their own men had been killed. Such a tragedy in Shortlands, the high home of the district! One of the young mistresses, persisting in dancing on the cabin roof of the launch, wilful young madam, drowned in the midst of the festival, with the young doctor! Everywhere on the Sunday morning, the colliers wandered about, discussing the calamity. At all the Sunday dinners of the people, there seemed a strange presence. It was as if the angel of death were very near, there was a sense of the supernatural in the air. The men had excited, startled faces, the women looked solemn, some of them had been crying. The children enjoyed the excitement at first. There was an intensity in the air, almost magical. Did all enjoy it? Did all enjoy the thrill?

Gudrun had wild ideas of rushing to comfort Gerald. She was thinking all the time of the perfect comforting, reassuring thing to say to him. She was shocked and frightened, but she put that away, thinking of how she should deport herself with Gerald: act her part. That was the real thrill: how she should act her part.

Ursula was deeply and passionately in love with Birkin, and she was capable of nothing. She was perfectly callous about all the talk of the accident, but her estranged air looked like trouble. She merely sat by herself, whenever she could, and longed to see him again. She wanted him to come to the house – she would not have it otherwise, he must come at once. She was waiting for him. She stayed indoors all day, waiting for him to knock at the door. Every minute, she glanced automatically at the window. He would be there.

Chapter Fifteen

Sunday Evening

As the day wore on, the life-blood seemed to ebb away from Ursula, and within the emptiness a heavy despair gathered. Her passion seemed to bleed to death, and there was nothing. She sat suspended in a state of complete nullity, harder to bear than death.

'Unless something happens,' she said to herself, in the perfect lucidity of final suffering, 'I shall die. I am at the end of my line of life.'

She sat crushed and obliterated in a darkness that was the border of death. She realised how all her life she had been drawing nearer and nearer to this brink, where there was no beyond, from which one had to leap like Sappho into the unknown. The knowledge of the imminence of death was like a drug. Darkly, without thinking at all, she knew that she was near to death. She had travelled all her life along the line of fulfilment, and it was nearly concluded. She knew all she had to know, she had experienced all she had to experience, she was fulfilled in a kind of bitter ripeness, there remained only to fall from the tree into death. And one must fulfil one's development to the end, must carry the adventure to its conclusion. And the next step was over the border into death. So it was then! There was a certain peace in the knowledge.

After all, when one was fulfilled, one was happiest in falling into death, as a bitter fruit plunges in its ripeness downwards. Death is a great consummation, a consummating experience. It is a development from life. That we know, while we are yet living. What then need we think for further? One can never see beyond the consummation. It is enough that death is a great and conclusive experience. Why should we ask what comes after the experience, when the experience is still unknown to us? Let us die, since the great experience is the one that follows now upon all the rest, death, which is the next great crisis in front of which we have arrived. If we wait, if we baulk the issue, we do but hang about the gates in undignified uneasiness. There it is, in front of us, as in front of Sappho, the illimitable space. Thereinto goes the journey. Have we not the courage to go on with our journey, must we cry 'I daren't'? On ahead we will go, into death, and whatever death may mean. If a man can see the next step to be taken, why should he fear the next but one? Why ask about the next but one? Of the next step we are certain. It is the step into death.

'I shall die – I shall quickly die,' said Ursula to herself, clear as if in a trance, clear, calm, and certain beyond human certainty. But somewhere behind, in the twilight, there was a bitter weeping and a hopelessness. That must not be attended to. One must go where the unfaltering spirit goes, there must be no baulking the issue, because of fear. No baulking the issue, no listening to the lesser voices. If the deepest desire be now, to go on into the unknown of death, shall one forfeit the deepest truth for one more shallow?

'Then let it end,' she said to herself. It was a decision. It was not a question of taking one's life – she would *never* kill herself, that was repulsive and violent. It was a question of *knowing* the next step. And the next step led into the space of death. Did it? – or was there—?

Her thoughts drifted into unconsciousness, she sat as if asleep beside the fire. And then the thought came back. The space of death! Could she give herself to it? Ah, yes – it was a sleep. She had had enough. So long she had held out and resisted. Now was the time to relinquish, not to resist any more.

In a kind of spiritual trance, she yielded, she gave way, and all was dark. She could feel, within the darkness, the terrible assertion of her body, the unutterable anguish of dissolution, the only anguish that is too much, the far-off awful nausea of dissolution set in within the body.

'Does the body correspond so immediately with the spirit?' she asked herself. And she knew, with the clarity of ultimate knowledge, that the body is only one of the manifestations of the spirit, the transmutation of the integral spirit is the transmutation of the physical body as well. 'Unless I set my will, unless I absolve myself from the rhythm of life, fix myself and remain static, cut off from living, absolved within my own will. But better die than live mechanically a life that is a repetition of repetitions. To die is to move on with the invisible. To die is also a joy, a joy of submitting to that which is greater than the known; namely, the pure unknown. That is a joy. But to live mechanised and cut off within the motion of the will, to live as an entity absolved from the unknown, that is shameful and ignominious. There is no ignominy in death. There is complete ignominy in an unre-plenished, mechanised life. Life indeed may be ignominious, shameful to the soul. But death is never a shame. Death itself, like the illimitable space, is beyond our sullying.'

To-morrow was Monday. Monday, the beginning of another school-week! Another shameful, barren school-week, mere routine and mechanical activity. Was not the adventure of death infinitely preferable? Was not death infinitely more lovely and noble than such a life? A life of barren routine, without inner meaning, without any real significance. How sordid life was, how it was a terrible shame to the soul, to live now! How much cleaner and more dignified to be dead! One could not bear any more of this shame of sordid routine and mechanical nullity. One might come to fruit in death. She had had enough. For where was life to be found? No flowers grow upon busy machinery, there is no sky to a routine, there is no space to a rotary motion. And all life was a rotary motion, mechanised, cut off from reality. There was nothing to look for from life – it was the same in all countries and all peoples. The only window was death. One could look out on to the great dark sky of death with emotion, as one had looked out of the class-room window as a child, and seen perfect freedom in the outside. Now one was not a child, and one knew that the soul was a prisoner within this sordid vast edifice of life, and there was no escape, save in death.

But what a joy! What a gladness to think that whatever humanity did, it could not seize hold of the kingdom of death, to nullify that. The sea they turned into a murderous alley and a soiled road of commerce, disputed like the dirty land of a city every inch of it. The air they claimed too, shared it up, parcelled it out to certain owners, they trespassed in the air to fight for it. Everything was gone, walled in, with spikes on top of the walls, and one must ignominiously creep between the spiky walls through a labyrinth of life.

But the great dark, illimitable kingdom of death, there humanity was put to scorn. So much they could do upon earth, the multifarious little gods that they were. But the kingdom of death put them all to scorn, they dwindled into their true vulgar silliness in face of it.

How beautiful, how grand and perfect death was, how good to look forward to. There one would wash off all the lies and ignominy and dirt that had been put upon one here, a perfect bath of cleanness and glad refreshment, and go unknown, unquestioned, unabased. After all, one was rich, if only in the promise of perfect death. It was a gladness above all, that this remained to look forward to, the pure inhuman otherness of death.

Whatever life might be, it could not take away death, the inhuman transcendent death. Oh, let us ask no question of it, what it is or is not. To know is human, and in death we do not know, we are not human. And the joy of this compensates for all the bitterness of knowledge and the sordidness of our humanity. In death we shall not be human, and we shall not know. The promise of this is our heritage, we look forward like heirs to their majority.

Ursula sat quite still and quite forgotten, alone by the fire in the drawing-room. The children were playing in the kitchen, all the others were gone to church. And she was gone into the ultimate darkness of her own soul.

She was startled by hearing the bell ring, away in the kitchen, the children came scudding along the passage in delicious alarm.

'Ursula, there's somebody.'

'I know. Don't be silly,' she replied. She too was startled, almost frightened. She dared hardly go to the door.

Birkin stood on the threshold, his rain-coat turned up to his ears. He had come now, now she was gone far away. She was aware of the rainy night behind him.

'Oh, is it you?' she said.

'I am glad you are at home,' he said in a low voice, entering the house.

'They are all gone to church.'

He took off his coat and hung it up. The children were peeping at him round the corner.

'Go and get undressed now, Billy and Dora,' said Ursula. 'Mother will be back soon, and she'll be disappointed if you're not in bed.'

The children, in a sudden angelic mood, retired without a word. Birkin and Ursula went into the drawing-room. The fire burned low. He looked at her and wondered at the luminous delicacy of her beauty, and the wide shining of her eyes. He watched from a distance, with wonder in his heart, she seemed transfigured with light.

'What have you been doing all day?' he asked her.

'Only sitting about,' she said.

He looked at her. There was a change in her. But she was separate from him. She remained apart, in a kind of brightness. They both sat silent in the soft light of the lamp. He felt he ought to go away again, he ought not to have come. Still he did not gather enough resolution to move. But he was *de trop*, her mood was absent and separate.

Then there came the voices of the two children calling shyly outside the door, softly, with self-excited timidity:

'Ursula! Ursula!'

She rose and opened the door. On the threshold stood the two children in their long nightgowns, with wide-eyed, angelic faces. They were being very good for the moment, playing the rôle perfectly of two obedient children.

'Shall you take us to bed!' said Billy, in a loud whisper.

'Why, you *are* angels to-night,' she said softly. 'Won't you come and say good-night to Mr. Birkin?'

The children merged shyly into the room, on bare feet. Billy's face was wide and grinning, but there was a great solemnity of being good in his round blue eyes. Dora, peeping from the floss of her fair hair, hung back like some tiny Dryad, that has no soul.

'Will you say good-night to me?' asked Birkin, in a voice that was strangely soft and smooth. Dora drifted away at once, like a leaf lifted on a breath of wind. But Billy went softly forward, slow and willing, lifting his pinched-up mouth implicitly to be kissed. Ursula watched the full, gathered lips of the man gently touch those of the boy, so gently. Then Birkin lifted his fingers and touched the boy's round, confiding cheek, with a faint touch of love. Neither spoke. Billy seemed angelic like a cherub boy, or like an acolyte, Birkin was a tall, grave angel looking down to him.

'Are you going to be kissed?' Ursula broke in, speaking to the little girl. But Dora edged away like a tiny Dryad that will not be touched.

'Won't you say good-night to Mr. Birkin? Go, he's waiting for you,' said Ursula. But the girl-child only made a little motion away from him.

'Silly Dora, silly Dora!' said Ursula.

Birkin felt some mistrust and antagonism in the small child. He could not understand it.

'Come then,' said Ursula. 'Let us go before mother comes.'

'Who'll hear us say our prayers?' asked Billy anxiously.

'Whom you like.'

'Won't you?'

'Yes, I will.'

'Ursula?'

'Well, Billy?'

'Is it *whom* you like?'

'That's it.'

'Well, what is *whom?*'

'It's the accusative of who.'

There was a moment's contemplative silence, then the confiding:

'Is it?'

Birkin smiled to himself as he sat by the fire. When Ursula came down he sat motionless, with his arms on his knees. She saw him, how he was motionless and ageless, like some crouching idol, some image of a deathly religion. He looked round at her, and his face, very pale and unreal, seemed to gleam with a whiteness almost phosphorescent.

'Don't you feel well?' she asked, in indefinable repulsion.

'I hadn't thought about it.'

'But don't you know without thinking about it?'

He looked at her, his eyes dark and swift, and he saw her revulsion. He did not answer her question.

'Don't you know whether you are unwell or not, without thinking about it?' she persisted.

'Not always,' he said coldly.

'But don't you think that's very wicked?'

'Wicked?'

'Yes. I think it's *criminal* to have so little connection with your own body that you don't even know when you are ill.'

He looked at her darkly.

'Yes,' he said.

'Why don't you stay in bed when you are seedy? You look perfectly ghastly.'

'Offensively so?' he asked ironically.

'Yes, quite offensive. Quite repelling.'

'Ah! Well, that's unfortunate.'

'And it's raining, and it's a horrible night. Really, you shouldn't be forgiven for treating your body like it - you *ought* to suffer, a man who takes as little notice of his body as that.'

'—takes as little notice of his body as that,' he echoed mechanically.

This cut her short, and there was silence.

The others came in from church, and the two had the girls to face, then the mother and Gudrun, and then the father and the boy.

'Good-evening,' said Brangwen, faintly surprised. 'Came to see me, did you?'

'No,' said Birkin, 'not about anything in particular, that is. The day was dismal, and I thought you wouldn't mind if I called in.'

'It *has* been a depressing day,' said Mrs. Brangwen sympathetically. At that moment the voices of the children were heard calling from upstairs: 'Mother! Mother!' She lifted her face and answered mildly into the distance: 'I shall come up to you in a minute, Doysie.' Then to Birkin: 'There is nothing fresh at Shortlands, I suppose? Ah,' she sighed, 'no, poor things, I should think not.'

'You've been over there to-day, I suppose?' asked the father.

'Gerald came round to tea with me, and I walked back with him. The house is over-excited and unwholesome, I thought.'

'I should think they were people who hadn't much restraint,' said Gudrun.

'Or too much,' Birkin answered.

'Oh yes, I'm sure,' said Gudrun, almost vindictively, 'one or the other.'

'They all feel they ought to behave in some unnatural fashion,' said Birkin. 'When people are in grief, they would do better to cover their faces and keep in retirement, as in the old days.'

'Certainly!' cried Gudrun, flushed and inflammable. 'What can be worse than this public grief – what is more horrible, more false! If *grief* is not private, and hidden, what is?'

'Exactly,' he said. 'I felt ashamed when I was there and they were all going about in a lugubrious false way, feeling they must not be natural or ordinary.'

'Well—' said Mrs. Brangwen, offended at this criticism, 'it isn't so easy to bear a trouble like that.'

And she went upstairs to the children.

He remained only a few minutes longer, then took his leave. When he was gone Ursula felt such a poignant hatred of him, that all her brain seemed turned into a sharp crystal of fine hatred. Her whole nature seemed sharpened and intensified into a pure dart of hate. She could not imagine what it was. It merely took hold of her, the most poignant and ultimate hatred, pure and clear and beyond thought. She could not think of it at all, she was translated beyond herself. It was like a possession. She felt she was possessed. And for several days she went about possessed by this exquisite force of hatred against him. It surpassed anything she had ever known before, it seemed to throw her out of the world into some terrible region where nothing of her old life held good. She was quite lost and dazed, really dead to her own life.

It was so completely incomprehensible and irrational. She did not know *why* she hated him, her hate was quite abstract. She had only realised with a shock that stunned her, that she was overcome by this pure transportation. He was the enemy, fine as a diamond, and as hard and jewel-like, the quintessence of all that was inimical.

She thought of his face, white and purely wrought, and of his eyes that had such a dark, constant will of assertion, and she touched her own forehead, to feel if she were mad, she was so transfigured in white flame of essential hate.

It was not temporal, her hatred, she did not hate him for this or for that; she did not want to do anything to him, to have any connection with him. Her relation was ultimate and utterly beyond words, the hate was so pure and gem-like. It was as if he were a beam of essential enmity, a beam of light that did not only destroy her, but denied her altogether, revoked her whole world. She saw him as a clear stroke of uttermost contradiction, a strange gem-like being whose existence defined her own non-existence. When she heard he was ill again, her hatred only intensified itself a few degrees, if that were possible. It stunned her and annihilated her, but she could not escape it. She could not escape this transfiguration of hatred that had come upon her.

Chapter Sixteen

Man to Man

He lay sick and unmoved, in pure opposition to everything. He knew how near to breaking was the vessel that held his life. He knew also how strong and durable it was. And he did not care. Better a thousand times take one's chance with death, than accept a life one did not want. But best of all to persist and persist and persist for ever, till one were satisfied in life.

He knew that Ursula was referred back to him. He knew his life rested with her. But he would rather not live than accept the love she proffered. The old way of love seemed a dreadful bondage, a sort of conscription. What it was in him he did not know, but the thought of love, marriage, and children, and a life lived together, in the horrible privacy of domestic and connubial satisfaction, was repulsive. He wanted something clearer, more open, cooler, as it were. The hot narrow intimacy between man and wife was abhorrent. The way they shut their doors, these married people, and shut themselves into their own exclusive alliance with each other, even in love, disgusted him. It was a whole community of mistrustful couples insulated in private houses or private rooms, always in couples, and no further life, no further immediate, no disinterested relationship admitted: a kaleidoscope of couples, disjoined, separatist, meaningless entities of married couples. True, he hated promiscuity even worse than marriage, and a liaison was only another kind of coupling, reactionary from the legal marriage. Reaction was a greater bore than action.

On the whole, he hated sex, it was such a limitation. It was sex that turned a man into a broken half of a couple, the woman into the other broken half. And he wanted to be single in himself, the woman single in herself. He wanted sex to revert to the level of the other appetites, to be regarded as a functional process, not as a fulfilment. He believed in sex marriage. But beyond this, he wanted a further conjunction, where man had being and woman had being, two pure beings, each constituting the freedom of the other, balancing each other like two poles of one force, like two angels, or two demons.

He wanted so much to be free, not under the compulsion of any need for unification, or tortured by unsatisfied desire. Desire and aspiration should find their object without all this torture, as now, in a world of plenty of water, simple thirst is inconsiderable, satisfied almost unconsciously. And he wanted to be with Ursula as free as with himself, single and clear and cool, yet balanced, polarised with her. The merging, the clutching, the mingling of love was become madly abhorrent to him.

But it seemed to him, woman was always so horrible and clutching, she had such a lust for possession, a greed of self-importance in love. She wanted to have, to own, to control, to be dominant. Everything must be referred back to her, to Woman, the Great Mother of everything, out of whom proceeded everything and to whom everything must finally be rendered up.

It filled him with almost insane fury, this calm assumption of the Magna Mater, that all was hers, because she had borne it. Man was hers because she had borne him. A Mater Dolorosa, she had borne him, a Magna Mater, she now claimed him again, soul and body, sex, meaning, and all. He had a horror of the Magna Mater, she was detestable.

She was on a very high horse again was woman, the Great Mother. Did he not know it in Hermione. Hermione, the humble, the subservient, what was she all the while but the Mater Dolorosa, in her subservience, claiming with horrible, insidious arrogance and female tyranny, her own again, claiming back the man she had borne in suffering By her very suffering and humility she bound her son with chains, she held him her everlasting prisoner.

And Ursula, Ursula was the same – or the inverse. She too was the awful, arrogant queen of life, as if she were a queen bee on whom all the rest depended. He saw the yellow flare in her eyes, he knew the unthinkable overweening assumption of primacy in her. She was unconscious of it herself. She was only too ready to knock her head on the ground before a man. But this was only when she was so certain of her man, that she could worship him as a woman worships her own infant, with a worship of perfect possession.

It was intolerable, this possession at the hands of woman. Always a man must be considered as the broken-off fragment of a woman, and the sex was the still aching scar of the laceration. Man must be added on to a woman, before he had any real place or wholeness.

And why? Why should we consider ourselves, men and women, as broken fragments of one whole? It is not true. We are not broken fragments of one whole? Rather we are the singling away into purity and clear being, of things that were mixed. Rather the sex is that which remains in us of the mixed, the unresolved. And passion is the further separating of this mixture, that which is manly being taken into the being of the man, that which is womanly passing to the woman, till the two are clear and whole as angels, the admixture of sex in the highest sense surpassed, leaving two single beings constellated together like two stars.

In the old age, before sex was, we were mixed, each one a mixture. The process of singling into individuality resulted into the great polarisation of sex. The womanly drew to one side, the manly to the other. But the separation was imperfect even then. And so our world-cycle passes. There is now to come the new day, when we are beings each of us, fulfilled in difference. The man is pure man, the woman pure woman, they are perfectly polarised. But there is no longer any of the horrible merging, mingling self-abnegation of love. There is only the pure duality of polarisation, each one free from any contamination of the other. In each, the individual is primal, sex is subordinate, but perfectly polarised. Each has a single, separate being, with its own laws. The man has his pure freedom, the woman hers. Each acknowledges the perfection of the polarised sex-circuit. Each admits the different nature in the other.

So Birkin meditated whilst he was ill. He liked sometimes to be ill enough to take to his bed. For then he got better very quickly, and things came to him clear and sure.

Whilst he was laid up, Gerald came to see him. The two men had a deep, uneasy feeling for each other. Gerald's eyes were quick and restless, his whole manner tense and impatient, he seemed strung up to some activity. According to conventionality, he wore black clothes, he looked formal, handsome and *comme il faut*. His hair was fair almost to whiteness, sharp like splinters of light, his face was keen and ruddy, his body seemed full of northern energy.

Gerald really loved Birkin, though he never quite believed in him. Birkin was too unreal; – clever, whimsical, wonderful, but not practical enough. Gerald felt that his own understanding was much sounder and safer. Birkin was delightful, a wonderful spirit, but after all, not to be taken seriously, not quite to be counted as a man among men.

'Why are you laid up again?' he asked kindly, taking the sick man's hand. It was always Gerald who was protective, offering the warm shelter of his physical strength.

'For my sins, I suppose,' Birkin said, smiling a little ironically.

'For your sins? Yes, probably that is so. You should sin less, and keep better in health?'

'You'd better teach me.'

He looked at Gerald with ironic eyes.

'How are things with you?' Asked Birkin.

'With me?' Gerald looked at Birkin, saw he was serious, and a warm light came into his eyes.

'I don't know that they're any different. I don't see how they could be. There's nothing to change.'

'I suppose you are conducting the business as successfully as ever, and ignoring the demand of the soul.'

'That's it,' said Gerald. 'At least as far as the business is concerned. I couldn't say about the soul, I'm sure.'

'No.'

'Surely you don't expect me to?' laughed Gerald.

'No. How are the rest of your affairs progressing, apart from the business?'

'The rest of my affairs? What are those? I couldn't say; I don't know what you refer to?'

'Yes, you do,' said Birkin. 'Are you gloomy or cheerful? And what about Gudrun Brangwen?'

'What about her?' A confused look came over Gerald. 'Well,' he added,

'I don't know. I can only tell you she gave me a hit over the face last time I saw her.'

'A hit over the face! What for?'

'That I couldn't tell you, either.'

'Really! But when?'

'The night of the party – when Diana was drowned. She was driving the cattle up the hill, and I went after her – you remember.'

'Yes, I remember. But what made her do that? You didn't definitely ask her for it, I suppose?'

'I? No, not that I know of. I merely said to her that it was dangerous to drive those Highland bullocks – as it *is*. She turned in such a way, and said – "I suppose you think I'm afraid of you and your cattle, don't you?" So I asked her "why"? and for answer she flung me a back-hander across the face.'

Birkin laughed quickly, as if it pleased him. Gerald looked at him, wondering, and began to laugh as well, saying:

'I didn't laugh at the time, I assure you. I was never so taken aback in my life.'

'And weren't you furious?'

'Furious? I should think I was. I'd have murdered her for two pins.'

'H'm!' ejaculated Birkin. 'Poor Gudrun, wouldn't she suffer afterwards for having given herself away!' He was hugely delighted.

'Would she suffer?' asked Gerald, also amused now.

Both men smiled in malice and amusement.

'Badly, I should think; seeing how self-conscious she is.'

'She is self-conscious, is she? Then what made her do it? For I certainly think it was quite uncalled-for, and quite unjustified.'

'I suppose it was a sudden impulse.'

'Yes, but how do you account for her having such an impulse? I'd done her no harm.'

Birkin shook his head.

'The Amazon suddenly came up in her, I suppose,' he said.

'Well,' replied Gerald, 'I'd rather it had been the Orinoco.'

They both laughed at the poor joke. Gerald was thinking how Gudrun had said she would strike the last blow too. But some reserve made him keep this back from Birkin.

'And you resent it?' Birkin asked.

'I don't resent it. I don't care a tinker's curse about it.' He was silent a moment, then he added, laughing, 'No, I'll see it through, that's all. She seemed sorry afterwards.'

'Did she? You've not met since that night?'

Gerald's face clouded.

'No,' he said. 'We've been – you can imagine how it's been, since the accident.'

'Yes. Is it calming down?'

'I don't know. It's a shock, of course. But I don't believe mother minds. I really don't believe she takes any notice. And what's so funny, she used to be all for the children – nothing mattered, nothing whatever mattered but the children. And now, she doesn't take any more notice than if it was one of the servants.'

'No? Did it upset *you* very much?'

'It's a shock. But I don't feel it very much, really. I don't feel any different. We've all got to die, and it doesn't seem to make any great difference, anyhow, whether you die or not. I can't feel any *grief*, you know. It leaves me cold. I can't quite account for it.'

'You don't care if you die or not?' asked Birkin.

Gerald looked at him with eyes blue as the blue-fibred steel of a weapon. He felt awkward, but indifferent. As a matter of fact, he did care terribly, with a great fear.

'Oh,' he said, 'I don't want to die, why should I? But I never trouble. The question doesn't seem to be on the carpet for me at all. It doesn't interest me, you know.'

'*Timor mortis conturbat me*,' quoted Birkin, adding – 'No, death doesn't really seem the point any more. It curiously doesn't concern one. It's like an ordinary to-morrow.'

Gerald looked closely at his friend. The eyes of the two men met, and an unspoken understanding was exchanged.

Gerald narrowed his eyes, his face was cool and unscrupulous as he looked at Birkin, impersonally, with a vision that ended in a point in space, strangely keen-eyed and yet blind.

'If death isn't the point,' he said, in a strangely abstract, cold, fine voice – 'what is?' He sounded as if he had been found out.

'What is?' re-echoed Birkin. And there was a mocking silence.

'There's a long way to go, after the point of intrinsic death, before we disappear,' said Birkin.

'There is,' said Gerald. 'But what sort of way?' He seemed to press the other man for knowledge which he himself knew far better than Birkin did.

'Right down the slopes of degeneration – mystic, universal degeneration. There are many stages of pure degradation to go through: age-long. We live on long after our death, and progressively, in progressive devolution.'

Gerald listened with a faint, fine smile on his face, all the time, as if, somewhere, he knew so much better than Birkin, all about this: as if his own knowledge were direct and personal, whereas Birkin's was a matter of observation and inference, not quite hitting the nail on the head: – though aiming near enough at it. But he was not going to give himself away. If Birkin could get at the secrets, let him. Gerald would never help him. Gerald would be a dark horse to the end.

'Of course,' he said, with a startling change of conversation, 'it is father who really feels it. It will finish him. For him the world collapses. All his care now is for Winnie – he must save Winnie. He says she ought to be sent away to school, but she won't hear of it, and he'll never do it. Of course she *is* in rather a queer way. We're all of us curiously bad at living. We can do things – but we can't get on with life at all. It's curious – a family failing.'

'She oughtn't to be sent away to school,' said Birkin, who was considering a new proposition.

'She oughtn't? Why?'

'She's a queer child – a special child, more special even than you. And in my opinion special children should never be sent away to school. Only moderately ordinary children should be sent to school – so it seems to me.'

'I'm inclined to think just the opposite. I think it would probably make her more normal if she went away and mixed with other children.'

'She wouldn't mix, you see. *You* never really mixed, did you? And she wouldn't be willing even to pretend to. She's proud, and solitary, and naturally apart. If she has a single nature, why do you want to make her gregarious?'

'No, I don't want to make her anything. But I think school would be good for her.'

'Was it good for you?'

Gerald's eyes narrowed uglily. School had been torture to him. Yet he had not questioned whether one should go through this torture. He seemed to believe in education through subjection and torment.

'I hated it at the time, but I can see it was necessary,' he said. 'It brought me into line a bit – and you can't live unless you do come into line somewhere.'

'Well,' said Birkin, 'I begin to think that you can't live unless you keep entirely out of the line. It's no good trying to toe the line, when your one impulse is to smash up the line. Winnie is a special nature, and for special natures you must give a special world.'

'Yes, but where's your special world?' said Gerald.

'Make it. Instead of chopping yourself down to fit the world, chop the world down to fit yourself. As a matter of fact, two exceptional people make another world. You and I, we make another, separate world. You don't *want* a world same as your brothers-in-law. It's just the special quality you value. Do you *want* to be normal or ordinary? It's a lie. You want to be free and extraordinary, in an extraordinary world of liberty.'

Gerald looked at Birkin with subtle eyes of knowledge. But he would never openly admit what he felt. He knew more than Birkin, in one direction – much more. And this gave him his gentle love for the other man, as if Birkin were in some way young, innocent, child-like; so amazingly clever, but incurably innocent.

'Yet you are so banal as to consider me chiefly a freak,' said Birkin pointedly.

'A freak!' exclaimed Gerald, startled. And his face opened suddenly, as if lighted with simplicity, as when a flower opens out of the cunning bud. 'No – I never consider you a freak.' And he watched the other man with strange eyes, that Birkin could not understand. 'I feel,' Gerald continued, 'that there is always an element of uncertainty about you – perhaps you are uncertain about yourself. But I'm never sure of you. You can go away and change as easily as if you had no soul.'

He looked at Birkin with penetrating eyes. Birkin was amazed. He thought he had all the soul in the world. He stared in amazement. And Gerald, watching, saw the amazing attractive goodliness of his eyes, a young, spontaneous goodness that attracted the other man infinitely, yet filled him with bitter chagrin, because he mistrusted it so much. He knew Birkin could do without him – could forget, and not suffer. This was always present in Gerald's consciousness, filling him with bitter unbelief: this consciousness of the young, animal-like spontaneity of detachment. It seemed almost like hypocrisy and lying, sometimes, oh, often, on Birkin's part, to talk so deeply and importantly.

Quite other things were going through Birkin's mind. Suddenly he saw himself confronted with another problem – the problem of love and eternal conjunction between two men. Of course this was necessary – it had been a necessity inside himself all his life – to love a man purely and fully. Of course he had been loving Gerald all along, and all along denying it.

He lay in the bed and wondered, whilst his friend sat beside him, lost in brooding. Each man was gone in his own thoughts.

'You know how the old German knights used to swear a *Blutbruderschaft*,' he said to Gerald, with quite a new happy activity in his eyes.

'Make a little wound in their arms, and rub each other's blood into the cut?' said Gerald.

'Yes – and swear to be true to each other, of one blood, all their lives. That is what we ought to do. No wounds, that is obsolete. But we ought to swear to love each other, you and I, implicitly, and perfectly, finally, without any possibility of going back on it.'

He looked at Gerald with clear, happy eyes of discovery. Gerald looked down at him, attracted, so deeply bondaged in fascinated attraction, that he was mistrustful, resenting the bondage, hating the attraction.

'We will swear to each other, one day, shall we?' pleaded Birkin. 'We will swear to stand by each other – be true to each other – ultimately – infallibly – given to each other, organically – without possibility of taking back.'

Birkin sought hard to express himself. But Gerald hardly listened. His face shone with a certain luminous pleasure. He was pleased. But he kept his reserve. He held himself back.

'Shall we swear to each other, one day?' said Birkin, putting out his hand towards Gerald.

Gerald just touched the extended fine, living hand, as if withheld and afraid.

'We'll leave it till I understand it better,' he said, in a voice of excuse.

Birkin watched him. A little sharp disappointment, perhaps a touch of contempt came into his heart.

'Yes,' he said. 'You must tell me what you think, later. You know what I mean? Not sloppy emotionalism. An impersonal union that leaves one free.'

They lapsed both into silence. Birkin was looking at Gerald all the time. He seemed now to see, not the physical, animal man, which he usually saw in Gerald, and which usually he liked so much, but the man himself, complete, and as if fated, doomed, limited. This strange sense of fatality in Gerald, as if he were limited to one form of existence, one knowledge, one activity, a sort of fatal halfness, which to himself seemed wholeness, always overcame Birkin after their moments of passionate approach, and filled him with a sort of contempt, or boredom. It was the insistence on the limitation which so bored Birkin in Gerald. Gerald could never fly away from himself, in real indifferent gaiety. He had a clog, a sort of monomania.

There was silence for a time. Then Birkin said, in a lighter tone, letting the stress of the contact pass:

'Can't you get a good governess for Winifred? – somebody exceptional?'

'Hermione Roddice suggested we should ask Gudrun to teach her to draw and to model in clay.You know Winnie is astonishingly clever with that plasticine stuff. Hermione declares she is an artist.' Gerald spoke in the usual animated, chatty manner, as if nothing unusual had passed. But Birkin's manner was full of reminder.

'Really! I didn't know that. Oh well, then, if Gudrun *would* teach her, it would be perfect – couldn't be anything better – if Winifred is an artist. Because Gudrun somewhere is one. And every true artist is the salvation of every other.'

'I thought they got on so badly, as a rule.'

'Perhaps. But only artists produce for each other the world that is fit to live in. If you can arrange *that* for Winifred, it is perfect.'

'But you think she wouldn't come?'

'I don't know. Gudrun is rather self-opinionated. She won't go cheap anywhere. Or if she does, she'll pretty soon take herself back. So whether she would condescend to do private teaching, particularly here, in Beldover, I don't know. But it would be just the thing. Winifred has got a special nature. And if you can put into her way the means of being self-sufficient, that is the best thing possible. She'll never get on with the ordinary life. You find it difficult enough yourself, and she is several skins thinner than you are. It is awful to think what her life will be like unless she does find a means of expression, some way of fulfilment. You can see what mere leaving it to fate brings. You can see how much marriage is to be trusted to – look at your own mother.'

'Do you think mother is abnormal?'

'No! I think she only wanted something more, or other than the common run of life. And not getting it, she has gone wrong perhaps.'

'After producing a brood of wrong children,' said Gerald gloomily.

'No more wrong than any of the rest of us,' Birkin replied. 'The most normal people have the worst subterranean selves, take them one by one.'

'Sometimes I think it is a curse to be alive,' said Gerald, with sudden impotent anger.

'Well,' said Birkin, 'why not! Let it be a curse sometimes to be alive – at other times it is anything but a curse. You've got plenty of zest in it really.'

'Less than you'd think,' said Gerald, revealing a strange poverty in his look at the other man.

There was silence, each thinking his own thoughts.

'I don't see what she has to distinguish between teaching at the Grammar School and coming to teach Win,' said Gerald.

'The difference between a public servant and a private one. The only nobleman to-day, king and only aristocrat, is the public, the public. You are quite willing to serve the public – but to be a private tutor—'

'I don't want to serve either—'

'No! And Gudrun will probably feel the same.'

Gerald thought for a few minutes. Then he said:

'At all events, father won't make her feel like a private servant. He will be fussy and grateful enough.'

'So he ought. And so ought all of you. Do you think you can hire a woman like Gudrun Brangwen with money? She is your equal like anything – probably your superior.'

'Is she?' said Gerald.

'Yes, and if you haven't the guts to know it, I hope she'll leave you to your own devices.'

'Nevertheless,' said Gerald, 'if she is my equal, I wish she weren't a teacher, because I don't think teachers as a rule are my equal.'

'Nor do I, damn them. But am I a teacher because I teach, or a parson because I preach?'

Gerald laughed. He was always uneasy on this score. He did not *want* to claim social superiority, yet he *would* not claim intrinsic personal superiority, because he would never base his standard of values on pure being. So he wobbled upon a tacit assumption of social standing. Now Birkin wanted him to accept the fact of intrinsic difference between human beings, which he did not intend to accept. It was against his social honour, his principle. He rose to go.

'I've been neglecting my business all this while,' he said, smiling.

'I ought to have reminded you before,' Birkin replied, laughing and mocking.

'I knew you'd say something like that,' laughed Gerald, rather uneasily. 'Did you?'

'Yes, Rupert. It wouldn't do for us all to be like you are – we should soon be in the cart. When I am above the world, I shall ignore all businesses.'

'Of course, we're not in the cart now,' said Birkin, satirically.

'Not as much as you make out. At any rate, we have enough to eat and drink—'

'And be satisfied,' added Birkin.

Gerald came near the bed and stood looking down at Birkin whose throat was exposed, whose tossed hair fell attractively on the warm brow, above the eyes that were so unchallenged and still in the satirical face. Gerald, full-limbed and turgid with energy, stood unwilling to go, he was held by the presence of the other man. He had not the power to go away.

'So,' said Birkin. 'Good-bye.' And he reached out his hand from under the bed-clothes, smiling with a glimmering look.

'Good-bye,' said Gerald, taking the warm hand of his friend in a firm grasp. 'I shall come again. I miss you down at the mill.'

'I'll be there in a few days,' said Birkin.

The eyes of the two men met again. Gerald's, that were keen as a hawk's, were suffused now with warm light and with unadmitted love, Birkin looked back as out of a darkness, unsounded and unknown, yet with a kind of warmth, that seemed to flow over Gerald's brain like a fertile sleep.

'Good-bye then. There's nothing I can do for you?'

'Nothing, thanks.'

Birkin watched the black-clothed form of the other man move out of the door, the bright head was gone, he turned over to sleep.

Chapter Seventeen

The Industrial Magnate

In Beldover, there was both for Ursula and for Gudrun an interval. It seemed to Ursula as if Birkin had gone out of her for the time, he had lost his significance, he scarcely mattered in her world. She had her own friends, her own activities, her own life. She turned back to the old ways with zest, away from him.

And Gudrun, after feeling every moment in all her veins conscious of Gerald Crich, connected even physically with him, was now almost indifferent to the thought of him. She was nursing new schemes for going away and trying a new form of life. All the time, there was something in her urging her to avoid the final establishing of a relationship with Gerald. She felt it would be wiser and better to have no more than a casual acquaintance with him.

She had a scheme for going to St. Petersburg, where she had a friend who was a sculptor like herself, and who lived with a wealthy Russian whose hobby was jewel-making. The emotional, rather rootless life of the Russians appealed to her. She did not want to go to Paris. Paris was dry, and essentially boring. She would like to go to Rome, Munich, Vienna, or to St. Petersburg or Moscow. She had a friend in St. Petersburg and a friend in Munich. To each of these she wrote, asking about rooms.

She had a certain amount of money. She had come home partly to save, and now she had sold several pieces of work, she had been praised in various shows. She knew she could become quite the 'go' if she went to London. But she knew London, she wanted something else. She had seventy pounds, of which nobody knew anything. She would move soon, as soon as she heard from her friends. Her nature, in spite of her apparent placidity and calm, was profoundly restless.

The sisters happened to call in a cottage in Willey Green to buy honey. Mrs. Kirk, a stout, pale, sharp-nosed woman, sly, honied, with something shrewish and cat-like beneath, asked the girls into her too cosy, too tidy kitchen. There was a cat-like comfort and cleanliness everywhere.

'Yes, Miss Brangwen,' she said, in her slightly whining, insinuating voice, 'and how do you like being back in the old place, then?'

Gudrun, whom she addressed, hated her at once.

'I don't care for it,' she replied abruptly.

'You don't? Ay, well, I suppose you found a difference from London. You like life, and big, grand places. Some of us has to be content with Willey Green and Beldover. And what do you think of our Grammar School, as there's so much talk about?'

'What do I think of it?' Gudrun looked round at her slowly. 'Do you mean, do I think it's a good school?'

'Yes. What is your opinion of it?'

'I *do* think it's a good school.'

Gudrun was very cold and repelling. She knew the common people hated the school.

'Ay, you do, then! I've heard so much, one way and the other. It's nice to know what those that's in it feel. But opinions vary, don't they? Mr. Crich up at Highclose is all for it. Ay, poor man, I'm afraid he's not long for this world. He's very poorly.'

'Is he worse?' asked Ursula.

'Eh, yes – since they lost Miss Diana. He's gone off to a shadow. Poor man, he's had a world of trouble.'

'Has he?' asked Gudrun, faintly ironic.

'He has, a world of trouble. And as nice and kind a gentleman as ever you could wish to meet. His children don't take after him.'

'I suppose they take after their mother?' said Ursula.

'In many ways.' Mrs. Kirk lowered her voice a little. 'She was a proud haughty lady when she came into these parts – my word, she was that! She mustn't be looked at, and it was worth your life to speak to her.' The woman made a dry, sly face.

'Did you know her when she was first married?'

'Yes, I knew her. I nursed three of her children. And proper little terrors they were, little fiends – that Gerald was a demon if ever there was one, a proper demon, ay, at six months old.' A curious malicious, sly tone came into the woman's voice.

'Really,' said Gudrun.

'That wilful, masterful – he'd mastered one nurse at six months. Kick, and scream, and struggle like a demon. Many's the time I've pinched his little bottom for him, when he was a child in arms. Ay, and he'd have been better if he'd had it pinched oftener. But she wouldn't have them corrected – no-o, wouldn't hear of it. I can remember the rows she had with Mr. Crich, my word. When he'd got worked up, properly worked up till he could stand no more, he'd lock the study door and whip them. But she paced up and down all the while like a tiger outside, like a tiger, with very murder in her face. She had a face that could *look* death. And when the door was opened, she'd go in with her hands lifted – 'What have you been doing to *my* children, you coward.' She was like one out of her mind. I believe he was frightened of her; he had to be driven mad before he'd lift a finger. Didn't the servants have a life of it! And didn't we used to be thankful when one of them caught it. They were the torment of your life.'

'Really!' said Gudrun.

'In every possible way. If you wouldn't let them smash their pots on the table, if you wouldn't let them drag the kitten about with a string round its neck, if you wouldn't give them whatever they asked for, every mortal thing

– then there was a shine on, and their mother coming in asking – "What's the matter with him? What have you done to him? What is it, darling?" And then she'd turn on you as if she'd trample you under her feet. But she didn't trample on me. I was the only one that could do anything with her demons – for she wasn't going to be bothered with them herself. No, *she* took no trouble for them. But they must just have their way, they mustn't be spoken to. And Master Gerald was the beauty. I left when he was a year and a half, I could stand no more. But I pinched his little bottom for him when he was in arms, I did, when there was no holding him, and I'm not sorry I did—'

Gudrun went away in fury and loathing. The phrase, 'I pinched his little bottom for him,' sent her into a white, stony fury. She could not bear it, she wanted to have the woman taken out at once and strangled. And yet there the phrase was lodged in her mind for ever, beyond escape. She felt, one day, she would *have* to tell him, to see how he took it. And she loathed herself for the thought.

But at Shortlands the life-long struggle was coming to a close. The father was ill and was going to die. He had bad internal pains, which took away all his attentive life, and left him with only a vestige of his consciousness. More and more a silence came over him, he was less and less acutely aware of his surroundings. The pain seemed to absorb his activity. He knew it was there, he knew it would come again. It was like something lurking in the darkness within him. And he had not the power, or the will, to seek it out and to know it. There it remained in the darkness, the great pain, tearing him at times, and then being silent. And when it tore him he crouched in silent subjection under it, and when it left him alone again, he refused to know of it. It was within the darkness, let it remain unknown. So he never admitted it, except in a secret corner of himself, where all his never-revealed fears and secrets were accumulated. For the rest, he had a pain, it went away, it made no difference. It even stimulated him, excited him.

But it gradually absorbed his life. Gradually it drew away all his potentiality, it bled him into the dark, it weaned him of life and drew him away into the darkness. And in this twilight of his life little remained visible to him. The business, his work, that was gone entirely. His public interests had disappeared as if they had never been. Even his family had become extraneous to him, he could only remember, in some slight non-essential part of himself, that such and such were his children. But it was historical fact, not vital to him. He had to make an effort to know their relation to him. Even his wife barely existed. She indeed was like the darkness, like the pain within him. By some strange association, the darkness that contained the pain and the darkness that contained his wife were identical. All his thoughts and understandings became blurred and fused, and now his wife and the consuming pain were the same dark secret power against him, that he never faced. He never drove the dread out of its lair within him. He only knew that there was a dark place, and something inhabiting this darkness which issued from time to time and rent him. But he dared not penetrate and drive the beast into the open. He had rather ignore its existence. Only, in his vague way, the dread was his wife, the destroyer, and it was the pain, the destruction, a darkness which was one and both.

He very rarely saw his wife. She kept her room. Only occasionally she came forth, with her head stretched forward, and in her low, possessed voice, she asked him how he was. And he answered her, in the habit of more than thirty years: 'Well, I don't think I'm any the worse, dear.' But he was frightened of her, underneath this safeguard of habit, frightened almost to the verge of death.

But all his life, he had been so constant to his lights, he had never broken down. He would die even now without breaking down, without knowing what his feelings were, towards her. All his life, he had said: 'Poor Christiana, she has such a strong temper.' With unbroken will, he had stood by this position with regard to her, he had substituted pity for all his hostility, pity had been his shield and his safeguard, and his infallible weapon. And still, in his consciousness, he was sorry for her, her nature was so violent and so impatient.

But now his pity, with his life, was wearing thin, and the dread almost amounting to horror, was rising into being. But before the armour of his pity really broke, he would die, as an insect when its shell is cracked. This was his final resource. Others would live on, and know the living death, the ensuing process of hopeless chaos. He would not. He denied death its victory.

He had been so constant to his lights, so constant to charity, and to his love for his neighbour. Perhaps he had loved his neighbour even better than himself – which is going one further than the commandment. Always, this flame had burned in his heart, sustaining him through everything, the welfare of the people. He was a large employer of labour, he was a great mine-owner. And he had never lost this from his heart, that in Christ he was one with his workmen. Nay, he had felt inferior to them, as if they through poverty and labour were nearer to God than he. He had always the unacknowledged belief that it was his workmen, the miners, who held in their hands the means of salvation. To move nearer to God, he must move towards his miners, his life must gravitate towards theirs. They were, unconsciously, his idol, his God made manifest. In them he worshipped the highest, the great, sympathetic, mindless Godhead of humanity.

And all the while, his wife had opposed him like one of the great demons of hell. Strange, like a bird of prey, with the fascinating beauty and abstraction of a hawk, she had beat against the bars of his philanthropy, and like a hawk in a cage, she had sunk into silence. By force of circumstance, because all the world combined to make the cage unbreakable, he had been too strong for her, he had kept her prisoner. And because she was his prisoner, his passion for her had always remained keen as death. He had always loved her, loved her with intensity. Within the cage, she was denied nothing, she was given all licence.

But she had gone almost mad. Of wild and overweening temper, she could not bear the humiliation of her husband's soft, half-appealing kindness to everybody. He was not deceived by the poor. He knew they came and sponged on him, and whined to him, the worst sort; the majority, luckily for him, were much too proud to ask for anything, much too independent to come knocking at his door. But in Beldover, as everywhere else, there were the whining, parasitic, foul human beings who come crawling after charity, and feeding on the living body of the public like lice. A kind of fire would go over Christiana Crich's brain, as she saw two more pale-faced, creeping women in objectionable black clothes, cringing lugubriously up the drive to the door. She wanted to set the dogs on them, 'Hi Rip! Hi Ring! Ranger! At 'em, boys, set 'em off.' But Crowther, the butler, with all the rest of the servants, was Mr. Crich's man. Nevertheless, when her husband was away, she would come down like a wolf on the crawling supplicants: 'What do you people want? There is nothing for you here. You have no business on the drive at all. Simpson, drive them away and let no more of them through the gate.'

The servants had to obey her. And she would stand watching with an eye like the eagle's, whilst the groom in clumsy confusion drove the lugubrious persons down the drive, as if they were rusty fowls, scuttling before him.

But they learned to know, from the lodge-keeper, when Mr. Crich was away, and they timed their visits. How many times, in the first years, would Crowther knock softly at the door: 'Person to see you, sir.'

'What name?'

'Grocock, sir?'

'What do they want?' The question was half impatient, half gratified. He liked hearing appeals to his charity.

'About a child, sir.'

'Show them into the library, and tell them they shouldn't come after eleven o'clock in the morning.'

'Why do you get up from dinner? – send them off,' his wife would say abruptly.

'Oh, I can't do that. It's no trouble just to hear what they have to say.'

'How many more have been here to-day? Why don't you establish open house for them? They would soon oust me and the children.'

'You know, dear, it doesn't hurt me to hear what they have to say. And if they really are in trouble – well, it is my duty to help them out of it.'

'It's your duty to invite all the rats in the world to gnaw at your bones.'

'Come, Christiana, it isn't like that. Don't be uncharitable.'

But she suddenly swept out of the room, and out to the study. There sat the meagre charity-seekers, looking as if they were at the doctor's.

'Mr. Crich can't see you. He can't see you at this hour. Do you think he is your property, that you can come whenever you like? You must go away, there is nothing for you here.'

The poor people rose in confusion. But Mr. Crich, pale and black-bearded and deprecating, came behind her, saying:

'Yes, I don't like you coming as late as this. I'll hear any of you in the morning part of the day, but I can't really do with you after. What's amiss then, Gittens. How is your Missis?'

'Why, she's sunk very low, Mester Crich, she's a'most gone, she is—'

Sometimes, it seemed to Mrs. Crich as if her husband were some subtle funeral bird, feeding on the miseries of the people. It seemed to her he was never satisfied unless there was some sordid tale being poured out to him, which he drank in with a sort of mournful, sympathetic satisfaction. He would have no *raison d'être* if there were no lugubrious miseries in the world, as an undertaker would have no meaning if there were no funerals.

Mrs. Crich recoiled back upon herself, she recoiled away from this world of creeping democracy. A band of tight, baleful exclusion fastened round her heart, her isolation was fierce and hard, her antagonism was passive but terribly pure, like that of a hawk in a cage. As the years went on, she lost more and more count of the world, she seemed rapt in some glittering abstraction, almost purely unconscious. She would wander about the house and about the surrounding country, staring keenly and seeing nothing. She rarely spoke, she had no connection with the world. And she did not even think. She was consumed in a fierce tension of opposition, like the negative pole of a magnet.

And she bore many children. For, as time went on, she never opposed her husband in word or deed. She took no notice of him, externally. She submitted to him, let him take what he wanted and do as he wanted with her. She was like a hawk that sullenly submits to everything. The relation between her and her husband was wordless and unknown, but it was deep, awful, a relation of utter interdestruction. And he, who triumphed in the world, he became more and more hollow in his vitality, the vitality was bled from within him, as by some haemorrhage. She was hulked like a hawk in a cage, but her heart was fierce and undiminished within her, though her mind was destroyed.

So to the last he would go to her and hold her in his arms sometimes, before his strength was all gone. The terrible white, destructive light that burned in her eyes only excited and roused him. Till he was bled to death, and then he dreaded her more than anything. But he always said to himself, how happy he had been, how he had loved her with a pure and consuming love ever since he had known her. And he thought of her as pure, chaste; the white flame which was known to him alone, the flame of her sex, was a white flower of snow to his mind. She was a wonderful white snow-flower, which he had desired infinitely. And now he was dying with all his ideas and interpretations intact. They would only collapse when the breath left his body. Till then they would be pure truths for him. Only death would show the perfect completeness of the lie. Till death, she was his white snow-flower. He had subdued her, and her subjugation was to him an infinite chastity in her, a virginity which he could never break, and which dominated him as by a spell.

She had let go the outer world, but within herself she was unbroken and unimpaired. She only sat in her room like a moping, dishevelled hawk, motionless, mindless. Her children, for whom she had been so fierce in her youth, now meant scarcely anything to her. She had lost all that, she was quite by herself. Only Gerald, the gleaming, had some existence for her. But of late years, since he had become head of the business, he too was forgotten. Whereas the father, now he was dying, turned for compassion to Gerald. There had always been opposition between the two of them. Gerald had feared and despised his father, and to a great extent had avoided him all through boyhood and young manhood. And the father had felt very often a real dislike of his eldest son, which, never wanting to give way to, he had refused to acknowledge. He had ignored Gerald as much as possible, leaving him alone.

Since, however, Gerald had come home and assumed responsibility in the firm, and had proved such a wonderful director, the father, tired and weary of all outside concerns, had put all his trust of these things in his son, implicitly, leaving everything to him, and assuming a rather touching dependence on the young enemy. This immediately roused a poignant pity and allegiance in Gerald's heart, always shadowed by contempt and by unadmitted enmity. For Gerald was in reaction against Charity; and yet he was dominated by it, it assumed supremacy in the inner life, and he could not confute it. So he was partly subject to that which his father stood for, but he was in reaction against it. Now he could not save himself. A certain pity and grief and tenderness for his father overcame him, in spite of the deeper, more sullen hostility.

The father won shelter from Gerald through compassion. But for love he had Winifred. She was his youngest child, she was the only one of his children whom he had ever closely loved. And her he loved with all the great, over-weening, sheltering love of a dying man. He wanted to shelter her infinitely, infinitely, to wrap her in warmth and love and shelter, perfectly. If he could save her she should never know one pain, one grief, one hurt. He had been so right all his life, so constant in his kindness and his goodness. And this was his last passionate righteousness, his love for the child Winifred. Some things troubled him yet. The world had passed away from him, as his strength ebbed. There were no more poor and injured and humble to protect and succour. These were all lost to him. There were no more sons and daughters to trouble him, and to weigh on him as an unnatural responsibility. These too had faded out of reality. All these things had fallen out of his hands, and left him free.

There remained the covert fear and horror of his wife, as she sat mindless and strange in her room, or as she came forth with slow, prowling step, her head bent forward. But this he put away. Even his life-long righteousness, however, would not quite deliver him from the inner horror. Still, he could keep it sufficiently at bay. It would never break forth openly. Death would come first.

Then there was Winifred! If only he could be sure about her, if only he could be sure. Since the death of Diana, and the development of his illness, his craving for surety with regard to Winifred amounted almost to obsession. It was as if, even dying, he must have some anxiety, some responsibility of love, of Charity, upon his heart.

She was an odd, sensitive, inflammable child, having her father's dark hair and quiet bearing, but being quite detached, momentaneous. She was like a changeling indeed, as if her feelings did not matter to her, really. She often seemed to be talking and playing like the gayest and most childish of children, she was full of the warmest, most delightful affection for a few things – for her father, and for her animals in particular. But if she heard that her beloved kitten Leo had been run over by the motor-car she put her head on one side, and replied, with a faint contraction like resentment on her face: 'Has he?' Then she took no more notice. She only disliked the servant who would force bad news on her, and wanted her to be sorry. She wished not to know, and that seemed her chief motive. She avoided her mother, and most of the members of her family. She *loved* her Daddy, because he wanted her always to be happy, and because he seemed to become young again, and irresponsible in her presence. She liked Gerald, because he was so self-contained. She loved people who would make life a game to her. She had an amazing instinctive critical faculty, and was a pure anarchist, a pure aristocrat at once. For she accepted her equals wherever she found them, and she ignored with blithe indifference her inferiors, whether they were her brothers and sisters, or whether they were wealthy guests of the house, or whether they were the common people or the servants. She was quite single and by herself, deriving from nobody. It was as if she were cut off from all purpose or continuity, and existed simply moment by moment.

The father, as by some strange final illusion, felt as if all his fate depended on his ensuring to Winifred her happiness. She who could never suffer, because she never formed vital connections, she who could lose the dearest things of her life and be just the same the next day, the whole memory dropped out, as if deliberately, she whose will was so strangely and easily free, anarchistic, almost nihilistic, who like a soulless bird flits on its own will, without attachment or responsibility beyond the moment, who in her every motion snapped the threads of serious relationship with blithe, free hands, really nihilistic, because never troubled, she must be the object of her father's final passionate solicitude.

When Mr. Crich heard that Gudrun Brangwen might come to help Winifred with her drawing and modelling he saw a road to salvation for his child. He believed that Winifred had talent, he had seen Gudrun, he knew that she was an exceptional person. He could give Winifred into her hands as into the hands of a right being. Here was a direction and a positive force to be lent to his child, he need not leave her directionless and defenceless. If he could but graft the girl on to some tree of utterance before he died, he would have fulfilled his responsibility. And here it could be done. He did not hesitate to appeal to Gudrun.

Meanwhile, as the father drifted more and more out of life, Gerald experienced more and more a sense of exposure. His father after all had stood for the living world to him. Whilst his father lived Gerald was not responsible for the world. But now his father was passing away, Gerald found himself left exposed and unready before the storm of living, like the mutinous first mate of a ship that has lost his captain, and who sees only a terrible chaos in front of him. He did not inherit an established order and a living idea. The whole unifying idea of mankind seemed to be dying with his father, the centralising force that had held the whole together seemed to collapse with his father, the parts were ready to go asunder in terrible disintegration. Gerald was as if left on board of a ship that was going asunder beneath his feet, he was in charge of a vessel whose timbers were all coming apart.

He knew that all his life he had been wrenching at the frame of life to break it apart. And now, with something of the terror of a destructive child, he saw himself on the point of inheriting his own destruction. And during the last months, under the influence of death, and of Birkin's talk, and of Gudrun's penetrating being, he had lost entirely that mechanical certainty that had been his triumph. Sometimes spasms of hatred came over him, against Birkin and Gudrun and that whole set. He wanted to go back to the dullest conservatism, to the most stupid of conventional people. He wanted to revert to the strictest Toryism. But the desire did not last long enough to carry him into action.

During his childhood and his boyhood he had wanted a sort of savagedom. The days of Homer were his ideal, when a man was chief of an army of heroes, or spent his years in wonderful Odyssey. He hated remorselessly the circumstances of his own life, so much that he never really saw Beldover and the colliery valley. He turned his face entirely away from the blackened mining region that stretched away on the right hand of Shortlands, he turned entirely to the country and the woods beyond Willey Water. It was true that the panting and rattling of the coal-mines could always be heard at Short-lands. But from his earliest childhood, Gerald had paid no heed to this. He had ignored the whole of the industrial sea which surged in coal-blackened tides against the grounds of the house. The world was really a wilderness where one hunted and swam and rode. He rebelled against all authority. Life was a condition of savage freedom.

Then he had been sent away to school, which was so much death to him. He refused to go to Oxford, choosing a German university. He had spent a certain time at Bonn, at Berlin, and at Frankfurt. There, a curiosity had been aroused in his mind. He wanted to see and to know, in a curious objective fashion, as if it were an amusement to him. Then he must try war. Then he must travel into the savage regions that had so attracted him.

The result was, he found humanity very much alike everywhere, and to a mind like his, curious and cold, the savage was duller, less exciting than the European. So he took hold of all kinds of sociological ideas, and ideas of reform. But they never went more than skin-deep, they were never more than a mental amusement. Their interest lay chiefly in the reaction against the positive order, the destructive reaction.

He discovered at last a real adventure in the coal-mines. His father asked him to help in the firm. Gerald had been educated in the science of mining, and it had never interested him. Now, suddenly, with a sort of exultation, he laid hold of the world.

There was impressed photographically on his consciousness the great industry. Suddenly, it was real, he was part of it. Down the valley ran the colliery railway, linking mine with mine. Down the railway ran the trains, short trains of heavily laden trucks, long trains of empty wagons, each one bearing in big white letters the initials:

'C. B. & Co.'

These white letters on all the wagons he had seen since his first childhood, and it was as if he had never seen them, they were so familiar, and so ignored. Now at last he saw his own name written on the wall. Now he had a vision of power.

So many wagons, bearing his initial, running all over the country. He saw them as he entered London in the train, he saw them at Dover. So far his power ramified. He looked at Beldover, at Selby, at Whatmore, at Lethley Bank, the great colliery villages which depended entirely on his mines. They were hideous and sordid, during his childhood they had been sores in his consciousness. And now he saw them with pride. Four raw new towns, and many ugly industrial hamlets were crowded under his dependence. He saw the stream of miners flowing along the causeways from the mines at the end of the afternoon, thousands of blackened, slightly distorted human beings with red mouths, all moving subjugate to his will. He pushed slowly in his motor-car through the little market-top on Friday nights in Beldover, through a solid mass of human beings that were making their purchases and doing their weekly spending. They were all subordinate to him. They were ugly and uncouth, but they were his instruments. He was the God of the machine. They made way for his motorcar automatically, slowly.

He did not care whether they made way with alacrity, or grudgingly. He did not care what they thought of him. His vision had suddenly crystallised. Suddenly he had conceived the pure instrumentality of mankind. There had been so much humanitarianism, so much talk of sufferings and feelings. It was ridiculous. The sufferings and feelings of individuals did not matter in the least. They were mere conditions, like the weather. What mattered was the pure instrumentality of the individual. As a man as of a knife: does it cut well? Nothing else mattered.

Everything in the world has its function, and is good or not good in so far as it fulfils this function more or less perfectly. Was a miner a good miner? Then he was complete. Was a manager a good manager? That was enough. Gerald himself, who was responsible for all this industry, was he a good director? If he were, he had fulfilled is life. The rest was by-play.

The mines were there, they were old. They were giving out, it did not pay to work the seams. There was talk of closing down two of them. It was at this point that Gerald arrived on the scene.

He looked around. There lay the mines. They were old, obsolete. They were like old lions, no more good. He looked again. Pah! the mines were nothing but the clumsy efforts of impure minds. There they lay, abortions of a half-trained mind. Let the idea of them be swept away. He cleared his brain of them, and thought only of the coal in the under earth. How much was there?

There was plenty of coal. The old workings could not get at it, that was all. Then break the neck of the old workings. The coal lay there in its seams, even though the seams were thin. There it lay, inert matter, as it had always lain, since the beginning of time, subject to the will of man. The will of man was the determining factor. Man was the arch-god of earth. His mind was obedient to serve his will. Man's will was the absolute, the only absolute.

And it was his will to subjugate Matter to his own ends. The subjugation itself was the point, the fight was the be-all, the fruits of victory were mere results. It was not for the sake of money that Gerald took over the mines. He did not care about money, fundamentally. He was neither ostentatious nor luxurious, neither did he care about social position, not finally. What he wanted was the pure fulfilment of his own will in the struggle with the natural conditions. His will was now, to take the coal out of the earth, profitably. The profit was merely the condition of victory, but the victory itself lay in the feat achieved. He vibrated with zest before the challenge. Every day he was in the mines, examining, testing, he consulted experts, he gradually gathered the whole situation into his mind, as a general grasps the plan of his campaign.

Then there was need for a complete break. The mines were run on an old system, an obsolete idea. The initial idea had been, to obtain as much money from the earth as would make the owners comfortably rich, would allow the workmen sufficient wages and good conditions, and would increase the wealth of the country altogether. Gerald's father, following in the second generation, having a sufficient fortune, had thought only of the men. The mines, for him, were primarily great fields to produce bread and plenty for all the hundreds of human beings gathered about them. He had lived and striven with his fellow owners to benefit the men every time. And the men had been benefited in their fashion. There were few poor, and few needy. All was plenty, because the mines were good and easy to work. And the miners, in those days, finding themselves richer than they might have expected, felt glad and triumphant. They thought themselves well off, they congratulated themselves on their good fortune, they remembered how their fathers had starved and suffered, and they felt that better times had come. They were grateful to those others, the pioneers, the new owners, who had opened out the pits, and let forth this stream of plenty.

But man is never satisfied, and so the miners, from gratitude to their owners, passed on to murmuring. Their sufficiency decreased with knowledge, they wanted more. Why should the master be so out-of-all-proportion rich?

There was a crisis when Gerald was a boy, when the Masters' Federation closed down the mines because the men would not accept a reduction. This lock-out had forced home the new conditions to Thomas Crich. Belonging to the Federation, he had been compelled by his honour to close the pits against his men. He, the father, the Patriarch, was forced to deny the means of life to his sons, his people. He, the rich man who would hardly enter heaven because of his possessions, must now turn upon the poor, upon those who were nearer Christ than himself, those who were humble and despised and closer to perfection, those who were manly and noble in their labours, and must say to them: 'Ye shall neither labour nor eat bread.'

It was this recognition of the state of war which really broke his heart. He wanted his industry to be run on love. Oh, he wanted love to be the directing power even of the mines. And now, from under the cloak of love, the sword was cynically drawn, the sword of mechanical necessity.

This really broke his heart. He must have the illusion and now the illusion was destroyed. The men were not against *him*, but they were against the masters. It was war, and willy-nilly he found himself on the wrong side, in his own conscience. Seething masses of miners met daily, carried away by a new religious impulse. The idea flew through them: 'All men are equal on earth,' and they would carry the idea to its material fulfilment. After all, is it not the teaching of Christ? And what is an idea, if not the germ of action in the material world. 'All men are equal in spirit, they are all sons of God. Whence then this obvious *disquality?*' It was a religious creed pushed to its material conclusion. Thomas Crich at least had no answer. He could but admit, according to his sincere tenets, that the disquality was wrong. But he could not give up his goods, which were the stuff of disquality. So the men would fight for their rights. The last impulses of the last religious passion left on earth, the passion for equality, inspired them.

Seething mobs of men marched about, their faces lighted up as for holy war, with a smoke of cupidity. How disentangle the passion for equality from the passion of cupidity, when begins the fight for equality of possessions? But the God was the machine. Each man claimed equality in the Godhead of the great productive machine. Every man equally was part of this Godhead. But somehow, somewhere, Thomas Crich knew this was false. When the machine is the Godhead, and production or work is worship, then the most mechanical mind is purest and highest, the representative of God on earth. And the rest are subordinate, each according to his degree.

Riots broke out, Whatmore pit-head was in flames. This was the pit farthest in the country, near the woods. Soldiers came. From the windows of Shortlands, on that fatal day, could be seen the flare of fire in the sky not far off, and now the little colliery train, with the workmen's carriages which were used to convey the miners to the distant Whatmore, was crossing the valley full of soldiers, full of red-coats. Then there was the far-off sound of firing, then the later news that the mob was dispersed, one man was shot dead, the fire was put out.

Gerald, who was a boy, was filled with the wildest excitement and delight. He longed to go with the soldiers to shoot the men. But he was not allowed to go out of the lodge gates. At the gates were stationed sentries with guns. Gerald stood near them in delight, whilst gangs of derisive miners strolled up and down the lanes, calling and jeering:

'Now then, three ha'porth o' coppers, let's see thee shoot thy gun.' Insults were chalked on the walls and the fences, the servants left.

And all this while Thomas Crich was breaking his heart, and giving away hundreds of pounds in charity. Everywhere there was free food, a surfeit of free food. Anybody could have bread for asking, and a loaf cost only three-ha'pence. Every day there was a free tea somewhere, the children had never had so many treats in their lives. On Friday afternoon great basketfuls of buns and cakes were taken into the schools, and great pitchers of milk, the schoolchildren had what they wanted. They were sick with eating too much cake and milk.

And then it came to an end, and the men went back to work. But it was never the same as before. There was a new situation created, a new idea reigned. Even in the machine, there should be equality. No part should be subordinate to any other part: all should be equal. The instinct for chaos had entered. Mystic equality lies in abstraction, not in having or in doing, which are processes. In function and process, one man, one part, must of necessity be subordinate to another. It is a condition of being. But the desire for chaos had risen, and the idea of mechanical equality was the weapon of disruption which should execute the will of men, the will for chaos.

Gerald was a boy at the time of the strike, but he longed to be a man, to fight the colliers. The father, however, was trapped between two half-truths, and broken. He wanted to be a pure Christian, one and equal with all men. He even wanted to give away all he had, to the poor. Yet he was a great promoter of industry, and he knew perfectly that he must keep his goods and keep his authority. This was as divine a necessity in him, as the need to give away all he possessed – more divine, even, since this was the necessity he acted upon. Yet because he did *not* act on the other ideal, it dominated him, he was dying of chagrin because he must forfeit it. He wanted to be a father of loving kindness and sacrificial benevolence. The colliers shouted to him about his thousands a year. They would not be deceived.

When Gerald grew up in the ways of the world, he shifted the position. He did not care about the equality. The whole Christian attitude of love and self-sacrifice was old hat. He knew that position and authority were the right thing in the world, and it was useless to cant about it. They were the right thing, for the simple reason that they were functionally necessary. They were not the be-all and the end-all. It was like being part of a machine. He himself happened to be a controlling, central part, the masses of men were the parts variously controlled. This was merely as it happened. As well get excited because a central hub drives a hundred outer wheels – or because the whole universe wheels round the sun. After all, it would be mere silliness to say that the moon and the earth and Saturn and Jupiter and Venus have just as much right to be the centre of the universe, each of them separately, as the sun. Such an assertion is made merely in the desire of chaos.

Without bothering to *think* to a conclusion, Gerald jumped to a conclusion. He abandoned the whole democratic-equality problem as a problem of silliness. What mattered was the great social productive machine. Let that work perfectly, let it produce a sufficiency of everything, let every man be given a rational portion, greater or less according to his functional degree or magnitude, and then, provision made, let the devil supervene, let every man look after his own amusements and appetites, so long as he interfered with nobody.

So Gerald set himself to work, to put the great industry in order. In his travels, and in his accompanying readings, he had come to the conclusion that the essential secret of life was harmony. He did not define to himself at all clearly what harmony was. The word pleased him, he felt he had come to his own conclusions. And he proceeded to put his philosophy into practice by forcing order into the established world, translating the mystic word harmony into the practical word organisation.

Immediately he *saw* the firm, he realised what he could do. He had a fight to fight with Matter, with the earth and the coal it enclosed. This was the sole idea, to turn upon the inanimate matter of the underground, and reduce it to his will. And for this fight with matter, one must have perfect instruments in perfect organisation, a mechanism so subtle and harmonious in its workings that it represents the single mind of man, and by its relentless repetition of given movement, will accomplish a purpose irresistibly, inhumanly. It was this inhuman principle in the mechanism he wanted to construct that inspired Gerald with an almost religious exaltation. He, the man, could interpose a perfect, changeless, godlike medium between himself and the Matter he had to subjugate. There were two opposites, his will and the resistant Matter of the earth. And between these he could establish the very expression of his will, the incarnation of his power, a great and perfect machine, a system, an activity of pure order, pure mechanical repetition, repetition *ad infinitum*, hence eternal and infinite. He found his eternal and his infinite in the pure machine-principle of perfect co-ordination into one pure, complex, infinitely repeated motion, like the spinning of a wheel; but a productive spinning, as the revolving of the universe may be called a productive spinning, a productive repetition through eternity, to infinity. And this is the God-motion, this productive repetition *ad infinitum*. And Gerald was the God of the machine, *Deus ex Machina*. And the whole productive will of man was the Godhead.

He had his life-work now, to extend over the earth a great and perfect system in which the will of man ran smooth and unthwarted, timeless, a Godhead in process. He had to begin with the mines. The terms were given: first the resistant Matter of the underground; then the instruments of its subjugation, instruments human and metallic; and finally his own pure will, his own mind. It would need a marvellous adjustment of myriad instruments, human, animal, metallic, kinetic, dynamic, a marvellous casting of myriad tiny wholes into one great perfect entirety. And then, in this case there was perfection attained, the will of the highest was perfectly fulfilled, the will of mankind was perfectly enacted; for was not mankind mystically contradistinguished against inanimate Matter, was not the history of mankind just the history of the conquest of the one by the other?

The miners were overreached. While they were still in the toils of divine equality of man, Gerald had passed on, granted essentially their case, and proceeded in his quality of human being to fulfil the will of mankind as a whole. He merely represented the miners in a higher sense when he perceived that the only way to fulfil perfectly the will of man was to establish the perfect, inhuman machine. But he represented them very essentially, they were far behind, out of date, squabbling for their material equality. The desire had already transmuted into this new and greater desire, for a perfect intervening mechanism between man and Matter, the desire to translate the Godhead into pure mechanism.

As soon as Gerald entered the firm, the convulsion of death ran through the old system. He had all his life been tortured by a furious and destructive demon, which possessed him sometimes like an insanity. This temper now entered like a virus into the firm, and there were cruel eruptions. Terrible and inhuman were his examinations into every detail; there was no privacy he would spare, no old sentiment but he would turn it over. The old grey managers, the old grey clerks, the doddering old pensioners, he looked at them, and removed them as so much lumber. The whole concern seemed like a hospital of invalid employees. He had no emotional qualms. He arranged what pensions were necessary, he looked for efficient substitutes, and when these were found, he substituted them for the old hands.

'I've a pitiful letter here from Letherington,' his father would say, in a tone of deprecation and appeal. 'Don't you think the poor fellow might keep on a little longer. I always fancied he did very well.'

'I've got a man in his place now, father. He'll be happier out of it, believe me. You think his allowance is plenty, don't you?'

'It is not the allowance that he wants, poor man. He feels it very much, that he is superannuated. Says he thought he had twenty more years of work in him yet.'

'Not of this kind of work I want. He doesn't understand.'

The father sighed. He wanted not to know any more. He believed the pits would have to be overhauled if they were to go on working. And after all, it would be worst in the long run for everybody, if they must close down. So he could make no answer to the appeals of his old and trusty servants, he could only repeat 'Gerald says'.

So the father drew more and more out of the light. The whole frame of the real life was broken for him. He had been right according to his lights. And his lights had been those of the great religion. Yet they seemed to have become obsolete, to be superseded in the world. He could not understand. He only withdrew with his lights into an inner room, into the silence. The beautiful candles of belief, that would not do to light the world any more, they would still burn sweetly and sufficiently in the inner room of his soul, and in the silence of his retirement.

Gerald rushed into the reform of the firm, beginning with the office. It was needful to economise severely, to make possible the great alterations he must introduce.

'What are these widows' coals?' he asked.

'We have always allowed all widows of men who worked for the firm a load of coals every three months.'

'They must pay cost price henceforward. The firm is not a charity institution, as everybody seems to think.'

Widows, these stock figures of sentimental humanitarianism, he felt a dislike at the thought of them. They were almost repulsive. Why were they not immolated on the pyre of the husband, like the sati in India? At any rate, let them pay the cost of their coals.

In a thousand ways he cut down the expenditure, in ways so fine as to be hardly noticeable to the men. The miners must pay for the cartage of their coals, heavy cartage too; they must pay for their tools, for the sharpening, for the care of lamps, for the many trifling things that made the bill of charges against every man mount up to a shilling or so in the week. It was not grasped very definitely by the miners, though they were sore enough. But it saved hundreds of pounds every week for the firm.

Gradually Gerald got hold of everything. And then began the great reform. Expert engineers were introduced in every department. An enormous electric plant was installed, both for lighting and for haulage underground, and for power. The electricity was carried into every mine. New machinery was brought from America, such as the miners had never seen before, great iron men, as the cutting machines were called, and unusual appliances. The working of the pits was thoroughly changed, all the control was taken out of the hands of the miners, the butty system was abolished. Everything was run on the most accurate and delicate scientific method, educated and expert men were in control everywhere, the miners were reduced to mere mechanical instruments. They had to work hard, much harder than before, the work was terrible and heart-breaking in its mechanicalness.

But they submitted to it all. The joy went out of their lives, the hope seemed to perish as they became more and more mechanised. And yet they accepted the new conditions. They even got a further satisfaction out of them. At first they hated Gerald Crich, they swore to do something to him, to murder him. But as time went on, they accepted everything with some fatal satisfaction. Gerald was their high priest, he represented the religion they really felt. His father was forgotten already. There was a new world, a new order, strict, terrible, inhuman, but satisfying in its very destructiveness. The men were satisfied to belong to the great and wonderful machine, even whilst it destroyed them. It was what they wanted. It was the highest that man had produced, the most wonderful and superhuman. They were exalted by belonging to this great and superhuman system which was beyond feeling or reason, something really godlike. Their hearts died within them, but their souls were satisfied. It was what they wanted. Otherwise Gerald could never have done what he did. He was just ahead of them in giving them what they wanted, this participation in a great and perfect system that subjected life to pure mathematical principles. This was a sort of freedom, the sort they really wanted. It was the first great step in undoing, the first great phase of chaos, the substitution of the mechanical principle for the organic, the destruction of the organic purpose, the organic unity, and the subordination of every organic unit to the great mechanical purpose. It was pure organic disintegration and pure mechanical organisation. This is the first and finest state of chaos.

Gerald was satisfied. He knew the colliers said they hated him. But he had long ceased to hate them. When they streamed past him at evening, their heavy boots slurring on the pavement wearily, their shoulders slightly distorted, they took no notice of him, they gave him no greeting whatever, they passed in a grey-black stream of unemotional acceptance. They were not important to him, save as instruments, nor he to them, save as a supreme instrument of control. As miners they had their being, he had his being as director. He admired their qualities. But as men, personalities, they were just accidents, sporadic little unimportant phenomena. And tacitly, the men agreed to this. For Gerald agreed to it in himself.

He had succeeded. He had converted the industry into a new and terrible purity. There was a greater output of coal than ever, the wonderful and delicate system ran almost perfectly. He had a set of really clever engineers, both mining and electrical, and they did not cost much. A highly educated man cost very little more than a workman. His managers, who were all rare men, were no more expensive than the old bungling fools of his father's days, who were merely colliers promoted. His chief manager, who had twelve hundred a year, saved the firm at least five thousand. The whole system was now so perfect that Gerald was hardly necessary any more.

It was so perfect that sometimes a strange fear came over him, and he did not know what to do. He went on for some years in a sort of trance of activity. What he was doing seemed supreme, he was almost like a divinity. He was a pure and exalted activity.

But now he had succeeded – he had finally succeeded. And one or twice lately, when he was alone in the evening and had nothing to do, he had suddenly stood up in terror, not knowing what he was. And he went to the mirror and looked long and closely at his own face, at his own eyes, seeking for something. He was afraid, in mortal dry fear, but he knew not what of. He looked at his own face. There it was, shapely and healthy and the same as ever, yet somehow, it was not real, it was a mask. He dared not touch it, for fear it should prove to be only a composition mask. His eyes were blue and keen as ever, and as firm in their sockets. Yet he was not sure that they were not blue false bubbles that would burst in a moment and leave clear annihilation. He could see the darkness in them, as if they were only bubbles of darkness. He was afraid that one day he would break down and be a purely meaningless babble lapping round a darkness.

But his will yet held good, he was able to go away and read, and think about things. He liked to read books about the primitive man, books of anthropology, and also works of speculative philosophy. His mind was very active. But it was like a bubble floating in the darkness. At any moment it might burst and leave him in chaos. He would not die. He knew that. He would go on living, but the meaning would have collapsed out of him, his divine reason would be gone. In a strangely indifferent, sterile way, he was frightened. But he could not react even to the fear. It was as if his centres of feeling were drying up. He remained calm, calculative and healthy, and quite freely deliberate, even whilst he felt, with faint, small but final sterile horror, that his mystic reason was breaking, giving way now, at this crisis.

And it was a strain. He knew there was no equilibrium. He would have to go in some direction, shortly, to find relief. Only Birkin kept the fear definitely off him, saved him his quick sufficiency in life, by the odd mobility and changeableness which seemed to contain the quintessence of faith. But then Gerald must always come away from Birkin, as from a Church service, back to the outside real world of work and life. There it was, it did not alter, and words were futilities. He had to keep himself in reckoning with the world of work and material life. And it became more and more difficult, such a strange pressure was upon him, as if the very middle of him were a vacuum, and outside were an awful tension.

He had found his most satisfactory relief in women. After a debauch with some desperate woman, he went on quite easy and forgetful. The devil of it was, it was so hard to keep up his interest in women nowadays. He didn't care about them any more. A Pussum was all right in her way, but she was an exceptional case, and even she mattered extremely little. No, women, in that sense, were useless to him any more. He felt that his *mind* needed acute stimulation, before he could be physically roused.

Chapter Eighteen

Rabbit

Gudrun knew that it was a critical thing for her to go to Shortlands. She knew it was equivalent to accepting Gerald Crich as a lover. And though she hung back, disliking the condition, yet she knew she would go on. She equivocated. She said to herself, in torment recalling the blow and the kiss, 'After all, what is it? What is a kiss? What even is a blow? It is an instant, vanished at once. I can go to Shortlands just for a time, before I go away, if only to see what it is like.' For she had an insatiable curiosity to see and to know everything.

She also wanted to know what Winifred was really like. Having heard the child calling from the steamer in the night, she felt some mysterious connection with her.

Gudrun talked with the father in the library. Then he sent for his daughter. She came accompanied by Mademoiselle.

'Winnie, this is Miss Brangwen, who will be so kind as to help you with your drawing and making models of your animals,' said the father.

The child looked at Gudrun for a moment with interest, before she came forward, and with face averted offered her hand. There was a complete *sang froid* and indifference under Winifred's childish reserve, a certain irresponsible callousness.

'How do you do?' said the child, not lifting her face.

'How do you do?' said Gudrun.

Then Winifred stood aside, and Gudrun was introduced to Mademoiselle.

'You have a fine day for your walk,' said Mademoiselle, in a bright manner.

'*Quite* fine,' said Gudrun.

Winifred was watching from her distance. She was as if amused, but rather unsure as yet what this new person was like. She saw so many new persons, and so few who became real to her. Mademoiselle was of no count whatever, the child merely put up with her, calmly and easily, accepting her little authority with faint scorn, compliant out of childish arrogance of indifference.

'Well, Winifred,' said the father, 'aren't you glad Miss Brangwen has come? She makes animals and birds in wood and in clay, that the people in London write about in the papers, praising them to the skies.'

Winifred smiled slightly.

'Who told you, Daddie?' she asked.

'Who told me? Hermione told me, and Rupert Birkin.'

'Do you know them?' Winifred asked of Gudrun, turning to her with faint challenge.

'Yes,' said Gudrun.

Winifred readjusted herself a little. She had been ready to accept Gudrun as a sort of servant. Now she saw it was on terms of friendship they were intended to meet. She was rather glad. She had so many half inferiors, whom she tolerated with perfect good-humour.

Gudrun was very calm. She also did not take these things very seriously. A new occasion was mostly spectacular to her. However, Winifred was a detached, ironic child, she would never attach herself. Gudrun liked her and was intrigued by her. The first meetings went off with a certain humiliating clumsiness. Neither Winifred nor her instructress had any social grace.

Soon, however, they met in a kind of make-believe world. Winifred did not notice human beings unless they were like herself, playful and slightly mocking. She would accept nothing but the world of amusement, and the serious people of her life were the animals she had for pets. On those she lavished, almost ironically, her affection and her companionship. To the rest of the human scheme she submitted with a faint bored indifference.

She had a Pekinese dog called Looloo, which she loved.

'Let us draw Looloo,' said Gudrun, 'and see if we can get his Looliness, shall we?'

'Darling!' cried Winifred, rushing to the dog, that sat with contemplative sadness on the hearth, and kissing its bulging brow. 'Darling one, will you be drawn? Shall its mummy draw its portrait?' Then she chuckled gleefully, and turning to Gudrun, said: 'Oh, let's!'

They proceeded to get pencils and paper, and were ready.

'Beautifullest,' cried Winifred, hugging the dog, 'sit still while its mummy draws its beautiful portrait.' The dog looked up at her with grievous resignation in its large, prominent eyes. She kissed it fervently, and said: 'I wonder what mine will be like. It's sure to be awful.'

As she sketched she chuckled to herself, and cried out at times:

'Oh, darling, you're so beautiful!'

And again chuckling, she rushed to embrace the dog, in penitence, as if she were doing him some subtle injury. He sat all the time with the resignation and fretfulness of ages on his dark velvety face. She drew slowly, with a wicked concentration in her eyes, her head on one side, an intense stillness over her. She was as if working the spell of some enchantment. Suddenly she had finished. She looked at the dog, and then at her drawing, and then cried, with real grief for the dog, and at the same time with a wicked exultation:

'My beautiful, why did they?'

She took her paper to the dog, and held it under his nose. He turned his head aside as in chagrin and mortification, and she impulsively kissed his velvety bulging forehead.

' 's a Loolie, 's a little Loozie! Look at his portrait, darling, look at his portrait, that his mother has done of him.' She looked at her paper and chuckled. Then, kissing the dog once more, she rose and came gravely to Gudrun, offering her the paper.

It was a grotesque little diagram of a grotesque little animal, so wicked and so comical, a slow smile came over Gudrun's face, unconsciously. And at her side Winifred chuckled with glee, and said:

'It isn't like him, is it? He's much lovelier than that. He's *so* beautiful – mmm, Looloo, my sweet darling.' And she flew off to embrace the chagrined little dog. He looked up at her with reproachful, saturnine eyes, vanquished in his extreme agedness of being. Then she flew back to her drawing, and chuckled with satisfaction.

'It isn't like him, is it?' she said to Gudrun.

'Yes, it's very like him,' Gudrun replied.

The child treasured her drawing, carried it about with her, and showed it, with a silent embarrassment, to everybody.

'Look,' she said, thrusting the paper into her father's hand.

'Why, that's Looloo!' he exclaimed. And he looked down in surprise, hearing the almost inhuman chuckle of the child at his side.

Gerald was away from home when Gudrun first came to Shortlands. But the first morning he came back he watched for her. It was a sunny, soft morning, and he lingered in the garden paths, looking at the flowers that had come out during his absence. He was clean and fit as ever, shaven, his fair hair scrupulously parted at the side, bright in the sunshine, his short, fair moustache closely clipped, his eyes with their humorous kind twinkle, which was so deceptive. He was dressed in black, his clothes sat well on his well-nourished body. Yet as he lingered before the flower-beds in the morning sunshine, there was a certain isolation, a fear about him, as of something wanting.

Gudrun came up quickly, unseen. She was dressed in blue, with woollen yellow stockings, like the Bluecoat boys. He glanced up in surprise. Her stockings always disconcerted him, the pale-yellow stockings and the heavy, heavy black shoes. Winifred, who had been playing about the garden with Mademoiselle and the dogs, came flitting towards Gudrun. The child wore a dress of black-and-white stripes. Her hair was rather short, cut round and hanging level in her neck.

'We're going to do Bismarck, aren't we?' she said, linking her hand through Gudrun's arm.

'Yes, we're going to do Bismarck. Do you want to?'

'Oh yes – oh, I do! I want most awfully to do Bismarck. He looks *so* splendid this morning, so *fierce*. He's almost as big as a lion.' And the child chuckled sardonically at her own hyperbole. 'He's a real king, he really is.'

'*Bon jour, Mademoiselle,*' said the little French governess, wavering up with a slight bow, a bow of the sort that Gudrun loathed, insolent.

'*Winifred veut tant faire le portrait de Bismarck*—! Oh, *mais toute la matinée* – 'We will do Bismarck this morning!' – *Bismarck, Bismarck, toujours Bismarck! C'est un lapin, n'est-ce pas, mademoiselle?*'

'*Oui, c'est un grand lapin blanc et noir. Vous ne l'avez pas vu?*' said Gudrun in her good, but rather heavy French.

'*Non, mademoiselle, Winifred n'a jamais voulu me le faire voir. Tant de fois je le lui ai demandé, Qu'est ce donc que ce Bismarck, Winifred?' Mais elle n'a pas voulu me le dire. Son Bismarck, c'était un mystère.*'

'*Oui, c'est un mysterè, vraiment un mysterè!* Miss Brangwen, say that Bismarck is a mystery,' cried Winifred.

'Bismarck, is a mystery, Bismarck, *c'est un mysterè, der Bismarck, er ist ein Wunder,*' said Gudrun, in mocking incantation.

'*Ja, er ist ein Wunder,*' repeated Winifred, with odd seriousness, under which lay a wicked chuckle.

'*Ist er auch ein Wunder?*' came the slightly insolent sneering of Mademoiselle.

'*Doch!*' said Winifred briefly, indifferent.

'*Doch ist er nicht ein König.* Beesmarck, he was not a king, Winifred, as you have said. He was only – *il n'était que chancelier.*'

'*Qu'est ce qu'un chancelier?*' said Winifred, with slightly contemptuous indifference.

'A chancelier is a chancellor, and a chancellor is, I believe, a sort of judge,' said Gerald, coming up and shaking hands with Gudrun. 'You'll have made a song of Bismarck soon,' said he.

Mademoiselle waited, and discreetly made her inclination, and her greeting.

'So they wouldn't let you see Bismarck, Mademoiselle?' he said.

'*Non, Monsieur.*'

'Ay, very mean of them. What are you going to do to him, Miss Brangwen? I want him sent to the kitchen and cooked.'

'Oh no,' cried Winifred.

'We're going to draw him,' said Gudrun.

'Draw him and quarter him and dish him up,' he said, being purposely fatuous.

'Oh no,' cried Winifred with emphasis, chuckling.

Gudrun detected the tang of mockery in him, and she looked up and smiled into his face. He felt his nerves caressed. Their eyes met in knowledge.

'How do you like Shortlands?' he asked.

'Oh, very much,' she said, with nonchalance.

'Glad you do. Have you noticed these flowers?'

He led her along the path. She followed intently. Winifred came, and the governess lingered in the rear. They stopped before some veined salpiglossis flowers.

'Aren't they wonderful?' she cried, looking at them absorbedly. Strange how her reverential, almost ecstatic admiration of the flowers caressed his nerves. She stooped down, and touched the trumpets, with infinitely fine and delicate-touching finger-tips. It filled him with ease to see her. When she rose, her eyes, hot with the beauty of the flowers, looked into his.

'What are they?' she asked.

'Sort of petunia, I suppose,' he answered. 'I don't really know them.'

'They are quite strangers to me,' she said.

They stood together in a false intimacy, a nervous contact. And he was in love with her.

She was aware of Mademoiselle standing near, like a little French beetle, observant and calculating. She moved away with Winifred, saying they would go back to find Bismarck.

Gerald watched them go, looking all the while at the soft, full, still body of Gudrun, in its silky cashmere. How silky and rich and soft her body must be. An excess of appreciation came over his mind, she was the all-desirable, the all-beautiful. He wanted only to come to her, nothing more. He was only this, this being that should come to her, and be given to her.

At the same time he was finely and acutely aware of Mademoiselle's neat, brittle finality of form. She was like some elegant beetle with thin ankles, perched on her high heels, her glossy black dress perfectly correct, her dark hair done high and admirably. How repulsive her completeness and her finality was! He loathed her.

Yet he did admire her. She was perfectly correct. And it did rather annoy him, that Gudrun came dressed in startling colours, like a macaw, when the family was in mourning. Like a macaw she was! He watched the lingering way she took her feet from the ground. And her ankles were pale yellow, and her dress a deep blue. Yet it pleased him. It pleased him very much. He felt the challenge in her very attire - she challenged the whole world. And he smiled as to the note of a trumpet.

Gudrun and Winifred went through the house to the back, where were the stables and the out-buildings. Everywhere was still and deserted. Mr Crich had gone out for a short drive, the stable-man had just led round Gerald's horse. The two girls went to the hutch that stood in a corner, and looked at the great black-and-white rabbit.

'Isn't he beautiful! Oh, do look at him listening! Doesn't he look silly!' she laughed quickly, then added: 'Oh, do let's do him listening, do let us, he listens with so much of himself; – don't you, darling Bismarck?'

'Can we take him out?' said Gudrun.

'He's very strong. He really is extremely strong.' She looked at Gudrun, her head on one side, in odd calculating mistrust.

'But we'll try, shall we?'

'Yes, if you like. But he's a fearful kicker!'

They took the key to unlock the door. The rabbit exploded in a wild rush round the hutch.

'He scratches most awfully sometimes,' cried Winifred in excitement. 'Oh, do look at him, isn't he wonderful!' The rabbit tore round the hutch in a flurry. 'Bismarck!' cried the child, in rousing excitement. 'How *dreadful* you are! You are beastly.' Winifred looked up at Gudrun with some misgiving in her wild excitement. Gudrun smiled sardonically with her mouth. Winifred made a strange crooning noise of unaccountable excitement. 'Now he's still!' she cried, seeing the rabbit settled down in a far corner of the hutch. 'Shall we take him now?' she whispered excitedly, mysteriously, looking up at Gudrun and edging very close. 'Shall we get him now?—' she chuckled wickedly to herself.

They unlocked the door of the hutch. Gudrun thrust in her arm and seized the great, lusty rabbit as it crouched still, she grasped its long ears. It set its four feet flat, and thrust back. There was a long scraping sound as it was hauled forward, and in another instant it was in mid-air, lunging wildly, its body flying like a spring coiled and released, as it lashed out, suspended from the ears. Gudrun held the black-and-white tempest at arms' length, averting her face. But the rabbit was magically strong, it was all she could do to keep her grap. She almost lost her presence of mind.

'Bismarck, Bismarck, you are behaving terribly,' said Winifred in a rather frightened voice. 'Oh, do put him down, he's beastly.'

Gudrun stood for a moment astounded by the thunderstorm that had sprung into being in her grip. Then her colour came up, a heavy rage came over her like a cloud. She stood shaken as a house in a storm, and utterly overcome. Her heart was arrested with fury at the mindlessness and the bestial stupidity of this struggle, her wrists were badly scored by the claws of the beast, a heavy cruelty welled up in her.

Gerald came round as she was trying to capture the flying rabbit under her arm. He saw, with subtle recognition, her sullen passion of cruelty.

'You should let one of the men do that for you,' he said, hurrying up.

'Oh, he's *so* horrid!' cried Winifred, almost frantic.

He held out his nervous, sinewy hand and took the rabbit by the ears from Gudrun.

'It's most *fearfully* strong,' she cried in a high voice, like the crying of a seagull, strange and vindictive.

The rabbit made itself into a ball in the air and lashed out, flinging itself into a bow. It really seemed demoniacal. Gudrun saw Gerald's body tighten, saw a sharp blindness come into his eyes.

'I know these beggars of old,' he said.

The long, demon-like beast lashed out again, spread on the air as if it were flying, looking something like a dragon, then closing up again, inconceivably powerful and explosive. The man's body, strung to its efforts, vibrated strongly. Then a sudden sharp, white-edged wrath came up in him. Swift as lightning he drew back and brought his free hand down like a hawk on the neck of the rabbit. Simultaneously, there came the unearthly abhorrent scream of a rabbit in the fear of death. It made one immense writhe, tore his wrists and his sleeves in a final convulsion, all its belly flashed white in a whirlwind of paws, and then he had slung it round and had it under his arm, fast. It cowered and skulked. His face was gleaming with a smile.

'You wouldn't think there was all that force in a rabbit,' he said, looking at Gudrun. And he saw her eyes black as night in her pallid face, she looked almost unearthly. The scream of the rabbit, after the violent tussle, seemed to have torn the veil of her consciousness. He looked at her, and the whitish, electric gleam in his face intensified.

'I don't really like him,' Winifred was crooning. 'I don't care for him as I do for Loozie. He's hateful really.'

A smile twisted Gudrun's face as she recovered. She knew she was revealed.

'Don't they make the most fearful noise when they scream?' she cried, the high note in her voice like a seagull's cry.

'Abominable,' he said.

'He shouldn't be so silly when he has to be taken out,' Winifred was saying, putting out her hand and touching the rabbit tentatively, as it skulked under his arm, motionless as if it were dead.

'He's not dead, is he, Gerald?' she asked.

'No, he ought to be,' he said.

'Yes, he ought!' cried the child, with a sudden flush of amusement. And she touched the rabbit with more confidence. 'His heart is beating *so* fast. Isn't he funny? He really is.'

'Where do you want him?' asked Gerald.

'In the little green court,' she said.

Gudrun looked at Gerald with strange, darkened eyes, strained with underworld knowledge, almost supplicating, like those of a creature which is at his mercy, yet which is his ultimate victor. He did not know what to say to her. He felt the mutual hellish recognition. And he felt he ought to say something to cover it. He had the power of lightning in his nerves, she seemed like a soft recipient of his magical, hideous white fire. He was unconfident, he had qualms of fear.

'Did he hurt you?' he asked.

'No,' she said.

'He's an insensible beast,' he said, turning his face away.

They came to the little court, which was shut in by old red walls in whose crevices wallflowers were growing. The grass was soft and fine and old, a level floor carpeting the court, the sky was blue overhead. Gerald tossed the rabbit down. It crouched still and would not move. Gudrun watched it with faint horror.

'Why doesn't it move?' she cried.

'It's skulking,' he said.

She looked up at him, and a slight sinister smile contracted her white face.

'Isn't it a *fool!*' she cried. 'Isn't it a sickening *fool?*' The vindictive mockery in her voice made his brain quiver. Glancing up at him, into his eyes, she revealed again the mocking, white-cruel recognition. There was a league between them, abhorrent to them both. They were implicated with each other in abhorrent mysteries.

'How many scratches have you?' he asked, showing his hard forearm, white and hard and torn in red gashes.

'How really vile!' she cried, flushing with a sinister vision. 'Mine is nothing.'

She lifted her arm and showed a deep red score down the silken white flesh.

'What a devil!' he exclaimed. But it was as if he had had knowledge of her in the long red rent of her forearm, so silken and soft. He did not want to touch her. He would have to make himself touch her, deliberately. The long, shallow red rip seemed torn across his own brain, tearing the surface of his ultimate consciousness, letting through the for ever unconscious, unthinkable red ether of the beyond, the obscene beyond.

'It doesn't hurt you very much, does it?' he asked, solicitous

'Not at all,' she cried.

And suddenly the rabbit, which had been crouching as if it were a flower, so still and soft, suddenly burst into life. Round and round the court it went, as if shot from a gun, round and round like a furry meteorite, in a tense hard circle that seemed to bind their brains. They all stood in amazement, smiling uncannily, as if the rabbit were obeying some unknown incantation. Round and round it flew, on the grass under the old red walls like a storm.

And then quite suddenly it settled down, hobbled among the grass, and sat considering, its nose twitching like a bit of fluff in the wind. After having considered for a few minutes, a soft bunch with a black, open eye, which perhaps was looking at them, perhaps was not, it hobbled calmly forward and began to nibble the grass with that mean motion of a rabbit's quick eating.

'It's mad,' said Gudrun. 'It is most decidedly mad.'

He laughed.

'The question is,' he said, 'what is madness? I don't suppose it is rabbit-mad.'

'Don't you think it is?' she asked.

'No. That's what it is to be a rabbit.'

There was a queer, faint, obscene smile over his face. She looked at him and saw him, and knew that he was initiate as she was initiate. This thwarted her, and contravened her, for the moment.

'God be praised we aren't rabbits,' she said in a high, shrill voice.

The smile intensified a little on his face.

'Not rabbits?' he said, looking at her fixedly.

Slowly her face relaxed into a smile of obscene recognition.

'Ah, Gerald,' she said in a strong, slow, almost man-like way. '—All that, and more.' Her eyes looked up at him with shocking nonchalance.

He felt again as if she had hit him across the face – or rather as if she had torn him across the breast, dully, finally. He turned aside.

'Eat, eat, my darling!' Winifred was softly conjuring the rabbit, and creeping forward to touch it. It hobbled away from her. 'Let its mother stroke its fur then, darling, because it is so mysterious—'

Chapter Nineteen

Moony

After his illness Birkin went to the south of France for a time. He did not write, nobody heard anything of him. Ursula, left alone, felt as if everything were lapsing out. There seemed to be no hope in the world. One was a tiny little rock with the tide of nothingness rising higher and higher. She herself was real, and only herself – just like a rock in a wash of flood-water. The rest was all nothingness. She was hard and indifferent, isolated in herself.

There was nothing for it now, but contemptuous, resistant indifference. All the world was lapsing into a grey wish-wash of nothingness, she had no contact and no connection anywhere. She despised and detested the whole show. From the bottom of her heart, from the bottom of her soul, she despised and detested people, adult people. She loved only children and animals: children she loved passionately, but coldly. They made her want to hug them, to protect them, to give them life. But this very love, based on pity and despair, was only a bondage and a pain to her. She loved best of all the animals, that were single and unsocial as she herself was. She loved the horses and cows in the field. Each was single and to itself, magical. It was not referred away to some detestable social principle. It was incapable of soulfulness and tragedy, which she detested so profoundly.

She could be very pleasant and flattering, almost subservient, to people she met. But no one was taken in. Instinctively each felt her contemptuous mockery of the human being in himself, or herself. She had a profound grudge against the human being. That which the word 'human' stood for was despicable and repugnant to her.

Mostly her heart was closed in this hidden, unconscious strain of contemptuous ridicule. She thought she loved, she thought she was full of love. This was her idea of herself. But the strange brightness of her presence, marvellous radiance of intrinsic vitality, was a luminousness of supreme repudiation, nothing but repudiation.

Yet, at moments, she yielded and softened, she wanted pure love, only pure love. This other, this state of constant unfailing repudiation, was a strain, a suffering also. A terrible desire for pure love overcame her again.

She went out one evening, numbed by this constant essential suffering. Those who are timed for destruction must die now. The knowledge of this reached a finality, a finishing in her. And the finality released her. If fate would carry off in death or downfall all those who were timed to go, why need she trouble, why repudiate any further. She was free of it all, she could seek a new union elsewhere.

Ursula set off to Willey Green, towards the mill. She came to Willey Water. It was almost full again, after its period of emptiness. Then she turned off through the woods. The night had fallen, it was dark. But she forgot to be afraid, she who had such great sources of fear. Among the trees, far from any human beings, there was a sort of magic peace. The more one could find a pure loneliness, with no taint of people, the better one felt. She was in reality terrified, horrified in her apprehension of people.

She started, noticing something on her right hand, between the tree-trunks. It was like a great presence, watching her, dodging her. She started violently. It was only the moon, risen through the thin trees. But it seemed so mysterious, with its white and deathly smile. And there was no avoiding it. Night or day, one could not escape the sinister face, triumphant and radiant like this moon, with a high smile. She hurried on, cowering from the white planet. She would just see the pond at the mill before she went home.

Not wanting to go through the yard, because of the dogs, she turned off along the hill-side to descend on the pond from above. The moon was transcendent over the bare, open space, she suffered from being exposed to it. There was a glimmer of nightly rabbits across the ground. The night was as clear as crystal, and very still. She could hear a distant coughing of a sheep.

So she swerved down to the steep, tree-hidden bank above the pond, where the alders twisted their roots. She was glad to pass into the shade out of the moon. There she stood, at the top of the fallen-away bank, her hand on the rough trunk of a tree, looking at the water, that was perfect in its stillness, floating the moon upon it. But for some reason she disliked it. It did not give her anything. She listened for the hoarse rustle of the sluice. And she wished for something else out of the night, she wanted another night, not this moon-brilliant hardness. She could feel her soul crying out in her, lamenting desolately.

She saw a shadow moving by the water. It would be Birkin. He had come back then, unawares. She accepted it without remark, nothing mattered to her. She sat down among the roots of the alder tree, dim and veiled, hearing the sound of the sluice like dew distilling audibly into the night. The islands were dark and half revealed, the reeds were dark also, only some of them had a little frail fire of reflection. A fish leaped secretly, revealing the light in the pond. This fire of the chill night breaking constantly on to the pure darkness, repelled her. She wished it were perfectly dark, perfectly, and noiseless and without motion. Birkin, small and dark also, his hair tinged with moonlight, wandered nearer. He was quite near, and yet he did not exist to her. He did not know she was there. Supposing he did something he would not wish to be seen doing, thinking he was quite private? But there, what did it matter? What did the small privacies matter? How could it matter, what he did? How can there be any secrets, we are all the same organisms? How can there be any secrecy, when everything is known to all of us?

He was touching unconsciously the dead husks of flowers as he passed by, and talking disconnectedly to himself.

'You can't go away,' he was saying. 'There *is* no away. You only withdraw upon yourself.'

He threw a dead flower-husk on to the water.

'An antiphony – they lie, and you sing back to them. There wouldn't have to be any truth, if there weren't any lies. Then one needn't assert anything—'

He stood still, looking at the water, and throwing upon it the husks of the flowers.

'Cybele – curse her! The accursed Syria Dea! Does one begrudge it her? What else is there—?'

Ursula wanted to laugh loudly and hysterically, hearing his isolated voice speaking out. It was so ridiculous.

He stood staring at the water. Then he stooped and picked up a stone, which he threw sharply at the pond. Ursula was aware of the bright moon leaping and swaying, all distorted, in her eyes. It seemed to shoot out arms of fire like a cuttle-fish, like a luminous polyp, palpitating strongly before her.

And his shadow on the border of the pond was watching for a few moments, then he stooped and groped on the ground. Then again there was a burst of sound, and a burst of brilliant light, the moon had exploded on the water, and was flying asunder in flakes of white and dangerous fire. Rapidly, like white birds, the fires all broken rose across the pond, fleeing in clamorous confusion, battling with the flock of dark waves that were forcing their way in. The furthest waves of light, fleeing out, seemed to be clamouring against the shore for escape, the waves of darkness came in heavily, running under towards the centre. But at the centre, the heart of all, was still a vivid, incandescent quivering of a white moon not quite destroyed, a white body of fire writhing and striving and not even now broken open, not yet violated. It seemed to be drawing itself together with strange, violent pangs, in blind effort. It was getting stronger, it was re-asserting itself, the inviolable moon. And the rays were hastening in in thin lines of light, to return to the strengthened moon, that shook upon the water in triumphant reassumption.

Birkin stood and watched, motionless, till the pond was almost calm, the moon was almost serene. Then, satisfied of so much, he looked for more stones. She felt his invisible tenacity. And in a moment again, the broken lights scattered in explosion over her face, dazzling her; and then, almost immediately, came the second shot. The moon leapt up white and burst through the air. Darts of bright light shot asunder, darkness swept over the centre. There was no moon, only a battlefield of broken lights and shadows, running close together. Shadows, dark and heavy, struck again and again across the place where the heart of the moon had been, obliterating it altogether. The white fragments pulsed up and down, and could not find where to go, apart and brilliant on the water like the petals of a rose that a wind has blown far and wide.

Yet again, they were flickering their way to the centre, finding the path blindly, enviously. And again, all was still, as Birkin and Ursula watched. The waters were loud on the shore. He saw the moon regathering itself insidiously, saw the heart of the rose intertwining vigorously and blindly, calling back the scattered fragments, winning home the fragments, in a pulse and in effort of return.

And he was not satisfied. Like a madness, he must go on. He got large stones, and threw them, one after the other, at the white-burning centre of the moon, till there was nothing but a rocking of hollow noise, and a pond surged up, no moon any more, only a few broken flakes tangled and glittering broadcast in the darkness, without aim or meaning, a darkened confusion, like a black and white kaleidoscope tossed at random. The hollow night was rocking and crashing with noise, and from the sluice came sharp, regular flashes of sound. Flakes of light appeared here and there, glittering tormented among the shadows, far off, in strange places; among the dripping shadow of the willow on the island. Birkin stood and listened and was satisfied.

Ursula was dazed, her mind was all gone. She felt she had fallen to the ground and was spilled out, like water on the earth. Motionless and spent she remained in the gloom. Though even now she was aware, unseeing, that in the darkness was a little tumult of ebbing flakes of light, a cluster dancing secretly in a round, twining and coming steadily together. They were gathering a heart again, they were coming once more into being. Gradually the fragments caught together re-united, heaving, rocking, dancing, falling back as in panic, but working their way home again persistently, making semblance of fleeing away when they had advanced, but always flickering nearer, a little closer to the mark, the cluster growing mysteriously larger and brighter, as gleam after gleam fell in with the whole, until a ragged rose, a distorted, frayed moon was shaking upon the waters again, re-asserted, renewed, trying to recover from its convulsion, to get over the disfigurement and the agitation, to be whole and composed, at peace.

Birkin lingered vaguely by the water. Ursula was afraid that he would stone the moon again. She slipped from her seat and went down to him, saying:

'You won't throw stones at it any more, will you?'

'How long have you been there?'

'All the time. You won't throw any more stones, will you?'

'I wanted to see if I could make it be quite gone off the pond,' he said.

'Yes, it was horrible, really. Why should you hate the moon? It hasn't done you any harm, has it?'

'Was it hate?' he said.

And they were silent for a few minutes.

'When did you come back?' she said.

'To-day.'

'Why did you never write?'

'I could find nothing to say.'

'Why was there nothing to say?'

'I don't know. Why are there no daffodils now?'

'No.'

Again there was a space of silence. Ursula looked at the moon. It had gathered itself together, and was quivering slightly.

'Was it good for you to be alone?' she asked.

'Perhaps. Not that I know much. But I got over a good deal. Did you do anything important?'

'No. I looked at England, and thought I'd done with it.'

'Why England?' he asked in surprise.

'I don't know, it came like that.'

'It isn't a question of nations,' he said. 'France is far worse.'

'Yes, I know. I felt I'd done with it all.'

They went and sat down on the roots of the trees, in the shadow. And being silent, he remembered the beauty of her eyes, which were sometimes filled with light, like spring, suffused with wonderful promise. So he said to her, slowly, with difficulty:

'There is a golden light in you, which I wish you would give me.' It was as if he had been thinking of this for some time.

She was startled, she seemed to leap clear of him. Yet also she was pleased.

'What kind of a light?' she asked.

But he was shy, and did not say any more. So the moment passed for this time. And gradually a feeling of sorrow came over her.

'My life is unfulfilled,' she said.

'Yes,' he answered briefly, not wanting to hear this.

'And I feel as if nobody could ever really love me,' she said.

But he did not answer.

'You think, don't you,' she said slowly, 'that I only want physical things? It isn't true. I want you to serve my spirit.'

'I know you do. I know you don't want physical things by themselves. But, I want you to give me – to give your spirit to me – that golden light which is you – which you don't know – give it me—'

After a moment's silence she replied:

'But how can I, you don't love me! You only want your own ends. You don't want to serve *me*, and yet you want me to serve you. It is so one-sided!'

It was a great effort to him to maintain this conversation, and to press for the thing he wanted from her, the surrender of her spirit.

'It is different,' he said. 'The two kinds of service are so different. I serve you in another way – not through *yourself* – somewhere else. But I want us to be together without bothering about ourselves – to be really together because we *are* together, as if it were a phenomenon, not a thing we have to maintain by our own effort.'

'No,' she said, pondering. 'You are just egocentric. You never have any enthusiasm, you never came out with any spark towards me. You want yourself, really, and your own affairs. And you want me just to be there, to serve you.'

But this only made him shut off from her.

'Ah, well,' he said, 'words make no matter, anyway. The thing *is* between us, or it isn't.'

'You don't even love me,' she cried.

'I do,' he said angrily. 'But I want—' His mind saw again the lovely light of spring transfused through her eyes, as through some wonderful window. And he wanted her to be with him there, in this world of proud indifference. But what was the good of telling her he wanted this company in proud indifference. What was the good of talking, anyway? It must happen beyond the sound of words. It was merely ruinous to try to work her by conviction. This was a paradisal bird that could never be netted, it must fly by itself to the heart.

'I always think I am going to be loved – and then I am let down. You *don't* love me, you know. You don't want to serve me. You only want yourself.'

A shiver of rage went over his veins, at this repeated: 'You don't want to serve me.' All the paradisal disappeared from him.

'No,' he said, irritated, 'I don't want to serve you, because there is nothing there to serve. What you want me to serve is nothing, mere nothing. It isn't even you, it is your mere female quality. And I wouldn't give a straw for your female ego – it's a rag doll.'

'Ha!' she laughed in mockery. 'That's all you think of me, is it? And then you have the impudence to say you love me!'

She rose in anger, to go home.

'You want the paradisal unknowing,' she said, turning round on him as he still sat half visible in the shadow. 'I know what that means, thank you. You want me to be your thing, never to criticise you or to have anything to say for myself. You want me to be a mere *thing* for you! No, thank you! *If* you want that, there are plenty of women who will give it to you. There are plenty of women who will lie down for you to walk over them – *go* to them then, if that's what you want – go to them.'

'No,' he said, outspoken with anger. 'I want you to drop your assertive *will*, your frightened apprehensive self-insistence, that is what I want. I want you to trust yourself so implicitly that you can let yourself go.'

'Let myself go!' she re-echoed in mockery. '*I* can let myself go easily enough. It is you who can't let yourself go, it is you who hang on to yourself as if it were your only treasure. *You – you* are the Sunday school teacher – *You* – you preacher.'

The amount of truth that was in this made him stiff and unheeding of her.

'I don't mean let yourself go in the Dionysic ecstatic way,' he said. 'I know you can do that. But I hate ecstasy, Dionysic or any other. It's like going round in a squirrel cage. I want you not to care about yourself, just to be there and not to care about yourself, not to insist – be glad and sure and indifferent.'

'Who insists?' she mocked. 'Who is it that keeps on insisting? It isn't *me*!'

There was a weary, mocking bitterness in her voice. He was silent for some time.

'I know,' he said. 'While ever either of us insists to the other, we are all wrong. But there we are, the accord doesn't come.'

They sat in stillness under the shadow of the trees by the bank. The night was white around them, they were in the darkness, barely conscious.

Gradually, the stillness and peace came over them. She put her hand tentatively on his. Their hands clasped softly and silently in peace.

'Do you really love me?' she said.

He laughed.

'I call that your war-cry,' he replied, amused.

'Why!' she cried, amused and really wondering.

'Your insistence – Your war-cry – "A Brangwen, A Brangwen" – an old battle-cry. Yours is "Do you love me? Yield knave, or die." '

'No,' she said, pleading, 'not like that. Not like that. But I must know that you love me, mustn't I?'

'Well then, know it and have done with it.'

'But do you?'

'Yes, I do. I love you, and I know it's final. It is final, so why say any more about it.'

She was silent for some moments, in delight and doubt.

'Are you sure?' she said, nestling happily near to him.

'Quite sure – so now have done – accept it and have done.'

She was nestled quite close to him.

'Have done with what?' she murmured happily.

'With bothering,' he said.

She clung nearer to him. He held her close, and kissed her softly, gently. It was such peace and heavenly freedom, just to fold her and kiss her gently, and not to have any thoughts or any desires or any will, just to be still with her, to be perfectly still and together, in a peace that was not sleep, but content in bliss. To be content in bliss, without desire or insistence anywhere, this was heaven: to be together in happy stillness.

For a long time she nestled to him, and he kissed her softly, her hair, her face, her ears, gently, softly, like dew falling. But this warm breath on her ears disturbed her again, kindled the old destructive fire. She cleaved to him, and he could feel his blood changing like quicksilver.

'But we'll be still, shall we?' he said.

'Yes,' she said, as if submissively.

And she continued to nestle against him.

But in a little while she drew away and looked at him.

'I must be going home,' she said.

'Must you – how sad,' he replied.

She leaned forward and put up her mouth to be kissed.

'Are you really sad?' she murmured, smiling.

'Yes,' he said, 'I wish we could stay as we were, always.'

'Always! Do you?' she murmured, as he kissed her. And then, out of a full throat, she crooned: 'Kiss me! Kiss me!' And she cleaved close to him. He kissed her many times. But he too had his idea and his will. He wanted only gentle communion, no other, no passion now. So that soon she drew away, put on her hat and went home.

The next day, however, he felt wistful and yearning. He thought he had been wrong, perhaps. Perhaps he had been wrong to go to her with an idea of what he wanted. Was it really only an idea, or was it the interpretation of a profound yearning? If the latter, how was it he was always talking about sensual fulfilment? The two did not agree very well.

Suddenly he found himself face to face with a situation. It was as simple as this: fatally simple. On the one hand, he knew he did not want a further sensual experience – something deeper, darker, than ordinary life could give. He remembered the African fetishes he had seen at Halliday's so often. There came back to him one, a statuette about two feet high, a tall, slim, elegant figure from West Africa, in dark wood, glossy and suave. It was a woman, with hair dressed high, like a melon-shaped dome. He remembered her vividly: she was one of his soul's intimates. Her body was long and elegant, her face was crushed tiny like a beetle's, she had rows of round heavy collars, like a column of quoits, on her neck. He remembered her: her astonishing cultured elegance, her diminished, beetle face, the astounding long elegant body, on short, ugly legs, with such protuberant buttocks, so weighty and unexpected below her slim long loins. She knew what he himself did not know. She had thousands of years of purely sensual, purely unspiritual knowledge behind her. It must have been thousands of years since her race had died, mystically: that is, since the relation between the senses and the outspoken mind had broken, leaving the experience all in one sort, mystically sensual. Thousands of years ago, that which was imminent in himself must have taken place in these Africans: the goodness, the holiness, the desire for creation and productive happiness must have lapsed, leaving the single impulse for knowledge in one sort, mindless progressive knowledge through the senses, knowledge arrested and ending in the senses, mystic knowledge in disintegration and dissolution, knowledge such as the beetles have, which live purely within the world of corruption and cold dissolution. This was why her face looked like a beetle's: this was why the Egyptians worshipped the ball-rolling scarab: because of the principle of knowledge in dissolution and corruption.

There is a long way we can travel, after the death-break: after that point when the soul in intense suffering breaks, breaks away from its organic hold like a leaf that falls. We fall from the connection with life and hope, we lapse from pure integral being, from creation and liberty, and we fall into the long, long African process of purely sensual understanding, knowledge in the mystery of dissolution.

He realised now that this is a long process – thousands of years it takes, after the death of the creative spirit. He realised that there were great mysteries to be unsealed, sensual, mindless, dreadful mysteries, far beyond the phallic cult. How far, in their inverted culture, had these West Africans gone beyond phallic knowledge? Very, very far. Birkin recalled again the female figure: the elongated, long, long body, the curious unexpected heavy buttocks, the long, imprisoned neck, the face with tiny features like a beetle's. This was far beyond any phallic knowledge, sensual subtle realities far beyond the scope of phallic investigation.

There remained this way, this awful African process, to be fulfilled. It would be done differently by the white races. The white races, having the Arctic north behind them, the vast abstraction of ice and snow, would fulfil a mystery of ice-destructive knowledge, snow-abstract annihilation. Whereas the West Africans, controlled by the burning death-abstraction of the Sahara, had been fulfilled in sun-destruction, the putrescent mystery of sun-rays.

Was this then all that remained? Was there left now nothing but to break off from the happy creative being, was the time up? Is our day of creative life finished? Does there remain to us only the strange, awful afterwards of the knowledge in dissolution, the African knowledge, but different in us, who are blond and blue-eyed from the north?

Birkin thought of Gerald. He was one of these strange white wonderful demons from the north, fulfilled in the destructive frost mystery. And was he fated to pass away in this knowledge, this one process of frost-knowledge, death by perfect cold? Was he a messenger, an omen of the universal dissolution into whiteness and snow?

Birkin was frightened. He was tired too, when he had reached this length of speculation. Suddenly his strange, strained attention gave way, he could not attend to these mysteries any more. There was another way, the way of freedom. There was the paradisal entry into pure, single being, the individual soul taking precedence over love and desire for union, stronger than any pangs of emotion, a lovely state of free proud singleness, which accepted the obligation of the permanent connection with others, and with the other, submits to the yoke and leash of love, but never forfeits its own proud individual singleness, even while it loves and yields.

There was the other way, the remaining way. And he must run to follow it. He thought of Ursula, how sensitive and delicate she really was, her skin so over-fine, as if one skin were wanting. She was really so marvellously gentle and sensitive. Why did he ever forget it? He must go to her at once.

He must ask her to marry him. They must marry at once, and so make a definite pledge, enter into a definite communion. He must set out at once and ask her, this moment. There was no moment to spare.

He drifted on swiftly to Beldover, half unconscious of his own movement. He saw the town on the slope of the hill, not straggling, but as if walled-in with the straight, final streets of miners' dwellings, making a great square, and it looked like Jerusalem to his fancy. The world was all strange and transcendent.

Rosalind opened the door to him. She started slightly, as a young girl will, and said:

'Oh, I'll tell father.'

With which she disappeared, leaving Birkin in the hall, looking at some reproductions from Picasso, lately introduced by Gudrun. He was admiring the almost wizard, sensuous apprehension of the earth, when Will Brangwen appeared, rolling down his shirt-sleeves.

'Well,' said Brangwen, 'I'll get a coat.' And he too disappeared for a moment. Then he returned and opened the door of the drawing-room, saying:

'You must excuse me, I was just doing a bit of work in the shed. Come inside, will you?'

Birkin entered and sat down. He looked at the bright, reddish face of the other man, at the narrow brow and the very bright eyes, and at the rather sensual lips that unrolled wide and expansive under the black cropped moustache. How curious it was that this was a human being! What Brangwen thought himself to be, how meaningless it was, confronted with the reality of him. Birkin could see only a strange, inexplicable, almost patternless collection of passions and desires and suppressions and traditions and mechanical ideas, all cast unfused and disunited into this slender, bright-faced man of nearly fifty, who was as unresolved now as he was at twenty, and as uncreated. How could he be the parent of Ursula, when he was not created himself. He was not a parent. A slip of living flesh had been transmitted through him, but the spirit had not come from him. The spirit had not come from any ancestor, it had come out of the unknown. A child is the child of the mystery, or it is uncreated.

'The weather's not so bad as it has been,' said Brangwen, after waiting a moment. There was no connection between the two men.

'No,' said Birkin. 'It was full moon two days ago.'

'Oh! You believe in the moon then, affecting the weather?'

'No, I don't think I do. I don't really know enough about it.'

'You know what they say? "The moon and the weather may change together, but the change of the moon won't change the weather."'

'Is that it?' said Birkin. 'I hadn't heard it.'

There was a pause. Then Birkin said:

'Am I hindering you? I called to see Ursula, really. Is she at home?'

'I don't believe she is. I believe she's gone to the library. I'll just see.'

Birkin could hear him inquiring in the dining-room.

'No,' he said, coming back. 'But she won't be long. You wanted to speak to her?'

Birkin looked across at the other man with curious calm, clear eyes.

'As a matter of fact,' he said, 'I wanted to ask her to marry me.'

A point of light came in the golden-brown eyes of the elder man.

'O-oh?' he said, looking at Birkin, then dropping his eyes before the calm, steadily watching look of the other. 'Was she expecting you then?'

'No,' said Birkin.

'No? I didn't know anything of this sort was on foot—' Brangwen smiled awkwardly.

Birkin looked back at him, and said to himself: 'I wonder why it should be "on foot"!' Aloud he said:

'No, it's perhaps rather sudden.' At which, thinking of his relationship with Ursula, he added – 'but I don't know—'

'Quite sudden, is it? Oh!' said Brangwen, rather baffled and annoyed.

'In one way,' replied Birkin, '—not in another.'

There was a moment's pause, after which Brangwen said:

'Well, she pleases herself—'

'Oh yes!' said Birkin calmly.

A vibration came into Brangwen's strong voice as he replied:

'Though I shouldn't want her to be in too big a hurry, either. It's no good looking round afterwards, when it's too late.'

'Oh, it need never be too late,' said Birkin, 'as far as that goes.'

'How do you mean?' asked the father.

'If one repents being married, the marriage is at an end,' said Birkin.

'You think so?'

'Yes.'

'Ay, well, that may be your way of looking at it.'

Birkin, in silence, thought to himself: 'So it may. As for *your* way of looking at it, William Brangwen, it needs a little explaining.'

'I suppose,' said Brangwen, 'you know what sort of people we are? What sort of a bringing-up she's had?'

' "She" ' thought Birkin to himself, remembering his childhood's corrections, 'is the cat's mother.'

'Do I know what sort of a bringing-up she's had?' he said aloud.

He seemed to annoy Brangwen intentionally.

'Well,' he said, 'she's had everything that's right for a girl to have – as far as possible, as far as we could give it her.'

'I'm sure she has,' said Birkin, which caused a perilous full-stop. The father was becoming exasperated. There was something naturally irritant to him in Birkin's mere presence.

'And I don't want to see her going back on it all,' he said, in a clanging voice.

'Why?' said Birkin.

This monosyllable exploded in Brangwen's brain like a shot.

'Why! *I* don't believe in your new-fangled ways and new-fangled ideas – in and out like a frog in a gallipot. It would never do for me.'

Birkin watched him with steady emotionless eyes. The radical antagonism in the two men was rousing.

'Yes, but are my ways and ideas new-fangled?' asked Birkin.

'Are they?' Brangwen caught himself up. 'I'm not speaking of you in

particular,' he said. 'What I mean is that my children have been brought up
to think and do according to the religion I was brought up in myself, and
I don't want to see them going away from *that*.'

There was a dangerous pause.

'And beyond that—?' asked Birkin.

The father hesitated, he was in a nasty position.

'Eh? What do you mean? All I want to say is that my daughter' – he
tailed off into silence, overcome by futility. He knew that in some way he
was off the track.

'Of course,' said Birkin, 'I don't want to hurt anybody or influence
anybody. Ursula does exactly as she pleases.'

There was a complete silence, because of the utter failure in mutual
understanding. Birkin felt bored. Her father was not a coherent human
being, he was a roomful of old echoes. The eyes of the younger man rested
on the face of the elder. Brangwen looked up, and saw Birkin looking at
him. His face was covered with inarticulate anger and humiliation and sense
of inferiority in strength.

'And as for beliefs, that's one thing,' he said. 'But I'd rather see my
daughters dead to-morrow than that they should be at the beck and call of
the first man that likes to come and whistle for them.'

A queer painful light came into Birkin's eyes.

'As to that,' he said, 'I only know that it's much more likely that it's I
who am the beck and call of the woman, than she at mine.'

Again there was a pause. The father was somewhat bewildered.

'I know,' he said, 'she'll please herself – she always has done. I've done
my best for them, but that doesn't matter. They've got themselves to please,
and if they can help it they'll please nobody *but* themselves. But she's a right
to consider her mother, and me as well—'

Brangwen was thinking his own thoughts.

'And I tell you this much, I would rather bury them than see them getting
into a lot of loose ways such as you see everywhere nowadays. I'd rather
bury them—'

'Yes, but, you see,' said Birkin slowly, rather wearily, bored again by this
new turn, 'they won't give either you or me the chance to bury them, because
they're not to be buried.'

Brangwen looked at him in a sudden flare of impotent anger.

'Now, Mr. Birkin,' he said, 'I don't know what you've come here for, and
I don't know what you're asking for. But my daughters are my daughters
– and it's *my* business to look after them while I can.'

Birkin's brows knitted suddenly, his eyes concentrated in mockery. But
he remained perfectly stiff and calm. There was a pause.

'I've nothing against your marrying Ursula,' Brangwen began at length.
'It's got nothing to do with me, she'll do as she likes, me or no me.'

Birkin turned away, looking out of the window and letting go his
consciousness. After all, what good was this? It was hopeless to keep it up.
He would sit on till Ursula came home, then speak to her, then go away.
He would not accept trouble at the hands of her father. It was all unnecessary,
and he himself need not have provoked it.

The two men sat in complete silence, Birkin almost unconscious of his own whereabouts. He had come to ask her to marry him – well then, he would wait on, and ask her. As for what she said, whether she accepted or not, he did not think about it. He would say what he had come to say, and that was all he was conscious of. He accepted the complete insignificance of this household for him. But everything now was as if fated. He could see one thing ahead, and no more. From the rest, he was absolved entirely for the time being. It had to be left to fate and chance to resolve the issues.

At length they heard the gate. They saw her coming up the steps with a bundle of books under her arm. Her face was bright and abstracted as usual, with the abstraction, that look of being not quite *there*, not quite present to the facts of reality, that galled her father so much. She had a maddening faculty of assuming a light of her own, which excluded the reality, and within which she looked radiant as if in sunshine.

They heard her go into the dining-room and drop her armful of books on the table.

'Did you bring me that Girl's Own?' cried Rosalind.

'Yes, I brought it. But I forgot which one it was you wanted.'

'You would,' cried Rosalind angrily. 'It's right for a wonder.'

Then they heard her say something in a lowered tone.

'Where?' cried Ursula.

Again her sister's voice was muffled.

Brangwen opened the door and called in his strong, brazen voice:

'Ursula.'

She appeared in a moment, wearing her hat.

'Oh, how do you do!' she cried, seeing Birkin, and all dazzled as if taken by surprise. He wondered at her, knowing she was aware of his presence. She had her queer, radiant, breathless manner, as if confused by the actual world, unreal to it, having a complete bright world of her self alone.

'Have I interrupted a conversation?' she asked.

'No, only a complete silence,' said Birkin.

'Oh,' said Ursula vaguely, absent. Their presence was not vital to her, she was withheld, she did not take them in. It was a subtle insult that never failed to exasperate her father.

'Mr. Birkin came to speak to *you*, not to me,' said her father.

'Oh, did he!' she exclaimed vaguely, as if it did not concern her. Then, recollecting herself, she turned to him rather radiantly, but still quite superficially, and said: 'Was it anything special?'

'I hope so,' he said ironically.

'—To propose to you, according to all accounts,' said her father.

'Oh,' said Ursula.

'Oh,' mocked her father, imitating her. 'Have you nothing more to say?'

She winced as if violated.

'Did you really come to propose to me?' she asked of Birkin, as if it were a joke.

'Yes,' he said. 'I suppose I came to propose.' He seemed to fight shy of the last word.

'Did you?' she cried, with her vague radiance. He might have been saying anything whatsoever. She seemed pleased.

'Yes,' he answered. 'I wanted to – I wanted you to agree to marry me.'

She looked at him. His eyes were flickering with mixed lights, wanting something of her, yet not wanting it. She shrank a little, as if she were exposed to his eyes, and as if it were a pain to her. She darkened, her soul clouded over, she turned aside. She had been driven out of her own radiant, single world. And she dreaded contact, it was almost unnatural to her at these times.

'Yes,' she said vaguely, in a doubting, absent voice.

Birkin's heart contracted swiftly, in a sudden fire of bitterness. It all meant nothing to her. He had been mistaken again. She was in some self-satisfied world of her own. He and his hopes were accidentals, violations to her. It drove her father to a pitch of mad exasperation. He had had to put up with this all his life from her.

'Well, what do you say?' he cried.

She winced. Then she glanced down at her father, half frightened, and she said:

'I didn't speak, did I?' as if she were afraid she might have committed herself.

'No,' said her father, exasperated. 'But you needn't look like an idiot. You've got your wits, haven't you?'

She ebbed away in silent hostility.

'I've got my wits, what does that mean?' she repeated in a sullen voice of antagonism.

'You heard what was asked you, didn't you?' cried her father in anger.

'Of course I heard.'

'Well then, can't you answer?' thundered her father.

'Why should I?'

At the impertinence of this retort, he went stiff. But he said nothing.

'No,' said Birkin, to help out the occasion, 'there's no need to answer at once. You can say when you like.'

Her eyes flashed with a powerful light.

'Why should I say anything?' she cried. 'You do this off your *own* bat, it has nothing to do with me. Why do you both want to bully me?'

'Bully you! Bully you!' cried her father in bitter, rancorous anger. 'Bully you! Why, it's a pity you can't be bullied into some sense and decency. Bully you! *You'll* see to that, you self-willed creature.'

She stood suspended in the middle of the room, her face glimmering and dangerous. She was set in satisfied defiance. Birkin looked up at her. He too was angry.

'But no one is bullying you,' he said in a very soft dangerous voice also.

'Oh yes' she cried. 'You both want to force me into something.'

'That is an illusion of yours,' he said ironically.

'Illusion!' cried her father. 'A self-opinionated fool, that's what she is.'

Birkin rose, saying:

'However, we'll leave it for the time being.'

And without another word, he walked out of the house.

'You fool! You fool!' her father cried to her, with extreme bitterness. She left the room, and went upstairs, singing to herself. But she was terribly fluttered, as after some dreadful fight. From her window, she could see Birkin going up the road. He went in such a blithe drift of rage that her mind wondered over him. He was ridiculous, but she was afraid of him. She was as if escaped from some danger.

Her father sat below, powerless in humiliation and chagrin. It was as if he were possessed with all the devils, after one of these unaccountable conflicts with Ursula. He hated her as if his only reality were in hating her to the last degree. He had all hell in his heart. But he went away, to escape himself. He knew he must despair, yield, give in to despair, and have done.

Ursula's face closed, she completed herself against them all. Recoiling upon herself, she became hard and self-completed, like a jewel. She was bright and invulnerable, quite free and happy, perfectly liberated in her self-possession. Her father had to learn not to see her blithe obliviousness, or it would have sent him mad. She was so radiant with all things in her possession of perfect hostility.

She would go on now for days like this, in this bright frank state of seemingly pure spontaneity, so essentially oblivious of the existence of anything but herself, but so ready and facile in her interest. Ah, it was a bitter thing for a man to be near her, and her father cursed his fatherhood. But he must learn not to see her, not to know.

She was perfectly stable in resistance when she was in this state: so bright and radiant and attractive in her pure opposition, so very pure, and yet mistrusted by everybody, disliked on every hand. It was her voice, curiously clear and repellent, that gave her away. Only Gudrun was in accord with her. It was at these times that the intimacy between the two sisters was most complete, as if their intelligence were one. They felt a strong, bright bond of understanding between them, surpassing everything else. And during all these days of blind bright abstraction and intimacy of his two daughters, the father seemed to breathe an air of death, as if he were destroyed in his very being. He was irritable to madness, he could not rest, his daughters seemed to be destroying him. But he was inarticulate and helpless against them. He was forced to breathe the air of his own death. He cursed them in his soul, and only wanted that they should be removed from him.

They continued radiant in their easy female transcendency, beautiful to look at. They exchanged confidences, they were intimate in their revelations to the last degree, giving each other at last every secret. They withheld nothing, they told everything, till they were over the border of evil. And they armed each other with knowledge, they extracted the subtlest flavours from the apple of knowledge. It was curious how their knowledge was complementary, that of each to that of the other.

Ursula saw her men as sons, pitied their yearning and admired their courage, and wondered over them as a mother wonders over her child, with a certain delight in their novelty. But to Gudrun, they were the opposite camp. She feared them and despised them, and respected their activities even overmuch.

'Of course,' she said easily, 'there is a quality of life in Birkin which is quite remarkable. There is an extraordinary rich spring of life in him, really amazing, the way he can give himself to things. But there are so many things in life that he simply doesn't know. Either he is not aware of their existence at all, or he dismisses them as merely negligible – things which are vital to the other person. In a way, he is not clever enough, he is too intense in spots.'

'Yes,' cried Ursula, 'too much of a preacher. He is really a priest.'

'Exactly! He can't hear what anybody else has to say – he simply cannot hear. His own voice is so loud.'

'Yes. He cries you down.'

'He cries you down,' repeated Gudrun. 'And by mere force of violence. And of course it is hopeless. Nobody is convinced by violence. It makes talking to him impossible – and living with him I should think would be more than impossible.'

'You don't think one could live with him?' asked Ursula.

'I think it would be too wearing, too exhausting. One would be shouted down every time, and rushed into his way without any choice. He would want to control you entirely. He cannot allow that there is any other mind than his own. And then the real clumsiness of his mind is its lack of self-criticism. No, I think it would be perfectly intolerable.'

'Yes,' assented Ursula vaguely. She only half agreed with Gudrun. 'The nuisance is,' she said, 'that one would find almost any man intolerable after a fortnight.'

'It's perfectly dreadful,' said Gudrun. 'But Birkin – he is too positive. He couldn't bear it if you called your soul your own. Of him that is strictly true.'

'Yes,' said Ursula. 'You must have *his* soul.'

'Exactly! And what can you conceive more deadly?' This was all so true, that Ursula felt jarred to the bottom of her soul with ugly distaste.

She went on, with the discord jarring and jolting through her, in the most barren of misery.

Then there started a revulsion from Gudrun. She finished life off so thoroughly, she made things so ugly and so final. As a matter of fact, even if it were as Gudrun said, about Birkin, other things were true as well. But Gudrun would draw two lines under him and cross him out like an account that is settled. There he was, summed up, paid for, settled, done with. And it was such a lie. This finality of Gudrun's, this dispatching of people and things in a sentence, it was all such a lie. Ursula began to revolt from her sister.

One day as they were walking along the lane, they saw a robin sitting on the top twig of a bush, singing shrilly. The sisters stood to look at him. An ironical smile flickered on Gudrun's face.

'Doesn't he feel important?' smiled Gudrun.

'Doesn't he!' exclaimed Ursula, with a little ironical grimace. 'Isn't he a little Lloyd George of the air?'

'Isn't he! Little Lloyd George of the air! That's just what they are,' cried Gudrun in delight. Then for days, Ursual saw the persistent, obtrusive birds as stout, short politicians lifting up their voices from the platform, little men who must make themselves heard at any cost.

But even from this there came the revulsion. Some yellow-hammers suddenly shot along the road in front of her. And they looked to her so uncanny and inhuman, like flaring yellow barbs shooting through the air on some weird, living errand, that she said to herself: 'After all, it is impudence to call them little Lloyd Georges. They are really unknown to us, they are the unknown forces. It is impudence to look at them as if they were the same as human beings. They are of another world. How stupid anthropomorphism is! Gudrun is really impudent, insolent, making herself the measure of everything, making everything come down to human standards. Rupert is quite right, human beings are boring, painting the universe with their own image. The universe is non-human, thank God.' It seemed to her irreverence, destructive of all true life, to make little Lloyd Georges of the birds. It was such a lie towards the robins, and such a defamation. Yet she had done it herself. But under Gudrun's influence: so she exonerated herself.

So she withdrew away from Gudrun and from that which she stood for, she turned in spirit towards Birkin again. She had not seen him since the fiasco of his proposal. She did not want to, because she did not want the question of her acceptance thrust upon her. She knew what Birkin meant when he asked her to marry him; vaguely, without putting it into speech, she knew. She knew what kind of love, what kind of surrender he wanted. And she was not at all sure that it was the kind of love she herself wanted. She was not at all sure that it was this mutual unison in separateness that she wanted. She wanted unspeakable intimacies. She wanted to have him, utterly, finally to have him as her own, oh, so unspeakably, in intimacy. To drink him down – ah, like a life-draught. She made great professions, to herself, of her willingness to warm his foot-soles between her breasts, after the fashion of that nauseous Meredith poem. But only on condition that he, her lover, loved her absolutely, with complete self-abandon. And subtly enough, she knew he would never abandon himself *finally* to her. He did not believe in final self-abandonment. He said it openly. It was his challenge. She was prepared to fight him for it. For she believed in an absolute surrender to love. She believed that love far surpassed the individual. He said the individual was *more* than love, or than any relationship. For him, the bright, single soul accepted love as one of its conditions, a condition of its own equilibrium. She believed that love was *everything*. Man must render himself up to her. He must be quaffed to the dregs by her. Let him be *her man* utterly, and she in return would be his humble slave – whether she wanted it or not.

Chapter Twenty

Gladiatorial

After the fiasco of the proposal, Birkin had hurried blindly away from Beldover, in a whirl of fury. He felt he had been a complete fool, that the whole scene had been a farce of the first water. But that did not trouble him at all. He was deeply, mockingly angry that Ursula persisted always in this old cry: 'Why do you want to bully me?' and in her bright, insolent abstraction.

He went straight to Shortlands. There he found Gerald standing with his back to the fire, in the library, as motionless as a man is who is completely and emptily restless, utterly hollow. He had done all the work he wanted to do – and now there was nothing. He could go out in the car, he could run to town. But he did not want to go out in the car, he did not want to run to town, he did not want to call on the Thirlbys. He was suspended motionless, in an agony of inertia, like a machine that is without power.

This was very bitter to Gerald, who had never known what boredom was, who had gone from activity to activity, never at a loss. Now, gradually, everything seemed to be stopping in him. He did not want any more to do the things that offered. Something dead within him just refused to respond to any suggestion. He cast over in his mind what it would be possible to do to save himself from this misery of nothingness, relieve the stress of this hollowness. And there were only three things left that would rouse him, make him live. One was to drink or smoke hashish, the other was to be soothed by Birkin, and the third was women. And there was no one for the moment to drink with. Nor was there a woman. And he knew Birkin was out. So there was nothing to do but to bear the stress of his own emptiness.

When he saw Birkin his face lit up in a sudden, wonderful smile.

'By God, Rupert,' he said, 'I'd just come to the conclusion that nothing in the world mattered except somebody to take the edge off one's being alone: the right somebody.'

The smile in his eyes was very astonishing as he looked at the other man. It was the pure gleam of relief. His face was pallid and even haggard.

'The right woman, I suppose you mean,' said Birkin spitefully.

'Of course, for choice. Failing that, an amusing man.'

He laughed as he said it. Birkin sat down near the fire.

'What were you doing?' he asked.

'I? Nothing. I'm in a bad way just now, everything's on edge, and I can neither work nor play. I don't know whether it's a sign of old age, I'm sure.'

'You mean you are bored?'

'Bored, I don't know. I can't apply myself. And I feel the devil is either very present inside me or dead.'

Birkin glanced up and looked in his eyes.

'You should try hitting something,' he said.

Gerald smiled.

'Perhaps,' he said. 'So long as it was something worth hitting.'

'Quite!' said Birkin in his soft voice. There was a long pause during which each could feel the presence of the other.

'One has to wait,' said Birkin.

'Ah, God! Waiting! What are we waiting for?'

'Some old Johnny says there are three cures for *ennui*, sleep, drink, and travel,' said Birkin.

'All cold eggs,' said Gerald. 'In sleep, you dream, in drink you curse, and in travel you yell at a porter. No, work and love are the two. When you're not at work you should be in love.'

'Be it then,' said Birkin.

'Give me the object,' said Gerald. 'The possibilities of love exhaust themselves.'

'Do they? And then what?'

'Then you die,' said Gerald.

'So you ought,' said Birkin.

'I don't see it,' replied Gerald. He took his hands out of his trousers pockets and reached for a cigarette. He was tense and nervous. He lit the cigarette over a lamp, reaching forward and drawing steadily. He was dressed for dinner, as usual in the evening, although he was alone.

'There's a third one even to your two,' said Birkin. 'Work, love, and fighting. You forget the fight.'

'I suppose I do,' said Gerald. 'Did you ever do any boxing—?'

'No, I don't think I did,' said Birkin.

'Ay—' Gerald lifted his head and blew the smoke slowly into the air.

'Why?' said Birkin.

'Nothing. I thought we might have a round. It is perhaps true that I want something to hit. It's a suggestion.'

'So you think you might as well hit me?' said Birkin.

'You? Well—! Perhaps—! In a friendly kind of way, of course.'

'Quite!' said Birkin bitingly.

Gerald stood leaning back against the mantelpiece. He looked down at Birkin, and his eyes flashed with a sort of terror like the eyes of a stallion, that are bloodshot and overwrought, turned glancing backwards in a stiff terror.

'I feel that if I don't watch myself, I shall find myself doing something silly,' he said.

'Why not do it?' said Birkin coldly.

Gerald listened with quick impatience. He kept glancing down at Birkin, as if looking for something from the other man.

'I used to do some Japanese wrestling,' said Birkin. 'A Jap lived in the same house with me in Heidelberg, and he taught me a little. But I was never much good at it.'

'You did!' exclaimed Gerald. 'That's one of the things I've never ever seen done. You mean jiu-jitsu, I suppose?'

'Yes. But I am no good at those things – they don't interest me.'

'They don't? They do me. What's the start?'

'I'll show you what I can, if you like,' said Birkin.

'You will?' A queer, smiling look tightened Gerald's face for a moment as he said, 'Well, I'd like it very much.'

'Then we'll try jiu-jitsu. Only you can't do much in a starched shirt.'

'Then let us strip, and do it properly. Hold a minute—' He rang the bell and waited for the butler.

'Bring a couple of sandwiches and a syphon,' he said to the man, 'and then don't trouble me any more tonight – or let anybody else.'

The man went. Gerald turned to Birkin with his eyes lighted.

'And you used to wrestle with a Jap?' he said. 'Did you strip?'

'Sometimes.'

'You did! What was he like then as a wrestler?'

'Good, I believe. I am no judge. He was very quick and slippery and full of electric fire. It is a remarkable thing what a curious sort of fluid force they seem to have in them, those people – not like a human grip – like a polyp—'

Gerald nodded.

'I should imagine so,' he said, 'to look at them. They repel me, rather.'

'Repel and attract, both. They are very repulsive when they are cold, and they look grey. But when they are hot and roused, there is a definite attraction – a curious kind of full electric fluid – like eels.'

'Well—, yes—, probably.'

The man brought in the tray and set it down.

'Don't come in any more,' said Gerald.

The door closed.

'Well then,' said Gerald; 'shall we strip and begin? Will you have a drink first?'

'No, I don't want one.'

'Neither do I.'

Gerald fastened the door and pushed the furniture aside. The room was large, there was plenty of space, it was thickly carpeted. Then he quickly threw off his clothes and waited for Birkin. The latter, white and thin, came over to him. Birkin was more a presence than a visible object; Gerald was aware of him completely, but not really visually. Whereas Gerald himself was concrete and noticeable, a piece of pure final substance.

'Now,' said Birkin, 'I will show you what I learned and what I remember. You let me take you so—' And his hands closed on the naked body of the other man. In another moment, he had Gerald swung over lightly and balanced against his knee, head downwards. Relaxed, Gerald sprang to his feet with eyes glittering.

'That's smart,' he said. 'Now try again.'

So the two men began to struggle together. They were very dissimilar. Birkin was tall and narrow, his bones were very thin and fine. Gerald was much heavier and more plastic. His bones were strong and round, his limbs were rounded, all his contours were beautifully and fully moulded. He seemed to stand with a proper, rich weight on the face of the earth, whilst Birkin seemed to have the centre of gravitation in his own middle. And Gerald had a rich, frictional kind of strength, rather mechanical, but sudden and invincible, whereas Birkin was abstract as to be almost intangible. He impinged invisibly upon the other man, scarcely seeming to touch him, like a garment, and then suddenly piercing in a tense fine grip that seemed to penetrate into the very quick of Gerald's being.

They stopped, they discussed methods, they practised grips and throws, they became accustomed to each other, to each other's rhythm, they got a kind of mutual physical understanding. And then again they had a real struggle. They seemed to drive their white flesh deeper and deeper against each other, as if they would break into a oneness. Birkin had a great subtle energy, that would press upon the other man with an uncanny force, weigh him like a spell put upon him. Then it would pass, and Gerald would heave free, with white, heaving, dazzling movements.

So the two men entwined and wrestled with each other, working nearer and nearer. Both were white and clear, but Gerald flushed smart red where he was touched, and Birkin remained white and tense. He seemed to penetrate into Gerald's more solid, more diffuse bulk, to interfuse his body through the body of the other, as if to bring it subtly into subjection, always seizing with some rapid necromantic foreknowledge every motion of the other flesh, converting and counteracting it, playing upon the limbs and trunk of Gerald like some hard wind. It was as if Birkin's whole physical intelligence interpenetrated into Gerald's body, as if his fine, sublimated energy entered into the flesh of the fuller man, like some potency, casting a fine net, a prison, through the muscles into the very depths of Gerald's physical being.

So they wrestled swiftly, rapturously, intent and mindless at last, two essential white figures working into a tighter, closer oneness of struggle, with a strange, octopus-like knotting and flashing of limbs in the subdued light of the room; a tense white knot of flesh gripped in silence between the walls of old brown books. Now and again came a sharp gasp of breath, or a sound like a sigh, then the rapid thudding of movement on the thickly-carpeted floor, then the strange sound of flesh escaping under flesh. Often, in the white interlaced knot of violent living being that swayed silently, there was no head to be seen, only the swift, tight limbs, the solid white backs, the physical junction of two bodies clinched into oneness. Then would appear the gleaming, ruffled head of Gerald, as the struggle changed, then for a moment the dun-coloured, shadow-like head of the other man would lift up from the conflict, the eyes wide and dreadful and sightless.

At length Gerald lay back inert on the carpet, his breast rising in great slow panting, whilst Birkin kneeled over him, almost unconscious. Birkin was much more exhausted. He caught little, short breaths, he could scarcely breathe any more. The earth seemed to tilt and sway, and a complete darkness was coming over his mind. He did not know what happened. He slid forward quite unconscious over Gerald, and Gerald did not notice. Then he was half conscious again, aware only of the strange tilting and sliding of the world. The world was sliding, everything was sliding off into the darkness. And he was sliding, endlessly, endlessly away.

He came to consciousness again, hearing an immense knocking outside. What could be happening, what was it, the great hammer-stroke resounding through the house? He did not know. And then it came to him that it was his own heart beating. But that seemed impossible, the noise was outside. No, it was inside himself, it was his own heart. And the beating was painful, so strained, surcharged. He wondered if Gerald heard it. He did not know whether he were standing or lying or falling.

When he realised that he had fallen prostrate upon Gerald's body he wondered, he was surprised. But he sat up, steadying himself with his hand and waiting for his heart to become stiller and less painful. It hurt very much, and took away his consciousness.

Gerald, however, was still less conscious than Birkin. They waited dimly, in a sort of not-being, for many uncounted, unknown minutes.

'Of course—' panted Gerald, 'I didn't have to be rough – with you – I had to keep back – my force—'

Birkin heard the sound as if his own spirit stood behind him, outside him, and listened to it. His body was in a trance of exhaustion, his spirit heard thinly. His body could not answer. Only he knew his heart was getting quieter. He was divided entirely between his spirit, which stood outside, and knew, and his body, that was a plunging, unconscious stroke of blood.

'I could have thrown you – using violence—' panted Gerald. 'But you beat me right enough.'

'Yes,' said Birkin, hardening his throat and producing the words in the tension there, 'you're much stronger than I – you could beat me – easily.'

Then he relaxed again to the terrible plunging of his heart and his blood.

'It surprised me,' panted Gerald, 'what strength you've got. Almost supernatural.'

'For a moment,' said Birkin.

He still heard as if it were his own disembodied spirit hearing, standing at some distance behind him. It drew nearer, however, his spirit. And the violent striking of blood in his chest was sinking quieter, allowing his mind to come back. He realised that he was leaning with all his weight on the soft body of the other man. It startled him, because he thought he had withdrawn. He recovered himself and sat up. But he was still vague and unestablished. He put out his hand to steady himself. It touched the hand of Gerald, that was lying out on the floor. And Gerald's hand closed warm and sudden over Birkin's, they remained exhausted and breathless, the one hand clasped closely over the other. It was Birkin whose hand, in swift response, had closed in a strong, warm clasp over the hand of the other. Gerald's clasp had been sudden and momentaneous.

The normal consciousness, however, was returning, ebbing back. Birkin could breathe almost naturally again. Gerald's hand slowly withdrew, Birkin slowly, dazedly rose to his feet and went towards the table. He poured out a whisky and soda. Gerald also came for a drink.

'It was a real set-to, wasn't it?' said Birkin, looking at Gerald with darkened eyes.

'God, yes,' said Gerald. He looked at the delicate body of the other man, and added? 'It wasn't too much for you, was it?'

'No. One ought to wrestle and strive and be physically close. It makes one sane.'

'You do think so.'

'I do. Don't you?'

'Yes,' said Gerald.

There were long spaces of silence between their words. The wrestling had some deep meaning to them – an unfinished meaning.

'We are mentally, spiritually intimate, therefore we should be more or less physically intimate too – it is more whole.'

'Certainly it is,' said Gerald. Then he laughed pleasantly adding: 'It's rather wonderful to me.' He stretched out his arms handsomely.

'Yes,' said Birkin. 'I don't know why one should have to justify oneself.'

'No.'

The two men began to dress.

'I think also that you are beautiful,' said Birkin to Gerald, 'and that is enjoyable too. One should enjoy what is given.'

'You think I am beautiful – how do you mean, physically?' asked Gerald, his eyes glistening.

'Yes. You have a northern kind of beauty, like light refracted from snow – and a beautiful, plastic form. Yes, that is there to enjoy as well. We should enjoy everything.'

Gerald laughed in his throat, and said

'That's certainly one way of looking at it. I can say this much, I feel better. It has certainly helped me. Is this the *Bruderschaft* you wanted?'

'Perhaps. Do you think this pledges anything?'

'I don't know,' laughed Gerald.

'At any rate, one feels freer and more open now – and that is what we want.'

'Certainly,' said Gerald.

They drew to the fire, with the decanters and the glasses and the food.

'I always eat a little before I go to bed,' said Gerald. 'I sleep better.'

'I should not sleep so well,' said Birkin.

'No? There you are, we are not alike. I'll put a dressing-gown on.' Birkin remained alone, looking at the fire. His mind had reverted to Ursula. She seemed to return again into his consciousness. Gerald came down wearing a gown of broad-barred, thick black-and-green silk, brilliant and striking.

'You are very fine,' said Birkin, looking at the full robe.

'It was a caftan in Bokhara,' said Gerald. 'I like it.'

'I like it too.'

Birkin was silent, thinking how scrupulous Gerald was in his attire, how expensive too. He wore silk socks, and studs of fine workmanship, and silk underclothing, and silk braces. Curious! This was another of the differences between them. Birkin was careless and unimaginative about his own appearance.

'Of course you,' said Gerald, as if he had been thinking; 'there's something curious about you. You're curiously strong. One doesn't expect it, it is rather surprising.'

Birkin laughed. He was looking at the handsome figure of the other man, blond and comely in the rich robe, and he was half thinking of the difference between it and himself – so different; as far, perhaps, apart as man from woman, yet in another direction. But really it was Ursula, it was the woman who was gaining ascendance over Birkin's being at this moment. Gerald was becoming dim again, lapsing out of him.

'Do you know,' he said suddenly, 'I went and proposed to Ursula Brangwen to-night, that she should marry me.'

He saw the blank shining wonder come over Gerald's face.

'You did?'

'Yes. Almost formally – speaking first to her father, as it should be, in the world – though that was accident – or mischief.'

Gerald only stared in wonder, as if he did not grasp.

'You don't mean to say that you seriously went and asked her father to let you marry her?'

'Yes,' said Birkin, 'I did.'

'What, had you spoken to her before about it, then?'

'No, not a word. I suddenly thought I would go there and ask her – and her father happened to come instead of her – so I asked him first.'

'If you could have her?' concluded Gerald.

'Ye-es, that.'

'And you didn't speak to her?'

'Yes. She came in afterwards. So it was put to her as well.'

'It was! And what did she say then? You're an engaged man?'

'No – she only said she didn't want to be bullied into answering.'

'She what?'

'Said she didn't want to be bullied into answering.'

' "Said she didn't want to be bullied into answering!" Why, what did she mean by that?'

Birkin raised his shoulders. 'Can't say,' he answered. 'Didn't want to be bothered just then, I suppose.'

'But is this really so? And what did you do then?'

'I walked out of the house and came here.'

'You came straight here?'

'Yes.'

Gerald stared in amazement and amusement. He could not take it in.

'But is this really true, as you say it now?'

'Word for word.'

'It is?'

He leaned back in his chair, filled with delight and amusement.

'Well, that's good,' he said. 'And so you came here to wrestle with your good angel, did you?'

'Did I?' said Birkin.

'Well, it looks like it. Isn't that what you did?'

Now Birkin could not follow Gerald's meaning.

'And what's going to happen?' said Gerald. 'You're going to keep open the proposition, so to speak.'

'I suppose so. I vowed to myself I would see them all to the devil. But I suppose I shall ask her again, in a little while.'

Gerald watched him steadily.

'So you're fond of her then?' he asked.

'I think – I love her,' said Birkin, his face going very still and fixed.

Gerald glistened for a moment with pleasure, as if it were something done specially to please him. Then his face assumed a fitting gravity, and he nodded his head slowly.

'You know,' he said, 'I always believed in love – true love. But where does one find it nowadays?'

'I don't know,' said Birkin.

'Very rarely,' said Gerald. Then, after a pause, 'I've never felt it myself – not what I should call love. I've gone after women – and been keen enough over some of them. But I've never felt *love*. I don't believe I've ever felt as much *love* for a woman as I have for you – not *love*. You understand what I mean?'

'Yes. I'm sure you've never loved a woman.'

'You feel that, do you? And do you think I ever shall? You understand what I mean?' He put his hand to his breast, closing his fist there, as if he would draw something out. 'I mean that – that— I can't express what it is, but I know it.'

'What is it, then?' asked Birkin.

'You see, I can't put it into words. I mean, at any rate, something abiding, something that can't change—'

His eyes were bright and puzzled.

'Now do you think I shall ever feel that for a woman?' he said anxiously.

Birkin looked at him and shook his head.

'I don't know,' he said. 'I could not say.'

Gerald had been on the *qui vive*, as awaiting his fate. Now he drew back in his chair.

'No,' he said, 'and neither do I, and neither do I.'

'We are different, you and I,' said Birkin. 'I can't tell your life.'

'No,' said Gerald, 'no more can I. But I tell you – I begin to doubt it.'

'That you will ever love a woman?'

'Well – yes – what you would truly call love—'

'You doubt it?'

'Well – I begin to.'

There was a long pause.

'Life has all kinds of things,' said Birkin. 'There isn't only one road.'

'Yes, I believe that too. I believe it. And mind you, I don't care how it is with me – I don't care how it is – so long as I don't feel—' he paused, and a blank, barren look passed over his face, to express his feeling – 'so long as I feel I've *lived*, somehow – and I don't care how it is – but I want to feel that—'

'Fulfilled,' said Birkin.

'We-ell, perhaps it is fulfilled; I don't use the same words as you.'

'It is the same.'

Chapter Twenty-one

Threshold

Gudrun was away in London, having a little show of her work with a friend, and looking round, preparing for flight from Beldover. Come what might, she would be on the wing in a very short time. She received a letter from Winifred Crich, ornamented with drawings.

'Father also has been to London, to be examined by the doctors. It made him very tired. They say he must rest a very great deal, so he is mostly in bed. He brought me a lovely tropical parrot in faïence, of Dresden ware, also a man ploughing, and two mice climbing up a stalk, also in faïence. The mice were Copenhagen ware. They are the best, but mice don't shine so much, otherwise they are very good, their tails are slim and long. They all shine nearly like glass. Of course it is the glaze, but I don't like it. Gerald likes the man ploughing the best, his trousers are torn, he is ploughing with an ox, being, I suppose, a German peasant. It is all grey and white, white shirt and grey trousers, but very shiny and clean. Mr. Birkin likes the girl best, under the hawthorn blossom, with a lamb, and with daffodils painted on her skirts, in the drawing-room. But that is silly, because the lamb is not a real lamb, and she is silly too.

'Dear Miss Brangwen, are you coming back soon, you are very much missed here. I enclose a drawing of father sitting up in bed. He says he hopes you are not going to forsake us. Oh dear, Miss Brangwen, I am sure you won't. Do come back and draw the ferrets, they are the most lovely noble darlings in the world. We might carve them in holly-wood, playing against a background of green leaves. Oh, do let us, for they are most beautiful.

'Father says we might have a studio. Gerald says we could easily have a beautiful one over the stables, it would only need windows to be put in the slant of the roof, which is a simple matter. Then you could stay here all day and work, and we could live in the studio, like two real artists, like the man in the picture in the hall, with the frying-pan and the walls all covered with drawings. I long to be free, to live the free life of an artist. Even Gerald told father that only an artist is free, because he lives in a creative world of his own—'

Gudrun caught the drift of the family intentions, in this letter. Gerald wanted her to be attached to the household at Shortlands, he was using Winifred as his stalking-horse. The father thought only of his child, he saw a rock of salvation in Gudrun. And Gudrun admired him for his perspicacity.

The child, moreover, was really exceptional. Gudrun was quite content. She was quite willing, given a studio, to spend her days at Shortlands. She disliked the Grammar School already thoroughly, she wanted to be free. If a studio were provided, she would be free to go on with her work, she would await the turn of events with complete serenity. And she was really interested in Winifred, she would be quite glad to understand the girl.

So there was quite a little festivity on Winifred's account, the day Gudrun returned to Shortlands.

'You should make a bunch of flowers to give to Miss Brangwen when she arrives,' Gerald said, smiling to his sister.

'Oh no,' cried Winifred, 'it's silly.'

'Not at all. It is a very charming and ordinary attention.'

'Oh, it *is* silly,' protested Winifred, with all the extreme *mauvaise honte* of her years. Nevertheless, the idea appealed to her. She wanted very much to carry it out. She flitted round the green-houses and the conservatory looking wistfully at the flowers on their stems. And the more she looked, the more she *longed* to have a bunch of the blossoms she saw, the more fascinated she became with her little vision of ceremony, and the more consumedly shy and self-conscious she grew, till she was almost beside herself. She could not get the idea out of her mind. It was as if some haunting challenge prompted her, and she had not enough courage to take it up. So again she drifted into the green-houses, looking at the lovely roses in their pots, and at the virginal cyclamens, and at the mystic white clusters of a creeper. The beauty, oh, the beauty of them, and oh, the paradisal bliss, if she should have a perfect bouquet and could give it to Gudrun the next day. Her passion and her complete indecision almost made her ill.

At last she slid to her father's side.

'Daddie—' she said.

'What, my precious?'

But she hung back, the tears almost coming to her eyes, in her sensitive confusion. Her father looked at her, and his heart ran hot with tenderness, an anguish of poignant love.

'What do you want to say to me, my love?'

'Daddie—!' her eyes smiled laconically – 'isn't it silly if I give Miss Brangwen some flowers when she comes?'

The sick man looked at the bright, knowing eyes of his child, and his heart burned with love.

'No, darling, that's not silly. It's what they do to queens.'

This was not very reassuring to Winifred. She half suspected that queens in themselves were a silliness. Yet she so wanted her little romantic occasion.

'Shall I then?' she asked.

'Give Miss Brangwen some flowers? Do, Birdie. Tell Wilson I say you are to have what you want.'

The child smiled a small, subtle, unconscious smile to herself, in anticipation of her way.

'But I won't get them till to-morrow,' she said.

'Not till to-morrow, Birdie. Give me a kiss then—'

Winifred silently kissed the sick man, and drifted out of the room. She

again went the round of the green-houses and the conservatory, informing
the gardener, in her high, peremptory, simple fashion, of what she wanted,
telling him all the blooms she had selected.

'What do you want these for?' Wilson asked.

'I want them,' she said. She wished servants did not ask questions.

'Ay, you've said as much. But what do you want them for, for decoration,
or to send away, or what?'

'I want them for a presentation bouquet.'

'A presentation bouquet! Who's coming then? – the Duchess of Portland?'

'No.'

'Oh, not her? Well, you'll have a rare poppy-show if you put all the
things you've mentioned into your bouquet.'

'Yes, I want a rare poppy-show.'

'You do! Then there's no more to be said.'

The next day Winifred, in a dress of silvery velvet and holding a gaudy
bunch of flowers in her hand, waited with keen impatience in the schoolroom,
looking down the drive for Gudrun's arrival. It was a wet morning. Under
her nose was the strange fragrance of hot-house flowers, the bunch was like
a little fire to her, she seemed to have a strange new fire in her heart. This
slight sense of romance stirred her like an intoxicant.

At last she saw Gudrun coming, and she ran downstairs to warn her
father and Gerald. They, laughing at her anxiety and gravity, came with
her into the hall. The man-servant came hastening to the door, and there
he was, relieving Gudrun of her umbrella, and then of her raincoat. The
welcoming party hung back till their visitor entered the hall.

Gudrun was flushed with the rain, her hair was blown in loose little curls,
she was like a flower just opened in the rain, the heart of the blossom just
newly visible, seeming to emit a warmth of retained sunshine. Gerald winced
in spirit, seeing her so beautiful and unknown. She was wearing a soft blue
dress, and her stockings were of dark red.

Winifred advanced with odd, stately formality.

'We are so glad you've come back,' she said. 'These are your flowers.' She
presented the bouquet.

'Mine!' cried Gudrun. She was suspended for a moment, then a vivid
flush went over her, she was as if blinded for a moment with a flame of
pleasure. Then her eyes, strange and flaming, lifted and looked at the father,
and at Gerald. And again Gerald shrank in spirit, as if it would be more
than he could bear, as her hot, exposed eyes rested on him. There was
something so revealed, she was revealed beyond bearing, to his eyes. He
turned his face aside. And he felt he would not be able to avert her. And he
writhed under the imprisonment.

Gudrun put her face into the flowers.

'But how beautiful they are!' she said, in a muffled voice. Then, with a
strange, suddenly revealed passion, she stooped and kissed Winifred.

Mr. Crich went forward with his hand held out to her.

'I was afraid you were going to run away from us,' he said playfully.

Gudrun looked up at him with a luminous, roguish, unknown face.

'Really!' she replied. 'No, I didn't want to stay in London.'

Her voice seemed to imply that she was glad to get back to Shortlands, her tone was warm and subtly caressing.

'That is a good thing,' smiled the father. 'You see, you are very welcome here among us.'

Gudrun only looked into his face with dark-blue, warm, shy eyes. She was unconsciously carried away by her own power.

'And you look as if you came home in every possible triumph,' Mr. Crich continued, holding her hand.

'No,' she said, glowing strangely. 'I haven't had any triumph till I came here.'

'Ah, come, come! We're not going to hear any of those tales. Haven't we read notices in the newspaper, Gerald?'

'You came off pretty well,' said Gerald to her, shaking hands. 'Did you sell anything?'

'No,' she said, 'not much.'

'Just as well,' he said.

'She wondered what he meant. But she was all aglow with her reception, carried by this little flattering ceremonial on her behalf.

'Winifred,' said the father, 'have you a pair of shoes for Miss Brangwen? You had better change at once—'

Gudrun went out with her bouquet in her hand.

'Quite a remarkable young woman,' said the father to Gerald, when she had gone.

'Yes,' replied Gerald briefly, as if he did not like the observation.

Mr. Crich liked Gudrun to sit with him for half an hour. Usually he was ashy and wretched, with all the life gnawed out of him. But as soon as he rallied, he liked to make believe that he was just as before, quite well and in the midst of life – not of the outer world, but in the midst of a strong essential life. And to this belief, Gudrun contributed perfectly. With her, he could get by stimulation those precious half-hours of strength and exaltation and pure freedom, when he seemed to live more than he had ever lived.

She came to him as he lay propped up in the library. His face was like yellow wax, his eyes darkened, as it were sightless. His black beard, now streaked with grey, seemed to spring out of the waxy flesh of a corpse. Yet the atmosphere about him was energetic and playful. Gudrun subscribed to this perfectly. To her fancy, he was just an ordinary man. Only his rather terrible appearance was photographed upon her soul, away beneath her consciousness. She knew that, in spite of his playfulness, his eyes could not change from their darkened vacancy, they were the eyes of a man who is dead.

'Ah, this is Miss Brangwen,' he said, suddenly rousing as she entered, announced by the man-servant. 'Thomas, put Miss Brangwen a chair here – that's right.' He looked at her soft, fresh face with pleasure. It gave him the illusion of life. 'Now, you will have a glass of sherry and a little piece of cake. Thomas—'

'No, thank you,' said Gudrun. And as soon as she had said it, her heart sank horribly. The sick man seemed to fall into a gap of death, at her contradiction. She ought to play up to him, not to contravene him. In an instant she was smiling her rather roguish smile.

'I don't like sherry very much,' she said. 'But I like almost anything else.' The sick man caught at this straw instantly.

'Not sherry! No! Something else! What then? What is there, Thomas?'

'Port wine – curaçao—'

'I would love some curaçao—' said Gudrun, looking at the sick man confidingly.

'You would. Well then, Thomas, curaçao – and a little cake or a biscuit?'

'A biscuit,' said Gudrun. She did not want anything, but she was wise.

'Yes.'

He waited till she was settled with her little glass and her biscuit. Then he was satisfied.

'You have heard the plan,' he said with some excitement, 'for a studio for Winifred over the stables?'

'No!' exclaimed Gudrun, in mock wonder.

'Oh! – I thought Winnie wrote it to you in her letter!'

'Oh – yes – of course. But I thought perhaps it was only her own little idea—' Gudrun smiled subtly, indulgently. The sick man smiled also, elated.

'Oh no. It is a real project. There is a good room under the roof of the stables – with sloping rafters. We had thought of converting it into a studio.'

'How *very* nice that would be!' cried Gudrun, with excited warmth. The thought of the rafters stirred her.

'You think it would? Well, it can be done.'

'But how perfectly splendid for Winifred! Of course, it is just what is needed, if she is to work at all seriously. One must have one's workshop, otherwise one never ceases to be an amateur."

'Is that so? Yes. Of course, I should like you to share it with Winifred.'

'Thank you *so* much.'

Gudrun knew all these things already, but she must look shy and very grateful, as if overcome.

'Of course, what I should like best would be if you could give up your work at the Grammar School and just avail yourself of the studio, and work there – well, as much or as little as you liked—'

He looked at Gudrun with dark, vacant eyes. She looked back at him as if full of gratitude. These phrases of a dying man were so complete and natural, coming like echoes through his dead mouth.

'And as to your earnings – you don't mind taking from me what you have taken from the Education Committee, do you? I don't want you to be a loser.'

'Oh,' said Gudrun, 'if I can have the studio and work there, I can earn money enough, really I can.'

'Well,' he said, pleased to be the benefactor, 'we can see about all that. You wouldn't mind spending your days here?'

'If there were a studio to work in,' said Gudrun, 'I could ask for nothing better.'

'Is that so?'

He was really very pleased. But already he was getting tired. She could see the grey, awful semi-consciousness of mere pain and dissolution coming over him again, the torture coming into the vacancy of his darkened eyes. It was not over yet, this process of death. She rose softly, saying:

'Perhaps you will sleep. I must look for Winifred.'

She went out, telling the nurse that she had left him. Day by day the tissue of the sick man was further and further reduced, nearer and nearer the process came, towards the last knot which held the human being in its unity. But this knot was hard and unrelaxed, the will of the dying man never gave way. He might be dead in nine-tenths, yet the remaining tenth remained unchanged, till it too was torn apart. With his will he held the unit of himself firm, but the circle of his power was ever and ever reduced, it would be reduced to a point at last, then swept away.

To adhere to life, he must adhere to human relationships, and he caught at every straw. Winifred, the butler, the nurse, Gudrun, these were the people who meant all to him, in these last resources. Gerald, in his father's presence, stiffened with repulsion. It was so, to a less degree, with all the other children except Winifred. They could not see anything but the death, when they looked at their father. It was as if some subterranean dislike overcame them. They could not see the familiar face, hear the familiar voice. They were overwhelmed by the antipathy of visible and audible death. Gerald could not breathe in his father's presence. He must get out at once. And so, in the same way, the father could not bear the presence of his son. It sent a final irritation through the soul of the dying man.

The studio was made ready, Gudrun and Winifred moved in. They enjoyed so much the ordering and the appointing of it. And now they need hardly be in the house at all. They had their meals in the studio, they lived there safely. For the house was becoming dreadful. There were two nurses in white, flitting silently about, like heralds of death. The father was confined to his bed, there was a come and go of *sotto-voce* sisters and brothers and children.

Winifred was her father's constant visitor. Every morning, after breakfast, she went into his room when he was washed and propped up in bed, to spend half an hour with him.

'Are you better, Daddie?' she asked him invariably.

And invariably he answered:

'Yes, I think I'm a little better, pet.'

She held his hand in both her own, lovingly and protectively. And this was very dear to him.

She ran in again as a rule at lunch-time, to tell him the course of events, and every evening, when the curtains were drawn, and his room was cosy, she spent a long time with him. Gudrun was gone home, Winifred was alone in the house; she liked best to be with her father. They talked and prattled at random, he always as if he were well, just the same as when he was going about. So that Winifred, with a child's subtle instinct for avoiding the painful things, behaved as if nothing serious was the matter. Instinctively, she withheld her attention, and was happy. Yet in her remoter soul, she knew as well as the adults knew: perhaps better.

Her father was quite well in his make-belief with her. But when she went away, he relapsed under the misery of his dissolution. But still there were these bright moments, though as his strength waned, his faculty for attention grew weaker, and the nurse had to send Winifred away, to save him from exhaustion.

He never admitted that he was going to die. He knew it was so, he knew it was the end. Yet even to himself he did not admit it. He hated the fact, mortally. His will was rigid. He could not bear being overcome by death. For him there was no death. And yet, at times, he felt a great need to cry out and to wail and complain. He would have liked to cry aloud to Gerald, so that his son should be horrified out of his composure. Gerald was instinctively aware of this, and he recoiled, to avoid any such thing. This uncleanness of death repelled him too much. One should die quickly, like the Romans, one should be master of one's fate in dying as in living. He was convulsed in the clasp of this death of his father's, as in the coils of the great serpent of Laocoön. The great serpent had got the father, and the son was dragged into the embrace of horrifying death along with him. He resisted always. And in some strange way he was a tower of strength to his father.

The last time the dying man asked to see Gudrun he was grey with near death. Yet he must see someone, he must, in the intervals of consciousness, catch into connection with the living world, lest he should have to accept his own situation. Fortunately he was most of his time dazed and half gone. And he spent many hours dimly thinking of the past, as it were, dimly re-living his old experiences. But there were times even to the end when he was capable of realising what was happening to him in the present, the death that was on him. And these were the times when he called in outside help, no matter whose. For to realise this death that he was dying was a death beyond death, never to be borne. It was an admission never to be made.

Gudrun was shocked by his appearance, and by the darkened, almost disintegrated eyes, that still were unconquered and firm.

'Well,' he said in his weakened voice, 'and how are you and Winifred getting on?'

'Oh, very well indeed,' replied Gudrun.

There were slight dead gaps in the conversation, as if the ideas called up were only elusive straws floating on the dark chaos of the sick man's dying.

'The studio answers all right?' he said.

'Splendid. It couldn't be more beautiful and perfect,' said Gudrun.

She waited for what he would say next.

'And you think Winifred has the making of a sculptor?'

It was strange how hollow the words were, meaningless.

'I'm sure she has. She will do good things one day.'

'Ah! Then her life won't be altogether wasted, you think?'

Gudrun was rather surprised.

'Sure it won't!' she exclaimed softly.

'That's right.'

Again Gudrun waited for what he would say.

'You find life pleasant, it is good to live, isn't it?' he asked, with a pitiful faint smile that was almost too much for Gudrun.

'Yes,' she smiled – she would lie at random – 'I get a pretty good time, I believe.'

'That's right. A happy nature is a great asset.'

Again Gudrun smiled, though her soul was dry with repulsion. Did one have to die like this – having the life extracted forcibly from one, whilst one smiled and made conversation to the end? Was there no other way? Must one go through all the horror of this victory over death, the triumph of the integral will, that would not be broken till it disappeared utterly? One must, it was the only way. She admired the self-possession and the control of the dying man exceedingly. But she loathed the death itself. She was glad the everyday world held good, and she need not recognise anything beyond.

'You are quite all right here? – nothing we can do for you? – nothing you find wrong in your position?'

'Except that you are too good to me,' said Gudrun.

'Ah, well, the fault of that lies with yourself,' he said, and he felt a little exultation, that he had made this speech. He was still so strong and living! But the nausea of death began to creep back on him, in reaction.

Gudrun went away, back to Winifred. Mademoiselle had left, Gudrun stayed a good deal at Shortlands, and a tutor came in to carry on Winifred's education. But he did not live in the house, he was connected with the Grammar School.

One day, Gudrun was to drive with Winifred and Gerald and Birkin to town in the car. It was a dark, showery day. Winifred and Gudrun were ready and waiting at the door. Winifred was very quiet, but Gudrun had not noticed. Suddenly the child asked, in a voice of unconcern:

'Do you think my father's going to die, Miss Brangwen?'

Gudrun started.

'I don't know,' she replied.

'Don't you truly?'

'Nobody knows for certain. He *may* die, of course.'

The child pondered for a few moments, then she asked:

'But do you *think* he will die?'

It was put almost like a question in geography or science, insistent, as if she would force an admission from the adult. The watchful, slightly triumphant child was almost diabolical.

'Do I think he will die?' repeated Gudrun. 'Yes, I do.'

But Winifred's large eyes were fixed on her, and the girl did not move.

'He is very ill,' said Gudrun.

A small smile came over Winifred's face, subtle and sceptical.

'*I* don't believe he will,' the child asserted mockingly, and she moved away into the drive. Gudrun watched the isolated figure, and her heart stood still. Winifred was playing with a little rivulet of water, absorbedly as if nothing had been said.

'I've made a proper dam,' she said, out of the moist distance.

Gerald came to the door from out of the hall behind.

'It is just as well she doesn't choose to believe it,' he said.

Gudrun looked at him. Their eyes met; and they exchanged a sardonic understanding.

'Just as well,' said Gudrun.

He looked at her again, and a fire flickered up in his eyes.

'Best to dance while Rome burns, since it must burn, don't you think?' he said.

She was rather taken aback. But, gathering herself together, she replied: 'Oh – better dance than wail, certainly.'

'So I think.'

And they both felt the subterranean desire to let go, to fling away everything, and lapse into a sheer unrestraint, brutal and licentious. A strange black passion surged up pure in Gudrun. She felt strong. She felt her hands so strong, as as if she could tear the world asunder with them. She remembered the abandonments of Roman licence, and her heart grew hot. She knew she wanted this herself also – or something, something equivalent. Ah, if that which was unknown and suppressed in her were once let loose, what an orgiastic and satisfying event it would be. And she wanted it, she trembled slightly from the proximity of the man, who stood just behind her, suggestive of the same black licentiousness that rose in herself. She wanted it with him, this unacknowledged frenzy. For a moment the clear perception of this preoccupied her, distinct and perfect in its final reality. Then she shut it off completely, saying:

'We might as well go down to the lodge after Winifred – we can get in the car there.'

'So we can,' he answered, going with her.

They found Winifred at the lodge admiring the litter of pure-bred white puppies. The girl looked up, and there was a rather ugly, unseeing cast in her eyes as she turned to Gerald and Gudrun. She did not want to see them.

'Look!' she cried. 'Three new puppies! Marshall says this one seems perfect. Isn't it a sweetling? But it isn't so nice as its mother.' She turned to caress the fine white bull-terrier bitch that stood uneasily near her.

'My dearest Lady Crich,' she said, 'you are beautiful as an angel on earth. Angel – angel – don't you think she's good enough and beautiful enough to go to heaven, Gudrun? They will be in heaven, won't they – and *especially* my darling Lady Crich! Mrs. Marshall, I say!'

'Yes, Miss Winifred?' said the woman, appearing at the door.

'Oh, do call this one Lady Winifred, if she turns out perfect, will you? Do tell Marshall to call it Lady Winifred.'

'I'll tell him – but I'm afraid that's a gentleman puppy, Miss Winifred.'

'Oh *no!*' There was the sound of a car. 'There's Rupert!' cried the child, and she ran to the gate.

Birkin, driving his car, pulled up outside the lodge gate.

'We're ready!' cried Winifred. 'I want to sit in front with you, Rupert. May I?'

'I'm afraid you'll fidget about and fall out,' he said.

'No, I won't. I do want to sit in front next to you. It makes my feet so lovely and warm, from the engines.'

Birkin helped her up, amused at sending Gerald to sit by Gudrun in the body of the car.

'Have you any news, Rupert?' Gerald called, as they rushed along the lanes.'

'News?' exclaimed Birkin.

'Yes.' Gerald looked at Gudrun, who sat by his side, and he said, his eyes narrowly laughing, 'I want to know whether I ought to congratulate him, but I can't get anything definite out of him.'

Gudrun flushed deeply.

'Congratulate him on what?' she asked.

'There was some mention of an engagement – at least, he said something to me about it.'

Gudrun flushed darkly.

'You mean with Ursula?' she said, in challenge.

'Yes. That is so, isn't it?'

'I don't think there's any engagement,' said Gudrun coldly.

'That so? Still no developments, Rupert?' he called.

'Where? Matrimonial? No.'

'How's that?' called Gudrun.

Birkin glanced quickly round. There was irritation in his eyes also.

'Why?' he replied. 'What do you think of it, Gudrun?'

'Oh,' she cried, determined to fling her stone also into the pool, since they had begun, 'I don't think she wants an engagement. Naturally, she's a bird that prefers the bush.' Gudrun's voice was clear and gong-like. It reminded Rupert of her father's, so strong and vibrant.

'And I,' said Birkin, his face playful but yet determined, 'I want a binding contract, and am not keen on love, particularly free love.'

They were both amused. *Why* this public avowal? Gerald seemed suspended a moment, in amusement.

'Love isn't good enough for you?' he called.

'No!' shouted Birkin.

'Ha, well, that's being over-refined,' said Gerald, and the car ran through the mud.

'What's the matter, really?' said Gerald, turning to Gudrun.

This was an assumption of a sort of intimacy that irritated Gudrun almost like an affront. It seemed to her that Gerald was deliberately insulting her, and infringing on the decent privacy of them all.

'What is it?' she said, in her high, repellent voice. 'Don't ask me! – I know nothing about *ultimate* marriage, I assure you: or even penultimate.'

'Only the ordinary unwarrantable brand!' replied Gerald. 'Just so – same here. I am no expert on marriage and degrees of ultimateness. It seems to be a bee that buzzes loudly in Rupert's bonnet.'

'Exactly! But that is his trouble, exactly! Instead of wanting a woman for herself, he wants his *ideas* fulfilled. Which, when it comes to actual practice, is not good enough.'

'Oh no. Best go slap for what's womanly in woman, like a bull at a gate.' Then he seemed to glimmer in himself. 'You think love is the ticket, do you?' he asked.

'Certainly, while it lasts – you only can't insist on permanency,' came Gudrun's voice, strident above the noise.

'Marriage or no marriage, ultimate or penultimate or just so-so? – take the love as you find it.'

'As you please, or as you don't please,' she echoed. 'Marriage is a social arrangement, I take it, and has nothing to do with the question of love.'

His eyes were flickering on her all the time. She felt as if he were kissing her freely and malevolently. It made the colour burn in her cheeks, but her heart was quite firm and unfailing.

'You think Rupert is off his head a bit?' Gerald asked.

Her eyes flashed with acknowledgment.

'As regards a woman, yes,' she said, 'I do. There *is* such a thing as two people being in love for the whole of their lives – perhaps. But marriage is neither here nor there, even then. If they are in love, well and good. If not – why break eggs about it!'

'Yes,' said Gerald. 'That's how it strikes me. But what about Rupert?'

'I can't make out – neither can he nor anybody. He seems to think that if you marry you can get through marriage into a third heaven, or something – all very vague.'

'Very! And who wants a third heaven? As a matter of fact, Rupert has a great yearning to be *safe* – to tie himself to the mast.'

'Yes. It seems to me he's mistaken there too,' said Gudrun. 'I'm sure a mistress is more likely to be faithful than a wife – just because she is her *own* mistress. No – he says he believes that a man and wife can go further than any other two beings – but *where*, is not explained. They can know each other, heavenly and hellish, but particularly hellish, so perfectly that they go beyond heaven and hell – into – there it all breaks down – into nowhere.'

'Into Paradise, he says,' laughed Gerald.

Gudrun shrugged her shoulders. '*Je m'en fiche* of your Paradise!' she said.

'Not being a Mohammedan,' said Gerald. Birkin sat motionless, driving the car, quite unconscious of what they said. And Gudrun, sitting immediately behind him, felt a sort of ironic pleasure in thus exposing him.

'He says,' she added, with a grimace of irony, 'that you can find an eternal equilibrium in marriage, if you accept the unison, and still leave yourself separate, don't try to fuse.'

'Doesn't inspire me,' said Gerald.

'That's just it,' said Gudrun.

'I believe in love, in a real *abandon*, if you're capable of it,' said Gerald.

'So do I,' said she.

'And so does Rupert, too – though he is always shouting.'

'No,' said Gudrun. 'He won't abandon himself to the other person. You can't be sure of him. That's the trouble, I think.'

'Yet he wants marriage! Marriage – *et puis?*'

'*Le paradis!*' mocked Gudrun.

Birkin, as he drove, felt a creeping of the spine, as if somebody were threatening his neck. But he shrugged with indifference. It began to rain. Here was a change. He stopped the car and got down to put up the hood.

Chapter Twenty-two

Woman to Woman

They came to the town, and left Gerald at the railway station. Gudrun and Winifred were to come to tea with Birkin, who expected Ursula also. In the afternoon, however, the first person to turn up was Hermione. Birkin was out, so she went in the drawing-room, looking at his books and papers, and playing on the piano. Then Ursula arrived. She was surprised, unpleasantly so, to see Hermione, of whom she had heard nothing for some time.

'It is a surprise to see you,' she said.

'Yes,' said Hermione – 'I've been away at Aix—'

'Oh, for your health?'

'Yes.'

The two women looked at each other. Ursula resented Hermione's long, grave, downward-looking face. There was something of the stupidity and the unenlightened self-esteem of a horse in it. 'She's got a horse-face,' Ursula said to herself, 'she runs between blinkers.' It did seem as if Hermione, like the moon, had only one side to her penny. There was no obverse. She stared out all the time on the narrow, but to her, complete world of the extant consciousness. In the darkness, she did not exist. Like the moon, one half of her was lost to life. Her self was all in her head, she did not know what it was spontaneously to run or move, like a fish in the water, or a weasel in the grass. She must always *know*.

But Ursula only suffered from Hermione's one-sidedness. She only felt Hermione's cool evidence, which seemed to put her down as nothing. Hermione, who brooded and brooded till she was exhausted, with the ache of her effort at consciousness, spent and ashen in her body, who gained so slowly and with such effort her final and barren conclusions of knowledge, was apt, in the presence of other women, whom she thought simply female, to wear the conclusions of her bitter assurance like jewels which conferred on her an unquestionable distinction, established her in a higher order of life. She was apt, mentally, to condescend to women such as Ursula, whom she regarded as purely emotional. Poor Hermione, it was her one possession, this aching certainty of hers, it was her only justification. She must be confident here, for God knows, she felt rejected and deficient enough elsewhere. In the life of thought, of the spirit, she was one of the elect. And she wanted to be universal. But there was a devastating cynicism at the bottom of her. She did not believe in her own universals – they were sham. She did not believe in the inner life – it was a trick, not a reality. She did not believe in the spiritual world – it was an affectation. In the last resort, she believed in Mammon, the flesh, and the devil – these at least were not sham. She was a priestess without belief, without conviction, suckled in a creed outworn, and condemned to the reiteration of mysteries that were not divine to her. Yet there was no escape. She was a leaf upon a dying tree. What help was there then, but to fight still for the old, withered truths, to die for the old outworn belief, to be a sacred and inviolate priestess of desecrated mysteries? The old great truths *had* been true. And she was a leaf of the old great tree of knowledge that was withering now. To the old and last truth then she must be faithful even though cynicism and mockery took place at the bottom of her soul.

'I am so glad to see you,' she said to Ursula, in her slow voice, that was like an incantation. 'You and Rupert have become quite friends?'

'Oh yes,' said Ursula. 'He is always somewhere in the background.'

Hermione paused before she answered. She saw perfectly well the other woman's vaunt: it seemed truly vulgar.

'Is he?' she said slowly, and with perfect equanimity. 'And do you think you will marry?'

The question was so calm and mild, so simple and bare and dispassionate that Ursula was somewhat taken aback, rather attracted. It pleased her almost like a wickedness. There was some delightful naked irony in Hermione.

'Well,' replied Ursula, '*He* wants to, awfully, but I'm no so sure.'

Hermione watched her with slow, calm eyes. She noted this new expression of vaunting. How she envied Ursula a certain unconscious positivity! even her vulgarity!

'Why aren't you sure?' she asked, in her easy sing-song. She was perfectly at her ease, perhaps even rather happy in this conversation. 'You don't really love him?'

Ursula flushed a little at the mild impertinence of this question. And yet she could not definitely take offence. Hermione seemed so calmly and sanely candid. After all, it was rather great to be able to be so sane.

'He says it isn't love he wants,' she replied.

'What is it then?' Hermione was slow and level.

'He wants me really to accept him in marriage.'

Hermione was silent for some time, watching Ursula with slow, pensive eyes.

'Does he?' she said at length, without expression. Then, rousing, 'And what is it you don't want? You don't want marriage?'

'No – I don't – not really. I don't want to give the sort of *submission* he insists on. He wants me to give myself up – and I simply don't feel that I *can* do it.'

Again there was a long pause before Hermione replied:

'Not if you don't want to.' Then again there was silence. Hermione shuddered with a strange desire. Ah, if only he had asked *her* to subserve him, to be his slave! She shuddered with desire.

'You see, I can't—'

'But exactly in what does—'

They had both begun at once, they both stopped. Then Hermione, assuming priority of speech, resumed as if wearily:

'To what does he want you to submit?'

'He says he wants me to accept him non-emotionally, and finally— I really don't know *what* he means. He says he wants the demon part of himself to be mated - physically - not the human being. You see, he says one thing one day, and another the next - and he always contradicts himself—'

'And always thinks about himself, and his own dissatisfaction,' said Hermione slowly.

'Yes,' cried Ursula. 'As if there were no one but himself concerned. That makes it so impossible.'

But immediately she began to retract.

'He insists on my accepting God knows what in *him*,' she resumed. 'He wants me to accept *him* as - as an absolute— But it seems to me he doesn't want to *give* anything. He doesn't want real warm intimacy - he won't have it - he rejects it. He won't let me think, really, and he won't let me *feel* - he hates feelings.'

There was a long pause, bitter for Hermione. Ah, if only he would have made this demand of her? Her he *drove* into thought, drove inexorably into knowledge - and then execrated her for it.

'He wants me to sink myself,' Ursula resumed, 'not to have any being of my own—'

'Then why doesn't he marry an odalisk?' said Hermione in her mild sing-song, 'if it is that he wants.' Her long face looked sardonic and amused.

'Yes' said Ursula vaguely. After all, the tiresome thing was, he did not want an odalisk, he did not want a slave. Hermione would have been his slave - there was in her a horrible desire to prostrate herself before a man - a man who worshipped her, however, and admitted her as the supreme thing. He did not want an odalisk. He wanted a woman to *take* something from him, to give herself up so much that she could take the last realities of him, the last facts, the last physical facts, physical and unbearable.

And if she did, would he acknowledge her? Would he be able to acknowledge her through everything, or would he use her just as his instrument, use her for his own private satisfaction, not admitting her? That was what the other men had done. They had wanted their own show, and they would not admit her, they turned all she was into nothingness. Just as Hermione now betrayed herself as a woman. Hermione was like a man, she believed only in men's things. She betrayed the woman in herself. And Birkin, would he acknowledge, or would he deny her?

'Yes,' said Hermione, as each woman came out of her own separate reverie. 'It would be a mistake - I think it would be a mistake—'

'To marry him?' asked Ursula.

'Yes,' said Hermione slowly - 'I think you need a man - soldierly, strong-willed—' Hermione held out her hand and clenched it with rhapsodic intensity. 'You should have a man like the old heroes - you need to stand behind him as he goes into battle, you need to *see* his strength, and to *hear* his shout— You need a man physically strong, and virile in his will, *not* a sensitive man—' There was a break, as if the pythoness had uttered the oracle, and now the woman went on, in a rhapsody-wearied voice: 'And you see, Rupert isn't this, he isn't. He is frail in health and body, he needs great, great care. Then he is so changeable and unsure of himself – it requires the greatest patience and understanding to help him. And I don't think you are patient. You would have to be prepared to suffer – dreadfully. I can't *tell* you how much suffering it would take to make him happy. He lives an *intensely* spiritual life, at times – too, too wonderful. And then come the reactions. I can't speak of what I have been through with him. We have been together so long, I really do know him, I *do* know what he is. And I feel I must say it; I feel it would be perfectly *disastrous* for you to marry him – for you even more than for him.' Hermione lapsed into bitter reverie. 'He is so uncertain, so unstable – he wearies, and then reacts. I couldn't *tell* you what his reactions are. I couldn't *tell* you the agony of them. That which he affirms and loves one day – a little later he turns on it in a fury of destruction. He is never constant, always this awful, dreadful reaction. Always the quick change from good to bad, bad to good. And nothing is so devastating, nothing—'

'Yes,' said Ursula humbly, 'you must have suffered.'

An unearthly light came on Hermione's face. She clenched her hand like one inspired.

'And one must be willing to suffer – willing to suffer for him hourly, daily – if you are going to help him, if he is to keep true to anything at all—'

'And I don't *want* to suffer hourly and daily,' said Ursula. 'I don't, I should be ashamed. I think it is degrading not to be happy.'

Hermione stopped and looked at her a long time.

'Do you?' she said at last. And this utterance seemed to her a mark of Ursula's far distance from herself. For to Hermione suffering was the greatest reality, come what might. Yet she too had a creed of happiness.

'Yes,' she said. 'One *should* be happy—' But it was a matter of will.

'Yes,' said Hermione, listlessly now, 'I can only feel that it would be disastrous, disastrous – at least, to marry in a hurry. Can't you be together without marriage? Can't you go away and live somewhere without marriage? I do feel that marriage would be fatal for both of you. I think for you even more than for him – and I think of his health—'

'Of course,' said Ursula, '*I* don't care about marriage – it isn't really important to me – it's he who wants it.'

'It is his idea for the moment,' said Hermione, with that weary finality and a sort of *si jeunesse savait* infallibility.

There was a pause. Then Ursula broke into faltering challenge.

'You think I'm merely a physical woman, don't you?'

'No, indeed,' said Hermione. 'No, indeed! But I think you are vital and young – it isn't a question of years, or even of experience – it is almost a question of race. Rupert is race-old, he comes of an old race – and you seem to me so young, you come of a young, inexperienced race.'

'Do I!' said Ursula. 'But I think he is awfully young, on one side.'

'Yes, perhaps – childish in many respects. Nevertheless—'

They both lapsed into silence. Ursula was filled with deep resentment and a touch of hopelessness. 'It isn't true,' she said to herself, silently addressing her adversary. 'It isn't true. And it is *you* who want a physically strong, bullying man, not I. It is you who want an unsensitive man, not I. You *don't* know anything about Rupert, not really, in spite of the years you have had with him. You don't give him a woman's love, you give him an ideal love, and that is why he reacts away from you. You don't know. You only know the dead things. Any kitchen-maid would know something about him, you don't know. What do you think your knowledge is but dead understanding, that doesn't mean a thing. You are so false, and untrue, how could you know anything? What is the good of your talking about love – you untrue spectre of a woman! How can you know anything, when you don't believe? You don't believe in yourself and your own womanhood, so what good is your conceited, shallow cleverness—!'

The two women sat on in antagonistic silence. Hermione felt injured, that all her good intention, all her offering, only left the other woman in vulgar antagonism. But then, Ursula could not understand, never would understand, could never be more than the usual jealous and unreasonable female, with a good deal of powerful female emotion, female attraction, and a fair amount of female understanding, but no mind. Hermione had decided long ago that where there was no mind, it was useless to appeal for reason – one had merely to ignore the ignorant. And Rupert – he had now reacted towards the strongly female, healthy, selfish woman – it was his reaction for the time being – there was no helping it all. It was all a foolish backward and forward, a violent oscillation that would at length be too violent for his coherency, and he would smash and be dead. There was no saving him. This violent and directionless reaction between animalism and spiritual truth would go on in him till he tore himself in two between the opposite directions, and disappeared meaninglessly out of life. It was no good – he too was without unity, without *mind*, in the ultimate stages of living; not quite man enough to make a destiny for a woman.

They sat on till Birkin came in and found them together. He felt at once the antagonism in the atmosphere, something radical and insuperable, and he bit his lip. But he affected a bluff manner.

'Hello, Hermione, are you back again? How do you feel?'

'Oh, better. And how are you – you don't look well—'

'Oh! – I believe Gudrun and Winnie Crich are coming in to tea. At least they said they were. We shall be a tea-party. What train did you come by, Ursula?'

It was rather annoying to see him trying to placate both women at once. Both women watched him, Hermione with deep resentment and pity for him, Ursula very impatient. He was nervous and apparently in quite good spirits, chattering the conventional commonplaces. Ursula was amazed and indignant at the way he made small-talk; he was adept as any *fat* in Christendom. She became quite stiff, she would not answer. It all seemed to her so false and so belittling. And still Gudrun did not appear.

'I think I shall go to Florence for the winter,' said Hermione at length.

'Will you?' he answered. 'But it is so cold there.'

'Yes, but I shall stay with Palestra. It is quite comfortable.'

'What takes you to Florence?'

'I don't know,' said Hermione slowly. Then she looked at him with her slow, heavy gaze. 'Barnes is starting his school of aesthetics, and Olandese is going to give a set of discourses on the Italian national policy—'

'Both rubbish,' he said.

'No, I don't think so,' said Hermione.

'Which do you admire, then?'

'I admire both. Barnes is a pioneer. And then I am interested in Italy, in her coming to national consciousness.'

'I wish she'd come to something different from national consciousness, then,' said Birkin; 'especially as it only means a sort of commercial-industrial consciousness. I hate Italy and her national rant. And I think Barnes is an amateur.'

Hermione was silent for some moments, in a state of hostility. But yet, she had got Birkin back again into her world! How subtle her influence was, she seemed to start his irritable attention into her direction exclusively, in one minute. He was her creature.

'No,' she said, 'you are wrong.' Then a sort of tension came over her, she raised her face like the pythoness inspired with oracles, and went on in rhapsodic manner: *'Il Sandro mi scrive che ha accolto il piu grande entusiasmo, tutti i giovani e fanciulle e ragazzi, sono tutti—'* She went on in Italian, as if, in thinking of the Italians she thought in their language.

He listened with a shade of distaste to her rhapsody, then he said:

'For all that, I don't like it. Their nationalism is just industrialism - that and a shallow jealousy I detest so much.'

'I think you are wrong - I think you are wrong—' said Hermione. 'It seems to me purely spontaneous and beautiful, the modern Italian's *passion*, for it is a passion, for Italy, L'Italia—'

'Do you know Italy well?' Ursula asked of Hermione. Hermione hated to be broken in upon in this manner. Yet she answered mildly:

'Yes, pretty well. I spent several years of my girlhood there with my mother. My mother died in Florence.'

'Oh.'

There was a pause, painful to Ursula and to Birkin. Hermione, however, seemed abstracted and calm. Birkin was white, his eyes glowed as if he were in a fever, he was far too overwrought. How Ursula suffered in this tense atmosphere of strained wills! Her head seemed bound round by iron bands.

Birkin rang the bell for tea. They could not wait for Gudrun any longer. When the door was opened, the cat walked in.

'Micio! Micio!' called Hermione in her slow, deliberate sing-song. The young cat turned to look at her, then, with his slow and stately walk he advanced to her side.

'Vieni - vieni quâ,' Hermione was saying in her strange caressive, protective voice, as if she were always the elder, the mother superior. *'Vieni dire Buon' Giorno alla zia. Mi ricordi, mi ricordi bene - non è vero, piccolo? E vero che mi ricordi? E vero?'* And slowly she rubbed his head, slowly and with ironic indifference.

'Does he understand Italian?' said Ursula, who knew nothing of the language.

'Yes,' said Hermione at length. 'His mother was Italian. She was born in my waste-paper basket in Florence on the morning of Rupert's birthday. She was his birthday present.'

Tea was brought in. Birkin poured out for them. It was strange how inviolable was the intimacy which existed between him and Hermione. Ursula felt that she was an outsider. The very tea-cups and the old silver was a bond between Hermione and Birkin. It seemed to belong to an old, past world which they had inhabited together, and in which Ursula was a foreigner. She was almost a parvenue in their old cultured milieu. Her convention was not their convention, their standards were not her standards. But theirs were established, they had the sanction and the grace of age. He and she together, Hermione and Birkin, were people of the same old tradition, the same withered deadening culture. And she, Ursula, was an intruder. So they always made her feel.

Hermione poured a little cream into a saucer. The simple way she assumed her rights in Birkin's room maddened and discouraged Ursula. There was a fatality about it, as if it were bound to be. Hermione lifted the cat and put the cream before him. He planted his two paws on the edge of the table and bent his gracious young head to drink.

'Sicuro che capisce italiano,' sang Hermione, 'non l'avrà dimenticato, la lingua della Mamma.'

She lifted the cat's head with her long, slow, white fingers, not letting him drink, holding him in her power. It was always the same, this joy in power she manifested, peculiarly in power over any male being. He blinked forbearingly, with a male, bored expression, licking his whiskers. Hermione laughed in her short, grunting fashion.

'Ecco, il bravo ragazzo, com' è superbo, questo!'

She made a vivid picture, so calm and strange with the cat. She had a true static impressiveness, she was a social artist in some ways.

The cat refused to look at her, indifferently avoided her fingers, and began to drink again, his nose down to the cream, perfectly balanced, as he lapped with his odd little click.

'It's bad for him, teaching him to eat at table,' said Birkin.

'Yes,' said Hermione, easily assenting.

Then, looking down at the cat, she resumed her old, mocking, humorous sing-song.

'Ti imparano fare brutte cose, brutte cose—'

She lifted the Mino's white chin on her forefinger slowly. The young cat looked round with a supremely forbearing air, avoided seeing anything, withdrew his chin, and began to wash his face with his paw. Hermione grunted her laughter, pleased.

'Bel giovanetto—' she said.

The cat reached forward again and put his fine white paw on the edge of the saucer. Hermione lifted it down with delicate slowness. This deliberate, delicate carefulness of movement reminded Ursula of Gudrun.

'No! Non è permesso di mettere il zampino nel tondinetto. Non piace al babbo. Un signor gatto così selvatico—!'

And she kept her finger on the softly planted paw of the cat, and her voice had the same whimsical, humorous note of bullying.

Ursula had her nose out of joint. She wanted to go away now. It all seemed no good. Hermione was established for ever, she herself was ephemeral and had not yet even arrived.

'I will go now,' she said suddenly.

Birkin looked at her almost in fear – he so dreaded her anger. 'But there is no need for such hurry,' he said.

'Yes,' she answered. 'I will go.' And turning to Hermione, before there was time to say any more, she held out her hand and said 'Good-bye'.

'Good-bye—' sang Hermione, detaining the hand. 'Must you really go now?'

'Yes, I think I'll go,' said Ursula, her face set and averted from Hermione's eyes.

'You think you will—'

But Ursula had got her hand free. She turned to Birkin with a quick, almost jeering 'Good-bye', and she was opening the door before he had time to do it for her.

When she got outside the house she ran down the road in fury and agitation. It was strange, the unreasoning rage and violence Hermione roused in her, by her very presence. Ursula knew she gave herself away to the other woman, she knew she looked ill-bred, uncouth, exaggerated. But she did not care. She only ran up the road, lest she should go back and jeer in the faces of the two she had left behind. For they outraged her.

Chapter Twenty-three

Excurse

Next day Birkin sought Ursula out. It happened to be the half-day at the Grammar School. He appeared towards the end of the morning, and asked her, would she drive with him in the afternoon. She consented. But her face was closed and unresponding, and his heart sank.

The afternoon was fine and dim. He was driving the motor-car, and she sat beside him. But still her face was closed against him, unresponding. When she became like this, like a wall against him, his heart contracted.

His life now seemed so reduced that he hardly cared any more. At moments it seemed to him he did not care a straw whether Ursula or Hermione or anybody else existed or did not exist. Why bother! Why strive for a coherent, satisfied life? Why not drift on in a series of accidents – like a picaresque novel? Why not? Why bother about human relationships? Why take them seriously – male or female? Why form any serious connections at all? Why not be casual, drifting along, taking all for what it was worth?

And yet, still, he was damned and doomed to the old effort at serious living.

'Look,' he said, 'what I bought.' The car was running along a broad white road between autumn trees.

He gave her a little bit of screwed-up paper. She took it and opened it.

'How lovely,' she cried.

She examined the gift.

'How perfectly lovely!' she cried again. 'But why do you give them me?' She put the question offensively.

His face flickered with bored irritation. He shrugged his shoulders slightly.

'I wanted to,' he said coolly.

'But why? Why should you?'

'Am I called on to find reasons?' he asked.

There was a silence, whilst she examined the rings that had been screwed up in the paper.

'I think they are *beautiful*,' she said, 'especially this. This is wonderful—'

It was a round opal, red and fiery, set in a circle of tiny rubies.

'You like that best?' he said.

'I think I do.'

'I like the sapphire,' he said.

'This?'

It was a rose-shaped, beautiful sapphire, with small brilliants.

'Yes,' she said, 'it is lovely.' She held it in the light. 'Yes, perhaps it *is* the best—'

'The blue—' he said.

'Yes, wonderful—'

He suddenly swung the car out of the way of a farm-cart. It tilted on the bank. He was a careless driver, yet very quick. But Ursula was frightened. There was always that something regardless in him which terrified her. She suddenly felt he might kill her, by making some dreadful accident with the motor-car. For a moment she was stony with fear.

'Isn't it rather dangerous, the way you drive?' she asked him.

'No, it isn't dangerous,' he said. And then, after a pause: 'Don't you like the yellow ring at all?'

It was a squarish topaz set in a frame of steel, or some other similar mineral, finely wrought.

'Yes,' she said, 'I do like it. But why did you buy these rings?'

'I wanted them. They are second-hand.'

'You bought them for yourself?'

'No. Rings look wrong on my hands.'

'Why did you buy them then?'

'I bought them to give to you.'

'But why? Surely you ought to give them to Hermione! You belong to her.'

He did not answer. She remained with the jewels shut in her hand. She wanted to try them on her fingers, but something in her would not let her. And, moreover, she was afraid her hands were too large, she shrank from the mortification of a failure to put them on any but her little finger. They travelled in silence through the empty lanes.

Driving in a motor-car excited her, she forgot his presence even.

'Where are we?' she asked suddenly.

'Not far from Worksop.'

'And where are we going?'

'Anywhere.'

It was the answer she liked.

She opened her hand to look at the rings. They gave her *such* pleasure, as they lay, the three circles, with their knotted jewels, entangled in her palm. She would have to try them on. She did so secretly, unwilling to let him see, so that he should not know her finger was too large for them. But he saw, nevertheless. He always saw, if she wanted him not to. It was another of his hateful, watchful characteristics.

Only the opal, with its thin wire loop, would go on her ring finger. And she was superstitious. No, there was ill-portent enough, she would not accept this ring from him in pledge.

'Look,' she said, putting forward her hand, that was half closed and shrinking. 'The others don't fit me.'

He looked at the red-glinting, soft stone on her over-sensitive skin.

'Yes,' he said.

'But opals are unlucky, aren't they?' she said wistfully.

'No. I prefer unlucky things. Luck is vulgar. Who wants what *luck* would bring? I don't.'

'But why?' she laughed.

And, consumed with a desire to see how the other rings would look on her hand, she put them on her little finger.

'They can be made a little bigger,' he said.

Yes,' she replied doubtfully. And she sighed. She knew that, in accepting the rings, she was accepting a pledge. Yet fate seemed more than herself. She looked again at the jewels. They were very beautiful to her eyes – not as ornament, or wealth, but as tiny fragments of loveliness.

'I'm glad you bought them,' she said, putting her hand, half unwillingly, gently on his arm.

He smiled slightly. He wanted her to come to him. But he was angry at the bottom of his soul, and indifferent. He knew she had a passion for him, really. But it was not finally interesting. There were depths of passion when one became impersonal and indifferent, unemotional. Whereas Ursula was still at the emotional personal level – always so abominably personal. He had taken her as he had never been taken himself. He had taken her at the roots of her darkness and shame – like a demon, laughing over the fountain of mystic corruption which was one of the sources of her being, laughing, shrugging, accepting, accepting finally. As for her, when would she so much go beyond herself as to accept him at the quick of death?

She now became quite happy. The motor-car ran on, the afternoon was soft and dim. She talked with lively interest, analysing people and their motives – Gudrun, Gerald. He answered vaguely. He was not very much interested any more in personalities and in people – people were all different, but they were all enclosed nowadays in a definite limitation, he said; there were only about two great ideas, two great streams of activity remaining, with various forms of reaction therefrom. The reactions were all varied in various people, but they followed a few great laws, and intrinsically there was no difference. They acted and reacted involuntarily according to a few great laws, and once the laws, the great principles, were known, people were no longer mystically interesting. They were all essentially alike, the differences were only variations on a theme. None of them transcended the given terms.

Ursula did not agree – people were still an adventure to her – but – perhaps not as much as she tried to persuade herself. Perhaps there was something mechanical, now, in her interest. Perhaps also her interest was destructive, her analysing was a real tearing to pieces. There was an under-space in her where she did not care for people and their idiosyncrasies, even to destroy them. She seemed to touch for a moment this under-silence in herself, she became still, and she turned for a moment purely to Birkin.

'Won't it be lovely to go home in the dark?' she said. 'We might have tea rather late – shall we? – and have high tea? Wouldn't that be rather nice?'

'I promised to be at Shortlands for dinner,' he said.

'But – it doesn't matter – you can go to-morrow—'

'Hermione is there,' he said, in rather an uneasy voice. 'She is going away in two days. I suppose I ought to say good-bye to her. I shall never see her again.'

Ursula drew away, closed in a violent silence. He knitted his brows, and his eyes began to sparkle again in anger.

'You don't mind, do you?' he asked irritably.

'No, I don't care. Why should I? Why should I mind?' Her tone was jeering and offensive.

'That's what I ask myself,' he said; 'why *should* you mind! But you seem to.' His brows were tense with violent irritation.

'I *assure* you I don't, I don't mind in the least. Go where you belong – it's what I want you to do.'

'Ah, you fool!' he cried, 'with your "go where you belong". It's finished between Hermione and me. She means much more to *you*, if it comes to that, than she does to me. For you can only revolt in pure reaction from her – and to be her opposite is to be her counterpart.'

'Ah, opposite!' cried Ursula. 'I know your dodges. I am not taken in by your word-twisting. You belong to Hermione and her dead show. Well, if you do, you do. I don't blame you. But then you've nothing to do with me.'

In his inflamed, overwrought exasperation he stopped the car, and they sat there, in the middle of the country lane, to have it out. It was a crisis of war between them, so they did not see the ridiculousness of their situation.

'If you weren't a fool, if only you weren't a fool,' he cried in bitter despair, 'you'd see that one could be decent, even when one has been wrong. I *was* wrong to go on all those years with Hermione – it was a deathly process. But after all, one can have a little human decency. But no, you would tear my soul out with your jealousy at the very mention of Hermione's name.'

'I jealous! *I* – jealous! You *are* mistaken if you think that. I'm not jealous in the least of Hermione, she is nothing to me, not *that!* And Ursula snapped her fingers. 'No, it's you who are a liar. It's you who must return, like a dog to his vomit. It is what Hermione *stands* for that I hate. I *hate* it. It is lies, it is false, it is death. But you want it, you can't help it, you can't help yourself. You belong to that old, deathly way of living – then go back to it. But don't come to me, for I've nothing to do with it.'

And in the stress of her violent emotion, she got down from the car and went to the hedgerow, picking unconsciously some flesh-pink spindleberries, some of which were burst, showing their orange seeds.

'Ah, you are a fool,' he cried bitterly, with some contempt.

'Yes, I am. I *am* a fool. And thank God for it. I'm too big a fool to swallow your cleverness. God be praised. You go to your women – go to them – they are your sort – you've always had a string of them trailing after you – and you always will. Go to your spiritual brides – but don't come to me as well, because I'm not having any, thank you. You're not satisfied, are you? Your spiritual brides can't give you what you want, they aren't common and fleshy enough for you, aren't they? So you come to me, and keep them in the background! You will marry me for daily use. But you'll keep yourself well provided with spiritual brides in the background. I know your dirty little game.' Suddenly a flame ran over her, and she stamped her foot madly on the road, and he winced, afraid that she would strike him. 'And I, I'm not spiritual enough, I'm not as spiritual as that Hermione—!' Her brows knitted, her eyes blazed like a tiger's. 'Then *go* to her, that's all I say, *go* to her, *go.* Ha, she spiritual – *spiritual,* she! A dirty materialist as she is. *She* spiritual? What does she care for, what is her spirituality? What *is* it?' Her fury seemed to blaze out and burn his face. He shrank a little. 'I tell you it's *dirt, dirt,* and nothing *but* dirt. And it's dirt you want, you crave for it. Spiritual! Is *that* spiritual, her bullying, her conceit, her sordid materialism? She's a fishwife, a fishwife, she is such a materialist. And all so sordid. What does she work out to, in the end, with all her social passion, as you call it. Social passion – what social passion has she? – show it me! – where is it? She wants petty, immediate *power,* she wants the illusion that she is a great woman, that is all. In her soul she's a devilish unbeliever, common as dirt. That's what she is at the bottom. And all the rest is pretence – but you love it. You love the sham spirituality, it's your food. And why? Because of the dirt underneath. Do you think I don't know the foulness of your sex life – and hers? – I do. And it's that foulness you want, you liar. Then have it, have it. You're such a liar.'

She turned away, spasmodically tearing the twigs of spindleberry from the hedge, and fastening them, with vibrating fingers, in the bosom of her coat.

He stood watching in silence. A wonderful tenderness burned in him at the sight of her quivering, so sensitive fingers: and at the same time he was full of rage and callousness.

'This is a degrading exhibition,' he said coolly.

'Yes, degrading indeed,' she said. 'But more to me than to you.'

'Since you choose to degrade yourself,' he said. Again the flash came over her face, the yellow lights concentrated in her eyes.

'*You!*' she cried. 'You! You truth-lover! You purity-monger! It *stinks*, your truth and your purity. It stinks of the offal you feed on, you scavenger dog, you eater of corpses. You are foul, *foul* – and you must know it. Your purity, your candour, your goodness – yes, thank you, we've had some. What you are is a foul, deathly thing, obscene, that's what you are, obscene and perverse. You, and love! You may well say, you don't want love. No, you want *yourself*, and dirt and death – that's what you want. You are so *perverse*, so death-eating. And then—'

'There's a bicycle coming,' he said, writhing under her loud denunciation. She glanced down the road.

'I don't care,' she cried.

Nevertheless she was silent. The cyclist, having heard the voices raised in altercation, glanced curiously at the man and the woman, and at the standing motor-car as he passed.

'– Afternoon,' he said cheerfully.

'Good-afternoon,' replied Birkin coldly.

They were silent as the man passed into the distance.

A clearer look had come over Birkin's face. He knew she was in the main right. He knew he was perverse, so spiritual on the one hand, and in some strange way, degraded on the other. But was she herself any better? Was anybody any better?

'It may all be true, lies and stink and all,' he said. 'But Hermione's spiritual intimacy is no rottener than your emotional-jealous intimacy. One can preserve the decencies, even to one's enemies: for one's own sake. Hermione is my enemy – to her last breath! That's why I must bow her off the field.'

'You! You and your enemies and your bows! A pretty picture you make of yourself. But it takes nobody in but yourself. I *jealous! I!* What I say,' her voice sprang into flame, 'I say because it is *true*, do you see, because you are *you*, a foul and false liar, a whited sepulchre. That's why I say it. And *you* hear it.'

'And be grateful,' he added, with a satirical grimace.

'Yes,' she cried, 'and if you have a spark of decency in you, be gràteful.'

'Not having a spark of decency, however—' he retorted.

'No,' she cried, 'you haven't a *spark*. And so you can go your way, and I'll go mine. It's no good, not the slightest. So you can leave me now, I don't want to go any farther with you – leave me—'

'You don't even know where you are,' he said.

'Oh, don't bother, I assure you I shall be all right. I've got ten shillings in my purse, and that will take me back from anywhere *you* have brought me to.' She hesitated. The rings were still on her fingers, two on her little finger, one on her ring finger. Still she hesitated.

'Very good,' he said. 'The only hopeless thing is a fool.'

'You are quite right,' she said.

Still she hesitated. Then an ugly, malevolent look came over her face, she pulled the rings from her fingers and tossed them at him. One touched his face, the others hit his coat, and they scattered into the mud.

'And take your rings,' she said, 'and go and buy yourself a female elsewhere – there are plenty to be had, who will be quite glad to share your spiritual mess – or to have your physical mess, and leave your spiritual mess to Hermione.'

With which she walked away, desultorily, up the road. He stood motionless, watching her sullen, rather ugly walk. She was sullenly picking and pulling at the twigs of the hedge as she passed. She grew smaller, she seemed to pass out of his sight. A darkness came over his mind. Only a small, mechanical speck of consciousness hovered near him.

He felt tired and weak. Yet also he was relieved. He gave up his old position. He went and sat on the bank. No doubt Ursula was right. It was true, really, what she said. He knew that his spirituality was concomitant of a process of depravity, a sort of pleasure in self-destruction. There really *was* a certain stimulant in self-destruction, for him – especially when it was translated spiritually. But then he knew it – he knew it, and had done. And was not Ursula's way of emotional intimacy, emotional and physical, was it not just as dangerous as Hermione's abstract spiritual intimacy? Fusion, fusion, this horrible fusion of two beings, which every woman and most men insisted on, was it not nauseous and horrible anyhow, whether it was a fusion of the spirit or of the emotional body? Hermione saw herself as the perfect Idea, to which all men must come: and Ursula was the perfect Womb, the bath of birth, to which all men must come! And both were horrible. Why could they not remain individuals, limited by their own limits? Why this dreadful all-comprehensiveness, this hateful tyranny? Why not leave the other being free, why try to absorb, or melt, or merge? One might abandon oneself utterly to the *moments*, but not to any other being.

He could not bear to see the rings lying in the pale mud of the road. He picked them up and wiped them unconsciously on his hands. They were the little tokens of the reality of beauty, the reality of happiness in warm creation. But he had made his hands all dirty and gritty.

There was a darkness over his mind. The terrible knot of consciousness that had persisted there like an obsession was broken, gone, his life was dissolved in darkness over his limbs and his body. But there was a point of anxiety in his heart now. He wanted her to come back. He breathed lightly and regularly like an infant, that breathes innocently, beyond the touch of responsibility.

She was coming back. He saw her drifting desultorily under the high hedge, advancing towards him slowly. He did not move, he did not look again. He was as if asleep, at peace, slumbering and utterly relaxed.

She came up and stood before him, hanging her head.

'See what a flower I found you,' she said, wistfully holding a piece of purple-red bell-heather under his face. He saw the clump of coloured bells, and the tree-like, tiny branch: also her hands, with their over-fine, oversensitive skin.

'Pretty!' he said, looking up at her with a smile, taking the flower. Everything had become simple again, quite simple, the complexity gone into nowhere. But he badly wanted to cry: except that he was weary and bored by emotion.

Then a hot passion of tenderness for her filled his heart. He stood up and looked into her face. It was new, and oh, so delicate in its luminous wonder and fear. He put his arms round her, and she hid her face on his shoulder.

It was peace, just simple peace, as he stood folding her quietly there on the open lane. It was peace at last. The old, detestable world of tension had passed away at last, his soul was strong and at ease.

She looked up at him. The wonderful yellow light in her eyes now was soft and yielded, they were at peace with each other. He kissed her softly, many, many times. A laugh came into her eyes.

'Did I abuse you?' she asked.

He smiled too, and took her hand, that was so soft and given.

'Never mind,' she said, 'it is all for the good.' He kissed her again, softly, many times.

'Isn't it?' she said.

'Certainly,' he replied. 'Wait! I shall have my own back.'

She laughed suddenly, with a wild catch in her voice, and flung her arms around him.

'You are mine, my love, aren't you?' she cried, straining him close.

'Yes,' he said softly.

His voice was so soft and final, she went very still, as if under a fate which had taken her. Yes, she acquiesced – but it was accomplished without her acquiescence. He was kissing her quietly, repeatedly, with a soft, still happiness that almost made her heart stop beating.

'My love!' she cried, lifting her face and looking with frightened, gentle wonder of bliss. Was it all real? But his eyes were beautiful and soft and immune from stress or excitement, beautiful and smiling lightly to her, smiling with her. She hid her face on his shoulder, hiding before him, because he could see her so completely. She knew he loved her, and she was afraid, she was in a strange element, a new heaven round about her. She wished he were passionate, because in passion she was at home. But this was so still and frail, as space is more frightening than force.

Again, quickly, she lifted her head.

'Do you love me?' she said quickly, impulsively.

'Yes,' he replied, not heeding her motion, only her stillness.

She knew it was true. She broke away.

'So you ought,' she said, turning round to look at the road. 'Did you find the rings?'

'Yes.'

'Where are they?'

'In my pocket.'

She put her hand into his pocket and took them out.

She was restless.

'Shall we go?' she said.

'Yes,' he answered. And they mounted to the car once more, and left behind them this memorable battle-field.

They drifted through the wild, late afternoon in a beautiful motion that was smiling and transcendent. His mind was sweetly at ease, the life flowed through him as from some new fountain, he was as if born out of the cramp of a womb.

'Are you happy?' she asked him, in her strange, delighted way.

'Yes,' he said.

'So am I,' she cried in sudden ecstasy, putting her arm round him and clutching him violently against her, as he steered the motor-car.

'Don't drive much more,' she said. 'I don't want you to be always doing something.'

'No,' he said. 'We'll finish this little trip, and then we'll be free.'

'We will, my love, we will,' she cried in delight, kissing him as he turned to her.

He drove on in a strange new wakefulness, the tension of his consciousness broken. He seemed to be conscious all over, all his body awake with a simple, glimmering awareness, as if he had just come awake, like a thing that is born, like a bird when it comes out of an egg, into a new universe.

They dropped down a long hill in the dusk, and suddenly Ursula recognised on her right hand, below in the hollow, the form of Southwell Minster.

'Are we here!' she cried with pleasure.

The rigid, sombre, ugly cathedral was settling under the gloom of the coming night, as they entered the narrow town, the golden lights showed like slabs of revelation in the shop-windows.

'Father came here with mother,' she said, 'when they first knew each other. He loves it – he loves the Minster. Do you?'

'Yes. It looks like quartz crystals sticking up out of the dark hollow. We'll have our high tea at the Saracen's Head.'

As they descended, they heard the Minster bells playing a hymn, when the hour had struck six.

'Glory to thee my God this night
For all the blessings of the light—'

So, to Ursula's ear, the tune fell out, drop by drop, from the unseen sky on to the dusky town. It was like dim, bygone centuries sounding. It was all so far off. She stood in the old yard of the inn, smelling of straw and stables and petrol. Above, she could see the first stars. What was it all? This was no actual world, it was the dream-world of one's childhood – a great circumscribed reminiscence. The world had become unreal. She herself was a strange, transcendent reality.

'Is it?' she replied, laughing, but unassured.

They sat together in a little parlour by the fire.

'What?'

'Everything – is everything true?'

'The best is true,' he said, grimacing at her.

'Is it?' she replied, laughing, but unassured.

She looked at him. He seemed still so separate. New eyes were opened in her soul. She saw a strange creature from another world in him. It was as if she were enchanted, and everything were metamorphosed. She recalled again the old magic of the Book of Genesis, where the sons of God saw the daughter of men, that they were fair. And he was one of these, one of these strange creatures from the beyond, looking down at her, and seeing she was fair.

He stood on the hearth-rug looking at her, at her face that was upturned exactly like a flower, a fresh, luminous flower, glinting faintly golden with the dew of the first light. And he was smiling faintly as if there were no speech in the world, save the silent delight of flowers in each other. Smilingly they delighted in each other's presence, pure presence, not to be thought of, even known. But his eyes had a faintly ironical contraction.

And she was drawn to him strangely, as in a spell. Kneeling on the hearth-rug before him, she put her arms round his loins, and put her face against his thighs. Riches! Riches! She was overwhelmed with a sense of a heavenful of riches.

'We love each other,' she said in delight.

'More than that,' he answered, looking down at her with his glimmering, easy face.

Unconsciously, with her sensitive finger-tips, she was tracing the back of his thighs, following some mysterious life-flow there. She had discovered something, something more than wonderful, more wonderful than life itself. It was the strange mystery of his life-motion, there, at the back of the thighs, down the flanks. It was a strange reality of his being, the very stuff of being, there in the straight downflow of the thighs. It was here she discovered him one of the sons of God such as were in the beginning of the world, not a man, something other, something more.

This was release at last. She had had lovers, she had known passion. But this was neither love nor passion. It was the daughters of men coming back to the sons of God, the strange inhuman sons of God who are in the beginning.

Her face was now one dazzle of released, golden light, as she looked up at him and laid her hands full on his thighs, behind, as he stood before her. He looked down at her with a rich bright brow like a diadem above his eyes. She was beautiful as a new marvellous flower opened at his knees, a paradisal flower she was, beyond womanhood, such a flower of luminousness. Yet something was tight and unfree in him. He did not like this crouching, this radiance – not altogether.

It was all achieved for her. She had found one of the sons of God from the Beginning, and he had found one of the first most luminous daughters of men.

She traced with her hands the line of his loins and thighs, at the back, and a living fire ran through her, from him, darkly. It was a dark flood of electric passion she released from him, drew into herself. She had established a rich new circuit, a new current of passional electric energy, between the two of them, released from the darkest poles of the body and established in perfect circuit. It was a dark fire of electricity that rushed from him to her, and flooded them both with rich peace, satisfaction.

'My love,' she cried, lifting her face to him, her eyes, her mouth open in transport.

'My love,' he answered, bending and kissing her, always kissing her.

She closed her hands over the full, rounded body of his loins, as he stooped over her, she seemed to touch the quick of the mystery of darkness that was bodily him. She seemed to faint beneath, and he seemed to faint, stooping over her. It was a perfect passing away for both of them, and at the same time the most intolerable accession into being, the marvellous fullness of immediate gratification, overwhelming, outflooding from the source of the deepest life-force, the darkest, deepest, strangest life-source of the human body, at the back and base of the loins.

After a lapse of stillness, after the rivers of strange dark fluid richness had passed over her, flooding, carrying away her mind and flooding down her spine and down her knees, past her feet, a strange flood, sweeping away everything and leaving her an essential new being, she was left quite free, she was free in complete ease, her complete self. So she rose, stilly and blithe, smiling at him. He stood before her, glimmering, so awfully real, that her heart almost stopped beating. He stood there in his strange, whole body, that had its marvellous fountains, like the bodies of the sons of God who were in the beginning. There were strange fountains of his body, more mysterious and potent than any she had imagined or known, more satisfying, ah, finally, mystically-physically satisfying. She had thought there was no source deeper than the phallic source. And now, behold, from the smitten rock of the man's body, from the strange marvellous flanks and thighs, deeper, further in mystery than the phallic source, came the floods of ineffable darkness and ineffable riches.

They were glad, and they could forget perfectly. They laughed and went to the meal provided. There was a venison pasty, of all things, a large broad-faced cut ham, eggs and cresses and red beetroot, and medlars and apple-tart, and tea.

'What *good* things!' she cried with pleasure. 'How noble it looks! – shall I pour out the tea?—'

She was usually nervous and uncertain at performing these public duties, such as giving tea. But to-day she forgot, she was at her ease, entirely forgetting to have misgivings. The tea-pot poured beautifully from a proud slender spout. Her eyes were warm with smiles as she gave him his tea. She had learned at last to be still and perfect.

'Everything is ours,' she said to him.

'Everything,' he answered.

She gave a queer little crowing sound of triumph.

'I'm so glad!' she cried, with unspeakable relief.

'So am I,' he said. 'But I'm thinking we'd better get out of our responsibilities as quick as we can.'

'What responsibilities?' she asked, wondering.

'We must drop our jobs, like a shot.'

A new understanding dawned into her face.

'Of course,' she said, 'there's that.'

'We must get out,' he said. 'There's nothing for it but to get out, quick.'

She looked at him doubtfully across the table.

'But where?' she said.

'I don't know,' he said. 'We'll just wander about for a bit.'

Again she looked at him quizzically.

'I should be perfectly happy at the Mill,' she said.

'It's very near the old thing,' he said. 'Let us wander a bit.'

His voice could be so soft and happy-go lucky, it went through her veins like an exhilaration. Nevertheless, she dreamed of a valley, and wild gardens, and peace. She had a desire too for splendour – an aristocratic extravagant splendour. Wandering seemed to her like restlessness, dissatisfaction.

'Where will you wander to?' she asked.

'I don't know. I feel as if I would just meet you and we'd set off – just towards the distance.'

'But where can one go?' she asked anxiously. 'After all, there *is* only the world, and none of it is very distant.'

'Still,' he said, 'I should like to go with you – nowhere. It would be rather wandering just to nowhere. That's the place to get to – nowhere. One wants to wander away from the world's somewheres, into our own nowhere.'

Still she meditated.

'You see, my love,' she said, 'I'm so afraid that while we are only people, we've got to take the world that's given – because there isn't any other.'

'Yes, there is,' he said. 'There's somewhere where we can be free – somewhere where one needn't wear much clothes – none even – where one meets a few people who have gone through enough, and can take things for granted – where you can be yourself, without bothering. There is somewhere – there are one or two people—'

'But where—?' she sighed.

'Somewhere – anywhere. Let's wander off. That's the thing to do – let's wander off.'

'Yes—' she said, thrilled at the thought of travel. But to her it was only travel.

'To be free,' he said. 'To be free, in a free place, with a few other people!'

'Yes,' she said wistfully. Those 'few other people' depressed her.

'It isn't really a locality, though,' he said. 'It's a perfected relation between you and me, and others – the perfect relation – so that we are free together.'

'It is, my love, isn't it,' she said. 'It's you and me. It's you and me, isn't it?' She stretched out her arms to him. He went across and stooped to kiss her face. Her arms closed round him again, her hands spread upon his shoulders, moving slowly there, moving slowly on his back, down his back slowly, with a strange recurrent, rhythmic motion, yet moving slowly down, pressing mysteriously over his loins, over his flanks. The sense of the awfulness of riches that could never be impaired flooded her mind like a swoon, a death in most marvellous possession, mystic-sure. She possessed him so utterly and intolerably that she herself lapsed out. And yet she was only sitting still in the chair, with her hands pressed upon him, and lost.

Again he softly kissed her.

'We shall never go apart again,' he murmured quietly. And she did not speak, but only pressed her hands firmer down upon the source of darkness in him.

They decided, when they woke again from the pure swoon, to write their resignations from the world of work there and then. She wanted this.

He rang the bell and ordered note-paper without a printed address. The waiter cleared the table.

'Now then,' he said, 'yours first. Put your home address, and the date – then "Director of Education, Town Hall – Sir—" Now then! – I don't know how one really stands – I suppose one could get out of it in less than a month – Anyhow, "Sir – I beg to resign my post as class-mistress in the Willey Green Grammar School. I should be very grateful if you would liberate me as soon as possible, without waiting for the expiration of the month's notice." That'll do. Have you got it? Let me look. "Ursula Brangwen." Good! Now I'll write mine. I ought to give them three months, but I can plead health. I can arrange it all right.'

He sat and wrote out his formal resignation.

'Now,' he said, when the envelopes were sealed and addressed, 'shall we post them here, both together? I know Jackie will say, "Here's a coincidence!" when he receives them in all their identity. Shall we let him say it, or not?'

'I don't care,' she said.

'No—?' he said, pondering.

'It doesn't matter, does it?' she said.

'Yes,' he replied. 'Their imaginations shall not work on us. I'll post yours here, mine after. I cannot be implicated in their imaginings.'

He looked at her with his strange, non-human singleness.

'Yes, you are right,' she said.

She lifted her face to him, all shining and open. It was as if he might enter straight into the source of her radiance. His face became a little distracted.

'Shall we go?' he said.

'As you like,' she replied.

They were soon out of the little town and running through the uneven lanes of the country. Ursula nestled near him, into his constant warmth, and watched the pale-lit revelation racing ahead, the visible night. Sometimes it was a wide old road, with grass-spaces on either side, flying magic and elfin in the greenish illumination, sometimes it was trees looming overhead, sometimes it was bramble bushes, sometimes the walls of a crew-yard and the butt of a barn.

'Are you going to Shortlands to dinner?' Ursula asked him suddenly. He started.

'Good God!' he said. 'Shortlands! Never again. Not that. Besides, we should be too late.'

'Where are we going then – to the Mill?'

'If you like. Pity to go anywhere on this good dark night. Pity to come out of it, really. Pity we can't stop in the good darkness. It is better than anything ever would be – this good immediate darkness.'

She sat wondering. The car lurched and swayed. She knew there was no leaving him, the darkness held them both and contained them, it was not to be surpassed. Besides, she had a full mystic knowledge of his suave loins of darkness, dark-clad and suave, and in this knowledge there was some of the inevitability and the beauty of fate, fate which one asks for, which one accepts in full.

He sat still like an Egyptian Pharaoh, driving the car. He felt as if he were seated in immemorial potency, like the great carven statues of real Egypt, as real and as fulfilled with subtle strength, as these are, with a vague inscrutable smile on the lips. He knew what it was to have the strange and magical current of force in his back and loins, and down his legs, force so perfect that it stayed him immobile, and left his face subtly, mindlessly smiling. He knew what it was to be awake and potent in that other basic mind, the deepest physical mind. And from this source he had a pure and magic control, magical, mystical, a force in darkness, like electricity.

It was very difficult to speak, it was so perfect to sit in this pure living silence, subtle, full of unthinkable knowledge and unthinkable force, upheld immemorially in timeless force, like the immobile, supremely potent Egyptians, seated for ever in their living, subtle silence.

'We need not go home,' he said. 'This car has seats that let down and make a bed, and we can lift the hood.'

She was glad and frightened. She cowered near to him.

'But what about them at home?' she said.

'Send a telegram.'

Nothing more was said. They ran on in silence. But with a sort of second consciousness he steered the car towards a destination. For he had the free intelligence to direct his own ends. His arms and his breast and his head were rounded and living like those of the Greek, he had not the unawakened straight arms of the Egyptian, nor the sealed, slumbering head. A lambent intelligence played secondarily above his pure Egyptian concentration in darkness.

They came to a village that lined along the road. The car crept slowly along, until he saw the post office. Then he pulled up.

'I will send a telegram to your father,' he said. 'I will merely say "Spending the night in town", shall I?'

'Yes,' she answered. She did not want to be disturbed into taking thought.

She watched him move into the post office. It was also a shop, she saw. Strange, he was. Even as he went into the lighted, public place he remained dark and magic, the living silence seemed the body of reality in him, subtle, potent, indiscoverable. There he was! In a strange uplift of elation she saw him, the being never to be revealed, awful in its potency, mystic and real. This dark, subtle reality of him, never to be translated, liberated her into perfection, her own perfect being. She too was dark and fulfilled in silence.

He came out, throwing some packages into the car.

'There is some bread, and cheese, and raisins, and apples, and hard chocolate,' he said, in his voice that was as if laughing, because of the unblemished stillness and force which was the reality in him. She would have to touch him. To speak, to see, was nothing. It was a travesty to look and to comprehend the man there. Darkness and silence must fall perfectly on her, then she could know mystically, in unrevealed touch. She must lightly, mindlessly connect with him, have the knowledge which is death of knowledge, the reality of surety in not knowing.

Soon they had run on again into the darkness. She did not ask where they were going, she did not care. She sat in a fullness and a pure potency that was like apathy, mindless and immobile. She was next to him, and hung in a pure rest, as a star is hung, balanced unthinkably. Still there remained a dark lambency of anticipation. She would touch him. With perfect fine finger-tips of reality she would touch the reality in him, the suave, pure, untranslatable reality of his loins of darkness. To touch, mindlessly in darkness to come in pure touching upon the living reality of him, his suave perfect loins and thighs of darkness, this was her sustaining anticipation.

And he too waited in the magical steadfastness of suspense, for her to take this knowledge of him as he had taken it of her. He knew her darkly, with the fullness of dark knowledge. Now she would know him, and he too would be liberated. He would be night-free, like an Egyptian, steadfast in perfectly suspended equilibrium, pure mystic nodality of physical being. They would give each other this star-equilibrium which alone is freedom.

She saw that they were running among trees – great old trees with dying bracken undergrowth. The palish, gnarled trunks showed ghostly, and like old priests in the hovering distance, the fern rose magical and mysterious. It was a night all darkness, with low cloud. The motor-car advanced slowly.

'Where are we?' she whispered.

'In Sherwood Forest.'

It was evident he knew the place. He drove softly, watching. Then they came to a green road between the trees. They turned cautiously round, and were advancing between the oaks of the forest, down a green lane. The green lane widened into a little circle of grass, where there was a small trickle of water at the bottom of a sloping bank. The car stopped.

'We will stay here,' he said, 'and put out the lights.'

He extinguished the lamps at once, and it was pure night, with shadows of trees like realities of other nightly being. He threw a rug on to the bracken, and they sat in stillness and mindless silence. There were faint sounds from the wood, but no disturbance, no possible disturbance, the world was under a strange ban, a new mystery had supervened. They threw off their clothes, and he gathered her to him, and found her, found the pure lambent reality of her for ever invisible flesh. Quenched, inhuman, his fingers upon her unrevealed nudity were the fingers of silence upon silence, the body of mysterious night upon the body of mysterious night, the night masculine and feminine, never to be seen with the eye, or known with the mind, only known as a palpable revelation of living otherness.

She had her desire of him, she touched, she received the maximum of unspeakable communication in touch, dark, subtle, positively silent, a magnificent gift and give again, a perfect acceptance and yielding, a mystery, the reality of that which can never be known, vital, sensual reality that can never be transmuted into mind content, but remains outside, living body of darkness and silence and subtlety, the mystic body of reality. She had her desire fulfilled. He had his desire fulfilled. For she was to him what he was to her, the immemorial magnificence of mystic, palpable, real otherness.

They slept the chilly night through under the hood of the car, a night of unbroken sleep. It was already high day when he awoke. They looked at each other and laughed, then looked away, filled with darkness and secrecy. Then they kissed and remembered the magnificence of the night. It was so magnificent, such an inheritance of a universe of dark reality, that they were afraid to seem to remember. They hid away the remembrance and the knowledge.

Chapter Twenty-four

Death and Love

Thomas Crich died slowly, terribly slowly. It seemed impossible to everybody that the thread of life could be drawn out so thin, and yet not break. The sick man lay unutterably weak and spent, kept alive by morphia and by drinks, which he sipped slowly. He was only half conscious – a thin strand of consciousness linking the darkness of death with the light of day. Yet his will was unbroken, he was integral, complete. Only he must have perfect stillness about him.

Any presence but that of the nurses was a strain and an effort to him now. Every morning Gerald went into the room, hoping to find his father passed away at last. Yet always he saw the same transparent face, the same dread dark hair on the waxen forehead, and the awful, inchoate dark eyes, which seemed to be decomposing into formless darkness, having only a tiny grain of vision within them.

And always, as the dark, inchoate eyes turned to him, there passed through Gerald's bowels a burning stroke of revolt, that seemed to resound through his whole being, threatening to break his mind with its clangour, and making him mad.

Every morning, the son stood there, erect and taut with life, gleaming in his blondness. The gleaming blondness of his strange, imminent being put the father into a fever of fretful irritation. He could not bear to meet the uncanny, downward look of Gerald's blue eyes. But it was only for a moment. Each on the brink of departure, the father and son looked at each other, then parted.

For a long time Gerald preserved a perfect *sang froid*, he remained quite collected. But at last, fear undermined him. He was afraid of some horrible collapse in himself. He had to stay and see this thing through. Some perverse will made him watch his father drawn over the borders of life. And yet, now, every day, the great red-hot stroke of horrified fear through the bowels of the son struck a further inflammation. Gerald went about all day with a tendency to cringe, as if there were the point of a sword of Damocles pricking the nape of his neck.

There was no escape – he was bound up with his father, he had to see him through. And the father's will never relaxed or yielded to death. It would have to snap when death at last snapped it – if it did not persist after a physical death. In the same way, the will of the son never yielded. He stood firm and immune, he was outside this death and this dying.

It was a trial by ordeal. Could he stand and see his father slowly dissolve and disappear in death, without once yielding his will, without once relenting before the omnipotence of death. Like a Red Indian undergoing torture, Gerald would experience the whole process of slow death without wincing or flinching. He even triumphed in it. He somehow *wanted* this death, even forced it. It was as if he himself were dealing the death, even when he most recoiled in horror. Still, he would deal it, he would triumph through death.

But in the stress of this ordeal, Gerald too lost his hold on the outer, daily life. That which was much to him, came to mean nothing. Work, pleasure – it was all left behind. He went on more or less mechanically with his business, but this activity was all extraneous. The real activity was this ghastly wrestling for death in his own soul. And his own will should triumph. Come what might, he would not bow down or submit or acknowledge a master. He had no master in death.

But as the fight went on, and all that he had been and was continued to be destroyed, so that life was a hollow shell all round him, roaring and clattering like the sound of the sea, a noise in which he participated externally, and inside this hollow shell was all the darkness and fearful space of death, he knew he would have to find reinforcements, otherwise he would collapse inwards upon the great dark void which circled at the centre of his soul. His will held his outer life, his outer mind, his outer being unbroken and unchanged. But the pressure was too great. He would have to find something to make good the equilibrium. Something must come with him into the hollow void of death in his soul, fill it up, and so equalise the pressure within to the pressure without. For day by day he felt more and more like a bubble filled with darkness, round which whirled the iridescence of his consciousness, and upon which the pressure of the outer world, the outer life, roared vastly.

In this extremity his instinct led him to Gudrun. He threw away everything now – he only wanted the relation established with her. He would follow her to the studio, to be near her, to talk to her. He would stand about the room, aimlessly picking up the implements, the lumps of clay, the little figures she had cast – they were whimsical and grotesque – looking at them without perceiving them. And she felt him following her, dogging her heels like a doom. She held away from him, and yet she knew he drew always a little nearer, a little nearer.

'I say,' he said to her one evening, in an odd, unthinking, uncertain way, 'won't you stay to dinner to-night? I wish you would.'

She started slightly. He spoke to her like a man making a request of another man.

'They'll be expecting me at home,' she said.

'Oh, they won't mind, will they?' he said. 'I should be awfully glad if you'd stay.

Her long silence gave consent at last.

'I'll tell Thomas, shall I?' he said.

'I must go almost immediately after dinner,' she said.

It was a dark, cold evening. There was no fire in the drawing-room, they sat in the library. He was mostly silent, absent, and Winifred talked little. But when Gerald did rouse himself, he smiled and was pleasant and ordinary with her. Then there came over him again the long blanks, of which he was not aware.

She was very much attracted by him. He looked so preoccupied, and his strange, blank silences, which she could not read, moved her and made her wonder over him, made her feel reverential towards him.

But he was very kind. He gave her the best things at the table, he had a bottle of slightly sweet, delicious golden wine brought out for dinner, knowing she would prefer it to the burgundy. She felt herself esteemed, needed almost.

As they took coffee in the library, there was a soft, very soft knocking at the door. He started, and called, 'Come in.' The timbre of his voice, like something vibrating at high pitch, unnerved Gudrun. A nurse in white entered, half hovering in the doorway like a shadow. She was very good-looking, but strangely enough, shy and self-mistrusting.

'The doctor would like to speak to you, Mr. Crich,' she said in her low, discreet voice.

'The doctor!' he said, starting up. 'Where is he?'

'He is in the dining-room.'

'Tell him I'm coming.'

He drank up his coffee and followed the nurse, who had dissolved like a shadow.

'Which nurse was that?' asked Gudrun.

'Miss Inglis – I like her best,' replied Winifred.

After a while Gerald came back, looking absorbed by his own thoughts, and having some of that tension and abstraction which is seen in a slightly drunken man. He did not say what the doctor had wanted him for, but stood before the fire, with his hands behind his back, and his face open and as if rapt. Not that he was really thinking – he was only arrested in pure suspense inside himself, and thoughts wafted through his mind without order.

'I must go now and see Mama,' said Winifred, 'and see Dadda before he goes to sleep.'

She bade them both good-night.

Gudrun also rose to take her leave.

'You needn't go yet, need you?' said Gerald, glancing quickly at the clock. 'It is early yet. I'll walk down with you when you go. Sit down, don't hurry away.'

Gudrun sat down, as if, absent as he was, his will had power over her. She felt almost mesmerised. He was strange to her, something unknown. What was he thinking, what was he feeling, as he stood there so rapt, saying nothing? He kept her – she could feel that. He would not let her go. She watched him in humble submissiveness.

'Had the doctor anything new to tell you?' she asked softly, at length, with that gentle, timid sympathy which touched a keen fibre in his heart. He lifted his eyebrows with a negligent indifferent expression.

'No – nothing new,' he replied, as if the question were quite casual, trivial. 'He says the pulse is very weak indeed, very intermittent – but that doesn't necessarily mean much, you know.'

He looked down at her. Her eyes were dark and soft and unfolded, with a stricken look that roused him.

'No,' she murmured at length. 'I don't understand anything about these things.'

'Just as well not,' he said. 'I say, won't you have a cigarette? – do!' He quickly fetched the box and held her a light. Then he stood before her on the hearth again.

'No,' he said, 'we've never had much illness in the house, either – not till father.' He seemed to meditate a while. Then looking down at her, with strangely communicative blue eyes that filled her with dread, he continued: 'It's something you don't reckon with, you know, till it is there. And then you realise that it was there all the time – it was always there – you understand what I mean? – the possibility of this incurable illness, this slow death.'

He moved his feet uneasily on the marble hearth and put his cigarette to his mouth, looking up at the ceiling.

'I know,' murmured Gudrun: 'it is dreadful.'

He smoked without knowing. Then he took the cigarette from his lips, bared his teeth, and putting the tip of his tongue between his teeth, spat off a grain of tobacco, turning slightly aside, like a man who is alone, or who is lost in thought.

'I don't know what the effect actually *is* on one,' he said, and again he looked down at her. Her eyes were dark and stricken with knowledge, looking into his. He saw her submerged, and he turned aside his face. "But I absolutely am not the same. There's nothing left, if you understand what I mean. You seem to be clutching at the void – and at the same time you are void yourself. And so you don't know what to *do*.'

'No,' she murmured. A heavy thrill ran down her nerves, heavy, almost pleasure, almost pain. 'What can be done?' she added.

He turned and flipped the ash from his cigarette on to the great marble hearth-stones, that lay bare in the room, without fender or bar.

'I don't know, I'm sure,' he replied. 'But I do think you've got to find some way of resolving the situation – not because you want to, but because you've *got* to, otherwise you're done. The whole of everything, and yourself included, is just on the point of caving in, and you are just holding it up with your hands. Well, it's a situation that obviously can't continue. You can't stand holding the roof up with your hands for ever. You know that sooner or later you'll *have* to let go. Do you understand what I mean? And so something's got to be done, or there's a universal collapse – as far as you yourself are concerned.'

He shifted slightly on the hearth, crunching a cinder under his heel. He looked down at it. Gudrun was aware of the beautiful old marble panels of the fireplace, swelling softly carved, round him and above him. She felt as if she were caught at last by fate, imprisoned in some horrible and fatal trap.

'But what *can* be done?' she murmured humbly. 'You must use me if I can be of any help at all – but how can I? I don't see how I *can* help you.'

He looked down at her critically.

'I don't want you to *help*,' he said, slightly irritated, 'because there's nothing to be *done*. I only want sympathy, do you see: I want somebody I can talk to sympathetically. That eases the strain. And there *is* nobody to talk to sympathetically. That's the curious thing. There *is* nobody. There's Rupert Birkin. But then he *isn't* sympathetic, he wants to *dictate*. And that is no use whatsoever.'

She was caught in a strange snare. She looked down at her hands.

Then there was the sound of the door softly opening. Gerald started. He was chagrined. It was his starting that really startled Gudrun. Then he went forward, with quick, graceful, intentional courtesy.

'Oh, mother!' he said. 'How nice of you to come down. How are you?'

The elderly woman, loosely and bulkily wrapped in a purple gown, came forward silently, slightly hulked, as usual. Her son was at her side. He pushed her up a chair, saying: 'You know Miss Brangwen, don't you?'

The mother glanced at Gudrun indifferently.

'Yes,' she said. Then she turned her wonderful, forget-me-not blue eyes up to her son, as she slowly sat down in the chair he had brought her.

'I came to ask you about your father,' she said, in her rapid, scarcely audible voice. 'I didn't know you had company.'

'No? Didn't Winifred tell you? Miss Brangwen stayed to dinner to make us a little more lively—'

Mrs. Crich turned slowly round to Gudrun and looked at her, but with unseeing eyes.

'I'm afraid it would be no treat to her.' Then she turned again to her son. 'Winifred tells me the doctor had something to say about your father. What is it?'

'Only that the pulse is very weak – misses altogether a good many times – so that he might not last the night out,' Gerald replied.

Mrs. Crich sat perfectly impassive, as if she had not heard. Her bulk seemed hunched in the chair, her fair hair hung slack over her ears. But her skin was clear and fine, her hands, as she sat with them forgotten and folded, were quite beautiful, full of potential energy. A great mass of energy seemed decaying up in that silent, hulking form.

She looked up at her son as he stood, keen and soldierly, near to her. Her eyes were most wonderfully blue, bluer than forget-me-nots. She seemed to have a certain confidence in Gerald, and to feel a certain motherly mistrust of him.

'How are *you*?' she muttered in her strangely quiet voice, as if nobody should hear but him. 'You're not getting into a state, are you? You're not letting it make you hysterical?'

The curious challenge in the last words startled Gudrun.

'I don't think so, mother,' he answered, rather coldly cheery. 'Somebody's got to see it through, you know.'

'Have they? Have they?' answered his mother rapidly. 'Why should *you* take it on yourself? What have you got to do, seeing it through. It will see itself through. You are not needed.'

'No, I don't suppose I can do any good,' he answered. 'It's just how it affects us, you see.'

'You like to be affected – don't you? It's quite nuts for you? You would have to be important. You have no need to stop at home. Why don't you go away!'

These sentences, evidently the ripened grain of many dark hours, took Gerald by surprise.

'I don't think it's any good going away now, mother, at the last minute,' he said coldly.

'You take care,' replied his mother. 'You mind *yourself* – that's your business. You take too much on yourself. You mind yourself, or you'll find yourself in Queer Street, that's what will happen to you. You're hysterical, always were.'

'I'm all right, mother,' he said. 'There's no need to worry about *me*, I assure you.'

'Let the dead bury their dead – don't go and bury yourself along with them – that's what I tell you. I know you well enough.'

He did not answer this, not knowing what to say. The mother sat bunched up in silence, her beautiful white hands, that had no rings whatsoever, clasping the pommels of her arm-chair.

'You can't do it,' she said, almost bitterly. 'You haven't the nerve. You're as weak as a cat, really – always were. Is this young woman staying here?'

'No,' said Gerald. 'She is going home to-night.'

'Then she'd better have the dog-cart. Does she go far?'

'Only to Beldover.'

'Ah!' The elderly woman never looked at Gudrun, yet she seemed to take knowledge of her presence.

'You are inclined to take too much on yourself, Gerald,' said the mother, pulling herself to her feet, with a little difficulty.

'Will you go, mother?' he asked politely.

'Yes, I'll go up again,' she replied. Turning to Gudrun, she bade her 'Good-night'. Then she went slowly to the door, as if she were unaccustomed to walking. At the door she lifted her face to him implicitly. He kissed her.

'Don't come any further with me,' she said in her barely audible voice. 'I don't want you any further.'

He bade her good-night, watched her across to the stairs and mount slowly. Then he closed the door and came back to Gudrun. Gudrun rose also, to go.

'A queer being, my mother,' he said.

'Yes,' replied Gudrun.

'She has her own thoughts.'

'Yes,' said Gudrun.

Then they were silent.

'You want to go?' he asked. 'Half a minute, I'll just have a horse put in—'

'No,' said Gudrun. 'I want to walk.'

He had promised to walk with her down the long, lonely mile of drive, and she wanted this.

'You might *just* as well drive,' he said.

'I'd *much rather* walk,' she asserted, with emphasis.

'You would! Then I will come along with you. You know where your things are? I'll put boots on.'

He put on a cap and an overcoat over his evening dress. They went out into the night.

'Let us light a cigarette,' he said, stopping in a sheltered angle of the porch. 'You have one too.'

So, with the scent of tobacco on the night air, they set off down the dark drive that ran between close-cut hedges through sloping meadows.

He wanted to put his arm round her. If he could put his arm round her, and draw her against him as they walked, he would equilibrate himself. For now he felt like a pair of scales, the half of which tips down and down into an indefinite void. He must recover some sort of balance. And here was the hope and the perfect recovery.

Blind to her, thinking only of himself, he slipped his arm softly round her waist, and drew her to him. Her heart fainted, feeling herself taken. But then, his arm was so strong, she quailed under its powerful close grasp. She died a little death, and was drawn against him as they walked down the stormy darkness. He seemed to balance her perfectly in opposition to himself, in their dual motion of walking. So, suddenly, he was liberated and perfect, strong, heroic.

He put his hand to his mouth and threw his cigarette away, a gleaming point, into the unseen hedge. Then he was quite free to balance her.

'That's better,' he said, with exultancy.

The exultation in his voice was like a sweetish, poisonous drug to her. Did she then mean so much to him! She sipped the poison.

'Are you happier?' she asked wistfully.

'Much better,' he said in the same exultant voice, 'and I was rather far gone.'

She nestled against him. He felt her all soft and warm, she was the rich, lovely substance of his being. The warmth and motion of her walk suffused through him wonderfully.

'I'm *so* glad if I help you,' she said.

'Yes,' he answered. 'There's nobody else could do it, if you wouldn't.'

'That is true,' she said to herself, with a thrill of strange, fatal elation.

As they walked, he seemed to lift her nearer and nearer to himself, till she moved upon the firm vehicle of his body. He was so strong, so sustaining, and he could not be opposed. She drifted along in a wonderful interfusion of physical motion, down the dark, blowy hill-side. Far across shone the little yellow lights of Beldover, many of them, spread in a thick patch on another dark hill. But he and she were walking in perfect, isolated darkness, outside the world.

'But how much do you care for me!' came her voice, almost querulous. 'You see, I don't know, I don't understand!'

'How much!' His voice rang with a painful elation. 'I don't know either

– but everything.' He was startled by his own declaration. It was true. So he stripped himself of every safeguard, in making this admission to her. He cared everything for her – she was everything.

'But I can't believe it,' said her low voice, amazed, trembling. She was trembling with doubt and exultance. This was the thing she wanted to hear, only this. Yet now she heard it, heard the strange clapping vibration of truth in his voice as he said it, she could not believe. She could not believe – she did not believe. Yet she believed, triumphantly, with fatal exultance.

'Why not?' he said. 'Why don't you believe it? It's true. It is true, as we stand at this moment—' he stood still with her in the wind; 'I care for nothing on earth, or in heaven, outside this spot where we are. And it isn't my own presence I care about, it is all yours. I'd sell my soul a hundred times – but I couldn't bear not to have you here. I couldn't bear to be alone. My brain would burst. It is true.' He drew her closer to him, with definite movement.

'No,' she murmured, afraid. Yet this was what she wanted. Why did she so lose courage?

They resumed their strange walk. They were such strangers – and yet they were so frightfully, unthinkably near. It was like a madness. Yet it was what she wanted, it was what she wanted. They had descended the hill, and now they were coming to the square arch where the road passed under the colliery railway. The arch, Gudrun knew, had walls of squared stone, mossy on one side with water that trickled down, dry on the other side. She had stood under it to hear the train rumble thundering over the logs overhead. And she knew that under this dark and lonely bridge the young colliers stood in the darkness with their sweethearts, in rainy weather. And so she wanted to stand under the bridge with *her* sweetheart, and be kissed under the bridge in the invisible darkness. Her steps dragged as she drew near.

So, under the bridge, they came to a standstill, and he lifted her upon his breast. His body vibrated taut and powerful as he closed upon her and crushed her, breathless and dazed and destroyed, crushed her upon his breast. Ah, it was terrible, and perfect. Under this bridge, the colliers pressed their lovers at their breast. And now, under the bridge, the master of them all pressed her to himself! And how much more powerful and terrible was his embrace than theirs, how much more concentrated and supreme his love was, than theirs in the same sort! She felt she would swoon, die, under the vibrating, inhuman tension of his arms and his body – she would pass away. Then the unthinkable high vibration slackened and became more undulating. He slackened and drew her with him to stand with his back to the wall.

She was almost unconscious. So the colliers' lovers would stand with their backs to the walls, holding their sweethearts and kissing them as she was being kissed. Ah, but would their kisses be fine and powerful as the kisses of the firm-mouthed master? Even the keen, short-cut moustache – the colliers would not have that.

And the colliers' sweethearts would, like herself, hang their heads back limp over their shoulder, and look out from the dark archway at the close patch of yellow lights on the unseen hill in the distance, or at the vague form of trees, and at the buildings of the colliery wood-yard, in the other direction.

His arms were fast around her, he seemed to be gathering her into himself, her warmth, her softness, her adorable weight, drinking in the suffusion of her physical being, avidly. He lifted her, and seemed to pour her into himself, like wine into a cup.

'This is worth everything,' he said in a strange, penetrating voice.

So she relaxed, and seemed to melt, to flow into him, as if she were some infinitely warm and precious suffusion filling into his veins, like an intoxicant. Her arms were round his neck, he kissed her and held her perfectly suspended, she was all slack and flowing into him, and he was the firm, strong cup that receives the wine of her life. So she lay cast upon him, stranded, lifted up against him, melting and melting under his kisses, melting into his limbs and bones, as if he were soft iron becoming surcharged with her electric life.

Till she seemed to swoon, gradually her mind went, and she passed away, everything in her was melted down and fluid, and she lay still, become contained by him, sleeping in him as lightning sleeps in a pure, soft stone. So she was passed away and gone in him, and he was perfected.

When she opened her eyes again and saw the patch of lights in the distance, it seemed to her strange that the world still existed, that she was standing under the bridge resting her head on Gerald's breast. Gerald – who was he? He was the exquisite adventure, the desirable unknown to her.

She looked up, and in the darkness saw his face above her, his shapely, male face. There seemed a faint, white light emitted from him, a white aura, as if he were a visitor from the unseen. She reached up, like Eve reaching to the apples on the tree of knowledge, and she kissed him, though her passion was a transcendent fear of the thing he was, touching his face with her infinitely delicate, encroaching, wondering fingers. Her fingers went over the mould of his face, over his features. How perfect and foreign he was – ah, how dangerous! Her soul thrilled with complete knowledge. This was the glistening, forbidden apple, this face of a man. She kissed him, putting her fingers over his face, his eyes, his nostrils, over his brows and his ears, to his neck, to know him, to gather him in by touch. He was so firm and shapely, with such satisfying, inconceivable shapeliness, strange yet unutterably clear. He was such an unutterable enemy, yet glistening with uncanny white fire. She wanted to touch him and touch him and touch him, till she had him all in her hands, till she had strained him into her knowledge. Ah, if she could have the precious *knowledge* of him, she would be filled, and nothing could deprive her of this. For he was so unsure, so risky in the common world of day.

'You are so *beautiful*,' she murmured in her throat.

He wondered, and was suspended. But she felt him quiver, and she came down involuntarily nearer upon him. He could not help himself. Her fingers had him under their power. The fathomless, fathomless desire they could evoke in him was deeper than death, where he had no choice.

But she knew now, and it was enough. For the time, her soul was destroyed with the exquisite shock of his invisible fluid lightning. She knew. And this knowledge was a death from which she must recover. How much more of him was there to know? Ah, much, much, many days harvesting for her large, yet perfectly subtle and intelligent hands upon the field of his living, radio-active body. Ah, her hands were eager, greedy for knowledge. But for the present it was enough, enough, as much as her soul could bear. Too much, and she would shatter herself, she would fill the fine vial of her soul too quickly, and it would break. Enough now – enough for the time being. There were all the after days when her hands, like birds, could feed upon the fields of his mystical plastic form – till then enough.

And even he was glad to be checked, rebuked, held back. For to desire is better than to possess, the finality of the end was dreaded as deeply as it was desired.

They walked on towards the town, towards where the lamps threaded singly, at long intervals, down the dark high-road of the valley. They came at length to the gate of the drive.

'Don't come any further,' she said.

'You'd rather I didn't?' he asked, relieved. He did not want to go up the public streets with her, his soul all naked and alight as it was.

'Much rather – good-night.' She held out her hand. He grasped it, then touched the perilous, potent fingers with his lips.

'Good-night,' he said. 'To-morrow.'

And they parted. He went home full of the strength and the power of living desire.

But the next day, she did not come, she sent a note that she was kept indoors by a cold. Here was a torment! But he possessed his soul in some sort of patience, writing a brief answer, telling her how sorry he was not to see her.

The day after this, he stayed at home – it seemed so futile to go down to the office. His father could not live the week out. And he wanted to be at home, suspended.

Gerald sat on a chair by the window in his father's room. The landscape outside was black and winter-sodden. His father lay grey and ashen on the bed, a nurse moved silently in her white dress, neat and elegant, even beautiful. There was a scent of eau-de-Cologne in the room. The nurse went out of the room, Gerald was alone with death, facing the winter-black landscape.

'Is there much more water in Denley?' came the faint voice, determined and querulous, from the bed. The dying man was asking about a leakage from Willey Water into one of the pits.

'Some more – we shall have to run off the lake,' said Gerald.

'Will you?' The faint voice filtered to extinction. There was dead stillness. The grey-faced, sick man lay with eyes closed, more dead than death. Gerald looked away. He felt his heart was seared, it would perish if this went on much longer.

Suddenly he heard a strange noise. Turning round, he saw his father's eyes wide open, strained and rolling in a frenzy of inhuman struggling. Gerald started to his feet, and stood transfixed in horror.

'Wha-a-ah-h-h!' came a horrible choking rattle from his father's throat, the fearful, frenzied eye, rolling awfully in its wild, fruitless search for help, passed blindly over Gerald, then up came the dark blood and mess pumping over the face of the agonised being. The tense body relaxed, the head fell aside, down the pillow.

Gerald stood transfixed, his soul echoing in horror. He would move, but he could not. He could not move his limbs. His brain seemed to re-echo, like a pulse.

The nurse in white softly entered. She glanced at Gerald, then at the bed. 'Ah!' came her soft whimpering cry, and she hurried forward to the dead man. 'Ah–h!' came the slight sound of her agitated distress, as she stood bending over the bedside. Then she recovered, turned, and came for towel and sponge. She was wiping the dead face carefully, and murmuring, almost whimpering, very softly: 'Poor Mr. Crich! – Poor Mr. Crich! – Oh, poor Mr. Crich!'

'Is he dead?' clanged Gerald's sharp voice.

'Oh yes, he's gone,' replied the soft, moaning voice of the nurse, as she looked up at Gerald's face. She was young and beautiful and quivering. A strange sort of grin went over Gerald's face, over the horror. And he walked out of the room.

He was going to tell his mother. On the landing he met his brother Basil.

'He's gone, Basil,' he said, scarcely able to subdue his voice, not to let an unconscious, frightening exultation sound through.

'What?' cried Basil, going pale.

Gerald nodded. Then he went on to his mother's room.

She was sitting in her purple gown, sewing, very slowly sewing, putting in a stitch, then another stitch. She looked up at Gerald with her blue, undaunted eyes.

'Father's gone,' he said.

'He's dead? Who says so?'

'Oh, you know, mother, if you see him.'

She put her sewing down and slowly rose.

'Are you going to see him?' he asked.

'Yes,' she said.

By the bedside the children already stood in a weeping group.

'Oh, mother!' cried the daughters, almost in hysterics, weeping loudly.

But the mother went forward. The dead man lay in repose, as if gently asleep, so gently, so peacefully, like a young man sleeping in purity. He was still warm. She stood looking at him in gloomy, heavy silence for some time.

'Ay,' she said bitterly, at length, speaking as if to the unseen witnesses of the air. 'You're dead.' She stood for some minutes in silence, looking down. 'Beautiful,' she asserted, 'beautiful as if life had never touched you – never touched you. God send I look different. I hope I shall look my years when I am dead. Beautiful, beautiful,' she crooned over him. 'You can see him in his teens, with his first beard on his face. A beautiful soul, beautiful—' Then there was a tearing in her voice as she cried: 'None of you look like this when you are dead! Don't let it happen again.' It was a strange, wild command from out of the unknown. Her children moved unconsciously together, in a nearer group, at the dreadful command in her voice. The colour was flushed bright in her cheek, she looked awful and wonderful. 'Blame me, blame me if you like, that he lies there like a lad in his teens, with his first beard on his face. Blame me if you like. But you none of you know.' She was silent in intense silence. Then there came in a low, tense voice: 'If I thought that the children I bore would lie looking like that in death, I'd strangle them when they were infants, yes—'

'No, mother,' came the strange, clarion voice of Gerald from the background, 'we are different, we don't blame you.'

She turned and looked full in his eyes. Then she lifted her hands in a strange half-gesture of mad despair.

'Pray!' she said strongly. 'Pray for yourselves to God, for there's no help for you from your parents.'

'Oh, mother!' cried her daughters wildly.

But she had turned and gone, and they all went quickly away from each other.

When Gudrun heard that Mr. Crich was dead, she felt rebuked. She had stayed away lest Gerald should think her too easy of winning. And now, he was in the midst of trouble, whilst she was cold.

The following day she went up as usual to Winifred, who was glad to see her, glad to get away into the studio. The girl had wept, and then, too frightened, had turned aside to avoid any more tragic eventuality. She and Gudrun resumed work as usual in the isolation of the studio, and this seemed an immeasurable happiness, a pure world of freedom, after the aimlessness and misery of the house. Gudrun stayed on till evening. She and Winifred had dinner brought up to the studio, where they ate in freedom, away from all the people in the house.

After dinner Gerald came up. The great high studio was full of shadow and a fragrance of coffee. Gudrun and Winifred had a little table near the fire at the far end, with a white lamp whose light did not travel far. They were a tiny world to themselves, the two girls surrounded by lovely shadows, the beams and rafters shadowy overhead, the benches and implements shadowy down the studio.

'You are cosy enough here,' said Gerald, going up to them.

There was a low brick fireplace, full of fire, an old blue Turkish rug, the little oak table with the lamp and the white-and-blue cloth and the dessert, and Gudrun making coffee in an odd brass coffee-maker, and Winifred scalding a little milk in a tiny saucepan.

'Have you had coffee?' said Gudrun.

'I have, but I'll have some more with you,' he replied.

'Then you must have it in a glass – there are only two cups,' said Winifred.

'It is the same to me,' he said, taking a chair and coming into the charmed circle of the girls. How happy they were, how cosy and glamorous it was with them, in a world of lofty shadows! The outside world, in which he had been transacting funeral business all the day, was completely wiped out. In an instant he snuffed glamour and magic.

They had all their things very dainty, two odd and lovely little cups, scarlet and solid gilt, and a little black jug with scarlet discs, and the curious coffee machine, whose spirit-flame flowed steadily, almost invisibly. There was the effect of rather sinister richness, in which Gerald at once escaped himself.

They all sat down, and Gudrun carefully poured out the coffee.

'Will you have milk?' she asked calmly, yet nervously poising the little black jug with its big red dots. She was always so completely controlled, yet so bitterly nervous.

'No, I won't,' he replied.

So, with a curious humility, she placed him the little cup of coffee, and herself took the awkward tumbler. She seemed to want to serve him.

'Why don't you give me the glass – it is so clumsy for you,' he said. He would much rather have had it, and seen her daintily served. But she was silent, pleased with the disparity, with her self-abasement.

'You are quite *en ménage*,' he said.

'Yes. We aren't really at home to visitors,' said Winifred.

'You're not? Then I'm an intruder?'

For once he felt his conventional dress was out of place, he was an outsider.

Gudrun was very quiet. She did not feel drawn to talk to him. At this stage, silence was best – or mere light words. It was best to leave serious things aside. So they talked gaily and lightly till they heard the man below lead out the horse, and call it to 'Back-back!' into the dog-cart that was to take Gudrun home. So she put on her things and shook hands with Gerald, without once meeting his eyes. And she was gone.

The funeral was detestable. Afterwards, at the tea-table, the daughters kept saying – 'He was a good father to us – the best father in the world' – or else – 'We shan't easily find another man as good as father was.'

Gerald acquiesced in all this. It was the right conventional attitude, and, as far as the world went, he believed in the conventions. He took it as a matter of course. But Winifred hated everything, and hid in the studio, and cried her heart out, and wished Gudrun would come.

Luckily everybody was going away. The Criches never stayed long at home. By dinner-time, Gerald was left quite alone. Even Winifred was carried off to London for a few days with her sister Laura.

But when Gerald was really left alone, he could not bear it. One day passed by, and another. And all the time he was like a man hung in chains over the edge of an abyss. Struggle as he might, he could not turn himself to the solid earth, he could not get footing. He was suspended on the edge of a void, writhing. Whatever he thought of, was the abyss – whether it were friends or strangers, or work or play, it all showed him only the same bottomless void, in which his heart swung perishing. There was no escape, there was nothing to grasp hold of. He must writhe on the edge of the chasm, suspended in chains of invisible physical life.

At first he was quiet, he kept still, expecting the extremity to pass away, expecting to find himself released into the world of the living, after this extremity of penance. But it did not pass, and a crisis gained upon him.

As the evening of the third day came on, his heart rang with fear. He could not bear another night. Another night was coming on, for another night he was to be suspended in chains of physical life, over the bottomless pit of nothingness. And he could not bear it. He could not bear it. He was frightened deeply, and coldly, frightened in his soul. He did not believe in his own strength any more. He could not fall into this infinite void and rise again. If he fell, he would be gone for ever. He must withdraw, he must seek reinforcements. He did not believe in his own single self any further than this.

After dinner, faced with the ultimate experience of his own nothingness, he turned aside. He pulled on his boots, put on his coat, and set out to walk in the night.

It was dark and misty. He went through the wood, stumbling and feeling his way to the Mill. Birkin was away. Good – he was half glad. He turned up the hill, and stumbled blindly over the wild slopes, having lost the path in the complete darkness. It was boring. Where was he going? No matter. He stumbled on till he came to a path again. Then he went on through another wood. His mind became dark, he went on automatically. Without thought or sensation, he stumbled unevenly on, out into the open again, fumbling for stiles, losing the path, and going along the hedges of the fields till he came to the outlet.

And at last he came to high road. It had distracted him to struggle blindly through the maze of darkness. But now, he must take a direction. And he did not even know where he was. But he must take a direction now. Nothing would be resolved by merely walking, walking away. He had to take a direction.

He stood still on the road that was high in the utterly dark night, and he did not know where he was. It was a strange sensation, his heart beating, and ringed round with the utterly unknown darkness. So he stood for some time.

Then he heard footsteps, and saw a small, swinging light. He immediately went towards this. It was a miner.

'Can you tell me,' he said, 'where this road goes?'

'Road? Ay, it goes ter Whatmore.'

'Whatmore? Oh, thank you, that's right. I thought I was wrong. Good-night.'

'Good-night,' replied the broad voice of the miner.

Gerald guessed where he was. At least, when he came to Whatmore, he would know. He was glad to be on a high road. He walked forward as in a sleep of decision.

That was Whatmore Village—? Yes, the King's Head – and there the hall gates. He descended the steep hill almost running. Winding through the hollow, he passed the Grammar School, and came to Willey Green Church. The churchyard! He halted.

Then in another moment he had clambered up the wall and was going among the graves. Even in this darkness he could see the heaped pallor of old white flowers at his feet. This then was the grave. He stooped down. The flowers were cold and clammy. There was a raw scent of chrysanthemums and tube-roses, deadened. He felt the clay beneath, and shrank, it was so horribly cold and sticky. He stood away in revulsion.

Here was one centre then, here in the complete darkness beside the unseen, raw grave. But there was nothing for him here. No, he had nothing to stay here for. He felt as if some of the clay were sticking cold and unclean on his heart. No, enough of this.

Where then? – home? Never! It was no use going there. That was less than no use. It could not be done. There was somewhere else to go. Where?

A dangerous resolve formed in his heart, like a fixed idea. There was Gudrun – she would be safe in her home. But he could get at her – he would get at her. He would not go back to-night till he had come to her, if it cost him his life. He staked his all on this throw.

He set off walking straight across the fields towards Beldover. It was so dark, nobody could ever see him. His feet were wet and cold, heavy with clay. But he went on persistently, like a wind, straight forward, as if to his fate. There were great gaps in his consciousness. He was conscious that he was at Winthorpe hamlet, but quite unconscious how he had got there. And then, as in a dream, he was in the long street of Beldover, with its street-lamps.

There was a noise of voices, and of a door shutting loudly, and being barred, and of men talking in the night. The 'Lord Nelson' had just closed, and the drinkers were going home. He had better ask one of these where she lived – for he did not know the side streets at all.

'Can you tell me where Somerset Drive is?' he asked of one of the uneven men.

'Where what?' replied the tipsy miner's voice.

'Somerset Drive.'

'Somerset Drive! – I've heard o' such a place, but I couldn't for my life say where it is. Who might you be wanting?'

'Mr. Brangwen – William Brangwen.'

'William Brangwen—?'

'Who teaches at the Grammar School at Willey Green – his daughter teaches there too.'

'O-o-o-oh, Brangwen! *Now* I've got you. Of *course*, William Brangwen! Yes, yes, he's got two lasses as teachers, aside hisself. Ay, that's him – that's him! Why, certainly I know where he lives, back your life I do! Yi – *what* place do they ca' it?'

'Somerset Drive,' repeated Gerald patiently. He knew his own colliers fairly well.

'Somerset Drive, for certain!' said the collier, swinging his arm as if catching something up. 'Somerset Drive – yi! I couldn't for my life lay hold o' the lercality o' the place. Yis, I know the place, to be sure I do—'

He turned unsteadily on his feet and pointed up the dark, nigh-deserted road.

'You go up theer – an' you ta'e th' first – yi, th' first turnin' on your left – o' that side – past Withamses tuffy shop—'

'*I* know,' said Gerald.

'Ay! You go down a bit, past wheer th' water-man lives – and then Somerset Drive, as they ca' it, branches off on 't right hand side – an' there's nowt but three houses in it, no more than three, I believe – an' I'm a'most certain as theirs is th' last – th' last o' th' three – you see—'

'Thank you very much,' said Gerald. 'Good-night.'

And he started off, leaving the tipsy man there standing rooted.

Gerald went past the dark shops and houses, most of them sleeping now, and twisted round to the little blind road that ended on a field of darkness. He slowed down as he neared his goal, not knowing how he should proceed. What if the house were closed in darkness?

But it was not. He saw a big lighted window, and heard voices, then a gate banged. His quick ears caught the sound of Birkin's voice, his keen eyes made out Birkin, with Ursula standing in a pale dress on the step of the garden path. Then Ursula stepped down and came along the road, holding Birkin's arm.

Gerald went across into the darkness and they dawdled past him, talking happily, Birkin's voice low, Ursula's high and distinct. Gerald went quickly to the house.

The blinds were drawn before the big lighted window of the dining-room. Looking up the path at the side he could see the door left open, shedding a soft, coloured light from the hall lamp. He went quickly and silently up the path, and looked up into the hall. There were pictures on the walls, and the antlers of a stag – and the stairs going up on one side – and just near the foot of the stairs the half opened door of the dining-room.

With heart drawn fine, Gerald stepped into the hall, whose floor was of coloured tiles, went quickly and looked into the large, pleasant room. In a chair by the fire, the father sat asleep, his head tilted back against the side of the big oak chimney-piece, his ruddy face seen foreshortened, the nostrils open, the mouth fallen a little. It would take the merest sound to wake him.

Gerald stood a second suspended. He glanced down the passage behind him. It was all dark. Again he was suspended. Then he went swiftly upstairs. His senses were so finely, almost supernaturally keen, that he seemed to cast his own will over the half-unconscious house.

He came to the first landing. There he stood, scarcely breathing. Again, corresponding to the door below, there was a door again. That would be the mother's room. He could hear her moving about in the candle-light. She would be expecting her husband to come up. He looked along the dark landing.

Then, silently, on infinitely careful feet, he went along the passage, feeling the wall with the extreme tips of his fingers. There was a door. He stood and listened. He could hear two people's breathing. It was not that. He went stealthily forward. There was another door, slightly open. The room was in darkness. Empty. Then there was the bathroom, he could smell the soap and the heat. Then at the end another bedroom – one soft breathing. This was she.

With an almost occult carefulness he turned the door-handle and opened the door an inch. It creaked slightly. Then he opened it another inch – then another. His heart did not beat, he seemed to create a silence about himself, an obliviousness.

He was in the room. Still the sleeper breathed softly. It was very dark. He felt his way forward inch by inch, with his feet and hands. He touched the bed, he could hear the sleeper. He drew nearer, bending close as if his eyes would disclose whatever there was. And then, very near to his face, to his fear, he saw the round, dark head of a boy.

He recovered, turned round, saw the door afar, a faint light revealed. And

Women in Love

he retreated swiftly, drew the door to without fastening it, and passed rapidly down the passage. At the head of the stairs he hesitated. There was still time to flee.

But it was unthinkable. He would maintain his will. He turned past the door of the parental bedroom like a shadow, and was climbing the second flight of stairs. They creaked under his weight – it was exasperating. Ah, what disaster, if the mother's door opened just beneath him, and she saw him! It would have to be, if it were so. He held the control still.

He was not quite up these stairs when he heard a quick running of feet below, the outer door was closed and locked, he heard Ursula's voice, then the father's sleepy exclamation. He pressed on swiftly to the upper landing.

Again a door was ajar, a room was empty. Feeling his way forward, with the tips of his fingers, travelling rapidly, like a blind man, anxious lest Ursula should come upstairs, he found another door. There, with his preternaturally fine senses alert, he listened. He heard someone moving in bed. This would be she.

Softly now, like one who has only one sense, the tactile sense, he turned the latch. It clicked. He held still. The bedclothes rustled. His heart did not beat. Then again he drew the latch back, and very gently pushed the door. It made a sticking noise as it gave.

'Ursula?' said Gudrun's voice, frightened. He quickly opened the door and pushed it behind him.

'Is it you, Ursula?' came Gudrun's frightened voice. He heard her sitting up in bed. In another moment she would scream.

'No, it's me,' he said, feeling his way towards her. 'It is I, Gerald.'

She sat motionless in her bed in sheer astonishment. She was too astonished, too much taken by surprise, even to be afraid.

'Gerald!' she echoed, in blank amazement. He had found his way to the bed, and his outstretched hand touched her warm breast blindly. She shrank away.

'Let me make a light,' she said, springing out.

He stood perfectly motionless. He heard her touch the match-box, he heard her fingers in their movement. Then he saw her in the light of a match, which she held to the candle. The light rose in the room, then sank to a small dimness, as the flame sank down on the candle, before it mounted again.

She looked at him as he stood near the other side of the bed. His cap was pulled low over his brow, his black overcoat was buttoned close up to his chin. His face was strange and luminous. He was inevitable as a supernatural being. When she had seen him, she knew. She knew there was something fatal in the situation, and she must accept it. Yet she must challenge him.

'How did you come up?' she asked.

'I walked up the stairs – the door was open.'

She looked at him.

'I haven't closed this door, either,' he said. She walked swiftly across the room and closed her door softly, and locked it. Then she came back.

She was wonderful, with startled eyes and flushed cheeks, and her plait of hair rather short and thick down her back, and her long, fine white night-dress falling to her feet.

She saw that his boots were all clayey, even his trousers were plastered with clay. And she wondered if he had made footprints all the way up. He was a very strange figure, standing in her bedroom, near the tossed bed.

'Why have you come?' she asked, almost querulous.

'I wanted to,' he replied.

And this she could see from his face. It was fate.

'You are so muddy,' she said in distaste, but gently.

He looked down at his feet.

'I was walking in the dark,' he replied. But he felt vividly elated. There was a pause. He stood on one side of the tumbled bed, she on the other. He did not even take his cap from his brows.

'And what do you want of me?' she challenged.

He looked aside and did not answer. Save for the extreme beauty and mystic attractiveness of this distinct, strange face, she would have sent him away. But his face was too wonderful and undiscovered to her. It fascinated her with the fascination of pure beauty, cast a spell on her, like nostalgia, an ache.

'What do you want of me?' she repeated in an estranged voice.

He pulled off his cap in a movement of dream-liberation and went across to her. But he could not touch her because she stood barefoot in her night-dress, and he was muddy and damp. Her eyes, wide and large and wondering, watched him, and asked him the ultimate question.

'I came – because I must,' he said. 'Why do you ask?'

She looked at him in doubt and wonder.

'I must ask,' she said.

He shook his head slightly.

'There is no answer,' he replied, with strange vacancy.

There was about him a curious and almost godlike air of simplicity and naïve directness. He reminded her of an apparition, the young Hermes.

'But why did you come to me?' she persisted.

'Because – it has to be so. If there weren't you in the world, then *I* shouldn't be in the world, either.'

She stood looking at him with large, wide, wondering, stricken eyes. His eyes were looking steadily into hers all the time, and he seemed fixed in an odd supernatural steadfastness. She sighed. She was lost now. She had no choice.

'Won't you take off your boots?' she said. 'They must be wet.'

He dropped his cap on a chair, unbuttoned his overcoat, lifting up his chin to unfasten the throat buttons. His short, keen hair was ruffled. He was so beautifully blond, like wheat. He pulled off his overcoat.

Quickly he pulled off his jacket, pulled loose his black tie, and was unfastening his studs, which were headed each with a pearl. She listened, watching, hoping no one would hear the starched linen crackle. It seemed to snap like pistol-shots.

He had come for vindication. She let him hold her in his arms, clasp her close against him. He found in her an infinite relief. Into her he poured all his pent-up darkness and corrosive death, and he was whole again. It was wonderful, marvellous, it was a miracle. This was the ever-recurrent miracle of his life, at the knowledge of which he was lost in an ecstasy of relief and wonder. And she, subject, received him as a vessel filled with his bitter potion of death. She had no power at this crises to resist. The terrible frictional violence of death filled her, and she received it in an ecstasy of subjection, in throes of acute, violent sensation.

As he drew nearer to her, he plunged deeper into her enveloping soft warmth, a wonderful creative heat that penetrated his veins and gave him life again. He felt himself dissolving and sinking to rest in the bath of her living strength. It seemed as if her heart in her breast were a second unconquerable sun, into the glow and creative strength of which he plunged further and further. All his veins, that were murdered and lacerated, healed softly as life came pulsing in, stealing invisibly into him as if it were the all-powerful effluence of the sun. His blood, which seemed to have been drawn back into death, came ebbing on the return, surely, beautifully, powerfully.

He felt his limbs growing fuller and flexible with life, his body gained an unknown strength. He was a man again, strong and rounded. And he was a child, so soothed and restored and full of gratitude.

And she, she was the great bath of life, he worshipped her. Mother and substance of all life she was. And he, child and man, received of her and was made whole. His pure body was almost killed. But the miraculous, soft effluence of her breast suffused over him, over his seared, damaged brain, like a healing lymph, like a soft, soothing flow of life itself, perfect as if he were bathed in the womb again.

His brain was hurt, seared, the tissue was as if destroyed. He had not known how hurt he was, how his tissue, the very tissue of his brain was damaged by the corrosive flood of death. Now, as the healing lymph of her effluence flowed through him, he knew how destroyed he was, like a plant whose tissue is burst from inwards by a frost.

He buried his small, hard head between her breasts and pressed her breasts against him with his hands. And she with quivering hands pressed his head against her, as he lay suffused out, and she lay fully conscious. The lovely creative warmth flooded through him like a sleep of fecundity within the womb. Ah, if only she would grant him the flow of this living effluence, he would be restored, he would be complete again. He was afraid she would deny him before it was finished. Like a child at the breast, he cleaved intensely to her, and she could not put him away. And his seared, ruined membrane relaxed, softened, that which was seared and stiff and blasted yielded again, became soft and flexible, palpitating with new life. He was infinitely grateful, as to God, or as an infant is at its mother's breast. He was glad and grateful like a delirium, as he felt his own wholeness come over him again, as he felt the full, unutterable sleep coming over him, the sleep of complete exhaustion and restoration.

But Gudrun lay wide awake, destroyed into perfect consciousness. She lay motionless, with wide eyes staring motionless into the darkness, whilst he was sunk away in sleep, his arms round her.

She seemed to be hearing waves break on a hidden shore, long, slow, gloomy waves, breaking with the rhythm of fate, so monotonously that it seemed eternal. This endless breaking of slow, sullen waves of fate held her life a possession, whilst she lay with dark, wide eyes looking into the darkness. She could see so far, as far as eternity – yet she saw nothing. She was suspended in perfect consciousness – and of what was she conscious?

This mood of extremity, when she lay staring into eternity, utterly suspended, and conscious of everything, to the last limits, passed and left her uneasy. She had lain so long motionless. She moved, she became self-conscious. She wanted to look at him, to see him.

But she dared not make a light, because she knew he would wake, and she did not want to break his perfect sleep, that she knew he had got of her.

She disengaged herself softly and rose up a little to look at him. There was a faint light, it seemed to her, in the room. She could just distinguish his features, as he slept the perfect sleep. In this darkness, she seemed to see him so distinctly. But he was far off, in another world. Ah, she could shriek with torment, he was so far off, and perfected, in another world. She seemed to look at him as at a pebble far away under clear dark water. And here was she, left with all the anguish of consciousness, whilst he was sunk deep into the other element of mindless, remote, living shadow-gleam. He was beautiful, far off, and perfected. They would never be together. Ah, this awful, inhuman distance which would always be interposed between her and the other being!

There was nothing to do but to lie still and endure. She felt an overwhelming tenderness for him, and a dark, under-stirring of jealous hatred, that he should lie so perfect and immune, in another world, whilst she was tormented with violent wakefulness, cast out in the outer darkness.

She lay in intense and vivid consciousness, an exhausting superconsciousness. The church clock struck the hours, it seemed to her, in quick succession. She heard them distinctly in the tension of her vivid consciousness. And he slept as if time were one moment, unchanging and unmoving.

She was exhausted, wearied. Yet she must continue in this state of violent active superconsciousness. She was conscious of everything – her childhood, her girlhood, all the forgotten incidents, all the unrealised influences and all the happenings she had not understood, pertaining to herself, to her family, to her friends, her lovers, her acquaintances, everybody. It was as if she drew a glittering rope of knowledge out of the sea of darkness, drew and drew and drew it out of the fathomless depths of the past, and still it did not come to an end, there was no end to it, she must haul and haul at the rope of glittering consciousness, pull it out phosphorescent from the endless depths of the unconsciousness, till she was weary, aching, exhausted, and fit to break, and yet she had not done.

Ah, if only she might wake him! She turned uneasily. When could she rouse him and send him away? When could she disturb him? And she relapsed into her activity of automatic consciousness, that would never end.

But the time was drawing near when she could wake him. It was like a release. The clock had struck four, outside in the night. Thank God the might had passed almost away. At five he must go, and she would be released. Then she could relax and fill her own place. Now she was driven up against his perfect sleeping motion like a knife white-hot on a grindstone. There was something monstrous about him, about his juxtaposition against her.

The last hour was the longest. And yet, at last it passed. Her heart leapt with relief – yes, there was the slow, strong stroke of the church clock – at last, after this night of eternity. She waited to catch each slow, fatal reverberation. 'Three—four—five!' There, it was finished. A weight rolled off her.

She raised herself, leaned over him tenderly, and kissed him. She was sad to wake him. After a few moments, she kissed him again. But he did not stir. The darling, he was so deep in sleep! What a shame to take him out of it. She let him lie a little longer. But he must go – he must really go.

With full over-tenderness she took his face between her hands and kissed his eyes. The eyes opened, he remained motionless, looking at her. Her heart stood still. To hide her face from his dreadful opened eyes, in the darkness, she bent down and kissed him, whispering:

'You must go, my love.'

But she was sick with terror, sick.

He put his arms round her. Her heart sank.

'But you must go, my love. It's late.'

'What time is it?' he said.

Strange, his man's voice. She quivered. It was an intolerable oppression to her.

'Past five o'clock,' she said.

But he only closed his arms round her again. Her heart cried within her in torture. She disengaged her self firmly.

'You really must go,' she said.

'Not for a minute,' he said.

She lay still, nestling against him, but unyielding.

'Not for a minute,' he repeated, clasping her closer.

'Yes,' she said, unyielding. 'I'm afraid if you stay any longer.'

There was a certain coldness in her voice that made him release her, and she broke away, rose and lit the candle. That then was the end.

He got up. He was warm and full of life and desire. Yet he felt a little bit ashamed, humiliated, putting on his clothes before her, in the candle-light. For he felt revealed, exposed to her, at a time when she was in some way against him. It was all very difficult to understand. He dressed himself quickly, without collar or tie. Still he felt full and complete, perfected. She thought it humiliating to see a man dressing: the ridiculous shirt, the ridiculous trousers and braces. But again an idea saved her.

'It is like a workman getting up to go to work,' thought Gudrun. 'And I am like a workman's wife.' But an ache like nausea was upon her: a nausea of him.

He pushed his collar and tie into his overcoat pocket. Then he sat down and pulled on his boots. They were sodden, as were his socks and trouser-bottoms. But he himself was quick and warm.

'Perhaps you ought to have put your boots on downstairs,' she said.

At once, without answering, he pulled them off again and stood holding them in his hand. She had thrust her feet into slippers, and flung a loose robe round her. She was ready. She looked at him as he stood waiting, his black coat buttoned to the chin, his cap pulled down, his boots in his hand. And the passionate almost hateful fascination revived in her for a moment. It was not exhausted. His face was so warm-looking, wide-eyed and full of newness, so perfect. She felt old, old. She went to him heavily to be kissed. He kissed her quickly. She wished his warm, expressionless beauty did not so fatally put a spell on her, compel her and subjugate her. It was a burden upon her, that she resented, but could not escape. Yet when she looked at his straight man's brows, and at his rather small, well-shaped nose, and at his blue, indifferent eyes, she knew her passion for him was not yet satisfied, perhaps never could be satisfied. Only now she was weary, with an ache like nausea. She wanted him gone.

They went downstairs quickly. It seemed they made a prodigious noise. He followed her as, wrapped in her vivid green wrap, she preceded him with the light. She suffered badly with fear, lest her people should be roused. He hardly cared. He did not care now who knew. And she hated this in him. One *must* be cautious. One must preserve oneself.

She led the way to the kitchen. It was neat and tidy, as the woman had left it. He looked up at the clock – twenty minutes past five! Then he sat down on a chair to put on his boots. She waited, watching his every movement. She wanted it to be over, it was a great nervous strain on her.

He stood up – she unbolted the back door and looked out. A cold, raw night, not yet dawn, with a piece of a moon in the vague sky. She was glad she need not go out.

'Good-bye then,' he murmured.

'I'll come to the gate,' she said.

And again she hurried on in front, to warn him of the steps. And at the gate, once more she stood on the step whilst he stood below her.

'Good-bye,' she whispered.

He kissed her dutifully and turned away.

She suffered torments hearing his firm tread going so distinctly down the road. Ah, the insensitiveness of that firm tread!

She closed the gate and crept quickly and noiselessly back to bed. When she was in her room, and the door closed, and all safe, she breathed freely, and a great weight fell off her. She nestled down in bed, in the groove his body had made, in the warmth he had left. And excited worn out, yet still satisfied, she fell soon into a deep, heavy sleep.

Gerald walked quickly through the raw darkness of the coming dawn. He met nobody. His mind was beautifully still and thoughtless, like a still pool, and his body full and warm and rich. He went quickly along towards Shortlands in a grateful self-sufficiency.

Chapter Twenty-five

Marriage or not

The Brangwen family was going to move from Beldover. It was necessary now for the father to be in town.

Birkin had taken out a marriage licence, yet Ursula deferred from day to day. She would not fix any definite time – she still wavered. Her month's notice to leave the Grammar School was in its third week. Christmas was not far off.

Gerald waited for the Ursula–Birkin marriage. It was something crucial to him.

'Shall we make it a double-barrelled affair?' he said to Birkin one day.

'Who for the second shot?' asked Birkin.

'Gudrun and me,' said Gerald, the venturesome twinkle in his eyes.

Birkin looked at him steadily, as if somewhat taken aback.

'Serious – or joking?' he asked.

'Oh, serious. Shall I? Shall Gudrun and I rush in along with you?'

'Do by all means,' said Birkin. 'I didn't know you'd got that length.'

'What length?' said Gerald, looking at the other man, and laughing. 'Oh yes, we've gone all the lengths.'

'There remains to put it on a broad social basis, and to achieve a high moral purpose,' said Birkin.

'Something like that: the length and breadth and height of it,' replied Gerald, smiling.

'Oh well,' said Birkin, 'it's a very admirable step to take, I should say.'

Gerald looked at him closely.

'Why aren't you enthusiastic?' he asked. 'I thought you were such dead nuts on marriage.'

Birkin lifted his shoulders.

'One might as well be dead nuts on noses. There are all sorts of noses, snub and otherwise—'

Gerald laughed.

'And all sorts of marriage, also snub and otherwise?' he said.

'That's it.'

'And you think if I marry, it will be snub?' asked Gerald quizzically, his head a little on one side.

Birkin laughed quickly.

'How do I know what it will be!' he said. 'Don't lambaste me with my own parallels—'

Gerald pondered a while.

'But I should like to know your opinion, exactly,' he said.

'On your marriage? – or marrying? Why should you want my opinion? I've got no opinions. I'm not interested in legal marriage, one way or another. It's a mere question of convenience.'

Still Gerald watched him closely.

'More than that, I think,' he said seriously. 'However, you may be bored by the ethics of marriage, yet really to marry, in one's own personal case, is something critical, final—'

'You mean there is something final in going to the registrar with a woman?'

'If you're coming back with her, I do,' said Gerald. 'It is in some way irrevocable.'

'Yes, I agree,' said Birkin.

'No matter how one regards legal marriage, yet to enter into the married state, in one's own personal instance, is final—'

'I believe it is,' said Birkin, 'somewhere.'

'The question remains, then, should one do it,' said Gerald.

Birkin watched him narrowly, with amused eyes.

'You are like Lord Bacon, Gerald,' he said. 'You argue it like a lawyer – or like Hamlet's to-be-or-not-to-be. If I were you I would *not* marry: but ask Gudrun, not me. You're not marrying me, are you?'

Gerald did not heed the latter part of this speech.

'Yes,' he said, 'one must consider it coldly. It is something critical. One comes to the point where one must take a step in one direction or another. And marriage is one direction—'

'And what is the other?' asked Birkin quickly.

Gerald looked up at him with hot, strangely-conscious eyes, that the other man could not understand.

'I can't say,' he replied. 'If I knew *that*—' He moved uneasily on his feet and did not finish.

'You mean if you knew the alternative?' asked Birkin. 'And since you don't know it, marriage is a *pis aller*.'

Gerald looked up at Birkin with the same hot, constrained eyes.

'One does have the feeling that marriage is a *pis aller*,' he admitted.

'Then don't do it,' said Birkin. 'I tell you,' he went on, 'the same as I've said before, marriage in the old sense seems to me repulsive. *Egoïsme à deux* is nothing to it. It's a sort of tacit hunting in couples: the world all in couples, each couple in its own little house, watching its own little interests, and stewing in its own little privacy – it's the most repulsive thing on earth.'

'I quite agree,' said Gerald. 'There's something inferior about it. But as I say, what's the alternative.'

'One should avoid this *home* instinct. It's not an instinct, it's a habit of cowardliness. One should never have a *home*.'

'I agree really,' said Gerald. 'But there's no alternative.'

'We've got to find one. I do believe in a permanent union between a man and a woman. Chopping about is merely an exhaustive process. But a permanent relation between a man and a woman isn't the last word – it certainly isn't.'

'Quite,' said Gerald.

'In fact,' said Birkin, 'because the relation between man and woman is made the supreme and exclusive relationship, that's where all the tightness and meanness and insufficiency comes in.'

'Yes, I believe you,' said Gerald.

'You've got to take down the love-and-marriage ideal from its pedestal. We want something broader. I believe in the *additional* perfect relationship between man and man – additional to marriage.'

'I can never see how they can be the same,' said Gerald.

'Not the same – but equally important, equally creative, equally sacred, if you like.'

'I know,' said Gerald, 'you believe something like that. Only I can't *feel* it, you see.' He put his hand on Birkin's arm, with a sort of deprecating affection. And he smiled as if triumphantly.

He was ready to be doomed. Marriage was like a doom to him. He was willing to condemn himself in marriage, to become like a convict condemned to the mines of the underworld, living no life in the sun, but having a dreadful subterranean activity. He was willing to accept this. And marriage was the seal of his condemnation. He was willing to be sealed thus in the underworld, like a soul damned but living for ever in damnation. But he would not make any pure relationship with any other soul. He could not. Marriage was not the committing of himself into a relationship with Gudrun. It was a committing of himself in acceptance of the established world, he would accept the established order, in which he did not livingly believe, and then he would retreat to the underworld for his life. This he would do.

The other way was to accept Rupert's offer of alliance, to enter into the bond of pure trust and love with the other man, and then subsequently with the woman. If he pledged himself with the man he would later be able to pledge himself with the woman: not merely in legal marriage, but in absolute, mystic marriage.

Yet he could not accept the offer. There was a numbness upon him, a numbness either of unborn, absent volition or of atrophy. Perhaps it was the absence of volition. For he was strangely elated at Rupert's offer. Yet he was still more glad to reject it, not to be committed.

Chapter Twenty-six

A Chair

There was a jumble market every Monday afternoon in the old market-place in town. Ursula and Birkin strayed down there one afternoon. They had been talking of furniture, and they wanted to see if there was any fragment they would like to buy, amid the heaps of rubbish collected on the cobble-stones.

The old market-square was not very large, a mere bare patch of granite setts, usually with a few fruit-stalls under a wall. It was in a poor quarter of the town. Meagre houses stood down one side, there was a hosiery factory, a great blank with myriad oblong windows at the end, a street of little shops with flagstone pavement down the other side, and, for a crowning monument, the public baths, of new red brick, with a clock-tower. The people who moved about seemed stumpy and sordid, the air seemed to smell rather dirty, there was a sense of many mean streets ramifying off into warrens of meanness. Now and again a great chocolate-and-yellow tramcar ground round a difficult bend under the hosiery factory.

Ursula was superficially thrilled when she found herself out among the common people, in the jumbled place piled with old bedding, heaps of old iron, shabby crockery in pale lots, muffled lots of unthinkable clothing. She and Birkin went unwillingly down the narrow aisle between the rusty wares. He was looking at the goods, she at the people.

She excitedly watched a young woman who was going to have a baby, and who was turning over a mattress and making a young man, down-at-heel and dejected, feel it also. So secretive and active and anxious the young woman seemed, so reluctant, slinking, the young man. He was going to marry her because she was having a child.

When they had felt the mattress, the young woman asked the old man seated on a stool among his wares how much it was. He told her, and she turned to the young man. The latter was ashamed and self-conscious. He turned his face away, though he left his body standing there, and muttered aside. And again the woman anxiously and actively fingered the mattress and added up in her mind and bargained with the old, unclean man. All the while the young man stood by, shamefaced and down-at-heel, submitting.

'Look,' said Birkin, 'there is a pretty chair.'

'Charming!' cried Ursula. 'Oh, charming.'

It was an arm-chair of simple wood, probably birch, but of such fine delicacy of grace, standing there on the sordid stones, it almost brought tears to the eyes. It was square in shape, of the purest, slender lines, and four short lines of wood in the back, that reminded Ursula of harp-strings.

'It was once,' said Birkin, 'gilded – and it had a cane seat. Somebody has nailed this wooden seat in. Look, here is a trifle of the red that underlay the gilt. The rest is all black, except where the wood is worn pure and glossy. It is the fine unity of the lines that is so attractive. Look, how they run and meet and counteract. But of course the wooden seat is wrong – it destroys the perfect lightness and unity in tension the cane gave. I like it though—'

'Ah yes,' said Ursula, 'so do I.'

'How much is it?' Birkin asked the man.

'Ten shillings.'

'And you will send it—'

It was bought.

'So beautiful, so pure!' Birkin said. 'It almost breaks my heart.' They walked along between the heaps of rubbish. 'My beloved country – it had something to express even when it made that chair.'

'And hasn't it now?' asked Ursula. She was always angry when he took this tone.

'No, it hasn't. When I see that clear, beautiful chair, and I think of England, even Jane Austen's England – it had living thoughts to unfold even then, and pure happiness in unfolding them. And now, we can only fish among the rubbish-heaps for the remnants of their old expression. There is no production in us now, only sordid and foul mechanicalness.'

'It isn't true,' cried Ursula. 'Why must you always praise the past at the expense of the present? *Really*, I don't think so much of Jane Austen's England. It was materialistic enough, if you like—'

'It could afford to be materialistic,' said Birkin, 'because it had the power to be something other – which we haven't. We are materialistic because we haven't the power to be anything else – try as we may, we can't bring off anything but materialism: mechanism, the very soul of materialism.'

Ursula was subdued into angry silence. She did not heed what he said. She was rebelling against something else.

'And I hate your past. I'm sick of it,' she cried. 'I believe I even hate that old chair, though it *is* beautiful. It isn't *my* sort of beauty. I wish it had been smashed up when its day was over, not left to preach the beloved past to us. I'm sick of the beloved past.'

'Not so sick as I am of the accursed present,' he said.

'Yes, just the same. I hate the present – but I don't want the past to take its place – I don't want that old chair.'

He was rather angry for a moment. Then he looked at the sky shining beyond the tower of the public baths, and he seemed to get over it all. He laughed.

'All right,' he said, 'then let us not have it. I'm sick of it all, too. At any rate, one can't go on living on the old bones of beauty.'

'One can't,' she cried. 'I *don't* want old things.'

'The truth is, we don't want things at all,' he replied. 'The thought of a house and furniture of my own is hateful to me.'

This startled her for a moment. Then she replied:

'So it is to me. But one must live somewhere.'

'Not somewhere – anywhere,' he said. 'One should just live anywhere – not have a definite place. I don't want a definite place. As soon as you get a room, and it is *complete*, you want to run from it. Now my rooms at the Mill are quite complete, I want them at the bottom of the sea. It is a horrible tyranny of a fixed milieu, where each piece of furniture is a commandment-stone.'

She clung to his arm as they walked away from the market.

'But what are we going to do?' she said. 'We must live somehow. And I do want some beauty in my surroundings. I want a sort of natural *grandeur* even, *splendour*.'

'You'll never get it in houses and furniture – or even clothes. Houses and furniture and clothes, they are all terms of an old base world, a detestable society of man. And if you have a Tudor house and old, beautiful furniture, it is only the past perpetuated on top of you, horrible. And if you have a perfect modern house done for you by Poiret, it is something else perpetuated on top of you. It is all horrible. It is all possessions, possessions, bullying you and turning you into a generalisation. You have to be like Rodin, Michael Angelo, and leave a piece of raw rock unfinished to your figure. You must leave your surroundings sketchy, unfinished, so that you are never contained, never confined, never dominated from the outside.'

She stood in the street contemplating.

'And we are never to have a complete place of our own – never a home?' she said.

'Pray God, in this world, no,' he answered.

'But there's only this world,' she objected.

He spread out his hands with a gesture of indifference.

'Meanwhile, then, we'll avoid having things of our own,' he said.

'But you've just bought a chair,' she said.

'I can tell the man I don't want it,' he replied.

She pondered again. Then a queer little movement twitched her face.

'No,' she said, 'we don't want it. I'm sick of old things.'

'New ones as well,' he said.

They retraced their steps.

There – in front of some furniture, stood the young couple, the woman who was going to have a baby and the narrow-faced youth. She was fair, rather short, stout. He was of medium height, attractively built. His dark hair fell sideways over his brow from under his cap, he stood strangely aloof, like one of the damned.

'Let us give it to *them*,' whispered Ursula. 'Look, they are getting a home together.'

'*I* won't aid and abet them in it,' he said petulantly, instantly sympathising with the aloof, furtive youth, against the active, procreant female.

'Oh yes,' cried Ursula. 'It's right for them – there's nothing else for them.'

'Very well,' said Birkin, 'you offer it to them. I'll watch.'

Ursula went rather nervously to the young couple who were discussing an iron washstand – or rather, the man was glancing furtively and wonderingly, like a prisoner, at the abominable article, whilst the woman was arguing.

'We bought a chair,' said Ursula, ' and we don't want it. Would you have it? We should be glad if you would.'

The young couple looked round at her, not believing that she could be addressing them.

'Would you care for it?' repeated Ursula. 'It's really *very* pretty – but – but—' she smiled rather dazzlingly.

The young couple only stared at her, and looked significantly at each other to know what to do. And the man curiously obliterated himself, as if he could make himself invisible as a rat can.

'We wanted to *give* it to you,' explained Ursula, now overcome with confusion and dread of them. She was attracted by the young man. He was a still, mindless creature, hardly a man at all, a creature that the towns have produced, strangely pure-bred and fine in one sense, furtive, quick, subtle.

His lashes were dark and long and fine over his eyes, that had no mind in them, only a dreadful kind of subject, inward consciousness, glazed and dark. His dark brows and all his lines were finely drawn. He would be a dreadful, but wonderful lover to a woman, so marvellously contributed. His legs would be marvellously subtle and alive, under the shapeless trousers, he had some of the fineness and stillness and silkiness of a dark-eyed, silent rat.

Ursula had apprehended him with a fine *frisson* of attraction. The full-built woman was staring offensively. Again Ursula forgot him.

'Won't you have the chair?' she said.

The man looked at her with a sideways look of appreciation, yet far off, almost insolent. The woman drew herself up. There was a certain coster-monger richness about her. She did not know what Ursula was after, she was on her guard, hostile. Birkin approached, smiling wickedly at seeing Ursula so nonplussed and frightened.

'What's the matter?' he said, smiling. His eyelids had dropped slightly, there was about him the same suggestive, mocking secrecy that was in the bearing of the two city creatures. The man jerked his head a little on one side, indicating Ursula, and said, with curious amiable, jeering warmth:

'What she warnt? – eh?' An odd smile writhed his lips.

Birkin looked at him from under his slack, ironical eyelids.

'To give you a chair – that – with the label on it,' he said, pointing.

The man looked at the object indicated. There was a curious hostility in male, outlawed understanding between the two men.

'What's she warnt to give it *us* for, guv'nor,' he replied in a tone of free intimacy that insulted Ursula.

'Thought you'd like it – it's a pretty chair. We bought it and don't want it. No need for you to have it, don't be frightened,' said Birkin, with a wry smile.

The man glanced up at him, half inimical, half recognising.

'Why don't you want it for yourselves, if you've just bought it?' asked the woman coolly. ' 'Taint good enough for you, now you've had a look at it. Frightened it's got something in it, eh?'

She was looking at Ursula admiringly, but with some resentment.

'I'd never thought of that,' said Birkin. 'But no, the wood's too thin everywhere.'

'You see,' said Ursula, her face luminous and pleased. '*We* are just going to get married, and we thought we'd buy things. Then we decided just now, that we wouldn't have furniture, we'd go abroad.'

The full-built, slightly blowsy city girl looked at the fine face of the other woman with appreciation. They appreciated each other. The youth stood aside, his face expressionless and timeless, the thin line of the black moustache drawn strangely suggestive over his rather wide, closed mouth. He was impassive, abstract, like some dark suggestive presence, a gutter presence.

'It's all right to be some folks,' said the city girl, turning to her own young man. He did not look at her, but he smiled with the lower part of his face, putting his head aside in an odd gesture of assent. His eyes were unchanging, glazed with darkness.

'Cawsts something to chynge your mind,' he said in an incredibly low accent.

'Only ten shillings this time,' said Birkin.

The man looked up at him with a grimace of a smile, furtive, unsure.

'Cheap at 'arf a quid, guv'nor,' he said. 'Not like getting divawced.'

'We're not married yet,' said Birkin.

'No, no more aren't we,' said the young woman loudly. 'But we shall be a Saturday.'

Again she looked at the young man with a determined, protective look, at once overbearing and very gentle. He grinned sicklily, turning away his head. She had got his manhood, but Lord, what did he care! He had a strange furtive pride and slinking singleness.

'Good luck to you,' said Birkin.

'Same to you,' said the young woman. Then, rather tentatively: 'When's yours coming off, then?'

Birkin looked round at Ursula.

'It's for the lady to say,' he replied. 'We go to the registrar the moment she's ready.'

Ursula laughed, covered with confusion and bewilderment.

'No 'urry,' said the young man, grinning suggestive.

'Oh, don't break your neck to get there,' said the young woman. ' 'Slike when you're dead – you're a long time married.'

The young man turned aside as if this hit him.

'The longer the better, let us hope,' said Birkin.

'That's it, guv'nor,' said the young man admiringly. 'Enjoy it while it larsts – niver whip a dead donkey.'

'Only when he's shamming dead,' said the young woman, looking at her young man with caressive tenderness of authority.

'Aw, there's a difference,' he said satirically.

'What about the chair?' said Birkin.

'Yes, all right,' said the woman.

They trailed off to the dealer, the handsome but abject young fellow hanging a little aside.

'That's it,' said Birkin. 'Will you take it with you or have the address altered?'

'Oh, Fred can carry it. Make him do what he can for the dear old 'ome.'

'Mike use of 'im,' said Fred, grimly humorous, as he took the chair from the dealer. His movements were graceful, yet curiously abject, slinking.

' 'Ere's mother's cosy chair,' he said. 'Warnts a cushion.' And he stood it down on the market stones.

'Don't you think it's pretty?' laughed Ursula.

'Oh, I do,' said the young woman.

' 'Ave a sit in it, you'll wish you'd kept it,' said the young man.

Ursula promptly sat down in the middle of the market-place.

'Awfully comfortable,' she said. 'But rather hard. You try it.' She invited the young man to a seat. But he turned uncouthly, awkwardly aside, glancing up at her with quick bright eyes, oddly suggestive, like a quick, live rat.

'Don't spoil him,' said the young woman. 'He's not used to arm-chairs, 'e isn't.'

The young man turned away and said, with averted grin:

'Only warnts legs on 'is.'

The four parted. The young woman thanked them.

'Thank you for the chair – it'll last till it gives way.'

'Keep it for an ornyment,' said the young man.

'Good afternoon – good afternoon,' said Ursula and Birkin.

'Goo'-luck to you,' said the young man, glancing and avoiding Birkin's eyes as he turned aside his head.

The two couples went asunder, Ursula clinging to Birkin's arm. When they had gone some distance, she glanced back and saw the young man going beside the full, easy young woman. His trousers sank over his heels, he moved with a sort of slinking evasion, more crushed with odd self-consciousness now he had the slim old arm-chair to carry, his arm over the back, the four fine, square tapering legs swaying perilously near the granite setts of the pavement. And yet he was somewhere indomitable and separate, like a quick, vital rat. He had a queer, subterranean beauty, repulsive too.

'How strange they are!' said Ursula.

'Children of men,' he said. 'They remind me of Jesus: "The meek shall inherit the earth." '

'But they aren't the meek,' said Ursula.

'Yes, I don't know why, but they are,' he replied.

They waited for the tram-car. Ursula sat on top and looked out on the town. The dusk was just dimming the hollows of crowded houses.

'And are they going to inherit the earth?' she said.

'Yes – they.'

'Then what are we going to do?' she asked. 'We're not like them – are we? We're not the meek?'

'No. We've got to live in the chinks they leave us.'

'How horrible!' cried Ursula. 'I don't want to live in chinks.'

'Don't worry,' he said. 'They are the children of men, they like market-places and street corners best. That leaves plenty of chinks.'

'All the world,' she said.

'Ah, no – but some room.'

The tram-car mounted slowly up the hill, where the ugly winter-grey masses of houses looked like a vision of hell that is cold and angular. They sat and looked. Away in the distance was an angry redness of sunset. It was all cold, somehow small, crowded, and like the end of the world.

'I don't mind it even then,' said Ursula, looking at the repulsiveness of it all. 'It doesn't concern me.'

'No more it does,' he replied, holding her hand. 'One needn't see. One goes one's way. In my world it is sunny and spacious—'

'It is, my love, isn't it?' she cried, hugging near to him on the top of the tram-car, so that the other passengers stared at them.

'And we will wander about on the face of the earth,' he said, 'and we'll look at the world beyond just this bit.'

There was a long silence. Her face was radiant like gold as she sat thinking.

'I don't want to inherit the earth,' she said. 'I don't want to inherit anything.'

He closed his hand over hers.

'Neither do I. I want to be disinherited.'

She clasped his fingers closely.

'We won't care about *anything*,' she said.

He sat still and laughed.

'And we'll be married, and have done with them,' she added.

Again he laughed.

'It's one way of getting rid of everything,' she said, 'to get married.'

'And one way of accepting the whole world,' he added.

'A whole other world, yes,' she said happily.

'Perhaps there's Gerald – and Gudrun—' he said.

'If there is there is, you see,' she said. 'It's no good our worrying. We can't really alter them, can we?'

'No,' he said. 'One has no right to try – not with the best intentions in the world.'

'Do you try to force them?' she asked.

'Perhaps,' he said. 'Why should I want him to be free, if it isn't his business?'

She paused for a time.

'We can't *make* him happy, anyhow,' she said. 'He'd have to be it of himself.'

'I know,' he said. 'But we want other people with us, don't we?'

'Why should we?' she asked.

'I don't know,' he said uneasily. 'One has a hankering after a sort of further fellowship.'

'But why?' she insisted. 'Why should you hanker after other people? Why should you need them?'

This hit him right on the quick. His brows knitted.

'Does it end with just our two selves?' he asked, tense.

'Yes – what more do you want? If anybody likes to come along, let them. But why must you run after them?'

His face was tense and unsatisfied.

'You see,' he said, 'I always imagine our being really happy with some few other people – a little freedom with people.'

She pondered for a moment.

'Yes, one does want that. But it must *happen*. You can't do anything for it with your will. You always seem to think you can *force* the flowers to come out. People must love us because they love us – you can't *make* them.'

'I know,' he said. 'But must one take no steps at all? Must one just go as if one were alone in the world – the only creature in the world?'

'You've got me,' she said. 'Why should you *need* others? Why must you force people to agree with you? Why can't you be single by yourself, as you are always saying? You try to bully Gerald – as you tried to bully Hermione. You must learn to be alone. And it's so horrid of you. You've got me. And yet you want to force other people to love you as well. You do try to bully them to love you. And even then you don't want their love.'

His face was full of real perplexity.

'Don't I?' he said. 'It's the problem I can't solve. I *know* I want a perfect and complete relationship with you: and we've nearly got it – we really have. But beyond that. *Do* I want a real, ultimate relationship with Gerald? Do I want a final, almost extra-human relationship with him – a relationship in the ultimate of me and him – or don't I?'

She looked at him for a long time with strange bright eyes, but she did not answer.

Chapter Twenty-seven

Flitting

That evening Ursula returned home very bright-eyed and wondrous – which irritated her people. Her father came home at supper-time, tired after the evening class, and the long journey home. Gudrun was reading, the mother sat in silence.

Suddenly Ursula said to the company at large in a bright voice: 'Rupert and I are going to be married to-morrow.'

Her father turned round stiffly.

'You what?' he said.

'To-morrow!' echoed Gudrun.

'Indeed!' said the mother.

But Ursula only smiled wonderfully and did not reply.

'Married to-morrow!' cried her father harshly. 'What are you talking about?'

'Yes,' said Ursula. 'Why not?' Those two words from her always drove him mad. 'Everything is all right – we shall go to the registrar's office—'

There was a second's hush in the room after Ursula's blithe vagueness.

'*Really*, Ursula!' said Gudrun.

'Might we ask why there has been all this secrecy?' demanded the mother, rather superbly.

'But there hasn't' said Ursula. 'You knew.'

'Who knew?' now cried the father. 'Who knew? What do you mean by your "you knew" ?'

He was in one of his stupid rages, she instantly closed against him.

'Of course you knew,' she said coolly. 'You knew we were going to get married.'

There was a dangerous pause.

'We knew you were going to get married, did we? Knew! Why, does anybody know anything about *you*, you shifty bitch!'

'Father!' cried Gudrun, flushing deep in violent remonstrance. Then in a cold but gentle voice, as if to remind her sister to be tractable: 'But isn't it a *fearfully* sudden decision, Ursula?' she asked.

'No, not really,' replied Ursula, with the same maddening cheerfulness. 'He's been *wanting* me to agree for weeks – he's had the licence ready. Only I – I wasn't ready in myself. Now I am ready – is there anything to be disagreeable about?'

'Certainly not,' said Gudrun, but in a tone of cold reproof. 'You are perfectly free to do as you like.'

' "Ready in yourself" – *yourself*, that's all that matters, isn't it! "I wasn't ready in myself," ' he mimicked her phrase offensively. 'You and *yourself*, you're of some importance, aren't you?'

She drew herself up and set back her throat, her eyes shining yellow and dangerous.

'I am to myself,' she said, wounded and mortified. 'I know I am not to anybody else. You only wanted to *bully* me – you never cared for my happiness.'

He was leaning forward watching her, his face intense like a spark.

'Ursula, what are you saying? Keep your tongue still,' cried her mother.

Ursula swung round and the lights in her eyes flashed.

'No, I won't,' she cried. 'I won't hold my tongue and be bullied. What does it matter which day I get married – what does it *matter*! It doesn't affect anybody but myself.'

Her father was tense and gathered together like a cat about to spring.

'Doesn't it?' he cried, coming nearer to her. She shrank away.

'No, how can it?' she replied, shrinking but stubborn.

'It doesn't matter to *me*, then, what you do – what becomes of you?' he cried, in a strange voice like a cry.

The mother and Gudrun stood back as if hypnotised.

'No,' stammered Ursula. Her father was very near to her. 'You only want to—'

She knew it was dangerous, and she stopped. He was gathered together, every muscle ready.

'What?' he challenged.

'Bully me,' she muttered, and even as her lips were moving, his hand had caught her smack at the side of the face and she was sent up against the door.

'Father!' cried Gudrun in a high voice, 'it is impossible!'

He stood unmoving. Ursula recovered, her hand was on the door-handle. She slowly drew herself up. He seemed doubtful now.

'It's true,' she declared, with brilliant tears in her eyes, her head lifted up in defiance. 'What has your love meant, what did it ever mean? – bullying and denial – it did—'

He was advancing again with strange, tense movements, and clenched fist, and the face of a murderer. But swift as lightning she had flashed out of the door, and they heard her running upstairs.

He stood for a moment looking at the door. Then, like a defeated animal, he turned and went back to his seat by the fire.

Gudrun was very white. Out of the intense silence the mother's voice was heard saying, cold and angry:

'Well, you shouldn't take so much notice of her.'

Again the silence fell, each followed a separate set of emotions and thoughts.

Suddenly the door opened again: Ursula, dressed in hat and furs, with a small valise in her hand:

'Good-bye!' she said in her maddening, bright, almost mocking tone. 'I'm going.'

And in the next instant the door was closed, they heard the outer door, then her quick steps down the garden path, then the gate banged, and her light footfall was gone. There was a silence like death in the house.

Ursula went straight to the station, hastening heedlessly on winged feet. There was no train, she must walk on to the junction. As she went through the darkness, she began to cry, and she wept bitterly, with a dumb, heart-broken, child's anguish, all the way on the road, and in the train. Time passed unheeded and unknown, she did not know where she was, nor what was taking place. Only she wept from fathomless depths of hopeless, hopeless grief, the terrible grief of a child, that knows no extenuation.

Yet her voice had the same defensive brightness as she spoke to Birkin's landlady at the door.

'Good evening! Is Mr. Birkin in? Can I see him?'

'Yes, he's in. He's in his study.'

Ursula slipped past the woman. His door opened. He had heard her voice.

'Hello!' he exclaimed in surprise, seeing her standing there with the valise in her hand, and marks of tears on her face. She was one who wept without showing many traces, like a child.

'Do I look a sight?' she said, shrinking.

'No – why? Come in.' He took the bag from her hand and they went into the study.

There – immediately, her lips began to tremble like those of a child that remembers again, and the tears came rushing up.

'What's the matter?' he asked, taking her in his arms. She sobbed violently on his shoulder whilst he held her still, waiting.

'What's the matter?' he said again, when she was quieter. But she only pressed her face farther into his shoulder, in pain, like a child that cannot tell.

'What is it, then?' he asked.

Suddenly she broke away, wiped her eyes, regained her composure, and went and sat in a chair.

'Father hit me,' she announced, sitting bunched up, rather like a ruffled bird, her eyes were bright.

'What for?' he said.

She looked away and would not answer. There was a pitiful redness about her sensitive nostrils and her quivering lips.

'Why?' he repeated in his strange, soft, penetrating voice.

She looked round at him rather defiantly.

'Because I said I was going to be married to-morrow, and he bullied me.'

'Why did he bully you?'

Her mouth dropped again, she remembered the scene once more, the tears came up.

'Because I said he didn't care – and he doesn't; it's only his domineeringness that's hurt—' she said, her mouth pulled awry by her weeping all the time she spoke, so that he almost smiled, it seemed so childish. Yet it was not childish, it was a mortal conflict, a deep wound.

'It isn't quite true,' he said. 'And even so, you shouldn't *say* it.'

'It *is* true – it *is* true,' she wept, 'and I won't be bullied by his pretending it's love – when it *isn't* – he doesn't care, how can he – no, he can't—'

He sat in silence. She moved him beyond himself.

'Then you shouldn't rouse him, if he can't,' replied Birkin quietly.

'And I *have* loved him, I have,' she wept. 'I've loved him always, and he's always done this to me, he has—'

'It's been a love of opposition, then' he said. 'Never mind – it will be all right. It's nothing desperate.'

'Yes,' she wept, 'it is, it is.'

'Why?'

'I shall never see him again—'

'Not immediately. Don't cry, you had to break with him, it had to be – don't cry.'

He went over to her and kissed her fine, fragile hair, touching her wet cheeks gently.

'Don't cry,' he repeated, 'don't cry any more.'

He held her head close against him, very close and quiet.

At last she was still. Then she looked up, her eyes wide and frightened.

'Don't you want me?' she asked.

'Want you?' His darkened, steady eyes puzzled her and did not give her play.

'Do you wish I hadn't come?' she asked, anxious now again for fear she might be out of place.

'No,' he said. 'I wish there hadn't been the violence – so much ugliness – but perhaps it was inevitable.'

She watched him in silence. He seemed deadened.

'But where shall I stay?' she asked, feeling humiliated.

He thought for a moment.

'Here, with me,' he said. 'We're married as much to-day as we shall be to-morrow.'

'But—'

'I'll tell Mrs. Varley,' he said. 'Never mind now.'

He sat looking at her. She could feel his darkened steady eyes looking at her all the time. It made her a little bit frightened. She pushed her hair off her forehead nervously.

'Do I look ugly?' she said.

And she blew her nose again.

A small smile came round his eyes.

'No,' he said, 'fortunately.'

And he went across to her and gathered her like a belonging in his arms. She was so tenderly beautiful, he could not bear to see her, he could only bear to hide her against himself. Now, washed all clean by her tears, she was new and frail like a flower just unfolded, a flower so new, so tender, so made perfect by inner light, that he could not bear to look at her, he must hide her against himself, cover his eyes against her. She had the perfect candour of creation, something translucent and simple, like a radiant, shining flower that moment unfolded in primal blessedness. She was so new, so wonder-clear, so undimmed. And he was so old, so steeped in heavy memories. Her soul was new, undefined and glimmering with the unseen. And his soul was dark and gloomy, it had only one grain of living hope, like a grain of mustard seed. But this one living grain in him matched the perfect youth in her.

'I love you,' he whispered as he kissed her, and trembled with pure hope, like a man who is born again to a wonderful, lively hope far exceeding the bounds of death.

She could not know hwo much it meant to him, how much he meant by the few words. Almost childish, she wanted proof, and statement, even over-statement, for everything seemed still uncertain, unfixed to her.

But the passion of gratitude with which he received her into his soul, the extreme, unthinkable gladness of knowing himself living and fit to unite with her, he, who was so nearly dead, who was so near to being gone with the rest of his race down the slope of mechanical death, could never be understood by her. He worshipped her as age worships youth, he gloried in her because, in his one grain of faith, he was young as she, he was her proper mate. This marriage with her was his resurrection and his life.

All this she could not know. She wanted to be made much of, to be adored. There were infinite distances of silence between them. How could he tell her of the immanence of her beauty, that was not form, or weight, or colour, but something like a strange, golden light! How could he know himself what her beauty lay in, for him. He said. 'Your nose is beautiful, your chin is adorable.' But it sounded like lies, and she was disappointed, hurt. Even when he said, whispering with truth, 'I love you, l love you,' it was not the real truth. It was something beyond love, such a gladness of having surpassed oneself, of having transcended the old existence. How could he say 'I' when he was something new and unknown, not himself at all? This I, this old formula of the age, was a dead letter.

In the new, superfine bliss, a peace superseding knowledge, there was no I and you, there was only the third, unrealised wonder, the wonder of existing not as oneself, but in a consummation of my being and of her being in a new one, a new, paradisal unit regained from the duality. How can I say 'I love you' when I have ceased to be, and you have ceased to be: we are both caught up and transcended into a new oneness where everything is silent, because there is nothing to answer, all is perfect and at one. Speech travels between the separate parts. But in the perfect One there is perfect silence of bliss.

They were married by law on the next day, and she did as he bade her, she wrote to her father and mother. Her mother replied, not her father.

She did not go back to school. She stayed with Birkin in his rooms, or at the Mill, moving with him as he moved. But she did not see anybody, save Gudrun and Gerald. She was all strange and wondering as yet, but relieved as by dawn.

Gerald sat talking to her one afternoon in the warm study down at the Mill. Rupert had not yet come home.

'Are you happy?' Gerald asked her, with a smile.

'Very happy!' she cried, shrinking a little in her brightness.

'Yes, one can see it.'

'Can one?' cried Ursula in surprise.

He looked up at her with a communicative smile.

'Oh yes, plainly.'

She was pleased. She meditated a moment.

'And can you see that Rupert is happy as well?'

He lowered his eyelids and looked aside.

'Oh yes,' he said.

'Really!'

'Oh yes.'

He was very quiet, as if it were something not to be talked about by him. He seemed sad.

She was very sensitive to suggestion. She asked the question he wanted her to ask.

'Why don't you be happy as well?' she said. 'You could be just the same.'

He paused a moment.

'With Gudrun?' he asked.

'Yes!' she cried, her eyes glowing. But there was a strange tension, an emphasis, as if they were asserting their wishes, against the truth.

'You think Gudrun would have me, and we should be happy?' he said.

'Yes, I'm *sure*!' she cried.

Her eyes were round with delight. Yet underneath she was constrained, she knew her own insistence.

'Oh, I'm *so* glad,' she added.

He smiled.

'What makes you glad?' he said.

'For *her* sake,' she replied. 'I'm sure you'd – you're the right man for her.'

'You are?' he said. 'And do you think she would agree with you?'

'Oh yes!' she exclaimed hastily. Then, upon reconsideration, very uneasy: 'Though Gudrun isn't so very simple, is she? One doesn't know her in five minutes, does one? She's not like me in that.' She laughed at him with her strange, open, dazzled face.

'You think she's not much like you?' Gerald asked.

She knitted her brows.

'Oh, in many ways she is. But I never know what she will do when anything new comes.'

'You don't?' said Gerald. He was silent for some moments. Then he moved tentatively. 'I was going to ask her, in any case, to go away with me at Christmas,' he said in a very small, cautious voice.

'Go away with you? For a time, you mean?'

'As long as she likes,' he said, with a deprecating movement.

They were both silent for some minutes.

'Of course,' said Ursula at last, 'she *might* just be willing to rush into marriage. You can see.'

'Yes,' smiled Gerald. 'I can see. But in case she won't – do you think she would go abroad with me for a few days – or for a fortnight?'

'Oh yes,' said Ursula. 'I'd ask her.'

'Do you think we might all go together?'

'All of us?' Again Ursula's face lighted up. 'It would be rather fun, don't you think?'

'Great fun,' he said.

'And then you could see,' said Ursula.

'What?'

'How things went. I think it is best to take the honeymoon before the wedding – don't you?'

She was pleased with this *mot*. He laughed.

'In certain cases,' he said. 'I'd rather it were so in my own case.'

'Would you!' exclaimed Ursula. Then doubtingly, 'Yes, perhaps you're right. One should please oneself.'

Birkin came in a little later, and Ursula told him what had been said.

'Gudrun!' exclaimed Birkin. 'She's a born mistress, just as Gerald is a born lover – *amant en titre*. If as somebody says all women are either wives or mistresses, then Gudrun is a mistress.'

'And all men either lovers or husbands,' cried Ursula. 'But why not both?'

'The one excludes the other,' he laughed.

'Then I want a lover,' cried Ursula.

'No, you don't,' he said.

'But I do,' she wailed.

He kissed her and laughed.

It was two days after this that Ursula was to go to fetch her things from the house in Beldover. The removal had taken place, the family had gone. Gudrun had rooms in Willey Green.

Ursula had not seen her parents since her marriage. She wept over the rupture, yet what was the good of making it up! Good or not good, she could not go to them. So her things had been left behind and she and Gudrun were to walk over for them in the afternoon.

It was a wintry afternoon, with red in the sky, when they arrived at the house. The windows were dark and blank, already the place was frightening. A stark, void entrance-hall struck a chill to the hearts of the girls.

'I don't believe I dare have come in alone,' said Ursula. 'It frightens me.'

'Ursula!' cried Gudrun. 'Isn't it amazing! Can you believe you lived in this place and never felt it? How I lived here a day without dying of terror, I cannot conceive!'

They looked in the big dining-room. It was a good-sized room, but now a cell would have been lovelier. The large bay windows were naked, the floor was stripped, and a border of dark polish went round the tract of pale boarding. In the faded wall-paper were dark patches where furniture had stood, where pictures had hung. The sense of walls, dry, thin, flimsy-seeming walls, and a flimsy flooring, pale with its artificial black edges, was neutralising to the mind. Everything was null to the senses, there was enclosure without substance, for the walls were dry and papery. Where were they standing, on earth, or suspended in some cardboard box? In the hearth was burnt paper and scraps of half-burnt paper.

'Imagine that we passed our days here!' said Ursula.

'I know,' cried Gudrun. 'It is too appalling. What must we be like, if we are the contents of *this*!'

'Vile!' said Ursula. 'It really is.'

And she recognised half-burnt covers of *Vogue* – half-burnt representations of women in gowns – lying under the grate.

They went to the drawing-room. Another piece of shut-in air; without weight or substance, only a sense of intolerable papery imprisonment in nothingness. The kitchen did look more substantial, because of the red-tiled floor and the stove, but it was cold and horrid.

The two girls tramped hollowly up the bare stairs. Every sound re-echoed under their hearts. They tramped down the bare corridor. Against the wall of Ursula's bedroom were her things – a trunk, a work-basket, some books, loose coats, a hat-box, standing desolate in the universal emptiness of the dusk.

'A cheerful sight, aren't they?' said Ursula, looking down at her forsaken possessions.

'Very cheerful,' said Gudrun.

The two girls set to, carrying everything down to the front door. Again and again they made the hollow, re-echoing transit. The whole place seemed to resound about them with a noise of hollow, empty futility. In the distance the empty, invisible rooms sent forth a vibration almost of obscenity. They almost fled with the last articles into the out-of-door.

But it was cold. They were waiting for Birkin, who was coming with the car. They went indoors again, and upstairs to their parents' front bedroom, whose windows looked down on the road, and across the country at the black-barred sunset, black and red barred, without light.

They sat down in the window-seat to wait. Both girls were looking over the room. It was void, with a meaninglessness that was almost dreadful.

'Really,' said Ursula, 'this room *couldn't* be sacred, could it?'

Gudrun looked over it with slow eyes.

'Impossible,' she replied.

'When I think of their lives – father's and mother's, their love, and their marriage, and all of us children, and our bringing-up – would you have such a life, Prune?'

'I wouldn't, Ursula.'

'It all seems so *nothing* – their two lives – there's no meaning in it. Really, if they had *not* met, and *not* married, and not lived together – it wouldn't have mattered, would it?'

'Of course – you can't tell,' said Gudrun.

'No. But if I thought my life was going to be like it – Prune,' she caught Gudrun's arm, 'I should run.'

Gudrun was silent for a few moments.

'As a matter of fact, one cannot contemplate the ordinary life – one cannot contemplate it,' replied Gudrun. 'With you, Ursula, it is quite different. You will be out of it all, with Birkin. He's a special case. But with the ordinary man, who has his life fixed in one place, marriage is just impossible. There may be, and there *are*, thousands of women who want it, and could conceive of nothing else. But the very thought of it sends me *mad*. One must be free, above all, one must be free. One may forfeit everything else, but one must be free – one must not become 7, Pinchbeck Street – or Somerset Drive – or Shortlands. No man will be sufficient to make that good – no man! To marry, one must have a free lance or nothing, a comrade-in-arms, a Glücksritter. A man with a position in the social world – well, it is just impossible, impossible!'

'What a lovely word – a Glücksritter!' said Ursula. 'So much nicer than a soldier of fortune.'

'Yes, isn't it?' said Gudrun. 'I'd tilt the world with a Glücksritter. But a home, an establishment! Ursula, what would it mean? – think!'

'I know,' said Ursula. 'We've had one home – that's enough for me.'

'Quite enough,' said Gudrun.

'The little grey home in the west,' quoted Ursula ironically.

'Doesn't it sound grey, too,' said Gudrun grimly.

They were interrupted by the sound of the car. There was Birkin. Ursula was surprised that she felt so lit up, that she became suddenly so free from the problems of grey homes in the west.

They heard his heels click on the hall pavement below.

'Hello!' he called, his voice echoing alive through the house. Ursula smiled to herself. *He* was frightened of the place too.

'Hello! Here we are,' she called downstairs. And they heard him quickly running up.

'This is a ghostly situation,' he said.

'These houses don't have ghosts – they've never had any personality, and only a place with personality can have a ghost,' said Gudrun.

'I suppose so. Are you both weeping over the past?'

'We are,' said Gudrun, grimly.

Ursula laughed.

'Not weeping that it's gone, but weeping that it ever *was*,' she said.

'Oh,' he replied, relieved.

He sat down for a moment. There was something in his presence, Ursula thought, lambent and alive. It made even the impertinent structure of this null house disappear.

'Gudrun says she could not bear to be married and put into a house,' said Ursula meaningful – they knew this referred to Gerald.

He was silent for some moments.

'Well,' he said, 'if you know beforehand you couldn't stand it, you're safe.'

'Quite!' said Gudrun.

'Why *does* every woman think her aim in life is to have a hubby and a little grey home in the west? Why is this the goal of life? Why should it be?' said Ursula.

'*Il faut avoir le respect de ses bêtises,*' said Birkin.

'But you needn't have the respect for the *bêtise* before you've committed it,' laughed Ursula.

'Ah then, *des bêtises du papa?*'

'*Et de la maman,*' added Gudrun satirically.

'*Et des voisins,*' said Ursula.

They all laughed, and rose. It was getting dark. They carried the things to the car. Gudrun locked the door of the empty house. Birkin had lighted the lamps of the automobile. It all seemed very happy, as if they were setting out.

'Do you mind stopping at Coulsons. I have to leave the key there,' said Gudrun.

'Right,' said Birkin, and they moved off.

They stopped in the main street. The shops were just lighted, the last miners were passing home along the causeways, half-visible shadows in their grey pit-dirt, moving through the blue air. But their feet rang harshly in manifold sound, along the pavement.

How pleased Gudrun was to come out of the shop, and enter the car, and be borne swiftly away into the down-hill of palpable dusk, with Ursula and Birkin! What an adventure life seemed at the moment! How deeply, how suddenly she envied Ursula! Life for her was so quick, and an open door – so reckless as if not only this world, but the world that was gone and the world to come were nothing to her. Ah, if she could be *just like that*, it would be perfect.

For always, except in her moments of excitement, she felt a want within herself. She was unsure. She had felt that now, at last, in Gerald's strong and violent love, she was living fully and finally. But when she compared herself with Ursula, already her soul was jealous, unsatisfied. She was not satisfied – she was never to be satisfied.

What was she short of now? It was marriage – it was the wonderful stability of marriage. She did want it, let her say what she might. She had been lying. The old idea of marriage was right even now – marriage and the home. Yet her mouth gave a little grimace at the words. She thought of Gerald and Shortlands – marriage and the home! Ah well, let it rest! He meant a great deal to her – but—! Perhaps it was not in her to marry. She was one of life's outcasts, one of the drifting lives that have no root. No, no – it could not be so. She suddenly conjured up a rosy room, with herself in a beautiful gown, and a handsome man in evening dress who held her in his arms in the firelight, and kissed her. This picture she entitled 'Home'. It would have done for the Royal Academy.

'Come with us to tea – *do*,' said Ursula, as they ran nearer to the cottage of Willey Green.

'Thanks awfully – but I *must* go in—' said Gudrun. She wanted very much to go on with Ursula and Birkin. That seemed like life indeed to her. Yet a certain perversity would not let her.

'Do come – yes, it would be so nice,' pleaded Ursula.

'I'm awfully sorry – I should love to – but I can't – really—'

She descended from the car in trembling haste.

'Can't you really?' came Ursula's regretful voice.

'No, really I can't,' responded Gudrun's pathetic, chagrined words out of the dusk.

'All right, are you?' called Birkin.

'Quite!' said Gudrun. 'Good-night!'

'Good-night,' they called.

'Come whenever you like, we shall be glad,' called Birkin.

'Thank you very much,' called Gudrun, in the strange, twanging voice of lonely chagrin that was very puzzling to him. She turned away to her cottage gate, and they drove on. But immediately she stood to watch them, as the car ran vague into the distance. And as she went up the path to her strange house, her heart was full of incomprehensible bitterness.

In her parlour was a long-case clock, and inserted into its dial was a ruddy, round, slant-eyed, joyous-painted face, that wagged over with the most ridiculous ogle when the clock ticked, and back again with the same absurd glad-eye at the next tick. All the time the absurd smooth, brown-ruddy face gave her an obtrusive 'glad-eye'. She stood for minutes, watching it, till a sort of maddened disgust overcame her, and she laughed at herself hollowly. And still it rocked, and gave her the glad-eye from one side, then from the other, from one side, then from the other. Ah, how unhappy she was! In the midst of her most active happiness, ah, how unhappy she was! She glanced at the table. Gooseberry jam, and the same home-made cake with too much soda in it! Still, gooseberry jam was good, and one so rarely got it.

All the evening she wanted to go to the Mill. But she coldly refused to allow herself. She went the next afternoon instead. She was happy to find Ursula alone. It was a lovely, intimate secluded atmosphere. They talked endlessly and delightedly. 'Aren't you *fearfully* happy here?' said Gudrun to her sister glancing at her own bright eyes in the mirror. She always envied, almost with resentment, the strange positive fullness that subsisted in the atmosphere around Ursula and Birkin.

'How really beautifully this room is done,' she said aloud. 'This hard plaited matting – what a lovely colour it is, the colour of cool light!'

And it seemed to her perfect.

'Ursula,' she said at length, in a voice of question and detachment, 'did you know that Gerald Crich had suggested our going away all together at Christmas?'

'Yes, he's spoken to Rupert.'

A deep flush dyed Gudrun's cheek. She was silent a moment, as if taken aback, and not knowing what to say.

'But don't you think,' she said at last, it is *amazingly cool*!'

Ursula laughed.

'I like him for it,' she said.

Gudrun was silent. It was evident that, whilst she was almost mortified by Gerald's taking the liberty of making such a suggestion to Birkin, yet the idea itself attracted her strongly.

'There's a rather lovely simplicity about Gerald, I think,' said Ursula, 'so defiant, somehow! Oh, I think he's *very* lovable.'

Gudrun did not reply for some moments. She had still to get over the feeling of insult at the liberty taken with her freedom.

'What did Rupert say – do you know?' she asked.

'He said it would be most awfully jolly,' said Ursula.

Again Gudrun looked down, and was silent.

'Don't you think it would?' said Ursula, tentatively. She was never quite sure how many defences Gudrun was having round herself.

Gudrun raised her face with difficulty and held it averted.

'I think it *might* be awfully jolly, as you say,' she replied. 'But don't you think it was an unpardonable liberty to take – to talk of such things to Rupert – who after all – you see what I mean, Ursula – they might have been two men arranging an outing with some little *type* they'd picked up. Oh, I think it's unforgivable, quite!' She used the French word '*type.*'

Her eyes flashed, her soft face was flushed and sullen. Ursula looked on, rather frightened, frightened most of all because she thought Gudrun seemed rather common, really like a little *type*. But she had not the courage quite to think this – not right out.

'Oh no,' she cried, stammering. 'Oh no – not at all like that – oh no! No, I think it's rather beautiful, the friendship between Rupert and Gerald. They just are simple – they say anything to each other, like brothers.'

Gudrun flushed deeper. She not *bear* it that Gerald gave her away – even to Birkin.

'But do you think even brothers have any right to exchange confidences of that sort?' she asked, with deep anger.

'Oh yes,' said Ursula. 'There's never anything said that isn't perfectly straightforward. No, the thing that's amazed me most in Gerald – how perfectly simple and direct he can be! And you know, it takes rather a big man. Most of them *must* be indirect, they are such cowards.'

But Gudrun was still silent with anger. She wanted the absolute secrecy kept, with regard to her movements.

'Won't you go?' said Ursula. 'Do, we might all be so happy! There is something I *love* about Gerald – he's *much* more lovable than I thought him. He's free, Gudrun, he really is.'

Gudrun's mouth was still closed, sullen and ugly. She opened it at length.

'Do you know where he proposes to go?' she asked.

'Yes – to the Tyrol, where he used to go when he was in Germany – a lovely place where students go, small and rough and lovely, for winter sport!'

Through Gudrun's mind went the angry thought – 'they know everything.'

'Yes,' she said aloud, 'about forty kilometres from Innsbruck, isn't it?'

'I don't know exactly where – but it would be lovely, don't you think, high in the perfect snow—?'

'Very lovely!' said Gudrun, sarcastically.

Ursula was put out.

'Of course,' she said, 'I think Gerald spoke to Rupert so that it shouldn't seem like an outing with a *type*—'

'I know, of course,' said Gudrun, 'that he quite commonly does take up with that sort.'

'Does he!' said Ursula. 'Why how do you know?'

'I know of a model in Chelsea,' said Gudrun coldly.

Now Ursula was silent.

'Well,' she said at last, with a doubtful laugh, 'I hope he has a good time with her.' At which Gudrun looked more glum.

Chapter Twenty-eight

Gudrun in the Pompadour

Christmas drew near, all four prepared for flight. Birkin and Ursula were busy packing their few personal things, making them ready to be sent off, to whatever country and whatever place they might choose at last. Gudrun was very much excited. She loved to be on the wing.

She and Gerald, being ready first, set off via London and Paris to Innsbruck, where they would meet Ursula and Birkin. In London they stayed one night. They went to the music-hall, and afterwards to the Pompadour Café.

Gudrun hated the Café, yet she always went back to it, as did most of the artists of her acquaintance. She loathed its atmosphere of petty vice and petty jealousy and petty art. Yet she always called in again, when she was in town. It was as if she *had* to return to this small, slow central whirlpool of disintegration and dissolution: just give it a look.

She sat with Gerald drinking some sweetish liqueur, and staring with black, sullen looks at the various groups of people at the tables. She would greet nobody, but young men nodded to her frequently, with a kind of sneering familiarity. She cut them all. And it gave her pleasure to sit there, cheeks flushed, eyes black and sullen, seeing them all objectively, as put away from her, like creatures in some menagerie of apish degraded souls. God, what a foul crew they were! Her blood beat black and thick in her veins with rage and loathing. Yet she must sit and watch, watch. One or two people came to speak to her. From every side of the Café, eyes turned half furtively, half jeeringly at her, men looking over their shoulders, women under their hats.

The old crowd was there, Carlyon in his corner with his pupils and his girl, Halliday and Libidnikov and the Pussum – they were all there. Gudrun watched Gerald. She watched his eyes linger a moment on Halliday, on Halliday's party. These last were on the look-out – they nodded to him, he nodded again. They giggled and whispered among themselves. Gerald watched them with the steady twinkle in his eyes. They were urging Minette to something.

She at last rose. She was wearing a curious dress of dark silk with long pale rays, a curious rayed effect. She was thinner, her eyes were perhaps wider, more disintegrated. Otherwise she was just the same. Gerald watched her with the same steady twinkle in his eyes as she came across. She held out her thin fair hand to him.

'How are you?' she said.

He shook hands with her, but remained seated, and let her stand near him, against the table. She nodded coldly to Gudrun, whom she did not know to speak to, but well enough by sight and reputation.

'I am very well,' said Gerald. 'And you?'

'Oh I'm all wight. What about Wupert?'

'Rupert? He's very well, too.'

'Yes, I don't mean that. What about him being married?'

'Oh – yes, he is married.'

Minette's eyes had a hot flash.

'Oh, he's weally bwought if off then, has he? When was he married?'

'A week or two ago.'

'Weally! He's never written.'

'No.'

'No. Don't you think it's too bad?'

This last was in a tone of challenge. Minette let it be known by her tone, that she was aware of Gudrun's listening.

'I suppose he didn't feel like it,' replied Gerald.

'But why didn't he?' pursued Minette.

This was received in silence. There was an ugly, mocking persistence in the small, beautiful figure of the short-haired girl, as she stood near Gerald.

'Are you staying in town long?' she asked.

'To-night only.'

'Oh, only to-night. Are you coming over to speak to Julius?'

'Not to-night.'

'Oh very well. I'll tell him then.' Then came her touch of diablerie. 'You're looking awf'lly fit.'

'Yes – I feel it.' Gerald was quite calm and easy, a spark of satiric amusement in his eye.

'Are you having a good time?'

This was a direct blow for Gudrun, spoken in a level, toneless voice of callous ease.

'Yes,' he replied, quite colourlessly.

'I'm awf'lly sorry you aren't coming round. You aren't very faithful to your fwiends.'

'Not very,' he said.

She nodded them both 'Good-night', and went back slowly to her own set. Gudrun watched her curious walk, stiff and jerking at the loins. They heard her level, toneless voice distinctly.

'He won't come over; – he is otherwise engaged,' it said. There was more laughter and lowered voices and mockery at the table.

'Is she a friend of yours?' said Gudrun, looking calmly at Gerald.

'I've stayed at Halliday's with Birkin,' he said, meeting her slow, calm eyes. And she knew that Minette was one of his mistresses – and he knew she knew.

She looked round, and called for the waiter. She wanted an iced cocktail, of all things. This amused Gerald – he wondered what was up.

The Halliday party was tipsy, and malicious. They were talking out loudly about Birkin, ridiculing him on every point, particularly on his marriage.

'Oh, *don't* make me think of Birkin,' Halliday was squealing. 'He makes me perfectly sick. He is as bad as Jesus. "Lord, *what* must I do to be saved!" '

He giggled to himself tipsily.

'Do you remember,' came the quick voice of the Russian, 'the letters he used to send. "Desire is holy—" '

'Oh yes!' cried Halliday. 'Oh, how perfectly splendid. Why, I've got one in my pocket. I'm sure I have.'

He took out various papers from his pocket book.

'I'm sure I've – *hic! Oh dear!* – got one.'

Gerald and Gudrun were watching absorbedly.

'Oh yes, how perfectly – *hic!* – splendid! Don't make me laugh, Minette, it gives me the hiccup. Hic!—' They all giggled.

'What did he say in that one?' Minette asked, leaning forward, her close fair hair falling and swinging against her face. There was something curiously indecent about her small, longish, fair skull, particularly when the ears showed.

'Wait – oh, do wait! *No-o,* I won't give it to you, I'll read it aloud. I'll read you the choice bits – hic! Oh dear! Do you think if I drink water it would take off this hiccup? *Hic!* Oh, I feel perfectly helpless.'

'Isn't that the letter about uniting the dark and the light – and the Flux of Corruption?' asked Maxim, in his precise, quick voice.

'I believe so,' said Minette.

'Oh, is it? I'd forgotten – *hic!* – it was that one,' Halliday said, opening the letter. '*Hic!* Oh yes. How perfectly splendid! This is one of the best. "There is a phrase in every race—" ' he read in the sing-song, slow, distinct voice of a clergyman reading the Scriptures, ' "when the desire for destruction overcomes every other desire. In the individual, this desire is ultimately a desire for destruction in the self" – *hic!*—' he paused and looked up.

'I hope he's going ahead with the destruction of himself,' said the quick voice of the Russian. Halliday giggled, and lolled his head back, vaguely.

'There's not much to destroy in him,' said Minette. 'He's so thin already, there's only a fag-end to start on.'

'Oh, isn't it beautiful! I love reading it! I believe it has cured my hiccup!' squealed Halliday. 'Do let me go on. "It is a desire for the reduction-process in oneself, a reducing back to the origin, a return along the Flux of Corruption, to the original rudimentary conditions of being—!" Oh, but I *do* think it is wonderful. It almost supersedes the Bible—'

'Yes – Flux of Corruption,' said the Russian, 'I remember that phrase.'

'Oh, he was always talking about Corruption,' said Minette. 'He must be corrupt himself, to have it so much on his mind.'

'Exactly!' said the Russian.

'Do let me go on! Oh, this is a perfectly wonderful piece! But do listen to this. "And in the great retrogression, the reducing back of the created body of life, we get knowledge, and beyond knowledge, the phosphorescent ecstasy of acute sensation." Oh, I do think these phrases are too absurdly wonderful. Oh, but don't you think they *are* – they're nearly as good as Jesus. "And if, Julius, you want this ecstasy of reduction with Minette, you must go on till it is fulfilled. But surely there is in you also, somewhere, the living desire for positive creation, relationships in ultimate faith, when all this process of active corruption, with all its flowers of mud, is transcended, and more or less finished—" I do wonder what the flowers of mud are. Minette, you are a flower of mud.'

'Thank you – and what are you?'

'Oh, I'm another, surely, according to this letter! We're all flowers of mud – *Fleurs* – *hic! du mal!* It's perfectly wonderful, Birkin harrowing Hell – harrowing the Pompadour – *Hic!*'

'Go on – go on,' said Maxim. 'What comes next? It's really very interesting.'

'I think it's awful cheek to write like that,' said Minette.

'Yes – yes, so do I,' said the Russian. 'He is a megolamaniac, of course, it is a form of religious mania. He thinks he is the Saviour of man – go on reading.'

'Surely,' Halliday intoned, ' "surely goodness and mercy hath followed me all the days of my life—" ' he broke off and giggled. Then he began again, intoning like a clergyman. ' "Surely there will come an end in us to this desire – for the constant going apart – this passion for putting asunder – everything – ourselves, reducing ourselves part from part – reacting in intimacy only for destruction – using sex as a great reducing agent, reducing the two great elements of male and female from their highly complex unity – reducing the old ideas, going back to the savages for our sensations – always seeking to *lose* ourselves in some ultimate black sensation, mindless and infinite – burning only with destructive fires, ranging on with the hope of being burnt out utterly—" '

'I want to go,' said Gudrun to Gerald, as she signalled the waiter. Her eyes were flashing, her cheeks were flushed. The strange effect of Birkin's letter read aloud in a perfect clerical sing-song, clear and resonant, phrase by phrase, made the blood mount into her head as if she were mad.

She rose, whilst Gerald was paying the bill, and walked over to Halliday's table. They all glanced up at her.

'Excuse me,' she said. 'Is that a genuine letter you are reading?'

'Oh yes,' said Halliday. 'Quite genuine.'

'May I see?'

Smiling foolishly he handed it to her, as if hypnotised.

'Thank you,' she said.

And she turned and walked out of the Café with the letter, all down the brilliant room, between the tables, in her measured fashion. It was some moments before anybody realised what was happening.

From Halliday's table came half articulate cries, then somebody booed, then all the far end of the place began booing after Gudrun's retreating form. She was fashionably dressed in blackish-green and silver, her hat was brilliant green, like the sheen on an insect, but the brim was soft dark green, a falling edge with fine silver, her coat was dark green, lustrous, with a high collar of grey fur, and great fur cuffs, the edge of her dress showed silver and black velvet, her stockings and shoes were silver grey. She moved with slow, fashionable indifference to the door. The porter opened obsequiously for her, and at her nod, hurried to the edge of the pavement and whistled for a taxi. The two lights of a vehicle almost immediately curved round towards her, like two eyes.

Gerald had followed in wonder, amid all the booing, not having caught her misdeed. He heard Minette's voice saying:

'Go and get it back from her. I never heard of such a thing! Go and get it back from her. Tell Gerald Crich – there he goes – go and make him give it up.'

Gudrun stood at the door of the taxi, which the man held open for her.

'To the hotel?' she asked, as Gerald came out, hurriedly.

'Where you like,' he answered.

'Right!' she said. Then to the driver, 'Wagstaff's – Barton Street.'

The driver bowed his head, and put down the flag.

Gudrun entered the taxi, with the deliberate cold movement of a woman who is well-dressed and contemptuous in her soul. Yet she was frozen with overwrought feelings. Gerald followed her.

'You've forgotten the man,' she said coolly, with a slight nod of her hat. Gerald gave the porter a shilling. The man saluted. They were in motion.

'What was all the row about?' asked Gerald, in wondering excitement.

'I walked away with Birkin's letter,' she said, and he saw the crushed paper in her hand.

His eyes glittered with satisfaction.

'Ah!' he said. 'Splendid! A set of jackasses!'

'I could have *killed* them!' she cried in passion. '*Dogs!* – they are dogs! Why is Rupert such a *fool* as to write such letters to them? Why does he give himself away to such canaille? It's a thing that *cannot be borne.*'

Gerald wondered over her strange passion.

And she could not rest any longer in London. They must go by the morning train from Charing Cross. As they drew over the bridge, in the train, having glimpses of the river between the great iron girders, she cried:

'I feel I could *never* see this foul town again – I couldn't *bear* to come back to it.'

Chapter Twenty-nine

Continental

Ursula went on in an unreal suspense, the last weeks before going away. She was not herself – she was not anything. She was something that is going to be – soon – soon – very soon. But as yet, she was only imminent.

She went to see her parents. It was a rather stiff, sad meeting, more like a verification of separateness than a reunion. But they were all vague and indefinite with one another, stiffened in the fate that moved them apart.

She did not really come to until she was on the ship crossing from Dover to Ostend. Dimly she had come down to London with Birkin, London had been a vagueness, so had the train journey to Dover. It was all like a sleep.

And now, at last, as she stood in the stern of the ship, in a pitch-dark, rather blowy night, feeling the motion of the sea, and watching the small, rather desolate little lights that twinkled on the shores of England, as on the shores of nowhere, watched them sinking smaller and smaller on the profound and living darkness, she felt her soul stirring to awake from its anaesthetic sleep.

'Let us go forward, shall we?' said Birkin. He wanted to be at the tip of their projection. So they left off looking at the faint sparks that glimmered out of nowhere, in the far distance, called England, and turned their faces to the unfathomed night in front.

They went right to the bows of the softly plunging vessel. In the complete obscurity, Birkin found a comparatively sheltered nook, where a great rope was coiled up. It was quite near the very point of the ship, near the black, unpierced space ahead. Here they sat down, folded together, folded round with the same rug, creeping in nearer and ever nearer to one another, till it seemed they had crept right into each other, and become one substance. It was very cold, and the darkness was palpable.

One of the ship's crew came along the deck, dark as the darkness, not really visible. They then made out the faintest pallor of his face. He felt their presence, and stopped, unsure – then bent forward. When his face was near them, he saw the faint pallor of their faces. Then he withdrew like a phantom. And they watched him without making any sound.

They seemed to fall away into the profound darkness. There was no sky, no earth, only one unbroken darkness, into which, with a soft, sleeping motion, they seemed to fall like one closed seed of life falling through dark, fathomless space.

They had forgotten where they were, forgotten all that was and all that had been, conscious only in their heart, and there conscious only of this pure trajectory through the surpassing darkness. The ship's prow cleaved on, with a faint noise of cleavage, into the complete night, without knowing, without seeing, only surging on.

In Ursula the sense of the unrealised world ahead triumphed over everything. In the midst of this profound darkness, there seemed to glow on her heart the effulgence of a paradise unknown and unrealised. Her heart was full of the most wonderful light, golden like honey of darkness, sweet like the warmth of day, a light which was not shed on the world, only on the unknown paradise towards which she was going, a sweetness of habitation, a delight of living quite unknown, but hers infallibly. In her transport she lifted her face suddenly to him, and he touched it with his lips. So cold, so fresh, so sea-clear her face was, it was like kissing a flower that grows near the surf.

But he did not know the ecstasy of bliss in fore-knowledge that she knew. To him, the wonder of this transit was overwhelming. He was falling through a gulf of infinite darkness, like a meteorite plunging across the chasm between the worlds. The world was torn in two, and he was plunging like an unlit star through the ineffable rift. What was beyond was not yet for him. He was overcome by the trajectory.

In a trance he lay enfolding Ursula round about. His face was against her fine, fragile hair, he breathed its fragrance with the sea and the profound night. And his soul was at peace; yielded, as he fell into the unknown. This was the first time that an utter and absolute peace had entered his heart, now, in this final transit out of life.

When there came some stir on the deck, they roused. They stood up. How stiff and cramped they were in the night-time! And yet the paradisal glow on her heart, and the unutterable peace of darkness in his, this was the all-in-all.

They stood up and looked ahead. Low lights were seen down the darkness. This was the world again. It was not the bliss of her heart, nor the peace of his. It was the superficial unreal world of fact. Yet not quite the old world. For the peace and the bliss in their hearts was enduring.

Strange and desolate above all things, like disembarking from the Styx into the desolated underworld, was this landing at night. There was the raw, half-lighted, covered-in vastness of the dark place, boarded and hollow underfoot, with only desolation everywhere. Ursula had caught sight of the big, pallid, mystic letters 'OSTEND' standing in the darkness. Everybody was hurrying with a blind, insect-like intentness through the dark grey air, porters were calling in un-English English, then trotting with heavy bags, their colourless blouses looking ghostly as they disappeared; Ursula stood at a long, low, zinc-covered barrier along with hundreds of other spectral people, and all the way down the vast, raw darkness was this low stretch of open bags and spectral people, whilst, on the other side of the barrier, pallid officials in peaked caps and moustaches were turning the underclothing in the bags, then scrawling a chalk-mark.

It was done. Birkin snapped the hand-bags, off they went, the porter coming behind. They were through a great doorway, and in the open night again – ah, a railway platform! Voices were still calling in inhuman agitation through the dark-grey air, spectres were running along the darkness between the train.

'Köln – Berlin—' Ursula made out on the boards hung on the high train on one side.

'Here we are,' said Birkin. And on her side she saw: 'Elsass – Lothringen – Luxembourg, Metz – Basle.'

'That was it, Basle!'

The porter came up.

'*A Bâle – deuxième classe? – Voilà!*' And he clambered into the high train. They followed. The compartments were already some of them taken. But many were dim and empty. The luggage was stowed, the porter was tipped.

'*Nous avons encore—*?' said Birkin, looking at his watch and at the porter.

'*Encore une demi-heure.*' With which, in his blue blouse, he disappeared. He was ugly and insolent.

'Come,' said Birkin. 'It is cold. Let us eat.'

There was a coffee-wagon on the platform. They drank hot, watery coffee and ate the long rolls, split, with ham between, which were such a wide bite that it almost dislocated Ursula's jaw; and they walked beside the high trains. It was all so strange, so extremely desolate, like the underworld, grey, grey, dirt grey, desolate, forlorn, nowhere – grey, dreary nowhere.

At last they were moving through the night. In the darkness Ursula made out the flat fields, the wet, flat, dreary darkness of the Continent. They pulled up surprisingly soon – Bruges! Then on through the level darkness, with glimpses of sleeping farms and thin poplar trees and deserted high-roads. She sat dismayed, hand in hand with Birkin. He pale, immobile like a *revenant* himself, looked sometimes out of the window, sometimes closed his eyes. Then his eyes opened again, dark as the darkness outside.

A flash of a few lights on the darkness – Ghent station! A few more spectres moving outside on the platform – then the bell – then motion again through the level darkness. Ursula saw a man with a lantern come out of a farm by the railway and cross to the dark farm-buildings. She thought of the Marsh, the old, intimate farm life at Cossethay. My God, how far was she projected from her childhood, how far was she still to go! In one lifetime one travelled through aeons. The great chasm of memory from her childhood in the intimate country surroundings of Cossethay and the Marsh Farm – she remembered the servant Tilly, who used to give her bread and butter sprinkled with brown sugar in the old living-room where the grandfather clock had two pink roses in a basket painted above the figures on the face – and now when she was travelling into the unknown with Birkin, an utter stranger – was so great, that it seemed she had no identity, that the child she had been, playing in Cossethay churchyard, was a little creature of history, not really herself.

They were at Brussels – half an hour for breakfast. They got down. On the great station clock it said six o'clock. They had coffee and rolls and honey in the vast desert refreshment-room, so dreary, always so dreary, dirty, so spacious, such desolation of space. But she washed her face and hands in hot water and combed her hair – that was a blessing.

Soon they were in the train again and moving on. The greyness of dawn began. There were several people in the compartment, large florid Belgian business-men with long brown beards, talking incessantly in an ugly French she was too tired to follow.

It seemed the train ran by degrees out of the darkness into a faint light, then beat after beat into the day. Ah, how weary it was! Faintly, the trees showed, like shadows. Then a house, white, had a curious distinctness. How was it? Then she saw a village – there were always houses passing.

This was an old world she was still journeying through, winter-heavy and dreary. There was plough-land and pasture, and copses of bare trees, copses of bushes, and homesteads naked and work-bare. No new earth had come to pass.

She looked at Birkin's face. It was white and still and eternal, too eternal. She linked her fingers imploringly in his under the cover of her rug. His fingers responded, his eyes looked back at her. How dark, like a night, his eyes were, like another world beyond! Oh, if he were the world as well, if only the world were he! If only he could call a world into being, that should be their own world!

The Belgians left, the train ran on, through Luxembourg, through Alsace-Lorraine, through Metz. But she was blind, she could see no more. Her soul did not look out.

They came at last to Basle, to the hotel. It was all a drifting trance, from which she never came to. They went out in the morning before the train departed. She saw the street, the river, she stood on the bridge. But it all meant nothing. She remembered some shops – one full of pictures, one with orange velvet and ermine. But what did these signify? – nothing.

She was not at ease till they were in the train again. Then she was relieved. So long as they were moving onwards, she was satisfied. They came to Zürich, then, before very long, ran under the mountains that were deep in snow. At last she was drawing near. This was the other world now.

Innsbruck was wonderful, deep in snow, and evening. They drove in an open sledge over the snow: the train had been so hot and stifling. And the hotel, with the golden light glowing under the porch, seemed like a home.

They laughed with pleasure when they were in the hall. The place seemed full and busy.

'Do you know if Mr. and Mrs. Crich – English – from Paris, have arrived?' Birkin asked in German.

The porter reflected a moment, and was just going to answer when Ursula caught sight of Gudrun sauntering down the stairs, wearing her dark glossy coat with grey fur.

'Gudrun! Gudrun!' she called, waving up the well of the staircase. 'Shu-hu!'

Gudrun looked over the rail, and immediately lost her sauntering, diffident air. Her eyes flashed.

'Really – Ursula!' she cried. And she began to move downstairs as Ursula ran up. They met at a turn and kissed with laughter and exclamations inarticulate and stirring.

'But!' cried Gudrun, mortified. 'We thought it was *tomorrow* you were coming! I wanted to come to the station.'

'No, we've come to-day!' cried Ursula. 'Isn't it lovely here!'

'Adorable!' said Gudrun. 'Gerald's just gone out to get something. Ursula, aren't you *fearfully* tired?'

'No, not so very. But I look a filthy sight, don't I?'

'No, you don't. You look almost perfectly fresh. I like that fur cap *immensely!*' She glanced over Ursula, who wore a big soft coat with a collar of deep, soft, blond fur and a soft blond cap of fur.

'And you!' cried Ursula. 'What do you think *you* look like!'

Gudrun assumed an unconcerned, expressionless face.

'Do you like it?' she said.

'It's *very* fine!' cried Ursula, perhaps with a touch of satire.

'Go up – or come down,' said Birkin. For there the sisters stood, Gudrun with her hand on Ursula's arm, on the turn of the stairs half-way to the first landing, blocking the way, and affording full entertainment to the whole of the hall below, from the door porter to the plump Jew in black clothes.

The two young women slowly mounted, followed by Birkin and the waiter.

'First floor?' asked Gudrun, looking back over her shoulder.

'Second, Madam – the lift!' the waiter replied. And he darted to the elevator to forestall the two women. But they ignored him, as, chattering without heed, they set to mount the second flight. Rather chagrined, the waiter followed.

It was curious, the delight of the sisters in each other, at this meeting. It was as if they met in exile and united their solitary forces against all the world. Birkin looked on with some mistrust and wonder.

When they had bathed and changed, Gerald came in. He looked shining like the sun on frost.

'Go with Gerald and smoke,' said Ursula to Birkin. 'Gudrun and I want to talk.'

Then the sisters sat in Gudrun's bedroom and talked clothes and experiences. Gudrun told Ursula the experience of the Birkin letter in the café. Ursula was shocked and frightened.

'Where is the letter?' she asked.

'I kept it,' said Gudrun.

'You'll give it me, won't you?' she said.

But Gudrun was silent for some moments before she replied:

'Do you really want it, Ursula?'

'I want to read it,' said Ursula.

'Certainly,' said Gudrun.

Even now she could not admit, to Ursula, that she wanted to keep it as a memento or a symbol. But Ursula knew, and was not pleased. So the subject was switched off.

'What did you do in Paris?' asked Ursula.

'Oh,' said Gudrun laconically – 'the usual things. We had a *fine* party one night in Fanny Bath's studio.'

'Did you? And you and Gerald were there! Who else? Tell me about it.'

'Well,' said Gudrun. 'There's nothing particular to tell. You know Fanny is *frightfully* in love with that painter, Billy Macfarlane. He was there – so

Fanny spared nothing, she spent *very* freely. It was really remarkable! Of course, everybody got fearfully drunk – but in an interesting way, not like that filthy London crowd. The fact is these were all people that matter, which makes all the difference. There was a Roumanian, a fine chap. He got completely drunk, and climbed to the top of a high studio ladder, and gave the most marvellous address – really, Ursula, it was wonderful! He began in French – *La vie, c'est une affaire d'âmes impériales* – in a most beautiful voice – he was a fine-looking chap – but he had got into Roumanian before he had finished, and not a soul understood. But Donald Gilchrist was worked to a frenzy. He dashed his glass to the ground and declared, by God, he was glad he had been born, by God, it was a miracle to be alive. And do you know, Ursula, so it was—' Gudrun laughed rather hollowly.

'But how was Gerald among them all?' asked Ursula.

'Gerald! Oh, my word, he came out like a dandelion in the sun! *He's* a whole saturnalia in himself, once he is roused. I shouldn't like to say whose waist his arm did not go round. Really, Ursula, he seems to reap the women like a harvest. There wasn't one that would have resisted him. It was too amazing! Can you understand it?'

Ursula reflected, and a dancing light came into her eyes.

'Yes,' she said. 'I can. He is such a whole-hogger.'

'Whole-hogger! I should think so!' exclaimed Gudrun. 'But it is true, Ursula, every woman in the room was ready to surrender to him. Chanticleer isn't in it – even Fanny Bath, who is *genuinely* in love with Billy Macfarlane! I never was more amazed in my life! And you know, afterwards – I felt I was a whole *roomful* of women. I was no more myself to him than I was Queen Victoria. I was a whole roomful of women at once. It was most astounding! But my eye, I'd caught a Sultan that time—'

Gudrun's eyes were flashing, her cheek was hot, she looked strange, exotic, satiric. Ursula was fascinated at once – and yet uneasy.

They had to get ready for dinner. Gudrun came down in a daring gown of vivid green silk and tissue of gold, with green velvet bodice and a strange black-and-white band round her hair. She was really brilliantly beautiful and everybody noticed her. Gerald was in that full-blooded, gleaming state when he was most handsome. Birkin watched them with quick, laughing, half-sinister eyes, Ursula quite lost her head. There seemed a spell, almost a blinding spell, cast round their table, as if they were lighted up more strongly than the rest of the dining-room.

'Don't you love to be in this place?' cried Gudrun. 'Isn't the snow wonderful! Do you notice how it exalts everything? It is simply marvellous. One really does feel *übermenschlich* – more than human.'

'One does,' cried Ursula. 'But isn't that partly the being out of England?'

'Oh, of course,' cried Gudrun. 'One could never feel like this in England, for the simple reason that the damper is *never* lifted off one, there. It is quite impossible really to let go, in England, of that I am assured.'

And she turned again to the food she was eating. She was fluttering with vivid intensity.

'It's quite true,' said Gerald, 'it never is *quite* the same in England. But perhaps we don't want it to be – perhaps it's like bringing the light a little too near the powder-magazine, to let go altogether, in England. One is afraid what might happen, if *everybody else* let go.'

'My God!' cried Gudrun. 'But wouldn't it be wonderful if all England *did* suddenly go off like a display of fireworks.'

'It couldn't,' said Ursula. 'They are all too damp, the powder is damp in them.'

'I'm not so sure of that,' said Gerald.

'Nor I,' said Birkin. 'When the English really begin to go off, *en masse*, it'll be time to shut your ears and run.'

'They never will,' said Ursula.

'We'll see,' he replied.

'Isn't it marvellous,' said Gudrun, 'how thankful one can be, to be out of one's country. I cannot believe myself, I am so transported, the moment I set foot on a foreign shore. I say to myself: "Here steps a new creature into life." '

'Don't be too hard on poor old England,' said Gerald. 'Though we curse it, we love it really.'

To Ursula there seemed a fund of cynicism in these words.

'We may,' said Birkin. 'But it's a damnably uncomfortable love: like a love for an aged parent who suffers horribly from a complication of diseases, for which there is no hope.'

Gudrun looked at him with dilated dark eyes.

'You think there is no hope?' she asked in her pertinent fashion.

But Birkin backed away. He would not answer such a question.

'Any hope of England's becoming real? God knows. It's a great actual unreality now, an aggregation into unreality. It might be real, if there were no Englishmen.'

'You think the English will have to disappear?' persisted Gudrun. It was strange, her pointed interest in his answer. It might have been her own fate she was inquiring after. Her dark, dilated eyes rested on Birkin, as if she could conjure the truth of the future out of him, as out of some instrument of divination.

He was pale. Then, reluctantly, he answered:

'Well – what else is in front of them but disappearance? They've got to disappear from their own special brand of Englishness, anyhow.'

Gudrun watched him as if in a hypnotic state, her eyes wide and fixed on him.

'But in what way do you mean, disappear?—' she persisted.

'Yes, do you mean a change of heart?' put in Gerald.

'I don't mean anything, why should I?' said Birkin. 'I'm an Englishman, and I've paid the price of it. I can't talk about England – I can only speak for myself.'

'Yes,' said Gudrun slowly, 'you love England immensely, *immensely*, Rupert.'

'And leave her,' he replied.

'No, not for good. You'll come back,' said Gerald, nodding sagely.

'They say the lice crawl off a dying body,' said Birkin, with a glare of bitterness. 'So I leave England.'

'Ah, but you'll come back,' said Gudrun, with a sardonic smile.

'*Tant pis pour moi*,' he replied.

'Isn't he angry with his mother country!' laughed Gerald, amused.

'Ah, a patriot!' said Gudrun, with something like a sneer.

Birkin refused to answer any more.

Gudrun watched him still for a few seconds. Then she turned away. It was finished, her spell of divination in him. She felt already purely cynical. She looked at Gerald. He was wonderful like a piece of radium to her. She felt she could consume herself and know *all*, by means of this fatal, living metal. She smiled to herself at her fancy. And what would she do with herself when she had destroyed herself? For if spirit, if integral being is destructible, Matter is indestructible.

He was looking bright and abstracted, puzzled, for the moment. She stretched out her beautiful arm, with its fluff of green tulle, and touched his chin with her subtle, artist's fingers.

'What are they then?' she asked, with a strange, knowing smile.

'What?' he replied, his eyes suddenly dilating with wonder.

'Your thoughts.'

Gerald looked like a man coming awake.

'I think I had none,' he said.

'Really!' she said, with grave laughter in her voice.

And to Birkin it was as if she killed Gerald, with that touch.

'Ah, but,' cried Gudrun, 'let us drink to Britannia – let us drink to Britannia.'

It seemed there was wild despair in her voice. Gerald laughed and filled the glasses.

'I think Rupert means,' he said, 'that *nationally* all Englishmen must die, so that they can exist individually and—'

'Super-nationally—' put in Gudrun, with a slight ironic grimace, raising her glass.

The next day they descended at the tiny railway station of Hohenhausen at the end of the tiny valley railway. It was snow everywhere, a white, perfect cradle of snow, new and frozen, sweeping up on either side, black crags, and white sweeps of silver towards the blue pale heavens.

As they stepped out on the naked platform, with only snow around and above, Gudrun shrank as if it chilled her heart.

'My God, Jerry,' she said, turning to Gerald with sudden intimacy, 'you've done it now.'

'What?'

She made a faint gesture, indicating the world on either hand.

'Look at it!'

She seemed afraid to go on. He laughed.

They were in the heart of the mountains. From high above, on either side, swept down the white fold of snow, so that one seemed small and tiny in a valley of pure concrete heaven, all strangely radiant and changeless and silent.

'It makes one feel so small and alone,' said Ursula, turning to Birkin and laying her hand on his arm.

'You're not sorry you've come, are you?' said Gerald to Gudrun.

She looked doubtful. They went out of the station between banks of snow.

'Ah,' said Gerald, sniffing the air in elation, 'this is perfect. There's our sledge. We'll walk a bit – we'll run up the road.'

Gudrun, always doubtful, dropped her heavy coat on the sledge, as he did his, and they set off. Suddenly she threw up her head and set off scudding along the road of snow, pulling her cap down over her ears. Her blue, bright dress fluttered in the wind, her thick scarlet stockings were brilliant above the whiteness. Gerald watched her: she seemed to be rushing towards her fate, and leaving him behind. He let her get some distance, then, loosening his limbs, he went after her.

Everywhere was deep and silent snow. Great snow-eaves weighed down the broad-roofed Tyrolese houses that were sunk to the window-sashes in snow. Peasant women, full-skirted, wearing each a cross-over shawl and thick snow-boots, turned in the way to look at the soft, determined girl running with such heavy fleetness from the man who was overtaking her, but not gaining any power over her.

They passed the inn with its painted shutters and balcony, a few cottages, half buried in the snow; then the snow-buried silent saw-mill by the roofed bridge, which crossed the hidden stream, over which they ran into the very depth of the untouched sheets of snow. It was a silence and a sheer whiteness exhilarating to madness. But the perfect silence was most terrifying, isolating the soul, surrounding the heart with frozen air.

'It's a marvellous place, for all that,' said Gudrun, looking into his eyes with a strange, meaning look. His soul leapt.

'Good,' he said.

A fierce electric energy seemed to flow over all his limbs, his muscles were surcharged, his hands felt hard with strength. They walked along rapidly up the snow-road, that was marked by withered branches of trees stuck in at intervals. He and she were separate, like opposite poles of one fierce energy. But they felt powerful enough to leap over the confines of life into the forbidden places and back again.

Birkin and Ursula were running along also over the snow. He had disposed of the luggage, and they had a little start of the sledges. Ursula was excited and happy, but she kept turning suddenly to catch hold of Birkin's arm, to make sure of him.

'This is something I never expected,' she said. 'It is a different world, here.'

They went on into a snow meadow. There they were overtaken by the sledge that came tinkling through the silence. It was another mile before they came upon Gudrun and Gerald on the steep up-climb, beside the pink, half-buried shrine.

Then they passed into a gulley, where were walls of black rock and a river filled with snow, and a still blue sky above. Through a covered bridge they went, drumming roughly over the boards, crossing the snow-bed once more, then slowly up and up, the horses walking swiftly, the driver cracking his long whip as he walked beside, and calling his strange wild *hue-hue!*, the walls of rock passing slowly by till they emerged again between slopes and masses of snow. Up and up, gradually they went, through the cold shadow-radiance of the afternoon, silenced by the imminence of the mountains, the luminous, dazing sides of snow that rose above them and fell away beneath.

They came forth at last in a little high table-land of snow, where stood the last peaks of snow like the heart petals of an open rose. In the midst of the last deserted valleys of heaven stood a lonely building with brown wooden walls and white heavy roof, deep and deserted in the waste of snow, like a dream. It stood like a rock that had rolled down from the last steep slopes, a rock that had taken the form of a house, and was now half buried. It was unbelievable that one could live there uncrushed by all this terrible waste of whiteness and silence and clear, upper, ringing cold.

Yet the sledges ran up in fine style, people came to the door laughing and excited, the floor of the hostel rang hollow, the passage was wet with snow, it was a real, warm interior.

The newcomers tramped up the bare wooden stairs, following the serving woman. Gudrun and Gerald took the first bedroom. In a moment they found themselves alone in a bare, smallish, close-shut room that was all of golden-coloured wood, floor, walls, ceiling, door, all of the same warm gold panelling of oiled pine. There was a window opposite the door, but low down, because the roof sloped. Under the slope of the ceiling were the table with wash-hand-bowl and jug, and across, another table with mirror. On either side the door were two beds piled high with an enormous blue-checked overbolster, enormous.

This was all – no cupboard, none of the amenities of life. Here they were shut up together in this cell of golden-coloured wood, with two blue checked beds. They looked at each other and .laughed, frightened by this naked nearness of isolation.

A man knocked and came in with the luggage. He was a sturdy fellow with flattish cheek-bones, rather pale, and with coarse fair moustache. Gudrun watched him put down the bags in silence, then tramp heavily out.

'It isn't too rough, is it?' Gerald asked.

The bedroom was not very warm, and she shivered slightly.

'It is wonderful,' she equivocated. 'Look at the colour of this panelling – it's wonderful, like being inside a nut.'

He was standing watching her, feeling his short-cut moustache, leaning back slightly and watching her with his keen, undaunted eyes, dominated by the constant passion, that was like a doom upon him.

She went and crouched down in front of the window, curious.

'Oh, but this—!' she cried involuntarily, almost in pain.

In front was a valley shut in under the sky, the last huge slopes of snow and black rock, and at the end, like the navel of the earth, a white-folded wall, and two peaks glimmering in the late light. Straight in front ran the cradle of silent snow, between the great slopes that were fringed with a little roughness of pine trees, like hair, round the base. But the cradle of.snow ran on to the eternal closing-in, where the walls of snow and rock rose impene-trable, and the mountain peaks above were in heaven immediate. This was the centre, the knot, the navel of the world, where the earth belonged to the skies, pure, unapproachable, impassable.

It filled Gudrun with a strange rapture. She crouched in front of the window, clenching her face in her hands, in a sort of trance. At last she had arrived, she had reached her place. Here at last she folded her venture and settled down like a crystal in the navel of snow and was gone.

Gerald bent above her and was looking out over her shoulder. Already he felt he was alone. She was gone. She was completely gone, and there was icy vapour round his heart. He saw the blind valley, the great cul-de-sac of snow and mountain peaks under the heaven. And there was no way out. The terrible silence and cold and the glamorous whiteness of the dusk wrapped him round, and she remained crouching before the window, as at a shrine, a shadow.

'Do you like it?' he asked in a voice that sounded detached and foreign. At least she might acknowledge he was with her. But she only averted her soft, mute face a little from his gaze. And he knew that there were tears in her eyes, her own tears, tears of her strange religion, that put him to nought.

Quite suddenly, he put his hand under her chin and lifted up her face to him. Her dark blue eyes, in their wetness of tears, dilated as if she was startled in her very soul. They looked at him through their tears in terror and a little horror. His light blue eyes were keen, small-pupilled and unnatural in their vision. Her lips parted as she breathed with difficulty.

The passion came up in him, stroke after stroke, like the ringing of a bronze bell, so strong and unflawed and indomitable. His knees tightened to bronze as he hung above her soft face, whose lips parted and whose eyes dilated in a strange violation. In the grasp of his hand her chin was unutterably soft and silken. He felt strong as winter, his hands were living metal, invincible and not to be turned aside. His heart rang like a bell clanging inside him.

He took her up in his arms. She was soft and inert, motionless. All the while her eyes, in which the tears had not yet dried, were dilated as if in a kind of swoon of fascination and helplessness. He was super-humanly strong and unflawed, as if invested with supernatural force.

He lifted her close and folded her against him. Her softness, her inert, relaxed weight lay against his own surcharged, bronze-like limbs in a heaviness of desirability that would destroy him, if he were not fulfilled. She moved convulsively, recoiling away from him. His heart went up like a flame of ice, he closed over her like steel. He would destroy her rather than be denied.

But the overweening power of his body was too much for her. She relaxed again, and lay loose and soft, panting in a little delirium. And to him, she was so sweet, she was such bliss of release, that he would have suffered a whole eternity of torture rather than forgo one second of this pang of unsurpassable bliss.

'My God,' he said to her, his face drawn and strange, transfigured, 'what next?'

She lay perfectly still, with a still, child-like face and dark eyes, looking at him. She was lost, fallen right away.

'I shall always love you,' he said, looking at her.

But she did not hear. She lay, looking at him as at something she could never understand, never: as a child looks at a grown-up person, without hope of understanding, only submitting.

He kissed her, kissed her eyes shut, so that she could not look any more. He wanted something now, some recognition, some sign, some admission. But she only lay silent and childlike and remote, like a child that is overcome and cannot understand, only feels lost. He kissed her again, giving up.

'Shall we go down and have coffee and *Kuchen?*' he asked.

The twilight was falling slate-blue at the window. She closed her eyes, closed away the monotonous level of dead wonder, and opened them again to the everyday world.

'Yes,' she said briefly, regaining her will with a click. She went again to the window. Blue evening had fallen over the cradle of snow and over the great pallid slopes. But in the heaven the peaks of snow were rosy, glistening like transcendent, radiant spikes of blossom in the heavenly upper world, so lovely and beyond.

Gudrun saw all their loveliness, she *knew* how immortally beautiful they were, great pistils of rose-coloured, snow-fed fire in the blue twilight of the heaven. She could *see* it, she knew it, but she was not of it. She was divorced, debarred, a soul shut out.

With a last look of remorse, she turned away, and was doing her hair. He had unstrapped the luggage and was waiting, watching her. She knew he was watching her. It made her a little hasty and feverish in her precipitation.

They went downstairs, both with a strange other-world look on their faces, and with a glow in their eyes. They saw Birkin and Ursula sitting at the long table in a corner, waiting for them.

'How good and simple they look together,' Gudrun thought jealously. She envied them some spontaneity, a childish sufficiency to which she herself could never approach. They seemed such children to her.

'Such good *Kranzkuchen!*' cried Ursula greedily. 'So good!'

'Right,' said Gudrun. 'Can we have *Kaffee mit Kranzkuchen?*' she added to the waiter.

And she seated herself on the bench beside Gerald. Birkin, looking at them, felt a pain of tenderness for them.

'I think the place is really wonderful, Gerald,' he said; '*prachtvoll* and *wunderbar* and *wunderschön* and *unbeschreiblich* and all the other German adjectives.'

Gerald broke into a slight smile.

'*I* like it,' he said.

The tables, of white scrubbed wood, were placed round three sides of the room, as in a *Gasthaus.* Birkin and Ursula sat with their backs to the wall, which was of oiled wood, and Gerald and Gudrun sat in the corner next them, near to the stove. It was a fairly large place, with a tiny bar, just like a country inn, but quite simple and bare, and all of oiled wood, ceilings and walls and floor, the only furniture being the tables and benches going round three sides, the great green stove, and the bar and the doors on the fourth side. The windows were double, and quite uncurtained. It was early evening.

The coffee came – hot and good – and a whole ring of cake.

'A whole *Kuchen!*' cried Ursula. 'They give you more than us! I want some of yours.'

There were other people in the place, ten altogether, so Birkin had found out: two artists, three students, a man and wife, and a Professor and two daughters – all Germans. The four English people, being newcomers, sat in their coign of vantage to watch. The Germans peeped in at the door, called a word to the waiter, and went away again. It was not meal-time, so they did not come into this dining-room, but betook themselves, when their boots were changed, to the *Reunionsaal.*

The English visitors could hear the occasional twanging of a zither, the strumming of a piano, snatches of laughter and shouting and singing, a faint vibration of voices. The whole building being of wood, it seemed to carry every sound, like a drum, but instead of increasing each particular noise, it decreased it, so that the sound of the zither seemed tiny, as if a diminutive zither were playing somewhere, and it seemed the piano must be a small one, like a little spinet.

The host came when the coffee was finished. He was a Tyrolese, broad, rather flat-cheeked, with a pale, pock-marked skin and flourishing moustaches.

'Would you like to go to the *Reunionsaal* to be introduced to the other ladies and gentlemen?' he asked, bending forward and smiling, showing his large, strong teeth. His blue eyes went quickly from one to the other – he was not quite sure of his ground with these English people. He was unhappy too because he spoke no English and he was not sure whether to try his French.

'Shall we go to the *Reunionsaal*, and be introduced to the other people?' repeated Gerald, laughing.

There was a moment's hesitation.

'I suppose we'd better – better break the ice,' said Birkin.

The women rose, rather flushed. And the *Wirt's* black, beetle-like, broad-shouldered figure went on ignominiously in front, towards the noise. He opened the door and ushered the four strangers into the play-room.

Instantly a silence fell, a slight embarrassment came over the company. The newcomers had a sense of many blond faces looking their way. Then the host was bowing to a short, energetic-looking man with large moustaches, and saying in a low voice:

'*Herr Professor, darf ich vorstellen—*'

The Herr Professor was prompt and energetic. He bowed low to the English people, smiling, and began to be a comrade at once.

'*Nehmen die Herrschaften teil an unserer Unterhaltung?*' he said, with a vigorous suavity, his voice curling up in the question.

The four English people smiled, lounging with an attentive uneasiness in the middle of the room. Gerald, who was spokesman, said that they would willingly take part in the entertainment. Gudrun and Ursula, laughing, excited, felt the eyes of all the men upon them, and they lifted their heads and looked nowhere, and felt royal.

The Professor announced the names of those present, *sans cérémonie*. There was a bowing to the wrong people and to the right people. Everybody was there except the man and wife. The two tall, clear-skinned, athletic daughters of the professor, with their plain-cut, dark blue blouses and loden skirts, their rather long, strong necks, their clear blue eyes and carefully banded hair, and their blushes, bowed and stood back; the three students bowed very low, in the humble hope of making an impression of extreme good breeding; then there was a thin, dark-skinned man with full eyes, an odd creature, like a child, and like a troll, quick, detached; he bowed slightly; his companion, a large fair young man, stylishly dressed, blushed to the eyes and bowed very low.

It was over.

'Herr Loerke was giving us a recitation in the Cologne dialect,' said the Professor.

'He must forgive us for interrupting him,' said Gerald, 'we should like very much to hear it.'

There was instantly a bowing and an offering of seats. Gudrun and Ursula, Gerald and Birkin sat in the deep sofas against the wall. The room was of naked oiled panelling, like the rest of the house. It had a piano, sofas and chairs, and a couple of tables with books and magazines. In its complete absence of decoration, save for the big, blue stove, it was cosy and pleasant.

Herr Loerke was the little man with the boyish figure and the round, full, sensitive-looking head, and the quick, full eyes, like a mouse's. He glanced swiftly from one to the other of the strangers, and held himself aloof.

'Please go on with the recitation,' said the Professor suavely, with his slight authority. Loerke, who was sitting hunched on the piano-stool, blinked and did not answer.

'It would be a great pleasure,' said Ursula, who had been getting the sentence ready, in German, for some minutes.

Then, suddenly, the small, unresponding man swung aside, towards his previous audience and broke forth, exactly as he had broken off; in a controlled, mocking voice, giving an imitation of a quarrel between an old Cologne woman and a railway guard.

His body was slight and unformed, like a boy's, but his voice was mature, sardonic, its movement had the flexibility of essential energy, and of a mocking penetrating understanding. Gudrun could not understand a word of his monologue, but she was spell-bound watching him. He must be an artist, nobody else could have such fine adjustment and singleness. The Germans were doubled up with laughter, hearing his strange droll words, his droll phrases of dialect. And in the midst of their paroxysms, they glanced with deference at the four English strangers, the elect. Gudrun and Ursula were forced to laugh. The room rang with shouts of laughter. The blue eyes of the Professor's daughters were swimming over with laughter-tears, their clear cheeks were flushed crimson with mirth, their father broke out in the most astonishing peals of hilarity, the students bowed their heads on their knees in excess of joy. Ursula looked round amazed, the laughter was bubbling out of her involuntarily. She looked at Gudrun. Gudrun looked at her, and the two sisters burst out laughing, carried away. Loerke glanced at them swiftly, with his full eyes. Birkin was sniggering involuntarily. Gerald Crich sat erect, with a glistening look of amusement on his face. And the laughter crashed out again, in wild paroxysms, the Professor's daughters were reduced to shaking helplessness, the veins of the Professors's neck were swollen, his face was purple, he was strangled in ultimate, silent spasms of laughter. The students were shouting half-articulated words that tailed off in helpless explosions. Then suddenly the rapid patter of the artist ceased, there were little whoops of subsiding mirth, Ursula and Gudrun were wiping their eyes, and the Professor was crying loudly.

'*Das war ausgezeichnet, das war famos—*'

'*Wirklich famos,*' echoed his exhausted daughters, faintly.

'And we couldn't understand it,' cried Ursula.

'*Oh leider, leider!*' cried the Professor.

'You couldn't understand it?' cried the Students, let loose at last in speech with the newcomers. '*Ja, das ist wirklich schade, das ist schade, gnädige Frau. Wissen Sie—*'

The mixture was made, the newcomers were stirred into the party, like new ingredients, the whole room was alive. Gerald was in his element, he talked freely and excitedly, his face glistened with a strange amusement. Perhaps even Birkin, in the end, would break forth. He was shy and withheld, though full of attention.

Ursula was prevailed upon to sing 'Annie Lowrie', as the Professor called it. There was a hush of *extreme* deference. She had never been so flattered in her life. Gudrun accompanied her on the piano, playing from memory.

Ursula had a beautiful ringing voice, but usually no confidence, she spoiled everything. This evening she felt conceited and untrammelled. Birkin was well in the background, she shone almost in reaction, the Germans made her feel fine and infallible, she was liberated into overweening self-confidence. She felt like a bird flying in the air, as her voice soared out, enjoying herself extremely in the balance and flight of the song, like the motion of a bird's wings that is up in the wind, sliding and playing on the air, she played with sentimentality, supported by rapturous attention. She was very happy, singing that song by herself, full of a conceit of emotion and power, working upon all those people, and upon herself, exerting herself with gratification, giving immeasurable gratification to the Germans.

At the end, the Germans were all touched with admiring, delicious melancholy, they praised her in soft, reverent voices, they could not say too much.

'*Wie schön, wie rührend! Ach, die Schottischen Lieder, sie haben so viel Stimmung! Aber die gnädige Frau hat eine wunderbare Stimme; die gnädige Frau ist wirklich eine Künstlerin, aber wirklich!*'

She was dilated and brilliant, like a flower in the morning sun. She felt Birkin looking at her, as if he were jealous of her, and her breasts thrilled, her veins were all golden. She was as happy as the sun that has just opened above clouds. And everybody seemed so admiring and radiant, it was perfect.

After dinner she wanted to go out for a minute, to look at the world. The company tried to dissuade her – it was so terribly cold. But just to look, she said.

They all four wrapped up warmly, and found themselves in a vague, unsubstantial outdoors of dim snow and ghosts of an upper-world, that made strange shadows before the stars. It was indeed cold, bruisingly, frighteningly, unnaturally cold. Ursula could not believe the air in her nostrils. It seemed conscious, malevolent, purposive in its intense murderous coldness.

Yet it was wonderful, an intoxication, a silence of dim, unrealised snow, of the invisible intervening between her and the visible, between her and the flashing stars. She could see Orion sloping up. How wonderful he was, wonderful enough to make one cry aloud.

And all around was this cradle of snow, and there was firm snow underfoot, that struck with heavy cold through her bootsoles. It was night, and silence. She imagined she could hear the stars. She imagined distinctly she could hear the celestial, musical motion of the stars, quite near at hand. She seemed like a bird flying amongst their harmonious motion.

And she clung close to Birkin. Suddenly she realised she did not know what he was thinking. She did not know where he was ranging.

'My love!' she said, stopping to look at him.

His face was pale, his eyes dark, there was a faint spark of starlight on them. And he saw her face soft and upturned to him, very near. He kissed her softly.

'What then?' he asked.

'Do you love me?' she asked.

'Too much,' he answered quietly.

She clung a little closer.

'Not too much,' she pleaded.

'Far too much,' he said, almost sadly.

'And does it make you sad, that I am everything to you?' she asked, wistful. He held her close to him, kissing her, and saying, scarcely audible:

'No, but I feel like a beggar – I feel poor.'

She was silent, looking at the stars now. Then she kissed him.

'Don't be a beggar,' she pleaded, wistfully. 'It isn't ignominious that you love me.'

'It is ignominious to feel poor, isn't it?' he replied.

'Why? Why should it be?' she asked. He only stood still, in the terribly cold air that moved invisibly over the mountain tops, folding her round with his arms.

'I couldn't bear this cold, eternal place without you,' he said. 'I couldn't bear it, it would kill the quick of my life.'

She kissed him again, suddenly.

'Do you hate it?' she asked, puzzled, wondering.

'If I couldn't come near to you, if you weren't here, I should hate it. I couldn't bear it,' he answered.

'But the people are nice,' she said.

'I mean the stillness, the cold, the frozen eternality,' he said.

She wondered. Then her spirit came home to him, nestling unconscious in him.

'Yes, it is good we are warm and together,' she said.

And they turned home again. They saw the golden lights of the hotel glowing out in the night of snow-silence, small in the hollow, like a cluster of yellow berries. It seemed like a bunch of sun-sparks, tiny and orange in the midst of the snow-darkness. Behind, was a high shadow of a peak, blotting out the stars, like a ghost.

They drew near to their home. They saw a man come from the dark building, with a lighted lantern which swung golden, and made that his dark feet walked in a halo of snow. He was a small, dark figure in the darkened snow. He unlatched the door of an outhouse. A smell of cows, hot, animal, almost like beef, came out on the heavily cold air. There was a glimpse of two cattle in their dark stalls, then the door was shut again, and not a chink of light showed. It had reminded Ursula again of home, of the Marsh, of her childhood, and of the journey to Brussels, and, strangely, of Anton Skrebensky.

Oh, God, could one bear it, this past which was gone down the abyss? Could she bear, that it ever had been! She looked round this silent, upper world of snow and stars and powerful cold. There was another world, like views on a magic lantern; The Marsh, Cossethay, Ilkeston, lit up with a common, unreal light. There was a shadowy unreal Ursula, a whole shadow-play of an unreal life. It was as unreal, and circumscribed, as a magic-lantern show. She wished the slides could all be broken. She wished it could be gone for ever, like a lantern-slide which was broken. She wanted to have no past. She wanted to have come down from the slopes of heaven to this place, with Birkin, not to have toiled out of the murk of her childhood and her upbringing, slowly, all soiled. She felt that memory was a dirty trick played upon her. What was this decree, that she should 'remember'! Why not a bath of pure oblivion, a new birth, without any recollections or blemish of a past life. She was with Birkin, she had just come into life, here in the high snow, against the stars. What had she to do with parents and antecedents? She knew herself new and unbegotten, she had no father, no mother, no anterior connections, she was herself, pure and silvery, she belonged only to the oneness with Birkin, a oneness that struck deeper notes, sounding into the heart of the universe, the heart of reality, where she had never existed before.

Even Gudrun was a separate unit, separate, separate, having nothing to do with this self, this Ursula, in her new world of reality. That old shadow-world, the actuality of the past – ah, let it go! She rose free on the wings of her new condition.

Gudrun and Gerald had not come in. They had walked up the valley straight in front of the house, not like Ursula and Birkin, on to the little hill at the right. Gudrun was driven by a strange desire. She wanted to plunge on and on, till she came to the end of the valley of snow. Then she wanted to climb the wall of white finality, climb over, into the peaks that sprang up like sharp petals in the heart of the frozen, mysterious navel of the world. She felt that there, over the strange blind, terrible wall of rocky snow, there in the navel of the mystic world, among the final cluster of peaks, there, in the infolded navel of it all, was her consummation. If she could but come there, alone, and pass into the infolded navel of eternal snow and of uprising, immortal peaks of snow and rock, she would be a oneness with all, she would be herself the eternal, infinite silence, the sleeping, timeless, frozen centre of the All.

They went back to the house, to the Reunionsaal. She was curious to see what was going on. The men there made her alert, roused her curiosity. It was a new taste of life for her, they were so prostrate before her, yet so full of life.

The party was boisterous; they were dancing all together, dancing the *Schuhplatteln*, the Tyrolese dance of the clapping hands and tossing the partner in the air at the crisis. The Germans were all proficient – they were from Munich chiefly. Gerald also was quite passable. There were three zithers twanging away in a corner. It was a scene of great animation and confusion. The Professor was initiating Ursula into the dance, stamping, clapping, and swinging her high, with amazing force and zest. When the crisis came even Birkin was behaving manfully with one of the Professor's fresh, strong daughters, who was exceedingly happy. Everybody was dancing, there was the most boisterous turmoil.

Gudrun looked on with delight. The solid wooden floor resounded to the knocking heels of the men, the air quivered with the clapping hands and the zither music, there was a golden dust about the hanging lamps.

Suddenly the dance finished, Loerke and the students rushed out to bring in drinks. There was an excited clamour of voices, a clinking of mug-lids, a great crying of '*Prosit – Prosit!*' Loerke was everywhere at once, like a gnome, suggesting drinks for the women, making an obscure, slightly risky joke with the men, confusing and mystifying the waiter.

He wanted very much to dance with Gudrun. From the first moment he had seen her, he wanted to make a connection with her. Instinctively she felt this, and she waited for him to come up. But a kind of sulkiness kept him away from her, so she thought he disliked her.

'Will you *schuhpletteln, gnädige Frau?*' said the large, fair youth, Loerke's companion. He was too soft, too humble for Gudrun's taste. But she wanted to dance, and the fair youth, who was called Leitner, was handsome enough in his uneasy, slightly abject fashion, a humility that covered a certain fear. She accepted him as a partner.

The zithers sounded out again, the dance began. Gerald led them, laughing, with one of the Professor's daughters. Ursula danced with one of the students, Birkin with the other daughter of the Professor, the Professor with Frau Kramer, and the rest of the men danced together, with quite as much zest as if they had had women partners.

Because Gudrun had danced with the well-built, soft youth, his companion, Loerke, was more pettish and exasperated than ever, and would not even notice her existence in the room. This piqued her, but she made up to herself by dancing with the Professor, who was strong as a mature well-seasoned bull, and as full of coarse energy. She could not bear him, critically, and yet she enjoyed being rushed through the dance, and tossed up into the air, on his coarse, powerful impetus. The Professor enjoyed it too, he eyed her with strange, large blue eyes, full of galvanic fire. She hated him for the seasoned, semi-paternal animalism with which he regarded her, but she admired his weight of strength.

The room was charged with excitement and strong, animal emotion. Loerke was kept away from Gudrun, to whom he wanted to speak, as by a hedge of thorns, and he felt a sardonic ruthless hatred for this young love-companion, Leitner, who was his penniless dependant. He mocked the youth, with an acid ridicule, that made Leitner red in the face and impotent with resentment.

Gerald, who had now got the dance perfectly, was dancing again with the younger of the Professor's daughters, who was almost dying of virgin excitement, because she thought Gerald so handsome, so superb. He had her in his power, as if she were a palpitating bird, a fluttering, flushing, bewildered creature. And it made him smile, as she shrank convulsively between his hands, violently, when he must throw her into the air. At the end, she was so overcome with prostrate love for him, that she could scarcely speak sensibly at all.

Birkin was dancing with Ursula. There were odd little fires playing in his eyes, he seemed to have turned into something wicked and flickering, mocking, suggestive, quite impossible. Ursula was frightened of him, and fascinated. Clear, before her eyes, as in a vision, she could see the sardonic licentious mockery of his eyes, he moved towards her with subtle, animal, indifferent approach. The strangeness of his hands, which came quick and cunning, inevitably to the vital place beneath her breasts, and, lifting with mocking, suggestive impulse, carried her through the air as if without strength, through black magic, made her swoon with fear. For a moment she revolted, it was horrible. She would break the spell. But before the resolution had formed she had submitted again, yielded to her fear. He knew all the time what he was doing, she could see it in his smiling, concentrated eyes. It was his responsibility, she would leave it to him.

When they were alone in the darkness, she felt the strange licentiousness of him hovering upon her. She was troubled and repelled. Why should he turn like this.

'What is it?' she asked in dread.

But his face only glistened on her, unknown, horrible. And yet she was fascinated. Her impulse was to repel him violently, break from this spell of mocking brutishness. But she was too fascinated, she wanted to submit, she wanted to know. What would he do to her?

He was so attractive, and so repulsive at once. The sardonic suggestivity that flickered over his face and looked from his narrowed eyes, made her want to hide, to hide herself away from him and watch him from somewhere unseen.

'Why are you like this?' she demanded again, rousing against him with sudden force and animosity.

The flickering fires in his eyes concentrated as he looked into her eyes. Then the lids drooped with a faint motion of satiric contempt. Then they rose again to the same remorseless suggestivity. And she gave way, he might do as he would. His licentiousness was repulsively attractive. But he was self-responsible, she would see what it was.

They might do as they liked – this she realised as she went to sleep. How could anything that gave one satisfaction be excluded? What was degrading? Who cared? Degrading things were real, with a different reality. And he was so unabashed and unrestrained. Wasn't it rather horrible, a man who could be so soulful and spiritual, now to be so – she balked at her own thoughts and memories: then she added – so bestial? So bestial, they two! – so degraded! She winced. But after all, why not? She exulted as well. Why not be bestial, and go the whole round of experience? She exulted in it. She was bestial. How good it was to be really shameful! There would be no shameful thing she had not experienced. Yet she was unabashed, she was herself. Why not? She was free, when she knew everything, and no dark shameful things were denied her.

Gudrun, who had been watching Gerald in the *Reunionsaal*, suddenly thought:

'He should have all the women he can – it is his nature. It is absurd to call him monogamous – he is naturally promiscuous. That is his nature.'

The thought came to her involuntarily. It shocked her somewhat. It was as if she had seen some new *Mene! Mene!* upon the wall. Yet it was merely true. A voice seemed to have spoken it to her so clearly, that for the moment she believed in inspiration.

'It is really true,' she said to herself again.

She knew quite well she had believed it all along. She knew it implicitly. But she must keep it dark – almost from herself. She must keep it completely secret. It was knowledge for her alone, and scarcely even to be admitted to herself.

The deep resolve formed in her, to combat him. One of them must triumph over the other. Which should it be? Her soul steeled itself with strength. Almost she laughed within herself, at her confidence. It woke a certain keen, half contemptuous pity, tenderness for him: she was so ruthless.

Everybody retired early. The Professor and Loerke went into a small lounge to drink. They both watched Gudrun go along the landing by the railing upstairs.

'*Ein schönes Frauenzimmer*,' said the Professor.

'*Ja!*' asserted Loerke, shortly.

Gerald walked with his queer, long wolf-steps across the bedroom to the window, stooped and looked out, then rose again, and turned to Gudrun, his eyes sharp with an abstract smile. He seemed very tall to her, she saw the glisten of his whitish eyebrows, that met between his brows.

'How do you like it?' he said.

He seemed to be laughing inside himself, quite unconsciously. She looked at him. He was a phenomenon to her, not a human being: a sort of creature, greedy.

'I like it very much,' she replied.

'Who do you like best downstairs?' he asked, standing tall and glistening above her, with his glistening stiff hair erect.

'Who do I like best?' she repeated, wanting to answer his question, and finding it difficult to collect herself. 'Why I don't know, I don't know enough about them yet, to be able to say. Who do *you* like best?'

'Oh, I don't care – I don't like or dislike any of them. It doesn't matter about me. I wanted to know about you.'

'But why?' she asked, going rather pale. The abstract, unconscious smile in his eyes was intensified.

'I wanted to know,' he said.

She turned aside, breaking the spell. In some strange way, she felt he was getting power over her.

'Well, I can't tell you already,' she said.

She went to the mirror to take out the hairpins from her hair. She stood before the mirror every night for some minutes, brushing her fine dark hair. It was part of the inevitable ritual of her life.

He followed her, and stood behind her. She was busy with bent head, taking out the pins and shaking her warm hair loose. When she looked up, she saw him in the glass, standing behind her, watching unconsciously, not consciously seeing her, and yet watching, with fine-pupilled eyes that *seemed* to smile, and which were not really smiling.

She started. It took all her courage for her to continue brushing her hair, as usual, for her to pretend she was at her ease. She was far, far from being at her ease with him. She beat her brains wildly for something to say to him.

'What are your plans for to-morrow?' she asked nonchalantly, whilst her heart was beating so furiously, her eyes were so bright with strange nervousness, she felt he could not but observe. But she knew also that he was completely blind, blind as a wolf looking at her. It was a strange battle between her ordinary consciousness and his uncanny, black-art consciousness.

'I don't know,' he replied, 'what would you like to do?'

He spoke emptily, his mind was sunk away.

'Oh,' she said, with easy protestation, 'I'm ready for anything – anything will be fine for *me*, I'm sure.'

And to herself she was saying: 'God, why am I so nervous – why are you so nervous, you fool. If he sees it I'm done for for ever – you *know* you're done for for ever, if he sees the absurd state you're in.'

And she smiled to herself as if it were all child's play. Meanwhile her heart was plunging, she was almost fainting. She could see him, in the mirror, as he stood there behind her, tall and over-arching – blond and terribly frightening. She glanced at his reflection with furtive eyes, willing to give anything to save him from knowing she could see him. He did not know she could see his reflection. He was looking unconsciously, glisteningly down at her head, from which the hair fell loose, as she brushed it with wild, nervous hand. She held her head aside and brushed and brushed her hair madly. For her life, she could not turn round and face him. For her life, *she could not.* And the knowledge made her almost sink to the ground in a faint, helpless, spent. She was aware of his frightening, impending figure standing close behind her, she was aware of his hard, strong, unyielding chest, close upon her back. And she felt she could not bear it any more, in a few minutes she would fall down at his feet, grovelling at his feet, and letting him destroy her.

The thought pricked up all her sharp intelligence and presence of mind. She dared not turn round to him – and there he stood motionless, unbroken. Summoning all her strength, she said, in a full, resonant, nonchalant voice that was forced out with all her remaining self-control:

'Oh, would you mind looking in that bag behind there and giving me my—'

Here her power fell inert. 'My what – my what—?' she screamed in silence to herself.

But he had started round, surprised and startled that she should ask him to look in her bag, which she always kept so *very* private to herself. She turned now, her face white, her dark eyes blazing with uncanny, overwrought excitement. She saw him stooping to the bag, undoing the loosely buckled strap, unattentive.

'Your what?' he asked.

'Oh, a little enamel box – yellow – with a design of a cormorant plucking her breast—'

She went towards him, stooping her beautiful, bare arm, and deftly turned some of her things, disclosing the box, which was exquisitely painted.

'That is it, see,' she said, taking it from under his eyes.

And he was baffled now. He was left to fasten up the bag, whilst she swiftly did up her hair for the night, and sat down to unfasten her shoes. She would not turn her back to him any more.

He was baffled, frustrated, but unconscious. She had the whip hand over him now. She knew he had not realised her terrible panic. Her heart was beating heavily still. Fool, fool that she was, to get into such a state! How she thanked God for Gerald's obtuse blindness. Thank God he could see nothing.

She sat slowly unlacing her shoes, and he too commenced to undress. Thank God that crisis was over. She felt almost fond of him now, almost in love with him.

'Ah, Gerald,' she laughed, caressively, teasingly. 'Ah, what a fine game you played with the Professor's daughter – didn't you now?'

'What game?' he asked, looking round.

'*Isn't* she in love with you – oh *dear*, isn't she in love with you!' said Gudrun, in her gayest, most attractive mood.

'I shouldn't think so,' he said.

'Shouldn't think so!' she teased. 'Why the poor girl is lying at this moment overwhelmed, dying with love for you. She thinks you're *wonderful* – oh marvellous, beyond what man has ever been. *Really*, isn't it funny?'

'Why funny, what is funny?' he asked.

'Why to see you working it on her,' she said, with a half reproach that confused the male conceit in him. 'Really, Gerald, the poor girl—!'

'I did nothing to her,' he said.

'Oh, it was too shameful, the way you simply swept her off her feet.'

'That was *Schuhplatteln*,' he replied, with a bright grin.

'Ha–ha–ha!' laughed Gudrun.

Her mockery quivered through his muscles with curious re-echoes. When he slept he seemed to crouch down in the bed, lapped up in his own strength, that yet was hollow.

And Gudrun slept strongly, a victorious sleep. Suddenly, she was almost fiercely awake. The small timber room glowed with the dawn, that came upwards from the low window. She could see down the valley when she lifted her head: the snow with a pinkish, half-revealed magic, the fringe of pine trees at the bottom of the slope. And one tiny figure moved over the vaguely-illuminated space.

She glanced at his watch; it was seven o'clock. He was still completely asleep. And she was so hard awake, it was almost frightening – a hard, metallic wakefulness. She lay looking at him.

He slept in the subjection of his own health and defeat. She was overcome by a sincere regard for him. Till now, she was afraid before him. She lay and thought about him, what he was, what he represented in the world. A fine, independent will, he had. She thought of the revolution he had worked in the mines, in so short a time. She knew that if he were confronted with any problem, any hard actual difficulty, he would overcome it. If he laid hold of any idea, he would carry it through. He had the faculty of making order out of confusion. Only let him grip hold of a situation, and he would bring to pass an inevitable conclusion.

For a few moments she was borne away on the wild wings of ambition. Gerald, with his force of will and his power for comprehending the actual world, should be set to solve the problems of the day, the problem of industrialism in the modern world. She knew he would, in the course of time, effect the changes he desired, he could reorganise the industrial system. She knew he could do it. As an instrument, in these things, he was marvellous, she had never seen any man with his potentiality. He was unaware of it, but she knew.

He only needed to be hitched on, he needed that his hand should be set to the task, because he was so unconscious. And this she could do. She would marry him, he would go into Parliament in the Conservative interest, he would clear up the great muddle of labour and industry. He was so superbly fearless, masterful, he knew that every problem could be worked out, in life as in geometry. And he would care neither about himself nor about anything but the pure working out of the problem. He was very pure, really.

Her heart beat fast, she flew away on wings of elation, imagining a future. He would be a Napoleon of peace, or a Bismarck – and she the woman behind him. She had read Bismarck's letters, and had been deeply moved by them. And Gerald would be freer, more dauntless than Bismarck.

But even as she lay in fictitious transport, bathed in the strange, false sunshine of hope in life, something seemed to snap in her, and a terrible cynicism began to gain upon her, blowing in like a wind. Everything turned to irony with her: the last flavour of everything was ironical. When she felt her pang of undeniable reality, this was when she knew the hard irony of hopes and ideas.

She lay and looked at him, as he slept. He was sheerly beautiful, he was a perfect instrument. To her mind, he was a pure, inhuman, almost superhuman instrument. His instrumentality appealed so strongly to her, she wished she were God, to use him as a tool.

And at the same instant, came the ironical question: 'What for?' She thought of the colliers' wives, with their linoleum and their lace curtains and their little girls in high-laced boots. She thought of the wives and daughters of the pit-managers, their tennis-parties, and their terrible struggles to be superior each to the other, in the social scale. There was Shortlands with its meaningless distinction, the meaningless crowd of the Criches. There was London, the House of Commons, the extant social world. My God!

Young as she was, Gudrun had touched the whole pulse of social England. She had no ideas of rising in the world. She knew, with the perfect cynicism of cruel youth, that to rise in the world meant to have one outside show instead of another, the advance was like having a spurious half-crown instead of a spurious penny. The whole coinage of valuation was spurious. Yet, of course, her cynicism knew well enough that, in a world where spurious coin was current, a bad sovereign was better than a bad farthing. But rich and poor, she despised both alike.

Already she mocked at herself for her dreams. They could be fulfilled easily enough. But she recognised too well, in her spirit, the mockery of her own impulses. What did she care, that Gerald had created a richly-paying industry out of an old worn-out concern? What did she care? The worn-out concern and the rapid, splendidly organised industry, they were bad money. Yet, of course, she cared a great deal, outwardly – and outwardly was all that mattered, for inwardly was a bad joke.

Everything was intrinsically a piece of irony to her. She leaned over Gerald and said in her heart, with compassion:

'Oh, my dear, my dear, the game isn't worth even you. You are a fine thing really – why should you be used on such a poor show!'

Her heart was breaking with pity and grief for him. And at the same moment, a grimace came over her mouth, of mocking irony at her own unspoken tirade. Ah, what a farce it was! She thought of Parnell and Katherine O'Shea. Parnell! After all, who can take the nationalisation of Ireland seriously? Who can take political Ireland really seriously, whatever it does? And who can take political England seriously? Who can? Who can care a straw, really, how the old patched-up Constitution is tinkered at any more? Who cares a button for our national ideas, any more than for our national bowler hat? Aha, it is all old hat, it is all old bowler hat!

That's all it is, Gerald, my young hero. At any rate, we'll spare ourselves the nausea of stirring the old broth any more. You be beautiful, my Gerald, and reckless. There *are* perfect moments. Wake up, Gerald, wake up, convince me of the perfect moments. Oh convince me, I need it.

He opened his eyes, and looked at her. She greeted him with a mocking, enigmatic smile in which was a poignant gaiety. Over his face went the reflection of the smile, he smiled, too, purely unconsciously.

That filled her with extraordinary delight, to see the smile cross his face, reflected from her face. She remembered that was how a baby smiled. It filled her with extraordinary radiant delight.

'You've done it,' she said.

'What?' he asked, dazed.

'Convinced me.'

And she bent down, kissing him passionately, passionately, so that he was bewildered. He did not ask her of what he had convinced her, though he meant to. He was glad she was kissing him. She seemed to be feeling for his very heart to touch the quick of him. And he wanted her to touch the quick of his being, he wanted that most of all.

Outside, somebody was singing in a manly, reckless, handsome voice:

'Mach mir auf, mach mir auf, du Stolze,
Mach mir ein Feuer von Holze.
Vom Regen bin ich nass
Vom Regen bin ich nass—'

Gudrun knew that that song would sound through her eternity, sung in a manly, reckless, mocking voice. It marked one of her supreme moments, the supreme pangs of her nervous gratification. There it was, fixed in eternity for her.

The day came fine and bluish. There was a light wind blowing among the mountain-tops, keen as a rapier where it touched, carrying with it a fine dust of snow powder. Gerald went out with the fine, blind face of a man who is in his state of fulfilment. Gudrun and he were in perfect static unity this morning, but unseeing and unwitting. They went out with a toboggan, leaving Ursula and Birkin to follow.

Gudrun was all scarlet and royal blue – a scarlet jersey and cap, and a royal blue skirt and stockings. She went gaily over the white snow, with Gerald beside her, in white and grey, pulling the little toboggan. They grew small in the distance of snow, climbing the steep slope.

For Gudrun herself, she seemed to pass altogether into the whiteness of the snow, she became a pure, thoughtless crystal. When she reached the top of the slope, in the wind, she looked round, and saw peak beyond peak of rock and snow, bluish, transcendent in heaven. And it seemed to her like a garden, with the peaks for pure flowers, and her heart gathering them. She had no separate consciousness for Gerald.

She held on to him as they went sheering down over the keen slope. She felt as if her senses were being whetted on some fine grindstone that was keen as flame. The snow sprinted on either side, like sparks from a blade that is being sharpened, the whiteness round about ran swifter, swifter, in pure flame the white slope flew against her, and she fused like one molten, dancing globule, rushed through a white intensity. Then there was a great swerve at the bottom when they swung, as it were, in a fall to earth in the diminishing motion.

They came to rest. But when she rose to her feet, she could not stand. She gave a strange cry, turned and clung to him, sinking her face on his breast, fainting in him. Utter oblivion came over her as she lay for a few moments abandoned against him.

'What is it?' he was saying. 'Was it too much for you?'

But she heard nothing.

When she came to, she stood up and looked round astonished. Her face was white, her eyes brilliant and large.

'What is it?' he repeated. 'Did it upset you?'

She looked at him with her brilliant eyes that seemed to have undergone some transfiguration, and she laughed, with a terrible merriment.

'No,' she cried, with triumphant joy. 'It was the complete moment of my life.'

And she looked at him with her dazzling, overweening laughter, like one possessed. A fine blade seemed to enter his heart, but he did not care, or take any notice.

But they climbed up the slope again, and they flew down through the white flame again splendidly, splendidly. Gudrun was laughing and flashing, powdered with snow-crystals, Gerald worked perfectly. He felt he could guide the toboggan to a hairbreadth, almost he could make it pierce into the air and right into the very heart of the sky. It seemed to him the flying sledge was but his strength spread out, he had but to move his arms, the motion was his own. They explored the great slopes, to find another slide. He felt there must be something better than they had known. And he found what he desired, a perfect long, fierce sweep, sheering past the foot of a rock and into the trees at the base. It was dangerous, he knew. But then he knew also he would direct the sledge between his fingers.

The first days passed in an ecstasy of physical motion, sleighing, ski-ing, skating, moving in an intensity of speed and white light that surpassed life itself, and carried the souls of the human beings beyond into an inhuman abstraction of velocity and weight and eternal, frozen snow.

Gerald's eyes became hard and strange, and as he went by on his skis he was more like some powerful, fateful sigh than a man, his muscles elastic in a perfect, soaring trajectory, his body projected in pure flight, mindless, soulless, whirling along one perfect line of force.

Luckily there came a day of snow, when they must all stay indoors: otherwise Birkin said they would all lose their faculties, and begin to utter themselves in cries and shrieks, like some strange, unknown species of snow-creatures.

It happened in the afternoon that Ursula sat in the *Reunionsaal* talking to Loerke. The latter had seemed unhappy lately. He was lively and full of mischievous humour, as usual.

But Ursula had thought he was sulky about something. His partner, too, the big, fair, good-looking youth, was ill at ease, going about as if he belonged to nowhere, and was kept in some sort of subjection, against which he was rebelling.

Loerke had hardly talked to Gudrun. His associate, on the other hand, had paid her constantly a soft, over-deferential attention. Gudrun wanted to talk to Loerke. He was a sculptor, and she wanted to hear his view of his art. And his figure attracted her. There was the look of a little wastrel about him that intrigued her, and an old man's look that interested her, and then, beside this, an uncanny singleness, a quality of being by himself, not in contact with anybody else, that marked out an artist to her. He was a chatterer, a magpie, a maker of mischievous word-jokes, that were sometimes very clever, but which often were not. And she could see in his brown, gnome's eyes the black look of inorganic misery which lay behind all his small buffoonery.

His figure interested her – the figure of a boy, almost a street arab. He made no attempt to conceal it. He always wore a simple loden suit, with knee breeches. His legs were thin, and he made no attempt to disguise the fact: which was of itself remarkable in a German. And he never ingratiated himself anywhere, not in the slightest, but kept to himself, for all his apparent playfulness.

Leitner, his companion, was a great sportsman, very handsome with his big limbs and his blue eyes. Loerke would go tobogganing or skating in little snatches, but he was indifferent. And his fine, thin nostrils, the nostrils of a pure-bred street arab, would quiver with contempt at Leitner's splothering gymnastic displays. It was evident that the two men who had travelled and lived together, sharing the same bedroom, had now reached the stage of loathing. Leitner hated Loerke with an injured, writhing, impotent hatred, and Loerke treated Leitner with a fine-quivering contempt and sarcasm. Soon the two would have to go apart.

Already they were rarely together. Leitner ran attaching himself to somebody or other, always deferring, Loerke was a good deal alone. Out of doors he wore a Westphalian cap, a close brown velvet head with big brown velvet flaps down over his ears, so that he looked like a lop-eared rabbit or a troll. His face was brown-red, with a dry, bright skin, that seemed to crinkle with his mobile expressions. His eyes were arresting – brown, full, like a rabbit's or like a troll's, or like the eyes of a lost being, having a strange, dumb, depraved look of knowledge and a quick spark of uncanny fire. Whenever Gudrun had tried to talk to him he had shied away unresponsive, looking at her with his watchful dark eyes, but entering into no relation with her. He had made her feel that her slow French and her slower German were hateful to him. As for his own inadequate English, he was much too awkward to try it at all. But he understood a good deal of what was said, nevertheless. And Gudrun, piqued, left him alone.

This afternoon, however, she came into the lounge as he was talking to Ursula. His fine, black hair somehow reminded her of a bat, thin as it was on his full, sensitive-looking head, and worn away at the temples. He sat hunched up, as if his spirit were bat-like. And Gudrun could see he was making some slow confidence to Ursula, unwilling, a slow, grudging, scanty self-revelation. She went and sat by her sister.

He looked at her, then looked away again, as if he took no notice of her. But as a matter of fact, she interested him deeply.

'Isn't it interesting, Prune,' said Ursula, turning to her sister, 'Herr Loerke is doing a great frieze for a factory in Cologne, for the outside, the street.'

She looked at him, at his thin, brown, nervous hands, that were prehensile, and somehow like talons, like 'griffes', inhuman.

'What *in?*' she asked.

'*Aus was?*' repeated Ursula.

'*Granit,*' he replied.

It had become immediately a laconic series of question and answer between fellow craftsmen.

'What is the relief?' asked Gudrun.

'Alto relievo.'

'And at what height?'

It was very interesting to Gudrun to think of his making the great granite frieze for a great granite factory in Cologne. She got from him some notion of the design. It was a representation of a fair, with peasants and artisans in an orgy of enjoyment, drunk and absurd in their modern dress, whirling ridiculously in roundabouts, gaping at shows, kissing and staggering and rolling in knots, swinging in swing-boats, and firing down shooting-galleries, a frenzy of chaotic motion.

There was a swift discussion of technicalities. Gudrun was very much impressed.

'But how wonderful, to have such a factory!' cried Ursula. 'Is the whole building fine?'

'Oh yes,' he replied. 'The frieze is part of the whole architecture. Yes, it is a colossal thing.'

Then he seemed to stiffen, shrugged his shoulders, and went on:

'Sculpture and architecture must go together. The day for irrelevant statues, as for wall pictures, is over. As a matter of fact, sculpture is always part of an architectural conception. And since churches are all museum stuff, since industry is our business, now, then let us make our places of industry our art – our factory area our Parthenon, *ecco!*'

Ursula pondered.

'I suppose,' she said, 'there is no *need* for our great works to be so hideous.'

Instantly he broke into motion.

'There you are!' he cried, 'there you are! There is not only *no need* for our places of work to be ugly, but their ugliness ruins the work, in the end. Men will not go on submitting to such intolerable ugliness. In the end it will hurt too much, and they will wither because of it. And this will wither the *work* as well. They will think the work itself is ugly: the machines, the very act of labour. Whereas the machinery and the acts of labour are extremely, maddeningly beautiful. But this will be the end of our civilisation, when people will not work because work has become so intolerable to their senses, it nauseates them too much, they would rather starve. *Then* we shall see the hammer used only for smashing, then we shall see it. Yet here we are – we have the opportunity to make beautiful factories, beautiful machine-houses – we have the opportunity—'

Gudrun could only partly understand. She could have cried with vexation.

'What does he say?' she asked Ursula. And Ursula translated, stammering and brief. Loerke watched Gudrun's face to see her judgment.

'And do you think then,' said Gudrun, 'that art should serve industry?'

'Art should *interpret* industry as art once interpreted religion,' he said.

'But does your fair interpret industry?' she asked him.

'Certainly. What is man doing when he is at a fair like this? He is fulfilling the counterpart of labour – the machine works him instead of he the machine. He enjoys the mechanical motion in his own body.'

'But is there nothing but work – mechanical work?' said Gudrun.

'Nothing but work!' he repeated, leaning forward, his eyes two darknesses, with needle-points of light. 'No, it is nothing but this, serving a machine, or enjoying the motion of a machine – motion, that is all. You have never worked for hunger, or you would know what god governs us.'

Gudrun quivered and flushed. For some reason she was almost in tears.

'No, I have not worked for hunger,' she replied, 'but I have worked!'

'*Travaillé – lavorato?*' he asked. '*E che lavoro – che lavoro? Quel travail est-ce que vous avez fait?*'

He broke into a mixture of Italian and French, instinctively using a foreign language when he spoke to her.

'You have never worked as the world works,' he said to her, with sarcasm.

'Yes,' she said. 'I have. And I do – I work now for my daily bread.'

He paused, looked at her steadily, then dropped the subject entirely. She seemed to him to be trifling.

'But have *you* ever worked as the world works?' Ursula asked him.

He looked at her untrustful.

'Yes,' he replied, with a surly bark. 'I have known what it was to lie in bed for three days, because I had nothing to eat.'

Gudrun was looking at him with large, grave eyes that seemed to draw the confession from him as the marrow from his bones. All his nature held him back from confessing. And yet her large, grave eyes upon him seemed to open some valve in his veins, and involuntarily he was telling.

'My father was a man who did not like work, and we had no mother. We lived in Austria, Polish Austria. How did we live? Ha! – somehow! Mostly in a room with three other families – one set in each corner – and the w.c. in the middle of the room – a pan with a plank on it – ha! I had two brothers and a sister – and there might be a woman with my father. He was a free being, in his way – would fight with any man in the town – a garrison town – and was a little man too. But he wouldn't work for anybody – set his heart against it, and wouldn't.'

'And how did you live then?' asked Ursula.

He looked at her – then, suddenly, at Gudrun.

'Do you understand?' he asked.

'Enough,' she replied.

Their eyes met for a moment. Then he looked away. He would say no more.

'And how did you become a sculptor?' asked Ursula.

'How did I become a sculptor—' He paused. *Dunque*—' he resumed in a changed manner, and beginning to speak French – 'I became old enough – I used to steal from the market-place. Later I went to work – imprinted the stamp on clay bottles before they were baked. It was an earthenware bottle factory. There I began making models. One day I had had enough. I lay in the sun and did not go to work. Then I walked to Munich – then I walked to Italy – begging, begging everything.

'The Italians were very good to me – they were good and honourable to me. From Bozen to Rome, almost every night I had a meal and a bed, perhaps of straw, with some peasant. I love the Italian people with all my heart.

'*Dunque, adesso – maintenant –* I earn a thousand pounds in a year, or I earn two thousand—'

He looked down at the ground, his voice tailing off into silence.

Gudrun looked at his fine, thin, shiny skin, reddish-brown from the sun, drawn tight over his full temples; and at his thin hair—, and at the thick, coarse, brush-like moustache, cut short about his mobile, rather shapeless mouth.

'How old are you?' she asked.

He looked up at her with his full, elfin eyes startled.

Wie alt?' he repeated. And he hesitated. It was evidently one of his reticences.

'How old are *you?'* he replied, without answering.

'I am twenty-six,' she answered.

'Twenty-six,' he repeated, looking into her eyes. He paused. Then he said:

'Und Ihr Herr Gemahl, wie alt is er?'

'Who?' asked Gudrun.

'Your husband,' said Ursula, with a certain irony.

'I haven't got a husband,' said Gudrun in English. In German she answered:

'He is thirty-one.'

But Loerke was watching closely, with his uncanny, full, suspicious eyes. Something in Gudrun seemed to accord with him. He was really like one of the 'little people' who have no soul, who has found his mate in a human being. But he suffered in his discovery. She too was fascinated by him, fascinated, as if some strange creature, a rabbit or a bat, or a brown seal, had begun to talk to her. But also, she knew what he was unconscious of, his tremendous power of understanding, of apprehending her living motion. He did not know his own power. He did not know how, with his full, submerged, watchful eyes, he could look into her and see her, what she was, see her secrets. He would only want her to be herself – he knew her verily, with a subconscious, sinister knowledge, devoid of illusions and hopes.

To Gudrun, there was in Loerke the rock bottom of all life. Everybody else had their illusion, must have their illusion, their before and after. But he, with a perfect stoicism, did without any before and after, dispensed with all illusion. He did not deceive himself in the last issue. In the last issue he cared about nothing, he was troubled about nothing, he made not the slightest attempt to be at one with anything. He existed a pure, unconnected will, stoical and momentaneous. There was only his work.

It was curious, too, how his poverty, the degradation of his earlier life, attracted her. There was something insipid and tasteless to her in the idea of a gentleman, a man who had gone the usual course through school and university. A certain violent sympathy, however, came up in her for this mud-child. He seemed to be the very stuff of the underworld of life. There was no going beyond him.

Ursula too was attracted by Loerke. In both sisters he commanded a certain homage. But there were moments when to Ursula he seemed indescribably inferior, false, a vulgarism.

Both Birkin and Gerald disliked him, Gerald ignoring him with some contempt, Birkin exasperated.

'What do the women find so impressive in that little brat?' Gerald asked.

'God alone knows,' replied Birkin, 'unless it's some sort of appeal he makes to them, which flatters them and has such a power over them.'

Gerald looked up in surprise.

'*Does* he make an appeal to them?' he asked.

'Oh yes,' replied Birkin. 'He is the perfectly subjected being, existing almost like a criminal. And the women rush towards that, like a current of air towards a vacuum.'

'Funny they should rush to that,' said Gerald.

'Makes one mad, too,' said Birkin. 'But he has the fascination of pity and repulsion for them, a little obscene monster of the darkness that he is.'

Gerald stood still, suspended in thought.

'What *do* women want at the bottom?' he asked.

Birkin shrugged his shoulders.

'God knows,' he said. 'Some satisfaction in basic repulsion, it seems to me. They seem to creep down some ghastly tunnel of darkness, and will never be satisfied till they've come to the end.'

Gerald looked out into the mist of fine snow that was blowing by. Everywhere was blind to-day, horribly blind.

'And what *is* the end?' he asked.

Birkin shook his head.

'I've not got there yet, so I don't know. Ask Loerke, he's pretty near. He is a good many stages farther than either you or I can go.'

'Yes, but stages farther in what?' cried Gerald, irritated.

Birkin sighed, and gathered his brows into a knot of anger.

'Stages farther in social hatred,' he said. 'He lives like a rat in the river of corruption, just where it falls over into the bottomless pit. He's farther on than we are. He hates the ideal more acutely. He *hates* the ideal utterly, yet it still dominates him. I expect he is a Jew – or part Jewish.'

'Probably,' said Gerald.

'He is a gnawing little negation, gnawing at the roots of life.'

'But why does anybody care about him?' cried Gerald.

'Because they hate the ideal also in their souls. They want to explore the sewers, and he's the wizard rat that swims ahead.'

Still Gerald stood and stared at the blind haze of snow outside.

'I don't understand your terms really,' he said in a flat, doomed voice. 'But it sounds a rum sort of desire.'

I suppose we want the same,' said Birkin. 'Only we want to take a quick jump downwards, in a sort of ecstasy – and he ebbs with the stream, the sewer stream.'

Meanwhile Gudrun and Ursula waited for the next opportunity to talk to Loerke. It was no use beginning when the men were there. Then they could get into no touch with the isolated little sculptor. He had to be alone with them. And he preferred Ursula to be there, as a sort of transmitter to Gudrun.

'Do you do nothing but architectural sculpture?' Gudrun asked him one evening.

'Not now,' he replied. 'I have done all sorts – except portraits – I never did portraits. But other things—'

'What kind of things?' asked Gudrun.

He paused a moment, then rose and went out of the room. He returned almost immediately with a little roll of paper, which he handed to her. She unrolled it. It was a photogravure reproduction of a statuette, signed F. Loerke.

'That is quite an early thing – *not* mechanical,' he said, 'more popular.'

The statuette was of a naked girl, small, finely made, sitting on a great naked horse. The girl was young and tender, a mere bud. She was sitting sideways on the horse, her face in her hands, as if in shame and grief, in a little abandon. Her hair, which was short and must be flaxen, fell forward, divided, half covering her hands.

Her limbs were young and tender. Her legs, scarcely formed yet, the legs of a maiden just passing towards cruel womanhood, dangled childishly over the side of the powerful horse, pathetically, the small feet folded one over the other, as if to hide. But there was no hiding. There she was exposed naked on the naked flank of the horse.

The horse stood stock still, stretched in a kind of start. It was a massive, magnificent stallion, rigid with pent-up power. Its neck was arched and terrible, like a sickle, its flanks were pressed back, rigid with power.

Gudrun went pale, and a darkness came over her eyes, like shame, she looked up with a certain supplication, almost slave-like. He glanced at her and jerked his head a little.

'How big is it?' she asked in a toneless voice, persisting in appearing casual and unaffected.

'How big?' he replied, glancing again at her. 'Without pedestal – so high' – he measured with his hand – 'with pedestal, so—'

He looked at her steadily. There was a little brusque, turgid contempt for her in his swift gesture, and she seemed to cringe a little.

'And what is it done in?' she asked, throwing back her head and looking at him with affected coldness.

He still gazed at her steadily, and his dominance was not shaken.

'Bronze – green bronze.'

'Green bronze!' repeated Gudrun, coldly accepting his challenge. She was thinking of the slender, immature, tender limbs of the girl, smooth and cold in green bronze.

'Yes, beautiful,' she murmured, looking up at him with a certain dark homage.

He closed his eyes and looked aside, triumphant.

'Why,' said Ursula, 'did you make the horse so stiff? It is as stiff as a block.'

'Stiff?' he repeated, in arms at once.

'Yes. *Look* how stock and stupid and brutal it is. Horses are sensitive, quite delicate and sensitive, really.'

He raised his shoulders, spread his hands in a shrug of slow indifference, as much as to inform her she was an amateur and an impertinent nobody.

'*Wissen Sie,*' he said, with an insulting patience and condescension in his voice, 'that horse is a certain *form*, part of a whole form. It is part of a work of art, a piece of form. It is not a picture of a friendly horse to which you give a lump of sugar, do you see – it is part of a work of art, it has no relation to anything outside that work of art.'

Ursula, angry at being treated quite so insultingly *de haut en bas*, from the height of esoteric art to the depth of general exoteric amateurism, replied, hotly, flushing and lifting her face.

'But it *is* a picture of a horse, nevertheless.'

He lifted his shoulders in another shrug.

'As you like – it is not a picture of a cow, certainly.'

Here Gudrun broke in, flushed and brilliant, anxious to avoid any more of this, any more of Ursula's foolish persistence in giving herself away.

'What do you mean by "it is a picture of a horse"?' she cried at her sister. 'What do you mean by a horse? You mean an idea you have in *your* head, and which you want to see represented. There is another idea altogether, quite another idea. Call it a horse if you like, or say it is not a horse. I have just as much right to say that *your* horse isn't a horse, that it is a falsity of your own make-up.'

Ursula wavered, baffled. Then her words came.

'But why does he have this idea of a horse?' she said. 'I know it is his idea. I know it is a picture of himself, really—'

Loerke snorted with rage.

'A picture of myself!' he repeated in derision. '*Wissen sie, gnädige Frau*, that is a *Kunstwerk*, a work of art. It is a work of art, it is a picture of nothing, of absolutely nothing. It has nothing to do with anything but itself, it has no relation with the everyday world of this and other, there is no connection between them, absolutely none, they are two different and distinct planes of existence, and to translate one into the other is worse than foolish, it is a darkening of all counsel, a making confusion everywhere. Do you see, you *must not* confuse the relative work of action with the absolute world of art. That you *must not do.*'

'That is quite true,' cried Gudrun, let loose in a sort of rhapsody. 'The two things are quite and permanently apart, they have nothing to do with one another. *I* and my art, they have *nothing* to do with each other. My art stands in another world, I am in this world.'

Her face was flushed and transfigured. Loerke, who was sitting with his head ducked, like some creature at bay, looked up at her swiftly, almost furtively, and murmured:

'*Ja – so ist es, so ist es.*'

Ursula was silent after this outburst. She was furious. She wanted to poke a hole into them both.

'It isn't a word of it true, of all this harangue you have made me,' she replied flatly. 'The horse is a picture of your own stock, stupid brutality, and the girl was a girl you loved and tortured and then ignored.'

He looked up at her with a small smile of contempt in his eyes. He would not trouble to answer this last charge.

Gudrun too was silent in exasperated contempt. Ursula *was* such an insufferable outsider, rushing in where angels would fear to tread. But then – fools must be suffered, if not gladly.

But Ursula was persistent too.

'As for your world of art and your world of reality,' she replied, 'you have to separate the two, because you can't bear to know what you are. You can't bear to realise what a stock, stiff, hide-bound brutality you *are* really, so you say "it's the world of art". The world of art is only the truth about the real world, that's all – but you are too far gone to see it.'

She was white and trembling, intent. Gudrun and Loerke sat in stiff dislike of her. Gerald too, who had come up in the beginning of the speech, stood looking at her in complete disapproval and opposition. He felt she was undignified, she put a sort of vulgarity over the esotericism which gave man his last distinction. He joined his forces with the other two. They all three wanted her to go away. But she sat on in silence, her soul weeping, throbbing violently, her fingers twisting her handkerchief.

The others maintained a dead silence, letting the display of Ursula's obtrusiveness pass by. Then Gudrun asked, in a voice that was quite cool and casual, as if resuming a casual conversation:

'Was the girl a model?'

'*Nein, sie war kein Modell. Sie war eine kleine Malschülerin.*'

'An art student!' replied Gudrun.

And how the situation revealed itself to her! She saw the girl art student, unformed and of pernicious recklessness, too young, her straight flaxen hair cut short, hanging just into her neck, curving inwards slightly, because it was rather thick; and Loerke, the well-known master-sculptor, and the girl, probably well brought up and of good family, thinking herself so great to be his mistress. Oh, how well she knew the common callousness of it all. Dresden, Paris, or London, what did it matter? She knew it.

'Where is she now?' Ursula asked.

Loerke raised his shoulders to convey his complete ignorance and indifference.

'That is already six years ago,' he said; 'she will be twenty-three years old, no more good.'

Gerald had picked up the picture and was looking at it. It attracted him also. He saw on the pedestal that the piece was called 'Lady Godiva'.

'But this isn't Lady Godiva,' he said, smiling good-humouredly. 'She was the middle-aged wife of some Earl or other, who covered herself with her long hair.'

'*A la* Maud Allan,' said Gudrun, with a mocking grimace.

'Why Maud Allan?' he replied. 'Isn't it so? I always thought the legend was that.'

'Yes, Gerald dear, I'm quite *sure* you've got the legend perfectly.'

She was laughing at him, with a little, mock-caressive contempt.

'To be sure, I'd rather see the woman than the hair,' he laughed in return.

'Wouldn't you just!' mocked Gudrun.

Ursula rose and went away, leaving the three together.

Gudrun took the picture again from Gerald, and sat looking at it closely.

'Of course,' she said, turning to tease Loerke now, 'you *understood* your little *Malschülerin*.'

He raised his eyebrows and his shoulders in a complacent shrug.

'The little girl?' asked Gerald, pointing to the figure.

Gudrun was sitting with the picture in her lap. She looked up at Gerald, full into his eyes, so that he seemed to be blinded.

'*Didn't* he understand her!' she said to Gerald in a slightly mocking, humorous playfulness. 'You've only to look at the feet – *aren't* they darling, so pretty and tender – oh, they're really wonderful, they are really—'

She lifted her eyes slowly, with a hot, flaming look into Loerke's eyes. His soul was filled with her burning recognition, he seemed to grow more uppish and lordly.

Gerald looked at the small, sculptured feet. They were turned together, half covering each other in pathetic shyness and fear. He looked at them a long time, fascinated. Then, in some pain, he put the picture away from him. He felt full of barrenness.

'What was her name?' Gudrun asked Loerke.

'Annette von Weck,' Loerke replied, reminiscent. '*Ja, sie war hübsch.* She was pretty – but she was tiresome. She was a nuisance – not for a minute would she keep still – not until I'd slapped her hard and made her cry – then she'd sit for five minutes.'

He was thinking over the work, his work, the all important to him.

'Did you really slap her?' asked Gudrun coolly.

He glanced back at her, reading her challenge.

'Yes, I did,' he said, nonchalant, 'harder than I have ever beat anything in my life. I had to, I had to. It was the only way I got the work done.'

Gudrun watched him with large, dark-filled eyes for some moments. She seemed to be considering his very soul. Then she looked down in silence.

'Why did you have such a young Godiva then?' asked Gerald. 'She is so small, besides, on the horse – not big enough for it – such a child.'

A queer spasm went over Loerke's face.

'Yes,' he said. 'I don't like them any bigger, any older. Then they are beautiful at sixteen, seventeen, eighteen – after that, they are no use to me.'

There was a moment's pause.

'Why not?' asked Gerald.

Loerke shrugged his shoulders.

'I don't find them interesting – or beautiful – they are no good to me, for my work.'

'Do you mean to say a woman isn't beautiful after she is twenty?' asked Gerald.

'For me, no. Before twenty, she is small and fresh and tender and slight. After that – let her be what she likes, she has nothing for me. The Venus of Milo is a bourgeoise – so are they all.'

'And you don't care for women at all after twenty?' asked Gerald.

'They are no good to me, they are of no use in my art,' Loerke repeated impatiently. 'I don't find them beautiful.'

'You are an epicure,' said Gerald, with a slight sarcastic laugh.

'And what about men?' asked Gudrun suddenly.

'Yes, they are good at all ages,' replied Loerke. 'A man should be big and powerful – whether he is old or young is of no account, so he has the size, something of massiveness and – and stupid form.'

Ursula went out alone into the world of pure, new snow. But the dazzling whiteness seemed to beat upon her till it hurt her, she felt the cold was slowly strangling her soul. Her head felt dazed and numb.

Suddenly she wanted to go away. It occurred to her like a miracle, that she might go away into another world. She had felt so doomed up here in the eternal snow, as if there were no beyond.

Now suddenly, as by a miracle she remembered that away beyond, below her, lay the dark fruitful earth, that towards the south there were stretches of land dark with orange trees and cypress, grey with olives, that ilex trees lifted wonderful plumy tufts in shadow against a blue sky. Miracle of miracles! – this utterly silent, frozen world of the mountain-tops was not universal! One might leave it and have done with it. One might go away.

She wanted to realise the miracle at once. She wanted at this instant to have done with the snow world, the terrible, static ice-built mountain-tops. She wanted to see the dark earth, to smell its earthy fecundity, to see the patient wintry vegetation, to feel the sunshine touch a response in the buds.

She went back gladly to the house, full of hope. Birkin was reading, lying in bed.

'Rupert,' she said, bursting in on him. 'I want to go away.'

He looked up at her slowly.

'Do you?' he replied mildly.

She sat by him and put her arms round his neck. It surprised her that he was so little surprised.

'Don't *you?*' she asked troubled.

'I hadn't thought about it,' he said. 'But I'm sure I do.'

She sat up, suddenly erect.

'I hate it,' she said. 'I hate the snow, and the unnaturalness of it, the unnatural light it throws on everybody, the ghastly glamour, the unnatural feelings it makes everybody have.'

He lay still and laughed, meditating.

'Well,' he said, 'we can go away – we can go to-morrow. We'll go to-morrow to Verona, and find Romeo and Juliet, and sit in the amphitheatre – shall we?'

Suddenly she hid her face against his shoulder with perplexity and shyness. He lay so untrammelled.

'Yes,' she said softly, filled with relief. She felt her soul had new wings, now he was so uncaring. 'I shall love to be Romeo and Juliet,' she said. 'My love!'

'Though a fearfully cold wind blows in Verona,' he said, 'from out of the Alps. We shall have the smell of the snow in our noses.'

She sat up and looked at him.

'Are you glad to go?' she asked, troubled.

His eyes were inscrutable and laughing. She hid her face against his neck, clinging close to him, pleading:

'Don't laugh at me – don't laugh at me.'

'Why how's that?' he laughed, putting his arms round her.

'Because I don't want to be laughed at,' she whispered.

He laughed more, as he kissed her delicate, finely perfumed hair.

'Do you love me?' she whispered, in wild seriousness.

'Yes,' he answered, laughing.

Suddenly she lifted her mouth to be kissed. Her lips were taut and quivering and strenuous, his were soft, deep and delicate. He waited a few moments in the kiss. Then a shade of sadness went over his soul.

'Your mouth is so hard,' he said, in faint reproach.

'And yours is so soft and nice,' she said gladly.

'But why do you always grip your lips?' he asked, regretful.

'Never mind,' she said swiftly. 'It is my way.'

She knew he loved her; she was sure of him. Yet she could not let go a certain hold over herself, she could not bear him to question her. She gave herself up in delight to being loved by him. She knew that, in spite of his joy when she abandoned herself, he was a little bit saddened too. She could give herself up to his activity. But she could not be herself, she *dared* not come forth quite nakedly to his nakedness, abandoning all adjustment, lapsing in pure faith with him. She abandoned herself to *him*, or she took hold of him and gathered her joy of him. And she enjoyed him fully. But they were never *quite* together, at the same moment, one was always a little left out. Nevertheless she was glad in hope, glorious and free, full of life and liberty. And he was still and soft and patient, for the time.

They made their preparations to leave the next day. First they went to Gudrun's room, where she and Gerald were just dressed ready for the evening indoors.

'Prune,' said Ursula, 'I think we shall go away to-morrow. I can't stand the snow any more. It hurts my skin and my soul.'

'Does it really hurt your soul, Ursula?' asked Gudrun, in some surprise. 'I can't believe quite it hurts your skin – it is *terrible*. But I thought it was *admirable* for the soul.'

'No, not for mine. It just injures it,' said Ursula.

'Really!' cried Gudrun.

There was a silence in the room. And Ursula and Birkin could feel that Gudrun and Gerald were relieved by their going.

'You will go south?' said Gerald, a little ring of uneasiness in his voice.

'Yes,' said Birkin, turning away. There was a queer, indefinable hostility between the two men, lately. Birkin was on the whole dim and indifferent, drifting along in a dim, easy flow, unnoticing and patient, since he came abroad, whilst Gerald on the other hand, was intense and gripped into white light, *agonistes*. The two men revoked one another.

Gerald and Gudrun were very kind to the two who were departing, solicitous for their welfare as if they were two children. Gudrun came to Ursula's bedroom with three pairs of the coloured stockings for which she was notorious, and she threw them on the bed. But these were thick silk stockings, vermilion, cornflower blue, and grey, bought in Paris. The grey ones were knitted, seamless and heavy. Ursula was in raptures. She knew Gudrun must be feeling *very* loving, to give away such treasures.

'I can't take them from, Prune,' she cried. 'I can't possibly deprive you of them – the jewels.'

'*Aren't* they jewels!' cried Gudrun, eyeing her gifts with an envious eye. '*Aren't* they real lambs!'

'Yes, you *must* keep them,' said Ursula.

'I don't *want* them, I've got three more pairs. I *want* you to keep them – I want you to have them. They're yours, there—'

And with trembling, excited hands she put the coveted stockings under Ursula's pillow.

'One gets the greatest joy of all out of really lovely stockings,' said Ursula.

'One does,' replied Gudrun; 'the greatest joy of all.'

And she sat down in the chair. It was evident she had come for a last talk. Ursula, not knowing what she wanted, waited in silence.

'Do you *feel*, Ursula,' Gudrun began, rather sceptically, 'that you are going-away-for-ever, never-to-return, sort of thing?'

'Oh, we shall come back,' said Ursula. 'It isn't a question of train journeys.'

'Yes, I know. But spiritually, so to speak, you are going away from us all?'

Ursula quivered.

'I don't know a bit what is going to happen,' she said. 'I only know we are going somewhere.'

Gudrun waited.

'And you are glad?' she asked.

Ursula meditated for a moment.

'I believe I am *very* glad,' she replied.

But Gudrun read the unconscious brightness on her sister's face, rather than the uncertain tones of her speech.

'But don't you think you'll *want* the old connection with the world – father and the rest of us, and all that it means, England and the world of thought – don't you think you'll *need* that, really to make a world?'

Ursula was silent, trying to imagine.

'I think,' she said at length, involuntarily, 'that Rupert is right – one wants a new space to be in, and one falls away from the old.'

Gudrun watched her sister with impassive face and steady eyes.

'One wants a new space to be in, I quite agree,' she said. 'But *I* think that a new world is a development from this world, and that to isolate oneself with one other person, isn't to find a new world at all, but only to secure oneself in one's illusions.'

Ursula looked out of the window. In her soul she began to wrestle, and she was frightened. She was always frightened of words, because she knew that mere word-force could always make her believe what she did not believe.

'Perhaps,' she said, full of mistrust, of herself and everybody. 'But,' she added, 'I do think that one can't have anything new whilst one cares for the old – do you know what I mean? – even fighting the old is belonging to it. I know, one is tempted to stop with the world, just to fight it. But then it isn't worth it.'

Gudrun considered herself.

'Yes,' she said. 'In a way, one is of the world if one lives in it. But isn't it really an illusion to think you can get out of it? After all, a cottage in the Abruzzi, or wherever it may be, isn't a new world. No, the only thing to do with the world is to see it through.'

Ursula looked away. She was so frightened of argument.

'But there *can* be something else, can't there?' she said. 'One can see it through in one's soul, long enough before it sees itself through in actuality. And then, when one has seen one's soul, one is something else.'

'*Can* one see it through in one's soul?' asked Gudrun. 'If you mean that you can see to the end of what will happen, I don't agree. I really can't agree. And anyhow, you can't suddenly fly off on to a new planet, because you think you can see to the end of this.'

Ursula suddenly straightened herself.

'Yes,' she said. 'Yes – one knows. One has no more connections here. One has a sort of other self, that belongs to a new planet, not to this. You've got to hop off.'

Gudrun reflected for a few moments. Then a smile of ridicule, almost of contempt, came over her face.

'And what will happen when you find yourself in space?' she cried in derision. 'After all, the great ideas of the world are the same there. You above everybody can't get away from the fact that love, for instance, is the supreme thing, in space as well as on earth.'

'No,' said Ursula, 'it isn't. Love is too human and little. I believe in something inhuman, of which love is only a little part. I believe what we must fulfil comes out of the unknown to us, and it is something infinitely more than love. It isn't so merely *human*.'

Gudrun looked at Ursula with steady, balancing eyes. She admired and despised her sister so much, both! Then, suddenly she averted her face, saying coldly, uglily:

'Well, I've got no further than love, yet.'

Over Ursula's mind flashed the thought: 'Because you never *have* loved, you can't get beyond it.'

Gudrun rose, came over to Ursula and put her arm round her neck.

'Go and find your new world, dear,' she said, her voice clanging with false benignity. 'After all, the happiest voyage is the quest of Rupert's Blessed Isles.'

Her arm rested round Ursula's neck, her fingers on Ursula's cheek for a few moments. Ursula was supremely uncomfortable meanwhile. There was an insult in Gudrun's protective patronage that was really too hurting. Feeling her sister's resistance, Gudrun drew awkwardly away, turned over the pillow, and disclosed the stockings again.

'Ha-ha!' she laughed, rather hollowly. 'How we do talk indeed – new worlds and old—!'

And they passed to the familiar worldly subjects.

Gerald and Birkin had walked on ahead, waiting for the sledge to overtake them, conveying the departing guests.

'How much longer will you stay here?' asked Birkin, glancing up at Gerald's very red, almost blank face.

'Oh, I can't say,' Gerald replied. 'Till we get tired of it.'

'You're not afraid of the snow melting first?' asked Birkin.

Gerald laughed.

'Does it melt?' he said.

'Things are all right with you then?' said Birkin.

Gerald screwed up his eyes a little.

'All right?' he said. 'I never know what those common words mean. All right and all wrong, don't they become synonymous, somewhere?'

'Yes, I suppose. How about going back?' asked Birkin.

'Oh, I don't know. We may never get back. I don't look before and after,' said Gerald.

'*Nor* pine for what is not,' said Birkin.

Gerald looked into the distance, with the small-pupilled, abstract eyes of a hawk.

'No. There's something final about this. And Gudrun seems like the end to me. I don't know – but she seems so soft, her skin like silk, her arms heavy and soft. And it withers my consciousness, somehow, it burns the pith of my mind.' He went on a few paces, staring ahead, his eyes fixed, looking like a mask used in ghastly religions of the barbarians. 'It blasts your soul's eye,' he said, 'and leaves you sightless. Yet you *want* to be sightless, you *want* to be blasted, you don't want it any different.'

He was speaking as if in a trance, verbal and blank. Then suddenly he braced himself up with a kind of rhapsody, and looked at Birkin with vindictive, cowed eyes saying:

'Do you know what it is to suffer when you are with a woman? She's so beautiful, so perfect, you find her *so good*, it tears you like a silk, and every stroke and bit cuts hot – ha, that perfection, when you blast yourself, you blast yourself! And then—' he stopped on the snow and suddenly opened his clenched hands— 'it's nothing – your brain might have gone charred as rags – and—' he looked round into the air with a queer histrionic movement— 'it's blasting – you understand what I mean – it is a great experience, something final – and then – you're shrivelled as if struck by electricity.' He walked on in silence. It seemed like bragging, but like a man in extremity bragging truthfully.

'Of course,' he resumed, 'I wouldn't *not* have had it! It's a complete experience. And she's a wonderful woman. But – how I hate her somewhere! It's curious—'

Birkin looked at him, at his strange, scarcely conscious face. Gerald seemed blank before his own words.

'But you've had enough now?' said Birkin. 'You have had your experience. Why work on an old wound?'

'Oh,' said Gerald, 'I don't know. It's not finished—'

And the two walked on.

'I've loved you, as well as Gudrun, don't forget,' said Birkin bitterly. Gerald looked at him strangely, abstractedly.

'Have you?' he said, with icy scepticism. 'Or do you think you have?' He was hardly responsible for what he said.

The sledge came. Gudrun dismounted and they all made their farewell. They wanted to go apart, all of them. Birkin took his place, and the sledge drove away leaving Gudrun and Gerald standing on the snow, waving. Something froze Birkin's heart, seeing them standing there in the isolation of the snow, growing smaller and more isolated.

Chapter Thirty

Snowed Up

When Ursula and Birkin were gone, Gudrun felt herself free in her contest with Gerald. As they grew more used to each other, he seemed to press upon her more and more. At first she could manage him, so that her own will was always left free. But very soon, he began to ignore her female tactics, he dropped his respect for her whims and her privacies, he began to exert his own will blindly, without submitting to hers.

Already a vital conflict had set in, which frightened them both. But he was alone, whilst already she had begun to cast round for external resource.

When Ursula had gone, Gudrun felt her own existence had become stark and elemental. She went and crouched alone in her bedroom, looking out of the window at the big, flashing stars. In front was the faint shadow of the mountain-knot. That was the pivot. She felt strange and inevitable, as if she were centred upon the pivot of all existence, there was no further reality.

Presently Gerald opened the door. She knew he would not be long before he came. She was rarely alone, he pressed upon her like a frost, deadening her.

'Are you alone in the dark?' he said. And she could tell by his tone he resented it, he resented this isolation she had drawn round herself. Yet, feeling static and inevitable, she was kind towards him.

'Would you like to light the candle?' she asked.

He did not answer, but came and stood behind her, in the darkness.

'Look,' she said, 'at that lovely star up there. Do you know its name?'

He crouched beside her, to look through the low window.

'No,' he said. 'It is very fine.'

'*Isn't* it beautiful! Do you notice how it darts different coloured fires – it flashes really superbly—'

They remained in silence. With a mute, heavy gesture she put her hand on his knee, and took his hand.

'Are you regretting Ursula?' he asked.

'No, not at all,' she said. Then, in a slow mood, she asked:

'How much do you love me?'

He stiffened himself further against her.

'How much do you think I do?' he asked.

'I don't know,' she replied.

'But what is your opinion?' he asked.

There was a pause. At length, in the darkness, came her voice, hard and indifferent:

'Very little indeed,' she said coldly, almost flippant.

His heart went icy at the sound of her voice.

'Why don't I love you?' he asked, as if admitting the truth of her accusation, yet hating her for it.

'I don't know why you don't – I've been good to you. You were in a *fearful* state when you came to me.'

Her heart was beating to suffocate her, yet she was strong and unrelenting.

'When was I in a fearful state?' he asked.

'When you first came to me. I *had* to take pity on you. But it was never love.'

It was that statement 'It was never love', which sounded in his ears with madness.

'Why must you repeat it so often, that there is no love?' he said in a voice strangled with rage.

'Well you don't *think* you love, do you?' she asked.

He was silent with cold passion of anger.

'You don't think you *can* love me, do you?' she repeated almost with a sneer.

'No,' he said.

'You know you never *have* loved me, don't you?'

'I don't know what you mean by the word "love",' he replied.

'Yes, you do. You know all right that you have never loved me. Have you, do you think?'

'No,' he said, prompted by some barren spirit of truthfulness and obstinacy.

'And you never *will* love me,' she said finally, 'will you?'

There was a diabolic coldness in her, too much to bear.

'No,' he said.

'Then,' she replied, 'what have you against me?'

He was silent in cold, frightened rage and despair. 'If only I could kill her,' his heart was whispering repeatedly. 'If only I could kill her – I should be free.'

It seemed to him that death was the only severing of this Gordian knot.

'Why do you torture me?' he said.

She flung her arms round his neck.

'Ah, I don't want to torture you,' she said pityingly, as if she were comforting a child. The impertinence made his veins go cold, he was insensible. She held her arms round his neck, in a triumph of pity. And her pity for him was as cold as stone, its deepest motive was hate of him, and fear of his power over her, which she must always counterfoil.

'Say you love me,' she pleaded. 'Say you will love me for ever – won't you – won't you?'

But it was her voice only that coaxed him. Her senses were entirely apart from him, cold and destructive of him. It was her overbearing *will* that insisted.

'Won't you say you'll love me always?' she coaxed. 'Say it, even if it isn't true – say it Gerald, do.'

'I will love you always,' he repeated, in real agony, forcing the words out.

She gave him a quick kiss.

'Fancy your actually having said it,' she said with a touch of raillery.

He stood as if he had been beaten.

'Try to love me a little more, and to want me a little less,' she said, in a half contemptuous, half coaxing tone.

The darkness seemed to be swaying in waves across his mind, great waves of darkness plunging across his mind. It seemed to him he was degraded at the very quick, made of no account.

'You mean you don't want me?' he said.

'You are so insistent, and there is so little grace in you, so little fineness. You are so crude. You break me – you only waste me – it is horrible to me.'

'Horrible to you?' he repeated.

'Yes. Don't you think I might have a room to myself, now Ursula has gone? You can say you want a dressing-room.'

'You do as you like – you can leave altogether if you like,' he managed to articulate.

'Yes, I know that,' she replied. 'So can you. You can leave me whenever you like – without notice even.'

The great tides of darkness were swinging across his mind, he could hardly stand upright. A terrible weariness overcame him, he felt he must lie on the floor. Dropping off his clothes, he got into bed, and lay like a man suddenly overcome by drunkenness, the darkness lifting and plunging as if her were lying upon a black, giddy sea. He lay still in this strange, horrific reeling for some time, purely unconscious.

At length she slipped from her own bed and came over to him. He remained rigid, his back to her. He was all but unconscious.

She put her arms round his terrifying, insentient body, and laid her cheek against his hard shoulder.

'Gerald,' she whispered. 'Gerald.'

There was no change in him. She caught him against her. She pressed her breasts against his shoulders, she kissed his shoulder, through the sleeping jacket. Her mind wondered, over his rigid, unliving body. She was bewildered, and insistent, only her will was set for him to speak to her.

'Gerald, my dear!' she whispered, bending over him, kissing his ear.

Her warm breath playing, flying rhythmically over his ear, seemed to relax the tension. She could feel his body gradually relaxing a little, losing its terrifying, unnatural rigidity. Her hands clutched his limbs, his muscles, going over him spasmodically.

The hot blood began to flow again through his veins, his limbs relaxed.

'Turn round to me,' she whispered, forlorn with insistence and triumph.

So at last he was given again, warm and flexible. He turned and gathered her in his arms. And feeling her soft against him, so perfectly and wondrously soft and recipient, his arms tightened on her. She was as if crushed, powerless in him. His brain seemed hard and invincible now like a jewel, there was no resisting him.

His passion was awful to her, tense and ghastly, and impersonal, like a destruction, ultimate. She felt it would kill her. She was being killed.

'My God, my God,' she cried, in anguish, in his embrace, feeling her life being killed within her. And when he was kissing her, soothing her, her breath came slowly, as if she were really spent, dying.

'Shall I die, shall I die?' she repeated to herself.

And in the night, and in him, there was no answer to the question.

And yet, next day, the fragment of her which was not destroyed remained intact and hostile, she did not go away, she remained to finish the holiday, admitting nothing. He scarcely ever left her alone, but followed her like a shadow, he was like a doom upon her, a continual 'thou shalt', 'thou shalt not'. Sometimes it was he who seemed strongest, whilst she was almost gone, creeping near the earth like a spent wind; sometimes it was the reverse. But always it was this eternal see-saw, one destroyed that the other might exist, one ratified because the other was nulled.

'In the end,' she said to herself, 'I shall go away from him.'

'I can be free of her,' he said to himself in his paroxysms of suffering.

And he set himself to be free. He even prepared to go away, to leave her in the lurch. But for the first time there was a flaw in his will.

'Where shall I go?' he asked himself.

'Can't you be self-sufficient?' he replied to himself, putting himself upon his pride.

'Self-sufficient!' he repeated.

It seemed to him that Gudrun was sufficient unto herself, closed round and completed, like a thing in a case. In the calm, static reason of his soul, he recognised this, and admitted it was her right, to be closed round upon herself, self-complete, without desire. He realised it, he admitted it, it only needed one last effort on his own part, to win for himself the same completeness. He knew that it only needed one convulsion of his will for him to be able to turn upon himself also, to close upon himself as a stone fixes upon itself, and is impervious, self-completed, a thing isolated.

This knowledge threw him into a terrible chaos. Because, however much he might mentally *will* to be immune and self-complete, the desire for this state was lacking, and he could not create it. He could see that, to exist at all, he must be perfectly free of Gudrun, leave her if she wanted to be left, demand nothing of her, have no claim upon her.

But then, to have no claim upon her, he must stand by himself, in sheer nothingness. And his brain turned to nought at the idea. It was a state of nothingness. On the other hand, he might give in, and fawn to her. Or, finally, he might kill her. Or he might become just indifferent, purposeless, dissipated, momentaneous. But his nature was too serious, not gay enough or subtle enough for mocking licentiousness.

A strange rent had been torn in him; like a victim that is torn open and given to the heavens, so he had been torn apart and given to Gudrun. How should he close again? This wound, this strange, infinitely-sensitive opening of his soul, where he was exposed, like an open flower, to all the universe, and in which he was given to his complement, the other, the unknown, this wound, this disclosure, this unfolding of his own covering, leaving him incomplete, limited, unfinished, like an open flower under the sky, this was his cruellest joy. Why then should he forgo it? Why should he close up and become impervious, immune, like a partial thing in a sheath, when he had broken forth, like a seed that has germinated, to issue forth in being, embracing the unrealised heavens.

He would keep the unfinished bliss of his own yearning even through the torture she inflicted upon him. A strange obstinacy possessed him. He would not go away from her whatever she said or did. A strange, deathly yearning carried him along with her. She was the determining influence of his very being, though she treated him with contempt, repeated rebuffs and denials, still he would never be gone, since in being near her, even, he felt the quickening, the going forth in him, the release, the knowledge of his own limitation and the magic of the promise, as well as the mystery of his own destruction and annihilation.

She tortured the open heart of him even as he turned to her. And she was tortured herself. It may have been her will was stronger. She felt, with horror, as if he tore at the bud of her heart, tore it open, like an irreverent persistent being. Like a boy who pulls off a fly's wings, or tears open a bud to see what is in the flower, he tore at her privacy, at her very life, he would destroy her as an immature bud, torn open, is destroyed.

She might open towards him, a long while hence, in her dreams, when she was a pure spirit. But now she was not to be violated and ruined. She closed against him fiercely.

They climbed together, at evening, up the high slope, to see the sun set. In the finely breathing, keen wind they stood and watched the yellow sun sink in crimson and disappear. Then in the east the peaks and ridges glowed with living rose, incandescent like immortal flowers against a brown-purple sky, a miracle, whilst down below the world was a bluish shadow, and above, like an annunciation, hovered a rosy transport in mid-air.

To her it was so beautiful, it was a delirium. she wanted to gather the glowing, eternal peaks to her breast, and die. He saw them, saw they were beautiful. But there arose no clamour in his breast, only a bitterness that was visionary in itself. He wished the peaks were grey and unbeautiful, so that she should not get her support from them. Why did she betray the two of them so terribly, in embracing the glow of the evening? Why did she leave him standing there, with the ice-wind blowing through his heart, like death, to gratify herself among the rosy snow-tips?

'What does the twilight matter?' he said. 'Why do you grovel before it? Is it so important to you?'

She winced in violation and in fury.

'Go away,' she cried, 'and leave me to it. It is beautiful, beautiful,' she sang in strange, rhapsodic tones. 'It is the most beautiful thing I have ever seen in my life. Don't try to come between it and me. Take yourself away, you are out of place—'

He stood back a little, and left her standing there, statue-like, transported into the mystic glowing east. Already the rose was fading, large white stars were flashing out. He waited. He would forgo everything but the yearning.

'That was the most perfect thing I have ever seen,' she said in cold, brutal tones, when at last she turned round to him. 'It amazes me that you should want to destroy it. If you can't see it yourself, why try to debar me?' But in reality, he had destroyed it for her, she was straining after a dead effect.

'One day,' he said, softly, looking up at her, 'I shall destroy *you*, as you stand looking at the sunset; because you are such a liar.'

There was a soft, voluptuous promise to himself in the words. She was
chilled but arrogant.

'Ha!' she said. 'I am not afraid of your threats!'

She denied herself to him, she kept her room rigidly private to herself.
But he waited on, in a curious patience, belonging to his yearning for her.

'In the end,' he said to himself with real voluptuous promise, 'when it
reaches that point, I shall do away with her.' And he trembled delicately in
every limb, in anticipation, as he trembled in his most violent accesses of
passionate approach to her, trembling with too much desire.

She had a curious sort of allegiance with Loerke, all the while now,
something insidious and traitorous. Gerald knew of it. But in the unnatural
state of patience, and the unwillingness to harden himself against her, in
which he found himself, he took no notice, although her soft kindliness to
the other man, whom he hated as a noxious insect, made him shiver again
with an access of the strange shuddering that came over him repeatedly.

He left her alone only when he went ski-ing, a sport he loved, and which
she did not practise. Then he seemed to sweep out of life, to be a projectile
into the beyond. And often, when he went away, she talked to the little
German sculptor. They had an invariable topic, in their art.

They were almost of the same ideas. He hated Mestrovic, was not satisfied
with the Futurists, he liked the West African wooden figures, the Aztec art,
Mexican and Central American. He saw the grotesque, and a curious sort
of mechanical motion intoxicated him, a confusion in nature. They had a
curious game with each other, Gudrun and Loerke, of infinite suggestivity,
strange and leering, as if they had some esoteric understanding of life, that
they alone were initiated into the fearful central secrets, that the world dared
not know. Their whole correspondence was in a strange, barely comprehen-
sible suggestivity, they kindled themselves at the subtle lust of the Egyptians
or the Mexicans. The whole game was one of subtle inter-suggestivity, and
they wanted to keep it on the plane of suggestion. From their verbal and
physical nuances they got the highest satisfaction in the nerves, from a queer
interchange of half-suggested ideas, looks, expressions and gestures, which
were quite intolerable, though incomprehensible, to Gerald. He had no terms
in which to think of their commerce, his terms were much too gross.

The suggestion of primitive art was their refuge, and the inner mysteries
of sensation their object of worship. Art and Life were to them the Reality
and the Unreality.

'Of course,' said Gudrun, 'life doesn't *really* matter – it is one's art which
is central. What one does in one's life has *peu de rapport*, it doesn't signify
much.

'Yes, that is so, exactly,' replied the sculptor. 'What one does in one's art,
that is the breath of one's being. What one does in one's life, that is a
bagatelle for the outsiders to fuss about.'

It was curious what a sense of elation and freedom Gudrun found in this
communication. She felt established for ever. Of course Gerald was *bagatelle*.
Love was one of the temporal things in her life, except in so far as she was
an artist. She thought of Cleopatra – Cleopatra must have been an artist;
she reaped the essential from a man, she harvested the ultimate sensation,

and threw away the husk; and Mary Stuart, and the great Rachel, panting with her lovers after the theatre, these were the exoteric exponents of love. After all, what was the lover but fuel for the transport of this subtle knowledge, for a female art, the art of pure, perfect knowledge in sensuous understanding.

One evening Gerald was arguing with Loerke about Italy and Tripoli. The Englishman was in a strange, inflammable state, the German was excited. It was a contest of words, but it meant a conflict of spirit between the two men. And all the while Gudrun could see in Gerald an arrogant English contempt for a foreigner. Although Gerald was quivering, his eyes flashing, his face flushed, in his argument there was a brusqueness, a savage contempt in his manner, that made Gudrun's blood flare up, and made Loerke keen and mortified. For Gerald came down like a sledge-hammer with his assertions, anything the little German said was merely contemptible rubbish.

At last Loerke turned to Gudrun, raising his hands in helpless irony, a shrug of ironical dismissal, something appealing and child-like.

'*Sehen sie, gnädige Frau*—' he began.

'*Bitte sagen Sie nicht immer, gnädige Frau,*' cried Gudrun, her eyes flashing, her cheeks burning. She looked like a vivid Medusa. Her voice was loud and clamorous, the other people in the room were startled.

'Please don't call me Mrs. Crich,' she cried aloud.

The name, in Loerke's mouth particularly, had been an intolerable humiliation and constraint upon her these many days.

The two men looked at her in amazement. Gerald went white at the cheek-bones.

'What shall I say, then?' asked Loerke, with soft, mocking insinuation.

'*Sagen Sie nur nicht das,*' she muttered, her cheeks flushed crimson. 'Not that, at least.'

She saw, by the dawning look on Loerke's face, that he had understood. She was *not* Mrs. Crich! So-o-, that explained a great deal.

'*Soll ich Fräulein sagen?*' he asked malevolently.

'I am not married,' she said, with some hauteur.

Her heart was fluttering now, beating like a bewildered bird. She knew she had dealt a cruel wound, and she could not bear it.

Gerald sat erect, perfectly still, his face pale and calm, like the face of a statue. He was unaware of her, or of Loerke or anybody. He sat perfectly still in an unalterable calm. Loerke, meanwhile, was crouching and glancing up from under his ducked head.

Gudrun was tortured for something to say, to relieve the suspense. She twisted her face in a smile and glanced knowingly, almost sneering, at Gerald.

'Truth is best,' she said to him, with a grimace.

But now again she was under his domination; now, because she had dealt him this blow; because she had destroyed him, and she did not know how he had taken it. She watched him. He was interesting to her. She had lost her interest in Loerke.

Gerald rose at length and went over in a leisurely still movement to the professor. The two began a conversation on Goethe.

She was rather piqued by the simplicity of Gerald's demeanour this evening. He did not seem angry or disgusted, only he looked curiously innocent and pure, really beautiful. Sometimes it came upon him, this look of clear distance, and it always fascinated her.

She waited, troubled, throughout the evening. She thought he would avoid her, or give some sign. But he spoke to her simply and unemotionally, as he would to anyone else in the room. A certain peace, an abstraction possessed his soul.

She went to his room, hotly, violently in love with him. He was so beautiful and inaccessible. He kissed her, he was a lover to her. And she had extreme pleasure of him. But he did not come to, he remained remote and candid, unconscious. She wanted to speak to him. But this innocent, beautiful state of unconsciousness that had come upon him prevented her. She felt tormented and dark.

In the morning, however, he looked at her with a little aversion, some horror and some hatred darkening into his eyes. She withdrew on to her old ground. But still he would not gather himself together against her.

Loerke was waiting for her now. The little artist, isolated in his own complete envelope, felt that here at last was a woman from whom he could get something. He was uneasy all the while, waiting to talk with her, subtly contriving to be near her. Her presence filled him with keenness and excitement, he gravitated cunningly towards her, as if she had some unseen force of attraction.

He was not in the least doubtful of himself, as regards Gerald. Gerald was one of the outsiders. Loerke only hated him for being rich and proud and of fine appearance. All these things, however, riches, pride of social standing, handsome physique, were externals. When it came to the relation with a woman such as Gudrun, he, Loerke, had an approach and a power that Gerald never dreamed of.

How should Gerald hope to satisfy a woman of Gudrun's calibre? Did he think that pride or masterful will or physical strength would help him? Loerke knew a secret beyond these things. The greatest power is the one that is subtle and adjusts itself, not one which blindly attacks. And he, Loerke, had understanding where Gerald was a calf. He, Loerke, could penetrate into depths far out of Gerald's knowledge. Gerald was left behind like a postulant in the ante-room of this temple of mysteries, this woman. But he, Loerke, could he not penetrate into the inner darkness, find the spirit of the woman in its inner recess, and wrestle with it there, the central serpent that is coiled at the core of life.

What was it, after all, that a woman wanted? Was it mere social effect, fulfilment of ambition in the social world, in the community of mankind? Was it even a union in love and goodness? Did she want 'goodness'? Who but a fool would accept this of Gudrun? This was but the street view of her wants. Cross the threshold, and you found her completely, completely cynical about the social world and its advantages. Once inside the house of her soul, and there was a pungent atmosphere of corrosion, an inflamed darkness of sensation, and a vivid, subtle, critical consciousness, that saw the world distorted, horrific.

What then, what next? Was it sheer blind force of passion that would satisfy her now? Not this, but the subtle thrills of extreme sensation in reduction. It was an unbroken will reacting against her unbroken will in a myriad subtle thrills of reduction, the last subtle activities of analysis and breaking down, carried out in the darkness of her, whilst the outside form, the individual, was utterly unchanged, even sentimental in its poses.

But between two particular people, any two people on earth, the range of pure sensational experience is limited. The climax of sensual reaction, once reached in any direction, is reached finally, there is no going on. There is only repetition possible, or the going apart of the two protagonists, or the subjugating of the one will to the other, or death.

Gerald had penetrated all the outer places of Gudrun's soul. He was to her the most crucial instance of the existing world, the *ne plus ultra* of the world of man as it existed for her. In him she knew the world, and had done with it. Knowing him finally she was the Alexander seeking new worlds. But there *were* no new worlds, there were no more *men*, there were only creatures, little, ultimate *creatures* like Loerke. The world was finished now, for her. There was only the inner, individual darkness, sensation within the ego, the obscene religious mystery of ultimate reduction, the mystic frictional activities of diabolic reducing down, disintegrating the vital organic body of life.

All this Gudrun knew in her subconsciousness, not in her mind. She knew her next step – she knew what she should move on to when she left Gerald. She was afraid of Gerald, that he might kill her. But she did not intend to be killed. A fine thread still united her to him. It should not be *her* death which broke it. She had farther to go, a farther, slow, exquisite experience to reap, unthinkable subtleties of sensation to know, before she was finished.

Of the last series of subtleties, Gerald was not capable. He could not touch the quick of her. But where his ruder blows could not penetrate, the fine, insinuating blade of Loerke's insect-like comprehension could. At least, it was time for her now to pass over to the other, the creature, the final craftsman. She knew that Loerke, in his innermost soul, was detached from everything, for him there was neither heaven nor earth nor hell. He admitted no allegiance, he gave no adherence anywhere. He was single and, by abstraction from the rest, absolute in himself.

Whereas in Gerald's soul there still lingered some attachment to the rest, to the whole. And this was his limitation. He was limited, *borné*, subject to his necessity, in the last issue, for goodness, for righteousness, for oneness with the ultimate purpose. That the ultimate purpose might be the perfect and subtle experience of the process of death, the will being kept unimpaired, that was not allowed in him. And this was his limitation.

There was a hovering triumph in Loerke, since Gudrun had denied her marriage with Gerald. The artist seemed to hover like a creature on the wing, waiting to settle. He did not approach Gudrun violently, he was never ill-timed. But carried on by a sure instinct in the complete darkness of his soul, he corresponded mystically with her, imperceptibly, but palpably.

For two days, he talked to her, continued the discussions of art, of life, in which they both found such pleasure. They praised the bygone things, they took a sentimental, childish delight in the achieved perfections of the past. Particularly they liked the late eighteenth century, the period of Goethe and of Shelley, and Mozart.

They played with the past, and with the great figures of the past, a sort of little game of chess, or marionettes, all to please themselves. They had all the great men for their marionettes, and they two were the God of the show, working it all. As for the future, that they never mentioned except one laughed out some mocking dream of the destruction of the world by a ridiculous catastrophe of man's invention: a man invented such a perfect explosive that it blew the earth in two, and the two halves set off in different directions through space, to the dismay of the inhabitants: or else the people of the world divided into two halves, and each half decided *it* was perfect and right, the other half was wrong and must be destroyed; so another end of the world. Or else, Loerke's dream of fear, the world went cold, and snow fell everywhere, and only white creatures, Polar bears, white foxes, and men like awful white snow-birds, persisted in ice cruelty.

Apart from these stories, they never talked of the future. They delighted most either in mocking imaginations of destruction or in sentimental, fine marionette shows of the past. It was a sentimental delight to reconstruct the world of Goethe at Weimar, or of Schiller and poverty and faithful love, or to see again Jean Jacques in his quakings, or Voltaire at Ferney, or Frederick the Great reading his own poetry.

They talked together for hours, of literature and sculpture and painting, amusing themselves with Flaxman and Blake and Fuseli, with tenderness, and with Feuerbach and Böcklin. It would take them a lifetime, they felt, to live again, *in petto*, the lives of the great artists. But they preferred to stay in the eighteenth and the nineteenth centuries.

They talked in a mixture of languages. The ground-work was French, in either case. But he ended most of his sentences in a stumble of English and a conclusion of German, she skilfully wove herself to her end in whatever phrase came to her. She took a peculiar delight in this conversation. It was full of odd, fantastic expression, of double meanings, of evasions, of suggestive vagueness. It was a real physical pleasure to her to make this thread of conversation out of the different-coloured strands of three languages.

And all the while they two were hovering, hesitating round the flame of some invisible declaration. He wanted it, but was held back by some inevitable reluctance. She wanted it also, but she wanted to put it off, to put it off indefinitely, she still had some pity for Gerald, some connection with him. And the most fatal of all, she had the reminiscent sentimental compassion for herself in connection with him. Because of what *had* been, she felt herself held to him by immortal, invisible threads – because of what *had* been, because of his coming to her that first night, into her own house, in his extremity, because—

Gerald was gradually overcome with a revulsion of loathing for Loerke. He did not take the man seriously, he despised him merely, except as he felt in Gudrun's veins the influence of the little creature. It was this that drove

Gerald wild, the feeling in Gudrun's veins of Loerke's presence, Loerke's being, flowing dominant through her.

'What makes you so smitten with that little vermin?' he asked, really puzzled. For he, man-like, could not see anything attractive or important *at all* in Loerke. Gerald expected to find some handsomeness or nobleness to account for a woman's subjection. But he saw none here, only an insect-like repulsiveness.

Gudrun flushed deeply. It was these attacks she would never forgive.

'What do you mean?' she replied. 'My God, what a mercy I am *not* married to you!'

Her voice of flouting and contempt scotched him. He was brought up short. But he recovered himself.

'Tell me, only tell me,' he reiterated in a dangerous, narrowed voice – 'tell me what it is that fascinates you in him.'

'I am not fascinated,' she said, with cold, repelling innocence.

'Yes, you are. You are fascinated by that little dry snake, like a bird gaping ready to fall down its throat.'

She looked at him with black fury.

'I don't choose to be discussed by you,' she said.

'It doesn't matter whether you choose or not,' he replied, 'that doesn't alter the fact that you are ready to fall down and kiss the feet of that little insect. And I don't want to prevent you – do it, fall down and kiss his feet. But I want to know what it is that fascinates you – what is it?'

She was silent, suffused with black rage.

'How *dare* you come brow-beating me,' she cried, 'how dare you, you little squire, you bully. What right have you over me, do you think?'

His face was white and gleaming, she knew by the light in his eyes that she was in his power – the wolf. And because she was in his power, she hated him with a power that she wondered did not kill him. In her will she killed him as he stood, effaced him.

'It is not a question of right,' said Gerald, sitting down on a chair. She watched the change in his body. She saw his clenched, mechanical body moving there like an obsession. Her hatred of him was tingled with fatal contempt.

'It's not a question of my right over you – though I *have* some right, remember. I want to know, I only want to know what it is that subjugates you to that little scum of a sculptor downstairs, what it is that brings you down like a humble maggot, in worship of him. I want to know what you creep after.'

She stood over against the window, listening. Then she turned round.

'Do you?' she said, in her most easy, most cutting voice. 'Do you want to know what it is in him? It's because he has some understanding of a woman, because he is not stupid. That's why it is.'

A queer, sinister, animal-like smile came over Gerald's face.

'But what understanding is it?' he said. 'The understanding of a flea, a hopping flea with a proboscis. Why should you crawl abject before the understanding of a flea?'

There passed through Gudrun's mind Blake's representation of the soul of a flea. She wanted to fit it to Loerke. Blake was a clown too. But it was necessary to answer Gerald.

'Don't you think the understanding of a flea is more interesting than the understanding of a fool?' she asked.

'A fool!' he repeated.

'A fool, a conceited fool – a *Dummkopf*,' she replied, adding the German word.

'Do you call me a fool?' he replied. 'Well, wouldn't I rather be the fool I am than that flea downstairs?'

She looked at him. A certain blunt, blind stupidity in him palled on her soul, limiting her.

'You give yourself away by that last,' she said.

He sat and wondered.

'I shall go away soon,' he said.

She turned on him.

'Remember,' she said, 'I am completely independent of you – completely. You make your arrangements. I make mine.'

He pondered this.

'You mean we are strangers from this minute?' he asked.

She halted and flushed. He was putting her in a trap, forcing her hand. She turned round on him.

'Strangers,' she said, 'we can never be. But if you *want* to make any movement apart from me, then I wish you to know you are perfectly free to do so. Do not consider me in the slightest.'

Even so slight an implication that she needed him and was depending on him still was sufficient to rouse his passion. As he sat a change came over his body, the hot, molten stream mounted involuntarily through his veins. He groaned inwardly, under its bondage, but he loved it. He looked at her with clear eyes, waiting for her.

She knew at once, and was shaken with cold revulsion. *How* could he look at her with those clear, warm, waiting eyes, waiting for her, even now? What had been said between them, was it not enough to put them worlds asunder, to freeze them for ever apart! And yet he was all transfused and roused, waiting for her.

It confused her. Turning her head aside, she said:

'I shall always *tell* you, whenever I am going to make any change—'

And with this she moved out of the room.

He sat suspended in a fine recoil of disappointment, that seemed gradually to be destroying his understanding. But the unconscious state of patience persisted in him. He remained motionless, without thought or knowledge, for a long time. Then he rose and went downstairs to play at chess with one of the students. His face was open and clear, with a certain innocent *laisser-aller* that troubled Gudrun most, made her almost afraid of him, whilst she disliked him deeply for it.

It was after this that Loerke, who had never yet spoken to her personally, began to ask her of her state.

'You are not married at all, are you?' he asked.

She looked full at him.

'Not in the least,' she replied, in her measured way. Loerke laughed, wrinkling up his face oddly. There was a thin wisp of his hair straying on his forehead, she noticed that his skin was of a clear brown colour, his hands, his wrists. And his hands seemed closely prehensile. He seemed like topaz, so strangely brownish and pellucid.

'Good,' he said.

Still it needed some courage for him to go on.

'Was Mrs. Birkin your sister?' he asked.

'Yes.'

'And was *she* married?'

'She was married.'

'Have you parents, then?'

'Yes,' said Gudrun, 'we have parents.'

And she told him, briefly, laconically, her position. He watched her closely, curiously, all the while.

'So!' he exclaimed, with some surprise. 'And the Herr Crich, is he rich?'

'Yes, he is rich, a coal owner.'

'How long has your friendship with him lasted?'

'Some months.'

There was a pause.

'Yes, I am surprised,' he said at length. 'The English, I thought they were so – cold. And what do you think to do when you leave here?'

'What do I think to do?' she repeated.

'Yes. You cannot go back to the teaching. No' – he shrugged his shoulders – 'that is impossible. Leave that to the *canaille* who can do nothing else. You, for your part – you know, you are a wonderful woman, *eine seltsame Frau*. Why deny it – why make any question of it? You are an extraordinary woman, why should you follow the ordinary course, the ordinary life?'

Gudrun sat looking at her hands, flushed. She was pleased that he said, so simply, that she was a remarkable woman. He would not say that to flatter her – he was far too self-opinionated and objective by nature. He said it as he would say a piece of sculpture was remarkable, because he knew it was so.

And it gratified her to hear it from him. Other people had such a passion to make everything of one degree, of one pattern. In England it was chic to be perfectly ordinary. And it was a relief to her to be acknowledged extraordinary. Then she need not fret about the common standards.

'You see,' she said, 'I have no money whatsoever.'

'Ach, money!' he cried, lifting his shoulders. 'When one is grown up, money is lying about at one's service. It is only when one is young that it is rare. Take no thought for money – that always lies to hand.'

'Does it?' she said, laughing.

'Always. The Gerald will give you a sum if you ask him for it—'

She flushed deeply.

'I will ask anybody else,' she said, with some difficulty – 'but not him.'

Loerke looked closely at her.

'Good,' he said. 'Then let it be somebody else. Only don't go back to that England, that school. No, that is stupid.'

Again there was a pause. He was afraid to ask her outright to go with him, he was not even quite sure he wanted her; and she was afraid to be asked. He begrudged his own isolation, was *very* chary of sharing his life, even for a day.

'The only other place I know is Paris,' she said, 'and I can't stand that.'

She looked with her wide, steady eyes full at Loerke. He lowered his head and averted his face.

'Paris, no!' he said. 'Between the *religion d'amour*, and the latest 'ism, and the new turning to Jesus, one had better ride on a carrousel all day. But come to Dresden. I have a studio there – I can give you work – oh, that would be easy enough. I haven't seen any of your things, but I believe in you. Come to Dresden – that is a fine town to be in, and as good a life as you can expect of a town. You have everything there, without the foolishness of Paris or the beer of Munich.'

He sat and looked at her coldly. What she liked about him was that he spoke to her simple and flat, as to himself. He was a fellow craftsman, a fellow being to her, first.

'No – Paris,' he resumed, 'it makes me sick. Pah – *l'amour*. I detest it. *L'amour, l'amore, die Liebe* – I detest it in every language. Women and love, there is no greater tedium,' he cried.

She was slightly offended. And yet this was her own basic feeling. Men and love – there was no greater tedium.

'I think the same,' she said.

'A bore,' he repeated. 'What does it matter whether I wear this hat or another. So love. I needn't wear a hat at all, only for convenience. Neither need I love except for convenience. I tell you what, *gnädige Frau*—' and he leaned towards her – then he made a quick odd gesture, as of striking something aside – '*gnädige Fräulein*, never mind – I tell you what, I would give everything, everything, all your love, for a little companionship in intelligence—' his eyes flickered darkly, evilly at her. 'You understand?' he asked, with a faint smile. 'It wouldn't matter if she were a hundred years old, a thousand – it would be all the same to me, so that she can *understand*.' He shut his eyes with a little snap.

Again Gudrun was rather offended. Did he not think her good-looking, then? Suddenly she laughed.

'I shall have to wait about eighty years to suit you at that,' she said. 'I am ugly enough, aren't I?'

He looked at her with an artist's sudden, critical, estimating eye.

'You are beautiful,' he said, 'and I am glad of it. But it isn't that – it isn't that,' he cried, with emphasis that flattered her. 'It is that you have a certain wit, it is the kind of understanding. For me, I am little, *chétif*, insignificant. Good! Do not ask me to be strong and handsome, then. But it is the *me*' – he put his fingers to his mouth oddly – 'it is the *me* that is looking for a mistress, and my *me* is waiting for the *thee* of the mistress, for the match to my particular intelligence. You understand?'

'Yes,' she said, 'I understand.'

'As for the other, this *amour*' – he made a gesture, dashing his hand aside, as if to dash away something troublesome – 'it is unimportant, unimportant.

Does it matter whether I drink white wine this evening or whether I drink nothing? It *does not matter*, it does not matter. So this love, this *amour*, this *baiser*. Yes or no, *soit ou soit pas*, to-day, to-morrow, or never, it is all the same, it does not matter – no more than the white wine.'

He ended with an odd dropping of the head in a desperate negation. Gudrun watched him steadily. She had gone pale.

Suddenly she stretched over and seized his hand in her own.

'That is true,' she said, in rather a high, vehement voice, 'that is true for me too. It is the understanding that matters.'

He looked up at her almost frightened, furtive. Then he nodded a little sullenly. She let go his hand: he had made not the lightest response. And they sat in silence.

'Do you know,' he said, suddenly looking at her with dark, self-important, prophetic eyes, 'your fate and mine, they will run together till—' and he broke off in a little grimace.

'Till when?' she asked, blanched, her lips going white. She was terribly susceptible to these evil prognostications, but he only shook his head.

'I don't know,' he said, 'I don't know.'

Gerald did not come in from his ski-ing until nightfall, he missed the coffee and cake that she took at four o'clock. The snow was in perfect condition, he had travelled a long way, by himself, among the snow ridges, on his skis, he had climbed high, so high that he could see over the top of the pass five miles distant, could see the Marienhütte, the hostel on the crest of the pass, half buried in snow, and over into the deep valley beyond, to the dusk of the pine trees. One could go that way home; but he shuddered with nausea at the thought of home; – one could travel on skis down there, and come to the old imperial road, below the pass. But why come to any road? He revolted at the thought of finding himself in the world again. He must stay up there in the snow for ever. He had been happy by himself, high up there alone, travelling swiftly on skis, taking far flights and skimming past the dark rocks veined with brilliant snow.

But he felt something icy gathering at his heart. This strange mood of patience and innocence which had persisted in him for some days was passing away, he would be left again a prey to the horrible passions and tortures.

So he came down reluctantly, snow-burned, snow-estranged, to the house in the hollow, between the knuckles of the mountain-tops. He saw its lights shining yellow, and he held back, wishing he need not go in to confront those people, to hear the turmoil of voices and to feel the confusion of other presences. He was isolated as if there were a vacuum round his heart, or a sheath of pure ice.

The moment he saw Gudrun something jolted in his soul. She was looking rather lofty and superb, smiling slowly and graciously to the Germans. A sudden desire leapt in his heart to kill her. He thought, what a perfect voluptuous fulfilment it would be to kill her. His mind was absent all the evening, estranged by the snow and his passion. But he kept the idea constant within him, what a perfect voluptuous consummation it would be to strangle her, to strangle every spark of life out of her, till she lay completely inert, soft, relaxed for ever, a soft heap lying dead between his hands, utterly dead. Then he would have had her finally and for ever; there would be such a perfect voluptuous finality.

Gudrun was unaware of what he was feeling, he seemed so quiet and amiable, as usual. His amiability even made her feel brutal towards him.

She went into his room when he was partially undressed. She did not notice the curious, glad gleam of pure hatred, with which he looked at her. She stood near the door, with her hand behind her.

'I have been thinking, Gerald,' she said, with an insulting nonchalance, 'that I shall not go back to England.'

'Oh,' he said, 'where will you go then?'

But she ignored his question. She had her own logical statement to make, and it must be made as she had thought it.

'I can't see the use of going back,' she continued. 'It is over between me and you—'

She paused for him to speak. But he said nothing. He was only talking to himself, saying: 'Over, is it? I believe it is over. But it isn't finished. Remember, it isn't finished. We must put some sort of a finish on it. There must be a conclusion, there must be finality.'

So he talked to himself, but aloud he said nothing whatever.

'What has been, has been,' she continued. 'There is nothing that I regret. I hope you regret nothing—'

She waited for him to speak.

'Oh, I regret nothing,' he said, accommodatingly.

'Good then,' she answered, 'good then. Then neither of us cherishes any regrets, which is as it should be.'

'Quite as it should be,' he said aimlessly.

She paused to gather up her thread again.

'Our attempt has been a failure,' she said. 'But we can try again elsewhere.'

A little flicker of rage ran through his blood. It was as if she were rousing him, goading him. Why must she do it?

'Attempt at what?' he asked.

'At being lovers, I suppose,' she said, a little baffled, yet so trivial she made it all seem.

'Our attempt at being lovers has been a failure?' he repeated aloud.

To himself he was saying, 'I ought to kill her here. There is only this left, for me to kill her.' A heavy, overcharged desire to bring about her death possessed him. She was unaware.

'Hasn't it?' she asked. 'Do you think it has been a success?'

Again the insult of the flippant question ran through his blood like a current of fire.

'It had some of the elements of success, our relationship,' he replied. 'It – might have come off.'

But he paused before concluding the last phrase. Even as he began the sentence, he did not believe in what he was going to say. He knew it never could have been a success.

'No,' she replied. 'You cannot love.'

'And you?' he asked.

Her wide, dark-filled eyes were fixed on him like two moons of darkness. 'I couldn't love *you*,' she said, with stark, cold truth.

A blinding flash went over his brain, his body jolted. His heart had burst into flame. His consciousness was gone into his wrists, into his hands. He was one blind, incontinent desire to kill her. His wrists were bursting, there would be no satisfaction till his hands had closed on her.

But even before his body swerved forward on her, a sudden, cunning comprehension was expressed on her face, and in a flash she was out of the door. She ran in one flash to her room and locked herself in. She was afraid, but confident. She knew her life trembled on the edge of an abyss. But she was curiously sure of her footing. She knew her cunning could outwit him.

She trembled, as she stood in her room, with excitement and awful exhilaration. She knew she could outwit him. She could depend on her presence of mind, and on her wits. But it was a fight to the death, she knew it now. One slip, and she was lost. She had a strange, tense, exhilarated sickness in her body, as one who is in peril of falling from a great height, but who does not look down, does not admit the fear.

'I will go away the day after to-morrow,' she said.

She only did not want Gerald to think that she was afraid of him, that she was running away because she was afraid of him. She was not afraid of him, fundamentally. She knew it was her safeguard to avoid his physical violence. But even physically she was not afraid of him. She wanted to prove it to him. When she had proved it, that, whatever he was, she was not afraid of him; when she had proved *that*, she could leave him for ever. But meanwhile the fight between them, terrible as she knew it to be, was inconclusive. And she wanted to be confident in herself. However many terrors she might have, she would be unafraid, uncowed by him. He could never cow her, nor dominate her, nor have any right over her; this she would maintain until she had proved it. Once it was proved, she was free of him for ever.

But she had not proved it yet, neither to him nor to herself. And this was what still bound her to him. She was bound to him, she could not live beyond him. She sat up in bed, closely wrapped up, for many hours, thinking endlessly to herself. It was as if she would never have done weaving the great provision of her thoughts.

'It isn't as if he really loved me,' she said to herself. 'He doesn't. Every woman he comes across he wants to make her in love with him. He doesn't even know that he is doing it. But there he is, before every woman he unfurls his male attractiveness, displays his great desirability, he tries to make every woman think how wonderful it would be to have him for a lover. His very ignoring of the women is part of the game. He is never *unconscious* of them. He should have been a cockerel, so he could strut before fifty females, all his subjects. But really, his Don Juan does *not* interest me. I could play Dona Juanita a million times better than he plays Juan. He bores me, you know. His maleness bores me. Nothing is so boring, so inherently stupid and stupidly conceited. Really, the fathomless conceit of these men, it is ridiculous – the little strutters.

'They are all alike. Look at Birkin. Built out of the limitation of conceit they are, and nothing else. Really, nothing but their ridiculous limitation and intrinsic insignificance could make them so conceited.

'As for Loerke, there is a thousand times more in him than in Gerald. Gerald is so limited, there is a dead end to him. He would grind on at the old mills for ever. And really, there is no corn between the millstones any more. They grind on and on, when there is nothing to grind – saying the same things, believing the same things, acting the same things. Oh, my God, it would wear out the patience of a stone.

'I don't worship Loerke, but at any rate, he is a free individual. He is not stiff with conceit of his own maleness. He is not grinding dutifully at the old mills. Oh God, when I think of Gerald, and his work – those offices at Beldover, and the mines – it makes my heart sick. What *have* I to do with it – and him thinking he can be a lover to a woman! One might as well ask it of a self-satisfied lamp-post. These men, with their eternal jobs – and their eternal mills of God that keep on grinding at nothing! It is too boring, just boring. However did I come to take him seriously at all!

'At least in Dresden, one will have one's back to it all. And there will be amusing things to do. It will be amusing to go to these eurhythmic displays, and the German opera, the German theatre. It *will* be amusing to take part in German Bohemian life. And Loerke *is* an artist, he is a free individual. One will escape from so much, that is the chief thing, escape so much hideous boring repetition of vulgar actions, vulgar phrases, vulgar postures. I don't delude myself that I shall find an elixir of life in Dresden. I know I shan't. But I shall get away from people who have their own homes and their own children and their own acquaintances and their own this and their own that. I shall be among people who *don't* own things and who haven't got a home and a domestic servant in the background, who *haven't* got a standing and a status and a degree and a circle of friends of the same. Oh God, the wheels within wheels of people, it makes one's head tick like a clock, with a very madness of dead mechanical monotony and meaninglessness. How I *hate* life, how I hate it. How I hate the Geralds, that they can offer one nothing else.

'Shortlands! – Heavens! Think of living there, one week, then the next, and *then the third*—

'No, I won't think of it – it is too much—'

And she broke off, really terrified, really unable to bear any more.

The thought of the mechanical succession of day following day, day following day, *ad infinitum*, was one of the things that made her heart palpitate with a real approach of madness. The terrible bondage of this tick-tack of time, this twitching of the hands of the clock, this eternal repetition of hours and days – oh God, it was too awful to contemplate. And there was no escape from it, no escape.

She almost wished Gerald were with her to save her from the terror of her own thoughts. Oh, how she suffered, lying there alone, confronted by the terrible clock, with its eternal tick-tack. All life, all life resolved itself into this: tick-tack, tick-tack, tick-tack; then the striking of the hour; then the tick-tack, tick-tack, and the twitching of the clock-fingers.

Gerald could not save her from it. He, his body, his motion, his life – it was the same ticking, the same twitching across the dial, a horrible mechanical twitching forward over the face of the hours. What were his kisses, his embraces. She could hear their tick-tack, tick-tack.

Ha – ha – she laughed to herself, so frightened that she was trying to laugh it off – ha – ha, how maddening it was, to be sure, to be sure!

Then, with a fleeting self-conscious motion, she wondered if she would be very much surprised, on rising in the morning, to realise that her hair had turned white. She had *felt* it turning white so often, under the intolerable burden of her thoughts, and her sensations. Yet there it remained, brown as ever, and there she was herself, looking a picture of health.

Perhaps she was healthy. Perhaps it was only her unabateable health that left her so exposed to the truth. If she were sickly she would have her illusions, imaginations. As it was, there was no escape. She must always see and know and never escape. She could never escape. There she was, placed before the clock-face of life. And if she turned round as in a railway station, to look at the bookstall, still she could see, with her very spine, she could see the clock, always the great white clock-face. In vain she fluttered the leaves of books, or made statuettes in clay. She knew she was not *really* reading. She was not *really* working. She was watching the fingers twitch across the eternal, mechanical, monotonous clock-face of time. She never really lived, she only watched. Indeed, she was like a little, twelve-hour clock, *vis-à-vis* with the enormous clock of eternity – there she was, like Dignity and Impudence, or Impudence and Dignity.

The picture pleased her. Didn't her face really look like a clock dial – rather roundish and often pale, and impassive. She would have got up to look in the mirror, but the thought of the sight of her own face, that was like a twelve-hour clock dial, filled her with such deep terror, that she hastened to think of something else.

Oh, why wasn't somebody kind to her? Why wasn't there somebody who would take her in their arms, and hold her to their breast, and give her rest, pure, deep, healing rest. Oh, why wasn't there somebody to take her in their arms and fold her safe and perfect, for sleep. She wanted so much this perfect enfolded sleep. She lay always so unsheathed in sleep. She would lie always unsheathed in sleep, unrelieved, unsaved. Oh, how could she bear it, this endless unrelief, this eternal unrelief.

Gerald! Could he fold her in his arms and sheathe her in sleep? Ha! He needed putting to sleep himself – poor Gerald. That was all he needed. What did he do, he made the burden for her greater, the burden of her sleep was the more intolerable, when he was there. He was an added weariness upon her unripening nights, her unfruitful slumbers. Perhaps he got some repose from her. Perhaps he did. Perhaps this was what he was always dogging her for, like a child that is famished, crying for the breast. Perhaps this was the secret of his passion, his for ever unquenched desire for her – that he needed her to put him to sleep, to give him repose.

What then! Was she his mother? Had she asked for a child, whom she must nurse through the nights, for her lover. She despised him, she despised him, she hardened her heart. An infant crying in the night, this Don Juan.

Ooh, but how she hated the infant crying in the night. She would murder it gladly. She would stifle it and bury it, as Hetty Sorrell did. No doubt Hetty Sorrell's infant cried in the night - no doubt Arthur Donnithorne's infant would. Ha - the Arthur Donnithornes, the Geralds of this world. So manly by day, yet all the while, such a crying of infants in the night. Let them turn into mechanisms, let them. Let them become instruments, pure machines, pure wills, that work like clockwork, in perpetual repetition. Let them be this, let them be taken up entirely in their work, let them be perfect parts of a great machine, having a slumber of constant repetition. Let Gerald manage his firm. There he would be satisfied, as satisfied as a wheel-barrow that goes backwards and forwards along a plank all day - she had seen it.

The wheel-barrow - the one humble wheel - the unit of the firm. Then the cart, with two wheels; then the truck, with four; then the donkey-engine, with eight, then the winding-engine, with sixteen, and so on, till it came to the miner, with a thousand wheels, and then the electrician, with three thousand, and the underground manager, with twenty thousand, and the general manager with a hundred thousand little wheels working away to complete his make-up, and then Gerald, with a million wheels and cogs and axles.

Poor Gerald, such a lot of little wheels to his make-up! He was more intricate than a chronometer-watch. But oh heavens, what weariness! What weariness, God above! A chronometer-watch - a beetle - her soul fainted with utter ennui, from the thought. So many wheels to count and consider and calculate! Enough, enough - there was an end to man's capacity for complications, even. Or perhaps there was no end.

Meanwhile Gerald sat in his room, reading. When Gudrun was gone, he was left stupefied with arrested desire. He sat on the side of the bed for an hour, stupefied, little strands of consciousness appearing and reappearing. But he did not move, for a long time he remained inert, his head dropped on his breast.

Then he looked up and realised that he was going to bed. He was cold. Soon he was lying down in the dark.

But what he could not bear was the darkness. The solid darkness confronting him drove him mad. So he rose, and made a light. He remained seated for a while, staring in front. He did not think of Gudrun, he did not think of anything.

Then suddenly he went downstairs for a book. He had all his life been in terror of the nights that should come, when he could not sleep. He knew that this would be too much for him, to have to face nights of sleeplessness and of horrified watching the hours.

So he sat for hours in bed, like a statue, reading. His mind, hard and acute, read on rapidly, his body understood nothing. In a state of rigid unconsciousness, he read on through the night, till morning, when, weary and disgusted in spirit, disgusted most of all with himself, he slept for two hours.

Then he got up, hard and full of energy. Gudrun scarcely spoke to him, except at coffee when she said:

'I shall be leaving to-morrow.'

'We will go together as far as Innsbruck, for appearance's sake?' he asked.

'Perhaps,' she said.

She said 'Perhaps' between the sips of her coffee. And the sound of her taking her breath in the word was naueous to him. He rose quickly to be away from her.

He went and made arrangements for the departure on the morrow. Then, taking some food, he set out for the day on the skis. Perhaps, he said to the *Wirt*, he would go up to the Marienhütte, perhaps to the village below.

To Gudrun this day was full of a promise like spring. She felt an approaching release, a new fountain of life rising up in her. It gave her pleasure to dawdle through her packing, it gave her pleasure to dip into books, to try on her different garments, to look at herself in the glass. She felt a new lease of life was come upon her, and she was happy like a child, very attractive and beautiful to everybody, with her soft, luxuriant figure, and her happiness. Yet underneath was death itself.

In the afternoon she had to go out with Loerke. Her tomorrow was perfectly vague before her. This was what gave her pleasure. She might be going to England with Gerald, she might be going to Dresden with Loerke, she might be going to Munich, to a girl-friend she had there. Anything might come to pass on the morrow. And to-day was the white, snowy iridescent threshold of all possibility. All possibility – that was the charm to her, the lovely, iridescent, indefinite charm – pure illusion. All possibility – because death was inevitable, and *nothing* was possible but death.

She did not want things to materialise, to take any definite shape. She wanted, suddenly, at one moment of the journey to-morrow, to be wafted into an utterly new course, by some utterly unforeseen event, or motion. So that, although she wanted to go out with Loerke for the last time into the snow, she did not want to be serious or business-like.

And Loerke was not a serious figure. In his brown velvet cap, that made his head as round as a chestnut, with the brown velvet flaps loose and wild over his ears, and a wisp of elf-like, thin black hair blowing above his full, elf-like dark eyes, the shiny, transparent brown skin crinkling up into odd grimaces on his small-featured face, he looked an odd little boy-man, a bat. But in his figure, in the greeny loden suit, he looked *chétif* and puny, still strangely different from the rest.

He had taken a little toboggan, for the two of them, and they trudged between the blinding slopes of snow, that burned their now hardening faces, laughing in an endless sequence of quips and jests and polyglot fancies. The fancies were the reality to both of them, they were both so happy, tossing about the little coloured balls of verbal humour and whimsicality. Their natures seemed to sparkle in full interplay, they were enjoying a pure game. And they wanted to keep it on the level of a game, their relationship: *such* a fine game.

Loerke did not take the tobogganing very seriously. He put no fire and intensity into it, as Gerald did. Which pleased Gudrun. She was weary, oh so weary of Gerald's gripped intensity of physical motion. Loerke let the sledge go wildly, and gaily, like a flying leaf, and when, at a bend, he pitched both her and him out into the snow, he only waited for them both to pick themselves up unhurt off the keen white ground, to be laughing and pert as a pixie. She knew he would be making ironical, playful remarks as he wandered in hell – if he were in the humour. And that pleased her immensely. It seemed like a rising above the dreariness of actuality, the monotony of contingencies.

They played till the sun went down, in pure amusement, careless and timeless. Then, as the little sledge twirled riskily to rest at the bottom of the slope:

'Wait!' he said suddenly, and he produced from somewhere a large thermos flask, a packet of Keks, and a bottle of Schnapps.

'Oh, Loerke,' she cried. 'What an inspiration! What a *comble de joie* indeed! What is the Schnapps?'

He looked at it, and laughed.

'*Heidelbeer!*' he said.

'No! From the bilberries under the snow.. Doesn't it look as if it were distilled from snow. Can you—' she sniffed, and sniffed at the bottle – 'can you smell bilberries? Isn't it wonderful? It is exactly as if one could smell them through the snow.'

She stamped her foot lightly on the ground. He kneeled down and whistled, and put his ear to the snow. As he did so his black eyes twinkled up.

'Ha! Ha!' she laughed, warmed by the whimsical way in which he mocked at her verbal extravagances. He was always teasing her, mocking her ways. But as he in his mockery was even more absurd than she in her extravagances, what could one do but laugh and feel liberated.

She could feel their voices, hers and his, ringing silvery like bells in the frozen, motionless air of the first twilight. How perfect it was, how *very* perfect it was, this silvery isolation and interplay.

She sipped the hot coffee, whose fragrance flew around them like bees murmuring around flowers, in the snowy air, she drank tiny sips of the *Heidelbeerwasser*, she ate the cold, sweet, creamy wafers. How good everything was! How perfect everything tasted and smelled and sounded, here in this utter stillness of snow and falling twilight.

'You are going away to-morrow?' his voice came at last.

'Yes.'

There was a pause, when the evening seemed to rise in its silent, ringing pallor infinitely high, to the infinite which was near at hand.

'*Wohin?*'

That was the question – *wohin?* Wither? *Wohin?* What a lovely word! She *never* wanted it answered. Let it chime for ever.

'I don't know,' she said, smiling at him.

He caught the smile from her.

'One never does,' he said.

'One never does,' she repeated.

There was a silence, wherein he ate biscuits rapidly, as a rabbit eats leaves.

'But,' he laughed, 'Where will you take a ticket to?'

'Oh heaven!' she cried. 'One must take a ticket.'

Here was a blow. She saw herself at the wicket, at the railway station. Then a relieving thought came to her. She breathed freely.

'But one needn't go,' she cried.

'Certainly not,' he said.

'I mean one needn't go where one's ticket says.'

That struck him. One might take a ticket, so as not to travel to the destination it indicated. One might break off, and avoid the destination. A point located. That was an idea!

'Then take a ticket to London,' he said. 'One should never go there.'

'Right,' she answered.

He poured a little coffee into a tin can.

'You won't tell me where you will go?' he asked.

'Really and truly,' she said, 'I don't know. It depends which way the wind blows.'

He looked at her quizzically, then he pursed up his lips, like Zephyrus, blowing across the snow.

'It goes towards Germany,' he said.

'I believe so,' she laughed.

Suddenly, they were aware of a vague white figure near them. It was Gerald. Gudrun's heart leapt in sudden terror, profound terror. She rose to her feet.

'They told me where you were,' came Gerald's voice, like a judgment in the whitish air of twilight.

'*Maria!*' You come like a ghost,' exclaimed Loerke.

Gerald did not answer. His presence was unnatural and ghostly to them.

Loerke shook the flask – then he held it inverted over the snow. Only a few brown drops trickled out.

'All gone!' he said.

To Gerald, the smallish, odd figure of the German was distinct and objective, as if seen through field glasses. And he disliked the small figure exceedingly, he wanted it removed.

Then Loerke rattled the box which held the biscuits.

'Biscuits there are still,' he said.

And reaching from his seated posture in the sledge, he handed them to Gudrun. She fumbled, and took one. He would have held them to Gerald, but Gerald so definitely did not want to be offered a biscuit, that Loerke, rather vaguely, put the box aside. Then he took up the small bottle and held it to the light.

'Also there is some Schnapps,' he said to himself.

Then suddenly, he elevated the bottle gallantly in the air, a strange, grotesque figure leaning towards Gudrun, and said:

'*Gnädiges Fräulein*,' he said, '*wohl—*'

There was a crack, the bottle was flying, Loerke had started back, the three stood quivering in violent emotion.

Loerke turned to Gerald, a devilish leer on his bright-skinned face.

'Well done!' he said, in a satirical demoniac frenzy. '*C'est le sport, sans doute.*'

The next instant he was sitting ludicrously in the snow, Gerald's fist having rung against the side of his head. But Loerke pulled himself together, rose, quivering, looking full at Gerald, his body weak and furtive, but his eyes demoniacal with satire.

'*Vive le héros, vive—*'

But he flinched as, in a black flash, Gerald's fist came upon him, banged into the other side of his head, and sent him aside like a broken straw.

But Gudrun moved forward. She raised her clenched hand high, and brought it down, with a great downward stroke on to the face and on to the breast of Gerald.

A great astonishment burst upon him, as if the air had broken. Wide, wide his soul opened, in wonder, feeling the pain. Then it laughed, turning, with strong hands outstretched, at last to take the apple of his desire. At last he could finish his desire.

He took the throat of Gudrun between his hands, that were hard and indomitably powerful. And her throat was beautifully, so beautifully soft, save that, within, he could feel the slippery chords of her life. And this he crushed, this he could crush. What bliss! Oh what bliss, at last, what satisfaction, at last! The pure zest of satisfaction filled his soul. He was watching the unconsciousness come into her swollen face, watching the eyes roll back. How ugly she was! What a fulfilment, what a satisfaction! How good this was, oh how good it was, what a God-given gratification, at last! He was unconscious of her fighting and struggling. The struggling was her reciprocal lustful passion in this embrace, the more violent it became, the greater the frenzy of delight, till the zenith was reached, the crisis, the struggle was overborne, her movement became softer, appeased.

Loerke roused himself on the snow, too dazed and hurt to get up. Only his eyes were conscious.

'*Monsieur!*' he said in his thin, roused voice: '*Quand vous aurez fini—*'

A revulsion of contempt and disgust came over Gerald's soul. The disgust went to the very bottom of him, a nausea. Ah, what was he doing, to what depths was he letting himself go! As if he cared about her enough to kill her, to have her life on his hands!

A weakness ran over his body, a terrible relaxing, a thaw, a decay of strength. Without knowing, he had let go his grip, and Gudrun had fallen to her knees. Must he see, must he know?

A fearful weakness possessed him, his joints were turned to water. He drifted, as on a wind, veered, and went drifting away.

'I didn't want it, really,' was the last confession of disgust in his soul, as he drifted up the slope, weak, finished, only sheering off unconsciously from any further contact. 'I've had enough – I want to go to sleep. I've had enough.' He was sunk under a sense of nausea.

He was weak, but he did not want to rest, he wanted to go on and on, to the end. Never again to stay, till he came to the end, that was all the desire that remained to him. So he drifted on and on, unconscious and weak, not thinking of anything, so long as he could keep in action.

The twilight spread a weird, unearthly light overhead, bluish-rose in colour, the cold blue night sank on the snow. In the valley below, behind, in the great bed of snow, were two small figures; Gudrun dropped on her knees, like one executed, and Loerke sitting propped up near her. That was all.

Gerald stumbled on up the slope of snow, in the bluish darkness, always climbing, always unconsciously climbing, weary though he was. On his left was a steep slope with black rocks and fallen masses of rock and veins of snow slashing in and about the blackness of rock, veins of snow slashing vaguely in and about the blackness of rock. Yet there was no sound, all this made no noise.

To add to his difficulty, a small bright moon shone brilliantly just ahead, on the right, a painful brilliant thing that was always there, unremitting, from which there was no escape. He wanted so to come to the end – he had had enough. Yet he did not sleep.

He surged painfully up, sometimes having to cross a slope of black rock, that was blown bare of snow. Here he was afraid of falling, very much afraid of falling. And high up here, on the crest, moved a wind that almost overpowered him with a sleep-heavy iciness. Only it was not here, the end, and he must still go on. His indefinite nausea would not let him stay.

Having gained one ridge, he saw the vague shadow of something higher in front. Always higher, always higher. He knew he was following the track towards the summit of the slopes, where was the Marienhütte, and the descent on the other side. But he was not really conscious. He only wanted to go on, to go on whilst he could, to move, to keep going, that was all, to keep going, until it was finished. He had lost all his sense of place. And yet in the remaining instinct of life, his feet sought the track where the skis had gone.

He slithered down a sheer snow slope. That frightened him. He had no alpenstock, nothing. But having come safely to rest, he began to walk on in the illuminated darkness. It was as cold as sleep. He was between two ridges in a hollow. So he swerved. Should he climb the other ridge or wander along the hollow? How frail the thread of his being was stretched! He would perhaps climb the ridge. The snow was firm and simple. He went along. There was something standing out of the snow. He approached with dimmest curiosity.

It was a half-buried crucifix, a little Christ under a little sloping hood at the top of a pole. He sheered away. Somebody was going to murder him. He had a great dread of being murdered. But it was a dread which stood outside him like his own ghost.

Yet why be afraid? It was bound to happen. To be murdered! He looked round in terror at the snow, the rocking, pale, shadowy slopes of the upper world. He was bound to be murdered, he could see it. This was the moment when the death was uplifted, and there was no escape.

Lord Jesus, was it then bound to be – Lord Jesus! He could feel the blow descending, he knew he was murdered. Vaguely wandering forward, his hands lifted as if to feel what would happen, he was waiting for the moment when he would stop, when it would cease. It was not over yet.

He had come to the hollow basin of snow, surrounded by sheer slopes and precipices, out of which rose a track that brought one to the top of the mountain. But he wandered unconsciously, till he slipped and fell down, and as he fell something broke in his soul, and immediately he went to sleep.

Chapter Thirty-one

Exeunt

When they brought the body home the next morning, Gudrun was shut up in her room. From her window she saw men coming along with a burden over the snow. She sat still and let the minutes go by.

There came a tap at her door. She opened. There stood a woman, saying softly, oh, far too reverently:

'They have found him, madam!'

'*Il est mort?*'

'Yes – hours ago.'

Gudrun did not know what to say. What should she say? What should she feel? What should she do? What did they expect of her? She was coldly at a loss.

'Thank you,' she said, and she shut the door of her room. The woman went away mortified. Not a word, not a tear – ha! Gudrun was cold, a cold woman.

Gudrun sat on in her room, her face pale and impassive. What was she to do! She could not weep and make a scene. She could not alter herself. She sat motionless, hiding from people. Her one motive was to avoid actual contact with events. She only wrote out a long telegram to Ursula and Birkin.

In the afternoon, however, she rose suddenly to look for Loerke. She glanced with apprehension at the door of the room that had been Gerald's. Not for worlds would she enter there.

She found Loerke sitting alone in the lounge. She went straight up to him.

'It isn't true, is it?' she said.

He looked up at her. A small smile of misery twisted his face. He shrugged his shoulders.

'True?' he echoed.

'We haven't killed him?' she asked.

He disliked her coming to him in such a manner. He raised his shoulders wearily.

'It has happened,' he said.

She looked at him. He sat crushed and frustrated for the time being, quite as emotionless and barren as herself. My God! this was a barren tragedy, barren, barren.

She returned to her room to wait for Ursula and Birkin. She wanted to get away, only to get away. She could not think or feel until she had got away, till she was loosened from this position.

The day passed, the next day came. She heard the sledge, saw Ursula and Birkin alight, and she shrank from these also.

Ursula came straight up to her.

'Gudrun!' she cried, the tears running down her cheeks. And she took her sister in her arms. Gudrun hid her face on Ursula's shoulder, but still she could not escape the cold devil of irony that froze her soul.

'Ha, ha!' she thought, 'this is the right behaviour.'

But she could not weep, and the sight of her cold, pale, impassive face soon stopped the fountain of Ursula's tears. In a few moments, the sisters had nothing to say to each other.

'Was it very vile to be dragged back here again?' Gudrun asked at length.

Ursula looked up in some bewilderment.

'I never thought of it,' she said.

'I felt a beast, fetching you,' said Gudrun. 'But I simply couldn't see people. That is too much for me.'

'Yes,' said Ursula, chilled.

Birkin tapped and entered. His face was white and expressionless. She knew he knew. He gave her his hand, saying:

'The end of *this* trip, at any rate.'

Gudrun glanced at him, afraid.

There was silence between the three of them, nothing to be said. At length Ursula asked in a small voice:

'Have you seen him?'

He looked back at Ursula with a hard, cold look, and did not trouble to answer.

'Have you seen him?' she repeated.

'I have,' he said coldly.

Then he looked at Gudrun.

'Have you done anything?' he said.

'Nothing,' she replied, 'nothing.'

She shrank in cold disgust from making any statement.

'Loerke says that Gerald came to you when you were sitting on the sledge at the bottom of the Rudelbahn, that you had words, and Gerald walked away. What were the words about? I had better know, so that I can satisfy the authorities, if necessary.'

Gudrun looked up at him, white, childlike, mute with trouble.

'There weren't even any words,' she said. 'He knocked Loerke down and stunned him, he half strangled me, then he went away.'

To herself she was saying:

'A pretty little sample of the eternal triangle!' And she turned ironically away, because she knew that the fight had been between Gerald and herself and that the presence of the third party was a mere contingency – an inevitable contingency perhaps, but a contingency none the less. But let them have it as an example of the eternal triangle, the trinity of hate. It would be simpler for them.

Birkin went away, his manner cold and abstracted. But she knew he would do things for her, nevertheless, he would see her through. She smiled slightly to herself, with contempt. Let him do the work, since he was so extremely *good* at looking after other people.

Birkin went again to Gerald. He had loved him. And yet he felt chiefly disgust at the inert body lying there. It was so inert, so coldly dead, a carcase, Birkin's bowels seemed to turn to ice. He had to stand and look at the frozen dead body that had been Gerald.

It was the frozen carcase of a dead male. Birkin remembered a rabbit which he had once found frozen like a board on the snow. It had been rigid like a dried board when he picked it up. And now this was Gerald, stiff as a board, curled up as if for sleep, yet with the horrible hardness somehow evident. It filled him with horror. The room must be made warm, the body must be thawed. The limbs would break like glass or like wood if they had to be straightened.

He reached and touched the dead face. And the sharp, heavy bruise of ice bruised his living bowels. He wondered if he himself were freezing too, freezing from the inside. In the short blond moustache the life breath was frozen into a block of ice beneath the silent nostrils. And this was Gerald!

Again he touched the sharp, almost glittering fair hair of the frozen body. It was icy-cold, hair icy-cold, almost venomous. Birkin's heart began to freeze. He had loved Gerald. Now he looked at the shapely, strange-coloured face, with the small, fine, pinched nose and the manly cheeks, saw it frozen like an ice pebble – yet he had loved it. What was one to think or feel? His brain was beginning to freeze, his blood was turning to ice-water. So cold, so cold, a heavy, bruising cold pressing on his arms from outside, and a heavier cold congealing within him, in his heart and in his bowels.

He went over the snow slopes to see where the death had been. At last he came to the great shallow among the precipices and slopes, near the summit of the pass. It was a grey day, the third day of greyness and stillness. All was white, icy, pallid, save for the scoring of black rocks that jutted like roots sometimes, and sometimes were in naked faces. In the distance a slope sheered down from a peak, with many black rock-slides.

It was like a shallow pot lying among the stone and snow of the upper world. In this pot Gerald had gone to sleep. At the far end, the guides had driven iron stakes deep into the snow-wall, so that, by means of the great rope attached, they could haul themselves up the massive snow-front, out on to the jagged summit of the pass, naked to heaven, where the Marienhütte hid among the naked rocks. Round about, spiked, slashed snow-peaks pricked the heaven.

Gerald might have found this rope. He might have hauled himself up to the crest. He might have heard the dogs in the Marienhütte, and found shelter. He might have gone on down the steep, steep fall of the south side, down into the dark valley with its pines, on to the great Imperial road leading south to Italy.

He might! And what then? The Imperial road! The south? Italy? What then? Was it a way out? It was only a way in again. Birkin stood high in the painful air, looking at the peaks and the way south. Was it any good going south, to Italy? Down the old, old Imperial road?

He turned away. Either the heart would break or cease to care. Best cease to care. Whatever the mystery which has brought forth man and the universe, it is a non-human mystery, it has its own great ends, man is not the criterion. Best leave it all to the vast, creative, non-human mystery. Best strive with oneself only, not with the universe.

'God cannot do without man.' It was a saying of some great French religious teacher. But surely this is false. God can do without man. God could do without the ichthyosauri and the mastodon. These monsters failed creatively to develop, so God, the creative mystery, dispensed with them. In the same way the mystery could dispense with man, should he too fail creatively to change and develop. The eternal creative mystery could dispose of man, and replace him with a finer created being. Just as the horse has taken the place of the mastodon.

It was very consoling to Birkin to think this. If humanity ran into a cul-de-sac, and expended itself, the timeless creative mystery would bring forth some other being, finer, more wonderful, some new, more lovely race, to carry on the embodiment of creation. The game was never up. The mystery of creation was fathomless, infallible, inexhaustible, for ever. Races came and went, species passed away, but ever new species arose, more lovely, or equally lovely, always surpassing wonder. The fountain-head was incorruptible and unsearchable. It had no limits. It could bring forth miracles, create utter new races and new species in its own hour, new forms of consciousness, new forms of body, new units of being. To be man was as nothing compared to the possibilities of the creative mystery. To have one's pulse beating direct from the mystery, this was perfection, unutterable satisfaction. Human or inhuman mattered nothing. The perfect pulse throbbed with indescribable being, miraculous unborn species.

Birkin went home again to Gerald. He went into the room and sat down on the bed. Dead, dead and cold!

'Imperial Caesar dead and turned to clay
Would stop a hole to keep the wind away.'

There was no response from that which had been Gerald. Strange, congealed, icy substance – no more. No more!

Terribly weary, Birkin went away, about the day's business. He did it all quietly, without bother. To rant, to rave, to be tragic, to make situations – it was all too late. Best be quiet, and bear one's soul in patience and in fullness.

But when he went in again, at evening, to look at Gerald between the candles, because of his heart's hunger, suddenly his heart contracted, his own candle all but fell from his hand, as, with a strange whimpering cry, the tears broke out. He sat down in a chair, shaken by a sudden access. Ursula, who had followed him, recoiled aghast from him as he sat with sunken head and body convulsively shaken, making a strange, horrible sound of tears.

'I didn't want it to be like this – I didn't want it to be like this,' he cried
to himself. Ursula could but think of the Kaiser's: '*Ich habe es nicht gewollt.*'
She looked almost with horror on Birkin.

Suddenly he was silent. But he sat with his head dropped to hide his face.
Then furtively he wiped his face with his fingers. Then suddenly he lifted
his head and looked straight at Ursula with dark, almost vengeful eyes.

'He should have loved me,' he said. 'I offered him.'

She, afraid, white, with mute lips, answered:

'What difference would it have made!'

'It would!' he said. 'It would.'

He forgot her and turned to look at Gerald. With head oddly lifted, like
a man who draws his head back from an insult, half haughtily, he watched
the cold, mute, material face. It had a bluish cast. It sent a shaft like ice
through the heart of the living man. Cold, mute, material! Birkin remembered
how once Gerald had clutched his hand with a warm, momentaneous grip
of final love. For one second – then let go again, let go for ever. If he had
kept true to that clasp, death would not have mattered. Those who die, and
dying still can love, still believe, do not die. They live still in the beloved.
Gerald might still have been living in the spirit with Birkin, even after death.
He might have lived with his friend, a further life.

But now he was dead, like clay, like bluish, corruptible ice. Birkin looked
at the pale fingers, the inert mass. He remembered a dead stallion he had
seen: a dead mass of maleness, repugnant. He remembered also the beautiful
face of one whom he had loved, and who had died still having the faith to
yield to the mystery. That dead face was beautiful, no one could call it cold,
mute, material. No one could remember it without gaining faith in the
mystery, without the soul's warming with new, deep life trust.

And Gerald! The denier! He left the heart cold, frozen, hardly able to
beat. Gerald's father had looked wistful, to break the heart: but not this last
terrible look of cold, mute Matter. Birkin watched and watched.

Ursula stood aside watching the living man stare at the frozen face of the
dead man. Both faces were unmoved and unmoving. The candle-flames
flickered in the frozen air in the intense silence.

'Haven't you seen enough?' she said.

He got up.

'It's a bitter thing to me,' he said.

'What – that he's dead?' she said.

His eyes just met hers. He did not answer.

'You've got me,' she said.

He smiled and kissed her.

'If I die,' he said, 'you'll know I haven't left you.'

'And me?' she cried.

'And you won't have left me,' he said. 'We shan't have any need to
despair, in death.'

She took hold of his hand.

'But need you despair over Gerald?' she said.

'Yes,' he answered.

They went away. Gerald was taken to England to be buried. Birkin and

Ursula accompanied the body, along with one of Gerald's brothers. It was the Crich brothers and sisters who insisted on the burial in England. Birkin wanted to leave the dead man in the Alps, near the snow. But the family was strident, loudly insistent.

Gudrun went to Dresden. She wrote no particulars of herself. Ursula stayed at the Mill with Birkin for a week or two. They were both very quiet.

'Did you need Gerald?' she asked one evening.

'Yes,' he said.

'Aren't I enough for you?' she asked.

'No,' he said. 'You are enough for me, as far as a woman is concerned. You are all women to me. But I wanted a man friend, as eternal as you and I are eternal.'

'Why aren't I enough?' she said. 'You are enough for me. I don't want anybody else but you. Why isn't it the same with you?'

'Having you, I can live all my life without anybody else, any other sheer intimacy. But to make it complete, really happy, I wanted eternal union with a man too: another kind of love,' he said.

'I don't believe it,' she said. 'It's an obstinacy, a theory, a perversity.'

'Well—' he said.

'You can't have two kinds of love. Why should you!'

'It seems as if I can't,' he said. 'Yet I wanted it.'

'You can't have it, because it's false, impossible,' she said.

'I don't believe that,' he answered.

The
Ladybird

The Ladybird

How many swords had Lady Beveridge in her pierced heart! Yet there always seemed room for another. Since she had determined that her heart of pity and kindness should never die. If it had not been for this determination she herself might have died of sheer agony, in the years 1916 and 1917, when her boys were killed, and her brother, and death seemed to be mowing with wide swaths through her family. But let us forget.

Lady Beveridge loved humanity, and come what might, she would continue to love it. Nay, in the human sense, she would love her enemies. Not the criminals among the enemy, the men who committed atrocities. But the men who were enemies through no choice of their own. She would be swept into no general hate.

Somebody had called her the soul of England. It was not ill said, though she was half Irish. But of an old, aristocratic, loyal family famous for its brilliant men. And she, Lady Beveridge, had for years as much influence on the tone of English politics as any individual alive. The close friend of the real leaders in the House of Lords and in the Cabinet, she was content that the men should act, so long as they breathed from her as from the rose of life the pure fragrance of truth and genuine love. She had no misgiving regarding her own spirit.

She, she would never lower her delicate silken flag. For instance, throughout all the agony of the war she never forgot the enemy prisoners; she was determined to do her best for them. During the first years she still had influence. But during the last years of the war power slipped out of the hands of her and her sort, and she found she could do nothing any more: almost nothing. Then it seemed as if the many swords had gone home into the heart of this little, unyielding Mater Dolorosa. The new generation jeered at her. She was a shabby, old-fashioned little aristocrat, and her drawing-room was out of date.

But we anticipate. The years 1916 and 1917 were the years when the old spirit died for ever in England. But Lady Beveridge struggled on. She was being beaten.

It was in the winter of 1917 – or in the late autumn. She had been for a fortnight sick, stricken, paralysed by the fearful death of her youngest boy. She felt she *must* give in, and just die. And then she remembered how many others were lying in agony.

So she rose, trembling, frail, to pay a visit to the hospital where lay the enemy sick and wounded, near London. Countess Beveridge was still a privileged woman. Society was beginning to jeer at this little, worn bird of an out-of-date righteousness and aesthetic. But they dared not think ill of her.

She ordered the car and went alone. The Earl, her husband, had taken his gloom to Scotland. So, on a sunny, wan November morning Lady Beveridge descended at the hospital, Hurst Place. The guard knew her, and saluted as she passed. Ah, she was used to such deep respect! It was strange that she felt it so bitterly, when the respect became shallower. But she did. It was the beginning of the end to her.

The matron went with her into the ward. Alas, the beds were all full, and men were even lying on pallets on the floor. There was a desperate, crowded dreariness and helplessness in the place: as if nobody wanted to make a sound or utter a word. Many of the men were haggard and unshaven, one was delirious, and talking fitfully in the Saxon dialect. It went to Lady Beveridge's heart. She had been educated in Dresden, and had had many dear friendships in the city. Her children also had been educated there. She heard the Saxon dialect with pain.

She was a little, frail, bird-like woman, elegant, but with that touch of the blue-stocking of the 'Nineties which was unmistakable. She fluttered delicately from bed to bed, speaking in perfect German, but with a thin, English intonation: and always asking if there was anything she could do. The men were mostly officers and gentlemen. They made little requests which she wrote down in a book. Her long, pale, rather worn face, and her nervous little gestures somehow inspired confidence.

One man lay quite still, with his eyes shut. He had a black beard. His face was rather small and sallow. He might be dead. Lady Beveridge looked at him earnestly, and fear came into her face.

'Why, Count Dionys!' she said, fluttered. 'Are you asleep?'

It was Count Johann Dionys Psanek, a Bohemian. She had known him when he was a boy, and only in the spring of 1914 he and his wife had stayed with Lady Beveridge in her country house in Leicestershire.

His black eyes opened: large, black, unseeing eyes, with curved black lashes. He was a small man, small as a boy, and his face too was rather small. But all the lines were fine, as if they had been fired with a keen male energy. Now the yellowish swarthy paste of his flesh seemed dead, and the fine black brows seemed drawn on the face of one dead. The eyes, however, were alive: but only just alive, unseeing and unknowing.

'You know me, Count Dionys? You know me, don't you?' said Lady Beveridge, bending forward over the bed.

There was no reply for some time. Then the black eyes gathered a look of recognition, and there came the ghost of a polite smile.

'Lady Beveridge.' The lips formed the words. There was practically no sound.

'I am so glad you can recognise me. And I am so sorry you are hurt. I am so sorry.'

The black eyes watched her from that terrible remoteness of death, without changing.

'There is nothing I can do for you? Nothing at all?' she said, always speaking German.

And after a time, and from a distance, came the answer from his eyes, a look of weariness, of refusal, and a wish to be left alone; he was unable to strain himself into consciousness. His eyelids dropped.

'I am so sorry,' she said. 'If ever there is anything I can do— '

The eyes opened again, looking at her. He seemed at last to hear, and it was as if his eyes made the last weary gesture of a polite bow. Then slowly his eyelids closed again.

Poor Lady Beveridge felt another sword-thrust of sorrow in her heart, as she stood looking down at the motionless face, and at the black fine beard. The black hairs came out of his skin thin and fine, not very close together. A queer, dark, aboriginal little face he had, with a fine little nose: not an Aryan, surely. And he was going to die.

He had a bullet through the upper part of his chest, and another bullet had broken one of his ribs. He had been in hospital five days.

Lady Beveridge asked the matron to ring her up if anything happened. Then she drove away, saddened. Instead of going to Beveridge House, she went to her daughter's flat near the park – near Hyde Park. Lady Daphne was poor. She had married a commoner, son of one of the most famous politicians in England, but a man with no money. And Earl Beveridge had wasted most of the large fortune that had come to him, so that the daughter had very little, comparatively.

Lady Beveridge suffered, going in the narrow doorway into the rather ugly flat. Lady Daphne was sitting by the electric fire in the small yellow drawing-room, talking to a visitor. She rose at once, seeing her little mother.

'Why, mother, ought you to be out? I'm sure not.'

'Yes, Daphne darling. Of course I ought to be out.'

'How are you?' The daughter's voice was slow and sonorous, protective, sad. Lady Daphne was tall, only twenty-five years old. She had been one of the beauties, when the war broke out, and her father had hoped she would make a splendid match. Truly, she had married fame: but without money. Now, sorrow, pain, thwarted passion had done her great damage. Her husband was missing in the East. Her baby had been born dead. Her two darling brothers were dead. And she was ill, always ill.

A tall, beautifully-built girl, she had the fine stature of her father. Her shoulders were still straight. But how thin her white throat! She wore a simple black frock stitched with coloured wool round the top, and held in a loose coloured girdle: otherwise no ornaments. And her face was lovely, fair, with a soft exotic white complexion and delicate pink cheeks. Her hair was soft and heavy, of a lovely pallid gold colour, ash-blond. Her hair, her complexion were so perfectly cared for as to be almost artificial, like a hot-house flower.

But alas, her beauty was a failure. She was threatened with phthisis, and was far too thin. Her eyes were the saddest part of her. They had slightly reddened rims, nerve-worn, with heavy, veined lids that seemed as if they did not want to keep up. The eyes themselves were large and of a beautiful green-blue colour. But they were full, languid, almost glaucous.

Standing as she was, a tall, finely-built girl, looking down with affectionate care on her mother, she filled the heart with ashes. The little pathetic mother, so wonderful in her way, was not really to be pitied for all her sorrow. Her life was in her sorrows, and her efforts on behalf of the sorrows of others. But Daphne was not born for grief and philanthropy. With her splendid frame, and her lovely, long, strong legs, she was Artemis or Atalanta rather than Daphne. There was a certain width of brow and even of chin that spoke a strong, reckless nature, and the curious, distraught slant of her eyes told of a wild energy dammed up inside her.

That was what ailed her: her own wild energy. She had it from her father, and from her father's desperate race. The earldom had begun with a riotous, dare-devil border soldier, and this was the blood that flowed on. And alas, what was to be done with it?

Daphne had married an adorable husband: truly an adorable husband. Whereas she needed a dare-devil. But in her *mind* she hated all dare-devils: she had been brought up by her mother to admire only the good.

So, her reckless, anti-philanthropic passion could find no outlet – and *should* find no outlet, she thought. So her own blood turned against her, beat on her own nerves, and destroyed her. It was nothing but frustration and anger which made her ill, and made the doctors fear consumption. There it was, drawn on her rather wide mouth: frustration, anger, bitterness. There it was the same in the roll of her green-blue eyes, a slanting, averted look: the same anger furtively turning back on itself. This anger reddened her eyes and shattered her nerves. And yet her whole will was fixed in her adoption of her mother's creed, and in condemnation of her handsome, proud, brutal father, who had made so much misery in the family. Yes, her will was fixed in the determination that life should be gentle and good and benevolent. Whereas her blood was reckless, the blood of dare-devils. Her will was the stronger of the two. But her blood had its revenge on her. So it is with strong natures to-day: shattered from the inside.

'You have no news, darling?' asked the mother.

'No. My father-in-law had information that British prisoners had been brought into Hasrun, and that details would be forwarded by the Turks. And there was a rumour from some Arab prisoners that Basil was one of the British brought in wounded.'

'When did you hear this?'

'Primrose came in this morning.'

'Then we can hope, dear.'

'Yes.'

Never was anything more dull and bitter than Daphne's affirmative of hope. Hope had become almost a curse to her. She wished there need be no such thing. Ha, the torment of hoping, and the *insult* to one's soul. Like the importunate widow dunning for her deserts. Why could it not all be just clean disaster, and have done with it? This dilly-dallying with despair was worse than despair. She had hoped so much: ah, for her darling brothers she had hoped with such anguish. And the two she loved best were dead. So were most others she had hoped for, dead. Only this uncertainty about her husband still rankling.

'You feel better, dear?' said the little, unquenched mother.

'Rather better,' came the resentful answer.

'And your night?'

'No better.'

There was a pause.

'You are coming to lunch with me, Daphne darling?'

'No, mother dear. I promised to lunch at the Howards with Primrose. But I needn't go for a quarter of an hour. Do sit down.'

Both women seated themselves near the electric fire. There was that bitter pause, neither knowing what to say. Then Daphne roused herself to look at her mother.

'Are you sure you were fit to go out?' she said. 'What took you out so suddenly?'

'I went to Hurst Place, dear. I had the men on my mind, after the way the newspapers have been talking.'

'Why ever do you read the newspapers!' blurted Daphne, with a certain burning, acid anger. 'Well,' she said, more composed. 'And do you feel better now you've been?'

'So many people suffer besides ourselves, darling.'

'I know they do. Makes it all the worse. It wouldn't matter if it were only just us. At least, it would matter, but one could bear it more easily. To be just one of a crowd all in the same state.'

'And some even worse, dear.'

'Oh, quite! And the worse it is for all, the worse it is for one.'

'Is that so, darling? Try not to see too darkly. I feel if I can give just a little bit of myself to help the others – you know – it alleviates me. I feel that what I can give to the men lying there, Daphne, I give to my own boys. I can only help them now through helping others. But I can still do that, Daphne, my girl.'

And the mother put her little white hand into the long, white, cold hand of her daughter. Tears came to Daphne's eyes, and a fearful stony grimace to her mouth.

'It's so wonderful of you that you can feel like that,' she said.

'But you feel the same, my love. I know you do.'

'No, I don't. Everyone I see suffering these same awful things, it makes me wish more for the end of the world. And I quite see that the world won't end— '

'But it will get better, dear. This time it's like a great sickness – like a terrible pneumonia tearing the breast of the world.'

'Do you believe it will get better? I don't.'

'It will get better. Of course it will get better. It is perverse to think otherwise, Daphne. Remember what *has* been before, even in Europe. Ah, Daphne, we must take a bigger view.'

'Yes, I suppose we must.'

The daughter spoke rapidly, from the lips, in a resonant, monotonous tone. The mother spoke from the heart.

'And Daphne, I found an old friend among the men at Hurst Place.'

'Who?'

'Little Count Dionys. You remember him?'

'Quite. What's wrong?'

'Wounded rather badly – through the chest. So ill.'

'Did you speak to him?'

'Yes. I recognised him in spite of his beard.'

'Beard!'

'Yes – a black beard. I suppose he could not be shaven. It seems strange that he is still alive, poor man.'

'Why strange? He isn't old. How old is he?'

'Between thirty and forty. But so ill, so wounded, Daphne. And so small. So small, so sallow – *smorto*, you know the Italian word. The way dark people look. There is something so distressing in it.'

'Does he look *very* small now – uncanny?' asked the daughter.

'No, not uncanny. Something of the terrible far-awayness of a child that is very ill and can't tell you what hurts it. Poor Count Dionys, Daphne. I didn't know, dear, that his eyes were so black, and his lashes so curved and long. I had never thought of him as beautiful.'

'Nor I. Only a little comical. Such a dapper little man.'

'Yes. And yet now, Daphne, there is something remote and in a sad way heroic in his dark face. Something primitive.'

'What did he say to you?'

'He couldn't speak to me. Only with his lips, just my name.'

'So bad as that?'

'Oh yes. They are afraid he will die.'

'Poor Count Dionys. I liked him. He was a bit like a monkey, but he had his points. He gave me a thimble on my seventeenth birthday. Such an amusing thimble.'

'I remember, dear.'

'Unpleasant wife, though. Wonder if he minds dying far away from her. Wonder if she knows.'

'I think not. They didn't even know his name properly. Only that he was a colonel of such and such a regiment.'

'Fourth Cavalry,' said Daphne. 'Poor Count Dionys. Such a lovely name, I always thought: Count Johann Dionys Psanek. Extraordinary dandy he was. And an amazingly good dancer, small, yet electric. Wonder if he minds dying.'

'He was so full of life, in his own little animal way. They say small people are always conceited. But he doesn't look conceited now, dear. Something ages old in his face – and, yes, a certain beauty, Daphne.'

'You mean long lashes.'

'No. So still, so solitary – and ages old, in his race. I suppose he must belong to one of those curious little aboriginal races of Central Europe. I felt quite new beside him.'

'How nice of you,' said Daphne.

Nevertheless, next day Daphne telephoned to Hurst Place to ask for news of him. He was about the same. She telephoned every day. Then she was told he was a little stronger. The day she received the message that her husband was wounded and a prisoner in Turkey, and that his wounds were healing, she forgot to telephone for news of the little enemy Count. And the following day she telephoned that she was coming to the hospital to see him.

He was awake, more restless, more in physical excitement. They could see the nausea of pain round his nose. His face seemed to Daphne curiously hidden behind the black beard, which nevertheless was thin, each hair coming thin and fine, singly, from the sallow, slightly translucent skin. In the same way his moustache made a thin black line round his mouth. His eyes were wide open, very black, and of no legible expression. He watched the two women coming down the crowded, dreary room, as if he did not see them. His eyes seemed too wide.

It was a cold day, and Daphne was huddled in a black sealskin coat with a skunk collar pulled up to her ears, and a dull gold cap with wings pulled down on her brow. Lady Beveridge wore her sable coat, and had that odd, untidy elegance which was natural to her, rather like a ruffled chicken.

Daphne was upset by the hospital. She looked from right to left in spite of herself, and everything gave her a dull feeling of horror: the terror of these sick, wounded enemy men. She looked tall and obtrusive in her furs by the bed, her little mother at her side.

'I hope you don't mind my coming!' she said in German to the sick man. Her tongue felt rusty, speaking the language.

'Who is it then?' he asked.

'It is my daughter, Lady Daphne. You remembered *me*, Lady Beveridge! This is my daughter, whom you knew in Saxony. She was so sorry to hear you were wounded.'

The black eyes rested on the little lady. Then they returned to the looming figure of Daphne. And a certain fear grew on the low, sick brow. It was evident the presence loomed and frightened him. He turned his face aside. Daphne noticed how his fine black hair grew uncut over his small, animal ears.

'You don't remember me, Count Dionys?' she said dully.

'Yes,' he said. But he kept his face averted.

She stood there feeling confused and miserable, as if she had made a *faux pas* in coming.

'Would you rather be left alone?' she said. 'I'm sorry.'

Her voice was monotonous. She felt suddenly stifled in her closed furs, and threw her coat open, showing her thin white throat and plain black slip dress on her flat breast. He turned again unwillingly to look at her. He looked at her as if she were some strange creature standing near him.

'Good-bye,' she said. 'Do get better.'

She was looking at him with a queer, slanting, downward look of her heavy eyes as she turned away. She was still a little red round the eyes, with nervous exhaustion.

'You are so tall,' he said, still frightened.

'I was always tall,' she replied, turning half to him again.

'And I, small,' he said.

'I am so glad you are getting better,' she said.

'I am not glad,' he said.

'Why? I'm sure you are. Just as we are glad because we want you to get better.'

'Thank you,' he said. 'I have wished to die.'

'Don't do that, Count Dionys. Do get better,' she said, in the rather deep, laconic manner of her girlhood. He looked at her with a farther look of recognition. But his short, rather pointed nose was lifted with the disgust and weariness of pain, his brows were tense. He watched her with that curious flame of suffering which is forced to give a little outside attention, but which speaks only to itself.

'Why did they not let me die?' he said. 'I wanted death now.'

'No,' she said. 'You mustn't. You must live. If we *can* live we must.'

'I wanted death,' he said.

'Ah, well,' she said, 'even death we can't have when we want it, or when we think we want it.'

'That is true,' he said, watching her with the same wide black eyes. 'Please to sit down. You are too tall as you stand.'

It was evident he was a little frightened still by her looming, overhanging figure.

'I am sorry I am too tall,' she said, taking a chair which a man-nurse had brought her. Lady Beveridge had gone away to speak with the men. Daphne sat down, not knowing what to say further. The pitch-black look in the Count's wide eyes puzzled her.

'Why do you come here? Why does your lady mother come?' he said.

'To see if we can do anything,' she answered.

'When I am well, I will thank your ladyship.'

'All right,' she replied. 'When you are well I will let my lord the Count thank me. Please do get well.'

'We are enemies,' he said.

'Who? You and I and my mother?'

'Are we not? The most difficult thing is to be sure of anything. If they had let me die!'

'That is at least ungrateful, Count Dionys.'

'*Lady Daphne!* Yes. *Lady Daphne!* Beautiful, the name is. You are always called Lady Daphne? I remember you were so bright a maiden.'

'More or less,' she said, answering his question.

'Ach! We should all have new names now. I thought of a name for myself, but I have forgotten it. No longer Johann Dionys. That is shot away. I am Karl or Wilhelm or Ernst or Georg. Those are names I hate. Do you hate them?'

'I don't like them – but I don't hate them. And you mustn't leave off being Count Johann Dionys. If you do I shall have to leave off being Daphne. I like your name so much.'

'Lady Daphne! Lady Daphne!' he repeated. 'Yes, it rings well, it sounds beautiful to me. I think I talk foolishly. I hear myself talking foolishly to you.' He looked at her anxiously.

'Not at all,' she said.

'Ach! I have a head on my shoulders that is like a child's windmill, and

I can't prevent its making foolish words. Please to go away, not to hear me. I can hear myself.'

'Can't I do anything for you?' she asked.

'No, no! No, no! If I could be buried deep, very deep down, where everything is forgotten! But they draw me up, back to the surface. I would not mind if they buried me alive, if it were very deep, and dark, and the earth heavy above.'

'Don't say that,' she replied, rising.

'No, I am saying it when I don't wish to say it. Why am I here? Why am I here? Why have I survived into this? Why can I not stop talking?'

He turned his face aside. The black, fine, elfish hair was so long, and pushed up in tufts from the smooth brown nape of his neck. Daphne looked at him in sorrow. He could not turn his body. He could only move his head. And he lay with his face hard averted, the fine hair of his beard coming up strange from under his chin and from his throat, up to the socket of his ear. He lay quite still in this position. And she turned away, looking for her mother. She had suddenly realised that the bonds, the connections between him and his life in the world had broken, and he lay there a bit of loose, palpitating humanity, shot away from the body of humanity.

It was ten days before she went to the hospital again. She had wanted never to go again, to forget him, as one tries to forget incurable things. But she could not forget him. He came again and again into her mind. She had to go back. She had heard that he was recovering very slowly.

He looked really better. His eyes were not so wide open, they had lost that black, inky exposure which had given him such an unnatural look, unpleasant. He watched her guardedly. She had taken off her furs, and wore only her dress and a dark, soft feather toque.

'How are you?' she said, keeping her face averted, unwilling to meet his eyes.

'Thank you, I am better. The nights are not so long.'

She shuddered, knowing what long nights meant. He saw the worn look in her face too, the reddened rims of her eyes.

'Are you not well? Have you some trouble?' he asked her.

'No, no,' she answered.

She had brought a handful of pinky, daisy-shaped flowers.

'Do you care for flowers?' she asked.

He looked at them. Then he slowly shook his head.

'No,' he said. 'If I am on horseback, riding through the marshes or through the hills, I like to see them below me. But not here. Not now. Please do not bring flowers into this grave. Even in gardens, I do not like them. When they are upholstery to human life.'

'I will take them away again,' she said.

'Please do. Please give them to the nurse.'

Daphne paused.

'Perhaps,' she said, 'you wish I would not come to disturb you.'

He looked into her face.

'No,' he said. 'You are like a flower behind a rock, near an icy water. No,

you do not live too much. I am afraid I cannot talk sensibly. I wish to hold
my mouth shut. If I open it, I talk this absurdity. It escapes from my mouth.'
  'It is not so very absurd,' she said.
  But he was silent – looking away from her.
  'I want you to tell me if there is really nothing I can do for you,' she said.
  'Nothing,' he answered.
  'If I can write any letter for you.'
  'None,' he answered.
  'But your wife and your two children. Do they know where you are?'
  'I should think not.'
  'And where are they?'
  'I do not know. Probably they are in Hungary.'
  'Not at your home?'
  'My castle was burnt down in a riot. My wife went to Hungary with the
children. She has her relatives there. She went away from me. I wished it
too. Alas for her, I wished to be dead. Pardon me the personal tone.'
  Daphne looked down at him – the queer, obstinate little fellow.
  'But you have somebody you wish to tell – somebody you want to hear
from?'
  'Nobody. Nobody. I wish the bullet had gone through my heart. I wish
to be dead. It is only I have a devil in my body that will not die.'
  She looked at him as he lay with closed, averted face.
  'Surely it is not a devil which keeps you alive,' she said. 'It is something
good.'
  'No, a devil,' he said.
  She sat looking at him with a long, slow, wondering look.
  'Must one hate a devil that makes one live?' she asked.
  He turned his eyes to her with a touch of a satiric smile.
  'If one lives, no,' he said.
  She looked away from him the moment he looked at her. For her life she
could not have met his dark eyes direct.
  She left him, and he lay still. He neither read nor talked throughout the
long winter nights and the short winter days. He only lay for hours with
black, open eyes, seeing everything around with a touch of disgust, and
heeding nothing.
  Daphne went to see him now and then. She never forgot him for long. He
seemed to come into her mind suddenly, as if by sorcery.
  One day he said to her:
  'I see you are married. May I ask you who is your husband?'
  She told him. She had had a letter also from Basil. The Count smiled
slowly.
  'You can look forward,' he said, 'to a happy reunion and new, lovely
children, Lady Daphne. Is it not so?'
  'Yes, of course,' she said.
  'But you are ill,' he said to her.
  'Yes – rather ill.'
  'Of what?'
  'Oh!' she answered fretfully, turning her face aside. 'They talk about

lungs.' She hated speaking of it. 'Why, how do you know I am ill?' she added quickly.

Again he smiled slowly.

'I see it in your face, and hear it in your voice. One would say the Evil One had cast a spell on you.'

'Oh no,' she said hastily. 'But do I look ill?'

'Yes. You look as if something had struck you across the face, and you could not forget it.'

'Nothing has,' she said. 'Unless it's the war.'

'The war!' he repeated.

'Oh, well, don't let us talk of it,' she said.

Another time he said to her:

'The year has turned – the sun must shine at last, even in England. I am afraid of getting well too soon. I am a prisoner, am I not? But I wish the sun would shine. I wish the sun would shine on my face.'

'You won't always be a prisoner. The war will end. And the sun *does* shine even in the winter in England,' she said.

'I wish it would shine on my face,' he said.

So that when in February there came a blue, bright morning, the morning that suggests yellow crocuses and the smell of a mezereon tree and the smell of damp, warm earth, Daphne hastily got a taxi and drove out to the hospital.

'You have come to put me in the sun,' he said the moment he saw her.

'Yes, that's what I came for,' she said.

She spoke to the matron, and had his bed carried out where there was a big window that came low. There he was put full in the sun. Turning, he could see the blue sky and the twinkling tops of purplish, bare trees.

'The world! The world!' he murmured.

He lay with his eyes shut, and the sun on his swarthy, transparent, immobile face. The breath came and went through his nostrils invisibly. Daphne wondered how he could lie so still, how he could look so immobile. It was true as her mother had said: he looked as if he had been cast in the mould when the metal was white hot, all his lines were so clean. So small, he was, and in his way perfect.

Suddenly his dark eyes opened and caught her looking.

'The sun makes even anger open like a flower,' he said.

'Whose anger?' she said.

'I don't know. But I can make flowers, looking through my eyelashes. Do you know how?'

'You mean rainbows?'

'Yes, flowers.'

And she saw him, with a curious smile on his lips, looking through his almost closed eyelids at the sun.

'The sun is neither English nor German nor Bohemian,' he said. 'I am a subject of the sun. I belong to the fire-worshippers.'

'Do you?' she replied.

'Yes, truly, by tradition.' He looked at her smiling. 'You stand there like a flower that will melt,' he added.

She smiled slowly at him with a slow, cautious look of her eyes, as if she feared something.

'I am much more solid than you imagine,' she said.

Still he watched her.

'One day,' he said, 'before I go, let me wrap your hair round my hands, will you?' He lifted his thin, short, dark hands. 'Let me wrap your hair round my hands, like a bandage. They hurt me. I don't know what it is. I think it is all the gun explosions. But if you let me wrap your hair round my hands. You know, it is the hermetic gold – but so much of water in it, of the moon. That will soothe my hands. One day, will you?'

'Let us wait till the day comes,' she said.

'Yes,' he answered, and was still again.

'It troubles me,' he said after a while, 'that I complain like a child, and ask for things. I feel I have lost my manhood for the time being. The continual explosions of guns and shells! It seems to have driven my soul out of me like a bird frightened away at last. But it will come back, you know. And I am so grateful to you; you are good to me when I am soulless, and you don't take advantage of me. Your soul is quiet and heroic.'

'Don't,' she said. 'Don't talk!'

The expression of shame and anguish and disgust crossed his face.

'It is because I can't help it,' he said. 'I have lost my soul, and I can't stop talking to you. I can't stop. But I don't talk to anyone else. I try not to talk, but I can't prevent it. Do you draw the words out of me?'

Her wide, green-blue eyes seemed like the heart of some curious, full-open flower, some Christmas rose with its petals of snow and flush. Her hair glinted heavy, like water-gold. She stood there passive and indomitable with the wide-eyed persistence of her wintry, blond nature.

Another day when she came to see him, he watched her for a time, then he said:

'Do they all tell you you are lovely, you are beautiful?'

'Not quite all,' she replied.

'But your husband?'

'He has said so.'

'Is he gentle? Is he tender? Is he a dear lover?'

She turned her face aside, displeased.

'Yes,' she replied curtly.

He did not answer. And when she looked again he was lying with his eyes shut, a faint smile seeming to curl round his short, transparent nose. She could faintly see the flesh through his beard, as water through reeds. His black hair was brushed smooth as glass, his black eyebrows glinted like a curve of black glass on the swarthy opalescence of his brow.

Suddenly he spoke, without opening his eyes.

'You have been very kind to me,' he said.

'Have I? Nothing to speak of.'

He opened his eyes and looked at her.

'Everything finds its mate,' he said. 'The ermine and the pole-cat and the buzzard. One thinks so often that only the dove and the nightingale and the stag with his antlers have gentle mates. But the pole-cat and the ice-bears of the north have their mates. And a white she-bear lies with her cubs under a rock as a snake lies hidden, and the male bear slowly swims back from the sea, like a clot of snow or a shadow of a white cloud passing on the speckled sea. I have seen her too, and I did not shoot her, nor him when he landed with fish in his mouth, wading wet and slow and yellow-white over the black stones.'

'You have been in the North Sea?'

'Yes. And with the Eskimo in Siberia, and across the Tundras. And a white sea-hawk makes a nest on a high stone, and sometimes looks out with her white head over the edge of the rocks. It is not only a world of men, Lady Daphne.'

'Not by any means,' said she.

'Else it were a sorry place.'

'It is bad enough,' said she.

'Foxes have their holes. They have even their mates, Lady Daphne, that they bark to and are answered. And an adder finds his female. Psanek means an outlaw; did you know?'

'I did not.'

'Outlaws, and brigands, have often the finest woman-mates.'

'They do,' she said.

'I will be Psanek, Lady Daphne. I will not be Johann Dionys any more. I will be Psanek. The law has shot me through.'

'You might be Psanek and Johann and Dionys as well,' she said.

'With the sun on my face? Maybe,' he said, looking to the sun.

There were some lovely days in the spring of 1918. In March the Count was able to get up. They dressed him in a simple, dark-blue uniform. He was not very thin, only swarthy-transparent, now his beard was shaven and his hair was cut. His smallness made him noticeable, but he was masculine, perfect in his small stature. All the smiling dapperness that had made him seem like a monkey to Daphne when she was a girl had gone now. His eyes were dark and haughty; he seemed to keep inside his own reserves, speaking to nobody if he could help it, neither to the nurses nor the visitors nor to his fellow-prisoners, fellow-officers. He seemed to put a shadow between himself and them, and from across this shadow he looked with his dark, beautifully-fringed eyes, as a proud little beast from the shadow of its lair. Only to Daphne he laughed and chatted.

She sat with him one day in March on the terrace of the hospital, on a morning when white clouds went endlessly and magnificently about a blue sky, and the sunshine felt warm after the blots of shadow.

'When you had a birthday, and you were seventeen, didn't I give you a thimble?' he asked her.

'Yes. I have it still.'

'With a gold snake at the bottom, and a Mary-beetle of green stone at the top, to push the needle with.'

'Yes.'

'Do you ever use it?'

'No. I sew so rarely.'

'Would it displease you to sew something for me?'

'You won't admire my stitches. What would you wish me to sew?'

'Sew me a shirt that I can wear. I have never before worn shirts from a shop, with a maker's name inside. It is very distasteful to me.'

She looked at him – his haughty little brows.

'Shall I ask my maid to do it?' she said.

'Oh, please, no! Oh, please, no, do not trouble. No, please, I would not want it unless you sewed it yourself, with the Psanek thimble.'

She paused before she answered. Then came her slow:

'Why?'

He turned and looked at her with dark, searching eyes.

'I have no reason,' he said, rather haughtily.

She left the matter there. For two weeks she did not go to see him. Then suddenly one day she took the bus down Oxford Street and bought some fine white flannel. She decided he must wear flannel.

That afternoon she drove out to Hurst Place. She found him sitting on the terrace, looking across the garden at the red suburb of London smoking fumily in the near distance, interrupted by patches of uncovered ground and a flat, tin-roofed laundry.

'Will you give me measurements for your shirt?' she said.

'The number of the neck-band of this English shirt is fifteen. If you ask the matron she will give you the measurement. It is a little too large, too long in the sleeves, you see,' and he shook his shirt cuff over his wrist. 'Also too long altogether.'

'Mine will probably be unwearable when I've made them,' said she.

'Oh no. Let your maid direct you. But please do not let her sew them.'

'Will you tell me why you want me to do it?'

'Because I am a prisoner, in other people's clothes, and I have nothing of my own. All the things I touch are distasteful to me. If your maid sews for me, it will still be the same. Only you might give me what I want, something that buttons round my throat and on my wrists.'

'And in Germany – or in Austria?'

'My mother sewed for me. And after her, my mother's sister, who was the head of my house.'

'Not your wife?'

'Naturally not. She would have been insulted. She was never more than a guest in my house. In my family there are old traditions – but with me they have come to an end. I had best try to revive them.'

'Beginning with traditions of shirts?'

'Yes. In our family the shirt should be made and washed by a woman of our own blood: but when we marry, by the wife. So when I married I had sixty shirts, and many other things – sewn by my mother and my aunt, all with my initial, and the ladybird, which is our crest.'

'And where did they put the initial?'

'Here!' He put his finger on the back of his neck, on the swarthy, transparent skin. 'I fancy I can feel the embroidered ladybird still. On our linen we had no crown: only the ladybird.'

She was silent, thinking.

'You will forgive what I ask you?' he said, 'since I am a prisoner and can do no other, and since fate has made you so that you understand the world as I understand it. It is not really indelicate, what I ask you. There will be a ladybird on your finger when you sew, and those who wear the ladybird understand.'

'I suppose,' she mused, 'it is as bad to have your bee in your shirt as in your bonnet.'

He looked at her with round eyes.

'Don't you know what it is to have a bee in your bonnet?' she said.

'No.'

'To have a bee buzzing among your hair! To be out of your wits,' she smiled at him.

'So!' he said. 'Ah, the Psaneks have had a ladybird in their bonnets for many hundred years.'

'Quite, quite mad,' she said.

'It may be,' he answered. 'But with my wife I was quite sane for ten years. Now give me the madness of the ladybird. The world I was sane about has gone raving. The ladybird I was mad with is wise still.'

'At least, when I sew the shirts, if I sew them,' she said, 'I shall have the ladybird at my finger's end.'

'You want to laugh at me.'

'But surely you know you are funny, with your family insect.'

'My family insect? Now you want to be rude to me.'

'How many spots must it have?'

'Seven.'

'Three on each wing. And what do I do with the odd one?'

'You put that one between its teeth, like the cake for Cerberus.'

'I'll remember that.'

When she brought the first shirt, she gave it to the matron. Then she found Count Dionys sitting on the terrace. It was a beautiful spring day. Near at hand were tall elm trees and some rooks cawing.

'What a lovely day!' she said. 'Are you liking the world any better?'

'The world?' he said, looking up at her with the same old discontent and disgust on his fine, transparent nose.

'Yes,' she replied, a shadow coming over her face.

'Is this the world – all those little red-brick boxes in rows, where couples of little people live, who decree my destiny?'

'You don't like England?'

'Ah, England! Little houses like little boxes, each with its domestic Englishman and his domestic wife, each ruling the world because all are alike, so alike.'

'But England isn't all houses.'

'Fields then! Little fields with innumerable hedges. Like a net with an irregular mesh, pinned down over this island and everything under the net. Ah, Lady Daphne, forgive me. I am ungrateful. I am so full of bile, of spleen, you say. My only wisdom is to keep my mouth shut.'

'Why do you hate everything?' she said, her own face going bitter.

'Not everything. If I were free! If I were outside the law. Ah, Lady Daphne, how does one get outside the law?'

'By going inside oneself,' she said. 'Not outside.'

His face took on a greater expression of disgust.

'No, no. I am a man, I am a man, even if I am little. I am not a spirit, that coils itself inside a shell. In my soul is anger, anger, anger. Give me room for my anger. Give me room for that.'

His black eyes looked keenly into her. She rolled her eyes as if in a half-trance. And in a monotonous, tranced voice she said:

'Much better get over your anger. And *why* are you angry?'

'There is no why. If it were love, you would not ask me, *why do you love?* But it is anger, anger, anger. What else can I call it? And there is no why.'

Again he looked at her with his dark, sharp, questioning, tormented eyes.

'Can't you get rid of it?' she said, looking aside.

'If a shell exploded and blew me into a thousand fragments,' he said, 'it would not destroy the anger that is in me. I know that. No, it will never dissipate. And to die is no release. The anger goes on gnashing and whimpering in death. Lady Daphne, Lady Daphne, we have used up all the love, and this is what is left.'

'Perhaps *you* have used up all your love,' she replied. 'You are not everybody.'

'I know it. I speak for me and you.'

'Not for me,' she said rapidly.

He did not answer, and they remained silent.

At length she turned her eyes slowly to him.

'Why do you say you speak for me?' she said, in an accusing tone.

'Pardon me. I was hasty.'

But a faint touch of superciliousness in his tone showed he meant what he had said. She mused, her brow cold and stony.

'And why do you tell *me* about your anger?' she said. 'Will that make it better?'

'Even the adder finds his mate. And she has as much poison in her mouth as he.'

She gave a little sudden squirt of laughter.

'Awfully poetic thing to say about me,' she said.

He smiled, but with the same corrosive quality.

'Ah,' he said, 'you are not a dove. You are a wild-cat with open eyes, half dreaming on a bough, in a lonely place, as I have seen her. And I ask myself – What are her memories, then?'

'I wish I were a wild-cat,' she said suddenly.

He eyed her shrewdly, and did not answer.

'You want more war?' she said to him bitterly.

'More trenches? More Big Berthas, more shells and poison-gas, more machine-drilled science-manoeuvred so-called armies? Never. Never. I would rather work in a factory that makes boots and shoes. And I would rather deliberately starve to death than work in a factory that makes boots and shoes.

'Then what do you want?'

'I want my anger to have room to grow.'

'How?'

'I do not know. That is why I sit here, day after day. I wait.'

'For your anger to have room to grow?'

'For that.'

'Good-bye, Count Dionys.'

'Good-bye, Lady Daphne.'

She had determined never to go and see him again. She had no sign from him. Since she had begun the second shirt, she went on with it. And then she hurried to finish it, because she was starting a round of visits that would end in the summer sojourn in Scotland. She intended to post the shirt. But after all, she took it herself.

She found Count Dionys had been removed from Hurst Place to Voynich Hall, where other enemy officers were interned. The being thwarted made her more determined. She took the train next day to go to Voynich Hall.

When he came into the ante-room where he was to receive her, she felt at once the old influence of his silence and his subtle power. His face had still that swarthy-transparent look of one who is unhappy, but his bearing was proud and reserved. He kissed her hand politely, leaving her to speak.

'How are you?' she said. 'I didn't know you were here. I am going away for the summer.'

'I wish you a pleasant time,' he said. They were speaking English.

'I brought the other shirt,' she said. 'It is finished at last.'

'That is a greater honour than I dared expect,' he said.

'I'm afraid it may be more honourable than useful. The other didn't fit, did it?'

'Almost,' he said. 'It fitted the spirit, if not the flesh,' he smiled.

'I'd rather it had been the reverse, for once,' she said. 'Sorry.'

'I would not have it one stitch different.'

'Can we sit in the garden?'

'I think we may.'

They sat on a bench. Other prisoners were playing croquet not far off. But these two were left comparatively alone.

'Do you like it better here?' she said.

'I have nothing to complain of,' he said.

'And the anger?'

'It is doing well, I thank you,' he smiled.

'You mean getting better?'

'Making strong roots,' he said, laughing.

'Ah, so long as it only makes roots!' she said.

'And your ladyship, how is she?'

'My ladyship is rather better,' she replied.

'Much better, indeed,' he said, looking into her face.

'Do you mean I *look* much better?' she asked quickly.

'Very much. It is your beauty you think of. Well, your beauty is almost itself again.'

'Thanks.'

'You brood on your beauty as I on my anger. Ah, your ladyship, be wise, and make friends with your anger. That is the way to let your beauty blossom.'

'I was not unfriendly with you, was I?' she said.

'With me?' His face flickered with a laugh. 'Am I your anger? Your vicar in wrath? So then, be friends with the angry me, your ladyship. I ask nothing better.'

'What is the use,' she said, 'being friends with the *angry* you? I would much rather be friends with the happy you.'

'That little animal is extinct,' he laughed. 'And I am glad of it.'

'But what remains? Only the angry you? Then it is no use my trying to be friends.'

'You remember, dear Lady Daphne, that the adder does not suck his poison all alone, and the pole-cat knows where to find his she-pole-cat. You remember that each one has his own dear mate,' he laughed. 'Dear, deadly mate.'

'And what if I do remember those bits of natural history, Count Dionys?'

'The she-adder is dainty, delicate, and carries her poison lightly. The wild-cat has wonderful green eyes that she closes with memory like a screen. The ice-bear hides like a snake with her cubs, and her snarl is the strangest thing in the world.'

'Have you ever heard me snarl?' she asked suddenly.

He only laughed, and looked away.

They were silent. And immediately the strange thrill of secrecy was between them. Something had gone beyond sadness into another, secret, thrilling communion which she would never admit.

'What do you do all day here?' she asked.

'Play chess, play this foolish croquet, play billiards, and read, and wait, and remember.'

'What do you wait for?'

'I don't know.'

'And what do you remember?'

'Ah, that. Shall I tell you what amuses me? Shall I tell you a secret?'

'Please don't, if it's anything that matters.'

'It matters to nobody but me. Will you hear it?'

'If it does not implicate me in any way.'

'It does not. Well, I am a member of a certain old secret society – no, don't look at me, nothing frightening – only a society like the free-masons.'

'And?'

'And – well, as you know, one is initiated into certain so-called secrets and rites. My family has always been initiated. So I am an initiate too. Does it interest you?'

'Why, of course.'

'Well. I was always rather thrilled by these secrets. Or some of them. Some seemed to me far-fetched. The ones that thrilled me even never had any relation to actual life. When you knew me in Dresden and Prague, you would not have thought me a man invested with awful secret knowledge, now would you?'

'Never.'

'No. It was just a little exciting side-show. And I was a grimacing little society man. But now they become true. It becomes true.'

'The secret knowledge?'

'Yes.'

'What, for instance?'

'Take actual fire. It will bore you. Do you want to hear?'

'Go on.'

'This is what I was taught. The true fire is invisible. Flame, and the red fire we see burning, has its back to us. It is running away from us. Does that mean anything to you?'

'Yes.'

'Well then, the yellowness of sunshine – light itself – that is only the glancing aside of the real original fire. You know that is true. There would be no light if there was no refraction, no bits of dust and stuff to turn the dark fire into visibility. You know that's a fact. And that being so, even the sun is dark. It is only his jacket of dust that makes him visible. You know that too. And the true sunbeams coming towards us flow darkly, a moving darkness of the genuine fire. The sun is dark, the sunshine flowing to us is dark. And light is only the inside-turning away of the sun's directness that was coming to us. Does that interest you at all?'

'Yes,' she said dubiously.

'Well, we've got the world inside out. The true living world of fire is dark, throbbing, darker than blood. Our luminous world that we go by is only the reverse of this.'

'Yes, I like that,' she said.

'Well! Now listen. The same with love. This white love that we have is the same. It is only the reverse, the whited sepulchre of the true love. True love is dark, a throbbing together in darkness, like the wild-cat in the night, when the green screen opens and her eyes are on the darkness.'

'No, I don't see that,' she said in a slow, clanging voice.

'You, and your beauty – that is only the inside-out of you. The real you is the wild-cat invisible in the night, with red fire perhaps coming out of its wide, dark eyes. Your beauty is your whited sepulchre.'

'You mean cosmetics,' she said. 'I've got none on to-day – not even powder.'

He laughed.

'Very good,' he said. 'Consider me. I used to think myself small but handsome, and the ladies used to admire me moderately, never very much. A trim little fellow, you know. Well, that was just the inside-out of me. I am a black tom-cat howling in the night, and it is then that fire comes out of me. This me you look at is my whited sepulchre. What do you say?'

She was looking into his eyes. She could see the darkness swaying in the depths. She perceived the invisible, cat-like fire stirring deep inside them, felt it coming towards her. She turned her face aside. Then he laughed, showing his strong white teeth, that seemed a little too large, rather dreadful.

She rose to go.

'Well,' she said. 'I shall have the summer in which to think about the world inside-out. Do write if there is anything to say. Write to Thoresway. Good-bye?'

'Ah, your eyes!' he said. 'They are like jewels of stone.'

Being away from the Count, she put him out of her mind. Only she was sorry for him a prisoner in that sickening Voynich Hall. But she did not write. Nor did he.

As a matter of fact, her mind was now much more occupied with her husband. All arrangements were being made to effect his exchange. From month to month she looked for his return. And so she thought of him.

Whatever happened to her, she thought about it, thought and thought a great deal. The consciousness of her mind was like tablets of stone weighing her down. And whoever would make a new entry into her must break these tablets of stone piece by piece. So it was that in her own way she thought often enough of the Count's world inside-out. A curious latency stirred in her consciousness that was not yet an idea.

He said her eyes were like jewels of stone. What a horrid thing to say! What did he want her eyes to be like? He wanted them to dilate and become all black pupil, like a cat's at night. She shrank convulsively from the thought, and tightened her breast.

He said her beauty was her whited sepulchre. Even that, she knew what he meant. The invisibility of her he wanted to love. But ah, her pearl-like beauty was so dear to her, and it was so famous in the world.

He said her white love was like moonshine, harmful, the reverse of love. He meant Basil, of course. Basil always said she was the moon. But then Basil loved her for that. The ecstasy of it! She shivered, thinking of her husband. But it had also made her nerve-worn, her husband's love. Ah, nerve-worn.

What then would the Count's love be like? Something so secret and different. She would not be lovely and a queen to him. He hated her loveliness. The wild-cat has its mate. The little wild-cat that he was. Ah!

She caught her breath, determined not to think. When she thought of Count Dionys she felt the world slipping away from her. She would sit in front of a mirror, looking at her wonderful cared-for face that had appeared in so many society magazines. She loved it so, it made her feel so vain. And she looked at her blue-green eyes – the eyes of the wild-cat on a bough. Yes, the lovely blue-green iris drawn tight like a screen. Supposing it should relax. Supposing it should unfold, and open out the dark depths, the dark, dilated pupil! Supposing it should?

Never! She always caught herself back. She felt she might be killed before she could give way to that relaxation that the Count wanted of her. She could not. She just could not. At the very thought of it some hypersensitive nerve started with a great twinge in her breast; she drew back, forced to keep her guard. Ah no, Monsieur le Comte, you shall never take her ladyship off her guard.

She disliked the thought of the Count. An impudent little fellow. An impertinent little fellow! A little madman, really. A little outsider. No, no. She would think of her husband: an adorable, tall, well-bred Englishman, so easy and simple, and with the amused look in his blue eyes. She thought of the cultured, casual trail of his voice. It set her nerves on fire. She thought of his strong, easy body – beautiful, white-fleshed, with the fine springing of warm-brown hair like tiny flames. He was the Dionysos, full of sap, milk and honey, and northern golden wine: he, her husband. Not that little unreal Count. Ah, she dreamed of her husband, of the love-days, and the honeymoon, the lovely, simple intimacy. Ah, the marvellous revelation of that intimacy, when he left himself to her so generously. Ah, she was his wife for this reason, that he had given himself to her so greatly, so generously. Like an ear of corn he was there for her gathering – her husband, her own, lovely, English husband. Ah, when would he come again, when would he come again!

She had letters from him – and how he loved her. Far away, his life was all hers. All hers, flowing to her as the beam flows from a white star right down to us, to our heart. Her lover, her husband.

He was now expecting to come home soon. It had all been arranged. 'I hope you won't be disappointed in me when I do get back,' he wrote. 'I am afraid I am no longer the plump and well-looking young man I was. I've got a big scar at the side of my mouth, and I'm as thin as a starved rabbit, and my hair's going grey. Doesn't sound attractive, does it? And it isn't attractive. But once I can get out of this infernal place, and once I can be with you again, I shall come in for my second blooming. The very thought of being quietly in the same house with you, quiet and in peace, makes me realise that if I've been through hell, I have known heaven on earth and can hope to know it again. I am a miserable brute to look at now. But I have faith in you. You will forgive my appearance, and that alone will make me feel handsome.'

She read this letter many times. She was not afraid of his scar or his looks. She would love him all the more.

Since she had started making shirts – those two for the Count had been an enormous labour, even though her maid had come to her assistance forty times: but since she had started making shirts, she thought she might continue. She had some good suitable silk: her husband liked silk underwear.

But still she used the Count's thimble. It was gold outside and silver inside, and was too heavy. A snake was coiled round the base, and at the top, for pressing the needle, was inlet a semi-translucent apple-green stone, perhaps jade, carved like a scarab, with little dots. It was too heavy. But then she sewed so slowly. And she liked to feel her hand heavy, weighted. And as she sewed she thought about her husband, and she felt herself in love with him. She thought of him, how beautiful he was, and how she would love him now he was thin: she would love him all the more. She would love to trace his bones, as if to trace his living skeleton. The thought made her rest her hands in her lap, and drift into a muse. Then she felt the weight of the thimble on her finger, and took it off, and sat looking at the green stone. The ladybird. The ladybird. And if only her husband would come soon, soon. It was wanting him that made her so ill. Nothing but that. She had wanted him so badly. She wanted now. Ah, if she could go to him now, and find him, wherever he was, and see him and touch him and take all his love.

As she mused, she put the thimble down in front of her, took up a little silver pencil from her work-basket, and on a bit of blue paper that had been the band of a small skein of silk she wrote the lines of the silly little song:

'*Wenn ich ein Vöglein wär*'
Und auch zwei Flüglein hätt'
Flög' ich zu dir — '

That was all she could get on her bit of pale-blue paper.

'If I were a little bird
And had two little wings
I'd fly to thee — '

Silly enough, in all conscience. But she did not translate it, so it did not seem quite so silly.

At that moment her maid announced Lady Bingham – her husband's sister. Daphne crumpled up the bit of paper in a flurry, and in another minute Primrose, his sister, came in. The newcomer was not a bit like a primrose, being long-faced and clever, smart, but not a bit elegant, in her new clothes.

'Daphne dear, what a domestic scene! I suppose it's rehearsal. Well, you may as well rehearse, he's with Admiral Burns on the *Ariadne*. Father just heard from the Admiralty: quite fit. He'll be here in a day or two. Splendid, isn't it? And the war is going to end. At least it seems like it. You'll be safe of your man now, dear. Thank heaven when it's all over. What are you sewing?'

'A shirt,' said Daphne.

'A shirt! Why, how clever of you. I should never know which end to begin. Who showed you?'

'Millicent.'

'And how did *she* know? She's no business to know how to sew shirts: nor cushions nor sheets either. Do let me look. Why, how perfectly marvellous you are! – every bit by hand too. Basil isn't worth it, dear, really he isn't. Let him order his shirts in Oxford Street. Your business is to be beautiful, not to sew shirts. What a dear little pin-poppet, or rather needle-woman! I say, a satire on us, that is. But what a darling, with mother-of-pearl wings to her skirts! And darling little gold-eyed needles inside her. You screw her head off, and you find she's full of pins and needles. Woman for you! Mother says won't you come to lunch to-morrow. And won't you come to Brassey's to tea with me at this minute. Do, there's a dear. I've got a taxi.'

Daphne bundled her sewing loosely together.

When she tried to do a bit more, two days later, she could not find her thimble. She asked her maid, whom she could absolutely trust. The girl had not seen it. She searched everywhere. She asked her nurse – who was now her housekeeper – and footman. No, nobody had seen it. Daphne even asked her sister-in-law.

'Thimble, darling? No, I don't remember a thimble. I remember a dear little needle-lady, whom I thought such a precious satire on us women. I didn't notice a thimble.'

Poor Daphne wandered about in a muse. She did not want to believe it lost. It had been like a talisman to her. She tried to forget it. Her husband was coming, quite soon, quite soon. But she could not raise herself to joy. She had lost her thimble. It was as if Count Dionys accused her in her sleep of something, she did not quite know what.

And though she did not really want to go to Voynich Hall, yet like a fatality she went, like one doomed. It was already late autumn, and some lovely days. This was the last of the lovely days. She was told that Count Dionys was in the small park, finding chestnuts. She went to look for him. Yes, there he was in his blue uniform stooping over the brilliant yellow leaves of the sweet chestnut tree, that lay around him like a fallen nimbus of glowing yellow, under his feet, as he kicked and rustled, looking for the chestnut burrs. And with his short, brown hands he was pulling out the small chestnuts and putting them in his pockets. But as she approached he peeled a nut to eat it. His teeth were white and powerful.

'You remind me of a squirrel laying in a winter store,' said she.

'Ah, Lady Daphne – I was thinking, and did not hear you.'

'I thought you were gathering chestnuts – even eating them.'

'Also!' he laughed. He had a dark, sudden charm when he laughed, showing his rather large white teeth. She was not quite sure whether she found him a little repulsive.

'Were you *really* thinking?' she said, in her slow, resonant way.

'Very truly.'

'And weren't you enjoying the chestnut a bit?'

'Very much. Like sweet milk. Excellent, excellent.' He had the fragments of the nut between his teeth, and bit them finely. 'Will you take one too.' He held out the little, pointed brown nuts on the palm of his hand.

She looked at them doubtfully.

'Are they as tough as they always were?' she said.

'No, they are fresh and good. Wait, I will peel one for you.'

They strayed about through the thin clump of trees.

'You have had a pleasant summer; you are strong?'

'Almost *quite* strong,' said she. 'Lovely summer, thanks. I suppose it's no good asking you if you have been happy?'

'Happy?' He looked at her direct. His eyes were black, and seemed to examine her. She always felt he had a little contempt of her. 'Oh yes,' he said, smiling. 'I have been very happy.'

'So glad.'

They drifted a little farther, and he picked up an apple-green chestnut burr out of the yellow-brown leaves, handling it with sensitive fingers that still suggested paws to her.

'How did you succeed in being happy?' she said.

'How shall I tell you? I felt that the same power which put up the mountains could pull them down again – no matter how long it took.'

'And was that all?'

'Was it not enough?'

'I should say decidedly too little.'

He laughed broadly, showing the strong, negroid teeth.

'You do not know all it means,' he said.

'The thought that the mountains were going to be pulled down?' she said. 'It will be so long after my day.'

'Ah, you are bored,' he said. 'But I – I found the God who pulls things down: especially the things that men have put up. Do they not say that life is a search after God, Lady Daphne? I have found my God.'

'The god of destruction,' she said, blanching.

'Yes – not the devil of destruction, but the god of destruction. The blessed god of destruction. It is strange' – he stood before her, looking up at her – 'but I have found my God. The god of anger, who throws down the steeples and the factory chimneys. Ah, Lady Daphne, he is a man's God, he is a man's God. I have found my God, Lady Daphne.'

'Apparently. And how are you going to serve him?'

A naïve glow transfigured his face.

'Oh, I will help. With my heart I will help while I can do nothing with my hands. I say to my heart: Beat, hammer, beat with little strokes. Beat, hammer of God, beat them down. Beat it all down.'

Her brows knitted, her face took on a look of discontent.

'Beat what down?' she asked harshly.

'The world, the world of man. Not the trees – these chestnuts, for example' – he looked up at them, at the tufts and loose pinions of yellow – 'not these – nor the chattering sorcerers, the squirrels – nor the hawk that comes. Not those.'

'You mean beat England?' she said.

'Ah, no. Ah, no. Not England any more than Germany – perhaps not as much. Not Europe any more than Asia.'

'Just the end of the world?'

'No, no. No, no. What grudge have I against a world where little chestnuts are so sweet as these! Do you like yours? Will you take another?'

'No, thanks.'

'What grudge have I against a world where even the hedges are full of berries, bunches of black berries that hang down, and red berries that thrust up. Never would I hate the world. But the world of man. Lady Daphne' – his voice sank to a whisper – '*I hate it*. Zzz!' he hissed. 'Strike, little heart! Strike, strike, hit, smite! Oh, Lady Daphne!' – his eyes dilated with a ring of fire.

'What?' she said, scared.

'I believe in the power of my red, dark heart. God has put the hammer in my breast – the little eternal hammer. Hit – hit – hit! It hits on the world of man. It hits, it hits! And it hears the thin sound of cracking. The thin sound of cracking. Hark!'

He stood still and made her listen. It was late afternoon. The strange laugh of his face made the air seem dark to her. And she could easily have believed that she heard a faint, fine shivering, cracking, through the air, a delicate crackling noise.

'You hear it? Yes? Oh, may I live long! May I live long, so that my hammer may strike and strike, and the cracks go deeper, deeper! Ah, the world of man! Ah, the joy, the passion in every heart-beat! Strike home, strike true, strike sure. Strike to destroy it. Strike! Strike! To destroy the world of man. Ah, God. Ah, God, prisoner of peace. Do I not know you, Lady Daphne? Do I not? Do I not?'

She was silent for some moments, looking away at the twinkling lights of a station beyond.

'Not the white plucked lily of your body. I have gathered no flower for my ostentatious life. But in the cold dark, your lily root, Lady Daphne. Ah, yes, you will know it all your life, that I know where your root lies buried, with its sad, sad quick of life. What does it matter!'

They had walked slowly towards the house. She was silent. Then at last she said, in a peculiar voice:

'And you would never want to kiss me?'

'Ah, no!' he answered sharply.

She held out her hand.

'Good-bye, Count Dionys,' she drawled, fashionably. He bowed over her hand, but did not kiss it.

'Good-bye, Lady Daphne.'

She went away, with her brow set hard. And henceforth she thought only of her husband, of Basil. She made the Count die out of her. Basil was coming, he was near. He was coming back from the East, from war and death. Ah, he had been through awful fire of experience. He would be something new, something she did not know. He was something new, a stronger love who had been through terrible fire, and had come out strange and new, like a god. Ah, new and terrible his love would be, pure and intensified by the awful fire of suffering. A new lover – a new bridegroom – a new, supernatural wedding-night. She shivered in anticipation, waiting for her husband. She hardly noticed the wild excitement of the Armistice. She was waiting for something more wonderful to her.

And yet the moment she heard his voice on the telephone, her heart contracted with fear. It was his well-known voice, deliberate, diffident, almost drawling, with the same subtle suggestion of deference, and the rather exaggerated Cambridge intonation, up and down. But there was a difference, a new icy note that went through her veins like death.

'Is that you, Daphne? I shall be with you in half an hour. Is that all right for you? Yes, I've just landed, and shall come straight to you. Yes, a taxi. Shall I be too sudden for you, darling? No? Good, oh, good! Half an hour, then! I say, Daphne? There won't be anyone else there, will there? Quite alone! Good! I can ring up Dad afterwards. Yes, splendid, splendid. Sure you're all right, my darling? I'm at death's door till I see you. Yes. Good-bye – half an hour. Good-bye.'

When Daphne had hung up the receiver she sat down almost in a faint. What was it that so frightened her? His terrible, terrible altered voice, like cold, blue steel. She had no time to think. She rang for her maid.

'Oh, my lady, it isn't bad news?' cried Millicent, when she caught sight of her mistress white as death.

'No, good news. Major Apsley will be here in half an hour. Help me to dress. Ring to Murry's first to send in some roses, red ones, and some lilac-coloured iris – two dozen of each, at once.'

Daphne went to her room. She didn't know what to wear, she didn't know how she wanted her hair dressed. She spoke hastily to her maid. She chose a violet-coloured dress. She did not know what she was doing. In the middle of dressing the flowers came, and she left off to put them in the bowls. So that when she heard his voice in the hall, she was still standing in front of the mirror reddening her lips and wiping it away again.

'Major Apsley, my lady!' murmured the maid, in excitement.

'Yes, I can hear. Go and tell him I shall be *one* minute.'

Daphne's voice had become slow and sonorous, like bronze, as it always did when she was upset. Her face looked almost haggard, and in vain she dabbed with the rouge.

'How does he look?' she asked curtly, when her maid came back.

'A long scar here,' said the maid, and she drew her finger from the left-hand corner of her mouth into her cheek, slanting downwards.

'Make him look very different?' asked Daphne.

'Not so *very* different, my lady,' said Millicent gently. 'His eyes are the same, I think.' The girl also was distressed.

'All right,' said Daphne. She looked at herself in a long, last look as she turned away from the mirror. The sight of her own face made her feel almost sick. She had seen so much of herself. And yet even now she was fascinated by the heavy droop of her lilac-veined lids over her slow, strange, large, green-blue eyes. They *were* mysterious-looking. And she gave herself a long, sideways glance, curious and Chinese. How was it possible there was a touch of the Chinese in her face? – she so purely an English blonde, an Aphrodite of the foam, as Basil had called her in poetry. Ah well! She left off her thoughts and went through the hall to the drawing-room.

He was standing nervously in the middle of the room in his uniform. She hardly glanced at his face – and saw only the scar.

'Hullo, Daphne,' he said, in a voice full of the expected emotion. He stepped forward and took her in his arms, and kissed her forehead.

'So glad! So glad it's happened at last,' she said, hiding her tears.

'So glad what has happened, darling?' he asked, in his deliberate manner.

'That you're back.' Her voice had the bronze resonance, she spoke rather fast.

'Yes, I'm back, Daphne darling – as much of me as there is to bring back.'

'Why?' she said. 'You've come back whole, surely?' She was frightened.

'Yes, apparently I have. Apparently. But don't let's talk of that. Let's talk of you, darling. How are you? Let me look at you. You are thinner, you are older. But you are more wonderful than ever. Far more wonderful.'

'How?' said she.

'I can't exactly say how. You were only a girl. Now you are a woman. I suppose it's all that's happened. But you are wonderful as a woman, Daphne darling – more wonderful than all that's happened. I couldn't have believed you'd be so wonderful. I'd forgotten – or else I'd never known. I say, I'm a lucky chap really. Here I am, alive and well, and I've got you for a wife. It's brought you out like a flower. I say, darling, there is more now that Venus of the foam – grander. How beautiful you are! But you look like the beauty of all life – as if you were moon-mother of the world – Aphrodite.

God is good to me after all, darling. I ought never to utter a single complaint. How lovely you are – how lovely you are, my darling! I'd forgotten you – and I thought I knew you so well. Is it true that you belong to me? Are you really mine?'

They were seated on the yellow sofa. He was holding her hand, and his eyes were going up and down, from her face to her throat and breast. The sound of his words, and the strong, cold desire in his voice excited her, pleased her, and made her heart freeze. She turned and looked into his light blue eyes. They had no longer the amused light, nor the young look. They burned with a hard, focused light, whitish.

'It's all right. You are mine, aren't you, Daphne darling?' came his cultured, musical voice, that had always the well-bred twang of diffidence.

She looked back into his eyes.

'Yes, I am yours,' she said, from the lips.

'Darling! Darling!' he murmured, kissing her hand.

Her heart beat suddenly so terribly, as if her breast would be ruptured, and she rose in one movement and went across the room. She leaned her hand on the mantelpiece and looked down at the electric fire. She could hear the faint, faint noise of it. There was silence for a few moments.

Then she turned and looked at him. He was watching her intently. His face was gaunt, and there was a curious deathly sub-pallor, though his cheeks were not white. The scar ran livid from the side of his mouth. It was not so very big. But it seemed like a scar in him himself, in his brain, as it were. In his eyes was that hard, white, focused light that fascinated her and was terrible to her. He was different. He was like death; like risen death. She felt she dared not touch him. White death was still upon him. She could tell that he shrank with a kind of agony from contact. 'Touch me not, I am not yet ascended unto the Father.' Yet for contact he had come. Something, someone seemed to be looking over his shoulder. His own young ghost looking over his shoulder. Oh, God! She closed her eyes, seeming to swoon. He remained leaning forward on the sofa, watching her.

'Aren't you well, darling?' he asked. There was a strange, incomprehensible coldness in his very fire. He did not move to come near her.

'Yes, I'm well. It is only that after all it is so sudden. Let me get used to you,' she said, turning aside her face from him. She felt utterly like a victim of his white, awful face.

'I suppose I must be a bit of a shock to you,' he said. 'I hope you won't leave off loving me. It won't be that, will it?'

The strange coldness in his voice! And yet the white, uncanny fire.

'No, I shan't leave off loving you,' she admitted, in a low tone, as if almost ashamed. She *dared* not have said otherwise. And the saying it made it true.

'Ah, if you're sure of that,' he said. 'I'm a pretty unlovely sight to behold, I know, with this wound-scar. But if you can forgive it me, darling. Do you think you can?' There was something like compulsion in his tone.

She looked at him, and shivered slightly.

'I love you – more than before,' she said hurriedly.

'Even the scar?' came his terrible voice, inquiring.

She glanced again, with that slow, Chinese side-look, and felt she would die.

'Yes,' she said, looking away at nothingness. It was an awful moment to her. A little, slightly imbecile smile widened on his face.

He suddenly knelt at her feet, and kissed the toe of her slipper, and kissed the instep, and kissed the ankle in the thin, black stocking.

'I knew,' he said in a muffled voice. 'I knew you would make good. I knew if I had to kneel, it was before you. I knew you were divine, you were the one – Cybele – Isis. I knew I was your slave. I knew. It has all been just a long initiation. I had to learn how to worship you.'

He kissed her feet again and again, without the slightest self-consciousness, or the slightest misgiving. Then he went back to the sofa, and sat there looking at her, saying:

'It isn't love, it is worship. Love between me and you will be a sacrament, Daphne. That's what I had to learn. You are beyond me. A mystery to me. My God, how great it all is. How marvellous!'

She stood with her hand on the mantelpiece, looking down and not answering. She was frightened – almost horrified: but she was thrilled deep down to her soul. She really felt she could glow white and fill the universe like the moon, like Astarte, like Isis, like Venus. The grandeur of her own pale power. The man religiously worshipped her, not merely amorously. She was ready for him – for the sacrament of his supreme worship.

He sat on the sofa with his hands spread on the yellow brocade and pushing downwards behind him, down between the deep upholstery of the back and the seat. He had long, white hands with pale freckles. And his fingers touched something. With his long white fingers he groped and brought it out. It was the lost thimble. And inside it was the bit of screwed-up blue paper.

'I say, is that *your* thimble?' he asked.

She started, and went hurriedly forward for it.

'Where was it?' she said, agitated.

But he did not give it to her. He turned it round and pulled out the bit of blue paper. He saw the faint pencil marks on the screwed-up ball, and unrolled the band of paper, and slowly deciphered the verse.

'Wenn ich ein Vöglein wär'
Und auch zwei Flüglein hätt'
Flög' ich zu dir — '

'How awfully touching that is,' he said. 'A *Vöglein* with two little *Flüglein*! But what a precious darling child you are! Whom did you want to fly to, if you were a *Vöglein*?' He looked up at her with a curious smile.

'I can't remember,' she said, turning aside her head.

'I hope it was to me,' he said. 'Anyhow, I shall consider it was, and shall love you all the more for it. What a darling child! A *Vöglein* if you please, with two little wings! Why, how beautifully absurd of you, darling!'

He folded the scrap of paper carefully, and put it in his pocket-book, keeping the thimble all the time between his knees.

'Tell me when you lost it, Daphne,' he said, examining the bauble.

'About a month ago – or two months.'

'About a month ago – or two months. And what were you sewing? Do you mind if I ask? I like to think of you then. I was still in that beastly El Hasrun. What were you sewing, darling, two months ago, when you lost your thimble?'

'A shirt.'

'I say, a shirt! Whose shirt?'

'Yours.'

'There. Now we've run it to earth. Were you really sewing a shirt for me! Is it finished? Can I put it on at this minute?'

'That one isn't finished, but the first one is.'

'I say, darling, let me go and put it on. To think I should have it next my skin! I shall feel you all round me, all over me. I say how marvellous that will be! Won't you come?'

'Won't you give me the thimble?' she said.

'Yes, of course. What a noble thimble too! Who gave it you?'

'Count Dionys Psanek.'

'Who was he?'

'A Bohemian Count, in Dresden. He once stayed with us in Thoresway – with a tall wife. Didn't you meet them?'

'I don't think I did. I don't think I did. I don't remember. What was he like?'

'A little man with black hair and a rather low, dark forehead – rather dressy.'

'No, I don't remember him at all. So he gave it you. Well, I wonder where he is now? Probably rotted, poor devil.'

'No, he's interned in Voynich Hall. Mother and I have been to see him several times. He was awfully badly wounded.'

'Poor little beggar! In Voynich Hall! I'll look at him before he goes. Odd thing, to give you a thimble. Odd gift! You were a girl then, though. Do you think he had it made, or do you think he found it in a shop?'

'I think it belonged to the family. The ladybird at the top is part of their crest – and the snake as well, I think.'

'A ladybird! Funny thing for a crest. Americans would call it a bug. I must look at him before he goes. And you were sewing a shirt for me! And then you posted me this little letter into the sofa. Well, I'm awfully glad I received it, and that it didn't go astray in the post, like so many things. "*Wenn ich ein Vöglein wär*" – you perfect child! But that is the beauty of a woman like you: you are so superb and beyond worship, and then such an exquisite naïve child. Who could help worshipping you and loving you: immortal and mortal together. What, you want the thimble? Here! Wonderful, wonderful white fingers. Ah, darling, you are more goddess than child, you long, limber Isis with sacred hands. White, white, and immortal! Don't tell me your hands could die, darling: your wonderful Proserpine fingers. They are immortal as February and snowdrops. If you lift your hands the spring comes. I *can't* help kneeling before you, darling. I am no more than a sacrifice to you, an offering. I *wish* I could die in giving myself to you, give you all my blood on your altar, for ever.'

She looked at him with a long, slow look, as he turned his face to her. His face was white with ecstasy. And she was not afraid. Somewhere, saturnine, she knew it was absurd. But she chose not to know. A certain swoon-sleep was on her. With her slow, green-blue eyes she looked down on his ecstasised face, almost benign. But in her right hand unconsciously she held the thimble fast, she only gave him her left hand. He took her hand and rose to his feet in that curious priestly ecstasy which made him more than a man or a soldier, far, far more than a lover to her.

Nevertheless, his home-coming made her begin to be ill again. Afterwards, after his love, she had to bear herself in torment. To her shame and her heaviness, she knew she was not strong enough, or pure enough, to bear this awful out-pouring adoration-lust. It was not her fault she felt weak and fretful afterwards, as if she wanted to cry and be fretful and petulant, wanted someone to save her. She could not turn to Basil, her husband. After his ecstasy of adoration-lust for her, she recoiled from him. Alas, she was not the goddess, the superb person he named her. She was flawed with the fatal humility of her age. She could not harden her heart and burn her soul pure of this humility, this misgiving. She could not finally believe in her own woman-godhead – only in her own female mortality.

That fierce power of being alone, even with your lover, the fierce power of the woman *in excelsis* – alas, she could not keep it. She could rise to the height for the time, the incandescent, transcendent, moon-fierce womanhood. But alas, she could not stay intensified and resplendent in her white, womanly powers, her female mystery. She relaxed, she lost her glory, and became fretful. Fretful and ill and never to be soothed. And then naturally her man became ashy and somewhat acrid, while she ached with nerves, and could not eat.

Of course she began to dream about Count Dionys: to yearn wistfully for him. And it was absolutely a fatal thought to her that he was going away. When she thought that – that he was leaving England soon – going away into the dark for ever – then the last spark seemed to die in her. She felt her soul perish, whilst she herself was worn and soulless like a prostitute. A prostitute goddess. And her husband, the gaunt, white, intensified priest of her, who never ceased from being before her like a lust.

'To-morrow,' she said to him, gathering her last courage and looking at him with a side look, 'I want to go to Voynich Hall.'

'What, to see Count Psanek? Oh, good! Yes, very good! I'll come along as well. I should like very much to see him. I suppose he'll be getting sent back before long.'

It was a fortnight before Christmas, very dark weather. Her husband was in khaki. She wore her black furs and a black lace veil over her face, so that she seemed mysterious. But she lifted her veil and looped it behind, so that it made a frame for her face. She looked very lovely like that – her face pure like the most white hellebore flower, touched with winter pink, amid the blackness of her drapery and furs. Only she was rather too much like the picture of a modern beauty: too much the actual thing. She had half an idea that Dionys would hate her for her effective loveliness. He would see it and hate it. The thought was like a bitter balm to her. For herself, she loved her loveliness almost with obsession.

The Count came cautiously forward, glancing from the lovely figure of Lady Daphne to the gaunt well-bred Major at her side. Daphne was so beautiful in her dark furs, the black lace of her veil thrown back over her close-fitting, dull-gold-threaded hat, and her face fair like a winter flower in a cranny of darkness. But on her face, that was smiling with a slow self-satisfaction of beauty and of knowledge that she was dangling the two men, and setting all the imprisoned officers wildly on the alert, the Count could read that acridity of dissatisfaction and of inefficiency. And he looked away to the livid scar on the Major's cheek.

'Count Dionys, I wanted to bring my husband to see you. May I introduce him to you? Major Apsley – Count Dionys Psanek.'

The two men shook hands rather stiffly.

'I can sympathise with you being fastened up in this place,' said Basil in his slow, easy fashion. 'I hated it, I assure you, out there in the East.'

'But your conditions were much worse than mine,' smiled the Count.

'Well, perhaps they were. But prison is prison, even if it were heaven itself.'

'Lady Apsley has been the one angel of my heaven,' smiled the Count.

'I'm afraid I was as inefficient as most angels,' said she.

The small smile never left the Count's dark face. It was true as she said, he was low-browed, the black hair growing low on his brow, and his eyebrows making a thick bow above his dark eyes, which had again long black lashes. So that the upper part of his face seemed very dusky-black. His nose was small and somewhat translucent. There was a touch of mockery about him, which was intensified even by his small, energetic stature. He was still carefully dressed in the dark-blue uniform, whose shabbiness could not hinder the dark flame of life which seemed to glow through the cloth from his body. He was not thin – but still had a curious swarthy translucency of skin in his low-browed face.

'What would you have been more?' he laughed, making equivocal dark eyes at her.

'Oh, of course, a delivering angel – a cinema heroine,' she replied, closing her eyes and turning her face aside.

All the while the white-faced, tall Major watched the little man with a fixed, half-smiling scrutiny. The Count seemed to notice. He turned to the Englishman.

'I am glad that I can congratulate you, Major Apsley, on your safe and happy return to your home.'

'Thanks. I hope I may be able to congratulate you in the same way before long.'

'Oh yes,' said the Count. 'Before long I shall be shipped back.'

'Have you any news of your family?' interrupted Daphne.

'No news,' he replied briefly, with sudden gravity.

'It seems you'll find a fairish mess out in Austria,' said Basil.

'Yes, probably. It is what we had to expect,' replied the Count.

'Well, I don't know. Sometimes things do turn out for the best. I feel that's as good as true in my case,' said the Major.

'Things have turned out for the best?' said the Count, with an intonation of polite enquiry.

'Yes. Just for me personally, I mean – to put it quite selfishly. After all, what we've learned is that a man can only speak for himself. And I feel it's been dreadful, but it's not been lost. It was like an ordeal one had to go through,' said Basil.

'You mean the war?'

'The war and everything that went with it.'

'And when you've been through the ordeal?' politely enquired the Count.

'Why, you arrive at a higher state of consciousness, and therefore of life. And so, of course, at a higher plane of love. A surprisingly higher plane of love, that you had never suspected the existence of before.'

The Count looked from Basil to Daphne, who was posing her head a little self-consciously.

'Then indeed the war has been a valuable thing,' he said.

'Exactly!' cried Basil. 'I am another man.'

'And Lady Apsley?' queried the Count.

'Oh' – her husband faced round to her – 'she is *absolutely* another woman – and *much* more wonderful, more marvellous.'

The Count smiled and bowed slightly.

'When we knew her ten years ago, we should have said then that it was impossible,' said he, 'for her to be more wonderful.'

'Oh, quite!' returned the husband. 'It always seems impossible. And the impossible is always happening. As a matter of fact, I think the war has opened another circle of life to us – a wider ring.'

'It may be so,' said the Count.

'You don't feel it so yourself?' The Major looked with his keen, white attention into the dark, low-browed face of the other man. The Count looked smiling at Daphne.

'I am only a prisoner still, Major, therefore I feel my ring quite small.'

'Yes, of course you do. Of course. Well, I do hope you won't be a prisoner much longer. You must be dying to get back into your own country.'

'Yes, I shall be glad to be free. Also,' he smiled, 'I shall miss my prison and my visits from the angels.'

Even Daphne could not be sure he was mocking her. It was evident the visit was unpleasant to him. She could see he did not like Basil. Nay, more, she could feel that the presence of her tall, gaunt, idealistic husband, was hateful to the little swarthy man. But he passed it all off in smiles and polite speeches.

On the other hand, Basil was as if fascinated by the Count. He watched him absorbedly all the time, quite forgetting Daphne. She knew this. She knew that she was quite gone out of her husband's consciousness, like a lamp that has been carried away into another room. There he stood completely in the dark, as far as she was concerned, and all his attention focused on the other man. On his pale, gaunt face was a fixed smile of amused attention.

'But don't you get awfully bored,' he said, 'between the visits?'

The Count looked up with an affectation of frankness.

'No, I do not,' he said. 'I can brood, you see, on the things that come to pass.'

'I think that's where the harm comes in,' replied the Major. 'One sits and broods, and is cut off from everything, and one loses one's contact with reality. That's the effect it had on me, being a prisoner.'

'Contact with reality – what is that?'

'Well – contact with anybody, really – or anything.'

'Why must one have contact?'

'Well, because one must,' said Basil.

The Count smiled slowly.

'But I can sit and watch fate flowing, like black water, deep down in my own soul,' he said. 'I feel that there, in the dark of my own soul, things are happening.'

'That may be. But whatever happens, it is only one thing, really. It is a contact between your own soul and the soul of one other being, or of many other beings. Nothing else can happen to man. That's how I figured it out for myself. I may be wrong. But that's how I figured it out when I was wounded and a prisoner.'

The Count's face had gone dark and serious.

'But is this contact an aim in itself?' he asked.

'Well' – said the Major – he had taken his degree in philosophy – 'it seems to me it is. It results inevitably in some form of activity. But the cause and the origin and the life-impetus of all action, activity, whether constructive or destructive, seems to me to be in the dynamic contact between human beings. You bring to pass a certain dynamic contact between men, and you get war. Another sort of dynamic contact, and you get them all building a cathedral, as they did in the Middle Ages.'

'But was not the war, or the cathedral, the real aim, and the emotional contact just the means?' said the Count.

'I don't think so,' said the Major, his curious white passion beginning to glow through his face. The three were seated in a little card-room, left alone by courtesy by the other men. Daphne was still draped in her dark, too-becoming drapery. But alas, she sat now ignored by both men. She might just as well have been an ugly little nobody, for all the notice that was taken of her. She sat in the window-seat of the dreary small room with a look of discontent on her exotic, rare face, that was like a delicate white and pink hot-house flower. From time to time she glanced with long, slow looks from man to man: from her husband, whose pallid, intense, white glowing face was pressed forward across the table to the Count, who sat back in his chair, as if in opposition, and whose dark face seemed clubbed together in a dark, unwilling stare. Her husband was *quite* unaware of anything but his own white identity. But the Count still had a grain of secondary consciousness which hovered round and remained aware of the woman in the window-seat. The whole of his face, and his forward-looking attention was concentrated on Basil. But somewhere at the back of him he kept track of Daphne. She sat uneasy, in discontent, as women always do sit when men are locked together in a combustion of words. At the same time, she followed the argument. It was curious that, while her sympathy at this moment was with the Count, it was her husband whose words she believed to be true. The contact, the emotional contact was the real thing, the so-called 'aim' was only a by-product. Even wars and cathedrals, in her mind, were only by-products. The real thing was what the warriors and cathedral-builders had had in common, as a great uniting feeling: the thing they felt for one another, and for their women in particular, of course.

'There are a great many kinds of contact, nevertheless,' said Dionys.

'Well, do you know,' said the Major, 'it seems to me there is really only one supreme contact, the contact of love. Mind you, the love may take on an infinite variety of forms. And in my opinion, no form of love is wrong, so long as it *is* love, and you yourself *honour* what you are doing. Love has an extraordinary variety of forms! And that is all that there is in life, it seems to me. But I grant you, if you deny the *variety* of love you deny love altogether. If you try to specialise love into one set of accepted feelings, you wound the very soul of love. Love *must* be multiform, else it is just tyranny, just death.'

'But why call it all *love*?' said the Count.

'Because it seems to me it *is* love: the great power that draws human beings together, no matter what the result of the contact may be. Of course there is hate, but hate is only the recoil of love.'

'Do you think the old Egypt was established on love?' asked Dionys.

'Why, of course! And perhaps the most multiform, the most comprehensive love that the world has seen. All that we suffer from now is that our way of love is narrow, exclusive, and therefore not love at all; more like death and tyranny.'

The Count slowly shook his head, smiling slowly and as if sadly.

'No,' he said. 'No. It is no good. You must use another word than love.'

'I don't agree at all,' said Basil.

'What word then?' blurted Daphne.

The Count looked at her.

'Obedience, submission, faith, belief, responsibility, power,' he said slowly, picking out the words slowly, as if searching for what he wanted, and never quite finding it. He looked with his quiet dark eyes into her eyes. It was curious, she disliked his words intensely, but she liked him. On the other hand, she believed absolutely what her husband said, yet her physical sympathy was against him.

'Do you agree, Daphne?' asked Basil.

'Not a bit,' she replied, with a heavy look at her husband.

'Nor I,' said Basil. 'It seems to me, if you love, there is no obedience nor submission, except to the soul of love. If you mean obedience, submission, and all the rest, to the soul of love itself, I quite agree. But if you mean obedience, submission of one person to another, and one man having power over others – I don't agree, and never shall. It seems to me just there where we have gone wrong. Kaiser Wilhelm II wanted power — '

'No, no,' said the Count. 'He was a mountebank. He had no conception of the sacredness of power.'

'He proved himself very dangerous.'

'Oh yes. But peace can be even more dangerous still.'

'Tell me, then. Do you believe that you, as an aristocrat, should have feudal power over a few hundreds of other men, who happen to be born serfs, or not aristocrats?'

'Not as a hereditary aristocrat, but as a *man* who is by nature an aristocrat,' said the Count, 'it is my sacred duty to hold the lives of other men in my hands, and to shape the issue. But I can never fulfil my destiny till men will willingly put their lives in my hands.'

'You don't expect them to, do you?' smiled Basil.

'At this moment, no.'

'Or at any moment!' The Major was sarcastic.

'At a certain moment the men who are really living will come beseeching to put their lives into the hands of the greater men among them, beseeching the greater men to take the sacred responsibility of power.'

'Do you think so? Perhaps you mean men will at last begin to choose leaders whom they will *love*,' said Basil. 'I wish they would.'

'No, I mean that they will at last yield themselves before men who are greater than they: become vassals by choice.'

'Vassals!' exclaimed Basil, smiling. 'You are still in the feudal ages, Count.'

'Vassals. Not to any hereditary aristocrat – Hohenzollern or Hapsburg or Psanek,' smiled the Count. 'But to the man whose soul is born single, able to be alone, to choose and to command. At last the masses will come to such men and say: "You are greater than we. Be our lords. Take our life and our death in your hands, and dispose of us according to your will. Because we see a light in your face, and a burning on your mouth."'

The Major smiled for many moments, really piqued and amused, watching the Count, who did not turn a hair.

'I say, you must be awfully naïve, Count, if you believe the modern masses are ever going to behave like that. I assure you, they never will.'

'If they did,' said the Count, 'would you call it a new reign of love, or something else?'

'Well, of course, it would contain an element of love. There would have to be an element of love in their feeling for their leaders.'

'Do you think so? I thought that love assumed an equality in difference. I thought that love gave to every man the right to judge the acts of other men – "This was not an act of love, therefore it was wrong." Does not democracy, and love, give to every man this right?'

'Certainly,' said Basil.

'Ah, but my chosen aristocrat would say to those who chose him: "If you choose me, you give up forever your right to judge me. If you have truly chosen to follow me, you have thereby rejected all your rights to criticise me. You can no longer either approve or disapprove of me. You have performed the sacred act of choice. Henceforth you can only obey."'

'They wouldn't be able to help criticising, for all that,' said Daphne, blurting in her say.

He looked at her slowly, and for the first time in her life she was doubtful of what she was saying.

'The day of Judas,' he said, 'ends with the day of love.'

Basil woke up from a sort of trance.

'I think, of course, Count,' he said, 'that it's an awfully amusing idea. A retrogression slap back to the Dark Ages.'

'Not so,' said the Count. 'Men–the mass of men–were never before free to perform the sacred art of choice. To-day – soon – they may be free.'

'Oh, I don't know. Many tribes chose their kings and chiefs.'

'Men have never before been quite free to choose: and to know what they are doing.'

'You mean they've only made themselves free in order voluntarily to saddle themselves with new lords and masters?'

'I do mean that.'

'In short, life is just a vicious circle?'

'Not at all. An ever-widening circle, as you say. Always more wonderful.'

'Well, it's all frightfully interesting and amusing – don't you think so, Daphne? By the way, Count, where would women be? Would they be allowed to criticise their husbands?'

'Only before marriage,' smiled the Count. 'Not after.'

'Splendid!' said Basil. 'I'm all for that bit of your scheme, Count. I hope you're listening, Daphne.'

'Oh yes. But then I've only married *you*. I've got my right to criticise all the other men,' she said in a dull, angry voice.

'Exactly. Clever of you! So the Count won't get off! Well now, what do you think of the Count's aristocratic scheme for the future, Daphne? Do you approve?'

'Not at all. But then little men have always wanted power,' she said cruelly.

'Oh, big men as well, for that matter,' said Basil, conciliatory.

'I have been told before,' smiled the Count, 'little men are always bossy. I am afraid I have offended Lady Daphne?'

'No,' she said. 'Not really. I'm amused, really. But I always dislike any suggestion of bullying.'

'Indeed, so do I,' said he.

'The Count didn't mean bullying, Daphne,' said Basil. 'Come, there is really an allowable distinction between responsible power and bullying.'

'When men put their heads together about it,' said she.

She was haughty and angry, as if she were afraid of losing something. The Count smiled mischievously at her.

'You are offended, Lady Daphne? But why? You are safe from any spark of my dangerous and extensive authority.'

Basil burst into a roar of laughter.

'It *is* rather funny, you to be talking of power and of not being criticised,' he said. 'But I should like to hear more: I would like to hear more.'

As they drove home, he said to his wife:

'You know I like that little man. He's a quaint little bantam. And he sets one thinking.'

Lady Daphne froze to four degrees below zero, under the north wind of this statement, and not another word was to be thawed out of her.

Curiously enough, it was now Basil who was attracted by the Count, and Daphne who was repelled. Not that she was so bound up in her husband. Not at all. She was feeling rather sore against men altogether. But as so often happens, in this life based on the wicked triangle, Basil could only follow his enthusiasm for the Count in his wife's presence. When the two men were alone together, they were awkward, resistant, they could hardly get out a dozen words to one another. When Daphne was there, however, to complete the circuit of the opposing currents, things went like a house on fire.

This, however, was not much consolation to Lady Daphne. Merely to sit as a passive medium between two men who are squibbing philosophical nonsense to one another: no, it was not good enough! She almost hated the Count: low-browed little fellow, belonging to the race of prehistoric slaves. But her grudge against her white-faced, spiritually intense husband was sharp as vinegar. Let down: she was let down between the pair of them.

What next? Well, what followed was entirely Basil's fault. The winter was passing: it was obvious the war was really over, that Germany was finished. The Hohenzollern had fizzled out like a very poor squib, the Hapsburg was popping feebly in obscurity, the Romanov was smudged out without a sputter. So much for imperial royalty. Henceforth democratic peace.

The Count, of course, would be shipped back now like returned goods that had no market any more. There was a world peace ahead. A week or two, and Voynich Hall would be empty.

Basil, however, could not let matters follow their simple course. He was awfully intrigued by the Count. He wanted to entertain him as a guest before he went. And Major Apsley could get anything in reason, at this moment. So he obtained permission for the poor little Count to stay a fortnight at Thoresway, before being shipped back to Austria. Earl Beveridge, whose soul was black as ink since the war, would never have allowed the little alien enemy to enter his house, had it not been for the hatred which had been aroused in him, during the last two years, by the degrading spectacle of the so-called patriots who had been howling their mongrel indecency in the public face. These mongrels had held the Press and the British public in abeyance for almost two years. Their one aim was to degrade and humiliate anything that was proud or dignified remaining in England. It was almost the worst nightmare of all, this coming to the top of a lot of public filth which was determined to suffocate the souls of all dignified men.

Hence, the Earl, who never intended to be swamped by unclean scum, whatever else happened to him, stamped his heels in the ground and stood on his own feet. When Basil said to him, would he allow the Count to have a fortnight's decent peace in Thoresway before all was finished, Lord Beveridge gave a slow consent, scandal or no scandal. Indeed, it was really to defy scandal that he took such a step. For the thought of his dead boys was bitter to him: and the thought of England fallen under the paws of smelly mongrels was bitterer still.

Lord Beveridge was at Thoresway to receive the Count, who arrived escorted by Basil. The English Earl was a big, handsome man, rather heavy, with a dark, sombre face that would have been haughty if haughtiness had not been made so ridiculous. He was a passionate man, with a passionate man's sensitiveness, generosity, and instinctive overbearing. But *his* dark passionate nature, and his violent sensitiveness had been subjected now to fifty-five years subtle repression, condemnation, repudiation, till he had almost come to believe in his own wrongness. His little, frail wife, all love for humanity, she was the genuine article. Himself, he was labelled selfish, sensual, cruel, etc., etc. So by now he always seemed to be standing aside, in the shadow, letting himself be obliterated by the pallid rabble of the democratic hurry. That was the impression he gave, of a man standing back, half-ashamed, half-haughty, semi-hidden in the dark background.

He was a little on the defensive as Basil came in with the Count.

'Ah – how do you do, Count Psanek?' he said, striding largely forward and holding out his hand. Because he was the father of Daphne, the Count felt a certain tenderness for the taciturn Englishman.

'You do me too much honour, my lord, receiving me in your house,' said the small Count proudly.

The Earl looked at him slowly, without speaking: seemed to look down on him, in every sense of the words.

'We are still men, Count. We are not beasts altogether.'

'You wish to say that my countrymen are so very nearly beasts, Lord Beveridge?' smiled the Count, curling his fine nose.

Again the Earl was slow in replying.

'You have a low opinion of my manners, Count Psanek.'

'But perhaps a just appreciation of your meaning, Lord Beveridge,' smiled the Count, with the same reckless little look of contempt on his nose.

Lord Beveridge flushed dark, with all his native anger offended.

'I am glad Count Psanek makes my own meaning clear to me,' he said.

'I beg your pardon a thousand times, my lord, if I give offence in doing so,' replied the Count.

The Earl went black, and felt a fool. He turned his back on the Count. And then he turned round again, offering his cigar-case.

'Will you smoke?' he said. There was kindness in his tone.

'Thank you,' said the Count, taking a cigar.

'I dare say,' said Lord Beveridge, 'that all men are beasts in some way. I am afraid I have fallen into the common habit of speaking by rote, and not what I really mean. Won't you take a seat?'

'It is only as a prisoner that I have learned that I am *not* truly a beast. No, I am myself. I am not a beast,' said the Count, seating himself.

The Earl eyed him curiously.

'Well,' he said, smiling, 'I suppose it is best to come to a decision about it.'

'It is necessary, if one is to be safe from vulgarity.'

The Earl felt a twinge of accusation. With his agate-brown, hard-looking eyes he watched the black-browed little Count.

'You are probably right,' he said.

But he turned his face aside.

They were five people at dinner – Lady Beveridge was there as hostess.

'Ah, Count Dionys,' she said with a sigh, 'do you really feel that the war is over?'

'Oh yes,' he replied quickly. 'This war is over. The armies will go home. *Their* cannon will not sound any more. Never again like this.'

'Ah, I hope so,' he sighed.

'I am sure,' he said.

'You think there'll be no more war?' said Daphne.

For some reason she had made herself very fine, in her newest dress of silver and black and pink-chenille, with bare shoulders, and her hair fashionably done. The Count in his shabby uniform turned to her. She was nervous, hurried. Her slim white arm was near him, with the bit of silver at the shoulder. Her skin was white like a hot-house flower. Her lips moved hurriedly.

'Such a war as this there will never be again,' he said.

'What makes you so sure?' she replied, glancing into his eyes.

'The machine of war has got out of our control. We shall never start it again, till it has fallen to pieces. We shall be afraid.'

'Will everybody be afraid?' said she, looking down and pressing back her chin.

'I think so.'

'We will hope so,' said Lady Beveridge.

'Do you mind if I ask you, Count,' said Basil, 'what you feel about the way the war has ended? The way it has ended for *you*, I mean.'

'You mean that Germany and Austria have lost the war? It was bound to be. We have all lost the war. All Europe.'

'I agree there,' said Lord Beveridge.

'We've all lost the war?' said Daphne, turning to look at him.

There was pain on his dark, low-browed face. He suffered having the sensitive woman beside him. Her skin had a hot-house delicacy that made his head go round. Her shoulders were broad, rather thin, but the skin was white and so sensitive, so hot-house delicate. It affected him like the perfume of some white, exotic flower. And she seemed to be sending her heart towards him. It was as if she wanted to press her breast to his. From the breast she loved him, and sent out love to him. And it made him unhappy; he wanted to be quiet, and to keep his honour before these hosts.

He looked into her eyes, his own eyes dark with knowledge and pain. She, in her silence and her brief words seemed to be holding them all under her spell. She seemed to have cast a certain muteness on the table, in the midst of which she remained silently master, leaning forward to her plate, and silently mastering them all.

'Don't I think we've all lost the war?' he replied, in answer to her question. 'It was a war of suicide. Nobody could win it. It was suicide for all of us.'

'Oh, I don't know,' she replied. 'What about America and Japan?'

'They don't count. They only helped *us* to commit suicide. They did not enter vitally.'

There was such a look of pain on his face, and such a sound of pain in his voice, that the other three closed their ears, shut off from attending. Only Daphne was making him speak. It was she who was drawing the soul out of him, trying to read the future in him as the augurs read the future in the quivering entrails of the sacrificed beast. She looked direct into his face, searching his soul.

'You think Europe has committed suicide?' she said.

'Morally.'

'Only morally?' came her slow, bronze-like words, so fatal.

'That is enough,' he smiled.

'Quite,' she said, with a slow droop of her eyelids. Then she turned away her face. But he felt the heart strangling inside his breast. What was she doing now? What was she thinking? She filled him with uncertainty and with uncanny fear.

'At least,' said Basil, 'those infernal guns are quiet.'

'For ever,' said Dionys.

'I wish I could believe you, Count,' said the Major.

The talk became more general – or more personal. Lady Beveridge asked Dionys about his wife and family. He knew nothing save that they had gone to Hungary in 1916, when his own house was burnt down. His wife might even have gone to Bulgaria with Prince Bogorik. He did not know.

'But your children, Count!' cried Lady Beveridge.

'I do not know. Probably in Hungary, with their grandmother. I will go when I get back.'

'But have you never *written*? – never enquired?'

'I could not write. I shall know soon enough – everything.'

'You have no son?'

'No. Two girls.'

'Poor things!'

'Yes.'

'I say, isn't it an odd thing to have a ladybird on your crest?' asked Basil, to cheer up the conversation.

'Why queer? Charlemagne had bees. And it is a Marienkäfer – a Mary-beetle. The beetle of Our Lady. I think it is quite a heraldic insect, Major,' smiled the Count.

'You're proud of it?' said Daphne, suddenly turning to look at him again, with her slow, pregnant look.

'I am, you know. It has such a long genealogy – our spotted beetle. Much longer than the Psaneks. I think, you know, it is a descendant of the Egyptian scarabeus, which is a very mysterious emblem. So I connect myself with the Pharoahs: just through my ladybird.'

'You feel your ladybird has crept through so many ages,' she said.

'Imagine it!' he laughed.

'The scarab *is* a piquant insect,' said Basil.

'Do you know Fabre?' put in Lord Beveridge. 'He suggests that the beetle rolling a little ball of dung before him, in a dry old field, must have suggested to the Egyptians the First Principle that set the globe rolling. And so the scarab became the symbol of the creative principle – or something like that.'

'That the earth is a tiny ball of dry dung is good,' said Basil.

'Between the claws of a ladybird,' added Daphne.

'That is what it is, to go back to one's origin,' said Lady Beveridge.

'Perhaps they meant that it was the principle of decomposition which first set the ball rolling,' said the Count.

'The ball would have to be *there* first,' said Basil.

'Certainly. But it hadn't started to roll. Then the principle of decomposition started it.' The Count smiled as if it were a joke.

'I am no Egyptologist,' said Lady Beveridge, 'so I can't judge.'

The Earl and Countess Beveridge left next day. Count Dionys was left with the two young people in the house. It was a beautiful Elizabethan mansion, not very large, but with those magical rooms that are all a twinkle of small-paned windows, looking out from the dark panelled interior. The interior was cosy, panelled to the ceiling, and the ceiling moulded and touched with gold. And then the great square bow of the window with its little panes intervening like magic between oneself and the world outside, the crest in stained glass crowning its colour, the broad window-seat cushioned in faded green. Dionys wandered round the house like a little ghost, through the succession of small and large twinkling sitting-rooms and lounge rooms in front, down the long, wide corridor with the wide stair-head at each end, and up the narrow stairs to the bedrooms above, and on to the roof.

It was early spring, and he loved to sit on the leaded, pale-grey roof that had its queer seats and slopes, a little pale world in itself. Then to look down over the garden and the sloping lawn to the ponds massed round with trees, and away to the elms and furrows and hedges of the shires. On the left of the house was the farmstead, with ricks and great-roofed barns and dark-red cattle. Away to the right, beyond the park, was a village among trees, and the spark of a grey church spire.

He liked to be alone, feeling his soul heavy with its own fate. He would sit for hours watching the elm trees standing in rows like giants, like warriors across the country. The Earl had told him that the Romans had brought these elms to Britain. And he seemed to see the spirit of the Romans in them still. Sitting there alone in the spring sunshine, in the solitude of the roof, he saw the glamour of this England of hedgerows and elm trees, and the labourers with slow horses slowly drilling the sod, crossing the brown furrow: and the roofs of the village, with the church steeple rising beside a big black yew tree: and the chequer of fields away to the distance.

And the charm of the old manor around him, the garden with its grey stone walls and yew hedges – broad, broad yew hedges – and a peacock pausing to glitter and scream in the busy silence of an English spring, when celandines open their yellow under the hedges, and violets are in the secret, and by the broad paths of the garden polyanthus and crocuses vary the velvet and flame, and bits of yellow wallflower shake raggedly, with a wonderful triumphance, out of the cracks of the wall. There was a fold somewhere near, and he could hear the treble bleat of the growing lambs, and the deeper, contented baa-ing of the ewes.

This was Daphne's home, where she had been born. She loved it with an ache of affection. But now it was hard to forget her dead brothers. She wandered about in the sun, with two old dogs paddling after her. She talked with everybody – gardener, groom, stableman, with the farm-hands. That filled a large part of her life – straying round talking with the work-people. They were, of course, respectful to her – but not at all afraid of her. They knew she was poor, that she could not afford a car, nor anything. So they talked to her very freely: perhaps a little too freely. Yet she let it be. It was her one passion at Thoresway to hear the dependants talk and talk – about everything. The curious feeling of intimacy across a breach fascinated her. Their lives fascinated her: what they thought, what they *felt*. These, what they felt. That fascinated her. There was a gamekeeper she could have loved – an impudent, ruddy-faced, laughing, ingratiating fellow; she could have loved him, if he had not been isolated beyond the breach of his birth, her culture, her consciousness. Her *consciousness* seemed to make a great gulf between her and the lower classes, the unconscious classes. She accepted it as her doom. She could never meet in real contact anyone but a super-conscious, finished being like herself: or like her husband. Her father had some of the unconscious blood-warmth of the lower classes. But he was like a man who is damned. And the Count, of course. The Count had something that was hot and invisible, a dark flame of life that might warm the cold white fire of her own blood. But—

They avoided each other. All three, they avoided one another. Basil, too, went off alone. Or he immersed himself in poetry. Sometimes he and the Count played billiards. Sometimes all three walked in the park. Often Basil and Daphne walked to the village, to post. But truly, they avoided one another, all three. The days slipped by.

At evening they sat together in the small west room that had books and a piano and comfortable shabby furniture of faded rose-coloured tapestry: a shabby room. Sometimes Basil read aloud: sometimes the Count played the piano. And they talked. And Daphne stitch by stitch went on with a big embroidered bedspread, which she might finish if she lived long enough. But they always went to bed early. They were nearly always avoiding one another.

Dionys had a bedroom in the east bay – a long way from the rooms of the others. He had a habit, when he was quite alone, of singing, or rather crooning to himself the old songs of his childhood. It was only when he felt he was quite alone: when other people seemed to fade out of him, and all the world seemed to dissolve into darkness, and there was nothing but himself, his own soul, alive in the middle of his own small night, isolate for ever. Then, half unconscious, he would croon in a small, high-pitched, squeezed voice, a sort of high dream-voice, the songs of his childhood dialect. It was a curious noise: the sound of a man who is alone in his own blood: almost the sound of a man who is going to be executed.

Daphne heard the sound one night when she was going downstairs again with the corridor lantern to find a book. She was a bad sleeper, and her nights were a torture to her. She, too, like a neurotic, was nailed inside her own fretful self-consciousness. But she had a very keen ear. So she started as she heard the small, bat-like sound of the Count's singing to himself. She stood in the midst of the wide corridor, that was wide as a room, carpeted with a faded lavender-coloured carpet, with a piece of massive dark furniture at intervals by the wall, and an oak arm-chair and sometimes a faded, reddish Oriental rug. The big horn lantern which stood at nights at the end of the corridor she held in her hand. The intense 'peeping' sound of the Count, like a witchcraft, made her forget everything. She could not understand a word, of course. She could not understand the noise even. After listening for a long time, she went on downstairs. When she came back again he was still, and the light was gone from under his door.

After this, it became almost an obsession to her to listen for him. She waited with fretful impatience for ten o'clock, when she could retire. She waited more fretfully still for the maid to leave her, and for her husband to come and say goodnight. Basil had the room across the corridor. And then in resentful impatience she waited for the sounds of the house to become still. Then she opened her door to listen.

And far away, as if from far, far away in the unseen, like a ventriloquist sound or a bat's uncanny peeping, came the frail, almost inaudible sound of the Count's singing to himself before he went to bed. It *was* inaudible to anyone but herself. But she, by concentration, seemed to hear super-naturally. She had a low arm-chair by the door, and there, wrapped in a huge old black silk shawl, she sat and listened. At first she could not hear. That is, she could hear the sound. But it was only a sound. And then, gradually, gradually she began to follow the thread of it. It was like a thread which she followed out of the world: out of the world. And as she went, slowly, by degrees, far, far away, down the thin thread of his singing, she knew peace – she knew forgetfulness. She could pass beyond the world, away beyond where her soul balanced like a bird on wings, and was perfected.

So it was, in her upper spirit. But underneath was a wild, wild yearning, actually to go, actually to be given. Actually to go, actually to die the death, actually to cross the border and be gone, to be gone. To be gone from this herself, from this Daphne, to be gone from father and mother, brothers and husband, and home and land and world: to be gone. To be gone to the call from the beyond: the call. It was the Count calling. He was calling her. She was sure he was calling her. Out of herself, out of her world, he was calling her.

Two nights she sat just inside her room, by the open door, and listened. Then when he finished she went to sleep, a queer, light, bewitched sleep. In the day she was bewitched. She felt strange and light, as if pressure had been removed from around her. Some pressure had been clamped round her all her life. She had never realised it till now; now it was removed, and her feet felt so light, and her breathing delicate and exquisite. There had always been a pressure against her breathing. Now she breathed delicate and exquisite, so that it was a delight to breathe. Life came in exquisite breaths, quickly, as if it delighted to come to her.

The third night he was silent – though she waited and waited till the small hours of the morning. He was silent, he did not sing. And then she knew the terror and blackness of the feeling that he might never sing any more. She waited like one doomed, throughout the day. And when the night came she trembled. It was her greatest nervous terror, lest her spell should be broken, and she should be thrown back to what she was before.

Night came, and the kind of swoon upon her. Yes, and the call from the night. The call! She rose helplessly and hurried down the corridor. The light was under his door. She sat down in the big oak arm-chair that stood near his door, and huddled herself tight in her black shawl. The corridor was dim with the big, star-studded, yellow lantern-light. Away down she could see the lamp-light in her doorway; she had left her door ajar.

But she saw nothing. Only she wrapped herself close in the black shawl, and listened to the sound from the room. It called. Oh, it called her! Why could she not go? Why could she not cross through the closed door.

Then the noise ceased. And then the light went out, under the door of his room. Must she go back? Must she go back? Oh, impossible. As impossible as that the moon should go back on her tracks, once she has risen. Daphne sat on, wrapped in her black shawl. If it must be so, she would sit on through eternity. Return she never could.

And then began the most terrible song of all. It began with a rather dreary, slow, horrible sound, like death. And then suddenly came a real call – fluty, and a kind of whistling and a strange whirr at the changes, most imperative, and utterly inhuman. Daphne rose to her feet. And at the same moment up rose the whistling throb of a summons out of the death moan.

Daphne tapped low and rapidly at the door. 'Count! Count!' she whispered. The sound inside ceased. The door suddenly opened. The pale, obscure figure of Dionys.

'Lady Daphne!' he said in astonishment, automatically standing aside.

'You called,' she murmured rapidly, and she passed intent into his room.

'No, I did not call,' he said gently, his hand on the door still.

'Shut the door,' she said abruptly.

He did as he was bid. The room was in complete darkness. There was no moon outside. She could not see him.

'Where can I sit down?' she said abruptly.

'I will take you to the couch,' he said, putting out his hand and touching her in the dark. She shuddered.

She found the couch and sat down. It was quite dark.

'What are you singing?' she said rapidly.

'I am so sorry. I did not think anyone could hear.'

'What was it you were singing?'

'A song of my country.'

'Had it any words?'

'Yes, it is a woman who was a swan, and who loved a hunter by the marsh. So she became a woman and married him and had three children. Then in the night one night the king of the swans called to her to come back, or else he would die. So slowly she turned into a swan again, and slowly she opened her wide, wide wings, and left her husband and her children.'

There was silence in the dark room. The Count had been really startled,

startled out of his mood of the song into the day-mood of human convention. He was distressed and embarrassed by Daphne's presence in his dark room. She, however, sat on and did not make a sound. He, too, sat down in a chair by the window. It was everywhere dark. A wind was blowing in gusts outside. He could see nothing inside his room: only the faint, faint strip of light under the door. But he could feel her presence in the darkness. It was uncanny, to feel her near in the dark, and not to see any sign of her, nor to hear any sound.

She had been wounded in her bewitched state by the contact with the every-day human being in him. But now she began to relapse into her spell, as she sat there in the dark. And he, too, in the silence, felt the world sinking away from him once more, leaving him once more alone on a darkened earth, with nothing between him and the infinite dark space. Except now her presence. Darkness answering to darkness, and deep answering to deep. An answer, near to him, and invisible.

But he did not know what to do. He sat still and silent as she was still and silent. The darkness inside the room seemed alive like blood. He had no power to move. The distance between them seemed absolute.

Then suddenly, without knowing, he went across in the dark, feeling for the end of the couch. And he sat beside her on the couch. But he did not touch her. Neither did she move. The darkness flowed about them thick like blood, and time seemed dissolved in it. They sat with the small, invisible distance between them, motionless, speechless, thoughtless.

Then suddenly he felt her finger-tips touch his arm, and a flame went over him that left him no more a man. He was something seated in flame, in flame unconscious, seated erect, like an Egyptian King-god in the statues. Her finger-tips slid down him, and she herself slid down in a strange, silent rush, and he felt her face against his closed feet and ankles, her hands pressing his ankles. He felt her brow and hair against his ankles, her face against his feet, and there she clung in the dark, as if in space below him. He still sat erect and motionless. Then he bent forward and put his hand on her hair.

'Do you come to me?' he murmured. 'Do you come to me?'

The flame that enveloped him seemed to sway him silently.

'Do you really come to me?' he repeated. 'But we have nowhere to go.'

He felt his bare feet wet with her tears. Two things were struggling in him, the sense of eternal solitude, like space, and the rush of dark flame that would throw him out of his solitude towards her.

He was thinking too. He was thinking of the future. He had no future in the world: of that he was conscious. He had no future in this life. Even if he lived on, it would only be a kind of enduring. But he felt that in the after-life the inheritance was his. He felt the after-life belonged to him.

Future in the world he could not give her. Life in the world he had not to offer her. Better go on alone. Surely better go on alone.

But then the tears on his feet: and her face that would face him as he left her! No, no. The next life was his. He was master of the after-life. Why fear for this life? Why not take the soul she offered him? Now and for ever, for the life that would come when they both were dead. Take her into the underworld. Take her into the dark Hades with him, like Francesca and Paolo. And in hell hold her fast, queen of the underworld, himself master of the underworld. Master of the life to come. Father of the soul that would come after.

'Listen,' he said to her softly. 'Now you are mine. In the dark you are mine. And when you die you are mine. But in the day you are not mine, because I have no power in the day. In the night, in the dark, and in death, you are mine. And that is for ever. No matter if I must leave you. I shall come again from time to time. In the dark you are mine. But in the day I cannot claim you. I have no power in the day, and no place. So remember. When the darkness comes, I shall always be in the darkness of you. And as long as I live, from time to time I shall come to find you, when I am able to, when I am not a prisoner. But I shall have to go away soon. So don't forget – you are the night wife of the ladybird, while you live and even when you die.'

Later, when he took her back to her room, he saw her door still ajar.

'You shouldn't leave a light in your room,' he murmured.

In the morning there was a curious remote look about him. He was quieter than ever, and seemed very far away. Daphne slept late. She had a strange feeling as if she had slipped off all her cares. She did not care, she did not grieve, she did not fret any more. All that had left her. She felt she could sleep, sleep, sleep – for ever. Her face, too, was very still, with a delicate look of virginity that she had never had before. She had always been Aphrodite, the self-conscious one. And her eyes, the green-blue, had been like slow, living jewels, resistant. Now they had unfolded from the hard flower-bud, and had the wonder, and the stillness of a quiet night.

Basil noticed it at once.

'You're different, Daphne,' he said. 'What are you thinking about?'

'I wasn't thinking,' she said, looking at him with candour.

'What were you doing then?'

'What does one do when one doesn't think? Don't make me puzzle it out, Basil.'

'Not a bit of it, if you don't want to.'

But he was puzzled by her. The sting of his ecstatic love for her seemed to have left him. Yet he did not know what else to do but to make love to her. She went very pale. She submitted to him, bowing her head because she was his wife. But she looked at him with fear, with sorrow, with real suffering. He could feel the heaving of her breast, and knew she was weeping. But there were no tears on her face, she was only death-pale. Her eyes were shut.

'Are you in pain?' he asked her.

'No, no!' She opened her eyes, afraid lest she had disturbed him. She did not want to disturb him.

He was puzzled. His own ecstatic, deadly love for her had received a check. He was out of the reckoning.

He watched her when she was with the Count. Then she seemed so meek – so maidenly – so different from what he had known of her. She was so still, like a virgin girl. And it was this quiet, intact quality of Virginity in her which puzzled him most, puzzled his emotions and his ideas. He became suddenly ashamed to make love to her. And because he was ashamed, he said to her as he stood in her room that night:

'Daphne, are you in love with the Count?'

He was standing by the dressing-table, uneasy. She was seated in a low chair by the tiny dying wood fire. She looked up at him with wide, slow eyes. Without a word, with wide, soft, dilated eyes she watched him. What was it that made him feel all confused. He turned his face aside, away from her wide, soft eyes.

'Pardon me, dear. I didn't intend to ask such a question. Don't take any notice of it,' he said. And he strode away and picked up a book. She lowered her head and gazed abstractedly into the fire, without a sound. Then he looked at her again, at her bright hair that the maid had plaited for the night. Her plait hung down over her soft pinkish wrap. His heart softened to her as he saw her sitting there. She seemed like his sister. The excitement of desire had left him, and now he seemed to see clear and feel true for the first time in his life. She was like a dear, dear sister to him. He felt that she was his blood-sister, nearer to him than he had imagined any woman could be. So near – so dear – and all the sex and the desire gone. He didn't want it – he hadn't wanted it. This new pure feeling was so much more wonderful.

He went to her side.

'Forgive me, darling,' he said, 'for having questioned you.'

She looked up at him with the wide eyes, without a word. His face was good and beautiful. Tears came to her eyes.

'You have the right to question me,' she said sadly.

'No,' he said. 'No, darling. I have no right to question you. Daphne! Daphne, darling! It shall be as *you* wish, between us. Shall it? Shall it be as you wish?'

'You are the husband, Basil,' she said sadly.

'Yes, darling. But' – he went on his knees beside her – 'perhaps, darling, something has changed in us. I feel as if I ought never to touch you again – as if I never *wanted* to touch you – in that way. I feel it was wrong, darling. Tell me what you think.'

'Basil, don't be angry with me.'

'It isn't anger; it's pure love, darling – it is.'

'Let us not come any nearer to one another than this, Basil – physically – shall we?' she said. 'And don't be angry with me, will you?'

'Why,' he said. 'I think myself the sexual part has been a mistake. I had rather love you – as I love now. I *know* that this is true love. The other was always a bit whipped up. I *know* I love you now, darling: now I'm free from that other. But what if it comes upon me, that other, Daphne?'

'I am always your wife,' she said quietly. 'I am always your wife. I want always to obey you, Basil: what you wish.'

'Give me your hand, dear.'

She gave him her hand. But the look in her eyes at the same time warned him and frightened him. He kissed her hand and left her.

It was to the Count she belonged. This had decided itself in her down to the depths of her soul. If she could not marry him and be his wife in the world, it had nevertheless happened to her for ever. She could no more question it. Question had gone out of her.

Strange how different she had become – a strange new quiescence. The last days were slipping past. He would be going away – Dionys: he with the still remote face, the man she belonged to in the dark and in the light, for ever. He would be going away. He said it must be so. And she acquiesced. The grief was deep, deep inside her. He must go away. Their lives could not be one life, in this world's day. Even in her anguish she knew it was so. She knew he was right. He was for her infallible. He spoke the deepest soul in her.

She never *saw* him as a lover. When she saw him, he was the little officer, a prisoner, quiet, claiming nothing in all the world. And when she went to him as his lover, his wife, it was always dark. She only knew his voice and his contact in darkness. 'My wife in darkness,' he said to her. And in this too she believed him. She would not have contradicted him, no, not for anything on earth: lest, contradicting him she should lose the dark treasure of stillness and bliss which she kept in her breast even when her heart was wrung with the agony of knowing he must go.

No, she had found this wonderful thing after she had heard him singing: she had suddenly collapsed away from her old self into this darkness, this peace, this quiescence that was like a full dark river flowing eternally in her soul. She had gone to sleep from the *nuit blanche* of her days. And Basil, wonderful, had changed almost at once. She feared him, lest he might change back again. She would always have him to fear. But deep inside her she only feared for this love of hers for the Count: this dark, everlasting love that was like a full river flowing for ever inside her. Ah, let that not be broken.

She was so still inside her. She could sit so still, and feel the day slowly, richly changing to night. And she wanted nothing, she was short of nothing. If only Dionys need not go away! If only he need not go away!

But he said to her, the last morning:

'Don't forget me. Always remember me. I leave my soul in your hands and your womb. Nothing can ever separate us, unless we betray one another. If you have to give yourself to your husband, do so, and obey him. If you are true to me, innerly, innerly true, he will not hurt us. He is generous, be generous to him. And never fail to believe in me. Because even on the other side of death I shall be watching for you. I shall be king in Hades when I am dead. And you will be at my side. You will never leave me any more, in the after-death. So don't be afraid in life. Don't be afraid. If you have to cry tears, cry them. But in your heart of hearts know that I shall come again, and that I have taken you for ever. And so, in your heart of hearts be still, be still, since you are the wife of the ladybird.' He laughed as he left her, with his own beautiful, fearless laugh. But they were strange eyes that looked after him.

He went in the car with Basil back to Voynich Hall.

'I believe Daphne will miss you,' said Basil.

The Count did not reply for some moments.

'Well, if she does,' he said, 'there will be no bitterness in it.'

'Are you sure?' smiled Basil.

'Why – if we are sure of anything,' smiled the Count.

'She's changed, isn't she?'

'Is she?'

'Yes, she's quite changed since you came, Count.'

'She does not seem to me so very different from the girl of seventeen whom I knew.'

'No – perhaps not. I didn't know her then. But she's very different from the wife I have known.'

'A regrettable difference?'

'Well – no, not as far as she goes. She is much quieter inside herself. You know, Count, something of me died in the war. I feel it will take me an eternity to sit and think about it all.'

'I hope you may think it out to your satisfaction, Major.'

'Yes, I hope so too. But that is how it has left me – feeling as if I needed eternity now to brood about it all, you know. Without the need to act – or even to love, really. I suppose love is action.'

'Intense action,' said the Count.

'Quite so. I know really how I feel. I only ask of life to spare me from further effort of action of any sort – even love. And then to fulfil myself, brooding through eternity. Of course, I don't mind *work*, mechanical action. That in itself is a form of inaction.'

'A man can only be happy following his own inmost need,' said the Count.

'Exactly!' said Basil. 'I will lay down the law for nobody, not even for myself. And live my day— '

'Then you will be happy in your own way. I find it so difficult to keep from laying the law down for myself,' said the Count. 'Only the thought of death and the after life saves me from doing it any more.'

'As the thought of eternity helps me,' said Basil. 'I suppose it amounts to the same thing.'

The Man
Who Died

Chapter One

There was a peasant near Jerusalem who acquired a young gamecock which looked a shabby little thing, but which put on brave feathers as spring advanced, and was resplendent with arched and orange neck by the time the fig trees were letting out leaves from their end-tips.

This peasant was poor, he lived in a cottage of mud-brick, and had only a dirty little inner courtyard with a tough fig tree for all his territory. He worked hard among the vines and olives and wheat of his master, then came home to sleep in the mud-brick cottage by the path. But he was proud of his young rooster. In the shut-in yard were three shabby hens which laid small eggs, shed the few feathers they had, and made a disproportionate amount of dirt. There was also, in a corner under a straw roof, a dull donkey that often went out with the peasant to work, but sometimes stayed at home. And there was the peasant's wife, a black-browed youngish woman who did not work too hard. She threw a little grain, or the remains of the porridge mess, to the fowls, and she cut green fodder with a sickle for the ass.

The young cock grew to a certain splendour. By some freak of destiny, he was a dandy rooster, in that dirty little yard with three patchy hens. He learned to crane his neck and give shrill answers to the crowing of other cocks, beyond the walls, in a world he knew nothing of. But there was a special fiery colour to his crow, and the distant calling of the other cocks roused him to unexpected outbursts.

'How he sings,' said the peasant, as he got up and pulled his day-shirt over his head.

'He is good for twenty hens,' said the wife.

The peasant went out and looked with pride at his young rooster. A saucy, flamboyant bird, that has already made the final acquaintance of the three tattered hens. But the cockerel was tipping his head, listening to the challenge of far-off unseen cocks, in the unknown world. Ghost voices, crowing at him mysteriously out of limbo. He answered with a ringing defiance, never to be daunted.

'He will surely fly away one of these days,' said the peasant's wife.

So they lured him with grain, caught him, though he fought with all his wings and feet, and they tied a cord round his shank, fastening it against the spur; and they tied the other end of the cord to the post that held up the donkey's straw pent-roof.

The young cock, freed, marched with a prancing stride of indignation away from the humans, came to the end of his string, gave a tug and a hitch of his tied leg, fell over for a moment, scuffled frantically on the unclean earthen floor, to the horror of the shabby hens, then with a sickening lurch, regained his feet, and stood to think. The peasant and the peasant's wife laughed heartily, and the young cock heard them. And he knew, with a gloomy, foreboding kind of knowledge that he was tied by the leg.

He no longer pranced and ruffled and forged his feathers. He walked within the limits of his tether sombrely. Still he gobbled up the best bits of food. Still, sometimes, he saved an extra-best bit for his favourite hen of the moment. Still he pranced with quivering, rocking fierceness upon such of his harem as came nonchalantly within range, and gave off the invisible lure. And still he crowed defiance to the cock-crows that showered up out of limbo, in the dawn.

But there was now a grim voracity in the way he gobbled his food, and a pinched triumph in the way he seized upon the shabby hens. His voice, above all, had lost the full gold of its clangour. He was tied by the leg, and he knew it. Body, soul and spirit were tied by that string.

Underneath, however, the life in him was grimly unbroken. It was the cord that should break. So one morning, just before the light of dawn, rousing from his slumbers with a sudden wave of strength, he leaped forward on his wings, and the string snapped. He gave a wild, strange squawk, rose in one lift to the top of the wall, and there he crowed a loud and splitting crow. So loud, it woke the peasant.

At the same time, at the same hour before dawn, on the same morning, a man awoke from a long sleep in which he was tied up. He woke numb and cold, inside a carved hole in the rock. Through all the long sleep his body had been full of hurt, and it was still full of hurt. He did not open his eyes. Yet he knew that he was awake, and numb, and cold, and rigid, and full of hurt, and tied up. His face was banded with cold bands, his legs were bandaged together. Only his hands were loose.

He could move if he wanted: he knew that. But he had no want. Who would want to come back from the dead? A deep, deep nausea stirred in him, at the premonition of movement. He resented already the fact of the strange, incalculable moving that had already taken place in him: the moving back into consciousness. He had not wished it. He had wanted to stay outside, in the place where even memory is stone dead.

But now, something had returned to him, like a returned letter, and in that return he lay overcome with a sense of nausea. Yet suddenly his hands moved. They lifted up, cold, heavy and sore. Yet they lifted up, to drag away the cloth from his face, and push at the shoulder-bands. Then they fell again, cold, heavy, numb, and sick with having moved even so much, unspeakably unwilling to move further.

With his face cleared and his shoulders free, he lapsed again, and lay dead, resting on the cold nullity of being dead. It was the most desirable. And almost, he had it complete: the utter cold nullity of being outside.

Yet when he was most nearly gone, suddenly, driven by an ache at the wrists, his hands rose and began pushing at the bandages of his knees, his feet began to stir, even while his breast lay cold and dead still.

And at last, the eyes opened. On to the dark. The same dark! Yet perhaps there was a pale chink, of the all-disturbing light, prising open the pure dark. He could not lift his head. The eyes closed. And again it was finished.

Then suddenly he leaned up, and the great world reeled. Bandages fell away. And narrow walls of rock closed upon him, and gave the new anguish of imprisonment. There were chinks of light. With a wave of strength that came from revulsion, he leaned forward, in that narrow well of rock, and leaned frail hands on the rock near the chinks of light.

Strength came from somewhere, from revulsion; there was a crash and a wave of light, and the dead man was crouching in his lair, facing the animal onrush of light. Yet it was hardly dawn. And the strange, piercing keenness of daybreak's sharp breath was on him. It meant full awakening.

Slowly, slowly he crept down from the cell of rock with the caution of the bitterly wounded. Bandages and linen and perfume fell away, and he crouched on the ground against the wall of rock, to recover oblivion. But he saw his hurt feet touching the earth again, with unspeakable pain, the earth they had meant to touch no more, and he saw his thin legs that had died, and pain unknowable, pain like utter bodily disillusion, filled him so full that he stood up, with one torn hand on the ledge of the tomb.

To be back! To be back again, after all that! He saw the linen swathing-bands fallen round his dead feet, and stooping, he picked them up, folded them, and laid them back in the rocky cavity from which he had emerged. Then he took the perfumed linen sheet, wrapped it round him as a mantle, and turned away, to the wanness of the chill dawn.

He was alone; and having died, was even beyond loneliness.

Filled still with the sickness of unspeakable disillusion, the man stepped with wincing feet down the rocky slope, past the sleeping soldiers, who lay wrapped in their woollen mantles under the wild laurels. Silent, on naked scarred feet, wrapped in a white linen shroud, he glanced down for a moment on the inert, heap-like bodies of the soldiers. They were repulsive, a slow squalor of limbs, yet he felt a certain compassion. He passed on towards the road, lest they should wake.

Having nowhere to go, he turned from the city that stood on her hills. He slowly followed the road away from the town, past the olives, under which purple anemones were drooping in the chill of dawn, and rich-green herbage was pressing thick. The world, the same as ever, the natural world, thronging with greenness, a nightingale winsomely, wistfully, coaxingly calling from the bushes beside a runnel of water, in the world, the natural world of morning and evening, forever undying, from which he had died.

He went on, on scarred feet, neither of this world nor of the next. Neither here nor there, neither seeing nor yet sightless, he passed dimly on, away from the city and its precincts, wondering why he should be travelling, yet driven by a dim, deep nausea of disillusion, and a resolution of which he was not even aware.

Advancing in a kind of half-consciousness under the dry stone wall of the olive orchard, he was roused by the shrill, wild crowing of a cock just near him, a sound which made him shiver as if electricity had touched him. He saw a black and orange cock on a bough above the road, then running through the olives of the upper level a peasant in a grey woollen shirt-tunic. Leaping out of greenness, came the black and orange cock with the red comb, his tail-feathers streaming lustrous.

'O, stop him, master!' called the peasant. 'My escaped cock!'

The man addressed, with a sudden flicker of smile, opened his great white wings of a shroud in front of the leaping bird. The cock fell back with a squawk and a flutter, the peasant jumped forward, there was a terrific beating of wings and whirring of feathers, then the peasant had the escaped cock safely under his arm, its wings shut down, its face crazily craning forward, its round eyes goggling from its white chops.

'It's my escaped cock!' said the peasant, soothing the bird with his left hand, as he looked perspiringly up into the face of the man wrapped in white linen.

The peasant changed countenance, and stood transfixed, as he looked into the dead-white face of the man who had died. That dead-white face, so still, with the black beard growing on it as if in death; and those wide-open, black, sombre eyes, that had died! and those washed scars on the waxy forehead! The slow-blooded man of the field let his jaw drop, in childish inability to meet the situation.

'Don't be afraid,' said the man in the shroud. 'I am not dead. They took me down too soon. So I have risen up. Yet if they discover me, they will do it all over again . . .'

He spoke in a voice of old disgust. Humanity! Especially humanity in authority! There was only one thing it could do. He looked with black, indifferent eyes into the quick, shifty eyes of the peasant. The peasant quailed, and was powerless under the look of deathly indifference and strange, cold resoluteness. He could only say the one thing he was afraid to say:

'Will you hide in my house, master?'

'I will rest there. But if you tell anyone, you know what will happen. You will have to go before a judge.'

'Me! I shan't speak. Let us be quick!'

The peasant looked round in fear, wondering sulkily why he had let himself in for this doom. The man with scarred feet climbed painfully up to the level of the olive garden, and followed the sullen, hurrying peasant across the green wheat among the olive trees. He felt the cool silkiness of the young wheat under his feet that had been dead, and the roughishness of its separate life was apparent to him. At the edges of rocks, he saw the silky, silvery-haired buds of the scarlet anemone bending downwards. And they, too, were in another world. In his own world he was alone, utterly alone. These things around him were in a world that had never died. But he himself had died, or had been killed from out of it, and all that remained now was the great void nausea of utter disillusion.

They came to a clay cottage, and the peasant waited dejectedly for the other man to pass.

'Pass!' he said. 'Pass! We have not been seen.'

The man in white linen entered the earthen room, taking with him the aroma of strange perfumes. The peasant closed the door, and passed through the inner doorway into the yard, where the ass stood within the high walls, safe from being stolen. There the peasant, in great disquietude, tied up the cock. The man with the waxen face sat down on a mat near the hearth, for he was spent and barely conscious. Yet he heard outside the whispering of the peasant to his wife, for the woman had been watching from the roof.

Presently they came in, and the woman hid her face. She poured water, and put bread and dried figs on a wooden platter.

'Eat master!' said the peasant. 'Eat! No one has seen.'

But the stranger had no desire for food. Yet he moistened a little bread in the water, and ate it, since life must be. But desire was dead in him, even for food and drink. He had risen without desire, without even the desire to live, empty save for the all-overwhelming disillusion that lay like nausea where his life had been. Yet perhaps, deeper even than disillusion, was a desireless resoluteness, deeper even than consciousness.

The peasant and his wife stood near the door, watching. They saw with terror the livid wounds on the thin, waxy hands and the thin feet of the stranger, and the small lacerations in the still dead forehead. They smelled with terror the scent of rich perfumes that came from him, from his body. And they looked at the fine, snowy, costly linen. Perhaps really he was a dead king, from the region of terrors. And he was still cold and remote in the region of death, with perfumes coming from his transparent body as if from some strange flower.

Having with difficulty swallowed some of the moistened bread, he lifted his eyes to them. He saw them as they were: limited, meagre in their life, without any splendour of gesture and of courage. But they were what they were, slow, inevitable parts of the natural world. They had no nobility, but fear made them compassionate.

And the stranger had compassion on them again, for he knew that they would respond best to gentleness, giving back a clumsy gentleness again.

'Do not be afraid,' he said to them gently. 'Let me stay a little while with you. I shall not stay long. And then I shall go away for ever. But do not be afraid. No harm will come to you through me.'

They believed him at once, yet the fear did not leave them. And they said: 'Stay, master, while ever you will. Rest! Rest quietly!'

But they were afraid.

So he let them be, and the peasant went away with the ass. The sun had risen bright, and in the dark house with the door shut, the man was again as if in the tomb. So he said to the woman: 'I would lie in the yard.'

And she swept the yard for him, and laid him a mat, and he lay down under the wall in the morning sun. There he saw the first green leaves spurting like flames from the ends of the enclosed fig tree, out of the bareness to the sky of spring above. But the man who had died could not look, he only lay quite still in the sun, which was not yet too hot, and had no desire in him, not even to move. But he lay with his thin legs in the sun, his black, perfumed hair falling into the hollows of his neck, and his thin, colourless arms utterly inert. As he lay there, the hens clucked, and scratched, and the escaped cock, caught and tied by the leg again, cowered in a corner.

The peasant woman was frightened. She came peeping, and, seeing him never move, feared to have a dead man in the yard. But the sun had grown stronger, he opened his eyes and looked at her. And now she was frightened of the man who was alive, and spoke nothing.

He opened his eyes, and saw the world again bright as glass. It was life, in which he had no share any more. But it shone outside him, blue sky, and a bare fig tree with little jets of green leaf. Bright as glass, and he was not of it, for desire had failed.

Yet he was there, and not extinguished. The day passed in a kind of coma, and at evening he went into the house. The peasant man came home, but he was frightened, and had nothing to say. The stranger, too, ate of the mess of beans, a little. Then he washed his hands and turned to the wall, and was silent. The peasants were silent too. They watched their guest sleep. Sleep was so near death he could still sleep.

Yet when the sun came up, he went again to lie in the yard. The sun was the one thing that drew him and swayed him, and he still wanted to feel the cool air of the morning in his nostrils, see the pale sky overhead. He still hated to be shut up.

As he came out, the young cock crowed. It was a diminished, pinched cry, but there was that in the voice of the bird stronger than chagrin. It was the necessity to live, and even to cry out the triumph of life. The man who had died stood and watched the cock who had escaped and been caught, ruffling himself up, rising forward on his toes, throwing up his head, and parting his beak in another challenge from life to death. The brave sounds rang out, and thought they were diminished by the cord round the bird's leg, they were not cut off. The man who had died looked nakedly on life, and saw a vast resoluteness everywhere flinging itself up in stormy or subtle wave-crests, foam-tips emerging out of the blue invisible, a black and orange cock or the green flame-tongues out of the extremes of the fig tree. They came forth, these things and creatures of spring, glowing with desire and with assertion. They came like crests of foam, out of the blue flood of the invisible desire, out of the vast invisible sea of strength, and they came coloured and tangible, evanescent, yet deathless in their coming. The man who had died looked on the great swing into existence of things that had not died, but he saw no longer their tremulous desire to exist and to be. He heard instead their ringing, ringing, defiant challenge to all other things existing.

The man lay still, with eyes that had died now wide open and darkly still, seeing the everlasting resoluteness of life. And the cock, with the flat, brilliant glance, glanced back at him, with a bird's half-seeing look. And always the man who had died saw not the bird alone, but the short, sharp wave of life of which the bird was the crest. He watched the queer, beaky motion of the creature as it gobbled into itself the scraps of food; its glancing of the eye of life, ever alert and watchful, over-weening and cautious, and the voice of its life, crowing triumph and assertion, yet strangled by a cord of circumstance. He seemed to hear the queer speech of very life, as the cock triumphantly imitated the clucking of the favourite hen, when she had laid an egg, a clucking which still had, in the male bird, the hollow chagrin of the cord round his leg. And when the man threw a bit of bread to the cock, it called with an extraordinary cooing tenderness, tousling and saving the morsel for the hens. The hens ran up greedily, and carried the morsel away beyond the reach of the string.

Then, walking complacently after them, suddenly the male bird's leg would hitch at the end of his tether, and he would yield with a kind of collapse. His flag fell, he seemed to diminish, he would huddle in the shade. And he was young, his tail-feathers, glossy as they were, were not fully grown. It was not till evening again that the tide of life in him made him forget. Then when his favourite hen came strolling unconcernedly near him, emitting the lure, he pounced on her with all his feathers vibrating. And the man who had died watched the unsteady, rocking vibration of the bent bird, and it was not the bird he saw, but one wave-tip of life overlapping for a minute another, in the tide of the swaying ocean of life. And the destiny of life seemed more fierce and compulsive to him even than the destiny of death. The doom of death was a shadow compared to the raging destiny of life, the determined surge of life.

At twilight the peasant came home with the ass, and he said: 'Master! It is said that the body was stolen from the garden, and the tomb is empty, and the soldiers are taken away, accursed Romans! And the women are there to weep.'

The man who had died looked at the man who had not died.

'It is well,' he said. 'Say nothing, and we are safe.'

And the peasant was relieved. He looked rather dirty and stupid, and even as much flaminess as that of the young cock, which he had tied by the leg, would never glow in him. He was without fire. But the man who had died thought to himself:

'Why, then, should he be lifted up? Clods of earth are turned over for refreshment, they are not to be lifted up. Let the earth remain earthy, and hold its own against the sky. I was wrong to seek to lift it up. I was wrong to try to interfere. The ploughshare of devastation will be set in the soil of Judea, and the life of this peasant will be overturned like the sods of the field. No man can save the earth from tillage. It is tillage, not salvation . . .'

So he saw the man, the peasant, with compassion; but the man who had died no longer wished to interfere in the soul of the man who had not died, and who could never die, save to return to earth. Let him return to earth in his own good hour, and let no one try to interfere when the earth claims her own.

So the man with scars let the peasant go from him, for the peasant had no rebirth in him. Yet the man who had died said to himself: 'He is my host.'

And at dawn, when he was better, the man who had died rose up, and on slow, sore feet retraced his way to the garden. For he had been betrayed in a garden, and buried in a garden. And as he turned round the screen of laurels, near the rockface, he saw a woman hovering by the tomb, a woman in blue and yellow. She peeped again into the mouth of the hole, that was like a deep cupboard. But still there was nothing. And she wrung her hands and wept. And as she turned away, she saw the man in white, standing by the laurels, and she gave a cry, thinking it might be a spy, and she said:

'They have taken him away!'

So he said to her:

'Madeleine!'

Then she reeled as if she would fall, for she knew him. And he said to her:

'Madeleine! Do not be afraid. I am alive. They took me down too soon, so I came back to life. Then I was sheltered in a house.'

She did not know what to say, but fell at his feet to kiss them.

'Don't touch me, Madeleine,' he said. 'Not yet! I am not yet healed and in touch with men.'

So she wept because she did not know what to do. And he said:

'Let us go aside, among the bushes, where we can speak unseen.'

So in her blue mantle and her yellow robe, she followed him among the trees, and he sat down under a myrtle bush. And he said:

'I am not yet quite come to. Madeleine, what is to be done next?'

'Master!' she said. 'Oh, we have wept for you! And will you come back to us?'

'What is finished is finished, and for me the end is past,' he said. 'The stream will run till no more rains fill it, then it will dry up. For me, that life is over.'

'And will you give up your triumph?' she said sadly.

'My triumph,' he said, 'is that I am not dead. I have out-lived my mission and know no more of it. It is my triumph. I have survived the day and the death of my interference, and am still a man. I am young still, Madeleine, not even come to middle age. I am glad all that is over. It had to be. But now I am glad it is over, and the day of my interference is done. The teacher and the saviour are dead in me; now I can go about my business, into my own single life.'

She heard him, and did not fully understand. But what he said made her feel disappointed.

'But you will come back to us?' she said, insisting.

'I don't know what I shall do,' he said. 'When I am healed, I shall know better. But my mission is over, and my teaching is finished, and death has saved me from my own salvation. Oh, Madeleine, I want to take my single way in life, which is my portion. My public life is over, the life of my self-importance. Now I can wait on life, and say nothing, and have no one betray me. I wanted to be greater than the limits of my hands and feet, so I brought betrayal on myself. And I know I wronged Judas, my poor Judas. For I have died, and now I know my own limits. Now I can live without striving to sway others any more. For my reach ends in my finger-tips, and my stride is no longer than the ends of my toes. Yet I would embrace multitudes, I who have never truly embraced even one. But Judas and the high priests saved me from my own salvation, and soon I can turn to my destiny like a bather in the sea at dawn, who has just come down to the shore alone.'

'Do you want to be alone henceforward?' she asked. 'And was your mission nothing? Was it all untrue?'

'Nay!' he said. 'Neither were your lovers in the past nothing. They were much to you, but you took more than you gave. Then you came to me for salvation from your own excess. And I, in my mission, I too ran to excess. I gave more than I took, and that also is woe and vanity. So Pilate and the high priests saved me from my own excessive salvation. Don't run to excess now in living, Madeleine. It only means another death.'

She pondered bitterly, for the need for excessive giving was in her, and she could not bear to be denied.

'And will you not come back to us?' she said. 'Have you risen for yourself alone?'

He heard the sarcasm in her voice, and looked at her beautiful face which still was dense with excessive need for salvation from the woman she had been, the female who had caught men at her will. The cloud of necessity was on her, to be saved from the old, wilful Eve, who had embraced many men and taken more than she gave. Now the other doom was on her. She wanted to give without taking. And that, too, is hard, and cruel to the warm body.

'I have not risen from the dead in order to seek death again,' he said.

She glanced up at him, and saw the weariness settling again on his waxy face, and the vast disillusion in his dark eyes, and the underlying indifference. He felt her glance, and said to himself:

'Now my own followers will want to do me to death again, for having risen up different from their expectation.'

'But you will come to us, to see us, us who love you?' she said.

He laughed a little and said:

'Ah, yes.' Then he added: 'Have you a little money? Will you give me a little money? I owe it.'

She had not much, but it pleased her to give it to him.

'Do you think,' he said to her, 'that I might come and live with you in your house?'

She looked up at him with large blue eyes, that gleamed strangely.

'Now?' she said with peculiar triumph.

And he, who shrank now from triumph of any sort, his own or another's, said:

'Not now! Later, when I am healed, and . . . and I am in touch with the flesh.'

The words faltered in him. And in his heart he knew he would never go to live in her house. For the flicker of triumph had gleamed in her eyes; the greed of giving. But she murmured in a humming rapture:

'Ah, you know I would give up everything to you.'

'Nay!' he said. 'I didn't ask that.'

A revulsion from all the life he had known came over him again, the great nausea of disillusion, and the spear-thrust through his bowels. He crouched under the myrtle bushes, without strength. Yet his eyes were open. And she looked at him again, and she saw that it was not the Messiah. The Messiah had not risen. The enthusiasm and the burning purity were gone, and the rapt youth. His youth was dead. This man was middle-aged and disillusioned, with a certain terrible indifference, and a resoluteness which love would never conquer. This was not the Master she had so adored, the young, flamy, unphysical exalter of her soul. This was nearer to the lovers she had known of old, but with a greater indifference to the personal issue, and a lesser susceptibility.

She was thrown out of the balance of her rapturous, anguished adoration. This risen man was the death of her dream.

'You should go now,' he said to her. 'Do not touch me, I am in death. I shall come again here, on the third day. Come if you will, at dawn. And we will speak again.'

She went away, perturbed and shattered. Yet as she went, her mind discarded the bitterness of the reality, and she conjured up rapture and wonder, that the Master was risen and was not dead. He was risen, the Saviour, the exalter, the wonder-worker! He was risen, but not as man; as pure God, who should not be touched by flesh, and who should be rapt away into Heaven. It was the most glorious and most ghostly of the miracles.

Meanwhile the man who had died gathered himself together at last, and slowly made his way to the peasants' house. He was glad to go back to them, and away from Madeleine and his own associates. For the peasants had the inertia of earth and would let him rest, and as yet, would put no compulsion on him.

The woman was on the roof, looking for him. She was afraid that he had gone away. His presence in the house had become like gentle wine to her. She hastened to the door, to him.

'Where have you been?' she said. 'Why did you go away?'

'I have been to walk in a garden, and I have seen a friend, who gave me a little money. It is for you.'

He held out his thin hand, with the small amount of money, all that Madeleine could give him. The peasant's wife's eyes glistened, for money was scarce, and she said:

'Oh, master! And is it truly mine?'

'Take it!' he said. 'It buys bread, and bread brings life.'

So he lay down in the yard again, sick with relief at being alone again. For with the peasants he could be alone, but his own friends would never let him be alone. And in the safety of the yard, the young cock was dear to him, as it shouted in the helpless zest of life, and finished in the helpless humiliation of being tied by the leg. This day the ass stood swishing her tail under the shed. The man who had died lay down and turned utterly away from life, in the sickness of death in life.

But the woman brought wine and water, and sweetened cakes, and roused him, so that he ate a little, to please her. The day was hot, and as she crouched to serve him, he saw her breasts sway from her humble body, under her smock. He knew she wished he would desire her, and she was youngish, and not unpleasant. And he, who had never known a woman, would have desired her if he could. But he could not want her, though he felt gently towards her soft, crouching, humble body. But it was her thoughts, her consciousness, he could not mingle with. She was pleased with the money, and now she wanted to take more from him. She wanted the embrace of his body. But her little soul was hard, and short-sighted, and grasping, her body had its little greed, and no gentle reverence of the return gift. So he spoke a quiet pleasant word to her and turned away. He could not touch the little, personal body, the little, personal life of this woman, nor in any other. He turned away from it without hesitation.

Risen from the dead, he had realised at last that the body, too, has its little life, and beyond that, the greater life. He was virgin, in recoil from the little, greedy life of the body. But now he knew that virginity is a form of greed; and that the body rises again to give and to take, to take and to give, ungreedily. Now he knew that he had risen for the woman, or women, who knew the greater life of the body, not greedy to give, not greedy to take, and with whom he could mingle his body. But having died, he was patient, knowing there was time, an eternity of time. And he was driven by no greedy desire, either to give himself to others, or to grasp anything for himself. For he had died.

The peasant came home from work and said:

'Master, I thank you for the money. But we did not want it. And all I have is yours.'

But the man who had died was sad, because the peasant stood there in the little, personal body, and his eyes were cunning and sparkling with the hope of greater rewards in money later on. True, the peasant had taken him in free, and had risked getting no reward. But the hope was cunning in him. Yet even this was as men are made. So when the peasant would have helped him to rise, for night had fallen, the man who had died said:

'Don't touch me, brother. I am not yet risen to the Father.'

The sun burned with greater splendour, and burnished the young cock brighter. But the peasant kept the string renewed, and the bird was a prisoner. Yet the flame of life burned up to a sharp point in the cock, so that it eyed askance and haughtily the man who had died. And the man smiled and held the bird dear, and he said to it:

'Surely thou art risen to the Father, among birds.'

And the young cock, answering, crowed.

When at dawn on the third morning the man went to the garden, he was absorbed, thinking of the greater life of the body, beyond the little, narrow, personal life. So he came through the thick screen of laurel and myrtle bushes, near the rock, suddenly, and he saw three women near the tomb. One was Madeleine, and one was the woman who had been his mother, and the third was a woman he knew, called Joan. He looked up, and saw them all, and they saw him, and they were all afraid.

He stood arrested in the distance, knowing they were there to claim him back, bodily. But he would in no wise return to them. Pallid, in the shadow of a grey morning that was blowing to rain, he saw them, and turned away. But Madeleine hastened towards him.

'I did not bring them,' she said. 'They have come of themselves. See, I have brought you money! . . . Will you not speak to them?'

She offered him some gold pieces, and he took them, saying:

'May I have this money? I shall need it. I cannot speak to them, for I am not yet ascended to the Father. And I must leave you now.'

'Ah! Where will you go?' she cried.

He looked at her, and saw she was clutching for the man in him who had died and was dead, the man of his youth and his mission, of his chastity and his fear, of his little life, his giving without taking.

'I must go to my Father!' he said.

'And you will leave us? There is your mother!' she cried, turning round with the old anguish, which yet was sweet to her.

'But now I must ascend to my Father,' he said, and he drew back into the bushes, and so turned quickly, and went away, saying to himself:

'Now I belong to no one and have no connection, and mission or gospel is gone from me. Lo! I cannot make even my own life, and what have I to save? . . . I can learn to be alone.'

So he went back to the peasants' house, to the yard where the young cock was tied by the leg with a string. And he wanted no one, for it was best to be alone; for the presence of people made him lonely. The sun and the subtle salve of spring healed his wounds, even the gaping wound of disillusion through his bowels was closing up. And his need of men and women, his fever to have them and to be saved by them, this too was healing in him. Whatever came of touch between himself and the race of men, henceforth, should come without trespass or compulsion. For he said to himself:

'I tried to compel them to live, so they compelled me to die. It is always so, with compulsion. The recoil kills the advance. Now is my time to be alone.'

Therefore he went no more to the garden, but lay still and saw the sun, or walked at dusk across the olive slopes, among the green wheat, that rose a palm-breadth higher every sunny day. And always he thought to himself:

'How good it is to have fulfilled my mission, and to be beyond it. Now I can be alone, and leave all things to themselves, and the fig tree may be barren if it will, and the rich may be rich. My way is my own alone.'

So the green jets of leaves unspread on the fig tree, with the bright, translucent, green blood of the tree. And the young cock grew brighter, more lustrous with the sun's burnishing; yet always tied by the leg with a string. And the sun went down more and more in pomp, out of the gold and red-flushed air. The man who had died was aware of it all, and he thought:

'The Word is but the midge that bites at evening. Man is tormented with words like midges, and they follow him right into the tomb. But beyond the tomb they cannot go. Now I have passed the place where words can bite no more and the air is clear, and there is nothing to say, and I am alone within my own skin, which is the walls of all my domain.'

So he healed of his wounds, and enjoyed his immortality of being alive without fret. For in the tomb he had slipped that noose which we call care. For in the tomb he had left his striving self, which cares and asserts itself. Now his uncaring self healed and became whole within his skin, and he smiled to himself with pure aloneness, which is one sort of immortality.

Then he said to himself: 'I will wander the earth, and say nothing. For nothing is so marvellous as to be alone in the phenomenal world, which is raging, and yet apart. And I have not seen it, I was too much blinded by my confusion within it. Now I will wander among the stirring of the phenomenal world, for it is the stirring of all things among themselves which leaves me purely alone.'

So he communed with himself, and decided to be a physician. Because the power was still in him to heal any man or child who touched his compassion. Therefore he cut his hair and his beard after the right fashion, and smiled to himself. And he bought himself shoes, and the right mantle, and put the right cloth over his head, hiding all the little scars. And the peasant said:

'Master, will you go forth from us?'

'Yes, for the time is come for me to return to men.'

So he gave the peasant a piece of money, and said to him:

'Give me the cock that escaped and is now tied by the leg. For he shall go forth with me.'

So for a piece of money the peasant gave the cock to the man who had died, and at dawn the man who had died set out into the phenomenal world, to be fulfilled in his own loneliness in the midst of it. For previously he had been too much mixed up in it. Then he had died. Now he must come back, to be alone in the midst. Yet even now he did not go quite alone, for under his arm, as he went, he carried the cock, whose tail fluttered gaily behind, and who craned his head excitedly, for he too was adventuring out for the first time into the wider phenomenal world, which is the stirring of the body of cocks also. And the peasant woman shed a few tears, but then went indoors, being a peasant, to look again at the pieces of money. And it seemed to her, a gleam came out of the pieces of money, wonderful.

The man who had died wandered on, and it was a sunny day. He looked around as he went, and stood aside as the pack-train passed by, towards the city. And he said to himself:

'Strange is the phenomenal world, dirty and clean together! And I am the same. Yet I am apart! And life bubbles variously. Why should I have wanted it to bubble all alike? What a pity I preached to them! A sermon is so much more likely to cake into mud, and to close the fountains, than is a psalm or a song. I made a mistake. I understand that they executed me for preaching to them. Yet they could not finally execute me, for now I am risen in my own aloneness, and inherit the earth, since I lay no claim on it. And I will be alone in the seethe of all things; first and foremost, for ever, I shall be alone. But I must toss this bird into the seethe of phenomena, for he must ride his wave. How hot he is with life! Soon, in some place, I shall leave him among the hens. And perhaps one evening I shall meet a woman who can lure my risen body, yet leave me my aloneness. For the body of my desire has died, and I am not in touch anywhere. Yet how do I know! All at least is life. And this cock gleams with bright aloneness, though he answers the lure of hens. And I shall hasten on to that village on the hill ahead of me; already I am tired and weak, and want to close my eyes to everything.'

Hastening a little with the desire to have finished going, he overtook two men going slowly, and talking. And being soft-footed, he heard they were speaking of himself. And he remembered them, for he had known them in his life, the life of his mission. So he greeted them, but did not disclose himself in the dusk, and they did not know him. He said to them:

'What then of him who would be king, and was put to death for it?'

They answered suspiciously: 'Why ask you of him?'

'I have known him, and thought much about him,' he said.

So they replied: 'He has risen.'

'Yea! And where is he, and how does he live?'

'We know not, for it is not revealed. Yet he is risen, and in a little while will ascend unto the Father.'

'Yea! And where then is his Father?'

'Know ye not? You are then of the Gentiles! The Father is in Heaven, above the cloud and the firmament.'

'Truly? Then how will he ascend?'

'As Elijah the Prophet, he shall go up in a glory.'

'Even into the sky.'

'Into the sky.'

'Then is he not risen in the flesh?'

'He is risen in the flesh.'

'And will he take flesh up into the sky?'

'The Father in Heaven will take him up.'

The man who had died said no more, for his say was over, and words beget words, even as gnats. But the man asked him: 'Why do you carry a cock?'

'I am a healer,' he said, 'and the bird hath virtue.'

'You are not a believer?'

'Yea! I believe the bird is full of life and virtue.'

They walked on in silence after this, and he felt they disliked his answer. So he smiled to himself, for a dangerous phenomenon in the world is a man of narrow belief, who denies the right of his neighbour to be alone. And as they came to the outskirts of the village, the man who had died stood still in the gloaming and said in his old voice:

'Know ye me not?'

And they cried in fear: 'Master!'

'Yea!' he said, laughing softly. And he turned suddenly away, down a side lane, and was gone under the wall before they knew.

So he came to an inn where the asses stood in the yard. And he called for fritters, and they were made for him. So he slept under a shed. But in the morning he was wakened by a loud crowing, and his cock's voice ringing in his ears. So he saw the rooster of the inn walking forth to battle, with his hens, a goodly number, behind him. Then the cock of the man who had died sprang forth, and a battle began between the birds. The man of the inn ran to save his rooster, but the man who had died said:

'If my bird wins I will give him thee. And if he lose, thou shalt eat him.'

So the birds fought savagely, and the cock of the man who had died killed the common cock of the yard. Then the man who had died said to his young cock:

'Thou at least hast found thy kingdom, and the females to thy body. Thy aloneness can take on splendour, polished by the lure of thy hens.'

And he left his bird there, and went on deeper into the phenomenal world, which is a vast complexity of entanglements and allurements. And he asked himself a last question:

'From what, and to what, could this infinite whirl be saved?'

So he went his way, and was alone. But the way of the world was past belief, as he saw the strange entanglement of passions and circumstance and compulsion everywhere, but always the dread insomnia of compulsion. It was fear, the ultimate fear of death, that made men mad. So always he must move on, for if he stayed, his neighbours wound the strangling of their fear and bullying round him. There was nothing he could touch, for all, in a mad assertion of the ego, wanted to put a compulsion on him, and violate his intrinsic solitude. It was the mania of cities and societies and hosts, to lay a compulsion upon a man, upon all men. For men and women alike were mad with the egoistic fear of their own nothingness. And he thought of his own mission, how he had tried to lay the compulsion of love on all men. And the old nausea came back on him. For there was no contact without a subtle attempt to inflict a compulsion. And already he had been compelled even into death. The nausea of the old wound broke out afresh, and he looked again on the world with repulsion, dreading its mean contacts.

Chapter Two

The wind came cold and strong from inland, from the invisible snows of Lebanon. But the temple, facing south and west, towards Egypt, faced the splendid sun of winter as he curved down towards the sea, the warmth and radiance flooded in between the pillars of painted wood. But the sea was invisible, because of the trees, though its dashing sounded among the hum of pines. The air was turning golden to afternoon. The woman who served Isis stood in her yellow robe, and looked up at the steep slopes coming down to the sea, where the olive trees silvered under the wind like water splashing. She was alone save for the goddess. And in the winter afternoon the light stood erect and magnificent off the invisible sea, filling the hills of the coast. She went towards the sun, through the grove of Mediterranean pine trees and evergreen oaks, in the midst of which the temple stood, on a little, tree-covered tongue of land between two bays.

It was only a very little way, and then she stood among the dry trunks of the outermost pines, on the rocks under which the sea smote and sucked, facing the open where the bright sun gloried in winter. The sea was dark, almost indigo, running away from the land, and crested with white. The hand of the wind brushed it strangely with shadow, as it brushed the olives of the slopes with silver. And there was no boat out.

The three boats were drawn high up on the steep shingle of the little bay, by the small grey tower. Along the edge of the shingle ran a high wall, inside which was a garden occupying the brief flat of the bay, then rising in terraces up the steep slope of the coast. And there, some little way up, within another wall, stood the low white villa, white and alone as the coast, overlooking the sea. But higher, much higher up, where the olives had given way to pine trees again, ran the coast road, keeping to the height to be above the gullies that came down to the bays.

Upon it all poured the royal sunshine of the January afternoon. Or rather, all was part of the great sun, glow and substance and immaculate loneliness of the sea, and pure brightness.

Crouching in the rocks above the dark water, which only swung up and down, two slaves, half naked, were dressing pigeons for the evening meal. They pierced the throat of a blue, live bird, and let the drops of blood fall into the heaving sea, with curious concentration. They were performing some sacrifice, or working some incantation. The woman of the temple, yellow and white and alone like a winter narcissus, stood between the pines of the small, humped peninsula where the temple secretly hid, and watched.

A black-and-white pigeon, vividly white, like a ghost escaped over the low dark sea, sped out, caught the wind, tilted, rode, soared and swept over the pine trees, and wheeled away, a speck, inland. It had escaped. The priestess heard the cry of the boy slave, a garden slave of about seventeen. He raised his arms to heaven in anger as the pigeon wheeled away, naked and angry and young he held out his arms. Then he turned and seized the girl in an access of rage, and beat her with his fist that was stained with pigeon's blood. And she lay down with her face hidden, passive and quivering. The woman who owned them watched. And as she watched, she saw another onlooker, a stranger, in a low, broad hat, and a cloak of grey homespun, a dark bearded man standing on the little causeway of a rock that was the neck of her temple peninsula. By the blowing of his dark-grey cloak she saw him. And he saw her, on the rocks like a white-and-yellow narcissus, because of the flutter of her white linen tunic, below the yellow mantle of wool. And both of them watched the two slaves.

The boy suddenly left off beating the girl. He crouched over her, touching her, trying to make her speak. But she lay quite inert, face down on the smoothed rock. And he put his arms round her and lifted her, but she slipped back to earth like one dead, yet far too quickly for anything dead. The boy, desperate, caught her by the hips and hugged her to him, turning her over there. There she seemed inert, all her fight was in her shoulders. He twisted her over, intent and unconscious, and pushed his hands between her thighs, to push them apart. And in an instant he was covering her in the blind, frightened frenzy of a boy's first passion. Quick and frenzied his young body quivered naked on hers, blind, for a minute. Then it lay quite still, as if dead.

And then, in terror, he peeped up. He peeped round, and drew slowly to his feet, adjusting his loin-rag. He saw the stranger, and then he saw, on the rocks beyond, the lady of Isis, his mistress. And as he saw her, his whole body shrank and cowed, and with a strange cringing motion he scuttled lamely towards the door in the wall.

The girl sat up and looked after him. When she had seen him disappear, she too looked round. And she saw the stranger and the priestess. Then with a sullen movement she turned away, as if she had seen nothing, to the four dead pigeons and the knife, which lay there on the rock. And she began to strip the small feathers, so that they rose on the wind like dust.

The priestess turned away. Slaves! Let the overseer watch them. She was not interested. She went slowly through the pines again, back to the temple, which stood in the sun in a small clearing at the centre of the tongue of land. It was a small temple of wood, painted all pink and white and blue, having at the front four wooden pillars rising like stems to the swollen lotus-bud of Egypt at the top, supporting the roof and open, spiky lotus-flowers of the outer frieze, which went round under the eaves. Two low steps of stone led up to the platform before the pillars, and the chamber behind the pillars was open. There a low stone altar stood, with a few embers in its hollow, and the dark stain of blood in its end groove.

She knew her temple so well, for she had built it at her own expense, and tended it for seven years. There it stood, pink and white, like a flower in the little clearing, backed by blackish evergreen oaks; and the shadow of afternoon was already washing over its pillar bases.

She entered slowly, passing through to the dark inner chamber, lighted by a perfumed oil-flame. And once more she pushed shut the door, and once more she threw a few grains of incense on a brazier before the goddess, and once more she sat down before her goddess, in the almost-darkness, to muse, to go away into the dreams of the goddess.

It was Isis; but not Isis, Mother of Horus. It was Isis Bereaved, Isis in Search. The goddess, in painted marble, lifted her face and strode, one thigh forward, through the frail fluting of her robe, in the anguish of bereavement and of search. She was looking for the fragments of the dead Osiris, dead and scattered asunder, dead, torn apart, and thrown in fragments over the wide world. And she must find his hands and his feet, his heart, his thighs, his head, his belly, she must gather him together and fold her arms round the re-assembled body till it became warm again, and roused to life, and could embrace her, and could fecundate her womb. And the strange rapture and anguish of search went on through the years, as she lifted her throat and her hollowed eyes looked inward, in the tormented ecstasy of seeking, and the delicate navel of her bud-like belly showed through the frail, girdled robe with the eternal asking, asking, of her search. And through the years she found him bit by bit, heart and head and limbs and body. And yet she had not found the last reality, the final clue to him, that alone could bring him really back to her. For she was Isis of the subtle lotus, the womb which waits submerged and in bud, waits for the touch of that other inward sun that streams its rays from loins of the male Osiris.

This was the mystery the woman had served alone for seven years, since she was twenty, till now she was twenty-seven. Before, when she was young, she had lived in the world, in Rome, in Ephesus, in Egypt. For her father had been one of Anthony's captains and comrades, had fought with Anthony and had stood with him when Caesar was murdered, and through to the days of shame. Then he had come again across to Asia, out of favour with Rome, and had been killed in the mountains beyond Lebanon. The widow, having no favour to hope for from Octavius, had retired to her small property on the coast under Lebanon, taking her daughter from the world, a girl of nineteen, beautiful but unmarried.

When she was young the girl had known Caesar, and had shrunk from his eagle-like rapacity. The golden Anthony had sat with her many a half-hour, in the splendour of his great limbs and glowing manhood, and talked with her of the philosophies and the gods. For he was fascinated as a child by the gods, though he mocked at them, and forgot them in his own vanity. But he said to her:

'I have sacrificed two doves for you, to Venus, for I am afraid you make no offering to the sweet goddess. Beware you will offend her. Come, why is the flower of you so cool within? Does never a ray nor a glance find its way through? Ah, come, a maid should open to the sun, when the sun leans towards her to caress her.'

And the big, bright eyes of Anthony laughed down on her, bathing her in his glow. And she felt the lovely glow of his male beauty and his amorousness bathe all her limbs and her body. But it was as he said: the very flower of her womb was cool, was almost cold, like a bud in shadow of frost, for all the flooding of his sunshine. So Anthony, respecting her father, who loved her, had left her.

And it had always been the same. She saw many men, young and old. And on the whole, she liked the old ones best, for they talked to her still and sincere, and did not expect her to open like a flower to the sun of their maleness. Once she asked a philospher: 'Are all women born to be given to men?' To which the old man answered slowly:

'Rare women wait for the re-born man. For the lotus, as you know, will not answer to all the bright heat of the sun. But she curves her dark, hidden head in the depths, and stirs not. Till, in the night, one of these rare, invisible suns that have been killed and shine no more, rises among the stars in unseen purple, and like the violet, sends its rare purple rays out into the night. To these the lotus stirs as to a caress, and rises upwards through the flood, and lifts up her bent head, and opens with an expansion such as no other flower knows, and spreads her sharp rays of bliss, and offers her soft, gold depths such as no other flower possesses, to the penetration of the flooding, violet-dark sun that has died and risen and makes no show. But for the golden brief day-suns of show such as Anthony, and for the hard winter suns of power, such as Caesar, the lotus stirs not, nor will ever stir. Those will only tear open the bud. Ah, I tell you, wait for the re-born and wait for the bud to stir.'

So she had waited. For all the men were soldiers or politicians in the Roman spell, assertive, manly, splendid apparently but of an inward mean-ness, an inadequacy. And Rome and Egypt alike had left her alone, unroused. And she was a woman to herself, she would not give herself for a surface glow, nor marry for reasons. She would wait for the lotus to stir.

And then, in Egypt, she had found Isis, in whom she spelled her mystery. She had brought Isis to the shores of Sidon, and lived with her in the mystery of search; whilst her mother, who loved affairs, controlled the small estate and the slaves with a free hand.

When the woman had roused from her muse and risen to perform the last brief ritual to Isis, she replenished the lamp and left the sanctuary, locking the door. In the outer world, the sun had already set, and twilight was chill among the humming trees, which hummed still, though the wind was abating.

A stranger in the dark, broad hat rose from the corner of the temple steps, holding his hat in the wind. He was dark-faced, with a black pointed beard. 'Oh, madam, whose shelter may I implore?' he said to the woman, who stood in her yellow mantle on a step above him, beside a pink-and-white painted pillar. Her face was rather long and pale, her dusky blonde hair was held under a thin gold net. She looked down on the vagabond with indifference. It was the same she had seen watching the slaves.

'Why come you down from the road?' she asked.

'I saw the temple like a pale flower on the coast, and would rest among the trees of the precincts, if the lady of the goddess permits.'

'It is Isis in Search,' she said, answering his first question.

'The goddess is great,' he replied.

She looked at him still with mistrust. There was a faint, remote smile in the dark eyes lifted to her, though the face was hollow with suffering. The vagabond divined her hesitation, and was mocking her.

'Stay here upon the steps,' she said. 'A slave will show you the shelter.'

'The lady of Egypt is gracious.'

She went down the rocky path of the humped peninsula in her gilded sandals. Beautiful were her ivory feet, beneath the white tunic, and above the saffron mantle her dusky-blonde head bent as with endless musings. A woman entangled in her own dream. The man smiled a little, half bitterly, and sat again on the step to wait, drawing his mantle round him, in the cold twilight.

At length a slave appeared, also in hodden grey.

'Seek ye the shelter of our lady?' he said insolently.

'Even so.'

'Then come.'

With the brusque insolence of a slave waiting on a vagabond, the young fellow led through the trees and down into a little gully in the rock, where, almost in darkness, was a small cave, with a litter of the tall heaths that grew on the waste places of the coast, under the stone-pines. The place was dark, but absolutely silent from the wind. There was still a faint odour of goats.

'Here sleep!' said the slave. 'For the goats come no more on this half-island. And there is water!' He pointed to a little basin of rock where the maidenhair fern fringed a dripping mouthful of water.

Having scornfully bestowed his patronage, the slave departed. The man who had died climbed out to the tip of the peninsula, where the wave thrashed. It was rapidly getting dark, and the stars were coming out. The wind was abating for the night. Inland, the steep grooved up-slope was dark to the long wavering outline of the crest against the translucent sky. Only now and then a lantern flickered towards the villa.

The man who had died went back to the shelter. There he took bread from his leather pouch, dipped it in the water of the tiny spring, and slowly ate. Having eaten and washed his mouth, he looked once more at the bright stars in the pure windy sky, then settled the heath for his bed. Having laid his hat and his sandals aside, and put his pouch under his cheek for a pillow, he slept, for he was very tired. Yet during the night the cold woke him, pinching wearily through his weariness. Outside was brilliantly starry, and still windy. He sat and hugged himself in a sort of coma, and towards dawn went to sleep again.

In the morning the coast was still chill in shadow, though the sun was up behind the hills, when the woman came down from the villa towards the goddess. The sea was fair and pale blue, lovely in newness, and at last the wind was still. Yet the waves broke white in the many rocks, and tore in the shingle of the little bay. The woman came slowly, towards her dream. Yet she was aware of an interruption.

As she followed the little neck of rock on to her peninsula, and climbed the slope between the trees to the temple, a slave came down and stood, making his obeisance. There was a faint insolence in his humility. 'Speak!' she said.

'Lady, the man is there, he still sleeps. Lady, may I speak?'

'Speak!' she said, repelled by the fellow.

'Lady, the man is an escaped malefactor.'

The slave seemed to triumph in imparting the unpleasant news.

'By what sign?'

'Behold his hands and feet! Will the lady look on him?'

'Lead on!'

The slave led quickly over the mound of the hill down to the tiny ravine. There he stood aside, and the woman went into the crack towards the cave. Her heart beat a little. Above all, she must preserve her temple inviolate.

The vagabond was asleep with his cheek on his scrip, his mantle wrapped round him, but his bare, soiled feet curling side by side, to keep each other warm, and his hand lying clenched in sleep. And in the pale skin of his feet usually covered by sandal-straps, she saw the scars, and in the palm of the loose hand.

She had no interest in men, particularly in the servile class. Yet she looked at the sleeping face. It was worn, hollow, and rather ugly. But, a true priestess, she saw the other kind of beauty in it, the sheer stillness of the deeper life. There was even a sort of majesty in the dark brows, over the still, hollow cheeks. She saw that his black hair, left long, in contrast to the Roman fashion, was touched with grey at the temples, and the black pointed beard had threads of grey. But that must be suffering or misfortune, for the man was young. His dusky skin had the silvery glisten of youth still.

There was a beauty of much suffering, and the strange calm candour of finer life in the whole delicate ugliness of the face. For the first time, she was touched on the quick at the sight of a man, as if the tip of a fine flame of living had touched her. It was the first time. Men had roused all kinds of feeling in her, but never had touched her with the flame-tip of life.

She went back under the rock to where the slave waited.

'Know!' she said. 'This is no malefactor, but a free citizen of the east. Do not disturb him. But when he comes forth bring him to me; tell him I would speak with him.'

She spoke coldly, for she found slaves invariably repellent, a little repulsive. They were so embedded in the lesser life, and their appetites and their small consciousness were a little disgusting. So she wrapped her dream round her and went to the temple, where a slave girl brought winter roses and jasmine for the altar. But to-day, even in her ministrations, she was disturbed.

The sun rose over the hill, sparkling, the light fell triumphantly on the little pine-covered peninsula of the coast, and on the pink temple, in the pristine newness. The man who had died woke up, and put on his sandals. He put on his hat too, slung his scrip under his mantle, and went out, to see the morning in all its blue and its new gold. He glanced at the little yellow-and-white narcissus sparkling gaily in the rocks. And he saw the slave waiting for him like a menace.

'Master!' said the slave. 'Our lady would speak with you at the house of Isis.'

'It is well,' said the wanderer.

He went slowly, staying to look at the pale blue sea like a flower in unruffled bloom, and the white fringes among the rocks, like white rock-flowers, the hollow slopes sheering up high from the shore, grey with olive trees and green with bright young wheat, and set with the white, small villa. All fair and pure in the January morning.

The sun fell on the corner of the temple, he sat down on the step in the sunshine, in the infinite patience of waiting. He had come back to life, but not the same life that he had left, the life of little people and the little day. Re-born, he was in the other life, the greater day of the human consciousness. And he was alone and apart from the little day, and out of contact with the daily people. Not yet had he accepted the irrevocable *noli me tangere* which separates the re-born from the vulgar. The separation was absolute, as yet here at the temple he felt peace, the hard, bright pagan peace with hostility of slaves beneath.

The woman came into the dark inner doorway of the temple from the shrine, and stood there, hesitating. She could see the dark figure of the man, sitting in that terrible stillness that was portentous to her, had something almost menacing in its patience.

She advanced across the outer chamber of the temple, and the man, becoming aware of her, stood up. She addressed him in Greek, but he said:

'Madam, my Greek is limited. Allow me to speak vulgar Syrian.'

'Whence come you? Whither go you?' she asked, with a hurried preoccupation of a priestess.

'From the east beyond Damascus – and I go west as the road goes,' he replied slowly.

She glanced at him with sudden anxiety and shyness.

'But why do you have the marks of a malefactor?' she asked abruptly.

'Did the Lady of Isis spy upon me in my sleep?' he asked, with a grey weariness.

'The slave warned me – your hands and feet—' she said.

He looked at her. Then he said:

'Will the Lady of Isis allow me to bid her farewell, and go up to the road?'

The wind came in a sudden puff, lifting his mantle and his hat. He put up his hand to hold the brim, and she saw again the thin brown hand with its scar.

'See! The scar!' she said, pointing.

'Even so!' he said. 'But farewell, and to Isis my homage and my thanks for sleep.'

He was going. But she looked up at him with her wondering blue eyes.

'Will you not look at Isis?' she said, with sudden impulse. And something stirred in him, like pain.

'Where then?' he said.

'Come!'

He followed her into the inner shrine, into the almost-darkness. When his eyes got used to the faint glow of the lamp, he saw the goddess striding like a ship, eager in the swirl of her gown, and he made his obeisance.

'Great is Isis!' he said. 'In her search she is greater than death. Wonderful is such walking in a woman, wonderful the goal. All men praise thee, Isis, thou greater than the mother unto man.'

The woman of Isis heard, and threw incense on the brazier. Then she looked at the man.

'Is it well with thee here?' she asked him. 'Has Isis brought thee home to herself?'

He looked at the priestess in wonder and trouble.

'I know not,' he said.

But the woman was pondering that this was the lost Osiris. She felt it in the quick of her soul. And her agitation was intense.

He would not stay in the close, dark, perfumed shrine. He went out again to the morning, to the cold air. He felt something approaching to touch him, and all his flesh was still woven with pain and the wild commandment: *Noli me tangere!* Touch me not! Oh, don't touch me!

The woman followed into the open with timid eagerness. He was moving away.

'Oh, stranger, do not go! Oh, stay a while with Isis!'

He looked at her, at her face open like a flower, as if a sun had risen in her soul. And again his loins stirred.

'Would you detain me, girl of Isis?' he said.

'Stay! I am sure you are Osiris!' she said.

He laughed suddenly. 'Not yet!' he said. Then he looked at her wistful face. 'But I will sleep another night in the cave of the goats, if Isis wills it,' he added.

She put her hands together with a priestess's childish happiness.

'Ah! Isis will be glad!' she said.

So he went down to the shore in great trouble, saying to himself: 'Shall I give myself into this touch? Shall I give myself into this touch? Men have tortured me to death with their touch. Yet this girl of Isis is a tender flame of healing. I am a physician, yet I have no healing like the flame of this tender girl. The flame of this tender girl! Like the first pale crocus of the spring. How could I have been blind to the healing and the bliss in the crocus-like body of a tender woman! Ah, tenderness! More terrible and lovely than the death I died—'

He pried small shell-fish from the rocks, and ate them with relish and wonder for the simple taste of the sea. And inwardly he was tremulous, thinking: 'Dare I come into touch? For this is farther than death. I have dared to let them lay hands on me and put me to death. But dare I come into this tender touch of life? Oh, this is harder—'

But the woman went into the shrine again, and sat rapt in pure muse, through the long hours, watching the swirling stride of the yearning goddess, and the navel of the bud-like belly, like a seal on the virgin urge of the search. And she gave herself to the woman-flow and to the urge of Isis in Search.

Towards sundown she went on the peninsula to look for him. And she found him gone towards the sun, as she had gone the day before, and sitting on the pine-needles at the foot of the tree, where she had stood when first she saw him. Now she approached tremulously and slowly, afraid lest he did not want her. She stood near him unseen, till suddenly he glanced up at her from under his broad hat, and saw the westering sun on her netted hair. He was startled, yet he expected her.

'Is that your home?' he said, pointing to the white, low villa on the slope of olives.

'It is my mother's house. She is a widow, and I am her only child.'

'And are these all her slaves?'

'Except those that are mine.'

Their eyes met for a moment.

'Will you too sit to see the sun go down?' he said.

He had not risen to speak to her. He had known too much pain. So she sat on the dry brown pine-needles, gathering her saffron mantle round her knees. A boat was coming in, out of the open glow into the shadow of the bay, and slaves were lifting small nets, their babble coming off the surface of the water.

'And this is home to you,' he said.

'But I serve Isis in Search,' she replied.

He looked at her. She was like a soft, musing cloud, somehow remote. His soul smote him with passion and compassion.

'Mayst thou find thy desire, maiden,' he said, with sudden earnestness.

'And art thou not Osiris?' she asked.

He flushed suddenly.

'Yes, if thou wilt heal me!' he said. 'For the death aloofness is still upon me, and I cannot escape it.'

She looked at him for a moment in fear from the soft blue sun of her eyes. Then she lowered her head, and they sat in silence in the warmth and glow of the western sun: the man who had died, and the woman of the pure search.

The sun was curving down to the sea, in grand winter splendour. It fell on the twinkling, naked bodies of the slaves, with their ruddy broad hams and their small black heads, as they ran spreading the nets on the pebble beach. The all-tolerant Pan watched over them. All-tolerant Pan should be their god for ever.

The woman rose as the sun's rim dipped, saying:

'If you will stay, I will send down victual and covering.'

'The lady your mother, what will she say?'

The woman of Isis looked at him strangely, but with a tinge of misgiving. 'It is my own,' she said.

'It is good,' he said, smiling faintly and foreseeing difficulties.

He watched her go, with her absorbed, strange motion of the self-dedicate. Her dun head was a little bent, the white linen swung about her ivory ankles. And he saw the naked slaves stand to look at her, with a certain wonder, and even a certain mischief. But she passed intent through the door in the wall, on the bay.

The man who had died sat on at the foot of the tree overlooking the strand, for on the little shore everything happened. At the small stream which ran in round the corner of the property wall, women slaves were still washing linen, and now and again came the hollow chock! chock! chock! as they beat it against the smooth stones in the dark little hollow of the pool. There was a smell of olive refuse on the air; and sometimes still the faint rumble of the grindstone that was milling the olives, inside the garden, and the sound of the slave calling to the ass at the mill. Then through the doorway a woman stepped, a grey-haired woman in a mantle of whitish wool, and there followed her a bare-headed man in a toga, a Roman: probably her steward or overseer. They stood on the high shingle above the sea, and cast round a rapid glance. The broad-hammed, ruddy-bodied slaves bent absorbed and abject over the nets, picking them clean, the women washing linen thrust their palms with energy down on the wash, the old slave bent absorbed at the water's edge, washing the fish and the polyps of the catch. And the woman and the overseer saw it all in one glance. They also saw, seated at the foot of the tree on the rocks of the peninsula, the strange man silent and alone. And the man who had died saw that they spoke of him. Out of the little sacred world of the peninsula he looked on the common world, and saw it still hostile.

The sun was touching the sea, across the tiny bay stretched the shadow of the opposite humped headland. Over the shingle, now blue and cold in shadow, the elderly woman trod heavily, in shadow too, to look at the fish spread in the flat basket of the old man crouching at the water's edge: a naked old slave with fat hips and shoulders, on whose soft, fairish-orange body the last sun twinkled, then died. The old slave continued cleaning the fish absorbedly, not looking up: as if the lady were the shadow of twilight falling on him.

Then from the gateway stepped two slave-girls with flat baskets on their heads, and from one basket the terra-cotta wine-jar and the oil-jar poked up, leaning slightly. Over the massive shingle, under the wall, came the girls, and the woman of Isis in her saffron mantle stepped in twilight after them. Out at sea, the sun still shone. Here was shadow. The mother with grey head stood at the sea's edge and watched the daughter, all yellow and white, with dun blonde head, swinging unseeing and unheeding after the slave-girls, towards the neck of rock of the peninsula; the daughter, travelling in her absorbed other-world. And not moving from her place, the elderly mother watched that procession of three file up the rise of the headland, between the trees, and disappear, shut in by trees. No slave had lifted a head to look. The grey-haired woman still watched the trees where her daughter had disappeared. Then she glanced again at the foot of the tree, where the man who had died was still sitting, inconspicuous now, for the sun had left him; and only the far blade of the sea shone bright. It was evening. Patience! Let destiny move!

The mother plodded with a stamping stride up the shingle: not long and swinging and rapt, like the daughter, but short and determined. Then down the rocks opposite came two naked slaves trotting with huge bundles of dark green on their shoulders, so their broad, naked legs twinkled underneath like insects' legs, and their heads were hidden. They came trotting across the shingle, heedless and intent on their way, when suddenly the man, the Roman-looking overseer, addressed them, and they stopped dead. They stood invisible under their loads, as if they might disappear altogether, now they were arrested. Then a hand came out and pointed to the peninsula. Then the two green-heaped slaves trotted on, towards the temple precincts. The grey-haired woman joined the man, and slowly the two passed through the door again, from the shingle of the sea to the property of the villa. Then the old, fat-shouldered slave rose, pallid in the shadow, with his tray of fish from the sea, and the woman rose from the pool, dusky and alive, piling the wet linen in a heap on to the flat baskets, and the slaves who had cleaned the net gathered its whitish folds together. And the old slave with the fish-basket on his shoulder, and the women slaves with the heaped baskets of wet linen on their heads, and the two slaves with the folded net, and the slave with oars on his shoulders, and the boy with the folded sail on his arm, gathered in a naked group near the door, and the man who had died heard the low buzz of their chatter. Then as the wind wafted cold, they began to pass through the door.

It was the life of the little day, the life of little people. And the man who had died said to himself: 'Unless we encompass it in the greater day, and set the little life in the circle of the greater life, all is disaster.'

Even the tops of the hills were in shadow. Only the sky was still upwardly radiant. The sea was a vast milky shadow. The man who had died rose a little stiffly and turned into the grove.

There was no one at the temple. He went on to his lair in the rock. There, the slave-men had carried out the old heath of the bedding, swept the rock floor, and were spreading with nice art the myrtle, then the rougher heath, then the soft, bushy heath-tips on top, for a bed. Over it all they put a well-tanned white ox-skin. The maids had laid folded woollen covers at the head of the cave, and the wine-jar, the oil-jar, a terra-cotta drinking-cup and a basket containing bread, salt, cheese, dried figs and eggs stood neatly arranged. There was also a little brazier of charcoal. The cave was suddenly full, and a dwelling-place.

The woman of Isis stood in the hollow by the tiny spring.

Only one slave at a time could pass. The girl-slaves waited at the entrance to the narrow place. When the man who had died appeared, the woman sent the girls away. The men-slaves still arranged the bed, making the job as long as possible. But the woman of Isis dismissed them too. And the man who had died came to look at his house.

'Is it well?' the woman asked him.

'It is very well,' the man replied. 'But the lady, your mother, and he who is no doubt the steward, watched while the slaves brought the goods. Will they not oppose you?'

'I have my own portion! Can I not give of my own? Who is going to oppose me and the gods?' she said, with a certain soft fury, touched with exasperation. So that he knew that her mother would oppose her, and that the spirit of the little life would fight against the spirit of the greater. And he thought: 'Why did the woman of Isis relinquish her portion in the daily world? She should have kept her goods fiercely!'

'Will you eat and drink?' she said. 'On the ashes are warm eggs. And I will go up to the meal at the villa. But in the second hour of the night I shall come down to the temple. O, then, will you come too to Isis?' She looked at him, and a queer glow dilated her eyes. This was her dream, and it was greater than herself. He could not bear to thwart her or hurt her in the least thing now. She was in the full glow of her woman's mystery.

'Shall I wait at the temple?' he said.

'O, wait at the second hour and I shall come.' He heard the humming supplication in her voice and his fibres quivered.

'But the lady, your mother?' he said gently.

The woman looked at him, startled.

'She will not thwart me!' she said.

So he knew that the mother would thwart the daughter, for the daughter had left her goods in the hands of her mother, who would hold fast to this power.

But she went, and the man who had died lay reclining on his couch, and ate the eggs from the ashes, and dipped his bread in oil, and ate it, for his flesh was dry: and he mixed wine and water, and drank. And so he lay still, and the lamp made a small bud of light.

He was absorbed and enmeshed in new sensations. The woman of Isis was lovely to him, not so much in form as in the wonderful womanly glow of her. Suns beyond suns had dipped her in mysterious fire, the mysterious fire of a potent woman, and to touch her was like touching the sun. Best of all was her tender desire for him, like sunshine, so soft and still.

'She is like sunshine upon me,' he said to himself, stretching his limbs. 'I have never before stretched my limbs in such sunshine, as her desire for me. The greatest of all gods granted me this.'

At the same time he was haunted by the fear of the outer world. 'If they can, they will kill us,' he said to himself. 'But there is a law of the sun which protects us.'

And again he said to himself: 'I have risen naked and branded. But if I am naked enough for this contact, I have not died in vain. Before I was clogged.'

He rose and went out. The night was chill and starry, and of a great wintry splendour. 'There are destinies of splendour,' he said to the night, 'after all our doom of littleness and meanness and pain.'

So he went up silently to the temple, and waited in darkness against the inner wall, looking out on a grey darkness, stars, and rims of trees. And he said again to himself: 'There are destinies of splendour, and there is a greater power.'

So at last he saw the light of her silk lanthorn swinging, coming intermittent between the trees, yet coming swiftly. She was alone, and near, the light softly swishing on her mantle-hem. And he trembled with fear and with joy, saying to himself: 'I am almost more afraid of this touch than I was of death. For I am more nakedly exposed to it.'

'I am here, Lady of Isis,' he said softly out of the dark.

'Ah!' she cried, in fear also, yet in rapture. For she was given to her dream.

She unlocked the door of the shrine, and he followed after her. Then she latched the door shut again. The air inside was warm and close and perfumed. The man who had died stood by the closed door and watched the woman. She had come first to the goddess. And dim-lit, the goddess-statue stood surging forward, a little fearsome like a great woman-presence urging.

The priestess did not look at him. She took off her saffron mantle and laid it on a low couch. In the dim light she was bare-armed, in her girdled white tunic. But she was still hiding herself away from him. He stood back in shadow and watched her softly fan the brazier and fling on incense. Faint clouds of sweet aroma arose on the air. She turned to the statue in the ritual of approach, softly swaying forward with a slight lurch, like a moored boat, tipping towards the goddess.

He watched the strange rapt woman, and he said to himself: 'I must leave her alone in her rapture, her female mysteries.' So she tipped in her strange forward-swaying rhythm before the goddess. Then she broke into a murmur of Greek, which he could not understand. And, as she murmured, her swaying softly subsided, like a boat on a sea that grows still. And as he watched her, he saw her soul in its aloneness, and its female difference. He said to himself: 'How different she is from me, how strangely different! She is afraid of me, and my male difference. She is getting herself naked and clear of her fear. How sensitive and softly alive she is, with a life so different from mine! How beautiful with a soft, strange courage, of life, so different from my courage of death! What a beautiful thing, like the heart of a rose, like the core of a flame. She is making herself completely penetrable. Ah! how terrible to fail her, or to trespass on her!'

She turned to him, her face glowing from the goddess.

'You are Osiris, aren't you?' she said naïvely.

'If you will,' he said.

'Will you let Isis discover you? Will you not take off your things?'

He looked at the woman, and lost his breath. And his wounds, and especially the death-wound through his belly, began to cry again.

'It has hurt so much!' he said. 'You must forgive me if I am still held back.'

But he took off his cloak and his tunic and went naked towards the idol, his breast panting with the sudden terror of overwhelming pain, memory of overwhelming pain, and grief too bitter.

'They did me to death!' he said in excuse of himself, turning his face to her for a moment.

And she saw the ghost of the death in him as he stood there thin and stark before her, and suddenly she was terrified, and she felt robbed. She felt the shadow of the grey, grisly wing of death triumphant.

'Ah, Goddess,' he said to the idol in the vernacular. 'I would be so glad to live, if you would give me my clue again.'

For here again he felt desperate, faced by the demand of life, and burdened still by his death.

'Let me anoint you!' the woman said to him softly. 'Let me anoint the scars! Show me, and let me anoint them!'

He forgot his nakedness in this re-evoked old pain. He sat on the edge of the couch, and she poured a little ointment into the palm of his hand. And as she chafed his hand, it all came back, the nails, the holes, the cruelty, the unjust cruelty against him who had offered only kindness. The agony of injustice and cruelty came over him again, as in his death-hour. But she chafed the palm, murmuring: 'What was torn becomes a new flesh, what was a wound is full of fresh life; this scar is the eye of the violet.'

And he could not help smiling at her, in her naïve priestess's absorption. This was her dream, and he was only a dream-object to her. She would never know or understand what he was. Especially she would never know the death that was gone before in him. But what did it matter? She was different. She was woman: her life and her death were different from him. Only she was good to him.

When she chafed his feet with oil and tender, tender healing, he could not refrain from saying to her:

'Once a woman washed my feet with tears, and wiped them with her hair, and poured on precious ointment.'

The woman of Isis looked up at him from her earnest work, interrupted again.

'Were they hurt then?' she said. 'Your feet?'

'No, no! It was while they were whole.'

'And did you love her?'

'Love had passed in her. She only wanted to serve,' he replied. 'She had been a prostitute.'

'And did you let her serve you?' she asked.

'Yea.'

'Did you let her serve you with the corpse of her love?'

'Ay!'

Suddenly it dawned on him: I asked them all to serve me with the corpse of their love. And in the end I offered them only the corpse of my love. This is my body – take and eat – my corpse—

A vivid shame went through him. 'After all,' he thought, 'I wanted them to love with dead bodies. If I had kissed Judas with live love, perhaps he would never have kissed me with death. Perhaps he loved me in the flesh, and I willed that he should love me bodilessly, with the corpse of love—'

There dawned on him the reality of the soft, warm love which is in touch, and which is full of delight. 'And I told them, blessed are they that mourn,' he said to himself. 'Alas, if I mourned even this woman here, now I am in death, I should have to remain dead, and I want so much to live. Life has brought me to this woman with warm hands. And her touch is more to me now than all my words. For I want to live—'

'Go then to the goddess!' she said softly, gently pushing him towards Isis. And as he stood there dazed and naked as an unborn thing, he heard the woman murmuring to the goddess, murmuring, murmuring with a plaintive appeal. She was stooping now, looking at the scar in the soft flesh of the socket of his side, a scar deep and like an eye sore with endless weeping, just in the soft socket above the hip. It was here that his blood had left him, and his essential seed. The woman was trembling softly and murmuring in Greek. And he in the recurring dismay of having died, and in the anguished perplexity of having tried to force life, felt his wounds crying aloud, and the deep places of the body howling again: 'I have been murdered, and I lent myself to murder. They murdered me, but I lent myself to murder—'

The woman, silent now, but quivering, laid oil in her hand and put her palm over the wound in his right side. He winced, and the wound absorbed his life again, as thousands of times before. And in the dark, wild pain and panic of his consciousness rang only one cry: 'Oh, how can she take this death out of me? She can never know! She can never understand! She can never equal it! . . .'

In silence, she softly rhythmically chafed the scar with oil. Absorbed now in her priestess's task, softly, softly gathering power, while the vitals of the man howled in panic. But as she gradually gathered power, and passed in a girdle round him to the opposite scar, gradually warmth began to take the place of the cold terror, and he felt: 'I am going to be warm again, and I am going to be whole! I shall be warm like the morning. I shall be a man. It doesn't need understanding. It needs newness. She brings me newness—'

And he listened to the faint, ceaseless wail of distress of his wounds, sounding as if for ever under the horizons of his consciousness. But the wail was growing dim, more dim.

He thought of the woman toiling over him: 'She does not know! She does not realise the death in me. But she has another consciousness. She comes to me from the opposite end of the night.'

Having chafed all his lower body with oil, having worked with her slow intensity of a priestess, so that the sound of his wounds grew dimmer and dimmer, suddenly she put her breast against the wound in his left side, and her arms round him, folding over the wound in his right side, and she pressed him to her, in a power of living warmth, like the folds of a river. And the wailing died out altogether, and there was a stillness, and darkness in his soul, unbroken, dark stillness, wholeness.

Then slowly, slowly, in the perfect darkness of his inner man, he felt the stir of something coming. A dawn, a new sun. A new sun was coming up in him, in the perfect inner darkness of himself. He waited for it breathless, quivering with a fearful hope . . . 'Now I am not myself. I am something new . . .'

And as it rose, he felt, with a cold breath of disappointment, the girdle of the living woman slip down from him, the warmth and the glow slipped from him, leaving him stark. She crouched, spent, at the feet of the goddess, hiding her face.

Stooping, he laid his hand softly on her warm, bright shoulder, and the shock of desire went through him, shock after shock, so that he wondered if it were another sort of death: but full of magnificence.

Now all his consciousness was there in the crouching, hidden woman. He stooped beside her and caressed her softly, blindly, murmuring inarticulate things. And his death and his passion of sacrifice were all as nothing to him now, he knew only the crouching fullness of the woman there, the soft white rock of life. ... 'On this rock I built my life.' The deep-folded, penetrable rock of the living woman! The woman hiding her face. Himself bending over, powerful and new like dawn.

He crouched to her, and he felt the blaze of his manhood and his power rise up in his loins, magnificent.

'I am risen!'

Magnificent, blazing indomitable in the depths of his loins, his own sun dawned, and sent its fire running along his limbs, so that his face shone unconsciously.

He untied the string on the linen tunic and slipped the garment down, till he saw the white glow of her white-gold breasts. And he touched them, and he felt his life go molten. 'Father!' he said, 'why did you hide this from me?' And he touched her with the poignancy of wonder, and the marvellous piercing transcendence of desire. 'Lo!' he said, 'this is beyond prayer.' It was the deep, interfolded warmth, warmth living and penetrable, the woman, the heart of the rose! My mansion is the intricate warm rose, my joy is this blossom!

She looked up at him suddenly, her face like a lifted light, wistful, tender, her eyes like many wet flowers. And he drew her to his breast with a passion of tenderness and consuming desire, and the last thought: 'My hour is upon me, I am taken unawares—'

So he knew her, and was one with her.

Afterwards, with a dim wonder, she touched the great scars in his sides with her finger-tips, and said:

'But they no longer hurt?'

'They are suns!' he said. 'They shine from your touch. They are my atonement with you.'

And when they left the temple, it was the coldness before dawn. As he closed the door, he looked again at the goddess, and he said: 'Lo, Isis is a kindly goddess; and full of tenderness. Great gods are warm-hearted, and have tender goddesses.'

The woman wrapped herself in her mantle and went home in silence, sightless, brooding like the lotus softly shutting again, with its gold core full of fresh life. She saw nothing, for her own petals were a sheath to her. Only she thought: 'I am full of Osiris. I am full of the risen Osiris! ...'

But the man looked at the vivid stars before dawn, as they rained down to the sea, and the dog-star green towards the sea's rim. And he thought:

'How plastic it is, how full of curves and folds like an invisible rose of dark-petalled openness that shows where the dew touches its darkness! How full it is, and great beyond all gods. How it leans around me, and I am part of it, the great rose of Space. I am like a grain of its perfume, and the woman is a grain of its beauty. Now the world is one flower of many petalled darknesses, and I am in its perfume as in a touch.'

So, in the absolute stillness and fullness of touch, he slept in his cave while the dawn came. And after the dawn, the wind rose and brought a storm, with cold rain. So he stayed in his cave in the peace and the delight of being in touch, delighting to hear the sea, and the rain on the earth, and to see one white-and-gold narcissus bowing wet, and still wet. And he said: 'This is the great atonement, the being in touch. The grey sea and the rain, the wet narcissus and the woman I wait for, the invisible Isis and the unseen sun are all in touch, and at one.'

He waited at the temple for the woman, and she came in the rain. But she said to him:

'Let me sit awhile with Isis. And come to me, will you come to me, in the second hour of night?'

So he went back to the cave and lay in stillness and in the joy of being in touch, waiting for the woman who would come with the night, and consummate again the contact. Then when night came great yearning, too, was upon her, to be in touch, to be in touch with him, nearer.

So the days came, and the nights came, and days came again, and the contact was perfected and fulfilled. And he said: 'I will ask her nothing, not even her name, for a name would set her apart.'

And she said to herself: 'He is Osiris. I wish to know no more.'

Plum blossom blew from the trees, the time of the narcissus was past, anemones lit up the ground and were gone, the perfume of bean-field was in the air. All changed, the blossom of the universe changed its petals and swung round to look another way. The spring was fulfilled, a contact was established, the man and the woman were fulfilled of one another, and departure was in the air.

One day he met her under the trees, when the morning sun was hot, and the pines smelled sweet, and on the hills the last pear bloom was scattering. She came slowly towards him, and in her gentle lingering, her tender hanging back from him, he knew a change in her.

'Hast thou conceived?' he asked her.

'Why?' she said.

'Thou art like a tree whose green leaves follow the blossom, full of sap. And there is a withdrawing about thee.'

'It is so,' she said. 'I am with young by thee. Is it good?'

'Yea!' he said. 'How should it not be good? So the nightingale calls no more from the valley-bed. But where wilt thou bear the child, for I am naked of all but life?'

'We will stay here,' she said.

'But the lady, your mother?'

A shadow crossed her brow. She did not answer.

'What when she knows?' he said.

'She begins to know.'

'And would she hurt you?'

'Ah, not me! What I have is all my own. And I shall be big with Osiris. . . . But thou, do you watch her slaves.'

She looked at him, and the peace of her maternity was troubled by anxiety.

'Let not your heart be troubled!' he said. 'I have died in the death once.'

So he knew the time was come again for him to depart. He would go alone, with his destiny. Yet not alone, for the touch would be upon him, even as he left his touch on her. And invisible suns would go with him.

Yet he must go. For here on the bay the little life of jealousy and property was resuming sway again, as the suns of passionate fecundity relaxed their sway. In the name of property, the widow and her slaves would seek to be revenged on him for the bread he had eaten, and the living touch he had established, the woman he had delighted in. But he said: 'Not twice! They shall not now profane the touch in me. My wits against theirs.'

So he watched. And he knew they plotted. So he moved from the little cave and found another shelter, a tiny cove of sand by the sea, dry and secret under the rocks.

He said to the woman:

'I must go now soon. Trouble is coming to me from the slaves. But I am a man, and the world is open. But what is between us is good, and is established. Be at peace. And when the nightingale calls again from your valley-bed, I shall come again, sure as spring.'

She said: 'O, don't go! Stay with me on half the island, and I will build a house for you and me under the pine trees by the temple, where we can live apart.'

Yet she knew that he would go. And even she wanted the coolness of her own air around her, and the release from anxiety.

'If I stay,' he said, 'they will betray me to the Romans and to their justice. But I will never be betrayed again. So when I am gone, live in peace with the growing child. And I shall come again: all is good between us, near or apart. The suns come back in their seasons: and I shall come again.'

'Do not go yet,' she said. 'I have set a slave to watch at the neck of the peninsula. Do not go yet, till the harm shows.'

But as he lay in his little cove, on a calm, still night, he heard the soft knock of oars, and the bump of a boat against the rock. So he crept out to listen. And he heard the Roman overseer say:

'Lead softly to the goat's den. And Lysippus shall throw the net over the malefactor while he sleeps, and we will bring him before justice, and the Lady of Isis shall know nothing of it. . . .'

The man who had died caught a whiff of flesh from the oiled and naked slaves as they crept up, then the faint perfume of the Roman. He crept nearer to the sea. The slave who sat in the boat sat motionless, holding the oars, for the sea was quite still. And the man who had died knew him.

So out of the deep cleft of a rock he said, in a clear voice:

'Art thou not that slave who possessed the maiden under the eyes of Isis? Art thou not the youth? Speak!'

The youth stood up in the boat in terror. His movement sent the boat bumping against the rock. The slave sprang out in wild fear, and fled up the rocks. The man who had died quickly seized the boat and stepped in, and pushed off. The oars were yet warm with the unpleasant warmth of the hands of the slaves. But the man pulled slowly out, to get into the current which set down the coast, and would carry him in silence. The high coast was utterly dark against the starry night. There was no glimmer from the peninsula: the priestess came no more at night. The man who had died rowed slowly on, with the current, and laughed to himself: 'I have sowed the seed of my life and my resurrection, and put my touch forever upon the choice woman of this day, and I carry her perfume in my flesh like essence of roses. She is dear to me in the middle of my being. But the gold and flowing serpent is coiling up again, to sleep at the root of my tree.'

'So let the boat carry me. To-morrow is another day.'

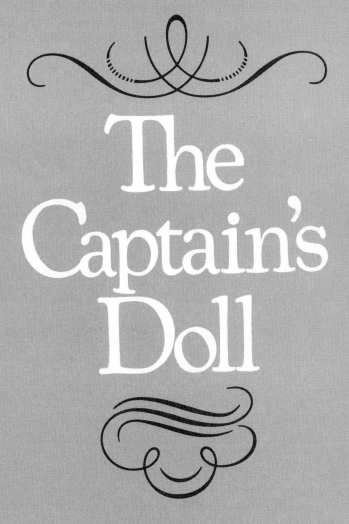

The Captain's Doll

Chapter One

'Hannele!'
   '*Ja–a.*'
   '*Wo bist du?*'
   '*Hier.*'
   '*Wo dann?*'
Hannele did not lift her head from her work. She sat in a low chair under a reading-lamp, a basket of coloured silk pieces beside her, and in her hands a doll, or mannikin, which she was dressing. She was doing something to the knee of the mannikin, so that the poor little gentleman flourished head downwards with arms wildly tossed out. And it was not at all seemly, because the doll was a Scotch soldier in tight-fitting tartan trews.

There was a tap at the door, and the same voice, a woman's, calling:
   'Hannele?'
   '*Ja–a!*'
   'Are you here? Are you alone?' asked the voice in German.
   'Yes – come in.'
Hannele did not sound very encouraging. She turned round her doll as the door opened, and straightened his coat. A dark-eyed young woman peeped in through the door, with a roguish coyness. She was dressed fashionably for the street, in a thick cape-wrap, and a little black hat pulled down to her ears.

'Quite, quite alone!' said the newcomer, in a tone of wonder. 'Where is he, then?'
   'That I don't know,' said Hannele.
   'And you sit here alone and wait for him? But no! That I call courage! Aren't you afraid?' Mitchka strolled across to her friend.
   'Why shall I be afraid?' said Hannele curtly.
   'But no! And what are you doing? Another puppet? He is a good one, though! Ha – ha – ha! *Him!* It is him! No – no – that is too beautiful! No – that is too beautiful, Hannele. It is him – exactly him. Only the trousers.'
   'He wears those trousers too,' said Hannele, standing her doll on her knee. It was a perfect portrait of an officer of a Scottish regiment, slender, delicately made, with a slight, elegant stoop of the shoulders and close-fitting tartan trousers. The face was beautifully modelled, and a wonderful portrait, dark-skinned, with a little, close-cut, dark moustache, and wide-open dark eyes,

and that air of aloofness and perfect diffidence which marks an officer and a gentleman.

Mitchka bent forward, studying the doll. She was a handsome woman with a warm, dark golden skin and clear black eyebrows over her russet-brown eyes.

'No,' she whispered to herself, as if awe-struck. 'That is him. That is him. Only not the trousers. Beautiful, though, the trousers. Has he really such beautiful fine legs?'

Hannele did not answer.

'Exactly him. Just as finished as he is. Just as complete. He is just like that: finished off. Has he seen it?'

'No,' said Hannele.

'What will he say, then?' She started. Her quick ear had caught a sound on the stone stairs. A look of fear came to her face. She flew to the door and out of the room, closing the door to behind her.

'Who is it?' her voice was heard calling anxiously down the stairs.

The answer came in German. Mitchka immediately opened the door again and came back to join Hannele.

'Only Martin,' she said.

She stood waiting. A man appeared in the doorway – erect, military.

'Ah! Countess Hannele,' he said in his quick, precise way, as he stood on the threshold in the distance. 'May one come in?'

'Yes, come in,' said Hannele.

The man entered with a quick, military step, bowed, and kissed the hand of the woman who was sewing the doll. Then, much more intimately, he touched Mitchka's hands with his lips.

Mitchka meanwhile was glancing round the room. It was a very large attic, with the ceiling sloping and then bending in two handsome movements towards the walls. The light from the dark-shaded reading-lamp fell softly on the huge white-washed vaulting of the ceiling, on the various objects round the walls, and made a brilliant pool of colour where Hannele sat in her soft, red dress, with her basket of silks.

She was a fair woman with dark-blond hair and a beautiful fine skin. Her face seemed luminous, a certain quick gleam of life about it as she looked up at the man. He was handsome, clean-shaven, with very blue eyes strained a little too wide. One could see the war in his face.

Mitchka was wandering round the room, looking at everything, and saying: 'Beautiful! But beautiful! Such good taste! A man, and such good taste! No, they don't need a woman. No, look here, Martin, the Captain Hepburn has arranged all this room himself. Here you have the man. Do you see? So simple, yet so elegant. He needs a woman.'

The room was really beautiful, spacious, pale, soft-lighted. It was heated by a large stove of dark-blue tiles, and had very little furniture save large peasant cupboards or presses of painted wood, and a huge writing-table, on which were writing materials and some scientific apparatus and a cactus plant with fine scarlet blossoms. But it was a man's room. Tobacco and pipes were on a little tray, on the pegs in the distance hung military overcoats and belts, and two guns on a bracket. Then there were two telescopes, one mounted on a stand near a window. Various astronomical apparatus lay upon the table.

'And he reads the stars. Only think – he is an astronomer and reads the stars. Queer, queer people, the English!'

'He is Scottish,' said Hannele.

'Yes, Scottish,' said Mitchka. 'But, you know, I am afraid when I am with him. He is at a closed end. I don't know where I can get to with him. Are you afraid of him too, Hannele? Ach, like a closed road!'

'Why should I be?'

'Ah, you! Perhaps you don't know when you should be afraid. But if he were to come and find us here? No, no – let us go. Let us go, Martin. Come, let us go. I don't want the Captain Hepburn to come and find me in his room. Oh no!' Mitchka was busily pushing Martin to the door, and he was laughing with the queer, mad laugh in his strained eyes. 'Oh no! I don't like. I don't like it,' said Mitchka, trying her English now. She spoke a few sentences prettily. 'Oh no, Sir Captain, I don't want that you come. I don't like it, to be here when you come. Oh no. Not at all. I go. I go, Hannele. I go, my Hannele. And you will really stay here and wait for him? But when will he come? You don't know? Oh dear, I don't like it, I don't like it. I do not wait in the man's room. No, no – Never – *jamais* – *jamais, voyez-vous*. Ach, you poor Hannele! And he has got wife and children in England? Nevair! No, nevair shall I wait for him.'

She had bustlingly pushed Martin through the door and settled her wrap and taken a mincing, elegant pose, ready for the street, and waved her hand and made wide, scared eyes at Hannele, and was gone. The Countess Hannele picked up the doll again and began to sew its shoe. What living she now had she earned making these puppets.

But she was restless. She pressed her arms into her lap, as if holding them bent had wearied her. Then she looked at the little clock on his writing-table. It was long after dinner-time – why hadn't he come? She sighed rather exasperated. She was tired of her doll.

Putting aside her basket of silks, she went to one of the windows. Outside the stars seemed white, and very near. Below was the dark agglomeration of the roofs of houses, a fume of light came up from beneath the darkness of roofs, and a faint breakage of noise from the town far below. The room seemed high, remote, in the sky.

She went to the table and looked at his letter-clip with letters in it, and at his sealing-wax and his stamp-box, touching things and moving them a little, just for the sake of the contrast, not really noticing what she touched. Then she took a pencil, and in stiff Gothic characters began to write her name – Johanna zu Rassentlow – time after time her own name – and then once, bitterly, curiously, with a curious sharpening of her nose: Alexander Hepburn.

But she threw the pencil down, having no more interest in her writing. She wandered to where the large telescope stood near a farther window, and stood for some minutes with her fingers on the barrel, where it was a little brighter from his touching it. Then she drifted restlessly back to her chair.

She had picked up her puppet when she heard him on the stairs. She lifted her face and watched as he entered.

'Hello, you there!' he said quietly, as he closed the door behind him. She glanced at him swiftly, but did not move nor answer.

He took off his overcoat with quick, quiet movements, and went to hang it up on the pegs. She heard his step, and looked again. He was like the doll, a tall, slender, well-bred man in uniform. When he turned, his dark eyes seemed very wide open. His black hair was growing grey at the temples – the first touch.

She was sewing her doll. Without saying anything, he wheeled round the chair from the writing-table, so that he sat with his knees almost touching her. Then he crossed one leg over the other. He wore fine tartan socks. His ankles seemed slender and elegant, his brown shoes fitted as if they were part of him. For some moments he watched her as she sat sewing. The light fell on her soft, delicate hair, that was full of strands of gold and of tarnished gold and shadow. She did not look up.

In silence he held out his small, naked-looking brown hand for the doll. On his fore-arm were black hairs.

She glanced up at him. Curious how fresh and luminous her face looked in contrast to his.

'Do you want to see it?' she asked, in natural English.

'Yes,' he said.

She broke off her thread of cotton and handed him the puppet. He sat with one leg thrown over the other, holding the doll in one hand and smiling inscrutably with his dark eyes. His hair, parted perfectly on one side, was jet black and glossy.

'You've got me,' he said at last, in his amused, melodious voice.

'What?' she said.

'You've got me,' he repeated.

'I don't care,' she said.

'What – You don't care?' His face broke into a smile. He had an odd way of answering, as if he were only half attending, as if he were thinking of something else.

'You are very late, aren't you?' she ventured.

'Yes. I am rather late.'

'Why are you?'

'Well, as a matter of fact, I was talking with the Colonel.'

'About me?'

'Yes. It was about you.'

She went pale as she sat looking up into his face. But it was impossible to tell whether there was distress on his dark brow or not.

'Anything nasty?' she said.

'Well, yes. It was rather nasty. Not about you, I mean. But rather awkward for me.'

She watched him. But still he said no more.

'What was it?' she said.

'Oh, well – only what I expected. They seem to know rather too much about you – about you and me, I mean. Not that anybody cares one bit, you know, unofficially. The trouble is, they are apparently going to have to take official notice.'

'Why?'

'Oh, well – it appears my wife has been writing letters to the Major-General. He is one of her family acquaintances – known her all his life. And I suppose she's been hearing rumours. In fact, I know she has. She said so in her letter to me.'

'And what do you say to her then?'

'Oh, I tell her I'm all right – not to worry.'

'You don't expect *that* to stop her worrying, do you?' she asked.

'Oh, I don't know. Why should she worry?' he said.

'I think she might have some reason,' said Hannele. 'You've not seen her for a year. And if she adores you— '

'Oh, I don't think she adores me. I think she quite likes me.'

'Do you think you matter as little as that to her?'

'I don't see why not. Of course she likes to feel *safe* about me.'

'But now she doesn't feel safe?'

'No – exactly. Exactly. That's the point. That's where it is. The Colonel advises me to go home on leave.'

He sat gazing with curious, bright, dark, unseeing eyes at the doll which he held by one arm. It was an extraordinary likeness of himself, true even to the smooth parting of his hair and his peculiar way of fixing his dark eyes.

'For how long?' she asked.

'I don't know. For a month,' he replied, first vaguely, then definitely.

'For a month!' She watched him, and seemed to see him fade from her eyes.

'And will you go?' she asked.

'I don't know. I don't know.' His head remained bent, he seemed to muse rather vaguely. 'I don't know,' he repeated. 'I can't make up my mind what I shall do.'

'Would you like to go?' she asked.

He lifted his brows and looked at her. Her heart always melted in her when he looked straight at her with his black eyes and that curious, bright, unseeing look that was more like second sight than direct human vision. She never knew what he saw when he looked at her.

'No,' he said simply. 'I don't *want* to go. I don't think I've any desire at all to go to England.'

'Why not?' she asked.

'I can't say.' Then again he looked at her, and a curious white light seemed to shine on his eyes, as he smiled slowly with his mouth, and said: 'I suppose you ought to know, if anybody does.'

A glad, half-frightened look came on her face.

'You mean you don't want to leave me?' she asked, breathless.

'Yes. I suppose that's what I mean.'

'But you aren't sure?'

'Yes, I am, I'm quite sure,' he said, and the curious smile lingered on his face, and the strange light shone on his eyes.

'That you don't want to leave me?' she stammered, looking aside.

'Yes, I'm quite sure I don't want to leave you,' he repeated. He had a curious, very melodious Scottish voice. But it was the incomprehensible smile on his face that convinced and frightened her. It was almost a gargoyle smile, a strange, lurking, changeless-seeming grin.

She was frightened, and turned aside her face. When she looked at him again, his face was like a mask, with strange, deep-graven lines and a glossy dark skin and a fixed look – as if carved half grotesquely in some glossy stone. His black hair on his smooth, beautifully-shaped head seemed changeless.

'Are you rather tired?' she asked him.

'Yes, I think I am.' He looked at her with black, unseeing eyes and a mask-like face. Then he glanced aside as if he heard something. Then he rose with his hand on his belt, saying: 'I'll take off my belt and change my coat, if you don't mind.'

He walked across the room, unfastening his broad, brown belt. He was in well-fitting, well-cut khaki. He hung up his belt and came back to her wearing an old, light tunic, which he left unbuttoned. He carried his slippers in one hand. When he sat down to unfasten his shoes, she noticed again how black and hairy his fore-arm was, how naked his brown hand seemed. His hair was black and smooth and perfect on his head, like some close helmet, as he stooped down.

He put on his slippers, carried his shoes aside, and resumed his chair, stretching luxuriously.

'There,' he said. 'I feel better now.' And he looked at her. 'Well,' he said, 'and how are you?'

'Me?' she said. 'Do I matter?' She was rather bitter.

'Do you matter?' he repeated, without noticing her bitterness. 'Why, what a question! Of course you are of the very highest importance. What? Aren't you?' And smiling his curious smile – it made her for a moment think of the fixed sadness of monkeys, of those Chinese carved soapstone apes. He put his hand under her chin, and gently drew his finger along her cheek. She flushed deeply.

'But I'm not as important as you, am I?' she asked defiantly.

'As important as me! Why, bless you, I'm not important a bit. I'm not important a bit!' – the odd, straying sound of his words mystified her. What did he really mean?

'And I'm even less important than that,' she said bitterly.

'Oh no, you're not. Oh no, you're not. You're very important. You're very important indeed, I assure you.'

'And your wife?' – the question came rebelliously. 'Your wife? Isn't she important?'

'My wife? My wife?' He seemed to let the word stray out of him as if he did not quite know what it meant. 'Why, yes, I suppose she is important in her own sphere.'

'What sphere?' blurted Hannele, with a laugh.

'Why, her own sphere, of course. Her own house, her own home, and her two children: that's her sphere.'

'And you? – where do you come in?'

'At present I don't come in,' he said.

'But isn't that just the trouble,' said Hannele. 'If you have a wife and a home, it's your business to belong to it, isn't it?'

'Yes, I suppose it is, if I want to,' he replied.

'And you *do* want to?' she challenged.

'No, I don't,' he replied.

'Well, then?' she said.

'Yes, quite,' he answered. 'I admit it's a dilemma.'

'But what will you *do*?' she insisted.

'Why, I don't know. I don't know yet. I haven't made up my mind what I'm going to do.'

'Then you'd better begin to make it up,' she said.

'Yes, I know that. I know that.'

He rose and began to walk uneasily up and down the room. But the same vacant darkness was on his brow. He had his hands in his pockets. Hannele sat feeling helpless. She couldn't help being in love with the man: with his hands, with his strange, fascinating physique, with his incalculable presence. She loved the way he put his feet down, she loved the way he moved his legs as he walked, she loved the mould of his loins, she loved the way he dropped his head a little, and the strange, dark vacancy of his brow, his not-thinking. But now the restlessness only made her unhappy. Nothing would come of it. Yet she had driven him to it.

He took his hands out of his pockets and returned to her like a piece of iron returning to a magnet. He sat down again in front of her and put his hands out to her, looking into her face.

'Give me your hands,' he said softly, with that strange, mindless, soft, suggestive tone which left her powerless to disobey. 'Give me your hands, and let me feel that we are together. Words mean so little. They mean nothing. And all that one thinks and plans doesn't amount to anything. Let me feel that we are together, and I don't care about all the rest.'

He spoke in his slow, melodious way, and closed her hands in his. She struggled still for voice.

'But you'll *have* to care about it. You'll *have* to make up your mind. You'll just *have* to,' she insisted.

'Yes, I suppose I shall. I suppose I shall. But now that we are together, I won't bother. Now that we are together, let us forget it.'

'But when we *can't* forget it any more?'

'Well – then I don't know. But – to-night – it seems to me – we might just as well forget it.'

The soft, melodious, straying sound of his voice made her feel helpless. She felt that he never answered her. Words of reply seemed to stray out of him, in the need to say *something*. But he himself never spoke. There he was, a continual blank silence in front of her.

She had a battle with herself. When he put his hand again on her cheek, softly, with the most extraordinary soft half-touch, as a kitten's paw sometimes touches one, like a fluff of living air, then, if it had not been for the magic of that almost indiscernible caress of his hand, she would have stiffened herself and drawn away and told him she could have nothing to do with him, while he was so half-hearted and unsatisfactory. She wanted to tell him these things. But when she began he answered invariably in the same soft, straying voice, that seemed to spin gossamer threads all over her, so that she could neither think nor act nor even feel distinctly. Her soul groaned rebelliously in her. And yet, when he put his hand softly under her chin, and lifted her face and smiled down on her with that gargoyle smile of his – she let him kiss her.

'What are you thinking about to-night?' he said. 'What are you thinking about?'

'What did your Colonel say to you, exactly?' she replied, trying to harden her eyes.

'Oh, that!' he answered. 'Never mind that. That is of no significance whatever.'

'But what *is* of any significance?' she insisted. She almost hated him.

'What is of any significance? Well, nothing to me, outside of this room at this minute. Nothing in time or space matters to me.'

'Yes, *this minute!*' she repeated bitterly. 'But then there's the future. *I've* got to live in the future.'

'The future! The future! The future is used up every day. The future to me is like a big tangle of black thread. Every morning you begin to untangle one loose end – and that's your day. And every evening you break off and throw away what you've untangled, and the heap is so much less: just one thread less, one day less. That's all the future matters to me.'

'Then nothing matters to you. And I don't matter to you. As you say, only an end of waste thread,' she resisted him.

'No, there you're wrong. You aren't the future to me.'

'What am I then? – the past?'

'No, not any of those things. You're nothing. As far as all that goes, you're nothing.'

'Thank you,' she said sarcastically, 'if I'm nothing.'

But the very irrelevancy of the man overcame her. He kissed her with half discernible, dim kisses, and touched her throat. And the meaninglessness of him fascinated her and left her powerless. She could ascribe no meaning to him, none whatever. And yet his mouth, so strange in kissing, and his hairy forearms, and his slender, beautiful breast with black hair – it was all like a mystery to her, as if one of the men from Mars were loving her. And she was heavy and spellbound, and she loved the spell that bound her. But also she didn't love it.

Chapter Two

Countess zu Rassentlow had a studio in one of the main streets. She was really a refugee. And nowadays you can be a grand-duke and a pauper, if you are a refugee. But Hannele was not a pauper, because she and her friend Mitchka had the studio where they made these dolls, and beautiful cushions of embroidered coloured wools, and such-like objects of feminine art. The dolls were quite famous, so the two women did not starve.

Hannele did not work much in the studio. She preferred to be alone in her own room, which was another fine attic, not quite so large as the captain's, under the same roof. But often she went to the studio in the afternoon, and if purchasers came, then they were offered a cup of tea.

The Alexander doll was never intended for sale. What made Hannele take it to the studio one afternoon, we do not know. But she did so, and stood it on a little bureau. It was a wonderful little portrait of an officer and gentleman, the physique modelled so that it made you hold your breath.

'And *that* – that is genius!' cried Mitchka. 'That is a *chef d'oeuvre!* That is thy masterpiece, Hannele. That is really marvellous. And beautiful! A beautiful man, what! But no, that is *too* real. I don't understand how you *dare*. I always thought you were *good*, Hannele, so much better-natured than I am. But now you frighten me. I am afraid you are wicked, do you know. It frightens me to think that you are wicked. *Aber nein!* But you won't leave him there?'

'Why not?' said Hannele, satiric.

Mitchka made big dark eyes of wonder, reproach, and fear.

'But you *must* not,' she said.

'Why not?'

'No, that you *may* not do. You love the man.'

'What then?'

'You can't leave his puppet standing there.'

'Why can't I?'

'But you are really wicked. *Du bist wirklich bös.* Only think! – and he is an English officer.'

'He isn't sacrosanct even then.'

'They will expel you from the town. They will deport you.'

'Let them, then.'

'But no! What will you do? That would be horrible if we had to go to Berlin or to Munich and begin again. Here everything has happened so well.'

'I don't care,' said Hannele.

Mitchka looked at her friend and said no more. But she was angry. After some time she turned and uttered her ultimatum.

'When you are not there,' she said, 'I shall put the puppet away in a drawer. I shall show it to nobody, nobody. And I must tell you, it makes me afraid to see it there. It makes me afraid. And you have no right to get me into trouble, do you see. It is not I who look at the English officers. I don't like them, they are too cold and finished off for me. I shall never bring trouble on *myself* because of the English officers.'

'Don't be afraid,' said Hannele. 'They won't trouble *you*. They know everything we do, well enough. They have their spies everywhere. Nothing will happen to you.'

'But if they make you go away – and I am planted here with the studio—'

It was no good, however; Hannele was obstinate.

So, one sunny afternoon there was a ring at the door: a little lady in white, with a wrinkled face that still had its prettiness.

'Good afternoon!' – in rather lardy-dardy, middle-class English. 'I wonder if I may see your things in your studio.'

'Oh yes!' said Mitchka. 'Please to come in.'

Entered the little lady in her finery and her crumpled prettiness. She would not be very old: perhaps younger than fifty. And it was odd that her face had gone so crumpled, because her figure was very trim, her eyes were bright, and she had pretty teeth when she laughed. She was very fine in her clothes: a dress of thick knitted white silk, a large ermine scarf with the tails only at the ends, and a black hat over which dripped a trail of green feathers of the osprey sort. She wore rather a lot of jewellery, and two bangles tinkled over her white kid gloves as she put up her fingers to touch her hair, whilst she stood complacently and looked round.

'You've got a *charming* studio – *charming* – perfectly delightful! I couldn't imagine anything more delightful.'

Mitchka gave a slight ironic bow, and said in her odd, plangent English: 'Oh yes. We like it very much also.'

Hannele, who had dodged behind a screen, now came quickly forth.

'Oh, how do you do!' smiled the elderly lady. 'I heard there were two of you. Now which is which, if I may be so bold? this' – and she gave a winsome smile and pointed a white kid finger at Mitchka – 'is the—?'

'Annamaria von Prielau-Carolath,' said Mitchka, slightly bowing.

'Oh!' – and the white kid finger jerked away. 'Then this— '

'Johanna zu Rassentlow,' said Hannele, smiling.

'Ah, yes! Countess von Rassentlow! And this is Baroness von – von – but I shall never remember even if you tell me, for I'm awful at names. Anyhow, I shall call one *Countess* and the other *Baroness*. That will do, won't it, for poor me! Now I should like awfully to see your things, if I may. I want to buy a little present to take back to England with me. I suppose I shan't have to pay the world in duty on things like these, shall I?'

'Oh no,' said Mitchka. 'No duty. Toys, you know, they – there is— ' Her English stammered to an end, so she turned to Hannele.

'They don't charge duty on toys, and the embroideries they don't notice,' said Hannele.

'Oh, well. Then I'm all right,' said the visitor. 'I hope I can buy something really nice! I see a perfectly lovely jumper over there, perfectly delightful. But a little too gay for me, I'm afraid. I'm not quite so young as I was, alas.' She smiled her winsome little smile, showing her pretty teeth and the old pearls in her ears shook.

'I've heard so much about your dolls. I hear they're perfectly exquisite, quite works of art. May I see some, please?'

'Oh yes,' came Mitchka's invariable answer, this exclamation being the foundation-stone of all her English.

There were never more than three or four dolls in stock. This time there were only two. The famous captain was hidden in his drawer.

'Perfectly beautiful! Perfectly wonderful!' murmured the little lady, in an artistic murmur. 'I think they're perfectly delightful. It's wonderful of you, Countess, to make them. It is you who make them, is it not? Or do you both do them together?'

Hannele explained, and the inspection and the rhapsody went on together. But it was evident that the little lady was a cautious buyer. She went over the things very carefully, and thought more than twice. The dolls attracted her – but she thought them expensive, and hung fire.

'I do wish,' she said wistfully, 'there had been a larger selection of the dolls. I feel, you know, there might have been one which I *just loved*. Of course these are *darlings* – darlings they are: and worth every *penny*, considering the work there is in them. And the art, of course. But I have a feeling, don't you know how it is, that if there had been just one or two more, I should have found one which I *absolutely* couldn't live without. Don't you know how it is? One is so foolish, of course. What does Goethe say – "*Dort wo du nicht bist . . .* "? My German isn't even a beginning, so you must excuse it. But it means you always feel you would be happy somewhere else, and not just where you are. Isn't that it? Ah, well, it's so very often true – so very often. But not always, thank goodness.' She smiled an odd little smile to herself, pursed her lips, and resumed: 'Well now, that's how I feel about the dolls. If only there had been one or two more. Isn't there a single one?'

She looked winsomely at Hannele.

'Yes,' said Hannele, 'there is one. But it is ordered. It isn't for sale.'

'Oh, do you think I might see it? I'm sure it's lovely. Oh, I'm dying to see it. You know what woman's curiosity is, don't you?' – she laughed her tinkling little laugh. 'Well, I'm afraid I'm all woman, unfortunately. One is so much harder if one has a touch of the man in one, don't you think, and more able to bear things. But I'm afraid I'm all woman.' She sighed and became silent.

Hannele went quietly to the drawer and took out the captain. She handed him to the little woman. The latter looked frightened. Her eyes became round and childish, her face went yellowish. Her jewels tinkled nervously as she stammered:

'Now *that* – isn't that— ' and she laughed a little, hysterical laugh.

She turned round, as if to escape.

'Do you mind if I sit down,' she said. 'I think the standing— ' and she subsided into a chair. She kept her face averted. But she held the puppet fast, her small, white fingers with their heavy jewelled rings clasped round his waist.

'You know,' rushed in Mitchka, who was terrified. 'You know, that is a life picture of one of the Englishmen, of a gentleman, you know. A life picture, you know.'

'A portrait,' said Hannele brightly.

'Yes,' murmured the visitor vaguely. 'I'm sure it is. I'm sure it is a very clever portrait indeed.'

She fumbled with a chain, and put up a small gold lorgnette before her eyes, as if to screen herself. And from behind the screen of her lorgnette she peered at the image in her hand.

'But,' she said, 'none of the English officers, or rather Scottish, wear the close-fitting tartan trews any more – except for fancy dress.'

Her voice was vague and distant.

'No, they don't now,' said Hannele. 'But that is the correct dress. I think they are so handsome, don't you?'

'Well. I don't know. It depends' – and the little woman laughed shakily.

'Oh yes,' said Hannele. 'It needs well-shapen legs.'

'Such as the original of your doll must have had – quite,' said the lady.

'Oh yes,' said Hannele. 'I think his legs are very handsome.'

'Quite!' said the lady. 'Judging from his portrait, as you call it. May I ask the name of the gentleman – if it is not too indiscreet?'

'Captain Hepburn,' said Hannele.

'Yes, of course it is. I knew him at once. I've known him for many years.'

'Oh, please,' broke in Mitchka. 'Oh, please, do not tell him you have seen it! Oh, please! Please do not tell anyone!'

The visitor looked up with a grey little smile.

'But why not?' she said. 'Anyhow, I can't tell him at once, because I hear he is away at present. You don't happen to know when he will be back?'

'I believe to-morrow,' said Hannele.

'To-morrow!'

'And please!' pleaded Mitchka, who looked lovely in her pleading distress, 'please not to tell anybody that you have seen it.'

'Must I promise?' smiled the little lady wanly. 'Very well, then, I won't tell him I've seen it. And now I think I must be going. Yes, I'll just take the cushion-cover, thank you. Tell me again how much it is, please.'

That evening Hannele was restless. He had been away on some duty for three days. He was returning that night – should have been back in time for dinner. But he had not arrived, and his room was locked and dark. Hannele had heard the servant light the stove some hours ago. Now the room was locked and blank as it had been for three days.

Hannele was most uneasy because she seemed to have forgotten him in the three days whilst he had been away. He seemed to have quite disappeared out of her. She could hardly even remember him. He had become so insignificant to her she was dazed.

Now she wanted to see him again, to know if it was really so. She felt that he was coming. She felt that he was already putting out some influence towards her. But what? And was he real? Why had she made his doll? Why had his doll been so important, if he was nothing? Why had she shown it to that funny little woman this afternoon? Why was she herself such a fool, getting herself into tangles in this place where it was so unpleasant to be entangled? Why was she entangled, after all? It was all so unreal. And particularly *he* was unreal: as unreal as a person in a dream, whom one has never heard of in actual life. In actual life, her own German friends were real. Martin was real: German men were real to her. But this other, he was simply not there. He didn't really exist. He was a nullus, in reality. A nullus – and she had somehow got herself complicated with him.

Was it possible? Was it possible she had been so closely entangled with an absolute nothing? Now he was absent she couldn't even *imagine* him. He had gone out of her imagination, and even when she looked at his doll she saw nothing but a barren puppet. And yet for this dead puppet she had been compromising herself, now, when it was so risky for her to be compromised.

Her own German friends – her own German men – they were men, they were real beings. But this English officer, he was neither fish, flesh, fowl, nor good red herring, as they say. He was just a hypothetical presence. She felt that if he never came back, she would be just as if she had read a rather peculiar but false story, a *tour de force* which works up one's imagination all falsely.

Nevertheless, she was uneasy. She had a lurking suspicion that there might be something else. So she kept uneasily wandering out to the landing, and listening to hear if he might be coming.

Yes – there was a sound. Yes, there was his slow step on the stairs, and the slow, straying purr of his voice. And instantly she heard his voice she was afraid again. She knew there *was* something there. And instantly she felt the reality of his presence, she felt the unreality of her own German men friends. The moment she heard the peculiar, slow melody of his foreign voice everything seemed to go changed in her, and Martin and Otto and Albrecht, her German friends, seemed to go pale and dim as if one could almost see through them, like unsubstantial things.

This was what she had to reckon with, this recoil from one to the other. When he was present, he seemed so terribly real. When he was absent he was completely vague, and her own men of her own race seemed so absolutely the only reality.

But he was talking. Who was he talking to? She heard the steps echo up the hollows of the stone staircase slowly, as if wearily, and voices slowly, confusedly mingle. The slow, soft trail of his voice – and then the peculiar, quick tones – yes, of a woman. And not one of the maids, because they were speaking English. She listened hard. The quick, and yet slightly hushed, slightly sad-sounding voice of a woman who talks a good deal, as if talking to herself. Hannele's quick ears caught the sound of what she was saying: 'Yes, I thought the Baroness a perfectly beautiful creature, perfectly lovely. But so extraordinarily like a Spaniard. Do you remember, Alec, at Malaga? I always thought they fascinated you then, with their mantillas. Perfectly lovely she would look in a mantilla. Only perhaps she is too open-hearted, too impulsive, poor thing. She lacks the Spanish reserve. Poor thing, I feel sorry for her. For them both, indeed. It must be very hard to have to do these things for a living, after you've been accustomed to be made much of for your own sake, and for your aristocratic title. It's very hard for them, poor things. Baroness, Countess, it sounds just a little ridiculous, when you're buying woollen embroideries from them. But I suppose, poor things, they can't help it. Better drop the titles altogether, I think— '

'Well, they do, if people will let them. Only English and American people find it so much easier to say Baroness or Countess than Fräulein von Prielau-Carolath, or whatever it is.'

'They could say simply Fräulein, as we do to our governesses – or as we used to, when we *had* German governesses,' came the voice of *her*.

'Yes, we *could*,' said his voice.

'After all, what is the good, what is the good of titles if you have to sell dolls and woollen embroideries – not so very beautiful, either.'

'Oh, quite! Oh, quite! I think titles are perhaps a mistake, anyhow. But they've always had them,' came his slow, musical voice, with its sing-song note of hopeless indifference. He sounded rather like a man talking out of his sleep.

Hannele caught sight of the tail of blue-green crane feathers veering round a turn in the stairs away below, and she beat a hasty retreat.

Chapter Three

There was a little platform out on the roof, where he used sometimes to stand his telescope and observe the stars or the moon: the moon when possible. It was not a very safe platform, just a little ledge of the roof, outside the window at the end of the top corridor: or rather, the top landing, for it was only the space between the attics. Hannele had the one attic-room at the back, he had the room we have seen, and a little bedroom which was really only a lumber-room. Before he came, Hannele had been alone under the roof. His rooms were then lumber-room and laundry-room, where the clothes were dried. But he had wanted to be high up, because of his stars, and this was the place that pleased him.

Hannele heard him quite late in the night, wandering about. She heard him also on the ledge outside. She could not sleep. He disturbed her. The moon was risen, large and bright in the sky. She heard the bells from the cathedral slowly strike two: two great drops of sound in the livid night. And again, from outside on the roof, she heard him clear his throat. Then a cat howled.

She rose, wrapped herself in a dark wrap, and went down the landing to the window at the end. The sky outside was full of moonlight. He was

squatted like a great cat peering up his telescope, sitting on a stool, his knees
wide apart. Quite motionless he sat in that attitude, like some leaden figure
on the roof. The moonlight glistened with a gleam of plumbago on the great
slope of black tiles. She stood still in the window, watching. And he remained
fixed and motionless at the end of the telescope.

She tapped softly on the window-pane. He looked round, like some tom-
cat staring round with wide night eyes. Then he reached down his hand and
pulled the window open.

'Hello,' he said quietly. 'You not asleep?'

'Aren't *you* tired?' she replied, rather resentful.

'No, I was as wide awake as I could be. *Isn't* the moon fine to-night!
What? Perfectly amazing. Wouldn't you like to come up and have a look
at her?'

'No, thank you,' she said hastily, terrified at the thought.

He resumed his posture, peering up the telescope.

'Perfectly amazing,' he said, murmuring. She waited for some time,
bewitched likewise by the great October moon and the sky full of resplendent
white-green light. It seemed like another sort of day-time. And there he
straddled on the roof like some cat! It was exactly like day in some other
planet.

At length he turned round to her. His face glistened faintly, and his eyes
were dilated like a cat's at night.

'You know I had a visitor?' he said.

'Yes.'

'My wife.'

'Your *wife!*' – she looked up really astonished. She had thought it might
be an acquaintance – perhaps his aunt – or even an elder sister. 'But she's
years older than you,' she added.

'Eight years,' he said. 'I'm forty-one.'

There was a silence.

'Yes,' he mused. 'She arrived suddenly, by surprise, yesterday, and found
me away. She's staying in the hotel, in the Vier Jahreszeiten.'

There was a pause.

'Aren't you going to stay with her?' asked Hannele.

'Yes, I shall probably join her to-morrow.'

There was a still longer pause.

'Why not to-night?' asked Hannele.

'Oh, well – I put it off for to-night. It meant all the bother of my wife
changing her room at the hotel – and it was late – and I was all mucky after
travelling.'

'But you'll go to-morrow?'

'Yes, I shall go to-morrow. For a week or so. After that I'm not sure what
will happen.'

There was quite a long pause. He remained seated on his stool on the
roof, looking with dilated, blank, black eyes at nothingness. She stood below
in the open window space, pondering.

'Do you want to go to her at the hotel?' asked Hannele.

'Well, I don't, particularly. But I don't mind, really. We're very good friends. Why, we've been friends for eighteen years – we've been married seventeen. Oh, she's a nice little woman. I don't want to hurt her feelings. I wish her no harm, you know. On the contrary, I wish her all the good in the world.'

He had no idea of the blank amazement in which Hannele listened to these stray remarks.

'But— ' she stammered. 'But doesn't she expect you to make *love* to her?'

'Oh yes, she expects that. You bet she does: womanlike.'

'And you?' – the question had a dangerous ring.

'Why, I don't mind, really, you know, if it's only for a short time. I'm used to her. I've always been fond of her, you know – and so if it gives her any pleasure – why, I like her to get what pleasure out of life she can.'

'But *you* – you *yourself*! Don't *you* feel anything?' Hannele's amazement was reaching the point of incredulity. She began to feel that he was making it up. It was all so different from her own point of view. To sit there so quiet and to make such statements in all good faith: no, it was impossible.

'I don't consider I count,' he said naïvely.

Hannele looked aside. If that wasn't lying, it was imbecility, or worse. She had for the moment nothing to say. She felt he was a sort of psychic phenomenon like a grasshopper or a tadpole or an ammonite. Not to be regarded from a human point of view. No, he just wasn't normal. And she had been fascinated by him! It was only sheer, amazed curiosity that carried her on to her next question.

'But do you *never* count, then?' she asked, and there was a touch of derision, of laughter in her tone. He took no offence.

'Well – very rarely,' he said. 'I count very rarely. That's how life appears to me. One matters so *very* little.'

She felt quite dizzy with astonishment. And he called himself a man!

'But if you matter so very little, what do you do anything at all for?' she asked.

'Oh, one has to. And then, why not? Why not do things, even if oneself hardly matters. Look at the moon. It doesn't matter in the least to the moon whether I exist or whether I don't. So why should it matter to me?'

After a blank pause of incredulity she said:

'I could die with laughter. It seems to me all so ridiculous – no, I can't believe it.'

'Perhaps it is a point of view,' he said.

There was a long and pregnant silence: we should not like to say pregnant with what.

'And so I don't mean anything to you at all?' she said.

'I didn't say that,' he replied.

'Nothing means anything to you,' she challenged.

'I don't say that.'

'Whether it's your wife – or me – or the moon – *toute la même chose*.'

'No – no – that's hardly the way to look at it.'

She gazed at him in such utter amazement that she felt something would really explode in her if she heard another word. Was this a man? – or what was it? It was too much for her, that was all.

'Well, good-bye,' she said. 'I hope you will have a nice time at the Vier Jahreszeiten.'

So she left him still sitting on the roof.

'I suppose,' she said to herself, 'that is love *à l'anglaise*. But it's more than I can swallow.'

Chapter Four

'Won't you come and have tea with me – do! Come right along now. Don't you find it bitterly cold? Yes – well now – come in with me and we'll have a cup of nice, hot tea in our little sitting-room. The weather changes so suddenly, and really one needs a little reinforcement. But perhaps you don't take tea?'

'Oh yes. I got so used to it in England,' said Hannele.

'Did you now! Well now, were you long in England?'

'Oh yes— '

The two women had met in the Domplatz. Mrs. Hepburn was looking extraordinarily like one of Hannele's dolls, in a funny little cape of odd striped skins, and a little dark-green skirt, and a rather fuzzy sort of hat. Hannele looked almost huge beside her.

'But now you will come in and have tea, won't you? Oh, please do. Never mind whether it's *de rigueur* or not. I *always* please myself *what* I do. I'm afraid my husband gets some shocks sometimes – but that we can't help. I won't have anybody laying down the law to me.' She laughed her winsome little laugh. 'So now come along in, and we'll see if there aren't hot scones as well. I love a hot scone for tea in cold weather. And I hope you do. That is, if there are any. We don't know yet.' She tinkled her little laugh. 'My husband may or may not be in. But that makes no difference to you and me, does it? There, it's just striking half-past four. In England we always have tea at half-past. My husband *adores* his tea. I don't suppose our man is five minutes off the half-past, ringing the gong for tea, not once in twelve months. My husband doesn't mind at all if dinner is a little late. But he gets – quite – well, quite "ratty" if tea is late.' She tinkled a laugh. 'Though I shouldn't say that. He is the soul of kindness and patience. I don't think I've ever known him do an unkind thing – or hardly say an unkind word. But I doubt if he will be in to-day.'

He *was* in, however, standing with his feet apart and his hands in his trouser pockets in the little sitting-room upstairs in the hotel. He raised his eyebrows the smallest degree, seeing Hannele enter.

'Ah, Countess Hannele – my wife has brought you along! Very nice, very nice! Let me take your wrap. Oh yes, certainly . . . '

'Have you rung for tea, dear?' asked Mrs. Hepburn.

'Er – yes. I said as soon as you came in they were to bring it.'

'Yes – well. Won't you ring again, dear, and say for *three*.'

'Yes – certainly. Certainly.'

He rang, and stood about with his hands in his pockets waiting for tea.

'Well now,' said Mrs. Hepburn, as she lifted the teapot, and her bangles tinkled, and her huge rings of brilliants twinkled, and her big ear-rings of clustered seed-pearls bobbed against her rather withered cheek, 'isn't it charming of Countess zu – Countess zu— '

'Rassentlow,' said he. 'I believe most people say Countess Hannele. I know we always do among ourselves. We say Countess Hannele's shop.'

'Countess Hannele's shop! Now, isn't that perfectly delightful: such a romance in the very sound of it. You take cream?'

'Thank you,' said Hannele.

The tea passed in a cloud of chatter, while Mrs. Hepburn manipulated the tea-pot, and lit the spirit-flame, and blew it out, and peeped into the steam of the tea-pot, and couldn't see whether there was any more tea or not – and – 'At home I *know* – I was going to say to a teaspoonful – how much tea there is in the pot. But this tea-pot – I don't know what it's made of – it isn't silver, I know that – it is so heavy in itself that it's deceived me several times already. And my husband is a greedy man, a greedy man – he likes at least three cups – and four if he can get them, or five! Yes, dear, I've plenty of tea to-day. You shall have even five, if you don't mind the last two weak. Do let me fill your cup, Countess Hannele. I think it's a *charming* name.'

'There's a play called *Hannele*, isn't there?' said he.

When he had had his five cups, and his wife had got her cigarette perched in the end of a long, long, slim, white holder, and was puffing like a little Chinawoman from the distance, there was a little lull.

'Alec, dear,' said Mrs. Hepburn. 'You won't forget to leave that message for me at Mrs. Rackham's. I'm so afraid it will be forgotten.'

'No, dear, I won't forget. Er – would you like me to go round now?'

Hannele noticed how often he said 'er' when he was beginning to speak to his wife. But they *were* such good friends, the two of them.

'Why, if you *would*, dear, I should feel perfectly comfortable. But I don't want you to hurry one bit.'

'Oh, I may as well go now.'

And he went. Mrs. Hepburn detained her guest.

'He *is* so charming to me,' said the little woman. 'He's really wonderful. And he always has been the same – invariably. So that if he *did* make a little slip – well, you know, I don't have to take it so seriously.'

'No,' said Hannele, feeling as if her ears were stretching with astonishment.

'It's the war. It's just the war. It's had a terribly deteriorating effect on the men.'

'In what way?' said Hannele.

'Why, morally. Really, there's hardly one man left the same as he was before the war. Terribly degenerated.'

'Is that so?' said Hannele.

'It is indeed. Why, isn't it the same with the German men and officers?'

'Yes, I think so,' said Hannele.

'And I'm sure so, from what I hear. But of course it is the women who are to blame in the first place. We poor women! We are a guilty race, I am afraid. But I never throw stones. I know what it is myself to have temptations. I have to flirt a little – and when I was younger – well, the men didn't escape me, I assure you. And I was *so* often scorched. But never *quite* singed. My husband never minded. He knew I was *really* safe. Oh yes, I have always been faithful to him. But still – I have been *very* near the flame.' And she laughed her winsome little laugh.

Hannele put her fingers to her ears to make sure they were not falling off.

'Of course during the war it was terrible. I know that in a certain hospital it was quite impossible for a girl to stay on if she kept straight. The matrons and sisters just turned her out. They wouldn't have her unless she was one of themselves. And you know what that means. Quite like the convent in Balzac's story – you know which I mean, I'm sure.' And the laugh tinkled gaily.

'But then, what can you expect, when there aren't enough men to go round! Why, I had a friend in Ireland. She and her husband had been an ideal couple, an *ideal* couple. Real playmates. And you can't say more than that, can you? Well, then, he became a major during the war. And she was so looking forward, poor thing, to the perfectly lovely times they would have together when he came home. She is like me, and is lucky enough to have a little income of her own – not a great fortune – but – well— Well now, what was I going to say? Oh yes, she was looking forward to the perfectly lovely times they would have when he came home: building on her dreams, poor thing, as we unfortunate women always do. I suppose we shall never be cured of it.' A little tinkling laugh. 'Well now, not a bit of it. Not a bit of it.' Mrs. Hepburn lifted her heavily-jewelled little hand in a motion of protest. It was curious, her hands were pretty and white, and her neck and breast, now she wore a little tea-gown, were also smooth and white and pretty, under the medley of twinkling little chains and coloured jewels. Why should her face have played her this nasty trick of going all crumpled? However, it was so.

'Not one bit of it,' reiterated the little lady. 'He came home quite changed. She said she could hardly recognise him for the same man. Let me tell you one little incident. Just a trifle, but significant. He was coming home – this was some time after he was free from the army – he was coming home from London, and he told her to meet him at the boat: gave her the time and everything. Well, she went to the boat, poor thing, and he didn't come. She waited, and no word of explanation or anything. So she couldn't make up her mind whether to go next day and meet the boat again. However, she decided she wouldn't. So of course, on that boat he arrived. When he got home, he said to her: "Why didn't you meet the boat?" "Well," she said, "I went yesterday, and you didn't come." "Then why didn't you meet it again to-day?" Imagine it, the sauce! And they had been real playmates. Heart-breaking, isn't it? "Well," she said in self-defence, "why didn't you come yesterday?" "Oh," he said, "I met a woman in town whom I liked, and she asked me to spend the night with her, so I did." Now what do you think of that? Can you conceive of such a thing?'

'Oh no,' said Hannele. 'I call that unnecessary brutality.'

'Exactly! So terrible to say such a thing to her! The brutality of it! Well, that's how the world is to-day. I'm thankful my husband isn't that sort. I don't say he's perfect. But whatever else he did, he'd never be unkind, and he *couldn't* be brutal. He just couldn't. He'd never tell me a lie – I know *that*. But callous brutality, no, thank goodness, he hasn't a spark of it in him. I'm the wicked one, if either of us is wicked.' The little laugh tinkled. 'Oh, but he's been perfect to me, perfect. Hardly a cross word. Why, on our wedding night, he kneeled down in front of me and promised, with God's help, to make my life happy. And I must say, as far as possible, he's kept his word. It has been his one aim in life, to make my life happy.'

The little lady looked away with a bright, musing look towards the window. She was being a heroine in a romance. Hannele could see her being a heroine, playing the chief part in her own life romance. It is such a feminine occupation, that no woman takes offence when she is made audience.

'I'm afraid I've more of the woman than the mother in my composition,' resumed the little heroine. 'I adore my two children. The boy is at Winchester, and my little girl is in a convent in Brittany. Oh, they are perfect darlings, both of them. But the man is first in my mind, I'm afraid. I fear I'm rather old-fashioned. But never mind. I can see the attractions in other men – can't I indeed! There was a perfectly exquisite creature – he was a very clever engineer – but much, much more than *that*. But never mind.' The little heroine sniffed as if there were perfume in the air, folded her jewelled hands, and resumed: 'However – I know what it is myself to flutter round the flame. You know I'm Irish myself, and we Irish can't help it. Oh, I wouldn't be English for anything. Just that little touch of imagination, you know . . . ' The little laugh tinkled. 'And that's what makes me able to sympathise with my husband even when, perhaps, I shouldn't. Why, when he was at home with me, he never gave a thought, not a thought to another woman. I must say, he used to make *me* feel a little guilty sometimes. But there! I don't think he ever thought of another woman as being flesh and blood, after he knew me. I could tell. Pleasant, courteous, charming – but other women were not flesh and blood to him, they were just people, callers – that kind of thing. It used to amaze me, when some perfectly lovely creature came, whom I should have been head over heels in love with in a minute – and he, he was charming, delightful; he could see her points, but she was no more to him than, let me say, a pot of carnations or a beautiful old piece of *punto di Milano*. Not flesh and blood. Well, perhaps one can feel too safe. Perhaps one needs a tiny pinch of salt of jealousy. I believe one does. And I have not had one jealous moment for seventeen years. So that, *really*, when I heard a whisper of something going on here, I felt almost pleased. I felt exonerated for my own little peccadilloes, for one thing. And I felt he was perhaps a little more human. Because, after all, it is nothing but human to fall in love, if you are alone for a long time and in the company of a beautiful woman – and if you're an attractive man yourself.'

Hannele sat with her eyes propped open and her ears buttoned back with amazement, expecting the next revelations.

'Why, of course,' she said, knowing she was expected to say something.

'Yes, of course,' said Mrs. Hepburn, eyeing her sharply. 'So I thought I'd better come and see how far things had gone. I had nothing but a hint to go on. I knew no name – nothing. I had just a hint that she was German, and a refugee aristocrat – and that he used to call at the studio.' The little lady eyed Hannele sharply, and gave a breathless little laugh, clasping her hands nervously. Hannele sat absolutely blank: really dazed.

'Of course,' resumed Mrs. Hepburn, 'that was enough. That was quite a sufficient clue. I'm afraid my intentions when I called at the studio were not as pure as they might have been. I'm afraid I wanted to see something more than the dolls. But when you showed me *his* doll, then I knew. Of course there wasn't a shadow of doubt after that. And I saw at once that she loved him, poor thing. She was *so* agitated. And no idea who I was. And you were so unkind to show me the doll. Of course, you had no idea who you were showing it to. But for her, poor thing, it was such a trial. I could see how she suffered. And I must say she's very lovely – she's very, very lovely, with her golden skin and her reddish amber eyes and her beautiful, beautiful carriage. And such a naïve, impulsive nature. Gives everything away in a minute. And then her deep voice – *"Oh yes – Oh, please!"* – such a child. And such an aristocrat, that lovely turn of her head, and her simple, elegant dress. Oh, she's very charming. And she's just the type I always knew would attract him, if he hadn't got me. I've thought about it many a time – many a time. When a woman is older than a man, she does think these things – especially if he has his attractive points too. And when I've dreamed of the woman he would love if he hadn't got me, it has always been a Spanish type. And the Baroness is extraordinarily Spanish in her appearance. She must have had some noble Spanish ancestor. Don't you think so?'

'Oh yes,' said Hannele. 'There were such a lot of Spaniards in Austria, too, with the various emperors.'

'With Charles V, exactly. Exactly. That's how it must have been. And so she has all the Spanish beauty, and all the German feeling. Of course, for myself, I miss the *reserve*, the haughtiness. But she's very, very lovely, and I'm sure I could never *hate* her. I couldn't even if I tried. And I'm not going to try. But I think she's much too dangerous for my husband to see much of her. Don't you agree, now?'

'Oh, but really,' stammered Hannele. 'There's nothing in it, really.'

'Well,' said the little lady, cocking her head shrewdly aside, 'I shouldn't like there to be any *more* in it.'

And there was a moment's dead pause. Each woman was reflecting. Hannele wondered if the little lady was just fooling her.

'Anyhow,' continued Mrs. Hepburn, 'the spark is there, and I don't intend the fire to spread. I am going to be very, very careful, myself, not to fan the flames. The last thing I should think of would be to make my husband scenes. I believe it would be fatal.'

'Yes,' said Hannele, during the pause.

'I am going very carefully. You think there isn't much in it – between him and the Baroness?'

'No – no – I'm sure there isn't,' cried Hannele, with a full voice of conviction. She was almost indignant at being slighted so completely herself, in the little lady's suspicions.

'Hm! – mm!' hummed the little woman, sapiently nodding her head slowly up and down. 'I'm not so sure! I'm not so sure that it hasn't gone pretty far.'

'Oh *no*!' cried Hannele, in real irritation of protest.

'Well,' said the other. 'In any case, I don't intend it to go any further.'

There was dead silence for some time.

'There's more in it than you say. There's more in it than you say,' ruminated the little woman. 'I know *him*, for one thing. I know he's got a cloud on his brow. And I know it hasn't left his brow for a single minute. And when I told him I had been to the studio, and showed him the cushion-cover, I knew he felt guilty. I am not so easily deceived. We Irish all have a touch of second sight, I believe. Of course I haven't challenged him. I haven't even mentioned the doll. By the way, *who* ordered the doll? Do you mind telling me?'

'No, it wasn't ordered,' confessed Hannele.

'Ah – I thought not – I thought not!' said Mrs. Hepburn, lifting her finger. 'At least, I knew no outsider had ordered it. Of course I knew.' And she smiled to herself.

'So,' she continued, 'I had too much sense to say anything about it. I don't believe in stripping wounds bare. I believe in gently covering them and letting them heal. But I *did* say I thought her a lovely creature.' The little lady looked brightly at Hannele.

'Yes,' said Hannele.

'And he was very vague in his manner. "Yes, not bad," he said. I thought to myself: Aha, my boy, you don't deceive me with your *not bad*. She's very much more than not bad. I said so, too. I wanted, of course, to let him know I had a suspicion.'

'And do you think he knew?'

'Of course he did. Of course he did. "She's much too dangerous," I said, "to be in a town where there are so many strange men: married and unmarried." And then he turned round to me and gave himself away, oh, so plainly. "Why?" he said. But such a haughty, distant tone. I said to myself: "It's time, my dear boy, you were removed out of the danger zone." But I answered him: Surely somebody is bound to fall in love with her. Not at all, he said, she keeps to her own countrymen. You don't tell *me*, I answered him, with her pretty broken English! It is a wonder the two of them are allowed to stay in the town. And then again he rounded on me. Good gracious! he said. Would you have them turned out just because they're beautiful to look at, when they have nowhere else to go, and they make their bit of a livelihood here? I assure you, he hasn't rounded on me in that overbearing way, not once before, in all our married life. So I just said quietly: I should like to protect *our own men*. And he didn't say anything more. But he looked at me under his brows and went out of the room.'

There was a silence. Hannele waited with her hands in her lap, and Mrs.

Hepburn mused, with her hands in *her* lap. Her face looked yellow, and *very* wrinkled.

'Well now,' she said, breaking again suddenly into life. 'What are we to do? I mean what is to be done? You are the Baroness's nearest friend. And I wish her *no* harm, none whatever.'

'What can we do?' said Hannele, in the pause.

'I have been urging my husband for some time to get his discharge from the army,' said the little woman. 'I knew he could have it in three months' time. But like so many more men, he has no income of his own, and he doesn't want to feel dependent. Perfect nonsense! So he says he wants to stay on in the army. I have never known him before go against my real wishes.'

'But it *is* better for a man to be independent,' said Hannele.

'I know it is. But it is also better for him to be *at home*. And I could get him a post in one of the observatories. He could do something in meteorological work.'

Hannele refused to answer any more.

'Of course,' said Mrs. Hepburn, 'if he *does* stay on here, it would be much better if the Baroness left the town.'

'I'm sure she will never leave of her own choice,' said Hannele.

'I'm sure she won't either. But she might be made to see that it would be very much *wiser* of her to move of her own free will.'

'Why?' said Hannele.

'Why, because she might any time be removed by the British authorities.'

'Why should she?' said Hannele.

'I think the women who are a menace to our men should be removed.'

'But she is *not* a menace to your men.'

'Well, I have my own opinion on that point.'

Which was a decided deadlock.

'I'm sure I've kept you an awful long time with my chatter,' said Mrs. Hepburn. 'But I did want to make everything as simple as possible. As I said before, I can't feel any ill-will against her. Yet I can't let things just go on. Heaven alone knows when they may end. Of course if I can persuade my husband to resign his commission and come back to England – anyhow, we will see. I'm sure I am the last person in the world to bear malice.'

The tone in which she said it conveyed a dire threat.

Hannele rose from her chair.

'Oh, and one other thing,' said her hostess, taking out a tiny lace handkerchief and touching her nose delicately with it. 'Do you think' – dab, dab – 'that I might have that *doll* – you know—?'

'That—?'

'Yes, of my husband' – the little lady rubbed her nose with her kerchief.

'The price is three guineas,' said Hannele.

'Oh, indeed!' – the tone was very cold. 'I thought it was not for sale.'

Hannele put on her wrap.

'You'll send it round – will you? – if you will be so kind.'

'I must ask my friend first.'

'Yes, of course. But I'm sure she will be so kind as to send it me. It is a little – er – indelicate, don't you think!'

'No,' said Hannele. 'No more than a painted portrait.'

'Don't you?' said her hostess coldly. 'Well, even a painted portrait I think I should like in my own possession. This *doll*— '

Hannele waited, but there was no conclusion.

'Anyhow,' she said, 'the price is three guineas: or the equivalent in marks.'

'Very well,' said the little lady, 'you shall have your three guineas when I get the doll.'

Chapter Five

Hannele went her way pondering. A man never is quite such an abject specimen as his wife makes him look, talking about 'my husband'. Therefore, if any woman wishes to rescue her husband from the clutches of another female, let her only invite this female to tea and talk quite sincerely about 'my husband, you know'. Every man has made a ghastly fool of himself with a woman at some time or other. No woman ever forgets. And most women will give the show away, with real pathos, to another woman. For instance, the picture of Alec at his wife's feet on his wedding night, vowing to devote himself to her life-long happiness – this picture strayed across Hannele's mind time after time, whenever she thought of her dear captain. With disastrous consequences to the captain. Of course if he had been at her own feet, then Hannele would have thought it almost natural: almost a necessary part of the show of love. But at the feet of that other little woman! And what was that other little woman wearing? Her wedding night! Hannele hoped before heaven it wasn't some awful little nightie of frail flowered silk. Imagine it, that little lady! Perhaps in a chic little boudoir cap of *punto di Milano*, and this slip of frail flowered silk: and the man, perhaps, in his braces! Oh, merciful heaven, save us from other people's indiscretions. No, let us be sure it was in proper evening dress – twenty years ago – very low cut, with a full skirt gathered behind and trailing a little, and a little feather erection in her high-dressed hair, and all those jewels: pearls of course: and he in a dinner-jacket and a white waistcoat: probably in an hotel bedroom in Lugano or Biarritz. And she? Was she standing with one small hand on his shoulder? – or was she seated on the couch in the bedroom? Oh, dreadful thought! And yet it was almost inevitable, that scene. Hannele had never been married, but she had come quite near enough to the realisation of the event to know that such a scene *was* practically inevitable. An indispensable part of any honeymoon. Him on his knees, with his heels up?

And how black and tidy his hair must have been then! and no grey at the temples at all. Such a good-looking bridegroom. Perhaps with a white rose in his button-hole still. And she could see him kneeling there, in his new black trousers and a wing collar. And she could see his head bowed. And she could hear his plangent, musical voice saying: 'With God's help, I will make your life happy. I will live for that and for nothing else.' And then the little lady must have had tears in her eyes, and she must have said, rather superbly: 'Thank you, dear. I'm perfectly sure of it.'

Ach! Ach! Husbands should be left to their own wives: and wives should be left to their own husbands. And *no* stranger should ever be made a party to these terrible bits of connubial staging. Nay, thought Hannele, that scene was really true. It actually took place. And with the man of that scene I have been in love! With the devoted husband of that little lady. Oh God, oh God, how was it possible! Him on his knees, on his knees, with his heels up!

Am I a perfect fool? she thought to herself. Am I really just an idiot, gaping with love for him? How *could* I? How could I? The very way he says: 'Yes, dear!' to her! The way he does what she tells him! The way he fidgets about the room with his hands in his pockets! The way he goes off when she sends him away because she wants to talk to me. And he knows she wants to talk to me. And he knows what she *might* have to say to me. Yet he goes off on his errand without a question, like a servant. 'I will do whatever you wish, darling.' He must have said those words time after time to the little lady. And fulfilled them, also. Performed all his pledges and his promises.

Ach! Ach! Hannele wrung her hands to think of *herself* being mixed up with him. And he had seemed to her so manly. He seemed to have so much silent male passion in him. And yet – the little lady! 'My husband has *always* been *perfectly sweet* to me.' Think of it! On his knees too. And his 'Yes, dear! Certainly. Certainly.' Not that he was afraid of the little lady. He was just committed to her, as he might have been committed to gaol, or committed to paradise.

Had she been dreaming, to be in love with him? Oh, she wished so much she had never been. She *wished* she had never given herself away. To him! – given herself away to him! – and so abjectly. Hung upon his words and his motions, and looked up to him as if he were Caesar. So he had seemed to her: like a mute Caesar. Like Germanicus. Like – she did not know what.

How had it all happened? What had taken her in? Was it just his good looks? No, not really. Because they were the kind of staring good looks she didn't really care for. He must have had charm. He must have charm. Yes, he *had* charm. When it worked.

His charm had not worked on her now for some time – never since that evening after his wife's arrival. Since then he had seemed to her – rather awful. Rather awful – stupid – an ass – a limited, rather vulgar person. That was what he seemed to her when his charm wouldn't work. A limited, rather inferior person. And in a world of *Schiebers* and profiteers and vulgar, pretentious persons, this was the worst thing possible. A limited, inferior, slightly pretentious individual! The husband of the little lady! And oh heaven, she was so deeply implicated with him! He had not, however, spoken with her in private since his wife's arrival. Probably he would never speak with her in private again. She hoped to heaven, never again. The awful thing was the past, that which had been between him and her. She shuddered when she thought of it The husband of the little lady!

But surely there was something to account for it! Charm, just charm. He had a charm. And then, oh, heaven, when the charm left off working! It had left off so completely at this moment, in Hannele's case, that her very mouth tasted salt. What *did* it all amount to?

What was his charm, after all? How could it have affected her? She began to think of him again, at his best: his presence, when they were alone high up in that big, lonely attic near the stars. His room! – the big white-washed walls, the first scent of tobacco, the silence, the sense of the stars being near, the telescopes, the cactus with fine scarlet flowers: and above all, the strange, remote, insidious silence of his presence, that was so congenial to her also. The curious way he had of turning his head to listen – to listen to what? – as if he heard something in the stars. The strange look, like destiny, in his wide-open, almost staring black eyes. The beautiful lines of his brow, that seemed always to have a certain cloud on it. The slow elegance of his straight, beautiful legs as he walked, and the exquisiteness of his dark, slender chest. She could feel the charm mounting over her again. She could feel the snake biting her heart. She could feel the arrows of desire rankling.

But then – and she turned from her thoughts back to this last little tea-party in the Vier Jahreszeiten. She thought of his voice: 'Yes, dear. Certainly. Certainly I will.' And she thought of the stupid, inferior look on his face. And the something of a servant-like way in which he went out to do his wife's bidding.

And then the charm was gone again, as the glow of sunset goes off a burning city and leaves it a sordid industrial hole. So much for charm!

So much for charm. She had better have stuck to her own sort of men, Martin, for instance, who was a gentleman and a daring soldier, and a queer sort and pleasant to talk to. Only he hadn't any *magic*. Magic? The very word made her writhe. Magic? Swindle. Swindle, that was all it amounted to. Magic!

And yet – let us not be too hasty. If the magic had *really* been there, on those evenings in that great lofty attic. Had it? Yes. Yes, she was bound to admit it. There had been magic. If there had been magic in his presence and in his contact, the husband of the little lady— But the distaste was in her mouth again.

So she started afresh, trying to keep a tight hold on the tail of that all-too-evanescent magic of his. Dear, it slipped so quickly into disillusion. Nevertheless. If it had existed it did exist. And if it did exist, it was worth having. You could call it an illusion if you liked. But an illusion which is a real experience is worth having. Perhaps this disillusion was a greater illusion than the illusion itself. Perhaps all this disillusion of the little lady and the husband of the little lady was falser than the illusion and magic of those few evenings. Perhaps the long disillusion of life was falser than the brief moments of real illusion. After all – the delicate darkness of his breast, the mystery that seemed to come with him as he trod slowly across the floor of his room, after changing his tunic— Nay, nay, if she could keep the illusion of his charm, she would give all disillusion to the devils. Nay, only let her be under the spell of his charm. Only let the spell be upon her. It was all she yearned for. And the thing she had to fight was the vulgarity of disillusion. The vulgarity of the little lady, the vulgarity of the husband of the little lady, the vulgarity of his insincerity, his 'Yes, dear. Certainly! Certainly!' – this was what she had to fight. He *was* vulgar and horrible, then. But also, the queer figure that sat alone on the roof watching the stars! The wonderful red flower of the cactus. The mystery that advanced with him as he came across the room after changing his tunic. The glamour and sadness of him, his silence, as he stooped unfastening his boots. And the strange gargoyle smile, fixed, when he caressed her with his hand under the chin! Life is all a choice. And if she chose the glamour, the magic, the charm, the illusion, the spell! Better death than that other, the husband of the little lady. When all was said and done, was he as much the husband of the little lady as he was that queer, delicate-breasted Caesar of her own knowledge? Which was he?

No, she was *not* going to send her the doll. The little lady should never have the doll.

'What a doll she would make herself! Heavens, what a wizened jewel!

Chapter Six

Captain Hepburn still called occasionally at the house for his post. The maid always put his letters in a certain place in the hall, so that he should not have to climb the stairs.

Among his letters – that is to say, along with another letter, for his correspondence was very meagre – he one day found an envelope with a crest. Inside this envelope two letters.

'Dear Captain Hepburn,

'I had the enclosed letter from Mrs. Hepburn. I don't intend her to have the doll which is your portrait, so I shall not answer this note. Also I don't see why she should try to turn us out of the town. She talked to me after tea that day, and it seems she believes that Mitchka is your lover. I didn't say anything at all – except that it wasn't true. But she needn't be afraid of me. I don't want you to trouble yourself. But you may as well *know* how things are.

'JOHANNA Z. R.'

The other letter was on his wife's well-known heavy paper, and in her well-known large, 'aristocratic' hand.

'My dear Countess.

'I wonder if there has been some mistake, or some misunderstanding. Four days ago you said you would send round that *doll* we spoke of, but I have seen no sign of it yet. I thought of calling at the studio, but did not wish to disturb the Baroness. I should be very much obliged if you could send the doll at once, as I do not feel easy while it is out of my possession. You may rely on having a cheque by return.

'Our old family friend, Major-General Barlow, called on me yesterday, and we had a most interesting conversation on our *Tommies*, and the protection of their morals here. It seems we have full power to send away any person or persons deemed undesirable, with twenty-four hours' notice to leave. But of course all this is done as quietly and with the intention of causing as little scandal as possible.

'Please let me have the doll by to-morrow, and perhaps some hint as to your future intentions.

'With very best wishes from one who only seeks to be your friend.

'Yours very sincerely,

'EVANGELINE HEPBURN.'

Chapter Seven

And then a dreadful thing happened: really a very dreadful thing. Hannele read of it in the evening newspaper of the town – the *Abendblatt*. Mitchka came rushing up with the paper at ten o'clock at night, just when Hannele was going to bed.

Mrs. Hepburn had fallen out of her bedroom window, from the third floor of the hotel, down on to the pavement below, and was killed. She was dressing for dinner. And apparently she had in the morning washed a certain little camisole, and put it on the window-sill to dry. She must have stood on a chair reaching for it when she fell out of the window. Her husband, who was in the dressing-room, heard a queer little noise, a short of choking cry, and came into her room to see what it was. And she wasn't there. The window was open, and the chair by the window. He looked round, and thought she had left the room for a moment, so returned to his shaving. He was half shaved when one of the maids rushed in. When he looked out of the window down into the street he fainted, and would have fallen too if the maid had not pulled him in in time.

The very next day the captain came back to his attic. Hannele did not know, until quite late at night when he tapped on her door. She knew his soft tap immediately.

'Won't you come over for a chat?' he said.

She paused for some moments before she answered. And then perhaps surprise made her agree: surprise and curiosity.

'Yes, in a minute,' she said, closing her door in his face.

She found him sitting quite still, not even smoking, in his quiet attic. He did not rise, but just glanced round with a faint smile. And she thought his face seemed different, more flexible. But in the half-light she could not tell. She sat at some little distance from him.

'I suppose you've heard,' he said.

'Yes.'

After a long pause, he resumed:

'Yes. It seems an impossible thing to have happened. Yet it *has* happened.'

Hannele's ears were sharp. But strain them as she might, she could not catch the meaning of his voice.

'A terrible thing. A *very* terrible thing,' she said.

'Yes.'

'Do you think she fell quite accidentally?' she said.

'Must have done. The maid was in just a minute before, and she seemed as happy as possible. I suppose reaching over that broad window-ledge, her brain must suddenly have turned. I can't imagine why she didn't call me. She could never bear even to look out of a high window. Turned her ill instantly if she saw a space below her. She used to say she couldn't really look at the moon, it made her feel as if she would fall down a dreadful height. She never dared do more than glance at it. She always had the feeling, I suppose, of the awful space beneath her, if she were on the moon.'

Hannele was not listening to his words, but to his voice. There was something a little automatic in what he said. But then that is always so when people have had a shock.

'It must have been terrible for you too,' she said.

'Ah, yes. At the time it was awful. Awful. I felt the smash right inside me, you know.'

'Awful!' she repeated.

'But now,' he said, 'I feel very strangely happy about it. I feel happy about it. I feel happy for her sake, if you can understand that. I feel she has got out of some great tension. I feel she's free now for the first time in her life. She was a gentle soul, and an original soul, but she was like a fairy who is condemned to live in houses and sit on furniture and all that, don't you know. It was never her nature.'

'No?' said Hannele, herself sitting in blank amazement.

'I always felt she was born in the wrong period – or on the wrong planet. Like some sort of delicate creature you take out of a tropical forest the moment it is born, and from the first moment teach it to perform tricks. You know what I mean. All her life she performed the tricks of life, clever little monkey she was at it too. Beat me into fits. But her own poor little soul, a sort of fairy soul, those queer Irish creatures, was cooped up inside her all her life, tombed in. There it was, tombed in, while she went through all the tricks of life that you have to go through if you are born to-day.'

'But,' stammered Hannele, 'what would she have done if she *had* been free?'

'Why, don't you see, there *is* nothing for her to do in the world to-day. Take her language, for instance. She never ought to have been speaking English. I don't know what language she ought to have spoken. Because if you take the Irish language, they only learn it back from English. They think in English, and just put Irish words on top. But English was never her language. It bubbled off her lips, so to speak. And she had no other language. Like a starling that you've made talk from the very beginning, and so it can only shout these talking noises, don't you know. It can't whistle its own whistling to save its life. Couldn't do it. It's lost it. All its own natural mode of expressing itself has collapsed, and it can only be artificial.'

There was a long pause.

'Would she have been wonderful, then, if she had been able to talk in some unknown language?' said Hannele jealously.

'I don't say she would have been wonderful. As a matter of fact, we think a talking starling is much more wonderful than an ordinary starling. I don't myself, but most people do. And she would have been a sort of starling. And she would have had her own language and her own ways. As it was, poor thing, she was always arranging herself and fluttering and chattering inside a cage. And she never knew she was in the cage, any more than we know we are inside our own skins.'

'But,' said Hannele, with a touch of mockery, 'how do you know you haven't made it all up – just to console yourself?'

'Oh, I've thought it long ago,' he said.

'Still,' she blurted, 'you may have invented it all – as a sort of consolation for – for – for your life.'

'Yes, I may,' he said. 'But I don't think so. It was her eyes. Did you ever notice her eyes? I often used to catch her eyes. And she'd be talking away, all the language bubbling off her lips. And her eyes were so clear and bright and different. Like a child's that is listening to something, and is going to be frightened. She was always listening – and waiting – for something else. I tell you what, she was exactly like that fairy in the Scotch song, who is in love with a mortal, and sits by the high road in terror waiting for him to come, and hearing the plovers and the curlews. Only nowadays motor-lorries go along the moor roads, and the poor thing is struck unconscious, and carried into our world in a state of unconsciousness, and when she comes round, she tries to talk our language and behave as we behave, and she can't remember anything else, so she goes on and on, till she falls with a crash, back to her own world.'

Hannele was silent, and so was he.

'You loved her then?' she said at length.

'Yes. But in this way. When I was a boy I caught a bird, a black-cap, and I put it in a cage. And I loved that bird. I don't know why, but I loved it. I simply loved that bird. All the gorse, and the heather, and the rock, and the hot smell of yellow gorse blossom, and the sky that seemed to have no end to it, when I was a boy, everything that I almost was *mad* with, as boys are, seemed to me to be in that little, fluttering black-cap. And it would peck its seed as if it didn't quite know what else to do; and look round about, and begin to sing. But in quite a few days it turned its head aside and died. Yes, it died. I never had the feeling again that I got from that black-cap when I was a boy – not until I saw her. And then I felt it all again. I felt it all again. And it was the same feeling. I knew, quite soon I knew, that she would die. She would peck her seed and look round in the cage just the same. But she would die in the end. Only it would last much longer. But she would die in the cage, like the black-cap.'

'But she loved the cage. She loved her clothes and her jewels. She must have loved her house and her furniture and all that with a perfect frenzy.'

'She did. She did. But like a child with play-things. Only they were big, marvellous play-things to her. Oh yes, she was never away from them. She never forgot her things – her trinkets and her furs and her furniture. She never got away from them for a minute. And everything in her mind was mixed up with them.'

'Dreadful!' said Hannele.

'Yes, it was dreadful,' he answered.

'Dreadful,' repeated Hannele.

'Yes, quite. Quite! And it got worse. And her way of talking got worse. As if it bubbled off her lips. But her eyes never lost their brightness, they never lost that faery look. Only I used to see fear in them. Fear of everything – even all the things she surrounded herself with. Just like my black-cap used to look out of his cage – so bright and sharp, and yet as if he didn't know that it was just the cage that was between him and the outside. He thought it was inside himself, the barrier. He thought it was part of his own nature to be shut in. And she thought it was part of her own nature. And so they both died.'

'What I can't see,' said Hannele, 'is what she would have done outside her cage. What other life could she have, except her *bibelots* and her furniture and her talk?'

'Why, none. There *is* no life outside for human beings.'

'Then there's nothing,' said Hannele.

'That's true. In a great measure, there's nothing.'

'Thank you,' said Hannele.

There was a long pause.

'And perhaps I was to blame. Perhaps I ought to have made some sort of a move. But I didn't know what to do. For my life, I didn't know what to do, except try to make her happy. She had enough money – and I didn't think it mattered if she shared it with me. I always had a garden – and the astronomy. It's been an immense relief to me watching the moon. It's been wonderful. Instead of looking inside the cage, as I did at my bird, or at her – I look right out – into freedom – into freedom.'

'The moon, you mean?' said Hannele.

'Yes, the moon.'

'And that's your freedom?'

'That's where I've found the greatest sense of freedom,' he said.

'Well, I'm not going to be jealous of the moon,' said Hannele at length.

'Why should you? It's not a thing to be jealous of.'

In a little while, she bade him good-night and left him.

Chapter Eight

The chief thing that the captain knew, at this juncture, was that a hatchet had gone through the ligatures and veins that connected him with the people of his affection, and that he was left with the bleeding ends of all his vital human relationships. Why it should be so he did not know. But then one never can know the whys and the wherefores of one's passional changes.

He only knew that it was so. The emotional flow between him and all the people he knew and cared for was broken, and for the time being he was conscious only of the cleavage. The cleavage that had occurred between him and his fellow-men, the cleft that was now between him and them. It was not the fault of anybody or anything. He could neither reproach himself nor them. What had happened had been preparing for a long time. Now suddenly the cleavage. There had been a long, slow weaning away: and now this sudden silent rupture.

What it amounted to principally was that he did not want even to see Hannele. He did not want to think of her even. But neither did he want to see anybody else, or to think of anybody else. He shrank with a feeling almost of disgust from his friends and acquaintances, and their expressions of sympathy. It affected him with instantaneous disgust when anybody wanted to share emotions with him. He did not want to share emotions or feelings of any sort. He wanted to be by himself, essentially, even if he was moving about among other people.

So he went to England to settle his own affairs, and out of duty to see his children. He wished his children all the well in the world – everything except any emotional connection with himself. He decided to take his girl away from the convent at once, and put her into a jolly English school. His boy was all right where he was.

The captain had now an income sufficient to give him his independence, but not sufficient to keep up his wife's house. So he prepared to sell the house and most of the things in it. He decided also to leave the army as soon as he could be free. And he thought he would wander about for a time, till he came upon something he wanted.

So the winter passed, without his going back to Germany. He was free of the army. He drifted along, settling his affairs. They were of no very great importance. And all the time he never wrote once to Hannele. He could not get over his disgust that people insisted on his sharing their emotions. He could not bear their emotions, neither their activities. Other people might have all the emotions and feelings and earnestness and busy activities they liked. Quite nice even that they had such a multifarious commotion for themselves. But the moment they approached him to spread their feelings over him or to entangle him in their activities a helpless disgust came up in him, and until he could get away he felt sick, even physically.

This was no state of mind for a lover. He could not even think of Hannele. Anybody else he felt he need not think about. He was deeply, profoundly thankful that his wife was dead. It was an end of pity now; because, poor thing, she had escaped and gone her own way into the void, like a flown bird.

Chapter Nine

Nevertheless, a man hasn't finished his life at forty. He may, however, have finished one great phase of his life.

And Alexander Hepburn was not the man to live alone. All our troubles, say somebody wise, come upon us because we cannot be alone. And that is all very well. We must all be *able* to be alone, otherwise we are just victims. But when we *are* able to be alone, then we realise that the only thing to do is to start a new relationship with another – or even the same – human being. That people should all be stuck up apart, like so many telegraph-poles, is nonsense.

So with our dear captain. He had his convulsion into a sort of telegram-pole isolation: which was absolutely necessary for him. But then he began to bud with a new yearning for – for what? For love?

It was a question he kept nicely putting to himself. And really, the nice young girls of eighteen or twenty attracted him very much: so fresh, so impulsive, and looking up to him as if he were something wonderful. If only he could have married two or three of them, instead of just one!

Love! When a man has no particular ambition, his mind turns back perpetually, as a needle towards the pole. That tiresome word Love. It means so many things. It meant the feeling he had had for his wife. He had loved her. But he shuddered at the thought of having to go through such love again. It meant also the feeling he had for the awfully nice young things he met here and there: fresh, impulsive girls ready to give all their hearts away. Oh yes, he could fall in love with half a dozen of them. But he knew he'd better not.

At last he wrote to Hannele: and got no answer. So he wrote to Mitchka and still got no answer. So he wrote for information – and there was none forthcoming, except that the two women had gone to Munich.

For the time being he left it at that. To him, Hannele did not exactly represent rosy love. Rather a hard destiny. He did not adore her. He did not feel one bit of adoration for her. As a matter of fact, not all the beauties and virtues of woman put together with all the gold in the Indies would have tempted him into the business of adoration any more. He had gone on his knees, once, vowing with faltering tones to try and make the adored one happy. And now – never again. Never.

The temptation this time was to be adored. One of those fresh young things would have adored him as if he were a god. And there was something *very* alluring about the thought. Very – very alluring. To be god-almighty in your own house, with a lovely young thing adoring you, and you giving off beams of bright effulgence like a Gloria! Who wouldn't be tempted: at the age of forty? And this was why he dallied.

But in the end he suddenly took the train to Munich. And when he got there he found the town beastly uncomfortable, the Bavarians rude and disagreeable, and no sign of the missing females, not even in the Café Stéphanie. He wandered round and round.

And then one day, oh heaven, he saw his doll in a shop window: a little art shop. He stood and stared quite spell-bound.

'Well, if that isn't the devil,' he said. 'Seeing yourself in a shop window!'

He was so disgusted that he would not go into the shop.

Then, every day for a week did he walk down that little street and look at himself in the shop window. Yes, there he stood, with one hand in his pocket. And the figure had one hand in its pocket. There he stood, with his cap pulled rather low over his brow. And the figure had its cap pulled low over its brow. But, thank goodness, his own cap now was a civilian tweed. But there he stood, his head rather forward, gazing with fixed dark eyes. And himself in little, that wretched figure, stood there with its head rather forward, staring with fixed dark eyes. It was such a real little *man* that it fairly staggered him. The oftener he saw it, the more it staggered him. And the more he hated it. Yet it fascinated him, and he came again to look.

And it was always there. A lonely little individual lounging there with one hand in its pocket, and nothing to do, among the bric-à-brac and the *bibelots*. Poor devil, stuck so incongruously in the world. And yet losing none of his masculinity.

A male little devil, for all his forlornness. But such an air of isolation, or not-belonging. Yet taut and male, in his tartan trews. And what a situation to be in! – lounging with his back against a little Japanese lacquer cabinet, with a few old pots on his right hand and a tiresome brass ink-tray on his left, while pieces of not-very-nice filet lace hung their length up and down the background. Poor little devil: it was like a deliberate satire.

And then one day it was gone. There was the cabinet and the filet lace and the tiresome ink-stand tray: and the little gentleman wasn't there. The captain at once walked into the shop.

'Have you sold that doll? – that unknown soldier?' he added, without knowing quite what he was saying.

The doll was sold.

'Do you know who bought it?'

The girl looked at him very coldly, and did not know.

'I once knew the lady who made it. In fact, the doll was *me*,' he said.

The girl now looked at him with sudden interest.

'Don't you think it was like me?' he said.

'Perhaps' – she began to smile.

'It was me. And the lady who made it was a friend of mine. Do you know her name?'

'Yes.'

'Gräfin zu Rassentlow,' he cried, his eyes shining.

'Oh yes. But her dolls are famous.'

'Do you know where she is? Is she in Munich?'

'That I don't know.'

'Could you find out?'

'I don't know. I can ask.'

'Or the Baroness von Prielau-Carolath.'

'The Baroness is dead.'

'Dead!'

'She was shot in a riot in Salzburg. They say a lover— '

'How do you know?'

'From the newspapers.'

'Dead! Is it possible. Poor Hannele.'

There was a pause.

'Well,' he said, 'if you would enquire about the address – I'll call again.'

Then he turned back from the door.

'By the way, do you mind telling me how much you sold the doll for?'

The girl hesitated. She was by no means anxious to give away any of her trade details. But at length she answered reluctantly:

'Five hundred marks.'

'So cheap,' he said. 'Good-day. Then I will call again.'

Chapter Ten

Then again he got a trace. It was in the Chit-Chat column of the *Muenchener Neue Zeitung*: under Studio-Comments. 'Theodor Worpswede's latest picture is a still-life, containing an entertaining group of a doll, two sunflowers in a glass jar, and a poached egg on toast. The contrast between the three substances is highly diverting and instructive, and this is perhaps one of the most interesting of Worpswede's works. The doll, by the way, is one of the creations of our fertile Countess Hannele. It is the figure of an English, or rather Scottish, officer in the famous tartan trousers which, clinging closely to the legs of the lively Gaul, so shocked the eminent Julius Caesar and his cohorts. We, of course, are no longer shocked, but full of admiration for the creative genius of our dear Countess. The doll itself is a masterpiece, and has begotten another masterpiece in Theodor Worpswede's Still-life. We have heard, by the way, a rumour of Countess zu Rassentlow's engagement. Apparently the Herr Regierungsrat von Poldi, of that most beautiful of summer resorts, Kaprun, in the Tyrol, is the fortunate man— '

Chapter Eleven

The captain bought the Still-life. This new version of himself along with the poached egg and the sunflowers was rather frightening. So he packed up for Austria, for Kaprun, with his picture, and had a fight to get the beastly thing out of Germany, and another fight to get it into Austria. Fatigued and furious he arrived in Salzburg, seeing no beauty in anything. Next day he was in Kaprun.

It was an elegant and fashionable watering-place before the war; a lovely little lake in the midst of the Alps, an old Tyrolese town on the water-side, green slopes sheering up opposite, and away beyond a glacier. It was still crowded and still elegant. But alas, with a broken, bankrupt, desperate elegance, and almost empty shops.

The captain felt rather dazed. He found himself in an hotel full of Jews of the wrong, rich sort, and wondered what next. The place was beautiful, but the life wasn't.

Chapter Twelve

The Herr Regierungsrat was not at first sight prepossessing. He was approaching fifty, and had gone stout and rather loose, as so many men of his class and race do. Then he wore one of those dreadful full-bottom coats, a kind of poor relation to our full-skirted frock-coat: it would best be described as a family coat. It flapped about him as he walked, and he looked at first glance lower middle-class.

But he wasn't. Of course, being in office in the collapsed Austria, he was a republican. But by nature he was a monarchist, nay, an imperialist, as every true Austrian is. And he was a true Austrian. And as such he was much finer and subtler than he looked. As one got used to him, his rather fat face, with its fine nose and slightly bitter, pursed mouth, came to have a resemblance to the busts of some of the late Roman emperors. And as one was with him, one came gradually to realise that out of all his baggy bourgeois appearance came something of a *grand geste*. He could not help it. There was something sweeping and careless about his soul: big, rather assertive, and ill-bred-seeming; but, in fact, not ill-bred at all, only a little bitter and a good deal indifferent to his surroundings. He looked at first sight so common and *parvenu*. And then one had to realise that he was a member of a big, old empire, fallen into a sort of epicureanism, and a little bitter. There was no littleness, no meanness, and no real coarseness. But he was a great talker, and relentless towards his audience.

Hannele was attracted to him by his talk. He began as soon as dinner appeared: and he went on, carrying the decanter and the wine-glass with him out on to the balcony of the villa, over the lake, on and on until midnight. The summer night was still and warm: the lake lay deep and full, and the old town twinkled away across. There was the faintest tang of snow in the air, from the great glacier-peaks that were hidden in the night opposite. Sometimes a boat with a lantern twanged a guitar. The clematis flowers were quite black, like leaves, dangling from the terrace.

It was so beautiful, there in the very heart of the Tyrol. The hotels glittered with lights: electric light was still cheap. There seemed a fullness and a loveliness in the night. And yet for some reason it was all terrible and devastating: the life-spirit seemed to be squirming, bleeding all the time.

And on and on talked the Herr Regierungsrat, with all the witty volubility of the more versatile Austrian. He was really very witty, very human, and with a touch of salty cynicism that remained one of a real old Roman of the Empire. That subtle stoicism, that unsentimental epicureanism, that kind of reckless hopelessness, of course, fascinated the women. And particularly Hannele. He talked on and on – about his work before the war, when he held an important post and was one of the governing class – then about the war – then about the hopelessness of the present: and in it all there seemed a bigness, a carelessness based on indifference and hopelessness that laughed at its very self. The real old Austria had always fascinated Hannele. As represented in the witty, bitter-indifferent Herr Regierungsrat it carried her away.

And he, of course, turned instinctively to her, talking in his rapid, ceaseless fashion, with a laugh and a pause to drink and a new start taken. She liked the sound of his Austrian speech; its racy carelessness, its salty indifference to standards of correctness. Oh yes, here was the *grand geste* still lingering.

He turned his large breast towards her, and made a quick gesture with his flat, well-shaped hand, blurted out another subtle, rough-seeming romance, pursed his mouth, and emptied his glass once more. Then he looked at his half-forgotten cigar and started again.

There was something almost boyish and impulsive about him: the way he turned to her, and the odd way he seemed to open his big breast to her. And again he seemed almost eternal, sitting there in his chair with knees planted apart. It was as if he would never rise again, but would remain sitting for ever, and talking. He seemed as if he had no legs, save to sit with. As if to stand on his feet and walk would not be natural to him.

Yet he rose at last, and kissed her hand with the grand gesture that France or Germany have never acquired: carelessness, profound indifference to other people's standards, and then such a sudden stillness, as he bent and kissed her hand. Of course she felt a queen in exile.

And perhaps it is more dangerous to feel yourself a queen in exile than a queen *in situ*. She fell in love with him, with this large, stout, loose widower of fifty, with two children. He had no money except some Austrian money that was worth nothing outside Austria. He could not even go to Germany. There he was, fixed in this hollow in the middle of the Tyrol.

But he had an ambition still, old Roman of the decadence that he was. He had year by year and without making any fuss collected the material for a very minute and thorough history of his own district: the Chiemgau and the Pinzgau. Hannele found that his fund of information on this subject was inexhaustible, and his intelligence was so delicate, so human, and his scope seemed so wide, that she felt a touch of reverence for him. He wanted to write this history. And she wanted to help him.

For, of course, as things were he would never write it. He was Regierungsrat: that is, he was the petty local governor of his town and immediate district. The Amthaus was a great old building, and there young ladies in high heels flirted among masses of papers with bare-kneed young gentlemen in Tyrolese costume, and occasionally they parted to take a pleasant, interesting attitude and write a word or two, after which they fluttered together for a little more interesting diversion. It was extraordinary how many finely built, handsome young people of an age fitted for nothing but love-affairs ran the governmental business of this department. And the Herr Regierungsrat sailed in and out of the big, old room, his wide coat flying like wings and making the papers flutter, his rather wine-reddened, old-Roman face smiling with its bitter look. And of course it was a witticism he uttered first, even if Hungary was invading the frontier or cholera was in Vienna.

When he was on his legs, he walked nimbly, briskly, and his coat-bottoms always flew. So he waved through the town, greeting somebody at every few strides and grinning, and yet with a certain haughty reserve. Oh yes, there was a certain salty *hauteur* about him which made the people trust him. And he spoke the vernacular so racily.

Hannele felt she would like to marry him. She would like to be near him. She would like him to write his history. She would like him to make her feel a queen in exile. No one had ever *quite* kissed her hand as he kissed it: with that sudden stillness and strange, chivalric abandon of himself. How he would abandon himself to her! – terribly – wonderfully – perhaps a little horribly. His wife, whom he had married late, had died after seven years of marriage. Hannele could understand that too. One or the other must die.

She became engaged. But something made her hesitate before marriage. Being in Austria was like being on a wrecked ship that *must* sink after a certain short length of time. And marrying the Herr Regierungsrat was like marrying the doomed captain of the doomed ship. The sense of fatality was part of the attraction.

And yet she hesitated. The summer weeks passed. The strangers flooded in and crowded the town, and ate up the food like locusts. People no longer counted the paper money, they weighed it by the kilogram. Peasants stored it in a corner of the meal-bin, and mice came and chewed holes in it. Nobody knew where the next lot of food was going to come from: yet it always came. And the lake teemed with bathers. When the captain arrived he looked with amazement on the crowds of strapping, powerful fellows who bathed all day long, magnificent blond flesh of men and women. No wonder the old Romans stood in astonishment before the huge blond limbs of the savage Germans.

Well, the life was like a madness. The hotels charged fifteen hundred kronen a day: the women, old and young, paraded in the peasant costume, in flowery cotton dresses with gaudy, expensive silk aprons: the men wore the Tyrolese costume, bare knees and little short jackets. And for the men, the correct thing was to have the leathern hose and the blue linen jacket as old as possible. If you had a hole in your leathern seat, so much the better.

Everything so physical. Such magnificent naked limbs and naked bodies, and in the streets, in the hotels, everywhere, bare, white arms of women and bare, brown, powerful knees and thighs of men. The sense of flesh everywhere, and the endless ache of flesh. Even in the peasants who rowed across the lake, standing and rowing with a slow, heavy, gondolier motion at the one curved oar, there was the same endless ache of physical yearning.

Chapter Thirteen

It was August when Alexander met Hannele. She was walking under a chintz parasol, wearing a dress of blue cotton with little red roses, and a red silk apron. She had no hat, her arms were bare and soft, and she had white stockings under her short dress. The Herr Regierungsrat was at her side, large, nimble, and laughing with a new witticism.

Alexander, in a light summer suit and Panama hat, was just coming out of the bank, shoving twenty thousand kronen into his pocket. He saw her coming across from the Amtsgericht, with the Herr Regierungsrat at her side, across the space of sunshine. She was laughing, and did not notice him.

She did not notice till he had taken off his hat and was saluting her. Then what she saw was the black, smooth, shining head, and she went pale. His black, smooth, close head – and all the blue Austrian day seemed to shrivel before her eyes.

'How do you do, Countess! I hoped I should meet you.'

She heard his slow, sad-clanging, straying voice again, and she pressed her hand with the umbrella stick against her breast. She had forgotten it – forgotten his peculiar, slow voice. And now it seemed like a noise that sounds in the silence of night. Ah, how difficult it was, that suddenly the world could split under her eyes, and show this darkness inside. She wished he had not come.

She presented him to the Herr Regierungsrat, who was stiff and cold. She asked where the captain was staying. And then, not knowing what else to say, she said:

'Won't you come to tea?'

She was staying in a villa across the lake. Yes, he would come to tea.

He went. He hired a boat and a man to row him across. It was not far. There stood the villa, with its brown balconies one above the other, the bright red geraniums and white geraniums twinkling all round, the trees of purple clematis tumbling at one corner. All the green window doors were open: but nobody about. In the little garden by the water's edge the rose trees were tall and lank, drawn up by the dark green trees of the background. A white table with chairs and garden seats stood under the shadow of a big willow tree, and a hammock with cushions swung just behind. But no one in sight. There was a little landing bridge on to the garden: and a fairly large boat-house at the garden end.

The captain was not sure that the boat-house belonged to the villa. Voices were shouting and laughing from the water's surface, bathers swimming. A tall, naked youth with a little red cap on his head and a tiny red loin-cloth round his slender young hips was standing on the steps of the boat-house calling to the three women who were swimming near. The dark-haired woman with the white cap swam up to the steps and caught the boy by the ankle. He cried and laughed and remonstrated, and poked her in the breast with his foot.

'*Nein, nein, Hardu!*' she cried as he tickled her with his toe. '*Hardu! Hardu! Hör' auf!* – Leave off!'. – and she fell with a crash back into the water. The youth laughed a loud, deep laugh of a lad whose voice is newly broken.

'*Was macht er dann?*' cried a voice from the waters. 'What is he doing?' It was a dark-skinned girl swimming swiftly, her big dark eyes watching amused from the water surface.

'*Jetze Hardu hör auf. Nein. Jetzt ruhig!* Now leave off! Now be quiet.' And the dark-skinned woman was climbing out in the sunshine on to the pale, raw-wood steps of the boat-house, the water glistening on her dark-blue, stockinette, soft-moulded back and loins: while the boy, with his foot stretched out, was trying to push her back into the water. She clambered out, however, and sat on the steps in the sun, panting slightly. She was dark and attractive-looking, with a mature beautiful figure, and handsome, strong women's legs.

In the garden appeared a black-and-white maid-servant with a tray.

'*Kaffee, gnädige Frau!*'

The voice came so distinct over the water.

'*Hannele! Hannele! Kaffee!*' called the woman on the steps of the bathing-house.

'*Tante Hannele! Kaffee!*' called the dark-eyed girl, turning round in the water, then swimming for home.

'*Kaffee! Kaffee!*' roared the youth, in anticipation.

'*Ja – a! Ich kom – mm,*' sang Hannele's voice from the water.

The dark-eyed girl, her hair tied up in a silk bandana, had reached the steps and was climbing out, a slim young fish in her close dark suit. The three stood clustered on the steps, the elder woman with one arm over the naked shoulders of the youth, the other arm over the shoulders of the girl. And all in chorus sang:

'*Hannele! Hannele! Hannele!* Wir warten auf dich.'

The boatman had left off rowing, and the boat was drifting slowly in. The family became quiet, because of the intrusion. The attractive-looking woman turned and picked up her blue bath-robe, of a mid-blue colour that became her. She swung it round her as if it were an opera cloak. The youth stared at the boat.

The captain was watching Hannele. With a white kerchief tied round her silky, brownish hair, she was swimming home. He saw her white shoulders and her white, wavering legs below in the clear water. Round the boat fishes were suddenly jumping.

The three on the steps beyond stood silent, watching the intruding boat with resentment. The boatman twisted his head round and watched them. The captain, who was facing them, watched Hannele. She swam slowly and easily up, caught the rail of the steps, and stooping forward, climbed slowly out of the water. Her legs were large and flashing white and looked rich, the rich, white thighs with the blue veins behind, and the full, rich softness of her sloping loins.

'*Ach! Schön! 'S war schön! Das Wasser ist gut,*' her voice was heard, half singing as she took her breath. 'It was lovely.'

'*Heiss,*' said the woman above. '*Zu warm.* Too warm.'

The youth made way for Hannele, who drew herself erect at the top of the steps, looking round, panting a little and putting up her hands to the knot of her kerchief on her head. Her legs were magnificent and white.

'*Kuck de Leut, die da bleiben,*' said the woman in the blue wrap, in a low voice. 'Look at the people stopping there.'

'*Ja!*' said Hannele negligently. Then she looked. She started as if in fear, looked round, as if to run away, looked back again, and met the eyes of the captain, who took off his hat.

She cried in a loud, frightened voice:

'Oh, but – I thought it was *to-morrow!*'

'No – to-day,' came the quiet voice of the captain over the water.

'*To-day!* Are you *sure?*' she cried, calling to the boat.

'Quite sure. But we'll make it to-morrow if you like,' he said.

'To-day! To-day!' she repeated in bewilderment. 'No! Wait a minute.' And she ran into the boat-house.

'*Was ist es?*' asked the dark woman, following her. 'What is it?'

'A friend – a visitor – Captain Hepburn,' came Hannele's voice.

The boatman now rowed slowly to the landing-stage. The dark woman, huddled in her blue wrap as in an opera-cloak, walked proudly and unconcernedly across the background of the garden and up the steps to the first balcony. Hannele, her feet slip-slopping in loose slippers, clutching an old yellow wrap round her, came to the landing-stage and shook hands.

'I am so sorry. It is so stupid of me. I was sure it was to-morrow,' she said.

'No, it was to-day. But I wish for your sake it had been to-morrow,' he replied.

'No. No. It doesn't matter. You won't mind waiting a minute, will you? You mustn't be angry with me for being so stupid.'

So she went away, the heelless slippers flipping up to her naked heels. Then the big-eyed, dusky girl stole into the house: and then the naked youth, who went with sangfroid. He would make a fine, handsome man: and he knew it.

Chapter Fourteen

Hepburn and Hannele were to make a small excursion to the glacier which stood there always in sight, coldly grinning in the sky. The weather had been very hot, but this morning there were loose clouds in the sky. The captain rowed over the lake soon after dawn. Hannele stepped into the little craft, and they pulled back to the town. There was a wind ruffling the water, so that the boat leaped and chuckled. The glacier, in a recess among the folded mountains, looked cold and angry. But morning was very sweet in the sky, and blowing very sweet with a faint scent of the second hay from the low lands at the head of the lake. Beyond stood naked grey rock like a wall of mountains, pure rock, with faint, thin slashes of snow. Yesterday it had rained on the lake. The sun was going to appear from behind the Breitsteinhorn, the sky with its clouds floating in blue light and yellow radiance was lovely and cheering again. But dark clouds seemed to spout up from the Pinzgau valley. And once across the lake, all was shadow, when the water no longer gave back the sky-morning.

The day was a feast day, a holiday. Already so early three young men from the mountains were bathing near the steps of the Badeanstalt. Handsome, physical fellows, with good limbs rolling and swaying in the early morning water. They seemed to enjoy it too. But to Hepburn it was always as if a dark wing were stretched in the sky, over these mountains, like a doom. And these three young, lusty, naked men swimming and rolling in the shadow.

Hepburn's was the first boat stirring. He made fast in the hotel boat-house, and he and Hannele went into the little town. It was deep in shadow, though the light of the sky, curdled with cloud, was bright overhead. But dark and chill and heavy lay the shadow in the black-and-white town, like a sediment.

The shops were all shut, but peasants from the hills were already strolling about in their holiday dress: the men in their short leather trousers, like football drawers, and bare brown knees and great boots: their little grey jackets faced with green, and their green hats with the proud chamois-brush behind. They seemed to stray about like lost souls, and the proud chamois-brush behind their hats, this proud, cocky, perking-up tail, like a mountain-buck with his tail up, was belied by the lost-soul look of the men, as they loitered about with their hands shoved in the front pockets of their trousers. Some women also were creeping about: peasant women, in the funny little black hats that had thick gold under the brim and long black streamers of ribbon, broad, black, water-wave ribbon starting from a bow under the brim behind and streaming right to the bottom of the skirt. These women, in their thick, dark dresses with tight bodices and massive, heavy, full skirts, and bright or dark aprons, strode about with the heavy stride of the mountain women, the heavy, quick, forward-leaning motion. They were waiting for the town-day to begin.

Hepburn had a knapsack on his back, with food for the day. But bread was wanting. They found the door of the bakery open, and got a loaf: a long, hot loaf of pure white bread, beautiful sweet bread. It cost seventy kronen. To Hepburn it was always a mystery where this exquisite bread came from, in a lost land.

In the little square where the clock stood were bunches of people, and a big motor-omnibus, and a motor-car that would hold about eight people. Hepburn had paid his seven hundred kronen for the two tickets. Hannele tied up her head in a thin scarf and put on her thick coat. She and Hepburn sat in front by the peaked driver. And at seven o'clock away went the car, swooping out of the town, past the handsome old Tyrolese Schloss, or manor, black-and-white, with its little black spires pricking up, past the station, and under the trees by the lake-side. The road was not good, but they ran at a great speed, out past the end of the lake, where the reeds grew, out into the open valley mouth, where the mountains opened in two clefts. It was cold in the car. Hepburn buttoned himself up to the throat and pulled his hat down on his ears. Hannele's scarf fluttered. She sat without saying anything, erect, her face fine and keen, watching ahead. From the deep Pinzgau Valley came the river roaring and raging, a glacier river of pale, seething ice-water. Over went the car, over the log bridge, darting towards the great slopes opposite. And then a sudden immense turn, a swerve under the height of the mountain-side, and again a darting lurch forward, under the pear trees of the high-road, past the big old ruined castle that so magnificently watched the valley mouth, and the foaming river; on, rushing under the huge roofs of the balconied peasant houses of a village, then swinging again to take another valley mouth, there where a little village clustered all black and white on a knoll, with a white church that had a black steeple, and a white castle with black spines, and clustering, ample black-and-white houses of the Tyrol. There is a grandeur even in the peasant houses, with their great wide passage halls where the swallows build, and where one could build a whole English cottage.

So the motor-car darted up this new, narrow, wilder, more sinister valley. A herd of almost wild young horses, handsome reddish things, burst around the car, and one great mare with full flanks went crashing up the road ahead, her heels flashing to the car, while her foal whinneyed and screamed from behind. But no, she could not turn from the road. On and on she crashed, forging ahead, the car behind her. And then at last she did swerve aside, among the thin alder trees by the wild river-bed.

'If it isn't a cow, it's a horse,' said the driver, who was thin and weaselish and silent, with his ear-flaps over his ears.

But the great mare had shaken herself in a wild swerve, and screaming and whinneying was plunging back to her foal. Hannele had been frightened.

The car rushed on, through water-meadows, along a naked, white bit of mountain road. Ahead was a darkness of mountain front and pine trees. To the right was the stony, furious, lion-like river, tawny-coloured here, and the slope up beyond. But the road for the moment was swinging fairly level through the stunned water-meadows of the savage valley. There were gates to open, and Hepburn jumped down to open them, as if he were the foot-boy. The heavy Jews of the wrong sort, seated behind, of course did not stir.

At a house on a knoll the driver sounded his horn, and out rushed children crying Papa! Papa! – then a woman with a basket. A few brief words from the weaselish man, who smiled with warm, manly blue eyes at his children, then the car leaped forward. The whole bearing of the man was so different when he was looking at his own family. He could not even say thank you when Hepburn opened the gates. He hated and even despised his human cargo of middle-class people. Deep, deep is class-hatred, and it begins to swallow all human feeling in its abyss. So, stiff, silent, thin, capable, and neuter towards his fares, sat the little driver with the flaps over his ears, and his thin nose cold.

The car swept round, suddenly, into the trees: and into the ravine. The river shouted at the bottom of a gulf. Bristling pine trees stood around. The air was black and cold and for ever sunless. The motor-car rushed on, in this blackness, under the rock-walls and the fir trees.

Then it suddenly stopped. There was a huge motor-omnibus ahead, drab and enormous-looking. Tourists and trippers of last night coming back from the glacier. It stood like a great rock. And the smaller motor-car edged past, tilting into the rock gutter under the face of stone.

So, after a while of this valley of the shadow of death, lurching in steep loops upwards, the motor-car scrambling wonderfully, struggling past trees and rock upwards, at last they came to the end. It was a huge inn or tourist hotel of brown wood: and here the road ended in a little wide bay surrounded and overhung by trees. Beyond was a garage and a bridge over a roaring river: and always the overhung darkness of trees and the intolerable steep slopes immediately above.

Hannele left her big coat. The sky looked blue above the gloom. They set out across the hollow-sounding bridge, over the everlasting mad rush of ice-water, to the immediate upslope of the path, under dark trees. But a little old man in a sort of sentry-box wanted fifty or sixty kronen: apparently for the upkeep of the road, a sort of toll.

The other tourists were coming – some stopping to have a drink first. The second omnibus had not yet arrived. Hannele and Hepburn were the first two, treading slowly up that dark path, under the trees. The grasses hanging on the rock face were still dewy. There were a few wild raspberries, and a tiny tuft of bilberries with black berries here and there, and a few tufts of unripe cranberries. The many hundreds of tourists who passed up and down did not leave much to pick. Some mountain harebells, like bells of blue water, hung coldly glistening in their darkness. Sometimes the hairy mountain-bell, pale-blue and bristling, stood alone, curving his head right down, stiff and taut. There was an occasional big, moist, lolling daisy.

So the two climbed slowly up the steep ledge of a road. This valley was just a mountain cleft, cleft sheer in the hard, living rock, with black trees like hair flourishing in this secret, naked place of the earth. At the bottom of the open wedge for ever roared the rampant, insatiable water. The sky from above was like a sharp wedge forcing its way into the earth's cleavage, and that eternal ferocious water was like the steel edge of the wedge, the terrible tip biting in into the rocks' intensity. Who could have thought that the soft sky of light, and the soft foam of water could thrust and penetrate into the dark, strong earth? But so it was. Hannele and Hepburn, toiling up the steep little ledge of a road that hung half-way down the gulf, looked back, time after time, back down upon the brown timbers and shingle roofs of the hotel, that now, away below, looked damp and wedged in like boulders. Then back at the next tourists struggling up. Then down at the water, that rushed like a beast of prey. And then, as they rose higher, they looked up also at the livid great sides of rock, livid, bare rock that sloped from the sky-ridge in a hideous sheer swerve downwards.

In his heart of hearts Hepburn hated it. He hated it, he loathed it, it seemed almost obscene, this livid, naked slide of rock, unthinkably huge and massive, sliding down to this gulf where bushes grew like hair in the darkness and water roared. Above, there were thin slashes of snow.

So the two climbed slowly on, up the eternal side of that valley, sweating with the exertion. Sometimes the sun, now risen high, shone full on their side of the gulley. Tourists were trickling downhill too: two maidens with bare arms and bare heads and huge boots: men tourists with great knapsacks and edelweiss in their hats: giving *Bergheil* for a greeting. But the captain said Good-day. He refused this *Bergheil* business. People swarming touristy on these horrible mountains made him feel almost sick.

He and Hannele also were not in good company together. There was a sort of silent hostility between them. She hated the effort of climbing; but the high air, the cold in the air, the savage cat-howling sound of the water, those awful flanks of livid rock, all this thrilled and excited her to another sort of savageness. And he, dark, rather slender and feline, with something of the physical suavity of a delicate-footed race, he hated beating his way up the rock, he hated the sound of the water, it frightened him, and the high air bit him in his chest, like a viper.

'Wonderful! Wonderful!' she cried, taking great breaths in her splendid chest.

'Yes. And horrible. Detestable,' he said.

She turned with a flash, and the high strident sound of the mountain in her voice.

'If you don't like it,' she said, rather jeering, 'why ever did you come?'

'I had to try,' he said.

'And if you don't like it,' she said, 'why should you try to spoil it for me?'

'I hate it,' he answered.

They were climbing more into the height, more into the light, into the open, in the full sun. The valley cleft was sinking below them. Opposite was only the sheer, livid slide of the naked rock, tipping from the pure sky. At a certain angle they could see away beyond the lake lying far off and small, the wall of those other rocks like a curtain of stone, dim and diminished to the horizon. And the sky with curdling clouds and blue sunshine intermittent.

'Wonderful, wonderful, to be high up,' she said, breathing great breaths.

'Yes,' he said. 'It *is* wonderful. But very detestable. I want to live near the sea-level. I am no mountain-topper.'

'Evidently not,' she said.

'*Bergheil!*' cried a youth with bare arms and bare chest, bare head, terrific fanged boots, a knapsack and an alpenstock, and all the bronzed wind and sun of the mountain snow in his skin and his faintly bleached hair. With his great heavy knapsack, his rumpled thick stockings, his ghastly fanged boots, Hepburn found him repulsive.

'*Guten Tag,*' he answered coldly.

'*Grüss Gott,*' said Hannele.

And the young Tannhäuser, the young Siegfried, this young Balder beautiful strode climbing down the rocks, marching and swinging with his alpenstock. And immediately after the youth came a maiden, with hair on the wind and her shirt-breast open, striding in corduroy breeches, rumpled worsted stockings, thick boots, a knapsack and an alpenstock. She passed without greeting. And our pair stopped in angry silence and watched her dropping down the mountain-side.

Chapter Fifteen

Ah, well, everything comes to an end, even the longest up-climb. So, after much sweat and effort and crossness, Hepburn and Hannele emerged on to the rounded bluff where the road wound out of that hideous great valley cleft into upper regions. So they emerged more on the level, out of the trees as out of something horrible, on to a naked, great bank of rock and grass.

'Thank the Lord!' said Hannele.

So they trudged on round the bluff, and then in front of them saw what is always, always wonderful, one of those shallow, upper valleys, naked, where the first waters are rocked. A flat, shallow, utterly desolate valley, wide as a wide bowl under the sky, with rock slopes and grey stone-slides and precipices all round, and the zig-zag of snow-stripes and ice-roots descending, and then rivers, streams and rivers rushing from many points downwards, down out of the ice-roots and the snow-dagger-points, waters rushing in newly-liberated frenzy downwards, down in waterfalls and cascades and threads, down into the wide, shallow bed of the valley, strewn with rocks and stones innumerable, and not a tree, not a visible bush.

Only, of course, two hotels or restaurant places. But these no more than low, sprawling, peasant-looking places lost among the stones, with stones on their roofs so that they seemed just a part of the valley bed. There was the valley, dotted with rock and rolled-down stone, and these two house-places, and woven with innumerable new waters, and one hoarse stone-tracked river in the desert, and the thin road-track winding along the desolate flat, past first one house, then the other, over one stream, then another, on to the far rock-face above which the glacier seemed to loll like some awful great tongue put out.

'Ah, it is wonderful!' he said, as if to himself.

And she looked quickly at his face, saw the queer, blank, sphinx-look with which he gazed out beyond himself. His eyes were black and set, and he seemed so motionless, as if he were eternal facing these upper facts.

She thrilled with triumph. She felt he was overcome.

'It *is* wonderful,' she said.

'Wonderful. And forever wonderful,' he said.

'Ah, in *winter*— ' she cried.

His face changed, and he looked at her.

'In winter you couldn't get up here,' he said.

They went on. Up the slopes cattle were feeding: came that isolated tong-tong-tong of cow-bells, dropping like the slow clink of ice on the arrested air. The sound always woke in him a primeval, almost hopeless melancholy. Always made him feel *navré*. He looked round. There was no tree, no bush, only great grey rocks and pale boulders scattered in place of trees and bushes. But yes, clinging on one side like a dark, close beard were the alpenrose shrubs.

'In May,' he said, 'that side there must be all pink with alpenroses.'

'I *must* come. I *must* come!' she cried.

There were tourists dotted along the road: and two tiny low carts drawn by silky, long-eared mules. These carts went right down to meet the motor-cars, and to bring up provisions for the Glacier Hotel: for there was still another big hotel ahead. Hepburn was happy in that upper valley, that first rocking cradle of early water. He liked to see the great fangs and slashes of ice and snow thrust down into the rock, as if the ice had bitten into the flesh of the earth. And from the fang-tips the hoarse water crying its birth-cry, rushing down.

By the turfy road and under the rocks were many flowers: wonderful harebells, big and cold and dark, almost black, and seeming like purple-dark ice: then little tufts of tiny pale-blue bells, as if some fairy frog had been blowing spume-bubbles out of the ice: then the bishops-crosier of the stiff, bigger, hairy mountain-bell: then many stars of pale-lavender gentian, touched with earth colour: and then monkshood, yellow, primrose yellow monkshood and sudden places full of dark monkshood. That dark-blue, black-blue, terrible colour of the strange rich monkshood made Hepburn look and look and look again. How did the ice come by that lustrous blue-purple intense darkness? – and by that royal poison? – that laughing-snake gorgeousness of much monkshood.

Chapter Sixteen

By one of the loud streams, under a rock in the sun, with scented minty or thyme flowers near, they sat down to eat some lunch. It was about eleven o'clock. A thin bee went in and out the scented flowers and the eyebright. The water poured with all the lust and greed of unloosed water over the stones. He took a cupful for Hannele, bright and icy, and she mixed it with the red Hungarian wine.

Down the road strayed the tourists like pilgrims, and at the closed end of the valley they could be seen, quite tiny, climbing the cut-out road that went up like a stairway. Just by their movements you perceived them. But on the valley-bed they went like rolling stones, little as stones. A very elegant mule came stepping by, following a middle-aged woman in tweeds and a tall, high-browed man in knickerbockers. The mule was drawing a very amusing little cart, a chair, rather like a round office-chair upholstered in red velvet, and mounted on two wheels. The red velvet had gone gold and orange and like fruit-juice, being old: really a lovely colour. And the muleteer, a little shabby creature, waddled beside excitedly.

'*Ach*,' cried Hannele, 'that looks almost like before the war: almost as peaceful.'

'Except that the chair is too shabby, and that they all feel exceptional,' he remarked.

There in that upper valley there was no sense of peace. The rush of the waters seemed like weapons, and the tourists all seemed in a sort of frenzy, in a frenzy to be happy, or to be thrilled. It was a feeling that desolated the heart.

The two sat in the changing sunshine under their rock, with the mountain flowers scenting the snow-bitter air, and they ate their eggs and sausage and cheese, and drank the bright-red Hungarian wine. It seemed lovely: almost like before the war: almost the same feeling of eternal holiday, as if the world was made for man's everlasting holiday. But not quite. Never again quite the same. The world is not made for man's everlasting holiday.

As Alexander was putting the bread back into his shoulder-sack, he exclaimed:

'Oh, look here!'

She looked, and saw him drawing out a flat package wrapped in paper: evidently a picture.

'A picture!' she cried.

He unwrapped the thing and handed it to her. It was Theodor Worpswede's *Stilleben*; not very large, painted on a board.

Hannele looked at it and went pale.

'It's *good*,' she cried, in an equivocal tone.

'Quite good,' he said.

'Especially the poached egg,' she said.

'Yes, the poached egg is almost living.'

'But where did you find it?'

'Oh, I found it in the artist's studio.' And he told her how he had traced her.

'How extraordinary!' she cried. 'But why did you buy it?'

'I don't quite know.'

'Did you *like* it?'

'No, not quite that.'

'You could *never* hang it up.'

'No, never,' he said.

'But do you think it is good as a work of art?'

'I think it is quite clever as a painting. I don't like the spirit of it, of course. I'm too catholic for that.'

'No. No,' she faltered. 'It's rather horrid really. That's why I wonder why you bought it.'

'Perhaps to prevent anyone else's buying it,' he said.

'Do you mind very much, then?' she asked.

'No, I don't mind very much. I didn't quite like it that you sold the doll,' he said.

'I needed the money,' she said quietly.

'Oh, quite.'

There was a pause for some moments.

'I felt you'd sold *me*,' she said, quiet and savage.

'When?'

'When your wife appeared. And when you *disappeared*.'

Again there was a pause: his pause this time.

'I did write to you,' he said.

'When?'

'Oh – March, I believe.'

'Oh yes. I had that letter.' Her voice was just as quiet, and even savager.

So there was a pause that belonged to both of them. Then she rose.

'I want to be going,' she said. 'We shall never get to the glacier at this rate.'

He packed up the picture, slung on his knapsack, and they set off. She stooped now and then to pick the starry, earth-lavender gentians from the roadside. As they passed the second of the valley hotels, they saw the man and wife sitting at a little table outside eating bread and cheese, while the mule-chair with its red velvet waited aside on the grass. They passed a whole grove of black-purple nightshade on the left, and some long, low cattle-huts which, with the stones on their roofs, looked as if they had grown up as stones grow in such places through the grass. In the wild, desert place some black pigs were snouting.

So they wound into the head of the valley, and saw the steep face ahead, and high up, like vapour or foam dripping from the fangs of a beast, waterfalls vapouring down from the deep fangs of ice. And there was one end of the glacier, like a great bluey-white fur just slipping over the slope of the rock.

As the valley closed in again the flowers were very lovely, especially the big, dark, icy bells, like harebells, that would sway so easily, but which hung dark and with that terrible motionlessness of upper mountain flowers. And the road turned to get on to the long slant in the cliff face, where it climbed like a stair. Slowly, slowly the two climbed up. Now again they saw the valley below, behind. The mule-chair was coming, hastening, the lady seated tight facing backwards, as the chair faced, and wrapped in rugs. The tall, fair, middle-aged husband in knickerbockers strode just behind, bareheaded.

Alexander and Hannele climbed slowly, slowly up the slant, under the dripping rock-face where the white and veined flowers of the grass of Parnassus still rose straight and chilly in the shadow, like water which had taken on itself white flower-flesh. Above they saw the slipping edge of the glacier, like a terrible great paw, bluey. And from the skyline dark grey clouds were fuming up, fuming up as if breathed black and icily out from some ice-cauldron.

'It is going to rain,' said Alexander.

'Not much,' said Hannele shortly.

'I hope not,' said he.

And still she would not hurry up that steep slant, but insisted on standing to look. So the dark, ice-black clouds fumed solid, and the rain began to fly on a cold wind. The mule-chair hastened past, the lady sitting comfortably with her back to the mule, a little pheasant-trimming in her tweed hat, while her Tannhäuser husband reached for his dark, cape-frilled mantle.

Alexander had his dust-coat, but Hannele had nothing but a light knitted jersey-coat, such as women wear indoors. Over the hollow crest above came the cold, steel rain. They pushed on up the slope. From behind came another mule, and a little old man hurrying, and a little cart like a hand-barrow, on which were hampers with cabbage and carrots and peas and joints of meat, for the hotel above.

'*Wird es viel sein?*' asked Alexander of the little gnome. 'Will it be much?'

'*Was meint der Herr?*' replied the other. 'What does the gentleman say?'

'*Der Regen, wird es lang dauern?* Will the rain last long?'

'*Nein. Nein. Dies ist kein langer Regen.*'

So, with his mule which had to stand exactly at that spot to make droppings, the little man resumed his way, and Hannele and Alexander were the last on the slope. The air smelt steel-cold of rain, and of hot droppings. Alexander watched the rain beat on the shoulders and on the blue skirt of Hannele.

'It is a pity you left your big coat down below,' he said.

'What good is it saying so now!' she replied, pale at the nose with anger.

'Quite,' he said, as his eyes glowed and his brow blackened. 'What good suggesting anything at any time, apparently?'

She turned round on him in the rain, as they stood perched nearly at the summit of that slanting cliff-climb, with a glacier-paw hung almost invisible above, and waters gloating aloud in the gulf below. She faced him, and he faced her.

'What have you ever suggested to me?' she said, her face naked as the rain itself with an ice-bitter fury. 'What have you ever suggested to me?'

'When have you ever been open to suggestion?' he said, his face dark and his eyes curiously glowing.

'I? I? Ha! Haven't I waited for you to suggest something? And all you can do is to come here with a picture to reproach me for having sold your doll. Ha! I'm glad I sold it. A foolish barren effigy it was too, a foolish staring thing. What should I do but sell it. Why should I keep it, do you imagine?'

'Why do you come here with me to-day, then?'

'Why do I come here with you to-day?' she replied. 'I come to see the mountains, which are wonderful, and give me strength. And I come to see the glacier. Do you think I come here to see *you*? Why should I? You are always in some hotel or other away below.'

'You came to see the glacier and the mountains *with* me,' he replied.

'Did I? Then I made a mistake. You can do nothing but find fault even with God's mountains.'

A dark flame suddenly went over his face.

'Yes,' he said, 'I hate them, I hate them. I hate their snow and their affectations.'

'*Affectation*!' she laughed. 'Oh! Even the mountains are affected for you, are they?'

'Yes,' he said. 'Their loftiness and their uplift. I hate their uplift. I hate people prancing on mountain-tops and feeling exalted. I'd like to make them all stop up there, on their mountain-tops, and chew ice to fill their stomachs. I wouldn't let them down again, I wouldn't. I hate it all, I tell you; I hate it.'

She looked in wonder on his dark, glowing, ineffectual face. It seemed to her like a dark flame burning in the daylight and in the ice-rains: very ineffectual and unnecessary.

'You must be a little mad,' she said superbly, 'to talk like that about the mountains. They are so much bigger than you.'

'No,' he said. 'No! They are not.'

'What!' she laughed aloud. 'The mountains are not bigger than you? But you are extraordinary.'

'They are not bigger than me,' he cried. 'Any more than you are bigger than me if you stand on a ladder. They are not bigger than me. They are less than me.'

'Oh! Oh!' she cried in wonder and ridicule. 'The mountains are less than you.'

'Yes,' he cried, 'they are less.'

He seemed suddenly to go silent and remote as she watched him. The speech had gone out of his face again, he seemed to be standing a long way off from her, beyond some border-line. And in the midst of her indignant amazement she watched him with wonder and a touch of fascination. To what country did he belong then? – to what dark, different atmosphere.

'You must suffer from megalomania,' she said. And she said what she felt.

But he only looked at her out of dark, dangerous, haughty eyes.

They went on their way in the rain in silence. He was filled with a passionate silence and imperiousness, a curious, dark, masterful force that supplanted thought in him. And she, who always pondered, went pondering: 'Is he mad? What does he mean? Is he a madman? He wants to bully me. He wants to bully me into something. What does he want to bully me into? Does he want me to love him?'

At this final question she rested. She decided that what he wanted was that she should love him. And this thought flattered her vanity and her pride and appeased her wrath against him. She felt quite mollified towards him.

But what a way he went about it! He wanted her to love him. Of this she was sure. He had always wanted her to love him, even from the first. Only he had not made up his *mind* about it. He had not made up his mind. After his wife had died he had gone away to make up his mind. Now he had made it up. He wanted her to love him. And he was offended, mortally offended because she had sold his doll.

So, this was the conclusion to which Hannele came. And it pleased her, and it flattered her. And it made her feel quite warm towards him, as they walked in the rain. The rain, by the way, was abating. The spume over the hollow crest to which they were approaching was thinning considerably. They could again see the glacier paw hanging out a little beyond. The rain was going to pass. And they were not far now from the hotel, and the third level of Lammerboden.

He wanted her to love him. She felt again quite glowing and triumphant inside herself, and did not care a bit about the rain on her shoulders. He wanted her to love him. Yes, that was how she had to put it. He didn't want to *love* her. No. He wanted *her* to love *him*.

But then, of course, woman-like, she took his love for granted. So many men had been so very ready to love her. And this one – to her amazement, to her indignation, and rather to her secret satisfaction – just blackly insisted that *she* must love *him*. Very well – she would give him a run for his money. That was it: he blackly insisted that *she* must love *him*. What he felt was not to be considered. *She* must love *him*. And be bullied into it. That was what it amounted to. In his silent, black, overbearing soul, he wanted to compel her, he wanted to have power over her. He wanted to make her love him so that he had power over her. He wanted to bully her, physically, sexually, and from the inside.

And she! Well, she was just as confident that she was not going to be bullied. She would love him: probably she would: most probably she did already. But she was not going to be bullied by him in any way whatsoever. No, he must go down on his knees to her if he wanted her love. And then she would love him. Because she *did* love him. But a dark-eyed little master and bully she would never have.

And this was her triumphant conclusion. Meanwhile the rain had almost ceased, they had almost reached the rim of the upper level, towards which they were climbing, and he was walking in that silent diffidence which made her watch him because she was not sure what he was feeling, what he was thinking, or even what he was. He was a puzzle to her: eternally incomprehensible in his feelings and even his sayings. There seemed to her no logic and no reason in what he felt and said. She could never tell what his next mood would come out of. And this made her uneasy, made her watch him. And at the same time it piqued her attention. He had some of the fascination of the incomprehensible. And his curious inscrutable face – it wasn't really only a meaningless mask, because he had seen it half an hour ago melt with a quite incomprehensible and rather, to her mind, foolish passion. Strange, black, inconsequential passion. Asserting with that curious dark ferocity that he was bigger than the mountains. Madness! Madness! Megalomania.

But because he gave himself away, she forgave him and even liked him. And the strange passion of his, that gave out incomprehensible flashes, *was* rather fascinating to her. She felt just a tiny bit sorry for him. But she wasn't going to be bullied by him. She wasn't going to give in to him and his black passion. No, never. It must be love on equal terms or nothing. For love on equal terms she was quite ready. She only waited for him to offer it.

Chapter Seventeen

In the hotel was a buzz of tourists. Alexander and Hannele sat in the restaurant drinking hot coffee and milk, and watching the maidens in cotton frocks and aprons and bare arms, and the fair youth with maidenly necks and huge voracious boots, and the many Jews of the wrong sort and the wrong shape. These Jews were all being very Austrian, in Tyrol costume that didn't sit on them, assuming the whole gesture and intonation of aristocratic Austria, so that you might think they *were* Austrian aristocrats, if you weren't properly listening, or if you didn't look twice. Certainly they were lords of the Alps, or at least lords of the Alpine hotels this summer, let prejudice be what it might. Jews of the wrong sort. And yet even they imparted a wholesome breath of sanity, disillusion, unsentimentality to the excited '*Bergheil*' atmosphere. Their dark-eyed, sardonic presence seemed to say to the maidenly-necked mountain youths: 'Don't sprout wings of the spirit too much, my dears.'

The rain had ceased. There was a wisp of sunshine from a grey sky. Alexander left the knapsack, and the two went out into the air. Before them lay the last level of the up-climb, the Lammerboden. It was a rather gruesome hollow between the peaks, a last shallow valley about a mile long. At the end the enormous static stream of the glacier poured in from the blunt mountain-top of ice. The ice was dull, sullen-coloured, melted on the surface by the very hot summer: and so it seemed a huge, arrested, sodden flood, ending in a wave-wall of stone-speckled ice upon the valley bed of rocky débris. A gruesome descent of stone and blocks of rock, the little valley bed, with a river raving through. On the left rose the grey rock, but the glacier was there, sending down great paws of ice. It was like some great, deep-furred ice-bear lying spread upon the top heights, and reaching down terrible paws of ice into the valley: like some immense sky-bear fishing in the earth's solid hollows from above. Hepburn it just filled with terror. Hannele too it scared, but it gave her a sense of ecstasy. Some of the immense, furrowed paws of ice held down between the rock were vivid blue in colour, but of a frightening, poisonous blue, like crystal copper sulphate. Most of the ice was a sullen, semi-translucent greeny grey.

The two set off to walk through the massy, desolate stone-bed, under rocks and over waters, to the main glacier. The flowers were even more beautiful on this last reach. Particularly the dark harebells were large and almost black and ice-metallic: one could imagine they gave a dull ice-chink. And the glass of Parnassus stood erect, white-veined big cups held terribly naked and open to their ice air.

From behind the great blunt summit of ice that blocked the distance at the end of the valley, a pale-grey, woolly mist or cloud was fusing up, exhaling huge, like some grey-dead aura into the sky, and covering the top of the glacier. All the way along the valley people were threading, strangely insignificant, among the grey dishevel of stone and rock, like insects. Hannele and Alexander went ahead quickly, along the tiring track.

'Are you glad now that you came?' she said, looking at him triumphant.

'Very glad I came,' he said. His eyes were dilated with excitement that was ordeal or mystic battle rather than the *Bergheil* ecstasy. The curious vibration of his excitement made the scene strange, rather horrible to her. She too shuddered. But it still seemed to her to hold the key to all glamour and ecstasy, the great silent, living glacier. It seemed to her like a grand beast.

As they came near they saw the wall of ice: the glacier end, thick crusted and speckled with stone and dirt débris. From underneath, secret in stones, water rushed out. When they came quite near, they saw the great monster was sweating all over, trickles and rivulets of sweat running down his sides of pure, slush-translucent ice. There it was, the glacier, ending abruptly in the wall of ice under which they stood. Near to, the ice was pure, but water-logged, all the surface rather rotten from the hot summer. It was sullenly translucent, and of a watery, darkish bluey-green colour. But near the earth it became again bright coloured, gleams of green like jade, gleams of blue like thin, pale sapphire, in little caverns above the wet stones where the walls trickled for ever.

Alexander wanted to climb on to the glacier. It was his one desire – to stand upon it. So under the pellucid wet wall they toiled among rocks upwards, to where the guide-track mounted the ice. Several other people were before them – mere day tourists – and all uncertain about venturing any farther. For the ice-slope rose steep and slithery, pure, sun-locked, sweating ice. Still, it was like a curved back. One could scramble on to it, and on up to the first level, like the flat on top of some huge paw.

There stood the little cluster of people, facing the uphill of sullen, pure, sodden-looking ice. They were all afraid: naturally. But being human, they all wanted to go beyond their fear. It was strange that the ice looked so pure, like flesh. Not bright, because the surface was soft like a soft, deep epidermis. But pure ice away down to immense depths.

Alexander, after some hesitation, began gingerly to try the ice. He was frightened of it. And he had no stick, and only smooth-soled boots. But he had a great desire to stand on the glacier. So, gingerly and shakily, he began to struggle a few steps up the pure slope. The ice was soft on the surface, he could kick his heel in it and get a little sideways grip. So, staggering and going sideways he got up a few yards, and was on the naked ice-slope.

Immediately the youths and the fat man below began to tackle it too: also two maidens. For some time, however, Alexander gingerly and scramblingly led the way. The slope of ice was steeper, and rounded, so that it was difficult to stand up in any way. Sometimes he slipped, and was clinging with burnt finger-ends to the soft ice mass. Then he tried throwing his coat down, and getting a foot-hold on that. Then he went quite quickly by bending down and getting a little grip with his fingers, and going ridiculously as on four legs.

Hannele watched from below, and saw the ridiculous exhibition, and was frightened and amused, but more frightened. And she kept calling, to the great joy of the Austrians down below:

'Come back. Do come back.'

But when he got on to his feet again he only waved his hand at her, half crossly, as she stood away down there in her blue frock. The other fellows with sticks and nail-boots had now taken heart and were scrambling like crabs past our hero, doing better than he.

He had come to a rift in the ice. He sat near the edge and looked down. Clean, pure ice, fused with pale colour, and fused into intense copper-sulphate blue away down in the crack. It was not like crystal, but fused as one fuses a borax bead under a blow-flame. And keenly, wickedly blue in the depths of the crack.

He looked upwards. He had not half mounted the slope. So on he went, upon the huge body of the soft-fleshed ice, slanting his way sometimes on all fours, sometimes using his coat, usually hitting-in with the side of his heel. Hannele down below was crying him to come back. But two other youths were now almost level with him. ˙

So he struggled on till he was more or less over the brim. There he stood and looked at the ice. It came down from above in a great hollow world of ice. A world, a terrible place of hills and valleys and slopes, all motionless, all of ice. Away above the grey mist-cloud was looming bigger. And near at hand were long, huge cracks, side by side, like gills in the ice. It would seem as if the ice breathed through these great ridged gills. One could look down into the series of gulfs, fearful depths, and the colour burning that acid, intense blue, intenser as the crack went deeper. And the crests of the open gills ridged and grouped pale blue above the crevices. It seemed as if the ice breathed there.

The wonder, the terror, and the bitterness of it. Never a warm leaf to unfold, never a gesture of life to give off. A world sufficient unto itself in lifelessness, all this ice.

He turned to go down, though the youths were passing beyond him. And seeing the naked translucent ice heaving downwards in a vicious curve, always the same dark translucency underfoot, he was afraid. If he slipped, he would certainly slither the whole way down, and break some of his bones. Even when he sat down he had to cling with his finger-nails in the ice, because if he had started to slide he would have slid the whole way down on his trouser-seat, precipitously, and have landed heaven knows how.

Hannele was watching from below. And he was frightened, perched, seated on the shoulder of ice and not knowing how to get off. Above he saw the great blue gills of ice ridging the air. Down below were two blue cracks – then the last wet level claws of ice upon the stones. And there stood Hannele and the three or four people who had got so far.

However, he found that by striking in his heels sideways with sufficient sharpness he could keep his footing, no matter how steep the slope. So he started to jerk his way zig-zag downwards.

As he descended, arrived a guide with a black beard and all the paraphernalia of ropes and pole and bristling boots. He and his gentlemen began to strike their way up the ice. With those bristling nails like teeth in one's boots, it was quite easy: and a pole to press on to.

Hannele, who had got sick of waiting, and who was also frightened, had gone scuttling on the return journey. He hurried after her, thankful to be off the ice, but excited and gratified. Looking round, he saw the guide and the man on the ice watching the ice-world and the weather. Then they too turned to come down. The day wasn't safe.

Chapter Eighteen

Pondering, rather thrilled, they threaded their way through the desert of rock and rushing water back to the hotel. The sun was shining warmly for a moment, and he felt happy, though his finger-ends were bleeding a little from the ice.

'But one day,' said Hannele, 'I should love to go with a guide right up, high, right into the glacier.'

'No,' said he. 'I've been far enough. I prefer the world where cabbages will grow on the soil. Nothing grows on glaciers.'

'They say there are glacier fleas, which only live on glaciers,' she said.

'Well, to me the ice didn't look good to eat, even for a flea.'

'You never know,' she laughed. 'But you're glad you've been aren't you?'

'Very glad. Now I need never go again.'

'But you *did* think it wonderful?'

'Marvellous. And awful, to my mind.'

Chapter Nineteen

They ate venison and spinach in the hotel, then set off down again. Both felt happier. She gathered some flowers and put them in her handkerchief so they should not die. And again they sat by the stream, to drink a little wine.

But the fume of cloud was blowing up again, thick from behind the glacier. Hannele was uneasy. She wanted to get down. So they went fairly quickly. Many other tourists were hurrying downwards also. The rain began – a sharp handful of drops flung from beyond the glacier. So Hannele and he did not stay to rest, but dropped easily down the steep, dark valley towards the motor-car terminus.

There they had tea, rather tired but comfortably so. The big hotel restaurant was hideous, and seemed sordid. So in the gloom of a grey, early twilight they went out again and sat on a seat, watching the tourists and the trippers and the motor-car men. There were three Jews from Vienna: and the girl had a huge white woolly dog, as big as a calf, and white and woolly and silky and amiable as a toy. The men, of course, came patting it and admiring it, just as men always do, in life and in novels. And the girl, holding the leash, posed and leaned backwards in the attitude of heroines on novel-covers. She said the white cool monster was a Siberian steppe-dog. Alexander wondered what the steppes made of such a wuffer. And the three Jews pretended they were elegant Austrians out of popular romances.

'Do you think,' said Alexander, 'you will marry the Herr Regierungsrat?'

She looked round, making wide eyes.

'It looks like it, doesn't it?' she said.

'Quite,' he said.

Hannele watched the woolly white dog. So of course it came wagging its ever-amiable hindquarters towards her. She looked at it still, but did not touch it.

'What makes you ask such a question?' she said.

'I can't say. But even so, you haven't really answered. Do you really fully intend to marry the Herr Regierungsrat? Is that your final intention at this moment?'

She looked at him again.

'But before I answer,' she said, 'oughtn't I to know why you ask?'

'Probably you know already,' he said.

'I assure you I don't.'

He was silent for some moments. The huge, woolly dog stood in front of him and breathed enticingly, with its tongue out. He only looked at it blankly.

'Well,' he said, 'if you were not going to marry the Herr Regierungsrat, I should suggest that you marry me.'

She stared away at the auto-garage, a very faint look of amusement, or pleasure, or ridicule on her face: or all three. And a certain shyness.

'But why?' she said.

'Why what?' he returned.

'Why should you suggest that I should marry you?'

'*Why?*' he replied, in his lingering tones. '*Why?* Well, for what purpose does a man usually ask a woman to marry him?'

'For what *purpose!*' she repeated, rather haughtily.

'For what reason, then!' he corrected.

She was silent for some moments. Her face was closed and a little numb-looking, her hands lay very still in her lap. She looked away from him, across the road.

'There is usually only one reason,' she replied, in a rather small voice.

'Yes?' he replied curiously. 'What would you say that was?'

She hesitated. Then she said, rather stiffly:

'Because he really loved her, I suppose. That seems to me the only excuse for a man asking a woman to marry him.'

Followed a dead silence, which she did not intend to break. He knew he would have to answer, and for some reason he didn't want to say what was obviously the thing to say.

'Leaving aside the question of whether you love me or I love you—' he began.

'I certainly *won't* leave it aside,' she said.

'And I certainly won't consider it,' he said, just as obstinately.

She turned now and looked full at him, with amazement, ridicule, and anger in her face.

'I really think you must be mad,' she said.

'I doubt if you do think that,' he replied. 'It is only a method of retaliation, that is. I think you understand my point very clearly.'

'Your point!' she cried. 'Your point! Oh, so you have a point in all this palavering?'

'Quite!' said he.

She was silent with indignation for some time. Then she said angrily:

'I assure you I do *not* see your point. I don't see any point at all. I see only impertinence.'

'Very good,' he replied. 'The point is whether we marry on a basis of love.'

'Indeed! Marry! We, marry! I don't think that is by any means the point.'

He took his knapsack from under the seat between his feet. And from the knapsack he took the famous picture.

'When,' he said, 'we were supposed to be in love with one another, you made that doll of me, didn't you?' And he sat looking at the odious picture.

'I never for one moment deluded myself that you *really* loved me,' she said bitterly.

'Take the other point, whether *you* loved *me* or not,' said he.

'How could I love you when I couldn't believe in your love for me?' she cried.

He put the picture down between his knees again.

'All this about love,' he said, 'is very confusing and very complicated.'

'Very! In *your* case. Love to me is simple enough,' she said.

'Is it? Is it? And was it simple love which made you make that doll of me?'

'Why shouldn't I make a doll of you? Does it do you any harm? And *weren't* you a doll, good heavens! You *were* nothing but a doll. So what hurt does it do you?'

'Yes, it does. It does me the greatest possible damage,' he replied.

She turned on him with wide-open eyes of amazement and rage.

'Why? Pray why? Can you tell me why?'

'Not quite, I can't,' he replied, taking up the picture and holding it in front of him. She turned her face from it as a cat turns its nose away from a lighted cigarette. 'But when I look at it – when I look at this – then I *know* that there's no love between you and me.'

'Then why are you talking at me in this shameful way?' she flashed at him, tears of anger and mortification rising to her eyes. 'You want your little revenge on me, I suppose, because I made that doll of you.'

'That may be so, in a small measure,' he said.

'That is *all*. That is all and everything,' she cried. 'And that is all you came back to me for – for this petty revenge. Well, you've had it now. But please don't speak to me any more. I shall see if I can go home in the big omnibus.'

She rose and walked away. He saw her hunting for the motor-bus conductor. He saw her penetrate into the yard of the garage. And he saw her emerge again, after a time, and take the path to the river. He sat on in front of the hotel. There was nothing else to do.

The tourists who had arrived in the big bus now began to collect. And soon the huge, drab vehicle itself rolled up and stood big as a house before the hotel door. The passengers began to scramble into their seats. The two men of the white dog were going: but the woman of the white dog, and the dog, were staying behind. Hepburn wondered if Hannele had managed to get herself transferred. He doubted it, because he knew the omnibus was crowded.

Moreover, he had her ticket.

The passengers were packed in. The conductor was collecting the tickets. And at last the great bus rolled away. The bay of the road-end seemed very empty. Even the woman with the white dog had gone. Soon the other car, the Luxus, so-called, must appear. Hepburn sat and waited. The evening was falling chilly, the trees looked gruesome.

At last Hannele sauntered up again, unwillingly.

'I think,' she said, 'you have my ticket.'

'Yes, I have,' he replied.

'Will you give it me, please?'

He gave it to her. She lingered a moment. Then she walked away.

There was the sound of a motor-car. With a triumphant purr the Luxus came steering out of the garage yard and drew up at the hotel door. Hannele came hastening also. She went straight to one of the hinder doors – she and Hepburn had their seats in front, beside the driver. She had her foot on the step of the back seat. And then she was afraid. The little sharp-faced driver – there was no conductor – came round looking at the car. He looked at her with his sharp, metallic eye of a mechanic.

'Are all the people going back who came?' she asked, shrinking.

'*Jawohl.*'

'It is full – this car?'

'*Jawohl.*'

'There's no other place?'

'*Nein.*'

Hannele shrank away. The driver was absolutely laconic.

Six of the passengers were here: four were already seated. Hepburn sat still by the hotel door, Hannele lingered in the road by the car, and the little driver, with a huge woollen muffler round his throat, was running round and in and out looking for the two missing passengers. Of course there were two missing passengers. No, he could not find them. And off he trotted again, silently, like a weasel after two rabbits. And at last, when everybody was getting cross, he unearthed them and brought them scuttling to the car.

Now Hannele took her seat, and Hepburn beside her. The driver snapped up the tickets and climbed in past them. With a vindictive screech the car glided away down the ravine. Another beastly trip was over, another infernal joyful holiday done with.

'I think,' said Hepburn, 'I may as well finish what I had to say.'

'What?' cried Hannele, fluttering in the wind of the rushing car.

'I may as well finish what I had to say,' shouted he, his breath blown away.

'Finish then,' she screamed, the ends of her scarf flickering behind her.

'When my wife died,' he said loudly, 'I knew I couldn't love any more.'

'Oh – h!' she screamed ironically.

'In fact,' he shouted, 'I realised that, as far as I was concerned, love was a mistake.'

'*What* was a mistake?' she screamed.

'Love,' he bawled.

'Love!' she screamed. 'A mistake?' Her tone was derisive.

'For me personally,' he said, shouting.

'Oh, only for you personally,' she cried, with a pouf of laughter.

The car gave a great swerve, and she fell on the driver. Then she righted herself. It gave another swerve, and she fell on Alexander. She righted herself angrily. And now they ran straight on: and it seemed a little quieter.

'I realised,' he said, 'that I had always made a mistake, undertaking to love.'

'It must have been an undertaking for *you*,' she cried.

'Yes, I'm afraid it was. I never really wanted it. But I thought I did. And that's where I made my mistake.'

'Whom have you ever loved? – even as an undertaking?' she asked.

'To begin with, my mother: and that was a mistake. Then my sister: and that was a mistake. Then a girl I had known all my life: and that was a mistake. Then my wife: and that was my most terrible mistake. And then I began the mistake of loving you.'

'Undertaking to love me, you mean,' she said. 'But then you never did properly undertake it. You never really *undertook* to love me.'

'Not quite, did I?' said he.

And she sat feeling angry that he had never made the undertaking.

'No,' he continued. 'Not quite. That is why I came back to you. I don't want to love you. I don't want marriage on a basis of love.'

'On a basis of what, then?'

'I think you know without my putting it into words,' he said.

'Indeed, I assure you I don't. You are much too mysterious,' she replied.

Talking in a swiftly-running motor-car is a nerve-wracking business. They both had a pause, to rest, and to wait for a quieter stretch of road.

'It isn't very easy to put it into words,' he said. 'But I tried marriage once on a basis of love, and I must say it was a ghastly affair in the long run. And I believe it would be so, for me, *whatever* woman I had.'

'There must be something wrong with you, then,' said she.

'As far as love goes. And yet I want marriage. I want marriage. I want a woman to honour and obey me.'

'If you are quite reasonable and *very* sparing with your commands,' said Hannele. 'And very careful how you give your orders.'

'In fact, I want a sort of patient Griselda. I want to be honoured and obeyed. I don't want love.'

'How Griselda managed to honour that fool of a husband of hers, even if she obeyed him, is more than I can say,' said Hannele. 'I'd like to know what she *really* thought of him. Just what any woman thinks of a bullying fool of a husband.'

'Well,' said he, 'that's no good to me.'

They were silent now until the car stopped at the station. There they descended and walked on under the trees by the lake.

'Sit on a seat,' he said, 'and let us finish.'

Hannele, who was really anxious to hear what he should say, and who, woman-like, was fascinated by a man when he began to give away his own inmost thoughts – no matter how much she might jeer afterwards – sat down by his side. It was a grey evening, just falling dark. Lights twinkled across the lake, the hotel over there threaded its strings of light. Some little boats came rowing quietly to shore. It was a grey, heavy evening, with that special sense of dreariness with which a public holiday usually winds up.

'Honour and obedience: and the proper physical feelings,' he said. 'To me that is marriage. Nothing else.'

'But what are the proper physical feelings but love?' asked Hannele.

'No,' he said. 'A woman wants you to adore her, and be in love with her – and I shan't. I will not do it again, if I live a monk for the rest of my days. I will neither adore you nor be in love with you.'

'You won't get a chance, thank you. And what do you call the proper physical feelings, if you are not in love? I think you want something vile.'

'If a woman honours me – absolutely from the bottom of her nature honours me – and obeys me because of that, I take it, my desire for her goes very much deeper than if I was in love with her, or if I adored her.'

'It's the same thing. If you love, then everything is there – all the lot: your honour and obedience and everything. And if love isn't there, nothing is there,' she said.

'That isn't true,' he replied. 'A woman may love you, she may adore you, but she'll never honour you nor obey you. The most loving and adoring woman to-day could any minute start and make a doll of her husband – as you made of me.'

'Oh, that eternal doll! What makes it stick so in your mind?'

'I don't know. But there it is. It wasn't malicious. It was flattering, if you like. But it just sticks in me like a thorn: like a thorn. And there it is, in the world, in Germany somewhere. And you can say what you like, but *any* woman, to-day, no matter *how* much she loves her man – she could start any minute and make a doll of him. And the doll would be her hero: and her hero would be no more than her doll. My wife might have done it. She did do it, in her mind. She had her doll of me right enough. Why, I heard her talk about me to other women. And her doll was a great deal sillier than the one you made. But it's all the same. If a woman loves you, she'll make a doll out of you. She'll never be satisfied till she's made your doll. And when she's got your doll, that's all she wants. And that's what love means. And so, I won't be loved. And I won't love. I won't have anybody loving me. It is an insult. I feel I've been insulted for forty years: by love, and the women who've loved me. I won't be loved. And I won't love. I'll be honoured and I'll be obeyed: or nothing.'

'Then it'll most probably be nothing,' said Hannele sarcastically. 'For I assure you I've nothing but love to offer.'

'Then keep your love,' said he.

She laughed shortly.

'And you?' she cried. 'You! Even suppose you *were* honoured and obeyed. I suppose all you've got to do is to sit there like a sultan and sup it up.'

'Oh no, I have many things to do. And woman or no woman, I'm going to start to do them.'

'What, pray?'

'Why, nothing very exciting. I'm going to East Africa to join a man who's breaking his neck to get his three thousand acres of land under control. And when I've done a few more experiments and observations, and got all the necessary facts, I'm going to do a book on the moon. Woman or no woman, I'm going to do that.'

'And the woman? – supposing you get the poor thing.'

'Why, she'll come along with me, and we'll set ourselves up out there.'

'And she'll do all the honouring and obeying and house-keeping incidentally, while you ride about in the day and stare at the moon in the night.'

He did not answer. He was staring away across the lake.

'What will you do for the woman, poor thing, while she's racking herself to pieces honouring you and obeying you and doing frightful housekeeping in Africa: because I know it can be *awful:* awful.'

'Well,' he said slowly, 'she'll be my wife, and I shall treat her as such. If the marriage service says love and cherish – well, in that sense I shall do so.'

'Oh!' cried Hannele. 'What, *love* her? Actually love the poor thing?'

'Not in that sense of the word, no. I shan't adore her or be in love with her. But she'll be my wife, and I shall love and cherish her as such.'

'Just because she's your wife. Not because she's herself. Ghastly fate for any miserable woman,' said Hannele.

'I don't think so. I think it's her highest fate.'

'To be your wife?'

'To be a wife – and to be loved and shielded as a wife – not as a flirting woman.'

'To be loved and cherished just because you're his wife! No, thank you. All I can admire is the conceit and impudence of it.'

'Very well, then – there it is,' he said, rising.

She rose too, and they went on towards where the boat was tied.

As they were rowing in silence over the lake, he said:

'I shall leave to-morrow.'

She made no answer. She sat and watched the lights of the villa draw near. And then she said:

'I'll come to Africa with you. But I won't promise to honour and obey you.'

'I don't want you otherwise,' he said, very quietly.

The boat was drifting to the little landing-stage. Hannele's friends were hallooing to her from the balcony.

'Hallo!' she cried. '*Ja. Da bin ich. Ja, 's war wunderschön.*'

Then to him she said:

'You'll come in?'

'No,' he said, 'I'll row straight back.'

From the villa they were running down the steps to meet Hannele.

'But won't you have me even if I love you?' she asked him.

'You must promise the other,' he said. 'It comes in the marriage service.'

'*Hat's geregnet? Wie war das Wetter? Warst du auf dem Gletscher?*' cried the voices from the garden.

'*Nein – kein Regen. Wunderschön! Ja, er war ganz auf dem Gletscher,*' cried Hannele in reply. And to him, *sotto voce*:

'Don't be a solemn ass. Do come in.'

'No,' he said, 'I don't want to come in.'

'Do you want to go away to-morrow? Go if you *do*. But, anyway, I won't say it *before* the marriage service. I needn't, need I?'

She stepped from the boat on to the plank.

'Oh,' she said, turning round, 'give me that picture, please, will you? I want to burn it.'

He handed it to her.

'And come to-morrow, will you?' she said.

'Yes, in the morning.'

He pulled back quickly into the darkness.

The Rainbow

TO ELSE

Chapter One

How Tom Brangwen Married a Polish Lady

Part I

The Brangwens had lived for generations on the Marsh Farm, in the meadows where the Erewash twisted sluggishly through alder trees, separating Derbyshire from Nottinghamshire. Two miles away, a church-tower stood on a hill, the houses of the little country town climbing assiduously up to it. Whenever one of the Brangwens in the fields lifted his head from his work, he saw the church-tower at Ilkeston in the empty sky. So that as he turned again to the horizontal land, he was aware of something standing above him and beyond him in the distance.

There was a look in the eyes of the Brangwens as if they were expecting something unknown, about which they were eager. They had that air of readiness for what would come to them, a kind of surety, an expectancy, the look of an inheritor.

They were fresh, blond, slow-speaking people, revealing themselves plainly, but slowly, so that one could watch the change in their eyes from laughter to anger, blue, lit-up laughter, to a hard blue-staring anger; through all the irresolute stages of the sky when the weather is changing.

Living on rich land, on their own land, near to a growing town, they had forgotten what it was to be in straitened circumstances. They had never become rich, because there were always children, and the patrimony was divided every time. But always, at the Marsh, there was ample.

So the Brangwens came and went without fear of necessity, working hard because of the life that was in them, not for want of the money. Neither were they thriftless. They were aware of the last halfpenny, and instinct made them not waste the peeling of their apple, for it would help to feed the cattle. But heaven and earth was teeming around them, and how should this cease? They felt the rush of the sap in spring, they knew the wave which cannot halt, but every year throws forward the seed to begetting, and, falling back, leaves the young-born on the earth. They knew the intercourse between heaven and earth, sunshine drawn into the breast and bowels, the rain sucked up in the daytime, nakedness that comes under the wind in autumn, showing the birds' nests no longer worth hiding. Their life and interrelations were such; feeling the pulse and body of the soil, that opened to their furrow for the grain, and became smooth and supple after their ploughing, and clung to their feet with a weight that pulled like desire, lying hard and unresponsive when the crops were to be shorn away. The young corn waved and was silken, and the lustre slid along the limbs of the men who saw it. They took the udder of the cows, the cows yielded milk and pulse against the hands of the men, the pulse of the blood of the teats of the cows beat into the pulse of the hands of the men. They mounted their horses, and held life between the grip of their knees, they harnessed their horses at the wagon, and, with hand on the bridle-rings, drew the heaving of the horses after their will.

In autumn the partridges whirred up, birds in flocks blew like spray across the fallow, rooks appeared on the grey, watery heavens, and flew cawing into the winter. Then the men sat by the fire in the house where the women moved about with surety, and the limbs and the body of the men were impregnated with the day, cattle and earth and vegetation and the sky, the men sat by the fire and their brains were inert, as their blood flowed heavy with the accumulation from the living day.

The women were different. On them too was the drowse of blood-intimacy, calves sucking and hens running together in droves, and young geese palpitating in the hand while the food was pushed down their throttle. But the women looked out from the heated, blind intercourse of farm-life, to the spoken world beyond. They were aware of the lips and the mind of the world speaking and giving utterance, they heard the sound in the distance, and they strained to listen.

It was enough for the men, that the earth heaved and opened its furrow to them, that the wind blew to dry the wet wheat, and set the young ears of corn wheeling freshly round about; it was enough that they helped the cow in labour, or ferreted the rats from under the barn, or broke the back of a rabbit with a sharp knock of the hand. So much warmth and generating and pain and death did they know in their blood, earth and sky and beast and green plants, so much exchange and interchange they had with these, that they lived full and surcharged, their senses full fed, their faces always turned to the heat of the blood, staring into the sun, dazed with looking towards the source of generation, unable to turn round.

But the woman wanted another form of life than this, something that was not blood-intimacy. Her house faced out from the farm-buildings and fields, looked out to the road and the village with church and Hall and the world beyond. She stood to see the far-off world of cities and governments and the active scope of man, the magic land to her, where secrets were made known and desires fulfilled. She faced outwards to where men moved dominant and creative, having turned their back on the pulsing heat of creation, and with this behind them, were set out to discover what was beyond, to enlarge their own scope and range and freedom; whereas the Brangwen men faced inwards to the teeming life of creation, which poured unresolved into their veins.

Looking out, as she must, from the front of her house towards the activity of man in the world at large, whilst her husband looked out to the back at sky and harvest and beast and land, she strained her eyes to see what man had done in fighting outwards to knowledge, she strained to hear how he uttered himself in his conquest, her deepest desire hung on the battle that she heard, far off, being waged on the edge of the unknown. She also wanted to know, and to be of the fighting host.

At home, even so near as Cossethay, was the vicar, who spoke the other, magic language, and had the other, finer bearing, both of which she could perceive, but could never attain to. The vicar moved in worlds beyond where her own menfolk existed. Did she not know her own menfolk: fresh, slow, full-built men, masterful enough, but easy, native to the earth, lacking outwardness and range of motion. Whereas the vicar, dark and dry and small beside her husband, had yet a quickness and a range of being that made Brangwen, in his large geniality, seem dull and local. She knew her husband. But in the vicar's nature was that which passed beyond her knowledge. As Brangwen had power over the cattle so the vicar had power over her husband. What was it in the vicar, that raised him above the common men as man is raised above the beast? She craved to know. She craved to achieve this higher being, if not in herself, then in her children. That which makes a man strong even if he be little and frail in body, just as any man is little and frail beside a bull, and yet stronger than the bull, what was it? It was not money nor power nor position. What power had the vicar over Tom Brangwen – none. Yet strip them and set them on a desert island, and the vicar was the master. His soul was master of the other man's. And why – why? She decided it was a question of knowledge.

The curate was poor enough, and not very efficacious as a man, either, yet he took rank with those others, the superior. She watched his children being born, she saw them running as tiny things beside their mother. And already they were separate from her own children, distinct. Why were her own children marked below the others? Why should the curate's children inevitably take precedence over her children, why should dominance be given them from the start? It was not money, nor even class. It was education and experience, she decided.

It was this, this education, this higher form of being, that the mother wished to give to her children, so that they too could live the supreme life on earth. For her children, at least the children of her heart, had the complete nature that should take place in equality with the living, vital people in the land, not be left behind obscure among the labourers. Why must they remain obscured and stifled all their lives, why should they suffer from lack of freedom to move? How should they learn the entry into the finer, more vivid circle of life?

Her imagination was fired by the squire's lady at Shelly Hall, who came to church at Cossethay with her little children, girls in tidy capes of beaver fur, and smart little hats, herself like a winter rose, so fair and delicate. So fair, so fine in mould, so luminous, what was it that Mrs. Hardy felt which she, Mrs. Brangwen, did not feel? How was Mrs. Hardy's nature different from that of the common women of Cossethay, in what was it beyond them? All the women of Cossethay talked eagerly about Mrs. Hardy, of her husband, her children, her guests, her dress, of her servants and her housekeeping. The lady of the Hall was the living dream of their lives, her life was the epic that inspired their lives. In her they lived imaginatively, and in gossiping of her husband who drank, of her scandalous brother, of Lord William Bentley her friend, member of Parliament for the division, they had their own

Odyssey enacting itself, Penelope and Ulysses before them, and Circe and the swine and the endless web.

So the women of the village were fortunate. They saw themselves in the lady of the manor, each of them lived her own fulfilment of the life of Mrs. Hardy. And the Brangwen wife of the Marsh aspired beyond herself, towards the further life of the finer woman, towards the extended being she revealed, as a traveller in his self-contained manner reveals far-off countries present in himself. But why should a knowledge of far-off countries make a man's life a different thing, finer, bigger? And why is a man more than the beast and the cattle that serve him? It is the same thing.

The male part of the poem was filled in by such men as the vicar and Lord William, lean, eager men with strange movements, men who had command of the further fields, whose lives ranged over a great extent. Ah, it was something very desirable to know, this touch of the wonderful men who had the power of thought and comprehension. The women of the village might be much fonder of Tom Brangwen, and more at their ease with him, yet if their lives had been robbed of the vicar, and of Lord William, the leading shoot would have been cut away from them, they would have been heavy and uninspired and inclined to hate. So long as the wonder of the beyond was before them, they could get along, whatever their lot. And Mrs. Hardy, and the vicar, and Lord William, these moved in the wonder of the beyond, and were visible to the eyes of Cossethay in their motion.

Part II

About 1840, a canal was constructed across the meadows of the Marsh Farm, connecting the newly-opened collieries of the Erewash Valley. A high embankment travelled along the fields to carry the canal, which passed close to the homestead, and, reaching the road, went over in a heavy bridge.

So the Marsh was shut off from Ilkeston, and enclosed in the small valley bed, which ended in a bushy hill and the village spire of Cossethay.

The Brangwens received a fair sum of money from this trespass across their land. Then, a short time afterwards, a colliery was sunk on the other side of the canal, and in a while the Midland Railway came down the valley at the foot of the Ilkeston hill, and the invasion was complete. The town grew rapidly, the Brangwens were kept busy producing supplies, they became richer, they were almost tradesmen.

Still the Marsh remained remote and original, on the old, quiet side of the canal embankment, in the sunny valley where slow water wound along in company of stiff alders, and the road went under ash-trees past the Brangwens' garden gate.

But, looking from the garden gate down the road to the right, there, through the dark archway of the canal's square aqueduct, was a colliery spinning away in the near distance, and further, red, crude houses plastered on the valley in masses, and beyond all, the dim smoking hill of the town.

The homestead was just on the safe side of civilisation, outside the gate. The house stood bare from the road, approached by a straight garden path, along which at spring the daffodils were thick in green and yellow. At the sides of the house were bushes of lilac and guelder-rose and privet, entirely hiding the farm buildings behind.

At the back a confusion of sheds spread into the home-close from out of two or three indistinct yards. The duck-pond lay beyond the furthest wall, littering its white feathers on the padded earthen banks, blowing its stray soiled feathers into the grass and the gorse bushes below the canal embankment, which rose like a high rampart near at hand, so that occasionally a man's figure passed in silhouette, or a man and a towing horse traversed the sky.

At first the Brangwens were astonished by all this commotion around them. The building of a canal across their land made them strangers in their own place, this raw bank of earth shutting them off disconcerted them. As they worked in the fields, from beyond the now familiar embankment came the rhythmic run of the winding engines, startling at first, but afterwards a narcotic to the brain. Then the shrill whistle of the trains re-echoed through the heart, with fearsome pleasure, announcing the far-off come near and imminent.

As they drove home from town, the farmers of the land met the blackened colliers trooping from the pit-mouth. As they gathered the harvest, the west wind brought a faint, sulphurous smell of pit-refuse burning. As they pulled the turnips in November, the sharp clink-clink-clink-clink-clink of empty trucks shunting on the line, vibrated in their hearts with the fact of other activity going on beyond them.

The Alfred Brangwen of this period had married a woman from Heanor, a daughter of the 'Black Horse'. She was a slim, pretty, dark woman, quaint in her speech, whimsical, so that the sharp things she said did not hurt. She was oddly a thing to herself, rather querulous in her manner, but intrinsically separate and indifferent, so that her long lamentable complaints, when she raised her voice against her husband in particular and against everybody else after him, only made those who heard her wonder and feel affectionately towards her, even while they were irritated and impatient with her. She railed long and loud about her husband, but always with a balanced, easy-flying voice and a quaint manner of speech that warmed his belly with pride and male triumph while he scowled with mortification at the things she said.

Consequently Brangwen himself had a humorous puckering at the eyes, a sort of fat laugh, very quiet and full, and he was spoilt like a lord of creation. He calmly did as he liked, laughed at their railing, excused himself in a teasing tone that she loved, followed his natural inclinations, and sometimes, pricked too near the quick, frightened and broke her by a deep, tense fury which seemed to fix on him and hold him for days, and which she would give anything to placate in him. They were two very separate beings, vitally connected, knowing nothing of each other, yet living in their separate ways from one root.

There were four sons and two daughters. The eldest boy ran away early to sea, and did not come back. After this the mother was more the node and centre of attraction in the home. The second boy, Alfred, whom the mother admired most, was the most reserved. He was sent to school in Ilkeston and made some progress. But in spite of his dogged, yearning effort, he could not get beyond the rudiments of anything, save of drawing. At this, in which he had some power, he worked, as if it were his hope. After much grumbling and savage rebellion against everything, after much trying and shifting about, when his father was incensed against him and his mother almost despairing, he became a draughtsman in a lace-factory in Nottingham.

He remained heavy and somewhat uncouth, speaking with broad Derbyshire accent, adhering with all his tenacity to his work and to his town position, making good designs, and becoming fairly well-off. But at drawing, his hand swung naturally in big, bold lines, rather lax, so that it was cruel for him to pedgill away at the lace designing, working from the tiny squares of his paper, counting and plotting and niggling. He did it stubbornly, with anguish, crushing the bowels within him, adhering to his chosen lot whatever it should cost. And he came back into life set and rigid, a rare-spoken, almost surly man.

He married the daughter of a chemist, who affected some social superiority, and he became something of a snob, in his dogged fashion, with a passion for outward refinement in the household, mad when anything clumsy or gross occurred. Later, when his three children were growing up, and he seemed a staid, almost middle-aged man, he turned after strange women, and became a silent, inscrutable follower of forbidden pleasure, neglecting his indignant bourgeois wife without a qualm.

Frank, the third son, refused from the first to have anything to do with learning. From the first he hung round the slaughter-house which stood away in the third yard at the back of the farm. The Brangwens had always killed their own meat, and supplied the neighbourhood. Out of this grew a regular butcher's business in connection with the farm.

As a child Frank had been drawn by the trickle of dark blood that ran across the pavement from the slaughter-house to the crew-yard, by the sight of the man carrying across to the meat-shed a huge side of beef, with the kidneys showing, embedded in their heavy laps of fat.

He was a handsome lad with soft brown hair and regular features something like a later Roman youth. He was more easily excitable, more readily carried away than the rest, weaker in character. At eighteen he married a little factory girl, a pale, plump, quiet thing with sly eyes and a wheedling voice, who insinuated herself into him and bore him a child every year and made a fool of him. When he had taken over the butchery business, already a growing callousness to it, and a sort of contempt made him neglectful of it. He drank, and was often to be found in his public house blathering away as if he knew everything, when in reality he was a noisy fool.

Of the daughters, Alice, the elder, married a collier and lived for a time stormily in Ilkeston, before moving away to Yorkshire with her numerous young family. Effie, the younger, remained at home.

The last child, Tom, was considerably younger than his brothers, so had belonged rather to the company of his sisters. He was his mother's favourite. She roused herself to determination, and sent him forcibly away to a grammar-school in Derby when he was twelve years old. He did not want to go, and his father would have given way, but Mrs. Brangwen had set her heart on it. Her slender, pretty, tightly-covered body, with full skirts, was now the centre of resolution in the house, and when she had once set upon anything, which was not often, the family failed before her.

So Tom went to school, an unwilling failure from the first. He believed his mother was right in decreeing school for him, but he knew she was only right because she would not acknowledge his constitution. He knew, with a child's deep, instinctive foreknowledge of what is going to happen to him, that he would cut a sorry figure at school. But he took the infliction as inevitable, as if he were guilty of his own nature, as if his being were wrong, and his mother's conception right. If he could have been what he liked, he would have been that which his mother fondly but deludedly hoped he was. He would have been clever, and capable of becoming a gentleman. It was her aspiration for him, therefore he knew it as the true aspiration for any boy. But you can't make a silk purse out of a sow's ear, as he told his mother very early, with regard to himself; much to her mortification and chagrin.

When he got to school, he made a violent struggle against his physical inability to study. He sat gripped, making himself pale and ghastly in his effort to concentrate on the book, to take in what he had to learn. But it was no good. If he beat down his first repulsion, and got like a suicide to the stuff, he went very little further. He could not learn deliberately. His mind simply did not work.

In feeling he was developed, sensitive to the atmosphere around him, brutal perhaps, but at the same time delicate, very delicate. So he had a low opinion of himself. He knew his own limitation. He knew that his brain was a slow hopeless good-for-nothing. So he was humble.

But at the same time his feelings were more discriminating than those of most of the boys, and he was confused. He was more sensuously developed, more refined in instinct than they. For their mechanical stupidity he hated them, and suffered cruel contempt for them. But when it came to mental things, then he was at a disadvantage. He was at their mercy. He was a fool. He had not the power to controvert even the most stupid argument, so that he was forced to admit things he did not in the least believe. And having admitted them, he did not know whether he believed them or not; he rather thought he did.

But he loved anyone who could convey enlightenment to him through feeling. He sat betrayed with emotion when the teacher of literature read, in a moving fashion, Tennyson's 'Ulysses', or Shelley's 'Ode to the West Wind'. His lips parted, his eyes filled with a strained, almost suffering light. And the teacher read on, fired by his power over the boy. Tom Brangwen was moved by this experience beyond all calculation, he almost dreaded it, it was so deep. But when, almost secretly and shamefully, he came to take the book himself, and began the words 'Oh wild west wind, thou breath of autumn's being,' the very fact of the print caused a prickly sensation of repulsion to go over his skin, the blood came to his face, his heart filled with a bursting passion of rage and incompetence. He threw the book down and walked over it and went out to the cricket field. And he hated books as if they were his enemies. He hated them worse than ever he hated any person.

He could not voluntarily control his attention. His mind had no fixed habits to go by, he had nothing to get hold of, nowhere to start from. For him there was nothing palpable, nothing known in himself, that he could apply to learning. He did not know how to begin. Therefore he was helpless when it came to deliberate understanding or deliberate learning.

He had an instinct for mathematics, but if this failed him, he was helpless as an idiot. So that he felt that the ground was never sure under his feet, he was nowhere. His final downfall was his complete inability to attend to a question put without suggestion. If he had to write a formal composition on the Army, he did at last learn to repeat the few facts he knew: 'You can join the army at eighteen. You have to be over five foot eight.' But he had all the time a living conviction that this was a dodge and that his commonplaces were beneath contempt. Then he reddened furiously, felt his bowels sink with shame, scratched out what he had written, made an agonised effort to think of something in the real composition style, failed, became sullen with rage and humiliation, put the pen down and would have been torn to pieces rather than attempt to write another word.

He soon got used to the Grammar School, and the Grammar School got used to him, setting him down as a hopeless duffer at learning, but respecting him for a generous, honest nature. Only one narrow, domineering fellow, the Latin master, bullied him and made the blue eyes mad with shame and rage. There was a horrid scene, when the boy laid open the master's head with a slate, and then things went on as before. The teacher got little sympathy. But Brangwen winced and could not bear to think of the deed, not even long after, when he was a grown man.

He was glad to leave school. It had not been unpleasant, he had enjoyed the companionship of the other youths, or had thought he enjoyed it, the time had passed very quickly, in endless activity. But he knew all the time that he was in an ignominious position, in this place of learning. He was aware of failure all the while, of incapacity. But he was too healthy and sanguine to be wretched, he was too much alive. Yet his soul was wretched almost to hopelessness.

He had loved one warm, clever boy who was frail in body, a consumptive type. The two had had an almost classic friendship, David and Jonathan, wherein Brangwen was the Jonathan, the server. But he had never felt equal with his friend, because the other's mind outpaced his, and left him ashamed, far in the rear. So the two boys went at once apart on leaving school. But Brangwen always remembered his friend that had been, kept him as a sort of light, a fine experience to remember.

Tom Brangwen was glad to get back to the farm, where he was in his own again. 'I have got a turnip on my shoulders, let me stick to th' fallow,' he said to his exasperated mother. He had too low an opinion of himself.

But he went about at his work on the farm gladly enough, glad of the active labour and the smell of the land again, having youth and vigour and humour, and a comic wit, having the will and the power to forget his own shortcomings, finding himself violent with occasional rages, but usually on good terms with everybody and everything.

When he was seventeen, his father fell from a stack and broke his neck. Then the mother and son and daughter lived on at the farm, interrupted by occasional loud-mouthed lamenting, jealous-spirited visitations from the butcher Frank, who had a grievance against the world, which he felt was always giving him less than his dues. Frank was particularly against the young Tom, whom he called a mardy baby, and Tom returned the hatred violently, his face growing red and his blue eyes staring. Effie sided with Tom against Frank. But when Alfred came, from Nottingham, heavy jowled and lowering, speaking very little, but treating those at home with some contempt, Effie and the mother sided with him and put Tom into the shade. It irritated the youth that his elder brother should be made something of a hero by the women, just because he didn't live at home and was a lace-designer and almost a gentleman. But Alfred was something of a Prometheus Bound, so the women loved him. Tom came later to understand his brother better.

As youngest son, Tom felt some importance when the care of the farm devolved on to him. He was only eighteen, but he was quite capable of doing everything his father had done. And of course, his mother remained as centre to the house.

The young man grew up very fresh and alert, with zest for every moment of life. He worked and rode and drove to market, he went out with companions and got tipsy occasionally and played skittles and went to the little travelling theatres. Once, when he was drunk at a public house, he went upstairs with a prostitute who seduced him. He was then nineteen.

The thing was something of a shock to him. In the close intimacy of the farm kitchen, the woman occupied the supreme position. The men deferred to her in the house, on all household points, on all points of morality and behaviour. The woman was the symbol for that further life which comprised religion and love and morality. The men placed in her hands their own conscience, they said to her 'Be my conscience-keeper, be the angel at the doorway guarding my outgoing and my incoming.' And the woman fulfilled her trust, the men rested implicitly in her, receiving her praise or her blame with pleasure or with anger, rebelling and storming, but never for a moment really escaping in their own souls from her prerogative. They depended on her for their stability. Without her, they would have felt like straws in the wind, to be blown hither and thither at random. She was the anchor and the security, she was the restraining hand of God, at times highly to be execrated.

Now when Tom Brangwen, at nineteen, a youth fresh like a plant, rooted in his mother and his sister, found that he had lain with a prostitute woman in a common public house, he was very much startled. For him there was until that time only one kind of woman – his mother and sister.

But now? He did not know what to feel. There was a slight wonder, a pang of anger, of disappointment, a first taste of ash and of cold fear lest this was all that would happen, lest his relations with woman were going to be no more than this nothingness; there was a slight sense of shame before the prostitute, fear that she would despise him for his inefficiency; there was a cold distaste for her, and a fear of her; there was a moment of paralysed horror when he felt he might have taken a disease from her; and upon all this startled tumult of emotion, was laid the steadying hand of common sense, which said it did not matter very much, so long as he had no disease. He soon recovered balance, and really it did not matter so very much.

But it had shocked him, and put a mistrust into his heart, and emphasised his fear of what was within himself. He was, however, in a few days going about again in his own careless, happy-go-lucky fashion, his blue eyes just as clear and honest as ever, his face just as fresh, his appetite just as keen.

Or apparently so. He had, in fact, lost some of his buoyant confidence, and doubt hindered his outgoing.

For some time after this, he was quieter, more conscious when he drank, more backward from companionship. The disillusion of his first carnal contact with woman, strengthened by his innate desire to find in a woman the embodiment of all his inarticulate, powerful religious impulses, put a bit in his mouth. He had something to lose which he was afraid of losing, which he was not even sure of possessing. This first affair did not matter much: but the business of love was, at the bottom of his soul, the most serious and terrifying of all to him.

He was tormented now with sex desire, his imagination reverted always to lustful scenes. But what really prevented his returning to a loose woman, over and above the natural squeamishness, was the recollection of the paucity of the last experience. It had been so nothing, so dribbling and functional, that he was ashamed to expose himself to the risk of a repetition of it.

He made a strong, instinctive fight to retain his native cheerfulness unimpaired. He had naturally a plentiful stream of life and humour, a sense of sufficiency and exuberance, giving ease. But now it tended to cause tension. A strained light came into his eyes, he had a slight knitting of the brows. His boisterous humour gave place to lowering silences, and days passed by in a sort of suspense.

He did not know there was any difference in him, exactly; for the most part he was filled with slow anger and resentment. But he knew he was always thinking of women, or a woman, day in, day out, and that infuriated him. He could not get free: and he was ashamed. He had one or two sweethearts, starting with them in the hope of speedy development. But when he had a nice girl, he found that he was incapable of pushing the desired development. The very presence of the girl beside him made it impossible. He could not think of her like that, he could not think of her actual nakedness. She was a girl and he liked her, and dreaded violently even the thought of uncovering her. He knew that, in these last issues of nakedness, he did not exist to her nor she to him. Again, if he had a loose girl, and things began to develop, she offended him so deeply all the time, that he never knew whether he was going to get away from her as quickly as possible, or whether he were going to take her out of inflamed necessity. Again he learnt his lesson: if he took her it was a paucity which he was forced to despise. He did not despise himself nor the girl. But he despised the net result in him of the experience – he despised it deeply and bitterly.

Then, when he was twenty-three, his mother died, and he was left at home with Effie. His mother's death was another blow out of the dark. He could not understand it, he knew it was no good his trying. One had to submit to these unforeseen blows that come unawares and leave a bruise that remains and hurts whenever it is touched. He began to be afraid of all that which was up against him. He had loved his mother.

After this, Effie and he quarrelled fiercely. They meant a very great deal to each other, but they were both under a strange, unnatural tension. He stayed out of the house as much as possible. He got a special corner for himself at the 'Red Lion' at Cossethay, and became a usual figure by the fire, a fresh, fair young fellow with heavy limbs and head held back, mostly silent, though alert and attentive, very hearty in his greeting of everybody he knew, shy of strangers. He teased all the women, who liked him extremely, and he was very attentive to the talk of the men, very respectful.

To drink made him quickly flush very red in the face, and brought out the look of self-consciousness and unsureness, almost bewilderment, in his blue eyes. When he came home in this state of tipsy confusion his sister hated him and abused him, and he went off his head, like a mad bull with rage.

He had still another turn with a light-o'-love. One Whitsuntide he went a jaunt with two other young fellows, on horseback, to Matlock and thence to Bakewell. Matlock was at that time just becoming a famous beauty-spot, visited from Manchester and from the Staffordshire towns. In the hotel where the young men took lunch, were two girls, and the parties struck up a friendship.

The Miss who made up to Tom Brangwen, then twenty-four years old, was a handsome, reckless girl neglected for an afternoon by the man who had brought her out. She saw Brangwen and liked him, as all women did, for his warmth and his generous nature, and for the innate delicacy in him. But she saw he was one who would have to be brought to the scratch. However, she was roused and unsatisfied and made mischievous, so she dared anything. It would be an easy interlude, restoring her pride.

She was a handsome girl with a bosom, and dark hair and blue eyes, a girl full of easy laughter, flushed from the sun, inclined to wipe her laughing face in a very natural and taking manner.

Brangwen was in a state of wonder. He treated her with his chaffing deference, roused, but very unsure of himself, afraid to death of being too forward, ashamed lest he might be thought backward, mad with desire yet restrained by instinctive regard for women from making any definite approach, feeling all the while that his attitude was ridiculous, and flushing deep with confusion. She, however, became hard and daring as he became confused, it amused her to see him come on.

'When must you get back?' she asked.

'I'm not particular,' he said.

There the conversation again broke down.

Brangwen's companions were ready to go on.

'Art commin', Tom,' they called, 'or art for stoppin'?'

'Ay, I'm commin',' he replied, rising reluctantly, an angry sense of futility and disappointment spreading over him.

He met the full, almost taunting look of the girl, and he trembled with unusedness.

'Shall you come an' have a look at my mare,' he said to her, with his hearty kindliness that was now shaken with trepidation.

'Oh, I should like to go,' she said, rising.

And she followed him, his rather sloping shoulders and his cloth riding-gaiters, out of the room. The young men got their horses out of the stable.

'Can you ride?' Brangwen asked her.

'I should like to if I could – I have never tried,' she said.

'Come then, an' have a try,' he said.

And he lifted her, he blushing, she laughing, into the saddle.

'I s'll slip off – it's not a lady's saddle,' she cried.

'Hold yer tight,' he said, and he led her out of the hotel gate.

The girl sat very insecurely, clinging fast. He put a hand on her waist, to support her. And he held her closely, he clasped her as in an embrace, he was weak with desire as he strode beside her.

The horse walked by the river.

'You want to sit straddle-leg,' he said to her.

'I know I do,' she said.

It was the time of very full skirts. She managed to get astride the horse, quite decently, showing an intent concern for covering her pretty leg.

'It's a lot's better this road,' she said, looking down at him.

'Ay, it is,' he said, feeling the marrow melt in his bones from the look in her eyes. 'I dunno why they have that side-saddle business, twistin' a woman in two.'

'Should us leave you then – you seem to be fixed up there?' called Brangwen's companions from the road.

He went red with anger.

'Ay – don't worry,' he called back.

'How long are yer stoppin'?' they asked.

'Not after Christmas,' he said.

And the girl gave a tinkling peal of laughter.

'All right – by-bye!' called his friends.

And they cantered off, leaving him very flushed, trying to be quite normal with the girl. But presently he had gone back to the hotel and given his horse into the charge of an ostler and had gone off with the girl into the woods, not quite knowing where he was or what he was doing. His heart thumped and he thought it the most glorious adventure, and was mad with desire for the girl.

Afterwards he glowed with pleasure. By Jove, but that was something like! He stayed the afternoon with the girl, and wanted to stay the night. She, however, told him this was impossible: her own man would be back by dark, and she must be with him. He, Brangwen, must not let on that there had been anything between them.

She gave him an intimate smile, which made him feel confused and gratified.

He could not tear himself away, though he had promised not to interfere with the girl. He stayed on at the hotel over night. He saw the other fellow at the evening meal: a small, middle-aged man with iron-grey hair and a curious face, like a monkey's, but interesting, in its way almost beautiful. Brangwen guessed that he was a foreigner. He was in company with another, an Englishman, dry and hard. The four sat at table, two men and two women. Brangwen watched with all his eyes.

He saw how the foreigner treated the women with courteous contempt, as if they were pleasing animals. Brangwen's girl had put on a ladylike manner, but her voice betrayed her. She wanted to win back her man. When dessert came on, however, the little foreigner turned round from his table and calmly surveyed the room, like one unoccupied. Brangwen marvelled over the cold, animal intelligence of the face. The brown eyes were round, showing all the brown pupil, like a monkey's, and just calmly looking, perceiving the other person without referring to him at all. These rested on Brangwen. The latter marvelled at the old face turned round on him, looking at him without considering it necessary to know him at all. The eyebrows of the round, perceiving, but unconcerned eyes were rather high up, with slight wrinkles above them, just as a monkey's had. It was an old, ageless face.

The man was most amazingly a gentleman all the time, an aristocrat. Brangwen stared fascinated. The girl was pushing her crumbs about on the cloth, uneasily, flushed and angry.

As Brangwen sat motionless in the hall afterwards, too much moved and lost to know what to do, the little stranger came up to him with a beautiful smile and manner, offering a cigarette and saying:

'Will you smoke?'

Brangwen never smoked cigarettes, yet he took the one offered, fumbling painfully with thick fingers, blushing to the roots of his hair. Then he looked with his warm blue eyes at the almost sardonic, lidded eyes of the foreigner. The latter sat down beside him, and they began to talk, chiefly of horses.

Brangwen loved the other man for his exquisite graciousness, for his tact and reserve, and for his ageless, monkey-like self-surety. They talked of horses, and of Derbyshire, and of farming. The stranger warmed to the young fellow with real warmth, and Brangwen was excited. He was transported at meeting this odd, middle-aged, dry-skinned man, personally. The talk was pleasant, but that did not matter so much. It was the gracious manner, the fine contact that was all.

They talked a long while together, Brangwen flushing like a girl when the other did not understand his idiom. Then they said good night, and shook hands. Again the foreigner bowed and repeated his good night.

'Good night, and *bon voyage*.'

Then he turned to the stairs.

Brangwen went up to his room and lay staring out at the stars of the summer night, his whole being in a whirl. What was it all? There was a life so different from what he knew it. What was there outside his knowl-

how much? What was this that he had touched? What was he in this new influence? What did everything mean? Where was life, in that which he knew or all outside him?

He fell asleep, and in the morning had ridden away before any other visitors were awake. He shrank from seeing any of them again, in the morning.

His mind was one big excitement. The girl and the foreigner: he knew neither of their names. Yet they had set fire to the homestead of his nature, and he would be burned out of cover. Of the two experiences, perhaps the meeting with the foreigner was the more significant. But the girl – he had not settled about the girl.

He did not know. He had to leave it there, as it was. He could not sum up his experiences.

The result of these encounters was, that he dreamed day and night, absorbedly, of a voluptuous woman and of the meeting with a small, withered foreigner of ancient breeding. No sooner was his mind free, no sooner had he left his own companions, than he began to imagine an intimacy with fine-textured, subtle-mannered people such as the foreigner at Matlock, and amidst this subtle intimacy was always the satisfaction of a voluptuous woman.

He went about absorbed in the interest and the actuality of this dream. His eyes glowed, he walked with his head up, full of the exquisite pleasure of aristocratic subtlety and grace, tormented with the desire for the girl.

Then gradually the glow began to fade, and the cold material of his customary life to show through. He resented it. Was he cheated in his illusion? He balked the mean enclosure of reality, stood stubbornly like a bull at a gate, refusing to re-enter the well-known round of his own life.

He drank more than usual to keep up the glow. But it faded more and more for all that. He set his teeth at the commonplace, to which he would not submit. It resolved itself starkly before him, for all that.

He wanted to marry, to get settled somehow, to get out of the quandary he found himself in. But how? He felt unable to move his limbs. He had seen a little creature caught in bird-lime, and the sight was a nightmare to him. He began to feel mad with rage of impotency.

He wanted something to get hold of, to pull himself out. But there was nothing. Steadfastly he looked at the young women, to find a one he could marry. But not one of them did he want. And he knew that the idea of a life among such people as the foreigner was ridiculous.

Yet he dreamed of it, and stuck to his dreams, and would not have the reality of Cossethay and Ilkeston. There he sat stubbornly in his corner at the 'Red Lion', smoking and musing and occasionally lifting his beer-pot, and saying nothing, for all the world like a gorping farm-labourer, as he said himself.

Then a fever of restless anger came upon him. He wanted to go away – right away. He dreamed of foreign parts. But somehow he had no contact with them. And it was a very strong root which held him to the Marsh, to his own house and land.

Then Effie got married, and he was left in the house with only Tilly, the cross-eyed woman-servant who had been with them for fifteen years. He felt things coming to a close. All the time, he had held himself stubbornly resistant to the action of the commonplace unreality which wanted to absorb him. But now he had to do something.

He was by nature temperate. Being sensitive and emotional, his nausea prevented him from drinking too much.

But, in futile anger, with the greatest of determination and apparent good humour, he began to drink in order to get drunk. 'Damn it,' he said to himself, 'you must have it one road or another – you can't hitch your horse to the shadow of a gate-post – if you've got legs you've got to rise off your backside some time or other.'

So he rose and went down to Ilkeston, rather awkwardly took his place among a gang of young bloods, stood drinks to the company, and discovered he could carry it off quite well. He had an idea that everybody in the room was a man after his own heart, that everything was glorious, everything was perfect. When somebody in alarm told him his coat pocket was on fire, he could only beam from a red, blissful face and say 'Iss-all-ri-ight – iss-al'-ri-ight – it's a' right – let it be, let it be—' and he laughed with pleasure, and was rather indignant that the others should think it unnatural for his coat pocket to burn: – it was the happiest and most natural thing in the world – what?

He went home talking to himself and to the moon, that was very high and small, stumbling at the flashes of moonlight from the puddles at his feet, wondering What the Hanover! then laughing confidently to the moon, assuring her this was first class, this was.

In the morning he woke up and thought about it, and for the first time in his life, knew what it was to feel really acutely irritable, in a misery of real bad temper. After bawling and snarling at Tilly, he took himself off for very shame, to be alone. And looking at the ashen fields and the putty roads, he wondered what in the name of Hell he could do to get out of this prickly sense of disgust and physical repulsion. And he knew that this was the result of his glorious evening.

And his stomach did not want any more brandy. He went doggedly across the fields with his terrier, and looked at everything with a jaundiced eye.

The next evening found him back again in his place at the 'Red Lion', moderate and decent. There he sat and stubbornly waited for what would happen next.

Did he, or did he not believe that he belonged to this world of Cossethay and Ilkeston? There was nothing in it he wanted. Yet could he ever get out of it? Was there anything in himself that would carry him out of it? Or was he a dunderheaded baby, not man enough to be like the other young fellows who drank a good deal and wenched a little without any question, and were satisfied.

He went on stubbornly for a time. Then the strain became too great for him. A hot, accumulated consciousness was always awake in his chest, his wrists felt swelled and quivering, his mind became full of lustful images, his eyes seemed blood-flushed. He fought with himself furiously, to remain

normal. He did not seek any woman. He just went on as if he were normal.
Till he must either take some action or beat his head against the wall.

Then he went deliberately to Ilkeston, in silence, intent and beaten. He
drank to get drunk. He gulped down the brandy, and more brandy, till his
face became pale, his eyes burning. And still he could not get free. He went
to sleep in drunken unconsciousness, woke up at four o'clock in the morning
and continued drinking. He *would* get free. Gradually the tension in him
began to relax. He began to feel happy. His riveted silence was unfastened,
he began to talk and babble. He was happy and at one with all the world,
he was united with all flesh in a hot blood-relationship. So, after three days
of incessant brandy-drinking, he had burned out the youth from his blood,
he had achieved this kindled state of oneness with all the world, which is the
end of youth's most passionate desire. But he had achieved his satisfaction
by obliterating his own individuality, that which it depended on his manhood
to preserve and develop.

So he became a bout-drinker, having at intervals these bouts of three or
four days of brandy-drinking, when he was drunk for the whole time. He
did not think about it. A deep resentment burned in him. He kept aloof from
any women, antagonistic.

When he was twenty-eight, a thick-limbed, stiff, fair man with fresh
complexion, and blue eyes staring very straight ahead, he was coming one
day down from Cossethay with a load of seed out of Nottingham. It was a
time when he was getting ready for another bout of drinking, so he stared
fixedly before him, watchful yet absorbed, seeing everything and aware of
nothing, coiled in himself. It was early in the year.

He walked steadily beside the horse, the load clanked behind as the hill
descended steeper. The road curved downhill before him, under banks and
hedges, seen only for a few yards ahead.

Slowly turning the curve at the steepest part of the slope, his horse
britching between the shafts, he saw a woman approaching. But he was
thinking for the moment of the horse.

Then he turned to look at her. She was dressed in black, was apparently
rather small and slight, beneath her long black cloak, and she wore a black
bonnet. She walked hastily, as if unseeing, her head rather forward. It was
her curious, absorbed, flitting motion, as if she was passing unseen by
everybody, that first arrested him.

She had heard the cart, and looked up. Her face was pale and clear, she
had thick dark eyebrows and a wide mouth, curiously held. He saw her face
clearly, as if by a light in the air. He saw her face so distinctly, that he
ceased to coil on himself, and was suspended.

'That's her,' he said involuntarily. As the cart passed by, splashing through
the thin mud, she stood back against the bank. Then, as he walked still
beside his britching horse, his eyes met hers. He looked quickly away,
pressing back his head, a pain of joy running through him. He could not
bear to think of anything.

He turned round at the last moment. He saw her bonnet, her shape in the
black cloak, the movement as she walked. Then she was gone round the
bend.

She had passed by. He felt as if he were walking again in a far world, not Cossethay, a far world, the fragile reality. He went on, quiet, suspended, rarefied. He could not bear to think or to speak, nor make any sound or sign, nor change his fixed motion. He could scarcely bear to think of her face. He moved within the knowledge of her, in the world that was beyond reality.

The feeling that they had exchanged recognition possessed him like a madness, like a torment. How could he be sure, what confirmation had he? The doubt was like a sense of infinite space, a nothingness, annihilating. He kept within his breast the will to surety. They had exchanged recognition.

He walked about in this state for the next few days. And then again like a mist it began to break to let through the common, barren world. He was very gentle with man and beast, but he dreaded the starkness of disillusion cropping through again.

As he was standing with his back to the fire after dinner a few days later, he saw the woman passing. He wanted to know that she knew him, that she was aware. He wanted it said that there was something between them. So he stood anxiously watching, looking at her as she went down the road. He called to Tilly.

'Who might that be?' he asked.

Tilly, the cross-eyed woman of forty, who adored him, ran gladly to the window to look. She was glad when he asked her for anything. She craned her head over the short curtain, the little tight knob of her black hair sticking out pathetically as she bobbed about.

'Oh why' – she lifted her head and peered with her twisted, keen brown eyes – 'why, you know who it is – it's her from th' vicarage – you know—'

'*How* do I know, you hen-bird,' he shouted.

Tilly blushed and drew her neck in and looked at him with her squinting, sharp, almost reproachful look.

'Why you do – it's the new housekeeper.'

'Ay – an' what by that?'

'Well, an' *what* by that?' rejoined the indignant Tilly.

'She's a woman, isn't she, housekeeper or no housekeeper? She's got more to her than that! Who is she – she's got a name?'

'Well, if she has, *I* don't know,' retorted Tilly, not to be badgered by this lad who had grown up into a man.

'What's her name?' he asked, more gently.

'I'm sure I couldn't tell you,' replied Tilly, on her dignity.

'An' is that all as you've gathered, as she's housekeeping at the vicarage?'

'I've 'eered mention of 'er name, but I couldn't remember it for my life.'

'Why, yer riddle-skulled woman o' nonsense, what have you got a head for?'

'For what other folks 'as got theirs for,' retorted Tilly, who loved nothing more than these tilts when he would call her names.

There was a lull.

'I don't believe as anybody could keep it in their head,' the woman-servant continued, tentatively.

'What?' he asked.

'Why, 'er name.'

'How's that?'

'She's fra some foreign parts or other.'

'Who told you that?'

'That's all I do know, as she is.'

'An' wheer do you reckon she's from, then?'

'I don't know. They do say as she hails fra th' Pole. I don't know,' Tilly hastened to add, knowing he would attack her.

'Fra th' Pole, why do *you* hail fra th' Pole? Who set up that menagerie confabulation?'

'That's what they say – *I* don't know—'

'Who says?'

'Mrs. Bentley says as she's fra th' Pole – else she *is* a Pole, or summat.' Tilly was only afraid she was landing herself deeper now.

'Who says she's a Pole?'

'They all say so.'

'Then what's brought her to these parts?'

'I couldn't tell you. She's got a little girl with her.'

'Got a little girl with her?'

'Of three or four, with a head like a fuzz-ball.'

'Black?'

'White – fair as can be, an' all of a fuzz.'

'Is there a father, then?'

'Not to my knowledge. I don't know.'

'What brought her here?'

'I couldn't say, without th' vicar axed her.'

'Is the child her child?'

'I s'd think so – they say so.'

'Who told you about her?'

'Why, Lizzie – a-Monday – we seed her goin' past.'

'You'd have to be rattling your tongues if anything went past.'

Brangwen stood musing. That evening he went up to Cossethay to the 'Red Lion', half with the intention of hearing more.

She was the widow of a Polish doctor, he gathered. Her husband had died, a refugee, in London. She spoke a bit foreign-like, but you could easily make out what she said. She had one little girl named Anna. Lensky was the woman's name, Mrs. Lensky.

Brangwen felt that here was the unreality established at last. He felt also a curious certainty about her, as if she were destined to him. It was to him a profound satisfaction that she was a foreigner.

A swift change had taken place on the earth for him, as if a new creation were fulfilled, in which he had real existence. Things had all been stark, unreal, barren, mere nullities before. Now they were actualities that he could handle.

He dared scarcely think of the woman. He was afraid. Only all the time he was aware of her presence not far off, he lived in her. But he dared not know her, even acquaint himself with her by thinking of her.

One day he met her walking along the road with her little girl. It was a child with a face like a bud of apple-blossom, and glistening fair hair like thistle-down sticking out in straight, wild, flamy pieces, and very dark eyes. The child clung jealously to her mother's side when he looked at her, staring with resentful black eyes. But the mother glanced at him again, almost vacantly. And the very vacancy of her look inflamed him. She had wide grey-brown eyes with very dark, fathomless pupils. He felt the fine flame running under his skin, as if all his veins had caught fire on the surface. And he went on walking without knowledge.

It was coming, he knew, his fate. The world was submitting to its transformation. He made no move: it would come, what would come.

When his sister Effie came to the Marsh for a week, he went with her for once to church. In the tiny place, with its mere dozen pews, he sat not far from the stranger. There was a fineness about her, a poignancy about the way she sat and held her head lifted. She was strange, from far off, yet so intimate. She was from far away, a presence, so close to his soul. She was not really there, sitting in Cossethay church beside her little girl. She was not living the apparent life of her days. She belonged to somewhere else. He felt it poignantly, as something real and natural. But a pang of fear for his own concrete life, that was only Cossethay, hurt him, and gave him misgiving.

Her thick dark brows almost met above her irregular nose, she had a wide, rather thick mouth. But her face was lifted to another world of life: not to heaven or death: but to some place where she still lived, in spite of her body's absence.

The child beside her watched everything with wide, black eyes. She had an odd little defiant look, her little red mouth was pinched shut. She seemed to be jealously guarding something, to be always on the alert for defence. She met Brangwen's near, vacant, intimate gaze, and a palpitating hostility, almost like a flame of pain, came into the wide, over-conscious dark eyes.

The old clergyman droned on, Cossethay sat unmoved as usual. And there was the foreign woman with the foreign air about her, inviolate, and the strange child, also foreign, jealously guarding something.

When the service was over, he walked in the way of another existence out of the church. As he went down the church-path with his sister, behind the woman and child, the little girl suddenly broke from her mother's hand, and slipped back with quick, almost invisible movement, and was picking at something almost under Brangwen's feet. Her tiny fingers were fine and quick, but they missed the red button.

'Have you found something?' said Brangwen to her.

And he also stooped for the button. But she had got it, and she stood back with it pressed against her little coat, her black eyes flaring at him, as if to forbid him to notice her. Then, having silenced him, she turned with a swift 'Mother—,' and was gone down the path.

The mother had stood watching impassive, looking not at the child, but at Brangwen. He became aware of the woman looking at him, standing there isolated yet for him dominant in her foreign existence.

He did not know what to do, and turned to his sister. But the wide grey eyes, almost vacant yet so moving, held him beyond himself.

'Mother, I may have it, mayn't I?' came the child's proud, silvery tones.

'Mother' – she seemed always to be calling her mother to remember her – 'mother' – and she had nothing to continue now her mother had replied 'Yes, my child.' But, with ready invention, the child stumbled and ran on, 'What are those people's names?'

Brangwen heard the abstract:

'I don't know, dear.'

He went on down the road as if he were not living inside himself, but somewhere outside.

'Who *was* that person?' his sister Effie asked.

'I couldn't tell you,' he answered unknowing.

'She's *somebody* very funny,' said Effie, almost in condemnation. 'That child's like one bewitched.'

'Bewitched – how bewitched?' he repeated.

'You can see for yourself. The mother's plain, I must say – but the child is like a changeling. She'd be about thirty-five.'

But he took no notice. His sister talked on.

'There's your woman for you,' she continued. 'You'd better marry *her*.'

But still he took no notice. Things were as they were.

Another day, at tea-time, as he sat alone at the table, there came a knock at the front door. It startled him like a portent. No one ever knocked at the front door. He rose and began slotting back the bolts, turning the big key. When he had opened the door, the strange woman stood on the threshold.

'Can you give me a pound of butter?' she asked, in a curious detached way of one speaking a foreign language.

He tried to attend to her question. She was looking at him questioningly. But underneath the question, what was there, in her very standing motionless, which affected him?

He stepped aside and she at once entered the house, as if the door had been opened to admit her. That startled him. It was the custom for everybody to wait on the doorstep till asked inside. He went into the kitchen and she followed.

His tea-things were spread on the scrubbed deal table, a big fire was burning, a dog rose from the hearth and went to her. She stood motionless just inside the kitchen.

'Tilly,' he called loudly, 'have we got any butter?'

The stranger stood there like a silence in her black cloak.

'Eh?' came the shrill cry from the distance.

He shouted his question again.

'We've got what's on t' table,' answered Tilly's shrill voice out of the dairy.

Brangwen looked at the table. There was a large pat of butter on a plate, almost a pound. It was round, and stamped with acorns and oak-leaves.

'Can't you come when you're wanted?' he shouted.

'Why, what d'you want?' Tilly protested, as she came peeking inquisitively through the other door.

She saw the strange woman, stared at her with cross-eyes, but said nothing.

'*Haven't* we any butter?' asked Brangwen again, impatiently, as if he could command some by his question.

'I tell you there's what's on t' table,' said Tilly, impatient that she was unable to create any to his demand. 'We haven't a morsel besides.'

There was a moment's silence.

The stranger spoke, in her curiously distinct, detached manner of one who must think her speech first.

'Oh, then thank you very much. I am sorry that I have come to trouble you.'

She could not understand the entire lack of manners, was slightly puzzled. Any politeness would have made the situation quite impersonal. But here it was a case of wills in confusion. Brangwen flushed at her polite speech. Still he did not let her go.

'Get summat an' wrap *that* up for her,' he said to Tilly, looking at the butter on the table.

And taking a clean knife, he cut off that side of the butter where it was touched.

His speech, the 'for her', penetrated slowly into the foreign woman and angered Tilly.

'Vicar has his butter fra Brown's by rights,' said the insuppressible servant-woman. 'We s'll be churnin' to-morrow mornin' first thing.'

'Yes' – the long-drawn foreign yes – 'yes,' said the Polish woman, 'I went to Mrs. Brown's. She hasn't any more.'

Tilly bridled her head, bursting to say that, according to the etiquette of people who bought butter, it was no sort of manners whatever coming to a place cool as you like and knocking at the front door asking for a pound as a stop-gap while your other people were short. If you go to Brown's you go to Brown's, an' my butter isn't just to make shift when Brown's has got none.

Brangwen understood perfectly this unspoken speech of Tilly's. The Polish lady did not. And as she wanted butter for the vicar, and as Tilly was churning in the morning, she waited.

'Sluther up now,' said Brangwen loudly after this silence had resolved itself out; and Tilly disappeared through the inner door.

'I am afraid that I should not come, so,' said the stranger, looking at him enquiringly, as if referring to him for what it was usual to do.

He felt confused.

'How's that?' he said, trying to be genial and being only protective.

'Do you—?' she began deliberately. But she was not sure of her ground, and the conversation came to an end. Her eyes looked at him all the while, because she could not speak the language.

They stood facing each other. The dog walked away from her to him. He bent down to it.

'And how's your little girl?' he asked.

'Yes, thank you, she is very well,' was the reply, a phrase of polite speech in a foreign language merely.

'Sit you down,' he said.

And she sat in a chair, her slim arms, coming through the slits of her cloak, resting on her lap.

'You're not used to these parts,' he said, still standing on the hearthrug with his back to the fire, coatless, looking with curious directness at the woman. Her self-possession pleased him and inspired him, set him curiously free. It seemed to him almost brutal to feel so master of himself and of the situation.

Her eyes rested on him for a moment, questioning, as she thought of the meaning of his speech.

'No,' she said, understanding. 'No – it is strange.'

'You find it middlin' rough?' he said.

Her eyes waited on him, so that he should say it again.

'Our ways are rough to you,' he repeated.

'Yes – yes, I understand. Yes, it is different, it is strange. But I was in Yorkshire—'

'Oh, well then,' he said, 'it's no worse here than what they are up there.'

She did not quite understand. His protective manner, and his sureness, and his intimacy, puzzled her. What did he mean? If he was her equal, why did he behave so without formality?

'No—' she said, vaguely, her eyes resting on him.

She saw his fresh and naïve, uncouth, almost entirely beyond relationship with her. Yet he was good-looking, with his fair hair and blue eyes full of energy, and with his healthy body that seemed to take equality with her. She watched him steadily. He was difficult for her to understand, warm, uncouth, and confident as he was, sure on his feet as if he did not know what it was to be unsure. What then was it that gave him this curious stability?

She did not know. She wondered. She looked round the room he lived in. It had a close intimacy that fascinated and almost frightened her. The furniture was old and familiar as old people, the whole place seemed so kin to him, as if it partook of his being, that she was uneasy.

'It is already a long time that you have lived in this house – yes?' she asked.

'I've always lived here,' he said.

'Yes – but your people – your family?'

'We've been here above *two* hundred years,' he said. Her eyes were on him all the time, wide-open and trying to grasp him. He felt that he was there for her.

'It is your own place, the house, the farm—?'

'Yes,' he said. He looked down at her and met her look. It disturbed her. She did not know him. He was a foreigner, they had nothing to do with each other. Yet his look disturbed her to knowledge of him. He was so strangely confident and direct.

'You live quite alone?'

'Yes – if you call it alone?'

She did not understand. It seemed unusual to her. What was the meaning of it?

And whenever her eyes, after watching him for some time, inevitably met his, she was aware of a heat beating up over her consciousness. She sat motionless and in conflict. Who was this strange man who was at once so near to her? What was happening to her? Something in his young, warm-twinkling eyes seemed to assume a right to her, to speak to her, to extend her his protection. But how? Why did he speak to her? Why were his eyes so certain, so full of light and confident, waiting for no permission nor signal?

Tilly returned with a large leaf and found the two silent. At once he felt it incumbent on him to speak, now the serving-woman had come back.

'How old is your little girl?' he asked.

'Four years,' she replied.

'Her father hasn't been dead long, then?' he asked.

'She was one year when he died.'

'Three years?'

'Yes, three years that he is dead – yes.'

Curiously quiet she was, almost abstracted, answering these questions. She looked at him again, with some maidenhood opening in her eyes. He felt he could not move, neither towards her nor away from her. Something about her presence hurt him, till he was almost rigid before her. He saw the girl's wondering look rise in her eyes.

Tilly handed her the butter and she rose.

'Thank you very much,' she said. 'How much is it?'

'We'll make th' vicar a present of it,' he said. 'It'll do for me goin' to church.'

'It 'ud look better of you if you went to church and took th' money for your butter,' said Tilly, persistent in her claim to him.

'You'd have to put in, shouldn't you?' he said.

'How much, please?' said the Polish woman to Tilly. Brangwen stood by and let be.

'Then, thank you very much,' she said.

'Bring your little girl down sometime to look at th' fowls and horses,' he said, – 'if she'd like it.'

'Yes, she would like it,' said the stranger.

And she went. Brangwen stood dimmed by her departure. He could not notice Tilly, who was looking at him uneasily, wanting to be reassured. He could not think of anything. He felt that he had made some invisible connection with the strange woman.

A daze had come over his mind, he had another centre of consciousness. In his breast, or in his bowels, somewhere in his body, there had started another activity. It was as if a strong light were burning there, and he was blind within it, unable to know anything, except that this transfiguration burned between him and her, connecting them, like a secret power.

Since she had come to the house he went about in a daze, scarcely seeing even the things he handled, drifting, quiescent, in a state of metamorphosis. He submitted to that which was happening to him, letting go his will, suffering the loss of himself, dormant always on the brink of ecstasy, like a creature evolving to a new birth.

She came twice with her child to the farm, but there was this lull between them, an intense calm and passivity like a torpor upon them, so that there was no active change took place. He was almost unaware of the child, yet by his native good humour he gained her confidence, even her affection, setting her on a horse to ride, giving her corn for the fowls.

Once he drove the mother and child from Ilkeston, picking them up on the road. The child huddled close to him as if for love, the mother sat very still. There was a vagueness, like a soft mist over all of them, and a silence as if their wills were suspended. Only he saw her hands, ungloved, folded in her lap, and he noticed the wedding-ring on her finger. It excluded him: it was a closed circle. It bound her life, the wedding-ring, it stood for her life in which he could have no part. Nevertheless, beyond all this, there was herself and himself which should meet.

As he helped her down from the trap, almost lifting her, he felt he had some right to take her thus between his hands. She belonged as yet to that other, to that which was behind. But he must care for her also. She was too living to be neglected.

Sometimes her vagueness, in which he was lost, made him angry, made him rage. But he held himself still as yet. She had no response, no being towards him. It puzzled and enraged him, but he submitted for a long time. Then, from the accumulated troubling of her ignoring him, gradually a fury broke out, destructive, and he wanted to go away, to escape her.

It happened she came down to the Marsh with the child whilst he was in this state. Then he stood over against her, strong and heavy in his revolt, and though he said nothing, still she felt his anger and heavy impatience grip hold of her, she was shaken again as out of a torpor. Again her heart stirred with a quick, out-running impulse, she looked at him, at the stranger who was not a gentleman yet who insisted on coming into her life, and the pain of a new birth in herself strung all her veins to a new form. She would have to begin again, to find a new being, a new form, to respond to that blind, insistent figure standing over against her.

A shiver, a sickness of new birth passed over her, the flame leaped up him, under his skin. She wanted it, this new life from him, with him, yet she must defend herself against it, for it was a destruction.

As he worked alone on the land, or sat up with his ewes at lambing time, the facts and material of his daily life fell away, leaving the kernel of his purpose clean. And then it came upon him that he would marry her and she would be his life.

Gradually, even without seeing her, he came to know her. He would have liked to think of her as of something given into his protection, like a child without parents. But it was forbidden him. He had to come down from this pleasant view of the case. She might refuse him. And besides, he was afraid of her.

But during the long February nights with the ewes in labour, looking out from the shelter into the flashing stars, he knew he did not belong to himself. He must admit that he was only fragmentary, something incomplete and subject. There were the stars in the dark heaven travelling, the whole host passing by on some eternal voyage. So he sat small and submissive to the greater ordering.

Unless she would come to him, he must remain as a nothingness. It was a hard experience. But, after her repeated obliviousness to him, after he had seen so often that he did not exist for her, after he had raged and tried to escape, and said he was good enough by himself, he was a man, and could stand alone, he must, in the starry multiplicity of the night humble himself, and admit and know that without her he was nothing.

He was nothing. But with her, he would be real. If she were now walking across the frosty grass near the sheep-shelter, through the fretful bleating of the ewes and lambs, she would bring him completeness and perfection. And if it should be so, that she should come to him! It should be so – it was ordained so.

He was a long time resolving definitely to ask her to marry him. And he knew, if he asked her, she must really acquiesce. She must, it could not be otherwise.

He had learned a little of her. She was poor, quite alone, and had had a hard time in London, both before and after her husband died. But in Poland she was a lady well born, a landowner's daughter.

All these things were only words to him, the fact of her superior birth, the fact that her husband had been a brilliant doctor, the fact that he himself was her inferior in almost every way of distinction. There was an inner reality, a logic of the soul, which connected her with him.

One evening in March, when the wind was roaring outside, came the moment to ask her. He had sat with his hands before him, leaning to the fire. And as he watched the fire, he knew almost without thinking that he was going this evening.

'Have you got a clean shirt?' he asked Tilly.

'You know you've got clean shirts,' she said.

'Ay, – bring me a white one.'

Tilly brought down one of the linen shirts he had inherited from his father, putting it before him to air at the fire. She loved him with a dumb, aching love as he sat leaning with his arms on his knees, still and absorbed, unaware of her. Lately, a quivering inclination to cry had come over her, when she did anything for him in his presence. Now her hands trembled as she spread the shirt. He was never shouting and teasing now. The deep stillness there was in the house made her tremble.

He went to wash himself. Queer little breaks of consciousness seemed to rise and burst like bubbles out of the depths of his stillness.

'It's got to be done,' he said as he stooped to take the shirt out of the fender, 'it's got to be done, so why balk it?' And as he combed his hair before the mirror on the wall, he retorted to himself, superficially: 'The woman's not speechless dumb. She's not clutterin' at the nipple. She's got the right to please herself, and displease whosoever she likes.'

This streak of common sense carried him a little further.

'Did you want anythink?' asked Tilly, suddenly appearing, having heard him speak. She stood watching him comb his fair beard. His eyes were calm and uninterrupted.

'Ay,' he said, 'where have you put the scissors?'

She brought them to him, and stood watching as, chin forward, he trimmed his beard.

'Don't go an' crop yourself as if you was at a shearin' contest,' she said, anxiously. He blew the fine-curled hair quickly off his lips.

He put on all clean clothes, folded his stock carefully, and donned his best coat. Then, being ready, as grey twilight was falling, he went across to the orchard to gather the daffodils. The wind was roaring in the apple trees, the yellow flowers swayed violently up and down, he heard even the fine whisper of their spears as he stooped to break the flattened, brittle stems of the flowers.

'What's to-do?' shouted a friend who met him as he left the garden gate.

'Bit of courtin', like,' said Brangwen.

And Tilly, in a great state of trepidation and excitement, let the wind whisk her over the field to the big gate, whence she could watch him go.

He went up the hill and on towards the vicarage, the wind roaring through the hedges, whilst he tried to shelter his bunch of daffodils by his side. He did not think of anything, only knew that the wind was blowing.

Night was falling, the bare trees drummed and whistled. The vicar, he knew, would be in his study, the Polish woman in the kitchen, a comfortable room, with her child. In the darkest of twilight, he went through the gate and down the path where a few daffodils stooped in the wind, and shattered crocuses made a pale, colourless ravel.

There was a light streaming on to the bushes at the back from the kitchen window. He began to hesitate. How could he do this? Looking through the window, he saw her seated in the rocking-chair with the child, already in its nightdress, sitting on her knee. The fair head with its wild, fierce hair was drooping towards the fire-warmth, which reflected on the bright cheeks and clear skin of the child, who seemed to be musing, almost like a grown-up person. The mother's face was dark and still, and he saw, with a pang, that she was away back in the life that had been. The child's hair gleamed like spun glass, her face was illuminated till it seemed like wax lit up from the inside. The wind boomed strongly. Mother and child sat motionless, silent, the child staring with vacant eyes into the fire, the mother looking into space. The little girl was almost asleep. It was her will which kept her eyes so wide.

Suddenly she looked round, troubled, as the wind shook the house, and Brangwen saw the small lips move. The mother began to rock, he heard the slight crunch of the rockers of the chair. Then he heard the low, monotonous murmur of a song in a foreign language. Then a great burst of wind, the mother seemed to have drifted away, the child's eyes were black and dilated. Brangwen looked up at the clouds which packed in great, alarming haste across the dark sky.

Then there came the child's high, complaining, yet imperative voice:

'Don't sing that stuff, mother; I don't want to hear it.'

The singing died away.

'You will go to bed,' said the mother.

He saw the clinging protest of the child, the unmoved far-awayness of the mother, the clinging, grasping effort of the child. Then suddenly the clear childish challenge:

'I want you to tell me a story.'

The wind blew, the story began, the child nestled against the mother, Brangwen waited outside, suspended, looking at the wild waving of the trees in the wind and the gathering darkness. He had his fate to follow, he lingered there at the threshold.

The child crouched distinct and motionless, curled in against her mother, the eyes dark and unblinking among the keen wisps of hair, like a curled-up animal asleep but for the eyes. The mother sat as if in shadow, the story went on as if by itself. Brangwen stood outside seeing the night fall. He did not notice the passage of time. The hand that held the daffodils was fixed and cold.

The story came to an end, the mother rose at last, with the child clinging round her neck. She must be strong, to carry so large a child so easily. The little Anna clung round her mother's neck. The fair, strange face of the child looked over the shoulder of the mother, all asleep but the eyes, and these, wide and dark, kept up the resistance and the fight with something unseen.

When they were gone, Brangwen stirred for the first time from the place where he stood, and looked round at the night. He wished it were really as beautiful and familiar as it seemed in these few moments of release. Along with the child, he felt a curious strain on him, a suffering, like a fate.

The mother came down again, and began folding the child's clothes. He knocked. She opened wondering, a little bit at bay, like a foreigner, uneasy.

'Good evening,' he said. 'I'll just come in a minute.'

A change went quickly over her face; she was unprepared. She looked down at him as he stood in the light from the window, holding the daffodils, the darkness behind. In his black clothes she again did not know him. She was almost afraid.

But he was already stepping on to the threshold, and closing the door behind him. She turned into the kitchen, startled out of herself by this invasion from the night. He took off his hat, and came towards her. Then he stood in the light, in his black clothes and his black stock, hat in one hand and yellow flowers in the other. She stood away, at his mercy, snatched out of herself. She did not know him, only she knew he was a man come for her. She could only see the dark-clad man's figure standing there upon her, and the gripped fist of flowers. She could not see the face and the living eyes.

He was watching her, without knowing her, only aware underneath of her presence.

'I come to have a word with you,' he said, striding forward to the table, laying down his hat and the flowers, which tumbled apart and lay in a loose heap. She had flinched from his advance. She had no will, no being. The wind boomed in the chimney, and he waited. He had disembarrassed his hands. Now he shut his fists.

He was aware of her standing there unknown, dread, yet related to him.

'I came up,' he said, speaking curiously matter-of-fact and level, 'to ask if you'd marry me. You are free, aren't you?'

There was a long silence, whilst his blue eyes, strangely impersonal, looked into her eyes to seek an answer to the truth. He was looking for the truth out of her. And she, as if hypnotised, must answer at length.

'Yes, I am free to marry.'

The expression of his eyes changed, became less impersonal, as if he were looking almost at her, for the truth of her. Steady and intent and eternal they were, as if they would never change. They seemed to fix and to resolve her. She quivered, feeling herself created, will-less, lapsing into him, into a common will with him.

'You want me?' she said.

A pallor came over his face.

'Yes,' he said.

Still there was no response and silence.

'No,' she said, not of herself. 'No, I don't know.'

He felt the tension breaking up in him, his fists slackened, he was unable to move. He stood there looking at her, helpless in his vague collapse. For the moment she had become unreal to him. Then he saw her come to him, curiously direct and as if without movement, in a sudden flow. She put her hand to his coat.

'Yes I want to,' she said, impersonally, looking at him with wide, candid, newly-opened eyes, opened now with supreme truth. He went very white as he stood, and did not move, only his eyes were held by hers, and he suffered. She seemed to see him with her newly-opened, wide eyes, almost of a child, and with a strange movement, that was agony to him, she reached slowly forward her dark face and her breast to him, with a slow insinuation of a kiss that made something break in his brain, and it was darkness over him for a few moments.

He had her in his arms, and, obliterated, was kissing her. And it was sheer, bleached agony to him, to break away from himself. She was there so small and light and accepting in his arms, like a child, and yet with such an insinuation of embrace, of infinite embrace, that he could not bear it, he could not stand.

He turned and looked for a chair, and keeping her still in his arms, sat down with her close to him, to his breast. Then, for a few seconds, he went utterly to sleep, asleep and sealed in the darkest sleep, utter, extreme oblivion.

From which he came to gradually, always holding her warm and close upon him, and she as utterly silent as he, involved in the same oblivion, the fecund darkness.

He returned gradually, but newly created, as after a gestation, a new birth, in the womb of darkness. Aerial and light everything was, new as a morning, fresh and newly-begun. Like a dawn the newness and the bliss filled in. And she sat utterly still with him, as if in the same.

Then she looked up at him, the wide, young eyes blazing with light. And he bent down and kissed her on the lips. And the dawn blazed in them, their new life came to pass, it was beyond all conceiving good, it was so good, that it was almost like a passing-away, a trespass. He drew her suddenly closer to him.

For soon the light began to fade in her, gradually, and as she was in his arms, her head sank, she leaned it against him, and lay still, with sunk head, a little tired, effaced because she was tired. And in her tiredness was a certain negation of him.

'There is the child,' she said, out of the long silence.

He did not understand. It was a long time since he had heard a voice. Now also he heard the wind roaring, as if it had just begun again.

'Yes,' he said, not understanding. There was a slight contraction of pain at his heart, a slight tension on his brows. Something he wanted to grasp and could not.

'You will love her?' she said.

The quick contraction, like pain, went over him again.

'I love her now,' he said.

She lay still against him, taking his physical warmth without heed. It was great confirmation for him to feel her there, absorbing the warmth from him, giving him back her weight and her strange confidence. But where was she, that she seemed so absent? His mind was open with wonder. He did not know her.

'But I am much older than you,' she said.

'How old?' he asked.

'I am thirty-four,' she said.

'I am twenty-eight,' he said.

'Six years.'

She was oddly concerned, even as if it pleased her a little. He sat and listened and wondered. It was rather splendid, to be so ignored by her, whilst she lay against him, and he lifted her with his breathing, and felt her weight upon his living, so he had a completeness and inviolable power. He did not interfere with her. He did not even know her. It was so strange that she lay there with her weight abandoned upon him. He was silent with delight. He felt strong, physically, carrying her on his breathing. The strange, inviolable completeness of the two of them made him feel as sure and as stable as God. Amused, he wondered what the vicar would say if he knew.

'You needn't stop here much longer, housekeeping,' he said.

'I like it also, here,' she said. 'When one has been in many places, it is very nice here.'

He was silent again at this. So close on him she lay, and yet she answered him from so far away. But he did not mind.

'What was your own home like, when you were little?' he asked.

'My father was a landowner,' she replied. 'It was near a river.'

This did not convey much to him. All was as vague as before. But he did not care, whilst she was so close.

'I am a landowner – a little one,' he said.

'Yes,' she said.

He had not dared to move. He sat there with his arms round her, her lying motionless on his breathing, and for a long time he did not stir. Then softly, timidly, his hand settled on the roundness of her arm, on the unknown. She seemed to lie a little closer. A hot flame licked up from his belly to his chest.

But it was too soon. She rose, and went across the room to a drawer, taking out a little tray-cloth. There was something quiet and professional about her. She had been a nurse beside her husband, both in Warsaw and in the rebellion afterwards. She proceeded to set a tray. It was as if she ignored Brangwen. He sat up, unable to bear a contradiction in her. She moved about inscrutably.

Then, as he sat there, all mused and wondering, she came near to him, looking at him with wide, grey eyes that almost smiled with a low light. But her ugly-beautiful mouth was still unmoved and sad. He was afraid.

His eyes, strained and roused with unusedness, quailed a little before her, he felt himself quailing and yet he rose, as if obedient to her, he bent and kissed her heavy, sad, wide mouth, that was kissed, and did not alter. Fear was too strong in him. Again he had not got her.

She turned away. The vicarage kitchen was untidy, and yet to him beautiful with the untidiness of her and her child. Such a wonderful remoteness there was about her, and then something in touch with him, that made his heart knock in his chest. He stood there and waited, suspended.

Again she came to him, as he stood in his black clothes, with blue eyes very bright and puzzled for her, his face tensely alive, his hair dishevelled. She came close up to him, to his intent, black-clothed body, and laid her hand on his arm. He remained unmoved. Her eyes, with a blackness of memory struggling with passion, primitive and electric away at the back of them, rejected him and absorbed him at once. But he remained himself. He breathed with difficulty, and sweat came out at the roots of his hair, on his forehead.

'Do you want to marry me?' she asked slowly, always uncertain.

He was afraid lest he could not speak. He drew breath hard, saying:

'I do.'

Then again, what was agony to him, with one hand lightly resting on his arm, she leaned forward a little, and with a strange, primeval suggestion of embrace, held him her mouth. It was ugly-beautiful, and he could not bear it. He put his mouth on hers, and slowly, slowly the response came, gathering force and passion, till it seemed to him she was thundering at him till he could bear no more. He drew away, white, unbreathing. Only, in his blue eyes, was something of himself concentrated. And in her eyes was a little smile upon a black void.

She was drifting away from him again. And he wanted to go away. It was intolerable. He could bear no more. He must go. Yet he was irresolute. But she turned away from him.

With a little pang of anguish, of denial, it was decided.

'I'll come an' speak to the vicar to-morrow,' he said, taking his hat.

She looked at him, her eyes expressionless and full of darkness. He could see no answer.

'That'll do, won't it?' he said.

'Yes,' she answered, mere echo without body or meaning.

'Good night,' he said.

'Good night.'

He left her standing there, expressionless and void as she was. Then she went on laying the tray for the vicar. Needing the table, she put the daffodils aside on the dresser without noticing them. Only their coolness, touching her hand, remained echoing there a long while.

They were such strangers, they must for ever be such strangers, that his passion was a clanging torment to him. Such intimacy of embrace, and such utter foreignness of contact! It was unbearable. He could not bear to be near her, and know the utter foreignness between them, know how entirely they were strangers to each other. He went out into the wind. Big holes were blown into the sky, the moonlight blew about. Sometimes a high moon, liquid-brilliant, scudded across a hollow space and took cover under electric, brown-irridescent cloud-edges. Then there was a blot of cloud, and shadow. Then somewhere in the night a radiance again, like a vapour. And all the sky was teeming and tearing along, a vast disorder of flying shapes and darkness and ragged fumes of light and a great brown circling halo, then the terror of a moon running liquid-brilliant into the open for a moment, hurting the eyes before she plunged under cover of cloud again.

Chapter Two

They Live at the Marsh

She was the daughter of a Polish landowner who, deeply in debt to the Jews, had married a German wife with money, and who had died just before the rebellion. Quite young, she had married Paul Lensky, an intellectual who had studied at Berlin, and had returned to Warsaw a patriot. Her mother had married a German merchant and gone away.

Lydia Lensky, married to the young doctor, became with him a patriot and an émancipée. They were poor, but they were very conceited. She learned nursing as a mark of her emancipation. They represented in Poland the new movement just begun in Russia. But they were very patriotic: and, at the same time, very 'European'.

They had two children. Then came the great rebellion. Lensky, very ardent and full of words, went about inciting his countrymen. Little Poles flamed down the streets of Warsaw, on the way to shoot every Muscovite. So they crossed into the south of Russia, and it was common for six little insurgents to ride into a Jewish village, brandishing swords and words, emphasising the fact that they were going to shoot every living Muscovite.

Lensky was something of a fire-eater also. Lydia, tempered by her German blood, coming of a different family, was obliterated, carried along in her husband's emphasis of declaration, and his whirl of patriotism. He was indeed a brave man, but no bravery could quite have equalled the vividness of his talk. He worked very hard, till nothing lived in him but his eyes. And Lydia, as if drugged, followed him like a shadow, serving, echoing. Sometimes she had her two children, sometimes they were left behind.

She returned once to find them both dead of diphtheria. Her husband wept aloud, unaware of everybody. But the war went on, and soon he was

back at his work. A darkness had come over Lydia's mind. She walked
always in a shadow, silenced, with a strange, deep terror having hold of her,
her desire was to seek satisfaction in dread, to enter a nunnery, to satisfy the
instincts of dread in her, through service of a dark religion. But she could
not.

Then came the flight to London. Lensky, the little, thin man, had got all
his life locked into a resistance and could not relax again. He lived in a sort
of insane irritability, touchy, haughty to the last degree, fractious, so that as
assistant doctor in one of the hospitals he soon became impossible. They
were almost beggars. But he kept still his great ideas of himself, he seemed
to live in a complete hallucination, where he himself figured vivid and lordly.
He guarded his wife jealously against the ignominy of her position, rushed
round her like a brandished weapon, an amazing sight to the English eye,
had her in his power, as if he hypnotised her. She was passive, dark, always
in shadow.

He was wasting away. Already when the child was born he seemed
nothing but skin and bone and fixed idea. She watched him dying, nursed
him, nursed the baby, but really took no notice of anything. A darkness was
on her, like remorse, or like a remembering of the dark, savage, mystic ride
of dread, of death, of the shadow of revenge. When her husband died, she
was relieved. He would no longer dart about her.

England fitted her mood, its aloofness and foreignness. She had known a
little of the language before coming, and a sort of parrot-mind made her
pick it up fairly easily. But she knew nothing of the English, nor of English
life. Indeed, these did not exist for her. She was like one walking in the
Underworld, where the shades throng intelligibly but have no connection
with one. She felt the English people as a potent, cold, slightly hostile host
amongst whom she walked isolated.

The English people themselves were almost deferential to her, the Church
saw that she did not want. She walked without passion, like a shade,
tormented into moments of love by the child. Her dying husband with his
tortured eyes and the skin drawn tight over his face, he was as a vision to
her, not a reality. In a vision he was buried and put away. Then the vision
ceased, she was untroubled, time went on grey, uncoloured, like a long
journey where she sat unconscious as the landscape unrolled beside her.
When she rocked her baby at evening, maybe she fell into a Polish slumber
song, or she talked sometimes to herself in Polish. Otherwise she did not
think of Poland, nor of that life to which she had belonged. It was a great
blot looming blank in its darkness. In the superficial activity of her life, she
was all English. She even thought in English. But her long blanks and
darknesses of abstraction were Polish.

So she lived for some time. Then, with slight uneasiness, she used half to
awake to the streets of London. She realised that there was something around
her, very foreign, she realised she was in a strange place. And then, she was
sent away into the country. There came into her mind now the memory of
her home where she had been a child, the big house among the land, the
peasants of the village.

She was sent to Yorkshire, to nurse an old rector in his rectory by the sea.

This was the first shake of the kaleidoscope that brought in front of her eyes something she must see. It hurt her brain, the open country and the moors. It hurt her and hurt her. Yet it forced itself upon her as something living, it roused some potency of her childhood in her, it had some relation to her.

There was green and silver and blue in the air about her now. And there was a strange insistence of light from the sea, to which she must attend. Primroses glimmered around, many of them, and she stooped to the disturbing influence near her feet, she even picked one or two flowers, faintly remembering in the new colour of life, what had been. All the day long, as she sat at the upper window, the light came off the sea, constantly, constantly, without refusal, till it seemed to bear her away, and the noise of the sea created a drowsiness in her, a relaxation like sleep. Her automatic consciousness gave way a little, she stumbled sometimes, she had a poignant, momentary vision of her living child, that hurt her unspeakably. Her soul roused to attention.

Very strange was the constant glitter of the sea unsheathed in heaven, very warm and sweet the graveyard, in a nook of the hill catching the sunshine and holding it as one holds a bee between the palms of the hands, when it is benumbed. Grey grass and lichens and a little church, and snowdrops among coarse grass, and a cupful of incredibly warm sunshine.

She was troubled in spirit. Hearing the rushing of the beck away down under the trees, she was startled, and wondered what it was. Walking down, she found the bluebells around her glowing like a presence, among the trees.

Summer came, the moors were tangled with harebells like water in the ruts of the roads, the heather came rosy under the skies, setting the whole world awake. And she was uneasy. She went past the gorse bushes shrinking from their presence, she stepped into the heather as into a quickening bath that almost hurt. Her fingers moved over the clasped fingers of the child, she heard the anxious voice of the baby, as it tried to make her talk, distraught.

And she shrank away again, back into her darkness, and for a long while remained blotted safely away from living. But autumn came with the faint red glimmer of robins singing, winter darkened the moors, and almost savagely she turned again to life, demanding her life back again, demanding that it should be as it had been when she was a girl, on the land at home, under the sky. Snow lay in great expanses, the telegraph posts strode over the white earth, away under the gloom of the sky. And savagely her desire rose in her again, demanding that this was Poland, her youth, that all was her own again.

But there were no sledges nor bells, she did not see the peasants coming out like new people, in their sheepskins and their fresh, ruddy, bright faces, that seemed to become new and vivid when the snow lit up the ground. It did not come to her, the life of her youth, it did not come back. There was a little agony of struggle, then a relapse into the darkness of the convent, where Satan and the devils raged round the walls, and Christ was white on the cross of victory.

She watched from the sick-room the snow whirl past, like flocks of shadows in haste, flying on some final mission out to a leaden inalterable sea, beyond the final whiteness of the curving shore, and the snow-speckled blackness of the rocks half submerged. But near at hand on the trees the snow was soft in bloom. Only the voice of the dying vicar spoke grey and querulous from behind.

By the time the snowdrops were out, however, he was dead. He was dead. But with curious equanimity the returning woman watched the snowdrops on the edge of the grass below, blown white in the wind, but not to be blown away. She watched them fluttering and bobbing, the white, shut flowers, anchored by a thread to the grey-green grass, yet never blown away, not drifting with the wind.

As she rose in the morning, the dawn was beating up white, gusts of light blown like a thin snowstorm from the east, blown stronger and fiercer, till the rose appeared, and the gold, and the sea lit up below. She was impassive and indifferent. Yet she was outside the enclosure of darkness.

There passed a space of shadow again, the familiarity of dread-worship, during which she was moved, oblivious, to Cossethay. There, at first, there was nothing – just grey nothing. But then one morning there was a light from the yellow jasmine caught her, and after that, morning and evening, the persistent ringing of thrushes from the shrubbery, till her heart, beaten upon, was forced to lift up its voice in rivalry and answer. Little tunes came into her mind. She was full of trouble almost like anguish. Resistant, she knew she was beaten, and from fear of darkness turned to fear of light. She would have hidden herself indoors, if she could. Above all, she craved for the peace and heavy oblivion of her old state. She could not bear to come to, to realise. The first pangs of this new parturition were so acute, she knew she could not bear it. She would rather remain out of life, than be torn, mutilated into this birth, which she could not survive. She had not the strength to come to life now, in England, so foreign, skies so hostile. She knew she would die like an early, colourless, scentless flower that the end of the winter puts forth mercilessly. And she wanted to harbour her modicum of twinkling life.

But a sunshiny day came full of the scent of a mezereon tree, when bees were tumbling into the yellow crocuses, and she forgot, she felt like somebody else, not herself, a new person, quite glad. But she knew it was fragile, and she dreaded it. The vicar put pea-flower into the crocuses, for his bees to roll in, and she laughed. Then night came, with brilliant stars that she knew of old, from her girlhood. And they flashed so bright, she knew they were victors.

She could neither wake nor sleep. As if crushed between the past and the future, like a flower that comes above-ground to find a great stone lying above it, she was helpless.

The bewilderment and helplessness continued, she was surrounded by great moving masses that must crush her. And there was no escape. Save in the old obliviousness, the cold darkness she strove to retain. But the vicar showed her eggs in the thrush's nest near the back door. She saw herself the mother-thrush upon the nest, and the way her wings were spread, so eager down upon her secret. The tense, eager, nesting wings moved her beyond endurance. She thought of them in the morning, when she heard the thrush whistling as he got up, and she thought, 'Why didn't I die out there, why was I brought here?'

She was aware of people who passed around her, not as persons, but as looming presences. It was very difficult for her to adjust herself. In Poland, the peasantry, the people, had been cattle to her, they had been her cattle that she owned and used. What were these people? Now she was coming awake, she was lost.

But she had felt Brangwen go by almost as if he had brushed her. She had tingled in body as she had gone on up the road. After she had been with him in the Marsh kitchen, the voice of her body had risen strong and insistent. Soon, she wanted him. He was the man who had come nearest to her for her awakening.

Always, however, between-whiles she lapsed into the old unconsciousness, indifference and there was a will in her to save herself from living any more. But she would wake in the morning one day and feel her blood running, feel herself lying open like a flower unsheathed in the sun, insistent and potent with demand.

She got to know him better, and her instinct fixed on him – just on him. Her impulse was strong against him, because he was not of her own sort. But one blind instinct led her, to take him, to leave him, and then to relinquish herself to him. It would be safety. She felt the rooted safety of him, and the life in him. Also he was young and very fresh. The blue, steady livingness of his eyes she enjoyed like morning. He was very young.

Then she lapsed again to stupor and indifference. This, however, was bound to pass. The warmth flowed through her, she felt herself opening, unfolding, asking, as a flower opens in full request under the sun, as the beaks of tiny birds open flat, to receive, to receive. And unfolded she turned to him, straight to him. And he came, slowly, afraid, held back by uncouth fear, and driven by a desire bigger than himself.

When she opened and turned to him, then all that had been and all that was, was gone from her, she was as new as a flower that unsheathes itself and stands always ready, waiting, receptive. He could not understand this. He forced himself, through lack of understanding, to the adherence to the line of honourable courtship and sanctioned, licensed marriage. Therefore, after he had gone to the vicarage and asked for her, she remained for some days held in this one spell, open, receptive to him, before him. He was roused to chaos. He spoke to the vicar and gave in the banns. Then he stood to wait.

She remained attentive and instinctively expectant before him, unfolded, ready to receive him. He could not act, because of self-fear and because of his conception of honour towards her. So he remained in a state of chaos.

And after a few days, gradually she closed again, away from him, was sheathed over, impervious to him, oblivious. Then a black, bottomless despair became real to him, he knew what he had lost. He felt he had lost it for good, he knew what it was to have been in communication with her, and to be cast off again. In misery, his heart like a heavy stone, he went about unliving.

Till gradually he became desperate, lost his understanding, was plunged in a revolt that knew no bounds. Inarticulate, he moved with her at the Marsh in violent, gloomy, wordless passion, almost in hatred of her. Till gradually she became aware of him, aware of herself with regard to him, her blood stirred to life, she began to open towards him, to flow towards him again. He waited till the spell was between them again, till they were together within one rushing, hastening flame. And then again he was bewildered, he was tied up as with cords, and could not move to her. So she came to him, and unfastened the breast of his waistcoat and his shirt, and put her hand on him, needing to know him. For it was cruel to her, to be opened and offered to him, yet not to know what he was, not even that he was there. She gave herself to the hour, but he could not, and he bungled in taking her.

So that he lived in suspense, as if only half his faculties worked, until the wedding. She did not understand. But the vagueness came over her again, and the days lapsed by. He could not get definitely into touch with her. For the time being, she let him go again.

He suffered very much from the thought of actual marriage, the intimacy and nakedness of marriage. He knew her so little. They were so foreign to each other, they were such strangers. And they could not talk to each other. When she talked, of Poland or of what had been, it was all so foreign, she scarcely communicated anything to him. And when he looked at her, an over-much reverence and fear of the unknown changed the nature of his desire into a sort of worship, holding her aloof from his physical desire, self-thwarting.

She did not know this, she did not understand. They had looked at each other, and had accepted each other. It was so, then there was nothing to balk at, it was complete between them.

At the wedding, his face was stiff and expressionless. He wanted to drink, to get rid of his forethought and afterthought, to set the moment free. But he could not. The suspense only tightened at his heart. The jesting and joviality and jolly, broad insinuation of the guests only coiled him more. He could not hear. That which was impending obsessed him, he could not get free.

She sat quiet, with a strange, still smile. She was not afraid. Having accepted him, she wanted to take him, she belonged altogether to the hour, now. No future, no past, only this, her hour. She did not even notice him, as she sat beside him at the head of the table. He was very near, their coming together was close at hand. What more!

As the time came for all the guests to go, her dark face was softly lighted, the bend of her head was proud, her grey eyes clear and dilated, so that the men could not look at her, and the women were elated by her, they served her. Very wonderful she was, as she bade farewell, her ugly wide mouth smiling with pride and recognition, her voice speaking softly and richly in the foreign accent, her dilated eyes ignoring one and all the departing guests. Her manner was gracious and fascinating, but she ignored the being of him or her to whom she gave her hand.

And Brangwen stood beside her, giving his hearty hand-shake to his friends, receiving their regard gratefully, glad of their attention. His heart was tormented within him, he did not try to smile. The time of his trial and his admittance, his Gethsemane and his Triumphal Entry in one, had come now.

Behind her, there was so much unknown to him. When he approached her, he came to such a terrible painful unknown. How could he embrace it and fathom it? How could he close his arms round all this darkness and hold it to his breast and give himself to it? What might not happen to him? If he stretched and strained for ever he would never be able to grasp it all, and to yield himself naked out of his own hands into the unknown power! How could a man be strong enough to take her, put his arms round her and have her, and be sure he could conquer this awful unknown next his heart? What was it then that she was, to which he must also deliver himself up, and which at the same time he must embrace, contain?

He was to be her husband. It was established so. And he wanted it more than he wanted life, or anything. She stood beside him in her silk dress, looking at him strangely, so that a certain terror, horror took possession of him, because she was strange and impending and he had no choice. He could not bear to meet her look from under her strange, thick brows.

'Is it late?' she said.

He looked at his watch.

'No – half-past eleven,' he said. And he made an excuse to go into the kitchen, leaving her standing in the room among the disorder and the drinking-glasses.

Tilly was seated beside the fire in the kitchen, her head in her hands. She started up when he entered.

'Why haven't you gone to bed?' he said.

'I thought I'd better stop an' lock up an' do,' she said. Her agitation quietened him. He gave her some little order, then returned, steadied now, almost ashamed, to his wife. She stood a moment watching him, as he moved with averted face. Then she said:

'You will be good to me, won't you?'

She was small and girlish and terrible, with a queer, wide look in her eyes. His heart leaped in him, in anguish of love and desire, he went blindly to her and took her in his arms.

'I want to,' he said as he drew her closer and closer in. She was soothed by the stress of his embrace, and remained quite still, relaxed against him, mingling in to him. And he let himself go from past and future, was reduced to the moment with her. In which he took her and was with her and there was nothing beyond, they were together in an elemental embrace beyond their superficial foreignness. But in the morning he was uneasy again. She was still foreign and unknown to him. Only, within the fear was pride, belief in himself as mate for her. And she, everything forgotten in her new hour of coming to life, radiated vigour and joy, so that he quivered to touch her.

It made a great difference to him, marriage. Things became so remote and of so little significance, as he knew the powerful source of his life, his eyes opened on a new universe, and he wondered in thinking of his triviality before. A new, calm relationship showed to him in the things he saw, in the cattle he used, the young wheat as it eddied in a wind.

And each time he returned home, he went steadily, expectantly, like a man who goes to a profound, unknown satisfaction. At dinner-time, he appeared in the doorway, hanging back a moment from entering, to see if she was there. He saw her setting the plates on the white-scrubbed table. Her arms were slim, she had a slim body and full skirts, she had a dark, shapely head with close-banded hair. Somehow it was her head, so shapely and poignant, that revealed her his woman to him. As she moved about clothed closely, full-skirted and wearing her little silk apron, her dark hair smoothly parted, her head revealed itself to him in all its subtle, intrinsic beauty, and he knew she was his woman, he knew her essence, that it was his to possess. And he seemed to live thus in contact with her, in contact with the unknown, the unaccountable and incalculable.

They did not take much notice of each other, consciously.

'I'm betimes,' he said.

'Yes,' she answered.

He turned to the dogs, or to the child if she was there. The little Anna played about the farm, flitting constantly in to call something to her mother, to fling her arms round her mother's skirts, to be noticed, perhaps caressed, then, forgetting, to slip out again.

Then Brangwen, talking to the child, or to the dog between his knees, would be aware of his wife, as, in her tight, dark bodice and her lace fichu, she was reaching up to the corner cupboard. He realised with a sharp pang that she belonged to him, and he to her. He realised that he lived by her. Did he own her? Was she here for ever? Or might she go away? She was not really his, it was not a real marriage, this marriage between them. She might go away. He did not feel like a master, husband, father of her children. She belonged elsewhere. Any moment, she might be gone. And he was ever drawn to her, drawn after her, with ever-raging, ever-unsatisfied desire. He must always turn home, wherever his steps were taking him, always to her, and he could never quite reach her, he could never quite be satisfied, never be at peace, because she might go away.

At evening, he was glad. Then, when he had finished in the yard, and come in and washed himself, when the child was put to bed, he could sit on the other side of the fire with his beer on the hob and his long white pipe in his fingers, conscious of her there opposite him, as she worked at her embroidery, or as she talked to him, and he was safe with her now, till morning. She was curiously self-sufficient and did not say very much. Occasionally she lifted her head, her grey eyes shining with a strange light, that had nothing to do with him or with this place, and would tell him about herself. She seemed to be back again in the past, chiefly in her childhood or her girlhood, with her father. She very rarely talked of her first husband. But sometimes, all shining-eyed, she was back at her own home, telling him about the riotous times, the trip to Paris with her father, tales of the mad acts of the peasants when a burst of religious, self-hurting fervour had passed over the country.

She would lift her head and say:

'When they brought the railway across the country, they made afterwards smaller railways, of shorter width, to come down to our town – a hundred miles. When I was a girl, Gisla, my German gouvernante, was very shocked and she would not tell me. But I heard the servants talking. I remember, it was Pierre, the coachman. And my father, and some of his friends, land-owners, they had taken a wagon, a whole railway wagon – that you travel in—'

'A railway-carriage,' said Brangwen.

She laughed to herself.

'I know it was a great scandal: yes – a whole wagon, and they had girls, you know, *filles*, naked, all the wagon-full, and so they came down to our village. They came through villages of the Jews, and it was a great scandal. Can you imagine? All the countryside! And my mother, she did not like it. Gisla said to me, "Madame, she must not know that you have heard such things."

'My mother, she used to cry, and she wished to beat my father, plainly beat him. He would say, when she cried because he sold the forest, the wood, to jingle money in his pocket, and go to Warsaw or Paris or Kiev, when she said he must take back his word, he must not sell the forest, he would stand and say, "I know, I have heard it all, I have heard it all before. Tell me some new thing. I know, I know, I know.' Oh, but can you understand, I loved him when he stood there under the door, saying only, "I know, I know, I know it all already." She could not change him, no, not if she killed herself for it. And she could change everybody else, but him, she could not change him—'

Brangwen could not understand. He had pictures of a cattle-truck full of naked girls riding from nowhere to nowhere, of Lydia laughing because her father made great debts and said, 'I know, I know'; of Jews running down the street shouting in Yiddish, 'Don't do it, don't do it,' and being cut down by demented peasants – she called them 'cattle' – whilst she looked on interested and even amused; of tutors and governesses and Paris and a convent. It was too much for him. And there she sat, telling the tales to the open space, not to him, arrogating a curious superiority to him, a distance between them, something strange and foreign and outside his life, talking, rattling, without rhyme or reason, laughing when he was shocked or astounded, condemning nothing, confounding his mind and making the whole world a chaos, without order or stability of any kind. Then, when they went to bed, he knew that he had nothing to do with her. She was back in her childhood, he was a peasant, a serf, a servant, a lover, a paramour, a shadow, a nothing. He lay still in amazement, staring at the room he knew so well, and wondering whether it was really there, the window, the chest of drawers, or whether it was merely a figment in the atmosphere. And gradually he grew into a raging fury against her. But because he was so much amazed, and there was as yet such a distance between them, and she was such an amazing thing to him, with all wonder opening out behind her, he made no retaliation on her. Only he lay still and wide-eyed with rage, inarticulate, not understanding, but solid with hostility.

And he remained wrathful and distinct from her, unchanged outwardly to her, but underneath a solid power of antagonism to her. Of which she became gradually aware. And it irritated her to be made aware of him as a separate power. She lapsed into a sort of sombre exclusion, a curious communion with mysterious powers, a sort of mystic, dark state which drove him and the child nearly mad. He walked about for days stiffened with resistance to her, stiff with a will to destroy her as she was. Then suddenly, out of nowhere, there was connection between them again. It came on him as he was working in the fields. The tension, the bond, burst, and the passionate flood broke forward into a tremendous, magnificent rush, so that he felt he could snap off the trees as he passed, and create the world afresh.

And when he arrived home, there was no sign between them. He waited and waited till she came. And as he waited, his limbs seemed strong and splendid to him, his hands seemed like passionate servants to him, goodly, he felt a stupendous power in himself, of life, and of urgent, strong blood.

She was sure to come at last, and touch him. Then he burst into flame for her, and lost himself. They looked at each other, a deep laugh at the bottom of their eyes, and he went to take of her again, wholesale, mad to revel in the inexhaustible wealth of her, to bury himself in the depths of her in an inexhaustible exploration, she all the while revelling in that he revelled in her, tossed all her secrets aside and plunged to that which was secret to her as well, whilst she quivered with fear and the last anguish of delight.

What did it matter who they were, whether they knew each other or not?

The hour passed away again, there was severance between them, and rage and misery and bereavement for her, and deposition and toiling at the mill with slaves for him. But no matter. They had had their hour, and should it chime again, they were ready for it, ready to renew the game at the point where it was left off, on the edge of the outer darkness, when the secrets within the woman are game for the man, hunted doggedly, when the secrets of the woman are the man's adventure, and they both give themselves to the adventure.

She was with child, and there was again the silence and distance between them. She did not want him nor his secrets nor his game, he was deposed, he was cast out. He seethed with fury at the small, ugly-mouthed woman who had nothing to do with him. Sometimes his anger broke on her, but she did not cry. She turned on him like a tiger, and there was battle.

He had to learn to contain himself again, and he hated it. He hated her that she was not there for him. And he took himself off, anywhere.

But an instinct of gratitude and a knowledge that she would receive him back again, that later on she would be there for him again, prevented his straying very far. He cautiously did not go too far. He knew she might lapse into ignorance of him, lapse away from him, farther, farther, farther, till she was lost to him. He had sense enough, premonition enough in himself, to be aware of this and to measure himself accordingly. For he did not want to lose her: he did not want her to lapse away.

Cold, he called her, selfish, only caring about herself, a foreigner with a bad nature, caring really about nothing, having no proper feelings at the bottom of her, and no proper niceness. He raged, and piled up accusations that had some measure of truth in them all. But a certain grace in him forbade him from going too far. He knew, and he quivered with rage and hatred, that she was all these vile things, that she was everything vile and detestable. But he had grace at the bottom of him, which told him that, above all things, he did not want to lose her, he was not going to lose her.

So he kept some consideration for her, he preserved some relationship. He went out more often, to the 'Red Lion' again, to escape the madness of sitting next to her when she did not belong to him, when she was as absent as any woman in indifference could be. He could not stay at home. So he went to the 'Red Lion'. And sometimes he got drunk. But he preserved his measure, some things between them he never forfeited.

A tormented look came into his eyes, as if something were always dogging him. He glanced sharp and quick, he could not bear to sit doing nothing. He had to go out, to find company, to give himself away there. For he had no other outlet, he could not work to give himself out, he had not the knowledge.

As the months of her pregnancy went on, she left him more and more alone, she was more and more unaware of him, his existence was annulled. And he felt bound down, bound, unable to stir, beginning to go mad, ready to rave. For she was quiet and polite, as if he did not exist, as one is quiet and polite to a servant.

Nevertheless she was great with his child, it was his turn to submit. She sat opposite him, sewing, her foreign face inscrutable and indifferent. He felt he wanted to break her into acknowledgment of him, into awareness of him. It was insufferable that she had so obliterated him. He would smash her into regarding him. He had a raging agony of desire to do so.

But something bigger in him withheld him, kept him motionless. So he went out of the house for relief. Or he turned to the little girl for her sympathy and her love, he appealed with all his power to the small Anna. So soon they were like lovers, father and child.

For he was afraid of his wife. As she sat there with bent head, silent, working or reading, but so unutterably silent that his heart seemed under the millstone of it, she became herself like the upper millstone lying on him, crushing him, as sometimes a heavy sky lies on the earth.

Yet he knew he could not tear her away from the heavy obscurity into which she was merged. He must not try to tear her into recognition of himself, and agreement with himself. It were disastrous, impious. So, let him rage as he might, he must withhold himself. But his wrists trembled and seemed mad, seemed as if they would burst.

When, in November, the leaves came beating against the window shutters, with a lashing sound, he started, and his eyes flickered with flame. The dog looked up at him, he sunk his head to the fire. But his wife was startled. He was aware of her listening.

'They blow up with a rattle,' he said.

'What?' she asked.

'The leaves.'

She sank away again. The strange leaves beating in the wind on the wood had come nearer than she. The tension in the room was overpowering, it was difficult for him to move his head. He sat with every nerve, every vein, every fibre of muscle in his body stretched on a tension. He felt like a broken arch thrust sickeningly out from support. For her response was gone, he thrust at nothing. And he remained himself, he saved himself from crashing down into nothingness, from being squandered into fragments, by sheer tension, sheer backward resistance.

During the last months of her pregnancy, he went about in a surcharged, imminent state that did not exhaust itself. She was also depressed, and sometimes she cried. It needed so much life to begin afresh, after she had lost so lavishly. Sometimes she cried. Then he stood stiff, feeling his heart would burst. For she did not want him, she did not want even to be made aware of him. By the very puckering of her face he knew that he must stand back, leave her intact, alone. For it was the old grief come back in her, the old loss, the pain of the old life, the dead husband, the dead children. This was sacred to her, and he must not violate her with his comfort. For what she wanted she would come to him. He stood aloof with turgid heart.

He had to see her tears come, fall over her scarcely moving face, that only puckered sometimes, down on to her breast, that was so still, scarcely moving. And there was no noise, save now and again, when, with a strange, somnambulant movement, she took her handkerchief and wiped her face and blew her nose, and went on with the noiseless weeping. He knew that any offer of comfort from himself would be worse than useless, hateful to her, jangling her. She must cry. But it drove him insane. His heart was scalded, his brain hurt in his head, he went away, out of the house.

His great and chiefest source of solace was the child. She had been at first aloof from him, reserved. However friendly she might seem one day, the next she would have lapsed to her original disregard of him, cold, detached, at her distance.

The first morning after his marriage he had discovered it would not be so easy with the child. At the break of dawn he had started awake hearing a small voice outside the door saying plaintively:

'Mother!'

He rose and opened the door. She stood on the threshold in her night-dress, as she had climbed out of bed, black eyes staring round and hostile, her fair hair sticking out in a wild fleece. The man and child confronted each other.

'I want my mother,' she said, jealously accenting the 'my'.

'Come on then,' he said gently.

'Where's my mother?'

'She's here – come on.'

The child's eyes, staring at the man with ruffled hair and beard, did not change. The mother's voice called softly. The little bare feet entered the room with trepidation.

'Mother!'

'Come, my dear.'

The small bare feet approached swiftly.

'I wondered where you were,' came the plaintive voice. The mother stretched out her arms. The child stood beside the high bed. Brangwen lightly lifted the tiny girl, with an 'up-a-daisy', then took his own place in the bed again.

'Mother!' cried the child, as in anguish.

'What, my pet?'

Anna wriggled close into her mother's arms, clinging tight, hiding from the fact of the man. Brangwen lay still, and waited. There was a long silence.

Then suddenly, Anna looked round, as if she thought he would be gone. She saw the face of the man lying upturned to the ceiling. Her black eyes stared antagonistic from her exquisite face, her arms clung tightly to her mother, afraid. He did not move for some time, not knowing what to say. His face was smooth and soft-skinned with love, his eyes full of soft light. He looked at her, scarcely moving his head, his eyes smiling.

'Have you just wakened up,' he said.

'Go away,' she retorted, with a little darting forward of the head, something like a viper.

'Nay,' he answered, '*I'm* not going. You can go.'

'Go away,' came the sharp little command.

'There's room for you,' he said.

'You can't send your father from his own bed, my little bird,' said her mother, pleasantly.

The child glowered at him, miserable in her impotence.

'There's room for you as well,' he said. 'It's a big bed enough.'

She glowered without answering, then turned and clung to her mother. She would not allow it.

During the day she asked her mother several times:

'When are we going home, mother?'

'We are at home, darling, we live here now. This is our house, we live here with your father.'

The child was forced to accept it. But she remained against the man. As night came on, she asked:

'Where are you going to sleep, mother?'

'I sleep with the father now.'

And when Brangwen came in, the child asked fiercely:

'*Why* do you sleep with *my* mother? My mother sleeps with me,' her voice quivering.

'You come as well, an' sleep with both of us,' he coaxed.

'Mother!' she cried, turning, appealing against him.

'But I must have a husband, darling. All women must have a husband.'

'And you like to have a father with your mother, don't you?' said Brangwen.

Anna glowered at him. She seemed to cogitate.

'No,' she cried fiercely at length, 'no, I don't *want*.' And slowly her face puckered, she sobbed bitterly. He stood and watched her, sorry. But there could be no altering it.

Which, when she knew, she became quiet. He was easy with her, talking to her, taking her to see the live creatures, bringing her the first chickens in his cap, taking her to gather the eggs, letting her throw crusts to the horse. She would easily accompany him, and take all he had to give, but she remained neutral still.

She was curiously, incomprehensibly jealous of her mother, always anxiously concerned about her. If Brangwen drove with his wife to Nottingham, Anna ran about happily enough, or unconcerned, for a long time. Then, as afternoon came on, there was only one cry - 'I want my mother, I want my mother—' and a bitter, pathetic sobbing that soon had the soft-hearted Tilly sobbing too. The child's anguish was that her mother was gone, gone.

Yet as a rule, Anna seemed cold, resenting her mother, critical of her. It was:

'I don't like you to do that, mother,' or, 'I don't like you to say that.' She was a sore problem to Brangwen and to all the people at the Marsh. As a rule, however, she was active, lightly flitting about the farmyard, only appearing now and again to assure herself of her mother. Happy she never seemed, but quick, sharp, absorbed, full of imagination and changeability. Tilly said she was bewitched. But it did not matter so long as she did not cry. There was something heart-rending about Anna's crying, her childish anguish seemed so utter and so timeless, as if it were a thing of all the ages.

She made playmates of the creatures of the farmyard, talking to them, telling them the stories she had from her mother, counselling them and correcting them. Brangwen found her at the gate leading to the paddock and to the duckpond. She was peering through the bars and shouting to the stately white geese, that stood in a curving line:

'You're not to call at people when they want to come. You must not do it.'

The heavy, balanced birds looked at the fierce little face and the fleece of keen hair thrust between the bars, and they raised their heads and swayed off, producing the long, can-canking, protesting noise of geese, rocking their ship-like, beautiful white bodies in a line beyond the gate.

'You're naughty, you're naughty,' cried Anna, tears of dismay and vexation in her eyes. And she stamped her slipper.

'Why, what are they doing?' said Brangwen.

'They won't let me come in,' she said, turning her flushed little face to him.

'Yi, they will. You can go in if you want to,' and he pushed open the gate for her.

She stood irresolute, looking at the group of bluey-white geese standing monumental under the grey, cold day.

'Go on,' he said.

She marched valiantly a few steps in. Her little body started convulsively at the sudden, derisive can-cank-ank of the geese. A blankness spread over her. The geese trailed away with uplifted heads under the low grey sky.

'They don't know you,' said Brangwen. 'You should tell 'em what your name is.'

'They're *naughty* to shout at me,' she flashed.

'They think you don't live here,' he said.

Later he found her at the gate calling shrilly and imperiously:

'My name is Anna, Anna Lensky, and I live here, because Mr. Brangwen's my father now. He *is*, yes he *is*. And I live here.'

This pleased Brangwen very much. And gradually, without knowing it herself, she clung to him, in her lost, childish, desolate moments, when it was good to creep up to something big and warm, and bury her little self in his big, unlimited being. Instinctively he was careful of her, careful to recognise her and to give himself to her disposal.

She was difficult of her affections. For Tilly, she had a childish, essential contempt, almost dislike, because the poor woman was such a servant. The child would not let the serving-woman attend to her, do intimate things for her, not for a long time. She treated her as one of an inferior race. Brangwen did not like it.

'Why aren't you fond of Tilly?' he asked.

'Because – because – because she looks at me with her eyes bent.'

Then gradually she accepted Tilly as belonging to the household, never as a person.

For the first weeks, the black eyes of the child were for ever on the watch. Brangwen, good-humoured but impatient, spoiled by Tilly, was an easy blusterer. If for a few minutes he upset the household with his noisy impatience, he found at the end the child glowering at him with intense black eyes, and she was sure to dart forward her little head, like a serpent, with her biting:

'Go away.'

'I'm *not* going away,' he shouted, irritated at last. 'Go yourself – hustle – stir thysen – hop.' And he pointed to the door. The child backed away from him, pale with fear. Then she gathered up courage, seeing him become patient.

'We don't live with *you*,' she said, thrusting forward her little head at him. 'You – you're – you're a bomakle.'

'A what?' he shouted.

Her voice wavered – but it came.

'A bomakle.'

'Ay, an' you're a comakle.'

She meditated. Then she hissed forwards her head.

'I'm not.'

'Not what?'

'A comakle.'

'No more am I a bomakle.'

He was really cross.

Other times she would say:

'My mother *doesn't* live here.'

'Oh, ay?'

'I want her to go away.'

'Then want's your portion,' he replied laconically.

So they drew nearer together. He would take her with him when he went out in the trap. The horse ready at the gate, he came noisily into the house, which seemed quiet and peaceful till he appeared to set everything awake.

'Now then, Topsy, pop into thy bonnet.'

The child drew herself up, resenting the indignity of the address.

'I can't fasten my bonnet myself,' she said haughtily.

'Not man enough yet,' he said, tying the ribbons under her chin with clumsy fingers.

She held up her face to him. Her little bright-red lips moved as he fumbled under her chin.

'You talk – nonsents,' she said, re-echoing one of his phrases.

'*That* face shouts for th' pump,' he said, and taking out a big red handkerchief, that smelled of strong tobacco, began wiping round her mouth.

'Is Kitty waiting for me?' she asked.

'Ay,' he said. 'Let's finish wiping your face – it'll pass wi' a cat-lick.'

She submitted prettily. Then, when he let her go, she began to skip, with a curious flicking up of one leg behind her.

'Now my young buck-rabbit,' he said. 'Slippy!'

She came and was shaken into her coat, and the two set off. She sat very close beside him in the gig, tucked tightly, feeling his big body sway, against her, very splendid. She loved the rocking of the gig, when his big, live body swayed upon her, against her. She laughed, a poignant little shrill laugh, and her black eyes glowed.

She was curiously hard, and then passionately tender-hearted. Her mother was ill, the child stole about on tip-toe in the bedroom for hours, being nurse, and doing the thing thoughtfully and diligently. Another day, her mother was unhappy. Anna would stand with her legs apart, glowering, balancing on the sides of her slippers. She laughed when the goslings wriggled in Tilly's hand, as the pellets of food were rammed down their throats with a skewer, she laughed nervously. She was hard and imperious with the animals, squandering no love, running about amongst them like a cruel mistress.

Summer came, and hay-harvest, Anna was a brown elfish mite dancing about. Tilly always marvelled over her, more than she loved her.

But always in the child was some anxious connection with the mother. So long as Mrs. Brangwen was all right, the little girl played about and took very little notice of her. But corn-harvest went by, the autumn drew on, and the mother, the later months of her pregnancy beginning, was strange and detached, Brangwen began to knit his brows, the old, unhealthy uneasiness, the unskinned susceptibility came on the child again. If she went to the fields with her father, then, instead of playing about carelessly, it was:

'I want to go home.'

'Home, why tha's nobbut this minute come.'

'I want to go home.'

'What for? What ails thee?'

'I want my mother.'

'Thy mother! Thy mother none wants thee.'

'I want to go home.'

There would be tears in a moment.

'Can ter find t'road, then?'

And he watched her scudding, silent and intent, along the hedge-bottom, at a steady, anxious pace, till she turned and was gone through the gateway. Then he saw her two fields off, still pressing forward, small and urgent. His face was clouded as he turned to plough up the stubble.

The year drew on, in the hedges the berries shone red and twinkling above bare twigs, robins were seen, great droves of birds dashed like spray from the fallow, rooks appeared, black and flapping down to earth, the ground was cold as he pulled the turnips, the roads were churned deep in mud. Then the turnips were pitted and work was slack.

Inside the house it was dark, and quiet. The child flitted uneasily round, and now and again came her plaintive, startled cry:

'Mother!'

Mrs. Brangwen was heavy and unresponsive, tired, lapsed back. Brangwen went on working out of doors.

At evening, when he came in to milk, the child would run behind him. Then, in the cosy cow-sheds, with the doors shut and the air looking warm by the light of the hanging lantern, above the branching horns of the cows, she would stand watching his hands squeezing rhythmically the teats of the placid beast, watch the froth and the leaping squirt of milk, watch his hand sometimes rubbing slowly, understandingly, upon a hanging udder. So they kept each other company, but at a distance, rarely speaking.

The darkest days of the year came on, the child was fretful, sighing as if some oppression were on her, running hither and thither without relief. And Brangwen went about at his work, heavy, his heart heavy as the sodden earth.

The winter nights fell early, the lamp was lighted before tea-time, the shutters were closed, they were all shut into the room with the tension and stress. Mrs. Brangwen went early to bed, Anna playing on the floor beside her. Brangwen sat in the emptiness of the downstairs room, smoking, scarcely conscious even of his own misery. And very often he went out to escape it.

Christmas passed, the wet, drenched, cold days of January recurred monotonously, with now and then a brilliance of blue flashing in, when Brangwen went out into a morning like crystal, when every sound rang again, and the birds were many and sudden and brusque in the hedges. Then an elation came over him in spite of everything, whether his wife were strange or sad, or whether he craved for her to be with him, it did not matter, the air rang with clear noises, the sky was like crystal, like a bell, and the earth was hard. Then he worked and was happy, his eyes shining, his cheeks flushed. And the zest of life was strong in him.

The birds pecked busily round him, the horses were fresh and ready, the bare branches of the trees flung themselves up like a man yawning, taut with energy, the twigs radiated off into the clear light. He was alive and full of zest for it all. And if his wife were heavy, separated from him, extinguished, then, let her be, let him remain himself. Things would be as they would be. Meanwhile he heard the ringing crow of a cockerel in the distance, he saw the pale shell of the moon effaced on a blue sky.

So he shouted to the horses, and was happy. If, driving into Ilkeston, a fresh young woman were going in to do her shopping, he hailed her, and reined in his horse, and picked her up. Then he was glad to have her near him, his eyes shone, his voice, laughing, teasing in a warm fashion, made the poise of her head more beautiful, her blood ran quicker. They were both stimulated, the morning was fine.

What did it matter that, at the bottom of his heart, was care and pain? It was at the bottom, let it stop at the bottom. His wife, her suffering, her coming pain – well, it must be so. She suffered, but he was out of doors, full in life, and it would be ridiculous, indecent, to pull a long face and to insist on being miserable. He was happy, this morning, driving to town, with the hoofs of the horse spanking the hard earth. Well he was happy, if half the world were weeping at the funeral of the other half. And it was a jolly girl sitting beside him. And Woman was immortal, whatever happened, whoever turned towards death. Let the misery come when it could not be resisted.

The evening arrived later very beautiful, with a rosy flush hovering above the sunset, and passing away into violet and lavender, with turquoise green north and south in the sky, and in the east, a great, yellow moon hanging heavy and radiant. It was magnificent to walk between the sunset and the moon, on a road where little holly trees thrust black into the rose and lavender, and starlings flickered in droves across the light. But what was the end of the journey? The pain came right enough, later on, when his heart and his feet were heavy, his brain dead, his life stopped.

One afternoon, the pains began, Mrs. Brangwen was put to bed, the midwife came. Night fell, the shutters were closed, Brangwen came in to tea, to the loaf and the pewter teapot, the child, silent and quivering, playing with glass beads, the house, empty, it seemed, or exposed to the winter night, as if it had no walls.

Sometimes there sounded, long and remote in the house, vibrating through everything, the moaning cry of a woman in labour. Brangwen, sitting downstairs, was divided. His lower, deeper self was with her, bound to her, suffering. But the big shell of his body remembered the sound of owls that used to fly round the farmstead when he was a boy. He was back in his youth, a boy, haunted by the sound of the owls, waking up his brother to speak to him. And his mind drifted away to the birds, their solemn, dignified faces, their flight so soft and broad-winged. And then to the birds his brother had shot, fluffy, dust-coloured, dead heaps of softness with faces absurdly asleep. It was a queer thing, a dead owl.

He lifted his cup to his lips, he watched the child with the beads. But his mind was occupied with owls, and the atmosphere of his boyhood, with his brothers and sisters. Elsewhere, fundamental, he was with his wife in labour, the child was being brought forth out of their one flesh. He and she, one flesh, out of which life must be put forth. The rent was not in his body, but it was of his body. On her the blows fell, but the quiver ran through to him, to his last fibre. She must be torn asunder for life to come forth, yet still they were one flesh, and still, from further back, the life came out of him to her, and still he was the unbroken that has the broken rock in its arms, their flesh was one rock from which the life gushed, out of her who was smitten and rent, from him who quivered and yielded.

He went upstairs to her. As he came to the bedside she spoke to him in Polish.

'Is it very bad?' he asked.

She looked at him, and oh, the weariness to her, of the effort to understand another language, the weariness of hearing him, attending to him, making out who he was, as he stood there fair-bearded and alien, looking at her. She knew something of him, of his eyes. But she could not grasp him. She closed her eyes.

He turned away, white to the gills.

'It's not so very bad,' said the midwife.

He knew he was a strain on his wife. He went downstairs.

The child glanced up at him, frightened.

'I want my mother,' she quavered.

'Ay, but she's badly,' he said mildly, unheeding.

She looked at him with lost, frightened eyes.

'Has she got a headache?'

'No – she's going to have a baby.'

The child looked round. He was unaware of her. She was alone again in terror.

'I want my mother,' came the cry of panic.

'Let Tilly undress you,' he said. 'You're tired.'

There was another silence. Again came the cry of labour.

'I want my mother,' rang automatically from the wincing, panic-stricken child, that felt cut off and lost in a horror of desolation.

Tilly came forward, her heart wrung.

'Come an' let me undress her then, pet-lamb,' she crooned. 'You s'll have your mother in th' mornin', don't you fret, my duckie; never mind, angel.'

But Anna stood upon the sofa, her back to the wall.

'I want my mother,' she cried, her little face quivering, and the great tears of childish, utter anguish falling.

'She's poorly, my lamb, she's poorly to-night, but she'll be better by mornin'. Oh, don't cry, don't cry, love, she doesn't want you to cry, precious little heart, no, she doesn't.'

Tilly took gently hold of the child's skirts. Anna snatched back her dress, and cried, in a little hysteria:

'No, you're not to undress me – I want my mother,' — and her child's face was running with grief and tears, her body shaken.

'Oh, but let Tilly undress you. Let Tilly undress you, who loves you, don't be wilful to-night. Mother's poorly, she doesn't want you to cry.'

The child sobbed distractedly, she could not hear.

'I want my mother,' she wept.

'When you're undressed, you s'll go up to see your mother – when you're undressed, pet, when you've let Tilly undress you, when you're a little jewel in your nightie, love. Oh, don't you cry, don't you—'

Brangwen sat stiff in his chair. He felt his brain going tighter. He crossed over the room, aware only of the maddening sobbing.

'Don't make a noise,' he said.

And a new fear shook the child from the sound of his voice. She cried mechanically, her eyes looking watchful through her tears, in terror, alert to what might happen.

'I want – my – mother,' quavered the sobbing, blind voice.

A shiver of irritation went over the man's limbs. It was the utter, persistent unreason, the maddening blindness of the voice and the crying.

'You must come and be undressed,' he said, in a quiet voice that was thin with anger.

And he reached his hand and grasped her. He felt her body catch in a convulsive sob. But he too was blind, and intent, irritated into mechanical action. He began to unfasten her little apron. She would have shrunk from him, but could not. So her small body remained in his grasp, while he fumbled at the little buttons and tapes, unthinking, intent, unaware of anything but the irritation of her. Her body was held taut and resistant, he pushed off the little dress and the petticoats, revealing the white arms. She kept stiff, overpowered, violated, he went on with his task. And all the while she sobbed, choking:

'I want my mother.'

He was unheedingly silent, his face stiff. The child was now incapable of understanding, she had become a little, mechanical thing of fixed will. She wept, her body convulsed, her voice repeating the same cry.

'Eh, dear o' me!' cried Tilly, becoming distracted herself. Brangwen, slow, clumsy, blind, intent, got off all the little garments, and stood the child naked in its shift upon the sofa.

'Where's her nightie?' he asked.

Tilly brought it, and he put it on her. Anna did not move her limbs to his desire. He had to push them into place. She stood, with fixed, blind will, resistant, a small, convulsed, unchangeable thing weeping ever and repeating the same phrase. He lifted one foot after the other, pulled off slippers and socks. She was ready.

'Do you want a drink?' he asked.

She did not change. Unheeding, uncaring, she stood on the sofa, standing back, alone, her hands shut and half lifted, her face, all tears, raised and blind. And through the sobbing and choking came the broken:

'I - want - my - mother.'

'Do you want a drink?' he said again.

There was no answer. He lifted the stiff, denying body between his hands. Its stiff blindness made a flash of rage go through him. He would like to break it.

He set the child on his knee, and sat again in his chair beside the fire, the wet, sobbing, inarticulate noise going on near his ear, the child sitting stiff, not yielding to him or anything, not aware.

A new degree of anger came over him. What did it all matter? What did it matter if the mother talked Polish and cried in labour, if this child were stiff with resistance, and crying? Why take it to heart? Let the mother cry in labour, let the child cry in resistance, since they would do so. Why should he fight against it, why resist? Let it be, if it were so. Let them be as they were, if they insisted.

And in a daze he sat, offering no fight. The child cried on, the minutes ticked away, a sort of torpor was on him.

It was some little time before he came to, and turned to attend to the child. He was shocked by her little wet, blinded face. A bit dazed, he pushed back the wet hair. Like a living statue of grief, her blind face cried on.

'Nay,' he said, 'not as bad as that. It's not as bad as that, Anna, my child. Come, what are you crying for so much? Come, stop now, it'll make you sick. I wipe you dry, don't wet your face any more. Don't cry any more wet tears, don't, it's better not to. Don't cry - it's not so bad as all that. Hush now, hush - let it be enough.'

His voice was queer and distant and calm. He looked at the child. She was beside herself now. He wanted her to stop, he wanted it all to stop, to become natural.

'Come,' he said, rising to turn away, 'we'll go an' supper-up the beast.'

He took a big shawl, folded her round, and went out into the kitchen for a lantern.

'You're never taking the child out, of a night like this,' said Tilly.

'Ay, it'll quieten her,' he answered.

It was raining. The child was suddenly still, shocked, finding the rain on its face, the darkness.

'We'll just give the cows their something-to-eat, afore they go to bed,' Brangwen was saying to her, holding her close and sure.

There was a trickling of water into the butt, a burst of rain-drops sputtering on to her shawl, and the light of the lantern swinging, flashing on a wet pavement and the base of a wet wall. Otherwise it was black darkness: one breathed darkness.

He opened the doors, upper and lower, and they entered into the high, dry barn, that smelled warm even if it were not warm. He hung the lantern on the nail and shut the door. They were in another world now. The light shed softly on the timbered barn, on the whitewashed walls, and the great heap of hay; instruments cast their shadows largely, a ladder rose to the dark arch of a loft. Outside there was the driving rain, inside, the softly-illuminated stillness and calmness of the barn.

Holding the child on one arm, he set about preparing the food for the cows, filling a pan with chopped hay and brewer's grains and a little meal. The child, all wonder, watched what he did. A new being was created in her for the new conditions. Sometimes, a little spasm, eddying from the bygone storm of sobbing, shook her small body. Her eyes were wide and wondering, pathetic. She was silent, quite still.

In a sort of dream, his heart sunk to the bottom, leaving the surface of him still, quite still, he rose with the panful of food, carefully balancing the child on one arm, the pan in the other hand. The silky fringe of the shawl swayed softly, grains and hay trickled to the floor; he went along a dimly-lit passage behind the mangers, where the horns of the cows pricked out of the obscurity. The child shrank, he balanced stiffly, rested the pan on the manger wall, and tipped out the food, half to this cow, half to the next. There was a noise of chains running, as the cows lifted or dropped their heads sharply; then a contented, soothing sound, a long snuffing as the beasts ate in silence.

The journey had to be performed several times. There was the rhythmic sound of the shovel in the barn, then the man returned walking stiffly between the two weights, the face of the child peering out from the shawl. Then the next time, as he stooped, she freed her arm and put it round his neck, clinging soft and warm, making all easier.

The beasts fed, he dropped the pan and sat down on a box, to arrange the child.

'Will the cows go to sleep now?' she said, catching her breath as she spoke.

'Yes.'

'Will they eat all their stuff up first?'

'Yes. Hark at them.'

And the two sat still listening to the snuffing and breathing of cows feeding in the sheds communicating with this small barn. The lantern shed a soft, steady light from one wall. All outside was still in the rain. He looked down at the silky folds of the paisley shawl. It reminded him of his mother. She used to go to church in it. He was back again in the old irresponsibility and security, a boy at home.

The two sat very quiet. His mind, in a sort of trance, seemed to become more and more vague. He held the child close to him. A quivering little shudder, re-echoing from her sobbing, went down her limbs. He held her closer. Gradually she relaxed, the eyelids began to sink over her dark, watchful eyes. As she sank to sleep, his mind became blank.

When he came to, as if from sleep, he seemed to be sitting in a timeless stillness. What was he listening for? He seemed to be listening for some sound a long way off, from beyond life. He remembered his wife. He must go back to her. The child was asleep, the eyelids not quite shut, showing a slight film of black pupil between. Why did she not shut her eyes? Her mouth was also a little open.

He rose quickly and went back to the house.

'Is she asleep?' whispered Tilly.

He nodded. The servant-woman came to look at the child who slept in the shawl, with cheeks flushed hot and red, and a whiteness, a wanness round the eyes.

'God-a-mercy!' whispered Tilly, shaking her head.

He pushed off his boots and went upstairs with the child. He became aware of the anxiety grasped tight at his heart, because of his wife. But he remained still. The house was silent save for the wind outside, and the noisy trickling and splattering of water in the water-butts. There was a slit of light under his wife's door.

He put the child into bed wrapped as she was in the shawl, for the sheets would be cold. Then he was afraid that she might not be able to move her arms, so he loosened her. The black eyes opened, rested on him vacantly, sank shut again. He covered her up. The last little quiver from the sobbing shook her breathing.

This was his room, the room he had had before he married. It was familiar. He remembered what it was to be a young man, untouched.

He remained suspended. The child slept, pushing her small fists from the shawl. He could tell the woman her child was asleep. But he must go to the other landing. He started. There was the sound of the owls – the moaning of the woman. What an uncanny sound! It was not human – at least to a man.

He went down to her room, entering softly. She was lying still, with eyes shut, pale, tired. His heart leapt, fearing she was dead. Yet he knew perfectly well she was not. He saw the way her hair went loose over her temples, her mouth was shut with suffering in a sort of grin. She was beautiful to him – but it was not human. He had a dread of her as she lay there. What had she to do with him? She was other than himself.

Something made him go and touch her fingers that were still grasped on the sheet. Her brown-grey eyes opened and looked at him. She did not know him as himself. But she knew him as the man. She looked at him as a woman in childbirth looks at the man who begot the child in her: an impersonal look, in the extreme hour, female to male. Her eyes closed again. A great, scalding peace went over him, burning his heart and his entrails, passing off into the infinite.

When her pains began afresh, tearing her, he turned aside, and could not look. But his heart in torture was at peace, his bowels were glad. He went downstairs, and to the door, outside, lifted his face to the rain, and felt the darkness striking unseen and steadily upon him.

The swift, unseen threshing of the night upon him silenced him and he was overcome. He turned away indoors, humbly. There was the infinite world, eternal, unchanging, as well as the world of life.

Chapter Three

Childhood of Anna Lensky

Tom Brangwen never loved his own son as he loved his step-child Anna. When they told him it was a boy, he had a thrill of pleasure. He liked the confirmation of fatherhood. It gave him satisfaction to know he had a son. But he felt not very much outgoing to the baby itself. He was its father, that was enough.

He was glad that his wife was mother of his child. She was serene, a little bit shadowy, as if she were transplanted. In the birth of the child she seemed to lose connection with her former self. She became now really English, really Mrs. Brangwen. Her vitality, however, seemed lowered.

She was still, to Brangwen, immeasurably beautiful. She was still passionate, with a flame of being. But the flame was not robust and present. Her eyes shone, her face glowed for him, but like some flower opened in the shade, that could not bear the full light. She loved the baby. But even this, with a sort of dimness, a faint absence about her, a shadowiness even in her mother-love. When Brangwen saw her nursing his child, happy, absorbed in it, a pain went over him like a thin flame. For he perceived how he must subdue himself in his approach to her. And he wanted again the robust, moral exchange of love and passion such as he had had at first with her, at one time and another, when they were matched at their highest intensity. This was the one experience for him now. And he wanted it, always, with remorseless craving.

She came to him again, with the same lifting of her mouth as had driven him almost mad with trammelled passion at first. She came to him again, and, his heart delirious in delight and readiness, he took her. And it was almost as before.

Perhaps it was quite as before. At any rate, it made him know perfection, it established in him a constant eternal knowledge.

But it died down before he wanted it to die down. She was finished, she could take no more. And he was not exhausted, he wanted to go on. But it could not be.

So he had to begin the bitter lesson, to abate himself, to take less than he wanted. For she was Woman to him, all other women were her shadows. For she had satisfied him. And he wanted it to go on. And it could not. However he raged, and, filled with suppression that became hot and bitter, hated her in his soul that she did not want him, however he had mad outbursts, and drank and made ugly scenes, still he knew, he was only kicking against the pricks. It was not, he had to learn, that she *would* not want him enough, as much as he demanded that she should want him. It was that she could not. She could only want him in her own way, and to her own measure. And she had spent much life before he found her as she was, the woman who could take him and give him fulfilment. She had taken him and given him fulfilment. She still could do so, in her own times and ways. But he must control himself, measure himself to her.

He wanted to give her all his love, all his passion, all his essential energy. But it could not be. He must find other things than her, other centres of living. She sat close and impregnable with the child. And he was jealous of the child.

But he loved her, and time came to give some sort of course to his troublesome current of life, so that it did not foam and flood and make misery. He formed another centre of love in her child, Anna. Gradually a part of his stream of life was diverted to the child, relieving the main flood to his wife. Also he sought the company of men, he drank heavily now and again.

The child ceased to have so much anxiety for her mother after the baby came. Seeing the mother with the baby boy, delighted and serene and secure, Anna was at first puzzled, then gradually she became indignant, and at last her little life settled on its own swivel, she was no more strained and distorted to support her mother. She became more childish, not so abnormal, not charged with cares she could not understand. The charge of the mother, the satisfying of the mother, had devolved elsewhere than on her. Gradually the child was freed. She became an independent, forgetful little soul, loving from her own centre.

Of her own choice, she then loved Brangwen most, or most obviously. For these two made a little life together, they had a joint activity. It amused him, at evening, to teach her to count, or to say her letters. He remembered for her all the little nursery rhymes and childish songs that lay forgotten at the bottom of his brain.

At first she thought them rubbish. But he laughed, and she laughed. They became to her a huge joke. Old King Cole she thought was Brangwen. Mother Hubbard was Tilly, her mother was the old woman who lived in a shoe. It was a huge, it was a frantic delight to the child, this nonsense, after her years with her mother, after the poignant folk-tales she had had from her mother, which always troubled and mystified her soul.

She shared a sort of recklessness with her father, a complete, chosen carelessness that had the laugh of ridicule in it. He loved to make her voice go high and shouting and defiant with laughter. The baby was dark-skinned and dark-haired, like the mother, and had hazel eyes. Brangwen called him the blackbird.

'Hallo,' Brangwen would cry, starting as he heard the wail of the child announcing it wanted to be taken out of the cradle, 'there's the blackbird tuning up.'

'The blackbird's singing,' Anna would shout with delight, 'the blackbird's singing.'

'When the pie was opened,' Brangwen shouted in his bawling bass voice, going over to the cradle, 'the bird began to sing.'

'Wasn't it a dainty dish to set before a king?' cried Anna, her eyes flashing with joy as she uttered the cryptic words, looking at Brangwen for confirmation. He sat down with the baby, saying loudly:

'Sing up, my lad, sing up.'

And the baby cried loudly, and Anna shouted lustily, dancing in wild bliss:

'Sing a song of sixpence
Pocketful of posies,
Ascha! Ascha!—'

Then she stopped suddenly in silence and looked at Brangwen again, her eyes flashing, as she shouted loudly and delightedly:

'I've got it wrong, I've got it wrong.'

'Oh, my sirs,' said Tilly entering, 'what a racket!'

Brangwen hushed the child and Anna flipped and danced on. She loved her wild bursts of rowdiness with her father. Tilly hated it, Mrs. Brangwen did not mind.

Anna did not care much for other children. She domineered them, she treated them as if they were extremely young and incapable, to her they were little people, they were not her equals. So she was mostly alone, flying round the farm, entertaining the farm-hands and Tilly and the servant-girl, whirring on and never ceasing.

She loved driving with Brangwen in the trap. Then, sitting high up and bowling along, her passion for eminence and dominance was satisfied. She was like a little savage in her arrogance. She thought her father important, she was installed beside him on high. And they spanked along, beside the high, flourishing hedge-tops, surveying the activity of the countryside. When people shouted a greeting to him from the road below, and Brangwen shouted jovially back, her little voice was soon heard shrilling along with his, followed by her chuckling laugh, when she looked up at her father with bright eyes, and they laughed at each other. And soon it was the custom for the passerby to sing out: 'How are ter, Tom? Well, my lady!' or else,

'Mornin', Tom, mornin', my Lass!' or else, 'You're off together then?' or else, 'You're lookin' rarely, you two.'

Anna would respond, with her father: 'How are you, John! *Good* mornin', William! Ay, makin' for Derby,' shrilling as loudly as she could. Though often, in response to 'You're off out a bit then,' she would reply, 'Yes, we are,' to the great joy of all. She did not like the people who saluted him and did not salute her.

She went into the public-house with him, if he had to call, and often sat beside him in the bar-parlour as he drank his beer or brandy. The landladies paid court to her, in the obsequious way landladies have.

'Well, little lady, an' what's your name?'

'Anna Brangwen,' came the immediate, haughty answer.

'Indeed it is! An' do you like driving in a trap with your father?'

'Yes,' said Anna, shy, but bored by these inanities. She had a touch-me-not way of blighting the inane inquiries of grown-up people.

'My word, she's a fawce little thing,' the landlady would say to Brangwen.

'Ay,' he answered, not encouraging comments on the child. Then there followed the present of a biscuit, or of cake, which Anna accepted as her dues.

'What does she say, that I'm a fawce little thing?' the small girl asked afterwards.

She means your're a sharp-shins.'

Anna hesitated. She did not understand. Then she laughed at some absurdity she found.

Soon he took her every week to market with him. 'I can come, can't I?' she asked every Saturday, or Thursday morning, when he made himself look fine in his dress of a gentleman farmer. And his face clouded at having to refuse her.

So at last, he overcame his own shyness, and tucked her beside him. They drove into Nottingham and put up at the 'Black Swan'. So far all right. Then he wanted to leave her at the inn. But he saw her face, and knew it was impossible. So he mustered his courage, and set off with her, holding her hand, to the cattle-market.

She stared in bewilderment, flitting silent at his side. But in the cattle-market she shrank from the press of men, all men, all in heavy, filthy boots, and leathern leggins. And the road underfoot was all nasty with cow-muck. And it frightened her to see the cattle in the square pens, so many horns, and so little enclosure, and such a madness of men and a yelling of drovers. Also she felt her father was embarrassed by her, and ill-at-ease.

He bought her a cake at the refreshment-booth, and set her on a seat. A man hailed him.

'*Good* morning, Tom. That thine, then?' – and the bearded farmer jerked his head at Anna.

'Ay,' said Brangwen, deprecating.

'I did-na know tha'd one that old.'

'No, it's my missis's.'

'Oh, that's it!' And the man looked at Anna as if she were some odd little cattle. She glowered with black eyes.

Brangwen left her there, in charge of the barman, whilst he went to see about the selling of some young stirks. Farmers, butchers, drovers, dirty, uncouth men from whom she shrank instinctively stared down at her as she sat on her seat, then went to get their drink, talking in unabated tones. All was big and violent about her.

'Whose child met that be?' they asked of the barman.

'It belongs to Tom Brangwen.'

The child sat on in neglect, watching the door for her father. He never came; many, many men came, but not he, and she sat like a shadow. She knew one did not cry in such a place. And every man looked at her inquisitively, she shut herself away from them.

A deep, gathering coldness of isolation took hold on her. He was never coming back. She sat on, frozen, unmoving.

When she had become blank and timeless he came, and she slipped off her seat to him, like one come back from the dead. He had sold his beast as quickly as he could. But all the business was not finished. He took her again through the hurtling welter of the cattle-market.

Then at last they turned and went out through the gate. He was always hailing one man or another, always stopping to gossip about land and cattle and horses and other things she did not understand, standing in the filth and the smell, among the legs and great boots of men. And always she heard the questions:

'What lass is that, then? I didn't know tha'd one o' that age.'

'It belongs to my missis.'

Anna was very conscious of her derivation from her mother, in the end, and of her alienation.

But at last they were away, and Brangwen went with her into a little dark, ancient eating-house in the Bridlesmith-Gate. They had cow's-tail soup, and meat and cabbage and potatoes. Other men, other people, came into the dark, vaulted place, to eat. Anna was wide-eyed and silent with wonder.

Then they went into the big market, into the corn exchange, then to shops. He bought her a little book off a stall. He loved buying things, odd things that he thought would be useful. Then they went to the 'Black Swan', and she drank milk and he brandy, and they harnessed the horse and drove off, up the Derby Road.

She was tired out with wonder and marvelling. But the next day, when she thought of it, she skipped, flipping her leg in the odd dance she did, and talked the whole time of what had happened to her, of what she had seen. It lasted her all the week. And the next Saturday she was eager to go again.

She became a familiar figure in the cattle-market, sitting waiting in the little booth. But she liked best to go to Derby. There her father had more friends. And she liked the familiarity of the smaller town, the nearness of the river, the strangeness that did not frighten her, it was so much smaller. She liked the covered-in market, and the old women. She liked the 'George Inn', where her father put up. The landlord was Brangwen's old friend, and Anna was made much of. She sat many a day in the cosy parlour talking to Mr. Wigginton, a fat man with red hair, the làndlord. And when the farmers all gathered at twelve o'clock for dinner, she was a little heroine.

At first she would only glower or hiss at these strange men with their uncouth accent. But they were good-humoured. She was a little oddity, with her fierce, fair hair like spun glass sticking out in a flamy halo round the apple-blossom face and the black eyes, and the men liked an oddity. She kindled their attention.

She was very angry because Marriott, a gentleman-farmer from Amber-gate, called her the little pole-cat.

'Why, you're a pole-cat,' he said to her.

'I'm not,' she flashed.

'You are. That's just how a pole-cat goes.'

She thought about it.

'Well, you're – you're—' she began.

'I'm what?'

She looked him up and down.

'You're a bow-leg man.'

Which he was. There was a roar of laughter. They loved her that she was indomitable.

'Ah,' said Marriott. 'Only a pole-cat says that.'

'Well, I *am* a pole-cat,' she flamed.

There was another roar of laughter from the men.

They loved to tease her.

'Well, me little maid,' Braithwaite would say to her, 'an' how's th' lamb's wool?'

He gave a tug at a glistening, pale piece of her hair.

'It's not lamb's wool,' said Anna, indignantly putting back her offended lock.

'Why, what'st ca' it then?'

'It's hair.'

'Hair! Wheriver dun they rear that sort?'

'Wheriver dun they?' she asked, in dialect, her curiosity overcoming her.

Instead of answering he shouted with joy. It was the triumph, to make her speak dialect.

She had one enemy, the man they called Nut-Nat, or Nat-Nut, a cretin, with inturned feet, who came flap-lapping along, shoulder jerking up at every step. This poor creature sold nuts in the public-houses where he was known. He had no roof to his mouth, and the men used to mock his speech.

The first time he came into the 'George' when Anna was there, she asked, after he had gone, her eyes very round:

'Why does he do that when he walks?'

' 'E canna 'elp 'isself, Duckie, it's th' make o' th' fellow.'

She thought about it, then she laughed nervously. And then she bethought herself, her cheeks flushed, and she cried:

'He's a *horrid* man.'

'Nay, he's non horrid; he canna help it if he wor struck that road.'

But when poor Nat came wambling in again, she slid away. And she would not eat his nuts, if the men bought them for her. And when the farmers gambled at dominoes for them, she was angry.

'They are dirty-man's nuts,' she cried.

So a revulsion started against Nat, who had not long after to go to the workhouse.

There grew in Brangwen's heart now a secret desire to make her a lady. His brother Alfred, in Nottingham, had caused a great scandal by becoming the lover of an educated woman, a lady, widow of a doctor. Very often, Alfred Brangwen went down as a friend to her cottage, which was in Derbyshire, leaving his wife and family for a day or two, then returning to them. And no-one dared gainsay him, for he was a strong-willed, direct man, and he said he was a friend of this widow.

One day Brangwen met his brother on the station.

'Where are *you* going to, then?' asked the younger brother.

'I'm going down to Wirksworth.'

'You've got friends down there, I'm told.'

'Yes.'

'I s'll have to be lookin' in when I'm down that road.'

'You please yourself.'

Tom Brangwen was so curious about the woman that the next time he was in Wirksworth he asked for her house.

He found a beautiful cottage on the steep side of a hill, looking clean over the town, that lay in the bottom of the basin, and away at the old quarries on the opposite side of the space. Mrs Forbes was in the garden. She was a tall woman with white hair. She came up the path taking off her thick gloves, laying down her shears. It was autumn. She wore a wide-brimmed hat.

Brangwen blushed to the roots of his hair, and did not know what to say.

'I thought I might look in,' he said, 'knowing you were friends of my brother's. I had to come to Wirksworth.'

She saw at once that he was a Brangwen.

'Will you come in?' she said. 'My father is lying down.'

She took him into a drawing-room, full of books, with a piano and a violin-stand. And they talked, she simply and easily. She was full of dignity. The room was of a kind Brangwen had never known; the atmosphere seemed open and spacious, like a mountain-top to him.

'Does my brother like reading?' he asked.

'Some things. He has been reading Herbert Spencer. And we read Browning sometimes.'

Brangwen was full of admiration, deep thrilling, almost reverential admiration. He looked at her with lit-up eyes when she said, 'we read'. At last he burst out, looking round the room:

'I didn't know our Alfred was this way inclined.'

'He is quite an unusual man.'

He looked at her in amazement. She evidently had a new idea of his brother: she evidently appreciated him. He looked again at the woman. She was about forty, straight, rather hard, a curious, separate creature. Himself, he was not in love with her, there was something chilling about her. But he was filled with boundless admiration.

At tea-time he was introduced to her father, an invalid who had to be helped about, but who was ruddy and well-favoured, with snowy hair and watery blue eyes, and a courtly naïve manner that again was new and strange to Brangwen so sauve, so merry, so innocent.

His brother was this woman's lover! It was too amazing. Brangwen went home despising himself for his own poor way of life. He was a clod-hopper and a boor, dull, stuck in the mud. More than ever he wanted to clamber out, to this visionary polite world.

He was well off. He was as well off as Alfred, who could not have above six hundred a year, all told. He himself made about four hundred, and could make more. His investments got better every day. Why did he not do something? His wife was a lady also.

But when he got to the Marsh, he realised how fixed everything was, how the other form of life was beyond him, and he regretted for the first time that he had succeeded to the farm. He felt a prisoner, sitting safe and easy and unadventurous. He might, with risk, have done more with himself. He could neither read Browning nor Herbert Spencer, nor have access to such a room as Mrs. Forbes's. All that form of life was outside him.

But then, he said he did not want it. The excitement of the visit began to pass off. The next day he was himself, and if he thought of the other woman, there was something about her and her place that he did not like, something cold something alien, as if she were not a woman, but an inhuman being who used up human life for cold, unliving purposes.

The evening came on, he played with Anna, and then sat alone with his own wife. She was sewing. He sat very still, smoking, perturbed. He was aware of his wife's quiet figure, and quiet dark head bent over her needle. It was too quiet for him. It was too peaceful. He wanted to smash the walls down, and let the night in, so that his wife should not be so secure and quiet, sitting there. He wished the air were not so close and narrow. His wife was obliterated from him, she was in her own world, quiet, secure, unnoticed, unnoticing. He was shut down by her.

He rose to go out. He could not sit still any longer. He must get out of this oppressive, shut-down, woman-haunt.

His wife lifted her head and looked at him.

'Are you going out?' she asked.

He looked down and met her eyes. They were darker than darkness, and gave deeper space. He felt himself retreating before her, defensive, whilst her eyes followed and tracked him down.

'I was just going up to Cossethay,' he said.

She remained watching him.

'Why do you go?' she said.

His heart beat fast, and he sat down, slowly.

'No reason particular,' he said, beginning to fill his pipe again, mechanically.

'Why do you go away so often,' she said.

'But you don't want me,' he replied.

She was silent for a while.

'You do not want to be with me any more,' she said.

It startled him. How did she know this truth? He thought it was his secret.

'Yi,' he said.

'You want to find something else,' she said.

He did not answer. 'Did he?' he asked himself.

'You should not want so much attention,' she said. 'You are not a baby.'

'I'm not grumbling,' he said. Yet he knew he was.

'You think you have not enough,' she said.

'How enough?'

'You think you have not enough in me. But how do you know me? What do you do to make me love you?'

He was flabbergasted.

'I never said I hadn't enough in you,' he replied. 'I didn't know you wanted making to love me. What do you want?'

'You don't make it good between us any more, you are not interested. You do not make me want you.'

'And you don't make me want *you*, do you now?' There was a silence. They were such strangers.

'Would you like to have another woman?' she asked.

His eyes grew round, he did not know where he was. How could she, his own wife, say such a thing? But she sat there, small and foreign and separate. It dawned upon him she did not consider herself his wife, except in so far as they agreed. She did not feel she had married him. At any rate, she was willing to allow he might want another woman. A gap, a space opened before him.

'No,' he said slowly. 'What other woman should I want?'

'Like your brother,' she said.

He was silent for some time, ashamed also.

'What of her?' he said. 'I didn't like the woman.'

'Yes, you liked her,' she answered persistently.

He stared in wonder at his own wife as she told him his own heart so callously. And he was indignant. What right had she to sit there telling him these things? She was his wife, what right had she to speak to him like this, as if she were a stranger.

'I didn't,' he said. 'I want no woman.'

'Yes, you would like to be like Alfred.'

His silence was one of angry frustration. He was astonished. He had told her of his visit to Wirksworth, but briefly, without interest, he thought.

As she sat with her strange dark face turned towards him, her eyes watched him, inscrutable, casting him up. He began to oppose her. She was again the active unknown facing him. Must he admit her? He resisted involuntarily.

'Why should you want to find a woman who is more to you than me?' she said.

The turbulence raged in his breast.

'I don't,' he said.

'Why do you?' she repeated. 'Why do you want to deny me?'

Suddenly, in a flash, he saw she might be lonely, isolated, unsure. She had seemed to him the utterly certain, satisfied, absolute, excluding him. Could she need anything?

'Why aren't you satisfied with me? – I'm not satisfied with you. Paul used to come to me and take me like a man does. You only leave me alone or take me like your cattle, quickly, to forget me again – so that you can forget me again.'

'What am I to remember about you?' said Brangwen.

'I want you to know there is somebody there besides yourself.'

'Well, don't I know it?'

'You come to me as if it was for nothing, as if I was nothing there. When Paul came to me, I *was* something to him – a woman, I was. To you I am nothing – it is like cattle – or nothing—'

'You make me feel as if *I* was nothing,' he said.

They were silent. She sat watching him. He could not move, his soul was seething and chaotic. She turned to her sewing again. But the sight of her bent before him held him and would not let him be. She was a strange, hostile, dominant thing. Yet not quite hostile. As he sat he felt his limbs were strong and hard, he sat in strength.

She was silent for a long time, stitching. He was aware, poignantly, of the round shape of her head, very intimate, compelling. She lifted her head and sighed. The blood burned in him, her voice ran to him like fire.

'Come here,' she said, unsure.

For some moments he did not move. Then he rose slowly and went across the hearth. It required an almost deathly effort of volition, or of acquiescence. He stood before her and looked down at her. Her face was shining again, her eyes were shining again like terrible laughter. It was to him terrible, how she could be transfigured. He could not look at her, it burnt his heart.

'My love!' she said.

And she put her arms round him as he stood before her, round his thighs. pressing him against her breast. And her hands on him seemed to reveal to him the mould of his own nakedness, he was passionately lovely to himself. He could not bear to look at her.

'My dear!' she said. He knew she spoke a foreign language. The fear was like bliss in his heart. He looked down. Her face was shining, her eyes were full of light, she was awful. He suffered from the compulsion to her. She was the awful unknown. He bent down to her, suffering, unable to let go, unable to let himself go, yet drawn, driven. She was now the transfigured, she was wonderful, beyond him. He wanted to go. But he could not as yet kiss her. He was himself apart. Easiest he could kiss her feet. But he was too ashamed for the actual deed, which were like an affront. She waited for him to meet her, not to bow before her and serve her. She wanted his active participation, not his submission. She put her fingers on him. And it was torture to him, that he must give himself to her actively, participate in her, that he must meet and embrace and know her, who was other than himself. There was that in him which shrank from yielding to her, resisted the relaxing towards her, opposed the mingling with her, even while he most desired it. He was afraid, he wanted to save himself.

There were a few moments of stillness. Then gradually, the tension, the withholding relaxed in him, and he began to flow towards her. She was beyond him, the unattainable. But he let go his hold on himself, he relinquished himself, and knew the subterranean force of his desire to come to her, to be with her, to mingle with her, losing himself to find her, to find himself in her. He began to approach her, to draw near.

His blood beat up in waves of desire. He wanted to come to her, to meet her. She was there, if he could reach her. The reality of her who was just beyond him absorbed him. Blind and destroyed, he pressed forward, nearer, nearer, to receive the consummation of himself, he received within the darkness which should swallow him and yield him up to himself. If he could come really within the blazing kernel of darkness, if really he could be destroyed, burnt away till he lit with her in one consummation, that were supreme, supreme.

Their coming together now, after two years of married life, was much more wonderful to them than it had been before. It was the entry into another circle of existence, it was the baptism to another life, it was the complete confirmation. Their feet trod strange ground of knowledge, their footsteps were lit-up with discovery. Wherever they walked, it was well, the world re-echoed round them in discovery. They went gladly and forgetful. Everything was lost, and everything was found. The new world was discovered, it remained only to be explored.

They had passed through the doorway into the further space, where movement was so big, that it contained bonds and constraints and labours, and still was complete liberty. She was the doorway to him, he to her. At last they had thrown open the doors, each to the other, and had stood in the doorways facing each other, whilst the light flooded out from behind on to each of their faces, it was the transfiguration, glorification, the admission.

And always the light of the transfiguration burned on in their hearts. He went his way, as before, she went her way, to the rest of the world there seemed no change. But to the two of them, there was the perpetual wonder of the transfiguration.

He did not know her any better, any more precisely, now that he knew her altogether. Poland, her husband, the war – he understood no more of this in her. He did not understand her foreign nature, half German, half Polish, nor her foreign speech. But he knew her, he knew her meaning, without understanding. What she said, what she spoke, this was a blind gesture on her part. In herself she walked strong and clear, he knew her, he saluted her, was with her. What was memory after all, but the recording of a number of possibilities which had never been fulfilled? What was Paul Lensky to her, but an unfulfilled possibility to which he, Brangwen, was the reality and the fulfilment? What did it matter, that Anna Lensky was born of Lydia and Paul? God was her father and her mother. He had passed through the married pair without fully making Himself known to them.

Now He was declared to Brangwen and to Lydia Brangwen, as they stood together. When at last they had joined hands, the house was finished, and the Lord took up his abode. And they were glad.

The days went on as before, Brangwen went out to his work, his wife nursed her child and attended in some measure to the farm. They did not think of each other – why should they? Only when she touched him, he knew her instantly, that she was with him, near him, that she was the gateway and the way out, that she was beyond, and that he was travelling in her through the beyond. Whither? – What does it matter? He responded always. When she called, he answered, when he asked, her response came at once, or at length.

Anna's soul was put at peace between them. She looked from one to the other, and she saw them established to her safety, and she was free. She played between the pillar of fire and the pillar of cloud in confidence, having the assurance on her right hand and the assurance on her left. She was no longer called upon to uphold with her childish might the broken end of the arch. Her father and her mother now met to the span of the heavens, and she, the child, was free to play in the space beneath, between.

Chapter Four

Girlhood of Anna Brangwen

When Anna was nine years old, Brangwen sent her to the dames' school in Cossethay. There she went, flipping and dancing in her inconsequential fashion, doing very much as she liked, disconcerting old Miss Coates by her indifference to respectability and by her lack of reverence. Anna only laughed at Miss Coates, liked her, and patronised her in superb, childish fashion.

The girl was at once shy and wild. She had a curious contempt for ordinary people, a benevolent superiority. She was very shy, and tortured with misery when people did not like her. On the other hand, she cared very little for anybody save her mother, whom she still rather resentfully worshipped, and her father, whom she loved and patronised, but upon whom she depended. These two, her mother and father, held her still in fee. But she was free of other people, towards whom, on the whole, she took the benevolent attitude. She deeply hated ugliness or intrusion or arrogance, however. As a child, she was as proud and shadowy as a tiger, and as aloof. She could confer favours, but, save from her mother and father, she could receive none. She hated people who came too near to her. Like a wild thing, she wanted her distance. She mistrusted intimacy.

In Cossethay and Ilkeston she was always an alien. She had plenty of acquaintances, but no friends. Very few people whom she met were significant to her. They seemed part of a herd, undistinguished. She did not take people very seriously.

She had two brothers, Tom, dark-haired, small, volatile, whom she was intimately related to but whom she never mingled with, and Fred, fair and responsive, whom she adored but did not consider as a real, separate thing. She was too much the centre of her own universe, too little aware of anything outside.

The first *person* she met, who affected her as a real, living person, whom she regarded as having definite existence, was Baron Skrebensky, her mother's friend. He also was a Polish exile, who had taken orders, and had received from Mr. Gladstone a small country living in Yorkshire.

When Anna was about ten years old, she went with her mother to spend a few days with the Baron Skrebensky. He was very unhappy in his red-brick vicarage. He was vicar of a country church, a living worth a little over two hundred pounds a year, but he had a large parish containing several collieries, with a new, raw, heathen population. He went to the north of England expecting homage from the common people, for he was an aristocrat. He was roughly, even cruelly received. But he never understood it. He remained a fiery aristocrat. Only he had to learn to avoid his parishioners.

Anna was very much impressed by him. He was a smallish man with a rugged, rather crumpled face and blue eyes set very deep and glowing. His wife was a tall, thin woman, of noble Polish family, mad with pride. He still spoke broken English, for he had kept very close to his wife, both of them forlorn in this strange, inhospitable country, and they always spoke in Polish together. He was disappointed with Mrs. Brangwen's soft, natural English, very disappointed that her child spoke no Polish.

Anna loved to watch him. She liked the big, new, rambling vicarage, desolate and stark on its hill. It was so exposed, so bleak and bold after the Marsh. The Baron talked endlessly in Polish to Mrs. Brangwen; he made furious gestures with his hands, his blue eyes were full of fire. And to Anna, there was a significance about his sharp, flinging movements. Something in her responded to his extravagance and his exuberant manner. She thought him a very wonderful person. She was shy of him, she liked him to talk to her. She felt a sense of freedom near him.

She never could tell how she knew it, but she did know that he was a knight of Malta. She could never remember whether she had seen his star, or cross, of his order or not, but it flashed in her mind, like a symbol. He at any rate represented to the child the real world, where kings and lords and princes moved and fulfilled their shining lives, whilst queens and ladies and princesses upheld the noble order.

She had recognised the Baron Skrebensky as a real person, he had had some regard for her. But when she did not see him any more, he faded and became a memory. But as a memory he was always alive to her.

Anna became a tall, awkward girl. Her eyes were still very dark and quick, but they had grown careless, they had lost their watchful, hostile look. Her fierce, spun hair turned brown, it grew heavier and was tied back. She was sent to a young ladies' school in Nottingham.

And at this period she was absorbed in becoming a young lady. She was intelligent enough, but not interested in learning. At first, she thought all the girls at school very ladylike and wonderful, and she wanted to be like them. She came to a speedy disillusion: they galled and maddened her, they were petty and mean. After the loose, generous atmosphere of her home, where little things did not count, she was always uneasy in the world, that would snap and bite at every trifle.

A quick change came over her. She mistrusted herself, she mistrusted the outer world. She did not want to go on, she did not want to go out into it, she wanted to go no further.

'What do *I* care about that lot of girls?' she would say to her father, contemptuously; 'they are nobody.'

The trouble was that the girls would not accept Anna at her measure. They would have her according to themselves or not at all. So she was confused, seduced, she became as they were for a time, and then, in revulsion, she hated them furiously.

'Why don't you ask some of your girls here?' her father would say.

'They're not coming here,' she cried.

'And why not?'

'They're bagatelle,' she said, using one of her mother's rare phrases.

'Bagatelles or billiards, it makes no matter, they're nice young lasses enough.'

But Anna was not to be won over. She had a curious shrinking from commonplace people, and particularly from the young lady of her day. She would not go into company because of the ill-at-ease feeling other people brought upon her. And she never could decide whether it were her fault or theirs. She half respected these other people, and continuous disillusion maddened her. She wanted to respect them. Still she thought the people she did not *know* were wonderful. Those she knew seemed always to be limiting her, tying her up in little falsities that irritated her beyond bearing. She would rather stay at home and avoid the rest of the world, leaving it illusory.

For at the Marsh life had indeed a certain freedom and largeness. There was no fret about money, no mean little precedence, nor care for what other people thought, because neither Mrs. Brangwen nor Brangwen could be sensible of any judgment passed on them from outside. Their lives were too separate.

So Anna was only easy at home, where the common sense and the supreme relation between her parents produced a freer standard of being than she could find outside. Where, outside the Marsh, could she find the tolerant dignity she had been brought up in? Her parents stood undiminished and unaware of criticism. The people she met outside seemed to begrudge her her very existence. They seemed to want to belittle her also. She was exceedingly reluctant to go amongst them. She depended upon her mother and her father. And yet she wanted to go out.

At school, or in the world, she was usually at fault, she felt usually that she ought to be slinking in disgrace. She never felt quite sure, in herself, whether she were wrong, or whether the others were wrong. She had not done her lessons: well, she did not see any reason why she *should* do her lessons, if she did not want to. Was there some occult reason why she should?

Were these people, schoolmistresses, representatives of some mystic Right, some Higher Good? They seemed to think so themselves. But she could not for her life see why a woman should bully and insult her because she did not know thirty lines of *As You Like It*. After all, *what* did it matter if she knew them or not? Nothing could persuade her that it was of the slightest importance. Because she despised inwardly the coarsely working nature of the mistress. Therefore she was always at outs with authority. From constant telling, she came almost to believe in her own badness, her own intrinsic inferiority. She felt that she ought always to be in a state of slinking disgrace, if she fulfilled what was expected of her. But she rebelled. She never really believed in her own badness. At the bottom of her heart she despised the other people, who carped and were loud over trifles. She despised them, and wanted revenge on them. She hated them whilst they had power over her.

Still she kept an ideal: a free, proud lady absolved from the petty ties, existing beyond petty considerations. She would see such ladies in pictures: Alexandra, Princess of Wales, was one of her models. This lady was proud and royal, and stepped indifferently over all small, mean desires: so thought Anna, in her heart. And the girl did up her hair high under a little slanting hat, her skirts were fashionably bunched up, she wore an elegant, skin-fitting coat.

Her father was delighted. Anna was very proud in her bearing, too naturally indifferent to smaller bonds to satisfy Ilkeston, which would have liked to put her down. But Brangwen was having no such thing. If she chose to be royal, royal she should be. He stood like a rock between her and the world.

After the fashion of his family, he grew stout and handsome. His blue eyes were full of light, twinkling and sensitive, his manner was deliberate, but hearty, warm. His capacity for living his own life without attention from his neighbours made them respect him. They would run to do anything for him. He did not consider them, but was open-handed towards them. so they made profit of their willingness. He liked people, so long as they remained in the background.

Mrs. Brangwen went on in her own way, following her own devices. She had her husband, her two sons and Anna. These staked out and marked her horizon. The other people were outsiders. Inside her own world, her life passed along like a dream for her, it lapsed, and she lived within its lapse, active and always pleased, intent. She scarcely noticed the outer things at all. What was outside was outside, non-existent. She did not mind if the boys fought, so long as it was out of her presence. But if they fought when she was by, she was angry, and they were afraid of her. She did not care if they broke a window of a railway carriage or sold their watches to have a revel at the Goose Fair. Brangwen was perhaps angry over these things. To the mother they were insignificant. It was odd little things that offended her. She was furious if the boys hung around the slaughter-house, she was displeased when the school reports were bad. It did not matter how many sins her boys were accused of, so long as they were not stupid, or inferior. If they seemed to brook insult, she hated them. And it was only a certain *gaucherie*, a gawkiness on Anna's part that irritated her against the girl.

Certain forms of clumsiness, grossness, made the mother's eyes glow with curious rage. Otherwise she was pleased, indifferent.

Pursuing her splendid-lady ideal, Anna became a lofty demoiselle of sixteen, plagued by family shortcomings. She was very sensitive to her father. She knew if he had been drinking, were he ever so little affected, and she could not bear it. He flushed when he drank, the veins stood out on his temples, there was a twinkling, cavalier boisterousness in his eye, his manner was jovially overbearing and mocking. And it angered her. When she heard his loud, roaring, boisterous mockery, an anger of resentment filled her. She was quick to forestall him, the moment he came in.

'You look a sight, you do, red in the face,' she cried.

'I might look worse if I was green,' he answered.

'Boozing in Ilkeston.'

'And what's wrong wi' Il'son?'

She flounced away. He watched her with amused, twinkling eyes, yet in spite of himself said that she flouted him.

They were a curious family, a law to themselves, separate from the world, isolated, a small republic set in invisible bounds. The mother was quite indifferent to Ilkeston and Cossethay, to any claims made on her from outside, she was very shy of any outsider, exceedingly courteous, winning even. But the moment the visitor had gone, she laughed and dismissed him, he did not exist. It had been all a game to her. She was still a foreigner, unsure of her ground. But alone with her own children and husband at the Marsh, she was mistress of a little native land that lacked nothing.

She had some beliefs somewhere, never defined. She had been brought up a Roman Catholic. She had gone to the Church of England for protection. The outward form was a matter of indifference to her. Yet she had some fundamental religion. It was as if she worshipped God as a mystery, never seeking in the least to define what He was.

And inside her, the subtle sense of the Great Absolute wherein she had her being was very strong. The English dogma never reached her: the language was too foreign. Through it all she felt the great Separator who held life in His hands, gleaming, imminent, terrible, the Great Mystery, immediate beyond all telling.

She shone and gleamed to the Mystery, Whom she knew through all her senses, she glanced with strange, mystic superstitions that never found expression in the English language, never mounted to thought in English. But so she lived, within a potent, sensuous belief that included her family and contained her destiny.

To this she had reduced her husband. He existed with her entirely indifferent to the general values of the world. Her very ways, the very mark of her eyebrows were symbols and indication to him. There, on the farm with her, he lived through a mystery of life and death and creation, strange, profound ecstasies and incommunicable satisfactions, of which the rest of the world knew nothing; which made the pair of them apart and respected in the English village, for they were also well-to-do.

But Anna was only half safe within her mother's unthinking knowledge. She had a mother-of-pearl rosary that had been her own father's. What it meant to her she could never say. But the string of moonlight and silver, when she had it between her fingers, filled her with strange passion. She learned at school a little Latin, she learned an Ave Maria and a Pater Noster, she learned how to say her rosary. But that was no good. 'Ave Maria, gratia plena, Dominus tecum, Benedicta tu in mulieribus et benedictus fructus ventris tui Jesus. Ave Maria, Sancta Maria, ora pro nobis peccatoribus, nunc et in hora mortis nostrae, Amen.'

It was not right, somehow. What these words meant when translated was not the same as the pale rosary meant. There was a discrepancy, a falsehood. It irritated her to say, 'Dominus tecum,' or, 'benedicta tu in mulieribus.' She loved the mystic words, 'Ave Maria, Sancta Maria;' she was moved by 'benedictus fructus ventris tui Jesus,' and by 'nunc et in hora mortis nostrae.' But none of it was quite real. It was not satisfactory, somehow.

She avoided her rosary, because, moving her with curious passion as it did, it *meant* only these not very significant things. She put it away. It was her instinct to put all these things away. It was her instinct to avoid thinking, to avoid it, to save herself.

She was seventeen, touchy, full of spirits, and very moody: quick to flush, and always uneasy, uncertain. For some reason or other, she turned more to her father, she felt almost flashes of hatred for her mother. Her mother's dark muzzle and curiously insidious ways, her mother's utter surety and confidence, her strange satisfaction, even triumph, her mother's way of laughing at things and her mother's silent overriding of vexatious propositions, most of all her mother's triumphant power maddened the girl.

She became sudden and incalculable. Often she stood at the window, looking out, as if she wanted to go. Sometimes she went, she mixed with people. But always she came home in anger, as if she were diminished, belittled, almost degraded.

There was over the house a kind of dark silence and intensity, in which passion worked its inevitable conclusions. There was in the house a sort of richness, a deep, inarticulate interchange which made other places seem thin and unsatisfying. Brangwen could sit silent, smoking in his chair, the mother could move about in her quiet, insidious way, and the sense of the two presences was powerful, sustaining. The whole intercourse was wordless, intense and close.

But Anna was uneasy. She wanted to get away. Yet wherever she went, there came upon her that feeling of thinness, as if she were made smaller, belittled. She hastened home.

There she raged and interrupted the strong, settled interchange. Sometimes her mother turned on her with a fierce, destructive anger, in which was no pity or consideration. And Anna shrank, afraid. She went to her father.

He would still listen to the spoken word, which fell sterile on the unheeding mother. Sometimes Anna talked to her father. She tried to discuss people, she wanted to know what was meant. But her father became uneasy. He did not want to have things dragged into consciousness. Only out of consideration for her he listened. And there was a kind of bristling rousedness in the room. The cat got up and stretching itself, went uneasily to the door. Mrs. Brangwen was silent, she seemed ominous. Anna could not go on with her fault-finding, her criticism, her expression of dissatisfactions. She felt even her father against her. He had a strong, dark bond with her mother, a potent intimacy that existed inarticulate and wild, following its own course, and savage if interrupted, uncovered.

Nevertheless Brangwen was uneasy about the girl, the whole house continued to be disturbed. She had a pathetic, baffled appeal. She was hostile to her parents, even whilst she lived entirely with them, within their spell.

Many ways she tried, of escape. She became an assiduous church-goer. But the *language* meant nothing to her: it seemed false. She hated to hear things expressed, put into words. Whilst the religious feelings were inside her they were passionately moving. In the mouth of the clergyman, they were false, indecent. She tried to read. But again the tedium and the sense of the falsity of the spoken word put her off. She went to stay with girl friends. At first she thought it splendid. But then the inner boredom came on, it seemed to her all nothingness. And she felt always belittled, as if never, never could she stretch her length and stride her stride.

Her mind reverted often to the torture cell of a certain Bishop of France, in which the victim could neither stand nor lie stretched out, never. Not that she thought of herself in any connection with this. But often there came into her mind the wonder, how the cell was built, and she could feel the horror of the crampedness, as something very real.

She was, however, only eighteen when a letter came from Mrs. Alfred Brangwen, in Nottingham, saying that her son William was coming to Ilkeston to take a place as junior draughtsman, scarcely more than apprentice, in a lace factory. He was twenty years old, and would the Marsh Brangwens be friendly with him.

Tom Brangwen at once wrote offering the young man a home at the Marsh. This was not accepted, but the Nottingham Brangwens expressed gratitude.

There had never been much love lost between the Nottingham Brangwens and the Marsh. Indeed, Mrs. Alfred, having inherited three thousand pounds, and having occasion to be dissatisfied with her husband, held aloof from all the Brangwens whatsoever. She affected, however, some esteem of Mrs. Tom, as she called the Polish woman, saying that at any rate she was a lady.

Anna Brangwen was faintly excited at the news of her Cousin Will's coming to Ilkeston. She knew plenty of young men, but they had never become real to her. She had seen in this young gallant a nose she liked, in that a pleasant moustache, in the other a nice way of wearing clothes, in one a ridiculous fringe of hair, in another a comical way of talking. They were objects of amusement and faint wonder to her, rather than real beings, the young men.

The only man she knew was her father; and, as he was something large, looming, a kind of Godhead, he embraced all manhood for her, and other men were just incidental.

She remembered her cousin Will. He had town clothes and was thin, with a very curious head, black as jet, with hair like sleek, thin fur. It was a curious head: it reminded her she knew not of what: of some animal, some mysterious animal that lived in the darkness under the leaves and never came out, but which lived vividly, swift and intense. She always thought of him with that black, keen, blind head. And she considered him odd.

He appeared at the Marsh one Sunday morning: a rather long, thin youth with a bright face and a curious self-possession among his shyness, a native unawareness of what other people might be, since he was himself.

When Anna came downstairs in her Sunday clothes, ready for church, he rose and greeted her conventionally, shaking hands. His manners were better than hers. She flushed. She noticed that he now had a thick fledge on his upper lip, a black, finely-shapen line marking his wide mouth. It rather repelled her. It reminded her of the thin, fine fur of his hair. She was aware of something strange in him.

His voice had rather high upper notes, and very resonant middle notes. It was queer. She wondered why he did it. But he sat very naturally in the Marsh living-room. He had some uncouthness, some natural self-possession of the Brangwens, that made him at home there.

Anna was rather troubled by the strange intimate, affectionate way her father had towards this young man. He seemed gentle towards him, he put himself aside in order to fill out the young man. This irritated Anna.

'Father,' she said abruptly, 'give me some collection.'

'What collection?' asked Brangwen.

'Don't be ridiculous,' she cried, flushing.

'Nay,' he said, 'what collection's this?'

'You know it's the first Sunday of the month.'

Anna stood confused. Why was he doing this, why was he making her conspicuous before this stranger?

'I want some collection,' she reasserted.

'So tha says,' he replied indifferently, looking at her, then turning again to this nephew.

She went forward, and thrust her hand into his breeches pocket. He smoked steadily, making no resistance, talking to his nephew. Her hand groped about in his pocket, and then drew out his leathern purse. Her colour was bright in her clear cheeks, her eyes shone. Brangwen's eyes were twinkling. The nephew sat sheepishly. Anna, in her finery, sat down and slid all the money into her lap. There was silver and gold. The youth could not help watching her. She was bent over the heap of money, fingering the different coins.

'I've a good mind to take half a sovereign,' she said, and she looked up with glowing dark eyes. She met the light-brown eyes of her cousin, close and intent upon her. She was startled. She laughed quickly, and turned to her father.

'I've a good mind to take half a sovereign, our Dad,' she said.

'Yes, nimble fingers,' said her father. 'You take what's your own.'

'Are you coming, our Anna?' asked her brother from the door.

She suddenly chilled to normal, forgetting both her father and her cousin.

'Yes, I'm ready,' she said, taking sixpence from the heap of money and sliding the rest back into the purse, which she laid on the table.

'Give it here,' said her father.

Hastily she thrust the purse into his pocket and was going out.

'You'd better go wi' 'em, lad, hadn't you?' said the father to the nephew.

Will Brangwen rose uncertainly. He had golden-brown, quick, steady eyes, like a bird's, like a hawk's, which cannot look afraid.

'Your Cousin Will'll come with you,' said the father.

Anna glanced at the strange youth again. She felt him waiting there for her to notice him. He was hovering on the edge of her consciousness, ready to come in. She did not want to look at him. She was antagonistic to him.

She waited without speaking. Her cousin took his hat and joined her. It was summer outside. Her brother Fred was plucking a sprig of flowery currant to put in his coat, from the bush at the angle of the house. She took no notice. Her cousin followed just behind her.

They were on the high road. She was aware of a strangeness in her being. It made her uncertain. She caught sight of the flowering currant in her brother's buttonhole.

'Oh, our Fred,' she cried. 'Don't wear that stuff to go to church.'

Fred looked down protectively at the pink adornment on his breast.

'Why, I like it,' he said.

'Then you're the only one who does, I'm sure,' she said.

And she turned to her cousin.

'Do *you* like the smell of it?' she asked.

He was there beside her, tall and uncouth and yet self-possessed. It excited her.

'I can't say whether I do or not,' he replied.

'Give it here, Fred, don't have it smelling in church,' she said to the little boy, her page.

Her fair, small brother handed her the flower dutifully. She sniffed it and gave it without a word to her cousin, for his judgment. He smelled the dangling flower curiously.

'It's a funny smell,' he said.

And suddenly she laughed, and a quick light came on all their faces, there was a blithe trip in the small boy's walk.

The bells were ringing, they were going up the summery hill in their Sunday clothes. Anna was very fine in a silk frock of brown and white stripes, tight along the arms and the body, bunched up very elegantly behind the skirt. There was something of the cavalier about Will Brangwen, and he was well dressed.

He walked along with the sprig of currant-blossom dangling between his fingers, and none of them spoke. The sun shone brightly on little showers of buttercup down the bank, in the fields the fool's-parsley was foamy, held very high and proud above a number of flowers that flitted in the greenish twilight of the mowing-grass below.

They reached the church. Fred led the way to the pew, followed by the cousin, then Anna. She felt very conspicuous and important. Somehow, this young man gave her away to other people. He stood aside and let her pass to her place, then sat next to her. It was a curious sensation, to sit next to him.

The colour came streaming from the painted window above her. It lit on the dark wood of the pew, on the stone, worn aisle, on the pillar behind her cousin, and on her cousin's hands, as they lay on his knees. She sat amid illumination, illumination and luminous shadow all around her, her soul very bright. She sat, without knowing it, conscious of the hands and motionless knees of her cousin. Something strange had entered into her world, something entirely strange and unlike what she knew.

She was curiously elated. She sat in a glowing world of unreality, very delightful. A brooding light, like laughter, was in her eyes. She was aware of a strange influence entering in to her, which she enjoyed. It was a dark enrichening influence she had not known before. She did not think of her cousin. But she was startled when his hands moved.

She wished he would not say the responses so plainly. It diverted her from her vague enjoyment. Why would he obtrude, and draw notice to himself? It was bad taste. But she went on all right till the hymn came. He stood up beside her to sing, and that pleased her. Then suddenly, at the very first word, his voice came strong and over-riding, filling the church. He was singing the tenor. Her soul opened in amazement. His voice filled the church! It rang out like a trumpet, and rang out again. She started to giggle over her hymn-book. But he went on, perfectly steady. Up and down rang his voice, going its own way. She was helplessly shocked into laughter. Between moments of dead silence in herself she shook with laughter. On came the laughter, seized her and shook her till the tears were in her eyes. She was amazed, and rather enjoyed it. And still the hymn rolled on, and still she laughed. She bent over her hymn-book crimson with confusion, but still her sides shook with laughter. She pretended to cough, she pretended to have a crumb in her throat. Fred was gazing up at her with clear blue eyes. She was recovering herself. And then a slur in the strong, blind voice at her side brought it all on again, in a gust of mad laughter.

She bent down to prayer in cold reproof of herself. And yet, as she knelt, little eddies of giggling went over her. The very sight of his knees on the praying cushion sent the little shock of laughter over her.

She gathered herself together and sat with prim, pure face, white and pink and cold as a christmas rose, her hands in her silk gloves folded on her lap, her dark eyes all vague, abstracted in a sort of dream, oblivious of everything.

The sermon rolled on vaguely, in a tide of pregnant peace.

Her cousin took out his pocket-handkerchief. He seemed to be drifted absorbed into the sermon. He put his handkerchief to his face. Then something dropped on to his knee. There lay the bit of flowering currant! He was looking down at it in real astonishment. A wild snort of laughter came from Anna. Everybody heard: it was torture. He had shut the crumpled flower in his hand and was looking up again with the same absorbed attention to the sermon. Another snort of laughter from Anna. Fred nudged her remindingly. Her cousin sat motionless. Somehow he was aware that his face was red. She could feel him. His hand, closed over the flower, remained quite still, pretending to be normal. Another wild struggle in Anna's breast, and the snort of laughter. She bent forward shaking with laughter. It was now no joke. Fred was nudge-nudging at her. She nudged him back fiercely. Then another vicious spasm of laughter seized her. She tried to ward it off in a little cough. The cough ended in a suppressed whoop. She wanted to die. And the closed hand crept away to the pocket. Whilst she sat in taut suspense, the laughter rushed back at her, knowing he was fumbling in his pocket to shove the flower away.

In the end, she felt weak, exhausted and thoroughly depressed. A blankness of wincing depression came over her. She hated the presence of the other people. Her face became quite haughty. She was unaware of her cousin any more.

When the collection arrived with the last hymn, her cousin was again singing resoundingly. And still it amused her. In spite of the shameful exhibition she had made of herself, it amused her still. She listened to it in a spell of amusement. And the bag was thrust in front of her, and her sixpence was mingled in the folds of her glove. In her haste to get it out, it flipped away and went twinkling in the next pew. She stood and giggled. She could not help it: she laughed outright, a figure of shame.

'What were you laughing about, our Anna?' asked Fred, the moment they were out of the church.

'Oh, I couldn't help it,' she said, in her careless, half-mocking fashion. 'I don't know *why* Cousin Will's singing set me off.'

'What was there in my singing to make you laugh?' he asked.

'It was so loud,' she said.

They did not look at each other, but they both laughed again, both reddening.

'What were you snorting and laughing for, our Anna?' asked Tom, the elder brother, at the dinner table, his hazel eyes bright with joy. 'Everybody stopped to look at you.' Tom was in the choir.

She was aware of Will's eyes shining steadily upon her, waiting for her to speak.

'It was Cousin Will's singing,' she said.

At which her cousin burst into a suppressed, chuckling laugh, suddenly showing all his small, regular, rather sharp teeth, and just as quickly closing his mouth again.

'Has he got such a remarkable voice on him then?' asked Brangwen.

'No, it's not that,' said Anna. 'Only it tickled me – I couldn't tell you why.'

And again a ripple of laughter went down the table.

Will Brangwen thrust forward his dark face, his eyes dancing, and said: 'I'm in the choir of St Nicholas.'

'Oh, you go to church then!' said Brangwen.

'Mother does – father doesn't,' replied the youth.

It was the little things, his movement, the funny tones of his voice, that showed up big to Anna. The matter-of-fact things he said were absurd in contrast. The things her father said seemed meaningless and neutral.

During the afternoon they sat in the parlour, that smelled of geranium, and they ate cherries, and talked. Will Brangwen was called on to give himself forth. And soon he was drawn out.

He was interested in churches, in church architecture. The influence of Ruskin had stimulated him to a pleasure in the medieval forms. His talk was fragmentary, he was only half articulate. But listening to him, as he spoke of church after church, of nave and chancel and transept, of rood-screen and font, of hatchet-carving and moulding and tracery, speaking always with close passion of particular things, particular places, there gathered in her heart a pregnant hush of churches, a mystery, a ponderous significance of bowed stone, a dim-coloured light through which something took place obscurely, passing into darkness: a high, delighted framework of the mystic screen, and beyond, in the furthest beyond, the altar. It was a very real experience. She was carried away. And the land seemed to be covered with a vast, mystic church, reserved in gloom, thrilled with an unknown Presence.

Almost it hurt her, to look out of the window and see the lilacs towering in the vivid sunshine. Or was this the jewelled glass?

He talked of Gothic and Renaissance and Perpendicular, and Early English and Norman. The words thrilled her.

'Have you been to Southwell?' he said. 'I was there at twelve o'clock at midday, eating my lunch in the churchyard. And the bells played a hymn.

'Ay, it's a fine Minster, Southwell, heavy. It's got heavy, round arches, rather low, on thick pillars. It's grand, the way those arches travel forward.

'There's a sedilia as well – pretty. But I like the main body of the church – and that north porch—'

He was very much excited and filled with himself that afternoon. A flame kindled round him, making his experience passionate and glowing, burningly real.

His uncle listened with twinkling eyes, half-moved. His aunt bent forward her dark face, half-moved, but held by other knowledge. Anna went with him.

He returned to his lodging at night treading quick, his eyes glittering, and his face shining darkly as if he came from some passionate, vital tryst.

The glow remained in him, the fire burned, his heart was fierce like a sun. He enjoyed his unknown life and his own self. And he was ready to go back to the Marsh.

Without knowing it, Anna was wanting him to come. In him she had escaped. In him the bounds of her experience were transgressed: he was the hole in the wall, beyond which the sunshine blazed on an outside world.

He came. Sometimes, not often, but sometimes, talking again, there recurred the strange, remote reality which carried everything before it. Sometimes, he talked of his father, whom he hated with a hatred that was burningly close to love, of his mother, whom he loved, with a love that was keenly close to hatred, or to revolt. His sentences were clumsy, he was only half articulate. But he had the wonderful voice, that could ring its vibration through the girl's soul, transport her into his feeling. Sometimes his voice was hot and declamatory, sometimes it had a strange, twanging, almost cat-like sound, sometimes it hesitated, puzzled, sometimes there was the break of a little laugh. Anna was taken by him. She loved the running flame that coursed through her as she listened to him. And his mother and his father became to her two separate people in her life.

For some weeks the youth came frequently, and was received gladly by them all. He sat amongst them, his dark face glowing, an eagerness and a touch of derisiveness on his wide mouth, something grinning and twisted, his eyes always shining like a bird's, utterly without depth. There was no getting hold of the fellow, Brangwen irritably thought. He was like a grinning young tom-cat, that came when he thought he would, and without cognisance of the other person.

At first the youth had looked towards Tom Brangwen when he talked; and then he looked towards his aunt, for her appreciation, valuing it more than his uncle's; and then he turned to Anna, because from her he got what he wanted, which was not in the elder people.

So that the two young people, from being always attendant on the elder, began to draw apart and establish a separate kingdom. Sometimes Tom Brangwen was irritated. His nephew irritated him. The lad seemed to him too special, self-contained. His nature was fierce enough, but too much abstracted, like a separate thing, like a cat's nature. A cat could lie perfectly peacefully on the hearthrug whilst its master or mistress writhed in agony a yard away. It had nothing to do with other people's affairs. What did the lad really care about anything, save his own instinctive affairs?

Brangwen was irritated. Nevertheless he liked and respected his nephew. Mrs. Brangwen was irritated by Anna, who was suddenly changed, under the influence of the youth. The mother liked the boy: he was not quite an outsider. But she did not like her daughter to be so much under the spell.

So that gradually the two young people drew apart, escaped from the elders, to create a new thing by themselves. He worked in the garden to propitiate his uncle. He talked churches to propitiate his aunt. He followed Anna like a shadow: like a long, persistent, unswerving black shadow he went after the girl. It irritated Brangwen exceedingly. It exasperated him beyond bearing, to see the lit-up grin, the cat-grin as he called it, on his nephew's face.

And Anna had a new reserve, a new independence. Suddenly she began to act independently of her parents, to live beyond them. Her mother had flashes of anger.

But the courtship went on. Anna would find occasion to go shopping in Ilkeston at evening. She always returned with her cousin; he walking with his head over her shoulder, a little bit behind her, like the Devil looking over Lincoln, as Brangwen noted angrily and yet with satisfaction.

To his own wonder, Will Brangwen found himself in an electric state of passion. To his wonder, he had stopped her at the gate as they came home from Ilkeston one night, and had kissed her, blocking her way and kissing her whilst he felt as if some blow were struck at him in the dark. And when they went indoors, he was acutely angry that her parents looked up scrutinisingly at him and her. What right had they there: why should they look up! Let them remove themselves, or look elsewhere.

And the youth went home with the stars in heaven whirling fiercely about the blackness of his head, and his heart fierce, insistent, but fierce as if he felt something baulking him. He wanted to smash through something.

A spell was cast over her. And how uneasy her parents were, as she went about the house unnoticing, not noticing them, moving in a spell as if she were invisible to them. She *was* invisible to them. It made them angry. Yet they had to submit. She went about absorbed, obscured for a while.

Over him too the darkness of obscurity settled. He seemed to be hidden in a tense, electric darkness, in which his soul, his life was intensely active, but without his aid or attention. His mind was obscured. He worked swiftly and mechanically, and he produced some beautiful things.

His favourite work was wood-carving. The first thing he made for her was a butter-stamper. In it he carved a mythological bird, a phoenix, something like an eagle, rising on symmetrical wings, from a circle of very beautiful flickering flames that rose upwards from the rim of the cup.

Anna thought nothing of the gift on the evening when he gave it to her. In the morning, however, when the butter was made, she fetched his seal in place of the old wooden stamper of oak-leaves and acorns. She was curiously excited to see how it would turn out. Strange, the uncouth bird moulded there, in the cup-like hollow, with curious, thick waverings running inwards from a smooth rim. She pressed another mould. Strange, to lift the stamp and see that eagle-beaked bird raising its breast to her. She loved creating it over and over again. And every time she looked, it seemed a new thing come to life. Every piece of butter became this strange, vital emblem.

She showed it to her mother and father.

'That is beautiful,' said her mother, a little light coming on to her face.

'Beautiful!' exclaimed the father, puzzled, fretted. 'Why, what sort of a bird does he call it?'

And this was the question put by the customers during the next weeks.

'What sort of a bird do you call *that*, as you've got on th' butter?'

When he came in the evening, she took him into the dairy to show him.

'Do you like it?' he asked, in his loud, vibrating voice that always sounded strange, re-echoing in the dark places of her being.

They very rarely touched each other. They liked to be alone together, near to each other, but there was still a distance between them.

In the cool dairy the candle-light lit on the large, white surfaces of the cream pans. He turned his head sharply. It was so cool and remote in there, so remote. His mouth was open in a little, strained laugh. She stood with her head bent, turned aside. He wanted to go near to her. He had kissed her once. Again his eye rested on the round blocks of butter, where the emblematic bird lifted its breast from the shadow cast by the candle flame. What was restraining him? Her breast was near him; his head lifted like an eagle's. She did not move. Suddenly, with an incredibly quick, delicate movement, he put his arms round her and drew her to him. It was quick, cleanly done, like a bird that swoops and sinks close, closer.

He was kissing her throat. She turned and looked at him. Her eyes were dark and flowing with fire. His eyes were hard and bright with a fierce purpose and gladness, like a hawk's. She felt him flying into the dark space of her flames, like a brand, like a gleaming hawk.

They had looked at each other, and seen each other strange, yet near, very near, like a hawk stooping, swooping, dropping into a flame of darkness. So she took the candle and they went back to the kitchen.

They went on in this way for some time, always coming together, but rarely touching, very seldom did they kiss. And then, often, it was merely a touch of the lips, a sign. But her eyes began to waken with a constant fire, she paused often in the midst of her transit, as if to recollect something, or to discover something.

And his face became sombre, intent, he did not really hear what was said to him.

One evening in August he came when it was raining. He came in with his jacket collar turned up, his jacket buttoned close, his face wet. And he looked so slim and definite, coming out of the chill rain, she was suddenly blinded with love for him. Yet he sat and talked with her father and mother, meaninglessly, whilst her blood seethed to anguish in her. She wanted to touch him now, only to touch him.

There was the queer, abstract look on her silvery radiant face that maddened her father, her dark eyes were hidden. But she raised them to the youth. And they were dark with a flare that made him quail for a moment.

She went into the second kitchen and took a lantern. Her father watched her as she returned.

'Come with me, Will,' she said to her cousin. 'I want to see if I put the brick over where that rat comes in.'

'You've no need to do that,' retorted her father. She took no notice. The youth was between the two wills. The colour mounted into the father's face, his blue eyes stared. The girl stood near the door, her head held slightly back, like an indication that the youth must come. He rose, in his silent, intent way, and was gone with her. The blood swelled in Brangwen's forehead veins.

It was raining. The light of the lantern flashed on the cobbled path and the bottom of the wall. She came to a small ladder, and climbed up. He reached her the lantern, and followed. Up there in the fowl-loft, the birds sat in fat bunches on the perches, the red combs shining like fire. Bright, sharp eyes opened. There was a sharp crawk of expostulation as one of the hens shifted over. The cock sat watching, his yellow neck-feathers bright as glass. Anna went across the dirty floor. Brangwen crouched in the loft watching. The light was soft under the red, naked tiles. The girl crouched in a corner. There was another explosive bustle of a hen springing from her perch.

Anna came back, stooping under the perches. He was waiting for her near the door. Suddenly she had her arms round him, was clinging close to him, cleaving her body against his, and crying, in a whispering, whimpering sound.

'Will, I love you, I love you, Will, I love you.' It sounded as if it were tearing her.

He was not even very much surprised. He held her in his arms, and his bones melted. He leaned back against the wall. The door of the loft was open. Outside, the rain slanted by in fine, steely, mysterious haste, emerging out of the gulf of darkness. He held her in his arms, and he and she together seemed to be swinging in big, swooping oscillations, the two of them clasped together up in the darkness. Outside the open door of the loft in which they stood, beyond them and below them, was darkness, with a travelling veil of rain.

'I love you, Will, I love you,' she moaned, 'I love you, Will.'

He held her as though they were one, and was silent.

In the house, Tom Brangwen waited a while. Then he got up and went out. He went down the yard. He saw the curious misty shaft coming from the loft door. He scarcely knew it was the light in the rain. He went on till the illumination fell on him dimly. Then looking up, through the blurr, he saw the youth and the girl together, the youth with his back against the wall, his head sunk over the head of the girl. The elder man saw them, blurred through the rain, but lit up. They thought themselves so buried in the night. He even saw the lighted dryness of the loft behind, and shadows and bunches of roosting fowls, up in the night, strange shadows cast from the lantern on the floor.

And a black gloom of anger, and a tenderness of self-effacement, fought in his heart. She did not understand what she was doing. She betrayed herself. She was a child, a mere child. She did not know how much of herself she was squandering. And he was blackly and furiously miserable. Was he then an old man, that he should be giving her away in marriage? Was he old? He was not old. He was younger than that young thoughtless fellow in whose arms she lay. Who knew her – he or that blind-headed youth? To whom did she belong, if not to himself?

He thought again of the child he had carried out at night into the barn, whilst his wife was in labour with the young Tom. He remembered the soft, warm weight of the little girl on his arm, round his neck. Now she would say he was finished. She was going away, to deny him, to leave an unendurable emptiness in him, a void that he could not bear. Almost he hated her. How dared she say he was old. He walked on in the rain, sweating with pain, with the horror of being old, with the agony of having to relinquish what was life to him.

Will Brangwen went home without having seen his uncle. He held his hot face to the rain, and walked on in a trance. 'I love you, Will, I love you.' The words repeated themselves endlessly. The veils had ripped and issued him naked into the endless space, and he shuddered. The walls had thrust him out and given him a vast space to walk in. Whither, through this darkness of infinite space, was he walking blindly? Where, at the end of all the darkness, was God the Almighty still darkly, seated, thrusting him on? 'I love you, Will, I love you.' He trembled with fear as the words beat in his heart again. And he dared not think of her face, of her eyes which shone, and of her strange, transfigured face. The hand of the Hidden Almighty, burning bright, had thrust out of the darkness and gripped him. He went on subject and in fear, his heart gripped and burning from the touch.

The days went by, they ran on dark-padded feet in silence. He went to see Anna, but again there had come a reserve between them. Tom Brangwen was gloomy, his blue eyes sombre. Anna was strange and delivered up. Her face in its delicate colouring was mute, touched dumb and poignant. The mother bowed her head and moved in her own dark world, that was pregnant again with fulfilment.

Will Brangwen worked at his wood-carving. It was a passion, a passion
for him to have the chisel under his grip. Verily the passion of his heart
lifted the fine bite of steel. He was carving, as he had always wanted, the
Creation of Eve. It was a panel in low relief, for a church. Adam lay asleep
as if suffering, and God, a dim, large figure, stooped towards him, stretching
forward His unveiled hand; and Eve, a small vivid, naked female shape, was
issuing like a flame towards the hand of God, from the torn side of Adam.

Now, Will Brangwen was working at the Eve. She was thin, a keen,
unripe thing. With trembling passion, fine as a breath of air, he sent the
chisel over her belly, her hard, unripe, small belly. She was a stiff little
figure, with sharp lines, in the throes and torture and ecstasy of her creation.
But he trembled as he touched her. He had not finished any of his figures.
There was a bird on a bough overhead, lifting its wings for flight, and a
serpent wreathing up to it. It was not finished yet. He trembled with passion,
at last able to create the new, sharp body of his Eve.

At the sides, at the far sides, at either end, were two Angels covering their
faces with their wings. They were like trees. As he went to the Marsh, in
the twilight, he felt that the Angels, with covered faces, were standing back
as he went by. The darkness was of their shadows and the covering of their
faces. When he went through the Canal bridge, the evening glowed in its
last deep colours, the sky was dark blue, the stars glittered from afar, very
remote and approaching above the darkening cluster of the farm, above the
paths of crystal along the edge of the heavens.

She waited for him like the glow of light, and as if his face were covered.
And he dared not lift his face to look at her.

Corn harvest came on. One evening they walked out through the farm
buildings at nightfall. A large gold moon hung heavily to the grey horizon,
trees hovered tall, standing back in the dusk, waiting. Anna and the young
man went on noiselessly by the hedge, along where the farm-carts had made
dark ruts in the grass. They came through a gate into a wide open field
where still much light seemed to spread against their faces. In the under-
shadow the sheaves lay on the ground where the reapers had left them, many
sheaves like bodies prostrate in shadowy bulk; others were riding hazily in
shocks, like ships in the haze of moonlight and of dusk, farther off.

They did not want to turn back, yet whither were they to go, towards the
moon? For they were separate, single.

'We will put up some sheaves,' said Anna. So they could remain there in
the broad, open place.

They went across the stubble to where the long rows of upreared shocks
ended. Curiously populous that part of the field looked, where the shocks
rode erect; the rest was open and prostrate.

The air was all hoary silver. She looked around her. Trees stood vaguely
at their distance, as if waiting like heralds, for the signal to approach. In
this space of vague crystal her heart seemed like a bell ringing. She was
afraid lest the sound should be heard.

'You take this row,' she said to the youth, and passing on, she stooped in
the next row of lying sheaves, grasping her hands in the tresses of the oats,
lifting the heavy corn in either hand, carrying it, as it hung heavily against

her, to the cleared space, where she set the two sheaves sharply down, bringing them together with a faint, keen clash. Her two bulks stood leaning together. He was coming, walking shadowily with the gossamer dusk, carrying his two sheaves. She waited near-by. He set his sheaves with a keen, faint clash, next to her sheaves. They rode unsteadily. He tangled the tresses of corn. It hissed like a fountain. He looked up and laughed.

Then she turned away towards the moon, which seemed glowingly to uncover her bosom every time she faced it. He went to the vague emptiness of the field opposite, dutifully.

They stooped, grasped the wet, soft hair of the corn, lifted the heavy bundles, and returned. She was always first. She set down her sheaves, making a pent-house with those others. He was coming shadowy across the stubble, carrying his bundles. She turned away, hearing only the sharp hiss of his mingling corn. She walked between the moon and his shadowy figure.

She took her two new sheaves and walked towards him, as he rose from stooping over the earth. He was coming out of the near distance. She set down her sheaves to make a new stook. They were unsure. Her hands fluttered. Yet she broke away, and turned to the moon, which laid bare her bosom, so she felt as if her bosom were heaving and panting with moonlight. And he had to put up her two sheaves, which had fallen down. He worked in silence. The rhythm of the work carried him away again, as she was coming near.

They worked together, coming and going, in a rhythm, which carried their feet and their bodies in tune. She stooped, she lifted the burden of sheaves, she turned her face to the dimness where he was, and went with her burden over the stubble. She hesitated, set down her sheaves, there was a swish and hiss of mingling oats, he was drawing near, and she must turn again. And there was the flaring moon laying bare her bosom again, making her drift and ebb like a wave.

He worked steadily, engrossed, threading backwards and forwards like a shuttle across the strip of cleared stubble, weaving the long line of riding shocks, nearer and nearer to the shadowy trees, threading his sheaves with hers.

And always, she was gone before he came. As he came, she drew away, as he drew away, she came. Were they never to meet? Gradually a low, deep-sounding will in him vibrated to her, tried to set her in accord, tried to bring her gradually to him, to a meeting, till they should be together, till they should meet as the sheaves that swished together.

And the work went on. The moon grew brighter, clearer, the corn glistened. He bent over the prostrate bundles, there was a hiss as the sheaves left the ground, a trailing of heavy bodies against him, a dazzle of moonlight on his eyes. And then he was setting the corn together at the stook. And she was coming near.

He waited for her, he fumbled at the stook. She came. But she stood back till he drew away. He saw her in shadow, a dark column, and spoke to her, and she answered. She saw the moonlight flash question on his face. But there was a space between them, and he went away, the work carried them, rhythmic.

Why was there always a space between them, why were they apart? Why, as she came up from under the moon, would she halt and stand off from him? Why was he held away from her? His will drummed persistently, darkly, it drowned everything else.

Into the rhythm of his work there came a pulse and a steadied purpose. He stooped, he lifted the weight, he heaved it towards her, setting it as in her, under the moonlit space. And he went back for more. Ever with increasing closeness he lifted the sheaves and swung striding to the centre with them, ever he drove her more nearly to the meeting, ever he did his share, and drew towards her, overtaking her. There was only the moving to and fro in the moonlight, engrossed, the swinging in the silence, that was marked only by the splash of sheaves, and silence, and a splash of sheaves. And ever the splash of his sheaves broke swifter, beating up to hers, and ever the splash of her sheaves recurred monotonously, unchanging, and ever the splash of his sheaves beat nearer.

Till at last, they met at the shock, facing each other, sheaves in hand. And he was silvery with moonlight, with a moonlit, shadowy face that frightened her. She waited for him.

'Put yours down,' she said.

'No, it's your turn.' His voice was twanging and insistent.

She set her sheaves against the shock. He saw her hands glisten among the spray of grain. And he dropped his sheaves and he trembled as he took her in his arms. He had overtaken her, and it was his privilege to kiss her. She was sweet and fresh with the night air, and sweet with the scent of grain. And the whole rhythm of him beat into his kisses, and still he pursued her, in his kisses, and still she was not quite overcome. He wondered over the moonlight on her nose! All the moonlight upon her, all the darkness within her! All the night in his arms, darkness and shine, he possessed of it all! All the night for him now, to unfold, to venture within, all the mystery to be entered, all the discovery to be made.

Trembling with keen triumph, his heart was white as a star as he drove his kisses nearer.

'My love!' she called, in a low voice, from afar. The low sound seemed to call to him from far off, under the moon, to him who was unaware. He stopped, quivered, and listened.

'My love,' came again the low, plaintive call, like a bird unseen in the night.

He was afraid. His heart quivered and broke. He was stopped.

'Anna,' he said, as if he answered her from a distance, unsure.

'My love.'

And he drew near, and she drew near.

'Anna,' he said, in wonder and the birthpain of love.

'My love,' she said, her voice growing rapturous. And they kissed on the mouth, in rapture and surprise, long, real kisses. The kiss lasted, there among the moonlight. He kissed her again, and she kissed him. And again they were kissing together. Till something happened in him, he was strange. He wanted her. He wanted her exceedingly. She was something new. They stood there folded, suspended in the night. And his whole being quivered with surprise, as from a blow. He wanted her, and he wanted to tell her so. But the shock was too great to him. He had never realised before. He trembled with irritation and unusedness, he did not know what to do. He held her more gently, gently, much more gently. The conflict was gone by. And he was glad, and breathless, and almost in tears. But he knew he wanted her. Something fixed in him for ever. He was hers. And he was very glad and afraid. He did not know what to do, as they stood there in the open, moonlit field. He looked through her hair at the moon, which seemed to swim liquid-bright.

She sighed, and seemed to wake up, then she kissed him again. Then she loosened herself away from him and took his hand. It hurt him when she drew away from his breast. It hurt him with a chagrin. Why did she draw away from him? But she held his hand.

'I want to go home,' she said, looking at him in a way he could not understand.

He held close to her hand. He was dazed and he could not move, he did not know how to move. She drew him away.

He walked helplessly beside her, holding her hand. She went with bent head. Suddenly he said, as the simple solution stated itself to him:

'We'll get married, Anna.'

She was silent.

'We'll get married, Anna, shall we?'

She stopped in the field again and kissed him, clinging to him passionately, in a way he could not understand. He could not understand. But he left it all now, to marriage. That was the solution now, fixed ahead. He wanted her, he wanted to be married to her, he wanted to have her altogether, as his own for ever. And he waited, intent, for the accomplishment. But there was all the while a slight tension of irritation.

He spoke to his uncle and aunt that night.

'Uncle,' he said, 'Anna and me think of getting married.'

'Oh ay!' said Brangwen.

'But how, you have no money?' said the mother.

The youth went pale. He hated these words. But he was like a gleaming, bright pebble, something bright and inalterable. He did not think. He sat there in his hard brightness, and did not speak.

'Have you mentioned it to your own mother?' asked Brangwen.

'No – I'll tell her on Saturday.'

'You'll go and see her?'

'Yes.'

There was a long pause.

'And what are you going to marry on – your pound a week?'

Again the youth went pale, as if the spirit were being injured in him.

'I don't know,' he said, looking at his uncle with his bright inhuman eyes, like a hawk's.

Brangwen stirred in hatred.

'It needs knowing,' he said.

'I shall have the money later on,' said the nephew. 'I will raise some now, and pay it back then.'

'Oh ay! – And why this desperate hurry? She's a child of eighteen, and you're a boy of twenty. You're neither of you of age to do as you like yet.'

Will Brangwen ducked his head and looked at his uncle with swift, mistrustful eyes, like a caged hawk.

'What does it matter how old she is, and how old I am?' he said. 'What's the difference between me now and when I'm thirty?'

'A big difference, let us hope.'

'But you have no experience – you have no experience, and no money. Why do you want to marry, without experience or money?' asked the aunt.

'What experience do I want, Aunt?' asked the boy.

And if Brangwen's heart had not been hard and intact with anger, like a precious stone, he would have agreed.

Will Brangwen went home strange and untouched. He felt he could not alter from what he was fixed upon, his will was set. To alter it he must be destroyed. And he would not be destroyed. He had no money. But he would get some from somewhere, it did not matter. He lay awake for many hours, hard and clear and unthinking, his soul crystallising more inalterably. Then he went fast asleep.

It was as if his soul had turned into a hard crystal. He might tremble and quiver and suffer, it did not alter.

The next morning Tom Brangwen, inhuman with anger spoke to Anna.

'What's this about wanting to get married?' he said.

She stood, paling a little, her dark eyes springing to the hostile, startled look of a savage thing that will defend itself, but trembles with sensitiveness.

'I do,' she said, out of her unconsciousness.

His anger rose, and he would have liked to break her.

'You do – you do – and what for?' he sneered with contempt. The old, childish agony, the blindness that could recognise nobody, the palpitating antagonism as of a raw, helpless, undefended thing came back on her.

'I do because I do,' she cried, in the shrill, hysterical way of her childhood. 'You are not my father – my father is dead – *you* are not my father.'

She was still a stranger. She did not recognise him. The cold blade cut down, deep into Brangwen's soul. It cut him off from her.

'And what if I'm not?' he said.

But he could not bear it. It had been so passionately dear to him, her 'Father – Daddie.'

He went about for some days as if stunned. His wife was bemused. She did not understand. She only thought the marriage was impeded for want of money and position.

There was a horrible silence in the house. Anna kept out of sight as much as possible. She could be for hours alone.

Will Brangwen came back, after stupid scenes at Nottingham. He too was pale and blank, but unchanging. His uncle hated him. He hated this youth, who was so inhuman and obstinate. Nevertheless, it was to Will Brangwen that the uncle, one evening, handed over the shares which he had transferred to Anna Lensky. They were for two thousand five hundred pounds. Will Brangwen looked at his uncle. It was a great deal of the Marsh capital here given away. The youth, however, was only colder and more fixed. He was abstract, purely a fixed will. He gave the shares to Anna.

After which she cried for a whole day, sobbing her eyes out. And at night, when she had heard her mother go to bed, she slipped down and hung in the doorway. Her father sat in his heavy silence, like a monument. He turned his head slowly.

'Daddy,' she cried from the doorway, and she ran to him sobbing as if her heart would break. 'Daddy – daddy – daddy.'

She crouched on the hearthrug with her arms round him and her face against him. His body was so big and comfortable. But something hurt her head intolerably. She sobbed almost with hysteria.

He was silent, with his hand on her shoulder. His heart was bleak. He was not her father That beloved image she had broken. Who was he then? A man put apart with those whose life has no more developments. He was isolated from her. There was a generation between them, he was old, he had died out from hot life. A great deal of ash was in his fire, cold ash. He felt the inevitable coldness, and in bitterness forgot the fire. He sat in his coldness of age and isolation. He had his own wife. And he blamed himself, he sneered at himself, for this clinging to the young, wanting the young to belong to him.

The child who clung to him wanted her child-husband. As was natural. And from him, Brangwen, she wanted help, so that her life might be properly fitted out. But love she did not want. Why should there be love between them, between the stout, middle-aged man and this child? How could there be anything between them, but mere human willingness to help each other? He was her guardian, no more. His heart was like ice, his face cold and expressionless. She could not move him any more than a statue.

She crept to bed, and cried. But she was going to be married to Will Brangwen, and then she need not bother any more. Brangwen went to bed with a hard, cold heart, and cursed himself. He looked at his wife. She was still his wife. Her dark hair was threaded with grey, her face was beautiful in its gathering age. She was just fifty. How poignantly he saw her! And he wanted to cut out some of his own heart, which was incontinent, and demanded still to share the rapid life of youth. How he hated himself.

His wife was so poignant and timely. She was still young and naïve, with some girl's freshness. But she did not want any more the fight, the battle, the control, as he, in his incontinence, still did. She was so natural, and he was ugly, unnatural, in his inability to yield place. How hideous, like greedy middle-age, which must stand in the way of life, like a large demon.

What was missing in his life, that, in his ravening soul, he was not satisfied? He had had that friend at school, his mother, his wife, and Anna? What had he done? He had failed with his friend, he had been a poor son; but he had known satisfaction with his wife, let it be enough; he loathed himself for the state he was in over Anna. Yet he was *not* satisfied. It was agony to know it.

Was his life nothing? Had he nothing to show, no work? He did not count his work, anybody could have done it. What had he known, but the long, marital embrace with his wife! Curious, that this was what his life amounted to! At any rate, it was something, it was eternal. He would say so to anybody, and be proud of it. He lay with his wife in his arms, and she was still his fulfilment, just the same as ever. And that was the be-all and the end-all. Yes, and he was proud of it.

But the bitterness, underneath, that there still remained an unsatisfied Tom Brangwen, who suffered agony because a girl cared nothing for him. He loved his sons – he had them also. But it was the further, the creative life with the girl, he wanted as well. Oh, and he was ashamed. He trampled himself to extinguish himself.

What weariness! There was no peace, however old one grew! One was never right, never decent, never master of oneself. It was as if his hope had been in the girl.

Anna quickly lapsed again into her love for the youth. Will Brangwen had fixed his marriage for the Saturday before Christmas. And he waited for her, in his bright, unquestioning fashion, until then. He wanted her, she was his, he suspended his being till the day should come. The wedding day, December the twenty-third, had come into being for him as an absolute thing. He lived in it.

He did not count the days. But like a man who journeys in a ship, he was suspended till the coming to port.

He worked at his carving, he worked in his office, he came to see her; all was but a form of waiting, without thought or question.

She was much more alive. She wanted to enjoy courtship. He seemed to come and go like the wind, without asking why or whither. But she wanted to enjoy his presence. For her, he was the kernel of life, to touch him alone was bliss. But for him, she was the essence of life. She existed as much when he was at his carving in his lodging in Ilkeston, as when she sat looking at him in the Marsh kitchen. In himself, he knew her. But his outward faculties seemed suspended. He did not see her with his eyes, nor hear her with his voice.

And yet he trembled, sometimes into a kind of swoon, holding her in his arms. They would stand sometimes folded together in the barn, in silence. Then to her, as she felt his young, tense figure with her hands, the bliss was intolerable, intolerable the sense that she possessed him. For his body was so keen and wonderful, it was the only reality in her world. In her world, there was this one tense, vivid body of a man, and then many other shadowy men, all unreal. In him, she touched the centre of reality. And they were together, he and she, at the heart of the secret. How she clutched him to her, his body the central body of all life. Out of the rock of his form the very fountain of life flowed.

But to him, she was a flame that consumed him. The flame flowed up his limbs, flowed through him, till he was consumed, till he existed only as an unconscious, dark transit of flame, deriving from her.

Sometimes, in the darkness, a cow coughed. There was, in the darkness, a slow sound of cud chewing. And it all seemed to flow round them and upon them as the hot blood flows through the womb, laving the unborn young.

Sometimes, when it was cold, they stood to be lovers in the stables, where the air was warm and sharp with ammonia. And during these dark vigils, he learned to know her, her body against his, they drew nearer and nearer together, the kisses came more subtly close and fitting. So when in the thick darkness a horse suddenly scrambled to its feet, with a dull, thunderous sound, they listened as one person listening, they knew as one person, they were conscious of the horse.

Tom Brangwen had taken them a cottage at Cossethay, on a twenty-one years' lease. Will Brangwen's eyes lit up as he saw it. It was the cottage next the church, with dark yew-trees, very black old trees, along the side of the house and the grassy front garden; a red, squarish cottage with a low slate roof, and low windows. It had a long dairy-scullery, a big flagged kitchen, and a low parlour, that went up one step from the kitchen. There were whitewashed beams across the ceilings, and odd corners with cupboards. Looking out through the windows, there was the grassy garden, the procession of black yew trees down one side, and along the other sides, a red wall with ivy separating the place from the highroad and the churchyard. The old, little church, with its small spire on a square tower, seemed to be looking back at the cottage windows.

'There'll be no need to have a clock,' said Will Brangwen, peeping out at the white clock-face on the tower, his neighbour.

At the back of the house was a garden adjoining the paddock, a cowshed with standing for two cows, pig-cotes and fowl-houses. Will Brangwen was very happy. Anna was glad to think of being mistress of her own place.

Tom Brangwen was now the fairy godfather. He was never happy unless he was buying something. Will Brangwen, with his interest in all wood-work, was getting the furniture. He was left to buy tables and round-staved chairs and the dressers, quite ordinary stuff, but such as was identified with his cottage.

Tom Brangwen, with more particular thought, spied out what he called handy little things for her. He appeared with a set of new-fangled cooking-pans, with a special sort of hanging lamp, though the rooms were so low, with canny little machines for grinding meat or mashing potatoes or whisking eggs.

Anna took a sharp interest in what he bought, though she was not always pleased. Some of the little contrivances, which he thought so canny, left her doubtful. Nevertheless she was always expectant, on market days there was always a long thrill of anticipation. He arrived with the first darkness, the copper lamps of his cart glowing. And she ran to the gate, as he, a dark, burly figure up in the cart, was bending over his parcels.

'It's cupboard love as brings you out so sharp,' he said, his voice resounding in the cold darkness. Nevertheless he was excited. And she, taking one of the cart lamps, poked and peered among the jumble of things he had brought, pushing aside the oil or implements he had got for himself.

She dragged out a pair of small, strong bellows, registered them in her mind, and then pulled uncertainly at something else. It had a long handle, and a piece of brown paper round the middle of it, like a waistcoat.

'What's this?' she said, poking.

He stopped to look at her. She went to the lamp-light by the horse, and

stood there bent over the new thing, while her hair was like bronze, her
apron white and cheerful. Her fingers plucked busily at the paper. She
dragged forth a little wringer, with clean indiarubber rollers. She examined
it critically, not knowing quite how it worked.

She looked up at him. He stood a shadowy presence beyond the light.

'How does it go?' she asked.

'Why, it's for pulpin' turnips,' he replied.

She looked at him. His voice disturbed her.

'Don't be silly. It's a little mangle,' she said. 'How do you stand it,
though?'

'You screw it on th' side o' your wash-tub.' He came and held it out to
her.

'Oh, yes!' she cried, with one of her little skipping movements, which still
came when she was suddenly glad.

And without another thought she ran off into the house, leaving him to
untackle the horse. And when he came into the scullery, he found her there,
with the little wringer fixed on the dolly-tub, turning blissfully at the handle,
and Tilly beside her, exclaiming:

'My word, that's a natty little thing! That'll save you luggin' your inside
out. That's the latest contraption, that is.'

And Anna turned away at the handle, with great gusto of possession.
Then she let Tilly have a turn.

'It fair runs by itself,' said Tilly, turning on and on. 'Your clothes'll nip
out on to th' line.'

Chapter Five

Wedding at the Marsh

It was a beautiful sunny day for the wedding, a muddy earth but a bright
sky. They had three cabs and two big closed-in vehicles. Everybody crowded
in the parlour in excitement. Anna was still upstairs. Her father kept taking
a nip of brandy. He was handsome in his black coat and grey trousers. His
voice was hearty but troubled. His wife came down in dark grey silk with
lace, and a touch of peacock-blue in her bonnet. Her little body was very
sure and definite. Brangwen was thankful she was there, to sustain him
among all these people.

The carriages! The Nottingham Mrs. Brangwen, in silk brocade, stands
in the doorway saying who must go with whom. There is a great bustle.
The front door is opened, and the wedding guests are walking down the
garden path, whilst those still waiting peer through the window, and the

little crowd at the gate gorps and stretches. How funny such dressed-up people look in the winter sunshine!

They are gone – another lot! There begins to be more room. Anna comes down blushing and very shy, to be viewed in her white silk and her veil. Her mother-in-law surveys her objectively, twitches the white train, arranges the folds of the veil and asserts herself.

Loud exclamations from the window that the bridegroom's carriage has just passed.

'Where's your hat, father, and your gloves?' cries the bride, stamping her white slipper, her eyes flashing through her veil. He hunts round – his hair is ruffled. Everybody has gone but the bride and her father. He is ready – his face very red and daunted. Tilly dithers in the little porch, waiting to open the door. A waiting woman walks round Anna, who asks:

'Am I all right?'

She is ready. She bridles herself and looks queenly. She waves her hand sharply to her father:

'Come here!'

He goes. She puts her hand very lightly on his arm, and holding her bouquet like a shower, stepping, oh, very graciously, just a little impatient with her father for being so red in the face, she sweeps slowly past the fluttering Tilly, and down the path. There are hoarse shouts at the gate, and all her floating foamy whiteness passes slowly into the cab.

Her father notices her slim ankle and foot as she steps up: a child's foot. His heart is hard with tenderness. But she is in ecstasies with herself for making such a lovely spectacle. All the way she sat flamboyant with bliss because it was all so lovely. She looked down solicitously at her bouquet: white roses and lilies-of-the-valley and tube-roses and maidenhair fern – very rich and cascade-like.

Her father sat bewildered with all this strangeness, his heart was so full it felt hard, and he couldn't think of anything.

The church was decorated for Christmas, dark with evergreens, cold and snowy with white flowers. He went vaguely down to the altar. How long was it since he had gone to be married himself? He was not sure whether he was going to be married now, or what he had come for. He had a troubled notion that he had to do something or other. He saw his wife's bonnet, and wondered why she wasn't there with him.

They stood before the altar. He was staring up at the east window, that glowed intensely, a sort of blue purple: it was deep blue glowing, and some crimson, and little yellow flowers held fast in veins of shadow, in a heavy web of darkness. How it burned alive in radiance among its black web.

'Who giveth this woman to be married to this man?' He felt somebody touch him. He started. The words still re-echoed in his memory, but were drawing off.

'Me,' he said hastily.

Ann bent her head and smiled in her veil. How absurd he was.

Brangwen was staring away at the burning blue window at the back of the altar, and wondering vaguely, with pain, if he ever should get old, if he ever should feel arrived and established. He was here at Anna's wedding.

Well, what right had he to feel responsible, like a father? He was still as unsure and unfixed as when he had married himself. His wife and he! With a pang of anguish he realised what uncertainties they both were. He was a man of forty-five. Forty-five! In five more years fifty. Then sixty – then seventy – then it was finished. My God – and one still was so unestablished!

How did one grow old – how could one become confident? He wished he felt older. Why, what difference was there, as far as he felt matured or completed, between him now and him at his own wedding? He might be getting married over again – he and his wife. He felt himself tiny, a little, upright figure on a plain circled round with the immense, roaring sky: he and his wife, two little, upright figures walking across this plain, whilst the heavens shimmered and roared about them. When did one come to an end? In which direction was it finished? There was no end, no finish, only this roaring vast space. Did one never get old, never die? That was the clue. He exulted strangely, with torture. He would go on with his wife, he and she like two children camping in the plain. What was sure but the endless sky? But that was so sure, so boundless.

Still the royal blue colour burned and blazed and sported itself in the web of darkness before him, unwearingly rich and splendid. How rich and splendid his own life was, red and burning and blazing and sporting itself in the dark meshes of his body: and his wife, how she glowed and burned dark within her meshes! Always it was so unfinished and unformed!

There was a loud noise of the organ. The whole party was trooping to the vestry. There was a blotted, scrawled book – and that young girl putting back her veil in her vanity, and laying her hand with the wedding-ring self-consciously conspicuous, and signing her name proudly because of the vain spectacle she made:

'Anna Theresa Lensky.'

'Anna Theresa Lensky' – what a vain, independent minx she was! The bridegroom, slender in his black swallow-tail and grey trousers, solemn as a young solemn cat, was writing seriously:

'William Brangwen.'

That looked more like it.

'Come and sign, father,' cried the imperious young hussy.

'Thomas Brangwen – clumsy-fist,' he said to himself as he signed.

Then his brother, a big, sallow fellow with black side-whiskers wrote:

'Alfred Brangwen.'

'How many more Brangwens?' said Tom Brangwen, ashamed of the too-frequent recurrence of his family name.

When they were out again in the sunshine, and he saw the frost hoary and blue among the long grass under the tomb-stones, the holly-berries overhead twinkling scarlet as the bells rang, the yew trees hanging their black, motionless, ragged boughs, everything seemed like a vision.

The marriage party went across the graveyard to the wall, mounted it by the little steps, and descended. Oh, a vain white peacock of a bride perching herself on the top of the wall and giving her hand to the bridegroom on the other side, to be helped down! The vanity of her white, slim, daintily-stepping feet, and her arched neck. And the regal impudence with which she seemed to dismiss them all, the others, parents and wedding guests, as she went with her young husband.

In the cottage big fires were burning, there were dozens of glasses on the table, and holly and mistletoe hanging up. The wedding party crowded in, and Tom Brangwen, becoming roisterous, poured out drinks. Everybody must drink. The bells were ringing away against the windows.

'Lift your glasses up,' shouted Tom Brangwen from the parlour, 'lift your glasses up, an' drink to the hearth an' home – hearth an' home, an' may they enjoy it.'

'Night an' day, an' may they enjoy it,' shouted Frank Brangwen, in addition.

'Hammer an' tongs, and may they enjoy it,' shouted Alfred Brangwen, the saturnine.

'Fill your glasses up, an' let's have it all over again,' shouted Tom Brangwen.

'Hearth an' home, an' may ye enjoy it.'

There was a ragged shout of the company in response.

'Bed an' blessin', an' may ye enjoy it,' shouted Frank Brangwen.

There was a swelling chorus in answer.

'Comin' and goin', an' may ye enjoy it,' shouted the saturnine Alfred Brangwen, and the men roared by now boldly, and the women said, 'Just hark, now!'

There was a touch of scandal in the air.

Then the party rolled off in the carriages, full speed back to the Marsh, to a large meal of the high-tea order, which lasted for an hour and a half. The bride and bridegroom sat at the head of the table, very prim and shining both of them, wordless, whilst the company raged down the table.

The Brangwen men had brandy in their tea, and were becoming unmanageable. The saturnine Alfred had glittering, unseeing eyes, and a strange, fierce way of laughing that showed his teeth. His wife glowered at him and jerked her head at him like a snake. He was oblivious. Frank Brangwen, the butcher, flushed and florid and handsome, roared echoes to his two brothers. Tom Brangwen, in his solid fashion, was letting himself go at last.

These three brothers dominated the whole company. Tom Brangwen wanted to make a speech. For the first time in his life, he must spread himself wordily.

'Marriage,' he began, his eyes twinkling and yet quite profound, for he was deeply serious and hugely amused at the same time, 'Marriage,' he said, speaking in the slow, full-mouthed way of the Brangwens, 'is what we're made for—'

'Let him talk,' said Alfred Brangwen, slowly and inscrutably, 'let him talk.' Mrs. Alfred darted indignant eyes at her husband.

'A man,' continued Tom Brangwen, 'enjoys being a man: for what purpose was he made a man, if not to enjoy it?'

'That a true word,' said Frank, floridly.

'And likewise,' continued Tom Brangwen, 'a woman enjoys being a woman: at least we surmise she does—'

'Oh, don't you bother—' called a farmer's wife.

'You may back your life they'd be summisin',' said Frank's wife.

'Now,' continued Tom Brangwen, 'for a man to be a man, it takes a woman—'

'It does that,' said a woman grimly.

'And for a woman to be a woman, it takes a man—' continued Tom Brangwen.

'All speak up, men,' chimed in a feminine voice.

'Therefore we have marriage,' continued Tom Brangwen.

'Hold, hold,' said Alfred Brangwen. 'Don't run us off our legs.'

And in dead silence the glasses were filled. The bride and bridegroom two children, sat with intent, shining faces at the head of the table, abstracted.

'There's no marriage in heaven,' went on Tom Brangwen; 'but on earth there is marriage.'

'That's the difference between 'em,' said Alfred Brangwen, mocking.

'Alfred,' said Tom Brangwen, 'keep your remarks till afterwards, and then we'll thank you for them. – There's very little else, on earth, but marriage. You can talk about making money, or saving souls. You can save your own soul seven times over, and you may have a mint of money, but your soul goes gnawin', gnawin', gnawin', and it says there's something it must have. In heaven there is no marriage. But on earth there *is* marriage, else heaven drops out, and there's no bottom to it.'

'Just hark you now,' said Frank's wife.

'Go on, Thomas,' said Alfred sardonically.

'*If* we've got to be Angels,' went on Tom Brangwen, haranguing the company at large, 'and if there is no such thing as a man nor a woman amongst them, then it seems to me as a married couple makes one Angel.'

'It's the brandy,' said Alfred Brangwen wearily.

'For,' said Tom Brangwen, and the company was listening to the conundrum, 'an Angel can't be *less* than a human being. And if it was only the soul of a man *minus* the man, then it would be less than a human being.'

'Decidedly,' said Alfred.

And a laugh went round the table. But Tom Brangwen was inspired.

'An Angel's got to be more than a human being,' he continued. 'So I say, an Angel is the soul of man and woman in one: they rise united at the Judgment Day, as one Angel—'

'Praising the Lord,' said Frank.

'Praising the Lord,' repeated Tom.

'And what about the women left over?' asked Alfred, jeering. The company was getting uneasy.

'That I can't tell. How do I know as there *is* anybody left over at the Judgment Day? Let that be. What I say is, that when a man's soul and a woman's soul unites together – that make an Angel—'

'I dunno about souls. I know as one plus one makes three, sometimes,' said Frank. But he had the laugh to himself.

'Bodies and souls, it's the same,' said Tom.

'And what about your missis, who was married afore you knew her?' asked Alfred, set on edge by this discourse.

'That I can't tell you. If I am to become an Angel, it'll be my married soul, and not my single soul. It'll not be the soul of me when I was a lad: for I hadn't a soul as would *make* an Angel then.'

'I can always remember,' said Frank's wife, 'when our Harold was bad, he did nothink but see an angel at th' back o' th' lookin'-glass. "Look, mother," 'e said, "at that angel!" "Theer isn't no angel, my duck," I said, but he wouldn't have it. I took th' lookin'-glass off'n th' dressin'-table, but it made no difference. He kep't on sayin' it was there. My word, it did give me a turn. I thought for sure as I'd lost him.'

'I can remember,' said another man, Tom's sister's husband, 'my mother gave me a good hidin' once, for sayin' I'd got an angel up my nose. She seed me pokin', an' she said: "What are you pokin' at your nose for – give over." "There's an angel up it," I said, an' she fetched me such a wipe. But there was. We used to call them thistle things "angels" as wafts about. An' I'd pushed one o' these up my nose, for some reason or other.'

'It's wonderful what children will get up their noses,' said Frank's wife. 'I c'n remember our Hemmie, she shoved one o' them bluebell things out o' th' middle of a bluebell, what they call "candles", up her nose, and oh, we had some work! I'd seen her stickin' 'em on the end of her nose, like, but I never thought she'd be so soft as to shove it right up. She was a gel of eight or more. Oh, my word, we got a crochet-hook an' I don't know what . . .'

Tom Brangwen's mood of inspiration began to pass away. He forgot all about it, and was soon roaring and shouting with the rest. Outside the wake came, singing the carols. They were invited into the bursting house. They had two fiddles and a piccolo. There in the parlour they played carols, and the whole company sang them at the top of its voice. Only the bride and bridegroom sat with shining eyes and strange, bright faces, and scarcely sang, or only with just moving lips.

The wake departed, and the guysers came. There was loud applause, and shouting and excitement as the old mystery play of St. George, in which every man present had acted as a boy, proceeded, with banging and thumping of club and dripping pan.

'By Jove, I got a crack once, when I was playin' Beelzebub,' said Tom Brangwen, his eyes full of water with laughing. 'It knocked all th' sense out of me as you'd crack an egg. But I tell you, when I come to, I played Old Johnny Roger with St. George, I did that.'

He was shaking with laughter. Another knock came at the door. There was a hush.

'It's th' cab,' said somebody from the door.

'Walk in,' shouted Tom Brangwen, and a red-faced grinning man entered.

'Now, you two, get yourselves ready an' off to blanket fair,' shouted Tom Brangwen. 'Strike a daisy, but if you're not off like a blink o' lightnin', you shanna go, you s'll sleep separate.'

Anna rose silently and went to change her dress. Will Brangwen would have gone out, but Tilly came with his hat and coat. The youth was helped on.

'Well, here's luck, my boy,' shouted his father.

'When th' fat's in th' fire, let it frizzle,' admonished his uncle Frank.

'Fair and *softly* does it, fair an' *softly* does it,' cried his aunt, Frank's wife, contrary.

'You don't want to fall over yourself,' said his uncle by marriage. 'You're not a bull at a gate.'

'Let a man have his own road,' said Tom Brangwen testily. 'Don't be so free of your advice – it's his wedding this time, not yours.'

''E don't want many sign-posts,' said his father. 'There's some roads a man has to be led, an' there's some roads a boss-eyed man can only follow wi' one eye shut. But this road can't be lost by a blind man nor a boss-eyed man nor a cripple – and he's neither, thank God.'

'Don't you be so sure o' your walkin' powers,' cried Frank's wife. 'There's many a man gets no further than half-way, nor can't to save his life, let him live for ever.'

'Why, how do you know?' said Alfred.

'It's plain enough in th' looks o' some,' retorted Lizzie, his sister-in-law.

The youth stood with a faint, half-hearing smile on his face. He was tense and abstracted. These things, or anything, scarcely touched him.

Anna came down, in her day dress, very elusive. She kissed everybody, men and women, Will Brangwen shook hands with everybody, kissed his mother, who began to cry, and the whole party went surging out to the cab.

The young couple were shut up, last injunctions shouted at them.

'Drive on,' shouted Tom Brangwen.

The cab rolled off. They saw the light diminish under the ash trees. Then the whole party, quietened, went indoors.

'They'll have three good fires burning,' said Tom Brangwen, looking at his watch. 'I told Emma to make 'em up at nine, an' then leave the door on th' latch. It's only half-past. They'll have three fires burning, an' lamps lighted, an' Emma will ha' warmed th' bed wi' th' warmin' pan. So I s'd think they'll be all right.'

The party was much quieter. They talked of the young couple.

'She said she didn't want a servant in,' said Tom Brangwen. 'The house isn't big enough, she'd always have the creature under her nose. Emma'll do what is wanted of her, an' they'll be to themselves.'

'It's best,' said Lizzie, 'you're more free.'

The party talked on slowly. Brangwen looked at his watch.

'Let's go an' give 'em a carol,' he said. 'We s'll find th' fiddles at the "Cock an' Robin".'

'Ay, come on,' said Frank.

Alfred rose in silence. The brother-in-law and one of Will's brothers rose also.

The five men went out. The night was flashing with stars. Sirius blazed like a signal at the side of the hill, Orion, stately and magnificent, was sloping along.

Tom walked with his brother, Alfred. The men's heels rang on the ground.

'It's a fine night,' said Tom.

'Ay,' said Alfred.

'Nice to get out.'

'Ay.'

The brothers walked close together, the bond of blood strong between them. Tom always felt very much the junior to Alfred.

'It's a long while since *you* left home,' he said.

'Ay,' said Alfred. 'I thought I was getting a bit oldish – but I'm not. It's the things you've got as gets worn out, it's not you yourself.'

'Why, what's worn out?'

'Most folks as I've anything to do with – as has anything to do with me. They all break down. You've got to go on by yourself, if it's only to perdition. There's nobody going alongside even there.'

Tom Brangwen meditated this.

'Maybe you was never broken in,' he said.

'No, I never was,' said Alfred proudly.

And Tom felt his elder brother despised him a little. He winced under it.

'Everybody's got a way of their own,' he said, stubbornly. 'It's only a dog as hasn't. An' them as can't take what they give an' give what they take, they must go by themselves, or get a dog as'll follow 'em.'

'They can do without the dog,' said his brother. And again Tom Brangwen was humble, thinking his brother was bigger than himself. But if he was, he was. And if it were finer to go alone, it was: he did not want to go for all that.

They went over the field, where a thin, keen wind blew round the ball of the hill, in the starlight. They came to the stile, and to the side of Anna's house. The lights were out, only on the blinds of the rooms downstairs, and of a bedroom upstairs, firelight flickered.

'We'd better leave 'em alone,' said Alfred Brangwen.

'Nay, nay,' said Tom. 'We'll carol 'em, for th' last time.'

And in a quarter of an hour's time, eleven silent, rather tipsy men scrambled over the wall, and into the garden by the yew trees, outside the windows where faint firelight glowered on the blinds. There came a shrill sound, two violins and a piccolo shrilling on the frosty air.

'In the fields with their flocks abiding.' A commotion of men's voices broke out singing in ragged unison.

Anna Brangwen had started up, listening, when the music began. She was afraid.

'It's the wake,' he whispered.

She remained tense, her heart beating heavily, possessed with strange, strong fear. Then there came the burst of men's singing, rather uneven. She strained still, listening.

'It's Dad,' she said, in a low voice. They were silent, listening.

'And my father,' he said.

She listened still. But she was sure. She sank down again into bed, into his arms. He held her very close, kissing her. The hymn rambled on outside, all the men singing their best, having forgotten everything else under the spell of the fiddles and the tune. The firelight glowed against the darkness in the room. Anna could hear her father singing with gusto.

'Aren't they silly,' she whispered.

And they crept closer, closer together, hearts beating to one another. And even as the hymn rolled on, they ceased to hear it.

Chapter Six

Anna Victrix

Will Brangwen had some weeks of holiday after his marriage, so the two took their honeymoon in full hands, alone in their cottage together.

And to him, as the days went by, it was as if the heavens had fallen, and he were sitting with her among the ruins, in a new world, everybody else buried, themselves two blissful survivors, with everything to squander as they would. At first, he could not get rid of a culpable sense of licence on his part. Wasn't there some duty outside, calling him and he did not come?

It was all very well at night, when the doors were locked and the darkness drawn round the two of them. Then they were the only inhabitants of the visible earth, the rest were under the flood. And being alone in the world, they were a law unto themselves, they could enjoy and squander and waste like conscienceless gods.

But in the morning, as the carts clanked by, and children shouted down the lane; as the hucksters came calling their wares, and the church clock struck eleven, and he and she had not got up yet, even to breakfast, he could not help feeling guilty, as if he were committing a breach of the law – ashamed that he was not up and doing.

'Doing what?' she asked. 'What is there to do? You will only lounge about.'

Still, even lounging about was respectable. One was at least in connection with the world, then. Whereas now, lying so still and peacefully, while the daylight came obscurely through the drawn blind, one was severed from the world, one shut oneself off in tacit denial of the world. And he was troubled.

But it was so sweet and satisfying lying there talking desultorily with her. It was sweeter than sunshine, and not so evanescent. It was even irritating the way the church-clock kept on chiming: there seemed no space between the hours, just a moment, golden and still, whilst she traced his features with her finger-tips, utterly careless and happy, and he loved her to do it.

But he was strange and unused. So suddenly, everything that had been before was shed away and gone. One day, he was a bachelor, living with the world. The next day, he was with her, as remote from the world as if the two of them were buried like a seed in darkness. Suddenly, like a chestnut falling out of a burr, he was shed naked and glistening on to a soft, fecund earth, leaving behind him the hard rind of worldly knowledge and experience. He heard it in the huckster's cries, the noise of carts, the calling of children. And it was all like the hard, shed rind, discarded. Inside, in the softness and stillness of the room, was the naked kernel, that palpitated in silent activity, absorbed in reality.

Inside the room was a great steadiness, a core of living eternity. Only far outside, at the rim, went on the noise and the destruction. Here at the centre the great wheel was motionless, centred upon itself. Here was a poised, unflawed stillness that was beyond time, because it remained the same, inexhaustible, unchanging, unexhausted.

As they lay close together, complete and beyond the touch of time or change, it was as if they were at the very centre of all the slow wheeling of space and the rapid agitation of life, deep, deep inside them all, at the centre where there is utter radiance, and eternal being, and the silence absorbed in praise: the steady core of all movements, the unawakened sleep of all wakefulness. They found themselves there, and they lay still, in each other's arms; for their moment they were at the heart of eternity, whilst time roared far off, for ever far off, towards the rim.

Then gradually they were passed away from the supreme centre, down the circles of praise and joy and gladness, further and further out, towards the noise and the friction. But their hearts had burned and were tempered by the inner reality, they were unalterably glad.

Gradually they began to wake up, the noises outside became more real. They understood and answered the call outside. They counted the strokes of the bell. And when they counted midday, they understood that it was midday, in the world, and for themselves also.

It dawned upon her that she was hungry. She had been getting hungrier for a lifetime. But even yet it was not sufficiently real to rouse her. A long way off she could hear the words, 'I am dying of hunger.' Yet she lay still, separate, at peace, and the words were unuttered. There was still another lapse.

And then, quite calmly, even a little surprised, she was in the present, and was saying:

'I am dying with hunger.'

'So am I,' he said calmly, as if it were of not the slightest significance. And they relapsed into the warm, golden stillness. And the minutes flowed unheeded past the window outside.

Then suddenly she stirred against him.

'My dear, I am dying of hunger,' she said.

It was a slight pain to him to be brought to.

'We'll get up,' he said, unmoving.

And she sank her head on to him again, and they lay still, lapsing. Half consciously, he heard the clock chime the hour. She did not hear.

'Do get up,' she murmured at length, 'and give me something to eat.'

'Yes,' he said, and he put his arms round her, and she lay with her face on him. They were faintly astonished that they did not move. The minutes rustled louder at the window.

'Let me go then,' he said.

She lifted her head from him, relinquishingly. With a little breaking away, he moved out of bed, and was taking his clothes. She stretched out her hand to him.

'You are so nice,' she said, and he went back for a moment or two.

Then actually he did slip into some clothes, and, looking round quickly at her, was gone out of the room. She lay translated again into a pale, clearer peace. As if she were a spirit, she listened to the noise of him downstairs, as if she were no longer of the material world.

It was half-past one. He looked at the silent kitchen, untouched from last night, dim with the drawn blind. And he hastened to draw up the blind, so people should know they were not in bed any later. Well, it was his own house, it did not matter. Hastily he put wood in the grate and made a fire. He exulted in himself, like an adventurer on an undiscovered island. The fire blazed up, he put on the kettle. How happy he felt! How still and secluded the house was! There were only he and she in the world.

But when he unbolted the door, and, half-dressed, looked out, he felt furtive and guilty. The world was there, after all. And he had felt so secure, as though this house were the Ark in the flood, and all the rest was drowned. The world was there: and it was afternoon. The morning had vanished and gone by, the day was growing old. Where was the bright, fresh morning? He was accused. Was the morning gone, and he had lain with blinds drawn, let it pass by unnoticed?

He looked again round the chill, grey afternoon. And he himself so soft and warm and glowing! There were two sprigs of yellow jasmine in the saucer that covered the milk-jug. He wondered who had been and left the sign. Taking the jug, he hastily shut the door. Let the day and the daylight drop out, let it go by unseen. He did not care. What did one day more or less matter to him. It could fall into oblivion unspent if it liked, this one course of daylight.

'Somebody has been·and found the door locked,' he said when he went upstairs with the tray. He gave her the two sprigs of jasmine. She laughed as she sat up in bed, childishly threading the flowers in the breast of her nightdress. Her brown hair stuck out like a nimbus, all fierce, round her softly glowing face. Her dark eyes watched the tray eagerly.

'How good!' she cried, sniffing the cold air. 'I'm glad you did a lot.' And she stretched out her hands eagerly for her plate – 'Come back to bed, quick – it's cold.' She rubbed her hands together sharply.

He put off what little clothing he had on, and sat beside her in the bed.

'You look like a lion, with your mane sticking out, and your nose pushed over your food,' he said.

She tinkled with laughter, and gladly ate her breakfast.

The morning was sunk away unseen, the afternoon was steadily going too, and he was letting it go. One bright transit of daylight gone by unacknowledged! There was something unmanly, recusant in it. He could not quite reconcile himself to the fact. He felt he ought to get up, go out quickly into the daylight, and work or spend himself energetically in the open air of the afternoon, retrieving what was left to him of the day.

But he did not go. Well, one might as well be hung for a sheep as for a lamb. If he had lost this day of his life, he had lost it. He gave it up. He was not going to count his losses. *She* didn't care. *She* didn't care in the least. Then why should he? Should he be behind her in recklessness and independence? She was superb in her indifference. He wanted to be like her.

She took her responsibilities lightly. When she spilled her tea on the pillow, she rubbed it carelessly with a handkerchief, and turned over the pillow. He would have felt guilty. She did not. And it pleased him. It pleased him very much to see how these things did not matter to her.

When the meal was over, she wiped her mouth on her handkerchief quickly, satisfied and happy, and settled down on the pillow again, with her fingers in his close, strange, fur-like hair.

The evening began to fall, the light was half alive, livid. He hid his face against her.

'I don't like the twilight,' he said.

'I love it,' she answered.

He hid his face against her, who was warm and like sunlight. She seemed to have sunlight inside her. Her heart beating seemed like sunlight upon him. In her was a more real day than the day could give: so warm and steady and restoring. He hid his face against her whilst the twilight fell, whilst she lay staring out with her unseeing dark eyes, as if she wandered forth untrammelled in the vagueness. The vagueness gave her scope and set her free.

To him, turned towards her heart-pulse, all was very still and very warm and very close, like noon-tide. He was glad to know this warm, full noon. It ripened him and took away his responsibility, some of his conscience.

They got up when it was quite dark. She hastily twisted her hair into a knot, and was dressed in a twinkling. Then they went downstairs, drew to the fire, and sat in silence, saying a few words now and then.

Her father was coming. She bundled the dishes away, flew round and tidied the room, assumed another character, and again seated herself. He sat thinking of his carving of Eve. He loved to go over his carving in his mind, dwelling on every stroke, every line. How he loved it now! When he went back to his Creation-panel again, he would finish his Eve, tender and sparkling. It did not satisfy him yet. The Lord should labour over her in a silent passion of Creation, and Adam should be tense as if in a dream of immortality, and Eve should take form glimmeringly, shadowily, as if the Lord must wrestle with His own soul for her, yet she was a radiance.

'What are you thinking about?' she asked.

He found it difficult to say. His soul became shy when he tried to communicate it.

'I was thinking my Eve was too hard and lively.'

'Why?'

'I don't know. She should be more—,' he made a gesture of infinite tenderness.

There was a stillness with a little joy. He could not tell her any more. Why could he not tell her any more? She felt a pang of disconsolate sadness. But it was nothing. She went to him.

Her father came, and found them both very glowing, like an open flower. He loved to sit with them. Where there was a perfume of love, anyone who came must breathe it. They were both quick and alive, lit up from the other-world, so that it was quite an experience for them, that anyone else could exist.

But still it troubled Will Brangwen a little, in his orderly, conventional mind, that the established rule of things had gone so utterly. One ought to get up in the morning and wash oneself and be a decent social being. Instead, the two of them stayed in bed till nightfall, and then got up, she never washed her face, but sat there talking to her father as bright and shameless as a daisy opened out of the dew. Or she got up at ten o'clock, and quite blithely went to bed again at three, or at half-past four, stripping him naked in the daylight, and all so gladly and perfectly, oblivious quite of his qualms. He let her do as she liked with him, and shone with strange pleasure. She was to dispose of him as she would. He was translated with gladness to be in her hands. And down went his qualms, his maxims, his rules, his smaller beliefs, she scattered them like an expert skittle-player. He was very much astonished and delighted to see them scatter.

He stood and gazed and grinned with wonder whilst his Tablets of Stone went bounding and bumping and splintering down the hill, dislodged for ever. Indeed, it was true as they said, that a man wasn't born before he was married. What a change indeed!

He surveyed the rind of the world: houses, factories, trams, the discarded rind; people scurrying about, work going on, all on the discarded surface. An earthquake had burst it all from inside. It was as if the surface of the world had been broken away entire: Ilkeston, streets, church, people, work, rule-of-the-day, all intact; and yet peeled away into unreality, leaving here exposed the inside, the reality: one's own being, strange feelings and passions and yearnings and beliefs and aspirations, suddenly become present, revealed, the permanent bedrock, knitted one rock with the woman one loved. It was confounding. Things are not what they seem! When he was a child, he had thought a woman was a woman merely by virtue of her skirts and petticoats. And now, lo, the whole world could be divested of its garment, the garment could lie there shed away intact, and one could stand in a new world, a new earth, naked in a new, naked universe. It was too astounding and miraculous.

This then was marriage! The old things didn't matter any more. One got up at four o'clock, and had broth at teatime and made toffee in the middle of the night. One didn't put on one's clothes or one did put on one's clothes. He still was not quite sure it was not criminal. But it was a discovery to find one might be so supremely absolved. All that mattered was that he should love her and she should love him and they should live kindled to one another, like the Lord in two burning bushes that were not consumed. And so they lived for the time.

She was less hampered than he, so she came more quickly to her fulness, and was sooner ready to enjoy again a return to the outside world. She was going to give a tea-party. His heart sank. He wanted to go on, to go on as they were. He wanted to have done with the outside world, to declare it finished for ever. He was anxious with a deep desire and anxiety that she should stay with him where they were in the timeless universe of free, perfect limbs and immortal breast, affirming that the old outward order was finished. The new order was begun to last for ever, the living life, palpitating from the gleaming core, to action, without crust or cover or outward lie. But no, he could not keep her. She wanted the dead world again – she wanted to walk on the outside once more. She was going to give a tea-party. It made him frightened and furious and miserable. He was afraid all would be lost that he had so newly come into: like the youth in the fairy tale, who was king for one day in the year, and for the rest a beaten herd: like Cinderella also, at the feast. He was sullen. But she blithely began to make preparations for her tea-party. His fear was too strong, he was troubled, he hated her shallow anticipation and joy. Was she not forfeiting the reality, the one reality, for all that was shallow and worthless? Wasn't she carelessly taking off her crown to be an artificial figure having other artificial women to tea: when she might have been perfect with him, and kept him perfect, in the land of intimate connection? Now he must be deposed, his joy must be destroyed, he must put on the vulgar, shallow death of an outward existence.

He ground his soul in uneasiness and fear. But she rose to a real outburst of house-work, turning him away as she shoved the furniture aside to her broom. He stood hanging miserable near. He wanted her back. Dread, and desire for her to stay with him, and shame at his own dependence on her drove him to anger. He began to lose his head. The wonder was going to pass away again. All the love, the magnificent new order was going to be lost, she would forfeit it all for the outside things. She would admit the outside world again, she would throw away the living fruit for the ostensible rind. He began to hate this in her. Driven by fear of her departure into a state of helplessness, almost of imbecility, he wandered about the house.

And she, with her skirts kilted up, flew round at her work, absorbed.

'Shake the rug then, if you must hang round,' she said.

And fretting with resentment, he went to shake the rug. She was blithely unconscious of him. He came back, hanging near to her.

'Can't you do anything?' she said, as if to a child, impatiently. 'Can't you do your wood-work?'

'Where shall I do it?' he asked, harsh with pain.

'Anywhere.'

How furious that made him.

'Or go for a walk,' she continued. 'Go down to the Marsh. Don't hang about as if you were only half there.'

He winced and hated it. He went away to read. Never had his soul felt so flayed and uncreated.

And soon he must come down again to her. His hovering near her, wanting her to be with him, the futility of him, the way his hands hung, irritated her beyond bearing. She turned on him blindly and destructively, he became a mad creature, black and electric with fury. The dark storms rose in him, his eyes glowed black and evil, he was fiendish in his thwarted soul.

There followed two black and ghastly days, when she was set in anguish against him, and he felt as if he were in a black, violent underworld, and his wrists quivered murderously. And she resisted him. He seemed a dark, almost evil thing, pursuing her, hanging on to her, burdening her. She would give anything to have him removed.

'You need some work to do,' she said. 'You ought to be at work. Can't you *do* something?'

His soul only grew the blacker. His condition now became complete, the darkness of his soul was thorough. Everything had gone: he remained complete in his own tense, black will. He was now unaware of her. She did not exist. His dark, passionate soul had recoiled upon itself, and now, clinched and coiled round a centre of hatred, existed in its own power. There was a curiously ugly pallor, an expressionlessness in his face. She shuddered from him. She was afraid of him. His will seemed grappled upon her.

She retreated before him. She went down to the Marsh, she entered again the immunity of her parents' love for her. He remained at Yew Cottage, black and clinched, his mind dead. He was unable to work at his wood-carving. He went on working monotonously at the garden, blindly, like a mole.

As she came home, up the hill, looking away at the town dim and blue on the hill, her heart relaxed and became yearning. She did not want to fight him any more. She wanted love – oh, love. Her feet began to hurry. She wanted to get back to him. Her heart became tight with yearning for him.

He had been making the garden in order, cutting the edges of the turf, laying the path with stones. He was a good, capable workman.

'How nice you've made it,' she said, approaching tentatively down the path.

But he did not heed, he did not hear. His brain was solid and dead.

'Haven't you made it nice?' she repeated, rather plaintively.

He looked up at her, with that fixed, expressionless face and unseeing eyes which shocked her, made her go dazed and blind. Then he turned away. She saw his slender, stooping figure groping. A revulsion came over her. She went indoors.

As she took off her hat in the bedroom, she found herself weeping bitterly, with some of the old, anguished, childish desolation. She sat still and cried on. She did not want him to know. She was afraid of his hard, evil moments, the head dropped a little, rigidly, in a crouching, cruel way. She was afraid of him. He seemed to lacerate her sensitive femaleness. He seemed to hurt her womb, to take pleasure in torturing her.

He came into the house. The sound of his footsteps in his heavy boots filled her with horror: a hard cruel, malignant sound. She was afraid he would come upstairs. But he did not. She waited apprehensively. He went out.

Where she was most vulnerable, he hurt her. Oh, where she was delivered over to him, in her very soft femaleness, he seemed to lacerate her and desecrate her. She pressed her hands over her womb in anguish, whilst the tears ran down her face. And why, and why? Why was he like this?

Suddenly she dried her tears. She must get the tea ready. She went downstairs and set the table. When the meal was ready, she called to him.

'I've mashed the tea, Will, are you coming?'

She herself could hear the sound of tears in her own voice, and she began to cry again. He did not answer, but went on with his work. She waited a few minutes, in anguish. Fear came over her, she was panic-stricken with terror, like a child; and she could not go home again to her father; she was held by the power in this man who had taken her.

She turned indoors so that he should not see her tears. She sat down to table. Presently he came into the scullery. His movements jarred on her, as she heard them. How horrible was the way he pumped, exacerbating, so cruel! How she hated to hear him! How he hated her! How his hatred was like blows upon her! The tears were coming again.

He came in, his face wooden and lifeless, fixed, persistent. He sat down to tea, his head dropped over his cup, uglily. His hands were red from the cold water, and there were rims of earth in his nails. He went on with his tea.

It was his negative insensitiveness to her that she could not bear, something clayey and ugly. His intelligence was self-absorbed. How unnatural it was to sit with a self-absorbed creature, like something negative ensconced opposite one. Nothing could touch him – he could only absorb things into his own self.

The tears were running down her face. Something startled him, and he was looking up at her with his hateful, hard, bright eyes, hard and unchanging as a bird of prey.

'What are you crying for?' came the grating voice.

She winced through her womb. She could not stop crying.

'What are you crying for?' came the question again, in just the same tone. And still there was silence, with only the sniff of her tears.

His eyes glittered, and as if with malignant desire. She shrank and became blind. She was like a bird being beaten down. A sort of swoon of helplessness came over her. She was of another order than he, she had no defence against him. Against such an influence, she was only vulnerable, she was given up.

He rose and went out of the house, possessed by the evil spirit. It tortured him and wracked him, and fought in him. And whilst he worked, in the deepening twilight, it left him. Suddenly he saw that she was hurt. He had only seen her triumphant before. Suddenly his heart was torn with compassion for her. He became alive again, in an anguish of compassion. He could not bear to think of her tears – he could not bear it. He wanted to go to her and pour out his heart's blood to her. He wanted to give everything to her, all his blood, his life, to the last dregs, pour everything away to her. He yearned with passionate desire to offer himself to her, utterly.

The evening star came, and the night. She had not lighted the lamp. His heart burned with pain and with grief. He trembled to go to her.

And at last he went, hesitating, burdened with a great offering. The hardness had gone out of him, his body was sensitive, slightly trembling. His hand was curiously sensitive, shrinking, as he shut the door. He fixed the latch almost tenderly.

In the kitchen was only the fireglow, he could not see her. He quivered with dread lest she had gone – he knew not where. In shrinking dread, he went through to the parlour, to the foot of the stairs.

'Anna,' he called.

There was no answer. He went up the stairs, in dread of the empty house – the horrible emptiness that made his heart ring with insanity. He opened the bedroom door, and his heart flashed with certainty that she had gone, that he was alone.

But he saw her on the bed, lying very still and scarcely noticeable, with her back to him. He went and put his hand on her shoulder, very gently, hesitating, in a great fear and self-offering. She did not move. He waited. The hand that touched her shoulder hurt him, as if she were sending it away. He stood dim with pain.

'Anna,' he said.

But still she was motionless, like a curled up, oblivious creature. His heart beat with strange throes of pain. Then, by a motion under his hand, he knew she was crying, holding herself hard so that her tears should not be known. He waited. The tension continued – perhaps she was not crying – then suddenly relapsed with a sharp catch of a sob. His heart flamed with love and suffering for her. Kneeling carefully on the bed, so that his earthy boots should not touch it, he took her in his arms to comfort her. The sobs gathered in her, she was sobbing bitterly. But not to him. She was still away from him.

He held her against his breast, whilst she sobbed, withheld from him, and all his body vibrated against her.

'Don't cry – don't cry,' he said, with an odd simplicity. His heart was calm and numb with a sort of innocence of love, now.

She still sobbed, ignoring him, ignoring that he held her. His lips were dry.

'Don't cry, my love,' he said, in the same abstract way. In his breast his heart burned like a torch, with suffering. He could not bear the desolateness of her crying. He would have soothed her with his blood. He heard the church clock chime, as if it touched him, and he waited in suspense for it to have gone by. It was quiet again.

'My love,' he said to her, bending to touch her wet face with his mouth. He was afraid to touch her. How wet her face was! His body trembled as he held her. He loved her till he felt his heart and all his veins would burst and flood her with his hot, healing blood. He knew his blood would heal and restore her.

She was becoming quieter. He thanked the God of mercy that at last she was becoming quieter. His head felt so strange and blazed. Still he held her close, with trembling arms. His blood seemed very strong, enveloping her.

And at last she began to draw near to him, she nestled to him. His limbs, his body, took fire and beat up in flames. She clung to him, she cleaved to his body. The flames swept him, he held her in sinews of fire. If she would kiss him! He bent his mouth down. And her mouth, soft and moist, received him. He felt his veins would burst with anguish of thankfulness, his heart was mad with gratefulness, he could pour himself out upon her for ever.

When they came to themselves, the night was very dark. Two hours had gone by. They lay still and warm and weak, like the new-born, together. And there was a silence almost of the unborn. Only his heart was weeping happily, after the pain. He did not understand, he had yielded, given way. There *was* no understanding. There could be only acquiescence and submission, and tremulous wonder of consummation.

The next morning, when they woke up, it had snowed. He wondered what was the strange pallor in the air, and the unusual tang. Snow was on the grass and the window-sill, it weighed down the black, ragged branches of the yews, and smoothed the graves in the churchyard.

Soon, it began to snow again, and they were shut in. He was glad, for then they were immune in a shadowy silence, there was no world, no time.

The snow lasted for some days. On the Sunday they went to church. They made a line of footprints across the garden, he left a flat snowprint of his hand on the wall as he vaulted over, they traced the snow across the churchyard. For three days they had been immune in a perfect love.

There were very few people in church, and she was glad. She did not care much for church. She had never questioned any beliefs, and she was, from habit and custom, a regular attendant at morning service. But she had ceased to come with any anticipation. To-day, however, in the strangeness of snow, after such consummation of love, she felt expectant again, and delighted. She was still in the eternal world.

She used, after she went to the High School, and wanted to be a lady, wanted to fulfil some mysterious ideal, always to listen to the sermon and to try to gather suggestions. That was all very well for a while. The vicar told her to be good in this way and in that. She went away feeling it was her highest aim to fulfil these injunctions.

But quickly this palled. After a short time, she was not very much interested in being good. Her soul was in quest of something, which was not just being good, and doing one's best. No, she wanted something else: something that was not her ready-made duty. Everything seemed to be merely a matter of social duty, and never of her *self*. They talked about her soul, but somehow never managed to rouse or to implicate her soul. As yet her soul was not brought in at all.

So that whilst she had an affection for Mr. Loverseed, the vicar, and a protective sort of feeling for Cossethay church, wanting always to help it and defend it, it counted very small in her life.

Not but that she was conscious of some unsatisfaction. When her husband was roused by the thought of the churches, then she became hostile to the ostensible church, she hated it for not fulfilling anything in her. The Church told her to be good: very well, she had no idea of contradicting what it said. The Church talked about her soul, about the welfare of mankind, as if the saving of her soul lay in her performing certain acts conducive to the welfare of mankind. Well and good – it was so, then.

Nevertheless, as she sat in church her face had a pathos and poignancy. Was this what she had come to hear: how by doing this thing and by not doing that, she could save her soul? She did not contradict it. But the pathos of her face gave the lie. There was something else she wanted to hear, it was something else she asked for from the Church.

But who was *she* to affirm it? And what was *she* doing with unsatisfied desires? She was ashamed. She ignored them and left them out of count as much as possible, her underneath yearnings. They angered her. She wanted to be like other people, decently satisfied.

He angered her more than ever. Church had an irresistible attraction for him. And he paid no more attention to that part of the service which was Church to her, than if he had been an angel or a fabulous beast sitting there.

He simply paid no heed to the sermon or to the meaning of the service. There was something thick, dark, dense, powerful about him that irritated her too deeply for her to speak of it. The Church teaching in itself meant nothing to him. 'And forgive us our trespasses as we forgive them that trespass against us' – it simply did not touch him. It might have been mere sounds, and it would have acted upon him in the same way. He did not want things to be intelligible. And he did not care about his trespasses, neither about the trespasses of his neighbour, when he was in church. Leave that care for weekdays. When he was in church, he took no more notice of his daily life. It was weekday stuff. As for the welfare of mankind – he merely did not realise that there was any such thing: except on weekdays, when he was good-natured enough. In church, he wanted a dark, nameless emotion, the emotion of all the great mysteries of passion.

He was not interested in the *thought* of himself or of her: oh, and how that irritated her! He ignored the sermon, he ignored the greatness of mankind, he did not admit the immediate importance of mankind. He did not care about himself as a human being. He did not attach any vital importance to his life in the drafting office, or his life among men. That was just merely the margin to the text. The verity was his connection with Anna and his connection with the Church, his real being lay in his dark emotional experience of the Infinite, of the Absolute. And the great mysterious, illuminated capitals to the text, were his feelings with the Church.

It exasperated her beyond measure. She could not get out of the Church the satisfaction he got. The thought of her soul was intimately mixed up with the thought of her own self. Indeed, her soul and her own self were one and the same in her. Whereas he seemed simply to ignore the fact of his own self, almost to refute it. He had a soul – a dark, inhuman thing caring nothing for humanity. So she conceived it. And in the gloom and the mystery of the Church his soul lived and ran free, like some strange, underground thing, abstract.

He was very strange to her, and, in this church spirit, in conceiving himself as a soul, he seemed to escape and run free of her. In a way, she envied it him, this dark freedom and jubilation of the soul, some strange entity in him. It fascinated her. Again she hated it. And again, she despised him, wanted to destroy it in him.

This snowy morning, he sat with a dark-bright face beside her, not aware of her, and somehow, she felt he was conveying to strange, secret places the love that sprang in him for her. He sat with a dark-rapt, half-delighted face, looking at a little stained window. She saw the ruby-coloured glass, with the shadow heaped along the bottom from the snow outside, and the familiar yellow figure of the lamb holding the banner, a little darkened now, but in the murky interior strangely luminous, pregnant.

She had always liked the little red and yellow window. The lamb, looking very silly and self-conscious, was holding up a forepaw, in the cleft of which was dangerously perched a little flag with a red cross. Very pale yellow, the lamb, with greenish shadows. Since she was a child she had liked this creature, with the same feeling she felt for the little woolly lambs on green legs that children carried home from the fair every year. She had always liked these toys, and she had the same amused, childish liking for this church lamb. Yet she had always been uneasy about it. She was never sure that this lamb with a flag did not want to be more than it appeared. So she half mistrusted it, there was a mixture of dislike in her attitude to it.

Now, by a curious gathering, knitting of his eyes, the faintest tension of ecstasy on his face, he gave her the uncomfortable feeling that he was in correspondence with the creature, the lamb in the window. A cold wonder came over her – her soul was perplexed. There he sat, motionless, timeless, with the faint, bright tension on his face. What was he doing? What connection was there between him and the lamb in the glass?

Suddenly it gleamed to her dominant, this lamb with the flag. Suddenly she had a powerful mystic experience, the power of the tradition seized on her, she was transported to another world. And she hated it, resisted it.

Instantly, it was only a silly lamb in the glass again. And dark, violent hatred of her husband swept up in her. What was he doing, sitting there gleaming, carried away, soulful?

She shifted sharply, she knocked him as she pretended to pick up her glove, she groped among his feet.

He came to, rather bewildered, exposed. Anybody but her would have pitied him. She wanted to rend him. He did not know what was amiss, what he had been doing.

As they sat at dinner, in their cottage, he was dazed by the chill of antagonism from her. She did not know why she was so angry. But she was incensed.

'Why do you never listen to the sermon?' she asked, seething with hostility and violation.

'I do,' he said.

'You don't – you don't hear a single word.'

He retired into himself, to enjoy his own sensation. There was something subterranean about him, as if he had an underworld refuge. The young girl hated to be in the house with him when he was like this.

After dinner, he retired into the parlour, continuing in the same state of abstraction, which was a burden intolerable to her. Then he went to the book-shelf and took down books to look at, that she had scarcely glanced over.

He sat absorbed over a book on the illuminations in old missals, and then over a book on paintings in churches: Italian, English, French and German. He had, when he was sixteen, discovered a Roman Catholic bookshop where he could find such things.

He turned the leaves in absorption, absorbed in looking, not thinking. He was like a man whose eyes were in his chest, she said of him later.

She came to look at the things with him. Half they fascinated her. She was puzzled, interested, and antagonistic.

It was when she came to pictures of the Pietà that she burst out.

'I do think they're loathsome,' she cried.

'What?' he said, surprised, abstracted.

'Those bodies with slits in them, posing to be worshipped.'

'You see, it means the Sacraments, the Bread,' he said slowly.

'Does it,' she cried. 'Then it's worse. *I* don't want to see your chest slit, not to eat your dead body, even if you offer it to me. Can't you see it's horrible?'

'It isn't me, it's Christ.'

'What if it is, it's you! And it's horrible, you wallowing in your own dead body, and thinking of eating it in the Sacrament.'

'You've to take it for what it means.'

'It means your human body put up to be slit and killed and then worshipped – what else?'

They lapsed into silence. His soul grew angry and aloof.

'And I think that lamb in Church,' she said, 'is the biggest joke in the parish—'

She burst into a 'Pouf' of ridiculing laughter.

'It might be, to those that see nothing in it,' he said. 'You know it's the symbol of Christ, of His innocence and sacrifice.'

'Whatever it means, it's a *lamb*,' she said. 'And I like lambs too much to treat them as if they had to mean something. As for the Christmas-tree flag – no—'

And again she poufed with mockery.

'It's because you don't know anything,' he said violently, harshly. 'Laugh at what you know, not at what you don't know.'

'What don't I know?'

'What things mean.'

'And what does it mean?'

He was reluctant to answer her. He found it difficult.

'*What* does it mean?' she insisted.

'It means the triumph of the Resurrection.'

She hesitated, baffled, a fear came upon her. What were these things? Something dark and powerful seemed to extend before her. Was it wonderful after all?

But no – she refused it.

'Whatever it may pretend to mean, what it *is* is a silly absurd toy-lamb with a Christmas-tree flag ledged on its paw – and if it wants to mean anything else, it must look different from that.'

He was in a state of violent irritation against her. Partly he was ashamed of his love for these things; he hid his passion for them. He was ashamed of the ecstasy into which he could throw himself with these symbols. And for a few moments he hated the lamb and the mystic pictures of the Eucharist, with a violent, ashy hatred. His fire was put out, she had thrown cold water on it. The whole thing was distasteful to him, his mouth was full of ashes. He went out cold with corpse-like anger, leaving her alone. He hated her. He walked through the white snow, under a sky of lead.

And she wept again, in bitter recurrence of the previous gloom. But her heart was easy – oh, much more easy.

She was quite willing to make it up with him when he came home again. He was black and surly, but abated. She had broken a little of something in him. And at length he was glad to forfeit from his soul all his symbols, to have her making love to him. He loved it when she put her head on his knee, and he had not asked her to or wanted her to, he loved her when she put her arms round him and made bold love to him, and he did not make love to her. He felt a strong blood in his limbs again.

And she loved the intent, far look of his eyes when they rested on her: intent, yet far, not near, not with her. And she wanted to bring them near. She wanted his eyes to come to hers, to know her. And they would not. They remained intent, and far, and proud, like a hawk's, naïve and inhuman as a hawk's. So she loved him and caressed him and roused him like a hawk, till he was keen and instant, but without tenderness. He came to her fierce and hard, like a hawk striking and taking her. He was no mystic any more, she was his aim and object, his prey. And she was carried off, and he was satisfied, or satiated at last.

Then immediately she began to retaliate on him. She too was a hawk. If she imitated the pathetic plover running plaintive to him, that was part of the game. When he, satisfied, moved with a proud, insolent slouch of the body and a half-contemptuous drop of the head, unaware of her, ignoring her very existence, after taking his fill of her and getting his satisfaction of her, her soul roused, its pinions became like steel, and she struck at him. When he sat on his perch glancing sharply round with solitary pride, pride eminent and fierce, she dashed at him and threw him from his station savagely, she goaded him from his keen dignity of a male, she harassed him from his unperturbed pride, till he was mad with rage, his light brown eyes burned with fury, they saw her now, like flames of anger they flared at her and recognised her as the enemy.

Very good, she was the enemy, very good. As he prowled round her, she watched him. As he struck at her, she struck back.

He was angry because she had carelessly pushed away his tools so that they got rusty.

'Don't leave them littering in my way, then,' she said.

'I shall leave them where I like,' he cried.

'Then I shall throw them where I like.'

They glowered at each other, he with rage in his hands, she with her soul fierce with victory. They were very well matched. They would fight it out.

She turned to her sewing. Immediately the tea-things were cleared away, she fetched out the stuff, and his soul rose in rage. He hated beyond measure to hear the shriek of calico as she tore the web sharply, as if with pleasure. And the run of the sewing-machine gathered a frenzy in him at last.

'Aren't you going to stop that row?' he shouted. 'Can't you do it in the daytime?'

She looked up sharply, hostile from her work.

'No, I can't do it in the daytime. I have other things to do. Besides, I like sewing, and you're not going to stop me doing it.'

Whereupon she turned back to her arranging, fixing, stitching, his nerves jumped with anger as the sewing-machine started and stuttered and buzzed.

But she was enjoying herself, she was triumphant and happy as the darting needle danced ecstatically down a hem, drawing the stuff along under its vivid stabbing, irresistibly. She made the machine hum. She stopped it imperiously, her fingers were deft and swift and mistress.

If he sat behind her stiff with impotent rage it only made a trembling vividness come into her energy. On she worked. At last he went to bed in a rage, and lay stiff, away from her. And she turned her back on him. And in the morning they did not speak, except in mere cold civilities.

And when he came home at night, his heart relenting and growing hot for love of her, when he was just ready to feel he had been wrong, and when he was expecting her to feel the same, there she sat at the sewing-machine, the whole house was covered with clipped calico, the kettle was not even on the fire.

She started up, affecting concern.

'Is it so late?' she cried.

But his face had gone stiff with rage. He walked through to the parlour, then he walked back and out of the house again. Her heart sank. Very swiftly she began to make his tea.

He went black-hearted down the road to Ilkeston. When he was in this state he never thought. A bolt shot across the doors of his mind and shut him in, a prisoner. He went back to Ilkeston, and drank a glass of beer. What was he going to do? He did not want to see anybody.

He would go to Nottingham, to his own town. He went to the station and took a train. When he got to Nottingham, still he had nowhere to go. However, it was more agreeable to walk familiar streets. He paced them with a mad restlessness, as if he were running amok. Then he turned to a book-shop and found a book on Bamberg Cathedral. Here was a discovery! here was something for him! He went into a quiet restaurant to look at his treasure. He lit up with thrills of bliss as he turned from picture to picture. He had found something at last, in these carvings. His soul had great satisfaction. Had he not come out to seek, and had he not found! He was in a passion of fulfilment. These were the finest carvings, statues, he had ever seen. The book lay in his hands like a doorway. The world around was only an enclosure, a room. But he was going away. He lingered over the lovely statues of women. A marvellous, finely-wrought universe crystallised out around him as he looked again, at the crowns, the twining hair, the woman-faces. He liked all the better the unintelligible text of the German. He preferred things he could not understand with the mind. He loved the undiscovered and the undiscoverable. He pored over the pictures intensely. And these were wooden statues, 'Holz' – he believed that meant wood. Wooden statues so shapen to his soul! He was a million times gladdened. How undiscovered the world was, how it revealed itself to his soul! What a fine, exciting thing his life was, at his hand! Did not Bamberg Cathedral make the world his own? He celebrated his triumphant strength and life and verity, and embraced the vast riches he was inheriting.

But it was about time to go home. He had better catch a train. All the time there was a steady bruise at the bottom of his soul, but so steady as to be forgettable. He caught a train for Ilkeston.

It was ten o'clock as he was mounting the hill to Cossethay, carrying his limp book on Bamberg Cathedral. He had not yet thought of Anna, not definitely. The dark finger pressing a bruise controlled him thoughtlessly.

Anna had started guiltily when he left the house. She had hastened preparing the tea, hoping he would come back. She had made some toast, and got all ready. Then he didn't come. She cried with vexation and disappointment. Why had he gone? Why couldn't he come back now? Why was it such a battle between them? She loved him – she did love him – why couldn't he be kinder to her, nicer to her?

She waited in distress – then her mood grew harder. He passed out of her thoughts. She had considered indignantly, what right he had to interfere with her sewing? She had indignantly refuted his right to interfere with her at all. She was not to be interfered with. Was she not herself, and he the outsider.

Yet a quiver of fear went through her. If he should leave her? She sat conjuring fears and sufferings, till she wept with very self-pity. She did not know what she would do if he left her, or if he turned against her. The thought of it chilled her, made her desolate and hard. And against him, the stranger, the outsider, the being who wanted to arrogate authority, she remained steadily fortified. Was she not herself? How could one who was not of her own kind presume with authority? She knew she was immutable, unchangeable, she was not afraid for her own being. She was only afraid of all that was not herself. It pressed round her, it came to her and took part in her, in form of her man, this vast, resounding, alien world which was not herself. And he had so many weapons, he might strike from so many sides.

When he came in at the door, his heart was blazed with pity and tenderness, she looked so lost and forlorn and young. She glanced up, afraid. And she was surprised to see him, shining-faced, clear and beautiful in his movements, as if he were clarified. And a startled pang of fear, and shame of herself went through her.

They waited for each other to speak.

'Do you want to eat anything?' she said.

'I'll get it myself,' he answered, not wanting her to serve him. But she brought out food. And it pleased him she did it for him. He was again a bright lord.

'I went to Nottingham,' he said mildly.

'To your mother?' she asked, in a flash of contempt.

'No – I didn't go home.'

'Who did you go to see?'

'I went to see nobody.'

'Then why did you go to Nottingham?'

'I went because I wanted to go.'

He was getting angry that she again rebuffed him when he was so clear and shining.

'And who did you see?'

'I saw nobody.'

'Nobody?'

'No – who should I see?'

'You saw nobody you knew?'

'No, I didn't,' he replied irritably.

She believed him, and her mood became cold.

'I bought a book,' he said, handing her the propitiatory volume.

She idly looked at the pictures. Beautiful, the pure women, with their clear-dropping gowns. Her heart became colder. What did they mean to *him?*

He sat and waited for her. She bent over the book.

'Aren't they nice?' he said, his voice roused and glad. Her blood flushed, but she did not lift her head.

'Yes,' she said. In spite of herself, she was compelled by him. He was strange, attractive, exerting some power over her.

He came over to her, and touched her delicately. Her heart beat with wild passion, wild raging passion. But she resisted as yet. It was always the unknown, always the unknown and she clung fiercely to her known self. But the rising flood carried her away.

They loved each other to transport again, passionately and fully.

'Isn't it more wonderful than ever?' she asked him, radiant like a newly opened flower, with tears like dew.

He held her closer. He was strange and abstracted.

'It is always more wonderful,' she asseverated, in a glad, child's voice, remembering her fear, and not quite cleared of it yet.

So it went on continually, the recurrence of love and conflict between them. One day it seemed as if everything was shattered, all life spoiled, ruined, desolate and laid waste. The next day it was all marvellous again, just marvellous. One day she thought she would go mad from his very presence, the sound of his drinking was detestable to her. The next day she loved and rejoiced in the way he crossed the floor, he was sun, moon and stars in one.

She fretted, however, at last, over the lack of stability. When the perfect hours came back, her heart did not forget that they would pass away again. She was uneasy. The surety, the surety, the inner surety, the confidence in the abidingness of love: that was what she wanted. And that she did not get. She knew also that he had not got it.

Nevertheless it was a marvellous world, she was for the most part lost in the marvellousness of it. Even her great woes were marvellous to her.

She could be very happy. And she wanted to be happy. She resented it when he made her unhappy. Then she could kill him, cast him out. Many days, she waited for the hour when he would be gone to work. Then the flow of her life, which he seemed to damn up, was let loose, and she was free. She was free, she was full of delight. Everything delighted her. She took up the rug and went to shake it in the garden. Patches of snow were on the fields, the air was light. She heard the ducks shouting on the pond, she saw them charge and sail across the water as if they were setting off on an invasion of the world. She watched the rough horses, one of which was clipped smooth on the belly, so that he wore a jacket and long stockings of brown fur, stand kissing each other in the wintry morning by the church-yard wall. Everything delighted her, now he was gone, the insulator, the obstruction removed, the world was all hers, in connection with her.

She was joyfully active. Nothing pleased her more than to hang out the washing in a high wind that came full-butt over the round of the hill, tearing the wet garments out of her hands, making flap-flap-flap of the waving stuff. She laughed and struggled and grew angry. But she loved her solitary days.

Then he came home at night, and she knitted her brows because of some endless contest between them. As he stood in the doorway her heart changed. It steeled itself. The laughter and zest of the day disappeared from her. She was stiffened.

They fought an unknown battle, unconsciously. Still they were in love with each other, the passion was there. But the passion was consumed in a battle. And the deep, fierce unnamed battle went on. Everything glowed intensely about them, the world had put off its clothes and was awful, with new, primal nakedness.

Sunday came when the strange spell was cast over her by him. Half she loved it. She was becoming more like him. All the week-days, there was a glint of sky and fields, the little church seemed to babble away to the cottages the morning through. But on Sundays, when he stayed at home, a deeply-coloured, intense gloom seemed to gather on the face of the earth, the church seemed to fill itself with shadow, to become big, a universe to her, there was a burning of blue and ruby, a sound of worship about her. And when the doors were opened, and she came out into the world, it was a world new-created, she stepped into the resurrection of the world, her heart beating to the memory of the darkness and the Passion.

If, as very often, they went to the Marsh for tea on Sundays, then she regained another, lighter world, that had never known the gloom and the stained glass and the ecstasy of chanting. Her husband was obliterated, she was with her father again, who was so fresh and free and all daylight. Her husband, with his intensity and his darkness, was obliterated. She left him, she forgot him, she accepted her father.

Yet, as she went home again with the young man, she put her hand on his arm tentatively, a little bit ashamed, her hand pleaded that he would not hold it against her, her recusancy. But he was obscured. He seemed to become blind, as if he were not there with her.

Then she was afraid. She wanted him. When he was oblivious of her, she almost went mad with fear. For she had become so vulnerable, so exposed. She was in touch so intimately. All things about her had become intimate, she had known them near and lovely, like presences hovering upon her. What if they should all go hard and separate again, standing back from her terrible and distinct, and she, having known them, should be at their mercy?

This frightened her. Always, her husband was to her the unknown to which she was delivered up. She was a flower that has been tempted forth into blossom, and has no retreat. He had her nakedness in his power. And who was he, what was he? A blind thing, a dark force, without knowledge. She wanted to preserve herself.

Then she gathered him to herself again and was satisfied for a moment. But as time went on, she began to realise more and more that he did not alter, that he was something dark, alien to herself. She had thought him just the bright reflex of herself. As the weeks and months went by she realised that he was a dark opposite to her, that they were opposites, not complements.

He did not alter, he remained separately himself, and he seemed to expect her to be part of himself, the extension of his will. She felt him trying to gain power over her, without knowing her. What did he want? Was he going to bully her?

What did she want herself? She answered herself, that she wanted to be happy, to be natural, like the sunlight and the busy daytime. And, at the bottom of her soul, she felt he wanted her to be dark, unnatural. Sometimes, when he seemed like the darkness covering and smothering her, she revolted almost in horror, and struck at him. She struck at him, and made him bleed, and he became wicked. Because she dreaded him and held him in horror, he became wicked, he wanted to destroy. And then the fight between them was cruel.

She began to tremble. He wanted to impose himself on her. And he began to shudder. She wanted to desert him, to leave him a prey to the open, with the unclean dogs of the darkness setting on to devour him. He must beat her, and make her stay with him. Whereas she fought to keep herself free of him.

They went their ways now shadowed and stained with blood, feeling the world far off, unable to give help. Till she began to get tired. After a certain point, she became impassive, detached utterly from him. He was always ready to burst out murderously against her. Her soul got up and left him, she went her way. Nevertheless in her apparent blitheness, that made his soul black with opposition, she trembled as if she bled.

And ever and again, the pure love came in sunbeams between them, when she was like a flower in the sun to him, so beautiful, so shining, so intensely dear that he could scarcely bear it. Then as if his soul had six wings of bliss he stood absorbed in praise, feeling the radiance from the Almighty beat through him like a pulse, as he stood in the upright flame of praise, transmitting the pulse of Creation.

And ever and again he appeared to her as the dread flame of power. Sometimes, when he stood in the doorway, his face lit up, he seemed like an Annunciation to her, her heart beat fast. And she watched him, suspended. He had a dark, burning being that she dreaded and resisted. She was subject to him as to the Angel of the Presence. She waited upon him and heard his will, and she trembled in his service.

Then all this passed away. Then he loved her for her childishness and for her strangeness to him, for the wonder of her soul which was different from his soul, and which made him genuine when he would be false. And she loved him for the way he sat loosely in a chair, or for the way he came through a door with his face open and eager. She loved his ringing, eager voice, and the touch of the unknown about him, his absolute simplicity.

Yet neither of them was quite satisfied. He felt, somewhere, that she did not respect him. She only respected him as far as he was related to herself. For what he was, beyond her, she had no care. She did not care for what he represented in himself. It is true, he did not know himself what he represented. But whatever it was she did not really honour it. She did no service to his work as a lace-designer, nor to himself as bread-winner. Because he went down to the office and worked every day – that entitled him to no respect or regard from her, he knew. Rather she despised him for it. And he almost loved her for this, though at first it maddened him like an insult.

What was much deeper, she soon came to combat his deepest feelings. What he thought about life and about society and mankind did not matter very much to her: he was right enough to be insignificant. This was again galling to him. She would judge beyond him on these things. But at length he came to accept her judgments, discovering them as if they were his own. It was not here the deep trouble lay. The deep root of his enmity lay in the fact that she jeered at his soul. He was inarticulate and stupid in thought. But to some things he clung passionately. He loved the Church. If she tried to get out of him, what he *believed*, then they were both soon in a white rage.

Did he believe the water turned to wine at Cana? She would drive him to the thing as a historical fact: so much rain-water – look at it – can it become grape-juice, wine? For an instant, he saw with the clear eyes of the mind and said no, his clear mind, answering her for a moment, rejected the idea. And immediately his whole soul was crying in a mad, inchoate hatred against this violation of himself. It *was* true for him. His mind was extinguished again at once, his blood was up. In his blood and bones, he wanted the scene, the wedding, the water brought forward from the firkins as red wine: and Christ saying to His mother: 'Woman, what have I to do with thee? – mine hour is not yet come.'

And then:

'His mother saith unto the servants, "Whatsoever he saith unto you, do it." '

Brangwen loved it, with his bones and blood he loved it, he could not let it go. Yet she forced him to let it go. She hated his blind attachments.

Water, natural water, could it suddenly and unnaturally turn into wine, depart from its being and at haphazard take on another being? Ah no, he knew it was wrong.

She became again the palpitating, hostile child, hateful, putting things to destruction. He became mute and dead. His own being gave him the lie. He knew it was so: wine was wine, water was water, for ever: the water had not become wine. The miracle was not a real fact. She seemed to be destroying him. He went out, dark and destroyed, his soul running its blood. And he tasted of death. Because his life was formed in these unquestioned concepts.

She, desolate again as she had been when she was a child, went away and sobbed. She did not care, she did not care whether the water had turned to wine or not. Let him believe it if he wanted to. But she knew she had won. And an ashy desolation came over her.

They were ashenly miserable for some time. Then the life began to come back. He was nothing if not dogged. He thought again of the chapter of St. John. There was a great biting pang. 'But thou hast kept the good wine until now.' 'The best wine!' The young man's heart responded in a craving, in a triumph, although the knowledge that it was not true in fact bit at him like a weasel in his heart. Which was stronger, the pain of the denial, or the desire for affirmation? He was stubborn in spirit, and abode by his desire. But he would not any more affirm the miracles as true.

Very well, it was not true, the water had not turned into wine. The water had not turned into wine. But for all that he would live in his soul as if the water *had* turned into wine. For truth of fact, it had not. But for his soul, it had.

'Whether it turned into wine or whether it didn't,' he said, 'it doesn't bother me. I take it for what it is.'

'And *what* is it?' she asked, quickly, hopefully.

'It's the Bible,' he said.

That answer enraged her, and she despised him. She did not actively question the Bible herself. But he drove her to contempt.

And yet he did not care about the Bible, the written letter. Although he could not satisfy her, yet she knew of herself that he had something real. He was not a dogmatist. He did not believe in *fact* that the water turned into wine. He did not want to make a fact out of it. Indeed, his attitude was without criticism. It was purely individual. He took that which was of value to him from the Written Word, he added to his spirit. His mind he let sleep.

And she was bitter against him, that he let his mind sleep. That which was human, belonged to mankind, he would not exert. He cared only for himself. He was no Christian. Above all, Christ had asserted the brotherhood of man.

She, almost against herself, clung to the worship of the human knowledge. Man must die in the body, but in his knowledge he was immortal. Such, somewhere, was her belief, quite obscure and unformulated. She believed in the omnipotence of the human mind.

He, on the other hand, blind as a subterranean thing, just ignored the human mind and ran after his own dark-souled desires, following his own tunnelling nose. She felt often she must suffocate. And she fought him off.

Then he, knowing he was blind, fought madly back again, frantic in sensual fear. He did foolish things. He asserted himself on his rights, he arrogated the old position of master of the house.

'You've a right to do as I want,' he cried.

'Fool!' she answered. 'Fool!'

'I'll let you know who's master,' he cried.

'Fool!' she answered. 'Fool! I've known my own father, who could put a dozen of you in his pipe and push them down with his finger-end. Don't I know what a fool you are!'

He knew himself what a fool he was, and was flayed by the knowledge. Yet he went on trying to steer the ship of their dual life. He asserted his position as the captain of the ship. And captain and ship bored her. He wanted to loom important as master of one of the innumerable domestic craft that make up the great fleet of society. It seemed to her a ridiculous armada of tubs jostling in futility. She felt no belief in it. She jeered at him as master of the house, master of their dual life. And he was black with shame and rage. He knew, with shame, how her father had been a man without arrogating any authority.

He had gone on the wrong tack, and he felt it hard to give up the expedition. There was great surging and shame. Then he yielded. He had given up the master-of-the-house idea.

There was something he wanted, nevertheless, some form of mastery. Ever and anon, after his collapses into the petty and the shameful, he rose up again, and, stubborn in spirit, strong in his power to start afresh, set out once more in his male pride of being to fulfil the hidden passion of his spirit.

It began well, but it ended always in war between them, till they were both driven almost to madness. He said, she did not respect him. She laughed in hollow scorn of this. For her it was enough that she loved him.

'Respect what?' she asked.

But he always answered the wrong thing. And though she cudgelled her brains, she could not come at it.

'Why don't you go on with your wood-carving?' she said. 'Why don't you finish your Adam and Eve?'

But she did not care for the Adam and Eve, and he never put another stroke to it. She jeered at the Eve, saying, 'She is like a little marionette. Why is she so small? You've made Adam as big as God, and Eve like a doll.'

'It is impudence to say that Woman was made out of Man's body,' she continued, 'when every man is born of woman. What impudence men have, what arrogance!'

In a rage one day, after trying to work on the board, and failing, so that his belly was a flame of nausea, he chopped up the whole panel and put it on the fire. She did not know. He went about for some days very quiet and subdued after it.

'Where is the Adam and Eve board?' she asked him.

'Burnt.'

She looked at him.

'But your carving?'

'I burned it.'

'When?'

She did not believe him.

'On Friday night.'

'When I was at the Marsh?'

'Yes.'

She said no more.

Then, when he had gone to work, she wept for a whole day, and was much chastened in spirit. So that a new, fragile flame of love came out of the ashes of this last pain.

Directly, it occurred to her that she was with child. There was a great trembling of wonder and anticipation through her soul. She wanted a child. Not that she loved babies so much, though she was touched by all young things. But she wanted to bear children. And a certain hunger in her heart wanted to unite her husband with herself, in a child.

She wanted a son. She felt, a son would be everything. She wanted to tell her husband. But it was such a trembling, intimate thing to tell him, and he was at this time hard and unresponsive. So that she went away and wept. It was such a waste of a beautiful opportunity, such a frost that nipped in the bud one of the beautiful moments of her life. She went about heavy and tremulous with her secret, wanting to touch him, oh, most delicately, and see his face, dark and sensitive, attend to her news. She waited and waited

for him to become gentle and still towards her. But he was always harsh and
he bullied her.

So that the buds shrivelled from her confidence, she was chilled. She went
down to the Marsh.

'Well,' said her father, looking at her and seeing her at the first glance,
'what's amiss wi' you now?'

The tears came at the touch of his careful love.

'Nothing,' she said.

'Can't you hit it off, you two?' he said.

'He's so obstinate,' she quivered; but her soul was obdurate itself.

'Ay, an' I know another who's all that,' said her father.

She was silent.

'You don't want to make yourselves miserable,' said her father; 'all about
nowt.'

'*He* isn't miserable,' she said.

'I'll back my life, if you can do nowt else, you can make him as miserable
as a dog. You'd be a dab hand at that, my lass.'

'*I* do nothing to make him miserable,' she retorted.

'Oh no – oh no! A packet o' butterscotch, you are.'

She laughed a little.

'You mustn't think I *want* him to be miserable,' she cried. 'I don't.'

'We quite readily believe it,' retorted Brangwen. 'Neither do you intend
him to be hopping for joy like a fish in a pond.'

This made her think. She was rather surprised to find that she did *not*
intend her husband to be hopping for joy like a fish in a pond.

Her mother came, and they all sat down to tea, talking casually.

'Remember, child,' said her mother, 'that everything is not waiting for
your hand just to take or leave. You mustn't expect it. Between two people,
the love itself is the important thing, and that is neither you nor him. It is
a third thing you must create. You mustn't expect it to be just your way.'

'Ha – nor do I. If I did I should soon find my mistake out. If *I* put my
hand out to take anything, my hand is very soon bitten, I can tell you.'

'Then you must mind where you put your hand,' said her father.

Anna was rather indignant that they took the tragedy of her young married
life with such equanimity.

'You love the man right enough,' said her father, wrinkling his forehead
in distress. 'That's all as counts.'

'I *do* love him, more shame to him,' she cried. 'I want to tell him – I've
been waiting for four days now to tell him—' her face began to quiver, the
tears came. Her parents watched her in silence. She did not go on.

'Tell him what?' said her father.

'That we're going to have an infant,' she sobbed, 'and he's never, never
let me, not once, every time I've come to him, he's been horrid to me, and
I wanted to tell him, I did. And he won't let me – he's cruel to me.'

She sobbed as if her heart would break. Her mother went and comforted
her, put her arms round her, and held her close. Her father sat with a queer,
wrinkled brow, and was rather paler than usual. His heart went tense with
hatred of his son-in-law.

So that, when the tale was sobbed out, and comfort administered and tea sipped, and something like calm restored to the little circle, the thought of Will Brangwen's entry was not pleasantly entertained.

Tilly was set to watch out for him as he passed by on his way home. The little party at table heard the woman-servant's shrill call:

'You've got to come in, Will. Anna's here.'

After a few moments, the youth entered.

'Are you stopping?' he asked in his hard, harsh voice.

He seemed like a blade of destruction standing there. She quivered to tears.

'Sit you down,' said Tom Brangwen, 'an' take a bit off your length.'

Will Brangwen sat down. He felt something strange in the atmosphere. He was dark browed, but his eyes had the keen, intent, sharp look, as if he could only see in the distance; which was a beauty in him, and which made Anna so angry.

'Why does he always deny me?' she said to herself. 'Why is it nothing to him, what I am?'

And Tom Brangwen, blue-eyed and warm, sat in opposition to the youth.

'How long are you stopping?' the young husband asked his wife.

'Not very long,' she said.

'Get your tea, lad,' said Tom Brangwen. 'Are you itchin' to be off the moment you enter?'

They talked of trivial things. Through the open door the level rays of sunset poured in, shining on the floor. A grey hen appeared stepping swiftly in the doorway, pecking, and the light through her comb and her wattles made an oriflamme tossed here and there, as she went, her grey body was like a ghost.

Anna, watching, threw scraps of bread, and she felt the child flame within her. She seemed to remember again forgotten, burning, far-off things.

'Where was I born, mother?' she asked.

'In London.'

'And was my father' – she spoke of him as if he were merely a strange name: she could never connect herself with him – 'was he dark?'

'He had dark-brown hair and dark eyes and a fresh colouring. He went bald, rather bald, when he was quite young,' replied her mother, also as if telling a tale which was just old imagination.

'Was he good-looking?'

'Yes – he was very good-looking – rather small. I have never seen an Englishman who looked like him.'

'Why?'

'He was' – the mother made a quick, running movement with her hands – 'his figure was alive and changing – it was never fixed. He was not in the least steady – like a running stream.'

It flashed over the youth – Anna too was like a running stream. Instantly he was in love with her again.

Tom Brangwen was frightened. His heart always filled with fear, fear of the unknown, when he heard his women speak of their bygone men as of strangers they had known in passing and had taken leave of again.

In the room, there came a silence and a singleness over all their hearts. They were separate people with separate destinies. Why should they seek each to lay violent hands of claim on the other?

The young people went home as a sharp little moon was setting in the dusk of spring. Tufts of trees hovered in the upper air, the little church pricked up shadowily at the tope of the hill, the earth was a dark blue shadow.

She put her hand lightly on his arm, out of her far distance. And out of the distance, he felt her touch him. They walked on, hand in hand, along opposite horizons, touching across the dusk. There was a sound of thrushes calling in the dark blue twilight.

'I think we are going to have an infant, Bill,' she said, from far off.

He trembled, and his fingers tightened on hers.

'Why?' he asked, his heart beating. 'You don't know?'

'I do,' she said.

They continued without saying any more, walking along opposite horizons, hand in hand across the intervening space, two separate people. And he trembled as if a wind blew on to him in strong gusts, out of the unseen. He was afraid. He was afraid to know he was alone. For she seemed fulfilled and separate and sufficient in her half of the world. He could not bear to know that he was cut off. Why could he not be always one with her? It was he who had given her the child. Why could she not be with him, one with him? Why must he be set in this separateness, why could she not be with him, close, close, as one with him? She must be one with him.

He held her fingers tightly in his own. She did not know what he was thinking. The blaze of light on her heart was too beautiful and dazzling, from the conception in her womb. She walked glorified, and the sound of the thrushes, of the trains in the valley, of the far-off, faint noises of the town, were her 'Magnificat'.

But he was struggling in silence. It seemed as though there were before him a solid wall of darkness that impeded him and suffocated him and made him mad. He wanted her to come to him, to complete him, to stand before him so that his eyes did not, should not meet the naked darkness. Nothing mattered to him but that she should come and complete him. For he was ridden by the awful sense of his own limitation. It was as if he ended uncompleted, as yet uncreated on the darkness, and he wanted her to come and liberate him into the whole.

But she was complete in herself, and he was ashamed of his need, his helpless need of her. His need, and his shame of need, weighed on him like a madness. Yet still he was quiet and gentle, in reverence of her conception, and because she was with child by him.

And she was happy in showers of sunshine. She loved her husband, as a presence, as a grateful condition. But for the moment her need was fulfilled, and now she wanted only to hold her husband by the hand in sheer happiness, without taking thought, only being glad.

He had various folios of reproductions, and among them a cheap print from Fra Angelico's 'Entry of the Blessed into Paradise'. This filled Anna with bliss. The beautiful, innocent way in which the Blessed held each other by the hand as they moved towards the radiance, the real, real, angelic melody, made her weep with happiness. The floweriness, the beams of light, the linking of hands, was almost too much for her, too innocent.

Day after day came shining through the door of Paradise, day after day she entered into the brightness. The child in her shone till she herself was a beam of sunshine; and how lovely was the sunshine that loitered and wandered out of doors, where the catkins on the big hazel bushes at the end of the garden hung in their shaken, floating aureole, where little fumes like fire burst out from the black yew trees as a bird settled clinging to the branches. One day bluebells were along the hedge-bottoms, then cowslips twinkled like manna, golden and evanescent on the meadows. She was full of a rich drowsiness and loneliness. How happy she was, how gorgeous it was to live: to have known herself, her husband, the passion of love and begetting; and to know that all this lived and waited and burned on around her, a terrible purifying fire, through which she had passed for once to come to this peace of golden radiance, when she was with child, and innocent, and in love with her husband and with all the many angels hand in hand. She lifted her throat to the breeze that came across the fields, and she felt it handling her like sisters fondling her, she drank it in perfume of cowslips and of apple-blossoms.

And in all the happiness a black shadow, shy, wild, a beast of prey, roamed and vanished from sight, and like strands of gossamer blown across her eyes, there was a dread for her.

She was afraid when he came home at night. As yet, her fear never spoke, the shadow never rushed upon her. He was gentle, humble, he kept himself withheld. His hands were delicate upon her, and she loved them. But there ran through her the thrill, crisp as pain, for she felt the darkness and other-world still in his soft, sheathed hands.

But the summer drifted in with the silence of a miracle, she was almost always alone. All the while, went on the long, lovely drowsiness, the maidenblush roses in the garden were all shed, washed away in a pouring rain, summer drifted into autumn, and the long, vague, golden days began to close. Crimson clouds fumed about the west, and as night came on, all the sky was fuming and steaming, and the moon, far above the swiftness of vapours, was white, bleared, the night was uneasy. Suddenly the moon would appear at a clear window in the sky, looking down from far above, like a captive. And Anna did not sleep. There was a strange, dark tension about her husband.

She became aware that he was trying to force his will upon her, something, there was something he wanted, as he lay there dark and tense. And her soul sighed in weariness.

Everything was so vague and lovely, and he wanted to wake her up to the hard, hostile reality. She drew back in resistance. Still he said nothing. But she felt his power persisting on her, till she became aware of the strain, she cried out against the exhaustion. He was forcing her, he was forcing her. And she wanted so much the joy and the vagueness and the innocence of her pregnancy. She did not want his bitter-corrosive love, she did not want it poured into her, to burn her. Why must she have it? Why, oh, why was he not content, contained?

She sat many hours by the window, in those days when he drove her most with the black constraint of his will, and she watched the rain falling on the yew trees. She was not sad, only wistful, blanched. The child under her heart was a perpetual warmth. And she was sure. The pressure was only upon her from the outside, her soul had no stripes.

Yet in her heart itself was always this same strain, tense, anxious. She was not safe, she was always exposed, she was always attacked. There was a yearning in her for a fulness of peace and blessedness. What a heavy yearning it was – so heavy.

She knew, vaguely, that all the time he was not satisfied, all the time he was trying to force something from her. Ah, how she wished she could succeed with him, in her own way! He was there, so inevitable. She lived in him also. And how she wanted to be at peace with him, at peace. She loved him. She would give him love, pure love. With a strange, rapt look in her face, she awaited his homecoming that night.

Then, when he came, she rose with her hands full of love, as of flowers, radiant, innocent. A dark spasm crossed his face. As she watched, her face shining and flower-like with innocent love, his face grew dark and tense, the cruelty gathered in his brows, his eyes turned aside, she saw the whites of his eyes as he looked aside from her. She waited, touching him with her hands. But from his body through her hands came the bitter-corrosive shock of his passion upon her, destroying her in blossom. She shrank. She rose from her knees and went away from him, to preserve herself. And it was great pain to her.

To him also it was agony. He saw the glistening, flower-like love in her face, and his heart was black because he did not want it. Not this – not this. He did not want flowery innocence. He was unsatisfied. The rage and storm of unsatisfaction tormented him ceaselessly. Why had she not satisfied him? He had satisfied her. She was satisfied, at peace, innocent round the doors of her own paradise.

And he was unsatisfied, unfulfilled, he raged in torment, wanting, wanting. It was for her to satisfy him: then let her do it. Let her not come with flowery handfuls of innocent love. He would throw these aside and trample the flowers to nothing. He would destroy her flowery, innocent bliss. Was he not entitled to satisfaction from her, and was not his heart all raging desire, his soul a black torment of unfulfilment. Let it be fulfilled in him, then, as it was fulfilled in her. He had given her her fulfilment. Let her rise up and do her part.

He was cruel to her. But all the time he was ashamed. And being ashamed, he was more cruel. For he was ashamed that he could not come to fulfilment without her. And he could not. And she would not heed him. He was shackled and in darkness of torment.

She beseeched him to work again, to do his wood-carving. But his soul was too black. He had destroyed his panel of Adam and Eve. He could not begin again, least of all now, whilst he was in this condition.

For her there was no final release, since he could not be liberated from himself. Strange and amorphous, she must go yearning on through the trouble, like a warm, glowing cloud blown in the middle of a storm. She felt so rich, in her warm vagueness, that her soul cried out on him, because he harried her and wanted to destroy her.

She had her moments of exaltation still, re-births of old exaltations. As she sat by her bedroom window, watching the steady rain, her spirit was somewhere far off.

She sat in pride and curious pleasure. When there was no one to exult with, and the unsatisfied soul must dance and play, then one danced before the Unknown.

Suddenly she realised that this was what she wanted to do. Big with child as she was, she danced there in the bedroom by herself, lifting her hands and her body to the Unseen, to the unseen Creator who had chosen her, to Whom she belonged.

She would not have had anyone know. She danced in secret, and her soul rose in bliss. She danced in secret before the Creator, she took off her clothes and danced in the pride of her bigness.

It surprised her, when it was over. She was shrinking and afraid. To what was she now exposed? She half wanted to tell her husband. Yet she shrank from him.

All the time she ran on by herself. She liked the story of David, who danced before the Lord, and uncovered himself exultingly. Why should he uncover himself to Michal, a common woman? He uncovered himself to the Lord.

'Thou comest to me with a sword and a spear and a shield, but I come to thee in the name of the Lord: – for the battle is the Lord's, and he will give you into our hands.'

Her heart rang to the words. She walked in her pride. And her battle was her own Lord's, her husband was delivered over.

In these days she was oblivious of him. Who was he, to come against her? No, he was not even the Philistine, the Giant. He was like Saul proclaiming his own kingship. She laughed in her heart. Who was he, proclaiming his kingship? She laughed in her heart with pride.

And she had to dance in exultation beyond him. Because he was in the house, she had to dance before her Creator in exemption from the man. On a Saturday afternoon, when she had a fire in the bedroom, again she took off her things and danced, lifting her knees and her hands in a slow, rhythmic exulting. He was in the house, so her pride was fiercer. She would dance his nullification, she would dance to her unseen Lord. She was exalted over him, before the Lord.

She heard him coming up the stairs, and she flinched. She stood with the firelight on her ankles and feet, naked in the shadowy, late afternoon, fastening up her hair. He was startled. He stood in the doorway, his brows black and lowering.

'What are you doing?' he said, gratingly. 'You'll catch a cold.'

And she lifted her hands and danced again, to annul him, the light glanced on her knees as she made her slow, fine movements down the far side of the room, across the firelight. He stood away near the door in blackness of shadow, watching, transfixed. And with slow, heavy movements she swayed backwards and forwards, like a full ear of corn, pale in the dusky afternoon, threading before the firelight, dancing his non-existence, dancing herself to the Lord, to exultation.

He watched, and his soul burned in him. He turned aside, he could not look, it hurt his eyes. Her fine limbs lifted and lifted, her hair was sticking out all fierce, and her belly, big, strange, terrifying, uplifted to the Lord. Her face was rapt and beautiful, she danced exulting before her Lord, and knew no man.

It hurt him as he watched as if he were at the stake. He felt he was being burned alive. The strangeness, the power of her in her dancing consumed him, he was burned, he could not grasp, he could not understand. He waited obliterated. Then his eyes became blind to her, he saw her no more. And through the unseeing veil between them he called to her, in his jarring voice:

'What are you doing that for?'

'Go away,' she said. 'Let me dance by myself.'

'That isn't dancing,' he said harshly. 'What do you want to do that for?'

'I don't do it for you,' she said. 'You go away.'

Her strange, lifted belly, big with his child! Had he no right to be there? He felt his presence a violation. Yet he had his right to be there. He went and sat on the bed.

She stopped dancing, and confronted him, again lifting her slim arms and twisting her hair. Her nakedness hurt her, opposed to him.

'I can do as I like in my bedroom,' she cried. 'Why do you interfere with me?'

And she slipped on a dressing-gown and crouched before the fire. He was more at ease now she was covered up. The vision of her tormented him all the days of his life, as she had been then, a strange, exalted thing having no relation to himself.

After this day, the door seemed to shut on his mind. His brow shut and became impervious. His eyes ceased to see, his hands were suspended. Within himself his will was coiled like a beast, hidden under the darkness, but always potent, working.

At first she went on blithely enough with him shut down beside her. But then his spell began to take hold of her. The dark, seething potency of him, the power of a creature that lies hidden and exerts its will to the destruction of the free-running creature, as the tiger lying in the darkness of the leaves steadily enforces the fall and death of the light creatures that drink by the waterside in the morning, gradually began to take effect on her. Though he lay there in his darkness and did not move, yet she knew he lay waiting for her. She felt his will fastening on her and pulling her down, even whilst he was silent and obscure.

She found that, in all her outgoings and her incomings, he prevented her. Gradually she realised that she was being borne down by him, borne down by the clinging, heavy weight of him, that he was pulling her down as a leopard clings to a wild cow and exhausts her and pulls her down.

Gradually she realised that her life, her freedom, was sinking under the silent grip of his physical will. He wanted her in his power. He wanted to devour her at leisure, to have her. At length she realised that her sleep was a long ache and a weariness and exhaustion, because of his will fastened upon her, as he lay there beside her, during the night.

She realised it all, and there came a momentous pause, a pause in her swift running, a moment's suspension in her life, when she was lost.

Then she turned fiercely on him, and fought him. He was not to do this to her, it was monstrous. What horrible hold did he want to have over her body? Why did he want to drag her down, and kill her spirit? Why did he want to deny her spirit? Why did he deny her spirituality, hold her for a body only? And was he to claim her carcase?

Some vast, hideous darkness he seemed to represent to her.

'What do you do to me?' she cried. 'What beastly thing do you do to me? You put a horrible pressure on my head, you don't let me sleep, you don't let me *live*. Every moment of your life you are doing something to me, something horrible, that destroys me. There is something horrible in you, something dark and beastly in your will. What do you want of me? What do you want to do to me?'

All the blood in his body went black and powerful and corrosive as he heard her. Black and blind with hatred of her he was. He was in a very black hell, and could not escape.

He hated her for what she said. Did he not give her everything, was she not everything to him? And the shame was a bitter fire in him, that she was everything to him, that he had nothing but her. And then that she should taunt him with it, that he could not escape! The fire went black in his veins. For try as he might, he could not escape. She was everything to him, she was his life and his derivation. He depended on her. If she were taken away, he would collapse as a house from which the central pillar is removed.

And she hated him, because he depended on her so utterly. He was horrible to her. She wanted to thrust him off, to set him apart. It was horrible that he should cleave to her, so close, so close, like a leopard that had leapt on her, and fastened.

He went on from day to day in a blackness of rage and shame and frustration. How he tortured himself, to be able to get away from her. But he could not. She was as the rock on which he stood, with deep, heaving water all round, and he was unable to swim. He *must* take his stand on her, he must depend on her.

What had he in life, save her? Nothing. The rest was a great heaving flood. The terror of the night of heaving, overwhelming flood, which was his vision of life without her, was too much for him. He clung to her fiercely and abjectly.

And she beat him off, she beat him off. Where could he turn, like a swimmer in a dark sea, beaten off from his hold, whither could he turn? He wanted to leave her, he wanted to be able to leave her. For his soul's sake, for his manhood's sake, he must be able to leave her.

But for what? She was the ark, and the rest of the world was flood. The only tangible, secure thing was the woman. He could leave her only for another woman. And where was the other woman, and who was the other woman? Besides, he would be just in the same state. Another woman would be woman, the case would be the same.

Why was she the all, the everything, why must he live only through her, why must he sink if he were detached from her? Why must he cleave to her in a frenzy as for his very life?

The only other way to leave her was to die. The only straight way to leave her was to die. His dark, raging soul knew that. But he had no desire for death.

Why could he not leave her? Why could he not throw himself into the hidden water to live or die, as might be? He could not, he could not. But supposing he went away, right away, and found work, and had a lodging again. He could be again as he had been before.

But he knew he could not. A woman, he must have a woman. And having a woman, he must be free of her. It would be the same position. For he could not be free of her.

For how can a man stand, unless he have something sure under his feet. Can a man tread the unstable water all his life, and call that standing? Better give in and drown at once.

And upon what could he stand, save upon a woman? Was he then like the old man of the seas, impotent to move save upon the back of another life? Was he impotent, or a cripple, or a defective, or a fragment?

It was black, mad, shameful torture, the frenzy of fear, the frenzy of desire, and the horrible, grasping back-wash of shame.

What was he afraid of? Why did life, without Anna, seem to him just a horrible welter, everything jostling in a meaningless, dark, fathomless flood? Why, if Anna left him even for a week, did he seem to be clinging like a madman to the edge of reality, and slipping surely, surely into the flood of unreality that would drown him. This horrible slipping into unreality drove him mad, his soul screamed with fear and agony.

Yet she was pushing him off from her, pushing him away, breaking his fingers from their hold on her, persistently, ruthlessly. He wanted her to have pity. And sometimes for a moment she had pity. But she always began again, thrusting him off, into the deep water, into the frenzy and agony of uncertainty.

She became like a fury to him, without any sense of him. Her eyes were bright with a cold, unmoving hatred. Then his heart seemed to die in its last fear. She might push him off into the deeps.

She would not sleep with him any more. She said he destroyed her sleep. Up started all his frenzy and madness of fear and suffering. She drove him away. Like a cowed, lurking devil he was driven off, his mind working cunningly against her, devising evil for her. But she drove him off. In his moments of intense suffering, she seemed to him inconceivable, a monster, the principle of cruelty.

However her pity might give way for moments, she was hard and cold as a jewel. He must be put off from her, she must sleep alone. She made him a bed in the small room.

And he lay there whipped, his soul whipped almost to death, yet unchanged. He lay in agony of suffering, thrown back into unreality, like a man thrown overboard into a sea, to swim till he sinks, because there is no hold, only a wide, weltering sea.

He did not sleep, save for the white sleep when a thin veil is drawn over the mind. It was not sleep. He was awake, and he was not awake. He could not be alone. He needed to be able to put his arms round her. He could not bear the empty space against his breast, where she used to be. He could not bear it. He felt as if he were suspended in space, held there by the grip of his will. If he relaxed his will would fall, fall through endless space, into the bottomless pit, always falling, will-less, helpless, non-existent, just dropping to extinction, falling till the fire of friction had burned out, like a falling star, then nothing, nothing, complete nothing.

He rose in the morning grey and unreal. And she seemed fond of him again, she seemed to make up to him a little.

'I slept well,' she said, with her slightly false brightness. 'Did you?'

'All right,' he answered.

He would never tell her.

For three or four nights he lay alone through the white sleep, his will unchanged, unchanged, still tense, fixed in its grip. Then, as if she were revived and free to be fond of him again, deluded by his silence and seeming acquiescence, moved also by pity, she took him back again.

Each night, in spite of all the shame, he had waited with agony for bedtime, to see if she would shut him out. And each night, as, in her false brightness, she said Good night, he felt he must kill her or himself. But she asked for her kiss, so pathetically, so prettily. So he kissed her, whilst his heart was ice.

And sometimes he went out. Once he sat for a long time in the church porch, before going in to bed. It was dark with a wind blowing. He sat in the church porch and felt some shelter, some security. But it grew cold, and he must go in to bed.

Then came the night when she said, putting her arms round him and kissing him fondly:

'Stay with me to-night, will you?'

And he had stayed without demur. But his will had not altered. He would have her fixed to him.

So that soon she told him again she must be alone.

'I don't *want* to send you away. I *want* to sleep with you. But I can't sleep, you don't let me sleep.'

His blood turned black in his veins.

'What do you mean by such a thing? It's an arrant lie. *I* don't let you sleep—'

'But you don't. I sleep so well when I'm alone. And I can't sleep when you're there. You do something to me, you put a pressure on my head. And I *must* sleep, now the child is coming.'

'It's something in yourself,' he replied, 'something wrong in you.'

Horrible in the extreme were these nocturnal combats, when all the world was asleep, and they two were alone, alone in the world, and repelling each other. It was hardly to be borne.

He went and lay down alone. And at length, after a grey and livid and ghastly period, he relaxed, something gave way in him. He let go, he did not care what became of him. Strange and dim he became to himself, to her, to everybody. A vagueness had come over everything, like a drowning. And it was an infinite relief to drown, a relief, a great, great relief.

He would insist no more, he would force her no more. He would force himself upon her no more. He would let go, relax, lapse, and what would be, should be.

Yet he wanted her still, he always, always wanted her. In his soul, he was desolate as a child, he was so helpless. Like a child on its mother, he depended on her for his living. He knew it, and he knew he could hardly help it.

Yet he must be able to be alone. He must be able to lie down alongside the empty space, and let be. He must be able to leave himself to the flood, to sink or live as might be. For he recognised at length his own limitation, and the limitation of his power. He had to give in.

There was a stillness, a wanness between them. Half at least of the battle was over. Sometimes she wept as she went about, her heart was very heavy. But the child was always warm in her womb.

They were friends again, new, subdued friends. But there was a wanness between them. They slept together once more, very quietly, and distinct, not one together as before. And she was intimate with him as at first. But he was very quiet, and not intimate. He was glad in his soul, but for the time being he was not alive.

He could sleep with her, and let her be. He could be alone now. He had just learned what it was to be able to be alone. It was right and peaceful. She had given him a new, deeper freedom. The world might be a welter of uncertainty, but he was himself now. He had come into his own existence. He was born for a second time, born at last unto himself, out of the vast body of humanity. Now at last he had a separate identity, he existed alone, even if he were not quite alone. Before he had only existed in so far as he had relations with another being. Now he had an absolute self – as well as a relative self.

But it was a very dumb, weak, helpless self, a crawling nursling. He went about very quiet, and in a way, submissive. He had an unalterable self at last, free, separate, independent.

She was relieved, she was free of him. She had given him to himself. She wept sometimes with tiredness and helplessness. But he was a husband. And she seemed, in the child that was coming, to forget. It seemed to make her warm and drowsy. She lapsed into a long muse, indistinct, warm, vague, unwilling to be taken out of her vagueness. And she rested on him also.

Sometimes she came to him with a strange light in her eyes, poignant, pathetic, as if she were asking for something. He looked and he could not understand. She was so beautiful, so visionary, the rays seemed to go out of his breast to her, like a shining. He was there for her, all for her. And she would hold his breast, and kiss it, and kiss it, kneeling beside him, she who was waiting for the hour of her delivery. And he would lie looking down at his breast, till it seemed that his breast was not himself, that he had left it lying there. Yet it was himself also, and beautiful and bright with her kisses.

He was glad with a strange, radiant pain. Whilst she kneeled beside him, and kissed his breast with a slow, rapt, half-devotional movement.

He knew she wanted something, his heart yearned to give it her. His heart yearned over her. And as she lifted her face, that was radiant and rosy as a little cloud, his heart still yearned over her, and, now from the distance, adored her. She had a flower-like presence which he adored as he stood far off, a stranger.

The weeks passed on, the time drew near, they were very gentle, and delicately happy. The insistent, passionate, dark soul, the powerful unsatisfaction in him seemed stilled and tamed, the lion lay down with the lamb in him.

She loved him very much indeed, and he waited near her. She was a precious, remote thing to him at this time, as she waited for her child. Her soul was glad with an ecstasy because of the coming infant. She wanted a boy: oh, very much she wanted a boy.

But she seemed so young and so frail. She was indeed only a girl. As she stood by the fire washing herself – she was proud to wash herself at this time – and he looked at her, his heart was full of extreme tenderness for her. Such fine, fine limbs, her slim, round arms like chasing lights, and her legs to simple and childish, yet so very proud. Oh, she stood on proud legs, with a lovely reckless balance of her full belly, and the adorable little roundnesses, and the breasts becoming important. Above it all, her face was like a rosy cloud shining.

How proud she was, what a lovely proud thing her young body! And she loved him to put his hand on her ripe fullness, so that he should thrill also with the stir and the quickening there. He was afraid and silent, but she flung her arms round his neck with proud, impudent joy.

The pains came on, and Oh – how she cried! She would have him stay with her. And after her long cries she would look at him, with tears in her eyes and a sobbing laugh on her face, saying:

'I don't mind it really.'

It was bad enough. But to her it was never deathly. Even the fierce, tearing pain was exhilarating. She screamed and suffered, but was all the time curiously alive and vital. She felt so powerfully alive and in the hands of such a masterly force of life, that her bottom-most feeling was one of exhilaration. She knew she was winning, winning, she was always winning, with each onset of pain she was nearer to victory.

Probably he suffered more than she did. He was not shocked or horrified. But he was screwed very tight in the vise of suffering.

It was a girl. The second of silence on her face when they said so showed him she was disappointed. And a great blazing passion of resentment and protest sprang up in his heart. In that moment he claimed the child.

But when the milk came, and the infant sucked her breast, she seemed to be leaping with extravagant bliss.

'It sucks me, it sucks me, it likes me – oh, it loves it!' she cried, holding the child to her breast with her two hands covering it, passionately.

And in a few moments, as she became used to her bliss, she looked at the youth with glowing, unseeing eyes, and said:

'Anna Victrix.'

He went away, trembling, and slept. To her, her pains were the wound-smart of a victor, she was the prouder.

When she was well again she was very happy. She called the baby Ursula. Both Anna and her husband felt they must have a name that gave them private satisfaction. The baby was tawny skinned, it had a curious downy skin, and wisps of bronze hair, and the yellow grey eyes that wavered, and then became golden-brown like the father's. So they called her Ursula because of the picture of the saint.

It was a rather delicate baby at first, but soon it became stronger, and was restless as a young eel. Anna was worn out with the day-long wrestling with its young vigour.

As a little animal, she loved and adored it and was happy. She loved her husband, she kissed his eyes and nose and mouth, and made much of him, she said his limbs were beautiful, she was fascinated by the physical form of him.

And she was indeed Anna Victrix. He could not combat her any more. He was out in the wilderness, alone with her. Having occasion to go to London, he marvelled, as he returned, thinking of naked, lurking savages on an island, how these had built up and created the great mass of Oxford Street or Piccadilly. How had helpless savages, running with their spears on the riverside, after fish, how had they come to rear up this great London, the ponderous, massive, ugly superstructure of a world of man upon a world of nature! It frightened and awed him. Man was terrible, awful in his works. The works of man were more terrible than man himself, almost monstrous.

And yet, for his own part, for his private being, Brangwen felt that the whole of the man's world was exterior and extraneous to his own real life with Anna. Sweep away the whole monstrous superstructure of the world of to-day, cities and industries and civilisation, leave only the bare earth with plants growing and waters running, and he would not mind, so long as he were whole, had Anna and the child and the new, strange certainty in his soul. Then, if he were naked, he would find clothing somewhere, he would make a shelter and bring food to his wife.

And what more? What more would be necessary? The great mass of activity in which mankind was engaged meant nothing to him. By nature, he had no part in it. What did he live for, then? For Anna only, and for the sake of living? What did he want on this earth? Anna only, and his children, and his life with his children and her? Was there no more?

He was attended by a sense of something more, something further, which gave him absolute being. It was as if now he existed in Eternity, let Time be what it might. What was there outside? The fabricated world, that he did not believe in? What should he bring to her, from outside? Nothing? Was it enough, as it was? He was troubled in his acquiescence. She was not with him. Yet he scarcely believed in himself, apart from her, though the whole Infinite was with him. Let the whole world slide down and over the edge of oblivion, he would stand alone. But he was unsure of her. And he existed also in her. So he was unsure.

He hovered near to her, never quite able to forget the vague, haunting uncertainty, that seemed to challenge him, and which he would not hear. A pang of dread, almost guilt, as of insufficiency, would go over him as he heard her talking to the baby. She stood before the window, with the month-old child in her arms, talking in a musical, young sing-song that he had not heard before, and which rang on his heart like a claim from the distance, or the voice of another world sounding its claim on him. He stood near, listening, and his heart surged, surged to rise and submit. Then it shrank back and stayed aloof. He could not move, a denial was upon him, as if he could not deny himself. He must, he must be himself.

'Look at the silly blue-caps, my beauty,' she crooned, holding up the infant to the window, where shone the white garden, and the blue-tits scuffling in the snow: 'Look at the silly blue-caps, my darling, having a fight in the snow! Look at them, my bird – beating the snow about with their wings, and shaking their heads. Oh, aren't they wicked things, wicked things! Look at their yellow feathers on the snow there! They'll miss them, won't they, when they're cold later on.

'Must we tell them to stop, must we say "stop it" to them, my bird? But they are naughty, naughty! Look at them!' Suddenly her voice broke loud and fierce, she rapped the pane sharply.

'Stop it,' she cried, 'stop it, you little nuisances. Stop it!' She called louder, and rapped the pane more sharply. Her voice was fierce and imperative.

'Have more sense,' she cried.

'There, now they're gone. Where have they gone, the silly things? What will they say to each other? What will they say, my lambkin? They'll forget, won't they, they'll forget all about it, out of their silly little heads, and their blue caps.'

After a moment, she turned her bright face to her husband.

'They were *really* fighting, they were really fierce with each other?' she said, her voice keen with excitement and wonder, as if she belonged to the birds' world, were identified with the race of birds.

'Ay, they'll fight, will blue-caps,' he said, glad when she turned to him with her glow from elsewhere. He came and stood beside her and looked out at the marks on the snow where the birds had scuffled, and at the yew trees' burdened, white and black branches. What was the appeal it made to him, what was the question of her bright face, what was the challenge he was called to answer? He did not know. But as he stood there he felt some responsibility which made him glad, but uneasy, as if he must put out his own light. And he could not move as yet.

Anna loved the child very much, oh, very much. Yet still she was not quite fulfilled. She had a slight expectant feeling, as of a door half opened. Here she was, safe and still in Cossethay. But she felt as if she were not in Cossethay at all. She was straining her eyes to something beyond. And from her Pisgah mount, which she had attained, what could she see? A faint, gleaming horizon, a long way off, and a rainbow like an archway, a shadow-door with faintly coloured coping above it. Must she be moving thither?

Something she had not, something she did not grasp, could not arrive at. There was something beyond her. But why must she start on the journey? She stood so safely on the Pisgah mountain.

In the winter, when she rose with the sunrise, and out of the back windows saw the east flaming yellow and orange above the green, flowing grass, while the great pear tree in between stood dark and magnificent as an idol, and under the dark pear tree, the little sheet of water spread smooth in burnished, yellow light, she said, 'It is here'. And when, at evening, the sunset came in a red glare through the big opening in the clouds, she said again, 'It is beyond'.

Dawn and sunset were the feet of the rainbow that spanned the day, and she saw the hope, the promise. Why should she travel any further?

Yet she always asked the question. As the sun went down in his fiery winter haste, she faced the blazing close of the affair, in which she had not played her fullest part, and she made her demand still: 'What are you doing, making this big shining commotion? What is it that you keep so busy about, that you will not let us alone?'

She did not turn to her husband, for him to lead her. He was apart from her, with her, according to her different conceptions of him. The child she might hold up, she might toss the child forward into the furnace, the child might walk there, amid the burning coals and the incandescent roar of heat, as the three witnesses walked with the angel in the fire.

Soon, she felt sure of her husband. She knew his dark face and the extent of its passion. She knew his slim, vigorous body, she said it was hers. Then there was no denying her. She was a rich woman enjoying her riches.

And soon again she was with child. Which made her satisfied and took away her discontent. She forgot that she had watched the sun climb up and pass his way, a magnificent traveller surging forward. She forgot that the moon had looked through a window of the high, dark night, and nodded like a magic recognition, signalled to her to follow. Sun and moon travelled on, and left her, passed her by, a rich woman enjoying her riches. She should go also. But she could not go, when they called, because she must stay at home now. With satisfaction she relinquished the adventure to the unknown. She was bearing her children.

There was another child coming, and Anna lapsed into vague content. If she were not the wayfarer to the unknown, if she were arrived now, settled in her builded house, a rich woman, still her doors opened under the arch of the rainbow, her threshold reflected the passing of the sun and moon, the great travellers, her house was full of the echo of journeying.

She was a door and a threshold, she herself. Through her another soul was coming, to stand upon her as upon the threshold, looking out, shading its eyes for the direction to take.

Chapter Seven

The Cathedral

During the first year of her marriage, before Ursula was born, Anna Brangwen and her husband went to visit her mother's friend, the Baron Skrebensky. The latter had kept a slight connection with Anna's mother, and had always preserved some officious interest in the young girl, because she was a pure Pole.

When Baron Skrebensky was about forty years old, his wife died, and left him raving, disconsolate. Lydia had visited him then, taking Anna with her. It was when the girl was fourteen years old. Since then she had not seen him. She remembered him as a small sharp clergyman who cried and talked and terrified her, whilst her mother was most strangely consoling, in a foreign language.

The little Baron never quite approved of Anna, because she spoke no Polish. Still, he considered himself in some way her guardian, on Lensky's behalf, and he presented her with some old, heavy Russian jewellery, the least valuable of his wife's relics. Then he lapsed out of the Brangwen's life again, though he lived only about thirty miles away.

Three years later came the startling news that he had married a young English girl of good family. Everybody marvelled. Then came a copy of 'The History of the Parish of Briswell, by Rudolph, Baron Skrebensky, Vicar of Briswell.' It was a curious book, incoherent, full of interesting exhumations. It was dedicated: 'To my wife, Millicent Maud Pearse, in whom I embrace the generous spirit of England.'

'If he embraces no more than the spirit of England,' said Tom Brangwen, 'it's a bad look-out for him.'

But paying a formal visit with his wife, he found the new Baroness a little, creamy-skinned, insidious thing with red-brown hair and a mouth that one must always watch, because it curved back continually in an incomprehensible, strange laugh that exposed her rather prominent teeth. She was not beautiful, yet Tom Brangwen was immediately under her spell. She seemed to snuggle like a kitten within his warmth, whilst she was at the same time elusive and ironical, suggesting the fine steel of her claws.

The Baron was almost dotingly courteous and attentive to her. She, almost mockingly, yet quite happy, let him dote. Curious little thing she was, she had the soft, creamy, elusive beauty of a ferret. Tom Brangwen was quite at a loss, at her mercy, and she laughed, a little breathlessly, as if tempted to cruelty. She did put fine torments on the elderly Baron.

When some months later she bore a son, the Baron Skrebensky was loud with delight.

Gradually she gathered a circle of acquaintances in the county. For she was of good family, half Venetian, educated in Dresden. The little foreign vicar attained to a social status which almost satisfied his maddened pride.

Therefore the Brangwens were surprised when the invitation came for Anna and her young husband to pay a visit to Briswell vicarage. For the Skrebenskys were now moderately well off, Millicent Skrebensky having some fortune of her own.

Anna took her best clothes, recovered her best high-school manner, and arrived with her husband. Will Brangwen, ruddy, bright, with long limbs and a small head, like some uncouth bird, was not changed in the least. The little Baroness was smiling, showing her teeth. She had a real charm, a kind of joyous coldness, laughing, delighted, like some weasel. Anna at once respected her, and was on her guard before her, instinctively attracted by the strange, childlike surety of the Baroness, yet mistrusting it, fascinated. The little baron was now quite white-haired, very brittle. He was wizened and wrinkled, yet fiery, unsubdued. Anna looked at his lean body, at his small, fine lean legs and lean hands as he sat talking, and she flushed. She recognised the quality of the male in him, his lean, concentrated age, his informed fire, his faculty for sharp, deliberate response. He was so detached, so purely objective. A woman was thoroughly outside him. There was no confusion. So he could give that fine, deliberate response.

He was something separate and interesting; his hard, intrinsic being, whittled down by age to an essentiality and a directness almost death-like, cruel, was yet so unswervingly sure in its action, so distinct in its surety, that she was attracted to him. She watched his cool, hard, separate fire, fascinated by it. Would she rather have it than her husband's diffuse heat, than his blind, hot youth?

She seemed to be breathing high, sharp air, as if she had just come out of a hot room. These strange Skrebenskys made her aware of another, freer element, in which each person was detached and isolated. Was not this her natural element? Was not the close Brangwen life stifling her?

Meanwhile the little baroness, with always a subtle light stirring of her full, lustrous, hazel eyes, was playing with Will Brangwen. He was not quick enough to see all her movements. Yet he watched her steadily, with unchanging, lit-up eyes. She was a strange creature to him. But she had no power over him. She flushed, and was irritated. Yet she glanced again and again at his dark, living face, curiously, as if she despised him. She despised his uncritical, unironical nature, it had nothing for her. Yet it angered her as if she were jealous. He watched her with deferential interest as he would watch a stoat playing. But he himself was not implicated. He was different in kind. She was all lambent, biting, flames, he was a red fire glowing steadily. She could get nothing out of him. So she made him flush darkly by assuming a biting, subtle class-superiority. He flushed, but still he did not object. He was too different.

Her little boy came in with the nurse. He was a quick, slight child, with fine preceptiveness, and a cool transitoriness in his interest. At once he treated Will Brangwen as an outsider. He stayed by Anna for a moment, acknowledged her, then was gone again, quick, observant, restless, with a glance of interest at everything.

The father adored him, and spoke to him in Polish. It was queer, the stiff, aristocratic manner of the father with the child, the distance in the relationship, the classic fatherhood on the one hand, the filial subordination on the other. They played together, in their different degrees very separate, two different beings, differing as it were in rank rather than in relationship. And the baroness smiled, smiled, smiled, always smiled, showing her rather protruding teeth, having always a mysterious attraction and charm.

Anna realised how different her own life might have been, how different her own living. Her soul stirred, she became as another person. Her intimacy with her husband passed away, the curious enveloping Brangwen intimacy, so warm, so close, so stifling, when one seemed always to be in contact with the other person, like a blood-relation, was annulled. She denied it, this close relationship with her young husband. He and she were not one. His heat was not always to suffuse her, suffuse her, through her mind and her individuality, till she was of one heat with him, till she had not her own self apart. She wanted her own life. He seemed to lap her and suffuse her with his being, his hot life, till she did not know whether she were herself, or whether she were another creature, united with him in a world of close blood-intimacy that closed over her and excluded her from all the cool outside.

She wanted her own, old, sharp self, detached, detached, active but not absorbed, active for her own part, taking and giving, but never absorbed. Whereas he wanted this strange absorption with her, which still she resisted. But she was partly helpless against it. She had lived so long in Tom Brangwen's love, beforehand.

From the Skrebensky's, they went to Will Brangwen's beloved Lincoln Cathedral, because it was not far off. He had promised her, that one by one, they should visit all the cathedrals of England. They began with Lincoln, which he knew well.

He began to get excited as the time drew near to set off. What was it that changed him so much? She was almost angry, coming as she did from the Skrebensky's. But now he ran on alone. His very breast seemed to open its doors to watch for the great church brooding over the town. His soul ran ahead.

When he saw the cathedral in the distance, dark blue lifted watchful in the sky, his heart leapt. It was the sign in heaven, it was the Spirit hovering like a dove, like an eagle over the earth. He turned his glowing, ecstatic face to her, his mouth opened with a strange, ecstatic grin.

'There she is,' he said.

The 'she' irritated her. Why 'she'? It was 'it'. What was the cathedral, a big building, a thing of the past, obsolete, to excite him to such a pitch? She began to stir herself to readiness.

They passed up the steep hill, he eager as a pilgrim arriving at the shrine. As they came near the precincts, with castle on one side and cathedral on the other, his veins seemed to break into fiery blossom, he was transported.

They had passed through the gate, and the great west front was before them, with all its breadth and ornament.

'It is a false front,' he said, looking at the golden stone and the twin towers, and loving them just the same. In a little ecstasy he found himself in the porch, on the brink of the unrevealed. He looked up to the lovely unfolding of the stone. He was to pass within to the perfect womb.

Then he pushed open the door, and the great, pillared gloom was before him, in which his soul shuddered and rose from her nest. His soul leapt, soared up into the great church. His body stood still, absorbed by the height. His soul leapt up into the gloom, into possession, it reeled, it swooned with a great escape, it quivered in the womb, in the hush and the gloom of fecundity, like seed of procreation in ecstasy.

She too was overcome with wonder and awe. She followed him in his progress. Here, the twilight was the very essence of life, the coloured darkness was the embryo of all light, and the day. Here, the very first dawn was breaking, the very last sunset sinking, and the immemorial darkness, whereof life's day would blossom and fall away again, re-echoed peace and profound immemorial silence.

Away from time, always outside of time! Between east and west, between dawn and sunset, the church lay like a seed in silence, dark before germination, silenced after death. Containing birth and death, potential with all the noise and transition of life, the cathedral remained hushed, a great, involved seed, whereof the flower would be radiant life inconceivable, but whose beginning and whose end were the circle of silence. Spanned round with the rainbow, the jewelled gloom folded music upon silence, light upon darkness, fecundity upon death, as a seed folds leaf upon leaf and silence upon the root and the flower, hushing up the secret of all between its parts, the death out of which it fell, the life into which it has dropped, the immortality it involves, and the death it will embrace again.

Here in the church, 'before' and 'after' were folded together, all was contained in oneness. Brangwen came to his consummation. Out of the doors of the womb he had come, putting aside the wings of the womb, and proceeding into the light. Through daylight and day-after-day he had come, knowledge after knowledge, and experience after experience, remembering the darkness of the womb, having prescience of the darkness after death. Then between-while he had pushed open the doors of the cathedral, and entered the twilight of both darkness, the hush of the two-fold silence where dawn was sunset, and the beginning and the end were one.

Here the stone leapt up from the plain of earth, leapt up in a manifold, clustered desire each time, up, away from the horizontal earth, through twilight and dusk and the whole range of desire, through the swerving, the declination, ah, to the ecstasy, the touch, to the meeting and the consummation, the meeting, the clasp, the close embrace, the neutrality, the perfect, swooning consummation, the timeless ecstasy. There his soul remained, at the apex of the arch, clinched in the timeless ecstasy, consummated.

And there was no time nor life nor death, but only this, this timeless consummation, where the thrust from earth met the thrust from earth and the arch was locked on the keystone of ecstasy. This was all, this was everything. Till he came to himself in the world below. Then again he gathered himself together, in transit, every jet of him strained and leaped, leaped clear into the darkness above, to the fecundity and the unique mystery, to the touch, the clasp, the consummation, the climax of eternity, the apex of the arch.

She too was overcome, but silenced rather than tuned to the place. She loved it as a world not quite her own, she resented his transports and ecstasies. His passion in the cathedral at first awed her, then made her angry. After all, there was the sky outside, and in here, in this mysterious half-night, when his soul leapt with the pillars upwards, it was not to the stars and the crystalline dark space, but to meet and clasp with the answering impulse of leaping stone, there in the dusk and secrecy of the roof. The far-off clinching and mating of the arches, the leap and thrust of the stone, carring a great roof overhead, awed and silenced her.

But yet – yet she remembered that the open sky was no blue vault, no dark dome hung with many twinkling lamps, but a space where stars were wheeling in freedom, with freedom above them always higher.

The cathedral roused her too. But she would never consent to the knitting of all the leaping stone in a great roof that closed her in, and beyond which was nothing, nothing, it was the ultimate confine. His soul would have liked it to be so: here, here is all, complete, eternal: motion, meeting, ecstasy, and no illusion of time, of night and day passing by, but only perfectly proportioned space and movement clinching and renewing, and passion surging its way into great waves to the altar, recurrence of ecstasy.

Her soul too was carried forward to the altar, to the threshold of Eternity, in reverence and fear and joy. But ever she hung back in the transit, mistrusting the culmination of the altar. She was not to be flung forward on the lift and lift of passionate flights, to be cast at last upon the altar steps as upon the shore of the unknown. There was a great joy and a verity in it. But even in the dazed swoon of the cathedral, she claimed another right. The altar was barren, its lights gone out. God burned no more in that bush. It was dead matter lying there. She claimed the right to freedom above her, higher than the roof. She had always a sense of being roofed in.

So that she caught at little things, which saved her from being swept forward headlong in the tide of passion that leaps on into the Infinite in a great mass, triumphant and flinging its own course. She wanted to get out of this fixed, leaping, forward-travelling movement, to rise from it as a bird rises with wet, limp feet from the sea, to lift herself as a bird lifts its breast and thrusts its body from the pulse and heave of a sea that bears it forward to an unwilling conclusion, tear herself away like a bird on wings, and in open space where there is clarity, rise up above the fixed, surcharged motion, a separate speck that hangs suspended, moves this way and that, seeing and answering before it sinks again, having chosen or found the direction in which it shall be carried forward.

And it was as if she must grasp at something, as if her wings were too weak to lift her straight off the heaving motion. So she caught sight of the wicked, odd little faces carved in stone, and she stood before them arrested.

These sly little faces peeped out of the grand tide of the cathedral like something that knew better. They knew quite well, these little imps that retorted on man's own illusion, that the cathedral was not absolute. They winked and leered, giving suggestion of the many things that had been left out of the great concept of the church. 'However much there is inside here, there's a good deal they haven't got in,' the little faces mocked.

Apart from the lift and spring of the great impulse towards the altar, these little faces had separate wills, separate motions, separate knowledge, which rippled back in defiance of the tide, and laughed in triumph of their own very littleness.

'Oh, look!' cried Anna. 'Oh, look how adorable, the faces! Look at her.'

Brangwen looked unwillingly. This was the voice of the serpent in his Eden. She pointed him to a plump, sly, malicious little face carved in stone.

'He knew her, the man who carved her,' said Anna. 'I'm sure she was his wife.'

'It isn't a woman at all, it's a man,' said Brangwen curtly.

'Do you think so? – No! That isn't a man. That is no man's face.'

Her voice sounded rather jeering. He laughed shortly, and went on. But she would not go forward with him. She loitered about the carvings. And he could not go forward without her. He waited impatient of this counter-action. She was spoiling his passionate intercourse with the cathedral. His brows began to gather.

'Oh, this is good!' she cried again. 'Here is the same woman – look! – only he's made her cross! Isn't it lovely! Hasn't he made her hideous to a degree?' She laughed with pleasure. 'Didn't he hate her? He must have been a nice man! Look at her – isn't it awfully good – just like a shrewish woman. He must have enjoyed putting her in like that. He got his own back on her, didn't he?'

'It's a man's face, no woman's at all – a monk's – clean shaven,' he said.

She laughed with a pouf! of laughter.

'You hate to think he put his wife in your cathedral, don't you?' she mocked, with a tinkle of profane laughter. And she laughed with malicious triumph.

She had got free from the cathedral, she had even destroyed the passion he had. She was glad. He was bitterly angry. Strive as he would, he could not keep the cathedral wonderful to him. He was disillusioned. That which had been his absolute, containing all heaven and earth, was become to him as to her, a shapely heap of dead matter – but dead, dead.

His mouth was full of ash, his soul was furious. He hated her for having destroyed another of his vital illusions. Soon he would be stark, stark, without one place wherein to stand, without one belief in which to rest.

Yet somewhere in him he responded more deeply to the sly little face that knew better, than he had done before to the perfect surge of his cathedral.

Nevertheless for the time being his soul was wretched and homeless, and he could not bear to think of Anna's ousting him from his beloved realities. He wanted his cathedral; he wanted to satisfy his blind passion. And he could not any more. Something intervened.

They went home again, both of them altered. She had some new reverence for that which he wanted, he felt that his cathedrals would never again be to him as they had been. Before, he had thought them absolute. But now he saw them crouching under the sky, with still the dark, mysterious world of reality inside, but as a world within a world, a sort of side show, whereas before they had been as a world to him within a chaos: a reality, an order, an absolute, within a meaningless confusion.

He had felt, before, that could he but go through the great door and look down the gloom towards the far-off, concluding wonder of the altar, that then, with the windows suspended around like tablets of jewels, emanating their own glory, then he had arrived. Here the satisfaction he had yearned after came near, towards this, the porch of the great Unknown, all reality gathered, and there, the altar was the mystic door, through which all and everything must move on to eternity.

But now, somehow, sadly and disillusioned, he realised that the doorway was no doorway. It was too narrow, it was false. Outside the cathedral were many flying spirits that could never be sifted through the jewelled gloom. He had lost his absolute.

He listened to the thrushes in the gardens and heard a note which the cathedrals did not include: something free and careless and joyous. He crossed a field that was all yellow with dandelions, on his way to work, and the bath of yellow glowing was something at once so sumptuous and so fresh, that he was glad he was away from his shadowy cathedral.

There was life outside the Church. There was much that the Church did not include. He thought of God, and of the whole blue rotunda of the day. That was something great and free. He thought of the ruins of the Grecian worship, and it seemed, a temple was never perfectly a temple, till it was ruined and mixed up with the winds and the sky and the herbs.

Still he loved the Church. As a symbol, he loved it. He tended it for what it tried to represent, rather than for that which it did represent. Still he loved it. The little church across his garden-wall drew him, he gave it loving attention. But he went to take charge of it, to preserve it. It was as an old, sacred thing to him. He looked after the stone and woodwork, mending the organ and restoring a piece of broken carving, repairing the church furniture. Later, he became choir-master also.

His life was shifting its centre, becoming more superficial. He had failed to become really articulate, failed to find real expression. He had to continue in the old form. But in spirit, he was uncreated.

Anna was absorbed in the child now, she left her husband to take his own way. She was willing now to postpone all adventure into unknown realities. She had the child, her palpable and immediate future was the child. If her soul had found no utterance, her womb had.

The church that neighboured with his house became very intimate and dear to him. He cherished it, he had it entirely in his charge. If he could find no new activity, he would be happy cherishing the old, dear form of worship. He knew this little, whitewashed church. In its shadowy atmosphere he sank back into being. He liked to sink himself in its hush as a stone sinks into water.

He went across his garden, mounted the wall by the little steps, and entered the hush and peace of the church. As the heavy door clanged to behind him, his feet re-echoed in the aisle, his heart re-echoed with a little passion of tenderness and mystic peace. He was also slightly ashamed, like a man who has failed, who lapses back for his fulfilment.

He loved to light the candles at the organ, and sitting there alone in the little glow, practise the hymns and chants for the service. The whitewashed arches retreated into darkness, the sound of the organ and the organ-pedals died away upon the unalterable stillness of the church, there were faint, ghostly noises in the tower, and then the music swelled out again, loudly, triumphantly.

He ceased to fret about his life. He relaxed his will, and let everything go. What was between him and his wife was a great thing, if it was not everything. She had conquered, really. Let him wait, and abide, wait and abide. She and the baby and himself, they were one. The organ rang out his protestation. His soul lay in the darkness as he pressed the keys of the organ.

To Anna, the baby was a complete bliss and fulfilment. Her desire sank into abeyance, her soul was in bliss over the baby. It was rather a delicate child, she had trouble to rear it. She never for a moment thought it would die. It was a delicate infant, therefore it behoved her to make it strong. She threw herself into the labour, the child was everything. Her imagination was all occupied here. She was a mother. It was enough to handle the new little limbs, the new little body, hear the new little voice crying in the stillness. All the future rang to her out of the sound of the baby's crying and cooing, she balanced the coming years of life in her hands, as she nursed the child. The passionate sense of fulfilment, of the future germinated in her, made her vivid and powerful. All the future was in her hands, in the hands of the woman. And before this baby was ten months old, she was again with child. She seemed to be in the fecund of storm life, every moment was full and busy with productiveness to her. She felt like the earth, the mother of everything.

Brangwen occupied himself with the church, he played the organ, he trained the choir-boys, he taught a Sunday-school class of youths. He was happy enough. There was an eager, yearning kind of happiness in him as he taught the boys on Sundays. He was all the time exciting himself with the proximity of some secret that he had not yet fathomed.

In the house, he served his wife and the little matriarchy. She loved him because he was the father of her children. And she always had a physical passion for him. So he gave up trying to have the spiritual superiority and control, or even her respect for his conscious or public life. He lived simply by her physical love for him. And he served the little matriarchy, nursing the child and helping with the housework, indifferent any more of his own dignity and importance. But his abandoning of claims, his living isolated upon his own interest, made him seem unreal, unimportant.

Anna was not publicly proud of him. But very soon she learned to be indifferent to public life. He was not what is called a manly man: he did not drink or smoke or arrogate importance. But he was her man, and his very indifference to all claims of manliness set her supreme in her own world with him. Physically, she loved him and he satisfied her. He went alone and subsidiary always. At first it had irritated her, the outer world existed so little to him. Looking at him with outside eyes, she was inclined to sneer at him. But her sneer changed to a sort of respect. She respected him, that he could serve her so simply and completely. Above all, she loved to bear his children. She loved to be the source of children.

She could not understand him, his strange, dark rages and his devotion to the church. It was the church *building* he cared for; and yet his soul was passionate for something. He laboured cleaning the stonework, repairing the woodwork, restoring the organ, and making the singing as perfect as possible. To keep the church fabric and the church-ritual intact was his business; to have the intimate sacred building utterly in his own hands, and to make the form of service complete. There was a little bright anguish and tension on his face, and in his intent movements. He was like a lover who knows he is betrayed, but who still loves, whose love is only the more intense. The church was false, but he served it the more attentively.

During the day, at his work in the office, he kept himself suspended. He did not exist. He worked automatically till it was time to go home.

He loved with a hot heart the dark-haired little Ursula, and he waited for the child to come to consciousness. Now the mother monopolised the baby. But his heart waited in its darkness. His hour would come.

In the long run, he learned to submit to Anna. She forced him to the spirit of her laws, whilst leaving him the letter of his own. She combated in him his devils. She suffered very much from his inexplicable and incalculable dark rages, when a blackness filled him, and a black wind seemed to sweep out of existence everything that had to do with him. She could feel herself, everything, being annihilated by him.

At first she fought him. At night, in this state, he would kneel down to say his prayers. She looked at his crouching figure.

'Why are you kneeling there, pretending to pray?' she said, harshly. 'Do you think anybody can pray, when they are in the vile temper you are in?'

He remained crouching by the bedside, motionless.

'It's horrible,' she continued, 'and such a pretence! What do you pretend you are saying? Who do you pretend you are praying to?'

He still remained motionless, seething with inchoate rage, when his whole nature seemed to disintegrate. He seemed to live with a strain upon himself, and occasionaly came these dark, chaotic rages, the lust for destruction. She then fought with him, and their fights were horrible, murderous. And then the passion between them came just as black and awful.

But little by little, as she learned to love him better, she would put herself aside, and when she felt one of his fits upon him, would ignore him, successfully leave him in his world, whilst she remained in her own. He had a black struggle with himself, to come back to her. For at last he learned that he would be in hell until he came back to her. So he struggled to submit to her, and she was afraid of the ugly strain in his eyes. She made love to him, and took him. Then he was grateful to her love, humble.

He made himself a woodwork shed, in which to restore things which were destroyed in the church. So he had plenty to do: his wife, his child, the church, the woodwork, and his wage-earning, all occupying him. If only there were not some limit to him, some darkness across his eyes! He had to give in to it at last himself. He must submit to his own inadequacy, aware of some limit to himself, of something unformed in his own black, violent temper, and to reckon with it. But as she was more gentle with him, it became quieter.

As he sat sometimes very still, with a bright, vacant face, Anna could see the suffering among the brightness. He was aware of some limit to himself, of something unformed in his very being, of some buds which were not ripe in him, some folded centres of darkness which would never develop and unfold whilst he was alive in the body. He was unready for fulfilment. Something undeveloped in him limited him, there was a darkness in him which he *could* not unfold, which would never unfold in him.

Chapter Eight

The Child

From the first, the baby stirred in the young father a deep, strong emotion he dared scarcely acknowledge, it was so strong and came out of the dark of him. When he heard the child cry, a terror possessed him, because of the answering echo from the unfathomed distances in himself. Must he know in himself such distances, perilous and imminent?

He had the infant in his arms, he walked backwards and forwards troubled by the crying of his own flesh and blood. This was his own flesh and blood crying! His soul rose against the voice suddenly breaking out from him, from the distances in him.

Sometimes in the night, the child cried and cried, when the night was heavy and sleep oppressed him. And half asleep, he stretched out his hand to put it over the baby's face to stop the crying. But something arrested his hand: the very inhumanness of the intolerable, continuous crying arrested him. It was so impersonal, without cause or object. Yet he echoed to it directly, his soul answered its madness. It filled him with terror, almost with frenzy.

He learned to acquiesce to this, to submit to the awful, obliterated sources which were the origin of his living tissue. He was not what he conceived himself to be! Then he was what he was, unknown, potent, dark.

He became accustomed to the child, he knew how to lift and balance the little body. The baby had a beautiful, rounded head that moved him passionately. He would have fought to the last drop to defend that exquisite, perfect round head.

He learned to know the little hands and feet, the strange, unseeing, golden-brown eyes, the mouth that opened only to cry, or to suck, or to show a queer, toothless laugh. He could almost understand even the dangling legs, which at first had created in him a feeling of aversion. They could kick in their queer little way, they had their own softness.

One evening, suddenly, he saw the tiny, living thing rolling naked in the mother's lap, and he was so sick, it was so utterly helpless and vulnerable and extraneous; in a world of hard surfaces and varying altitudes, it lay vulnerable and naked at every point. Yet it was quite blithe. And yet, in its blind, awful crying, was there not the blind, far-off terror of its own vulnerable nakedness, the terror of being so utterly delivered over, helpless at every point. He could not bear to hear it crying. His heart strained and stood on guard against the whole universe.

But he waited for the dread of these days to pass; he saw the joy coming. He saw the lovely, creamy, cool little ear of the baby, a bit of dark hair rubbed to a bronze floss, like bronze-dust. And he waited, for the child to become his, to look at him and answer him.

It had a separate being, but it was his own child. His flesh and blood vibrated to it. He caught the baby to his breast with his passionate, clapping laugh. And the infant knew him.

As the newly-opened, newly-dawned eyes looked at him, he wanted them to perceive him, to recognise him. Then he was verified. The child knew him, a queer contortion of laughter came on its face for him. He caught it to his breast, clapping with a triumphant laugh.

The golden-brown eyes of the child gradually lit up and dilated at the sight of the dark-glowing face of the youth. It knew its mother better, it wanted its mother more. But the brightest, sharpest little ecstasy was for the father.

It began to be strong, to move vigorously and freely, to make sounds like words. It was a baby girl now. Already it knew his strong hands, it exulted in his strong clasp, it laughed and crowed when he played with it.

And his heart grew red-hot with passionate feeling for the child. She was not much more than a year old when the second baby was born. Then he took Ursula for his own. She his first little girl. He had set his heart on her.

The second had dark blue eyes and a fair skin: it was more a Brangwen, people said. The hair was fair. But they forgot Anna's stiff blonde fleece of childhood. They called the newcomer Gudrun.

This time, Anna was stronger, and not so eager. She did not mind that the baby was not a boy. It was enough that she had milk and could suckle her child: Oh, oh, the bliss of the little life sucking the milk of her body! Oh, oh, oh the bliss, as the infant grew stronger, of the two tiny hands clutching, catching blindly yet passionately at her breast, of the tiny mouth seeking her in blind, sure, vital knowledge, of the sudden consummate peace as the little body sank, the mouth and throat sucking, sucking, sucking, drinking life from her to make a new life, almost sobbing with passionate joy of receiving its own existence, the tiny hands clutching frantically as the nipple was drawn back, not to be gainsaid. This was enough for Anna. She seemed to pass off into a kind of rapture of motherhood, her rapture of motherhood was everything.

So that the father had the elder baby, the weaned child, the golden-brown, wondering vivid eyes of the little Ursula were for him, who had waited behind the mother till the need was for him. The mother felt a sharp stab of jealousy. But she was still more absorbed in the tiny baby. It was entirely hers, its need was direct upon her.

So Ursula became the child of her father's heart. She was the little blossom, he was the sun. He was patient, energetic, inventive for her. He taught her all the funny little things, he filled her and roused her to her fullest tiny measure. She answered him with her extravagant infant's laughter and her call of delight.

Now there were two babies, a woman came in to do the housework. Anna was wholly nurse. Two babies were not too much for her. But she hated any form of work, now her children had come, except the charge of them.

When Ursula toddled about, she was an absorbed, busy child, always amusing herself, needing not much attention from other people. At evening, towards six o'clock, Anna very often went across the lane to the stile, lifted Ursula over into the field, with a: 'Go and meet Daddy.' Then Brangwen, coming up the steep round of the hill, would see before him on the brow of the path a tiny, tottering, wind-blown little mite with a dark head, who, as soon as she saw him, would come running in tiny, wild, windmill fashion, lifting her arms up and down to him, down the steep hill. His heart leapt up, he ran his fastest to her, to catch her, because he knew she would fall. She came fluttering on, wildly, with her little limbs flying. And he was glad when he caught her up in his arms. Once she fell as she came flying to him, he saw her pitch forward suddenly as she was running with her hands lifted to him; and when he picked her up, her mouth was bleeding. He could never bear to think of it, he always wanted to cry, even when he was an old man and she had become a stranger to him. How he loved that little Ursula! – his heart had been sharply seared for her, when he was a youth, first married.

When she was a little older, he would see her recklessly climbing over the bars of the stile, in her red pinafore, swinging in peril and tumbling over, picking herself up and flitting towards him. Sometimes she liked to ride on his shoulder, sometimes she preferred to walk with his hand, sometimes she would fling her arms round his legs for a moment, then race free again, whilst he went shouting and calling to her, a child along with her. He was still only a tall, thin, unsettled lad of twenty-two.

It was he who had made her her cradle, her little chair, her little stool, her high chair. It was he who would swing her up to table or who would make for her a doll out of an old table-leg, whilst she watched him, saying:

'Make her eyes, Daddy, make her eyes!'

And he made her eyes with his knife.

She was very fond of adorning herself, so he would tie a piece of cotton round her ear, and hang a blue bead on it underneath for an ear-ring. The ear-rings varied with a red bead, and a golden bead, and a little pearl bead. And as he came home at night, seeing her bridling and looking very self-conscious, he took notice and said:

'So you're wearing your best golden and pearl ear-rings, to-day?'

'Yes.'

'I suppose you've been to see the queen?'

'Yes, I have.'

'Oh, and what had she to say?'

'She said – she said – "You won't dirty your nice white frock." ' '

He gave her the nicest bits from his plate, putting them into her red, moist mouth. And he would make on a piece of bread-and-butter a bird, out of jam: which she ate with extraordinary relish.

After the tea-things were washed up, the woman went away, leaving the family free. Usually Brangwen helped in the bathing of the children. He held long discussions with his child as she sat on his knee and he unfastened her clothes. And he seemed to be talking really of momentous things, deep moralities. Then suddenly she ceased to hear, having caught sight of a glassie rolled into a corner. She slipped away, and was in no hurry to return.

'Come back here,' he said, waiting. She became absorbed, taking no notice.

'Come on,' he repeated, with a touch of command.

An excited little chuckle came from her, but she pretended to be absorbed.

'Do you hear, Milady?'

She turned with a fleeting, exulting laugh. He rushed on her, and swept her up.

'Who was it that didn't come!' he said, rolling her between his strong hands, tickling her. And she laughed heartily, heartily. She loved him that he compelled her with his strength and decision. He was all-powerful, the tower of strength which rose out of her sight.

When the children were in bed, sometimes Anna and he sat and talked, desultorily, both of them idle. He read very little. Anything he was drawn to read became a burning reality to him, another scene outside his window. Whereas Anna skimmed through a book to see what happened, then she had enough.

Therefore they would often sit together, talking desultorily. What was really between them they could not utter. Their words were only accidents in the mutual silence. When they talked, they gossiped. She did not care for sewing.

She had a beautiful way of sitting musing, gratefully, as if her heart were lit up. Sometimes she would turn to him, laughing, to tell him some little thing that had happened during the day. Then he would laugh, they would talk awhile, before the vital, physical silence was between them again.

She was thin but full of colour and life. She was perfectly happy to do just nothing, only to sit with a curious, languid dignity, so careless as to be almost regal, so utterly indifferent, so confident. The bond between them was undefinable, but very strong. It kept everyone else at a distance.

His face never changed whilst she knew him, it only became more intense. It was ruddy and dark in its abstraction, not very human, it had a strong, intent brightness. Sometimes, when his eyes met hers, a yellow flash from them caused a darkness to swoon over her consciousness, electric, and a slight strange laugh came on his face. Her eyes would turn languidly, then close, as if hypnotised. And they lapsed into the same potent darkness. He had the quality of a young black cat, intent, unnoticeable, and yet his presence gradually made itself felt, stealthily and powerfully took hold of her. He called, not to her, but to something in her, which responded subtly, out of her unconscious darkness.

So they were together in a darkness, passionate, electric, for ever haunting the back of the common day, never in the light. In the light, he seemed to sleep, unknowing. Only she knew him when the darkness set him free, and he could see with his gold-glowing eyes his intention and his desires in the dark. Then she was in a spell, then she answered his harsh, penetrating call with a soft leap of her soul, the darkness woke up, electric, bristling with an unknown, overwhelming insinuation.

By now they knew each other; she was the daytime, the daylight, he was the shadow, put aside, but in the darkness potent with an overwhelming voluptuousness.

She learned not to dread and to hate him, but to fill herself with him, to give herself to his black, sensual power, that was hidden all the daytime. And the curious rolling of the eyes, as if she were lapsing in a trance away from her ordinary consciousness became habitual with her, when something threatened and opposed her in life, the conscious life.

So they remained as separate in the light, and in the thick darkness, married. He supported her daytime authority, kept it inviolable at last. And she, in all the darkness, belonged to him, to his close, insinuating, hypnotic familiarity.

All his daytime activity, all his public life, was a kind of sleep. She wanted to be free, to belong to the day. And he ran avoiding the day in work. After tea, he went to the shed to his carpentry or his wood-carving. He was restoring the patched, degraded pulpit to its original form.

But he loved to have the child near him, playing by his feet. She was a piece of light that really belonged to him, that played within his darkness. He left the shed door on the latch. And when, with his second sense of another presence, he knew she was coming, he was satisfied, he was at rest. When he was alone with her, he did not want to take notice, to talk. He wanted to live unthinking, with her presence flickering upon him.

He always went in silence. The child would push open the shed door, and see him working by lamplight, his sleeves rolled back. His clothes hung about him, carelessly, like mere wrapping. Inside, his body was concentrated with a flexible, charged power all of its own, isolated. From when she was a tiny child Ursula could remember his forearm, with its fine black hairs and its electric flexibility, working at the bench through swift, unnoticeable movements, always ambushed in a sort of silence.

She hung a moment in the door of the shed, waiting for him to notice her. He turned, his black, curved eyebrows arching slightly.

'Hullo, Twittermiss!'

And he closed the door behind her. Then the child was happy in the shed that smelled of sweet wood and resounded to the noise of the plane or the hammer or the saw, yet was charged with the silence of the worker. She played on, intent and absorbed, among the shavings and the little nogs of wood. She never touched him: his feet and legs were near, she did not approach them.

She liked to flit out after him when he was going to church at night. If he were going to be alone, he swung her over the wall, and let her come.

Again she was transported when the door was shut behind them, and they two inherited the big, pale, void place. She would watch him as he lit the organ candles, wait whilst he began his practising his tunes, then she ran foraging here and there, like a kitten playing by herself in the darkness with eyes dilated. The ropes hung vaguely, twining on the floor, from the bells in the tower, and Ursula always wanted the fluffy, red-and-white, or blue-and-white rope-grips. But they were above her.

Sometimes her mother came to claim her. Then the child was seized with resentment. She passionately resented her mother's superficial authority. She wanted to assert her own detachment.

He, however, also gave her occasional cruel shocks. He let her play about in the church, she rifled foot-stools and hymn-books and cushions, like a bee among flowers, whilst the organ echoed away. This continued for some weeks. Then the charwoman worked herself up into a frenzy of rage, to dare to attack Brangwen, and one day descended on him like a harpy. He wilted away, and wanted to break the old beast's neck.

Instead he came glowering in fury to the house, and turned on Ursula.

'Why, you tiresome little monkey, can't you even come to church without pulling the place to bits?'

His voice was harsh and cat-like, he was blind to the child. She shrank away in childish anguish and dread. What was it, what awful thing was it?

The mother turned with her calm, almost superb manner.

'What has she done, then?'

'Done? She shall go in the church no more, pulling and littering and destroying.'

The wife slowly rolled her eyes and lowered her eyelids.

'What has she destroyed, then?'

He did not know.

'I've just had Mrs. Wilkinson at me,' he cried, 'with a list of things she's done.'

Ursula withered under the contempt and anger of the 'she', as he spoke of her.

'Send Mrs. Wilkinson here to me with a list of the things she's done,' said Anna. '*I* am the one to hear that.'

'It's not the things the child has done,' continued the mother, 'that have put you out so much, it's because you can't bear being spoken to by that old woman. But you haven't the courage to turn on *her* when she attacks you, you bring your rage here.'

He relapsed into silence. Ursula knew that he was wrong. In the outside, upper world, he was wrong. Already came over the child the cold sense of the impersonal world. There she knew her mother was right. But still her heart clamoured after her father, for him to be right, in his dark, sensuous underworld. But he was angry, and went his way in blackness and brutal silence again.

The child ran about absorbed in life, quiet, full of amusement. She did not notice things, nor changes nor alterations. One day she would find daisies in the grass, another day, apple-blossoms would be sprinkled white on the ground, and she would run among it, for pleasure because it was there. Yet again birds would be pecking at the cherries, her father would throw cherries down from the tree all round her on the garden. Then the fields were full of hay.

She did not remember what had been nor what would be, the outside things were there each day. She was always herself, the world outside was accidental. Even her mother was accidental to her: a condition that happened to endure.

Only her father occupied any permanent position in the childish consciousness. When he came back she remembered vaguely how he had gone away, when he went away she knew vaguely that she must wait for his coming back. Whereas her mother, returning from an outing, merely became present, there was no reason for connecting her with some previous departure.

The return or the departure of the father was the one event which the child remembered. When he came, something woke up in her, some yearning. She knew when he was out of joint or irritable or tired: then she was uneasy, she could not rest.

When he was in the house, the child felt full and warm, rich like a creature in the sunshine. When he was gone, she was vague, forgetful. When he scolded her even, she was often more aware of him than of herself. He was her strength and her greater self.

Ursula was three years old when another baby girl was born. Then the two small sisters were much together, Gudrun and Ursula. Gudrun was a quiet child who played for hours alone, absorbed in her fancies. She was brown-haired, fair-skinned, strangely placid, almost passive. Yet her will was indomitable, once set. From the first she followed Ursula's lead. Yet she was a thing to herself, so that to watch the two together was strange. They were like two young animals playing together but not taking real notice of each other. Gudrun was the mother's favourite – except that Anna always lived in her latest baby.

The burden of so many lives depending on him wore the youth down. He had his work in the office, which was done purely by effort of will: he had his barren passion for the church; he had three young children. Also at this time his health was not good. So he was haggard and irritable, often a pest in the house. Then he was told to go to his woodwork, or to the church.

Between him and the little Ursula there came into being a strange alliance. They were aware of each other. He knew the child was always on his side. But in his consciousness he counted it for nothing. She was always for him. He took it for granted. Yet his life was based on her, even whilst she was a tiny child, on her support and her accord.

Anna continued in her violent trance of motherhood, always busy, often harassed, but always contained in her trance of motherhood. She seemed to exist in her own violent fruitfulness, and it was as if the sun shone tropically on her. Her colour was bright, her eyes full of a fecund gloom, her brown hair tumbled loosely over her ears. She had a look of richness. No responsibility, no sense of duty troubled her. The outside, public life was less than nothing to her, really.

Whereas when, at twenty-six, he found himself father of four children, with a wife who lived intrinsically like the ruddiest lilies of the field, he let the weight of responsibility press on him and drag him. It was then that his child Ursula strove to be with him. She was with him, even as a baby of four, when he was irritable and shouted and made the household unhappy. She suffered from his shouting, but somehow it was not really him. She wanted it to be over, she wanted to resume her normal connection with him. When he was disagreeable, the child echoed to the crying of some need in him, and she responded blindly. Her heart followed him as if he had some tie with her, and some love which he could not deliver. Her heart followed him persistently, in its love.

But there was the dim, childish sense of her own smallness and inadequacy, a fatal sense of worthlessness. She could not do anything, she was not enough. She could not be important to him. This knowledge deadened her from the first.

Still she set towards him like a quivering needle. All her life was directed by her awareness of him, her wakefulness to his being. And she was against her mother.

Her father was the dawn wherein her consciousness woke up. But for him, she might have gone on like the other children, Gudrun and Theresa and Catherine, one with the flowers and insects and playthings, having no existence apart from the concrete object of her attention. But her father came too near to her. The clasp of his hands and the power of his breast woke her up almost in pain from the transient unconsciousness of childhood. Wide-eyed, unseeing, she was awake before she knew how to see. She was wakened too soon. Too soon the call had come to her, when she was a small baby, and her father held her close to his breast, her sleep-living heart was beaten into wakefulness by the striving of his bigger heart, by his clasping her to his body for love and for fulfilment, asking as a magnet must always ask. From her the response had struggled dimly, vaguely into being.

The children were dressed roughly for the country. When she was little, Ursula pattered about in little wooden clogs, a blue overall over her thick red dress, a red shawl crossed on her breast and tied behind again. So she ran with her father to the garden.

The household rose early. He was out digging by six o'clock in the morning, he went to his work at half-past eight. And Ursula was usually in the garden with him, though not near at hand.

At Eastertime one year, she helped him to set potatoes. It was the first time she had ever helped him. The occasion remained as a picture, one of her earliest memories. They had gone out soon after dawn. A cold wind was blowing. He had his old trousers tucked into his boots, he wore no coat nor waistcoat, his shirt-sleeves fluttered in the wind, his face was ruddy and intent, in a kind of sleep. When he was at work he neither heard nor saw. A long, thin man, looking still a youth, with a line of black moustache above his thick mouth, and his fine hair blown on his forehead, he worked away at the earth in the grey first light, alone. His solitariness drew the child like a spell.

The wind came chill over the dark-green fields. Ursula ran up and watched him push the setting-peg in at one side of his ready earth, stride across, and push it in the other side, pulling the line taut and clear upon the clods intervening. Then with a sharp cutting noise the bright spade came towards her, cutting a grip into the new, soft earth.

He struck his spade upright and straightened himself.

'Do you want to help me?' he said.

She looked up at him from out of her little woollen bonnet.

'Ay,' he said, 'you can put some taters in for me. Look – like that – these little sprits standing up – so much apart, you see.'

And stooping down he quickly, surely placed the spritted potatoes in the soft grip, where they rested separate and pathetic on the heavy cold earth.

He gave her a little basket of potatoes, and strode himself to the other end of the line. She saw him stooping, working towards her. She was excited, and unused. She put in one potato, then rearranged it, to make it sit nicely. Some of the sprits were broken, and she was afraid. The responsibility excited her like a string tying her up. She could not help looking with dread at the string buried under the heaped-back soil. Her father was working nearer, stooping, working nearer. She was overcome by her responsibility. She put potatoes quickly into the cold earth.

He came near.

'Not so close,' he said, stooping over her potatoes, taking some out and rearranging the others. She stood by with the painful terrified helplessness of childhood. He was so unseeing and confident, she wanted to do the thing and yet she could not. She stood by looking on, her little blue overall fluttering in the wind, the red woollen ends of her shawl blowing gustily. Then he went down the row, relentlessly, turning the potatoes in with his sharp spade-cuts. He took no notice of her, only worked on. He had another world from hers.

She stood helplessly stranded on his world. He continued his work. She knew she could not help him. A little bit forlorn, at last she turned away, and ran down the garden, away from him, as fast as she could go away from him, to forget him and his work.

He missed her presence, her face in her red woollen bonnet, her blue overall fluttering. She ran to where a little water ran trickling between grass and stones. That she loved.

When he came by he said to her:

'You didn't help me much.'

The child looked at him dumbly. Already her heart was heavy because of her own disappointment. Her mouth was dumb and pathetic. But he did not notice, he went his way.

And she played on, because of her disappointment persisting even the more in her play. She dreaded work, because she could not do it as he did it. She was conscious of the great breach between them. She knew she had no power. The grown-up power to work deliberately was a mystery to her.

He would smash into her sensitive child's world destructively. Her mother was lenient, careless. The children played about as they would all day. Ursula was thoughtless – why should she remember things? If across the garden she saw the hedge had budded, and if she wanted these greeny-pink, tiny buds for bread-and-cheese, to play at tea-party with, over she went for them.

Then suddenly, perhaps the next day, her soul would almost start out of her body as her father turned on her, shouting:

'Who's been tramplin' an' dancin' across where I've just sowed seed? I know it's you, nuisance! Can you find nowhere else to walk, but just over my seed beds? But it's like you, that is – no heed but to follow your own greedy nose.'

It had shocked him in his intent world to see the zigzagging lines of deep little footprints across his work. The child was infinitely more shocked. Her vulnerable little soul was flayed and trampled. *Why* were the footprints there? She had not wanted to make them. She stood dazzled with pain and shame and unreality.

Her soul, her consciousness seemed to die away. She became shut off and senseless, a little fixed creature whose soul had gone hard and unresponsive. The sense of her own unreality hardened her like a frost. She cared no longer.

And the sight of her face, shut and superior with self-asserting indifference, made a flame of rage go over him. He wanted to break her.

'I'll break your obstinate little face,' he said, through shut teeth, lifting his hand.

The child did not alter in the least. The look of indifference, complete glancing indifference, as if nothing but herself existed to her, remained fixed.

Yet far away in her, the sobs were tearing her soul. And when he had gone, she would go and creep under the parlour sofa, and lie clinched in the silent, hidden misery of childhood.

When she crawled out, after an hour or so, she went rather stiffly to play. She willed to forget. She cut off her childish soul from memory, so that the pain, and the insult should not be real. She asserted herself only. There was now nothing in the world but her own self. So very soon, she came to believe in the outward malevolence that was against her. And very early, she learned that even her adored father was part of this malevolence. And very early she learned to harden her soul in resistance and denial of all that was outside her, harden herself upon her own being.

She never felt sorry for what she had done, she never forgave those who had made her guilty. If he had said to her, 'Why, Ursula, did you trample my carefully-made bed?' that would have hurt her to the quick, and she would have done anything for him. But she was always tormented by the unreality of outside things. The earth was to walk on. Why must she avoid a certain patch, just because it was called a seed-bed? It was the earth to walk on. This was her instinctive assumption. And when he bullied her, she became hard, cut herself off from all connection, lived in the little separate world of her own violent will.

As she grew older, five, six, seven, the connection between her and her father was even stronger. Yet it was always straining to break. She was always relapsing on her own violent will into her own separate world of herself. This made him grind his teeth with bitterness, for he still wanted her. But she could harden herself into her own self's universe, impregnable.

He was very fond of swimming, and in warm weather would take her down to the canal, to a silent place, or to a big pond or reservoir, to bathe. He would take her on his back as he went swimming, and she clung close, feeling his strong movement under her, so strong, as if it would uphold all the world. Then he taught her to swim.

She was a fearless little thing, when he dared her. And he had a curious craving to frighten her, to see what she would do with him. He said, would she ride on his back whilst he jumped off the canal bridge down into the water beneath.

She would. He loved to feel the naked child clinging on to his shoulders. There was a curious fight between their two wills. He mounted the parapet of the canal bridge. The water was a long way down. But the child had a deliberate will set upon his. She held herself fixed to him.

He leapt, and down they went. The crash of the water as they went under struck through the child's small body, with a sort of unconsciousness. But she remained fixed. And when they came up again, and when they went to the bank, and when they sat on the grass side by side, he laughed, and said it was fine. And the dark-dilated eyes of the child looked at him wonderingly, darkly, wondering from the shock, yet reserved and unfathomable, so he laughed almost with a sob.

In a moment she was clinging safely on his back again, and he was swimming in deep water. She was used to his nakedness, and to her mother's nakedness, ever since she was born. They were clinging to each other, and making up to each other for the strange blow that had been struck at them. Yet still, on other days, he would leap again with her from the bridge, daringly, almost wickedly. Till at length, as he leapt, once, she dropped forward on to his head, and nearly broke his neck, so that they fell into the water in a heap, and fought for a few moments with death. He saved her, and sat on the bank, quivering. But his eyes were full of the blackness of death. It was as if death had cut between their two lives, and separated them.

Still they were not separate. There was this curious taunting intimacy between them. When the fair came, she wanted to go in the swingboats. He took her, and, standing up in the boat, holding on to the irons, began to drive higher, perilously higher. The child clung fast on her seat.

'Do you want to go any higher?' he said to her, and she laughed with her mouth, her eyes wide and dilated. They were rushing through the air.

'Yes,' she said, feeling as if she would turn into vapour, lose hold of everything, and melt away. The boat swung far up, then down like a stone, only to be caught sickeningly up again.

'Any higher?' he called, looking at her over his shoulder, his face evil and beautiful to her.

She laughed with white lips.

He sent the swingboat sweeping through the air in a great semi-circle, till it jerked and swayed at the high horizontal. The child clung on, pale, her eyes fixed on him. People below were calling. The jerk at the top had almost shaken them both out. He had done what he could – and he was attracting censure. He sat down, and let the swingboat swing itself out.

People in the crowd cried shame on him as he came out of the swingboat. He laughed. The child clung to his hand, pale and mute. In a while she was violently sick. He gave her lemonade, and she gulped a little.

'Don't tell your mother you've been sick,' he said. There was no need to ask that. When she got home, the child crept away under the parlour sofa, like a sick little animal, and was a long time before she crawled out.

But Anna got to know of this escapade, and was passionately angry and contemptuous of him. His golden-brown eyes glittered, he had a strange, cruel little smile. And as the child watched him, for the first time in her life a disillusion came over her, something cold and isolating. She went over to her mother. Her soul was dead towards him. It made her sick.

Still she forgot and continued to love him, but ever more coldly. He was at this time, when he was about twenty-eight years old, strange and violent in his being, sensual. He acquired some power over Anna, over everybody he came into contact with.

After a long bout of hostility, Anna at last closed with him. She had now four children, all girls. For seven years she had been absorbed in wifehood and motherhood. For years he had gone on beside her, never really encroaching upon her. Then gradually another self seemed to assert its being within him. He was still silent and separate. But she could feel him all the while coming near upon her, as if his breast and his body were threatening her, and he was always coming closer. Gradually he became indifferent of responsibility. He would do what pleased him, and no more.

He began to go away from home. He went to Nottingham on Saturdays, always alone, to the football match and to the music-hall, and all the time he was watching, in readiness. He never cared to drink. But with his hard, golden-brown eyes, so keen seeing with their tiny black pupils, he watched all the people, everything that happened, and he waited.

In the Empire one evening he sat next to two girls. He was aware of the one beside him. She was rather small, common, with a fresh complexion and an upper lip that lifted from her teeth, so that, when she was not conscious, her mouth was slightly open and her lips pressed outwards in a kind of blind appeal. She was strongly aware of the man next to her, so that all her body was still, very still. Her face watched the stage. Her arms went down into her lap, very self-conscious and still.

A gleam lit up in him: should he begin with her? Should he begin with her to live the other, the unadmitted life of his desire? Why not? He had always been so good. Save for his wife, he was a virgin. And why, when all women were different? Why, when he would only live once? He wanted the other life. His own life was barren, not enough. He wanted the other.

Her open mouth, showing the small, irregular, white teeth, appealed to him. It was open and ready. It was so vulnerable. Why should he not go in and enjoy what was there? The slim arm that went down so still and motionless to the lap, it was pretty. She would be small, almost like a child, and pretty. Her childishness whetted him keenly. She would be helpless between his hands.

'That was the best turn we've had,' he said to her, leaning over as he clapped his hands. He felt strong and unshakeable in himself, set over against all the world. His soul was keen and watchful, glittering with a kind of amusement. He was perfectly self-contained. He was himself, the absolute, the rest of the world was the object that should contribute to his being.

The girl started, turned round, her eyes lit up with an almost painful flash of a smile, the colour came deeply in her cheeks.

'Yes, it was,' she said, quite meaninglessly, and she covered her rather prominent teeth with her lips. Then she sat looking straight before her, seeing nothing, only conscious of the colour burning in her cheeks.

It pricked him with a pleasant sensation. His veins and his nerves attended to her, she was so young and palpitating.

'It's not such a good programme as last week's,' he said.

Again she half turned her face to him, and her clear, bright eyes, bright like shallow water, filled with light, frightened, yet involuntarily lighting and shaking with response.

'Oh, isn't it! I wasn't able to come last week.'

He noted the common accent. It pleased him. He knew what class she came of. Probably she was a warehouse-lass. He was glad she was a common girl.

He proceeded to tell her about the last week's programme. She answered at random, very confusedly. The colour burned in her cheek. Yet she always answered him. The girl on the other side sat remotely, obviously silent. He ignored her. All his address was for his own girl, with her bright, shallow eyes and her vulnerably opened mouth.

The talk went on, meaningless and random on her part, quite deliberate and purposive on his. It was a pleasure to him to make this conversation, an activity pleasant as a fine game of chance and skill. He was very quiet and pleasant-humoured, but so full of strength. She fluttered beside his steady pressure of warmth and his surety.

He saw the performance drawing to a close. His senses were alert and wilful. He would press his advantages. He followed her and her plain friend down the stairs to the street. It was raining.

'It's a nasty night,' he said. 'Shall you come and have a drink of something – a cup of coffee – it's early yet.'

'Oh, I don't think so,' she said, looking away into the night.

'I wish you would,' he said, putting himself as it were at her mercy. There was a moment's pause.

'Come to Rollins?' he said.

'No – not there.'

'To Carson's, then?'

There was a silence. The other girl hung on. The man was the centre of positive force.

'Will your friend come as well?'

There was another moment of silence, while the other girl felt her ground.

'No, thanks,' she said. 'I've promised to meet a friend.'

'Another time, then?' he said.

'Oh, thanks,' she replied, very awkward.

'Good night,' he said.

'See you later,' said his girl to her friend.

'Where?' said the friend.

'You know, Gertie,' replied his girl.

'All right, Jennie.'

The friend was gone into the darkness. He turned with his girl to the tea-shop. They talked all the time. He made his sentences in sheer, almost muscular pleasure of exercising himself with her. He was looking at her all the time, perceiving her, appreciating her, finding her out, gratifying himself with her. He could see distinct attractions in her; her eyebrows, with their particular curve, gave him keen aesthetic pleasure. Later on he would see her bright, pellucid eyes, like shallow water, and know those. And there remained the open, exposed mouth, red and vulnerable. That he reserved as yet. And all the while his eyes were on the girl, estimating and handling with pleasure her young softness. About the girl herself, who or what she was, he cared nothing, he was quite unaware that she was anybody. She was just the sensual object of his attention.

'Shall we go, then?' he said.

She rose in silence, as if acting without a mind, merely physically. He seemed to hold her in his will. Outside it was still raining.

'Let's have a walk,' he said. 'I don't mind the rain, do you?'

'No, I don't mind it,' she said.

He was alert in every sense and fibre, and yet quite sure and steady, and lit up, as if transfused. He had a free sensation of walking in his own darkness, not in anybody else's world at all. He was purely a world to himself, he had nothing to do with any general consciousness. Just his own senses were supreme. All the rest was external, insignificant, leaving him alone with this girl whom he wanted to absorb, whose properties he wanted to absorb into his own senses. He did not care about her, except that he wanted to overcome her resistance, to have her in his power, fully and exhaustively to enjoy her.

They turned into the dark streets. He held her umbrella over her, and put his arm round her. She walked as if she were unaware. But gradually, as he walked, he drew her a little closer, into the movement of his side and hip. She fitted in there very well. It was a real good fit, to walk with her like this. It made him exquisitely aware of his own muscular self. And his hand that grasped her side felt one curve of her, and it seemed like a new creation to him, a reality, an absolute, an existing tangible beauty of the absolute. It was like a star. Everything in him was absorbed in the sensual delight of this one small, firm curve in her body, that his hand, and his whole being, had lighted upon.

He led her into the Park, where it was almost dark. He noticed a corner between two walls, under a great overhanging bush of ivy.

'Let us stand here a minute,' he said.

He put down the umbrella, and followed her into the corner, retreating out of the rain. He needed no eyes to see. All he wanted was to know through touch. She was like a piece of palpable darkness. He found her in the darkness, put his arms round her and his hands upon her. She was silent and inscrutable. But he did not want to know anything about her, he only wanted to discover her. And through her clothing, what absolute beauty he touched.

'Take your hat off,' he said.

Silently, obediently, she shook off her hat and gave herself to his arms again. He liked her – he liked the feel of her – he wanted to know her more closely. He let his fingers subtly seek out her cheek and neck. What amazing beauty and pleasure, in the dark! His fingers had often touched Anna on the face and neck like that. What matter! It was one man who touched Anna, another who now touched this girl. He liked best his new self. He was given over altogether to the sensuous knowledge of this woman, and every moment he seemed to be touching absolute beauty, something beyond knowledge.

Very close, marvelling and exceedingly joyful in their discoveries, his hands pressed upon her, so subtly, so seekingly, so finely and desirously searching her out, that she too was almost swooning in the absolute of sensual knowledge. In utter sensual delight she clenched her knees, her thighs, her loins together! It was an added beauty to him.

But he was patiently working for her relaxation, patiently, his whole being fixed in the smile of latent gratification, his whole body electric with a subtle, powerful, reducing force upon her. So he came at length to kiss her, and she was almost betrayed by his insidious kiss. Her open mouth was too helpless and unguarded. He knew this, and his first kiss was very gentle, and soft, and assuring, so assuring. So that her soft, defenceless mouth became assured, even bold, seeking upon his mouth. And he answered her gradually, gradually, his soft kiss sinking in softly, softly, but ever more heavily, more heavily yet, till it was too heavy for her to meet, and she began to sink under it. She was sinking, sinking, his smile of latent gratification was becoming more tense, he was sure of her. He let the whole force of his will sink upon her to sweep her away. But it was too great a shock for her. With a sudden horrible movement she ruptured the state that contained them both.

'Don't – don't!

It was a rather horrible cry that seemed to come out of her, not to belong to her. It was some strange agony of terror crying out the words. There was something vibrating and beside herself in the noise. His nerves ripped like silk.

'What's the matter?' he said, as if calmly. 'What's the matter?'

She came back to him, but trembling, reservedly this time.

Her cry had given him gratification. But he knew he had been too sudden for her. He was now careful. For a while he merely sheltered her. Also there had broken a flaw into his perfect will. He wanted to persist, to begin again, to lead up to the point where he had let himself go on her, and then manage more carefully, successfully. So far she had won. And the battle was not over yet. But another voice woke in him and prompted him to let her go – let her go in contempt.

He sheltered her, and soothed her, and caressed her, and kissed her, and again began to come nearer, nearer. He gathered himself together. Even if he did not take her, he would make her relax, he would fuse away her resistance. So softly, softly, with infinite caressiveness he kissed her, and the whole of his being seemed to fondle her. Till, at the verge, swooning at the breaking point, there came from her a beaten, inarticulate, moaning cry:

'Don't - oh, don't!'

His veins fused with extreme voluptuousness. For a moment he almost lost control of himself, and continued automatically. But there was a moment of inaction, of cold suspension. He was not going to take her. He drew her to him and soothed her, and caressed her. But the pure zest had gone. She struggled to herself and realised he was not going to take her. And then, at the very last moment, when his fondling had come near again, his hot living desire despising her, against his cold sensual desire, she broke violently away from him.

'Don't,' she cried, harsh now with hatred, and she flung her hand across and hit him violently. 'Keep off of me.'

His blood stood still for a moment. Then the smile came again within him, steady, cruel.

'Why, what's the matter?' he said, with suave irony. 'Nobody's going to hurt you.'

'I know what *you* want,' she said.

'*I* know what I want,' he said. 'What's the odds?'

'Well, you're not going to have it off *me*.'

'Aren't I? Well, then I'm not. It's no use crying about it, is it?'

'No, it isn't,' said the girl, rather disconcerted by his irony.

'But there's no need to have a row about it. We can kiss good night just the same, can't we?'

She was silent in the darkness.

'Or do you want your hat and umbrella to go home this minute?'

Still she was silent. He watched her dark figure as she stood there on the edge of the faint darkness, and he waited.

'Come and say good night nicely, if we're going to say it,' he said.

Still she did not stir. He put his hand out and drew her into the darkness again.

'It's warmer in here,' he said; 'a lot cosier.'

His will had not yet relaxed from her. The moment of hatred exhilarated him.

'I'm going now,' she muttered, as he closed his hand over her.

'See how well you fit your place,' he said, as he drew her to her previous position, close upon him. 'What do you want to leave it for?'

And gradually the intoxication invaded him again, the zest came back. After all, why should he not take her?

But she did not yield to him entirely.

'Are you a married man?' she asked at length.

'What if I am?' he said.

She did not answer.

'I don't ask you whether *you're* married or not,' he said.

'You know jolly well I'm *not*,' she answered hotly. Oh, if she could only break away from him, if only she need not yield to him.

At length her will became cold against him. She had escaped. But she hated him for her escape more than for her danger. Did he despise her so coldly? And she was in torture of adherence to him still.

'Shall I see you next week – next Saturday?' he said, as they returned to the town. She did not answer.

'Come to the Empire with me – you and Gertie,' he said.

'I should look well, going with a married man,' she said.

'I'm no less of a man for being married, am I?' he said.

'Oh, it's a different matter altogether with a married man,' she said, in a ready-made speech that showed her chagrin.

'How's that?' he asked.

But she would not enlighten him. Yet she promised, without promising, to be at the meeting-place next Saturday evening.

So he left her. He did not know her name. He caught a train and went home.

It was the last train, he was very late. He was not home till midnight. But he was quite indifferent. He had no real relation with his home, not this man which he now was. Anna was sitting up for him. She saw the queer, absolved look on his face, a sort of latent, almost sinister smile, as if he were absolved from his 'good' ties.

'Where have you been?' she asked, puzzled, interested.

'To the Empire.'

'Who with?'

'By myself. I came home with Tom Cooper.'

She looked at him, and wondered what he had been doing. She was indifferent as to whether he lied or not.

'You have come home very strange,' she said. And there was an appreciative inflexion in the speech.

He was not affected. As for his humble, good self, he was absolved from it. He sat down and ate heartily. He was not tired. He seemed to take no notice of her.

For Anna the moment was critical. She kept herself aloof, and watched him. He talked to her, but with a little indifference, since he was scarcely aware of her. So, then she did not affect him. Here was a new turn of affairs! He was rather attractive, nevertheless. She liked him better than the ordinary mute, half-effaced, half-subdued man she usually knew him to be. So, he was blossoming out into his real self! It piqued her. Very good, let him blossom! She liked a new turn of affairs. He was a strange man come home to her. Glancing at him, she saw she could not reduce him to what he had been before. In an instant she gave it up. Yet not without a pang of rage, which would insist on their old, beloved love, their old, accustomed intimacy and her old, established supremacy. She almost rose up to fight for them. And looking at him, and remembering his father, she was wary. This was the new turn of affairs!

Very good, if she could not influence him in the old way, she would be level with him in the new. Her old defiant hostility came up. Very good, she too was out on her own adventure. Her voice, her manner changed, she was ready for the game. Something was liberated in her. She liked him. She liked this strange man come home to her. He was very welcome, indeed! She was very glad to welcome a stranger. She had been bored by the old husband. To his latent, cruel smile she replied with brilliant challenge. He expected her to keep the moral fortress. Not she! It was much too dull a part. She challenged him back with a sort of radiance, very bright and free, opposite to him. He looked at her, and his eyes glinted. She too was out in the field.

His senses pricked up and keenly attended to her. She laughed, perfectly indifferent and loose as he was. He came towards her. She neither rejected him nor responded to him. In a kind of radiance, superb in her inscrutability, she laughed before him. She too could throw everything overboard, love, intimacy, responsibility. What were her four children to her now? What did it matter that this man was the father of her four children?

He was the sensual male seeking his pleasure, she was the female ready to take hers: but in her own way. A man could turn into a free lance: so then could a woman. She adhered as little as he to the moral world. All that had gone before was nothing to her. She was another woman, under the instance of a strange man. He was a stranger to her, seeking his own ends. Very good. She wanted to see what this stranger would do now, what he was.

She laughed, and kept him at arm's length, whilst apparently ignoring him. She watched him undress as if he were a stranger. Indeed he was a stranger to her.

And she roused him profoundly, violently, even before he touched her. The little creature in Nottingham had but been leading up to this. They abandoned in one motion the moral position, each was seeking gratification pure and simple.

Strange his wife was to him. It was as if he were a perfect stranger, as if she were infinitely and essentially strange to him, the other half of the world, the dark half of the moon. She waited for his touch as if he were a marauder who had come in, infinitely unknown and desirable to her. And he began to discover her. He had an inkling of the vastness of the unknown sensual store of delights she was. With a passion of voluptuousness that made him dwell on each tiny beauty, in a kind of frenzy of enjoyment, he lit upon her: her beauty, the beauties, the separate, several beauties of her body.

He was quite ousted from himself, and sensually transported by that which he discovered in her. He was another man revelling over her. There was no tenderness, no love between them any more, only the maddening, sensuous lust for discovery and the insatiable, exorbitant gratification in the sensual beauties of her body. And she was a store, a store of absolute beauties that it drove him to contemplate. There was such a feast to enjoy, and he was only one man's capacity.

He lived in a passion of sensual discovery with her for some time – it was a duel: no love, no words, no kisses even, only the maddening perception of beauty consummate, absolute through touch. He wanted to touch her, to discover her, maddeningly he wanted to know her. Yet he must not hurry, or he missed everything. He must enjoy one beauty at a time. And the multitudinous beauties of her body, the many little rapturous places, sent him mad with delight, and with desire to be able to know more, to have strength to know more. For all was there.

He would say during the daytime:

'To-night I shall know the little hollow under her ankle, where the blue vein crosses.' And the thought of it, and the desire for it, made a thick darkness of anticipation.

He would go all the day waiting for the night to come, when he could give himself to the enjoyment of some luxurious absolute of beauty in her. The thought of the hidden resources of her, the undiscovered beauties and ecstatic places of delight in her body, waiting, only waiting for him to discover them, sent him slightly insane. He was obsessed. If he did not discover and make known to himself these delights, they might be lost for ever. He wished he had a hundred men's energies, with which to enjoy her. He wished he were a cat, to lick her with a rough, grating, lascivious tongue. He wanted to wallow in her, bury himself in her flesh, cover himself over with her flesh.

And she, separate, with a strange, dangerous, glistening look in her eyes received all his activities upon her as if they were expected by her, and provoked him when he was quiet to more, till sometimes he was ready to perish for sheer inability to be satisfied of her, inability to have had enough of her.

Their children became mere offspring to them, they lived in the darkness and death of their own sensual activities. Sometimes he felt he was going mad with a sense of Absolute Beauty, perceived by him in her through his senses. It was something too much for him. And in everything, was this same, almost sinister, terrifying beauty. But in the revelations of her body through contact with his body, was the ultimate beauty, to know which was almost death in itself, and yet for the knowledge of which he would have undergone endless torture. He would have forfeited anything, anything, rather than forego his right even to the instep of her foot, and the place from which the toes radiated out, the little, miraculous white plain from which ran the little hillocks of the toes, and the folded, dimpling hollows between the toes. He felt he would have died rather than forfeit this.

This was what their love had become, a sensuality violent and extreme as death. They had no conscious intimacy, no tenderness of love. It was all the lust and the infinite, maddening intoxication of the sense, a passion of death.

He had always, all his life, had a secret dread of Absolute Beauty. It had always been like a fetish to him, something to fear, really. For it was immoral and against mankind. So he had turned to the Gothic form, which always asserted the broken desire of mankind in its pointed arches, escaping the rolling, absolute beauty of the round arch.

But now he had given way, and with infinite sensual violence gave himself to the realisation of this supreme, immoral, Absolute Beauty, in the body of woman. It seemed to him, that it came to being in the body of woman, under his touch. Under his touch, even under his sight, it was there. But when he neither saw nor touched the perfect place, it was not perfect, it was not there. And he must make it exist.

But still the thing terrified him. Awful and threatening it was, dangerous to a degree, even whilst he gave himself to it. It was pure darkness, also. All the shameful things of the body revealed themselves to him now with a sort of sinister, tropical beauty. All the shameful, natural and unnatural acts of sensual voluptuousness which he and the woman partook of together, created together, they had their heavy beauty and their delight. Shame, what was it? It was part of extreme delight. It was that part of delight of which man is usually afraid. Why afraid? The secret, shameful things are most terribly beautiful.

They accepted shame, and were one with it in their most unlicensed pleasures. It was incorporated. It was a bud that blossomed into beauty and heavy, fundamental gratification.

Their outward life went on much the same, but the inward life was revolutionised. The children became less important, the parents were absorbed in their own living.

And gradually, Brangwen began to find himself free to attend to the outside life as well. His intimate life was so violently active, that it set another man in him free. And this new man turned with interest to public life, to see what part he could take in it. This would give him scope for new activity, activity of a kind for which he was now created and released. He wanted to be unanimous with the whole of purposive mankind.

At this time Education was in the forefront as a subject of interest. There was the talk of new Swedish methods, of handwork instruction, and so on. Brangwen embraced sincerely the idea of handwork in schools. For the first time, he began to take real interest in a public affair. He had at length, from his profound sensual activity, developed a real purposive self.

There was talk of night-schools, and of handicraft classes. He wanted to start a woodwork class in Cossethay, to teach carpentry and joinery and wood-carving to the village boys, two nights a week. This seemed to him a supremely desirable thing to be doing. His pay would be very little – and when he had it, he spent it all on extra wood and tools. But he was very happy and keen in his new public spirit.

He started his night-classes in woodwork when he was thirty years old. By this time he had five children, the last a boy. But boy or girl mattered very little to him. He had a natural blood-affection for his children, and he liked them as they turned up: boys or girls. Only he was fondest of Ursula. Somehow, she seemed to be at the back of his new night-school venture.

The house by the yew trees was in connection with the great human endeavour at last. It gained a new vigour thereby.

To Ursula, a child of eight, the increase in magic was considerable. She heard all the talk, she saw the parish room fitted up as a workshop. The parish room was a high, stone, barn-like, ecclesiastical building standing away by itself in the Brangwens' second garden, across the lane. She was always attracted by its age and its stranded obsoleteness. Now she watched preparations made, she sat on the flight of stone steps that came down from the porch to the garden, and heard her father and the vicar talking and planning and working. Then an inspector came, a very strange man, and stayed talking with her father all one evening. Everything was settled, and twelve boys enrolled their names. It was very exciting.

But to Ursula, everything her father did was magic. Whether he came from Ilkeston with news of the town, whether he went across to the church with his music or his tools on a sunny evening, whether he sat in his white surplice at the organ on Sundays, leading the singing with his strong tenor voice, or whether he were in the workshop with the boys, he was always a centre of magic and fascination to her, his voice, sounding out in command, cheerful, laconic, had always a twang in it that sent a thrill over her blood, and hypnotised her. She seemed to run in the shadow of some dark, potent secret of which she would not, of whose existence even she dared not become conscious, it cast such a spell over her, and so darkened her mind.

Chapter Nine

The Marsh and the Flood

There was always regular connection between the Yew Cottage and the Marsh, yet the two households remained separate, distinct.

After Anna's marriage, the Marsh became the home of the two boys, Tom and Fred. Tom was a rather short, good-looking youth, with crisp black hair and long black eyelashes and soft, dark, possessed eyes. He had a quick intelligence. From the High School he went to London to study. He had an instinct for attracting people of character and energy. He gave place entirely to the other person, and at the same time kept himself independent. He scarcely existed except through other people. When he was alone he was unresolved. When he was with another man, he seemed to add himself to the other, make the other bigger than life size. So that a few people loved him and attained a sort of fulfilment in him. He carefully chose these few.

He had a subtle, quick, critical intelligence, a mind that was like a scale or balance. There was something of a woman in all this.

In London he had been the favourite pupil of an engineer, a clever man, who became well-known at the time when Tom Brangwen had just finished his studies. Through this master the youth kept acquaintance with various individual, outstanding characters. He never asserted himself. He seemed to be there to estimate and establish the rest. He was like a presence that makes us aware of our own being. So that he was while still young connected with some of the most energetic scientific and mathematical people in London. They took him as an equal. Quiet and perceptive and impersonal as he was, he kept his place and learned how to value others in just degree. He was there like a judgment. Besides, he was very good-looking, of medium stature, but beautifully proportioned, dark, with fine colouring, always perfectly healthy.

His father allowed him a liberal pocket-money, besides which he had a sort of post as assistant to his chief. Then from time to time the young man appeared at the Marsh, curiously attractive, well-dressed, reserved, having by nature a subtle, refined manner. And he set the change in the farm.

Fred, the younger brother, was a Brangwen, large-boned, blue-eyed, English. He was his father's very son, the two men, father and son, were supremely at ease with one another. Fred was succeeding to the farm.

Between the elder brother and the younger existed an almost passionate love. Tom watched over Fred with a woman's poignant attention and self-less care. Fred looked up to Tom as to something miraculous, that which he himself would aspire to be, were he great also.

So that after Anna's departure, the Marsh began to take on a new tone. The boys were gentlemen; Tom had a rare nature and had risen high. Fred was sensitive and fond of reading, he pondered Ruskin and then the Agnostic writings. Like all the Brangwens, he was very much a thing to himself, though fond of people, and indulgent to them, having an exaggerated respect for them.

There was a rather uneasy friendship between him and one of the young Hardys at the Hall. The two households were different, yet the young men met on shy terms of equality.

It was young Tom Brangwen, with his dark lashes and beautiful colouring, his soft, inscrutable nature, his strange repose and his informed air, added to his position in London, who seemed to emphasise the superior foreign element in the Marsh. When he appeared, perfectly dressed, as if soft and affable, and yet quite removed from everybody, he created an uneasiness in people, he was reserved in the minds of the Cossethay and Ilkeston acquaintances to a different, remote world.

He and his mother had a kind of affinity. The affection between them was of a mute, distant character, but radical. His father was always uneasy and slightly deferential to his eldest son. Tom also formed the link that kept the Marsh in real connection with the Skrebenskys, now quite important people in their own district.

So a change in tone came over the Marsh. Tom Brangwen the father, as he grew older, seemed to mature into a gentleman-farmer. His figure lent itself: burly and handsome. His face remained fresh and his blue eyes as full of light, his thick hair and beard had turned gradually to a silky whiteness. It was his custom to laugh a great deal, in his acquiescent, wilful manner. Things had puzzled him very much, so he had taken the line of easy, good-humoured acceptance. He was not responsible for the frame of things. Yet he was afraid of the unknown in life.

He was fairly well-off. His wife was there with him, a different being from himself, yet somewhere vitally connected with him:—who was he to understand where and how? His two sons were gentlemen. They were men distinct from himself, they had separate beings of their own, yet they were connected with himself. It was all adventurous and puzzling. Yet one remained vital within one's own existence, whatever the off-shoots.

So, handsome and puzzled, he laughed and stuck to himself as the only thing he could stick to. His youngness and the wonder remained almost the same in him. He became indolent, he developed a luxuriant ease. Fred did most of the farm-work, the father saw to the more important transactions.

He drove a good mare, and sometimes he rode his cob. He drank in the hotels and the inns with better-class farmers and proprietors, he had well-to-do acquaintances among men. But one class suited him no better than another.

His wife, as ever, had no acquaintances. Her hair was threaded now with grey, her face grew older in form without changing in expression. She seemed the same as when she had come to the Marsh twenty-five years ago, save that her health was more fragile. She seemed always to haunt the Marsh rather than to live there. She was never part of the life. Something she represented was alien there, she remained a stranger within the gates, in some ways fixed and impervious, in some ways curiously refining. She caused the separateness and individuality of all the Marsh inmates, the friability of the household.

When young Tom Brangwen was twenty-three years old there was some breach between him and his chief which was never explained, and he went away to Italy, then to America. He came home for a while, then went to Germany; always the same good-looking, carefully-dressed, attractive young man, in perfect health, yet somehow outside of everything. In his dark eyes was a deep misery which he wore with the same ease and pleasantness as he wore his close-sitting clothes.

To Ursula he was a romantic, alluring figure. He had a grace of bringing beautiful presents: a box of expensive sweets, such as Cossethay had never seen; or he gave her a hair-brush and a long slim mirror of mother-of-pearl, all pale and glimmering and exquisite; or he sent her a little necklace of rough stones, amethyst and opal and brilliants and garnet. He spoke other languages easily and fluently, his nature was curiously gracious and insinuating. With all that, he was undefinably an outsider. He belonged to nowhere, to no society.

Anna Brangwen had left her intimacy with her father undeveloped since the time of her marriage. At her marriage it had been abandoned. He and she had drawn a reserve between them. Anna went more to her mother.

Then suddenly the father died.

It happened one springtime when Ursula was about eight years old, he, Tom Brangwen, drove off on a Saturday morning to the market in Nottingham, saying he might not be back till late, as there was a special show and then a meeting he had to attend. His family understood that he would enjoy himself.

The season had been rainy and dreary. In the evening it was pouring with rain. Fred Brangwen, unsettled, uneasy, did not go out, as was his wont. He smoked and read and fidgeted, hearing always the trickling of water outside. This wet, black night seemed to cut him off and make him unsettled, aware of himself, aware that he wanted something else, aware that he was scarcely living. There seemed to him to be no root to his life, no place for him to get satisfied in. He dreamed of going abroad. But his instinct knew that change of place would not solve his problem. He wanted change, deep, vital change of living. And he did not know how to get it.

Tilly, an old woman now, came in saying that the labourers who had been suppering up said the yard and everywhere was just a slew of water.

He heard in indifference. But he hated a desolate, raw wetness in the world. He would leave the Marsh.

His mother was in bed. At last he shut his book, his mind was blank, he walked upstairs intoxicated with depression and anger, and, intoxicated with depression and anger, locked himself into sleep.

Tilly set slippers before the kitchen fire, and she also went to bed, leaving the door unlocked. Then the farm was in darkness, in the rain.

At eleven o'clock it was still raining. Tom Brangwen stood in the yard of the 'Angel', Nottingham, and buttoned his coat.

'Oh, well,' he said cheerfully, 'it's rained on me before. Put 'er in, Jack, my lad, put her in – Tha'rt a rare old cock, Jacky-boy, wi' a belly on thee as does credit to thy drink, if not to thy corn. Co' up lass, let's get off ter th' old homestead. Oh, my heart, what a wetness in the night! There'll be no volcanoes after this. Hey, Jack, my beautiful young slender feller, which of us is Noah? It seems as though the water-works is bursted. Ducks and ayquatic fowl 'll be king o' the castle at this rate – dove an' olive branch an' all. Stand up then, gel, stand up, we're not stoppin' here all night, even if you thought we was. I'm dashed if the jumping rain wouldn't make anybody think they was drunk. Hey, Jack – does rain-water wash the sense in, or does it wash it out?' And he laughed to himself at the joke.

He was always ashamed when he had to drive after he had been drinking, always apologetic to the horse. His apologetic frame made him facetious. He was aware of his inability to walk quite straight. Nevertheless his will kept stiff and attentive, in all his fuddleness.

He mounted and bowled off through the gates of the inn-yard. The mare went well, he sat fixed, the rain beating on his face. His heavy body rode motionless in a kind of sleep, one centre of attention was kept fitfully burning, the rest was dark. He concentrated his last attention on the fact of driving along the road he knew so well. He knew it so well, he watched for it attentively, with an effort of will.

He talked aloud to himself, sententious in his anxiety, as if he were perfectly sober, whilst the mare bowled along and the rain beat on him. He watched the rain before the gig-lamps, the faint gleaming of the shadowy horse's body, the passing of the dark hedges.

'It's not a fit night to turn a dog out,' he said to himself, aloud. 'It's high time as it did a bit of clearing up, I'll be damned if it isn't. It was a lot of use putting those ten loads of cinders on th' road. They'll be washed to kingdom-come if it doesn't alter. Well, it's our Fred's look-out, if they are. He's top-sawyer as far as those things go. I don't see why I should concern myself. They can wash to kingdom-come and back again for what I care. I suppose they would be washed back again some day. That's how things are. Th' rain tumbles down just to mount up in clouds again. So they say. There's no more water on the earth than there was in the year naught. That's the story, my boy, if you understand it. There's no more to-day than there was a thousand years ago – nor no less either. You can't wear water out. No, my boy: it'll give you the go-by. Try to wear it out, and it takes its hook into vapour, it has its fingers at its nose to you. It turns into cloud and falleth as rain on the just and unjust. I wonder if I'm the just or the unjust.'

He started awake as the trap lurched deep into a rut. And he wakened to the point in his journey. He had travelled some distance since he was last conscious.

But at length he reached the gate, and stumbled heavily down, reeling, gripping fast to the trap. He descended into several inches of water.

'Be damned!' he said angrily. 'Be damned to the miserable slop.'

And he led the horse washing through the gate. He was quite drunk now, moving blindly, in habit. Everywhere there was water underfoot.

The raised causeway of the house and the farm-stead was dry, however. But there was a curious roar in the night which seemed to be made in the darkness of his own intoxication. Reeling, blinded, almost without consciousness he carried his parcels and the rug and cushions into the house, dropped them, and went out to put up the horse.

Now he was at home, he was a sleep-walker, waiting only for the moment of activity to stop. Very deliberately and carefully, he led the horse down the slope to the cart-shed. She shied and backed.

'Why, wha's amiss?' he hiccupped, plodding steadily on. And he was again in a wash of water, the horse splashed up water as he went. It was thickly dark, save for the gig-lamps, and they lit on a rippling surface of water.

'Well, that's a knock-out,' he said, as he came to the cart-shed, and was wading in six inches of water. But everything seemed to him amusing. He laughed to think of six inches of water being in the cart-shed.

He backed in the mare. She was restive. He laughed at the fun of untackling the mare with a lot of water washing round his feet. He laughed because it upset her. 'What's amiss, what's amiss, a drop o' water won't you!' As soon as he had undone the traces, she walked quickly away.

He hung up the shafts and took the gig-lamp. As he came out of the familiar jumble of shafts and wheels in the shed, the water, in little waves, came washing strongly against his legs. He staggered and almost fell.

'Well, what the deuce!' he said, staring round at the running water in the black, watery night.

He went to meet the running flood, sinking deeper and deeper. His soul was full of great astonishment. He *had* to go and look where it came from, though the ground was going from under his feet. He went on, down towards the pond, shakily, He rather enjoyed it. He was knee-deep, and the water was pulling heavily. He stumbled, reeled sickeningly.

Fear took hold of him. Gripping tightly to the lamp, he reeled, and looked round. The water was carrying his feet away, he was dizzy. He did not know which way to turn. The water was whirling, whirling, the whole black night was swooping in rings. He swayed uncertainly at the centre of all the attack, reeling in dismay. In his soul, he knew he would fall.

As he staggered something in the water struck his legs, and he fell. Instantly he was in the turmoil of suffocation. He fought in a black horror of suffocation, fighting, wrestling, but always borne down, borne inevitably down. Still he wrestled and fought to get himself free, in the unutterable struggle of suffocation, but he always fell again deeper. Something struck his head, a great wonder of anguish went over him, then the blackness covered him entirely.

In the utter darkness, the unconscious, drowning body was rolled along, the waters pouring, washing, filling in the place. The cattle woke up and rose to their feet, the dog began to yelp. And the unconscious, drowning body was washed along in the black, swirling darkness, passively.

Mrs. Brangwen woke up and listened. With preternaturally sharp senses she heard the movement of all the darkness that swirled outside. For a moment she lay still. Then she went to the window. She heard the sharp rain, and the deep running of water. She knew her husband was outside.

'Fred,' she called, 'Fred!'

Away in the night was a hoarse, brutal roar of a mass of water rushing downwards.

She went downstairs. She could not understand the multiplied running of water. Stepping down the step into the kitchen, she put her foot into water. The kitchen was flooded. Where did it come from? She could not understand.

Water was running in out of the scullery. She paddled through barefoot, to see. Water was bubbling fiercely under the outer door. She was afraid. Then something washed against her, something twined under her foot. It was the riding whip. On the table were the rug and the cushion and the parcel from the gig.

He had come home.

'Tom!' she called, afraid of her own voice.

She opened the door. Water ran in with a horrid sound. Everywhere was moving water, a sound of waters.

'Tom!' she cried, standing in her nightdress with the candle, calling into the darkness and the flood out of the doorway.

'Tom! Tom!'

And she listened. Fred appeared behind her, in trousers and shirt.

'Where is he?' he asked.

He looked at the flood, then at his mother. She seemed small and uncanny, elvish, in her nightdress.

'Go upstairs,' he said. 'He'll be in th' stable.'

'To-om! To-om!' cried the elderly woman, with a long, unnatural, penetrating call that chilled her son to the marrow. He quickly pulled on his boots and his coat.

'Go upstairs, mother,' he said; 'I'll go an' see where he is.'

'To-om! To-o-om!' rang out the shrill, unearthly cry of the small woman. There was only the noise of water and the mooing of uneasy cattle, and the long yelping of the dog, clamouring in the darkness.

Fred Brangwen splashed out into the flood with a lantern. His mother stood on a chair in the doorway, watching him go. It was all water, water, running, flashing under the lantern.

'Tom! Tom! To-o-om!' came her long, unnatural cry, ringing over the night. It made her son feel cold in his soul.

And the unconscious, drowning body of the father rolled on below the house, driven by the black water towards the high-road.

Tilly appeared, a skirt over her nightdress. She saw her mistress clinging on the top of a chair in the open doorway, a candle burning on the table.

'God's sake!' cried the old serving-woman. 'The cut's burst. That embankment's broke down. Whativer are we goin' to do!'

Mrs. Brangwen watched her son, and the lantern, go along the upper causeway to the stable. Then she saw the dark figure of a horse: then her son hung the lamp in the stable, and the light shone out faintly on him as he untackled the mare. The mother saw the soft blazed face of the horse thrust forward into the stable-door. The stables were still above the flood. But the water flowed strongly into the house.

'It's getting higher,' said Tilly. 'Hasn't master come in?'

Mrs. Brangwen did not hear.

'Isn't he the-ere?' she called, in her far-reaching, terrifying voice.

'No,' came the short answer out of the night.

'Go and loo-ok for him.'

His mother's voice nearly drove the youth mad.

He put the halter on the horse and shut the stable door. He came splashing back through the water, the lantern swinging.

The unconscious, drowning body was pushed past the house in the deepest current. Fred Brangwen came to his mother.

'I'll go to th' cart-shed,' he said.

'To-om, To-o-om!' rang out the strong, inhuman cry. Fred Brangwen's blood froze, his heart was very angry. He gripped his veins in a frenzy. Why was she yelling like this? He could not bear the sight of her, perched on a chair in her white nightdress in the doorway, elvish and horrible.

'He's taken the mare out of the trap, so he's all right,' he said, growling, pretending to be normal.

But as he descended to the cart-shed, he sank into a foot of water. He heard the rushing in the distance, he knew the canal had broken down. The water was running deeper.

The trap was there all right, but no signs of his father. The young man waded down to the pond. The water rose above his knees, it swirled and forced him. He drew back.

'Is he the-e-ere?' came the maddening cry of the mother.

'No,' was the sharp answer.

'To-om—To-o-om!' came the piercing, free, unearthly call. It seemed high and supernatural, almost pure. Fred Brangwen hated it. It nearly drove him mad. So awfully it sang out, almost like a song.

The water was flowing fuller into the house.

'You'd better go up to Beeby's and bring him and Arthur down, and tell Mrs. Beeby to fetch Wilkinson,' said Fred to Tilly. He forced his mother to go upstairs.

'I know your father is drowned,' she said, in a curious dismay.

The flood rose through the night till it washed the kettle off the hob in the kitchen. Mrs. Brangwen sat alone at a window upstairs. She called no more. The men were busy with the pigs and the cattle. They were coming with a boat for her.

Towards morning the rain ceased, the stars came out over the noise and the terrifying clucking and trickling of the water. Then there was a pallor in the east, the light began to come. In the ruddy light of the dawn she saw the waters spreading out, moving sluggishly, the buildings rising out of a waste of water. Birds began to sing, drowsily, and as if slightly hoarse with the dawn. It grew brighter. Up the second field was the great, raw gap in the canal embankment.

Mrs. Brangwen went from window to window, watching the flood. Somebody had brought a little boat. The light grew stronger, the red gleam was gone off the flood-waters, day took place. Mrs. Brangwen went from the front of the house to the back, looking out, intent and unrelaxing, on the pallid morning of spring.

She saw a glimpse of her husband's buff coat in the floods, as the water rolled the body against the garden hedge. She called to the men in the boat. She was glad he was found. They dragged him out of the hedge. They could not lift him into the boat. Fred Brangwen jumped into the water, up to his waist, and half carried the body of his father through the flood to the road. Hay and twigs and dirt were in the beard and hair. The youth pushed through the water crying loudly without tears, like a stricken animal. The mother at the window cried, making no trouble.

The doctor came. But the body was dead. They carried it up to Cossethay, to Anna's house.

When Anna Brangwen heard the news, she pressed back her head and rolled her eyes, as if something were reaching forward to bite at her throat. She pressed back her head, her mind was driven back to sleep. Since she had married and become a mother, the girl she had been was forgotten. Now, the shock threatened to break in upon her and sweep away all her intervening life, make her as a girl of eighteen again, loving her father. So she pressed back, away from the shock, she clung to her present life.

It was when they brought him to her house dead and in his wet clothes, his wet, sodden clothes, fully dressed as he came from market, yet all sodden and inert, that the shock really broke into her, and she was terrified. A big, soaked, inert heap, he was, who had been to her the image of power and strong life.

Almost in horror, she began to take the wet things from him, to pull off him the incongruous market-clothes of a well-to-do farmer. The children were sent away to the Vicarage, the dead body lay on the parlour floor, Anna quickly began to undress him, laid his fob and seals in a wet heap on the table. Her husband and the woman helped her. They cleared and washed the body, and laid it on the bed.

There, it looked still and grand. He was perfectly calm in death, and, now he was laid in line, inviolable, unapproachable. To Anna, he was the majesty of the inaccessible male, the majesty of death. It made her still and awe-stricken, almost glad.

Lydia Brangwen, the mother, also came and saw the impressive, inviolable body of the dead man. She went pale, seeing death. He was beyond change or knowledge, absolute, laid in line with the infinite. What had she to do with him? He was a majestic Abstraction, made visible now for a moment, inviolate, absolute. And who could lay claim to him, who could speak of him, of the him who was revealed in the stripped moment of transit from life into death? Neither the living nor the dead could claim him, he was both the one and the other, inviolable, inaccessibly himself.

'I shared life with you, I belong in my own way to eternity,' said Lydia Brangwen, her heart cold, knowing her own singleness.

'I did not know you in life. You are beyond me, supreme now in death,' said Anna Brangwen, awe-stricken, almost glad.

It was the sons who could not bear it. Fred Brangwen went about with a set, blanched face and shut hands, his heart full of hatred and rage for what had been done to his father, bleeding also with desire to have his father again, to see him, to hear him again. He could not bear it.

Tom Brangwen only arrived on the day of the funeral. He was quiet and controlled as ever. He kissed his mother, who was still dark-faced, inscrutable, he shook hands with his brother without looking at him, he saw the great coffin with its black handles. He even read the name-plate, 'Tom Brangwen, of the Marsh Farm. Born—. Died—.'

The good-looking, still face of the young man crinkled up for a moment in a terrible grimace, then resumed its stillness. The coffin was carried round to the church, the funeral bell tanged at intervals, the mourners carried their wreaths of white flowers. The mother, the Polish woman, went with dark, abstract face, on her son's arm. He was good-looking as ever, his face perfectly motionless and somehow pleasant. Fred walked with Anna, she strange and winsome, he with a face like wood, stiff, unyielding.

Only afterwards Ursula, flitting between the currant bushes down the garden, saw her Uncle Tom standing in his black clothes, erect and fashionable, but his fists lifted, and his face distorted, his lips curled back from his teeth in a horrible grin, like an animal which grimaces with torment, whilst his body panted quick, like a panting dog's. He was facing the open distance, panting, and holding still, then panting rapidly again, but his face never changing from its almost bestial look of torture, the teeth all showing, the nose wrinkled up, the eyes, unseeing, fixed.

Terrified, Ursula slipped away. And when her Uncle Tom was in the house again, grave and very quiet, so that he seemed almost to affect gravity, to pretend grief, she watched his still, handsome face, imagining it again in its distortion. But she saw the nose was rather thick, rather Russian, under its transparent skin, she remembered the teeth under the carefully cut moustache were small and sharp and spaced. She could see him, in all his elegant demeanour, bestial, almost corrupt. And she was frightened. She never forgot to look for the bestial, frightening side of him, after this.

He said 'Good-bye' to his mother and went away at once. Ursula almost shrank from his kiss now. She wanted it, nevertheless, and the little revulsion as well.

At the funeral, and after the funeral, Will Brangwen was madly in love with his wife. The death had shaken him. But death and all seemed to gather in him into a mad, overwhelming passion for his wife. She seemed so strange and winsome. He was almost beside himself with desire for her.

And she took him, she seemed ready for him, she wanted him.

The grandmother stayed a while at the Yew Cottage, till the Marsh was restored. Then she returned to her own rooms, quiet, and it seemed, wanting nothing. Fred threw himself into the work of restoring the farm. That his father was killed there, seemed to make it only the more intimate and the more inevitably his own place.

There was a saying that the Brangwens always died a violent death. To them all, except perhaps Tom, it seemed almost natural. Yet Fred went about obstinate, his heart fixed. He could never forgive the Unknown this murder of his father.

After the death of the father, the Marsh was very quiet. Mrs. Brangwen was unsettled. She could not sit all the evening peacefully, as she could before, and during the day she was always rising to her feet and hesitating, as if she must go somewhere, and were not quite sure whither.

She was seen loitering about the garden, in her little woollen jacket. She was often driven out in the gig, sitting beside her son and watching the countryside or the streets of the town, with a childish, candid, uncanny face, as if it all were strange to her.

The children, Ursula and Gudrun and Theresa went by the garden gate on their way to school. The grandmother would have them call in each time they passed, she would have them come to the Marsh for dinner. She wanted children about her.

Of her sons, she was almost afraid. She could see the sombre passion and desire and dissatisfaction in them, and she wanted not to see it any more. Even Fred, with his blue eyes and his heavy jaw, troubled her. There was no peace. He wanted something, he wanted love, passion, and he could not find them. But why must he trouble her? Why must he come to her with his seething and suffering and dissatisfactions? She was too old.

Tom was more restrained, reserved. He kept his body very still. But he troubled her even more. She could not but see the black depths of disintegration in his eyes, the sudden glance upon her, as if she could save him, as if he would reveal himself.

And how could age save youth? Youth must go to youth. Always the storm! Could she not lie in peace, these years, in the quiet, apart from life? No, always the swell must heave upon her and break against the barriers. Always she must be embroiled in the seethe and rage and passion, endless, endless, going on for ever. And she wanted to draw away. She wanted at last her own innocence and peace. She did not want her sons to force upon her any more the old brutal story of desire and offerings and deep, deep-hidden rage of unsatisfied men against women. She wanted to be beyond it all, to know the peace and innocence of age.

She had never been a woman to work much. So that now she would stand often at the garden-gate, watching the scant world go by. And the sight of children pleased her, made her happy. She had usually an apple or a few sweets in her pocket. She liked children to smile at her.

She never went to her husband's grave. She spoke of him simply, as if he were alive. Sometimes the tears would run down her face, in helpless sadness. Then she recovered, and was herself again, happy.

On wet days, she stayed in bed. Her bedroom was her city of refuge, where she could lie down and muse and muse. Sometimes Fred would read to her. But that did not mean much. She had so many dreams to dream over, such an unsifted store. She wanted time.

Her chief friend at this period was Ursula. The little girl and the musing, fragile woman of sixty seemed to understand the same language. At Cossethay all was activity and passion, everything moved upon poles of passion. Then there were four children younger than Ursula, a throng of babies, all the time many lives beating against each other.

So that for the eldest child, the peace of the grandmother's bedroom was exquisite. Here Ursula came as to a hushed, paradisal land, here her own existence became simple and exquisite to her as if she were a flower.

Always on Saturdays she came down to the Marsh, and always clutching a little offering, either a little mat made of strips of coloured, woven paper, or a tiny basket made in the kindergarten lesson, or a little crayon drawing of a bird.

When she appeared in the doorway, Tilly, ancient but still in authority, would crane her skinny neck to see who it was.

'Oh, it's you, is it?' she said. 'I thought we should be seein' you. My word, that's a bobby-dazzlin' posy you've brought!'

It was curious how Tilly preserved the spirit of Tom Brangwen, who was dead, in the Marsh. Ursula always connected her with her grandfather.

This day the child had brought a tight little nosegay of pinks, white ones, with a rim of pink ones. She was very proud of it, and very shy because of her pride.

'Your gran'mother's in her bed. Wipe your shoes well if you're goin' up, and don't go burstin' in on her like a skyrocket. My word, but that's a fine posy! Did you do it all by yourself, an' all?'

Tilly stealthily ushered her into the bedroom. The child entered with a strange, dragging hesitation characteristic of her when she was moved. Her grandmother was sitting up in bed, wearing a little grey woollen jacket.

The child hesitated in silence near the bed, clutching the nosegay in front of her. Her childish eyes were shining. The grandmother's grey eyes shone with a similar light.

'How pretty!' she said. 'How pretty you have made them! What a darling little bunch.'

Ursula, glowing, thrust them into her grandmother's hand, saying, 'I made them you.'

'That is how the peasants tied them at home,' said the grandmother, pushing the pinks with her fingers, and smelling them. 'Just such tight little bunches! And they make wreaths for their hair – they weave the stalks. Then they go round with wreaths in their hair, and wearing their best aprons.'

Ursula immediately imagined herself in this story-land.

'Did you used to have a wreath in your hair, grandmother?'

'When I was a little girl, I had golden hair, something like Katie's. Then I used to have a wreath of little blue flowers, oh, so blue, that come when the snow is gone. Andrey, the coachman, used to bring me the very first.'

They talked, and then Tilly brought the tea-tray, set for two. Ursula had a special green and gold cup kept for herself at the Marsh. There was thin bread and butter, and cress for tea. It was all special and wonderful. She ate very daintily, with little fastidious bites.

'Why do you have two wedding-rings, grandmother? – Must you?' asked the child, noticing her grandmother's ivory coloured hand with blue veins, above the tray.

'If I had two husbands, child.'

Ursula pondered a moment.

'Then you must wear both rings together?'

'Yes.'

'Which was my grandfather's ring?'

The woman hesitated.

'This grandfather whom you knew? This was his ring, the red one. The yellow one was your other grandfather's whom you never knew.'

Ursula looked interestedly at the two rings on the proffered finger.

'Where did he buy it you?' she asked.

'This one? In Warsaw, I think.'

'You didn't know my own grandfather then?'

'Not this grandfather.'

Ursula pondered this fascinating intelligence.

'Did he have white whiskers as well?'

'No, his beard was dark. You have his brows, I think.'

Ursula ceased and became self-conscious. She at once identified herself with her Polish grandfather.

'And did he have brown eyes?'

'Yes, dark eyes. He was a clever man, as quick as a lion. He was never still.'

Lydia still resented Lensky. When she thought of him, she was always younger than he, she was always twenty, or twenty-five, and under his domination. He incorporated her in his ideas as if she were not a person herself, as if she were just his aide-de-camp, or part of his baggage, or one among his surgical appliances. She still resented it. And he was always only thirty: he had died when he was thirty-four. She did not feel sorry for him. He was older than she. Yet she still ached in the thought of those days.

'Did you like my first grandfather best?' asked Ursula.

'I liked them both,' said the grandmother.

And, thinking, she became again Lensky's girl-bride. He was of good family, of better family even than her own, for she was half German. She was a young girl in a house of insecure fortune. And he, an intellectual, a clever surgeon and physician, had loved her. How she had looked up to him! She remembered her first transports when he talked to her, the important young man with the severe black beard. He had seemed so wonderful, such an authority. After her own lax household, his gravity and confident, hard authority seemed almost God-like to her. For she had never known it in her life, all her surroundings had been loose, lax, disordered, a welter.

'Mis Lydia, will you marry me?' he had said to her in German, in his grave, yet tremulous voice. She had been afraid of his dark eyes upon her. They did not see her, they were fixed upon her. And he was hard, confident. She thrilled with the excitement of it, and accepted. During the courtship, his kisses were a wonder to her. She always thought about them, and wondered over them. She never wanted to kiss him back. In her idea, the man kissed, and the woman examined in her soul the kisses she had received.

She had never quite recovered from her prostration of the first days, or nights, of marriage. He had taken her to Vienna, and she was utterly alone with him, utterly alone in another world, everything, everything foreign, even he foreign to her. Then came the real marriage, passion came to her, and she became his slave, he was her lord, her lord. She was the girl-bride, the slave, she kissed his feet, she had thought it an honour to touch his body, to unfasten his boots. For two years, she had gone on as his slave, crouching at his feet, embracing his knees.

Children had come, he had followed his ideas. She was there for him, just to keep him in condition. She was to him one of the baser or material conditions necessary for his welfare in prosecuting his ideas, of nationalism, of liberty, of science.

But gradually, at twenty-three, twenty-four, she began to realise that she too might consider these ideas. By his acceptance of her self-subordination, he exhausted the feeling in her. There were those of his associates who would discuss the ideas with her, though he did not wish to do so himself. She adventured into the minds of other men. His, then, was not the only male mind! She did not exist, then, just as his attribute! She began to perceive the attention of other men. An excitement came over her. She remembered now the men who had paid her court, when she was married, in Warsaw.

Then the rebellion broke out, and she was inspired too. She would go as a nurse at her husband's side. He worked like a lion, he wore his life out. And she followed him helplessly. But she disbelieved in him. He was so separate, he ignored so much. He counted too much on himself. His work, his ideas, – did nothing else matter?

Then the children were dead, and for her, everything became remote. He became remote. She saw him, she saw him go white when he heard the news, then frown, as if he thought, '*Why* have they died now, when I have no time to grieve?'

'He has no time to grieve,' she had said, in her remote, awful soul. 'He has no time. It is so important, what he does! He is then so self-important, this half-frenzied man! Nothing matters, but this work of rebellion! He has not time to grieve, nor to think of his children! He had not time even to beget them, really.'

She had let him go on alone. But, in the chaos, she had worked by his side again. And out of the chaos, she had fled with him to London.

He was a broken, cold man. He had no affection for her, nor for anyone. He had failed in *his* work, so everything had failed. He stiffened, and died.

She could not subscribe. He had failed, everything had failed, yet behind the failure was the unyielding passion of life. The individual effort might fail, but not the human joy. She belonged to the human joy.

He died and went his way, but not before there was another child. And this little Ursula was his grandchild. She was glad of it. For she still honoured him, though he had been mistaken.

She, Lydia Brangwen, was sorry for him now. He was dead – he had scarcely lived. He had never known her. He had lain with her, but he had never known her. He had never received what she could give him. He had gone away from her empty. So, he had never lived. So, he had died and passed away. Yet there had been strength and power in him.

She could scarcely forgive him that he had never lived. If it were not for Anna, and for this little Ursula, who had his brows, there would be no more left of him than of a broken vessel thrown away, and just remembered.

Tom Brangwen had served her. He had come to her, and taken from her. He had died and gone his way into death. But he had made himself immortal in his knowledge with her. So she had her place here, in life, and in immortality. For he had taken his knowledge of her into death, so that she had her place in death. 'In my father's house are many mansions.'

She loved both her husbands. To one she had been a naked little girl-bride, running to serve him. The other she loved out of fulfilment, because he was good and had given her being, because he had served her honourably, and become her man, one with her.

She was established in this stretch of life, she had come to herself. During her first marriage, she had not existed, except through him, he was the substance and she the shadow running at his feet. She was very glad she had come to her own self. She was grateful to Brangwen. She reached out to him in gratitude, into death.

In her heart she felt a vague tenderness and pity for her first husband, who had been her lord. He was so wrong when he died. She could not bear it, that he had never lived, never really become himself. And he had been her lord! Strange, it all had been! Why had he been her lord? He seemed now so far off, so without bearing on her.

'Which did you, grandmother?'

'What?'

'Like best.'

'I liked them both. I married the first when I was quite a girl. Then I loved your grandfather when I was a woman. There is a difference.'

They were silent for a time.

'Did you cry when my first grandfather died?' the child asked.

Lydia Brangwen rocked herself on the bed, thinking aloud.

'When we came to England, he hardly ever spoke, he was too much concerned to take any notice of anybody. He grew thinner and thinner, till his cheeks were hollow and his mouth stuck out. He wasn't handsome any more. I knew he couldn't bear being beaten. I thought everything was lost in the world. Only I had your mother a baby, it was no use my dying.

'He looked at me with his black eyes, almost as if he hated me, when he was ill, and said, "It only wanted this. It only wanted that I should leave you and a young child to starve in this London." I told him we should not starve. But I was young, and foolish, and frightened, which he knew.

'He was bitter, and he never gave way. He lay beating his brains, to see what he could do. "I don't know what you will do," he said. "I am no good, I am a failure from beginning to end. I cannot even provide for my wife and child!"

'But you see, it was not for him to provide for us. My life went on, though his stopped, and I married your grandfather.

'I ought to have known, I ought to have been able to say to him: "Don't be so bitter, don't die because this has failed. You are not the beginning and the end." But I was too young, he had never let me become myself, I thought he was truly the beginning and the end. So I let him take all upon himself. Yet all did not depend on him. Life must go on, and I must marry your grandfather, and have your Uncle Tom, and your Uncle Fred. We cannot take so much upon ourselves.'

The child's heart beat fast as she listened to these things. She could not understand, but she seemed to feel far-off things. It gave her a deep, joyous thrill, to know she hailed from far off, from Poland, and that dark-bearded impressive man. Strange, her antecedents were, and she felt fate on either side of her terrible.

Almost every day, Ursula saw her grandmother, and every time, they talked together. Till the grandmother's sayings and stories, told in the complete hush of the Marsh bedroom, accumulated with mystic significance, and became a sort of Bible to the child.

And Ursula asked her deepest childish questions of her grandmother.

'Will somebody love me, grandmother?'

'Many people love you, child. We all love you.'

'But when I am grown up, will somebody love me?'

'Yes, some man will love you, child, because it's your nature. And I hope it will be somebody who will love you for what you are, and not for what he wants of you. But we have a right to what we want.'

Ursula was frightened, hearing these things. Her heart sank, she felt she had no ground under her feet. She clung to her grandmother. Here was peace and security. Here, from her grandmother's peaceful room, the door opened on to the greater space, the past, which was so big, that all it contained seemed tiny, loves and births and deaths, tiny units and features within a vast horizon. That was a great relief, to know the tiny importance of the individual, within the great past.

Chapter Ten

The Widening Circle

It was very burdensome to Ursula, that she was the eldest of the family. By the time she was eleven, she had to take to school Gudrun and Theresa and Catherine. The boy, William, always called Billy, so that he should not be confused with his father, was a lovable, rather delicate child of three, so he stayed at home as yet. There was another baby girl, called Cassandra.

The children went for a time to the little church school just near the Marsh. It was the only place within reach, and being so small, Mrs. Brangwen felt safe in sending her children there, though the village boys did nickname Ursula 'Urtler', and Gudrun 'Good-runner', and Theresa 'Teapot'.

Gudrun and Ursula were co-mates. The second child, with her long, sleepy body and her endless chain of fancies, would have nothing to do with realities. She was not for them, she was for her own fancies. Ursula was the one for realities. So Gudrun left all such to her elder sister, and trusted in her implicitly, indifferently. Ursula had a great tenderness for her co-mate sister.

It was no good trying to make Gudrun responsible. She floated along like a fish in the sea, perfect within the medium of her own difference and being. Other existence did not trouble her. Only she believed in Ursula, and trusted to Ursula.

The eldest child was very much fretted by her responsibility for the other young ones. Especially Theresa, a sturdy, bold-eyed thing, had a faculty for warfare.

'Our Ursula, Billy Pillins has lugged my hair.'

'What did you say to him?'

'I said nothing.'

Then the Brangwen girls were in for a feud with the Pillinses, or Phillipses.

'You won't pull my hair again, Billy Pillins,' said Theresa, walking with her sisters, and looking superbly at the freckled, red-haired boy.

'Why shan't I?' retorted Billy Pillins.

'You won't because you dursn't,' said the tiresome Theresa.

'You come here, then, Tea-pot, an' see if I dursna.'

Up marched Tea-pot, and immediately Billy Pillins lugged her black, snaky locks. In a rage she flew at him. Immediately in rushed Ursula and Gudrun, and little Katie, in clashed the other Phillipses, Clem and Walter, and Eddie Anthony. Then there was a fray. The Brangwen girls were well-grown and stronger than many boys. But for pinafores and long hair, they would have carried easy victories. They went home, however, with hair lugged and pinafores torn. It was a joy to the Phillips boys to rip the pinafores of the Brangwen girls.

Then there was an outcry. Mrs. Brangwen *would* not have it; no, she would not. All her innate dignity and stand-offishness rose up. Then there was the vicar lecturing the school. 'It was a sad thing that the boys of Cossethay could not behave more like gentlemen to the girls of Cossethay. Indeed, what kind of boy was it that should set upon a girl, and kick her, and beat her, and tear her pinafore? That boy deserved severe castigation, and the name of *coward*, for no boy who was not a *coward* – etc., etc.'

Meanwhile much hang-dog fury in the Pillinses' hearts, much virtue in the Brangwen girls', particularly in Theresa's. And the feud continued, with periods of extraordinary amity, when Ursula was Clem Phillips's sweetheart, and Gudrun was Walter's, and Theresa was Billy's, and even the tiny Katie had to be Eddie Ant'ny's sweetheart. There was the closest union. At every possible moment the little gang of Brangwens and Phillipses flew together. Yet neither Ursula nor Gudrun would have any real intimacy with the Phillips boys. It was a sort of fiction to them, this alliance and this dubbing of sweethearts.

Again Mrs. Brangwen rose up.

'Ursula, I will *not* have you raking the roads with lads, so I tell you. Now stop it, and the rest will stop it.'

How Ursula *hated* always to represent the little Brangwen club. She could never be herself, no, she was always Ursula-Gudrun-Theresa-Catherine – and later even Billy was added on to her. Moreover, she did not want the Phillipses either. She was out of taste with them.

However, the Brangwen-Pillins coalition readily broke down, owing to the unfair superiority of the Brangwens. The Brangwens were rich. They had free access to the Marsh Farm. The school teachers were almost respectful to the girls, the vicar spoke to them on equal terms. The Brangwen girls presumed, they tossed their heads.

'*You're* not ivrybody, Urtler Brangwin, ugly-mug,' said Clem Phillips, his face going very red.

'I'm better than you, for all that,' retorted Urtler.

'You *think* you are – wi' a face like that – Ugly Mug, – Urtler Brangwin,' he began to jeer, trying to set all the others in cry against her. Then there was hostility again. How she *hated* their jeering. She became cold against the Phillipses. Ursula was very proud in her family. The Brangwen girls had all a curious blind dignity, even a kind of nobility in their bearing. By some result of breed and upbringing, they seemed to rush along their own lives without caring that they existed to other people. Never from the start did it occur to Ursula that other people might hold a low opinion of her. She thought that whosoever knew her, knew she was enough and accepted her as such. She thought it was a world of people like herself. She suffered bitterly if she were forced to have a low opinion of any person, and she never forgave that person.

This was maddening to many little people. All their lives, the Brangwens were meeting folk who tried to pull them down to make them seem little. Curiously, the mother was aware of what would happen, and was always ready to give her children the advantage of the move.

When Ursula was twelve, and the common school and the companionship of the village children, niggardly and begrudging, was beginning to affect her, Anna sent her with Gudrun to the Grammar School in Nottingham. This was a great release for Ursula. She had a passionate craving to escape from the belittling circumstances of life, the little jealousies, the little differences, the little meannesses. It was a torture to her that the Phillipses were poorer and meaner than herself, that they used mean little reservations, took petty little advantages. She wanted to be with her equals: but not by diminishing herself. She *did* want Clem Phillips to be her equal. But by some puzzling, painful fate or other, when he was really there with her, he produced in her a tight feeling in the head. She wanted to beat her forehead, to escape.

Then she found that the way to escape was easy. One departed from the whole circumstance. One went away to the Grammar School, and left the little school, the meagre teachers, the Phillipses whom she had tried to love but who had made her fail, and whom she could not forgive. She had an instinctive fear of petty people, as a deer is afraid of dogs. Because she was blind, she could not calculate nor estimate people. She must think that everybody was just like herself.

She measured by the standard of her own people: her father and mother, her grandmother, her uncles. Her beloved father, so utterly simple in his demeanour, yet with his strong, dark soul fixed like a root in unexpressed depths that fascinated and terrified her: her mother, so strangely free of all money and convention and fear, entirely indifferent to the world, standing by herself, without connection: her grandmother, who had come from so far and was centred in so wide an horizon: people must come up to these standards before they could be Ursula's people.

So even as a girl of twelve she was glad to burst the narrow boundary of Cossethay, where only limited people lived. Outside, was all vastness, and a throng of real, proud people whom she would love.

Going to school by train, she must leave home at a quarter to eight in the morning, and she did not arrive again till half-past five at evening. Of this she was glad, for the house was small and overfull. It was a storm of movement, whence there had been no escape. She hated so much being in charge.

The house was a storm of movement. The children were healthy and turbulent, the mother only wanted their animal well-being. To Ursula, as she grew a little older, it became a nightmare. When she saw, later, a Rubens picture with storms of naked babies, and found this was called 'Fecundity', she shuddered, and the world became abhorrent to her. She knew as a child what it was to live amidst storms of babies, in the heat and swelter of fecundity. And as a child, she was against her mother, passionately against her mother, she craved for some spirituality and stateliness.

In bad weather, home was a bedlam. Children dashed in and out of the rain, to the puddles under the dismal yew trees, across the wet flagstones of the kitchen, whilst the cleaning-woman grumbled and scolded; children were swarming on the sofa, children were kicking the piano in the parlour, to make it sound like a beehive, children were rolling on the hearthrug, legs in air, pulling a book in two between them, children, fiendish, ubiquitous, were stealing upstairs to find out where our Ursula was, whispering at bedroom doors, hanging on the latch, calling mysteriously, 'Ursula! Ursula!' to the girl who had locked herself in to read. And it was hopeless. The locked door excited their sense of mystery, she had to open to dispel the lure. These children hung on to her with round-eyed excited questions.

The mother flourished amid all this.

'Better have them noisy than ill,' she said.

But the growing girls, in turn, suffered bitterly. Ursula was just coming to the stage when Andersen and Grimm were being left behind for the 'Idylls of the King' and romantic love-stories.

'Elaine the fair Elaine the lovable,
Elaine the lily maid of Astolat,
High in her chamber in a tower to the east
Guarded the sacred shield of Launcelot.'

How she loved it! How she leaned in her bedroom window with her black, rough hair on her shoulders, and her warm face all rapt, and gazed across at the churchyard and the little church, which was a turreted castle, whence Launcelot would ride just now, would wave to her as he rode by, his scarlet cloak passing behind the dark yew trees and between the open space: whilst she, ah, she, would remain the lonely maid high up and isolated in the tower, polishing the terrible shield, weaving it a covering with a true device, and waiting, waiting, always remote and high.

At which point there would be a faint scuffle on the stairs, a light-pitched whispering outside the door, and a creaking of the latch: then Billy, excited, whispering:

'It's locked – it's locked.'

Then the knocking, kicking at the door with childish knees, and the urgent, childish:

'Ursula – our Ursula? Ursula? Eh, our Ursula?'

No reply.

'Ursula! Eh–our Ursula?' the name was shouted now. Still no answer.

'Mother, she won't answer,' came the yell. 'She's dead.'

'Go away – I'm not dead. What do you want?' came the angry voice of the girl.

'Open the door, our Ursula,' came the complaining cry. It was all over. She must open the door. She heard the screech of the bucket downstairs dragged across the flagstones as the woman washed the kitchen floor. And the children were prowling in the bedroom, asking:

'What were you doing? What had you locked the door for?' Then she discovered the key of the parish room, and betook herself there, and sat on some sacks with her books. There began another dream.

She was the only daughter of the old lord, she was gifted with magic. Day followed day of rapt silence, whilst she wandered ghost-like in the hushed, ancient mansion, or flitted along the sleeping terraces.

Here a grave grief attacked her: that her hair was dark. She *must* have fair hair and a white skin. She was rather bitter about her black mane.

Never mind, she would dye it when she grew up, or bleach it in the sun, till it was bleached fair. Meanwhile she wore a fair white coif of pure Venetian lace.

She flitted silently along the terraces, where jewelled lizards basked upon the stone, and did not move when her shadow fell upon them. In the utter stillness she heard the tinkle of the fountain, and smelled the roses whose blossoms hung rich and motionless. So she drifted, drifted on the wistful feet of beauty, past the water and the swans, to the noble park, where, underneath a great oak, a doe all dappled lay with her four fine feet together, her fawn nestling sun-coloured beside her.

Oh, and this doe was her familiar. It would talk to her, because she was a magician, it would tell her stories as if the sunshine spoke.

Then one day, she left the door of the parish room unlocked, careless and unheeding as she always was; the children found their way in, Katie cut her finger and howled, Billy hacked notches in the fine chisels, and did much damage. There was a great commotion.

The crossness of the mother was soon finished. Ursula locked up the room again, and considered all was over. Then her father came in with the notched tools, his forehead knotted.

'Who the deuce opened the door?' he cried in anger.

'It was Ursula who opened the door,' said her mother. He had a duster in his hand. He turned and flapped the cloth hard across the girl's face. The cloth stung, for a moment the girl was as if stunned. Then she remained motionless, her face closed and stubborn. But her heart was blazing. In spite of herself the tears surged higher, in spite of her they surged higher.

In spite of her, her face broke, she made a curious gulping grimace, and the tears were falling. So she went away, desolate. But her blazing heart was fierce and unyielding. He watched her go, and a pleasurable pain filled him, a sense of triumph and easy power, followed immediately by acute pity.

'I'm sure that was unnecessary – to hit the girl across the face,' said the mother coldly.

'A flip with the duster won't hurt her,' he said.

'Nor will it do her any good.'

For days, for weeks, Ursula's heart burned from this rebuff. She felt so cruelly vulnerable. Did he not know how vulnerable she was, how exposed and wincing? He, of all people, knew. And he wanted to do this to her. He wanted to hurt her right through her closest sensitiveness, he wanted to treat her with shame, to maim her with insult.

Her heart burnt in isolation, like a watchfire lighted. She did not forget, she did not forget, she never forgot. When she returned to her love for her father, the seed of mistrust and defiance burned unquenched, though covered up far from sight. She no longer belonged to him unquestioned. Slowly, slowly, the fire of mistrust and defiance burned in her, burned away her connection with him.

She ran a good deal alone, having a passion for all moving, active things. She loved the little brooks. Wherever she found a little running water, she was happy. It seemed to make her run and sing in spirit along with it. She could sit for hours by a brook or stream, on the roots of the alders, and watch the water hasten dancing over the stones, or among the twigs of a fallen branch. Sometimes, little fish vanished before they had become real, like hallucinations, sometimes wagtails ran by the water's brink, sometimes other little birds came to drink. She saw a kingfisher darting blue – and then she was very happy. The kingfisher was the key to the magic world: he was witness of the border of enchantment.

But she must move out of the intricately woven illusion of her life: the illusion of a father whose life was an Odyssey in an outer world; the illusion of her grandmother, of realities so shadowy and far-off that they became as mystic symbols: – peasant-girls with wreaths of blue flowers in their hair, the sledges and the depths of winter; the dark-bearded young grandfather, marriage and war and death; then the multitude of illusions concerning herself, how she was truly a princess of Poland, how in England she was under a spell, she was not really this Ursula Brangwen; then the mirage of her reading: out of the multicoloured illusion of this her life, she must move on, to the Grammar School in Nottingham.

She was shy, and she suffered. For one thing, she bit her nails, and had a cruel consciousness in her finger-tips, a shame, an exposure. Out of all proportion, this shame haunted her. She spent hours of torture, conjuring how she might keep her gloves on: if she might say her hands were scalded, if she might seem to forget to take off her gloves.

For she was going to inherit her own estate, when she went to the High School. There, each girl was a lady. There, she was going to walk among free souls, her co-mates and her equals, and all petty things would be put away. Ah, if only she did not bite her nails! If only she had not this blemish! She wanted so much to be perfect – without spot or blemish, living the high, noble life.

It was a grief to her that her father made such a poor introduction. He was brief as ever, like a boy saying his errand, and his clothes looked ill-fitting and casual. Whereas Ursula would have liked robes and a ceremonial of introduction to this, her new estate.

She made a new illusion of school. Miss Grey, the headmistress, had a certain silvery, school-mistressy beauty of character. The school itself had been a gentleman's house. Dark, sombre lawns separated it from the dark, select avenue. But its rooms were large and of good appearance, and from the back, one looked over lawns and shrubbery, over the trees and the grassy slope of the Arboretum, to the town which heaped the hollow with its roofs and cupolas and its shadows.

So Ursula seated herself upon the hill of learning, looking down on the smoke and confusion and the manufacturing, engrossed activity of the town. She was happy. Up here, in the Grammar School, she fancied the air was finer, beyond the factory smoke. She wanted to learn Latin and Greek and French and mathematics. She trembled like a postulant when she wrote the Greek alphabet for the first time.

She was upon another hill-slope, whose summit she had not scaled. There was always the marvellous eagerness in her heart, to climb and to see beyond. A Latin verb was virgin soil to her: she sniffed a new odour in it; it meant something, though she did not know what it meant. But she gathered it up: it was significant. When she knew that:

$$x^2 - y^2 = (x+y)\,(x-y)$$

then she felt that she had grasped something, that she was liberated into an intoxicating air, rare and unconditioned. And she was very glad as she wrote her French exercise:

'J'ai donné le pain à mon petit frère.'

In all these things there was the sound of a bugle to her heart, exhilarating, summoning her to perfect places. She never forgot her brown 'Longman's

First French Grammar', nor her 'Via Latina' with its red edges, nor her little grey Algebra book. There was always a magic in them.

At learning she was quick, intelligent, instinctive, but she was not 'thorough'. If a thing did not come to her instinctively, she could not learn And then, her mad rage of loathing for all lessons, her bitter contempt of all teachers and schoolmistresses, her recoil to a fierce, animal arrogance made her detestable.

She was a free, unabateable animal, she declared in her revolts: there was no law for her, nor any rule. She existed for herself alone. Then ensued a long struggle with everybody, in which she broke down at last, when she had run the full length of her resistance, and sobbed her heart out, desolate; and afterwards, in a chastened, washed-out, bodiless state, she received the understanding that would not come before, and went her way sadder and wiser.

Ursula and Gudrun went to school together. Gudrun was a shy, quiet, wild creature, a thin slip of a thing hanging back from notice or twisting past to disappear into her own world again. She seemed to avoid all contact, instinctively, and pursued her own intent way, pursuing half-formed fancies that had no relation to anyone else.

She was not clever at all. She thought Ursula clever enough for two. Ursula understood, so why should she, Gudrun, bother herself? The younger girl lived her religious, responsible life in her sister, by proxy. For herself, she was indifferent and intent as a wild animal, and as irresponsible.

When she found herself at the bottom of the class, she laughed, lazily, and was content, saying she was safe now. She did not mind her father's chagrin nor her mother's tinge of mortification.

'What do I pay for you to go to Nottingham for?' her father asked, exasperated.

'Well, Dad, you know you needn't pay for me,' she replied, nonchalant. 'I'm ready to stop at home.'

She was happy at home, Ursula was not. Slim and unwilling abroad, Gudrun was easy in her own house as a wild thing in its lair. Whereas Ursula, attentive and keen abroad, at home was reluctant, uneasy, unwilling to be herself, or unable.

Nevertheless Sunday remained the maximum day of the week for both. Ursula turned passionately to it, to the sense of eternal security it gave. She suffered anguish of fears during the week-days, for she felt strong powers that would not recognise her. There was upon her always a fear and a dislike of authority. She felt she could always do as she wanted if she managed to avoid a battle with Authority and the authorised Powers. But if she gave herself away, she would be lost, destroyed. There was always the menace against her.

This strange sense of cruelty and ugliness always imminent, ready to seize hold upon her this feeling of the grudging power of the mob lying in wait for her, who was the exception, formed one of the deepest influences of her life. Wherever she was, at school, among friends, in the street, in the train, she instinctively abated herself, made herself smaller, feigned to be less than she was, for fear that her undiscovered self should be seen, pounced upon, attacked by brutish resentment of the commonplace, the average Self.

She was fairly safe at school, now. She knew how to take her place there, and how much of herself to reserve. But she was free only on Sundays. When she was but a girl of fourteen, she began to feel a resentment growing against her in her own home. She knew she was the disturbing influence there. But as yet, on Sundays, she was free, really free, free to be herself, without fear or misgiving.

Even at its stormiest, Sunday was a blessed day. Ursula woke to it with a feeling of immense relief. She wondered why her heart was so light. Then she remembered it was Sunday. A gladness seemed to burst out around her, a feeling of great freedom. The whole world was for twenty-four hours revoked, put back. Only the Sunday world existed.

She loved the very confusion of the household. It was lucky if the children slept till seven o'clock. Usually, soon after six, a chirp was heard, a voice, an excited chirrup began, announcing the creation of a new day, there was a thudding of quick little feet, and the children were up and about, scampering in their shirts, with pink legs and glistening, flossy hair all clean from the Saturday's night bathing, their souls excited by their bodies' cleanliness.

As the house began to teem with rushing, half-naked clean children, one of the parents rose, either the mother, easy and slatternly, with her thick, dark hair loosely coiled and slipping over one ear, or the father, warm and comfortable, with ruffled black hair and shirt unbuttoned at the neck.

Then the girls upstairs heard the continual:

'Now then, Billy, what are you up to?' in the father's strong, vibrating voice: or the mother's dignified:

'I have said, Cassie, I will not have it.'

It was amazing how the father's voice could ring out like a gong, without his being in the least moved, and how the mother could speak like a queen holding an audience, though her blouse was sticking out all round and her hair was not fastened up and the children were yelling a pandemonium.

Gradually breakfast was produced, and the elder girls came down into the babel, whilst half-naked children flitted round like the wrong ends of cherubs, as Gudrun said, watching the bare little legs and the chubby tails appearing and disappearing.

Gradually the young ones were captured, and nightdresses finally removed, ready for the clean Sunday shirt. But before the Sunday shirt was slipped over the fleecy head, away darted the naked body, to wallow in the sheepskin which formed the parlour rug, whilst the mother walked after, protesting sharply, holding the shirt like a noose, and the father's bronze voice rang out, and the naked child wallowing on its back in the deep sheepskin announced gleefully:

'I'm bading in the sea, mother.'

'Why should I walk after you with your shirt?' said the mother. 'Get up now.'

'I'm bading in the sea, mother,' repeated the wallowing, naked figure.

'We say bathing, not bading,' said the mother, with her strange, indifferent dignity. 'I am waiting here with your shirt.'

At length shirts were on, and stockings were paired, and little trousers buttoned and little petticoats tied behind. The besetting cowardice of the family was its shirking of the garter question.

'Where are your garters, Cassie?'

'I don't know.'

'Well, look for them.'

But not one of the elder Brangwens would really face the situation. After Cassie had grovelled under all the furniture and blacked up all her Sunday cleanliness, to the infinite grief of everybody, the garter was forgotten in the new washing of the young face and hands.

Later, Ursula would be indignant to see Miss Cassie marching into church from Sunday school with her stocking sluthered down to her ankle, and a grubby knee showing.

'It's disgraceful!' cried Ursula at dinner. 'People will think we're pigs, and the children are *never* washed.'

'Never mind what people think,' said the mother superbly. '*I* see that the child is bathed properly, and if I satisfy myself I satisfy everybody. She can't keep her stocking up and no garter, and it isn't the child's fault she was let to go without one.'

The garter trouble continued in varying degrees, but till each child wore long skirts or long trousers, it was not removed.

On this day of decorum, the Brangwen family went to church by the high-road, making a detour outside all the garden-hedge, rather than climb the wall into the churchyard. There was no law of this, from the parents. The children themselves were the wardens of the Sabbath decency, very jealous and instant with each other.

It came to be, gradually, that after church on Sundays the house was really something of a sanctuary, with peace breathing like a strange bird alighted in the rooms. Indoors, only reading and tale-telling and quiet pursuits, such as drawing, were allowed. Out of doors, all playing was to be carried on unobtrusively. If there were noise, yelling or shouting, then some fierce spirit woke up in the father and the elder children, so that the younger were subdued, afraid of being excommunicated.

The children themselves preserved the Sabbath. If Ursula in her vanity sang:

> 'Il était un' bergère
> Et ron-ron-ron petit patapon,'

Theresa was sure to cry:

'*That's* not a Sunday song, our Ursula.'

'You don't know,' replied Ursula, superior. Nevertheless, she wavered. And her song faded down before she came to the end.

Because, though she did not know it, her Sunday was very precious to her. She found herself in a strange, undefined place, where her spirit could wander in dreams, unassailed.

The white-robed spirit of Christ passed between olive trees. It was a vision, not a reality. And she herself partook of the visionary being. There was the voice in the night calling, 'Samuel, Samuel!' And still the voice called in the night. But not this night, nor last night, but in the unfathomed night of Sunday, of the Sabbath silence.

There was Sin, the serpent, in whom was also wisdom. There was Judas with the money and the kiss.

But there was no *actual* Sin. If Ursula slapped Theresa across the face, even on a Sunday, that was not Sin, the everlasting. It was misbehaviour. If Billy played truant from Sunday school, he was bad, he was wicked, but he was not a Sinner.

Sin was absolute and everlasting: wickedness and badness were temporary and relative. When Billy, catching up the local jargon, called Cassie a 'sinner', everybody detested him. Yet when there came to the Marsh a flippetty-floppetty foxhound puppy, he was mischievously christened 'Sinner'.

The Brangwens shrank from applying their religion to their own immediate actions. They wanted the sense of the eternal and immortal, not a list of rules for everyday conduct. Therefore they were badly-behaved children, headstrong and arrogant, though their feelings were generous. They had, moreover – intolerable to their ordinary neighbours – a proud gesture, that did not fit with the jealous idea of the democratic Christian. So that they were always extraordinary, outside of the ordinary.

How bitterly Ursula resented her first acquaintance with evangelical teachings. She got a peculiar thrill from the application of salvation to her own personal case. 'Jesus died for *me*, He suffered for me.' There was a pride and a thrill in it, followed almost immediately by a sense of dreariness. Jesus with holes in His hands and feet: it was distasteful to her. The shadowy Jesus with the Stigmata: that was her own vision. But Jesus the actual man, talking with teeth and lips, telling one to put one's finger into His wounds, like a villager gloating in his sores, repelled her. She was enemy of those who insisted on the humanity of Christ. If He were just a man, living in ordinary human life, then she was indifferent.

But it was the jealousy of vulgar people which must insist on the humanity of Christ. It was the vulgar mind which would allow nothing extra-human, nothing beyond itself to exist. It was the dirty, desecrating hands of the revivalists which wanted to drag Jesus into this everyday life, to dress Jesus up in trousers and frock-coat, to compel Him to a vulgar equality of footing. It was the impudent suburban soul which would ask, 'What would Jesus do, if he were in my shoes?'

Against all this, the Brangwens stood at bay. If any one, it was the mother who was caught by, or who was most careless of the vulgar clamour. She would have nothing extra-human. She never really subscribed, all her life, to Brangwen's mystical passion.

But Ursula was with her father. As she became adolescent, thirteen, fourteen, she set more and more against her mother's practical indifference. To Ursula, there was something callous, almost wicked in her mother's attitude. What did Anna Brangwen, in these years, care for God or Jesus or Angels? She was the immediate life of to-day. Children were still being born to her, she was throng with all the little activities of her family. And almost instinctively she resented her husband's slavish service to the Church, his dark, subject hankering to worship an unseen God. What did the unrevealed God matter, when a man had a young family that needed fettling for? Let him attend to the immediate concerns of his life, not go projecting himself towards the ultimate.

But Ursula was all for the ultimate. She was always in revolt against babies and muddled domesticity. To her Jesus was another world, He was not of this world. He did not thrust His hands under her face and, pointing to His wounds, say:

'Look, Ursula Brangwen, I got these for your sake. Now do as you're told.'

To her, Jesus was beautifully remote, shining in the distance, like a white moon at sunset, a crescent moon beckoning as it follows the sun, out of our ken. Sometimes dark clouds standing very far off, pricking up into a clear yellow band of sunset, of a winter evening, reminded her of Calvary, sometimes the full moon rising blood-red upon the hill terrified her with the knowledge that Christ was now dead, hanging heavy and dead upon the Cross.

On Sundays, this visionary world came to pass. She heard the long hush, she knew the marriage of dark and light was taking place. In church, the Voice sounded, re-echoing not from this world, as if the Church itself were a shell that still spoke the language of creation.

'The Sons of God saw the daughters of men that they were fair: and they took them wives of all which they chose.

'And the Lord said, My spirit shall not always strive with Man, for that he also is flesh; yet his days shall be an hundred and twenty years.

'There were giants in the earth in those days; and also after that, when the Sons of God came in unto the daughters of men, and they bare children unto them, the same became mighty men which were of old, men of renown.'

Over this Ursula was stirred as by a call from far off. In those days, would not the Sons of God have found her fair, would she not have been taken to wife by one of the Sons of God? It was a dream that frightened her, for she could not understand it.

Who were the sons of God? Was not Jesus the only begotten Son? Was not Adam the only man created from God? Yet there were men not begotten by Adam. Who were these, and whence did they come? They too must derive from God. Had God many offspring, besides Adam and besides Jesus, children whose origin the children of Adam cannot recognise? And perhaps these children, these sons of God, had known no expulsion, no ignominy of the fall.

These came on free feet to the daughters of men, and saw they were fair, and took them to wife, so that the women conceived and brought forth men of renown. This was a genuine fate. She moved about in the essential days, when the sons of God came in unto the daughters of men.

Nor would any comparison of myths destroy her passion in the knowledge. Jove had become a bull, or a man, in order to love a mortal woman. He had begotten in her a giant, a hero.

Very good, so he had, in Greece. For herself, she was no Grecian woman.

Not Jove nor Pan nor any of those gods, not even Bacchus nor Apollo, could come to her. But the Sons of God who took to wife the daughters of men, these were such as should take her to wife.

She clung to the secret hope, the aspiration. She lived a dual life, one where the facts of daily life encompassed everything, being legion, and the other wherein the facts of daily life were superseded by the eternal truth. So utterly did she desire the Sons of God should come to the daughters of men; and she believed more in her desire and its fulfilment than in the obvious facts of life. The fact that a man was a man, did not state his descent from Adam, did not exclude that he was also one of the unhistoried, unaccountable Sons of God. As yet, she was confused, but not denied.

Again she heard the Voice:

'It is easier for a camel to go through the eye of a needle, than for a rich man to enter into heaven.'

But it was explained, the needle's eye was a little gateway for foot passengers, through which the great, humped camel with his load could not possibly squeeze himself: or perhaps, at a great risk, if he were a little camel, he might get through. For one could not absolutely exclude the rich man from heaven, said the Sunday school teachers.

It pleased her also to know, that in the East one must use hyperbole, or else remain unheard; because the Eastern man must see a thing swelling to fill all heaven, or dwindled to a mere nothing, before he is suitably impressed. She immediately sympathised with this Eastern mind.

Yet the words continued to have a meaning that was untouched either by the knowledge of gateways or hyperboles. The historical, or local, or psychological interest in the words was another thing. There remained unaltered the inexplicable value of the saying. What was this relation between a needle's eye, a rich man, and heaven? What sort of a needle's eye, what sort of a rich man, what sort of heaven? Who knows? It means the Absolute World, and can never be more than half interpreted in terms of the relative world.

But must one apply the speech literally? Was her father a rich man? Couldn't he get to heaven? Or was he only a half-rich man? Or was he merely a poor man? At any rate, unless he gave everything away to the poor, he would find it much harder to get to heaven. The needle's eye would be too tight for him. She almost wished he were penniless poor. If one were coming to the base of it, any man was rich who was not as poor as the poorest.

She had her qualms, when in imagination she saw her father giving away their piano and the two cows, and the capital at the bank, to the labourers of the district, so that they, the Brangwens, should be as poor as the Wherrys. And she did not want it. She was impatient.

'Very well,' she thought, 'we'll forego that heaven, that's all – at any rate the needle's eye sort.' And she dismissed the problem. She was *not* going to be as poor as the Wherrys, not for all the sayings on earth – the miserable squalid Wherrys.

So she reverted to the non-literal application of the scriptures. Her father very rarely read, but he had collected many books of reproductions, and he would sit and look at these, curiously intent, like a child, yet with a passion that was not childish. He loved the early Italian painters, but particularly Giotto and Fra Angelico and Filippo Lippi. The great compositions cast a spell over him. How many times had he turned to Raphael's 'Dispute of the Sacrament' or Fra Angelico's 'Last Judgment' or the beautiful, complicated renderings of the Adoration of the Magi, and always, each time, he received the same gradual fulfilment of delight. It had to do with the establishment of a whole mystical, architectural conception which used the human figure as a unit. Sometimes he had to hurry home, and go to the Fra Angelico 'Last Judgment'. The pathway of open graves, the huddled earth on either side, the seemly heaven arranged above, the singing process to paradise on the one hand, the stuttering descent to hell on the other, completed and satisfied him. He did not care whether or not he believed in devils or angels. The whole conception gave him the deepest satisfaction, and he wanted nothing more.

Ursula, accustomed to these pictures from her childhood, hunted out their detail. She adored Fra Angelico's flowers and light and angels, she liked the demons and enjoyed the hell. But the representation of the encircled God, surrounded by all the angels on high, suddenly bored her. The figure of the Most High bored her, and roused her resentment. Was this the culmination and the meaning of it all, this draped, null figure? The angels were so lovely, and the light so beautiful. And only for this, to surround such a banality for God!

She was dissatisfied, but not fit as yet to criticise. There was yet so much to wonder over. Winter came, pine branches were torn down in the snow, the green pine needles looked rich upon the ground. There was the wonderful, starry, straight track of a pheasant's footsteps across the snow imprinted so clear; there was the lobbing mark of the rabbit, two holes abreast, two holes following behind; the hare shoved deeper shafts, slanting, and his two hind feet came down together and made one large pit; the cat podded little holes, and birds made a lacy pattern.

Gradually there gathered the feeling of expectation. Christmas was coming. In the shed, at nights, a secret candle was burning, a sound of veiled voices was heard. The boys were learning the old mystery play of St. George and Beelzebub. Twice a week, by lamplight, there was choir practice in the church, for the learning of old carols Brangwen wanted to hear. The girls went to these practices. Everywhere was a sense of mystery and rousedness. Everybody was preparing for something.

The time came near, the girls were decorating the church, with cold fingers binding holly and fir and yew about the pillars, till a new spirit was in the church, the stone broke out into dark, rich leaf, the arches put forth their buds, and cold flowers rose to blossom in the dim, mystic atmosphere. Ursula must weave mistletoe over the door, and over the screen, and hang a silver dove from a sprig of yew, till dusk came down, and the church was like a grove.

In the cow-shed the boys were blacking their faces for a dress-rehearsal; the turkey hung dead, with opened, speckled wings, in the dairy. The time was come to make pies, in readiness.

The expectation grew more tense. The star was risen into the sky, the songs, the carols were ready to hail it. The star was the sign in the sky. Earth too should give a sign. As evening drew on, hearts beat fast with anticipation, hands were full of ready gifts. There were the tremulously expectant words of the church service, the night was past and the morning was come, the gifts were given and received, joy and peace made a flapping of wings in each heart, there was a great burst of carols, the Peace of the World had dawned, strife had passed away, every hand was linked in hand, every heart was singing.

It was bitter, though, that Christmas Day, as it drew on to evening, and night, became a sort of bank holiday, flat and stale. The morning was so wonderful, but in the afternoon and evening the ecstasy perished like a nipped thing, like a bud in a false spring. Alas, that Christmas was only a domestic feast, a feast of sweetmeats and toys! Why did not the grown-ups also change their everyday hearts, and give way to ecstasy? Where was the ecstasy?

How passionately the Brangwens craved for it, the ecstasy. The father was troubled, dark-faced and disconsolate, on Christmas night, because the passion was not there, because the day was become as every day, and hearts were not aflame. Upon the mother was a kind of absentness, as ever, as if she were exiled for all her life. Where was the fiery heart of joy, now the coming was fulfilled; where was the star, the Magi's transport, the thrill of new being that shook the earth?

Still it was there, even if it were faint and inadequate. The cycle of creation still wheeled in the Church year. After Christmas, the ecstasy slowly sank and changed. Sunday followed Sunday, trailing a fine movement, a finely developed transformation over the heart of the family. The heart that was big with joy, that had seen the star and had followed to the inner walls of the Nativity, that there had swooned in the great light, must now feel the light slowly withdrawing, a shadow falling, darkening. The chill crept in, silence came over the earth, and then all was darkness. The veil of the temple was rent, each heart gave up the ghost, and sank dead.

They moved quietly, a little wanness on the lips of the children, at Good Friday, feeling the shadow upon their hearts. Then, pale with a deathly scent, came the lilies of resurrection, that shone coldly till the Comforter was given.

But why the memory of the wounds and the death? Surely Christ rose with healed hands and feet, sound and strong and glad? Surely the passage of the cross and the tomb was forgotten? But no – always the memory of the wounds, always the smell of grave-clothes? A small thing was Resurrection, compared with the Cross and the death, in this cycle.

So the children lived the year of christianity, the epic of the soul of mankind. Year by year the inner, unknown drama went on in them, their hearts were born and came to fulness, suffered on the cross, gave up the ghost, and rose again to unnumbered days, untired, having at least this rhythm of eternity in a ragged, inconsequential life.

But it was becoming a mechanical action now, this drama: birth at Christmas for death at Good Friday. On Easter Sunday the life-drama was as good as finished. For the Resurrection was shadowy and overcome by the shadow of death, the Ascension was scarce noticed, a mere confirmation of death.

What was the hope and the fulfilment? Nay, was it all only a useless after-death, a wan, bodiless after-death? Alas, and alas for the passion of the human heart, that must die so long before the body was dead.

For from the grave, after the passion and the trial of anguish, the body rose torn and chill and colourless. Did not Christ say, 'Mary!' and when she turned with outstretched hands to him, did he not hasten to add, 'Touch me not; for I am not yet ascended to my father.'

Then how could the hands rejoice, or the heart be glad, seeing themselves repulsed. Alas, for the resurrection of the dead body! Alas, for the wavering, glimmering appearance of the risen Christ. Alas, for the Ascension into heaven, which is a shadow within death, a complete passing away.

Alas, that so soon the drama is over; that life is ended at thirty-three; that the half of the year of the soul is cold and historiless! Alas, that a risen Christ has no place with us! Alas, that the memory of the passion of Sorrow and Death and the Grave holds triumph over the pale fact of Resurrection!

But why? Why shall I not rise with my body whole and perfect, shining with strong life? Why, when Mary says: Rabboni, shall I not take her in my arms and kiss her and hold her to my breast? Why is the risen body deadly, and abhorrent with wounds?

The Resurrection is to life, not to death. Shall I not see those who have risen again walk here among men perfect in body and spirit, whole and glad in the flesh, living in the flesh, loving in the flesh, begetting children in the flesh, arrived at last to wholeness, perfect without scar or blemish, healthy without fear of ill health? Is this not the period of manhood and of joy and fulfilment, after the Resurrection? Who shall be shadowed by Death and the Cross, being risen, and who shall fear the mystic, perfect flesh that belongs to heaven?

Can I not, then, walk this earth in gladness, being risen from sorrow? Can I not eat with my brother happily, and with joy kiss my beloved, after my resurrection, celebrate my marriage in the flesh with feastings, go about my business eagerly, in the joy of my fellows? Is heaven impatient for me, and bitter against this earth, that I should hurry off, or that I should linger pale and untouched? Is the flesh which was crucified become a poison to the crowds in the street, or is it as a strong gladness and hope to them, as the first flower blossoming out of the earth's humus?

Chapter Eleven

First Love

As Ursula passed from girlhood towards womanhood, gradually the cloud of self-responsibility gathered upon her. She became aware of herself, that she was a separate entity in the midst of an unseparated obscurity, that she must go somewhere, she must become something. And she was afraid, troubled. Why, oh why must one grow up, why must one inherit this heavy, numbing responsibility of living an undiscovered life? Out of the nothingness and the undifferentiated mass, to make something of herself! But what? In the obscurity and pathlessness to take a direction! But whither? How take even one step? And yet, how stand still? This was torment indeed, to inherit the responsibility of one's own life.

The religion which had been another world for her, a glorious sort of play-world, where she lived, climbing the tree with the short-statured man, walking shakily on the sea like the disciple, breaking the bread into five thousand portions, like the Lord, giving a great picnic to five thousand people, now fell away from reality, and became a tale, a myth, an illusion, which, however much one might assert it to be true an historical fact, one knew was not true – at least, for this present-day life of ours. There could, within the limits of this life we know, be no Feeding of the Five Thousand. And the girl had come to the point where she held that that which one cannot experience in daily life is not true for oneself.

So, the old duality of life, wherein there had been a week-day world of people and trains and duties and reports, and besides that a Sunday world of absolute truth and living mystery, of walking upon the waters and being blinded by the face of the Lord, of following the pillar of cloud across the desert and watching the bush that crackled yet did not burn away, this old, unquestioned duality suddenly was found to be broken apart. The weekday world had triumphed over the Sunday world. The Sunday world was not real, or at least, not actual. And one lived by action.

Only the weekday world mattered. She herself, Ursula Brangwen, must know how to take the weekday life. Her body must be a weekday body, held in the world's estimate. Her soul must have a weekday value, known according to the world's knowledge.

Well, then, there was a weekday life to live, of action and deeds. And so there was a necessity to choose one's action and one's deeds. One was responsible to the world for what one did.

Nay, one was more than responsible to the world. One was responsible to oneself. There was some puzzling, tormenting residue of the Sunday world within her, some persistent Sunday self, which insisted upon a relationship with the now shed-away vision world. How could one keep up a relationship with that which one denied? Her task was now to learn the week-day life.

How to act, that was the question? Whither to go, how to become oneself? One was not oneself, one was merely a half-stated question. How to become oneself, how to know the question and the answer of oneself, when one was merely an unfixed something-nothing, blowing about like the winds of heaven, undefined, unstated.

She turned to the visions, which had spoken far-off words that ran along the blood like ripples of an unseen wind, she heard the words again, she denied the vision, for she must be a weekday person, to whom visions were not true, and she demanded only the weekday meaning of the words.

There *were* words spoken by the vision: and words must have a weekday meaning, since words were weekday stuff. Let them speak now: let them bespeak themselves in weekday terms. The vision should translate itself into weekday terms.

'Sell all thou hast, and give to the poor,' she heard on Sunday morning. That was plain enough, plain enough for Monday morning too. As she went down the hill to the station, going to school, she took the saying with her.

'Sell all thou hast, and give to the poor.'

Did she want to do that? Did she want to sell her pearl-backed brush and mirror, her silver candlestick, her pendant, her lovely little necklace, and go dressed in drab like the Wherrys: the unlovely uncombed Wherrys, who were the 'poor' to her? She did not.

She walked this Monday morning on the verge of misery. For she *did* want to do what was right. And she *didn't* want to do what the gospels said. She didn't want to be poor – really poor. The thought was a horror to her: to live like the Wherrys, so ugly, to be at the mercy of everybody.

'Sell that thou hast, and give to the poor.'

One could not do it in real life. How dreary and hopeless it made her!

Nor could one turn the other cheek. Theresa slapped Ursula on the face. Ursula, in a mood of Christian humility, silently presented the other side of her face. Which Theresa, in exasperation at the challenge, also hit. Whereupon Ursula, with boiling heart, went meekly away.

But anger, and deep, writhing shame tortured her, so she was not easy till she had again quarrelled with Theresa and had almost shaken her sister's head off.

'That'll teach you,' she said, grimly.

And she went away, unchristian but clean.

There was something unclean and degrading about this humble side of Christianity. Ursula suddenly revolted to the other extreme.

'I hate the Wherrys, and I wish they were dead. Why does my father leave us in the lurch like this, making us be poor and insignificant? Why is he not more? If we had a father as he ought to be, he would be Earl William Brangwen, and I should be the Lady Ursula? What right have *I* to be poor? crawling along the lane like vermin? If I had my rights I should be seated on horseback in a green riding-habit, and my groom would be behind me. And I should stop at the gates of the cottages, and enquire of the cottage woman who came out with a child in her arms, how did her husband, who had hurt his foot. And I would pat the flaxen head of the child, stooping from my horse, and I would give her a shilling from my purse, and order nourishing food to be sent from the hall to the cottage.'

So she rode in her pride. And sometimes, she dashed into flames to rescue a forgotten child; or she dived into the canal locks and supported a boy who was seized with cramp; or she swept up a toddling infant from the feet of a runaway horse: always imaginatively, of course.

But in the end there returned the poignant yearning from the Sunday world. As she went down in the morning from Cossethay and saw Ilkeston smoking blue and tender upon its hill, then her heart surged with far-off words:

'Oh, Jerusalem, Jerusalem – how often would I have gathered thy children together as a hen gathereth her chickens under her wings, and ye would not—'

The passion rose in her for Christ, for the gathering under the wings of security and warmth. But how did it apply to the weekday world? What could it mean, but that Christ should clasp her to his breast, as a mother clasps her child? And oh, for Christ, for him who could hold her to his breast and lose her there. Oh, for the breast of man, where she should have refuge and bliss for ever! All her senses quivered with passionate yearning.

Vaguely she knew that Christ meant something else: that in the vision-world He spoke of Jerusalem, something that did not exist in the everyday world. It was not houses and factories He would hold in His bosom: nor householders nor factory-workers nor poor people: but something that had no part in the weekday world, nor seen nor touched with weekday hands and eyes.

Yet she *must* have it in weekday terms – she must. For all her life was a weekday life, now, this was the whole. So he must gather her body to his breast, that was strong with a broad bone, and which sounded with the beating of the heart, and which was warm with the life of which she partook, the life of the running blood.

So she craved for the breast of the Son of Man, to lie there. And she was ashamed in her soul, ashamed. For whereas Christ spoke for the Vision to answer, she answered from the weekday fact. It was a betrayal, a transference of meaning, from the vision world, to the matter-of-fact world. So she was ashamed of her religious ecstasy, and dreaded lest any one should see it.

Early in the year, when the lambs came, and shelters were built of straw, and on her uncle's farm the men sat at night with a lantern and a dog, then again there swept over her this passionate confusion between the vision world and the weekday world. Again she felt Jesus in the countryside. Ah, he would lift up the lambs in his arms! Ah, and she was the lamb. Again, in the morning, going down the lane, she heard the ewe call, and the lambs came running, shaking and twinkling with new-born bliss. And she saw them stooping, nuzzling, groping to the udder, to find the teats, whilst the mother turned her head gravely and sniffed her own. And they were sucking, vibrating with bliss on their little, long legs, their throats sketched up, their new bodies quivering to the stream of blood-warm, loving milk.

Oh, and the bliss, the bliss! She could scarcely tear herself away to go to school. The little noses nuzzling at the udder, the little bodies so glad and sure, the little black legs, crooked, the mother standing still, yielding herself to their quivering attraction – then the mother walked calmly away.

Jesus – the vision world – the everyday world – all mixed inextricably in a confusion of pain and bliss. It was almost agony, the confusion, the inextricability. Jesus, the vision, speaking to her, who was non-visionary! And she would take his words of the spirit and make them to pander to her own carnality.

This was a shame to her. The confusing of the spirit world with the material world, in her own soul, degraded her. She answered the call of the spirit in terms of immediate, everyday desire.

'Come unto me, all ye that labour and are heavy-laden, and I will give you rest.'

It was the temporal answer she gave. She leapt with sensuous yearning to respond to Christ. If she could go to him really, and lay her head on his breast, to have comfort, to be made much of, caressed like a child!

All the time she walked in a confused heat of religious yearning. She wanted Jesus to love her deliciously, to take her sensuous offering, to give her sensuous response. For weeks she went in a muse of enjoyment.

And all the time she knew underneath that she was playing false, accepting the passion of Jesus for her own physical satisfaction. But she was in such a daze, such a tangle. How could she get free?

She hated herself, she wanted to trample on herself, destroy herself. How could one become free? She hated religion, because it lent itself to her confusion. She abused everything. She wanted to become hard, indifferent, brutally callous to everything but just the immediate need, the immediate satisfaction. To have a yearning towards Jesus, only that she might use him to pander to her own soft sensation, use him as a means of reacting upon herself, maddened her in the end. There was then no Jesus, no sentimentality. With all the bitter hatred of helplessness she hated sentimentality.

At this period came the young Skrebensky. She was nearly sixteen years old, a slim, smouldering girl, deeply reticent, yet lapsing into unreserved expansiveness now and then, when she seemed to give away her whole soul, but when in fact she only made another counterfeit of her soul for outward presentation. She was sensitive in the extreme, always tortured, always affecting a callous indifference to screen herself.

She was at this time a nuisance on the face of the earth, with her spasmodic passion and her slumberous torment. She seemed to go with all her soul in her hands, yearning, to the other person. Yet all the while, deep at the bottom of her was a childish antagonism of distrust. She thought she loved everybody and believed in everybody. But because she could not love herself nor believe in herself, she mistrusted everybody with the mistrust of a serpent or a captured bird. Her starts of revulsion and hatred were more inevitable than her impulses of love.

So she wrestled through her dark days of confusion, soulless, uncreated, unformed.

One evening, as she was studying in the parlour, her head buried in her hands, she heard new voices in the kitchen speaking. At once, from its apathy, her excitable spirit started and strained to listen. It seemed to crouch, to lurk under cover, tense, glaring forth unwilling to be seen.

There were two strange men's voices, one soft and candid, veiled with soft candour, the other veiled with easy mobility, running quickly. Ursula sat quite tense, shocked out of her studies, lost. She listened all the time to the sound of the voices, scarcely heeding the words.

The first speaker was her Uncle Tom. She knew the naïve candour covering the girding and savage misery of his soul. Who was the other speaker? Whose voice ran on so easy, yet with an inflamed pulse? It seemed to hasten and urge her forward, that other voice.

'I remember you,' the young man's voice was saying. 'I remember you from the first time I saw you, because of your dark eyes and fair face.'

Mrs. Brangwen laughed, shy and pleased.

'You were a curly-headed little lad,' she said.

'Was I? Yes, I know. They were very proud of my curls.'

And a laugh ran to silence.

'You were a very well-mannered lad, I remember,' said her father.

'Oh! did I ask you to stay the night? I always used to ask people to stay the night. I believe it was rather trying for my mother.'

There was a general laugh. Ursula rose. She had to go.

At the click of the latch everybody looked round. The girl hung in the doorway, seized with a moment's fierce confusion. She was going to be good-looking. Now she had an attractive gawkiness, as she hung a moment, not knowing how to carry her shoulders. Her dark hair was tied behind, her yellow-brown eyes shone without direction. Behind her, in the parlour, was the soft light of a lamp upon open books.

A superficial readiness took her to her Uncle Tom, who kissed her, greeting her with warmth, making a show of intimate possession of her, and at the same time leaving evident his own complete detachment.

But she wanted to turn to the stranger. He was standing back a little, waiting. He was a young man with very clear greyish eyes that waited until they were called upon, before they took expression.

Something in his self-possessed waiting moved her, and she broke into a confused, rather beautiful laugh as she gave him her hand, catching her breath like an excited child. His hand closed over hers very close, very near, he bowed, and his eyes were watching her with some attention. She felt proud – her spirit leapt to life.

'You don't know Mr. Skrebensky, Ursula,' came her Uncle Tom's intimate voice. She lifted her face with an impulsive flash to the stranger, as if to declare a knowledge, laughing her palpitating, excited laugh.

His eyes became confused with roused lights, his detached attention changed to a readiness for her. He was a young man of twenty-one, with a slender figure and soft brown hair brushed up on the German fashion straight from his brow.

'Are you staying long?' she asked.

'I've got a month's leave,' he said, glancing at Tom Brangwen. 'But I've various places I must go to – put in some time here and there.'

He brought her a strong sense of the outer world. It was as if she were set on a hill and could feel vaguely the whole world lying spread before her.

'What have you a month's leave from?' she asked.

'I'm in the Engineers – in the Army.'

'Oh!' she exclaimed, glad.

'We're taking *you* away from your studies,' said her Uncle Tom.

'Oh, no,' she replied quickly.

Skrebensky laughed, young and inflammable.

'She won't wait to be taken away,' said her father. But that seemed clumsy. She wished he would leave her to say her own things.

'Don't you like study?' asked Skrebensky, turning to her, putting the question from his own case.

'I like some things,' said Ursula. 'I like Latin and French – and grammar.'

He watched her, and all his being seemed attentive to her, then he shook his head.

'I don't,' he said. 'They say all the brains of the army are in the Engineers. I think that's why I joined them – to get the credit of other people's brains.'

He said this quizzically and with chagrin. And she became alert to him. It interested her. Whether he had brains or not, he was interesting. His directness attracted her, his independent motion. She was aware of the movement of his life over against hers.

'I don't think brains matter,' she said.

'What does matter then?' came her Uncle Tom's intimate, caressing, half-jeering voice.

She turned to him.

'It matters whether people have courage or not,' she said.

'Courage for what?' asked her uncle.

'For everything.'

Tom Brangwen gave a sharp little laugh. The mother and father sat silent, with listening faces. Skrebensky waited. She was speaking for him.

'Everything's nothing,' laughed her uncle.

She disliked him at that moment.

'She doesn't practise what she preaches,' said her father, stirring in his chair and crossing one leg over the other. 'She has courage for mighty little.'

But she would not answer. Skrebensky sat still, waiting. His face was irregular, almost ugly, flattish, with a rather thick nose. But his eyes were pellucid, strangely clear, his brown hair was soft and thick as silk, he had a slight moustache. His skin was fine, his figure slight, beautiful. Beside him, her Uncle Tom looked full-blown, her father seemed uncouth. Yet he reminded her of her father, only he was finer, and he seemed to be shining. And his face was almost ugly.

He seemed simply acquiescent in the fact of his own being, as if he were beyond any change or question. He was himself. There was a sense of fatality about him that fascinated her. He made no effort to prove himself to other people. Let it be accepted for what it was, his own being. In its isolation it made no excuse or explanation for itself.

So he seemed perfectly, even fatally established, he did not ask to be rendered before he could exist, before he could have relationship with another person.

This attracted Ursula very much. She was so used to unsure people who took on a new being with every new influence. Her Uncle Tom was always more or less what the other person would have him. In consequence, one never knew the real Uncle Tom, only a fluid, unsatisfactory flux with a more or less consistent appearance.

But, let Skrebensky do what he would, betray himself entirely, he betrayed himself always upon his own responsibility. He permitted no question about himself. He was irrevocable in his isolation.

So Ursula thought him wonderful, he was so finely constituted, and so distinct, self-contained, self-supporting. This, she said to herself, was a gentleman, he had a nature like fate, the nature of an aristocrat.

She laid hold of him at once for her dreams. Here was one such as those Sons of God who saw the daughters of men, that they were fair. He was no son of Adam. Adam was servile. Had not Adam been driven cringing out of his native place, had not the human race been a beggar ever since, seeking its own being? But Anton Skrebensky could not beg. He was in possession of himself, of that, and no more. Other people could not really give him anything nor take anything from him. His soul stood alone.

She knew that her mother and father acknowledged him. The house was changed. There had been a visit paid to the house. Once three angels stood in Abraham's doorway, and greeted him, and stayed and ate with him, leaving his household enriched for ever when they went.

The next day she went down to the Marsh according to invitation. The two men were not come home. Then, looking through the window, she saw the dogcart drive up, and Skrebensky leapt down. She saw him draw himself together, jump, laugh to her uncle, who was driving, then come towards her to the house. He was so spontaneous and revealed in his movements. He was isolated within his own clear, fine atmosphere, and as still as if fated.

His resting in his own fate gave him an appearance of indolence, almost of languor: he made no exuberant movement. When he sat down, he seemed to go loose, languid.

'We are a little late,' he said.

'Where have you been?'

'We went to Derby to see a friend of my father's.'

'Who?'

It was an adventure to her to put direct questions and get plain answers. She knew she might do it with this man.

'Why, he is a clergyman too – he is my guardian – one of them.'

Ursula knew that Skrebensky was an orphan.

'Where is really your home now?' she asked.

'My home? – I wonder. I am very fond of my colonel – Colonel Hepburn: then there are my aunts: but my real home, I suppose, is the army.'

'Do you like being on your own?'

His clear, greenish-grey eyes rested on her a moment, and, as he considered, he did not see her.

'I suppose so,' he said. 'You see my father – well, he was never acclimatised here. He wanted – I don't know what he wanted – but it was a strain. And my mother – I always knew she was too good to me. I could feel her being too good to me – my mother! Then I went away to school so early. And I must say, the outside world was always more naturally a home to me than the vicarage – I don't know why.'

'Do you feel like a bird blown out of its own latitude?' she asked, using a phrase she had met.

'No, no. I find everything very much as I like it.'

He seemed more and more to give her a sense of the vast world, a sense of distances and large masses of humanity. It drew her as a scent draws a bee from afar. But also it hurt her.

It was summer, and she wore cotton frocks. The third time he saw her she had on a dress with fine blue-and-white stripes, with a white collar, and a large white hat. It suited her golden, warm complexion.

'I like you best in that dress,' he said, standing with his head slightly on one side, and appreciating her in a perceiving, critical fashion.

She was thrilled with a new life. For the first time she was in love with a vision of herself: she saw as it were a fine little reflection of herself in his eyes. And she must act up to this: she must be beautiful. Her thoughts turned swiftly to clothes, her passion was to make a beautiful appearance. Her family looked on in amazement at the sudden transformation of Ursula. She became elegant, really elegant, in figured cotton frocks she made for herself, and hats she bent to her fancy. An inspiration was upon her.

He sat with a sort of languor in her grandmother's rocking-chair, rocking slowly, languidly, backward and forward, as Ursula talked to him.

'You are not poor, are you?' she said.

'Poor in money? I have about a hundred and fifty a year of my own – so I am poor or rich, as you like. I am poor enough, in fact.'

'But you will earn money?'

'I shall have my pay – I have my pay now. I've got my commission. That is another hundred and fifty.'

'You will have more, though?'

'I shan't have more than £200 a year for ten years to come. I shall always be poor, if I have to live on my pay.'

'Do you mind it?'

'Being poor? Not now – not very much. I may later. People – the officers, are good to me. Colonel Hepburn has a sort of fancy for me – he is a rich man, I suppose.'

A chill went over Ursula. Was he going to sell himself in some way?

'Is Colonel Hepburn married?'

'Yes – with two daughters.'

But she was too proud at once to care whether Colonel Hepburn's daughter wanted to marry him or not.

There came a silence. Gudrun entered, and Skrebensky still rocked languidly on the chair.

'You look very lazy,' said Gudrun.

'I am lazy,' he answered.

'You look really floppy,' she said.

'I am floppy,' he answered.

'Can't you stop?' asked Gudrun.

'No – it's the *perpetuum mobile.*'

'You look as if you hadn't a bone in your body.'

'That's how I like to feel.'

'I don't admire your taste.'

'That's my misfortune.'

And he rocked on.

Gudrun seated herself behind him, and as he rocked back, she caught his hair between her finger and thumb, so that it tugged him as he swung forward again. He took no notice. There was only the sound of the rockers on the floor. In silence, like a crab, Gudrun caught a strand of his hair each time he rocked back. Ursula flushed, and sat in some pain. She saw the irritation gathering on his brow.

At last he leapt up, suddenly, like a steel spring going off, and stood on the hearthrug.

'Damn it, *why* can't I rock?' he asked petulantly, fiercely.

Ursula loved him for his sudden, steel-like start out of the languor. He stood on the hearthrug fuming, his eyes gleaming with anger.

Gudrun laughed in her deep, mellow fashion.

'Men don't rock themselves,' she said.

'Girls don't pull men's hair,' he said.

Gudrun laughed again.

Ursula sat amused, but waiting. And he knew Ursula was waiting for him. It roused his blood. He had to go to her, to follow her call.

Once he drove her to Derby in the dog-cart. He belonged to the horsey set of the sappers. They had lunch in an inn, and went through the market, pleased with everything. He bought her a copy of *Wuthering Heights* from a bookstall. Then they found a little fair in progress and she said:

'My father used to take me in the swingboats.'

'Did you like it?' he asked.

'Oh, it was fine,' she said.

'Would you like to go now?'

'Love it,' she said, though she was afraid. But the prospect of doing an unusual, exciting thing was attractive to her.

He went straight to the stand, paid the money, and helped her to mount. He seemed to ignore everything but just what he was doing. Other people were mere objects of indifference to him. She would have liked to hang back, but she was more ashamed to retreat from him than to expose herself to the crowd or to dare the swingboat. His eyes laughed, and standing before her with his sharp, sudden figure, he set the boat swinging. She was not afraid, she was thrilled. His colour flushed, his eyes shone with a roused light, and she looked up at him, her face like a flower in the sun, so bright and attractive. So they rushed through the bright air, up at the sky as if flung from a catapult, then falling terribly back. She loved it. The motion seemed to fan their blood to fire, they laughed, feeling the flames.

After the swingboats, they went on the roundabouts to calm down, he twisting astride on his jerky wooden steed towards her, and always seeming at his ease, enjoying himself. A zest of antagonism to the convention made him fully himself. As they sat on the whirling carousal, with the music grinding out, she was aware of the people on the earth outside, and it seemed that he and she were riding carelessly over the faces of the crowd, riding for ever buoyantly, proudly, gallantly over the upturned faces of the crowd, moving on a high level, spurning the common mass.

When they must descend and walk away, she was unhappy, feeling like a giant suddenly cut down to ordinary level, at the mercy of the mob.

They left the fair, to return for the dog-cart. Passing the large church, Ursula most look in. But the whole interior was filled with scaffolding, fallen stone and rubbish were heaped on the floor, bits of plaster crunched underfoot, and the place re-echoed to the calling of secular voices and to blows of the hammer.

She had come to plunge in the utter gloom and peace for a moment, bringing all her yearning, that had returned on her uncontrolled after the reckless riding over the face of the crowd, in the fair. After pride, she wanted comfort, solace, for pride and scorn seemed to hurt her most of all.

And she found the immemorial gloom full of bits of falling plaster, and dust of floating plaster, smelling of old lime, having scaffolding and rubbish heaped about, dust cloths over the altar.

'Let us sit down a minute,' she said.

They sat unnoticed in the back pew, in the gloom, and she watched the dirty, disorderly work of bricklayers and plasterers. Workmen in heavy boots walking grinding down the aisles, calling out in a vulgar accent:

'Hi, mate, has them corner mouldin's come?'

There were shouts of coarse answer from the roof of the church. The place echoed desolate.

Skrebensky sat close to her. Everything seemed wonderful, if dreadful to her, the world tumbling into ruins, and she and he clambering unhurt, lawless over the face of it all. He sat close to her, touching her, and she was aware of his influence upon her. But she was glad. It excited her to feel the press of him upon her, as if his being were urging her to something.

As they drove home, he sat near to her. And when he swayed to the cart, he swayed in a voluptuous, lingering way, against her, lingering as he swung away to recover balance. Without speaking, he took her hand across, under the wrap, and with his unseeing face lifted to the road, his soul intent, he began with his one hand to unfasten the buttons of her glove, to push back her glove from her hand, carefully laying bare her hand. And the close-working, instinctive subtlety of his fingers upon her hand sent the young girl mad with voluptuous delight. His hand was so wonderful, intent as a living creature skilfully pushing and manipulating in the dark underworld, removing her glove and laying bare her palm, her fingers. Then his hand closed over hers, so firm, so close, as if the flesh knitted to one thing his hand and hers. Meanwhile his face watched the road and the ears of the horse, he drove with steady attention through the villages, and she sat beside him, rapt, glowing, blinded with a new light. Neither of them spoke. In outward attention they were entirely separate. But between them was the compact of his flesh with hers, in the hand-clasp.

Then, in a strange voice, affecting nonchalance and superficiality he said to her:

'Sitting in the church there reminded me of Ingram.'

'Who is Ingram?' she asked.

She also affected calm superficiality. But she knew that something forbidden was coming.

'He is one of the other men with me down at Chatham – a subaltern – but a year older than I am.'

'And why did the church remind you of him?'

'Well, he had a girl in Rochester, and they always sat in a particular corner in the cathedral for their love-making.'

'How nice!' she cried, impulsively.

They misunderstood each other.

'It had its disadvantages though. The verger made a row about it.'

'What a shame! Why shouldn't they sit in a cathedral?'

'I suppose they all think it a profanity – except you and Ingram and the girl.'

'I don't think it a profanity – I think it's right, to make love in a cathedral.'

She said this almost defiantly, in despite of her own soul.

He was silent.

'And was she nice?'

'Who? Emily? Yes, she was rather nice. She was a milliner, and she wouldn't be seen in the streets with Ingram. It was rather sad, really, because the verger spied on them, and got to know their names and them made a regular row. It was a common tale afterwards.'

'What did she do?'

'She went to London, into a big shop. Ingram still goes up to see her.'

'Does he love her?'

'It's a year and a half he's been with her now.'

'What was she like?'

'Emily? Little, shy-violet sort of girl with nice eyebrows.'

Ursula meditated this. It seemed like real romance of the outer world.

'Do all men have lovers?' she asked, amazed at her own temerity. But her hand was still fastened with his, and his face still had the same unchanging fixity of outward calm.

'They're always mentioning some amazing fine woman or other, and getting drunk to talk about her. Most of them dash up to London the moment they are free.'

'What for?'

'To some amazing fine woman or other.'

'What sort of woman?'

'Various. Her name changes pretty frequently, as a rule. One of the fellows is a perfect maniac. He keeps a suit-case always ready, and the instant he is at liberty, he bolts with it to the station, and changes in the train. No matter who is in the carriage, off he whips his tunic, and performs at least the top half of his toilet.'

Ursula quivered and wondered.

'Why is he in such a hurry?' she said.

Her throat was becoming hard and difficult.

'He's got a woman in his mind, I suppose.'

She was chilled, hardened. And yet this world of passions and lawlessness was fascinating to her. It seemed to her a splendid recklessness. Her adventure in life was beginning. It seemed very splendid.

That evening she stayed at the Marsh till after dark, and Skrebensky escorted her home. For she could not go away from him. And she was waiting, waiting for something more.

In the warm of the early night, with the shadows new about them, she felt in another, harder, more beautiful, less personal world. Now a new state should come to pass.

He walked near to her, and with the same, silent, intent approach put his arm round her waist, and softly, very softly, drew her to him, till his arm was hard and pressed in upon her: she seemed to be carried along, floating, her feet scarce touching the ground, borne upon the firm, moving surface of his body, upon whose side she seemed to lie, in a delicious swoon of motion. And whilst she swooned, his face bent nearer to her, her head was leaned on his shoulder, she felt his warm breath on her face. Then softly, oh softly, so softly that she seemed to faint away, his lips touched her cheek, and she drifted through strands of heat and darkness.

Still she waited, in her swoon and her drifting, waited, like the Sleeping Beauty in the story. She waited, and again his face was bent to hers, his lips came warm to her face, their footsteps lingered and ceased, they stood still under the trees, whilst his lips waited on her face, waited like a butterfly that does not move on a flower. She pressed her breast a little nearer to him, he moved, put both his arms around her, and drew her close.

And then, in the darkness, he bent to her mouth, softly, and touched her mouth with his mouth. She was afraid, she lay still on his arm, feeling his lips on her lips. She kept still, helpless. Then his mouth drew near, pressing open her mouth, a hot, drenching surge rose within her, she opened her lips to him, in pained, poignant eddies she drew him nearer, she let him come farther, his lips came and surging, surging, soft, oh soft, yet oh, like the powerful surge of water, irresistible, till with a little blind cry, she broke away.

She heard him breathing heavily, strangely, beside her. A terrible and magnificent sense of his strangeness possessed her. But she shrank a little now, within herself. Hesitating, they continued to walk on, quivering like shadows under the ash trees of the hill, where her grandfather had walked with his daffodils to make his proposal, and where her mother had gone with her young husband, walking close upon him as Ursula was now walking upon Skrebensky.

Ursula was aware of the dark limbs of the trees stretching overhead, clothed with leaves, and of fine ash leaves tressing the summer night.

They walked with their bodies moving in complex unity, close together. He held her hand, and they went the long way round by the road, to be farther. Always she felt as if she were supported off her feet, as if her feet were light as little breezes in motion.

He would kiss her again – but not again that night with the same deep-reaching kiss. She was aware now, aware of what a kiss might be. And so, it was more difficult to come to him.

She went to bed feeling all warm with electric warmth, as if the gush of dawn were within her, upholding her. And she slept deeply, sweetly, oh, so sweetly. In the morning she felt sound as an ear of wheat, fragrant and firm and full.

They continued to be lovers, in the first wondering state of unrealisation. Ursula told nobody; she was entirely lost in her own world.

Yet some strange affectation made her seek for a spurious confidence. She had at school a quiet, meditative, serious-souled friend called Ethel, and to Ethel must Ursula confide the story. Ethel listened absorbedly, with bowed, unbetraying head, whilst Ursula told her secret. Oh, it was so lovely, his gentle, delicate way of making love! Ursula talked like a practised lover.

'Do you think,' asked Ursula, 'it is wicked to let a man kiss you – *real* kisses, not flirting?'

'I should think,' said Ethel, 'it depends.'

'He kissed me under the ash trees on Cossethay hill – do you think it was wrong?'

'When?'

'On Thursday night when he was seeing me home – but real kisses – real—. He is an officer in the army.'

'What time was it?' asked the deliberate Ethel.

'I don't know – about half-past nine.'

There was a pause.

'*I* think it's wrong,' said Ethel, lifting her head with impatience. 'You don't know him.'

She spoke with some contempt.

'Yes, I do. He is half a Pole, and a Baron too. In England he is equivalent to a Lord. My grandmother was his father's friend.'

But the two friends were hostile. It was as if Ursula *wanted* to divide herself from her acquaintances, in asserting her connection with Anton, as she now called him.

He came a good deal to Cossethay, because her mother was fond of him. Anna Brangwen became something of a *grande dame* with Skrebensky, very calm, taking things for granted.

'Aren't the children in bed?' cried Ursula petulantly, as she came in with the young man.

'They will be in bed in half an hour,' said the mother.

'There is no peace,' cried Ursula.

'The children must *live*, Ursula,' said her mother.

And Skrebensky was against Ursula in this. Why should she be so insistent?

But then, as Ursula knew, he did not have the perpetual tyranny of young children about him. He treated her mother with great courtliness, to which Mrs. Brangwen returned an easy, friendly hospitality. Something pleased the girl in her mother's calm assumption of state. It seemed impossible to abate Mrs. Brangwen's position. She could never be beneath anyone in public relation. Between Brangwen and Skrebensky there was an unbridgeable silence. Sometimes the two men made a slight conversation, but there was no interchange. Ursula rejoiced to see her father retreating into himself against the young man.

She was proud of Skrebensky in the house. His lounging, languorous indifference irritated her and yet cast a spell over her. She knew it was the outcome of a spirit of *laissez-aller* combined with profound young vitality. Yet it irritated her deeply.

Notwithstanding, she was proud of him as he lounged in his lambent fashion in her home, he was so attentive and courteous to her mother and to herself all the time. It was wonderful to have his awareness in the room. She felt rich and augmented by it, as if she were the positive attraction and he the flow towards her. And his courtesy and his agreement might be all her mother's, but the lambent flicker of his body was for herself. She held it.

She must ever prove her power.

'I meant to show you my little wood-carving,' she said.

'I'm sure it's not worth showing, that,' said her father.

'Would you like to see it?' she asked, leaning towards the door.

And his body had risen from the chair, though his face seemed to want to agree with her parents.

'It is in the shed,' she said.

And he followed her out of the door, whatever his feelings might be.

In the shed they played at kisses, really played at kisses. It was a delicious, exciting game. She turned to him, her face all laughing, like a challenge. And he accepted the challenge at once. He twined his hand full of her hair, and gently, with his hand wrapped round with hair behind her head, gradually brough her face nearer to his, whilst she laughed breathless with challenge, and his eyes gleamed with answer, with enjoyment of the game. And he kissed her, asserting his will over her, and she kissed him back, asserting her deliberate enjoyment of him. Daring and reckless and dangerous they knew it was, their game, each playing with fire, not with love. A sort of defiance of all the world possessed her in it – she would kiss him just because she wanted to. And a dare-devilry in him, like a cynicism, a cut at everything he pretended to serve, retaliated in him.

She was very beautiful then, so wide opened, so radiant, so palpitating, exquisitely vulnerable and poignantly, wrongly, throwing herself to risk. It roused a sort of madness in him. Like a flower shaking and wide-opened in the sun, she tempted him and challenged him, and he accepted the challenge, something went fixed in him. And under all her laughing, poignant reck-lessness was the quiver of tears. That almost sent him mad, mad with desire, with pain, whose only issue was through possession of her body.

So, shaken, afraid, they went back to her parents in the kitchen, and dissimulated. But something was roused in both of them that they could not now allay. It intensified and heightened their senses, they were more vivid, and powerful in their being. But under it all was a poignant sense of transcience. It was a magnificent self-assertion on the part of both of them, he asserted himself before her, he felt himself infinitely male and infinitely irresistible, she asserted herself before him, she knew herself infinitely desirable, and hence infinitely strong. And after all, what could either of them get from such a passion but a sense of his or of her own maximum self, in contradistinction to all the rest of life? Wherein was something finite and sad, for the human soul at its maximum wants a sense of the infinite.

Nevertheless, it was begun now, this passion, and must go on, the passion of Ursula to know her own maximum self, limited and so defined against him. She could limit and define herself against him, the male, she could be her maximum self, female, oh female, triumphant for one moment in exquisite assertion against the male, in supreme contradistinction to the male.

The next afternoon, when he came, prowling, she went with him across to the church. Her father was gradually gathering in anger against him, her mother was hardening in anger against her. But the parents were naturally tolerant in action.

They went together across the churchyard, Ursula and Skrebensky, and ran to hiding in the church. It was dimmer in there than the sunny afternoon outside, but the mellow glow among the bowed stone was very sweet. The windows burned in ruby and in blue, they made magnificent arras to their bower of secret stone.

'What a perfect place for a *rendezvous*,' he said, in a hushed voice, glancing round.

She too glanced round the familiar interior. The dimness and stillness chilled her. But her eyes lit up with daring. Here, here she would assert her indomitable gorgeous female self, here. Here she would open her female flower like a flame, in this dimness that was more passionate than light.

They hung apart a moment, then wilfully turned to each other for the desired contact. She put her arms round him, she cleaved her body by his, and with her hands pressed upon his shoulders, on his back, she seemed to feel right through him, to know his young, tense body right through. And it was so fine, so hard, yet so exquisitely subject and under her control. She reached him her mouth and drank his full kiss, drank it fuller and fuller.

And it was so good, it was very, very good. She seemed to be filled with his kiss, filled as if she had drunk strong, glowing sunshine. She glowed all inside, the sunshine seemed to beat upon her heart underneath, she had drunk so beautifully.

She drew away, and looked at him radiant, exquisitely, glowingly beautiful, and satisfied, but radiant as an illumined cloud.

To him this was bitter, that she was so radiant and satisfied. She laughed upon him, blind to him, so full of her own bliss, never doubting but that he was the same as she was. And radiant as an angel she went with him out of the church, as if her feet were beams of light that walked on flowers for footsteps.

He went beside her, his soul clenched, his body unsatisfied. Was she going to make this easy triumph over him? For him, there was now no self-bliss, only pain and confused anger.

It was high summer, and the hay-harvest was almost over. It would be finished on Saturday. On Saturday, however, Skrebensky was going away. He could not stay any longer.

Having decided to go he became very tender and loving to her, kissing her gently, with such soft, sweet, insidious closeness that they were both of them intoxicated.

The very last Friday of his stay he met her coming out of school, and took her to tea in the town. Then he had a motor-car to drive her home.

Her excitement at riding in a motor-car was greatest of all. He too was very proud of this last *coup*. He saw Ursula kindle and flare up to the romance of the situation. She raised her head like a young horse snuffing with wild delight.

The car swerved round a corner, and Ursula was swung against Skrebensky. The contact made her aware of him. With a swift, foraging impulse she sought for his hand and clasped it in her own, so close, so combined, as if they were two children.

The wind blew in on Ursula's face, the mud flew in a soft, wild rush from the wheels, the country was blackish green, with the silver of new hay here and there, and masses of trees under a silver-gleaming sky.

Her hand tightened on his with a new consciousness, troubled. They did not speak for some time, but sat, hand-fast, with averted, shining faces.

And every now and then the car swung her against him. And they waited for the motion to bring them together. Yet they stared out of the windows, mute.

She saw the familiar country racing by. But now, it was no familiar country, it was wonderland. There was the Hemlock Stone standing on its grassy hill. Strange it looked on this wet, early summer evening, remote, in a magic land. Some rooks were flying out of the trees.

Ah, if only she and Skrebensky could get out, dismount into this enchanted land where nobody had ever been before! Then they would be enchanted people, they would put off the dull, customary self. If she were wandering there, on that hill-slope under a silvery, changing sky, in which many rooks melted like hurrying showers of blots! If they could walk past the wetted hay-swaths, smelling the early evening, and pass in to the wood where the honeysuckle scent was sweet on the cold tang in the air, and showers of drops fell when one brushed a bough, cold and lovely on the face!

But she was here with him in the car, close to him, and the wind was rushing on her lifted, eager face, blowing back the hair. He turned and looked at her, at her face clean as a chiselled thing, her hair chiselled back by the wind, her fine nose keen and lifted.

It was agony to him, seeing her swift and clean-cut and virgin. He wanted to kill himself, and throw his detested carcase to her feet. His desire to turn round on himself and rend himself was an agony to him.

Suddenly she glanced at him. He seemed to be crouching towards her, reaching, he seemed to wince between the brows. But instantly, seeing her lighted eyes and radiant face, his expression changed, his old reckless laugh shone to her. She pressed his hand in utter delight, and he abided. And suddenly she stooped and kissed his hand, bent her head and caught it to her mouth, in generous homage. And the blood burned in him. Yet he remained still, he made no move.

She started. They were swinging into Cossethay. Skrebensky was going to leave her. But it was all so magic, her cup was so full of bright wine, her eyes could only shine.

He tapped and spoke to the man. The car swung up by the yew trees. She gave him her hand and said good-bye, naïve and brief as a schoolgirl. And she stood watching him go, her face shining. The fact of his driving on meant nothing to her, she was so filled by her own bright ecstacy. She did not see him, go, for she was filled with light, which was of him. Bright with an amazing light as she was, how could she miss him.

In her bedroom she threw her arms in the air in clear pain of magnificence. Oh, it was her transfiguration, she was beyond herself. She wanted to fling herself into all the hidden brightness of the air. It was there, it was there, if she could but meet it.

But the next day she knew he had gone. Her glory had partly died down – but never from her memory. It was too real. Yet it was gone by, leaving a wistfulness. A deeper yearning came into her soul, a new reserve.

She shrank from touch and question. She was very proud, but very new, and very sensitive. Oh, that no one should lay hands on her!

She was happier running on by herself. Oh, it was a joy to run along the lanes without seeing things, yet being with them. It was such a joy to be alone with all one's riches.

The holidays came, when she was free. She spent most of her time running on by herself, curled up in a squirrel-place in the garden, lying in a hammock in the coppice, while the birds came near – near – so near. Oh, in rainy weather, she flitted to the Marsh, and lay hidden with her book in a hay-loft.

All the time, she dreamed of him, sometimes definitely, but when she was happiest, only vaguely. He was the warm colouring of her dreams, he was the hot blood beating within them.

When she was less happy, out of sorts, she pondered over his appearance, his clothes, the buttons with his regimental badge, which he had given her. Or she tried to imagine his life in barracks. Or she conjured up a vision of herself as she appeared in his eyes.

His birthday was in August, and she spent some pains on making him a cake. She felt that it would not be in good taste for her to give him a present.

Their correspondence was brief, mostly an exchange of post-cards, not at all frequent. But with her cake she must send him a letter.

'Dear Anton. The sunshine has come back specially for your birthday, I think.

'I made the cake myself, and wish you many happy returns of the day. Don't eat it if it is not good. Mother hopes you will come and see us when you are near enough.

> *'I am*
> *'Your sincere friend,*
> *'Ursula Brangwen.'*

It bored her to write a letter even to him. After all, writing words on paper had nothing to do with him or her.

The fine weather had set in, the cutting machine went on from dawn till sunset, chattering round the fields. She heard from Skrebensky; he too was on duty in the country, on Salisbury Plain. He was now a second lieutenant in a Field Troop. He would have a few days off shortly, and would come to the Marsh for the wedding.

Fred Brangwen was going to marry a schoolmistress out of Ilkeston as soon as corn-harvest was at an end.

The dim blue-and-gold of a hot, sweet autumn saw the close of the corn-harvest. To Ursula, it was as if the world had opened its softest purest flower, its chicory flower, its meadow saffron. The sky was blue and sweet, the yellow leaves down the lane seemed like free, wandering flowers as they chittered round the feet, making a keen, poignant, almost unbearable music to her heart. And the scents of autumn were like a summer madness to her. She fled away from the little, purple-red button-chrysanthemums like a frightened dryad, the bright yellow little chrysanthemums smelled so strong, her feet seemed to dither in a drunken dance.

Then her Uncle Tom appeared, always like the cynical Bacchus in the picture. He would have a jolly wedding, a harvest supper and a wedding feast in one: a tent in the home close, and a band for dancing, and a great feast out of doors.

Fred demurred, but Tom must be satisfied. Also Laura, a handsome, clever girl, the bride, she also must have a great and jolly feast. It appealed to her educated sense. She had been to Salisbury Training College, knew folk-songs and morris-dancing.

So the preparations were begun, directed by Tom Brangwen. A marquee was set up on the home close, two large bonfires were prepared. Musicians were hired, feast made ready.

Skrebensky was to come, arriving in the morning. Ursula had a new white dress of soft crêpe, and a white hat. She liked to wear white. With her black hair and clear golden skin, she looked southern, or rather tropical, like a Creole. She wore no colour whatsoever.

She trembled that day as she appeared to go down to the wedding. She was to be a bridesmaid. Skrebensky would not arrive till afternoon. The wedding was at two o'clock.

As the wedding-party returned home, Skrebensky stood in the parlour at the Marsh. Through the window he saw Tom Brangwen, who was the best man, coming up the garden path most elegant in cut-away coat and white slip and spats, with Ursula laughing on his arm. Tom Brangwen was handsome, with his womanish colouring and dark eyes and black close-cut moustache. But there was something subtly coarse and suggestive about him for all his beauty; his strange, bestial nostrils opened so hard and wide, and his well-shaped head almost disquieting in its nakedness, rather bald from the front, and all its soft fulness betrayed.

Skrebensky saw the man rather than the woman. She saw only the slender, unchangeable youth waiting there inscrutable, like her fate. He was beyond her, with his loose, slightly horsey appearance, that made him seem very manly and foreign. Yet his face was smooth and soft and impressionable.

She shook hands with him, and her voice was like the rousing of a bird startled by the dawn.

'Isn't it nice,' she cried, 'to have a wedding?'

There were bits of coloured confetti lodged on her dark hair.

Again the confusion came over him, as if he were losing himself and becoming all vague, undefined, inchoate. Yet he wanted to be hard, manly, horsey. And he followed her.

There was a light tea, and the guests scattered. The real feast was for the evening. Ursula walked out with Skrebensky through the stackyard to the fields, and up the embankment to the canal-side.

The new corn-stacks were big and golden as they went by, an army of white geese marched aside in braggart protest. Ursula was light as a white ball of down. Skrebensky drifted beside her, indefinite, his old form loosened, and another self, grey, vague, drifting out as from a bud. They talked lightly, of nothing.

The blue way of the canal wound softly between the autumn hedges, on towards the greenness of a small hill. On the left was the whole black agitation of colliery and railway and the town which rose on its hill, the church tower topping all. The round white dot of the clock on the tower was distinct in the evening light.

That way, Ursula felt, was the way to London, through the grim, alluring seethe of the town. On the other hand was the evening, mellow over the green water-meadows and the winding alder trees beside the river, and the pale stretches of stubble beyond. There the evening glowed softly, and even a pee-wit was flapping in solitude and peace.

Ursula and Anton Skrebensky walked along the ridge of the canal between. The berries on the hedges were crimson and bright red, above the leaves. The glow of evening and the wheeling of the solitary pee-wit and the faint cry of the birds came to meet the shuffling noise of the pits, the dark, fuming stress of the town opposite, and they two walked the blue strip of water-way, the ribbon of sky between.

He was looking, Ursula thought, very beautiful, because of a flush of sunburn on his hands and face. He was telling her how he had learned to shoe horses and select cattle fit for killing.

'Do you like to be a soldier?' she asked.

'I am not exactly a soldier,' he replied.

'But you only do things for wars,' she said.

'Yes.'

'Would you like to go to war?'

'I? Well, it would be exciting. If there were a war I would want to go.'

A strange, distracted feeling came over her, a sense of potent unrealities.

'Why would you want to go?'

'I should be doing something, it would be genuine. It's a sort of toy-life as it is.'

'But what would you be doing if you went to war?'

'I would be making railways or bridges, working like a nigger.'

'But you'd only make them to be pulled down again when the armies had done with them. It seems just as much a game.'

'If you call war a game.'

'What is it?'

'It's about the most serious business there is, fighting.'

A sense of hard separateness came over her.

'Why is fighting more serious than anything else?' she asked.

'You either kill or get killed – and I suppose it is serious enough, killing.'

'But when you're dead you don't matter any more,' she said.

He was silenced for a moment.

'But the result matters,' he said. 'It matters whether we settle the Mahdi or not.'

'Not to you – nor me – we don't care about Khartoum.'

'You want to have room to live in: and somebody has to make room.'

'But I don't want to live in the desert of Sahara – do you?' she replied, laughing with antagonism.

'*I* don't – but we've got to back up those who do.

'Why have we?'

'Where is the nation if we don't?'

'But we aren't the nation. There are heaps of other people who are the nation.'

'They might say *they* weren't either.'

'Well, if everybody said it, there wouldn't be a nation. But I should still be myself,' she asserted brilliantly.

'You wouldn't be yourself if there were no nation.'

'Why not?'

'Because you'd just be a prey to everybody and anybody.'

'How a prey?'

'They'd come and take everything you'd got.'

'Well, they couldn't take much even then. I don't care what they take. I'd rather have a robber who carried me off than a millionaire who gave me everything you can buy.'

'That's because you are a romanticist.'

'Yes, I am. I want to be romantic. I hate houses that never go away, and people just living in the houses. It's all so stiff and stupid. I hate soldiers, they are stiff and wooden. What do you fight for, really?'

'I would fight for the nation.'

'For all that, you aren't the nation. What would you do for yourself?'

'I belong to the nation and must do my duty by the nation.'

'But when it didn't need your services in particular – when there *is* no fighting? What would you do then?'

He was irritated.

'I would do what everybody else does.'

'What?'

'Nothing. I would be in readiness for when I was needed.'

The answer came in exasperation.

'It seems to me,' she answered, 'as if you weren't anybody – as if there weren't anybody there, where you are. Are you anybody, really? You seem like nothing to me.'

They had walked till they had reached a wharf, just above a lock. There an empty barge, painted with a red and yellow cabin hood, but with a long, coal-black hold, was lying moored. A man, lean and grimy, was sitting on a box against the cabin-side by the door, smoking, and nursing a baby that was wrapped in a drab shawl, and looking into the glow of evening. A woman bustled out, sent a pail dashing into the canal, drew her water, and bustled in again. Children's voices were heard. A thin blue smoke ascended from the cabin chimney, there was a smell of cooking.

Ursula, white as a moth, lingered to look. Skrebensky lingered by her. The man glanced up.

'Good evening,' he called, half impudent, half attracted. He had blue eyes which glanced impudently from his grimy face.

'Good evening,' said Ursula, delighted. '*Isn't* it nice, now?'

'Ay,' said the man, 'very nice.'

His mouth was red under his ragged, sandy moustache. His teeth were white as he laughed.

'Oh, but—' stammered Ursula, laughing, 'it *is*. Why do you say it as if it weren't?'

''Appen for them as is childt-nursin' it's none so rosy.'

'May I look inside your barge?' asked Ursula.

'There's nobody'll stop you; you come if you like.'

The barge lay at the opposite bank, at the wharf. It was the *Annabel*, belong to J. Ruth of Loughborough. The man watched Ursula closely from his keen, twinkling eyes. His fair hair was wispy on his grimed forehead. Two dirty children appeared to see who was talking.

Ursula glanced at the great lock gates. They were shut, and the water was sounding, spurting and trickling down in the gloom beyond. On this side the bright water was almost to the top of the gate. She went boldly across, and round to the wharf.

Stooping from the bank, she peeped into the cabin, where was a red glow of fire and the shadowy figure of a woman. She *did* want to go down.

'You'll mess your frock,' said the man, warningly.

'I'll be careful,' she answered. 'May I come?'

'Ay, come if you like.'

She gathered her skirts, lowered her foot to the side of the boat, and leapt down, laughing. Coal-dust flew up.

The woman came to the door. She was plump and sandy-haired, young, with an odd, stubby nose.

'Oh, you *will* make a mess of yourself,' she cried, surprised and laughing with a little wonder.

'I did want to see. Isn't it lovely living on a barge?' asked Ursula.

'I don't live on one altogether,' said the woman cheerfully.

'She's got her parlour an' her plush suite in Loughborough,' said her husband with just pride.

Ursula peeped into the cabin, where saucepans were boiling and some dishes were on the table. It was very hot. Then she came out again. The man was talking to the baby. It was a blue-eyed, fresh-faced thing with floss of red-gold hair.

'Is it a boy or a girl?' she asked.

'It's a girl – aren't you a girl, eh?' he shouted at the infant, shaking his head. Its little face wrinkled up into the oddest, funniest smile.

'Oh!' cried Ursula. 'Oh, the dear! Oh, how nice when she laughs!'

'She'll laugh hard enough,' said the father.

'What is her name?' asked Ursula.

'She hasn't got a name, she's not worth one,' said the man. 'Are you, you fag-end o' nothing?' he shouted to the baby. The baby laughed.

'No we've been that busy, we've never took her to th' registry office,' came the woman's voice. 'She was born on th' boat here.'

'But you know what you're going to call her?' asked Ursula.

'We did think of Gladys Em'ly,' said the mother.

'We thought of nowt o' th' sort,' said the father.

'Hark at him! What *do* you want?' cried the mother in exasperation.

'She'll be called Annabel after th' boat she was born on.'

'She's not, so there,' said the mother, viciously defiant.

The father sat in humorous malice, grinning.

'Well, you'll see,' he said.

And Ursula could tell, by the woman's vibrating exasperation, that he would never give way.

'They're all nice names,' she said. 'Call her Gladys Annabel Emily.'

'Nay, that's heavy-laden, if you like,' he answered.

'You see!' cried the woman. 'He's that *pig-headed!*'

'And she's so nice, and she laughs, and she hasn't even got a name,' crooned Ursula to the child.

'Let me hold her,' she added.

He yielded her the child, that smelt of babies. But it had such blue, wide, china blue eyes, and it laughed so oddly, with such a taking grimace, Ursula loved it. She cooed and talked to it. It was such as odd, exciting child.

'What's *your* name?' the man suddenly asked of her.

'My name is Ursula – Ursula Brangwen,' she replied.

'Ursula!' he exclaimed, dumbfounded.

'There was a Saint Ursula. It's a very old name,' she added hastily, in justification.

'Hey, mother!' he called.

There was no answer.

'Pem!' he called, 'can't y'hear?'

'What?' came the short answer.

'What about "Ursula"?' he grinned.

'What about *what?*' came the answer, and the woman appeared in the doorway, ready for combat.

'Ursula – it's the lass's name there,' he said, gently.

The woman looked the young girl up and down. Evidently she was attracted by her slim, graceful, new beauty, her effect of white elegance, and her tender way of holding the child.

'Why, how do you write it?' the mother asked, awkward now she was touched. Ursula spelled out her name. The man looked at the woman. A bright, confused flush came over the mother's face, a sort of luminous shyness.

'It's not a *common* name, is it!' she exclaimed, excited as by an adventure.

'Are you goin' to have it then?' he asked.

'I'd rather have it than Annabel,' she said, decisively.

'An' I'd rather have it than Gladys Em'ler,' he replied.

There was a silence, Ursula looked up.

'Will you really call her Ursula?' she asked.

'Ursula Ruth,' replied the man, laughing vainly, as pleased as if he had found something.

It was now Ursula's turn to be confused.

'It *does* sound awfully nice,' she said. 'I *must* give her something. And I haven't got anything at all.'

She stood in her white dress, wondering, down there in the barge. The lean man sitting near to her watched her as if she were a strange being, as if she lit up his face. His eyes smiled on her, boldly, and yet with exceeding admiration underneath.

'Could I give her my necklace?' she said.

It was the little necklace made of pieces of amethyst and topaz and pearl and crystal, strung at intervals on a little golden chain, which her Uncle Tom had given her. She was very fond of it. She looked at it lovingly, when she had taken it from her neck.

'Is it valuable?' the man asked her, curiously.

'I think so,' she replied.

'The stones and pearl are real; it is worth three or four pounds,' said Skrebensky from the wharf above. Ursula could tell he disapproved of her.

'I *must* give it to your baby – may I?' she said to the bargee.

He flushed, and looking away into the evening.

'Nay,' he said, 'it's not for me to say.'

'What would your father and mother say?' cried the woman curiously, from the door.

'It is my own,' said Ursula, and she dangled the little glittering string before the baby. The infant spread its little fingers. But it could not grasp. Ursula closed the tiny hand over the jewel. The baby waved the bright ends of the string. Ursula had given her necklace away. She felt sad. But she did not want it back.

The jewel swung from the baby's hand and fell in a little heap on the coal-dusty bottom of the barge. The man groped for it, with a kind of careful reverence. Ursula noticed the coarsened, blunted fingers groping at the little jewelled heap. The skin was red on the back of the hand, the fair hairs glistened stiffly. It was a thin, sinewy, capable hand nevertheless, and Ursula liked it. He took up the necklace carefully, and blew the coal-dust from it, as it lay in the hollow of his hand. He seemed still and attentive. He held out his hand with the necklace shining small in its hard, black hollow.

'Take it back,' he said.

Ursula hardened with a kind of radiance.

'No,' she said. 'It belongs to little Ursula.'

And she went to the infant and fastened the necklace round its warm, soft, weak little neck.

There was a moment of confusion, then the father bent over his child:

'What do you say?' he said. 'Do you say thank you? Do you say thank you, Ursula?'

'Her name's Ursula *now*,' said the mother, smiling a little bit ingratiatingly from the door. And she came out to examine the jewel on the child's neck.

'It *is* Ursula, isn't it?' said Ursula Brangwen.

The father looked up at her, with an intimate, half-gallant, half-impudent, but wistful look. His captive soul loved her: but his soul was captive, he knew, always.

She wanted to go. He set a little ladder for her to climb up to the wharf. She kissed the child, which was in its mother's arms, then she turned away. The mother was effusive. The man stood silent by the ladder.

Ursula joined Skrebensky. The two young figures crossed the lock, above the shining yellow water. The barge-man watched them go.

'I *loved* them,' she was saying. 'He was so gentle – oh, so gentle! And the baby was such a dear!'

'Was he gentle?' said Skrebensky. 'The woman had been a servant, I'm sure of that.'

Ursula winced.

'But I loved his impudence – it was so gentle underneath.'

She went hastening on, gladdened by having met the grimy, lean man with the ragged moustache. He gave her a pleasant warm feeling. He made her feel the richness of her own life. Skrebensky, somehow, had created a deadness round her, a sterility, as if the world were ashes.

They said very little as they hastened home to the big supper. He was envying the lean father of three children, for his impudent directness and his worship of the woman in Ursula, a worship of body and soul together, the man's body and soul wistful and worshipping the body and spirit of the girl, with a desire that knew the inaccessibility of its object, but was only glad to know that the perfect thing existed, glad to have had a moment of communion.

Why could not he himself desire a woman so? Why did he never really want a woman, not with the whole of him: never loved, never worshipped, only just physically wanted her.

But he would want her with his body, let his soul do as it would. A kind of flame of physical desire was gradually beating up in the Marsh, kindled by Tom Brangwen, and by the fact of the wedding of Fred, the shy, fair, stiff-set farmer with the handsome, half-educated girl. Tom Brangwen, with all his secret power, seemed to fan the flame that was rising. The bride was strongly attracted by him, and he was exerting his influence on another beautiful, fair girl, chill and burning as the sea, who said witty things which he appreciated, making her glint with more, like phosphorescence. And her greenish eyes seemed to rock a secret, and her hands like mother-of-pearl seemed luminous, transparent, as if the secret were burning visible in them.

At the end of supper, during dessert, the music began to play, violins, and flutes. Everybody's face was lit up. A glow of excitement prevailed. When the little speeches were over, and the port remained unreached for any more, those who wished were invited out to the open for coffee. The night was warm.

Bright stars were shining, the moon was not yet up. And under the stars burned two great, red, flameless fires, and round these lights and lanterns hung, the marquee stood open before a fire, with its lights inside.

The young people flocked out into the mysterious night. There was sound of laughter and voices, and a scent of coffee. The farm-buildings loomed dark in the background. Figures, pale and dark, flitted about, intermingling. The red fire glinted on a white or a silken shirt, the lanterns gleamed on the transient heads of the wedding guests.

To Ursula it was wonderful. She felt she was a new being. The darkness seemed to breathe like the sides of some great beast, the haystacks loomed half-revealed, a crowd of them, a dark, fecund lair just behind. Waves of delirious darkness ran through her soul. She wanted to let go. She wanted to reach and be amongst the flashing stars, she wanted to race with her feet and be beyond the confines of this earth. She was made to be gone. It was as if a hound were straining on the leash, ready to hurl itself after a nameless quarry into the dark. And she was the quarry, and she was also the hound. The darkness was passionate and breathing with immense, unperceived heaving. It was waiting to receive her in her flight. And how could she start – and how could she let go? She must leap from the known into the unknown. Her feet and hands beat like a madness, her breast strained as if in bonds.

The music began, and the bonds began to slip. Tom Brangwen was dancing with the bride, quick and fluid and as if in another element, inaccessible as the creatures that move in the water. Fred Brangwen went in with another partner. The music came in waves. One couple after another was washed and absorbed into the deep underwater of the dance.

'Come,' said Ursula to Skrebensky, laying her hand on his arm.

At the touch of her hand on his arm, his consciousness melted away from him. He took her into his arms, as if into the sure, subtle power of his will, and they became one movement, one dual movement, dancing on the slippery grass. It would be endless, this movement, it would continue for ever. It was his will and her will locked in a trance of motion, two wills locked in one motion, yet never fusing, never yielding one to the other. It was a glaucous, intertwining, delicious flux and contest in flux.

They were both absorbed into a profound silence, into a deep, fluid underwater energy that gave them unlimited strength. All the dancers were waving intertwined in the flux of music. Shadowy couples passed and repassed before the fire, the dancing feet danced silently by into the darkness. It was a vision of the depths of the underworld, under the great flood.

There was a wonderful rocking of the darkness, slowly, a great, slow swinging of the whole night, with the music playing lightly on the surface, making the strange, ecstatic, rippling on the surface of the dance, but underneath only one great flood heaving slowly backwards to the verge of oblivion, slowly forward to the other verge, the heart sweeping along each time, and tightening with anguish as the limit was reached, and the move-ment, at crises, turned and swept back.

As the dance surged heavily on, Ursula was aware of some influence looking in upon her. Something was looking at her. Some powerful, glowing sight was looking right into her, not upon her, but right at her. Out of the great distance, and yet imminent, the powerful, overwhelming watch was kept upon her. And she danced on and on with Skrebensky, while the great, white watching continued, balancing all in its revelation.

'The moon has risen,' said Anton, as the music ceased, and they found themselves suddenly stranded, like bits of jetsam on a shore. She turned, and saw a great white moon looking at her over the hill. And her breast opened to it, she was cleaved like a transparent jewel to its light. She stood filled with the full moon, offering herself. Her two breasts opened to make way for it, her body opened wide like a quivering anemone, a soft, dilated invitation touched by the moon. She wanted the moon to fill in to her, she wanted more, more communion with the moon, consummation. But Skrebensky put his arm round her, and led her away. He put a big, dark cloak round her, and sat holding her hand, whilst the moonlight streamed above the glowing fires.

She was not there. Patiently she sat, under the cloak, with Skrebensky holding her hand. But her naked self was away there beating upon the moonlight, dashing the moonlight with her breasts and her knees, in meeting, in communion. She half started, to go in actuality, to fling away her clothing and flee away, away from this dark confusion and chaos of people to the hill and the moon. But the people stood round her like stones, like magnetic stones, and she could not go, in actuality. Skrebensky, like a load-stone weighed on her, the weight of his presence detained her. She felt the burden of him, the blind, persistent, inert burden. He was inert, and he weighed upon her. She sighed in pain. Oh, for the coolness and entire liberty and brightness of the moon. Oh, for the cold liberty to be herself, to be entirely as she liked. She wanted to get right away. She felt like bright metal weighted down by dark, impure magnetism. He was the dross, people were the dross. If she could but get away to the clean free moonlight.

'Don't you like me to-night?' said his low voice, the voice of the shadow over her shoulder. She clenched her hands in the dewy brilliance of the moon, as if she were mad.

'Don't you like me to-night?' repeated the soft voice.

And she knew that if she turned, she would die. A strange rage filled her, a rage to tear things asunder. Her hands felt destructive, like metal blades of destruction.

'Let me alone,' she said.

A darkness, an obstinacy settled on him too, in a kind of inertia. He sat inert beside her. She threw off her cloak and walked towards the moon, silver-white herself. He followed her closely.

The music began again and the dance. He appropriated her. There was a fierce, white, cold passion in her heart. But he held her close, and danced with her. Always present, like a soft weight upon her, bearing her down, was his body against her as they danced. He held her very close, so that she could feel his body, the weight of him sinking, settling upon her, overcoming her life and energy, making her inert along with him, she felt his hands pressing behind her, upon her. But still in her body was the subdued, cold, indomitable passion. She liked the dance: it eased her, put her into a sort of trance. But it was only a kind of waiting, of using up the time that intervened between her and her pure being. She left herself against him, she let him exert all his power over her, to bear her down. She received all the force of his power. She even wished he might overcome her. She was cold and unmoved as a pillar of salt.

His will was set and straining with all its tension to encompass him and compel her. If he could only compel her. He seemed to be annihilated. She was cold and hard and compact of brilliance as the moon itself, and beyond him as the moonlight was beyond him, never to be grasped or known. If he could only set a bond round her and compel her!

So they danced four or five dances, always together, always his will becoming more tense, his body more subtle, playing upon her. And still he had not got her, she was hard and bright as ever, intact. But he must weave himself round her, enclose her, enclose her in a net of shadow, of darkness, so she would be like a bright creature gleaming in a net of shadows, caught. Then he would have her, he would enjoy her. How he would enjoy her, when she was caught.

At last, when the dance was over, she would not sit down, she walked away. He came with his arm round her, keeping her upon the movement of his walking. And she seemed to agree. She was bright as a piece of moonlight, as bright as a steel blade, he seemed to be clasping a blade that hurt him. Yet he would clasp her, if it killed him.

They went towards the stackyard. There he saw, with some thing like terror, the great new stacks of corn glistening and gleaming transfigured, silvery and present under the night-blue sky, throwing dark, substantial shadows, but themselves majestic and dimly present. She, like glimmering gossamer, seemed to burn among them, as they rose like cold fires to the silvery-bluish air. All was intangible, a burning of cold, glimmering, whitish-steely fires. He was afraid of the great moon-conflagration of the cornstacks rising above him. His heart grew smaller, it began to fuse like a bead. He knew he would die.

She stood for some moments out in the overwhelming luminosity of the moon. She seemed a beam of gleaming power. She was afraid of what she was. Looking at him, at his shadowy, unreal, wavering presence a sudden lust seized her, to lay hold of him and tear him and make him into nothing. Her hands and wrists felt immeasurably hard and strong, like blades. He waited there beside her like a shadow which she wanted to dissipate, destroy as the moonlight destroys a darkness, annihilate, have done with. She looked at him and her face gleamed bright and inspired. She tempted him.

And an obstinacy in him made him put his arm round her and draw her to the shadow. She submitted: let him try what he could do. Let him try what he could do. He leaned against the side of the stack, holding her. The stack stung him keenly with a thousand cold, sharp flames. Still obstinately he held her.

And timorously, his hands went over her, over the salt, compact brilliance of her body. If he could but have her, how he would enjoy her! If he could but net her brilliant, cold, salt-burning body in the soft iron of his own hands, net her, capture her, hold her down, how madly he would enjoy her. He strove subtly, but with all his energy, to enclose her, to have her. And always she was burning and brilliant and hard as salt, and deadly. Yet obstinately, all his flesh burning and corroding, as if he were invaded by some consuming, scathing poison, still he persisted, thinking at last he might overcome her. Even, in his frenzy, he sought for her mouth with his mouth, though it was like putting his face into some awful death. She yielded to him, and he pressed himself upon her in extremity, his soul groaning over and over:

'Let me come – let me come.'

She took him in the kiss, hard her kiss seized upon him, hard and fierce and burning corrosive as the moonlight. She seemed to be destroying him. He was reeling, summoning all his strength to keep his kiss upon her, to keep himself in the kiss.

But hard and fierce she had fastened upon him, cold as the moon and burning as a fierce salt. Till gradually his warm, soft iron yielded, yielded, and she was there fierce, corrosive, seething with his destruction, seething like some cruel, corrosive salt around the last substance of his being, destroying him, destroying him in the kiss. And her soul crystallised with triumph, and his soul was dissolved with agony and annihilation. So she held him there, the victim, consumed, annihilated. She had triumphed: he was not any more.

Gradually she began to come to herself. Gradually a sort of daytime consciousness came back to her. Suddenly the night was struck back into its old, accustomed, mild reality. Gradually she realised that the night was common and ordinary, that the great, blistering, transcendent night did not really exist. She was overcome with slow horror. Where was she? What was this nothingness she felt? The nothingness was Skrebensky. Was he really there? – who was he? He was silent, he was not there. What had happened? Had she been mad: what horrible thing had possessed her? She was filled with overpowering fear of herself, overpowering desire that it should not be, that other burning, corrosive self. She was seized with a frenzied desire that what had been should never be remembered, never be thought of, never be for one moment allowed possible. She denied it with all her might. With all her might she turned away from it. She was good, she was loving. Her heart was warm, her blood was dark and warm and soft. She laid her hand caressively on Anton's shoulder.

'Isn't it lovely?' she said, softly, coaxingly, caressingly. And she began to caress him to life again. For he was dead. And she intended that he should never know, never become aware of what had been. She would bring him back from the dead without leaving him one trace of fact to remember his annihilation by.

She exerted all her ordinary, warm self, she touched him, she did him homage of loving awareness. And gradually he came back to her, another man. She was soft and winning and caressing. She was his servant, his adoring slave. And she restored the whole shell of him. She restored the whole form and figure of him. But the core was gone. His pride was bolstered up, his blood ran once more in pride. But there was no core to him: as a distinct male he had no core. His triumphant, flaming, overweening heart of the intrinsic male would never beat again. He would be subject now, reciprocal, never the indomitable thing with a core of overweening, unabateable fire. She had abated that fire, she had broken him.

But she caressed him. She would not have him remember what had been. She would not remember herself.

'Kiss me, Anton, kiss me,' she pleaded.

He kissed her, but she knew he could not touch her. His arms were round her, but they had not got her. She could feel his mouth upon her, but she was not at all compelled by it.

'Kiss me,' she whispered, in acute distress, 'kiss me.'

And he kissed her as she bade him, but his heart was hollow. She took his kisses, outwardly. But her soul was empty and finished.

Looking away, she saw the delicate glint of oats dangling from the side of the stack, in the moonlight, something proud and royal, and quite impersonal. She had been proud with them, where they were, she had been also. But in this temporary warm world of the commonplace, she was a kind, good girl. She reached out yearningly for goodness and affection. She wanted to be kind and good.

They went home through the night that was all pale and glowing around, with shadows and glimmerings and presences. Distinctly, she saw the flowers in the hedge-bottoms, she saw the thin, raked sheaves flung white upon the thorny hedge.

How beautiful, how beautiful it was! She thought with anguish how wildly happy she was to-night, since he had kissed her. But as he walked with his arm round her waist, she turned with a great offering of herself to the night that glistened tremendous, a magnificent godly moon white and candid as a bridegroom, flowers silvery and transformed filling up the shadows.

He kissed her again, under the yew trees at home, and she left him. She ran from the intrusion of her parents at home, to her bedroom, where, looking out on the moonlit country, she stretched up her arms, hard, hard, in bliss, agony offering herself to the blond, debonair presence of the night.

But there was a wound of sorrow, she had hurt herself, as if she had bruised herself, in annihilating him. She covered up her two young breasts with her hands, covering them to herself; and covering herself with herself, she crouched in bed, to sleep.

In the morning the sun shone, she got up strong and dancing. Skrebensky was still at the Marsh. He was coming to church. How lovely, how amazing life was! On the fresh Sunday morning she went out to the garden, among the yellows and the deep-vibrating reds of autumn, she smelled the earth and felt the gossamer, the cornfields across the country were pale and unreal, everywhere was the intense silence of the Sunday morning, filled with unacquainted noises. She smelled the body of the earth, it seemed to stir its powerful flank beneath her as she stood. In the bluish air came the powerful exudation, the peace was the peace of strong, exhausted breathing, the reds and yellows and the white gleam of stubble were the quivers and motion of the last subsiding transports and clear bliss of fulfilment.

The church-bells were ringing when he came. She looked up in keen anticipation at his entry. But he was troubled and his pride was hurt. He seemed very much clothed, she was conscious of his tailored suit.

'Wasn't it lovely last night?' she whispered to him.

'Yes,' he said. But his face did not open nor become free.

The service and the singing in church that morning passed unnoticed by her. She saw the coloured glow of the windows, the forms of the worshippers. Only she glanced at the book of Genesis, which was her favourite book in the Bible.

'And God blessed Noah and his sons, and said unto them, Be fruitful and multiply and replenish the earth.

'And the fear of you and the dread of you shall be upon every beast of the earth, and upon every fowl of the air, upon all that moveth upon the earth, and upon all the fishes in the sea; into your hand are they delivered.

'Every moving thing that liveth shall be meat for you; even as the green herb have I given you all things.'

But Ursula was not moved by the history this morning. Multiplying and replenishing the earth bored her. Altogether it seemed merely a vulgar and stock-raising sort of business. She was left quite cold by man's stock-breeding lordship over beast and fishes.

'And you, be ye fruitful and multiply; bring forth abundantly in the earth, and multiply therein.'

In her soul she mocked at this multiplication, every cow becoming two cows, every turnip ten turnips.

'And God said; This is the token of the covenant which I make between me and you and every living creature that is with you, for perpetual generations;

'I do set my bow in the cloud, and it shall be a token of a covenant between me and the earth.

'And it shall come to pass, when I bring a cloud over the earth, that a bow shall be seen in the cloud;

'And I will remember my covenant, which is between me and you and every living creature of all flesh, and the waters shall no more become a flood to destroy all flesh.'

'Destroy all flesh,' why 'flesh' in particular? Who was this lord of flesh? After all, how big was the Flood? Perhaps a few dryads and fauns had just run into the hills and the farther valleys and woods, frightened, but most had gone on blithely unaware of any flood at all, unless the nymphs should tell them. It pleased Ursula to think of the naiads in Asia Minor meeting the nereids at the mouth of the streams, where the sea washed against the fresh, sweet tide, and calling to their sisters the news of Noah's Flood. They would tell amusing accounts of Noah in his ark. Some nymphs would relate how they had hung on the side of the ark, peeped in, and heard Noah and Shem and Ham and Japeth, sitting in their place under the rain, saying, how they four were the only men on earth now, because the Lord had drowned all the rest, so that they four would have everything to themselves, and be masters of every thing, sub-tenants under the great Proprietor.

Ursula wished she had been a nymph. She would have laughed through the window of the ark, and flicked drops of the flood at Noah, before she drifted away to people who were less important in their Proprietor and their Flood.

What was God, after all? If maggots in a dead dog be but God kissing carrion, what then is not God? She was surfeited of this God. She was weary of the Ursula Brangwen who felt troubled about God. What ever God was, He was, and there was no need for her to trouble about Him. She felt she had now all licence.

Skrebensky sat beside her, listening to the sermon, to the voice of law and order. 'The very hairs of your head are all numbered.' He did not believe it. He believed his own things were quite at his own disposal. You could do as you liked with your own things, so long as you left other people's alone.

Ursula caressed him and made love to him. Nevertheless he knew she wanted to react upon him and to destroy his being. She was not with him, she was against him. But her making love to him, her complete admiration of him, in open life, gratified him.

She caught him out of himself, and they were lovers, in a young, romantic, almost fantastic way. He gave her a little ring. They put it in Rhine wine, in their glass, and she drank, then he drank. They drank till the ring lay exposed at the bottom of the glass. Then she took the simple jewel, and tied it on a thread round her neck, where she wore it.

He asked her for a photograph when he was going away. She went in great excitement to the photographer, with five shillings. The result was an ugly little picture of herself with her mouth on one side. She wondered over it and admired it.

He saw only the live face of the girl. The picture hurt him. He kept it, he always remembered it, but he could scarcely bear to see it. There was a hurt to his soul in the clear, fearless face that was touched with abstraction. Its abstraction was certainly away from him.

Then war was declared with the Boers in South Africa, and everywhere was a fizz of excitement. He wrote that he might have to go. And he sent her a box of sweets.

She was slightly dazed at the thought of his going to the war, not knowing how to feel. It was a sort of romantic situation that she knew so well in fiction she hardly understood it in fact. Underneath a top elation was a sort of dreariness, deep, ashy disappointment.

However, she secreted the sweets under her bed, and ate them all herself, when she went to bed, and when she woke in the morning. All the time she felt very guilty and ashamed, but she simply did not want to share them.

That box of sweets remained stuck in her mind afterwards. Why had she secreted them and eaten them every one? Why? She did not feel guilty – she only knew she ought to feel guilty. And she could not make up her mind. Curiously monumental that box of sweets stood up, now it was empty. It was a crux for her. What was she to think of it?

The idea of war altogether made her feel uneasy, uneasy. When men began organised fighting with each other it seemed to her as if the poles of the universe were cracking, and the whole might go tumbling into the bottomless pit. A horrible bottomless feeling she had. Yet of course there was the minted superscription of romance and honour and even religion about war. She was very confused.

Skrebensky was busy, he could not come to see her. She asked for no assurance, no security. What was between them, was, and could not be altered by avowals. She knew that by instinct, she trusted to the intrinsic reality.

But she felt an agony of helplessness. She could do nothing. Vaguely she knew the huge powers of the world rolling and crashing together, darkly, clumsily, stupidly, yet colossal, so that one was brushed along almost as dust. Helpless, helpless, swirling like dust! Yet she wanted so hard to rebel, to rage, to fight. But with what?

Could she with her hands fight the face of the earth, beat the hills in their places? Yet her breast wanted to fight, to fight the whole world. And these two small hands were all she had to do it with.

The months went by, and it was Christmas – the snowdrops came. There was a little hollow in the wood near Cossethay, where snowdrops grew wild. She sent him some in a box, and he wrote her a quick little note of thanks – very grateful and wistful he seemed. Her eyes grew childlike and puzzled. Puzzled from day to day she went on, helpless, carried along by all that must happen.

He went about at his duties, giving himself up to them. At the bottom of his heart his self, the soul that aspired and had true hope of self-effectuation lay as dead, still-born, a dead weight in his womb. Who was he, to hold important his personal connection? What did a man matter personally? He was just a brick in the whole great social fabric, the nation, the modern humanity. His personal movements were small, and entirely subsidiary. The whole form must be ensured, not ruptured, for any personal reason whatsoever, since no pesonal reason could justify such a breaking. What did personal intimacy matter? One had to fill one's place in the whole, the great scheme of man's elaborate civilisation, that was all. The Whole mattered – but the unit, the person, had no importance, except as he represented the Whole.

So Skrebensky left the girl out and went his way, serving what he had to serve, and enduring what he had to endure, without remark. To his own intrinsic life, he was dead. And he could not rise again from the dead. His soul lay in the tomb. His life lay in the established order of things. He had his five senses too. They were to be gratified. Apart from this, he represented the great, established, extant Idea of life, and as this he was important and beyond question.

The good of the greatest number was all that mattered. That which was the greatest good for them all, collectively, was the greatest good for the individual. And so, every man must give himself to support the state, and so labour for the greatest good of all. One might make improvements in the state, perhaps, but always with a view to preserving it intact.

No highest good of the community, however, would give him the vital fulfilment of his soul. He knew this. But he did not consider the soul of the individual sufficiently important. He believed a man was important in so far as he represented all humanity.

He could not see, it was not born in him to see, that the highest good of
the community as it stands is no longer the highest good of even the average
individual. He thought that, because the community represents millions of
people, therefore it must be millions of times more important than any
individual, forgetting that the community is an abstraction from the many,
and is not the many themselves. Now when the statement of the abstract
good for the community has become a formula lacking in all inspiration or
value to the average intelligence, then the 'common good' becomes a general
nuisance, representing the vulgar, conservative materialism at a low level.

And by the highest good of the greatest number is chiefly meant the
material prosperity of all classes. Skrebensky did not really care about his
own material prosperity. If he had been penniless – well, he would have
taken his chances. Therefore how could he find his highest good in giving
up his life for the material prosperity of everybody else! What he considered
an unimportant thing for himself he could not think worthy of every sacrifice
on behalf of other people. And that which he would consider of the deepest
importance to himself as an individual – oh, he said, you mustn't consider
the community from that standpoint. No – no – we know what the community
wants; it wants something solid, it wants good wages, equal opportunities,
good conditions of living, that's what the community wants. It doesn't want
anything subtle or difficult. Duty is very plain – keep in mind the material,
the immediate welfare of every man, that's all.

So there came over Skrebensky a sort of nullity, which more and more
terrified Ursula. She felt there was something hopeless which she had to
submit to. She felt a great sense of disaster impending. Day after day was
made inert with a sense of disaster. She became morbidly sensitive, depressed,
apprehensive. It was anguish to her when she saw one rook slowly flapping
in the sky. That was a sign of ill-omen. And the foreboding became so black
and so powerful in her, that she was almost extinguished.

Yet what was the matter? At the worst he was only going away. Why did
she mind, what was it she feared? She did not know. Only she had a black
dread possessing her. When she went at night and saw the big, flashing stars
they seemed terrible, by day she was always expecting some charge to be
made against her.

He wrote in March to say that he was going to South Africa in a short
time, but before he went, he would snatch a day at the Marsh.

As if in a painful dream, she waited suspended, unresolved. She did not
know, she could not understand. Only she felt that all the threads of her fate
were being held taut, in suspense. She only wept sometimes as she went
about, saying blindly:

'I am so fond of him, I am so fond of him.'

He came. But why did he come? She looked at him for a sign. He gave
no sign. He did not even kiss her. He behaved as if he were an affable, usual
acquaintance. This was superficial, but what did it hide? She waited for
him, she wanted him to make some sign.

So the whole of the day they wavered and avoided contact, until evening.
Then, laughing, saying he would be back in six months' time and would tell
them all about it, he shook hands with her mother and took his leave.

Ursula accompanied him into the lane. The night was windy, the yew trees seethed and hissed and vibrated. The wind seemed to rush about among the chimneys and the church-tower. It was dark.

The wind blew Ursula's face, and her clothes cleaved to her limbs. But it was a surging, turgid wind, instinct with compressed vigour of life. And she seemed to have lost Skrebensky. Out there in the strong, urgent night she could not find him.

'Where are you?' she asked.

'Here,' came his bodiless voice.

And groping, she touched him. A fire like lightning drenched them.

'Anton?' she said.

'What?' he answered.

She held him with her hands in the darkness, she felt his body again with hers.

'Don't leave me – come back to me,' she said.

'Yes,' he said, holding her in his arms.

But the male in him was scotched by the knowledge that she was not under his spell nor his influence. He wanted to go away from her. He rested in the knowledge that to-morrow he was going away, his life was really elsewhere. His life was elsewhere – his life was elsewhere – the centre of his life was not what she would have. She was different – there was a breach between them. They were hostile worlds.

'You will come back to me?' she reiterated.

'Yes,' he said. And he meant it. But as one keeps an appointment, not as a man returning to his fulfilment.

So she kissed him, and went indoors, lost. He walked down to the Marsh abstracted. The contact with her hurt him, and threatened him. He shrank, he had to be free of her spirit. For she would stand before him, like the angel before Balaam, and drive him back with a sword from the way he was going, into a wilderness.

The next day she went to the station to see him go. She looked at him, she turned to him, but he was always so strange and null – so null. He was so collected. She thought it was that which made him null. Strangely nothing he was.

Ursula stood near him with a mute, pale face which he would rather not see. There seemed some shame at the very root of life, cold, dead shame for her.

The three made a noticeable group on the station; the girl in her fur cap and tippet and her olive green costume, pale, tense with youth, isolated, unyielding; the soldierly young man in a crush hat and a heavy overcoat, his face rather pale and reserved above his purple scarf, his whole figure neutral; then the elder man, a fashionable bowler hat pressed low over his dark brows, his face warm-coloured and calm, his whole figure curiously suggestive of full-blooded indifference; he was the eternal audience, the chorus, the spectator at the drama; in his own life he would have no drama.

The train was rushing up. Ursula's heart heaved, but the ice was frozen too strong upon it.

'Good-bye,' she said, lifting her hand, her face laughing with her peculiar, blind, almost dazzling laugh. She wondered what he was doing, when he stooped and kissed her. He should be shaking hands and going.

'Good-bye,' she said again.

He picked up his little bag and turned his back on her. There was a hurry along the train. Ah, here was his carriage. He took his seat. Tom Brangwen shut the door, and the two men shook hands as the whistle went.

'Good-bye – and good luck,' said Brangwen.

'Thank you – good-bye.'

The train moved off. Skrebensky stood at the carriage window, waving, but not really looking to the two figures, the girl and the warm-coloured, almost effeminately-dressed man. Ursula waved her handkerchief. The train gathered speed; it grew smaller and smaller. Still it ran in a straight line. The speck of white vanished. The rear of the train was small in the distance. Still she stood on the platform, feeling a great emptiness about her. In spite of herself her mouth was quivering: she did not want to cry: her heart was dead cold.

Her Uncle Tom had gone to an automatic machine, and was getting matches.

'Would you like some sweets?' he said, turning round.

Her face was covered with tears, she made curious, downward grimaces with her mouth, to get control. Yet her heart was not crying – it was cold and earthy.

'What kind would you like – any?' persisted her uncle.

'I should love some peppermint drops,' she said, in a strange, normal voice, from her distorted face. But in a few moments she had gained control of herself, and was still, detached.

'Let us go into the town,' he said, and he rushed her into a train, moving to the town station. They went to a café to drink coffee, she sat looking at people in the street, and a great wound was in her breast, a cold imperturbability in her soul.

This cold imperturbability of spirit continued in her now. It was as if some disillusion had frozen upon her, a hard disbelief. Part of her had gone cold, apathetic. She was too young, too baffled to understand, or even to know that she suffered much. And she was too deeply hurt to submit.

She had her blind agonies, when she wanted him, she wanted him. But from the moment of his departure, he had become a visionary thing of her own. All her roused torment and passion and yearning she turned to him.

She kept a diary, in which she wrote impulsive thoughts. Seeing the moon in the sky, her own heart surcharged, she went and wrote:

'If I were the moon, I know where I would fall down.'

It meant so much to her, that sentence – she put into it all the anguish of her youth and her young passion and yearning. She called to him from her heart wherever she went, her limbs vibrated with anguish towards him wherever she was, the radiating force of her soul seemed to travel to him, endlessly, endlessly, and in her soul's own creation, find him.

But who was he, and where did he exist? In her own desire only.

She received a post-card from him, and she put it in her bosom. It did not mean much to her, really. The second day, she lost it, and never even remembered she had had it, till some days afterwards.

The long weeks went by. There came the constant bad news of the war. And she felt as if all, outside there in the world, were a hurt, a hurt against her. And something in her soul remained cold, apathetic, unchanging.

Her life was always only partial at this time, never did she live completely. There was the cold, unliving part of her. Yet she was madly sensitive. She could not bear herself. When a dirty, red-eyed old woman came begging of her in the street, she started away as from an unclean thing. And then, when the old woman shouted acrid insults after her, she winced, her limbs palpitated with insane torment, she could not bear herself. Whenever she thought of the red-eyed old woman, a sort of madness ran in inflammation over her flesh and her brain, she almost wanted to kill herself.

And in this state, her sexual life flamed into a kind of disease within her. She was so overwrought and sensitive, that the mere touch of coarse wool seemed to tear her nerves.

Chapter Twelve

Shame

Ursula had only two more terms at school. She was studying for her matriculation examination. It was dreary work, for she had very little intelligence when she was disjointed from happiness. Stubbornness and a consciousness of impending fate kept her half-heartedly pinned to it. She knew that soon she would want to become a self-responsible person, and her dread was that she would be prevented. An all-containing will in her for complete independence, complete social independence, complete independence from any personal authority, kept her dullishly at her studies. For she knew that she had always her price of ransom – her femaleness. She was always a woman, and what she could not get because she was a human being, fellow to the rest of mankind, she would get because she was a female, other than the man. In her femaleness she felt a secret riches, a reserve, she had always the price of freedom.

However, she was sufficiently reserved about this last resource. The other things should be tried first. There was the mysterious man's world to be adventured upon, the world of daily work and duty, and existence as a working member of the community. Against this she had a subtle grudge. She wanted to make her conquest also of this man's world.

So she ground away at her work, never giving it up. Some things she liked. Her subjects were English, Latin, French, mathematics and history. Once she knew how to read French and Latin, the syntax bored her. Most tedious was the close study of English literature. Why should one remember the things one read? Something in mathematics, their cold absoluteness, fascinated her, but the actual practice was tedious. Some people in history puzzled her and made her ponder, but the political parts angered her, and she hated ministers. Only in odd streaks did she get a poignant sense of acquisition and enrichment and enlarging from her studies; one afternoon, reading *As You Like It*; once when, with her blood, she heard a passage of Latin, and she knew how the blood beat in a Roman's body; so that ever after she felt she knew the Romans by contact. She enjoyed the vagaries of English Grammar, because it gave her pleasure to detect the live movements of words and sentences; and mathematics, the very sight of the letters in Algebra, had a real lure for her.

She felt so much and so confusedly at this time, that her face got a queer, wondering, half-scared look, as if she were not sure what might seize upon her at any moment out of the unknown.

Odd little bits of information stirred unfathomable passion in her. When she knew that in the tiny brown buds of autumn were folded, minute and complete, the finished flowers of the summer nine months hence, tiny, folded up, and left there waiting, a flash of triumph and love went over her.

'I could never die while there was a tree,' she said passionately, sententiously, standing before a great ash in worship.

It was the people who, somehow, walked as an upright menace to her. Her life at this time was unformed, palpitating, essentially shrinking from all touch. She gave something to other people, but she was never herself, since she *had* no self. She was not afraid nor ashamed before trees, and birds, and the sky. But she shrank violently from people, ashamed she was not as they were, fixed, emphatic, but a wavering, undefined sensibility only, without form or being.

Gudrun was at this time a great comfort and shield to her. The younger girl was a lithe, *farouche* animal, who mistrusted all approach, and would have none of the petty secrecies and jealousies of schoolgirl intimacy. She would have no truck with the tame cats, nice or not, because she believed that they were all only untamed cats with a nasty, untrustworthy habit of tameness.

This was a great stand-back for Ursula, who suffered agonies when she thought a person disliked her, no matter how much she despised that other person. How could anyone dislike her, Ursula Brangwen? The question terrified her and was unanswerable. She sought refuge in Gudrun's natural, proud indifference.

It had been discovered that Gudrun had a talent for drawing. This solved the problem of the girl's indifference to all study. It was said to her, 'She can draw marvellously.'

Suddenly Ursula found a queer awareness existed between herself and her class-mistress, Miss Inger. The latter was a rather beautiful woman of twenty-eight, a fearless-seeming, clean type of modern girl whose very independence betrays her sorrow. She was clever, and expert in what she did, accurate, quick, commanding.

To Ursula she had always given pleasure, because of her clear, decided, yet graceful appearance. She carried her head high, a little thrown back, and Ursula thought there was a look of nobility in the way she twisted her smooth, brown hair upon her head. She always wore clean, attractive, well-fitting blouses, and a well-made skirt. Everything about her was so well-ordered, betraying a fine, clear spirit, that it was a pleasure to sit in her class.

Her voice was just as ringing and clear, and with unwavering, finely-touched modulation. Her eyes were blue, clear, proud, she gave one altogether the sense of a fine-mettled, scrupulously groomed person, and of an unyielding mind. Yet there was an infinite poignancy about her, a great pathos in her lonely, proudly closed mouth.

It was after Skrebensky had gone that there sprang up between the mistress and the girl that strange awareness, then the unspoken intimacy that sometimes connects two people who may never even make each other's acquaintance. Before, they had always been good friends, in the undistinguished way of the class-room, with the professional relationship of mistress and scholar always present. Now, however, another thing came to pass. When they were in the room together, they were aware of each other, almost to the exclusion of everything else. Winifred Inger felt a hot delight in the lessons when Ursula was present, Ursula felt her whole life begin when Miss Inger came into the room. Then, with the beloved, subtly-intimate teacher present, the girl sat as within the rays of some enrichening sun, whose intoxicating heat poured straight into her veins.

The state of bliss, when Miss Inger was present, was supreme in the girl, but always eager, eager. As she went home, Ursula dreamed of the school-mistress, made infinite dreams of things she could give her, of how she might make the elder woman adore her.

Miss Inger was a Bachelor of Arts, who had studied at Newnham. She was a clergyman's daughter, of good family. But what Ursula adored so much was her fine, upright, athletic bearing, and her indomitably poud nature. She was proud and free as a man, yet exquisite as a woman.

The girl's heart burned in her breast as she set off for school in the morning. So eager was her breast, so glad her feet, to travel towards the beloved. Ah, Miss Inger, how straight and fine was her back, how strong her loins, how calm and free her limbs!

Ursula craved ceaselessly to know if Miss Inger cared for her. As yet no definite sign had been passed between the two. Yet surely, surely Miss Inger loved her too, was fond of her, liked her at least more than the rest of the scholars in the class. Yet she was never certain. It might be that Miss Inger cared nothing for her. And yet, and yet, with blazing heart, Ursula felt that if only she could speak to her, touch her, she would know.

The summer term came, and with it the swimming class. Miss Inger was to take the swimming class. Then Ursula trembled and was dazed with passion. Her hopes were soon to be realised. She would see Miss Inger in her bathing dress.

The day came. In the great bath the water was glimmering pale emerald green, a lovely, glimmering mass of colour within the whitish marble-like confines. Overhead the light fell softly and the great green body of pure water moved under it as someone dived from the side.

Ursula, trembling, hardly able to contain herself, pulled off her clothes, put on her tight bathing-suit, and opened the door of her cabin. Two girls were in the water. The mistress had not appeared. She waited. A door opened. Miss Inger came out, dressed in a rust-red tunic like a Greek girl's tied round the waist, and a red silk handkerchief round her head. How lovely she looked! Her knees were so white and strong and proud, and she was firm-bodied as Diana. She walked simply to the side of the bath, and with a negligent movement, flung herself in. For a moment Ursula watched the white, smooth, strong shoulders, and the easy arms swimming. Then she too dived into the water.

Now, ah now, she was swimming in the same water with her dear mistress. The girl moved her limbs voluptuously, and swam by herself, deliciously, yet with a craving of unsatisfaction. She wanted to touch the other, to touch her, to feel her.

'I will race you, Ursula,' came the well-modulated voice.

Ursula started violently. She turned to see the warm, unfolded face of her mistress looking at her, to her. She was acknowledged. Laughing her own beautiful, startled laugh, she began to swim. The mistress was just ahead, swimming with easy strokes. Ursula could see the head put back, the water flickering upon the white shoulders, the strong legs kicking shadowily. And she swam blinded with passion. Ah, the beauty of the firm, white, cool flesh! Ah, the wonderful firm limbs. Ah, if she did not so despise her own thin, dusky fragment of a body, if only she too were fearless and capable. .

She swam on eagerly, not wanting to win, only wanting to be near her mistress, to swim in a race with her. They neared the end of the bath, the deep end. Miss Inger touched the pipe, swung herself round, and caught Ursula round the waist in the water, and held her for a moment.

'I won,' said Miss Inger, laughing.

There was a moment of suspense. Ursula's heart was beating so fast, she clung to the rail, and could not move. Her dilated, warm, unfolded, glowing face turned to the mistress, as if to her very sun.

'Good-bye,' said Miss Inger, and she swam away to the other pupils, taking professional interest in them.

Ursula was dazed. She could still feel the touch of the mistress's body against her own – only this, only this. The rest of the swimming time passed like a trance. When the call was given to leave the water, Miss Inger walked down the bath towards Ursula. Her rust-red, thin tunic was clinging to her, the whole body was defined, firm and magnificent, as it seemed to the girl.

'I enjoyed our race, Ursula, did you?' said Miss Inger.

The girl could only laugh with revealed, open, glowing face.

The love was now tacitly confessed. But it was some time before any further progress was made. Ursula continued in suspense, in inflamed bliss.

Then one day, when she was alone, the mistress came near to her, and touching her cheek with her fingers, said with some difficulty.

'Would you like to come to tea with me on Saturday, Ursula?'

The girl flushed all gratitude.

'We'll go to a lovely little bungalow on the Soar, shall we? I stay the week-ends there sometimes.'

Ursula was beside herself. She could not endure till the Saturday came, her thoughts burned up like a fire. If only it were Saturday, if only it were Saturday.

Then Saturday came, and she set out. Miss Inger met her in Sawley, and they walked about three miles to the bungalow. It was a moist, warm cloudy day.

The bungalow was a tiny, two-roomed shanty set on a steep bank. Everything in it was exquisite. In delicious privacy, the two girls made tea, and then they talked. Ursula need not be home till about ten o'clock.

The talk was led, by a kind of spell, to love. Miss Inger was telling Ursula of a friend, how she had died in child-birth, and what she had suffered; then she told of a prostitute, and of some of her experiences with men.

As they talked thus, on the little verandah of the bungalow, the night fell, there was a little warm rain.

'It is really stifling,' said Miss Inger.

They watched a train, whose lights were pale in the lingering twilight, rushing across the distance.

'It will thunder,' said Ursula.

The electric suspense continued, the darkness sank, they were eclipsed.

'I think I shall go and bathe,' said Miss Inger, out of the cloud-black darkness.

'At night?' said Ursula.

'It is best at night. Will you come?'

'I should like to.'

'It is quite safe – the grounds are private. We had better undress in the bungalow, for fear of the rain, then run down.'

Shyly, stiffly, Ursula went into the bungalow, and began to remove her clothes. The lamp was turned low, she stood in the shadow. By another chair Winifred Inger was undressing.

Soon the naked, shadowy figure of the elder girl came to the younger.

'Are you ready?' she said.

'One moment.'

Ursula could hardly speak. The other naked woman stood by, stood near, silent. Ursula was ready.

They ventured out into the darkness, feeling the soft air of night upon their skins.

'I can't see the path,' said Ursula.

'It is here,' said the voice, and the wavering, pallid figure was beside her, a hand grasping her arm. And the elder held the younger close against her, close, as they went down, and by the side of the water, she put her arms round her, and kissed her. And she lifted her in her arms, close, saying, softly:

'I shall carry you into the water.'

Ursula lay still in her mistress's arms, her forehead against the beloved, maddening breast.

'I shall put you in,' said Winifred.

But Ursula twined her body about her mistress.

After awhile the rain came down on their flushed, hot limbs, startling, delicious. A sudden, ice-cold shower burst in a great weight upon them. They stood up to it with pleasure. Ursula received the stream of it upon her breasts and her limbs. It made her cold, and a deep, bottomless silence welled up in her, as if bottomless darkness were returning upon her.

So the heat vanished away, she was chilled, as if from a waking up. She ran indoors, a chill, non-existent thing, wanting to get away. She wanted the light, the presence of other people, the external connection with the many. Above all she wanted to lose herself among natural surroundings.

She took her leave of her mistress and returned home. She was glad to be on the station with a crowd of Saturday-night people, glad to sit in the lighted, crowded railway carriage. Only she did not want to meet anybody she knew. She did not want to talk. She was alone, immune.

All this stir and seethe of lights and people was but the rim, the shores of a great inner darkness and void. She wanted very much to be on the seething, partially illuminated shore, for within her was the void reality of dark space.

For a time Miss Inger, her mistress, was gone; she was only a dark void, and Ursula was free as a shade walking in an underworld of extinction, of oblivion. Ursula was glad, with a kind of motionless, lifeless gladness, that her mistress was extinct, gone out of her.

In the morning, however, the love was there again, burning, burning. She remembered yesterday, and she wanted more, always more. She wanted to be with her mistress. All separation from her mistress was a restriction from living. Why could she not go to her to-day, to-day? Why must she pace about revoked at Cossethay whilst her mistress was elsewhere? She sat down and wrote a burning, passionate love-letter: she could not help it.

The two women became intimate. Their lives seemed suddenly to fuse into one, inseparable. Ursula went to Winifred's lodging, she spent there her only living hours. Winifred was very fond of water, – of swimming, of rowing. She belonged to various athletic clubs. Many delicious afternoons the two girls spent in a light boat on the river, Winifred always rowing. Indeed, Winifred seemed to delight in having Ursula in her charge, in giving things to the girl, in filling and enrichening her life.

So that Ursula developed rapidly during the few months of her intimacy with her mistress. Winifred had had a scientific education. She had known many clever people. She wanted to bring Ursula to her own position of thought.

They took religion and rid it of its dogmas, its falsehoods. Winifred humanised it all. Gradually it dawned upon Ursula that all the religion she knew was but a particular clothing to a human aspiration. The aspiration was the real thing, – the clothing was a matter almost of national taste or need. The Greeks had a naked Apollo, the Christians a white-robed Christ, the Buddhists a royal prince, the Egyptians their Osiris. Religions were local and religion was universal. Christianity was a local branch. There was as yet no assimilation of local religions into universal religion.

In religion there were the two great motives of fear and love. The motive of fear was as great as the motive of love. Christianity accepted crucifixion to escape from fear; 'Do your worst to me, that I may have no more fear of the worst.' But that which was feared was not necessarily all evil, and that which was loved not necessarily all good. Fear shall become reverence, and reverence is submission in identification; love shall become triumph, and triumph is delight in identification.

So much she talked of religion, getting the gist of many writings. In philosophy she was brought to the conclusion that the human desire is the criterion of all truth and all good. Truth does not lie beyond humanity, but is one of the products of the human mind and feeling. There is really nothing to fear. The motive of fear in religion is base, and must be left to the ancient worshippers of power, worship of Moloch. We do not worship power, in our enlightened souls. Power is degenerated to money and Napoleonic stupidity.

Ursula could not help dreaming of Moloch. Her God was not mild and gentle, neither Lamb nor Dove. He was the lion and the eagle. Not because the lion and the eagle had power, but because they were proud and strong; they were themselves, they were not passive subjects of some shepherd, or pets of some loving woman, or sacrifices of some priest. She was weary to death of mild, passive lambs and monotonous doves. If the lamb might lie down with the lion, it would be a great honour to the lamb, but the lion's powerful heart would suffer no diminishing. She loved the dignity and self-possession of lions.

She did not see how lambs could love. Lambs could only be loved. They could only be afraid, and tremblingly submit to fear, and become sacrificial; or they could submit to love, and become beloveds. In both they were passive. Raging, destructive lovers, seeking the moment when fear is greatest, and triumph is greatest, the fear not greater than the triumph, the triumph not greater than the fear, these were no lambs nor doves. She stretched her own limbs like a lion or a wild horse, her heart was relentless in its desires. It would suffer a thousand deaths, but it would still be a lion's heart when it rose from death, a fiercer lion she would be, a surer, knowing herself different from and separate from the great, conflicting universe that was not herself.

Winifred Inger was also interested in the Women's Movement.

'The men will do no more – they have lost the capacity for doing,' said the elder girl. 'They fuss and talk, but they are really inane. They make everything fit into an old, inert idea. Love is a dead idea to them. They don't come to one and love one, they come to an idea, and they say "You are my idea," so they embrace themselves. As if I were any man's idea! As if I exist because a man has an idea of me! As if I will be betrayed by him, lend him my body as an instrument for his idea, to be a mere apparatus of his dead theory. But they are too fussy to be able to act; they are all impotent, they can't *take* a woman. They come to their own idea every time, and take that. They are like serpents trying to swallow themselves because they are hungry.'

Ursula was introduced by her friend to various women and men, educated, unsatisfied people, who still moved within the smug provincial society as if they were nearly as tame as their outward behaviour showed, but who were inwardly raging and mad.

It was a strange world the girl was swept into, like a chaos, like the end of the world. She was too young to understand it all. Yet the inoculation passed into her, through her love for her mistress.

The examination came, and then school was over. It was the long vacation. Winifred Inger went away to London. Ursula was left alone in Cossethay. A terrible, outcast, almost poisonous despair possessed her. It was no use doing anything, or being anything. She had no connection with other people. Her lot was isolated and deadly. There was nothing for her anywhere, but this black disintegration. Yet, within all the great attack of disintegration upon her, she remained herself. It was the terrible core of all her suffering, that she was always herself. Never could she escape that: she could not put off being herself.

She still adhered to Winifred Inger. But a sort of nausea was coming over her. She loved her mistress. But a heavy, clogged sense of deadness began to gather upon her, from the other woman's contact. And sometimes she thought Winifred was ugly, clayey. Her female hips seemed big and earthy, her ankles and her arms were too thick. She wanted some fine intensity, instead of this heavy cleaving of moist clay, the cleaves because it has no life of its own.

Winifred still loved Ursula. She had a passion for the fine flame of the girl, she served her endlessly, would have done anything for her.

'Come with me to London,' she pleaded to the girl. 'I will make it nice for you, – you shall do lots of things you will enjoy.'

'No,' said Ursula, stubbornly and dully. 'No, I don't want to go to London, I want to be by myself.'

Winifred knew what this meant. She knew that Ursula was beginning to reject her. The fine, unquenchable flame of the younger girl would consent no more to mingle with the perverted life of the elder woman. Winifred knew it would come. But she too was proud. At the bottom of her was a black pit of despair. She knew perfectly well that Ursula would cast her off.

And that seemed like the end of her life. But she was too hopeless to rage. Wisely, economising what was left of Ursula's love, she went away to London, leaving the beloved girl alone.

And after a fortnight, Ursula's letter became tender again, loving. Her Uncle Tom had invited her to go and stay with him. He was managing a big, new colliery in Yorkshire. Would Winifred come too?

For now Ursula was imagining marriage for Winifred. She wanted her to marry her Uncle Tom. Winifred knew this. She said she would come to Wiggiston. She would now let fate do as it liked with her, since there was nothing remaining to be done. Tom Brangwen also saw Ursula's intention. He too was at the end of his desires. He had done the things he had wanted to. They had all ended in a disintegrated lifelessness of soul, which he hid under an utterly tolerant good-humour. He no longer cared about anything on earth, neither man nor woman, nor God nor humanity. He had come to a stability of nullification. He did not care any more, neither about his body nor about his soul. Only he would preserve intact his own life. Only the simple, superficial fact of living persisted. He was still healthy, He lived. Therefore he would fill each moment. That had always been his creed. It was not instinctive easiness: it was the inevitable outcome of his nature. When he was in the absolute privacy of his own life, he did as he pleased, unscrupulous, without any ulterior thought. He believed neither in good nor evil. Each moment was like a separate little island, isolated from time, and blank, unconditioned by time.

He lived in a large new house of red brick, standing outside a mass of homogeneous red-brick dwellings, called Wiggiston. Wiggiston was only seven years old. It had been a hamlet of eleven houses on the edge of healthy, half-agricultural country. Then the great seam of coal had been opened. In a year Wiggiston appeared, a great mass of pinkish rows of thin, unreal dwellings of five rooms each. The streets were like visions of pure ugliness; a grey-black macadamised road, asphalt causeways, held in between a flat succession of wall, window, and door, a new-brick channel that began nowhere, and ended nowhere. Everything was amorphous, yet everything repeated itself endlessly. Only now and then, in one of the house-windows vegetables or small groceries were displayed for sale.

In the middle of the town was a large, open, shapeless space, or market-place, of black trodden earth, surrounded by the same flat material of dwellings, new red-brick becoming grimy, small oblong windows, and oblong doors, repeated endlessly, with just, at one corner, a great and gaudy public-house, and somewhere lost on one of the sides of the square, a large window opaque and darkish green, which was the post-office.

The place had the strange desolation of a ruin. Colliers hanging about in gangs and groups, or passing along the asphalt pavements heavily to work, seemed not like living people, but like spectres. The rigidity of the blank streets, the homogeneous amorphous sterility of the whole suggested death rather than life. There was no meeting place, no centre, no artery, no organic formation. There it lay, like the new foundations of a red-brick confusion rapidly spreading, like a skin-disease.

Just outside of this, on a little hill, was Tom Brangwen's big, red-brick house. It looked from the front upon the edge of the place, a meaningless squalor of ash-pits and closets and irregular rows of the backs of houses, each with its small activity made sordid by barren cohesion with the rest of the small activities. Farther off was the great colliery that went night and day. And all around was the country, green with two winding streams, ragged with gorse, and heath, the darker wood in the distance.

The whole place was just unreal, just unreal. Even now, when he had been there for two years, Tom Brangwen did not believe in the actuality of the place. It was like some gruesome dream, some ugly, dead, amorphous mood become concrete.

Ursula and Winifred were met by the motor-car at the raw little station, and drove through what seemed to them like the horrible raw beginnings of something. The place was a moment of chaos perpetuated, persisting, chaos fixed and rigid. Ursula was fascinated by the many men who were there – groups of men standing in the streets, four or five men walking in a gang together, their dogs running behind or before. They were all decently dressed, and most of them rather gaunt. The terrible gaunt repose of their bearing fascinated her. Like creatures with no more hope, but which still live and have passionate being, within some utterly unliving shell, they passed meaninglessly along, with strange, isolated dignity. It was as if a hard, horny shell enclosed them all.

Shocked and startled, Ursula was carried to her Uncle Tom's house. He was not yet at home. His house was simply, but well furnished. He had taken out a dividing wall, and made the whole front of the house into a large library, with one end devoted to his science. It was a handsome room, appointed as a laboratory and reading room, but giving the same sense of hard, mechanical activity, activity mechanical yet inchoate, and looking out on the hideous abstraction of the town, and at the green meadows and rough country beyond, and at the great, mathematical colliery on the other side.

They saw Tom Brangwen walking up the curved drive. He was getting stouter, but with his bowler hat worn well set down on his brows, he looked manly, handsome, curiously like any other man of action. His colour was as fresh, his health as perfect as ever, he walked like a man rather absorbed.

Winifred Inger was startled when he entered the library, his coat fastened and correct, his head bald to the crown, but not shiny, rather like something naked that one is accustomed to see covered, and his dark eyes liquid and formless. He seemed to stand in the shadow, like a thing ashamed. And the clasp of his hand was so soft and yet so forceful, that it chilled the heart. She was afraid of him, repelled by him, and yet attracted.

He looked at the athletic, seemingly fearless girl, and he detected in her a kinship with his own dark corruption. Immediately, he knew they were akin.

His manner was polite, almost foreign, and rather cold. He still laughed in his curious, animal fashion, suddenly wrinkling up his wide nose, and showing his sharp teeth. The fine beauty of his skin and his complexion, some almost waxen quality, hid the strange, repellent grossness of him, the slight sense of putrescence, the commonness which revealed itself in his rather fat thighs and loins.

Winifred saw at once the deferential, slightly servile, slightly cunning regard he had for Ursula, which made the girl at once so proud and so perplexed.

'But is this place as awful as it looks?' the young girl asked, a strain in her eyes.

'It is just what it looks,' he said. 'It hides nothing.'

'Why are the men so sad?'

'Are they sad?' he replied.

'They seem unutterably, unutterably sad,' said Ursula, out of a passionate throat.

'I don't think they are that. They just take it for granted.'

'What do they take for granted?'

'This – the pits and the place altogether.'

'Why don't they alter it?' she passionately protested.

'They believe they must alter themselves to fit the pits and the place, rather than alter the pits and the place to fit themselves. It is easier,' he said.

'And you agree with them,' burst out his niece, unable to bear it. 'You think like they do – that living human beings must be taken and adapted to all kinds of horrors. We could easily do without the pits.'

He smiled, uncomfortably, cynically. Ursula felt again the revolt of hatred from him.

'I suppose their lives are not really so bad,' said Winifred Inger, superior to the Zolaesque tragedy.

He turned with his polite, distant attention.

'Yes, they are pretty bad. The pits are very deep, and hot, and in some places wet. The men die of consumption fairly often. But they earn good wages.'

'How gruesome!' said Winifred Inger.

'Yes,' he replied gravely. It was his grave, solid, self-contained manner which made him so much respected as a colliery manager.

The servant came in to ask where they would have tea.

'Put it in the summer-house, Mrs. Smith,' he said.

The fair-haired, good-looking young woman went out.

'Is she married and in service?' asked Ursula.

'She is a widow. Her husband died of consumption a little while ago.' Brangwen gave a sinister little laugh. 'He lay there in the house-place at her mother's, and five or six other people in the house, and died very gradually. I asked her if his death wasn't a great trouble to her. "Well," she said, "he was very fretful towards the last, never satisfied, never easy, always fret-fretting, an' never knowing what would satisfy him. So in one way it was a relief when it was over – for him and for everybody." They had only been married two years, and she had one boy. I asked her if she hadn't been very happy. "Oh, yes, sir, we was very comfortable at first, till he took bad – oh, we was very comfortable – oh, yes – but, you see, you get used to it. I've had my father and two brothers go off just the same. You get used to it". '

'It's a horrible thing to get used to,' said Winifred Inger, with a shudder.

'Yes,' he said, still smiling. 'But that's how they are. She'll be getting married again directly. One man or another – it does not matter very much. They're all colliers.'

'What do you mean?' asked Ursula. 'They're all colliers?'

'It is with the women as with us,' he replied. 'Her husband was John Smith, loader. We reckoned him as a loader, he reckoned himself as a loader, and so she knew he represented his job. Marriage and home is a little side-show. The women know it right enough, and take if for what it's worth. One man or another, it doesn't matter all the world. The pit matters. Round the pit there will always be the side-shows, plenty of 'em.'

He looked round at the red chaos, the rigid, amorphous confusion of Wiggiston.

'Every man his own little side-show, his home, but the pit owns every man. The women have what is left. What's left of this man, or what is left of that – it doesn't matter altogether. The pit takes all that really matters.'

'It is the same everywhere,' burst out Winifred. 'It is the office, or the shop, or the business that gets the man, the woman gets the bit the shop can't digest. What is he at home, a man? He is a meaningless lump – a standing machine, a machine out of work.'

'They know they are sold,' said Tom Brangwen. 'That's where it is. They know they are sold to their job. If a woman talks her throat out, what difference can it make? The man's sold to his job. So the women don't bother. They take what they can catch – and *vogue la galère.*'

'Aren't they very strict here?' asked Miss Inger.

'Oh, no. Mrs. Smith has two sisters who have just changed husbands. They're not very particular – neither are they very interested. They go dragging along what is left from the pits. They're not interested enough to be very immoral – it all amounts to the same thing, moral or immoral – just a question of pit-wages. The most moral duke in England makes two hundred thousand a year out of these pits. He keeps the morality end up.'

Ursula sat black-souled and very bitter, hearing the two of them talk. There seemed something ghoulish even in their very deploring of the state of things. They seemed to take a ghoulish satisfaction in it. The pit was the great mistress. Ursula looked out of the window and saw the proud, demon-like colliery with her wheels twinkling in the heavens, the formless, squalid mass of the town lying aside. It was the squalid heap of side-shows. The pit was the main show, the *raison d'être* of all.

How terrible it was! There was a horrible fascination in it – human bodies and lives subjected in slavery to that symmetric monster of the colliery. There was a swooning, perverse satisfaction in it. For a moment she was dizzy.

Then she recovered, felt herself in a great loneliness, wherein she was sad but free. She had departed. No more would she subscribe to the great colliery, to the great machine which has taken us all captives. In her soul, she was against it, she disowned even its power. It had only to be forsaken to be inane, meaningless. And she knew it was meaningless. But it needed a great, passionate effort of will on her part, seeing the colliery, still to maintain her knowledge that it was meaningless.

But her Uncle Tom and her mistress remained there among the horde, cynically reviling the monstrous state and yet adhering to it, like a man who reviles his mistress, yet who is in love with her. She knew her Uncle Tom perceived what was going on. But she knew moreover that in spite of his criticism and condemnation, he still wanted the great machine. His only happy moments, his only moments of pure freedom were when he was serving the machine. Then, and then only, when the machine caught him up, was he free from the hatred of himself, could he act wholely, without cynicism and unreality.

His real mistress was the machine, and the real mistress of Winifred was the machine. She too, Winifred, worshipped the impure abstraction, the mechanisms of matter. There, there, in the machine, in service of the machine, was she free from the clog and degradation of human feeling. There, in the monstrous mechanism that held all matter, living or dead, in its service, did she achieve her consummation and her perfect unison, her immortality.

Hatred sprang up in Ursula's heart. If she could she would smash the machine. Her soul's action should be the smashing of the great machine. If she could destroy the colliery, and make all the men of Wiggiston out of work, she would do it. Let them starve and grub in the earth for roots, rather than serve such a Moloch as this.

She hated her Uncle Tom, she hated Winifred Inger. They went down to the summer-house for tea. It was a pleasant place among a few trees, at the end of a tiny garden, on the edge of a field. Her Uncle Tom and Winifred seemed to jeer at her, to cheapen her. She was miserable and desolate. But she would never give way.

Her coldness for Winifred should never cease. She knew it was over between them. She saw gross, ugly movements in her mistress, she saw a clayey, inert, unquickened flesh, that reminded her of the great prehistoric lizards. One day her Uncle Tom came in out of the broiling sunshine heated from walking. Then the perspiration stood out upon his head and brow, his hand was wet and hot and suffocating in its clasp. He too had something marshy about him – the succulent moistness and turgidity, and the same brackish, nauseating effect of a marsh, where life and decaying are one.

He was repellent to her, who was so dry and fine in her fire. Her very bones seemed to bid him keep his distance from her.

It was in these weeks that Ursula grew up. She stayed two weeks at Wiggiston, and she hated it. All was grey, dry ash, cold and dead and ugly. But she stayed. She stayed also to get rid of Winifred. The girl's hatred and her sense of repulsiveness in her mistress and in her uncle seemed to throw the other two together. They drew together as if against her.

In hardness and bitterness of soul, Ursula knew that Winifred was become her uncle's lover. She was glad. She had loved them both. Now she wanted to be rid of them both. Their marshy, bitter-sweet corruption came sick and unwholesome in her nostrils. Anything, to get out of the foetid air. She would leave them both for ever, leave for ever their strange, soft, half-corrupt element. Anything to get away.

One night Winifred came all burning into Ursula's bed, and put her arms round the girl, holding her to herself in spite of unwillingness, and said,

'Dear, my dear – shall I marry Mr. Brangwen – shall I?'

The clinging, heavy, muddy question weighed on Ursula intolerably.

'Has he asked you?' she said, using all her might of hard resistance.

'He's asked me,' said Winifred. 'Do you want me to marry him, Ursula?'

'Yes,' said Ursula.

The arms tightened more on her.

'I knew you did, my sweet – and I will marry him. You're *fond* of him, aren't you?'

'I've been *awfully* fond of him – ever since I was a child.'

'I know – I know. I can see what you like in him. He *is* a man by himself, he has something apart from the rest.'

'Yes,' said Ursula.

'But he's not like you, my dear – ha, he's not as good as you. There's something even objectionable in him – his thick thighs — '

Ursula was silent.

'But I'll marry him, my dear – it will be best. Now say you love me.'

A sort of profession was extorted out of the girl. Nevertheless her mistress went away sighing, to weep in her own chamber.

In two days' time Ursula left Wiggiston. Miss Inger went to Nottingham. There was an engagement between her and Tom Brangwen, which the uncle seemed to vaunt as if it were an assurance of his validity.

Brangwen and Winifred Inger continued engaged for another term. Then they married. Brangwen had reached the age when he wanted children. He wanted children. Neither marriage nor the domestic establishment meant anything to him. He wanted to propagate himself. He knew what he was doing. He had the instinct of a growing inertia, of a thing that chooses its place of rest in which to lapse into apathy, complete, profound indifference. He would let the machinery carry him; husband, father, pit-manager, warm clay lifted through the recurrent action of day after day by the great machine from which it derived its motion. As for Winifred, she was an educated woman, and of the same sort as himself. She would make a good companion. She was his mate.

Chapter Thirteen

The Man's World

Ursula came back to Cossethay to fight with her mother. Her schooldays were over. She had passed the matriculation examination. Now she came home to face that empty period between school and possible marriage.

At first she thought it would be just like holidays all the time, she would feel just free. Her soul was in chaos, blinded suffering, maimed. She had no will left to think about herself. For a time she must just lapse.

But very shortly she found herself up against her mother. Her mother had, at this time, the power to irritate and madden the girl continuously. There were already seven children, yet Mrs. Brangwen was again with child, the ninth she had borne. One had died of diphtheria in infancy.

Even this fact of her mother's pregnancy enraged the eldest girl. Mrs. Brangwen was so complacent, so utterly fulfilled in her breeding. She would not have the existence at all of anything but the immediate, physical, common things. Ursula inflamed in soul, was suffering all the anguish of youth's reaching for some unknown ordeal, that it can't grasp, can't even distinguish or conceive. Maddened, she was fighting all the darkness she was up against. And part of this darkness was her mother. To limit, as her mother did, everything to the ring of physical considerations, and complacently to reject the reality of anything else, was horrible. Not a thing did Mrs. Brangwen care about, but the children, the house, and a little local gossip. And she *would not* be touched, she would let nothing else live near her. She went about, big with child, slovenly, easy, having a certain lax dignity, taking her own time, pleasing herself, always, always doing things for the children, and feeling that she thereby fulfilled the whole of womanhood.

This long trance of complacent child-bearing had kept her young and undeveloped. She was scarcely a day older than when Gudrun was born. All these years nothing had happened save the coming of the children, nothing had mattered but the bodies of her babies. As her children came into consciousness, as they began to suffer their own fulfilment, she cast them off. But she remained dominant in the house. Brangwen continued in a kind of rich drowse of physical heat, in connection with his wife. They were neither of them quite personal, quite defined as individuals, so much were they pervaded by the physical heat of breeding and rearing their young.

How Ursula resented it, how she fought against the close, physical, limited life of herded domesticity! Calm, placid unshakeable as ever, Mrs. Brangwen went about in her dominance of physical maternity.

There were battles. Ursula would fight for things that mattered to her. She would have the children less rude and tyrannical, she *would* have a place in the house. But her mother pulled her down, pulled her down. With all the cunning instinct of a breeding animal, Mrs. Brangwen ridiculed and held cheap Ursula's passions, her ideas, her pronunciations. Ursula would try to insist, in her own home, on the right of women to take equal place with men in the field of action and work.

'Ay,' said the mother, 'there's a good crop of stockings lying ripe for mending. Let that be your field of action.'

Ursula disliked mending stockings, and this retort maddened her. She hated her mother bitterly. After a few weeks of enforced domestic life, she had had enough of her home. The commonness, the triviality, the immediate meaninglessness of it all drove her to frenzy. She talked and stormed ideas, she corrected and nagged at the children, she turned her back in silent contempt on her breeding mother, who treated her with supercilious indifference, as if she were a pretentious child not to be taken seriously.

Brangwen was sometimes dragged into the trouble. He loved Ursula, therefore he always had a sense of shame, almost of betrayal, when he turned on her. So he turned fiercely and scathingly, and with a wholesale brutality that made Ursula go white, mute, and numb. Her feelings seemed to be becoming deadened in her, her temper hard and cold.

Brangwen himself was in one of his states of flux. After all these years, he began to see a loophole of freedom. For twenty years he had gone on at this office as a draughtsman, doing work in which he had no interest, because it seemed his allotted work. The growing up of his daughters, their developing rejection of old forms set him also free.

He was a man of ceaseless activity. Blindly, like a mole, he pushed his way out of the earth that covered him, working always away from the physical element in which his life was captured. Slowly, blindly, gropingly, with what initiative was left to him, he made his way towards individual expression and individual form.

At last, after twenty years, he came back to his wood-carving, almost to the point where he had left off his Adam and Eve panel, when he was courting. But now he had knowledge and skill without vision. He saw the puerility of his young conceptions, he saw the unreal world in which they had been conceived. He now had a new strength in his sense of reality. He felt as if he were real, as if he handled real things. He had worked for many years at Cossethay, building the organ for the church, restoring the wood-work, gradually coming to a knowledge of beauty in the plain labours. Now he wanted again to carve things that were utterances of himself.

But he could not quite hitch on – always he was too busy, too uncertain, confused. Wavering, he began to study modelling. To his surprise he found he could do it. Modelling in clay, in plaster, he produced beautiful repro-ductions, really beautiful. Then he set-to to make a head of Ursula, in high relief, in the Donatello manner. In his first passion, he got a beautiful suggestion of his desire. But the pitch of concentration would not come. With a little ash in his mouth he gave up. He continued to copy, or to make designs by selecting motives from classic stuff. He loved the Della Robbia and Donatello as he had loved Fra Angelico when he was a young man. His work had some of the freshness, the naïve alertness of the early Italians. But it was only reproduction.

Having reached his limit in modelling, he turned to painting. But he tried water-colour painting after the manner of any other amateur. He got his results but was not much interested. After one or two drawings of his beloved church, which had the same alertness as his modelling, he seemed to be incongruous with the modern atmospheric way of painting, so that his church tower stood up, really stood and asserted its standing, but was ashamed of its own lack of meaning, he turned away again.

He took up jewellery, read Benvenuto Cellini, pored over reproductions of ornaments, and began to make pendants in silver and pearl and matrix. The first things he did, in his start of discovery, were really beautiful. Those later were more imitative. But, starting with his wife, he made a pendant each for all his womenfolk. Then he made rings and bracelets.

Then he took up beaten and chiselled metal work. When Ursula left school, he was making a silver bowl of lovely shape. How he delighted in it, almost lusted after it.

All this time his only connection with the real outer world was through his winter evening classes, which brought him into contact with state education. About all the rest, he was oblivious, and entirely indifferent – even about the war. The nation did not exist to him. He was in a private retreat of his own, that had neither nationality, nor any great adherent.

Ursula watched the newspapers, vaguely, concerning the war in South Africa. They made her miserable, and she tried to have as little to do with them as possible. But Skrebensky was out there. He sent her an occasional post-card. But it was as if she were a blank wall in his direction, without windows or outgoing. She adhered to the Skrebensky of her memory.

Her love for Winifred Inger wrenched her life as it seemed from the roots and native soil where Skrebensky had belonged to it, and she was aridly transplanted. He was really only a memory. She revived his memory with strange passion, after the departure of Winifred. He was to her almost the symbol of her real life. It was as if, through him, in him, she might return to her own self, which she was before she had loved Winifred, before this deadness had come upon her, this pitiless transplanting. But even her memories were the work of her imagination.

She dreamed of him and her as they had been together. She could not dream of him progressively, of what he was doing now, of what relation he would have to her now. Only sometimes she wept to think how cruelly she had suffered when he left her – ah, *how* she had suffered! She remembered what she had written in her diary:

'If I were the moon, I know where I would fall down.'

Ah, it was a dull agony to her to remember what she had been then. For it was remembering a dead self. All that was dead after Winifred. She knew the corpse of her young, loving self, she knew its grave. And the young loving self she mourned for had scarcely existed, it was the creature of her imagination.

Deep within her a cold despair remained unchanging and unchanged. No one would ever love her now – she would love no one. The body of love was killed in her after Winifred, there was something of the corpse in her. She would live, she would go on, but she would have no lovers, no love would want her any more. She herself would want no lover. The vividest little flame of desire was extinct in her for ever. The tiny, vivid germ that contained the bud of her real self, her real love, was killed, she would go on growing as a plant, she would do her best to produce her minor flowers, but her leading flower was dead before it was born, all her growth was the conveying of a corpse of hope.

The miserable weeks went on, in the poky house crammed with children. What was her life – a sordid, formless, disintegrated nothing; Ursula Brangwen a person without worth or importance, living in the mean village of Cossethay, within the sordid scope of Ilkeston. Ursula Brangwen, at seventeen, worthless and unvalued, neither wanted nor needed by anybody, and conscious herself of her own dead value. It would not bear thinking of.

But still her dogged pride held its own. She might be defiled, she might be a corpse that should never be loved, she might be a core-rotten stalk living upon the food that others provided, yet she would give in to nobody.

Gradually she became conscious that she could not go on living at home as she was doing, without place or meaning or worth. The very children that went to school held her uselessness in contempt. She must do something.

Her father said she had plenty to do to help her mother. From her parents she would never get more than a hit in the face. She was not a practical person. She thought of wild things, of running away and becoming a domestic servant, of asking some man to take her.

She wrote to the mistress of the High School for advice.

'I cannot see very clearly what you should do, Ursula,' came the reply, 'unless you are willing to become an elementary school teacher. You have matriculated, and that qualifies you to take a post as uncertificated teacher in any school, at a salary of about fifty pounds a year.

'I cannot tell you how deeply I sympathise with you in your desire to do something. You will learn that mankind is a great body of which you are one useful member, you will take your own place at the great task which humanity is trying to fulfil. That will give you a satisfaction and a self-respect which nothing else could give.'

Ursula's heart sank. It was a cold, dreary satisfaction to think of. Yet her cold will acquiesced. This was what she wanted.

'You have an emotional nature,' the letter went on, 'a quick natural response. If only you could learn patience and self-discipline, I do not see why you should not make a good teacher. The least you could do is to try. You need only serve a year, or perhaps two years, as uncertificated teacher. Then you would go to one of the training colleges, where I hope you would take your degree. I most strongly urge and advise you to keep up your studies always with the intention of taking a degree. That will give you a qualification and a position in the world, and will give you more scope to choose your own way.

'I shall be proud to see one of my girls win her own economical independence, which means so much more than it seems. I shall be glad indeed to know that one more of my girls had provided for herself the means of freedom to choose for herself.'

It all sounded grim and desperate. Ursula rather hated it. But her mother's contempt and her father's harshness had made her raw at the quick, she knew the ignominy of being a hanger-on, she felt the festering thorn of her mother's animal estimation.

At length she had to speak. Hard and shut down and silent within herself, she slipped out one evening to the work-shed. She heard the tap-tap-tap of the hammer upon the metal. Her father lifted his head as the door opened. His face was ruddy and bright with instinct, as when he was a youth, his black moustache was cut close over his wide mouth, his black hair was fine and close as ever. But there was about him an abstraction, a sort of instrumental detachment from human things. He was a worker. He watched his daughter's hard, expressionless face. A hot anger came over his breast and belly.

'What now?' he said.

'Can't I,' she answered, looking aside, not looking at him, 'can't I go out to work?'

'Go out to work, what for?'

His voice was so strong, and ready and vibrant. It irritated her.

'I want some other life than this.'

A flash of strong rage arrested all his blood for a moment.

'Some other life?' he repeated. 'Why, what other life do you want?'

She hesitated.

'Something else besides housework and hanging about. And I want to earn something.'

Her curious, brutal hardness of speech, and the fierce invincibility of her youth, which ignored him, made him also harden with anger.

'And how do you think *you're* going to earn anything?' he asked.

'I can become a teacher – I'm qualified by my matric.'

He wished her matric. in hell.

'And how much are you qualified to earn by your matric.?' he asked, jeering.

'Fifty pounds a year,' she said.

He was silent, his power taken out of his hand.

He had always hugged a secret pride in the fact that his daughters need not go out to work. With his wife's money and his own they had four hundred a year. They could draw on the capital if need be later on. He was not afraid for his old age. His daughters might be ladies.

Fifty pounds a year was a pound a week – which was enough for her to live on independently.

'And what sort of a teacher do you think *you'd* make? You haven't the patience of a Jack-gnat with your own brothers and sisters, let alone with a class of children. And I thought you didn't like dirty, board-school brats.'

'They're not all dirty.'

'You'd find they're not all clean.'

There was silence in the workshop. The lamplight fell on the burned silver bowl that lay between him, on mallet and furnace and chisel. Brangwen stood with a queer, cat-like light on his face, almost like a smile. But it was no smile.

'Can I try?' she said.

'You can do what the deuce you like, and go where you like.'

Her face was fixed and expressionless and indifferent. It always sent him to a pitch of frenzy to see it like that. He kept perfectly still.

Cold, without any betrayal of feeling, she turned and left the shed. He worked on, with all his nerves jangled. Then he had to put down his tools and go into the house.

In a bitter tone of anger and contempt he told his wife. Ursula was present. There was a brief altercation, closed by Mrs. Brangwen's saying, in a tone of biting superiority and indifference:

'Let her find out what it's like. She'll soon have had enough.'

The matter was left there. But Ursula considered herself free to act. For some days she made no move. She was reluctant to take the cruel step of finding work, for she shrank with extreme sensitiveness and shyness from new contact, new situations. Then at length a sort of doggedness drove her. Her soul was full of bitterness.

She went to the Free Library in Ilkeston, copied out addresses from the *Schoolmistress*, and wrote for application forms. After two days she rose early to meet the postman. As she expected, there were three long envelopes.

Her heart beat painfully as she went up with them to her bedroom. Her fingers trembled, she could hardly force herself to look at the long, official forms she had to fill in. The whole thing was so cruel, so impersonal. Yet it must be done.

'Name (surname first) ....'

In a trembling hand she wrote, 'Brangwen, – Ursula.'

'Age and date of birth: ....'

After a long time considering, she filled in that line.

'Qualifications, with date of Examination: ....'

With a little pride she wrote:

'London Matriculation Examination.'

'Previous experience and where obtained: ....'
Her heart sank as she wrote:
'None.'
Still there was much to answer. It took her two hours to fill in the three forms. Then she had to copy her testimonials from her head-mistress and from the clergyman.

At last, however, it was finished. She had sealed the three long envelopes. In the afternoon she went down to Ilkeston to post them. She said nothing of it all to her parents. As she stamped her long letters and put them into the box at the main post-office she felt as if already she was out of the reach of her father and mother, as if she had connected herself with the outer, greater world of activity, the man-made world.

As she returned home, she dreamed again in her own fashion her old, gorgeous dreams. One of her applications was to Gillingham, in Kent, one to Kingston-on-Thames, and one to Swanwick in Derbyshire.

Gillingham was such a lovely name, and Kent was the Garden of England. So that, in Gillingham, an old, old village by the hopfields, where the sun shone softly, she came out of school in the afternoon into the shadow of the plane trees by the gate, and turned down the sleepy road towards the cottage where cornflowers poked their blue heads through the old wooden fence, and phlox stood built up of blossom beside the path.

A delicate, silver-haired lady rose with delicate, ivory hands uplifted as Ursula entered the room, and:
'Oh, my dear, what do you think!'
'What is it, Mrs. Wetherall?'
Frederick had come home. Nay, his manly step was heard on the stair, she saw his strong boots, his blue trousers, his uniformed figure, and then his face, clean and keen as an eagle's, and his eyes lit up with the glamour of strange seas, ah, strange seas that had woven through his soul, as he descended into the kitchen.

This dream, with its amplifications, lasted her a mile of walking. Then she went to Kingston-on-Thames.

Kingston-on-Thames was an old historic place just south of London. There lived the well-born dignified souls who belonged to the metropolis, but who loved peace. There she met a wonderful family of girls living in a large old Queen Anne house, whose lawns sloped to the river, and in an atmosphere of stately peace she found herself among her soul's intimates. They loved her as sisters, they shared with her all noble thoughts.

She was happy again. In her musings she spread her poor, clipped wings, and flew into the pure empyrean.

Day followed day. She did not speak to her parents. Then came the return of her testimonials from Gillingham. She was not wanted, neither at Swanwick. The bitterness of rejection followed the sweets of hope. Her bright feathers were in the dust again.

Then, suddenly, after a fortnight, came an intimation from Kingston-on-Thames. She was to appear at the Education Office of that town on the following Thursday, for an interview with the Committee. Her heart stood still. She knew she would make the Committee accept her. Now she was afraid, now that her removal was imminent. Her heart quivered with fear and reluctance. But underneath her purpose was fixed.

She passed shadowily through the day, unwilling to tell her news to her mother, waiting for her father. Suspense and fear were strong upon her. She dreaded going to Kingston. Her easy dreams disappeared from the grasp of reality.

And yet, as the afternoon wore away, the sweetness of the dream returned again. Kingston-on-Thames – there was such sound of dignity to her. The shadow of history and the glamour of stately progress enveloped her. The palaces would be old and darkened, the place of kings obscured. Yet it was a place of kings for her – Richard and Henry and Wolsey and Queen Elizabeth. She divined great lawns with noble trees, and terraces whose steps the water washed softly, where the swans sometimes came to earth. Still she must see the stately, gorgeous barge of the Queen float down, the crimson carpet put upon the landing stairs, the gentlemen in their purple-velvet cloaks, bare-headed, standing in the sunshine grouped on either side waiting.

'Sweet Thames, run softly till I end my song.'

Evening came, her father returned home, sanguine and alert and detached as ever. He was less real than her fancies. She waited whilst he ate his tea. He took big mouthfuls, big bites, and ate unconsciously with the same abandon an animal gives to its food.

Immediately after tea he went over to the church. It was choir-practice, and he wanted to try the tunes on his organ.

The latch of the big door clicked loudly as she came after him, but the organ rolled more loudly still. He was unaware. He was practising the anthem. She saw his small, jet-black head and alert face between the candle-flames, his slim body sagged on the music-stool. His face was so luminous and fixed, the movements of his limbs seemed strange, apart from him. The sound of the organ seemed to belong to the very stone of the pillars, like sap running in them.

Then there was a close of music and silence.

'Father!' she said.

He looked round as if at an apparition. Ursula stood shadowily within the candle-light.

'What now?' he said, not coming to earth.

It was difficult to speak to him.

'I've got a situation,' she said, forcing herself to speak.

'You've got what?' he answered, unwilling to come out of his mood of organ-playing. He closed the music before him.

'I've got a situation to go to.'

Then he turned to her, still abstracted, unwilling.

'Oh, where's that?' he said.

'At Kingston-on-Thames. I must go on Thursday for an interview with the Committee.'

'You must go on Thursday?'

'Yes.'

And she handed him the letter. He read it by the light of the candles.

'*Ursula Brangwen, Yew Tree Cottage, Cossethay, Derbyshire.*

'*Dear Madam, You are requested to call at the above offices on Thursday next, the 10th, at 11.30 a.m., for an interview with the committee, referring to your application for the post of assistant mistress at the Wellingborough Green Schools.*'

It was very difficult for Brangwen to take in this remote and official information, glowing as he was within the quiet of his church and his anthem music.

'Well, you needn't bother me with it now, need you?' he said impatiently, giving her back the letter.

'I've got to go on Thursday,' she said.

He sat motionless. Then he reached more music, and there was a rushing sound of air, then a long, emphatic trumpet-note of the organ, as he laid his hands on the keys. Ursula turned and went away.

He tried to give himself again to the organ. But he could not. He could not get back. All the time a sort of string was tugging, tugging him elsewhere, miserably.

So that when he came into the house after choir-practice his face was dark and his heart black. He said nothing, however, until all the younger children were in bed. Ursula, however, knew what was brewing.

At length he asked:

'Where's that letter?'

She gave it to him. He sat looking at it. 'You are requested to call at the above offices on Thursday next—' It was a cold, official notice to Ursula herself and had nothing to do with him. So! She existed now as a separate social individual. It was for her to answer this note, without regard to him. He had even no right to interfere. His heart was hard and angry.

'You had to do it behind our backs, had you?' he said, with a sneer. And her heart leapt with hot pain. She knew she was free – she had broken away from him. He was beaten.

'You said, "let her try," ' she retorted, almost apologising to him.

He did not hear. He sat looking at the letter.

'Education Office, Kingston-on-Thames' – and then the typewritten 'Miss Ursula Brangwen, Yew Tree Cottage, Cossethay.' It was all so complete and so final. He could not but feel the new position Ursula held, as recipient of that letter. It was an iron in his soul.

'Well,' he said at length, 'you're not going.'

Ursula started and could find no words to clamour her revolt.

'If you think you're dancin' off to th' other side of London, you're mistaken.'

'Why not?' she cried, at once hard fixed in her will to go.

'That's why not,' he said.

And there was silence till Mrs. Brangwen came downstairs.

'Look here, Anna,' he said, handing her the letter.

She put back her head, seeing a typewritten letter, anticipating trouble from the outside world. There was the curious, sliding motion of her eyes, as if she shut off her sentient, maternal self, and a kind of hard trance, meaningless, took its place. Thus, meaningless, she glanced over the letter, careful not to take it in. She apprehended the contents with her callous, superficial mind. Her feeling self was shut down.

'What post is it?' she said.

'She wants to go and be a teacher in Kingston-on-Thames, at fifty pounds a year.'

'Oh, indeed.'

The mother spoke as if it were a hostile fact concerning some stranger. She would have let her go, out of callousness. Mrs. Brangwen would begin to grow up again only with her youngest child. Her eldest girl was in the way now.

'She's not going all that distance,' said the father.

'I have to go where they want me,' cried Ursula. 'And it's a good place to go to.'

'What do *you* know about the place?' said her father harshly.

'And it doesn't matter whether they want you or not, if your father says you are not to go,' said the mother calmly.

How Ursula hated her!

'You said I was to try,' the girl cried. 'Now I've got a place and I'm going to go.'

'You're not going all that distance,' said her father.

'Why don't you get a place at Ilkeston, where you can live at home?' asked Gudrun, who hated conflicts, who could not understand Ursula's uneasy way, yet who must stand by her sister.

'There aren't any places at Ilkeston,' cried Ursula. 'And I'd rather go right away.'

'If you'd asked about it, a place could have been got for you in Ilkeston. But you had to play Miss High-an'-mighty, and go your own way,' said her father.

'I've no doubt you'd rather go right away,' said her mother, very caustic. 'And I've no doubt you'd find other people didn't put up with you for very long either. You've too much opinion of yourself for your good.'

Between the girl and her mother was a feeling of pure hatred. There came a stubborn silence. Ursula knew she must break it.

'Well, they've written to me, and I s'll have to go,' she said.

'Where will you get the money from?' asked her father.

'Uncle Tom will give it me,' she said.

Again there was silence. This time she was triumphant.

Then at length her father lifted his head. His face was abstracted, he seemed to be abstracting himself, to make a pure statement.

'Well, you're not going all that distance away,' he said. 'I'll ask Mr. Burt about a place here. I'm not going to have you by yourself at the other side of London.'

'But I've *got* to go to Kingston,' said Ursula. 'They've sent for me.'

'They'll do without you,' he said.

There was a trembling silence when she was on the point of tears.

'Well,' she said, low and tense, 'you can put me off this, but I'm *going* to have a place. I'm *not* going to stop at home.'

'Nobody wants you to stop at home,' he suddenly shouted, going livid with rage.

She said no more. Her nature had gone hard and smiling in its own arrogance, in its own antagonistic indifference to the rest of them. This was the state in which he wanted to kill her. She went singing into the parlour.

'C'est la mère Michel qui a perdu son chat,
Qui cri par la fenêtre qu'est-ce qui le lui rendra—'

During the next days Ursula went about bright and hard, singing to herself, making love to the children, but her soul hard and cold with regard to her parents. Nothing more was said. The hardness and brightness lasted for four days. Then it began to break up. So at evening she said to her father:

'Have you spoken about a place for me?'

'I spoke to Mr. Burt.'

'What did he say?'

'There's a committee meeting to-morrow. He'll tell me on Friday.'

So she waited till Friday. Kingston-on-Thames had been an exciting dream. Here she could feel the hard, raw reality. So she knew that this would come to pass. Because nothing was ever fulfilled, she found, except in the hard limited reality. She did not want to be a teacher in Ilkeston, because she knew Ilkeston, and hated it. But she wanted to be free, so she must take her freedom where she could.

On Friday her father said there was a place vacant in Brinsley Street school. This could most probably be secured for her, at once, without the trouble of application.

Her heart halted. Brinsley Street was a school in a poor quarter, and she had had a taste of the common children of Ilkeston. They had shouted after her and thrown stones. Still, as a teacher, she would be in authority. And it was all unknown. She was excited. The very forest of dry, sterile brick had some fascination for her. It was so hard and ugly, so relentlessly ugly, it would purge her of some of her floating sentimentality.

She dreamed how she would make the little, ugly children love her. She would be so *personal*. Teachers were always so hard and impersonal. There was no vivid relationship. She would make everything personal and vivid, she would give herself, she would give, give, give all her great stores of wealth to her children, she would make them *so* happy, and they would prefer her to any teacher on the face of the earth.

At Christmas she would choose such fascinating Christmas cards for them, and she would give them such a happy party in one of the class-rooms.

The headmaster, Mr. Harby, was a short, thick-set, rather common man, she thought. But she would hold before him the light of grace and refinement, he would have her in such high esteem before long. She would be the gleaming sun of the school, the children would blossom like little weeds, the teachers like tall, hard plants would burst into rare flower.

The Monday morning came. It was the end of September, and a drizzle of fine rain like veils round her, making her seem intimate, a world to herself. She walked forward to the new land. The old was blotted out. The veil would be rent that hid the new world. She was gripped hard with suspense as she went down the hill in the rain, carrying her dinner-bag.

Through the thin rain she saw the town, a black, extensive mount. She must enter in upon it. She felt at once a feeling of repugnance and of excited fulfilment. But she shrank.

She waited at the terminus for the tram. Here it was beginning. Before her was the station to Nottingham, whence Theresa had gone to school half an hour before; behind her was the little church school she had attended when she was a child, when her grandmother was alive. Her grandmother had been dead two years now. There was a strange woman at the Marsh, with her Uncle Fred, and a small baby. Behind her was Cossethay, and blackberries were ripe on the hedges.

As she waited at the tram-terminus she reverted swiftly to her childhood; her teasing grandfather, with his fair beard and blue eyes, and his big, monumental body; he had got drowned, her grandmother, whom Ursula would sometimes say she had loved more than anyone else in the world: the little church school, the Phillips boys; one was a soldier in the Life Guards now, one was a collier. With a passion she clung to the past.

But as she dreamed of it, she heard the tram-car grinding round a bend, rumbling dully, she saw it draw into sight, and hum nearer. It sidled round the loop at the terminus, and came to a standstill, looming above her. Some shadowy grey people stepped from the far end, the conductor was walking in the puddles, swinging round the pole.

She mounted into the wet, comfortless tram, whose floor was dark with wet, whose windows were all steamed, and she sat in suspense. It had begun, her new existence.

One other passenger mounted – a sort of charwoman with a drab, wet coat. Ursula could not bear the waiting of the tram. The bell clanged, there was a lurch forward. The car moved cautiously down the wet street. She was being carried forward, into her new existence. Her heart burned with pain and suspense, as if something were cutting her living tissue.

Often, oh often the tram seemed to stop, and wet, cloaked people mounted and sat mute and grey in stiff rows opposite her, their umbrellas between their knees. The windows of the tram grew more steamy; opaque. She was shut in with these unliving, spectral people. Even yet it did not occur to her that she was one of them. The conductor came down issuing tickets. Each little ring in his clipper sent a pang of dread through her. But her ticket surely was different from the rest.

They were all going to work; she also was going to work. Her ticket was the same. She sat trying to fit in with them. But fear was at her bowels, she felt an unknown, terrible grip upon her.

At Bath Street she must dismount and change trams. She looked uphill. It seemed to lead to freedom. She remembered the many Saturday afternoons she had walked up to the shops. How free and careless she had been!

Ah, her tram was sliding gingerly downhill. She dreaded every yard of her conveyance. The car halted, she rose hastily.

She kept turning her head as the car ran on, because she was uncertain of the street. At last, her heart a flame of suspense, trembling, she rose. The conductor rang the bell brusquely.

She was walking down a small, mean, wet street, empty of people. The school squatted low within its railed, asphalt yard, that shone black with rain. The building was grimy, and horrible, dry plants were shadowily looking through the windows.

She entered the arched doorway of the porch. The whole place seemed to have a threatening expression, imitating the church's architecture, for the purpose of domineering, like a gesture of vulgar authority. She saw that one pair of feet had paddled across the flagstone floor of the porch. The place was silent, deserted, like an empty prison waiting the return of tramping feet.

Ursula went forward to the teachers' room that burrowed in a gloomy hole. She knocked timidly.

'Come in!' called a surprised man's voice. as from a prison cell. She entered the dark little room that never got any sun. The gas was lighted naked and raw. At the table a thin man in shirt-sleeves was rubbing a paper on a jelly-tray. He looked up at Ursula with his narrow, sharp face, said 'Good morning,' then turned away again, and stripped the paper off the tray, glancing at the violet-coloured writing transferred, before he dropped the curled sheet aside among a heap.

Ursula watched him fascinated. In the gaslight and gloom and the narrowness of the room, all seemed unreal.

'Isn't it a nasty morning," she said.

'Yes,' he said, 'it's not much of weather.'

But in here it seemed that neither morning nor weather really existed. This place was timeless. He spoke in an occupied voice, like an echo. Ursula did not know what to say. She took off her waterproof.

'Am I early?' she asked.

The man looked first at a little clock, then at her. His eyes seemed to be sharpened to needle-points of vision.

'Twenty-five past,' he said. 'You're the second to come. I'm first this morning.'

Ursula sat down gingerly on the edge of a chair, and watched his thin red hands rubbing away on the white surface of the paper, then pausing, pulling up a corner of the sheet, peering, and rubbing away again. There was a great heap of curled white-and-scribbed sheets on the table.

'Must you do so many?' asked Ursula.

Again the man glanced up sharply. He was about thirty or thirty-three years old, thin, greenish, with a long nose and a sharp face. His eyes were blue, and sharp as points of steel, rather beautiful, the girl thought.

'Sixty-three,' he answered.

'So many!' she said, gently. Then she remembered.

'But they're not all for your class, are they?' she added.

'Why aren't they?' he replied, a fierceness in his voice.

Ursula was rather frightened by his mechanical ignoring of her, and his directness of statement. It was something new to her. She had never been treated like this before, as if she did not count, as if she were addressing a machine.

'It *is* too many,' she said sympathetically.

'You'll get about the same,' he said.

That was all she received. She sat rather blank, not knowing how to feel. Still she liked him. He seemed to cross. There was a queer, sharp, keen-edge feeling about him that attracted her and frightened her at the same time. It was so cold, and against his nature.

The door opened, and a short, neutral-tinted young woman of about twenty-eight appeared.

'Oh, Ursula!' the newcomer exclaimed. 'You are here early! My word, I'll warrant you don't keep it up. That's Mr. Williamson's peg. *This is* yours. Standard Five teacher always has this. Aren't you going to take your hat off?'

Miss Violet Harby removed Ursula's waterproof from the peg on which it was hung, to one a little farther down the row. She had already snatched the pins from her own stuff hat, and jammed them through her coat. She turned to Ursula, as she pushed up her frizzed, flat, dun-coloured hair.

'Isn't it a beastly morning,' she exclaimed, 'beastly! And if there's one thing I hate above another it's a wet Monday morning; – pack of kids trailing in anyhow-nohow, and no holding 'em—'

She had taken a black pinafore from a newspaper package, and was tying it round her waist.

'You've brought an apron, haven't you?' she said jerkily, glancing at Ursula. 'Oh – you'll want one. You've no idea what a sight you'll look before half-past four, what with chalk and ink and kids' dirty feet. – Well, I can send a boy down to mamma's for one.'

'Oh, it doesn't matter,' said Ursula.

'Oh, yes – I can send easily,' cried Miss Harby.

Ursula's heart sank. Everybody seemed so cocksure and so bossy. How was she going to get on with such jolty, jerky, bossy people? And Miss Harby had not spoken a word to the man at the table. She simply ignored him. Ursula felt the callous crude rudeness between the two teachers.

The two girls went out into the passage. A few children were already clattering in the porch.

'Jim Richards,' called Miss Harby, hard and authoritative. A boy came sheepishly forward.

'Shall you go down to our house for me, eh?' said Miss Harby, in a commanding, condescending, coaxing voice. She did not wait for an answer. 'Go down and ask mamma to send me one of my school pinas, for Miss Brangwen – shall you?'

The boy muttered a sheepish 'Yes, miss,' and was moving away.

'Hey,' called Miss Harby. 'Come here – now what are you going for? What shall you say to mamma?'

'A school pina—' muttered the boy.

' "Please, Mrs. Harby, Miss Harby says will you send her another school pinafore for Miss Brangwen, because she's come without one." '

'Yes, miss,' muttered the boy, head ducked, and was moving off. Miss Harby caught him back, holding him by the shoulder.

'What are you going to say?'

'Please, Mrs. Harby, Miss Harby wants a pinny for Miss Brangwin,' muttered the boy very sheepishly.

'*Miss Brangwen!*' laughed Miss Harby, pushing him away. 'Here, you'd better have my umbrella – wait a minute."

The unwilling boy was rigged up with Miss Harby's umbrella, and set off.

'Don't take long over it,' called Miss Harby, after him. Then she turned to Ursula, and said brightly:

'Oh, he's a caution, that lad – but not bad, you know.'

'No,' Ursula agreed, weakly.

The latch of the door clicked, and they entered the big room. Ursula glanced down the place. Its rigid, long silence was official and chilling. Halfway down was a glass partition, the doors of which were open. A clock ticked re-echoing, and Miss Harby's voice sounded double as she said:

'This is the big room – Standard Five-Six-and-Seven. – Here's your place – Five—'

She stood in the near end of the great room. There was a small high teacher's desk facing a squadron of long benches, two high windows in the wall opposite.

It was fascinating and horrible to Ursula. The curious, unliving light in the room changed her character. She thought it was the rainy morning. Then she looked up again, because of the horrid feeling of being shut in a rigid, inflexible air, away from all feeling of the ordinary day; and she noticed that the windows were of ribbed, suffused glass.

The prison was round her now! She looked at the walls, colour washed, pale green and chocolate, at the large windows with frowsy geraniums against the pale glass, at the long rows of desks, arranged in a squadron, and dread filled her. This was a new world, a new life, with which she was threatened. But still excited, she climbed into her chair at her teacher's desk. It was high, and her feet could not reach the ground, but must rest on the step. Lifted up there, off the ground, she was in office. How queer, how queer it all was! How different it was from the mist of rain blowing over Cossethay. As she thought of her own village, a spasm of yearning crossed her, it seemed so far off, so lost to her.

She was here in this hard, stark reality – *reality*. It was queer that she should call this the reality, which she had never known till to-day, and which now so filled her with dread and dislike, that she wished she might go away. This was the reality, and Cossethay, her beloved, beautiful, well-known Cossethay, which was as herself unto her, that was minor reality. This prison of a school was reality. Here, then, she would sit in state, the queen of scholars! Here she would realise her dream of being the beloved teacher bringing light and joy to her children! But the desks before her had an abstract angularity that bruised her sentiment and made her shrink. She winced, feeling she had been a fool in her anticipations. She had brought her feelings and her generosity to where neither generosity nor emotion were wanted. And already she felt rebuffed, troubled by the new atmosphere, out of place.

She slid down, and they returned to the teacher's room. It was queer to feel that one ought to alter one's personality. She was nobody, there was no reality in herself, the reality was all outside of her, and she must apply herself to it.

Mr. Harby was in the teachers' room, standing before a big, open cupboard, in which Ursula could see piles of pink blotting-paper, heaps of shiny new books, boxes of chalk, and bottles of coloured inks. It looked a treasure store.

The schoolmaster was a short, sturdy man, with a fine head, and a heavy jowl. Nevertheless he was good-looking, with his shapely brows and nose, and his great hanging moustache. He seemed absorbed in his work, and took no notice of Ursula's entry. There was something insulting in the way he could be so actively unaware of another person, so occupied.

When he had a moment of absence, he looked up from the table and said good-morning to Ursula. There was a pleasant light in his brown eyes. He seemed very manly and incontrovertible, like something she wanted to push over.

'You had a wet walk,' he said to Ursula.

'Oh, I don't mind, I'm used to it,' she replied, with a nervous little laugh.

But already he was not listening. Her words sounded ridiculous and babbling. He was taking no notice of her.

'You will sign your name here,' he said to her, as if she were some child – 'and the time when you come and go.'

Ursula signed her name in the time book and stood back. No one took any further notice of her. She beat her brains for something to say, but in vain.

'I'd let them in now,' said Mr. Harby to the thin man, who was very hastily arranging his papers.

The assistant teacher made no sign of acquiescence, and went on with what he was doing. The atmosphere in the room grew tense. At the last moment Mr. Brunt slipped into his coat.

'You will go to the girls' lobby,' said the schoolmaster to Ursula, with a fascinating, insulting geniality, purely official and domineering.

She went out and found Miss Harby, and another girl teacher, in the porch. On the asphalt yard the rain was falling. A toneless bell tang-tang-tanged drearily overhead, monotonously, insistently. It came to an end. Then Mr. Brunt was seen, bare-headed, standing at the other gate of the school yard, blowing shrill blasts on a whistle and looking down the rainy, dreary street.

Boys in gangs and streams came trotting up, running past the master and with a loud clatter of feet and voices, over the yard to the boys' porch. Girls were running and walking through the other entrance.

In the porch where Ursula stood there was a great noise of girls, who were tearing off their coats and hats, and hanging them on the racks bristling with pegs. There was a smell of wet clothing, a tossing out of wet, draggled hair, a noise of voices and feet.

The mass of girls grew greater, the rage around the pegs grew steadier, the scholars tended to fall into little noisy gangs in the porch. Then Violet Harby clapped her hands, clapped them louder, with a shrill 'Quiet, girls, quiet?'

There was a pause. The hubbub died down but did not cease.

'What did I say?' cried Miss Harby, shrilly.

There was almost complete silence. Sometimes a girl, rather late, whirled into the porch and flung off her things.

'Leaders – in place,' commanded Miss Harby shrilly.

Pairs of girls in pinafores and long hair stood separate in the porch.

'Standard Four, Five, and Six – fall in,' cried Miss Harby.

There was a hubbub, which gradually resolved itself into three columns of girls, two and two, standing smirking in the passage. In among the peg-racks, other teachers were putting the lower classes into ranks.

Ursula stood by her own Standard Five. They were jerking their shoulders, tossing their hair, nudging, writhing, staring, grinning, whispering and twisting.

A sharp whistle was heard, and Standard Six, the biggest girls, set off, led by Miss Harby. Ursula, with her Standard Five, followed after. She stood beside a smirking, grinning row of girls, waiting in a narrow passage. What she was herself she did not know.

Suddenly the sound of a piano was heard, and Standard Six set off hollowly down the big room. The boys had entered by another door. The piano played on, a march tune, Standard Five followed to the door of the big room. Mr. Harby was seen away beyond at his desk. Mr. Brunt guarded the other door of the room. Ursula's class pushed up. She stood near them. They glanced and smirked and shoved.

'Go on,' said Ursula.

They tittered.

'Go on,' said Ursula, for the piano continued.

The girls broke loosely into the room. Mr. Harby, who had seemed immersed in some occupation, away at his desk, lifted his head and thundered: 'Halt!'

There was a halt, the piano stopped. The boys who were just starting through the other door, pushed back. The harsh, subdued voice of Mr. Brunt was heard, then the booming shout of Mr. Harby, from far down the room: 'Who told Standard Five girls to come in like that?'

Ursula crimsoned. Her girls were glancing up at her, smirking their accusation.

'I sent them in, Mr. Harby,' she said, in a clear, struggling voice. There was a moment of silence. Then Mr. Harby roared from the distance.

'Go back to your places, Standard Five girls.'

The girls glanced up at Ursula, accusing, rather jeering, fugitive. They pushed back. Ursula's heart hardened with ignominious pain.

'Forward – march,' came Mr. Brunt's voice, and the girls set off, keeping time with the ranks of boys.

Ursula faced her class, some fifty-five boys and girls, who stood filling the ranks of the desks. She felt utterly non-existent. She had no place nor being there. She faced the block of children.

Down the room she heard the rapid firing of questions. She stood before her class not knowing what to do. She waited painfully. Her block of children, fifty unknown faces, watched her, hostile, ready to jeer. She felt as if she were in torture over a fire of faces. And on every side she was naked of them. Of unutterable length and torture the seconds went by.

Then she gathered courage. She heard Mr. Brunt asking questions in mental arithmetic. She stood near to her class, so that her voice need not be raised too much, and faltering, uncertain, she said:

'Seven hats at twopence ha'penny each?'

A grin went over the faces of the class, seeing her commence. She was red and suffering. Then some hands shot up like blades, and she asked for the answer.

The day passed incredibly slowly. She never knew what to do, there came horrible gaps, when she was merely exposed to the children; and when, relying on some pert little girl for information, she had started a lesson, she did not know how to go on with it properly. The children were her masters. She deferred to them. She could always hear Mr. Brunt. Like a machine, always in the same hard, high, inhuman voice he went on with his teaching, oblivious of everything. And before this inhuman number of children she was always at bay. She could not get away from it. There it was, this class of fifty collective children, depending on her for command, for command it hated and resented. It made her feel she could not breathe: she must suffocate, it was so inhuman. They were so many, that they were not children. They were a squadron. She could not speak as she would to a child, because they were not individual children, they were a collective, inhuman thing.

Dinner-time came, and stunned, bewildered, solitary, she went into the teachers' room for dinner. Never had she felt such a stranger to life before. It seemed to her she had just disembarked from some strange horrible state where everything was as in hell, a condition of hard, malevolent system. And she was not really free. The afternoon drew at her like some bondage.

The first week passed in a blind confusion. She did not know how to teach, and she felt she never would know. Mr. Harby came down every now and then to her class, to see what she was doing. She felt so incompetent as he stood by, bullying and threatening, so unreal, that she wavered, became neutral and non-existent. But he stood there watching with the listening-genial smile of the eyes, that was really threatening; he said nothing, he made her go on teaching, she felt she had no soul in her body. Then he went away, and his going was like a derision. The class was his class. She was a wavering substitute. He thrashed and bullied, he was hated. But he was master. Though she was gentle and always considerate of her class, yet they belonged to Mr. Harby, and they did not belong to her. Like some invincible source of the mechanism he kept all power to himself. And the class owned his power. And in school it was power, and power alone that mattered.

Soon Ursula came to dread him, and at the bottom of her dread was a seed of hate, for she despised him, yet he was master of her. Then she began to get on. All the other teachers hated him, and fanned their hatred among themselves. For he was master of them and the children, he stood like a wheel to make absolute his authority over the herd. That seemed to be his one reason to life, to hold blind authority over the school. His teachers were his subjects as much as the scholars. Only, because they had some authority, his instinct was to detest them.

Ursula could not make herself a favourite with him. From the first moment she set hard against him. She set against Violet Harby also. Mr. Harby was, however, too much for her, he was something she could not come to grips with, something too strong for her. She tried to approach him as a young, bright girl usually approaches a man, expecting a little chivalrous courtesy. But the fact that she was a girl, a woman, was ignored or used as a matter for contempt against her. She did not know what she was, nor what she must be. She wanted to remain her own responsive, personal self.

So she taught on. She made friends with the Standard Three teacher, Maggie Schofield. Miss Schofield was about twenty years old, a subdued girl who held aloof from the other teachers. She was rather beautiful, meditative, and seemed to live in another, lovelier world.

Ursula took her dinner to school, and during the second week ate it in Miss Schofield's room. Standard Three classroom stood by itself and had windows on two sides, looking on to the playground. It was a passionate relief to find such a retreat in the jarring school. For there were pots of chrysanthemums and coloured leaves, and a big jar of berries: there were pretty little pictures on the wall, photogravure reproductions from Greuze, and Reynolds's 'Age of Innocence', giving an air of intimacy; so that the room, with its window space, its smaller, tidier desks, its touch of pictures and flowers, made Ursula at once glad. Here at last was a little personal touch, to which she could respond.

It was Monday. She had been at school a week and was getting used to the surroundings, though she was still an entire foreigner in herself. She looked forward to having dinner with Maggie. That was the bright spot in the day. Maggie was so strong and remote, walking with slow, sure steps down a hard road, carrying the dream within her. Ursula went through the class teaching as through a meaningless daze.

Her class tumbled out at midday in haphazard fashion. She did not realise what host she was gathering against herself by her superior tolerance, her kindness and her *laisser-aller*. They were gone, and she was rid of them, and that was all. She hurried away to the teachers' room.

Mr. Brunt was crouching at the small stove, putting a little rice pudding into the oven. He rose then, and attentively poked in a small saucepan on the hob with a fork. Then he replaced the saucepan lid.

'Aren't they done?' asked Ursula gaily, breaking in on his tense absorption.

She always kept a bright, blithe manner, and was pleasant to all the teachers. For she felt like the swan among the geese, of superior heritage and belonging. And her pride at being the swan in this ugly school was not yet abated.

'Not yet,' replied Mr. Brunt, laconic.

'I wonder if my dish is hot,' she said, bending down at the oven. She half expected him to look for her, but he took no notice. She was hungry and she poked her finger eagerly in the pot to see if her brussels sprouts and potatoes and meat were ready. They were not.

'Don't you think it's rather jolly bringing dinner?' she said to Mr. Brunt.

'I don't know as I do,' he said, spreading a serviette on a corner of the table, and not looking at her.

'I suppose it is too far for you to go home?'

'Yes,' he said. Then he rose and looked at her. He had the bluest, fiercest, most pointed eyes that she had ever met. He stared at her with growing fierceness.

'If I were you, Miss Brangwen,' he said, menacingly, 'I should get a bit tighter hand over my class.'

Ursula shrank.

'Would you?' she asked, sweetly, yet in terror. 'Aren't I strict enough?'

'Because,' he repeated, taking no notice of her, 'they'll get you down if you don't tackle 'em pretty quick. They'll pull you down, and worry you, till Harby gets you shifted – that's how it'll be. You won't be here another six weeks' – and he filled his mouth with food – 'if you don't tackle 'em and tackle 'em quick.'

'Oh, but—' Ursula said, resentfully, ruefully. The terror was deep in her.

'Harby'll not help you. This is what he'll do – he'll let you go on, getting worse and worse, till either you clear out or he clears you out. It doesn't matter to me, except that you'll leave a class behind you as *I* hope I shan't have to cope with.'

She heard the accusation in the man's voice, and felt condemned. But still, school had not yet become a definite reality to her. She was shirking it. It was reality, but it was all outside her. And she fought against Mr. Brunt's representation. She did not want to realise.

'Will it be so terrible?' she said, quivering, rather beautiful, but with a slight touch of condescension, because she would not betray her own trepidation.

'Terrible?' said the man, turning to his potatoes again. 'I dunno about terrible.'

'I do feel frightened,' said Ursula. 'The children seem so—'

'What?' said Miss Harby, entering at that moment.

'Why,' said Ursula, 'Mr. Brunt says I ought to tackle my class,' and she laughed uneasily.

'Oh, you have to keep order if you want to teach,' said Miss Harby, hard, superior, trite.

Ursula did not answer. She felt non valid before them.

'If you want to be let to *live*, you have,' said Mr. Brunt.

'Well, if you can't keep order, what good *are* you?' said Miss Harby.

'An' you've got to do it by yourself,' – his voice rose like the bitter cry of the prophets. 'You'll get no *help* from anybody.'

'Oh, indeed?' said Miss Harby. 'Some people can't be helped.' And she departed.

The air of hostility and disintegration, of wills working in antagonistic subordination, was hideous. Mr. Brunt, subordinate, afraid, acid with shame, frightened her. Ursula wanted to run. She only wanted to clear out, not to understand.

Then Miss Schofield came in, and with her another, more restful note.

Ursula at once turned for confirmation to the newcomer. Maggie remained personal within all this unclean system of authority.

'Is the big Anderson here?' she asked of Mr. Brunt. And they spoke of some affair about two scholars, coldly, officially.

Miss Schofield took her brown dish, and Ursula followed with her own. The cloth was laid in the pleasant Standard Three room, there was a jar with two or three monthly roses on the table.

'It is so nice in here, you *have* made it different,' said Ursula gaily. But she was afraid. The atmosphere of the school was upon her.

'The big room,' said Miss Schofield, 'ha, it's misery to be in it?'

She too spoke with bitterness. She too lived in the ignominious position of an upper servant hated by the master above and the class beneath. She was, she knew, liable to attack from either side at any minute, or from both at once, for the authorities would listen to the complaints of parents, and both would turn round on the mongrel authority, the teacher.

So there was a hard, bitter withholding in Maggie Schofield even as she poured out her savoury mess of big golden beans and brown gravy.

'It is vegetarian hot-pot,' said Miss Schofield. 'Would you like to try it?'

'I should love to,' said Ursula.

Her own dinner seemed coarse and ugly beside this savoury, clean dish.

'I've never eaten vegetarian things,' she said. 'But I should think they can be good.'

'I'm not really a vegetarian,' said Maggie, 'I don't like to bring meat to school.'

'No,' said Ursula, 'I don't think I do either.'

And again her soul rang an answer to a new refinement, a new liberty. If all vegetarian things were as nice as this, she would be glad to escape the slight uncleanness of meat.

'How good!' she cried.

'Yes,' said Miss Schofield, and she proceeded to tell her the receipt. The two girls passed on to talk about themselves. Ursula told all about the High School, and about her matriculation, bragging a little. She felt so poor here, in this ugly place. Miss Schofield listened with brooding, handsome face, rather gloomy.

'Couldn't you have got to some better place than this?' she asked at length.

'I didn't know what it was like,' said Ursula, doubtfully.

'Ah!' said Miss Schofield, and she turned aside her head with a bitter motion.

'Is it as horrid as it seems?' asked Ursula, frowning lightly, in fear.

'It *is*,' said Miss Schofield, bitterly. 'Ha! – it is *hateful!*'

Ursula's heart sank, seeing even Miss Schofield in the deadly bondage.

'It is Mr. Harby,' said Maggie Schofield, breaking forth. 'I don't think I *could* live again in the big room – Mr. Brunt's voice and Mr. Harby – ah—'

She turned aside her head with a deep hurt. Some things she could not bear.

'Is Mr. Harby really horrid?' asked Ursula, venturing into her own dread.

'He! – why, he's just a bully,' said Miss Schofield, raising her shamed dark eyes, that flamed with tortured contempt. 'He's not bad as long as you keep in with him, and refer to him, and do everything in his way – but – it's all so *mean*! It's just a question of fighting on both sides – and those great louts—'

She spoke with difficulty and with increased bitterness. She had evidently suffered. Her soul was raw with ignominy. Ursula suffered in response.

'But why is it so horrid?' she asked, helplessly.

'You can't do *anything*,' said Miss Schofield. 'He's against you on one side and he sets the children against you on the other. The children are simply awful. You've got to *make* them do everything. Everything, everything has got to come out of you. Whatever they learn, you've got to force it into them – and that's how it is.'

Ursula felt her heart fail inside her. Why must she grasp all this, why must she force learning on fifty-five reluctant children, having all the time an ugly, rude jealousy behind her, ready to throw her to the mercy of the herd of children, who would like to rend her as a weaker representative of authority. A great dread of her task possessed her. She saw Mr. Brunt, Miss Harby, Miss Schofield, all the school-teachers, drudging unwillingly at the graceless task of compelling many children into one disciplined, mechanical set, reducing the whole set to an automatic state of obedience and attention, and then of commanding their acceptance of various pieces of knowledge. The first great task was to reduce sixty children to one state of mind, or being. This state must be produced automatically, through the will of the teacher, and the will of the whole school authority, imposed upon the will of the children. The point was that the headmaster and the teachers should have one will in authority, which should bring the will of the children into accord. But the. headmaster was narrow and exclusive. The will of the teachers could not agree with his, their separate wills refused to be so subordinated. So there was a state of anarchy, leaving the final judgment to the children themselves, which authority should exist.

So there existed a set of separate wills, each straining itself to the utmost to exert its own authority. Children will never naturally acquiesce to sitting in a class and submitting to knowledge. They must be compelled by a stronger, wiser will. Against which will they must always strive to revolt. So that the first great effort of every teacher of a large class must be to bring the will of the children into accordance with his own will. And this he can only do by an abnegation of his personal self, and an application of a system of laws, for the purpose of achieving a certain calculable result, the imparting of certain knowledge. Whereas Ursula thought she was going to become the first wise teacher by making the whole business personal, and using no compulsion. She believed entirely in her own personality.

So that she was in a very deep mess. In the first place she was offering to a class a relationship which only one or two of the children were sensitive enough to appreciate so that the mass were left outsiders, therefore against her. Secondly, she was placing herself in passive antagonism to the one fixed authority of Mr. Harby, so that the scholars could more safely harry her. She did not know, but her instinct gradually warned her. She was tortured by the voice of Mr. Brunt. On it went, jarring, harsh, full of hate, but so monotonous, it nearly drove her mad: always the same set, harsh monotony. The man was become a mechanism working on and on and on. But the personal man was in subdued friction all the time. It was horrible – all hate! Must she be like this? She could feel the ghastly necessity. She must become the same – put away the personal self, become an instrument, an abstraction, working upon a certain material, the class, to achieve a set purpose of making them know so much each day. And she could not submit. Yet gradually she felt the invincible iron closing upon her. The sun was being blocked out. Often when she went out at playtime and saw a luminous blue sky with changing clouds, it seemed just a fantasy, like a piece of painted scenery. Her heart was so black and tangled in the teaching, her personal self was shut in prison, abolished, she was subjugate to a bad, destructive will. How then could the sky be shining? There was no sky, there was no luminous atmosphere of out-of-doors. Only the inside of the school was real – hard, concrete, real and vicious.

She would not yet, however, let school quite overcome her. She always said, 'It is not a permanency, it will come to an end.' She could always see herself beyond the place, see the time when she had let it. On Sundays and on holidays, when she was away at Cossethay or in the woods where the beech-leaves were fallen, she could think of St. Philip's Church School, and by an effort of will put it in the picture as a dirty little low-squatting building that made a very tiny mound under the sky, while the great beech-woods spread immense about her, and the afternoon was spacious and wonderful. Moreover the children, the scholars, they were insignificant little objects far away, oh, far away. And what power had they over her free soul? A fleeting thought of them, as she kicked her way through the beech-leaves, and they were gone. But her will was tense against them all the time.

All the while, they pursued her. She had never had such a passionate love of the beautiful things about her. Sitting on top of the tram-car, at evening, sometimes school was swept away as she saw a magnificent sky settling down. And her breast, her very hands, clamoured for the lovely flare of sunset. It was poignant almost to agony, her reaching for it. She almost cried aloud seeing the sundown so lovely.

For she was held away. It was no matter how she said to herself that school existed no more once she had left it. It existed. It was within her like a dark weight, controlling her movement. It was in vain the high-spirited, proud young girl flung off the school and its association with her. She was Miss Brangwen, she was Standard Five teacher, she had her most important being in her work now.

Constantly haunting her, like a darkness hovering over her heart and threatening to swoop down over it at every moment, was the sense that somehow, somehow she was brought down. Bitterly she denied unto herself that she was really a school-teacher. Leave that to the Violet Harbys. She herself would stand clear of the accusation. It was in vain she denied it.

Within herself some recording hand seemed to point mechanically to a negation. She was incapable of fulfilling her task. She could never for a moment escape from the fatal weight of the knowledge.

And so she felt inferior to Violet Harby. Miss Harby was a splendid teacher. She could keep order and inflict knowledge on a class with remarkable efficiency. It was no good Ursula's protesting to herself that she was infinitely, infinitely the superior of Violet Harby. She knew that Violet Harby succeeded where she failed, and this in a task which was almost a test of her. She felt something all the time wearing upon her, wearing her down. She went about in these first weeks trying to deny it, to say she was free as ever. She tried not to feel at a disadvantage before Miss Harby, tried to keep up the effect of her own superiority. But a great weight was on her, which Violet Harby could bear, and she herself could not.

Though she did not give in, she never succeeded. Her class was getting in worse condition, she knew herself less and less secure in teaching it. Ought she to withdraw and go home again? Ought she to say she had come to the wrong place, and so retire? Her very life was at test.

She went on doggedly, blindly, waiting for a crisis. Mr. Harby had now begun to persecute her. Her dread and hatred of him grew and loomed larger and larger. She was afraid he was going to bully her and destroy her. He began to persecute her because she could not keep her class in proper condition, because her class was the weak link in the chain which made up the school.

One of the offences was that her class was noisy and disturbed Mr. Harby, as he took Standard Seven at the other end of the room. She was taking composition on a certain morning, walking in among the scholars. Some of the boys had dirty ears and necks, their clothing smelled unpleasantly, but she could ignore it. She corrected the writing as she went.

'When you say "their fur is brown", how do you write "their"?' she asked.

There was a little pause; the boys were always jeeringly backward in answering. They had begun to jeer at her authority altogether.

'Please, miss, t-h-e-i-r', spelled a lad, loudly, with a note of mockery.

At that moment Mr. Harby was passing.

'Stand up, Hill?' he called, in a big voice.

Everybody started. Ursula watched the boy. He was evidently poor, and rather cunning. A stiff bit of hair stood straight off his forehead, the rest fitted close to his meagre head. He was pale and colourless.

'Who told you to call out?' thundered Mr. Harby.

The boy looked up and down, with a guilty air, and a cunning, cynical reserve.

'Please, sir, I was answering,' he replied, with the same humble insolence.

'Go to my desk.'

The boy set off down the room, the big black jacket hanging in dejected folds about him, his thin legs, rather knocked at the knees, going already with the pauper's crawl, his feet in their big boots scarcely lifted. Ursula watched him in his crawling, slinking progress down the room. He was one of *her* boys! When he got to the desk, he looked round, half furtively, with a sort of cunning grin and a pathetic leer at the big boys in Standard VII. Then, pitiable, pale, in his dejected garments, he lounged under the menace of the headmaster's desk, with one thin leg crooked at the knee and the foot stuck out sideways his hands in the low-hanging pockets of his man's jacket.

Ursula tried to get her attention back to the class. The boy gave her a little horror, and she was at the same time hot with pity for him. She felt she wanted to scream. She was responsible for the boy's punishment. Mr. Harby was looking at her handwriting on the board. He turned to the class.

'Pens down.'

The children put down their pens and looked up.

'Fold arms.'

They pushed back their books and folded arms.

Ursula, stuck among the back forms, could not extricate herself.

'*What* is your composition about?' asked the headmaster. Every hand shot up. 'The—' stuttered some voice in its eagerness to answer.

'I wouldn't advise you to call out,' said Mr. Harby. He would have a pleasant voice, full and musical, but for the detestable menace that always tailed in it. He stood unmoved, his eyes twinkling under his bushy black eyebrows, watching the class. There was something fascinating in him, as he stood, and again she wanted to scream. She was all jarred, she did not know what she felt.

'Well, Alice?' he said.

'The rabbit,' piped a girl's voice.

'A very easy subject for Standard Five.'

Ursula felt a slight shame of incompetence. She was exposed before the class. And she was tormented by the contradictoriness of everything. Mr. Harby stood so strong, and so male, with his black brows and clear forehead, the heavy jaw, the big, overhanging moustache: such a man, with strength and male power, and a certain blind, native beauty. She might have liked him as a man. And here he stood in some other capacity, bullying over such a trifle as a boy's speaking out without permission. Yet he was not a little, fussy man. He seemed to have some cruel, stubborn, evil spirit, he was imprisoned in a task too small and petty for him, which yet, in a servile acquiescence, he would fulfil, because he had to earn his living. He had no finer control over himself, only this blind, dogged, wholesale will. He would keep the job going, since he must. And this job was to make the children spell the word 'caution' correctly, and put a capital letter after a full-stop. So at this he hammered with his suppressed hatred, always suppressing himself, till he was beside himself. Ursula suffered, bitterly as he stood, short and handsome and powerful, teaching her class. It seemed such a miserable thing for him to be doing. He had a decent, powerful, rude soul. What did he care about the composition on 'The Rabbit'? Yet his will kept him there before the class, threshing the trivial subject. It was habit with him now, to be so little and vulgar, out of place. She saw the shamefulness of his position, felt the fettered wickedness in him which would blaze out into evil rage in the long run, so that he was like a persistent, strong creature tethered. It was really intolerable. The jarring was torture to her. She looked over the silent, attentive class that seemed to have crystallised into order and rigid, neutral form. This he had it in his power to do, to crystallise the children into hard, mute fragments, fixed under his will: his brute will, which fixed them by sheer force. She too must learn to subdue them to her will: she must. For it was her duty, since the school was such. He had crystallised the class into order. But to see him, a strong, powerful man, using all his power for such a purpose, seemed almost horrible. There was something hideous about it. The strange, genial light in his eye was really vicious, and ugly, his smile was one of torture. He could not be impersonal. He could not have a clear, pure purpose, he could only exercise his own brute will. He did not believe in the least in the education he kept inflicting year after year upon the children. So he must bully, only bully, even while it tortured his strong, wholesome nature with shame like a spur always galling. He was so blind and ugly and out of place. Ursula could not bear it as he stood there. The whole situation was wrong and ugly.

The lesson was finished, Mr. Harby went away. At the far end of the room she heard the whistle and the thud of the cane. Her heart stood still within her. She could not bear it, no, she could not bear it when the boy was beaten. It made her sick. She felt that she must go out of this school, this torture-place. And she hated the schoolmaster, thoroughly and finally. The brute, had he no shame? He should never be allowed to continue the atrocity of this bullying cruelty. Then Hill came crawling back, blubbering piteously. There was something desolate about this blubbering that nearly broke her heart. For after all, if she had kept her class in proper discipline, this would never have happened, Hill would never have called out and been caned.

She began the arithmetic lesson. But she was distracted. The boy Hill sat away on the back desk, huddled up, blubbering and sucking his hand. It was a long time. She dared not go near, nor speak to him. She felt ashamed before him. And she felt she could not forgive the boy for being the huddled, blubbering object, all wet and snivelled, which he was.

She went on correcting the sums. But there were too many children. She could not get round the class. And Hill was on her conscience. At last he had stopped crying, and sat bunched over his hands, playing quietly. Then he looked up at her. His face was dirty with tears, his eyes had a curious washed look, like the sky after rain, a sort of wanness. He bore no malice. He had already forgotten, and was waiting to be restored to the normal position.

'Go on with your work, Hill,' she said.

The children were playing over their arithmetic, and, she knew, cheating thoroughly. She wrote another sum on the blackboard. She could not get round the class. She went again to the front to watch. Some were ready. Some were not. What was she to do?

At last it was time for recreation. She gave the order to cease working, and in some way or other got her class out of the room. Then she faced the disorderly litter of blotted, uncorrected books, of broken rulers and chewed pens. And her heart sank in sickness. The misery was getting deeper.

The trouble went on and on, day after day. She had always piles of books to mark, myriads of errors to correct, a heart-wearying task that she loathed. And the work got worse and worse. When she tried to flatter herself that the composition grew more alive, more interesting, she had to see that the handwriting grew more and more slovenly, the books more filthy and disgraceful. She tried what she could, but it was of no use. But she was not going to take it seriously. Why should she? Why should she say to herself, that it mattered, if she failed to teach a class to write perfectly neatly? Why should she take the blame unto herself?

Pay day came, and she received four pounds two shillings and one penny. She was very proud that day. She had never had so much money before. And she had earned it all herself. She sat on the top of the tram-car fingering the gold and fearing she might lose it. She felt so established and strong, because of it. And when she got home she said to her mother:

'It is pay day to-day, mother.'

'Ay,' said her mother, coolly.

Then Ursula put down fifty shillings on the table.

'That is my board,' she said.

'Ay,' said her mother, letting it lie.

Ursula was hurt. Yet she had paid her scot. She was free. She paid for what she had. There remained moreover thirty-two shillings of her own. She would not spend any, she who was naturally a spendthrift, because she could not bear to damage her fine gold.

She had a standing ground now apart from her parents. She was something else besides the mere daughter of William and Anna Brangwen. She was independent. She earned her own living. She was an important member of the working community. She was sure that fifty shillings a month quite paid for her keep. If her mother received fifty shillings a month for each of the children, she would have twenty pounds a month and no clothes to provide. Very well then.

Ursula was independent of her parents. She now adhered elsewhere. Now, the 'Board of Education' was a phrase that rang significant to her, and she felt Whitehall far beyond her as her ultimate home. In the government, she knew which minister had supreme control over Education, and it seemed to her that, in some way, he was connected with her, as her father was connected with her.

She had another self, another responsibility. She was no longer Ursula Brangwen, daughter of William Brangwen. She was also Standard Five teacher in St. Philip's School. And it was a case now of being Standard Five teacher, and nothing else. For she could not escape.

Neither could she succeed. That was her horror. As the weeks passed on, there was no Ursula Brangwen, free and jolly. There was only a girl of that name obsessed by the fact that she could not manage her class of children. At week-ends there came days of passionate reaction, when she went mad with the taste of liberty, when merely to be free in the morning, to sit down at her embroidery and stitch the coloured silks was a passion of delight. For the prison house was always awaiting her! This was only a respite, as her chained heart knew well. So that she seized hold of the swift hours of the week-end, and wrung the last drop of sweetness out of them, in a little, cruel frenzy.

She did not tell anybody how this state was a torture to her. She did not confide, either to Gudrun or to her parents, how horrible she found it to be a school-teacher. But when Sunday night came, and she felt the Monday morning at hand, she was strung up tight with dreadful anticipation, because the strain and the torture was near again.

She did not believe that she could ever teach that great, brutish class, in that brutal school: ever, ever. And yet, if she failed, she must in some way go under. She must admit that the man's world was too strong for her, she could not take her place in it; she must go down before Mr. Harby. And all her life henceforth, she must go on, never having freed herself of the man's world, never having achieved the freedom of the great world of responsible work. Maggie had taken her place there, she had even stood level with Mr. Harby and got free of him: and her soul was always wandering in far-off valleys and glades of poetry. Maggie was free. Yet there was something like subjection in Maggie's very freedom. Mr. Harby, the man, disliked the reserved woman, Maggie. Mr. Harby, the schoolmaster, respected his teacher, Miss Schofield.

For the present, however, Ursula only envied and admired Maggie. She herself had still to get where Maggie had got. She had still to make her footing. She had taken up a position on Mr. Harby's ground, and she must keep it. For he was now beginning a regular attack on her, to drive her away out of his school. She could not keep order. Her class was a turbulent crowd, and the weak spot in the school's work. Therefore she must go, and someone more useful must come in her place, someone who could keep discipline.

The headmaster had worked himself into an obsession of fury against her. He only wanted her gone. She had come, she had got worse as the weeks went on, she was absolutely no good. His system, which was his very life in school, the outcome of his bodily movement, was attacked and threatened at the point where Ursula was included. She was the danger that threatened his body with a blow, a fall. And blindly, thoroughly, moving from strong instinct of opposition, he set to work to expel her.

When he punished one of her children as he had punished the boy Hill, for an offence against *himself*, he made the punishment extra heavy with the significance that the extra stroke came in because of the weak teacher who allowed all these things to be. When he punished for an offence against *her*, he punished lightly, as if offences against her were not significant. Which all the children knew, and they behaved accordingly.

Every now and again Mr. Harby would swoop down to examine exercise books. For a whole hour, he would be going round the class, taking book after book, comparing page after page, whilst Ursula stood aside for all the remarks and fault-finding to be pointed at her through the scholars. It was true, since she had come, the composition books had grown more and more untidy, disorderly, filthy. Mr. Harby pointed to the pages done before her régime, and to those done after, and fell into a passion of rage. Many children he sent out to the front with their books. And after he had thoroughly gone through the silent and quivering class he caned the worst offenders well, in front of the others, thundering in real passion of anger and chagrin.

'Such a condition in a class, I can't believe it! It is simply disgraceful! I can't think how you have been let to get like it! Every Monday morning I shall come down and examine these books. So don't think that because there is nobody paying any attention to you, that you are free to unlearn everything you ever learned, and go back till you are not fit for Standard Three. I shall examine all books every Monday—'

Then in a rage, he went away with his cane, leaving Ursula to confront a pale, quivering class, whose childish faces were shut in blank resentment, fear, and bitterness, whose souls were full of anger and contempt for *her* rather than of the master, whose eyes looked at her with the cold, inhuman accusation of children. And she could hardly make mechanical words to speak to them. When she gave an order they obeyed with an insolent off-handedness, as if to say: 'As for you, do you think we would obey *you*, but for the master?' She sent the blubbering, caned boys to their seats, knowing that they too jeered at her and her authority, holding her weakness responsible for what punishment had overtaken them. And she knew the whole position, so that even her horror of physical beating and suffering sank to a deeper pain, and became a moral judgment upon her, worse than any hurt.

She must, during the next week, watch over her books, and punish any fault. Her soul decided it coldly. Her personal desire was dead for that day at least. She must have nothing more of herself in school. She was to be Standard Five teacher only. That was her duty. In school, she was nothing but Standard Five teacher. Ursula Brangwen must be excluded.

So that, pale, shut, at last distant and impersonal, she saw no longer the child, how his eyes danced, or how he had a queer little soul that could not be bothered with shaping handwriting so long as he dashed down what he thought. She saw no children, only the task that was to be done. And keeping her eyes there, on the task, and not on the child, she was impersonal enough to punish where she could otherwise only have sympathised, understood, and condoned, to approve where she would have been merely uninterested before. But her interest had no place any more.

It was agony to the impulsive, bright girl of seventeen to become distant and official, having no personal relationship with the children. For a few days, after the agony of the Monday, she succeeded, and had some success with her class. But it was a state not natural to her, and she began to relax.

Then came another infliction. There were not enough pens to go round the class. She sent to Mr. Harby for more. He came in person.

'Not enough pens, Miss Brangwen?' he said, with the smile and calm of exceeding rage against her.

'No, we are six short,' she said, quaking.

'Oh, how is that?' he said, menacingly. Then, looking over the class, he asked:

'How many are there here to-day?'

'Fifty-two,' said Ursula, but he did not take any notice, counting for himself.

'Fifty-two,' he said. 'And how many pens are there, Staples?'

Ursula was now silent. He would not heed her if she answered, since he had addressed the monitor.

'That's a very curious thing,' said Mr. Harby, looking over the silent class with a slight grin of fury. All the childish faces looked up at him blank and exposed.

'A few days ago there were sixty pens for this class – now there are forty-eight. What is forty-eight from sixty, Williams?' There was a sinister suspense in the question. A thin, ferret-faced boy in a sailor suit started up exaggeratedly.

'Please, sir!' he said. Then a slow, sly grin came over his face. He did not know. There was a tense silence. The boy dropped his head. Then he looked up again, a little cunning triumph in his eyes. 'Twelve,' he said.

'I would advise you to attend,' said the headmaster dangerously. The boy sat down.

'Forty-eight from sixty is twelve: so there are twelve pens to account for. Have you looked for them, Staples?'

'Yes, sir.'

'Then look again.'

The scene dragged on. Two pens were found: ten were missing. Then the storm burst.

'Am I to have you thieving, besides your dirt and bad work and bad behaviour?' the headmaster began. 'Not content with being the worst-behaved and dirtiest class in the school, you are thieves into the bargain, are you? It is a very funny thing! Pens don't melt into the air: pens are not in the habit of mizzling away into nothing. What has become of them then? They must be somewhere. What has become of them? For they must be found, and found by Standard Five. They were lost by Standard Five, and they must be found.'

Ursula stood and listened, her heart hard and cold. She was so much upset, that she felt almost mad. Something in her tempted her to turn on the headmaster and tell him to stop, about the miserable pens. But she did not. She could not.

After every session, morning and evening, she had the pens counted. Still they were missing. And pencils and india-rubbers disappeared. She kept the class staying behind, till the things were found. But as soon as Mr. Harby had gone out of the room, the boys began to jump about and shout, and at last they bolted in a body from the school.

This was drawing near a crisis. She could not tell Mr. Harby because, while he would punish the class, he would make her the cause of the punishment, and her class would pay her back with disobedience and derision. Already there was a deadly hostility grown up between her and the children. After keeping in the class, at evening, to finish some work, she would find boys dodging behind her, calling after her: 'Brangwen, Brangwen – Proud-acre.'

When she went into Ilkeston of a Saturday morning with Gudrun, she heard again the voices yelling after her:

'Brangwen, Brangwen.'

She pretended to take no notice, but she coloured with shame at being held up to derision in the public street. She Ursula Brangwen of Cossethay, could not escape from the Standard Five teacher which she was. In vain she went out to buy ribbon for her hat. They called after her, the boys she tried to teach.

And one evening, as she went from the edge of the town into the country, stones came flying at her. Then the passion of shame and anger surpassed her. She walked on unheeding, beside herself. Because of the darkness she could not see who were those that threw. But she did not want to know.

Only in her soul a change took place. Never more, and never more would she give herself as individual to her class. Never would she, Ursula Brangwen, the girl she was, the person she was, come into contact with those boys. She would be Standard Five teacher, as far away personally from her class as if she had never set foot in St. Philip's school. She would just obliterate them all, and keep herself apart, take them as scholars only.

So her face grew more and more shut, and over her flayed, exposed soul of a young girl who had gone open and warm to give herself to the children, there set a hard, insentient thing, that worked mechanically according to a system imposed.

It seemed she scarcely saw her class the next day. She could only feel her will, and what she would have of this class which she must grasp into subjection. It was no good, any more, to appeal, to play upon the better feelings of the class. Her swift-working soul realised this.

She, as teacher, must bring them all as scholars, into subjection. And this she was going to do. All else she would forsake. She had become hard and impersonal, almost avengeful on herself as well as on them, since the stone throwing. She did not want to be a person, to be herself any more, after such humiliation. She would assert herself for mastery, be only teacher. She was set now. She was going to fight and subdue.

She knew by now her enemies in the class. The one she hated most was Williams. He was a sort of defective, not bad enough to be so classed. He could read with fluency, and had plenty of cunning intelligence. But he could not keep still. And he had a kind of sickness very repulsive to a sensitive girl, something cunning and etiolated and degenerate. Once he had thrown an ink-well at her, in one of his mad little rages. Twice he had run home out of class. He was a well-known character.

And he grinned up his sleeve at this girl-teacher, sometimes hanging round her to fawn on her. But this made her dislike him more. He had a kind of leech-like power.

From one of the children she took a supple cane, and this she determined to use when real occasion came. One morning, at composition, she said to the boy Williams:

'Why have you made this blot?'

'Please, miss, it fell off my pen,' he whined out, in the mocking voice that he was so clever in using. The boys near snorted with laughter. For Williams was an actor, he could tickle the feelings of his hearers subtly. Particularly he could tickle the children with him into ridiculing his teacher, or indeed, any authority of which he was not afraid. He had that peculiar gaol instinct.

'Then you must stay in and finish another page of composition,' said the teacher.

This was against her usual sense of justice, and the boy resented it derisively. At twelve o'clock she caught him slinking out.

'Williams, sit down,' she said.

And there she sat, and there he sat, alone, opposite to her, on the back desk, looking up at her with his furtive eyes every minute.

'Please, miss, I've got to go an errand,' he called out insolently.

'Bring me your book,' said Ursula.

The boy came out, flapping his book along the desks. He had not written a line.

'Go back and do the writing you have to do,' said Ursula. And she sat at her desk, trying to correct books. She was trembling and upset. And for an hour the miserable boy writhed and grinned in his seat. At the end of that time he had done five lines.

'As it is so late now,' said Ursula, 'you will finish the rest this evening.'

The boy kicked his way insolently down the passage.

The afternoon came again. Williams was there, glancing at her, and her heart beat thick, for she knew it was a fight between them. She watched him.

During the geography lesson, as she was pointing to the map with her cane, the boy continually ducked his whitish head under the desk, and attracted the attention of other boys.

'Williams,' she said, gathering her courage, for it was critical now to speak to him, 'what are you doing?'

He lifted his face, the sore-rimmed eyes half smiling. There was something intrinsically indecent about him. Ursula shrank away.

'Nothing,' he replied, feeling a triumph.

'What are you doing?' she repeated, her heart-beat suffocating her.

'Nothing,' replied the boy, insolently, aggrieved, comic.

'If I speak to you again, you must go down to Mr. Harby,' she said.

But this boy was a match even for Mr. Harby. He was so persistent, so cringing, and flexible, he howled so when he was hurt, that the master hated more the teacher who sent him than he hated the boy himself. For of the boy he was sick of the sight. Which Williams knew. He grinned visibly.

Ursula turned to the map again, to go on with the geography lesson. But there was a little ferment in the class. Williams' spirit infected them all. She heard a scuffle, and then she trembled inwardly. If they all turned on her this time, she was beaten.

'Please, miss—' called a voice in distress.

She turned round. One of the boys she liked was ruefully holding out a torn celluloid collar. She heard the complaint, feeling futile.

'Go in front, Wright,' she said.

She was trembling in every fibre. A big, sullen boy, not bad but very difficult, slouched out to the front. She went on with the lesson, aware that Williams was making faces at Wright, and that Wright was grinning behind her. She was afraid. She turned to the map again. And she was afraid.

'Please, miss, Williams—' came a sharp cry, and a boy on the back row was standing up, with drawn, pained brows, half a mocking grin on his pain, half real resentment against Williams – 'Please, miss, he's nipped me,' – and he rubbed his leg ruefully.

'Come in front, Williams,' she said.

The rat-like boy sat with his pale smile and did not move.

'Come in front,' she repeated, definite now.

'I shan't,' he cried, snarling, rat-like, grinning. Something went click in

Ursula's soul. Her face and eyes set, she went through the class straight. The boy cowered before her glowering, fixed eyes. But she advanced on him, seized him by the arm, and dragged him from his seat. He clung to the form. It was the battle between him and her. Her instinct had suddenly become calm and quick. She jerked him from his grip, and dragged him, struggling and kicking, to the front. He kicked her several times, and clung to the forms as he passed, but she went on. The class was on its feet in excitement. She saw it, and made no move.

She knew if she let go the boy he would dash to the door. Already he had run home once out of her class. So she snatched her cane from the desk, and brought it down on him. He was writhing and kicking. She saw his face beneath her, white, with eyes like the eyes of a fish, stony, yet full of hate and horrible fear. And she loathed him, the hideous writhing thing that was nearly too much for her. In horror lest he should overcome her, and yet at the heart quite calm, she brought down the cane again and again, whilst he struggled making inarticulate noises, and lunging vicious kicks at her. With one hand she managed to hold him, and now and then the cane came down on him. He writhed, like a mad thing. But the pain of the strokes cut through his writhing, vicious, coward's courage, bit deeper, till at last, with a long whimper that became a yell, he went limp. She let him go, and he rushed at her, his teeth and eyes glinting. There was a second of agonised terror in her heart: he was a beast thing. Then she caught him, and the cane came down on him. A few times, madly, in a frenzy, he lunged and writhed, to kick her. But again the cane broke him, he sank with a howling yell on the floor, and like a beaten beast lay there yelling.

Mr. Harby had rushed up towards the end of this performance.

'What's the matter?' he roared.

Ursula felt as if something were going to break in her.

'I've thrashed him,' she said, her breast heaving, forcing out the words on the last breath. The headmaster stood choked with rage, helpless. She looked at the writhing, howling figure on the floor.

'Get up,' she said. The thing writhed away from her. She took a step forward. She had realised the presence of the headmaster for one second, and then she was oblivious of it again.

'Get up,' she said. And with a little dart the boy was on his feet. His yelling dropped to a mad blubber. He had been in a frenzy.

'Go and stand by the radiator,' she said.

As if mechanically, blubbering, he went.

The headmaster stood robbed of movement or speech. His face was yellow, his hands twitched convulsively. But Ursula stood stiff not far from him. Nothing could touch her now: she was beyond Mr. Harby. She was as if violated to death.

The headmaster muttered something, turned, and went down the room, whence, from the far end, he was heard roaring in a mad rage at his own class.

The boy blubbered wildly by the radiator. Ursula looked at the class. There were fifty pale, still faces watching her, a hundred round eyes fixed on her in an attentive, expressionless stare.

'Give out the history readers,' she said to the monitors.

There was dead silence. As she stood there, she could hear again the ticking of the clock, and the chock of piles of books taken out of the low cupboard. Then came the faint flap of books on the desks. The children passed in silence, their hands working in unison. They were no longer a pack, but each one separated into a silent, closed thing.

'Take page 125, and read that chapter,' said Ursula.

There was a click of many books opened. The children found the page, and bent their heads obediently to read. And they read, mechanically.

Ursula, who was trembling violently, went and sat in her high chair. The blubbering of the boy continued. The strident voice of Mr. Brunt, the roar of Mr. Harby, came muffled through the glass partition. And now and then a pair of eyes rose from the reading-book, rested on her a moment, watchful, as if calculating impersonally, then sank again.

She sat still without moving, her eyes watching the class, unseeing. She was quite still, and weak. She felt that she could not raise her hand from the desk. If she sat there for ever, she felt she could not move again, nor utter a command. It was a quarter-past four. She almost dreaded the closing of the school, when she would be alone.

The class began to recover its ease, the tension relaxed, Williams was still crying. Mr. Brunt was giving orders for the closing of the lesson. Ursula got down.

'Take your place, Williams,' she said.

He dragged his feet across the room, wiping his face on his sleeve. As he sat down, he glanced at her furtively, his eyes still redder. Now he looked like some beaten rat.

At last the children were gone. Mr. Harby trod by heavily, without looking her way, or speaking. Mr. Brunt hesitated as she was locking her cupboard.

'If you settle Clarke and Letts in the same way, Miss Brangwen, you'll be all right,' he said, his blue eyes glancing down in a strange fellowship, his long nose pointing at her.

'Shall I?' she laughed nervously. She did not want anybody to talk to her.

As she went along the street, clattering on the granite pavement, she was aware of boys dodging behind her. Something struck her hand that was carrying her bag, bruising her. As it rolled away she saw that it was a potato. Her hand was hurt, but she gave no sign. Soon she would take the tram.

She was afraid, and strange. It was to her quite strange and ugly, like some dream where she was degraded. She would have died rather than admit it to anybody. She could not look at her swollen hand. Something had broken in her; she had passed a crisis. Williams was beaten, but at a cost.

Feeling too much upset to go home, she rode a little farther into the town, and got down from the tram at a small teashop. There, in the dark little place behind the shop, she drank her tea and ate bread-and-butter. She did not taste anything. The taking of tea was just a mechanical action, to cover over her existence. There she sat in the dark, obscure little place, without knowing. Only unconsciously she nursed the back of her hand, which was bruised.

When finally she took her way home, it was sunset red across the west.

She did not know why she was going home. There was nothing for her there. She had, true, only to pretend to be normal. There was nobody she could speak to, nowhere to go for escape. But she must keep on, under this red sunset, alone, knowing the horror in humanity, that would destroy her, and with which she was at war. Yet it had to be so.

In the morning again she must go to school. She got up and went without murmuring even to herself. She was in the hands of some bigger, stronger, coarser will.

School was fairly quiet. But she could feel the class watching her, ready to spring on her. Her instinct was aware of the class instinct to catch her if she were weak. But she kept cold and was guarded.

Williams was absent from school. In the middle of the morning there was a knock at the door: someone wanted the headmaster. Mr. Harby went out, heavily, angrily, nervously. He was afraid of irate parents. After a moment in the passage, he came again into school.

'Sturgess,' he called to one of his larger boys. 'Stand in front of the class and write down the name of anyone who speaks. Will you come this way, Miss Brangwen.'

He seemed vindictively to seize upon her.

Ursula followed him, and found in the lobby a thin woman with a whitish skin, not ill-dressed in a grey costume and a purple hat.

'I called about Vernon,' said the woman, speaking in a refined accent. There was about the woman altogether an appearance of refinement and of cleanliness, curiously contradicted by her half beggar's deportment, and a sense of her being unpleasant to touch, like something going bad inside. She was neither a lady nor an ordinary working man's wife, but a creature separate from society. By her dress she was not poor.

Ursula knew at once that she was Williams' mother, and that he was Vernon. She remembered that he was always clean, and well-dressed, in a sailor suit. And he had this same peculiar, half transparent unwholesomeness, rather like a corpse.

'I wasn't able to send him to school to-day,' continued the woman, with a false grace of manner. 'He came home last night so ill – he was violently sick – I thought I should have to send for the doctor. – You know he has a weak heart.'

The woman looked at Ursula with her pale, dead eyes.

'No,' replied the girl, 'I did not know.'

She stood still with repulsion and uncertainty. Mr. Harby, large and male, with his overhanging moustache, stood by with a slight, ugly smile at the corner of his eyes. The woman went on insidiously, not quite human:

'Oh, yes, he has had heart disease ever since he was a child. That is why he isn't very regular at school. And it is very bad to beat him. He was awfully ill this morning – I shall call on the doctor as I go back.'

'Who is staying with him now, then?' put in the deep voice of the schoolmaster, cunningly.

'Oh, I left him with a woman who comes in to help me – and who understands him. But I shall call in the doctor on my way home.'

Ursula stood still. She felt vague threats in all this. But the woman was so utterly strange to her, that she did not understand.

'He told me he had been beaten,' continued the woman, 'and when I undressed him to put him to bed, his body was covered with marks – I could show them to any doctor.'

Mr. Harby looked at Ursula to answer. She began to understand. The woman was threatening to take out a charge of assault on her son against her. Perhaps she wanted money.

'I caned him,' she said. 'He was so much trouble.'

'I'm sorry if he was troublesome,' said the woman, 'but he must have been shamefully beaten. I could show the marks to any doctor. I'm sure it isn't allowed, if it was known.'

'I caned him while he kept kicking me,' said Ursula, getting angry because she was half excusing herself. Mr. Harby standing there with the twinkle at the side of his eyes, enjoying the dilemma of the two women.

'I'm sure I'm sorry if he behaved badly,' said the woman. 'But I can't think he deserved beating as he has been. I can't send him to school, and really can't afford to pay the doctor. – Is it allowed for the teachers to beat the children like that, Mr. Harby?'

The headmaster refused to answer. Ursula loathed herself, and loathed Mr. Harby with his twinkling cunning and malice on the occasion. The other miserable woman watched her chance.

'It is an expense to me, and I have a great struggle to keep my boy decent.'

Ursula still would not answer. She looked out at the asphalt yard, where a dirty rag of paper was blowing.

'And it isn't allowed to beat a child like that, I am sure, especially when he is delicate.'

Ursula stared with a set face on the yard, as if she did not hear. She loathed all this, and had ceased to feel or to exist.

'Though I know he is troublesome sometimes – but I think it was too much. His body is covered with marks.'

Mr. Harby stood sturdy and unmoved, waiting now to have done, with the twinkling, tiny wrinkles of an ironical smile at the corners of his eyes. He felt himself master of the situation.

'And he was violently sick. I couldn't possibly send him to school to-day. He couldn't keep his head up.'

Yet she had no answer.

'You will understand, sir, why he is absent,' she said, turning to Mr. Harby.

'Oh, yes,' he said, rough and off-hand. Ursula detested him for his male triumph. And she loathed the woman. She loathed everything.

'You will try to have it remembered, sir, that he has a weak heart. He *is* so sick after these things.'

'Yes,' said the headmaster, 'I'll see about it.'

'I know he is troublesome,' the woman only addressed herself to the male now – 'but if you could have him punished without beating – he is really delicate.'

Ursula was beginning to feel upset. Harby stood in rather superb mastery, the woman cringing to him to tickle him as one tickles trout.

'I had come to explain why he was away this morning, sir. You will understand.'

She held out her hand. Harby took it and let it go, surprised and angry.

'Good morning,' she said, and she gave her gloved, seedy hand to Ursula. She was not ill-looking, and had a curious insinuating way, very distasteful yet effective.

'Good morning, Mr. Harby, and thank you.'

The figure in the grey costume and the purple hat was going across the school yard with a curious lingering walk. Ursula felt a strange pity for her, and revulsion from her. She shuddered. She went into the school again.

The next morning Williams turned up, looking paler than ever, very neat and nicely dressed in his sailor blouse. He glanced at Ursula with a half-smile: cunning, subdued, ready to do as she told him. There was something about him that made her shiver. She loathed the idea of having laid hands on him. His elder brother was standing outside the gate at playtime, a youth of about fifteen, tall and thin and pale. He raised his hat, almost like a gentleman. But there was something subdued, insidious about him too.

'Who is it?' said Ursula.

'It's the big Williams,' said Violet Harby roughly. '*She* was here yesterday, wasn't she?'

'Yes.'

'It's no good her coming – her character's not good enough for her to make any trouble.'

Ursula shrank from the brutality and the scandal. But it had some vague, horrid fascination. How sordid everything seemed! She felt sorry for the queer woman with the lingering walk, and those queer, insidious boys. The Williams in her class was wrong somewhere. How nasty it was altogether.

So the battle went on till her heart was sick. She had several more boys to subjugate before she could establish herself. And Mr. Harby hated her almost as if she were a man. She knew now that nothing but a thrashing would settle some of the big louts who wanted to play cat and mouse with her. Mr. Harby would not give them the thrashing if he could help it. For he hated the teacher, the stuck-up, insolent high-school miss with her independence.

'Now, Wright, what have you done this time?' he would say genially to the boy who was sent to him from Standard Five for punishment. And he left the lad standing, lounging, wasting his time.

So that Ursula would appeal no more to the headmaster, but, when she was driven wild, she seized her cane, and slashed the boy who was insolent to her, over head and ears and hands. And at length they were afraid of her, she had them in order.

But she had paid a great price out of her own soul, to do this. It seemed as if a great flame had gone through her and burnt her sensitive tissue. She who shrank from the thought of physical suffering in any form, had been forced to fight and beat with a cane and rouse all her instincts to hurt. And afterwards she had been forced to endure the sound of their blubbering and desolation, when she had broken them to order.

Oh, and sometimes she felt as if she would go mad. What did it matter, what did it matter if their books were dirty and they did not obey? She would rather, in reality, that they disobeyed the whole rules of the school, than that they should be beaten, broken, reduced to this crying, hopeless state. She would rather bear all their insults and insolences a thousand times than reduce herself and them to this. Bitterly she repented having got beside herself, and having tackled the boy she had beaten.

Yet it had to be so. She did not want to do it. Yet she had to. Oh, why, why had she leagued herself to this evil system where she must brutalise herself to live? Why had she become a school-teacher, why, why?

The children had forced her to the beatings. No, she did not pity them. She had come to them full of kindness and love, and they would have torn her to pieces. They chose Mr. Harby. Well then, they must know her as well as Mr. Harby, they must first be subjugate to her. For she was not going to be made nought, no, neither by them, nor by Mr. Harby, nor by all the system around her. She was not going to be put down, prevented from standing free. It was not to be said of her, she could not take her place and carry out her task. She would fight and hold her place in this state also, in the world of work and man's convention.

She was isolated now from the life of her childhood, a foreigner in a new life, of work and mechanical consideration. She and Maggie, in their dinner-hours and their occasional teas at the little restaurant, discussed life and ideas. Maggie was a great suffragette, trusting in the vote. To Ursula the vote was never a reality. She had within her the strange, passionate knowledge of religion and living far transcending the limits of the automatic system that contained the vote. But her fundamental, organic knowledge had as yet to take form and rise to utterance. For her, as for Maggie, the liberty of woman meant something real and deep. She felt that somewhere, in something, she was not free. And she wanted to be. She was in revolt. For once she were free she could get somewhere. Ah, the wonderful, real somewhere that was beyond her, the somewhere that she felt deep, deep inside her.

In coming out and earning her own living she had made a strong, cruel move towards freeing herself. But having more freedom she only became more profoundly aware of the big want. She wanted so many things. She wanted to read great, beautiful books, and be rich with them; she wanted to see beautiful things, and have the joy of them for ever; she wanted to know big, free people; and there remained always the want she could put no name to.

It was so difficult. There were so many things, so much to meet and surpass. And one never knew where one was going. It was a blind fight. She had suffered bitterly in this school of St. Philip's. She was like a young filly that has been broken in to the shafts, and has lost its freedom. And now she was suffering bitterly from the agony of the shafts. The agony, the galling, the ignominy of her breaking in. This wore into her soul. But she would never submit. To shafts like these she would never submit for long. But she would know them. She would serve them that she might destroy them.

She and Maggie went to all kinds of places together, to big suffrage meetings in Nottingham, to concerts, to theatres, to exhibitions of pictures. Ursula saved her money and bought a bicycle, and the two girls rode to Lincoln, to Southwell, and into Derbyshire. They had an endless wealth of things to talk about. And it was a great joy, finding, discovering.

But Ursula never told about Winifred Inger. That was a sort of secret side-show to her life, never to be opened. She did not even think of it. It was the closed door she had not the strength to open.

Once she was broken in to her teaching, Ursula began gradually to have a new life of her own again. She was going to college in eighteen months' time. Then she would take her degree, and she would – ah, she would perhaps be a big woman, and lead a movement. Who knows? – At any rate she would go to college in eighteen months' time. All that mattered now was work, work.

And till college, she must go on with this teaching in St. Philip's School, which was always destroying her, but which she could now manage, without spoiling all her life. She would submit to it for a time, since the time had a definite limit.

The class-teaching itself at last became almost mechanical. It was a strain on her, an exhausting wearying strain, always unnatural. But there was a certain amount of pleasure in the sheer oblivion of teaching, so much work to do, so many children to see after, so much to be done, that one's self was forgotten. When the work had become like habit to her, and her individual soul was left out, had its growth elsewhere, then she could be almost happy.

Her real, individual self drew together and became more coherent during these two years of teaching; during the struggle against the odds of class teaching. It was always a prison to her, the school. But it was a prison where her wild, chaotic soul became hard and independent. When she was well enough and not tired, then she did not hate the teaching. She enjoyed getting into the swing of work of a morning, putting forth all her strength, making the thing go. It was for her a strenuous form of exercise. And her soul was left to rest, it had the time of torpor in which to gather itself together in strength again. But the teaching hours were too long, the tasks too heavy, and the disciplinary condition of the school too unnatural for her. She was worn very thin and quivering.

She came to school in the morning seeing the hawthorn flowers wet, the little, rosy grains swimming in a bowl of dew. The larks quivered their song up into the new sunshine, and the country was so glad. It was a violation to plunge into the dust and greyness of the town.

So that she stood before her class unwilling to give herself up to the activity of teaching, to turn her energy, that longed for the country and for joy of early summer, into the dominating of fifty children and the transferring to them some morsels of arithmetic. There was a little absentness about her. She could not force herself into forgetfulness. A jar of buttercups and fool's-parsley in the window-bottom kept her away in the meadows, where in the lush grass the moon-daisies were half-submerged, and a spray of pink ragged robin. Yet before her were faces of fifty children. They were almost like big daisies in a dimness of the grass.

A brightness was on her face, a little unreality in her teaching. She could not quite see her children. She was struggling between two worlds, her own world of young summer and flowers, and this other world of work. And the glimmer of her own sunlight was between her and her class.

Then the morning passed with a strange far-awayness and quietness. Dinner-time came, when she and Maggie ate joyously, with all the windows open. And then they went out into St. Philip's churchyard, where was a shadowy corner under red hawthorn trees. And there they talked and read Shelley or Browning or some work about 'Woman and Labour'.

And when she went back to school, Ursula lived still in the shadowy corner of the graveyard, where pink-red petals lay scattered from the hawthorn tree, like myriad tiny shells on a beach, and a church bell sometimes rang sonorously, and sometimes a bird called out, whilst Maggie's voice went on low and sweet.

These days she was happy in her soul: oh, she was so happy, that she wished she could take her joy and scatter it in armfuls broadcast. She made her children happy, too, with a little tingling of delight. But to her, the children were not a school class this afternoon. They were flowers, birds, little bright animals, children, anything. They only were not Standard Five. She felt no responsibility for them. It was for once a game, this teaching. And if they got their sums wrong, what matter? And she would take a pleasant bit of reading. And instead of history with dates, she would tell a lovely tale. And for grammar, they could have a bit of written analysis that was not difficult, because they had done it before:

> 'She shall be sportive as a fawn
> That wild with glee across the lawn
> Or up the mountain springs.'

She wrote that from memory, because it pleased her.

So the golden afternoon passed away and she went home happy. She had finished her day of school, and was free to plunge into the glowing evening of Cossethay. And she loved walking home. But it had not been school. It had been playing at school beneath red hawthorn blossom.

She could not go on like this. The quarterly examination was coming, and her class was not ready. It irritated her that she must drag herself away from her happy self, and exert herself with all her strength to force, to compel this heavy class of children to work hard at arithmetic. They did not want to work, she did not want to compel them. And yet, some second conscience gnawed at her, telling her the work was not properly done. It irritated her almost to madness, and she let loose all the irritation in the class. Then followed a day of battle and hate and violence, when she went home raw, feeling the golden evening taken away from her, herself incarcerated in some dark, heavy place, and chained there with a consciousness of having done badly at work.

What good was it that it was summer, that right till evening, when the corncrakes called, the larks would mount up into the light, to sing once more before nightfall. What good was it all, when she was out of tune, when she must only remember the burden and shame of school that day.

And still, she hated school. Still she cried, she did not believe in it. Why should the children learn, and why should she teach them? It was all so much milling the wind. What folly was it that made life into this, the fulfilling of some stupid, factitious duty? It was all so made up, so unnatural. The school, the sums, the grammar, the quarterly examinations, the registers – it was all a barren nothing!

Why should she give her allegiance to this world, and let it so dominate her, that her own world of warm sun and growing, sap-filled life was turned into nothing? She was not going to do it. She was not going to be a prisoner in the dry, tyrannical man-world. She was not going to care about it. What did it matter if her class did ever so badly in the quarterly examination. Let it – what did it matter?

Nevertheless, when the time came, and the report on her class was bad, she was miserable, and the joy of the summer was taken away from her, she was shut up in gloom. She could not really escape from this world of system and work, out into her fields where she was happy. She must have her place in the working world, be a recognised member with full rights there. It was more important to her than fields and sun and poetry, at this time. But she was only the more its enemy.

It was a very difficult thing, she thought, during the long hours of intermission in the summer holidays, to be herself, her happy self that enjoyed so much to lie in the sun, to play and swim and be content, and also to be a school-teacher getting results out of a class of children. She dreamed fondly of the time when she need not be a teacher any more. But vaguely, she knew that responsibility had taken place in her for ever, and as yet her prime business was to work.

The autumn passed away, the winter was at hand. Ursula became more and more an inhabitant of the world of work, and of what is called life. She could not see her future, but a little way off, was college, and to the thought of this she clung fixedly. She would go to college, and get her two or three years' training, free of cost. Already she had applied and had her place appointed for the coming year.

So she continued to study for her degree. She would take French, Latin, English, mathematics and botany. She went to classes in Ilkeston, she studied at evening. For there was this world to conquer, this knowledge to acquire, this qualification to attain. And she worked with intensity, because of a want inside her that drove her on. Almost everything was subordinated now to this one desire to take her place in the world. What kind of place it was to be she did not ask herself. The blind desire drove her on. She must take her place.

She knew she would never be much of a success as an elementary school teacher. But neither had she failed. She hated it, but she had managed it.

Maggie had left St. Philip's School, and had found a more congenial post. The two girls remained friends. They met at evening classes, they studied and somehow encouraged a firm hope each in the other. They did not know whither they were making, nor what they ultimately wanted. But they knew they wanted now to learn, to know and to do.

They talked of love and marriage, and the position of woman in marriage. Maggie said that love was the flower of life, and blossomed unexpectedly and without law, and must be plucked where it was found, and enjoyed for the brief hour of its duration.

To Ursula this was unsatisfactory. She thought she still loved Anton Skrebensky. But she did not forgive him that he had not been strong enough to acknowledge her. He had denied her. How then could she love him? How then was love so absolute? She did not believe it. She believed that love was a way, a means, not an end in itself, as Maggie seemed to think. And always the way of love would be found. But whither did it lead?

'I believe there are many men in the world one might love – there is not only one man,' said Ursula.

She was thinking of Skrebensky. Her heart was hollow with the knowledge of Winifred Inger.

'But you must distinguish between love and passion,' said Maggie, adding, with a touch of contempt: 'Men will easily have a passion for you, but they won't love you.'

'Yes,' said Ursula, vehemently, the look of suffering, almost of fanaticism, on her face. 'Passion is only part of love. And it seems so much because it can't last. That is why passion is never happy.'

She was staunch for joy, for happiness, and permanency, in contrast with Maggie, who was for sadness, and the inevitable passing-away of things. Ursula suffered bitterly at the hands of life, Maggie was always single, always withheld, so she went in a heavy brooding sadness that was almost meat to her. In Ursula's last winter at St. Philip's the friendship of the two girls came to a climax. It was during this winter that Ursula suffered and enjoyed most keenly Maggie's fundamental sadness of enclosedness. Maggie enjoyed and suffered Ursula's struggles against the confines of her life. And then the two girls began to drift apart, as Ursula broke from that form of life wherein Maggie must remain enclosed.

Chapter Fourteen

The Widening Circle

Maggie's people, the Schofields, lived in the large gardener's cottage, that was half a farm, behind Belcote Hall. The hall was too damp to live in, so the Schofields were caretakers, gamekeepers, farmers, all in one. The father was gamekeeper and stock-breeder, the eldest son was market-gardener, using the big hall gardens, the second son was farmer and gardener. There was a large family, as at Cossethay.

Ursula loved to stay at Belcote, to be treated as a grand lady by Maggie's brothers. They were good-looking men. The eldest was twenty-six years old. He was the gardener, a man not very tall, but strong and well made, with brown, sunny, easy eyes and a face handsomely hewn, brown, with a long fair moustache which he pulled as he talked to Ursula.

The girl was excited because these men attended to her when she came near. She could make their eyes light up and quiver, she could make Anthony, the eldest, twist and twist his moustache. She knew she could move them almost at will with her light laughter and chatter. They loved her ideas, watched her as she talked vehemently about politics or economics. And she, while she talked, saw the golden-brown eyes of Anthony gleam like the eyes of a satyr as they watched her. He did not listen to her words, he listened to her. It excited her.

He was like a faun pleased when she would go with him over his hothouses, to look at the green and pretty plants, at the pink primulas nodding among their leaves, and cinarrias flaunting purple and crimson and white. She asked about everything, and he told her very exactly and minutely, in a queer pedantic way that made her want to laugh. Yet she was really interested in what he did. And he had the curious light in his face, like the light in the eyes of the goat that was tethered by the farmyard gate.

She went down with him into the warmish cellar, where already in the darkness the little yellow knobs of rhubarb were coming. He held the lantern down to the dark earth. She saw the tiny knob-end of the rhubarb thrusting upwards upon the thick red stem, thrusting itself like a knob of flame through the soft soil. His face was turned up to her, the light glittered on his eyes and his teeth as he laughed, with a faint, musical neigh. He looked handsome. And she heard a new sound in her ears, the faintly-musical, neighing laugh of Anthony, whose moustache twisted up, and whose eyes were luminous with a cold, steady, arrogant-laughing glare. There seemed a little prance of triumph in his movement, she could not rid herself of a movement of acquiescence, a touch of acceptance. Yet he was so humble, his voice was so caressing. He held his hand for her to step on when she must climb a wall. And she stepped on the living firmness of him, that quivered firmly under her weight.

She was aware of him as if in a mesmeric state. In her ordinary sense, she had nothing to do with him. But the peculiar ease and unnoticeableness of his entering the house, the power of his cold, gleaming light on her when he looked at her, was like a bewitchment. In his eyes, as in the pale grey eyes of a goat, there seemed some of that steady, hard fire of moonlight which has nothing to do with the day. It made her alert, and yet her mind went out like an extinguished thing. She was all senses, all her senses were alive.

Then she saw him on Sunday, dressed up in Sunday clothes, trying to impress her. And he looked ridiculous. She clung to the ridiculous effect of his stiff, Sunday clothes.

She was always conscious of some unfaithfulness to Maggie, on Anthony's score. Poor Maggie stood apart as if betrayed. Maggie and Anthony were enemies by instinct. Ursula had to go back to her friend brimming with affection and a poignancy of pity. Which Maggie received with a little stiffness. The poetry and books and learning took the place of Anthony, with his goats' movements and his cold, gleaming humour.

While Ursula was at Belcote, the snow fell. In the morning, a covering of snow weighed on the rhododendron bushes.

'Shall we go out?' said Maggie.

She had lost some of her leader's sureness, and was now tentative, a little in reserve from her friend.

They took the key of the gate and wandered into the park. It was a white world on which dark trees and tree masses stood under a sky keen with frost. The two girls went past the hall, that was shuttered and silent, their footprints marking the snow on the drive. Down the park, a long way off, a man was carrying armfuls of hay across the snow. He was a small, dark figure, like an animal moving in its unawareness.

Ursula and Maggie went on exploring, down to a tinkling, chilly brook, that had worn the snow away in little scoops, and ran dark between. They saw a robin glance its bright eyes and burst scarlet and grey into the hedge, then some pertly-marked blue-tits scuffled. Meanwhile the brook slid on coldly, chuckling to itself.

The girls wandered across the snowy grass to where the artificial fish-ponds lay under thin ice. There was a big tree with a thick trunk twisted with ivy, that hung almost horizontal over the ponds. Ursula climbed joyfully into this and sat amid bosses of bright ivy and dull berries. Some ivy leaves were like green spears held out, and tipped with snow. The ice was seen beneath them.

Maggie took out a book, and sitting lower down the trunk began to read Coleridge's 'Christabel'. Ursula half listened. She was wildly thrilled. Then she saw Anthony coming across the snow, with his confident, slightly strutting stride. His face looked brown and hard against the snow, smiling with a sort of tense confidence.

'Hello!' she called to him.

A response went over his face, his head was lifted in an answering, jerking gesture.

'Hello!' he said. 'You're like a bird in there.'

And Ursula's laugh rang out. She answered to the peculiar, reedy twang in his penetrating voice.

She did not think of Anthony, yet she lived in a sort of connection with him, in his world. One evening she met him as she was coming down the lane, and they walked side by side.

'I think it's so *lovely* here,' she cried.

'Do you?' he said. 'I'm glad you like it.'

There was a curious confidence in his voice.

'Oh, I love it. What more does one want than to live in this beautiful place, and make things grow in your garden. It is like the Garden of Eden.'

'Is it?' he said, with a little laugh. 'Yes – well, it's not so bad—' he was hesitating. The pale gleam was strong in his eyes, he was looking at her steadily, watching her, as an animal might. Something leaped in her soul. She knew he was going to suggest to her that she should be as he was.

'Would you like to stay here with me?' he asked, tentatively.

She blenched with fear and with the intense sensation of proffered licence suggested to her.

They had come to the gate.

'How?' she asked. 'You aren't alone here.'

'We could marry,' he answered, in the strange, coldly-gleaming insinuating tone that chilled the sunshine into moonlight. All substantial things seemed transformed. Shadows and dancing moonlight were real, and all cold, inhuman, gleaming sensations. She realised with something like terror that she was going to accept this. She was going inevitably to accept him. His hand was reaching out to the gate before them. She stood still. His flesh was hard and brown and final. She seemed to be in the grip of some insult.

'I couldn't,' she answered, involuntarily.

He gave the same brief, neighing little laugh, very sad and bitter now, and slotted back the bar of the gate. Yet he did not open. For a moment they both stood looking at the fire of sunset that quivered among the purple twigs of the trees. She saw his brown, hard, well-hewn face gleaming with anger and humiliation and submission. He was an animal that knows that it is subdued. Her heart flamed with sensation of him, of the fascinating thing he offered her, and with sorrow, and with an inconsolable sense of loneliness. Her soul was an infant crying in the night. He had no soul. Oh, and why had she? He was the cleaner.

She turned away, she turned round from him, and saw the east flushed strangely rose, the moon coming yellow and lovely upon a rosy sky, above the darkening, bluish snow. All this so beautiful, all this so lovely! He did not see it. He was one with it. But she saw it, and was one with it. Her seeing separated them infinitely.

They went on in silence down the path, following their different fates. The trees grew darker and darker, the snow made only a dimness in an unreal world. And like a shadow, the day had gone into a faintly luminous, snowy evening, while she was talking aimlessly to him, to keep him at a distance, yet to keep him near her, and he walked heavily. He opened the garden gate for her quietly, and she was entering into her own pleasances, leaving him outside the gate.

Then even whilst she was escaping, or trying to escape, this feeling of pain, came Maggie the next day, saying:

'I wouldn't make Anthony love you, Ursula, if you don't want him. It is not nice.'

'But, Maggie, I never made him love me,' cried Ursula, dismayed and suffering, and feeling as if she had done something base.

She liked Anthony, though. All her life, at intervals, she returned to the thought of him and of that which he offered. But she was a traveller, she was a traveller on the face of the earth, and he was an isolated creature living in the fulfilment of his own senses.

She could not help it, that she was a traveller. She knew Anthony, that he was not one. But oh, ultimately and finally, she must go on and on, seeking the goal that she knew she did draw nearer to.

She was wearing away her second and last cycle at St. Philip's. As the months went she ticked them off, first October, then November, December, January. She was careful always to subtract a month from the remainder, for the summer holidays. She saw herself travelling round a circle, only an arc of which remained to complete. Then, she was in the open, like a bird tossed into mid-air, a bird that had learned in some measure to fly.

There was college ahead; that was her mid-air, unknown, spacious. Come college, and she would have broken from the confines of all the life she had known. For her father was also going to move. They were all going to leave Cossethay.

Brangwen had kept his carelessness about his circumstances. He knew his work in the lace designing meant little to him personally, he just earned his wage by it. He did not know what meant much to him. Living close to Anna Brangwen, his mind was always suffused through with physical heat, he moved from instinct to instinct, groping, always groping on.

When it was suggested to him that he might apply for one of the posts as hand-work instructor, posts about to be created by the Nottingham Education Committee, it was as if a space had been given to him, into which he could remove from his hot, dusky enclosure. He sent in his application, confidently, expectantly. He had a sort of belief in his supernatural fate. The inevitable weariness of his daily work had stiffened some of his muscles, and made a slight deadness in his ruddy, alert face. Now he might escape.

He was full of the new possibilities, and his wife was acquiescent. She was willing now to have a change. She too was tired of Cossethay. The house was too small for the growing children. And since she was nearly forty years old, she began to come awake from her sleep of motherhood, her energy moved more outwards. The din of growing lives roused her from her apathy. She too must have her hand in making life. She was quite ready to move, taking all her brood. It would be better now if she transplanted them. For she had borne her last child, it would be growing up.

So that in her easy, unused fashion she talked plans and arrangements with her husband, indifferent really as to the method of the change, since a change was coming; even if it did not come in this way it would come in another.

The house was full of ferment. Ursula was wild with excitement. At last her father was going to be something, socially. So long, he had been a social cypher, without form or standing. Now he was going to be Art and Handwork Instructor for the County of Nottingham. That was really a status. It was a position. He would be a specialist in his way. And he was an uncommon man. Ursula felt they were all getting a foothold at last. He was coming to his own. Who else that she knew could turn out from his own fingers the beautiful things her father could produce? She felt he was certain of this new job.

They would move. They would leave this cottage at Cossethay which had grown too small for them; they would leave Cossethay, where the children had all been born, and where they were always kept to the same measure.

For the people who had known them as children along with the other village boys and girls would never, could never understand that they should grow up different. They had held 'Urtler Brangwen' one of themselves, and had given her her place in her native village, as in a family. And the bond was strong. But now, when she was growing to something beyond what Cossethay would allow or understand, the bond between her and her old associates was becoming a bondage.

"Ello, Urs'ler, 'ow are yer goin' on?' they said when they met her. And it demanded of her in the old voice the old response. And something in her must respond and belong to people who knew her. But something else denied bitterly. What was true of her ten years ago was not true now. And something else which she was, and must be, they could neither see nor allow. They felt it there nevertheless, something beyond them, and they were injured. They said she was proud and conceited, that she was too big for her shoes nowadays. They said, she needn't pretend, because they knew what she was. They had known her since she was born. They quoted this and that about her. And she was ashamed because she did feel different from the people she had lived amongst. It hurt her that she could not be at her ease with them any more. And yet – and yet – one's kite will rise on the wind as far as ever one has string to let it go. It tugs and tugs and will go, and one is glad the further it goes, even if everybody else is nasty about it. So Cossethay hampered her, and she wanted to go away, to be free to fly her kite as high as she liked. She wanted to go away, to be free to stand straight up to her own height.

So that when she knew that her father had the new post, and that the family would move, she felt like skipping on the face of the earth, and making psalms of joy. The old, bound shell of Cossethay was to be cast off, and she was to dance away into the blue air. She wanted to dance and sing.

She made dreams of the new place she would live in, where stately cultured people of high feeling would be friends with her, and she would live with the noble in the land, moving to a large freedom of feeling. She dreamed of a rich, proud, simple girl-friend, who had never known Mr. Harby and his like, nor ever had a note in her voice of bondaged contempt and fear, as Maggie had.

And she gave herself to all that she loved in Cossethay, passionately, because she was going away now. She wandered about to her favourite spots. There was a place where she went trespassing to find the snowdrops that grew wild. It was evening and the winter-darkened meadows were full of mystery. When she came to the woods an oak tree had been newly chopped down in the dell. Pale drops of flowers glimmered many under the hazels, and by the sharp, golden splinters of wood that were splashed about, the grey-green blades of snowdrop leaves pricked unheeding, the drooping still little flowers were without heed.

Ursula picked some lovingly, in an ecstasy. The golden chips of wood shone yellow like sunlight, the snowdrops in the twilight were like the first stars of night. And she, alone amongst them, was wildly happy to have found her way into such a glimmering dusk, to the intimate little flowers, and the splash of wood chips like sunshine over the twilight of the ground. She sat down on the felled tree and remained awhile remote.

Going home, she left the purplish dark of the trees for the open lane, where the puddles shone long and jewel-like in the ruts, the land about her was darkened, and the sky a jewel overhead. Oh, how amazing it was to her! It was almost too much. She wanted to run, and sing, and cry out for very wildness and poignancy, but she could not run and sing and cry out in such a way as to cry out the deep things in her heart, so she was still, and almost sad with loneliness.

At Easter she went again to Maggie's home, for a few days. She was, however shy and fugitive. She saw Anthony, how suggestive he was to look on, and how his eyes had a sort of supplicating light, that was rather beautiful. She looked at him, and she looked again, for him to become real to her. But it was her own self that was occupied elsewhere. She seemed to have some other being.

And she turned to spring and the opening buds. There was a large pear tree by a wall, and it was full, thronged with tiny, grey-green buds, myriads. She stood before it arrested with delight, and a realisation went deep into her heart. There was so great a host in array behind the cloud of pale, dim green, so much to come forth – so much sunshine to pour down.

So the weeks passed on, trance-like and pregnant. The pear tree at Cossethay burst into bloom against the cottage-end, like a wave burst into foam. Then gradually the bluebells came, blue as water, standing thin in the level places under the trees and bushes, flowing in more and more, till there was a flood of azure, and pale-green leaves burning, and tiny birds with fiery little song and flight. Then swiftly the flood sank and was gone, and it was summer.

There was to be no going to the seaside for a holiday. The holiday was the removal from Cossethay.

They were going to live near Willey Green, which place was most central for Brangwen. It was an old, quiet village on the edge of the thronged colliery-district. So that it served, in its quaintness of odd old cottages lingering in their sunny gardens, as a sort of bower or pleasaunce to the sprawling colliery-townlet of Beldover, a pleasant walk-round for the colliers on Sunday morning, before the public-houses opened.

In Willey Green stood the Grammar School where Brangwen was occupied for two days during the week, and where experiments in education were being carried on.

Ursula wanted to live in Willey Green on the remoter side, towards Southwell, and Sherwood Forest. There it was so lovely and romantic. But out into the world meant out into the world. Will Brangwen must become modern.

He brought, with his wife's money, a fairly large house in the new, red-brick part of Beldover. It was a villa built by the widow of the late colliery manager, and stood in a quiet, new little side-street near the large church.

Ursula was rather sad. Instead of having arrived at distinction they had come to new red-brick suburbia in a grimy, small town.

Mrs. Brangwen was happy. The rooms were splendidly large – a splendid dining-room, drawing-room and kitchen, besides a very pleasant study downstairs. Everything was admirably appointed. The widow had settled herself in lavishly. She was a native of Beldover, and had intended to reign almost queen. Her bathroom was white and silver, her stairs were of oak, her chimney-pieces were massive and oaken, with bulging, columnar supports.

'Good and substantial,' was the keynote. But Ursula resented the stout, inflated prosperity implied everywhere. She made her father promise to chisel down the bulging oaken chimney-pieces, chisel them flat. That sort of important paunch was very distasteful to her. Her father was himself long and loosely built. What had he to do with so much 'good and substantial' importance?

They bought a fair amount also of the widow's furniture. It was in common good taste – the great Wilton carpet, the large round table, the Chesterfield covered with glossy chintz in roses and birds. It was all really very sunny and nice, with large windows, and a view right across the shallow valley.

After all, they would be, as one of their acquaintances said, among the élite of Beldover. They would represent culture. And as there was no one of higher social importance than the doctors, the colliery-managers, and the chemists, they would shine, with their Della Robbia beautiful Madonna, their lovely reliefs from Donatello, their reproductions from Botticelli. Nay, the large photographs of the Primavera and the Aphrodite and the Nativity in the dining-room, the ordinary reception-room, would make dumb the mouth of Beldover.

And after all, it is better to be princess in Beldover than a vulgar nobody in the country.

There was great preparation made for the removal of the whole Brangwen family, ten in all. The house in Beldover was prepared, the house in Cossethay was dismantled. Come the end of the school-term the removal would begin.

Ursula left school at the end of July, when the summer holiday commenced. The morning outside was bright and sunny, and the freedom got inside the schoolroom this last day. It was as if the walls of the school were going to melt away. Already they seemed shadowy and unreal. It was breaking-up morning. Soon scholars and teachers would be outside, each going his own way. The irons were struck off, the sentence was expired, the prison was a momentary shadow halting about them. The children were carrying away books and inkwell, and rolling up maps. All their faces were bright with gladness and goodwill. There was a bustle of cleaning and clearing away all marks of this last term of imprisonment. They were all breaking free. Busily, eagerly, Ursula made up her totals of attendances in the register. With pride she wrote down the thousands: to so many thousands of children had she given another sessions's lessons. It looked tremendous. The excited hours passed slowly in suspense. Then at last it was over. For the last time, she stood before her children whilst they said their prayers and sang a hymn. Then it was over.

'Good-bye, children,' she said. 'I shall not forget you, and you must not forget me.'

'No, miss,' cried the children in chorus, with shining faces.

She stood smiling on them, moved, as they filed out. Then she gave her monitors their term sixpences, and they too departed. Cupboards were locked, blackboards washed, ink wells and dusters removed. The place stood bare and vacated. She had triumphed over it. It was a shell now. She had fought a good fight here, and it had not been altogether unenjoyable. She owed some gratitude even to this hard, vacant place, that stood like a memorial or a trophy. So much of her life had been fought for and won and lost here. Something of this school would always belong to her, something of her to it. She acknowledged it. And now came the leave-taking.

In the teachers' room the teachers were chatting and loitering, talking excitedly of where they were going: to the Isle of Man, to Llandudno, to Yarmouth. They were eager, and attached to each other, like comrades leaving a ship.

Then it was Mr. Harby's turn to make a speech to Ursula. He looked handsome, with his silver-grey temples and black brows, and his imperturbable male solidity.

'Well,' he said, 'we must say good-bye to Miss Brangwen and wish her all good fortune for the future. I suppose we shall see her again some time, and hear how she is getting on.'

'Oh, yes,' said Ursula, stammering, blushing, laughing. 'Oh, yes, I shall come and see you.'

Then she realised that this sounded too personal, and she felt foolish.

'Miss Schofield suggested these two books,' he said, putting a couple of volumes on the table: 'I hope you will like them.'

Ursula feeling very shy picked up the books. There was a volume of Swinburne's poetry, and a volume of Meredith's.

'Oh, I shall love them,' she said. 'Thank you very much – thank you all so much – it is so—'

She stuttered to an end, and very red, turned the leaves of the books eagerly, pretending to be taking the first pleasure, but really seeing nothing.

Mr. Harby's eyes were twinkling. He alone was at his ease, master of the situation. It was pleasing to him to make Ursula the gift, and for once extend good feeling to his teachers. As a rule, it was so difficult, each one was so strained in resentment under his rule.

'Yes,' he said, 'we hoped you would like the choice—'

He looked with his peculiar, challenging smile for a moment, then returned to his cupboards.

Ursula felt very confused. She hugged her books, loving them. And she felt that she loved all the teachers, and Mr. Harby. It was very confusing.

At last she was out. She cast one hasty glance over the school buildings squatting on the asphalt yard in the hot, glistening sun, one look down the well-known road, and turned her back on it all. Something strained in her heart. She was going away.

'Well, good luck,' said the last of the teachers, as she shook hands at the end of the road. 'We'll expect you back some day.'

He spoke in irony. She laughed, and broke away. She was free. As she sat on the top of the tram in the sunlight, she looked round her with tremendous delight. She had left something which had meant much to her. She would not go to school any more, and do the familiar things. Queer! There was a little pang amid her exultation, of fear, not of regret. Yet how she exulted this morning!

She was tremulous with pride and joy. She loved the two books. They were tokens to her, representing the fruit and trophies of her two years which, thank God, were over.

'To Ursula Brangwen, with best wishes for her future, and in warm memory of the time she spent in St. Philip's School,' was written in the headmaster's neat, scrupulous handwriting. She could see the careful hand holding the pen, the thick fingers with tufts of black hair on the back of each one.

He had signed, all the teachers had signed. She liked having all their signatures. She felt she loved them all. They were her fellow-workers. She carried away from the school a pride she could never lose. She had her place as comrade and sharer in the work of the school, her fellow teachers had signed to her, as one of them. And she was one of all workers, she had put in her tiny brick to the fabric man was building, she had qualified herself as co-builder.

Then the day for the home removal came. Ursula rose early, to pack up the remaining goods. The carts arrived, lent by her uncle at the Marsh, in the lull between hay and corn harvest. The goods roped in the cart, Ursula mounted her bicycle and sped away to Beldover.

The house was hers. She entered its clean-scrubbed silence. The dining-room had been covered with a thick rush matting, hard and of the beautiful, luminous, clean colour of sun-dried reeds. The walls were pale grey, the doors were darker grey. Ursula admired it very much, as the sun came through the large windows, streaming in.

She flung open doors and windows to the sunshine. Flowers were bright and shining round the small lawn, which stood above the road, looking over the raw field opposite, which would later be built upon. No one came. So she wandered down the garden at the back of the wall. The eight bells of the church rang the hour. She could hear the many sounds of the town about her.

At last, the cart was seen coming round the corner, familiar furniture piled undignified on top, Tom, her brother, and Theresa, marching on foot beside the mass, proud of having walked ten miles or more, from the tram terminus. Ursula poured out beer, and the men drank thirstily, by the door. A second cart was coming. Her father appeared on his motor bicycle. There was the staggering transport of furniture up the steps to the little lawn, where it was deposited all pellmell in the sunshine, very queer and discomforting.

Brangwen was a pleasant man to work with, cheerful and easy. Ursula loved deciding him where the heavy things should stand. She watched anxiously the struggle up the steps and through the doorways. Then the big things were in, the carts set off again. Ursula and her father worked away carrying in all the light things that remained upon the lawn, and putting them in place. Dinner time came. They ate bread and cheese in the kitchen.

'Well, we're getting on,' said Brangwen, cheerfully.

Two more loads arrived. The afternoon passed away in a struggle with the furniture, upstairs. Towards five o'clock, appeared the last loads, consisting also of Mrs. Brangwen and the younger children, driven by Uncle Fred in the trap. Gudrun had walked with Margaret from the station. The whole family had come.

'There!' said Brangwen, as his wife got down from the cart: 'Now we're all here.'

'Ay,' said his wife pleasantly.

And the very brevity, the silence of intimacy between the two made a home in the hearts of the children, who clustered round feeling strange in the new place.

Everything was at sixes and sevens. But a fire was made in the kitchen, the hearth-rug put down, the kettle set on the hob, and Mrs. Brangwen began towards sunset to prepare the first meal. Ursula and Gudrun were slaving in the bedrooms, candles were rushing about. Then from the kitchen came the smell of ham and eggs and coffee, and in the gaslight, the scrambled meal began. The family seemed to huddle together like a little camp in a strange place. Ursula felt a load of responsibility upon her, caring for the half-little ones. The smallest kept near the mother.

It was dark, and the children went sleepy but excited to bed. It was a long time before the sound of voices died out. There was a tremendous sense of adventure.

In the morning everybody was awake soon after dawn, the children crying: 'When I wakened up I didn't know where I was.'

There were the strange sounds of the town, and the repeated chiming of the big church bells, so much harsher and more insistent than the little bells of Cossethay. They looked through the windows past the other new red houses to the wooded hill across the valley. They had all a delightful sense of space and liberation, space and light and air.

But gradually all set to work. They were a careless, untidy family. Yet when once they set about to get the house in order, the thing went with felicity and quickness. By evening the place was roughly established.

They would not have a servant to live in the house, only a woman who could go home at night. And they would not even have the woman yet. They wanted to do as they liked in their own home, with no stranger in the midst.

Chapter Fifteen

The Bitterness of Ecstasy

A storm of industry raged on in the house. Ursula did not go to college till October. So, with a distinct feeling of responsibility, as if she must express herself in this house, she laboured arranging, re-arranging, selecting, contriving.

She could use her father's ordinary tools, both for woodwork and metal-work, so she hammered and tinkered. Her mother was quite content to have the things done. Brangwen was interested. He had a ready belief in his daughter. He himself was at work putting up his work-shed in the garden.

At last she had finished for the time being. The drawing-room was big and empty. It had the good Wilton carpet, of which the family was so proud, and the large couch and large chairs covered with shiny chintz, and the piano, a little sculpture in plaster that Brangwen had done, and not very much more. It was too large and empty-feeling for the family to occupy very much. Yet they liked to know it was there, large and empty.

The home was the dining-room. There the hard rush floor-covering made the ground light, reflecting light upon the bottom their hearts; in the window-bay was a broad, sunny seat, the table was so solid one could not jostle it, and the chairs so strong one could knock them over without hurting them. The familiar organ that Brangwen had made stood on one side, looking peculiarly small, the sideboard was comfortably reduced to normal propor-tions. This was the family living-room.

Ursula had a bedroom to herself. It was really a servants' bedroom, small and plain. Its window looked over the back garden at other back gardens, some of them old and very nice, some of them littered with packing-cases, then at the backs of the houses whose fronts were the shops in High Street, or the genteel homes of the under-manager or the chief cashier, facing the chapel.

She had six weeks still before going to college. In this time she nervously read over some Latin and some botany, and fitfully worked at some math-ematics. She was going into college as a teacher, for her training. But, having already taken her matriculation examination, she was entered for a university course. At the end of a year she would sit for the Intermediate Arts, then two years after for her B.A. So her case was not that of the ordinary school-teacher. She would be working among the private students who came only for pure education, not for mere professional training. She would be of the elect.

For the next three years she would be more or less dependent on her parents again. Her training was free. All college fees were paid by the government, she had moreover a few pounds grant every year. This would just pay for her train fares and her clothing. Her parents would only have to feed her. She did not want to cost them much. They would not be well off. Her father would earn only two hundred a year, and a good deal of her mother's capital was spent in buying the house. Still, there was enough to get along with.

Gudrun was attending the Art School at Nottingham. She was working particularly at sculpture. She had a gift for this. She loved making little models in clay, of children or of animals. Already some of these had appeared in the Students' Exhibition in the Castle, and Gudrun was a distinguished person. She was chafing at the Art School and wanted to go to London. But there was not enough money. Neither would her parents let her go so far.

Theresa had left the High School. She was a great strapping, bold hussy, indifferent to all higher claims. She would stay at home. The others were at school, except the youngest. When term started, they would all be transferred to the Grammar School at Willey Green.

Ursula was excited at making acquaintances in Beldover. The excitement soon passed. She had tea at the clergyman's, at the chemist's, at the other chemist's, at the doctor's, at the under-manager's – then she knew practically everybody. She could not take people very seriously, though at the time she wanted to.

She wandered the country, on foot and on her bicycle, finding it very beautiful in the forest direction, between Mansfield and Southwell and Worksop. But she was here only skirmishing for amusement. Her real exploration would begin in college.

Term began. She went into town each day by train. The cloistered quiet of the college began to close around her.

She was not at first disappointed. The big college built of stone, standing in the quiet street, with a rim of grass and lime trees all so peaceful: she felt it remote, a magic land. Its architecture was foolish, she knew from her father. Still, it was different from that of all other buildings. Its rather pretty, plaything, Gothic form was almost a style, in the dirty industrial town.

She liked the hall, with its big stone chimney-piece and its Gothic arches supporting the balcony above. To be sure the arches were ugly, the chimney-piece of cardboard-like carved stone, with its armorial decoration, looked silly just opposite the bicycle stand and the radiator, whilst the great notice-board with its fluttering papers seemed to slam away all sense of retreat and mystery from the far wall. Nevertheless, amorphous as it might be, there was in it a reminiscence of the wondrous, cloistral origin of education. Her soul flew straight back to the medieval times, when the monks of God held the learning of men and imparted it within the shadow of religion. In this spirit she entered college.

The harshness and vulgarity of the lobbies and cloak-rooms hurt her at first. Why was it not all beautiful? But she could not openly admit her criticism. She was on holy ground.

She wanted all the students to have a high, pure spirit, she wanted them to say only the real, genuine things, she wanted their faces to be still and luminous as the nuns' and the monks' faces.

Alas, the girls chattered and giggled and were nervous, they were dressed up and frizzed, the men looked mean and clownish.

Still, it was lovely to pass along the corridor with one's books in one's hands, to push the swinging, glass-panelled door, and enter the big room where the first lecture would be given. The windows were large and lofty, the myriad brown students' desks stood waiting, the great blackboard was smooth behind the rostrum.

Ursula sat beside her window, rather far back. Looking down, she saw the lime trees turning yellow, the tradesman's boy passing silent down the still, autumn-sunny street. There was the world, remote, remote.

Here, within the great, whispering sea-shell, that whispered all the while with reminiscence of all the centuries, time faded away, and the echo of knowledge filled the timeless silence.

She listened, she scribbled her notes with joy, almost with ecstasy, never for a moment criticising what she heard. The lecturer was a mouth-piece, a priest. As he stood, black-gowned, on the rostrum, some strands of the whispering confusion of knowledge that filled the whole place seemed to be singled out and woven together by him, till they became a lecture.

At first, she preserved herself from criticism. She would not consider the professors as men, ordinary men who ate bacon, and pulled on their boots before coming to college. They were the black-gowned priests of knowledge, serving for ever in a remote, hushed temple. They were the initiated, and the beginning and the end of the mystery was in their keeping.

Curious joy she had of the lectures. It was a joy to hear the theory of education, there was such freedom and pleasure in ranging over the very stuff of knowledge, and seeing how it moved and lived and had its being. How happy Racine made her! She did not know why. But as the big lines of the drama unfolded themselves, so steady, so measured, she felt a thrill as of being in the realm of the reality. Of Latin, she was doing Livy and Horace. The curious, intimate, gossiping tone of the Latin class suited Horace. Yet she never cared for him, nor even Livy. There was an entire lack of sternness in the gossipy class-room. She tried hard to keep her old grasp of the Roman spirit. But gradually the Latin became mere gossip-stuff and artificiality to her, a question of manners and verbosities.

Her terror was the mathematics class. The lecturer went so fast, her heart beat excitedly, she seemed to be straining every nerve. And she struggled hard, during private study, to get the stuff into control.

Then came the lovely, peaceful afternoons in the botany laboratory. There were few students. How she loved to sit on her high stool before the bench, with her pith and her razor and her material, carefully mounting her slides, carefully bringing her microscope into focus, then turning with joy to record her observation, drawing joyfully in her book, if the slide were good.

She soon made a college friend, a girl who had lived in Florence, a girl who wore a wonderful purple or figured scarf draped over a plain, dark dress. She was Dorothy Russell, daughter of a south-country advocate. Dorothy lived with a maiden aunt in Nottingham, and spent her spare moments slaving for the Women's Social and Political Union. She was quiet and intense, with an ivory face and dark hair looped plain over her ears.

Ursula was very fond of her, but afraid of her. She seemed so old and so relentless towards herself. Yet she was only twenty-two. Ursula always felt her to be a creature of fate, like Cassandra.

The two girls had a close, stern friendship. Dorothy worked at all things with the same passion, never sparing herself. She came closest to Ursula during the botany hours. For she could not draw. Ursula made beautiful and wonderful drawings of the sections under the miscroscope, and Dorothy always came to learn the manner of the drawing.

So the first year went by, in magnificent seclusion and activity of learning. It was strenuous as a battle, her college life, yet remote as peace.

She came to Nottingham in the morning with Gudrun. The two sisters were distinguished wherever they went, slim, strong girls, eager and extremely sensitive. Gudrun was the more beautiful of the two, with her sleepy, half-languid girlishness that looked so soft, and yet was balanced and inalterable underneath. She wore soft, easy clothing, and hats which fell by themselves into a careless grace.

Ursula was much more carefully dressed, but she was self-conscious, always falling into depths of admiration of somebody else, and modelling herself upon this other, and so producing a hopeless incongruity. When she dressed for practical purposes she always looked well. In winter, wearing a tweed coat-and-skirt and a small hat of black fur pulled over her eager, palpitant face, she seemed to move down the street in a drifting motion of suspense and exceeding sensitive receptivity.

At the end of the first year Ursula got through her Intermediate Arts examination, and there came a lull in her eager activities. She slackened off, she relaxed altogether. Worn nervous and inflammable by the excitement of the preparation for the examination, and by the sort of exaltation which carried her through the crisis itself, she now fell into a quivering passivity, her will all loosened.

The family went to Scarborough for a month. Gudrun and the father were busy at the handicraft holiday school there, Ursula was left a good deal with the children. But when she could, she went off by herself.

She stood and looked out over the shining sea. It was very beautiful to her. The tears rose hot in her heart.

Out of the far, far space there drifted slowly in to her a passionate, unborn yearning. 'There are so many dawns that have not yet risen.' It seemed as if, from over the ege of the sea, all the unrisen dawns were appealing to her, all her unborn soul was crying for the unrisen dawns.

As she sat looking out at the tender sea, with its lovely, swift glimmer, the sob rose in her breast, till she caught her lip suddenly under her teeth, and the tears were forcing themselves from her. And in her very sob, she laughed. Why did she cry? She did not want to cry. It was so beautiful that she laughed. It was so beautiful that she cried.

She glanced apprehensively round, hoping no one would see her in this state.

Then came a time when the sea was rough. She watched the water travelling in to the coast, she watched a big wave running unnoticed, to burst in a shock of foam against a rock, enveloping all in a great white beauty, to pour away again, leaving the rock emerged black and teeming. Oh, and if, when the wave burst into whiteness, it were only set free!

Sometimes she loitered along the harbour, looking at the sea-browned sailors, who, in their close blue jerseys, lounged on the harbour-wall, and laughed at her with impudent, communicative eyes.

There was established a little relation between her and them. She never would speak to them or know any more of them. Yet as she walked by and they leaned on the sea-wall, there was something between her and them, something keen and delightful and painful. She liked best the young one whose fair, salty hair tumbled over his blue eyes. He was so new and fresh and salt and not of this world.

From Scarborough she went to her Uncle Tom's. Winifred had a small baby, born at the end of the summer. She had become strange and alien to Ursula. There was an unmentionable reserve between the two women. Tom Brangwen was an attentive father, a very domestic husband. But there was something spurious about his domesticity, Ursula did not like him any more. Something ugly, blatant in his nature had come out now, making him shift everything over to a sentimental basis. A materialistic unbeliever, he carried it all off by becoming full of human feeling, a warm, attentive host, a generous husband, a model citizen. And he was clever enough to rouse admiration everywhere, and to take in his wife sufficiently. She did not love him. She was glad to live in a state of complacent self-deception with him, she worked according to him.

Ursula was relieved to go home. She had still two peaceful years before her. Her future was settled for two years. She returned to college to prepare for her final examination.

But during this year the glamour began to depart from college. The professors were not priests initiated into the deep mysteries of life and knowledge. After all, they were only middle-men handling wares they had become so accustomed to that they were oblivious of them. What was Latin? – So much dry goods of knowledge. What was the Latin class altogether but a sort of second-hand curio shop, where one bought curios and learned the market-value of curios; dull curios too, on the whole. She was as bored by the Latin curiosities as she was by Chinese and Japanese curiosities in the antique shops. 'Antiques' – the very word made her soul fall flat and dead.

The life went out of her studies, why, she did not know. But the whole thing seemed sham, spurious; spurious Gothic arches, spurious peace, spurious Latinity, spurious dignity of France, spurious naïveté of Chaucer. It was a second-hand dealer's shop, and one bought an equipment for an examination. This was only a little side-show to the factories of the town. Gradually the perception stole into her. This was no religious retreat, no perception of pure learning. It was a little apprentice-shop where one was further equipped for making money. The college itself was a little, slovenly laboratory for the factory.

A harsh and ugly disillusion came over her again, the same darkness and bitter gloom from which she was never safe now, the realisation of the permanent substratum of ugliness under everything. As she came to the college in the afternoon, the lawns were frothed with daisies, the lime trees hung tender and sunlit and green; and oh, the deep, white froth of the daisies was anguish to see.

For inside, inside the college, she knew she must enter the sham workshop. All the while, it was a sham store, a sham warehouse, with a single motive of material gain, and no productivity. It pretended to exist by the religious virtue of knowledge. But the religious virtue of knowledge was become a flunkey to the god of material success.

A sort of inertia came over her. Mechanically, from habit, she went on with her studies. But it was almost hopeless. She could scarcely attend to anything. At the Anglo-Saxon lecture in the afternoon, she sat looking down, out of the window, hearing no word, of Beowulf or of anything else. Down below, in the street, the sunny grey pavement went beside the palisade. A woman in a pink frock, with a scarlet sunshade, crossed the road, a little white dog running like a fleck of light about her. The woman with the scarlet sunshade came over the road, a lilt in her walk, a little shadow attending her. Ursula watched spell-bound. The woman with the scarlet sunshade and the flickering terrier was gone – and whither? Whither?

In what world of reality was the woman in the pink dress walking? To what warehouse of dead unreality was she herself confined?

What good was this place, this college? What good was Anglo-Saxon, when one only learned it in order to answer examination questions, in order that one should have a higher commercial value later on? She was sick with this long service at the inner commercial shrine. Yet what else was there? Was life all this, and this only? Everywhere, everything was debased to the same service. Everything went to produce vulgar things, to encumber material life.

Suddenly she threw over French. She would take honours in botany. This was the one study that lived for her. She had entered into the lives of the plants. She was fascinated by the strange laws of the vegetable world. She had here a glimpse of something working entirely apart from the purpose of the human world.

College was barren, cheap, a temple converted to the most vulgar, petty commerce. Had she not gone to hear the echo of learning pulsing back to the source of the mystery? – The source of mystery! And barrenly, the professors in their gowns offered commercial commodity that could be turned to good account in the examination room; ready-made stuff too, and not really worth the money it was intended to fetch; which they all knew.

All the time in the college now, save when she was labouring in her botany laboratory, for there the mystery still glimmered, she felt she was degrading herself in a kind of trade of sham jewjaws.

Angry and stiff, she went through her last term. She would rather be out again earning her own living. Even Brinsley Street and Mr. Harby seemed real in comparison. Her violent hatred of the Ilkeston School was nothing compared with the sterile degradation of college. But she was not going back to Brinsley Street either. She would take her B.A., and become a mistress in some Grammar School for a time.

The last year of her college career was wheeling slowly round. She could see ahead her examination and her departure. She had the ash of disillusion gritting under her teeth. Would the next move turn out the same? Always the shining doorway ahead; and then, upon approach, always the shining doorway was a gate into another ugly yard, dirty and active and dead. Always the crest of the hill gleaming ahead under heaven: and then, from the top of the hill only another sordid valley full of amorphous, squalid activity.

No matter! Every hill-top was a little different, every valley was somehow new. Cossethay and her childhood with her father; the Marsh and the little Church school near the Marsh, and her grandmother and her uncles; the High School at Nottingham and Anton Skrebensky; Anton Skrebensky and the dance in the moonlight between the fires; then the time she could not think of without being blasted, Winifred Inger, and the months before becoming a school-teacher; then the horrors of Brinsley Street, lapsing into comparative peacefulness, Maggie, and Maggie's brother, whose influence she could still feel in her veins, when she conjured him up; then college, and Dorothy Russell, who was now in France, then the next move into the world again!

Already it was a history. In every phase she was so different. Yet she was always Ursula Brangwen. But what did it mean, Ursula Brangwen? She did not know what she was. Only she was full of rejection, of refusal. Always, always she was spitting out of her mouth the ash and grit of disillusion, of falsity. She could only stiffen in rejection, in rejection. She seemed always negative in her action.

That which she was, positively, was dark and unrevealed, it could not come forth. It was like a seed buried in dry ash. This world in which she lived was like a circle lighted by a lamp. This lighted area, lit up by man's completest consciousness, she thought was all the world: that here all was disclosed for ever. Yet all the time, within the darkness she had been aware of points of light, like the eyes of wild beasts, gleaming, penetrating, vanishing. And her soul had acknowledged in a great heave of terror only the outer darkness. This inner circle of light in which she lived and moved, wherein the trains rushed and the factories ground out their machine-produce and the plants and the animals worked by the light of science and knowledge, suddenly it seemed like the area under an arc-lamp, wherein the moths and children played in the security of blinding light, not even knowing there was any darkness, because they stayed in the light.

But she could see the glimmer of dark movement just out of range, she saw the eyes of the wild beast gleaming from the darkness, watching the vanity of the camp fire and the sleepers; she felt the strange, foolish vanity of the camp, which said 'Beyond our light and our order there is nothing,' turning their faces always inward towards the sinking fire of illuminating consciousness, which comprised sun and stars, and the Creator, and the System of Righteousness, ignoring always the vast darkness that wheeled round about, with half-revealed shapes lurking on the edge.

Yea, and no man dared even throw a firebrand into the darkness. For if he did he was jeered to death by the others, who cried 'Fool, anti-social knave, why would you disturb us with bogeys? There *is* no darkness. We move and live and have our being within the light, and unto us is given the eternal light of knowledge, we comprise and comprehend the innermost core and issue of knowledge. Fool and knave, how dare you belittle us with the darkness?'

Nevertheless the darkness wheeled round about, with grey shadow-shapes of wild beasts, and also with dark shadow-shapes of the angels, whom the light fenced out, as it fenced out the more familiar beasts of darkness. And some, having for a moment seen the darkness, saw it bristling with the tufts of the hyena and the wolf; and some having given up their vanity of the light, having died in their own conceit, saw the gleam in the eyes of the wolf and the hyena, that it was the flash of the sword of angels, flashing at the door to come in, that the angels in the darkness were lordly and terrible and not to be denied, like the flash of fangs.

It was a little while before Easter, in her last year of college, when Ursula was twenty-two years old, that she heard again from Skrebensky. He had written to her once or twice from South Africa, during the first months of his service out there in the war, and since had sent her a post-card every now and then, at ever longer intervals. He had become a first lieutenant, and had stayed out in Africa. She had not heard of him now for more than two years.

Often her thoughts returned to him. He seemed like the gleaming dawn, yellow, radiant, of a long, grey, ashy day. The memory of him was like the thought of the first radiant hours of morning. And here was the blank grey ashiness of later daytime. Ah, if he had only remained true to her, she might have known the sunshine, without all this toil and hurt and degradation of a spoiled day. He would have been her angel. He held the keys of the sunshine. Still he held them. He could open to her the gates of succeeding freedom and delight. Nay, if he had remained true to her, he would have been the doorway to her, into the boundless sky of happiness and plunging, inexhaustible freedom which was the paradise of her soul. Ah, the great range he would have opened to her, the illimitable endless space for self-realisation and delight for ever.

The one thing she believed in was in the love she had held for him. It remained shining and complete, a thing to hark back to. And she said to herself, when present things seemed a failure:

'Ah, I was fond of him,' as if with him the leading flower of her life had died.

Now she heard from him again. The chief effect was pain. The pleasure, the spontaneous joy was not there any longer. But her *will* rejoiced. Her will had fixed itself to him. And the old excitement of her dreams stirred and woke up. He was come, the man with the wondrous lips that could send the kiss wavering to the very end of all space. Was he come back to her? She did not believe.

My dear Ursula, I am back in England again for a few months before going out again, this time to India. I wonder if you still keep the memory of our times together. I have still got the little photograph of you. You must be changed since then, for it is about six years ago. I am fully six years older, – I have lived through another life since I knew you at Cossethay. I wonder if you would care to see me. I shall come up to Derby next week, and I would call in Nottingham, and we might have tea together. Will you let me know? I shall look for your answer.

Anton Skrebensky

Ursula had taken this letter from the rack in the hall at college, and torn it open as she crossed to the Women's room. The world seemed to dissolve away from around her, she stood alone in clear air.

Where could she go, to be alone? She fled away, upstairs, and through the private way to the reference library. Seizing a book, she sat down and pondered the letter. Her heart beat, her limbs trembled. As in a dream, she heard one gong sound in the college, then, strangely, another. The first lecture had gone by.

Hurriedly she took one of her note-books and began to write.

Dear Anton, Yes, I still have the ring. I should be very glad to see you again. You can come here to college for me, or I will meet you somewhere in the town. Will you let me know? Your sincere friend—'

Trembling, she asked the librarian, who was her friend, if he would give her an envelope. She sealed and addressed her letter, and went out, bareheaded, to post it. When it was dropped into the pillar-box, the world became a very still, pale place, without confines. She wandered back to college, to her pale dream, like a first wan light of dawn.

Skrebensky came one afternoon the following week. Day after day, she had hurried swiftly to the letter-rack on her arrival at college in the morning, and during the intervals between lectures. Several times, swiftly, with secretive fingers, she had plucked his letter down from its public prominence, and fled across the hall holding it fast and hidden. She read her letters in the botany laboratory, where her corner was always reserved to her.

Several letters, and then he was coming. It was Friday afternoon he appointed. She worked over her microscope with feverish activity, able to give only half her attention, yet working closely and rapidly. She had on her slide some special stuff come up from London that day, and the professor was fussy and excited about it. At the same time, as she focused the light on her field, and saw the plant-animal lying shadowy in a boundless light, she was fretting over a conversation she had had a few days ago with Dr. Frankstone, who was a woman doctor of physics in the college.

'No, really,' Dr. Frankstone had said, 'I don't see why we should attribute some special mystery to life – do you? We don't understand it as we understand electricity, even, but that doesn't warrant our saying it is something special, something different in kind and distinct from everything else in the universe – do you think it does? May it not be that life consists in a complexity of physical and chemical activities, of the same order as the activities we already know in science? I don't see, really, why we should imagine there is a special order of life, and life alone—'

The conversation had ended on a note of uncertainty, indefinite, wistful. But the purpose, what was the purpose? Electricity had no soul, light and heat had no soul. Was she herself an impersonal force, or conjunction of forces, like one of these? She looked still at the unicellular shadow that lay within the field of light, under her microscope. It was alive. She saw it move – she saw the bright mist of its ciliary activity, she saw the gleam of its nucleus, as it slid across the plane of light. What then was its will? If it was a conjunction of forces, physical and chemical, what held these forces unified, and for what purpose were they unified?

For what purpose were the incalculable physical and chemical activities nodalised in this shadowy, moving speck under her microscope? What was the will which nodalised them and created the one thing she saw? What was its intention? To be itself? Was its purpose just mechanical and limited to itself?

It intended to be itself. But what self? Suddenly in her mind the world gleamed strangely, with an intense light, like the nucleus of the creature under the microscope. Suddenly she had passed away into an intensely-gleaming light of knowledge. She could not understand what it all was. She only knew that it was not limited mechanical energy, nor mere purpose of self-preservation and self-assertion. It was a consummation, a being infinite. Self was a oneness with the infinite. To be oneself was a supreme, gleaming triumph of infinity.

Ursula sat abstracted over her microscope, in suspense. Her soul was busy, infinitely busy, in the new world. In the new world, Skrebensky was waiting for her – he would be waiting for her. She could not go yet, because her soul was engaged. Soon she would go.

A stillness, like passing away, took hold of her. Far off, down the corridors, she heard the gong booming five o'clock. She must go. Yet she sat still.

The other students were pushing back their stools and putting their microscopes away. Everything broke into turmoil. She saw, through the window, students going down the steps, with books under their arms, talking, all talking.

A great craving to depart came upon her. She wanted also to be gone. She was in dread of the material world, and in dread of her own transfiguration. She wanted to run to meet Skrebensky – the new life, the reality.

Very rapidly she wiped her slides and put them back, cleared her place at the bench, active, active, active. She wanted to run to meet Skrebensky, hasten – hasten. She did not know what she was to meet. But it would be a new beginning. She must hurry.

She flitted down the corridor on swift feet, her razor and note-books and pencil in one hand, her pinafore over her arm. Her face was lifted and tense with eagerness. He might not be there.

Issuing from the corridor, she saw him at once. She knew him at once. Yet he was so strange. He stood with the curious self-effacing diffidence which so frightened her in well-bred young men whom she knew. He stood as if he wished to be unseen. He was very well-dressed. She would not admit to herself the chill like a sunshine of frost that came over her. This was he, the key, the nucleus to the new world.

He saw her coming swiftly across the hall, a slim girl in a white flannel blouse and dark skirt, with some of the abstraction and gleam of the unknown upon her, and he started, excited. He was very nervous. Other students were loitering about the hall.

She laughed, with a blind, dazzled face, as she gave him her hand. He too could not perceive her.

In a moment she was gone, to get her outdoor things. Then again, as when she had been at school, they walked out into the town to tea. And they went to the same tea-shop.

She knew a great difference in him. The kinship was there, the old kinship, but he had belonged to a different world from hers. It was as if they had cried a state of truce between him and her, and in this truce they had met. She knew, vaguely, in the first minute, that they were enemies come together in a truce. Every movement and word of his was alien to her being.

Yet still she loved the fine texture of his face, of his skin. He was rather browner, physically stronger. He was a man now. She thought his manliness made the strangeness in him. When he was only a youth, fluid, he was nearer to her. She thought a man must inevitably set into this strange separateness, cold otherness of being. He talked, but not to her. She tried to speak to him, but she could not reach him.

He seemed so balanced and sure, he made such a confident presence. He was a great rider, so there was about him some of a horseman's sureness and habitual definiteness of decision, also some of the horseman's animal darkness. Yet his soul was only the more wavering, vague. He seemed made up of a set of habitual actions and decisions. The vulnerable, variable quick of the man was inaccessible. She knew nothing of it. She could only feel the dark, heavy fixity of his animal desire.

This dumb desire on his part had brought him to her? She was puzzled, hurt by some hopeless fixity in him, that terrified her with a cold feeling of despair. What did he want? His desires were so underground. Why did he not admit himself? What did he want? He wanted something that should be nameless. She shrank in fear.

Yet she flashed with excitement. In his dark, subterranean male soul, he was kneeling before her, darkly exposing himself. She quivered, the dark flame ran over her. He was waiting at her feet. He was helpless, at her mercy. She could take or reject. If she rejected him, something would die in him. For him it was life or death. And yet, all must be kept so dark, the consciousness must admit nothing.

'How long,' she said, 'are you staying in England?'

'I am not sure – but not later than July, I believe.'

Then they were both silent. He was here, in England, for six months. They had a space of six months between them. He waited. The same iron rigidity, as if the world were made of steel, possessed her again. It was no use turning with flesh and blood to this arrangement of forged metal.

Quickly, her imagination adjusted itself to the situation.

'Have you an appointment in India?' she asked.

'Yes – I have just the six months' leave.'

'Will you like being out there?'

'I think so – there's a good deal of social life, and plenty going on –

hunting, polo – and always a good horse – and plenty of work, any amount of work.'

He was always side-tracking, always side-tracking his own soul. She could see him so well out there, in India – one of the governing class, superimposed upon an old civilisation, lord and master of a clumsier civilisation than his own. It was his choice. He would become again an aristocrat, invested with authority and responsibility, having a great helpless populace beneath him. One of the ruling class, his whole being would be given over to the fulfilling and the executing of the better idea of the state. And in India, there would be real work to do. The country did need the civilisation which he himself represented: it did need his roads and bridges, and the enlightenment of which he was part. He would go to India. But that was not her road.

Yet she loved him, the body of him, whatever his decisions might be. He seemed to want something of her. He was waiting for her to decide of him. It had been decided in her long ago, when he had kissed her first. He was her lover, though good and evil should cease. Her will never relaxed, though her heat and soul must be imprisoned and silenced. He waited upon her, and she accepted him. For he had come back to her.

A glow came into his face, into his fine, smooth skin, his eyes, gold-grey, glowed intimately to her. He burned up, he caught fire and became splendid, royal, something like a tiger. She caught his brilliant, burnished glamour. Her heart and her soul were shut away fast down below, hidden. She was free of them. She was to have her satisfaction.

She became proud and erect, like a flower, putting itself forth in its proper strength. His warmth invigorated her. His beauty of form, which seemed to glow out in contrast with the rest of people, made her proud. It was like deference to her, and made her feel as if she represented before him all the grace and flower of humanity. She was no mere Ursula Brangwen. She was Woman, she was the whole of Woman in the human order. All-containing, universal, how should she be limited to individuality?

She was exhilarated, she did not want to go away from him. She had her place by him. Who should take her away?

They came out of the café.

'Is there anything you would like to do?' he said. 'Is there anything we *can* do?'

It was a dark, windy night in March.

'There is nothing to do,' she said.

Which was the answer he wanted.

'Let us walk then – where shall we walk?' he asked.

'Shall we go to the river?' she suggested, timidly.

In a moment they were on the tram, going down to Trent Bridge. She was so glad. The thought of walking in the dark, far-reaching water-meadows, beside the full river, transported her. Dark water flowing in silence through the big, restless night made her feel wild.

They crossed the bridge, descended, and went away from the lights. In an instant, in the darkness, he took her hand and they went in silence, with subtle feet treading the darkness. The town fumed away on their left, there were strange lights and sounds, the wind rushed against the trees, and under the bridge. They walked close together, powerful in unison. He drew her very close, held her with a subtle, stealthy, powerful passion, as if they had a secret agreement which held good in the profound darkness. The profound darkness was their universe.

'It is like it was before,' she said.

Yet it was not in the least as it was before. Nevertheless his heart was perfectly in accord with her. They thought one thought.

'I knew I should come back,' he said at length.

She quivered.

'Did you always love me?' she asked.

The directness of the question overcame him, submerged him for a moment. The darkness travelled massively along.

'I had to come back to you,' he said, as if hypnotised. 'You were always at the back of everything.'

She was silent with triumph, like fate.

'I loved you,' she said, 'always.'

The dark flame leaped up in him. He must give her himself. He must give her the very foundations of himself. He drew her very close, and they went on in silence.

She started violently, hearing voices. They were near a stile across the dark meadows.

'It's only lovers,' he said to her softly.

She looked to see the dark figures against the fence, wondering that the darkness was inhabited.

'Only lovers will walk here to-night,' he said.

Then in a low, vibrating voice he told her about Africa, the strange darkness, the strange, blood fear.

'I am not afraid of the darkness in England,' he said. 'It is soft, and natural to me, it is my medium, especially when you are here. But in Africa it seems massive and fluid with terror – not fear of anything – just fear. One breathes it, like the smell of blood. The blacks know it. They worship it, really, the darkness. One almost likes it – the fear – something sensual.'

She thrilled again to him. He was to her a voice out of the darkness. He talked to her all the while, in low tones, about Africa, conveying something strange and sensual to her: the negro, with his loose, soft passion that could envelop one like a bath. Gradually he transferred to her the hot, fecund darkness that possessed his own blood. He was strangely secret. The whole world must be abolished. He maddened her with his soft, cajoling, vibrating tones. He wanted her to answer, to understand. A turgid, teeming night, heavy with fecundity in which every molecule of matter grew big with increase, secretly urgent with fecund desire, seemed to come to pass. She quivered, taut and vibrating, almost pained. And gradually, he ceased telling her of Africa, there came a silence, whilst they walked the darkness beside the massive river. Her limbs were rich and tense, she felt they must be vibrating with a low, profound vibration. She could scarcely walk. The deep vibration of the darkness could only be felt, not heard.

Suddenly, as they walked, she turned to him and held him fast, as if she were turned to steel.

'*Do* you love me?' she cried in anguish.

'Yes,' he said, in a curious, lapping voice, unlike himself. 'Yes, I love you.'

He seemed like the living darkness upon her, she was in the embrace of the strong darkness. He held her enclosed, soft, unutterably soft, and with the unrelaxing softness of fate, the relentless softness of fecundity. She quivered, and quivered, like a tense thing that is struck. But he held her all the time, soft, unending, like darkness closed upon her, omnipresent as the night. He kissed her, and she quivered as if she were being destroyed, shattered. The lighted vessel vibrated, and broke in her soul, the light fell, struggled, and went dark. She was all dark, will-less, having only the receptive will.

He kissed her, with his soft, enveloping kisses, and she responded to them completely, her mind, her soul gone out. Darkness cleaving to darkness, she hung close to him, pressed herself into soft flow of his kiss, pressed herself down, down to the source and core of his kiss, herself covered and enveloped in the warm, fecund flow of his kiss, that travelled over her, flowed over her, covered her, flowed over the last fibre of her, so they were one stream, one dark fecundity, and she clung at the core of him, with her lips holding open the very bottommost source of him.

So they stood in the utter, dark kiss, that triumphed over them both, subjected them, knitted them into one fecund nucleus of the fluid darkness.

It was bliss, it was the nucleolating of the fecund darkness. Once the vessel had vibrated till it was shattered, the light of consciousness gone, then the darkness reigned, and the unutterable satisfaction.

They stood enjoying the unmitigated kiss, taking it, giving to it endlessly, and still it was not exhausted. Their veins fluttered, their blood ran together as one stream.

Till gradually a sleep, a heaviness settled on them, a drowse, and out of the drowse, a small light of consciousness woke up. Ursula became aware of the night around her, the water lapping and running full just near, the trees roaring and soughing in gusts of wind.

She kept near to him, in contact with him, but she became ever more and more herself. And she knew she must go to catch her train. But she did not want to draw away from contact with him.

At length they roused and set out. No longer they existed in the unblemished darkness. There was the glitter of a bridge, the twinkle of lights across the river, the big flare of the town in front and on their right.

But still, dark and soft and incontestable, their bodies walked untouched by the lights, darkness, supreme and arrogant.

'The stupid lights,' Ursula said to herself, in her dark sensual arrogance. 'The stupid, artificial, exaggerated town, fuming its lights. It does not exist really. It rests upon the unlimited darkness, like a gleam of coloured oil on dark water, but what is it? – nothing, just nothing.'

In the tram, in the train, she felt the same. The lights, the civic uniform was a trick played, the people as they moved or sat were only dummies exposed. She could see, beneath their pale, wooden pretence of composure and civic purposefulness, the dark stream that contained them all. They were like little paper ships in their motion. But in reality each one was a dark, blind, eager wave urging blindly forward, dark with the same homogeneous desire. And all their talk and all their behaviour was sham, they were dressed-up creatures. She was reminded of the Invisible Man, who was a piece of darkness made visible only by his clothes.

During the next weeks, all the time she went about in the same dark richness, her eyes dilated and shining like the eyes of a wild animal, a curious half-smile which seemed to be gibing at the civic pretence of all the human life about her.

'What are you, you pale citizens?' her face seemed to say, gleaming. 'You subdued beast in sheep's clothing, you primeval darkness falsified to a social mechanism.'

She went about in the sensual sub-consciousness all the time, mocking at the ready-made, artificial daylight of the rest.

'They assume selves as they assume suits of clothing,' she said to herself, looking in mocking contempt at the stiffened, neutralised men. 'They think it better to be clerks or professors than to be the dark, fertile beings that exist in the potential darkness. What do you think you are?' her soul asked of the professor as she sat opposite him in class. 'What do you think you are, as you sit there in your gown and your spectacles? You are a lurking, blood-sniffing creature with eyes peering out of the jungle darkness, snuffing for your desires. That is what you *are*, though nobody would believe it, and you would be the very last to allow it.'

Her soul mocked at all this pretence. Herself, she kept on pretending. She dressed herself and made herself fine, she attended her lectures and scribbled her notes. But all in a mood of superficial, mocking facility. She understood well enough their two-and-two-make-four tricks. She was as clever as they were. But care! – did she care about their monkey tricks of knowledge or learning or civic deportment? She did not care in the least.

There was Skrebensky, there was her dark, vital self. Outside the college, the outer darkness, Skrebensky was waiting. On the edge of the night, he was attentive. Did he care?

She was free as a leopard that sends up its raucous cry in the night. She had the potent, dark stream of her own blood, she had the glimmering core of fecundity, she had her mate, her complement, her sharer in fruition. So, she had all, everything.

Skrebensky was staying in Nottingham all the time. He too was free. He knew no one in this town, he had no civic self to maintain. He was free. Their trams and markets and theatres and public meetings were a shaken kaleidoscope to him, he watched as a lion or a tiger may lie with narrowed eyes watching the people pass before its cage, the kaleidoscopic unreality of people, or a leopard lie blinking, watching the incomprehensible feats of the keepers. He despised it all – it was all non-existent. Their good professors, their good clergymen, their good political speakers, their good, earnest women – all the time he felt his soul was grinning, grinning at the sight of them. So many performing puppets, all wood and rag for the performance!

He watched the citizen, a pillar of society, a model, saw the stiff goat's legs, which have become almost stiffened to wood in the desire to make them puppet in their action, he saw the trousers formed to the puppet-action: man's legs, but man's legs become rigid and deformed, ugly, mechanical.

He was curiously happy, being alone, now. The glimmering grin was on his face. He had no longer any necessity to take part in the performing tricks of the rest. He had discovered the clue to himself, he had escaped from the show, like a wild beast escaped straight back into its jungle. Having a room in a quiet hotel, he hired a horse and rode out into the country, staying sometimes for the night in some village, and returning the next day.

He felt rich and abundant in himself. Everything he did was a voluptuous pleasure to him – either to ride on horseback, or to walk, or to lie in the sun, or to drink in a public-house. He had no use for people, nor for words. He had an amused pleasure in everything, a great sense of voluptuous richness in himself, and of the fecundity of the universal night he inhabited. The puppet shapes of people, their wood-mechanical voices, he was remote from them.

For there were always his meetings with Ursula. Very often, she did not go to college in the afternoon, but walked with him instead. Or he took a motor-car or a dog-cart and they drove into the country, leaving the car and going away by themselves into the woods. He had not taken her yet. With subtle, instinctive economy, they went to the end of each kiss, each embrace, each pleasure in intimate contact, knowing subconsciously that the last was coming. It was to be their final entry into the source of creation.

She took him home, and he stayed a week-end at Beldover with her family. She loved having him in the house. Strange how he seemed to come into the atmosphere of her family, with his laughing, insidious grace. They all loved him, he was kin to them. His raillery, his warm, voluptuous mocking presence was meat and joy to the Brangwen household. For this house was always quivering with darkness, they put off their puppet form when they came home, to lie and drowse in the sun.

There was a sense of freedom amongst them all, of the undercurrent of darkness among them all. Yet here, at home, Ursula resented it. It became distasteful to her. And she knew that if they understood the real relationship between her and Skrebensky, her parents, her father in particular, would go mad with rage. So subtly, she seemed to be like any other girl who is more or less courted by a man. And she was like any other girl. But in her, the antagonism to the social imposition was for the time complete and final.

She waited, every moment of the day, for his next kiss. She admitted it to herself in shame and bliss. Almost consciously, she waited. He waited, but, until the time came, more unconsciously. When the time came that he should kiss her again, a prevention was an annihilation to him. He felt his flesh go grey, he was heavy with a corpse-like inanition, he did not exist, if the time passed unfulfilled.

He came to her finally in a superb consummation. It was very dark, and again a windy, heavy night. They had come down the lane towards Beldover, down to the valley. They were at the end of their kisses, and there was the silence between them. They stood as at the edge of a cliff, with a great darkness beneath.

Coming out of the lane along the darkness, with the dark space spreading down to the wind, and the twinkling lights of the station below, the far-off windy chuff of a shunting train, the tiny clink-clink-clink of the wagons blown between the wind, the light of Beldover-edge twinkling upon the blackness of the hill opposite, the glow of the furnaces along the railway to the right, their steps began to falter. They would soon come out of the darkness into the lights. It was like turning back. It was unfulfilment. Two quivering, unwilling creatures, they lingered on the edge of the darkness, peering out at the lights and the machine-glimmer beyond. They could not turn back to the world – they could not.

So lingering along, they came to a great oak tree by the path. In all its budding mass it roared to the wind, and its trunk vibrated in every fibre, powerful, indomitable.

'We will sit down,' he said.

And in the roaring circle under the tree, that was almost invisible yet whose powerful presence received them, they lay a moment looking at the twinkling lights on the darkness opposite, saw the sweeping brand of a train past the edge of their darkened field.

Then he turned and kissed her, and she waited for him. The pain to her was the pain she wanted, the agony was the agony she wanted. She was caught up, entangled in the powerful vibration of the night. The man, what was he? – a dark, powerful vibration that encompassed her. She passed away as on a dark wind, far, far, away, into the pristine darkness of paradise, into the original immortality. She entered the dark fields of immortality.

When she rose, she felt strangely free, strong. She was not ashamed, – why should she be? He was walking beside her, the man who had been with her. She had taken him, they had been together. Whither they had gone, she did not know. But it was as if she has received another nature. She belonged to the eternal, changeless place into which they had leapt together.

Her soul was sure and indifferent of the opinion of the world of artificial light. As they went up the steps of the foot-bridge over the railway, and met the train-passengers, she felt herself belonging to another world, she walked past them immune, a whole darkness dividing her from them. When she went into the lighted dining-room at home, she was impervious to the lights and the eyes of her parents. Her everyday self was just the same. She merely had another, stronger self that knew the darkness.

This curious separate strength, that existed in darkness and pride of night, never forsook her. She had never been more herself. It could not occur to her that anybody, not even the young man of the world, Skrebensky, should have anything at all to do with her permanent self. As for her temporal, social self, she let it look after itself.

Her whole soul was implicated with Skrebensky – not the young man of the world, but the undifferentiated man he was. She was perfectly sure of herself, perfectly strong, stronger than all the world. The world was not strong – she was strong. The world existed only in a secondary sense: – she existed supremely.

She continued at college, in her ordinary routine, merely as a cover to her dark, powerful under-life. The fact of herself, and with her Skrebensky, was so powerful, that she took rest in the other. She sent to college in the morning, and attended her classes, flowering, and remote.

She had lunch with him in his hotel; every evening she spent with him, either in town, at his rooms, or in the country. She made the excuse at home of evening study for her degree. But she paid not the slightest attention to her study.

They were both absolute and happy and calm. The fact of their own consummate being made everything else so entirely subordinate that they were free. The only thing they wanted, as the days went by, was more time to themselves. They wanted the time to be absolutely their own.

The Easter vacation was approaching. They agreed to go right away. It would not matter if they did not come back. They were indifferent to the actual facts.

'I suppose we ought to get married,' he said, rather wistfully. It was so magnificently free and in a deeper world, as it was. To make public their connection would be to put it in range with all the things which nullified him, and from which he was for the moment entirely dissociated. If he married he would have to assume his social self. And the thought of assuming his social self made him at once diffident and abstract. If she were his social wife, if she were part of that complication of dead reality, then what had his under-life to do with her? One's social wife was almost a material symbol. Whereas now she was something more vivid to him than anything in conventional life could be. She gave the complete lie to all conventional life, he and she stood together, dark, fluid, infinitely potent, giving the living lie to the dead whole which contained them.

He watched her pensive, puzzled face.

'I don't think I want to marry you,' she said, her brow clouded.

It piqued him rather.

'Why not?' he asked.

'Let's think about it afterwards, shall we?' she said.

He was crossed, yet he loved her violently.

'You've got a *museau*, not a face,' he said.

'Have I?' she cried, her face lighting up like a pure flame. She thought she had escaped. Yet he returned – he was not satisfied.

'Why?' he asked, 'why don't you want to marry me?'

'I don't want to be with other people,' she said. 'I want to be like this. I'll tell you if ever I want to marry you.'

'All right,' he said.

He would rather the thing was left indefinite, and that she took the responsibility.

They talked of the Easter vacation. She thought only of complete enjoyment.

They went to an hotel in Piccadilly. She was supposed to be his wife. They bought a wedding-ring for a shilling, from a shop in a poor quarter.

They had revoked altogether the ordinary mortal world. Their confidence was like a possession upon them. They were possessed. Perfectly and supremely free they felt, proud beyond all question, and surpassing mortal conditions.

They were perfect, therefore nothing else existed. The world was a world of servants whom one civilly ignored. Wherever they went, they were the sensuous aristocrats, warm, bright, glancing with pure pride of the senses.

The effect upon other people was extraordinary. The glamour was cast from the young couple upon all they came into contact with, waiters or chance acquaintances.

'*Oui, Monsieur le baron*,' she would reply with a mocking courtesy to her husband.

So they came to be treated as titled people. He was an officer in the engineers. They were just married, going to India immediately.

Thus a tissue of romance was round them. She believed she was a young wife of a titled husband on the eve of departure for India. This, the social fact, was a delicious make-belief. The living fact was that he and she were man and woman, absolute and beyond all limitation.

The days went by – they were to have three weeks together – in perfect success. All the time, they themselves were reality, all outside was tribute to them. They were quite careless about money, but they did nothing very extravagant. He was rather surprised when he found that he had spent twenty pounds in a little under a week, but it was only the irritation of having to go to the bank. The machinery of the old system lasted for him, not the system. The money simply did not exist.

Neither did any of the old obligations. They came home from the theatre, had supper, then flitted about in their dressing-gowns. They had a large bedroom and a corner sitting-room high up, remote and very cosy. They ate all their meals in their own rooms, attended by a young German called Hans, who thought them both wonderful, and answered assiduously:

'*Gewiss, Herr Baron – bitte sehr, Frau Baronin.*'

Often, they saw the pink of dawn away across the park. The tower of Westminster Cathedral was emerging, the lamps of Piccadilly, stringing away beside the trees of the park, were becoming pale and moth-like, the morning traffic was clock-clocking down the shadowy road, which had gleamed all night like metal, down below, running far ahead into the night, beneath the lamps, and which was now vague, as in a mist, because of the dawn.

Then, as the flush of dawn became stronger, they opened the glass doors and went on to the giddy balcony, feeling triumphant as two angels in bliss, looking down at the still sleeping world, which would wake to a dutiful, rumbling, sluggish turmoil of unreality.

But the air was cold. They went into their bedroom, and bathed before going to bed, leaving the partition doors of the bath-room open, so that the vapour came into the bedroom and faintly dimmed the mirror. She was always in bed first. She watched him as he bathed, his quick, unconscious movements, the electric light glinting on his wet shoulders. He stood out of the bath, his hair all washed flat over his forehead, and pressed the water out of his eyes. He was slender, and, to her, perfect, a clean, straight-cut youth, without a grain of superfluous body. The brown hair on his body was soft and fine and adorable, he was all beautifully flushed, as he stood in the white bath-apartment.

He saw her warm, dark, lit-up face watching him from the pillow – yet he did not see it – it was always present, and was to him as his own eyes. He was never aware of the separate being of her. She was like his own eyes and his own heart beating to him.

So he went across to her, to get his sleeping suit. It was always a perfect adventure to go near to her. She put her arms round him, and snuffed his warm, softened skin.

'Scent,' she said.

'Soap,' he answered.

'Soap,' she repeated, looking up with bright eyes. They were both laughing, always laughing.

Soon they were fast asleep, asleep till midday, close together, sleeping one sleep. Then they awoke to the ever-changing reality of their state. They alone inhabited the world of reality. All the rest lived on a lower sphere.

Whatever they wanted to do, they did. They saw a few people – Dorothy, whose guest she was supposed to be, and a couple of friends of Skrebensky, young Oxford men, who called her Mrs. Skrebensky with entire simplicity. They treated her, indeed, with such respect, that she began to think she was really quite of the whole universe, of the old world as well as of the new. She forgot she was outside the pale of the old world. She thought she had brought it under the spell of her own, real world. And so she had.

In such ever-changing reality the weeks went by. All the time, they were an unknown world to each other. Every movement made by the one was a reality and an adventure to the other. They did not want outside excitements. They went to very few theatres, they were often in their sitting-room high up over Piccadilly, with windows open on two sides, and the door open on to the balcony, looking over the Green Park, or down upon the minute travelling of the traffic.

Then suddenly, looking at a sunset, she wanted to go. She must be gone. She must be gone at once. And in two hours' time they were at Charing Cross taking train for Paris. Paris was his suggestion. She did not care where it was. The great joy was in setting out. And for a few days she was happy in the novelty of Paris.

Then, for some reason, she must call in Rouen on the way back to London. He had an instinctive mistrust of her desire for the place. But, perversely, she wanted to go there. It was as if she wanted to try its effect upon her.

For the first time, in Rouen, he had a cold feeling of death; not afraid of any other man, but of her. She seemed to leave him. She followed after something that was not him. She did not want him. The old streets, the cathedral, the age and the monumental peace of the town took her away from him. She turned to it as if to something she had forgotten, and wanted. This was now the reality; this great stone cathedral slumbering there in its mass, which knew no transience nor heard any denial. It was majestic in its stability, its splendid absoluteness.

Her soul began to run by itself. He did not realise, nor did she. Yet in Rouen he had the first deadly anguish, the first sense of the death towards which they were wandering. And she felt the first heavy yearning, heavy,

heavy hopeless warning, almost like a deep, uneasy sinking into apathy, hopelessness.

They returned to London. But still they had two days. He began to tremble, he grew feverish with the fear of her departure. She had in her some fatal prescience, that made her calm. What would be, would be.

He remained fairly easy, however, still in his state of heightened glamour, till she had gone, and he had turned away from St. Pancras, and sat on the tram-car going up Pimlico to the 'Angel', to Moorgate Street on Sunday evening.

Then the cold horror gradually soaked into him. He saw the horror of the City Road, he realised the ghastly cold sordiness of the tram-car in which he sat. Cold, stark, ashen sterility had him surrounded. Where then was the luminous, wonderful world he belonged to by rights? How did he come to be thrown on this refuse-heap where he was?

He was as if mad. The horror of the brick buildings, of the tram-car, of the ashen-grey people in the street made him reeling and blind as if drunk. He went mad. He had lived with her in a close, living, pulsing world, where everything pulsed with rich being. Now he found himself struggling amid an ashen-dry, cold world of rigidity, dead walls and mechanical traffic, and creeping, spectre-like people. The life was extinct, only ash moved and stirred or stood rigid, there was a horrible, clattering activity, a rattle like the falling of dry slag, cold and sterile. It was as if the sunshine that fell were unnatural light exposing the ash of the town, as if the lights at night were the sinister gleam of decomposition.

Quite mad, beside himself, he went to his club and sat with a glass of whisky, motionless, as if turned to clay. He felt like a corpse that is inhabited with just enough life to make it appear as any other of the spectral, unliving beings which we call people in our dead language. Her absence was worse than pain to him. It destroyed his being.

Dead, he went on from lunch to tea. His face was all the time fixed and stiff and colourless, his life was a dry, mechanical movement. Yet even he wondered slightly at the awful misery that had overcome him. How could he be so ashlike and extinct? He wrote her a letter.

I have been thinking that we must get married before long. My pay will be more when I get out to India, we shall be able to get along. Or if you don't want to go to India, I could very probably stay here in England. But I think you would like India. You could ride, and you would know just everybody out there. Perhaps if you stay on to take your degree, we might marry immediately after that. I will write to your father as soon as I hear from you—

He went on, disposing of her. If only he could be with her! All he wanted now was to marry her, to be sure of her. Yet all the time he was perfectly, perfectly hopeless, cold, extinct, without emotion or connection.

He felt as if his life were dead. His soul was extinct. The whole being of him had become sterile, he was a spectre, divorced from life. He had no fullness, he was just a flat shape. Day by day the madness accumulated in him. The horror of not-being possessed him.

He went here, there, and everywhere. But whatever he did, he knew that only the cipher of him was there, nothing was filled in. He went to the theatre; what he heard and saw fell upon a cold surface of consciousness, which was now all that he was, there was nothing behind it, he could have no experience of any sort. Mechanical registering took place in him, no more. He had no being, no contents. Neither had the people he came into contact with. They were mere permutations of known quantities. There was no roundness or fullness in this world he now inhabited, everything was a dead shape mental arrangement, without life or being.

Much of the time, he was with friends and comrades. Then he forgot everything. Their activities made up for his own negation, they engaged his negative horror.

He only became happy when he drank, and he drank a good deal. Then he was just the opposite to what he had been. He became a warm, diffuse, glowing cloud, in a warm, diffuse formless fashion. Everything melted down into a rosy glow, and he was the glow, and everything was the glow, everybody else was the glow, and it was very nice, very nice. He would sing songs, it was *so* nice.

Ursula went back to Beldover shut and firm. She loved Skrebensky, of that she was resolved. She would allow nothing else.

She read his long, obsessed letter about getting married and going to India, without any particular response. She seemed to ignore what he said about marriage. It did not come home to her. He seemed, throughout the greater part of his letter, to be talking without much meaning.

She replied to him pleasantly and easily. She rarely wrote long letters.

India sounds lovely. I can just see myself on an elephant swaying between lanes of obsequious natives. But I don't know if father would let me go. We must see.

I keep living over again the lovely times we have had. But I don't think you liked me quite so much towards the end, did you? You did not like me when we left Paris. Why didn't you?

I love you very much. I love your body. It is so clear and fine. I am glad you do not go naked, or all the women would fall in love with you. I am very jealous of it, I love it so much.

He was more or less satisfied with this letter. But day after day he was walking about, dead, non-existent.

He could not come again to Nottingham until the end of April. Then he persuaded her to go with him for a weekend to a friend's house near Oxford. By this time they were engaged. He had written to her father, and the thing was settled. He brought her an emerald ring, of which she was very proud.

Her people treated her now with a little distance, as if she had already left them. They left her very much alone.

She went with him for the three days in the country house near Oxford. It was delicious, and she was very happy. But the thing she remembered most was when, getting up in the morning after he had gone back quietly to his own room, having spent the night with her, she found herself very rich in being alone, and enjoying to the full her solitary room, she drew up her blind and saw the plum trees in the garden below all glittering and snowy and delighted with the sunshine, in full bloom under a blue sky. They threw out their blossom, they flung it out under the blue heavens, the whitest blossom! How excited it made her.

She had to hurry through her dressing to go and walk in the garden under the plum trees, before anyone should come and talk to her. Out she slipped, and was paced like a queen in fairy pleasaunces. The blossom was silver-shadowy when she looked up from under the tree at the blue sky. There was a faint scent, a faint noise of bees, a wonderful quickness of happy morning.

She heard the breakfast gong and went indoors.

'Where have you been?' asked the others.

'I had to go out under the plum trees,' she said, her face glowing like a flower. 'It is so lovely.'

A shadow of anger crossed Skrebensky's soul. She had not wanted him to be there. He hardened his will.

At night there was a moon, and the blossom glistened ghostly, they went together to look at it. She saw the moonlight on his face as he waited near her, and his features were like silver and his eyes in shadow were unfathomable. She was in love with him. He was very quiet.

They went indoors and she pretended to be tired. So she went quickly to bed.

'Don't be long coming to me,' she whispered, as she was supposed to be kissing him good night.

And he waited, intent, obsessed, for the moment when he could come to her.

She enjoyed him, she made much of him. She liked to put her fingers on the soft skin of his sides, or on the softness of his back, when he made the muscles hard underneath, the muscles developed very strong through riding; and she had a great thrill of excitement and passion, because of the unimpressible hardness of his body, that was so soft and smooth under her fingers, that came to her with such absolute service.

She owned his body and enjoyed it with all the delight and carelessness of a possessor. But he had become gradually afraid of her body. He wanted her, he wanted her endlessly. But there had come a tension into his desire, a constraint which prevented his enjoying the delicious approach and the lovable close of the endless embrace. He was afraid. His will was always tense, fixed.

Her final examination was at midsummer. She insisted on sitting for it, although she had neglected her work during the past months. He also wanted her to go in for the degree. Then, he thought, she would be satisfied. Secretly he hoped she would fail, so that she would be more glad of him.

'Would you rather live in India or in England when we are married?' he asked her.

'Oh, in India, by far,' she said, with a careless lack of consideration which annoyed him.

Once she said, with heat:

'I shall be glad to leave England. Everything is so meagre and paltry, it is so unspiritual – I hate democracy.'

He became angry to hear her talk like this, he did not know why. Somehow, he could not bear it, when she attacked things. It was as if she were attacking him.

'What do you mean?' he asked her, hostile. 'Why do you hate democracy?'

'Only the greedy and ugly people come to the top in a democracy,' she said, 'because they're the only people who will push themselves there. Only degenerate races are democratic.'

'What do you want then – an aristocracy?' he asked, secretly moved. He always felt that by rights he belonged to the ruling aristocracy. Yet to hear her speak for his class pained him with a curious, painful pleasure. He felt he was acquiescing in something illegal, taking to himself some wrong, reprehensible advantages.

'I *do* want an aristocracy,' she cried. 'And I'd far rather have an aristocracy of birth than of money. Who are the aristocrats now – who are chosen as the best to rule? Those who have money and the brains for money. It doesn't matter what else they have: but they must have money-brains, – because they are ruling in the name of money.'

'The people elect the government,' he said.

'I know they do. But what are the people? Each one of them is a money-interest. I hate it, that anybody is my equal who has the same amount of money as I have. I *know* I am better than all of them. I hate them. They are not my equals. I hate equality on a money basis. It is the equality of dirt.'

Her eyes blazed at him, he felt as if she wanted to destroy him. She had gripped him and was trying to break him. His anger sprang up, against her. At least he would fight for his existence with her. A hard, blind resistance possessed him.

'I don't care about money,' he said, 'neither do I want to put my finger in the pie. I am too sensitive about my finger.'

'What is your finger to me?' she cried, in a passion, 'You with your dainty fingers, and your going to India because you will be one of the somebodies there! It's a mere dodge, your going to India.'

'In what way a dodge?' he cried, white with anger and fear.

'You think the Indians are simpler than us, and so you'll enjoy being near them and being a lord over them,' she said. 'And you'll feel so righteous, governing them for their own good. Who are you, to feel righteous? What are you righteous about, in your governing? Your governing stinks. What do you govern for, but to make things there as dead and mean as they are here!'

'I don't feel righteous in the least,' he said.

'Then what *do* you feel? It's all such a nothingness, what you feel and what you don't feel.'

'What do you feel yourself?' he said. 'Aren't you righteous in your own mind?'

'Yes, I am, because I'm against you, and all your old, dead things,' she cried.

She seemed, with the last words, uttered in hard knowledge, to strike down the flag that he kept flying. He felt cut off at the knees, a figure made worthless. A horrible sickness gripped him, as if his legs were really cut away, and he could not move, but remained a crippled trunk, dependent, worthless. The ghastly sense of helplessness as if he were a mere figure that did not exist vitally, made him mad, beside himself.

Now, even whilst he was with her, this death of himself came over him, when he walked about like a body from which all individual life is gone. In this state he neither heard nor saw nor felt, only the mechanism of his life continued.

He hated her, as far as, in this state, he could hate. His cunning suggested to him all the ways of making her esteem him. For she did not esteem him. He left her and did not write to her. He flirted with other women, with Gudrun.

This last made her very fierce. She was still fiercely jealous of his body. In passionate anger she upraided him because, not being man enough to satisfy one woman, he hung round others.

'Don't I satisfy you?' he asked of her, again going white to the throat.

'No,' she said. 'You've never satisfied me since the first week in London. You never satisfy me now. What does it mean to me, your having me—' She lifted her shoulders and turned aside her face in a motion of cold, indifferent worthlessness. He felt he would kill her.

When she had roused him to a pitch of madness, when she saw his eyes all dark and mad with suffering, then a great suffering overcame her soul, a great, inconquerable suffering. And she loved him. For, oh, she wanted to love him. Stronger than life or death was her craving to be able to love him.

And at such moments, when he was mad with her destroying him, when all his complacency was destroyed, all his everyday self was broken, and only the stripped, rudimentary, primal man remained, demented with torture, her passion to love him became love, she took him again, they came together in an overwhelming passion, in which he knew he satisfied her.

But it all contained a developing germ of death. After each contact, her anguished desire for him or for that which she never had from him was stronger, her love was more hopeless. After each contact his mad dependence on her was deepened, his hope of standing strong and taking her in his own strength was weakened. He felt himself a mere attribute of her.

Whitsuntide came, just before her examination. She was to have a few days of rest. Dorothy had inherited her patrimony, and had taken a cottage in Sussex. She invited them to stay with her.

They went down to Dorothy's neat, low cottage at the foot of the downs. Here they could do as they liked. Ursula was always yearning to go to the top of the downs. The white track wound up to the rounded summit. And she must go.

Up there, she could see the Channel a few miles away, the sea raised up and faintly glittering in the sky, the Isle of Wight a shadow lifted in the far distance, the river winding bright through the patterned plain to seaward, Arundel Castle a shadowy bulk, and then the rolling of the high, smooth downs, making a high, smooth land under heaven, acknowledging only the heavens in their great, sun-glowing strength, and suffering only a few bushes to trespass on the intercourse between their great, unabateable body and the changeful body of the sky.

Below she saw the villages and the woods of the weald, and the train running bravely, a gallant little thing, running with all the importance of the world over the water meadows and into the gap of the downs, waving its white steam, yet all the while so little. So little, yet its courage carried it from end to end of the earth, till there was no place where it did not go. Yet the downs, in magnificent indifference, bearing limbs and body to the sun, drinking sunshine and sea-wind and sea-wet cloud into its golden skin, with superb stillness and calm of being, was not the downs still more wonderful? The blind, pathetic, energetic courage of the train as it steamed tinily away through the patterned levels to the sea's dimness, so fast and so energetic, made her weep. Where was it going? It was going nowhere, it was just going. So blind, so without goal or aim, yet so hasty! She sat on an old prehistoric earth-work and cried, and the tears ran down her face. The train had tunnelled all the earth, blindly, and uglily.

And she lay face downwards on the downs, that were so strong, that cared only for their intercourse with the everlasting skies, and she wished she could become a strong mound smooth under the sky, bosom and limbs bared to all winds and clouds and bursts of sunshine.

But she must get up again and look down from her foothold of sunshine, down and away at the patterned, level earth, with its villages and its smoke and its energy. So shortsighted the train seemed, running to the distance, so terrifying in their littleness the villages, with such pettiness in their activity.

Skrebensky wandered dazed, not knowing where he was or what he was doing with her. All her passion seemed to be to wander up there on the downs, and when she must descend to earth, she was heavy. Up there she was exhilarated and free.

She would not love him in a house any more. She said she hated houses, and particularly she hated beds. There was something distasteful in his coming to her bed.

She would stay the night on the downs, up there, he with her. It was midsummer, the days were glamorously long. At about half-past ten, when the bluey-black darkness had at last fallen, they took rugs and climbed the steep track to the summit of the downs, he and she.

Up there, the stars were big, the earth below was gone into darkness. She was free up there with the stars. Far out they saw tiny yellow lights – but it was very far out, at sea, or on land. She was free up among the stars.

She took off her clothes, and made him take off all his, and they ran over the smooth, moonless turf, a long way, more than a mile from where they had left their clothing, running in the dark, soft wind, utterly naked, as naked as the downs themselves. Her hair was loose and blew about her shoulders, she ran swiftly, wearing sandals when she set off on the long run to the dew-pond.

In the round dew-pond the stars were untroubled. She ventured softly into the water, grasping at the stars with her hands.

And then suddenly she started back, running swiftly. He was there, beside her, but only on sufferance. He was a screen for her fears. He served her. She took him, she clasped him, clenching him close, but her eyes were open looking at the stars, it was as if the stars were lying with her and entering the unfathomable darkness of her womb, fathoming her at last. It was not him.

The dawn came. They stood together on a high place, an earthwork of the stone-age men, watching for the light. It came over the land. But the land was dark. She watched a pale rim on the sky, away against the darkened land. The darkness became bluer. A little wind was running in from the sea behind. It seemed to be running to the pale rift of the dawn. And she and he darkly, on an outpost of the darkness, stood watching for the dawn.

The light grew stronger, gushing up against the dark sapphire of the transparent night. The light grew stronger, whiter, then over it hovered a flush of rose. A flush of rose, and then yellow, pale, new-created yellow, the whole quivering and poising momentarily over the fountain on the sky's rim.

The rose hovered and quivered, burned, fused to flame, to a transient red, while the yellow urged out in great waves, thrown from the ever-increasing fountain, great waves of yellow flinging into the sky, scattering its spray over the darkness, which became bluer and bluer, paler, till soon it would itself be a radiance, which had been darkness.

The sun was coming. There was a quivering, a powerful terrifying swim of molten light. Then the molten source itself surged forth, revealing itself. The sun was in the sky, too powerful to look at.

And the ground beneath lay so still, so peaceful. Only now and again a cock crew. Otherwise, from the distant yellow hills to the pine trees at the foot of the downs, everything was newly washed into being, in a flood of new, golden creation.

It was so unutterably still and perfect with promise, the golden-lighted, distinct land, that Ursula's soul rocked and wept. Suddenly he glanced at her. The tears were running over her cheeks, her mouth was working strangely.

'What is the matter?' he asked.

After a moment's struggle with her voice.

'It is so beautiful,' she said, looking at the glowing, beautiful land. It was so beautiful, so perfect, and so unsullied.

He too realised what England would be in a few hours' time – a blind, sordid, strenuous activity, all for nothing, fuming with dirty smoke and running trains and groping in the bowels of the earth, all for nothing. A ghastliness came over him.

He looked at Ursula. Her face was wet with tears, very bright, like a transfiguration in the refulgent light. Nor was his the hand to wipe away the burning, bright tears. He stood apart, overcome by a cruel ineffectuality.

Gradually a great, helpless sorrow was rising in him. But as yet he was fighting it away, he was struggling for his own life. He became very quiet and unaware of the things about him, awaiting, as it were, her judgment on him.

They returned to Nottingham, the time of her examination came. She must go to London. But she would not stay with him in an hotel. She would go to a quiet little pension near the British Museum.

Those quiet residential squares of London made a great impression on her mind. They were very complete. Her mind seemed imprisoned in their quietness. Who was going to liberate her?

In the evening, her practical examinations being over, he went with her to dinner at one of the hotels down the river, near Richmond. It was golden and beautiful, with yellow water and white and scarlet-striped boat-awnings, and blue shadows under the trees.

'When shall we be married?' he asked her, quietly, simply, as if it were a mere question of comfort.

She watched the changing pleasure-traffic of the river. He looked at her golden, puzzled *museau*. The knot gathered in his throat.

'I don't know,' she said.

A hot grief gripped his throat.

'Why don't you know – don't you want to be married?' he asked her.

Her head turned slowly, her face, puzzled, like a boy's face, expressionless because she was trying to think, looked towards his face. She did not see him, because she was pre-occupied. She did not quite know what she was going to say.

'I don't think I want to be married,' she said, and her naïve, troubled, puzzled eyes rested a moment on his, then travelled away, pre-occupied.

'Do you mean never, or not just yet?' he asked.

The knot in his throat grew harder, his face was drawn as if he were being strangled.

'I mean never,' she said, out of some far self which spoke for once beyond her.

His drawn, strangled face watched her blankly for a few moments, then a strange sound took place in his throat. She started, came to herself, and, horrified, saw him. His head made a queer motion, the chin jerked back against the throat, the curious, crowing, hiccupping sound came again, his face twisted like insanity, and he was crying, crying blind and twisted as if something were broken which kept him in control.

'Tony – don't,' she cried, starting up.

It tore every one of her nerves to see him. He made groping movements to get out of his chair. But he was crying uncontrollably, noiselessly, with his face twisted like a mask, contorted and the tears running down the amazing grooves in his cheeks. Blindly, his face always this horrible working mask, he groped for his hat, for his way down from the terrace. It was eight o'clock, but still brightly light. The other people were staring. In great agitation, part of which was exasperation, she stayed behind, paid the waiter with a half-sovereign, took her yellow silk coat, then followed Skrebensky.

She saw him walking with brittle, blind steps along the path by the river. She could tell by the strange stiffness and brittleness of his figure that he was still crying. Hurrying after him, running, she took his arm.

'Tony,' she cried, 'don't! Why are you like this? What are you doing this for? Don't. It's not necessary.'

He heard, and his manhood was cruelly, coldly defaced. Yet it was no good. He could not gain control of his face. His face, his breast, were weeping violently, as if automatically. His will, his knowledge had nothing to do with it. He simply could not stop.

She walked holding his arm, silent with exasperation and perplexity and pain. He took the uncertain steps of a blind man, because his mind was blind with weeping.

'Shall we go home? Shall we have a taxi?' she said.

He could pay no attention. Very flustered, very agitated, she signalled indefinitely to a taxi-cab that was going slowly by. The driver saluted and drew up. She opened the door and pushed Skrebensky in, then took her own place. Her face was unlifted, the mouth closed down, she looked hard and cold and ashamed. She winced as the driver's dark red face was thrust round upon her, a full-blooded, animal face with black eyebrows and a thick, short-cut moustache.

'Where to, lady?' he said, his white teeth showing. Again for a moment she was flustered.

'Forty, Rutland Square,' she said.

He touched his cap and stolidly set the car in motion. He seemed to have a league with her to ignore Skrebensky.

The latter sat as if trapped within the taxi-cab, his face still working, whilst occasionally he made quick slight movements of the head, to shake away his tears. He never moved his hands. She could not bear to look at him. She sat with face uplifted and averted to the window.

At length, when she had regained some control over herself, she turned again to him. He was much quieter. His face was wet, and twitched occasionally, his hands still lay motionless. But his eyes were quite still, like a washed sky after rain, full of a wan light, and quite steady, almost ghostlike.

A pain flamed in her womb, for him.

'I didn't think I should hurt you,' she said, laying her hand very lightly, tentatively, on his arm. 'The words came without my knowing. They didn't mean anything, really.'

He remained quite still, hearing, but washed all wan and without feeling. She waited, looking at him, as if he were some curious, not-understandable creature.

'You won't cry again, will you, Tony?'

Some shame and bitterness against her burned him in the question. She noticed how his moustache was soddened wet with tears. Taking her handkerchief, she wiped his face. The driver's heavy, stolid back remained always turned to them, as if conscious but indifferent. Skrebensky sat motionless whilst Ursula wiped his face, softly, carefully, and yet clumsily, not as well as he would have wiped it himself.

Her handkerchief was too small. It was soon wet through. She groped in his pocket for his own. Then, with its more ample capacity, she carefully dried his face. He remained motionless all the while. Then she drew his cheek to hers and kissed him. His face was cold. Her heart was hurt. She saw the tears welling quickly to his eyes again. As if he were a child, she again wiped away his tears. By now she herself was on the point of weeping. Her underlip was caught between her teeth.

So she sat still, for fear of her own tears, sitting close by him, holding his hand warm and close and loving. Meanwhile the car ran on, and a soft, midsummer dusk began to gather. For a long while they sat motionless. Only now and again her hand closed more closely, lovingly, over his hand, then gradually relaxed.

The dusk began to fall. One or two lights appeared. The driver drew up to light his lamps. Skrebensky moved for the first time, leaning forward to watch the driver. His face had always the same still, clarified, almost childlike look, impersonal.

They saw the driver's strange, full, dark face peering into the lamps under drawn brows. Ursula shuddered. It was the face almost of an animal yet of a quick, strong, wary animal that had them within its knowledge, almost within its power. She clung closer to Skrebensky.

'My love?' she said to him, questioningly, when the car was again running in full motion.

He made no movement or sound. He let her hold his hand, he let her reach forward, in the gathering darkness, and kiss his still cheek. The crying had gone by – he would not cry any more. He was whole and himself again.

'My love,' she repeated, trying to make him notice her. But as yet he could not.

He watched the road. They were running by Kensington Gardens. For the first time his lips opened.

'Shall we get out and go into the park,' he asked.

'Yes,' she said, quietly, not sure what was coming.

After a moment he took the tube from its peg. She saw the stout, strong, self-contained driver lean his head.

'Stop at Hyde Park Corner.'

The dark head nodded, the car ran on just the same.

Presently they pulled up. Skrebensky paid the man. Ursula stood back.˙ She saw the driver salute as he received his tip, and then, before he set the car in motion, turn and look at her, with his quick, powerful, animal's look, his eyes very concentrated and the whites of his eyes flickering. Then he drove away into the crowd. He had let her go. She had been afraid.

Skrebensky turned with her into the park. A band was still playing and the place was thronged with people. They listened to the ebbing music, then went aside to a dark seat, where they sat closely, hand in hand.

Then at length, as out of the silence, she said to him, wondering:

'What hurt you so?'

She really did not know, at this moment.

'When you said you wanted never to marry me,' he replied, with a childish simplicity.

'But why did that hurt you so?' she said. 'You needn't mind everything I say so particularly.'

'I don't know – I didn't want to do it,' he said, humbly, ashamed.

She pressed his hand warmly. They sat close together, watching the soldiers go by with their sweethearts, the lights trailing in myriads down the great thoroughfares that beat on the edge of the park.

'I didn't know you cared so much,' she said, also humbly.

'I didn't,' he said. 'I was knocked over myself. – But I care – all the world.'

His voice was so quiet and colourless, it made her heart go pale with fear.

'My love!' she said, drawing near to him. But she spoke out of fear, not out of love.

'I care all the world – I care for nothing else – in life nor in death,' he said, in the same steady, colourless voice of essential truth.

'Than for what?' she murmured duskily.

'Than for you – to be with me.'

And again she was afraid. Was she to be conquered by this? She cowered close to him, very close to him. They sat perfectly still, listening to the great, heavy, beating sound of the town, the murmur of lovers going by, the footsteps of soldiers.

She shivered against him.

'You are cold?' he said.

'A little.'

'We will go and have some supper.'

He was now always quiet and decided and remote, very beautiful. He seemed to have some strange, cold power over her.

They went to a restaurant, and drank chianti. But his pale, wan look did not go away.

'Don't leave me to-night,' he said at length, looking at her, pleading. He was so strange and impersonal, she was afraid.

'But the people of my place,' she said, quivering.

'I will explain to them – they know we are engaged.'

She sat pale and mute. He waited.

'Shall we go?' he said at length.

'Where?'

'To an hotel.'

Her heart was hardened. Without answering, she rose to acquiesce. But she was now cold and unreal. Yet she could not refuse him. It seemed like fate, a fate she did not want.

They went to an Italian hotel somewhere, and had a sombre bedroom with a very large bed, clean, but sombre. The ceiling was painted with a bunch of flowers in a big medallion over the bed. She thought it was pretty.

He came to her, and cleaved to her very close, like steel cleaving and clinching on to her. Her passion was roused, it was fierce but cold. But it was fierce, and extreme, and good, their passion this night. He slept with her fast in his arms. All night long he held her fast against him. She was passive, acquiescent. But her sleep was not very deep nor very real.

She woke in the morning to a sound of water dashed on a courtyard, to sunlight streaming through a lattice. She thought she was in a foreign country. And Skrebensky was there an incubus upon her.

She lay still, thinking, whilst his arm was round her, his head against her shoulders, his body against hers, just behind her. He was still asleep.

She watched the sunshine coming in bars through the *persiennes*, and her immediate surroundings again melted away.

She was in some other land, some other world, where the old restraints had dissolved and vanished, where one moved freely, not afraid of one's fellow men, nor wary, nor on the defensive, but calm, indifferent, at one's ease. Vaguely, in a sort of silver light, she wandered at large and at ease. The bonds of the world were broken. This world of England had vanished away. She heard a voice in the yard below calling:

'O Giovann' – O'-O'-O'Giovann'—!'

And she knew she was in a new country, in a new life. It was very delicious to lie thus still, with one's soul wandering freely and simply in the silver light of some other, simpler, more finely natural world.

But always there was a foreboding waiting to command her. She became more aware of Skrebensky. She knew he was waking up. She must modify her soul, depart from her further world, for him.

She knew he was awake. He lay still, with a concrete stillness, not as when he slept. Then his arm tightened almost convulsively upon her, and he said, half timidly:

'Did you sleep well?'

'Very well.'

'So did I.'

There was a pause.

'And do you love me?' he asked.

She turned and looked at him searchingly. He seemed outside her.

'I do,' she said.

But she said it out of complacency and a desire not to be harried. There was a curious breach of silence between them, which frightened him.

They lay rather late, then he rang for breakfast. She wanted to be able to go straight downstairs and away from the place, when she got up. She was happy in this room, but the thought of the publicity of the hall downstairs rather troubled her.

A young Italian, a Sicilian, dark and slightly pock-marked, buttoned up in a sort of grey tunic, appeared with the tray. His face had an almost African imperturbability, impassive, incomprehensible.

'One might be in Italy,' Skrebensky said to him, genially. A vacant look, almost like fear, came on the fellow's face. He did not understand.

'This is like Italy,' Skrebensky explained.

The face of the Italian flashed with a non-comprehending smile, he finished setting out the tray, and was gone. He did not understand: he would understand nothing: he disappeared from the door like a half-domesticated wild animal. It made Ursula shudder slightly, the quick, sharp-sighted, intent animality of the man.

Skrebensky was beautiful to her this morning, his face softened and transfused with suffering and with love, his movements very still and gentle. He was beautiful to her, but she was detached from him by a chill distance. Always she seemed to be bearing up against the distance that separated them. But he was unaware. This morning he was transfused and beautiful. She admired his movements, the way he spread honey on his roll, or poured out the coffee.

When breakfast was over, she lay still again on the pillow, whilst he went through his toilet. She watched him, as he sponged himself, and quickly dried himself with the towel. His body was beautiful, his movements intent and quick, she admired him and she appreciated him without reserve. He seemed completed now. He aroused no fruitful fecundity in her. He seemed added up, finished. She knew him all round, not on any side did he lead into the unknown. Poignant, almost passionate appreciation she felt for him, but none of the dreadful wonder, none of the rich fear, the connection with the unknown, or the reverence of love. He was, however, unaware this morning. His body was quiet and fulfilled, his veins complete with satisfaction, he was happy, finished.

Again she went home. But this time he went with her. He wanted to stay by her. He wanted her to marry him. It was already July. In early September he must sail for India. He could not bear to think of going alone. She must come with him. Nervously, he kept beside her.

Her examination was finished, her college career was over. There remained for her now to marry or to work again. She applied for no post. It was concluded she would marry. India tempted her – the strange, strange land. But with the thought of Calcutta, or Bombay, or of Simla, and of the European population, India was no more attractive to her than Nottingham.

She had failed in her examination: she had gone down: she had not taken her degree. It was a blow to her. It hardened her soul.

'It doesn't matter,' he said. 'What are the odds, whether you are a Bachelor of Arts or not, according to the London University? All you know, you know, and if you are Mrs. Skrebensky, the B.A. is meaningless.'

Instead of consoling her, this made her harder, more ruthless. She was now up against her own fate. It was for her to choose between being Mrs. Skrebensky, even Baroness Skrebensky, wife of a lieutenant in the Royal Engineers, the Sappers, as he called them, living with the European population in India – or being Ursula Brangwen, spinster, school-mistress. She was qualified by her Intermediate Arts examination. She would probably even now get a post quite easily as assistant in one of the higher grade schools, or even in Willey Green School. Which was she to do?

She hated most of all entering the bondage of teaching once more. Very heartily she detested it. Yet at the thought of marriage and living with Skrebensky amid the European population in India, her soul was locked and would not budge. She had very little feeling about it: only there was a deadlock.

Skrebensky waited, she waited, everybody waited for the decision. When Anton talked to her, and seemed insidiously to suggest himself as a husband to her, she knew how utterly locked out he was. On the other hand, when she saw Dorothy, and discussed the matter, she felt she would marry him promptly, at once, as a sharp disavowal of adherence with Dorothy's views.

The situation was almost ridiculous.

'But do you love him?' asked Dorothy.

'It isn't a question of loving him,' said Ursula. 'I love him well enough – certainly more than I love anybody else in the world. And I shall never love anybody else the same again. We have had the flower of each other. But I don't *care* about love. I don't value it. I don't care whether I love or whether I don't, whether I have love or whether I haven't. What is it to me?'

And she shrugged her shoulders in fierce, angry contempt.

Dorothy pondered, rather angry and afraid.

'Then what *do* you care about?' she asked, exasperated.

'I don't know,' said Ursula. 'But something impersonal. Love – love – love – what does it mean – what does it amount to? So much personal gratification. It doesn't lead anywhere.'

'It isn't supposed to lead anywhere, is it?' said Dorothy, satirically. 'I thought it was the one thing which is an end in itself.'

'Then what does it matter to me?' cried Ursula. 'As an end in itself, I could love a hundred men, one after the other. Why should I end with a Skrebensky? Why should I not go on, and love all the types I fancy, one after another, if love is an end in itself? There are plenty of men who aren't Anton, whom I could love – whom I would like to love.'

'Then you don't love *him*,' said Dorothy.

'I tell you I do; – quite as much, and perhaps more than I should love any of the others. Only there are plenty of things that aren't in Anton that I would love in the other men.'

'What, for instance?'

'It doesn't matter. But a sort of strong understanding, in some men, and then a dignity, a directness, something unquestioned that there is in working men, and then a jolly, reckless passionateness that you see – a man who could really let go—'

Dorothy could feel that Ursula was already hankering after something else, something that this man did not give her.

'The question is, what *do* you want,' propounded Dorothy. 'Is it just other men?'

Ursula was silenced. This was her own dread. Was she just promiscuous?

'Because if it is,' continued Dorothy, 'you'd better marry Anton. The other can only end badly.'

So out of fear of herself Ursula was to marry Skrebensky.

He was very busy now, preparing to go to India. He must visit relatives and contract business. He was almost sure of Ursula now. She seemed to have given in. And he seemed to become again an important, self-assured man.

It was the first week in August, and he was one of a large party in a bungalow on the Lincolnshire coast. It was a tennis, golf, motor-car, motor-boat party, given by his great-aunt, a lady of social pretensions. Ursula was invited to spend the week with the party.

She went rather reluctantly. Her marriage was more of less fixed for the twenty-eighth of the month. They were to sail for India on September the fifth. One thing she knew, in her subconsciousness, and that was, she would never sail for India.

She and Anton, being important guests on account of the coming marriage, had rooms in the large bungalow. It was a big place, with a great central hall, two smaller writing-rooms, and then two corridors from which opened eight or nine bedrooms. Skrebensky was put on one corridor, Ursula on the other. They felt very lost, in the crowd.

Being lovers, however, they were allowed to be out alone together as much as they liked. Yet she felt very strange, in this crowd of strange people, uneasy, as if she had no privacy. She was not used to these homogeneous crowds. She was afraid.

She felt different from the rest of them, with their hard, easy, shallow intimacy, that seemed to cost them so little. She felt she was not pronounced enough. It was a kind of hold-your-own unconventional atmosphere. She did not like it. In crowds, in assemblies of people, she liked formality. She felt she did not produce the right effect. She was not effective: she was not beautiful: she was nothing. Even before Skrebensky she felt unimportant, almost inferior. He could take his part very well with the rest.

He and she went out into the night. There was a moon behind clouds, shedding a diffused light, gleaming now and again in bits of smoky mother-of-pearl. So they walked together on the wet, ribbed sands near the sea, hearing the run of the long, heavy waves, that made a ghostly whiteness and a whisper.

He was sure of himself. As she walked, the soft silk of her dress – she wore a blue shantung, full-skirted – blew away from the sea and flapped and clung to her legs. She wished it would not. Everything seemed to give her away, and she could not rouse herself to deny, she was so confused.

He would lead her away to a pocket in the sand-hills, secret amid the grey thorn-bushes and the grey, glassy grass. He held her close against him, felt all her firm, unutterably desirable mould of body through the fine fibre of the silk that fell about her limbs. The silk, slipping fierily on the hidden, yet revealed roundness and firmness of her body, her loins, seemed to run in him like fire, make his brain burn like brimstone. She liked it, the electric fire of the silk under his hands upon her limbs, the fire flew over her, as he drew nearer and nearer to discovery. She vibrated like a jet of electric, firm fluid in response. Yet she did not feel beautiful. All the time, she felt she was not beautiful to him, only exciting. She let him take her, and he seemed mad, mad with excited passion. But she, as she lay afterwards on the cold, soft sand, looking up at the blotted, faintly luminous sky, felt that she was as cold now as she had been before. Yet he, breathing heavily, seemed almost savagely satisfied. He seemed revenged.

A little wind wafted the sea grass and passed over her face. Where was the supreme fulfilment she would never enjoy? Why was she so cold, so unroused, so indifferent?

As they went home, and she saw the many, hateful lights of the bungalow, of several bungalows in a group, he said softly:

'Don't lock your door.'

'I'd rather, here,' she said.

'No, don't. We belong to each other. Don't let us deny it.'

She did not answer. He took her silence for consent.

He shared his room with another man.

'I suppose,' he said, 'it won't alarm the house if I go across to happier regions.'

'So long as you don't made a great row going, and don't try the wrong door,' said the other man, turning in to sleep.

Skrebensky went out in his wide-striped sleeping suit. He crossed the big dining hall, whose low firelight smelled of cigars and whisky and coffee, entered the other corridor and found Ursula's room. She was lying awake, wide-eyed and suffering. She was glad he had come, if only for consolation. It was consolation to be held in his arms, to feel his body against hers. Yet how foreign his arms and body were! Yet still, not so horribly foreign and hostile as the rest of the house felt to her.

She did not know how she suffered in this house. She was healthy and exorbitantly full of interest. So she played tennis and learned golf, she rowed out and swam in the deep sea, and enjoyed it very much indeed, full of zest. Yet all the time, among those others, she felt shocked and wincing, as if her violently-sensitive nakedness were exposed to the hard, brutal, material impact of the rest of the people.

The days went by unmarked, in a full, almost strenuous enjoyment of one's own physique. Skrebensky was one among the others, till evening came, and he took her for himself. She was allowed a great deal of freedom and was treated with a good deal of respect, as a girl on the eve of marriage, about to depart for another continent.

The trouble began at evening. Then a yearning for something unknown came over her, a passion for something she knew not what. She would walk the foreshore alone after dusk, expecting, expecting something, as if she had gone to a rendezvous. The salt, bitter passion of the sea, its indifference to the earth, its swinging, definite motion, its strength, its attack, and its salt burning, seemed to provoke her to a pitch of madness, tantalizing her with vast suggestion of fulfilment. And then, for personification, would come Skrebensky, Skrebensky, whom she knew, whom she was fond of, who was attractive, but whose soul could not contain her in its waves of strength, nor his breast compel her in burning, salty passion.

One evening they went out after dinner, across the low golf links to the dunes and the sea. The sky had small, faint stars, all was still and faintly dark. They walked together in silence, then ploughed, labouring, through the heavy loose sand of the gap between the dunes. They went in silence under the even, faint darkness, in the darker shadow of the sandhills.

Suddenly, cresting the heavy, sandy pass, Ursula lifted her head, and shrank back, momentarily frightened. There was a great whiteness confronting her, the moon was incandescent as a round furnace door, out of which came the high blast of moonlight, over the seaward half of the world, a dazzling, terrifying glare of white light. They shrank back for a moment into shadow, uttering a cry. He felt his chest laid bare, where the secret was heavily hidden. He felt himself fusing down to nothingness, like a bead that rapidly disappears in an incandescent flame.

'How wonderful!' cried Ursula, in low, calling tones. 'How wonderful!'

And she went forward, plunging into it. He followed behind. She too seemed to melt into the glare, towards the moon.

The sands were as ground silver, the sea moved in solid brightness, coming towards them, and she went to meet the advance of the flashing, buoyant water. She gave her breast to the moon, her belly to the flashing, heaving water. He stood behind, encompassed, a shadow ever dissolving.

She stood on the edge of the water, at the edge of the solid, flashing body of the sea, and the wave rushed over her feet.

'I want to go,' she cried, in a strong, dominant voice. 'I want to go.'

He saw the moonlight on her face, so she was like metal, he heard her ringing, metallic voice, like the voice of a harpy to him.

She prowled, ranging on the edge of the water like a possessed creature, and he followed her. He saw the froth of the wave followed by the hard, bright water swirl over her feet and her ankles, she swung out her arms, to balance, he expected every moment to see her walk into the sea, dressed as she was, and be carried swimming out.

But she turned, she walked to him.

'I want to go,' she cried again, in the high, hard voice, like the scream of gulls.

'Where?' he asked.

'I don't know.'

And she seized hold of his arm, held him fast, as if captive, and walked him a little way by the edge of the dazzling, dazing water.

Then there in the great flare of light, she clinched hold of him, hard, as if suddenly she had the strength of destruction, she fastened her arms round him and tightened him in her grip, whilst her mouth sought his in a hard, rending, ever-increasing kiss, till his body was powerless in her grip, his heart melted in fear from the fierce, beaked, harpy's kiss. The water washed again over their feet, but she took no notice. She seemed unaware, she seemed to be pressing in her beaked mouth till she had the heart of him. Then, at last, she drew away and looked at him – looked at him. He knew what she wanted. He took her by the hand and led her across the fore-shore, back to the sandhills. She went silently. He felt as if the ordeal of proof was upon him, for life or death. He led her to a dark hollow.

'No, here,' she said, going out to the slope full under the moonshine. She lay motionless, with wide-open eyes looking at the moon. He came direct to her, without preliminaries. She held him pinned down at the chest, awful. The fight, the struggle for consummation was terrible. It lasted till it was agony to his soul, till he succumbed, till he gave way as if dead, lay with his face buried, partly in her hair, partly in the sand, motionless, as if he would be motionless now for ever, hidden away in the dark, buried, only buried, he only wanted to be buried in the goodly darkness, only that, and no more.

He seemed to swoon. It was a long time before he came to himself. He was aware of an unusual motion of her breast. He looked up. Her face lay like an image in the moonlight, the eyes wide open, rigid. But out of the eyes, slowly, there rolled a tear, that glittered in the moonlight as it ran down her cheek.

He felt as if the knife were being pushed into his already dead body. With head strained back, he watched, drawn tense, for some minutes, watched the unaltering, rigid face like metal in the moonlight, the fixed, unseeing eye, in which slowly the water gathered, shook with glittering moonlight, then surcharged, brimmed over and ran trickling, a tear with its burden of moonlight, into the darkness, to fall in the sand.

He drew gradually away as if afraid, drew away – she did not move. He glanced at her – she lay the same. Could he break away? He turned, saw the open foreshore, clear in front of him, and he plunged away, on and on, ever farther from the horrible figure that lay stretched in the moonlight on the sands with the tears gathering and travelling on the motionless, eternal face.

He felt, if ever he must see her again, his bones must be broken, his body crushed, obliterated for ever. And as yet, he had the love of his own living body. He wandered on a long, long way, till his brain drew dark and he was unconscious with weariness. Then he curled in the deepest darkness he could find, under the sea-grass, and lay there without consciousness.

She broke from her tense cramp of agony gradually, though each movement was a goad of heavy pain. Gradually, she lifted her dead body from the sands, and rose at last. There was now no moon for her, no sea. All had passed away. She trailed her dead body to the house, to her room where she lay down inert.

Morning brought her a new access of superficial life. But all within her was cold, dead, inert. Skrebensky appeared at breakfast. He was white and obliterated. They did not look at each other nor speak to each other. Apart from the ordinary, trivial talk of civil people, they were separate, they did not speak of what was between them during the remaining two days of their stay. They were like two dead people who dare not recognise, dare not see each other.

Then she packed her bag and put on her things. There were several guests leaving together, for the same train. He would have no opportunity to speak to her.

He tapped at her bedroom door at the last minute. She stood with her umbrella in her hand. He closed the door. He did not know what to say.

'Have you done with me?' he asked her at length, lifting his head.

'It isn't me,' she said. 'You have done with me – we have done with each other.'

He looked at her, at the closed face, which he thought so cruel. And he knew he could never touch her again. His will was broken, he was seared, but he clung to the life of his body.

'Well, what have I done?' he asked, in a rather querulous voice.

'I don't know,' she said, in the same dull, feelingless voice. 'It is finished. It had been a failure.'

He was silent. The words still burned his bowels.

'Is it my fault?' he said, looking up at length, challenging the last stroke.

'You couldn't—' she began. But she broke down.

He turned away, afraid to hear more. She began to gather her bag, her handkerchief, her umbrella. She must be gone now. He was waiting for her to be gone.

At length the carriage came and she drove away with the rest. When she was out of sight, a great relief came over him, a pleasant banality. In an instant, everything was obliterated. He was childishly amiable and companionable all the day long. He was astonished that life could be so nice. It was better than it had been before. What a simple thing it was to be rid of her! How friendly and simple everything felt to him. What false thing had she been forcing on him?

But at night he dared not be alone. His room-mate had gone, and the hours of darkness were an agony to him. He watched the window in suffering and terror. When would this horrible darkness be lifted off him? Setting all his nerves, he endured it. He went to sleep with the dawn.

He never thought of her. Only his terror of the hours of night grew on him, obsessed him like a mania. He slept fitfully, with constant wakings of anguish. The fear wore away the core of him.

His plan was to sit up very late: drink in company until one or half-past one in the morning; then he would get three hours of sleep, of oblivion. It was light by five o'clock. But he was shocked almost to madness if he opened his eyes on the darkness.

In the daytime he was all right, always occupied with the thing of the moment, adhering to the trivial present, which seemed to him ample and satisfying. No matter how little and futile his occupations were, he gave himself to them entirely, and felt normal and fulfilled. He was always active, cheerful, gay, charming, trivial. Only he dreaded the darkness and silence of his own bedroom, when the darkness should challenge him upon his own soul. That he could not bear, as he could not bear to think about Ursula. He had no soul, no background. He never thought of Ursula, not once, he gave her no sign. She was the darkness, the challenge, the horror. He turned to immediate things. He wanted to marry quickly, to screen himself from the darkness, the challenge of his own soul. He would marry his Colonel's daughter. Quickly, without hesitation, pursued by his obsession for activity, he wrote to this girl, telling her his engagement was broken – it had been a temporary infatuation which he less than any one else could understand now it was over – and could he see his very dear friend soon? He would not be happy till he had an answer.

He received a rather surprised reply from the girl, but she would be glad to see him. She was living with her aunt. He went down to her at once, and proposed to her the first evening. He was accepted. The marriage took place quietly within fourteen days' time. Ursula was not notified of the event. In another week, Skrebensky sailed with his new wife to India.

Chapter Sixteen

The Rainbow

Ursula went home to Beldover faint, dim, closed up. She could scarcely speak or notice. It was as if her energy were frozen. Her people asked her what was the matter. She told them she had broken off the engagement with Skrebensky. They looked blank and angry. But she could not feel any more.

The weeks crawled by in apathy. He would have sailed for India now. She was scarcely interested. She was inert, without strength or interest.

Suddenly a shock ran through her, so violent, that she thought she was struck down. Was she with child? She had been so stricken under the pain of herself and of him, this had never occurred to her. Now like a flame it took hold of her limbs and body. Was she with child?

In the first flaming hours of wonder, she did not know what she felt. She was as if tied to the stake. The flames were licking her and devouring her. But the flames were also good. They seemed to wear her away to rest. What she felt in her heart and her womb she did not know. It was a kind of swoon.

Then gradually the heaviness of her heart pressed and pressed into consciousness. What was she doing? Was she bearing a child? Bearing a child? To what?

Her flesh thrilled, but her soul was sick. It seemed, this child, like the seal set on her own nullity. Yet she was glad in her flesh that she was with child. She began to think, that she would write to Skrebensky, that she would go out to him, and marry him, and live simply as a good wife to him. What did the self, the form of life matter? Only the living from day to day mattered, the beloved existence in the body, rich, peaceful, complete, with no beyond, no further trouble, no further complication. She had been wrong, she had been arrogant and wicked, wanting that other thing, that fantastic freedom, that illusory, conceited fulfilment which she had imagined she could not have with Skrebensky. Who was she to be wanting some fantastic fulfilment in her life? Was it not enough that she had her man, her children, her place of shelter under the sun? Was it not enough for her, as it had been for her mother? She would marry and love her husband and fill her place simply. That was the ideal.

Suddenly she saw her mother in a just and true light. Her mother was simple and radically true. She had taken the life that was given. She had not, in her arrogant conceit, insisted on creating life to fit herself. Her mother was right, profoundly right, and she herself had been false, trashy, conceited.

A great mood of humility came over her, and in this humility a bondaged sort of peace. She gave her limbs to the bondage, she loved the bondage, she called it peace. In this state she sat down to write to Skrebensky.

Since you left me I have suffered a great deal, and so have come to myself. I cannot tell you the remorse I feel for my wicked, perverse behaviour. It was given to me to love you, and to know your love for me. But instead of thankfully, on my knees, taking what God had given me, I must have the moon in my keeping, I must insist on having the moon for my own. Because I could not have it, everything else must go.

I do not know if you can ever forgive me. I could die with shame to think of my behaviour with you during our last times, and I don't know if I could ever bear to look you in the face again. Truly the best thing would be for me to die, and cover my fantasies for ever. But I find I am with child, so that cannot be.

It is your child, and for that reason I must revere it and submit my body entirely to its welfare, entertaining no thought of death, which once more is largely conceit. Therefore, because you once loved me, and because this child is your child, I ask you to have me back. If you will cable me one word, I will come to you as soon as I can. I swear to you to be a dutiful wife, and to serve you in all things. For now I only hate myself and my own conceited foolishness. I love you – I love the thought of you – you were natural and decent all through, whilst I was so false. Once I am with you again, I shall ask no more than to rest in your shelter all my life—

This letter she wrote, sentence by sentence, as if from her deepest, sincerest heart. She felt that now, now, she was at the depths of herself. This was her true self, forever. With this document she would appear before God at the Judgment Day.

For what had a woman but to submit? What was her flesh but for childbearing, her strength for her children and her husband, the giver of life? At last she was a woman.

She posted her letter to his club, to be forwarded to him in Calcutta. He would receive it soon after his arrival in India – within three weeks of his arrival there. In a month's time she would receive word from him. Then she would go.

She was quite sure of him. She thought only of preparing her garments and of living quietly, peacefully, till the time when she should join him again and her history would be concluded for ever. The peace held like an unnatural calm for a long time. She was aware, however, of a gathering restiveness, a tumult impending within her. She tried to run away from it. She wished she could hear from Skrebensky, in answer to her letter, so that her course should be resolved, she should be engaged in fulfilling her fate. It was this inactivity which made her liable to the revulsion she dreaded.

It was curious how little she cared about his not having written to her before. It was enough that she had sent her letter. She would get the required answer, that was all.

One afternoon in early October, feeling the seething rising to madness within her, she slipped out in the rain, to walk abroad, lest the house should suffocate her. Everywhere was drenched wet and deserted, the grimed houses glowed dull red, the butt houses burned scarlet in a gleam of light, under the glistening, blackish purple slates. Ursula went on towards Willey Green. She lifted her face and walked swiftly, seeing the passage of light across the shallow valley, seeing the colliery and its clouds of steam for a moment visionary in dim brilliance, away in the chaos of rain. Then the veils closed again. She was glad of the rain's privacy and intimacy.

Making on towards the wood, she saw the pale gleam of Willey Water through the cloud below, she walked the open space where hawthorn trees streamed like hair on the wind and round bushes were presences slowing through the atmosphere. It was very splendid, free and chaotic.

Yet she hurried to the wood for shelter. There, the vast booming overhead vibrated down and encircled her, tree-trunks spanned the circle of tremendous sound, myriads of tree-trunks, enormous and streaked black with water, thrust like stanchions upright between the roaring overhead and the sweeping of the circle underfoot. She glided between the tree-trunks afraid of them. They might turn and shut her in as she went through their martialled silence.

So she flitted along, keeping an illusion that she was unnoticed. She felt like a bird that has flown in through the window of a hall where vast warriors sit at the board. Between their grave, booming ranks she was hastening, assuming she was unnoticed, till she emerged, with beating heart, through the far window and out into the open, upon the vivid green, marshy meadow.

She turned under the shelter of the common, seeing the great veils of rain swinging with slow, floating waves across the landscape. She was very wet and a long way from home, far enveloped in the rain and the waving landscape. She must beat her way back through all this fluctuation, back to stability and security.

A solitary thing, she took the track straight across the wilderness, going back. The path was a narrow groove in the turf between high, sere, tussocky grass; it was scarcely more than a rabbit run. So she moved swiftly along, watching her footing, going like a bird on the wind, with no thought, contained in motion. But her heart had a small, living seed of fear, as she went through the wash of hollow space.

Suddenly she knew there was something else. Some horses were looming in the rain, not near yet. But they were going to be near. She continued her path, inevitably. They were horses in the lee of a clump of trees beyond, above her. She pursued her way with bent head. She did not want to lift her face to them. She did not want to know they were there. She went on in the wild track.

She knew the heaviness on her heart. It was the weight of the horses. But she would circumvent them. She would bear the weight steadily, and so escape. She would go straight on, and on, and be gone by.

Suddenly the weight deepened and her heart grew tense to hear it. Her breathing was laboured. But this weight also she could bear. She knew without looking that the horses were moving nearer. What were they? She felt the thud of their heavy hoofs on the ground. What was it that was drawing near her, what weight oppressing her heart? She did not know, she did not look.

Yet now her way was cut off. They were blocking her back. She knew they had gathered on a log bridge over the sedgy dike, a dark, heavy, powerfully heavy knot. Yet her feet went on and on. They would burst before her. They would burst before her. Her feet went on and on. And tense, and more tense became her nerves and her veins, they ran hot, they ran white hot, they must fuse and she must die.

But the horses had burst before her. In a sort of lightning of knowledge their movement travelled through her, the quiver and strain and thrust of their powerful flanks, as they burst before her and drew on, beyond.

She knew they had not gone, she knew they awaited her still. But she went on over the log bridge that their hoofs had churned and drummed, she went on, knowing things about them. She was aware of their breasts gripped, clenched narrow in a hold that never relaxed, she was aware of their red nostrils flaming with long endurance, and of their haunches, so rounded, so massive, pressing, pressing, pressing to burst the grip upon their breasts, pressing for ever till they went mad, running against the walls of time, and never bursting free. Their great haunches were smoothed and darkened with rain. But the darkness and wetness of rain could not put out the hard, urgent, massive fire that was locked within these flanks, never, never.

She went on, drawing near. She was aware of the great flash of hoofs, a bluish, iridescent flash surrounding a hollow of darkness. Large, large seemed the bluish, incandescent flash of the hoof-iron, large as a halo of lightning round the knotted darkness of the flanks. Like circles of lightning came the flash of hoofs from out of the powerful flanks.

They were awaiting her again. They had gathered under an oak tree, knotting their awful, blind, triumphing flanks together, and waiting, waiting. They were waiting for her approach. As if from a far distance she was drawing near, towards the line of twiggy oak trees where they made their intense darkness, gathered on a single bank.

She must draw near. But they broke away, they cantered round, making a wide circle to avoid noticing her, and cantered back into the open hillside behind her.

They were behind her. The way was open before her, to the gate in the high hedge in the near distance, so she could pass into the smaller, cultivated field, and so out to the highroad and the ordered world of man. Her way was clear. She lulled her heart. Yet her heart was couched with fear, couched with fear all along.

Suddenly she hesitated as if seized by lightning. She seemed to fall, yet found herself faltering forward with small steps. The thunder of horses galloping down the path behind her shook her, the weight came down upon her, down, to the moment of extinction. She could not look round, so the horses thundered upon her.

Cruelly, they swerved and crashed by on her left hand. She saw the fierce flanks crinkled and as yet inadequate, the great hoofs flashing bright as yet only brandished about her, and one by one the horses crashed by, intent, working themselves up.

They had gone by, brandishing themselves thunderously about her, enclosing her. They slackened their burst transport, they slowed down, and cantered together into a knot once more, in the corner by the gate and the trees ahead of her. They stirred, they moved uneasily, they settled their uneasy flanks into one group, one purpose. They were up against her.

Her heart was gone, she had no more heart. She knew she dare not draw near. That concentrated, knitted flank of the horse-group had conquered. It stirred uneasily, awaiting her, knowing its triumph. It stirred uneasily, with the uneasiness of awaiting triumph. Her heart was gone, her limbs were dissolved, she was dissolved like water. All the hardness and looming power was in the massive body of the horse-group.

Her feet faltered, she came to a standstill. It was the crisis. The horses stirred their flanks uneasily. She looked away, failing. On her left, two hundred yards down the slope, the thick hedge ran parallel. At one point there was an oak tree. She might climb into the boughs of that oak tree, and so round and drop on the other side of the hedge.

Shuddering, with limbs like water, dreaded every moment to fall, she began to work her way as if making a wide detour round the horse-mass. The horses stirred their flanks in a knot against her. She trembled forward as if in a trance.

Then suddenly, in a flame of agony, she darted, seized the rugged knots of the oak tree and began to climb. Her body was weak but her hands were as hard as steel. She knew she was strong. She struggled in a great effort till she hung on the bough. She knew the horses were aware. She gained her foot-hold on the bough. The horses were loosening their knot, stirring, trying to realise. She was working her way round to the other side of the tree. As they started to canter towards her, she fell in a heap on the other side of the hedge.

For some moments she could not move. Then she saw through the rabbit-cleared bottom of the hedge the great, working hoofs of the horses as they cantered near. She could not bear it. She rose and walked swiftly, diagonally across the field. The horses galloped along the other side of the hedge to the corner, where they were held up. She could feel them there in their huddled group all the while she hastened across the bare field. They were almost pathetic, now. Her will alone carried her, till, trembling, she climbed the fence under a leaning thorn tree that overhung the grass by the high-road. The use went from her, she sat on the fence leaning back against the trunk of the thorn tree, motionless.

As she sat there, spent, time and the flux of change passed away from her, she lay as if unconscious upon the bed of the stream, like a stone, unconscious, unchanging, unchangeable, whilst everything rolled by in transience, leaving her there, a stone at rest on the bed of the stream, inalterable and passive, sunk to the bottom of all change.

She lay still a long time, with her back against the thorn tree trunk, in her final isolation. Some colliers passed, tramping heavily up the wet road, their voices sounding out, their shoulders up to their ears, their figures blotched and spectral in the rain. Some did not see her. She opened her eyes languidly as they passed by. Then one man going along saw her. The whites of his eyes showed in his black face as he looked in wonderment at her. He hesitated in his walk, as if to speak to her, out of frightened concern for her. How she dreaded his speaking to her, dreaded his questioning her.

She slipped from her seat and went vaguely along the path – vaguely. It was a long way home. She had an idea that she must walk for the rest of her life, wearily, wearily. Step after step, step after step, and always along the wet, rainy road between the hedges. Step after step, step after step, the monotony produced a deep, cold sense of nausea in her. How profound was her cold nausea, how profound! That too plumbed the bottom. She seemed destined to find the bottom of all things to-day: the bottom of all things. Well, at any rate she was walking along the bottom-most bed – she was quite safe: quite safe, if she had to go on and on for ever, seeing this was the very bottom, and there was nothing deeper. There was nothing deeper, you see, so one could not but feel certain, passive.

She arrived home at last. The climb up the hill to Beldover had been very trying. Why must one climb the hill? Why must one climb? Why not stay below? Why force one's way up the slope? Why force one's way up and up, when one is at the bottom? Oh, it was very trying, very wearying, very burdensome. Always burdens, always, always burdens. Still, she must get to the top and go home to bed. She must go to bed.

She got in and went upstairs in the dusk without its being noticed she was in such a sodden condition. She was too tired to go downstairs again. She got into bed and lay shuddering with cold, yet too apathetic to get up or call for relief. Then gradually she became more ill.

She was very ill for a fortnight, delirious, shaken and racked. But always, amid the ache of delirium, she had a dull firmness of being, a sense of permanency. She was in some way like the stone at the bottom of the river, inviolable and unalterable, no matter what storm raged in her body. Her soul lay still and permanent, full of pain, but itself for ever. Under all her illness, persisted a deep, inalterable knowledge.

She knew, and she cared no more. Throughout her illness, distorted into vague forms, persisted the question of herself and Skrebensky, like a gnawing ache that was still superficial, and did not touch her isolated, impregnable core of reality. But the corrosion of him burned in her till it burned itself out.

Must she belong to him, must she adhere to him? Something compelled her, and yet it was not real. Always the ache, the ache of unreality, of her belonging to Skrebensky. What bound her to him when she was not bound to him? Why did the falsity persist? Why did the falsity gnaw, gnaw, gnaw at her, why could she not wake up to clarity, to reality. If she could but wake up, if she could but wake up, the falsity of the dream, of her connection with Skrebensky, would be gone. But the sleep, the delirium pinned her down. Even when she was calm and sober she was in its spell.

Yet she was never in its spell. What extraneous thing bound her to him? There was some bond put upon her. Why could she not break it through? What was it? What was it?

In her delirium she beat and beat at the question. And at last her weariness gave her the answer – it was the child. The child bound her to him. The child was like a bond round her brain, tightened on her brain. It bound her to Skrebensky.

But why, why did it bind her to Skrebensky? Could she not have a child of herself? Was not the child her own affair? all her own affair? What had it to do with him? Why must she be bound, aching and cramped with the bondage, to Skrebensky and Skrebensky's world? Anton's world: it became in her feverish brain a compression which enclosed her. If she could not get out of the compression she would go mad. The compression was Anton and Anton's world, not the Anton she possessed, but the Anton she did not possess, that which was owned by some other influence, by the world.

She fought and fought and fought all through her illness to be free of him and his world, to put it aside, to put it aside, into its place. Yet ever anew it gained ascendency over her, it laid new hold on her. Oh, the unutterable weariness of her flesh, which she could not cast off, nor yet extricate. If she could but extricate herself, if she could but disengage herself from feeling, from her body, from all the vast encumbrances of the world that was in contact with her, from her father, and her mother, and her lover, and all her acquaintance.

Repeatedly, in an ache of utter weariness she repeated: 'I have no father nor mother nor lover, I have no allocated place in the world of things, I do not belong to Beldover nor to Nottingham nor to England nor to this world, they none of them exist, I am trammelled and entangled in them, but they are all unreal. I must break out of it, like a nut from its shell which is an unreality.'

And again, to her feverish brain, came the vivid reality of acorns in February lying on the floor of a wood with their shells burst and discarded and the kernel issued naked to put itself forth. She was the naked, clear kernel thrusting forth the clear, powerful shoot, and the world was a bygone winter, discarded, her mother and father and Anton, and college and all her friends, all cast off like a year that has gone by, whilst the kernel was free and naked and striving to take new root, to create a new knowledge of Eternity in the flux of Time. And the kernel was the only reality, the rest was cast off into oblivion.

This grew and grew upon her. When she opened her eyes in the afternoon and saw the window of her room and the faint, smoky landscape beyond, this was all husk and shell lying by, all husk and shell, she could see nothing else, she was enclosed still, but loosely enclosed. There was a space between her and the shell. It was burst, there was a rift in it. Soon she would have her root fixed in a new Day, her nakedness would take itself the bed of a new sky and a new air, this old, decaying, fibrous husk would be gone.

Gradually she began really to sleep. She slept in the confidence of her new reality. She slept breathing with her soul the new air of a new world. The peace was very deep and enrichening. She had her root in new ground, she was gradually absorbed into growth.

When she woke at last it seemed as if a new day had come on the earth. How long, how long had she fought through the dust and obscurity, for this new dawn? How frail and fine and clear she felt, like the most fragile flower that opens in the end of winter. But the role of night was turned and the dawn was coming in.

Very far off was her old experience – Skrebensky, her parting with him – very far off. Some things were real; those first glamorous weeks. Before, these had seemed like hallucination. Now they seemed like common reality. The rest was unreal. She knew that Skrebensky had never become finally real. In the weeks of passionate ecstasy he had been with her in her desire, she had created him for the time being. But in the end he had failed and broken down.

Strange, what a void separated him and her. She liked him now, as she liked a memory, some bygone self. He was something of the past, finite. He was that which is known. She felt a poignant affection for him, as for that which is past. But, when she looked with her face forward, he was not. Nay, when she looked ahead, into the undiscovered land before her, what was there she could recognise but a fresh glow of light and inscrutable trees going up from the earth like smoke. It was the unknown, the unexplored, the undiscovered upon whose shore she had landed, alone, after crossing the void, the darkness which washed the New World and the Old.

There would be no child: she was glad. If there had been a child, it would have made little difference, however. She would have kept the child and herself, she would not have gone to Skrebensky. Anton belonged to the past.

There came the cablegram from Skrebensky: 'I am married.' An old pain and anger and contempt stirred in her. Did he belong so utterly to the cast-off past? She repudiated him. He was as he was. It was good that he was as he was. Who was she to have a man according to her own desire? It was not for her to create, but to recognise a man created by God. The man should come from the Infinite and she should hail him. She was glad she could not create her man. She was glad she had nothing to do with his creation. She was glad that this lay within the scope of that vaster power in which she rested at last. The man would come out of Eternity to which she herself belonged.

As she grew better, she sat to watch a new creation. As she sat at her window, she saw the people go by in the street below, colliers, women, children, walking each in the husk of an old fruition, but visible through the husk, the swelling and the heaving contour of the new germination. In the still, silenced forms of the colliers she saw a sort of suspense, a waiting in pain for the new liberation; she saw the same in the false hard confidence of the women. The confidence of the women was brittle. It would break quickly to reveal the strength and patient effort of the new germination.

In everything she saw she grasped and groped to find the creation of the living God, instead of the old, hard barren form of bygone living. Sometimes great terror possessed her. Sometimes she lost touch, she lost her feeling, she could only know the old horror of the husk which bound in her and all mankind. They were all in prison, they were all going mad.

She saw the stiffened bodies of the colliers, which seemed already enclosed in a coffin, she saw their unchanging eyes, the eyes of those who are buried alive: she saw the hard, cutting edges of the new houses, which seemed to spread over the hillside in their insentient triumph, the triumph of horrible, amorphous angles and straight lines, the expression of corruption triumphant and unopposed, corruption so pure that it is hard and brittle: she saw the dun atmosphere over the blackened hills opposite, the dark blotches of houses, slate roofed and amorphous, the old church-tower standing up in hideous obsoleteness above raw new houses on the crest of the hill, the amorphous, brittle, hard edged new houses advancing from Beldover to meet the corrupt new houses from Lethley, the houses of Lethley advancing to mix with the houses of Hainor, a dry, brittle, terrible corruption spreading over the face of the land, and she was sick with a nausea so deep that she perished as she sat. And then, in the blowing clouds, she saw a band of faint iridescence colouring in faint colours a portion of the hill. And forgetting, startled, she looked for the hovering colour and saw a rainbow forming itself. In one place it gleamed fiercely, and, her heart anguished with hope, she sought the shadow of iris where the bow should be. Steadily the colour gathered, mysteriously, from nowhere, it took presence upon itself, there was a faint, vast rainbow. The arc bended and strengthened itself till it arched indomitable, making great architecture of light and colour and the space of heaven, its pedestals luminous in the corruption of new houses on the low hill, its arch the top of heaven.

And the rainbow stood on the earth. She knew that the sordid people who crept hard-scaled and separate on the face of the world's corruption were living still, that the rainbow was arched in their blood and would quiver to life in their spirit, that they would cast off their horny covering of disintegration, that new, clean, naked bodies would issue to a new germination, to a new growth, rising to the light and the wind and the clean rain of heaven. She saw in the rainbow the earth's new architecture, the old, brittle corruption of houses and factories swept away, the world built up in a living fabric of Truth, fitting to the over-arching heaven.

TITLES IN THIS SERIES:

Richard Gordon
Doctor in the House
Doctor at Sea
Doctor at Large
Doctor in Love
Doctor in Clover
The Facemaker
The Medical Witness

Graham Greene
The Heart of the Matter
Stamboul Train
A Burnt-out Case
The Third Man
Loser Takes All
The Quiet American
The Power and the Glory

Ernest Hemingway*
For Whom the Bell Tolls
The Snows of Kilimanjaro
Fiesta
The Short Happy Life of Francis Macomber
Across the River and into the Trees
The Old Man and the Sea

Georgette Heyer
These Old Shades
Sprig Muslin
Sylvester
The Corinthian
The Convenient Marriage

Franz Kafka*
The Trial
America
In the Penal Settlement
Metamorphosis
The Castle
The Great Wall of China
Investigations of a Dog
Letter to his Father
The Diaries 1910-1923

Rudyard Kipling
The Jungle Book
The Second Jungle Book
Just So Stories
Puck of Pook's Hill
Stalky and Co.
Kim

D. H. Lawrence
Sons and Lovers
St. Mawr
The Fox
The White Peacock
Love among the Haystacks
The Virgin and the Gipsy
Lady Chatterley's Lover

D. H. Lawrence
Women in Love
The Ladybird
The Man Who Died
The Captain's Doll
The Rainbow

Norah Lofts
Jassy
Bless This House
Scent of Cloves
How Far to Bethlehem?

Robert Ludlum*
The Scarlatti Inheritance
The Osterman Weekend
The Matlock Paper
The Gemini Contenders

Thomas Mann*
Death in Venice
Tristan
Tonio Kröger
Doctor Faustus
Mario and the Magician
A Man and His Dog
The Black Swan
Confessions of Felix Krull, Confidence Man

W. Somerset Maugham
Cakes and Ale
The Painted Veil
Liza of Lambeth
The Razor's Edge
Theatre
The Moon and Sixpence

W. Somerset Maugham
Sixty-five Short Stories

Ed McBain*
Cop Hater
Give the Boys a Great Big Hand
Doll
Eighty Million Eyes
Hail, Hail, the Gang's All Here!
Sadie When She Died
Let's Hear it for the Deaf Man

James A. Michener*
The Source
The Bridges at Toko-Ri
Caravans
Sayonara

George Orwell
Animal Farm
Burmese Days
A Clergyman's Daughter
Coming up for Air
Keep the Aspidistra Flying
Nineteen Eighty-Four

Jean Plaidy
St. Thomas's Eve
Royal Road to Fotheringay
The Goldsmith's Wife
Perdita's Prince

Nevil Shute
A Town Like Alice
Pied Piper
The Far Country
The Chequer Board
No Highway

Georges Simenon
Ten Maigret Stories

Wilbur Smith
When the Lion Feeds
The Diamond Hunters
Eagle in the Sky
Gold Mine
Shout at the Devil

John Steinbeck*
The Grapes of Wrath
The Moon is Down
Cannery Row
East of Eden
Of Mice and Men

Mary Stewart
The Crystal Cave
The Hollow Hills
Wildfire at Midnight
Airs Above the Ground

Evelyn Waugh
Decline and Fall
Black Mischief
A Handful of Dust
Scoop
Put Out More Flags
Brideshead Revisited

H. G. Wells
The Time Machine
The Island of Dr. Moreau
The Invisible Man
The First Men in the Moon
The Food of the Gods
In the Days of the Comet
The War of the Worlds

Morris West
The Devil's Advocate
The Second Victory
Daughter of Silence
The Salamander
The Shoes of the Fisherman

Dennis Wheatley
The Devil Rides Out
The Haunting of Toby Jugg
Gateway to Hell
To the Devil – A Daughter

John Wyndham
The Day of the Triffids
The Kraken Wakes
The Chrysalids
The Seeds of Time
Trouble With Lichen
The Midwich Cuckoos

* Not currently available in Canada for copyright reasons